The
GODS
of
ENTROPY
and the Fifth Yin

DERYCK HOCKLEY

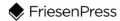 FriesenPress

Suite 300 - 990 Fort St
Victoria, BC, V8V 3K2
Canada

www.friesenpress.com

Copyright © 2020 by Deryck Hockley
First Edition — 2020

The author holds all rights to this (original and final edited:1996) book in this its present and existing form:

Many appreciated thanks to my professional editor for never showing up for work, not once.

A kiss, a hug (and a bik-ie) to my faithful friend and library assistant – her cuteness, Sheila Belle 'Beautiful Eyes' Hockley (aka: Sheila, Sheils, Seals, Zeals, and Sleaze (my Australian blue heeler, 2005–2015))who nevah evah failed to show up or failed to please:

And an acknowledgment (of course) to the patience with which my wife Gloria Mae has had through its long composition and years of editing; and with me in general.

No private, corporate or government entity contributed (in any way) to the writing of this novel; nor did the author receive any directional or financial support (cash-money, or credit in-kind) whatsoever in this its current and only intended form.

All rights reserved. No part of this publication may be reproduced in any form, or by any means, electronic or mechanical, including photocopying, recording, or any information browsing, storage, or retrieval system, without permission in writing from FriesenPress.

ISBN
978-1-5255-6835-0 (Hardcover)
978-1-5255-6836-7 (Paperback)
978-1-5255-6837-4 (eBook)

1. FICTION, VISIONARY & METAPHYSICAL

Distributed to the trade by The Ingram Book Company

TABLE OF CONTENTS

Author's note and disclaimer 1

Introduction 2

PREFIX TO THE THE FIRST EMPIRE
(Heraclitus & the commingling of Eastern & Western Philosophy) 10

Part One: The Fiest Empire 21

PREFIX TO THE SECOND EMPIRE
(all along the watchtower) 488

Part Two: Hoodwinked to Fund
the Holly Jolly, Juicy Deucy Empire 501

PREFIX TO THE THE THIRD EMPIRE
(Johnny Rocco) 811

Part Three: Mortgaging the Bank to Float the Tird Empire 823

> '...and (mother goddess Hera) set a watcher upon her (goddess Io), great and strong Argos, who with four eyes looks every way. And the goddess stirred in him unwearing strength: sleep never fell upon his eyes; but he kept sure watch always.'
>
> **Hesiod** (attributed — [*AEgimius*])

> 'The living spirit grows and even outgrows its earlier forms of expression; it freely chooses the men in whom it lives and who proclaim it.'
>
> **Carl Gustav Jung**

> 'Never have so many capable writers warned mankind against the dangers of wrong speech — and never have words been used more recklessly by politicians or taken more seriously by the public.'
>
> **Aldous Huxley**

In memory of my father
Douglas Horace Hockley BSM, RCA
(1905-1987)

In keeping with the noble spirit and the gentle nature of my father:
THIS NOVEL IS DEDICATED TO THE
HOI POLLOI OF THE WORLD.

By the same author:

Berbers and the High Atlas (2002)
(National Library of Canada ISBN 1-55395-164-6)

Author's note and disclaimer

Although an offence to one's personal convictions can often be a precursor to some sudden and further enlightenment, the author wishes to beg a pre-emptive pardon to readers who may feel hurt by imagining that their religious or ideological and philosophical convictions and their notion of the status quo of the phenomenon at large (along with their sense of history) are being roughly trodden upon by the material within. The author makes no further apology for his work.

Chief strategist T. H. Douglasson and his assistant Elizeus H. Cristi, along with our vague (and somewhat ephemeral) associates here at Arcas Enterprises, wish to acknowledge the Sick (***Slick***) Cow & the **Hollowed**-Earth alliances (whose distorted mythos permeate the world's societies at our peril) without which this philosophical, historical and satirical polemic would have no agenda. Further to that, we wish to tip our hats in jest to the quasi-*sacred* and the less than ***hallowed*** inspirations of the world…for what they are worth.

If the world and the events which occur in this novel bear any resemblance (or bear no resemblance whatsoever) to the world at large as perceived by you the reader, this occurrence is merely incidental (or at worst coincidental, which is unlikely). We recommend that while reading this prose you might fare better if you remain alert to that secret world of your heart, and although we apologize for the inconvenience of any intrusive and juxtaposition of reality (upon the wise reader) which may result from its reading, full and effectual accountability (as in life itself) must ultimately rest with the observing participant.

Despite character and place names that may be historically familiar or similar to the reader, all such identities (herein) are fictional.

Introduction

'This is a tale of arms and of a man:'
VIRGIL *(THE AENEID)*

...and those arms of which we speak not only remain intact still, but are now more expediently equipped than ever. As such, these same deadly clubs of vigour, force, ability and sway are as always (by way of some strong, unseen and ingenious reticence) affecting the status quo within the newness of time. This impedes the social and transcendental progress of the hoi polio that populates the narrative upon which we embark. The result is a disguised control that continues to debilitate and disable the status quo's learning curve that's needed for any proper, expedient social advancement: one which is not yet on the horizon. The impediment does this by providing calculated distortions and monstrously engineered malformation into certain factors that are intrinsic for the hoi polloi to shape progressive moral virtuosity. More noticeably, these anomalies help to shape their regressive ideology that happens to result in culturally conflicting mythos that thoroughly permeate the societies of the hoi polloi. For the lack of a true magician's binary art — an algorithm, per sé: *my kingdom for an algorithm* being the call sign — the remedy for this conundrum still remains distant and yet at large, at least for the time being. This plays havoc with the hoi polloi's destiny. And since no algorithm has been forthcoming to address this problem, it has had a disarming effect upon their world.

Meanwhile, Dyfed H. Lucifer, the protagonist and the hero (around whom this story line is centred), finds himself amid this phenomenon. But this hero is inclined as well to be more of a spin-off from his own antagonist alter-ego (of his own doing, of course) than being just himself, which is not necessarily a friendly trait that can place him behind the eight ball in the game of life. Besides, if one isn't careful, as a side affect it can easily put the run on personal fortitude. But that's another story.

At the moment Dyfed Lucifer fancies himself and is of the impression that he is all the rage. Apparently, he was a sensation in his own mind and a legend of his own time, and it can't be said that he didn't jolly well know it.

Dyfed is a person not unlike any of you, my readers (all three of you), and me. He is a self proclaimed, free (outside-the-box-as-possible) thinker, basically a self educated and independent intellectual who like all the others of that ilk (at one time or some point or another) have been quick to self awareness (on their own initiative); and it's just for this trait alone which everyone else is trying to play immediate catch-up.

In Dyfed H. Lucifer's case the third dimension was a world also full of convoluted mythos that he viewed as being fabricated from smoke and mirrors. Clearly, he had not attained self-knowledge, no matter how aware he thought he was. But this was also complicated by the true fact that he claimed to recall having materialized from the land of Logos[1]. This in itself (he believed) if it was not an entitlement exactly, it certainly permitted him to better interpret the phenomenon into which he had found himself

---

1 Logos is the word used by Heraclicus (540 – 480 BCE) to define the commonality and order of unity, a universal law or cosmic function.

immersed since birth. Certainly, his advantage over the melee of the hoi polloi in general was solely due to him having been infused with an advanced intuition, cognition and perception that was imposed upon him by genealogy and his childhood education; it was an advantage (he wrongly believed) which the general populace did not have. As it was, Dyfed was a long way from discovering that in most cases (at this point anyway) he was a very long way indeed from being correct in his estimations of what phenomenon was made, and accordingly fashioned, in the first place.

Dyfed's birthright had been acquired from his mother, a certain Queen Chloris Violet-Eye. In lieu of an absent (possibly minded) and unnamed father, he had been provided with a personal tutor — a wizard — named Manandan from whom he acquired scholastic instruction. As such, it was a combination between that wizard and his mother that furthered that condition of exalted adeptness upon our hero, Dyfed.

Manandan was also Chloris Violet-Eye's adopted over-seer or vizier. And like his liege and spiritual potentate (the beautiful Violet-Eye) Manandan was an ancient Hyperborean master of the fifth dimension. Although Violet-Eye had only arrived here recently herself upon the Isle of Peace to give a miraculous, unobstructed material birth to her son Dyfed, Manandan (along with other fellow Hyperborean Masters and a handful of local hoi polloi minions who through some merit or other had been taken in, house-trained and educated) had been here some time on an exercise to carry out investigation into human conditions in the third dimension. They were attaining (it seemed) a prognosis that indicated that because of a general unfolding of misaligned minds, the hoi polloi were (and would continue) failing to succeed (successfully) as a species. Apparently (for these poor mundane devils), their world (during this epoch) had gone all awry and they were being terribly wronged. They were not progressing, at least not as Mother Nature in her wisdom was most want to do. But was it actually caused by some bacterial infestation or radiation? This was something the Masters had long been wondering. Or was it a particular genome? It hadn't happened before, they knew that much.

At the moment it was safe to say that no one knew what was causing the hoi polloi's curious insanity that in turn produced a world in turmoil.

So it was, in the first year of the current era (of this the fifth age) we find ourselves among a syndicate staffed by thirteen Hyperborean masters, adepts and protagonist professors who formed a convocation of functionary agents of change that were made up of social philosophers, biochemists, biophysicists and particle physicists, along with plasma and genetic engineers, among others. So here they were, residing at a Hyperborean outpost adventure resort tucked out-of-the-way (and out of sight) on a remote and somewhat hidden island called the Isle of Peace located on the fringe of the third density that the inhabitants dubbed 'the Adventure, Rest and Recreation Resort' (ARRR).

Dyfed (having been born here) quickly became a product of each of the worlds in which he had one foot; that of the material or temporal realm and that of the ethereal or spiritual, at least partially so. Ultimately, this was his inheritance and in this he was presently unique. At least that was what he was told, or told himself: we don't know which.

As for Dyfed's father, a certain Apollo by name (although Dyfed believed himself of the Heraklian lineage), that man had supposedly been a Hyperborean king. Dyfed did not know his father, though not in the sense that it was confusion among many candidates. This legend concerning Dyfed's paternal ancestry may (however) have originated from Dyfed himself. Manandan took to alluding to Dyfed as the third wheel, or leg of regency, behind Violet-Eye and himself. The epithet — *Tripod* — soon became a cognomen or pet name for Dyfed as a child. Then, aside from being a prominent and uniquely local decorative motif vase pattern that was common to both the queen's and Manandan's separate households, the tripod (sometimes short for third leg) was the symbol that eventually appeared much later on the Isle of Peace's heraldic escutcheon, and eventually a symbol for the Isle itself and the ancient and forgotten people of its distant past.

As for the condition of the hoi polloi and their psyche world of the third dimension in which those little-minded unfortunates (often mis-referred to as large brained mammals[2] dwelled, over time the effects of these aforementioned conflicts of non logical and mythical entanglement (with its program for mind control and incitement toward waves of mass genocidal violence) had vastly contributed towards providing an opportunity for completely burying the true historical tale about humanity (and its destiny) under an avalanche of falsely authored (yet widely believed) chronicles, lists and annals. Seemingly un-orchestrated, this program of theirs' was of such a superior level of duplicity and was so grand, that the control mechanism for the hoi polloi's individual will was to be sophisticatedly constructed and supervised without obvious noticeability. But supervised by whom? The Haploids, of course! But as to the actual identities of who actually made up this deeply secretive cadré at large among the governing elite — those abominable and indomitable and secret power factor entities — no one yet knew for sure. And that was the question that the masters had recently turned their attention toward. As for the situation itself, it may not be, as once suspected, caused by a diseased and affected transgressor of reduced dimension co-efficiency that was causing this problem. So the problem then took them back to a more dangerous flaw. And then the question would become, what if that flaw was contagious in any way? Or was this just nothing more than a thrill addiction effect (attached only to the material world) that has a tendency to go awry? Originally, so Dyfed had learned from Manandan, it was thought that humanoid behavioural problem was caused by a faulty genome or some rogue bacteria.

Also, these chronicles (and tales to that effect) that had been unleashed over time were what had ultimately contributed immensely toward the belief in a wilfully fabricated false history of humanity's past. It had to do with the adage that one had to know their own past to know who they were and where they are going. But, conspiracy theories aside, the volition to conceal the truth about humanity's true presence among the general phenomena at large (via these chronicles, lists and annals) had been done specifically for whose benefit, exactly? Again, no one knew, at least not yet. We were back again to the sixty-four denarii question.

From the background of his lineage as well as what had been taught him by both his Mother and Manandan, Dyfed knew that the negative and curtailing influence of these same chronicles, lists and annals couldn't have surfaced on their own and were what had helped contribute to the current state of atrophy (complicated with an impoverishment of conscientiousness) which are known to hamper the properties of clarity, quiescence and purity among what are favourably referred to as 'large brained mammals'

---

2   Homo sapiens or hominids of wisdom.

(sic). And this disturbance (he knew) was unnaturally induced entropy. Furthermore, it was not one in harmony with the Universe's Holy vibration that in itself (whenever this Frankensteinian freak common to humanity did not occur) was contained by specific increments relative to the individual vibration, and was always in harmony. So, it was this unnatural condition acting within the great vibe (so he had been taught) that diminished the very estimation (and historical understanding) that the hoi polloi had [and have] about themselves (aside from it distributing a perversely distorted picture of their ancestors' possessions and passions in ages past). And this situation has inordinately fashioned many of the folks of this narrative into a squalid world of narrow-minded hostility, prejudice and entitlement that is beyond the abstract which has long since entered the realm of absurdity. At the time of our narrative, this condition of mature absurdity had undergone a complete and successful transfiguration into the veritable phenomenon of daily (cross-connected) human reality.

Due to the effects brought on by this impossible and unlikely paradox of induced nonsense, the hoi polloi's individual condition of reality (as seen from its present point) is scalar in nature while maintaining an on-going Quixote-type conflict with multiple vectors. This, Dyfed thought (as he matured) was vastly relevant to the current distemper that's affecting the hoi polloi's eternal well-being. Their true identity (which is their place of eternal security within the eternal moment of beginning less space/time) has now been nicely concealed from them without the possibility (for them) to gain an easy attained discernment for a relevant and well-needed correction, any time soon. Immersed in their current reality, their phenomenon is further complicated by their ignorance of what exactly they are. This is largely responsible for their inability to individually close the currently imposed distance from their original true self — the matrix of their eternal omniscient/omnipotent being — which is what some folks call their soul, others their mind or their potential for divine connection.

This non-secured security we speak about here is over and above anything that so called physical guardians can (or ever will) provide. Only the true non-self's self can provide this particular supreme condition of security. It is very much an individual's thing brought about by free self will whose divine source (called atman in Sanskrit and attan in Pali) is its intrinsic reagent.

It suffices to say that if peace and harmony were the bountiful, Blessed Star of reality (the great artificer of the golden light of truth, the mean (main) being [whose beginninglessness] trumps all nonsense which is not to be confused with some anatomical creator/destroyer space/time being); and if that Blessed Star (whose presence causes and casts the shadow which is the imposed realization of the unholy perishable self) is Azeus (also: Aba'al, Ajove, Ajehovah and Aallah) and is therefore potentially capable and able to witness the marriage of Happiness and Pleasure without envy, then (finally) the Blessed Star Azeus (et al) — once known also as Amun ('hidden one', as in — of ones' true self — hidden from the shadow-ego-self), also as Aton (Aten) which was also served by the namesakes Ra, Re or Thoth (Hermes) and a host of other avatars.

These have since become reshaped long after the era of the great hymn[3], that preverbal narrative construct of its time dedicated to Aten and whose composition is attributed to Pharaoh Amen-ho-tep (satisfied Amen) IV who is also known as Ak-hen-Aton. As such, it is clear and it is certain beyond any shadow of doubt that (in general) these

---

3   Taken from an unknown copy of the 14th century BCE hymn to Aten composed by Akhenaten.

hoi polloi of today (for whom we are here concerned) live no longer under the auspice of this aforementioned Azeus (without Zeus) or Aten, at all. Definitely not!

Rather, they exist within the sphere of the new and less than satisfactory programed construct of Zeus/Jove, also intrinsically related to Jehovah and Allah, the great lie which has distorted the natural order of the true/self with its malleable reflection (the ego/self) that exists in defined space/time. Zeus, along with its avatars, is the abominable misinterpretation, the false truth and the epitome of fake that exists beyond the pale of the maze (not to be confused with hidden), by which is meant secret. Its spot is concurrent and only perceived with the realization of the unholy shadow (the perishable self within the third dimension). This is solely the totem of one's lonely fear of the unconscious and is what some (Socrates for one)[4] have called 'perceiving the devil in the details' of the third dimension. Those who know themselves to be blessed by the narrative construct of the Blessed Star (Azeus) know that Azeus and the self are one and the same. Only those who know the true non-self and the eternal moment can understand that. The other sixty-four denarii question then is: "where does the true self dwell?'

Well, it dwells within the Blessed Star of the Eternal Moment of Beginning less Space/Time that is the genius of Azeus, of course — where else? For the concept of the shrine/temple among ancient religions was always meant to be the centre of the true self, and not a physical abode such as a temple. Azeus /Aba'al /Ajove / Ajehovah / Aallah and Atman is the centre off the true self.

But a facsimile (a resembling ego, which is no more than a pale reflection of a true self being) can also reside and abide briefly and flittingly within the shadowy platitude of the pretence prison of its own making. And that (in turn) created the evil genius of Zeus (et al) and is the domain of the replicated (and untrue) ego-self. This is the fake god that can be seen in all of today's religions and extracurricular activities.

The obverse side of the sixty-four denarii question (that is most often asked by the Sage or the Master) is: ...'which self are you earnestly striving for during this brief moment within this pale reflection of space/time?': an inquiry which (of course) must be followed by...'is that a rhetorical question?'

Coincidently, the phenomenon at large actually has no true and meaningful commonality whatsoever for the perceivers thereof, at least not until Azeus, Atman (et al) is finally realized.

And then there is the scalar/vector confusion; the apples to oranges comparison. This error of function is all too common. Anyway, the fantasy of Zeus that is pertinent to any given individual (assuming that there are more than one vibrating, individual spiritual sentient beings beyond the third dimensional reality), appears to manifest in a coordinating manner that makes it similar as to how it manifests with each and every other given individual. This is Nature at work.

It may also address the bracketed uncertainty above in this way: Call forth Azeus now (you minions of the mighty) and let your demeanour be loudly and proudly praised by It. Then let Zeus the devil — *Zeus the god of suffering and misery...the fake god...the false prophet...the in-debtor...the deceiver that was invented by the cunning and the wary (the true deceivers) from under whose rock that has somehow been morphed and promoted instead into and upon the pure and glistening mountain summit [called Mount*

---

4   Also, Jung referred to it as the *original, total unconsciousness* out of which the ego can rise and begin to develop.

Sapan, Zaphon, Hazzi, Hermon & Moriah] and the abode of the thunderbolt hurling incubus in charge of the clouds of storm, rain and fertility (stolen and misappropriated from certain characteristics of the true god-Azeus) from whence it all came about — go swiftly to hell and nev-ah ev-ah return.

So — once again, call forth Azeus whose real domain is with the self of self, not in the sunless sky of the eternal shades of night which is the shell of the self-ego without: for this thing is the god of death associated with the personal pronoun 'he' and known by many names. So — familiarize thyself with those names and be aware (beware) of them and note that they are recorded also in the chronicles, annals, and book of lists. Then having checked them off and cashed (cast) them out, oh true Lord — Azeus of the self-Amen — the Amen Azeus — the Blessed Star of the personalized spiritual benben — help us to repudiate and rebuke all others and never in weakness and gullibility embrace them again, for we do so at our peril. Help us — oh true lord Azeus — to remain without it; and deliver us for all time from falling back into the evil of its false debt: Amen.'

Please consult the sacred verse that's beyond sundry chronicles, annals, and books of lists: "*Help me, my Muse…help me…help me…help me focus and listen to you, my Muse for I have faith in God my Father from whom I am descended, who is the source of all things known and unknown*'.

It is believed (according to suggestions made in the exposé known as the Seventh Cosmos of Hieralias the Prophet) that this line is the actual title of what is often referred to as the Muse hymn. It is also the first line of the one hundred and eight paragraph prayer (six lines to a paragraph) that Hyperborean Masters once recited by memory in its entirety at their ceremony of confirmation in order to take up their diploma and to awaken to the potential of their true non self's self. Sadly, a full account of it's wording has been lost.

Devoid of any intentional plagiaries, the wording of this account of the Gods of Entropy is entirely the author's own work. However, in keeping with personal efforts to strive for that levelling agent of commonality, he has intentionally contrived (in the subjective sense) to put down words that conjure up images that hopefully allow the reader to flex their imagination and outwardly embrace contention; a touchstone that is needed here. The objective of this work is to make its features as familiar as possible to various cross sections of readers. Sadly, it would be wise to assume that there is nothing beyond that here to connect you with your present reality other than imagination: so use the latter with a generous will.

This tale is the abridged composition of the author's original unpublished trilogy (circa 1989): *The Many World Path's Interpretation of a Silver Goddess Loving, Non-Self Styled Bodhisattva's Quantum Leap through Space-Time as Seen from a One Incidental, Trans-Dimensional Non-substantive Actuality, Applied with a Dash* (a hint) *of Proper Time in Order to Remain Unshakenly Discontinuous and Unstirred within the Eternal Moment*. For the sole purpose of facilitating an obvious expedience toward story-title management — (under advice) the author permitted the work to be renamed: The Gods of Entropy & the Fifth Yin: surely, you can see the connection?

The humble purpose of this fable is to arouse the spirit and stir one's mind from its placid state into one of a contentious nature in order to perceive the light and life of loving creation beyond the shadows flickering on the cave wall around us. Hopefully, it will awaken the reader to an inner joy and alleviate them momentarily from any immediate lassitude. Lassitude, however, is the greatest hurdle in any author's expectation, for sadly it is the path of least resistance and the state of human weariness that we (the unenlightened) continually design and order up. In addition we insist (apparently) in adopting delusional rationalizations for phenomenon and in pretending toward pretentious identities for ourselves. These are all attachments that are dangerous illusions. All illusions are causational. As such, in employing them we immediately subject ourselves to a distracted state of uncontrollable individual causation. Yet, at the same time (which is every single moment of material existence) we must attempt always to affect a meaningful interface with a self-appointed, cause-deluded phenomenon that we've already brought into being and fashioned inappropriately around ourselves at some other past moment (now irrelevant) over which we no longer have any control. This sustains our self-afflicted distraction which unintentionally we generate each and every living moment that's not within the exceedingly guarded eternal space/moment of divinity itself. So, in our current state — the inversely proportional state of ignorance to self realization ratio reality (exponentially squared each and every moment within the perpetually passing phenomenon) — we move further apart from our true selves and each other, just as the universe (from our perspective) appears to be doing. This is just another dangerous illusional reality of our own creation. In any case, this form of spiritual-destroying entropy tends to play havoc with any poet's agenda to communicate intelligently.

Finally, it is now our duty to announce that this tale was consigned to the author over a period of time when he was very young. Later, he aspired to promote this tale and to relay its form to the best of his ability upon arriving at the level of proficiency when he deemed his literary skills to be sufficient in order to do justice to its impart. Being but a puerile youth at the time, he's not able to say who that mysterious imparter was. Apparently, this righteous teacher was wise and of a great age who lay partially beyond the author's scope of cognition and discernment. Still, they were able to communicate enough between them for him to detect in the former a certain recusancy toward the circumambient reality of the status quo at large. Furthermore, they loved each other and this emotion was the main conduit.

Curiously — somehow — this inosculate state of vibration that connected them sustained an existence between them long enough that contributed to the extraordinary way in which the author knew him at all. He realized that he knew him much like he knew himself. He called this teacher of personal righteousness, Parasolo (actually Parasolus), which was the name the teacher called him self.

Once, many years later when he was older, the author (by chance) came upon that same name. It read: *Parasolus: Comes di Victoria*. Essentially these words mean: '*greater than one unaccompanied, companion of victory*', although a civil servant (a bureaucratic attendant at the local land title's archival office who was facilitating the author's enquiries on another matter) demonstratively and boastfully (yet unknowingly and incorrectly) translated this now seldom used language of ancient *Amor* as — Count Parasolus of Victoria.

"I have a sense,' the storyteller has stated, 'that I could only beach upon Parasolo (that proprietor's state of being) by spiralling in a *Phi* curve through a strange vibrating torsion field comprised of a plasmatic substance best described as separated charged particles. The journey was a vague charter by means of floating dream fragments (bordering on nightmarishness) that danced upon shoals of light continually shifting through shadows. The environment crackled loud static sounds as experienced during faulty radio transmissions or when they're intercepted by ferocious electrical storms. Such conditions only throw confusion (while contributing at the same time to the inability) at the function ability of communication's usual path of fragility.'

So — for you psychos (with souped-up and tuned-in super normalities) who've finally climbed down from the old family tree — that spiky twig of material life — once decorated with glittering trinkets of mythos that were programmed into your twisted ancestral psyche; now that you have set your feet firmly upon the solid foundation of Logos (or even those of you who are still nothing more than squabbling babooning buffoons loudly jabbering nonsense and desperately force-feeding on proffered mythos and narrative constructs in panic stricken congregations among your tree's upper most branches all the while drenched in fear — along with its complimentary resultant — namely, loathing of others and also of the unknown), turn over a new leaf here; and in the name of the all pure self's non-self and your desperately needed endeavour to avert the conceptual non-presence in the hope that you will tune into the Omni-frequency of the multi dimensional companionship that meets on the level in the eternal moment — read on.

Neo-Parasolus: [Neo-Parasolus (Parasolo): Colonus in Imperium Britannia in Dominion de Canada in Americas: Comes de Victoria; Individual; Patriarch and Commander of *Aryan*[5] the Paisley (and the Good regiment of Tulip) and the would be sunderer of *Turan*[6] the false prophet that lies beyond the pale; and (besides all that) an indomitable pilgrim of life.]

---

5 Aryan is an Indo-Iranian word for a self-designated (cultural, metaphysical and non-racialized) civilized noble.
6 Turan are racialized folks designated as being of an ignoble culture: i.e.: from the Land of Tur.

PREFIX TO THE FIRST EMPIRE

"Fool!'… (my Muse told me one lazy day of missed opportunity. For goodness sake man!)[7] …'look in thy heart and write'.

Philip Sidney (Astrophel & Stella) [apology

---

[7] Author's bracketed explanatory additive.

(Heraclitus & the commingling of Eastern & Western Philosophy)

'At best, man is the noblest of animals;
separated from law and justice he is the worst!'
ARISTOTELES *(ALSO ARISTOTLE)*

Relative to the individual here in question (you pick a name: *pilgrim, hombre, companero,* the *wayfarer* or the *comrade of life*), our man here (in question, along with his reality at hand) felt his mind pause momentarily as he pondered the proverb cited above. The axiom, he knew, had issued from the wonder that was Aristoteles. It would seem that the question this statement posed (he thought) was how (exactly) do we define law and justice? At least defining it as far as it was useful and made sense in a sane society. Or specifically, what is it really that should be frowned upon in a society? Or how many definitions of law and justice have we managed to appoint over time, and what (exactly) should we peg as being against the law? Remember, too much is too much. Little is better when it comes to the law for as any specific ordination serving our society, the real law — that most viable codex of moral regulation that's made available — must be just and consensual while simultaneously being congruent to each and all without prejudice and equally balanced for each and every social level and station. Too many laws can't accomplish this, not with it being without prejudice and its condemnation ruling always to be set beyond reasonable doubt, it can't. So by design law must be congruent in proportion and in ratio with each human under the *'one law'* that's meant to nourish us, serve and protect us, never mind give us liberty. It needs to be capable of helping all of us pursue happiness and wealth equally, knowing at the same time that there will always be the rich side by side with the poor — the energetic alongside the lethargic — the intelligent next to the stupid — the industrious shoulder to shoulder with the idle — the gifted and the talented compared to the common — the beautiful to the beholder complimenting the ugly. Yet all must be judged equally in every way before this law where there are none who have special privilege or opportunity over others in any way, at any place or at any time.

And this, aside from the convoluted manner that would be needed to necessarily select a tailor-made deterrence imbued for the purpose of meting out measures for improvising impositions equally to each guilty individual in a totally unequal social phenomenon where truly nobody is actually equal to one another. Aristotles (our *pilgrim* noted) hadn't immediately provided any kind of restorative algorithm to this problem; at least not on this side of his slick and snazzy smarty-pants quip that was all about being the noblest and the most just of animals — had he?

As the *traveller* journeyed thoughtfully on his way the live-long day, he suddenly recalled the days of old when the shaking of the harnesses — that yoked the chariot steeds side by side — rose and fell until the thoroughfares drew dim and all the ways grew shady and dark. Now, with much more ease he handled the horses of the machine with gears via pedals, levers and handlebars; as for the day's shady dark, well that was now still pulled back from the sunny blue skies overhead for it was still morning. As he got on his way he adjusted himself on his seat as needed. This mode of relaxed travel gave him more viewing and sensing power and capability to have noted more closely the passing countryside in its environment than an enclosed vehicle did. He noted now that here and over there were some rare stands of tall, giant old growth trees alongside the road that towered over him as he passed by underneath upon his two wheeled chariot. Here eagles — those masters over all the prey they surveyed — had once upon a time stationed themselves. There, watching with sharp beady eyes the colour of golden corn, they had perched motionless high up among the tall stands of firs that aligned itself with the twists of the road as their sharp eyes closely surveyed the environment for rats, mice, squirrels or even marmots that moved and passed by beneath them. Occasionally, the *wayfarer* felt the whoosh of cool air as he passed by and over cold rushing streams and alongside weeping rocks and flows of waterfalls of gushing white that flushed out cold air that momentarily engulfed him.

But as to that original purpose of the road, he assumed it was for better accessibility to and from a farm somewhere with a manageable milk and honey land of healthy yet awkward and crafty smiling folks connecting to an urban or central market somewhere else down the road like *Joe* City that once thronged with oodles of pampered poodles whose disposition (quite different from *Joe* Countryside) was, by comparison (and persuasion), smooth, swank and slick. The folks there, unlike the former, felt quite entitled. Both of these communal endeavours, now either empty and hollow, had first languished and then disappeared into the misty annals of history that carelessness and neglect that had not bothered to be properly recorded in any way, was to eventually become recycled. Recycle was the name of the game back at Big Feverish Beaver Joe's un-bothered and out-of-the-way run-down garage and filling/service station back down the road a piece as far as yesterday.

The wayward traveller then fondly recalled the pink and baby-blue neon *OPEN* sign plastered against Beaver Joe's steamy, condensate saturated window panes of the one and only café in miles at this wood-chuck junction where he considered himself lucky to have been able to fill his single tank (and his strapped on pillion-style, red battered up old jerry-can) with gas. Either way, the *pilgrim* couldn't tell where he was at the moment. Who can? There were no road signs, and there were no signs either of the road having any amenities either now or once upon a time, no gas stations or restaurants, no nothin'. There hadn't even been a hotel, ever. Or so it seemed, for none of these facilities were seen lying abandoned and collapsing into the forest or the soil in ruinous decay anywhere along side this old road.

It was questionable whether the excavators of this road (those men of long ago) had followed the route of least resistance as they toiled to push the road forward and through. Some said they did this by starting at either one end or the other and pushed it through to its end. Another idea was that it began simultaneously from both its ends and two sets of engineers and excavators moved forward towards each other to meet somewhere in these coastal mountains in the middle. The *pilgrim* supposed the latter was likely, otherwise, he reasoned, they would have settled on an altitude mean and just burrowed straight through the mountains and spanned the gulches and ravines keeping all of it on the level. But they could have done both. He was glad, however, that they had decided to dip and dive and wind around even though he knew he was running low on benzene fuelled gas. The agents, operators, and practitioners of work who built this highway, intended it for those who travelled back then in the idea trend of that time. It was an era whose idea was of hard, unrelenting work from dawn until dusk where jolly good fun was communal, consensual as well as collective. The old school knew of no other. They were pioneers of policy, not necessarily for economical and manageable budgeted construction, or with an expedient land use in mind, either. Why bother with that? There was nothing but land lying around all over the place. Just cast your eyes down and around and have a gander, you can't miss it, though many do.

This winding road he travelled on was all he ever had or ever will have: or so it seemed, he thought. That is at least how he saw it. It was old (this road) and seldom (if ever) used any more, but it gave him a sense of security, even nostalgia and therefore it was a comfort road. Unfortunately, he had no comfort food to go with it; no ham and cheese sandwich in the pocket of his black leather-riding jacket. Today it was his road alone and (like everybody else) it was the only road he would ever take. That's what he thought, though most were in denial of even that, for they didn't understand the power of free will to be able to reason out choices for themselves that came from deep within that thinks itself into being.

Sitting astride his own in lined two wheeled chariot, watching, feeling, and inhaling the presence of the region in these parts as his pilgrimage unfolded before and around him, the *traveller* took notice of the unfolding reel of motion, as a part of (and parcel to) the phenomenon ahead as he motored blithely among it. He noted the area might give one the impression of open space. This was due to the fact that he was not in a box chariot but on a motorized bi-cycle. But the aforementioned effect described might also have been caused by the expansive sky, even though he was somewhat hemmed in by glaring and shiny stone faces that slanted upward with lofty cliffs of rock shining in the clear morning sunlight. Off from his right handlebar the land rose to a height above him much higher than it did on his left, but both were topped with bright green crusts of sepia-like deciduous and evergreen forests. Also, there, among the select sentinels of Douglas fir and yellow cedar he would spy gigantic whitened snags that were left overs from the old growth. These were the long limbering and denuded trunks and branches that appeared to him suddenly like long shanked lengths of whitened bones sticking out of the forest tops. As for the eagles and osprey that used to perch there, they existed here no longer. In any event, he saw none, just as he knew he wouldn't. It seemed that the only movement in the sky over the past few days had been the fast and noisy large helicopters controlled by agents of National Security. They filled the air with nitty-gritty bluster, turbulence and noise as they travelled at great speeds; appearing suddenly over hilltops they wobbled and warbled the air and shook the green forest canopies into pieces of flying bits. Instead of Cooper's and Northern goshawk, Bald eagle and White-tailed kite, it was now all Bell, Sikorsky and the giant Mi-26. He hadn't seen any of these in the last day and a half, though. Was he clear now? he wondered.

Soon these towering foliage and the crusts of the earth were being pushed further and further apart by the broadening and blueing sky above. But as the road was precarious, he dared not make any rash haste to speed up the space/time cycles of motion perception that ceaselessly unfolded endlessly before and around him now, at least not until the allotment of the here and now ended; though where and when that will be, no body he knew, knew.

As he motored across the road's rough and (in some places) broken surface, it took him through a winding journey of uneven terrain that had once, long before, been blasted out of the rugged lie of the land. This somewhat minor and superfluous change to the general countryside had come quickly and was abruptly terminated with exceedingly short sightedness. Natural change, on the other hand, generally comes ever so slowly and he could now see that it had left remnants of long ago that was washed up, lifted up and left over along the wayside all around him. But even natural change at a glacial pace isn't cast in granite, he had long before discovered. Glaciers, when they had been around, had had unknown multiple speeds once they were geared up and running madly in and out of existence as they were want to do over the eons. As all *hombres, pilgrims, companeros* and sundry *wayfaring comrades of life* do, he too hoped he was hurtling impetuously toward a moment of truth where time stood still and the beautiful were manifest — totally.

As to the road that the wayfarer navigated on this day, agents, operators, and practitioners of subsequent after-market travel never used it anymore. This was because long ago they had begun to use a newer highway. The part of the road that his journey took him on had been abandoned for a hundred years from public use. It had served more recently as a utility access for those local farmer's John Deere tractors and Mack trucks. It's purpose had become to access the silos and barns of the scattered rural domiciles' back forty. It was also used by the occasional unidentified (and unlicensed) off-road vehicles driven by disassociated, very reckless, deliriously madding recreational fun seekers. By the time that the light of current day shone down on these latter mentioned fun-bathers-in-the-sun on noisy dirt bikes, carousing buggies and hot chopped road hogs, this road had already grown to be ancient.

As for the question as to where the terminals for this crumbling concrete ribbon — this old chariot track upon which he was riding — were positioned, he could not say, a t least not for sure. He believed with all his might that this rough ribbon of road was bringing him closer to the flow of the Sto:lo River and the Bountiful Valley of his destination. That was all he allowed himself to believe for now. Still (he reminded himself), he might not yet be able to get there from here. No, he knew he wasn't out of the bush (woods, if you're a urbanite, and hadn't been properly introduced to the normal, unregimented group of trees that naturally cover Mother Earth) just yet, he decided. At that moment he then made a slight and conscious adjustment correction to his attitude. The more he did that, he found, the better equipped he was for life.

Something reminded the *traveller* just then to look down at the lens of his odometer. He was a wee bit uptight under the circumstances now for he had to carefully watch his speed. And it wasn't just because of the broken surface of the old road, either. It was because he was almost out of the benzene induced petroleum *gasoline* that kept his chariot on the move and upright. Soon it would sputter and quit on him, he knew that. And he was getting too old to walk any distance now. He then checked the time on his handy chronological mechanism on his wrist. At that moment, and for once, he was not being distracted outside the moment, although, he had to admit that he was accustomed to letting his mind wander. But at this moment (anyway) he was presently in the game and knew that he must stay alert and to keep an eye out (as they say).

With the security of a guess he reckoned then and there that he was making good time in the pursuit of his mission. Unfortunately, he had forgotten that he was actually unsure of just how much further he still had to go; not realizing at the time that that oversight turned his carefully calculated reckoning of estimated time of arrival (ETA) into something that was nothing less than sheer nonsense.

(The long and winding comfort road)

'I'm hurt but I'm not slain. I shall rest awhile and bleed a little. Then I shall rise up and fight again.'
ANDREW BARTON (MARINE PRIVATEER)

When agents, operators, and practitioners of subsequent travel later stopped using this road they had to for the newer world drove faster chariots powered with bigger infernal combustion engines. Some were fit-out with internal ignition and some with compression ignition engines that guzzled great quantities of refined fossilized crude oil fuel having further undergone catalytic reforming with an enhanced benzene pick-me-up. Fossilized fuel (the *voyager* reflected now) had been a godsend. It had saved the whales — at least for a short time. He believed that they were all extinct now. But way back a long time ago when the precious oil called triglyceride that was at a premium was being extracted from their blubbery bodies at industrial speed and a world wide scope, their tenability was in jeopardy. Being an ester (chemical compound) derived from glycerol, which couldn't be readily synthesized at the time, this compound which the whales' bodies produced naturally had been a prime element to smooth the way for a deranged civilization to use fellow mammals as a source of energy to light their streets in the great cities of their civilization. But this would last only so long as the whale species themselves held out, and according to grown-up reasoning that time-line was a fast shortening fuse. This oil was far from being the only source to light man's way in the dark during most of this time, but this choice to eliminate the whale mammal, those graceful, highly intelligent giants of the deep (without thought or notice) sounded the death-knell toward extinction for millions of sentient beings of one kind or another that belonged to the animal kingdom of Mother Good-Earth. So, you see, the invention of the infernal internal combustion engine then saved the whales from extinction in the nick of space/time, but delayed it only just for a little short period, which is what a nick is.

Who was it, the *pilgrim* wondered, who said that 'when the whales become extinct, of any consequence, we're next?'

But the reprieve of the whale slaughter soon became bitter sweet. Once an elementary petrochemical innate to crude oil called tetraethyl lead (an octane booster which helped to cause a knock less increase in engine compression) was added to the benzene, all hell broke loose. Soon airborne worldwide, this deadly lead molecule spread quickly across all the lands and seas of the Good-Earth to be absorbed therein so as to begin its resident invisible and silent poisoning of all life, especially mammals like whales, and us. Research had informed this *hombre* that certain human insanity and attitudes of senseless violence that once spiked within our society has now been attributed to coincide with this particular time frame beginning with the silent lead poisoning of all gentle animals. This deadly and colourless plague was once referred to briefly as an *Esso-sorr-ic* demon. It was a hoax, some said. Litigation quickly confirmed the hoax viewed through one shaft of light and falsified it as a hoax through another. All the while at that time (and only for awhile) court rulings acted as a sentinel guarding that and other monstrous infringements that continued nevertheless to be imposed and forced upon unsuspecting beings at large that live on planet good-earth. Just as with the destruction of animal life, such as those giants of the deep, the specifically privileged and entitled folks who ran the 'industry for profit' and benefited financial (and in no other way) by the mass tetraethyl lead-ing of a benzene poisoning act upon the all unwashed and unsuspecting, weren't sorry about it in the least. And never was there a scrap of repentance or remorse present in these individuals whatsoever, either for their shameless performance as a pathetic and disgusting human being or for the impending doom this caused for the trillions of bits of life that suffered due to this careless and reckless act.

Certainly Big Crude Inc.'s chief executive officer's fake front person, a certain Ethel Purpleopolous (a sister-in-law of the oligarch Hipparchia Philostropodousalouspolousadous and divorcee of the latter's brother, a certain Potamus Iapetus Purplebal, who was the founder and the real controlling agent of Big Crude) and its leading scientist Smidge Thomas Pennyweight, were the persons responsible for developing and patenting the poisonous chemical process that disseminated fearful harm. And this was accomplished by them before anyone else did (or could stop them). And as a result, a marked increase in senseless violence, madness, and irreversible psychological world insanity over and above the already obvious and natural hard-wired insanity of homo-sapiens [sic] (wise-hominids) quickly began to spread throughout. Obviously, everything here had become quite relative, and not for the first time. It appeared to be part of the dumbing down of humanity-plan that the Haploids were implementing.

But the folks during the time of the fun-in-the-sun-at-play-seekers in their trendy synthetic silk worm cocoon attire, along with (even, surprisingly) the John Deere and Mack driving farmers who wore caterpillar caps (or brimmed straw hay-seed sun-hats) whose big rough hands were usually clad (and glad) in light tan pig skin work gloves, no longer lived in a world of the old era of hard, unrelenting toil that lasted from dawn till dusk where jolly good fun was clean, consensual, and communally collective. Many of the latter still had a synthetic form of individualism even though they were absolutely and fully conditioned in the Haploid program that had existed BTEL (**b**efore **te**traethyl **l**ead). Now they slowly succumbed to this new development as the poison from the leaden tetraethyl lead first numbed and then rotted their brain in a fever of hatred for others and themselves and were in a mind for total self destruction and suicide faster than a football quarterback or hockey defenseman.

The *comrade of life* then let out a laugh as he let one of his leather bound arms drop from the handle grip to his side and then up onto his bent knee where he rested it. He drifted slightly, still deep within his mind, thinking now of his old opponent Wittgenstein from back in his reason-fencing days where they exercised their wits in the Wren library at Trinity College or at his own digs across the river at St. John's College. He then suddenly remembered an anecdote from long ago. The aforementioned Wittgenstein (pronounced here as Vit-gun-schtein) and he were once travelling together across rural Hungary and as they motored along in their luxuriously appointed rental chariot, the strangely precise philosopher (who the *pilgrim* had all along thought displayed no sense of humour whatsoever) said to him:

"Zo, led mi sey, mine dear Herr: — did you hear uff zee free men; one, zee mathematician, two, zee physicist, und free zee engineer? Vonce vile travelling just like uz in zee chariot, upon seeing seven vite svans in profile a-svimming in zee nearby pond, zee mathematician sez — 'look, it would appear dat zee svans in ziss country, zey are all vite in colour.' But zen zee physicist sez — 'correction mine Herr Mathematician, pleece. Uff all zee svans zat are in ziss country, I can zee only seven zat are vite.' Zen zee engineer looks around and ee sez — 'my dear Herr; another correction, pleece! I vould sey zat in dis country zare are certainly seven svans zat are vite, at least on vone side.'

At that alarming turn of internal events, the *pilgrim* jerked awake and turned his mind back to the codex of law which his friend and mentor, Dyfed Lucifer had drummed into his head, for no good reason, he supposed. For by his definition the occurrence of being ignoble must exist only within the human subsidiary of the ego. And despite being cloaked in the phenomenon of obscurity, ignobility appears nevertheless to unfold in a collateral continuum of cause and effect which is sadly all too real to the beholder though unnecessarily and needlessly so. Indeed, the universal axioms of all sanctimonious and corrective governing ideologies are founded on subsidiary laws and dependant on the ego and those beholders thereof: 'it's a laughable state which humans find themselves in, eh'? He then heard (once more) Wittgenstein's dirty, ragged laugh.

Earlier, the cool morning sun had thrown long tree shadows across the *pilgrim's* path that broke up the pattern of the road's deteriorating rough surface texture that was grainy like crumbs of bread. Dissident and dangerous weeds along with sharp grasses grew upward and cracked and split open the pavement now. They reached up from beneath the travelling *hombre* as he passed gently over them at a slowing pace. In places the pavement was broken right open and where once the bright paint of the smooth road surface markings were solid and shiny in white and yellow, now they were badly peeling and broken into separated shards over a surface that was crumbling like a layer of stale old cake or slices of pear on rolled out pastry. Here the enlightened *traveller* slowed down his pace a tad.

At his reduced speed he now noted that the sound of his side-valve (flathead) engine was throaty and commanding as it shot out sharp cuffs and clips of metallic sounding tiffs and phats amid its general throat-clearing rumble. This sound seemed to be reverberating all around him and bouncing off the shiny cliffs. He listened eagerly for any discrepancies of sound as the noisy vibration poured out from his engine. He noticed, too, that the tree shadows that had before been thrown across his path had now shrunk into stubbies as the sun-rays cascaded through the clear, pine scented air clearing the shoulder of a rocky crag and had climbed higher into the blue sky. He looked upon the brilliance of the lit up tippy-tops of Good Mother Earth's forested mantle and marvelled to have so recently emerged and escaped from the pit of hell dug deep into the desolation of the cool, arid Atacama Desert to find himself back here again, at last. Later, the flat dark silhouette shadow of himself and his motorized chariot became distorted and shorter and he felt more heat from the sun and from the earth beneath as the road suddenly rocked and rolled in his path. He swerved and weaved deliberately and without haste to avoid pot-holes and sluffs of fallen rocks that lay motionless and apart that were mostly scattered on just one side of the road or the other. Then he noticed that off from his left handlebar the giant and earthy forest was beginning to tumble and drop away as the sun-hot blue sky won out on the pushing match.

Suddenly the scraggly forested bush and low roadside brush fled and scattered like deer as the noisy vibrations now unrestrained and un-baffled poured out more effortlessly from his engine and out over the edge like a noisy flood of film. It reminded the *pilgrim* of a thin band of interlinking metallic and shifting waterfalls cascading down through the broken forest. It was like a chain reaction that diminished the further away it got but it scattered wider the faster it fled. Before him now a panorama of vistas had opened up. This enabled this *wayfaring comrade of life* to scan the wide panorama with his naked but goggle protected eye.

'My destination,' he said calmly to himself with some relief, 'is at hand, by George!' He heavily accented the last two words so that the word George was almost shouted out, its echo reverberating back from sheer rocky cliff walls that thrust up beyond his right handlebar. And there, before and below him (and instantly recognizable to him) was the Bountiful Valley that had just then come into view. 'There is no hurry, now' he thought to himself as he kicked his stand out from the side and turned off the engine. Then in a one, swift but fluid motion, he swung his right leg back and over the seat and stood tall beside his iron chariot. 'There has never been any hurry', he thought to himself. Here I am! In fact at this point he was a way ahead of tomorrow and had left today far behind back into yesterday. Tomorrow (as always) was now all that mattered, be-it the next artificial time change (a second or a minute, or a single rotation of the earth on it axis, or its revolution around Sol, King of Radiance every 365.25 earth rotations, or its complete axial precession of twenty-five thousand, eight hundred years) or (for the old believers) a summons from Azrael to the reckoning.

Currently the *companion* felt he was well placed and was pleased for feeling it. Now he could just wait for tomorrow to catch up. Everybody in the world at that moment was a few euphoria behind, anyway, he thought as he took a hand sized flask out of a pocket of his black leather jacket. Then unscrewing the lid he lifted it to his lips to take a short swig. And as for tomorrow, the mission (to which he was presently attending) would begin to come to its final completion. It was the beginning of the end.

It had been a mission (one that the *wayfarer* had chosen to accept many moons ago) that had also been initiated by his mentor and alter ego, Dyfed Lucifer. And tomorrow, apart from its embarkation and undertaking, was the only properly scheduled day he had had at any time since his mentor's mysterious but expected disappearance. And, as far as the *traveller* knew (from the extent of his long and knowledgeable past) tomorrow may also be his last scheduled day ever. This, however, had nothing to do with whether or not he might be suddenly and correctly identified as a felon by the authority of the world government's new order for breathing and getting on with his life without the necessary permits to do so, and therefore may and probably would be subject (at any time) to being seized and put into leg and hand irons. In truth the established order no longer needed that much of an excuse anymore to do any such thing, anyway. Either way, his scheduled days like any other *pilgrim companero hombre* were numbered. That much he knew for sure. And that's why it wasn't all coming to a close any time too soon. Once the great mammals of the sea became entrenched toward extinction, we're next. He remembered Dyfed said that to him once. And as far as those great mammals went, most of them had already gone the way of the dodo, the great auk and the passenger pigeon.

He removed his long wide riding gloves and his clear goggles, he pulled out and put on his shaded seeing-eye glasses. He removed his black leather all weather riding jacket and flung it over the motorcycle's seat. The weather was hot and still (and even hotter still now that he wasn't moving). He remained perfectly still beside his motorized chariot and looked around with his strangely alert, roaming silver eyes. The morning air was filled with the fragrance of late June and smell of his hot engine. Then with a single and sudden involuntary motion he breathed in the heavy thick air and caught a whiff of wild petunias that were growing amuck among the trees.

PART ONE

THE
FIEST
EMPIRE

(Dyfed, Prince of the Grove and of the Isle of Peace)

'Life's but a walking shadow, a poor player that struts and frets his hour upon the stage, and then is heard no more; it is a tale told by an idiot, full of sound and fury, signifying nothing.'
WILLIAM SHAKESPEARE *(MACBETH)*

It was said once, somewhere, that at the moment of Dyfed's birth to Queen Chloris Violet-Eye on the Isle of Peace, a vast wedge of migrating White Fronted geese (Anser albifrons) that had been nesting on a nearby sea marsh, lifted off to catch the first rays of golden Aurora (Dawn). In allowing the warming air heated by Radiance to expand under their wings for lift, the geese had risen high in the air by circling the isle five times to gain enough height to achieve their accustomed migration altitude. From here they disappeared above and beyond a sparkling coloured veil of fog that had recently been fabricated by a Master wizard to cordon off this blessed Isle from outside sight. This veil was the handy work of a magician named Lord Huge. This misty curtain around the Isle of Peace was in accordance to an ordinance from this enclave's chief administrator, a certain Master Manandan whose wish had been to cordon it off from the mounting eyes of prying and intrusive aliens. This was the word he used to refer to the common hoi polloi. But these particular eyes now also belonged to strangely adapted and resourceful sailors who began to ply these waters. And their presence was increasing upon the seas hereabouts. Manandan's intention had been to provide protection and security for the queen and her soon to be born prince from these suspicious foreigners. For it was their (his and the queen's) opinion that they (those foreign sea-going aliens) would bring nasty habits and frightfully ridiculous tales and hyperbole to the quietude of this luxurious resort whose initial function was for dimension travelling masters who wanted no more than to be free of bothering phenomenon other than what they sign up for. This resort (which was organized and operated by Manandan) had (quite recently) verily just begun to thrive around their newly arrived queen.

Chloris Violet-Eye had just arrived here at the invitation of Manandan. Already with child at the time of her arrival, apparently she had refused to give up the child to birth until she happened upon a place where she felt secure from the strange and dangerous world that un-expectantly had caught up and overtaken her. Her vizier and chief functionary (up until then) had been the aforementioned magician Lord Huge, the fabricator of rainbows and other marvels. But when she arrived un-expectantly as Manandan's guest, accompanied by her own vizier Lord Huge along with a hundred and eight attendants, Manandan the surprised host had immediately set down conditions for their residence here. He requested Lord Huge then to fashion in any way he felt fit, by any uncompromising mode of employ imaginable, a manner to secure the isle from unwanted visitors. In addition to that, Huge was to allow Master Manandan to supplant him in his role of the queen's chief functionary. This would allow him to take charge over her future son's education as well, which is what he had wanted.

The isle's council of senior Masters who met only once a year on the first Thursday after the first full moon following the vernal equinox, supported Master Manandan (the Chief Sage in residence) with an uproarious — so mote it be. After Lord Huge had agreed to the terms he set to and plied his art of conjure. Quickly he succeeded in fashioning a magical contraption that was in the form of a miraculous rainbow veil that formed a ring that totally obscured the Isle. Seen from the sea outside this veil, even light was reflected. Feeling secure and comfortable Queen Chloris Violet-Eye made ready to give birth.

These events all happened during the later stage of the fifth and final age. This was the Age of Pentangle whose current sector's mineral was of Iron. This had followed the sector of Tin (later referred to as Bronze. It was during this time that the hoi polloi, those humanoid and sentient beings that now existed on earth in the world of our narrative, had finally become utterly destitute, their ideas and their security from domination by others were now totally bankrupt. And it was into this same space/time (age), just when the race of third dimensional humanoid homo-sapiens were seething in unawareness in a mad and ravenous manner, that our hero Dyfed H. Lucifer was born to Queen Violet-Eye. Seemingly by happenstance (though truthfully by contrivance), only two hours after Violet had consented and the child she bore had been issued forth, two men in a coracle (having miraculously pierced the curtained veil, notwithstanding) were seen approaching the isle.

These two visitors were a certain King Pel, a fellow of the Kornovi folks, and his nephew, Prince Penrhyn, a long time administrator of the tin mines of the Dunmonii, and quite understandably they were quickly met on the beach by an alert and non-assuming Manandan and the rather perplexed and embarrassed Lord Huge (his good works, apparently, having failed). After learning that the two arrivals had come from afar to pay their respects and give homage to Queen Violet-Eye and her expectant son, Manandan told them that the child had been born just that same day at the hour when the geese had up and flown away on their migration north. As for the queen, she was still in confinement. The four of them, however, traipsed up the hill anyway to Violet's superb mansion set upon the ridge that had only just been completed and smelled of newly sealed marble, fresh cedar with much of the gleaming decoration paint still tacky upon the bric-a-brac. Indeed, outside in the not yet readied gardens, men in white overalls wearing yellow gloves were cleaning up and carting odds and ends, along with sawn off bits and left over pieces away to get Ugly and Clutter out of sight. On her part (upon hearing of the situation) Violet-Eye, in taking advantage of the excuse, immediately terminated her unnecessary confinement on the spot and granted the welcomed new arrivals a very punctual audience.

Much to Lord Huge's relief from embarrassment these folks who had just arrived (it turned out) were kindred spirits to those who safeguarded the resort on the Isle of Peace. Like the latter they too were masters and sages as sophisticated and polished as Manandan and Violet-Eye. And like the latter, they too brooked no truck with the likes of rough and roundish ashlars, common among the hoi polloi that were un-necessarily being pegged into square holes. When ushered in to her presence the new comers told the queen that they had arrived via the Emerald Isle to the west in a round about way from the land of Dyfed on the big island of Albion to the east. And they had come, they said, intent on serving her and to pledge allegiance and support for her child that they had learned was soon to be born to her here in the third dimension. This, they all knew, was indeed a very rare thing now a day.

They noted that she was looking radiant in young motherhood and both the king and the prince gazed fondly at her and the newly born child at her breast. Their timing had been impeccable, she told them. The prince then brought up the news of the queen's estranged brother, Daceneus. Apparently, having escaped death on numerous occasions (mostly from his own suffering and most miserably stricken citizens in the land of Dobruja), he was dead now of plague, along with his entire host at Munster, on the Emerald Isle to where he had fled. His death had been a boon to the Gangani of Leinster who, they told her, had been harried by her estranged brother. Surprised that he had even journeyed there, the queen was then told that Daceneus had sought that most westerly of lands to hide as far from their home in Dobruja (which lay between the river Dana and the Kara Sea that bordered Asia) and from the atrocities he had committed there. It was an uncomfortable subject and everyone knew anyway that she loathed her heretical brother.

King Pel then told her that they had been directed to the newly hidden Isle of Peace by a flourishing oracle that had been operating for some time in the land of the Republic of Dyfed that was run by sages and magicians and ruled over a sizable population of house-broken (and relatively well mannered) hoi polloi. The oracle sages were also part of the committee that ran the resort in that land. It was a resort that paralleled the one here on the Isle of Peace and was well known to folks like Manandan. This aforementioned oracle that was the centre of that tiny, self-administering state resort known as the Republic of Dyfed was on the tip of one of Albion's most westerly fingers of land. The difference between the Republic of Dyfed and the Isle of Peace resort was that Manandan prohibited any and all oracles to be opened here on the Isle of Peace. To Manandan oracles were a thing of the past and were paramount to primitive superstition, one of the diseases that had brought the hoi polloi to rack and ruin to begin with, in the present day.

The Republic of Dyfed was (as the crow flies) the land of Albion's closest colony to the Emerald Isle. And it was just over three degrees latitude south from the Isle of Peace that (with favourable winds) was a good day's sail. Anyway, the oracle there, they said, had delivered news of a Hyperborean man child about to be born to the revered Queen Violet-Eye, mistress of the Little Known Universe, and was rumoured to have been fathered by Apollo (another Hyperborean master) although one master thought it had been Herakles. And even if she didn't remember, they pretended she did. Anyway, it was on account of the name of the land from whence these two wise men had set out that Queen Violet-Eye had right there — Johnny of the spot — then given her new-born son the name Dyfed.

Dyfed started his adventure in the dazzling sunshine on the Isle of Peace, a land of once upon a time that was far away (though maybe not far enough) and set among the Emerald Sea. Here, upon this isle's promontories and along its warm sandy beaches, Dyfed began his life. He dipped and dived among the foam in the many sun-basked coves while the surf rolled in on white sea stags from the great blue and beyond. In the summer mornings he would roll his young supple form over the shiny white granules of sand in the hot sun, then later — with sparkling beach grit still clinging to his drying body — he might leisurely pick his little barefoot way through the forests and glens that smelled of tarragon, cedar, or pine as he wended his way back up toward his mother's shining white palace on the hill.

This luxurious abode — this eloquent sanctum sanctorum — fashioned together with love and harmony on a wide ridge of the hill that overlooked the sea, glistened and shone forth between its surrounding flora for all to see; even to the edge of the miraculous mist which, due to jolly bad luck and other evil portents, was about to become (and go) askew in Dyfed's youth. No longer, therefore, would it curtain this isle off from passing mariners at sea.

In the summer Dyfed's isle was a haven of heat with a sea breeze where sudden deluges occasionally slaked the thirsty earth. In that season the hot thick air was choked with fragrance and hummed with bird songs; that — as well as with the heady buzz of bees and other swarming insects as the warm salty zephyrs bent the long blades of grass along the brightly coloured hillsides. Just before the start of the cooler seasons, when the petals dropped and all the seed had blown; when the yellowy brown willow and the crispy oak leaves had begun to float to the ground in their zig zag course to be blown against the hedges of green laurel and mistletoe, dense flocks of Whooper swans (Cygnus) would begin to darkened the autumn sun with their arrival here from the far north in the land of ice. But here, on the Isle of Peace, the climate remained gentle. Elsewhere, just beyond this isle, when seasonal tempests blew and brought snow and sleet, here a soft rain fell. Elsewhere, where fog and drizzle dulled the brightness all around, or the sharp teeth of frosty winds bit and gnawed at the knuckles of the hand and the cheeks of the face, here the slanted sun-rays sparkled off the mild dampness, and balmy winds buffeted puffy tan coloured clouds that lit up with the sun as they slowly drifted across a light blue sky.

Later when Dyfed left his daytime play and his beachcombing in order to attend to his tutoring, he would walk out past the scented baths and through the terraced garden which were part of his mother's palatial mansion, and into the new morning. Here he walked alone and saw no one, for the grazing pastures for the cattle and sheep, the orchards and the tidy fields of wheat that were all attended by the queen's farmers and shepherds, remained some distance from the main dwelling, while the gardeners — who fussed with the vegetable plots and beds of fuchsias, worked within the nursery walls below the palace which looked back out over the sea.

Dyfed's passage to the tutorage would take him out through the gates of the twin lions and down the broad, golden brick road to the terminal at its far end that encompassed the entrance to Master Manandan's sanctuary. This enchanted spot enclosed this venerable old Sage's famous library, medicinal plot and arboretum. Manandan by now had become the boy's master tutor, and with the recent absence of Lord Huge, who had handed in his resignation and exiled himself from the Isle of Peace for the Orcadia archipelago in disgrace, Manandan (aside from being Queen Violet's chamberlain) had also become Queen Violet's sole mentor.

Although no other individual influenced young Dyfed more than Manandan, the youngster's prime benefactor was his mother. It was she who had quickened his essence and given him form. An almost divine yet pious figure, it was from Violet that Dyfed had received his distinguished looks and mark of inheritance as well as his finite moorings here upon the eternity of phenomenon's restless surface. A tall lithe woman, with milk white skin and hair the colour of the setting sun that tumbled in ringlets to her navel, Violet enjoyed the bounty of nature viewed through her beautiful, silvery, aquamarine eyes. She shunned the sedentary life of city-state. That state of affairs, she thought, brought out the foibles of blemish upon the human race and the destructive spoils of society about which she remained forever suspicious.

Dyfed would stroll on through passed the marble colonnade and enter Manandan's spacious tutelage that was part of his palace. This was the centre of his partitioned portion of the surrounding villa. It was extent, and though he and Violet lived in separate palaces, the short and steep driveway of yellow brick attached them. Both villas overlooked the resort's main ensemble. Through the large floor to ceiling windows of Manandan's tutorage Dyfed regularly acknowledged Golden Radiance whose chariot by this time of the morning had climbed into the sky and was now shining down upon a silver sea that lay beyond. Aside from the visual rays of Radiance, the audacious screech of gulls (family Laridae) and terns (related — subfamily Sterninae) permeated the silence as they swooped about in the warming air.

Manandan, a Hyperborean master, would soon appear. He was an imposing figure, tall and exalted and despite his age — which was very old — he retained a great physical strength. In addition, he bore enormous practical and intellectual skills that were well beyond the ordinary masters of the Little Known Universe, never mind those of the hoi polloi. In general there was about him a sense of magical power and a noble aura. Manandan spoke slowly and surprisingly softly for such an assertive individual. He was never haltering and could embark upon a lengthy discourse without faltering or becoming hesitant. With the utmost ease, he managed to proceed along a logical and progressive vein of thought, and it mattered little just how in depth the subject became, for he was able to lead it to a conclusion that would entertain and entirely enlighten all his listeners whether they be young, old, ignorant or profound, all sitting together side by side. He was a remarkable man and over an extremely lengthy lifespan Manandan had absorbed and retained knowledge in such a way that he was able to dispense it verbally in a concise, uncluttered manner which never failed to leave its mark upon his pupils or any other audient. His oratorical skills — able to be delivered in any number of tongues known to folks of two separate dimensions — were legend among his people (of which Dyfed, too, was considered one). And it was these skills and Manandan's vast knowledge that Dyfed was now being suffered to absorb.

Although Manandan's complexion was dark, he had silver eyes like his young pupil that were kind and understanding. Customarily, he dressed in the finest silks and linens and wore a flat tork in the shape of a disc around his neck that lit up and radiated the colours of the rainbow. His silvery, long wavy hair was well groomed and the thick strands that swept forward from his crown framed a smooth, almost sea blue brow. Although precious jewels (set in gobs of rich yellow gold) bedecked his silver locks, glittered among the folds of his cloak, and glistened upon his fingers, this timeless archetype of benevolence, this epitome of rumination and civility, had no use for wealth in the vulgar sense. It was Manandan's style and poise that captured the essence of what his person was all about, not his appearance. His style was a harmony and stability that was in a cosmic rhythm of order. He did not need any pretence nor any obtrusive display for glorification.

Dyfed had been a good student, inquisitive and bold as Manandan was approachable and understanding. He studied the natural philosophies, music and mathematics, geometry, metrology and applied mechanics of the cosmos kind before graduating into physics proper and universal plasmatic. Although he showed little inclination for the medicinal sciences that Manandan would have preferred, Dyfed loved the natural science which dealt with everything from the natural study of animals to natural philosophy. He studied metrology, astrology, archeo-astronomy, physics, music, mathematics and philosophy. He also studied communication, though he was never able to communicate with animals in quite the same marvellous way that Manandan was able.

But the main branch of the eternal, non-differentiated natural philosophy (which his master called 'Web of the Fates — the Past, Present and Future') was (under the circumstances) the area in which Dyfed would have done well to solicit for more improvement. Manandan could easily give of himself, but ultimately, cognizance in this rested squarely upon Dyfed's shoulders.

The web of the Fates was Manandan's terminology for the personal and collective state of man in relationship to himself and, as such, to each other in the historical and sociological sense. The Past, Present and Future, he taught, was synonymous with the three spheres of being that live side by side at the same time no matter where or when man is, other than in the fifth dimension. And that is just the beginning. Those of the so-called Past, he said many times, who are called the dead and live beneath the so-called mortals of the Present, who in turn live beneath the gods of the Future, are constant with the future. This becomes quite plain when one realizes that the present and the future are necessary for the past's fulfilment just as the past and the present are necessary for the fulfilment of the future. Each must remain in tune and in proportion with their two counterparts for any form of manifestation to occur. In another words, they rely on each other. If this condition should deteriorate, chaos will ensue at number of levels within the dimension. This is aside from the normalcy caused by the gods of Entropy This former condition is quite serious, and something of which humans in the third dimension of today should be cognitive. Without the right balance of harmony across the board, the third dimension could collapse. It was that simple. Harmony in this case is a perception. Without perception observation will not take place. And without observation, phenomenon will not exist for phenomena can't exist without being observed. There cannot be a universe without observers (obviously visa versa, although that point is moot). No observer, no universe, it's that simple. So, wherever and whatever you are you want perception in order to observe, even if you are alone in your own personal universe. It certainly beats the alternative. In the latter our embattled narrator was certainly on track.

History, Manandan further taught, was the residue (the web), that the Fates left in its trail, and at the same time cast in its path. It's a Zen thing that's supported mathematically, though once explained simply and in more detail by the monk Bodhidharma. Manandan therefore taught that history was equally present in the future in a similar sense that it was present in the past. History was absolute truth and the only alternative was fantasy. Fantasy was non-substantial and irrelevant nonsense, but it was also dangerous, too. Normally, fantasy is history's stand-in. In any case, as history (time) was equally present in the future and past (time) as it was in the moment, future history (time) was, therefore, inextricably fixed to that quasi landscape that humanity had already passed through during the first four worlds, just as history from those past worlds was fixed to those remaining in the future. These four worlds were actually four races of men who populated those worlds: the Golden race, the Silver race, the Bronze race, and the Iron race. Normally, a conceived chronological order does not work well here: so the reader will have to emblemize.

These races and their worlds took place irrespective of the lies believed by the majority of humanity who now fill history and file their own (think) content inscribed in the Universal Repository of Annals and Lists under the heading of 'the World's Chronological and Sacred past'. All of these lies have had (and continue to have) an indelible effect that caused (and continues to cause) further damaging effects in the substance of fantasy, just as truths do but in a much different way. These lies were introduced in two ways, Manandan told young Dyfed. One was a fantasy tale of events and the other was a fantasy make-believe world of fake in which folks were enticed to believe they existed in a manner in which they don't. This latter idea was caused by powerful suggestions and by manipulating the intrinsic touchstones which people use to feel the extent of the environment that surrounds them completely. Culture played a huge part in this and although Dyfed was unaware of foreign culture first hand, Manandan told him it was incomparable to anything he knew from their world. This idea of culture was caused by powerful suggestions and by manipulating the intrinsic touchstones which people used to feel the extent of the environment that surrounds them. These suggestions were referred to as mythos. The antithesis to this fantasy world was logos, though intelligent minds could work them together practically, Dyfed learned.

As far as the labyrinth of the so-called chronologically recorded historical texts, Manandan firmly told Dyfed to stay away from their agenda. Only truth mattered, he told him. Unlike falsehoods, truth needed no explanation per sé, for it was always a constant. Wood and petroleum float to the top of the sea of reality, though generally they are unobserved by the uninitiated: that as opposed to not being blatantly easy to spot.

"But in the world of the hoi polloi,' Manandan told Dyfed 'truth was almost another dimension. There was in the normal scheme of things, no such thing as truth. Truth only existed until it later became a fallacy or a lie that was relative: Even truth was relative here. Anyway, truth was certainly beyond the former's normal scope of comprehension: truth was also relegated to wine and children, not to mention fools.'

Dyfed came to write many of these words himself in order to illustrate the manner in which his master taught him to ward off the elements of disassociation, compounded — as it invariably was — with the destabilizing effect of illusion, a result of unnatural and contrary conditioning.

After the sciences, Manandan ventured to teach Dyfed about the world of men outside of their enclave there on the Isle of Peace. This was for his own benefit; for he was, after all, a son of a queen who was a Queen and a Mistress of the Hyperborean Masters of the Little Known Universe herself, and he a Prince of the Grove in his own right. This, however, entitled him to nothing in the world he saw around him now. Indeed, our young hero was quick to learn that there was quite a disconnect between his awareness and sense of presence and those ideas that helped him sketch out the phenomena at large compared to what his fellow humans outside his race discerned. Those unlucky fellows were the hoi polloi and they existed mainly outside this Isle of Peace, although some had been taken in and after being vetted and orientated, were given employment and were well treated here in the Isle of Peace resort.

"They live literally in another world to the one you sense around you,' Manandan warned Dyfed, 'despite the commonality of the phenomena in which we and they are all immersed together. And at this time, and for a long time to come, you too will be subject to that world of their making.' Manandan further explained that the outside race of men referred to a hoi polloi, were descended from those of their own ancient race. However, the ancestors of the hoi polloi had not been able to transcend beyond this dimension and become Masters as they — the Masters here today — had done long ago while the ancestors of the hoi polloi men were still hunter gathers within the Bronze Age. Dyfed, on the other hand, though he was one of the uninitiated Masters, was not one of them in the same way his mother or Manandan was.

'But you are not really one of the hoi polloi, either — exactly,' she told him. 'And since,' Manandan told him, 'we who are Masters desire to rectify the disgraceful and disastrous state of affairs among humans — namely, those hoi polloi here in this dimension — your birth here was for a purpose. But mark you! This is a dangerous mission that has been chosen for you to undertake if — in fact — you choose to comply. You aren't the first hybrid, but others have failed and were destroyed. And you must also know that you are going to be constantly in danger just like the hoi polloi whose lives are filled with remorse, suffering and misery. That is danger enough, but there is more.'

Manandan taught Dyfed that this phenomenon of the third dimension was fraught with shifting sands and illusions, but the human mind was responsible for this. Incredible as it may sound, the Great Mind, it must be stated — which is the source of all volitions within the human world and beyond — is virtually ignored, unnoticed, and unknown among the world of the third dimensional men. Yet there is nothing — not even phenomena — without it, and it governs and even controls its satellite mind, the mind of the human being. This is why there are no such thing as free will in the world of the ego, and the self ego centred. And in these present phenomena in which these hoi polloi find themselves, awareness is a conundrum, even for those most intelligent. The reason for this is the material human brain. It, too, has produced its own sense of presence — an effect of itself if you like — though it is severely disabled and atrophied compared to the Master Mind. This human brain has developed only to interpret its current phenomena in which the human imagines himself to be. It exists in a sort of insulated bubble. Communication of any kind between Master mind and Little mind is controlled one hundred per cent by the Master Mind. To reiterate: without the Master Mind there is nothing, not even phenomena. This is because without it you couldn't imagine any kind of phenomenon.

Manandan told Dyfed that the Master Mind absorbs everything that the inferior material brain perceives. However, it is capable of filtering correctly, something that the little mind is not capable of doing. The Master Mind can also withhold data from the Little Mind and it knows the Little mind completely, but not visa-versa. Indeed, because of the Little Mind's hugely diminished capabilities the Master Mind of every hoi polloi actively play tricks on its namesake. The Master Mind seems to take delight in doing this and often fools and plays around with this little brain to no en and which is like a puppet in a Punch and Judy show.

Now Manandan also talked about the Haploids of whom Dyfed must quickly become aware. To reiterate, they are ancient humanoid Homo sapiens (hoi polloi) but who are different from the Masters in that they did not graduate into advanced awareness to meld with the Master Mind, as did the Masters of the Little Known Universe. However, they do have a unique advantage over the hoi polloi. Somehow, so Manandan explained, a small faction of these undergraduates — freaks actually — did transcend (somewhat) due to some flaw or other. This gave them some limited capabilities of a higher order but they were degenerate and, for want of better terms were barren and infertile and their volitions were futile other than within the phenomenon of their own making and only for a very finite period of time. These are the Haploids. However, due to the aforementioned on-going incompetence of the gullible and illogical little mind provided by the material brain (the local host) of the hoi polloi, the Haploids (when in the same phenomena as the latter) could stump or pull the wool over the eyes of these hoi polloi with little effort. So now the hoi polloi not only had their own ill-equipped mind that generally ran the show for them in this current phenomenon, they also had the Master Mind downloading certain real factual data. This caused it some confusion. There was also the fantasy of phenomena itself to deal with. This made the hoi polloi's life here in this particular world uncomfortable and untenable in the long run. These of the Little Brain should never let their guard down too long or be inattentive to the phenomena around them lest trolls (which are actually their own lost potential) materialise out of thin air that's part and parcel of phenomena. For in that situation dangerous apparitions could quickly blend into their existence and make them suffer even more. We have given them the former name Haploid, but they are psychopaths on steroids. This was to be un fortuitous for him in his present state, for (as of yet) he had no proficiency to transcend into the security of the fifth dimension. But on his behalf they, the Masters, would help him work on that later, though it would not be easy.

There were still Haploids in the fifth dimension, Dyfed learned, but being somewhat fixed and compromised they posed no danger there that he knew of. They are only dangerous here in this world where, once returned here, they are eternally stuck and cannot return to the fifth dimension or advance anywhere else. This is the end for them.'

'Aside from Haploids there were the aforementioned trolls,' Manandan told Dyfed. 'They were a kind of material shadow, an unrealised potential which — having failed to graduate — existed only in the psyche of the subject. In this way only they were similar to Haploids but a troll is only dangerous to its own host, a specific human. When a subject encounters a troll, the troll is nothing more than themselves but is partially outside the host's dimension. But the hoi polloi don't know that. Visualising a troll is the terrifying spectre (in a moment of truth) of suddenly seeing ones' true self in an unguarded moment. Terrifying isn't an accurate word! In fact the troll is a potential that is a spin off from the Master Mind that can be very destructive to its host. Each and every sentient being we call a hoi polloi is a failed transcendent, hence the troll which is a ghost of its true self. These trolls are also a form of failed genius that, if things had panned out differently, could have had a Master Mind connection that paid out in dividends to the hoi polloi's condition — hence a Master.

Manandan explained to Dyfed that the Masters enjoy this third dimension because of its heightened sensitivity to forms and frictions. For this reason they favour its distraction for rest and recreation. "In essence,' he said, 'the habitant for the Masters who live here are basically resorts. The Isle of Peace is their capital while other satellite resorts, such as the one in the land of Dyfed (and other spots on the water/earth) are client resorts.'

Long ago they had come to notice that all humanoids were dejected and miserable beyond their ignorant state. They soon traced the reason to the hoi polloi's individual trolls; but more importantly they saw it to be the complication and co-existence of the Haploid presence. The Masters now wanted to amend this condition in favour of those poor sentient beings and to make them happy again. But that wouldn't happen they knew in a society plagued with sore anxiety and where the rolling thunders of war, the rainy skies of cultural/religions lies, and where heaps of hunger, debt, and scores of others miseries visit daily upon the human condition. 'We would right these wrongs at all costs, Dyfed,' said Manandan. 'And that's where you come in.'

Manandan further explained that due to the inferiority of the little mind that spun off the material brain of the hoi polloi, and through a long program designed to control the minds and actions of the same, the Haploids had used ingenious inventions that have proved successful. Apparently, Dyfed learned, the Haploids were the culprits who had indoctrinated the hoi polloi with what they call myths, religion and heavily edited and distorted history.

Dyfed came to write many of these words himself in order to illustrate the manner in which his master taught him to ward off the elements of disassociation, compounded as it always was with the destabilizing effect of illusion, a result of unnatural and contrary conditioning.

(Zeus the false prophet)

'Give whoso gives, and give not whoso gives not.'
HESIOD

Dyfed's tutoring under Manandan's watchful eye was extent. At certain stages Dyfed would not always sit attentively with his intelligent face upturned toward his master. Sometimes he would bolt away out into the sunlight and up the hill or along the palace's majestic corridors of polished stone toward the beach, desperately clutching at chunks of relative reality, as he went. Dyfed was a young, high spirited and natural human. Manandan would not fetch him or call Dyfed back who at this stage would be beyond any easy enticement to return to his studies. Dyfed, the old Master knew, needed to digest and process that which entered his realm.

But on one particular day Dyfed sat respectfully still and did not make a sound. He knew from his mother that his master was the greatest teacher in the world at large, and that he, Dyfed, had a golden opportunity — or was it responsibility — to learn and inwardly digest what he taught.

Manandan stopped and regarded the youthful Dyfed who was sitting stiffly upright pondering his aged tutor with wide-eyed amazement. The darkly tanned, grey haired man was quiet as he turned and looked out to sea. Suddenly, he extended an arm and pointed. Dyfed padded across the cool, smoothly polished marble floor in his bare feet and stood beside the tall, angular figure of Manandan who was gazing out the floor to ceiling windows toward the tiny harbour below. There in the direction that his mentor was pointing, Dyfed saw four large Amoran galleys oaring their way toward the stone quay close to the people's little village where most of the domesticated hoi polloi had gathered.

Dyfed knew that a dominant tribe of hoi polloi known as the Amorans had been impervious to Lord Huge's mist and that they had first set foot upon Violet and Manandan's isle during a midwinter storm that occurred roughly one degree of celestial time after Queen Violet had given birth to him.

The folks of Hellas acknowledged time in the third dimension according to the first Olympiad, so did the executives of the Amoran Empire: the returned Hyperborean Masters followed suit. So according to they're chronological order of solar cycles, Dyfed reckoned himself to be born in the year 666 and the Amoran intrusion onto the Isle of Peace Resort in the year 823. This was one hundred and fifty-seven solar years after Dyfed's birth, which according to how the Masters tally their spiritual age (a one to ten and a half ratio), Dyfed — as mentioned — was thirteen and unable yet to grow a beard.

Once the Amoran legions had penetrated the magic veil they continued to visit the isle each year. However, unlike other areas within the lands of Amoran domination, and because the isle was on the outer most fringe of their empire, the Amorans had intended — for the time being — to leave the inhabitants here in peace so as to continue on more or less as before. It wasn't a condition that the inhabitants of sages favoured, so quickly after their arrival preparations had begun for the Masters to vacate. He also knew that the Amorans called this isle most fair (upon which they lived) Mona, the Isle of the Moon.

One thing that Dyfed was not sure about was the amount of time that had elapsed from the moment his mother arrived on this isle to the day he was born. He knew only that although he had been conceived prior to her arrival here (perhaps during another era before she left there for the third dimension), she had refused to give him up to be born and had continued to carry him for a long time; at least until a time when certain and favourable events had unfolded: the protecting shield of the veil which Lord Huge had constructed was one such favourable event. Unfortunately, the veil hadn't lasted more than a moment or two in the grand scheme of timely things.

"Are they bringing Azeus, master?' enquired Dyfed. Azeus was his master's term for the pure mind, the absence of corruption, degeneration, and villainous-ness.

"No, Dyfed. They are bringing the impure and corrupt Zeus,' he laughed. 'Azeus for world order supreme still bides its time. Keep an eye out for the false prophet Zeus that turns up like a bad smell each and every generation, Dyfed. Continue to move toward the light of the free spirit that exist independently of everything, and which is your guide. Seek the wisdom of the Master Mind by the methods you have been taught. Seek Azeus, Dyvy me boy.'

"Is Amor the false navel, master?' asked Dyfed.

Manandan suddenly stared down at the young man. He contemplated him for a moment with his large light eyes beneath those hoary and bushy brows. He then looked back out to sea. A sudden deluge was pouring cloud water onto the smooth surface of the bay and onto the misty galleys manned by the men from Amor. As the torrent's journey moved inland toward the palace, the loud patter from the large sloppy raindrops beat heavily first onto the stone building followed then a few moments later onto the tree tops of the forest.

"Amor is a contender,' said Manandan, his voice partially drowned by the din of the rain, 'that is all. But Azeus will re-materialize in a time to come. It is just the beginning for the age is long. It is Amor that is the initiation of Zeus that is paving the way for this evil incubus. But it is clear and it is certain, Dyfed, that one day in the world to come, the ancient Hyperborean light will be rekindled anew. But that will happen only when the time has come to stamp out that which has truly become the world order of Zeus. When that day comes let every man and woman be prepared. Only then will the descendants of heroic men and women hold high the torch that will brighten the sky over Hesperia of the last light and lighten the land there once again and lay Zeus and the Last Men to rest wearing the mask of eternal death. The free state of Azeus, which only the truly free individual can envision, shall one day come to pass, but only within,' said Manandan. 'Only within.'

Dyfed's studies under Manandan continued until he was quite grown. When the lesson was over for the day, Dyfed, now quite tall and lithe, jumped with youthful anticipation as he ran out into the hot steaming air where the earth and stone smelled musty sweet from a recent downpour. Pungent was the forest smell that forced itself into his nostrils as he eagerly climbed the little hill close by. Dyfed was still in the newness of life and his heart was light for he perceived no evil. Here, as in all young temples of life, joy and harmony in its indigenous state lay within as was Natural, and having no conception of distress, the fragile and disarming condition of happiness-mature was still completely unknown to him.

Manandan the teacher, Manandan the wise watched as Dyfed exercised the freedom of his healthy individuality and choice as he climbed alone into the hilly forest behind the brick road. Manandan knew Dyfed as he knew himself and he neither pitied nor envied him but loved him instead. For Manandan knew that to evoke pity would be a form of denying not only Dyfed's future but his own personal past as well. And to be jealous of his innocence and to try and embark on a course to achieve that now unattainable state was mere foolishness. Manandan also knew that the state that dwelled in youngsters like Dyfed came from the immanence of their reincarnation. This happens only at the beginning of one's life journey on this level in this dimension. Hopefully, he thought, it would also occur upon the completion of Dyfed's life as well; but to strive to recreate it again at any point midway was pure folly.

Dyfed picked his way through the lushness that clothed this island jewel set here upon a watery waste that grew green from the edge of the cold, blue brine to the top of its highest hill. Fresh water, clear and milky white, cascaded in abundance around him as did all the other plums of sustenance that were manifested in profusion here in this bounteous garden of honey. Here all had been re-worked in preparation for its golden age by these Masters and no intrinsic law had been left undone nor any mode of quintessential value was left un-invented. But, unexplainably to Dyfed, now its dusk had prematurely begun to fall and the folks had begun to pack up and begin to extinguish its light. Now it slumbered, this ancient, de-populated remnant like some plentiful old tree whose fruit lay scattered unpicked upon the ground around it. Few men were left from the old world to seek sustenance from its ancient branches and its yield of knowledge. The new generations of hoi polloi now preferred the sweet new shoots that sprout up after a heavy rainfall or from a warm sprinkling of urine that trickles from the bladder of some horned creature.

On the hill beyond the palace, the warm wind dishevelled Dyfed's hair as he gazed with silver eyes over the shining sea that seemed to settle around the isle like beaten lead. The vaporous bubble that burst above had vanished into a column of mist and had blown out to sea to merge with a thick layer of brightly coloured cloud (the broken remnant of Lord Huge's handiwork) which now only partially encircled the island. Below, Amoran galleys from their new province in Albion lay anchored and motionless. He studied them momentarily then gazed out across the flat glittering expanse toward the eastern horizon where the encircling clouds had parted. There he could easily glimpse the purplish coloured contours of another land peeking at him from over the edge of the sea.

The world shaded suddenly as the sun dipped behind the cloud rim and a peewit, a Northern Lapwing (Vanellus vanellus of the plover family) shrieked overhead. Below, the men from the galleys came ashore. They asked many questions, as usual, and solicited opinions and points of view from the few hoi polloi who were about. What they gleaned, these armour clad men then carefully compiled and recorded in triplicate. Beyond that, they barked out orders and dealt roughly with those few local yokels left who were hoi polloi employees of the vacating resort. They visited and discussed topics with other new arrivals, supposedly learned men and women who — attracted here from abroad — had recently settled upon the isle. But Violet-Eye, Manandan and King Pel who remained un-discerned by the galley men and the others carefully avoided them. These soldiers from abroad hired the local light wicker chariots to cavort them around the countryside, and they embarked for this place or that, to ponder, to measure and to sketch. In time, these conquerors and compilers from Amor picked through and made an attempt to plunder the Isle of Peace. They remained unaware of the genuine article, however, and overlooked the real treasure troves. In the end, believing that they had gathered up, recorded, and collected all at was of any value, they came back only to break off the limbs and hack at the trunk of the old, old tree like juvenile delinquents. They had come, they had seen, but they had not benefited as they might have for they had failed to listen to the Isle of Peace's cosmic heartbeat and to time its rhythm. Despite their meticulousness they had failed to grasp the inner most workings and the very essence of the ancient heart of Hyperborean knowledge; the rhythm of the vibration of the universe: Ooommm.

Despite the great importance of this small island in respect to the will of the transcendent Masters (as already stated), until recently few people had ever actually lived here. Earlier in Dyfed's youth, the entire isle was his to roam at will. Sometimes he rode to the north where the tropical lowlands lavished in lush desolation, for few men other than Ayr the shepherd and his lord, Pan, ventured there. As Manandan's style of teaching was para-tactical, during the budding of the Hawthorn when Tethra was becalmed, Dyfed would often accompany Ayr and Prince Penrhyn to fish the teeming banks of the coastal waters in Manandan's little coracle. Never would they have come upon foreign vessels under sail or adrift in those waters as one would today. At other times he would accompany Manandan to the symbolic grave of King Golly who had later retired part time upon this isle just prior to transcendence It was then that he had supervised the erecting of the great stone structures here (which made this site important to the Masters) as well as elsewhere in this portion of the world. To the south of King golly's empty grave (that was used by the Masters for ceremonial purposes only) lay a meadow. It was at this place that the game scattered madly before arrows of pure energy which King Pel and Prince Penrhyn let loose from strange machines. To the west, close by the shore, was the great-hallowed burial mound of the hunter-gather ancients, now frequented by the initiates to the secret Lodge of Huge, which the artisan had founded originally in King Golly's memory. Here, during the festival of Shamain, the small group of islanders used to gather and feast while commiserating with the ancient artisans and philosophers from the realm of the Masters who were often summoned from the fifth dimension as guest speakers. Lord Huge presided as master of ceremonies during such occasions, and Manandan's unusual subservient role was that of high priest and acolyte to the Queen.

Manandan, like Lord Huge, was a gifted shaman, yet in turn was subservient to Violet-Eye, the priestess-queen. Subservient in this instance is the closest word of explanation. It did not mean inferior or subordinate to in any way. During this function a sacred dance was performed where all the participants held hands and followed Queen Violet's lead in a large spiral motion. Dyfed was second in sequence and his right hand tightly clasped that of his mother's while his left was held by Manandan as they danced and sang and spiralled into a great maze where followed the eating of a Eucharist, the root of life, followed by revelry that reflected a decorum descended from an ancient morality. This morality was considerably different from the one that the hoi polloi of today utilize. These old traditions practiced here on the Isle of Peace were the remnants from the previous world of the third density whose secrets had propelled them to transcend, and to which Dyfed was being exposed and initiated into now, belatedly, due to his post facto birth.

On occasions, Violet and Manandan related to the young Dyfed of the wondrous times during that aforementioned Chieftain Golly's primary tenure here, and of that event when Manandan himself had led a procession to lay the symbolic ashes of that ancient Master to rest, right here on this isle. These ancestors, Dyfed was told, were related to the race to whom lord Shirkuh — a direct ancestor of Dyfed's, somehow — belonged, and that they were the ancient race who had once constructed a vast and intricate culture which utilized a network of colossi both fragile and substantive, and tapped geomagnetic fields that reached out into the cosmos. They employed other arcane sciences as well before being overtaken by eternity's celestial clock that continually resets the stage anew to roll its course. This last event took place at the same time as the completion by those Masters of the Little Known Universe to master the transmutation of their space/time reality that effectively had elevated that race beyond the third dimension.

Following that, the phenomenal celestial instrument of chronology then funnelled darkness back into the great cities of light where now only the dim, non-graduates of their era remained. And this state of affairs now set those under-graduates, the leftover hoi polloi upon a nomadic path that swept out from that ancient world and brought about an atrophied race of men and woman. But the Masters, as earlier discussed, soon returned for furlong and enjoyment, at first keeping the vulgar and pathetic hoi polloi at bay while working on all sorts of gimmicks in trying to improve the latter's lot with their advanced science, but to no (or very little) avail. But momentous events overtook the world at that juncture and when the dust had cleared and the oceans and the land settled again, a strange affliction had over taken the hoi polloi. This was their own confusion about their Master Mind who appeared unto them as trolls. In addition, they had succumbed by this time to the power of a handful of Haploids of whom — until then — the Masters had been completely unaware. At that time it was discovered that Haploids — those freaks who by a quirk of nature had unaccountably transcended alongside the Masters (or behind them) — remained in an abnormal type flux in their falsely assumed position in the fifth dimension. But the moment their volition-mode responded to their choice favoured by their not so free will to re-enter the third density again (as the real Masters were able to do) …presto!…the Haploids discovered that they were flying blind, unaided now with an incomplete set of natural functionaries that were used unnaturally to plug all humanoids into a cognitive state of commonality in order to handle the *Idea of the Eye and the Hand* and be aware of basic realities as we know them to be.

And that brought us to the point of Dyfed's birth. The few Masters that had made the control command of Isle of Peace resort their temporary home had pretty much now quickly fled; they had evacuated back into the fifth dimension which by this time had left the aforementioned five persons — Queen Violet, Dyfed, Manandan, King Pel and Prince Penrhyn — to secure the portal, erase any final clues for the ability of transcendence and other sacred knowledge (apart from the stone monuments which none of the third dimensional folks understood anyway) and closed up the quietude and evacuated the resort while directing all the others to follow suit: Hence the arrival of King Pel and

Prince Penrhyn to assist Manandan in Dyfed's urgently needed education and eventually their evacuation. Then the mansions of Violet and Manandan were quickly demolished.

But for the time being (precious and short that it was), as prince to the island grove it was at the hallowed burial mound that Dyfed's initiation into the sacred knowledge of the ancient world occurred and where the ceremony for his investiture to this ancestral order would normally have taken place upon his arrival to manhood. But this last event, however, was not destined to take place, for the winds of change that churn the mills to which all humanity is ever subject, blew their turbulence from afar and came upon this gentle isle.

"Knowledge is a fragile thing which is not exactly a commodity but that which all higher life form is dependant upon,' Manandan told Dyfed lastly. 'Knowledge is a sacred and special enlightenment, and is not what men believe or what they want to believe, but what is. Enlightenment is relative. Knowledge that comes from the Great Vibration is degrees of perception and revelation working only partially in materialized cause and effect within the electrified mechanisms that fix the Little Known Universe. It is to understand the Sight of the Eye and the Feel of the Hand in order to correctly interpret what messages are received and used to fabricate one's Idea. These workings affect everything and everybody in the third material dimension and are all ultimately related no matter how far flung they seem to be from each other,' he said. Dyfed now knew that sometimes the understanding, the attainment of enhanced knowledge is sufficient in itself and the implementation of that comprehension far exceeded its immediate usefulness, which even in some hands becomes dangerous to the practitioners, not to mention to innocent bystanders as well. Ultimately, knowledge will be invaluable in the context of all things and will tie in and lead to relevant understandings and decision-making.

Manandan had once again had been gazing out the window as he spoke but now he paused and turned to regard Dyfed before continuing to expound some more. He was quite used to speaking in complex terms to the young men and women he had tutored over the ages, for initially the lesson is oratory skill. Dyfed was being furiously taught to remember and then eloquently deliver the information in specific terms. As time went on that eloquence would increase. It was not important just yet that he understand all of what it implied for his Master Mind knew everything that was needed. Its code only needed to be imprinted indelibly upon the student's young, impressionable little mind. Later, to the student of Manandan, his teachings' meaning would slowly become apparent, and any difficulties that he or she might have could be explained at that time. A lengthy but simple review of Dyfed's knowledge at the graduate level was able to reveal content, understanding and oratory skills all in one. This was an age-old system, well tried, and one that had provided excellence for a very long time. It was in this manner of tutoring that after his first few degrees in the celestial span of time, Dyfed had in fact learned a great deal more than he actively realized. This supposedly would reward him in later years. When faced with a quandary or a conundrum, his intellect was supposed to be able to mentally scan pertinent groups of information and reasoning already worked out in advance which would enable him to make quick, reliable decisions. But this was not blind faith, either, far from it. Faith was something you had to have about the origin of your true self and the Logos of Heraclitus; beyond that faith was for mythos, not logos.

As an adolescent, Dyfed had been taught the art of questioning. Questioning through a process of time honoured reasoning is much different then inanely questioning time honoured customs and elders in authority. Manandan had taught Dyfed that it was important that people's minds should remain uncluttered with irrelevant trappings for that condition impeded the thinking process that in most cases had a natural tendency to retain the most useless of trivialities. Also, one's Idea must be carefully examined to maintain its integrity and freedom from suggestibility and other programming pollutants. It was important, too, to position oneself with the Master Mind, or at least in its shadow, for that mind was fairly independent and was certainly illusive to being perceived. "Consider not only what you are being told,' Manandan said to Dyfed many times, 'but consider also what motive may be behind the telling. My telling will become apparent, but others' will upon you should be shielded and examined closely before acceptance is made. My motive in teaching you will become clearer in years to come.'

Manandan thought the future would bring massive enlightenment back to the earth. But along with it would come countless lies which will become difficult to cull because of the vast material at hand and only the very wary and those who can properly control their thinking process would remain the least affected by the immense and virtually impenetrable propaganda which would saturate the world's entire society. This, after all, had already been the case.

Manandan told his young pupil that long ago Lord Huge, who possessed all the arts, had held up a mirror in the face of Bel Disc the Relentless and had given him the third degree. But in the sacred dialect of Shamskar (the mother tongue which Dyfed spoke among the Masters) Lord Huge had received no answers in which to benefit the way of the sacred establishment. And even as Lord Huge had failed, he told Dyfed, he himself had approached the mystery of the future analytically through the Web of the Fates, and believed that the pseudo-establishment of the people at large would manifest as the anti-establishment; and that they, the establishment, the speakers of the truth in the sacred language of Shamskar and the practitioners of priest-kingship, could only fight a war of attrition in order to protect themselves and their civilization in this third density and on this level. In any event, declared Manandan, those Masters who remained here in this third density would be drastically reduced in numbers although the lion's share of their populace would remain — as always — beyond the pale. And in time, through decoy, vast numbers of the ordinary people, the hoi polloi, will be funnelled further and further away from the truth by the tyrannical leadership of the anti-establishment establishment to be controlled by the Haploids.

And these psychopaths will later claim divine right to rule and demand to be obeyed. They will enlist the populations of hoi polloi into their employ and impinge them with high debt. And that anti-establishment establishment will be manipulated and controlled by this silent and unknown Haploid power elite who, shielded by an illusionary body of authority, will wield vast privilege, prestige, jurisdiction, and might, along with prejudice and tendencies towards marginalization. And these acolytes of Zeus, he cautioned Dyfed, will attempt to turn even the Great Celestial Will that emanates from the Master Mind against those of sober minds and uncluttered intellects which exist here in the third density, and begrudge them the freedom of independent choice of thought and action. In its endeavour to have all mankind submit to Zeus, the conscripted peons who will take it upon themselves to promote the petty ordinances of the anti-establishment establishment, and bent on eroding individuality like ours, will beguile and coerce, bribe and finally command subordination and obedience from every vestige of humanity to bow to its authority,' said Manandan. "It will disallow any anti-antics that are capable of going against Zeus and their system, in any way.'

Meanwhile, as the subject Masters around his mother — these visiting and return third dimensional inheritors of Hyperborean civilization who in their own way were priests or magicians, astrologers, scribes and builders were men and women of science whose legacy eventually would fall into legend and myth (if they hadn't already) — had (as already stated) taken refuge in the fifth density from where they may look on. Now they were far and away from the sorrows and iron killing tools of the third dimensional psychopaths where even the Master's miraculous body torcs (toughened with towering technology) had become inadequate against such violent and sudden hatred.

What to do with Dyfed then, and how to launch him and float his being upon the troubled waters of this phenomenon was the conundrum that faced his mother Violet and Manandan. This had become the growing, sixty-four denarii question. There were places of relative safety, but would this advance Dyfed's position in his allotted career as a fifth columnist as he positioned himself to topple the neo-anti establishment establishment? These bloodlines of the people of that ancient civilization had never ceased in attempting to educate and civilize all their people, even those — who after the transmutation of the adept — had fallen into savage times. These hoi polloi had become known in these days as Kelts and northern Goths in their neck of the woods, yet many other names for folks existed throughout the world. Dyfed knew that many of the (related) locals had fled further afield to become known as the Dorians as well as bloodlines that even existed among the men from Amor. This latter mentioned clan or tribe of Amorans had been somewhat more successful (it was commonly thought) with fascism and extreme capitalism than the folks from Hellas had been. And it was this very program for which the Haploids were noted. And this program (Idea) of their Haploidic leaders (with the help of misused Hellenic oriented Ideas now second hand and handed down from the mind of Socrates and his apprentices Plato and Aristoteles) was plummeting the hoi polloi into debt and slavery. And this worsened humanity as their empire grew. They should have utilized the ideas and methods of Socrates more closely: But this was realized belatedly.

So, there it was. Amor, mostly unaffected by the might of vast empires among the far eastern peoples — such as the folks in the land of Ch'in — had become the Empire of the known world hereabouts. So the answer to the question of where to inject Dyfed was easy: to Amor, that's where. But how to get him safely from the Isle of Peace into protection and placement proximate to power in Amor, where he must begin his life's work, was the crux of the conundrum. Quick preparations were now underway. Apart from Violet, all other members of Dyfed's extended family (folks who by and large were descendants of Na Mima who like Dyfed were all cognitive as from whom they were somewhat specifically related and descended) were now unavailable to help out from their un-perceivable dimension. Manandan quickly set to work to set up a network that could deliver his candidate into the fray.

(Na Mima)

'Give a man a mask and he will tell you the truth.'
OSCAR WILDE (APOLOGIES TO THOSE WHO SAID IT BEFORE OSCAR DID)

To indulge in a short diversion for the purpose of clarity, this aforementioned Na Mima — who were ancestors to some species of modern man — arrived here a long, long time ago. Some came in the form of animals that were then quickly morphed into humans again. Others, like the priest-kings never altered their form. Legend has it that they were from the very distant past and Manandan told Dyfed that he (Dyfed) was a Na Mima, as was his mother. The Na Mima (with the sole exception of Dyfed) are not born here, in this dimension, he was told. This was a very strange concept but Manandan also told him that it involved something a little more complicated and Manandan reminded Dyfed that he had been conceived long before he was born here.

"You, Dyfed,' Manandan had said to him one day, 'are a descendant of these Na Mima, as is everybody else of our Warrior/Priest/King race who lives. Of course, whether they know it or not is another thing. But you are different for you know specifically who your personal Na Mima is and you know her as an experience within your life. This is unique. And you must resolve the fact that you also exist now both in the time of the past and somewhat in the present and future at the same time. You are unique also in that never before has one of us been born here in this situation as you have been. And it has also been my duty to make you unique in respect to the present and among those who will people the world you will inhabit in the future, as if it were truly your birth rite. This will be your affliction, albeit, somewhat to your fortune as well, I dare say.'

Dyfed asked no further questions, at that time. But there was one thing he wondered at. As a little boy he had asked for a torc, like the ones his mother's companions wore. This had been refused him although his uncle Penrhyn had given him a thin gold one later as a present. He wore it to this day but it was different then the torcs his folks wore. He had been given a play torc, as his family referred to it. It was flat and broad and quite heavy as it was an exquisite piece made from that heavy metal. It was similar, Dyfed had noted much later, to the torcs worn by the uninitiated, especially those folks known as the Kelts. But the differences that he noted in those men's torcs that matched his own from the torcs which Violet-Eye, Prince Penrhyn, King Pel, and Manandan wore, were vast. As stated the former's were made of flat gold in replication of the latter but which, he knew, were not magnetic nor did they attract and contain electricity as the other ones did. And his was not capable of sounds and holograph projections, and other wondrous things, either, that the masters were able to produce. These latter mentioned torcs which were worn by members of his family, were much larger and golden in colour, yet they appeared much shinier and being wafer thin were almost as light as a feather. They were magical, Dyfed knew, while his and those of the other foreign folks were simply jewellery; they were bling, though not necessarily anything as nasty as the bling worn by any of the old Tom, Dick and Harrys of the hoi polloi. No sir!

(To ascend or descend?
...that is not the right question)

'If society cannot help the many who are poor,
it cannot save the few who are rich.'
JOHN FITZGERALD KENNEDY

One day as Dyfed was walking in the grounds adjacent to the remnants that remained of Queen Violet's
garden he perceived Manandan to be deep in reflection. Close by had once been the site of the factory and academy of their resort that had once contained a number of laboratories, a state of the art foundry, numerous fabricating and processing plants including manufacturing vanadium battery piles. There had also been and an enormous power generating centre here, the last to be destroyed before the final exit. He thought of the life that had once teemed from here — its energy abounding. Here was where the apex of natural selection took place through breeding and education: Here concentrated forms of compact and organized energy, coagulated. It was a magnification where natural life forms absorb, breathe in, borrow, and utilize from the Earth/Ocean (and Universe at large). This used to happen here as the norm in order for advanced manifestations to automatically go on to manifest the next synapse signal…it was here that the willing and waiting Neuron was succoured before the inevitable expiration, the discharge, the throw-back and the kick-start whose excretion is (becomes) the expanded, diluted, and chaotic disorganization of entropy — energy changed. The resort had once hummed with Mechanical, Chemical, Kinetic, Electrical, Magnetic, Radiant, Heat, Thermal, Ionization, and even Nuclear energy which was at its centre by nature. This and more were what Dyfed's mind's eye was able to substantially detect by having to re-create it now from memory. At any old moment in his mind's eye he was capable of seeing the plots of lush agriculture…the library-quiet laboratories where masters of genetic engineering fashioned edible sides of beef, pig, venison, chicken and any number of naturally grown foodstuffs from composite carbon in large test-tube-like beds without the spilling of blood and the stopping of the heart of a single living creature in order to feed the people of the resort here on the Isle of Peace.

He then suddenly thought of Master Democritus, a friend and associate of Manandan's. This man (who had long since fled from this dimension) was the master who had intentionally let slip out (of the bag) the secret of the atom. Four centuries before the present it had been purposely placed back into the mix of the third dimension — its seed buried here within a fertile pocket — though the hoi polloi hadn't (as yet) picked up on it to any discernible degree. One day (Dyfed knew) Democritus would be erroneously dubbed among the hoi polloi as the father of the atomic theory. The masters had wanted it and had deemed it so. This was their intention all along in an effort to put power into the hands of the hoi polloi in order to eradicate the Haploids. Although it was a dangerous secret to provide to the world of the incredibly ignorant, certain Hyperborean laws provided standards and safety protection to guard against its misuse. But in the hands of the Haploids all bets were off and its power would be a lethal weapon. Fortunately, traditionally the Haploids (though more able in awareness than the hoi polloi due to their freak transcendence beyond the third dimension in which they became strangely fixed) were not considered to be scholars in any way and were greatly hampered by not being endearing. They could neither learn nor further themselves in the third dimension anymore than they had already done so. This was the only advantage the hoi polloi had over them, although it wasn't much. But would the latter be able to keep the secret from them? But at this time in history the point was moot.

Dyfed then drifted back once again into discerning (from a mind measured distance of the material phenomena at large which his awareness tapped into) the crackling of electrical gizmos and gadgets. Transformers, transducers, and capacitors channelled the circuitry of electronic flow where efficient protons were flushed from vats of acidity into proportionally controlled proton deficiencies of alkalinity. But in addition to this, these men of genius had used that same process with chemicals which are innate to the earth and of the ocean in situ; the mountain minerals, the rivers and mud flats: in this manner they were able to charge and recharge their outfits. In addition they tapped into the electro-magnetic charge of the planet itself while it whirled around the giant anode of Apollo-Radiance/Helios while continually (we hope) being bombarded by its (his) charged ions[8] via celestially controlled vibration of the astro-plasma. Dyfed's memory was of those curious regulated plasmas such as flames, lightning and electrical sparks, a regular occurrence around the Isle of Peace resort's control centre.

All these genius works done by the sages had now fallen silent and become deceased, though they wait to be revived to aid humanity's ability to make the transcending leap into the genius that is the Big Mind and the true self. Now the land around was quiet, its breath had been stopped, he thought, and the life which once teemed from it with the shouts of happy folks and the hollow sounds from the blows of distant anvils…the whine of mechanical machines running on the electricity of which the virtual Azeus' (Thor's) thunderbolts were made, the releasing of high pressures through valves, and the crackling of electrical transformers…all had fallen silent now and become deceased. Nor were there a trace left of any machinations — not a lathe nor a welder, nor a single phial, or containers of elements and chemicals, or a chart of sub-weights, not an inkling of the notion of an atomic weight, or even a length of conducting wire, an anode, a cathode, or an electronic chip fabricated of composites made by human Hyperborean hands, left exposed. Nothing was left now of their technology to turn up or to be discovered later. He remembered fondly that all during his life the entire site hummed and glowed inwards in the night as though crystalized in some form of soft, illuminating phosphorus gas.

Great flocks of swans were between nesting grounds at this time of the year and Dyfed who loved birds watched them pass high overhead with their necks arched forward followed by their large and powerful trailing bodies with wings set well back. Suddenly, as he watched, their graceful flight in formation took on an image that likened them to human souls fleeing the carnage of their past lives and sweeping in a wide flight pattern out over the ocean in great numbers on their way north. It was a strange vision and a lonely, desolate void suddenly and unaccountably overtook Dyfed's centre of being. He

---

8   Eye-ons — from the Hellenic present participle *'to go'*

shivered in unexplained repulsion as though a chilly gust had blown through his warm coat or churned up a dusty whirlwind that settled over his distant and future grave.

"Dyfed,' Manandan the sage said at length. 'The time has come for you to strike off in a new direction; enter a new sphere; migrate into another phase of life that I acutely detect will be one of great events. The time has come upon you much too rapidly but that is beyond our control now. I will venture to assert that equitability in all aspects of the age that you now face will be found wanting. However, if you live according to the beliefs that you were taught, you will succeed indeterminate and supple. If you do not, you will die and your identity will become collective with the brittle mediocrity that thrives upon the earth and you will sink into its faceless mass. Remember all that you have learned by me, and the gifts that your mother and your ancestors have given you. Honour yourself to whom you must first be true and treat others in similar fashion, and when you find a receptive soul teach them what you can. Remember, knowledge is always coupled with action. You are an intelligent lad, Dyvie, but remember that the world has become alien to our beliefs and unfortunately there is little that I can say now that will compensate for that other than to tell you that our culture can never be out dated for its nature is true realization. You must feel your way through life in this new age that is undergoing change by being sensitive to the universal rhythm. Never forget that as prince of the grove you are well equipped for this journey and that you will have allies in the authentic Lodge of Huge, among others, which you will encounter on your journey from time to time. Be on your guard at all times and keep your own council. Always remember that you are now in debt to no one: you have never been in debt, not even to your mother or me despite all we have done to further you and your cause of individuality. You must strive to keep that status, Dyvie, as you well know how, and pay as you go. But it is equally important never to allow any one, no matter how thoroughly they have convinced themselves or convinced others, to ever convince you that you owe them a debt in any way and of any kind, after or before the fact. Other than your compassion and empathy you owe absolutely nothing to anyone and you need not bow to any authority whatsoever. Do not be fooled by tricksters of any stripe that will attempt to flesh out the culture of false image in any of the civilizations you come across in the days of your life. Do not seek solace and protection within these states of relative order, or from any culture, other than the delicate one of true realization in which we have nurtured you. Indeed, always seek protection from them by the weapon of your marvellous mind, my surrogate son; for that mind is now, in part, a shaded mirror of the Master Mind which is the real you. That, and only that, is your culture and your true and ever lasting civilization. This is also your conscience. Remember, you share that conscience with immortality.'

However, despite these encouraging words Dyfed could see that Manandan was worried about his future.

"But master,' the lad replied after contemplating what Manandan had said. 'I have not had my investiture and I am loathe to leave my mother, this isle, and above all else you, who have given me great tools. Will my learning now cease?'

"I will no longer teach you, exactly, Dyfed,' he answered, 'but you have been taught to learn and so that factor will continue throughout your whole life. As far as your investiture, that is no longer necessary. You have learned of the placing of the building blocks of unity in the foundations of our great civilization and the secrets of its builders that came from a time long before the modern Kymri. Your mother has passed these down to you, while myself, King Pel, prince Penrhyn and even Lord Huge has played a role. We will now repair to the fifth dimension and you will forge on from here. Remember Dyvie, few people here now have knowledge of these ancient secrets. Remember also that if these are used wisely they can be put to great use. For the many events yet to come are simply the effects of the causes that you have learned in the web of the Fates. Take good care of your rhythm sense and always remember your heritage.'

As the now faint ghosts of the swan-souls faded from his awareness, Dyfed noticed that Manandan's eyes were moist with emotion. The image of his aesthetic and noble features, his dark angular head that at that moment was silhouetted against the late afternoon sky, struck a chord within Dyfed. With a sudden sense of alarm he realized that his master was saying goodbye. But this soft spoken and gentle man who regarded Dyfed with eyes that glistened like jewels from his ready tears quietly reassured him.

"You have learned well, Dyfed. You are strong. Remember to always stay away from fear for it is contagious. Learn from all things that take place around you and make note of them so as to discern their meaning in order to light the Path of the Way. Record all that you can but listen to your Great Mind which is the universe and feel its pulse which is the way of the hidden people of the stones, the steppe, the forest, and of the space between here and the moon. Go forward and in time you will be selected for a specialty.'

"I will miss you my Master,' Dyfed said, feeling a sore constriction growing in his throat as his silver eyes also filled up with hot tears that flowed down his cheeks. The tall youth and the aged sage embraced, and then slowly, without anything more exchanged between them, they walked silently on.

As the sun dropped down behind the headlands to the west they came out about midway onto the broad avenue of yellow brick that once connected their palaces. Here Dyfed waited as Manandan shuffled off down the approach and into the cool shadows where his residence had once been. Watching his ancient teacher there for the last time within this context, Dyfed sensed that Manandan had become a separate reality, undiscerned and unknown by the others who mottled this green grove like some blight of aphis. Around Manandan remained his aura, his intellectualism and his finesse. Manandan was fading from the third dimension and would soon be no more for those who could not see past this plane of reality.' Dyfed made a last glance in the direction of his mother's own vanished mansion. He then closed his eyes.

(You've a better view of the moon when your house is burnt to the ground)

'Death and sorrow will be the companions of our journey; hardship our garment; constancy and valour our only shield.'

SIR WINSTON SPENCER CHURCHILL

In the manner in which his people tallied one's age, Dyfed was now thirteen. At this point he left his benefactors (actually, they left him) and set out on his life's journey here in the third dimension where he had been born. It had been strange, he thought, that his loved ones who normally defied the definition of the third density phenomena in its space/time's reality, had also been dependent upon (and subject to) that same element of space/time. They had, of course, needed to. But it had been an intrinsic essence in their securing for themselves a measure of safety which allowed them leave it as readily as they had adopted it, and to be whisked away just in time from this place. In a sudden rush, it seemed, his mother and Manandan (along with their once large retinue of specialised sages) had suddenly up and disappeared without a 'by your leave'. They had returned to the Mysteries and its Nirvana (seemingly set somehow) upon the tenants of Orpheus. This had not necessarily been smoothed out across the poetic prose so dear to Aeschylus after being dignified by Heraclitus, Zeno and Epicurus, either. His mother's station of persona was located back before the corruption that was somewhere beyond in the fifth dimension. And such adepts as her and those who peopled the resort on the Isle of Peace only accessed this Valhalla palace of Nirvana. This, Dyfed knew, was accomplished via the logos of the bunny holes of nature (Physik) into to which (in a practical way) no non-adept could ascend nor descend. Discovered by the Hyperborean Masters, and utilized by them, as yet Dyfed (as an in-adept) was barred.

So, this resort was the only home Dyfed had ever known. And it was different for him, furthermore, for he wasn't leaving the dimension, he was going further afield in it. In any event, Dyfed now found himself more alone than he could ever have imagined and although he could do the alone thing standing on his head, he didn't like being smothered by and enclosed in a mob of stinky, babbling strangers; not one bit. He quickly discovered, though, he'd need to get used to it. Equipped and believing himself prepared, this local son now looked out with apprehension as a stranger would upon what had become a strange and alien land which (without an obvious opposing force) would endure as his phenomenon from now (the first day of the rest of his life) right to the very end of it. At any rate this stirred a condition that caused him a moment fraught with vivid emotions that welled up inside his heart almost to the point of panic. But Dyfed — in his present situation — wasn't stranded at all, exactly. He would endure. He knew that much. And once he got a grip, Manandan's tutoring (which had seen to that) kicked in and took over. And that (once it was seen to) just happened to be Dyfed's preparedness in all things. Quickly Dyfed was to find that (although at this point all bets were not off, in respect to this disjointed reality of the hoi polloi and their Haploid rulers) he needed to be creative. Filling and expanding the purpose of a third dimensional sentient being (he had discovered), that was something new to him in certain ways, always required special attention to the present. In his current surroundings it meant letting go of what he once had. He needed to concentrate in a different way than before because here in each moment the preverbal ball (a volition within the hoi polloi's mind) was somehow already moving into the next moment before it had fully grasped the last.

In his old world, of a day or two ago, connecting with others was a much subtler exercise. In his new reality everything was to be more relevant to each individual's volition such as their thinking method, their perception of you that was clouded by innumerable judgements and past fantasies which were attached to cause and effect, a decidedly nasty and debilitating third dimensional condition. Not a good situation, he thought. But Dyfed, with his quick mind, was easily able to handle it.

Here in this altered reality of the hoi polloi, one always needed to be attentive, Dyfed knew. Especially attentive to the sign of the times and all which that entailed (such as the subtle exchanges and especially volition decay). These occurred here constantly within all the avenues of life. And these avenues included folks' careers and preferences for pastimes and over all it embraced myriads of categories, divisions, and varieties of almost anything and everything. It included descriptions of all those anythings and everythings, along with persuasions which were frighteningly numerous; specifications, selections, and designations which were difficult to assemble and these were always changing. All of these filled or satisfied a desire and served its own purpose of sorts that impinged upon the host's every step along the domain of their life-journey. For the hoi polloi, what was relevant now in time became irrelevant and visa versa. To Dyfed it appeared to be an out of tune hurdy-gurdy in topsy-turvy time (that sounded decidedly like an disharmonic relative minor of G major), to put it bluntly.

But he also needed a certain vibration of drive in order to grasp the baton of vision that was necessary so as to complete that task set before him. And the destiny he chose was that of a task-journey of enshrining fellow and companionship to all. This then, if not the goal, would be the tool for his life's work.

He could suddenly feel the cool motion of breeze in the warm morning sun as he sped across the surface of the earth inhaling her fragrance and fumes mingling with the sweet strains from the V twin side-valve flathead. His immediate destiny (as of this day forward) was to alter, detour, and redirect the flow of reality of what and how things were, to refashion and to take up and actively commence in a fabricating a commonality of the Idea of ideas. This couldn't be done by pruning the tree but only by rerouting the thirsty roots of the entire forest…by rerouting blazing Radiance Apollo and the four strong winds, as well, so the forest would repent and grow straight and true. There was nothing for it now than to bite the bullet and mosey on over to the heart and soul of the dominant Idea, that centre of world centres itself and begin to infiltrate and influence its very heart. This was where his realization lay.

Dyfed had found his anima, and it was placed alongside a very shaky vector sheltered in self-induced transparent anonymity.

So what on earth was he doing again? Had he missed something? he wondered. It was ironic that the dominant (universally invigorating) place of wisdom and balance (along with the rule of good order) with which he yearned to retain (and was most comfortable; and for which he had become a trained affiliate) was that place back behind him. And that place was never to be revisited again other than in memory which lay within the fraternity of familiarity of his island resort: the home to Hyperborean dharma which is nothing more than good government, good rule and true law and fair justice for all. And the players didn't even have to be equal. They never were. But that was gone now, it was no longer intact… and it wasn't even to be found now in the ruins under his feet. Send in the philosophers… or no, maybe the clowns, after all certainly not the archaeologists. The resort (the shelter of his mother's nest) was closed, shut down, packed up, and relocated within without him and apart from him, forgotten about. There was no going back now. This situation — the current and scary condition of the dominant world hereabouts — was (ironically) what held out anything of value for him now. How ironic, he thought. It was this phenomenon and this phenomenon alone which was now solely capable of facilitating his life — any life or vocation he chose, or was chosen for him whether he liked it or not — for who really has any say in such matters, anyway? Somehow, somewhere out there far away in a strange and grainy world which Dyfed had not quite fully understood yet, never mind mastered, the landscape, its directors, and the rules which were to govern that vocation were somewhere out there just beyond his grasp. Getting them within his grasp was what must be done.

Dyfed was less than timorous about his future than he was regretful, for as the Prince of the Grove it wasn't going to be a walk in pastoral Arcadia, the bucolic home of Pan, and the land of nymphs that he had once seen around him. He knew too that he was to be so unlike any others who would also be seeking to master the character of state that he now sought. This thought caused him to pause. Were there any others like me, somewhere? he wondered. But there was no time to waste on superfluous notions. Destinations for the normally timorous folks like him, those who prefer to inhabit the rustic by-ways and shaded lanes far from the madding high streets would want to remain rural all of their lives. And the character of state he now sought after was just so much different and was the largest most populated jurisdiction of authority in the history of the world. And it was to the centre of this world empire that he had set his sights. And that centre was the city of Amor that, though illuminated and most organized, was not necessarily in all quarters a place of enlightenment, nor of the wisdom filled and personal security variety, anyway.

Yet, in this endeavour somehow then he was to have and hold commonality with folks with which he had (otherwise) nothing in common, whatsoever! But never mind, all roads led to Amor. That's what people told him. Now faced with the reality of the immediate future the suddenness of it begot him an overly anxious attitude. For the very concept of the logistics involved (not to mention the integrated corrective action which he was meant to provide, according to plan, by somehow being intrinsic in providing guidance by some form of divine right and authority to somehow manage to grasp hold of and place control of the world into his hands, was now hilariously bizarre, indeed — absurd. Welcome to the third dimension, he thought, with a forced existentialistic laugh; not that it was actually funny or anything. He lamented immensely over his overwhelming lack of experience and suddenly regretted having agreed to assume this or any other role of similar nature in the first place with the proverbial '*did I solicit thee, oh maker, from my clay to mould me man?*'[9] These were the things he pondered and wondered over. This then was the moment of humility whose nerve ends of consciousness were beyond all other emotions he had ever experienced. Self-diagnosing, he automatically realized he was suffering from aggravated panic. Fortunately, the duration of the anxiety lasted only the few seconds.

---

9   Epigram to Mary Shelley's novel Frankenstein (*Frankenschtein*).

(Dyfed Lucifer ventures in the direction of the First Empire)

'Transcendence is the only real alternative to extinction'
VACLAV HAVEL.

On the evening of his departure from the Isle of Peace, Dyfed waited, leaning against some squalid, ramshackle lean-tos hunched up near the harbour. He touched the torc that was worn only by the Hyperborean people which he now wore concealed under his shirt. But the hoi polloi milling around here upon ragged street on this late afternoon were not the variety that he had hoped to encounter. They were merely the untouchable unwashed minions. These squabbling, rambunctious, and sweating folks around him on this day were just another tribe among the great-unwashed multitude of the scum at large. Once, apart from their own imprisonment, they were free to fantasize. Now the great caldera of the Empire was enslaving folks so as to program them into their system. Dyfed, as expressly instructed by his mother and Manandan, had always kept his distance from all of these alien folks. Now he couldn't help but mingle.

On this day, expediently dressed with a cord around his neck that was attached to the torc that took the place of a thick notebook and pen, Dyfed stood well apart from these aforementioned foreign fellows.

He watched and gauged the rhythm of harmony in his effort to seamlessly blend and integrate himself in among them with the least amount of fuss and kerfuffle. His only worldly possessions were bundled (so as not to cause awe and suspicion) in a heavily stitched leather kit, rather than his first choice of some strong, lightweight material composed of molecular fullerenes of carbon. At thirteen Dyfed was already very tall and his slim body was strong and supplely tenacious. He could easily sling his heavily contained luggage cargo over his shoulder that presently slunk against the calves of his legs as he leaned back casually watching the action around him.

Now, swept-up in the game that was afoot, according to plan, he was currently being smothered with their pungent odour. Even the smell of their possessions subdued him and he was inundated with the peculiar sounds the people made…those harsh voices, their strange crackling laughter and other little animal noises which leaked out of them from time to time that was strangely familiar. It was growing late in the day and looking up he observed something that resembled a broad, silvery worn-out coin on the upper delta of the horizon. It was the last trace of radiation glowing from a sinking Helios Apollo that soon dropped beneath the world and dragged the cloak of a darkly lined gloaming with it. A new day has begun, he thought, and now began the long evening before the daylight. Dyfed watched as the faded silvery brightness of Sky shrank down into a tiny, shiny arc. It receded according to natural law just where the Radiance (Helios Apollo) had earlier dived beneath the earth and it quickly disappeared behind the dark contours of his island home. Momentarily, a shaggy darkness — like a noiseless, fluttering cloud of bats — quickly followed the patch of pale, silvery sky, and as the gloaming began to melt more into the shades, it pulled the raggedy, craggy pitch-inky-blackness after it.

Dyfed glanced around him, his flexed cognizance now strained mightily and attentively as it reached out beyond his normal periphery-sense. Most especially, his interest and focus was in gathering up the somewhat incomprehensible pieces, those building blocks of the hoi polloi's animated thoughts which (though comparatively to Dyfed's norm were rudimentarily constructed). But it was these that compiled the fuel and the energy for the topics of their conversations — their Ideas. As he looked out at these folks now he furtively consulted his notebook (torc). Squinting through the shade he scribbled away as he compiled, cross-referenced, and applied mental calculus. His Hyperborean trained mind remained fully in control as he had been taught to short-cut reasoning already figured out in advance. This training was meant to open a window for Dyfed into these creature's minds to see what lurked within — exposing any foibles of their mental character. It helped him, too, to understand their Idea, and to glimpse each one of these ideas as they fused together like goblets of condensate in the midst of fog. All these ideas (he gladly affirmed himself) were different from one another in so many various ways, not unlike that of his people. At least there was some structure to their intelligence, he decided. Nevertheless, his familiar building structure of thoughts was so much more lucid and advanced compared to theirs, he noted. He might technically be hoi polloi himself, since transcendence was as yet unknown to him, but his parentage, and his education, were descended directly from the Hyperborean sages.

To Dyfed's ears came guttural utterings and sharp exclamations, sighs and musings that accompanied and coloured the themes that poured out of these folks' minds. They provided for him a sketch of ample forms and flitting shadows of twist and jagged turns that they used adeptly to rough in the mysterious universe — the phenomenon — that existed around each and every one of them. This was done in their attempt to make any sense of it all, along with (and, most importantly, in conjunction with) their fellow travellers therein.

Dyfed knew that any sudden strangeness of his appearance…the instantaneousness of his unfamiliarity and his diverse ways with his queer and outlandish mannerisms to which they would be only partially accustomed…would impinge negatively upon their reality. Its effect, he thought — in a manner of jarring in on them like a red-hot lance, much like they had with him — would have, however, greater percussions for them than himself. The hoi polloi, he knew, were primitive and superstitious compared to him. His own elevated (perceived) awareness, he thought, would easily make allowances. Theirs, on the other hand, he believed, would not. Dyfed tried quickly to grasp each of their ideas — his Idea having the ability of prying them open like a oyster so as to expose the program of their comprehensions in order for him to prepare himself and them (on their behalf) for the shock they each may suffer from the differences between them and to shield it as much as possible. This was his safety net and was his tailor-made shield; his aegis, a friendly tool foremost among others for which Manandan had ingeniously provided him.

Dyfed did not speak. He did not call out or corner one or two of the higher social rank that lurked nearby and gregariously engage them, or distinguish himself before any of the melee of hoi polloi, in a hearty hail fellow well met, greet and meet posture of revealing shallowness. It was unbefitting of himself, he thought. It was beneath him. He was concentrating at the moment on a dirty scow that was loosely tied to the quay close to the rocky and pebbly beach where she lay slightly listing to starboard on the hard. For the last hours of daylight men had been busy loading her and now their feet were wet and muddy as they were almost finished shifting a ton of rubbish into the cargo hold. Dyfed knew the tide was rising, and in half an hour the laden down boat would be almost ready to float it self. Approaching one of the men organizing the loading, and showing him a glimpse of silver, Dyfed learned the scow's cargo was sailing due south. The man with alert eyes smiled a welcoming grin of uneven teeth as he accepted the silver and pointed to a spot down low near the bow where Dyfed should settle in. From his new perch he continued his watch, absorbing those strange sailors' unfamiliar, and discordant voices — the slow condensing of their ethereal thoughts — along with the squeaks and scrapes of placing objects into the scow.

Earlier, when the light was still prevalent on the land, he beheld the jerky actions of the savagely strong bodies of these docile yet rough men with their mixture of childish and maturely impatient dispositions. He watched as they postured (and positioned themselves) with each other and glimpsed their naturally acquired hierarchy in action. Though enthralled at the adventure ahead, he hadn't yet loosened that earlier moment of humility. It stuck with him still.

Aside from the sailors, a part of the awe of this surreal patch of babbling confusion was the very presence of the small trading vessel he was presently occupying. Until now, he had only seen vessels like it from a distance. It stunk of rubbish and filth, of course, and old leftover parts of the sea. This odd conveyance before and around him, one which had already ferried these crude, though intelligent, folks from somewhere to this shore, was to be his ticket to Amor, if not directly and non-stop as he had once hoped. This, possibly, though, was a blessing in disguise. So he wasn't about to turn his nose up at it. It was to be his passage-persona into the next corridor of his adopted world. For certain, no moon landing strategy was needed here to design, build, and put into function such a scow as this. Abhorrent to green men from Mars, perhaps, but to Dyfed, loading and launching this scow was certainly an event as entertaining as any other that was unfolding for him on that day.

Hardly (though) did these folk's Ideas resemble warlike Ares in any way, he thought, even if their docility concealed a savagery whose resolve was needed to steer and keep this rotting sieve of timbers afloat. Nonetheless, for all of that this leaky vessel was still a merchant runner, manned by competent merchantmen who could now deliver him into their midst for the first leg of his journey…to that mysterious place on the outside…on his way to the heart of the Empire.

So he observed them as they finished collecting treasures of other men's trash, those useless and garish pieces of leftover landfill that they stowed amidships. And there, beyond the gloaming in the steeping darkness at the level of the sea, just after the coming of the night and the shift of the tide, Dyfed listened to the ship's creaks as her list now seemed to right itself. Disorientation accompanied her groans and Dyfed felt motion awaken in her as the vessel began to rub against the rickety quay. The tide would soon turn back down and the currents would begin to run. Upon his clothes was the smell of rotten fish and filth. Looking up through the lug rigging at the mast top he saw a crescent moon on the wax as it emerged suddenly out of the cloudy folds of blackness and began riding a wild and lofty wind. The sight of Diana among the draft currents of the sky poignantly brought about a gladdening within his heart. Here was a touchstone to guide him that would remain no matter how the dimension, the landscape, the people, or how the furniture changed around him. Her light, this evening, though fraught with slanted rain amid fleeting summer storm clouds — only partially visible in the gloaming — managed to arrive and dance around him in intervals of hide and seek bathed in silver rays. This talisman would be the Idea of his beacon of cherished Insight as he moved forward in the gathering darkness toward that unknown terrain of his future.

Normally, Dyfed felt comfortable upon the heaving sea swells. But that was in the vessels that the Hyperboreans procured. He recalled, however, having looked aghast at the ships of Amor that recently had briefly visited here. The seaworthiness of this ankle washer (on the other hand), this tub in which he now had trusted his life came to be something of a dim light in comparison to those sleek and shallow drafted vessels of his own people in which he was accustomed to riding. But ultimately, he thought, it must somehow successfully plough the waves, no matter that it did it like the clumsy carcass of an old dead whale drifting with the tide.

Lying among the cargo within the sailing barge's belly, he smelled the piquant aromas that the vessel gave off. They mingled with the smell of the remnants of the village harbour still left over from the low tide. In dereliction the old familiar harbour now flooded had quickly attained an air of thorough unfamiliarity. He strained his senses beyond his immediate surroundings in order to capture the images of his island home for what might be the last time.

He listened now to the growing sound of the waves as they streamed in over the shallow mud flats. Their vibrations were magnified because of the darkness. Now he intentionally pushed his old memories of it away and as far from him as he could. Then suddenly the boat's motion was of a different nature and the darkened land that was still close at hand began to move against the recently lit dancing torches that decorated the tall poles mounted along the vessel's port gunwales. Slowly the dark mass moved away becoming more visible at first in the natural darkness as the night-loading torches were now snuffed out. Then it vanished altogether in the darkness that shrouded the sea.

Stifling his old memories of this isle and of his short life, Dyfed now felt very much alone. Then by the light of the swaying inboard lanterns he quickly caught the searching glances from the all too eager and dark, familiarizing eyes of the sailors. Suddenly, a jagged streak of lightening appeared suddenly high up out of the dark. Its preternatural state manifested simultaneously from top to bottom, stretching from some unseen cloud to some unseen land somewhere beyond the sea. Momentarily it lit up the sailors around him and the inside of the ship's hull with a strange, silvery glow. The sailors ignored this preternatural display and continually tripped purposely over his well-placed feet and breathed upon him their foul breaths as they huffed and puffed about their work. As the silhouettes of the rough men had finished the heavy job of heaving to and fro which it took to get the sailing barge rowed out of the harbour and on track, they seemed now to grind down and grow static, moving like stellar apparitions do in the night sky. As the clouds cleared and the stars danced around a languishing Diana above, the sea grew lethargic under the night heat. So the sailors' toul became less purposeful and more opinionated. Then their minds quietened down a bit and became pensive and curious. They were obviously comfortable at sea for they drank beer and crowded in on Dyfed, rubbing up against him, coughing in his direction and relieving themselves either over the side of the gunwales or uneasily into sloshing, easily spilled handheld pots. While amiably mumbling and grumbling together they smothered him with their dark stink. Confronting their hefty smiles and their dogma of communication, he politely refused some leftover gruel they offered up to him. They picked their noses and picked off scabs from their elbows and knees. They farted loudly and threw pots of piss overboard along with the devil only knows what else. One or two of them dropped off to sleep, snoring loudly, while others played a board game of knucklebones. Dyfed remained awake and ever watchful.

(The hoi polloi)

*'Ghoulies and ghosties…and long-leggedy beasties…
And things that go bump in the night…Good Lord deliver us.'*
SCOTTISH PRAYER

The weather had changed and Dyfed surveyed the smudge of a bustling village quite close to the water's edge through a cool rainy dawn. Not long before, under a low blanket of cloud, he had quietly disembarked alone over the scow's least smelly patch of gunwale. This cargo merchant's scow had anchored in a dark harbour set in a channel between Albion and a large low island to its west called Mona Minor. Other than the snorting and snoring of the chief petty officers along with the rest of the crew who still lay in a drunken slumber, the damp morning was quiet. Climbing over the gunwales with his own cargo on his back into what he thought was an unnecessary and annoying wetting, he waded ashore in the western district of Gwyneth in the land of Albion.

In the quiet and soggy darkness Dyfed made for a cluster row of drab wattle and daub buildings that were barely visible under the dismal darkness of overcast and a tepid drizzle. He now set out for them. He had planned to pass right on through this gathering of bivouacs, but tired and gritty of eye he decided first to find available digs until Dawn appeared and bothered Radiance into the state of wakefulness. Later, he would make arrangements to set out for Amor, whatever direction that might be. Suddenly he tripped over a snag that stuck up and caught him on the leg. Feeling around and squinting in the dark, he realized that he had stumbled into a muddy graveyard where lapped the seas at high tide which had sapped out one side of the greying clay. Due to sea spillage pouring into a large area of the graveyard it had been opened up this way and out from this door of earthly death the bones of ghosts were now being sucked out to sea. Dyfed was not used to graveyards. In his community there hadn't even been one. He had heard that here in the third dimension the hoi polloi appeared to live shorter lives than did those masters of the Little Known Universe with their adjusted physiology, of which he was part. Obviously, he thought, death dominated the minds of the hoi polloi. He never thought of death, at least not his own.

As he passed from this sodden cemetery of muck towards his potential digs he noticed the locals had given the burial place a name: 'The Beautiful Horrid' they called it.

Dyfed, who was now peckish and his stomach grumbling, was hoping for a decent full Amoran or Albionian breakfast: Either that or, at the very least, a place to dry off and change out of his wet clothes. But the only building he found available within sight that he thought might accommodate him was a small wooden right-angled structure piled high on top of a square stone structure which hugged the gloom of the morning. This building was pushed and shoved back from the water's edge and stood out among the row of wattle and daub structures that lay around it. Furthermore, on account of the early summer morning rain, all was surrounded now by something no less than a foot deep film of mud. A large pile of cut timber accompanied the inn in its misery. This timber was stacked beside the high path and lay between the inn and the sea quay.

The innkeeper, when he finally appeared, was irritated to be aroused so early in the middle of the night, as he put it. But Dyfed made a mental note that the inn owner employed an early warning system for incoming trespassers. It was a system comprised of an orchestral cacophony of yapping dogs probably donated by the township at large. They had already been announcing Dyfed's arrival for quite some time — back when he had first splashed ashore, actually, and stumbled into the graveyard with an expletive or two. When Dyfed's sharp command to quieten the dogs had finally allowed them their freedom to express their characteristic compulsion/obsession manoeuvre of circling themselves nose to tail numerous times over their own little nests before lying and quietening down, they then abided as such for what remained of the night.

Grumbling, the awakened innkeeper led Dyfed up some stone stairs to a dark room on the wooden framed second floor. Here he pointed to a bed in which Dyfed saw two people already sound asleep. Like a blind man, whose hearing becomes more acute, Dyfed heard the rain begin to pound heavier onto the building's roof. The innkeeper then immediately disappeared somewhere into the darkened inn. As Dyfed's eyes quickly grew accustomed to the darkness inside this room he noticed there was a second bed close by. An entire family inhabited this bed. The heavy downpour outside, and perhaps a little inside, too, suddenly subsided then stopped altogether.

The folks in the second bed, Dyfed noticed with his eyes squinted, were sound asleep except for one of the children — a little girl — who was awake, fully dressed, and playing on top of the blankets. This windowless room, whose only light now was that faint dawn that was just creeping through the spaces between the boards, was (as earlier stated) on the second floor of the inn. It had a disgusting smell of piss about it that lingered and adulterated the room. The first floor beneath was really a crawl space and barely the height of a short man. From the smell that wafted up Dyfed guessed it was full of chickens and pigs. This squat building constructed of wood, though taller than the others, was nasty and cramped compared to anything Dyfed was accustomed to. So here, just above the high tide mark in a hovel built with chickens and pigs in mind, Dyfed sat in the semi darkness on the edge of the damp bed in his cold, wet clothes. Behind him the two sleepers who may have been locally employed workmen, snored loudly.

His immediate thought was to quickly escape this hovel and camp elsewhere for free, Dyfed reflected. He could now see a slight light between the chinks of the building's siding for a tired, dry-eyed wet morning was quickly approaching. He rubbed his grainy dry eyes and found that despite being tired he was wide awake with sleep well beyond his grasp. He was also quite cold and the damp and the salty urine air in the room (mixed with the redolent smell of the freshly cut lumber that was stacked just outside) didn't help his attitude or his uneasy sense of confinement one bit. Furthermore, Dyfed was more aware than any among this crude, unspecialized specimen of their race of things about the physics of material phenomena. For enclosed in this hovel were the atoms of all the revolting bodily functions of the people in it: urine, faeces, semen, menstrual fluids, phlegm, intestinal gas, earwax and so forth. It was the toll one paid to experience this dimension, he had been told.

At precisely that same moment a tradesman (who having left his early bed to come down from the nearby hills) happened to rumble past the inn in the early light on his way into the still quiet town square. Dyfed clearly heard the hooves of the horse and the rumbling noise of the wooden wheels that sounded as if they were octagonal in shape instead of round. He heard them easily, even over the snoring and farting that was going on in the room, and despite the mud that softened the normal road wheel rattle.

He stood up from his seated position on the edge of the crowded bed in an effort to begin shuffling his way down the steep ladder to outside so as to pass the time of day elsewhere (with the newly arrived tradesman, perhaps) when suddenly the little girl of the second bed who had been playing and humming to herself climbed off it and running quickly over to him snatched his hand and pulled, trying in vain to lead him over to the other bed. She then started shouting…"come and play with me. Come and help me with my play dolls.' At that point everybody else in the family bed stirred and woke up and began rubbing their eyes.

"What's going on over there? said the bedded, clothed and hatted woman, presumably the little girl's mother. 'What are you doing there with my child? Oh no! You brute, get away from her you perverted filth. Coel, wake the fuck up you limp bastard, someone is fiddling with your daughter. Wake up and do something. Hey — you there, shoo, shoo,' she said waving her clothed arm outside the bedding In answer to the hawkish fish-wife's screeches, a large man rolled over in the bed and sat up, pulling the cover blanket off two other younger children as he did so. He rubbed his eyes as a little boy started to cry then shriek loudly upon being awakened. This in turn woke his brother who in foul disposition even bettered his brother in their competition for screeching the loudest. In addition, the two sleeping workmen who had been the appointed bedfellows to Dyfed's sleeping arrangements also woke.

"What is going on here? What are you doing there with my little girl you castrated swine?' cried the prospective father from the other bed. 'Get out of here. Don't leave off wanking to graduate to my little Ethel, you bastard.' But his voice never rivalled the shrieking of those little devils of his who were now sitting up bellowing at the tops of their voices. Nor did he better even the wailing that the girl had now set forth to help raise the rafters.

"I don't have any one to play with.' she screamed. 'Make him play with me, again,' she bawled obstinately between loud shrieks and unnatural sounding sops.

"Who are you?' said one of the sleeping workmen in an inquisitive and wonderment tone that could have come right out of some slap-stick comedy act. This man had suddenly sat straight up in the bed that Dyfed had momentarily sat on the edge of earlier. Dyfed noticed that he was starring off in slightly the wrong direction in the dark so as not to be able to actually look directly at anybody. He hadn't really seen Dyfed, or anything else going on yet, either; not through either of his stupid blurry looking eyes, he hadn't, anyway. Dyfed thought it might be fitting to suddenly howl in grotesque laughter at the spectacle. But he set out instead to leave it all behind him.

Momentarily, Dyfed would be long gone having fled the room and out the door where the rain had now stopped. He groped his way down the dangerously narrow, slippery outside stone stairs alongside the building that led down to the first floor stone walled around chicken coup and barnyard manger. From there it was just a few more steps across the bountiful, good muddy earth and into the new morning tripping over the dogs in plain sight as he craned his neck to look up and backward. The dogs only stirred now and nipped at him as he tripped and stepped on them. They may be eager greeters but the sleepyheads weren't keen to say their good-byes and hurry back now, ye' hear?

Here, under a suddenly clearing sky that had lightened considerably, a cleansing tonic of morning air forced itself through his befouled nostrils into his gasping lungs. Dyfed stopped at this point and turned his head to look back one more time at the hovel that appeared like some drab and nasty early morning stage set in a converted and collapsing flea market theatre. Shuddering in disbelief he wondered just what the devil it had all been about. Had he really dropped off for a time and that this had been nothing more than a dream? Certainly not, he assured himself. But who — in the blazing glow of Radiance Apollo (or was it more like the foul sulphuric flame of Lord Beelzebub's lighted farts) — had those incredulous apparitions back there actually been? 'Welcome to this world,' he thought: roll on Amor, please God.

(The harmonious blacksmith)

*'He who doth not love wine, women, and song —
remain a fool, his whole life long.'*
JOHANN STRAUSS II *(ATTRIBUTED)*

In the course of the next while, and before he reached the City of Amor at the centre of the empire, Dyfed would meet three men who would feature rather prominently during his life. The first of those men he happened to meet outside the inn that morning.

The man appeared as a tradesman, the one who had arrived earlier at the break of day by horse drawn wagon. Having heard the all hell broke loose ruckus from within yonder dwelling and wondering what foreboding disagreement could it be that caused such discourse of harmony so early, this man watched now as Dyfed emerged from it. Could it possibly be this calm though eye-catching youth? he wondered.

The tradesman was a blacksmith, and now he smiled to himself as he saw the tall, strapping young Dyfed who still wet from his morning swim ashore striding with a heavy satchel slung over his broad back. As Dyfed approached the blacksmith he said good morning to him in Cymraeg, the local tongue. The older man's curious eyes roamed the young prosperous looking man over as he asked him his name. Answering him Dyfed then in turn looked the blacksmith over from top to bottom.

"I can give you a hand at your labours,' he added after a moment. As the blacksmith quickly accepted Dyfed's offer of assistance, he helped off-load the heavy crated forge down from the cart. Without being prompted Dyfed then bellowed into existence a hot coal fire that was soon panting inside that heavy brick-lined, iron contraption which the blacksmith used to forge implements. Now, as the blacksmith took over, Dyfed milled around, watching and waiting. Soon the forge was belching out raw heat. The blacksmith then pulled up a stool for himself and a wooden box off the wagon for Dyfed to use which he placed close enough to the heat for the lad to sit and be able to dry himself off and keep warm until the sun rose higher and the day warmed.

"So,' said the blacksmith at length, as the pungent smell of burning coal saturated the morning air, 'you are Dyfed, the man of the fire. You are Dyfed Lucifer, then. And since I am the blacksmith, we are now kin.'

Since (at this time) Dyfed had no other worthy moniker to his name (his title of Prince was generally unused), it was this eponym that he now took away from this somewhat Mithraic baptism by fire. Now Dyfed, son of Violet-Eye, prince of the grove, became Dyfed Lucifer. It was to become his third dimensional name and the name for which he has been known ever since. He later added the initial H. This was meant either for Herakles or Hephaestus, both of whom could be related to him in some way.

As Dyfed watched, the blacksmith heated up some gruel brewed from fermented grain on the top of the iron forge while he stoked it. Then finding two fired pottered cups, the two of them sat sipping their hot breakfast beverage as the iron-monger kept on stoking the fire waiting for the first solicitation for business to awake from their beds and start their work day. Beyond the blacksmith and his new helper, the abandon all hope of the not-so-merry Inn Forlorn sat quiet once again. Its occupants, apparently, back again into sound slumber.

As he and Dyfed casually chatted, feeling each other out, the blacksmith abruptly assumed a smug look on his suddenly turned away face. Confidence ruled his moment. Meanwhile, he had noted that Dyfed had been busy studying his eyes. The blacksmith had attentive eyes that were centred on his creased and weathered face. Dyfed could see that they were eyes he used as tools for maximum advantage over his environment as they roamed around taking in his domain, feeling everybody and everything out, in all likelihood, much like he himself did. On Dyfed's part, though, he noticed that the blacksmith seemed calm and pensive while he watched the action of the fire. Now and then, he noted, the tall thin man would glance momentarily over to his tethered workhorse and then toward his wagon where his kit and working materials were stored. His hair was dark reddish brown with a tuft of greying by his ears. His expressive eyes were a very dark brown, but most unusual was his clean-shaven face and a lack of Keltic adornments that were worn on the hair and bodies of his fellow countrymen. His outward style was similar to the manner (so much as Dyfed had seen) of the foreign Amorans. But at this point Dyfed had seen only those few that had come to his island home. Dyfed further noted that all the while the man also watched him very closely. But he noted that the man was so much unlike the ruffians aboard the scow or the patron perverts at the inn.

Later, the dockyard and quays began to pick up noise, and men strolled by on their way to work. The blacksmith then got Dyfed to throw more coal into his forge furnace from a tightly meshed wicker basket. He then donned a heavy leather apron that shielded him from just below his neck down to just short of his ankles. Then he began his heavy work of hammering out hoops for oak barrels and rims for the common ash wood chariot and wagon wheels from the red-hot bars of molten metal he heated upon his anvil.

The blacksmith, as stated, spoke to Dyfed in Brythonic Keltic or Cymraeg. Dyfed had no difficulty there though the blacksmith could detect a slight alteration from the normal speech coming from Dyfed's tongue, but very little. But this told him that Dyfed was indeed a foreigner, just as he suspected. For his part, Dyfed had some satisfaction that the blacksmith's Ideas, along with his mental and physical mannerisms, were quite unlike the others outside of his family that he had met so far. This was a relief.

"You can accompany me from here, later, if you like,' the blacksmith said to Dyfed at length. 'Where are you headed?'

Dyfed replied that he was headed for the City of Amor and the centre of the Empire. Yes, he would gladly accept a ride.

"Then I cannot help you,' replied the blacksmith. 'I managed to escape from there myself once not too long ago,' he said, 'by the skin of my teeth, I might add. I'm not planning to return just now. It's too far away, and, anyway I'm no longer welcome there.'

"Then you are an enemy of Amor? Dyfed ventured to say. But the blacksmith simply contemplated him grimly for a moment and did not answer.

"What we will do here today is just donkey work with little skill involved,' he continued to say. 'Still, others can't do it and it pays for the corn and the beer to satisfy the belly and puts the roof over our heads and a fire in our hearth on the cold and wet nights.' Somehow Dyfed doubted the blacksmith's sincerity with respect to his pronouncement about the donkeywork, though he thought that millions of others certainly wouldn't have.

"This utilitarian craft that you apply here requires proficiency in skill and mastery,' Dyfed replied in disagreement, looking over at the leather clad older man with hammer in hand and posturing a stance as though he were Thor himself. And the man's face, reflecting the glow from the forge, appeared as though it was a mask of beaten copper that he wore. 'The Hellene philosopher, Aristoteles,' Dyfed added, 'who, fortunately (in view of his snotty attitude of entitlement for the likes of himself) and is now deceased, referred to crafts such as yours as the banausic arts. He also said that the industries of wage earners like you are of poor taste that debase our species and that banausic arts and wage earning industries in general sully the mind.' Here Dyfed laughed, his mirth showing clearly in his expressive silver eyes. 'Even Tully (Quintus Florens Tertullianus) agreed, and we still have Augustine and Boethius to hear from. I'm sure they will have the same complaint. And Tully,' Dyfed continued, 'having once sowed his seed among tinctured twats in complete abandon, has now, apparently, adopted dull celibacy as his companion, or so I'm told. Now he pushes the doctrine that original sin is born out of carnal lust coveted by ones natural parents. I say, what a fool. He is certainly on the losing end of his farcical logic, wouldn't you say? No, I suspect we have not yet got beyond that mind-set, not by a long shot,' he added.

Such an attitude from a refined young man such as this would have normally been a strange and unusual experience. But the lad's outburst seemed to intrigue the blacksmith. His eyes now narrowed and riveted closely upon the youth in front of him. Here they remained focussed for a long moment.

"You don't say?' was all the man said at last. It was said in the manner of an answer.

Just then men from the docks began arriving and the smithy deftly negotiated a good working day of commissions from them. Dyfed saw nobody come from the vessel he had arrived in. As the morning got warmer the air around the furnace got hotter and the sparks flew as the blacksmith pounded the heated red-hot hot bars. Using his hammer and tongs he pounded the metal bars again and again, back and forward into a long bar which he cut into uniform lengths. Then looping each length into a ring he pounded the ends together. The hot metal sizzled loudly when he dropped it into the grey, filmy water he had contained in a heavily pitched, oak wooden pail to cool.

Business was usually first come first serve. As he worked the blacksmith talked to Dyfed about his work and how he did such and such and why he did it. And as he listened intently Dyfed began to remove his outerwear due to the growing heat that his body couldn't keep up in throwing off. Soon he was down to being bare above the waist. The smithy, however, remained buttoned up to the neck and down to the gloves at his wrists in his heavy cloth shirt. And still over top of that in the front was his full length, thick leather apron held in place by its neck strap and mid-length tie strands. Even his head was covered in a large loosely woven, round floppy hat that he removed only to wipe the perspiration from his brow with a large clothe. But he did not remove it when he left off from his labour to discuss work with potential customers whose visits had now increased. Nor did he remove it when he stopped momentarily for a break and to sit a moment and drink some water from a pottered urn he kept wrapped in a thick, wet cloth. After sharing its contents with Dyfed he would replace the urn beneath the wagon-cart, away from the sun (now risen higher) and the heat from the forge.

Above, the gulls and crows circled in a blueing sky and shrieked at the world below them. They took to dropping small shellfish from quite some height that they picked up on the mud flats. This, apparently, was the easiest way for these armless creatures to break open the packaging. The crows and gulls would swoop down to the shelled carnage to peck out their measly but tasty meal. Then the ravens arrived, stealing from the others and teasing the dogs that yawned and stretched as Radiance rose and were now on the prowl for scraps. The ravens after driving the maddening dogs to distraction would hop away off to one side, laughing their throaty laugh, or fly up to a roost in order to eat among themselves. Alongside the daily routine in the life of the creatures of the earth, Dyfed also learned that the art of forging (which was fabricating) was a great skill. At length the blacksmith replied to Dyfed's earlier compliment, saying that it was an accurate observation that this art embodied a level of proficiency that should normally be more respected (as it was of old) and one that should have a higher pay scale attached and be of equal social importance to that of a democratic magistrate. But it must be much loftier than any facsimile overrated make-do among that profession which were now more common. He shot a long, hard look in Dyfed's direction as he spoke.

Dyfed pitched in to please the blacksmith who, he thought, might become disposed later to lift him away from this grubby little dirt hole and set him at least in the direction of the city of Amor. Now that this place had come to life Dyfed could see that the gathering hereabouts was a nasty little terminal port for fishing and importing or exporting materials like slate and timber that were destined for elsewhere by ship. Very close by to the immediate west was the island of Mona Major that was inhabited in part by a Druid coven (in fact a few of them). But as for this port, what with its wooden and mud huts it was nothing more than a hastily built commercial cenedl (village), that's all it was; it was so unlike Violet and Manandan's domain. It had no majestic apportionments, its array was not of any orderliness and its domesticated surroundings were not magical forests.

Dyfed watered the workhorse and the blacksmith had him pull four pre-fabricated wheel rims from the wagon whose circumferences were not yet welded together. The blacksmith adjusted the diameters of the wobbly iron rims by overlapping them until the distance between their circumferences matched the measurement that the customer had given him, plus the width of two fingers. Dyfed was instructed to mark them by notching the spot with a sharp pointed iron instrument. In his continuous dialogue to Dyfed as he worked, the blacksmith told the younger man…'measure twice cut once.' Later, when the ash wood frame and spokes arrived, the smithy would check the measurement again himself then cut, heat and pound them together. And then before cooling he would beat the hot rims onto the wheels.

As the time was approaching mid point between sun up and noon, and despite the heat, the cenedl still remained in shadow. This was due to a smallish mountain immediately to the east that over-shadowed the village and managed to keep Radiance Apollo's warming rays from beating directly down onto their necks at least till noon during this the hot season. Dyfed listened to the even rhythm and the timed metre of blows that the blacksmith unleashed onto the anvil. It was harmonious. He was now the companion of the harmonious blacksmith, Dyfed thought with amusement. He grew sleepy as he listened to the metered blows pounding onto the hot anvil blend with the cries of the gulls as they swooped around and around. Then exactly at halfway between sunup and noon the blacksmith looked up at the sun peeping over the hill. Then removing his apron he stopped for a break. Standing in the lee of his wagon and away from the glancing eyes of the Tud (the folk of the cenedl, as they are called in Cymraeg, the local language), the blacksmith momentarily removed his apron and then his over-shirt which he gave one, good, hard shake to dislodge any sweat and body heat before quickly replacing it. Dyfed noticed in those few moments that the man in true Prydainian (the generic name for the people of these isles) fashion had tattoos depicting animals and geometric designs covering both arms that disappeared up into the short sleeves of his undergarment. The ironsmith fetched some beer and some cold, cooked chicken legs, giving a large cup of beer and a couple of the drumsticks to Dyfed.

"Presumably you are versed in the arts of metallurgy as well as having mastery of the art of fabrication,' said Dyfed to the blacksmith. The latter thoughtfully regarded Dyfed for a moment before saying.

"I see, Davie, you are a man with a prestigious family link.' He eyed the tall youth closely.

"You shouldn't have needed the markings on my own skin to discern that,' retorted Dyfed casually. 'But I must say, it took me aback when I saw you half naked just now, for I initially took you for just a professional tradesman.' The blacksmith did not answer, but it was apparent that he was intending in choosing his words carefully before he spoke. Just then the sun fully cleared the rampart of the mountain and its rays burst in full force down onto the cenedl like from the passing of a cloud. As Dyfed and the blacksmith ate their chicken and drank their beer, the occupants of the yonder Inn Forlorn burst out from its confines. They spilled out of the door in single file overly dressed and into the hot sun.

Once outside, they stood together huddled a tight knot gazing in the direction of the blacksmith's contraptions. Suddenly they all began point toward Dyfed and the blacksmith. Shortly after, the innkeeper came out all bundled up as well and after conducting a short conference with the tight knot he began to walk directly toward Dyfed. The formerly gathered tight-knotted troop immediately followed in behind the innkeeper. Then with a hurried spurt it quickly caught up and closed ranks closely around the strutting innkeeper like a human shield. This human clump shortly came up very close to where Dyfed was sitting and then stretched out in a line behind the innkeeper, each stomping their feet as if they were cold or carefully spacing themselves as though they were on military parade. The innkeeper who had shown Dyfed to his crowded bed stood closest to Dyfed.

"Where is my money, honey boy?' the innkeeper demanded in his winey squeaky high voice which passed through a smirk that stretched across the lower part of his stupid face. With a sense of bemusement and in an effort to distance himself slightly from the confrontation, the blacksmith stood up with lunch still in hand and went over to lean against his cart, obviously curious and looking forward to the episode unfolding before him as he chewed away on his chicken leg.

Holding a chicken leg of his own, Dyfed fed it up into his mouth. He bit into the cold meat and tore the cartilage off the end of the drumstick with his teeth. He threw away the bare bone over his shoulder that caused a scuffle among the dogs behind him. He then carefully regarded the innkeeper and slowly chewed the meat off the cartilage that had a sharp piece of chicken bone sticking out between his lips like a bone needle. He swallowed the meat by delicately moving his tongue around it then spat out the cartilage and its sharp bone that flew passed the innkeeper's left ear, narrowly missing one of the former sleeping workmen who as second in line was standing very closely behind him. The workman suddenly backed up but tripped over a darting dog that was vying for the meat morsel that Dyfed had spat out. The man tumbled over backwards causing a commotion. Someone meant to kick the yelping dog but kicked the fallen man instead. The others laughed as the fallen man on his hands and knees then grabbed the cur by the neck. The dog turned and jumping forward bit the man's face. This was much to the irritation of the innkeeper whose own bone of contention he thought was of more importance.

"Your money?' Dyfed said, emphasising the word *your* and moving his eyes from the man-dog commotion below to appraise the innkeeper. And then with an obvious air of confidence as he stared into the innkeeper's cold dark eyes he said. 'What do I know about your money! Have you lost it? Are you accusing me of stealing your money, or are you just angry by detecting my comprehension of your stupidity for losing it?'

"No', the innkeeper stammered, getting angrier and turning red. 'The money you owe me,' he replied. 'The rent.'

"The rent? answered Dyfed. What rent? Why would I owe you rent? I didn't rent anything from you.'

"You rented a room from me last night,' he replied. 'You owe me...'

"I did no such thing,' Dyfed quickly interjected, applying a slight and incredulous laugh to start the retort off. 'Early this morning after I disembarked from that scow over there at anchor I looked over what you had to offer over here. It came up wanting and not to my liking. It was a chicken coup, not an inn...noisy with women and children, so I left, like any sensible man would.'

"There he is. That's him there,' said a voice off to Dyfed's left. The blacksmith was the first to turn and look over his shoulder and notice a captain from one of the sailing barges in the harbour approaching. Dyfed recognized him as the captain of the scow that had brought him here. He was striding with intent towards him while surrounded by three of the sailors from the vessel.

"Oi. Hey-up! You there,' shouted the captain. 'Mister Dyfed the marooned, formerly stranded on Mona Minor,' he added after a moment.

The innkeeper, who was now focussed on the approaching men, turned slightly to his right and pushing the one remaining sleeping workman (the one still on his feet) back with his right arm he regarded them as they approached. He then stepped forward in the direction towards the oncoming captain and sailors who were now almost on top of them. The innkeeper then quickly and loudly stated his position in his high, squeaky harsh voice in their general direction:

"This young man, here, owes me money. Whatever business you have with him will have to wait.'

"Stand aside sir,' said the captain gruffly in a deep voice. 'My name is Avaragus, and I'm the captain of the sailing barge belonging to the House of Thing, over there. And this man, here, while under my command, disobeyed my orders aboard about disembarking from my ship and, to be precise, owes me the price of a fine. And you? the captain then inquired. Who the hell, exactly are you?'

"I'm the local innkeeper here,' the other man squeaked, 'of the House of Inn, over there, if you please. He turned with a wheezing laugh, looking for plaudit from his line of accompanying morale bolsters and yes men. 'And this man here,' he continued, 'rented a room last night and then did a bunk, leaving me unpaid.'

"Don't be a stupid knot at the end of his rope,' said one of the sailors standing next to the captain. The sailor then shook his broad finger immediately in front of the innkeeper's face. 'He was aboard our ship from the night before last right up to first light this morning. Why would he rent a room from your hovel when he already had a comfortable place to sleep, a beverage to drink and good company of the likes of us to keep? Right boys?' He turned toward the other two sailors who then laughed and nodded their agreement in unison. Then with irritating sounds from their mouths, three of them pointed their shaking fingers into the innkeeper's face as he repeatedly tried to slap them away. The captain remained solemn. The blacksmith, Dyfed noted, watched with raised eyebrows and with an obvious, and growing amusement.

"He molested this young girl, here,' said the innkeeper, crossing his arms and pouting out his bottom lip, as though he had made some kind of final pronouncement to which all the others would have bow to.

"Now that is a serious accusation.' It was the smithy speaking this time, and as he spoke he pushed himself up to his full and great height from his casual and relaxed lean against the back of his wagon. Now his face was stern.

"Yes it is,' said Captain Avaragus, 'a very serious accusation, indeed. Sailor, go fetch the local magistrate, now; that is an order. He's from Gaul, I believe, so he may be drunk; but bring him here anyway.' Laughter emanated from the accompanying sailors.

"The magistrate won't come here,' interjected the smithy incredulously. 'He and his suite are in fact from Gaul and are bent on interpreting the Amoran law into Cymraeg. They've got their work cut out ahead of them. They're too busy.'

"They're Amorans,' shouted one of the inn dwellers, 'who've come here to spread their havoc.'

"No they're not,' interjected the blacksmith again. 'They are Amoran-like, but they are from Gaul, which is part of the Empire, as we are and soon to be more so, considering the riff-raff defending us. They are also of a particular cult, possibly wizards. The blacksmith turned and glanced at the island that loomed fairly close off shore beyond the quay across the narrow strait (channel) that looked more like a river. Anyway,' he said pointing to the innkeeper, 'both he and the magistrate are in way over their heads and neither seems to know it. We need to take this up with him at his office, now.'

So, off they went. The blacksmith watched as Dyfed, stripped naked to his waist, wearing a tall pointy hat with a wide brim, was quickly out striding those who followed; namely, Captain Avaragus of the sailing scow belonging to the House of Thing, and his three sailors; the overdressed innkeeper with a woollen hat propped on his head; the woman and her husband in heavy coats and their little girl and two little boys; the two formerly sleeping workmen, all of them warmly dressed, as well as the two customers from the harbour's warehouse who had just rolled over the ash wheels as the mob was on the move and had decided to tag along for a look-see. Finally the blacksmith made a move and tagged along at the rear. They went shuffling along closely together like a miniature Amoran infantry unit, with the expressed exception that they weren't well dressed. There were fourteen of them in between the blacksmith and Dyfed making sixteen of them in all, and they clumped and shuffled along together. Dyfed was well out ahead by now, though, and the smithy, trailing behind, wondered if the former knew where he was going, which of course he didn't.

Upon arriving at a medium sized building whose upper half was made of wood and set upon a stone foundation that rose to the height of the key-stone header atop the thick oak door, while he waited for the others to catch up Dyfed, read the words: Amoran Magistrate Authority. This was written both in Amoran and in the local language (their first published translation attempt) on the shingle outside. Then when they did arrive, Dyfed quickly jumped forward and strode ahead through the door first.

Once inside, and still ahead of the others, Dyfed noticed a fat, brown-eyed man in a cloak and tall hat, that wasn't pointy like his but roundish, sitting on a bench behind a table. He was in the midst of drinking from a tin cup when Dyfed burst in. Their eyes met. A moment or two later, when the formerly quiet line of people shuffling behind Dyfed, who had gathered outside the open door and suddenly in an unruly knot began their entrance (a noisy production of squeezing and elbowing their way in in an effort to force themselves through all at one time), the fat man in the cloak and roundish hat slammed the tin cup down hard on the table and immediately — and almost nimbly — jumped to his feet in alarm.

"What's going on here?' he demanded, still staring at Dyfed. The troop was finally followed by the silent and smiling smithy that strode in a few steps behind whistling a jaunty tune through his lips. Fortunately he was tall enough, like Dyfed, to be able to look over the heads of the others in order to view the proceedings from the back. There were two other men present in the room who were working with manuscripts. They had stopped what they were doing in a quiet and frozen pause — both with their necks cranked around — waiting (expectantly) with expressions of amazement on their faces.

"I'm here to press charges against this man, here,' said the innkeeper, pointing to Dyfed, who as the room filled up had been pushed further and further up against the desk in front of the magistrate.

"What charges?' asked the fat magistrate.

"Charges of molesting this little girl, here,' he replied, quickly reaching out and grabbing the little girl by the coat and roughly pulling her forward away from her mother through the tight crowd. It was much like the way a hunter pulls a dead rabbit out of a thick briar bush.

"Are you her father?' asked the magistrate, stumbling a bit with his speech.

"No, he is, I think,' answered the innkeeper, pointing to the man who was pressed up against him and was peering over his left shoulder with a stupid look on his face; then the former having realized his error, turned his head and pointed over his right shoulder instead. And this is her mother,' he volunteered without being pressed.

"Then who, exactly, are you, sir?' asked the magistrate.

"I'm the innkeeper,' he answered.

"And what then has all this got to do with you?'

"This man owes me money, your Excellency,' the innkeeper replied, pointing to Dyfed.

"Let me get this straight. This man over here allegedly owes you money so you are forcing charges of molestation upon him. Are her parents in any way involved in this accusation?' The magistrate looked back and forth between the man and woman that had been identified as the parents. But seeing no reaction, nor any intelligent light whatsoever dimly flickering behind their dark, dull eyes, nor receiving any word whatsoever from them, the magistrate then looked back at the innkeeper who he scrutinized closely with his dark, beady eyes.

"Bringing charges like this against a man is serious business,' said the fat magistrate. Do you know what you are doing and the penalty for defamation and false testimony?'

"Your Excellency,' Dyfed began in a drawl which, along with his body language, accented a notion of impatience with the obviously ludicrousness of the situation at hand. A situation, albeit, which the lad tempered in some brilliant way by expressing sympathy for his Excellency's rotten luck of having this problem fall on his desk in the first place. Although he was the victim here, Dyfed's tone seemed somehow to place himself in a similar if not the same category as the luckless magistrate who was now being faced with having to resolve this farce. But more than that (and to everybody's astonishment) Dyfed spoke in clear, fluent, and educated Amoran. 'This man is a greedy, highly confused, liar,' he continued. 'Ultimately, he suffers from only the devil knows what, which under the circumstances shouldn't surprise anyone. He is, besides, very likely a fool as well. He is here after money, that's all, your Excellency,' he said, adding a little laugh. 'There is no more depth to the man than that. Nor does lying deter him, for he is too shallow for that to adversely affect his conscience. You see, as I have said, he is greedy. He wants money, my money. He is lying about me owing him money, but he knows no other tried method of gain, and he is highly confused and a fool both for assuming he can get the better of me by using such a trust worthy Amoran official such as you, your Excellency. I, on the other hand, am Dyfed Lucifer,' he glanced momentarily at Smithy, the blacksmith. 'I have recently come from the Isle of Peace where I have been on business, and much anxious to be on my way, as I'm sure you can well appreciate my position,' he said. 'I'm on my way to the city of Amor, on personal business, of course. I'm likely never to return here, again; that's for sure.'

The magistrate had not been able to suppress his surprise to hear a young, half naked man — whose tribe, or race, he wasn't even remotely certain about — speaking the empire's official language, and most beautifully at that. That he should hear such words spoken with an educated fluency here, among the sticks in the back of beyond, downright amazed the magistrate. He could barely muster the diction of a sophomore, himself. The man began to eye Dyfed cautiously.

'And,' — Dyfed continued — 'as the captain over here and those three sailors over there have already attested (earlier), I was with them aboard ship from the Isle of Peace from the night before last until this morning's first light. And because of that fact, it may seem obvious that I was in no need of a room that the innkeeper here keeps insisting I rented from him without payment, which is the crux of this situation. But as I was tired from travel and wet, and it wasn't yet light, I at least looked over what the innkeeper had available early this morning. It wasn't to my liking. It was a room — apparently the room wherein some kind of molestation has allegedly taken place, perhaps a number of times — under the roof of the inn operated by this man here (the innkeeper). In addition, there were four other adults present in this room along with three children. It's just that he hasn't got to that part yet. Furthermore, I have molested nobody and my lack of attire is due to the heat of the day and a morning of hard work around the forge of the blacksmith who is over there. It was he who I was assisting out of courtesy and some curiosity due to my interest in metallurgy. Furthermore, I'm hoping he will deliver me away from this miserable, squalid little cenedl and set me on my journey along the path to Amor.'

Dyfed paused. When he continued again it was in the common Brythonic tongue that he spoke, interspersed with colloquiums in the local Cymraeg tongue. He used this dialect now for the sole purpose that the rest of the churls would be able to understand what he said, for they were too ignorant and too remote to speak the language of the empire.

'No, your Excellency, I did not molest that young girl, there. You see, early this morning — just before sunrise — after I had disembarked from yonder captain's vessel to whom I had paid in silver prior to sailing, and for which I have a receipt, I sought a room, as I have already said, at the inn in order to dry off, as I was cold and wet from wading ashore. The captain, you see, had not quite expedited his responsibility to deliver me to dry land, as agreed. So, I sought a room from that innkeeper, over there, so as to dry off. Alas, there was no room at the inn; at least there wasn't any bed to myself in what I will describe as a communal bedroom. So, the innkeeper there assigned me to a bed that was occupied by two men who were tightly wrapped up in the only blanket available. He indicated I could enjoy their company, if you please! There was a second and separate bed in that room in which this family over there were sound asleep, with the exception of that little girl here who was awake. Apart from myself who is here and who was cold and wet, it appeared that only the little girl and the innkeeper had been the ones awake in the inn when I arrived. The little girl had insisted that it was my turn now to play with her. The innkeeper, as I said, had just then left the room. Then, having heard the rumbling sounds of a blacksmith's cart outside, I now intended to pass the morning with a potential new friend who might provide heat to dry me off and assist my departure from this slovenly and decrepit cenedl; that being the kindly blacksmith who is still over there.'

The blacksmith's face suddenly lit up and he began smiling and grinning like an idiot towards the magistrate over the heads and shoulders of those in front of him.

"Hello, over here,' he said almost mockingly in the local dialect.

"Then,' continued Dyfed, 'an hour or so later — much work having been done by Smitty over there who had also given me some chores to help out — these nasty little people over here tramped out of the inn, rubbing the sleep out of their eyes as if having just awakened to the world, or sobered up perhaps, and marched up to me. Whereupon their chief spokesman, the innkeeper here, made libellous accusations against me on behalf of others over there who have as yet not spoken a word nor corroborated what the innkeeper has stated. Presumably, this is because — unlike the innkeeper — they know the penalty for libellous accusations, defamation and false testimony, your Excellency.'

Smitty the blacksmith noted that the magistrate stared long and hard at Dyfed as the young man spoke and even remained staring at him for a few moments after he had finished. Meanwhile the room remained exceedingly quiet. Since Dyfed spoke this time in the Brythonic tongue the fat magistrate only understood a smattering of what Dyfed had said, as he was a trained Amoran magistrate, not a linguist. It had been only recently his Amoran superiors had sent him here into the hinterland of Gwyneth from the city of Isis in Gaul. From here, apparently, he was bound for Viroconium and Caer Legion when the coast was clear. At least that is what his superiors had told him. The magistrate was warmly dressed in his long thick cloak and his heavy roundish hat that hung down past his ears, despite the warmth of the day. Perhaps this was because he had only recently arrived into the cool climate of Albion. He was from Massalia, he told Dyfed politely, where it was warmer than here, though he had studied in Mediolanum in Italia, near the heart of the Amoran Empire. It was a long journey from there to here and an even longer journey back, the magistrate lamented to himself every day about that.

He had realised at long last that only a green horn like him would have accepted such a dangerous border position as this. For his post was just beyond the empire's frontier, and therefore, essentially, behind enemy lines in the middle of nowhere surrounded by nasty little babbling barbarians. His only escape route was by sea, and that could be equally perilous. Yet here, judging by his somewhat cultured poise and manner was some kind of fellow countryman, at least in mind. A young, lean and clean fellow countryman without a shirt, albeit, but a countryman of some kind, none the less. And he was an Amoran for sure, and one who in addition spoke the local babble: if, of course, there was any intelligence in the local jabber and their chicken scratch for writing. The magistrate continued to regard Dyfed a moment more before he moved his eyes around and fixed them on the innkeeper.

"You brought this young man, who was looking for a room to get dry, to the bed in which two men — all wrapped up together in one blanket — occupied?' the magistrate asked the innkeeper in his halting, rudimentary, but decipherable Brythonic. He accompanied this with an over emphasized theatrical posture implying incredulousness. 'Are those two men here now?' he asked.

Dyfed noticed that the two sleeping workmen became very nervous and looked down at the floor while trying to obscure themselves and shrivel away to nothing like dried worms among the tight crowd around them. Meanwhile, the cramped room was getting warmer and warmer by the minute. The crowd then began to push away ever so slowly from the two sleeping workmen who, despite the crush, were left standing together slightly apart from the others. The magistrate cleared his voice.

"Did you men solicit, or did the innkeeper on your behalf solicit for you, for a fee, to deliver to you — in the course of last night — this handsome young man to your bed?'

Deadly silence followed.

"You, there, answer.'

"No, no, Excellency, your Worship. Definitely not,' said one of the sleeping workmen quickly, who it now appeared may be an unemployable, former workman whose forehead and cheeks were bleeding profusely into one eye and down his chin from four deep wounds inflicted by sharp canine teeth. 'Please, we are decent people here. We are not part of any of this trouble. We were awakened with these children over there screaming and that couple over here shouting and arguing about something, your Excellency. The innkeeper later brought this to our attention.'

"Then, if you two men are not part of this trouble, as you say,' — the fat magistrate paused — 'why are you here in an apparent attempt to bolster support for the innkeeper's claims against this young gentleman from the city of Amor? Are you in collusion with the innkeeper?' There was a sudden tramping of feet as the injured and bleeding sleeping workman (now very much wide awake) quickly turned about and scurried hurriedly from the room and out the door — followed by the sea captain and the three sailors. The sound of their feet sounded like a troop of stamping soldiers as they tramped out the door single file that was left open to the sunlight behind them. Then the woman who had said nothing the whole time suddenly picked up her two little boys and called her daughter to come. They too quickly retreated out of the magistrate's office behind the others, followed by her erstwhile husband who had also said nothing during the entire episode. Meanwhile, one of the two harbour warehouse labourers suddenly picked up the tune that the blacksmith had earlier been whistling upon entry, which in turn was then picked up by the other unemployed and rather simple workman. Then both of them looking bored and nonchalant, even confused — as though while shopping for nails and hammers they had mistakenly walked into a ladies undergarments shop instead — casually whistled themselves out the door together in tandem, followed by the remaining harbour warehouse labourer, where they walked under the noonday sun together. The last labourer out twirled around in a fancy pirouette manner to shut the door behind him.

"This man here,' said the blacksmith, 'recently journeyed from the isle of Peace, is in my employ, temporarily, Excellency.' Now, he too, spoke in perfect Amoran, which immediately added more confusion to the fat magistrate's face. 'I have reason, and a duty, to see that through no fault of his own he does not come a cropper over idle and malicious accusations such as what we've heard here, this morning. That's why I'm here. Though I barely know him at all, I am a good judge of character and do not find him wanting as such. It would be a shame if such a fine youth falls victim to libellous skulduggery to dog him for the remainder of his life, even if he were to survive a trial and not be beheaded or have his arms pulled out of their sockets or his chest cut open and his heart removed. Surely, Amor's justice will not fail him in this? your Excellency.'

The fat magistrate whipped the roundish hat off his baldhead and dropping it onto the table in front of him wiped his forehead with his thick sleeve. Now that the ship's Captain, the three sailors, the two labourers, the two sleeping workmen, the man and his wife and their three children had fled the sturdy shack, that left the innkeeper, Dyfed, the blacksmith, the magistrate and his two helpers with more air to breathe.

"Marcellus! Quick there, draw up the accusations brought by this man, here, against Dyfed Lucifer recently of the Isle of Peace, he said quickly in the Amoran tongue. Then switching to his staccato type Brythonic he said. 'What is your name, innkeeper? Cad did you say; Cad the innkeeper? Allright! Marcellus, copy out his complaint,' the magistrate resumed in Amoran, 'and the statement that this young man has given in answer to what Cad the innkeeper has claimed. However, since there has been no proof,' the magistrate glanced at the blacksmith, 'no charge will be brought against this young man.' And so it went; and later Dyfed and the innkeeper were dismissed but not before a nominal fee was levied to both men. The charge, it was said, was merely an administration fee owed to those doing the administering. Dyfed protested the fee on his part as he was the victim of accusation, but Smitty put a large calloused hand softly on Dyfed's shoulder and said.

"If you would accept some kindly advice, master Dyfed, from a well intentioned blacksmith, drop that appeal and pay. There's a good lad.'

Meanwhile, Cad the innkeeper paid his fee and fled out the door without a sound. Smitty waited for Dyfed to pay, then they left the small room together. The magistrate, along with his two office companions who had pocketed the paid fees, followed them to the door like weary hosts who thought that their late night guests would never leave. There, and in a bumbling commotion (in which all three hosts seemed to participate in together) they closed the door behind Dyfed and the smithy. Then, appearing exhausted and out of breath they leaned back against the closed door with a collective sigh of relief. The magistrate then tore up the complaint.

Later that afternoon, Dyfed left the little town sitting atop Smitty the Harmonious Blacksmith's cart.

(A shabby little cenedl between the shrubs somewhere on the side of a hill)

'Home is the sailor home from the sea, and the hunter home from the hill'
ROBERT LOUIS STEVENSON

After a sleepless night beneath Smitty's cart — when Dawn's first light rose up and frightened the darkness of night away — Dyfed Lucifer and Smitty set out again, turning away from the direction of the land of the Tegeing, known to the Amorans as Decangli. Now they travelled south passed the shoulder of a great white mountain that dominated Gwyneth (also Gwynedd) that was known in this land as Pen Llithrig y wrach.

Lying awake before rising, Dyfed had not been stingy in his reflection upon his introduction to this strange land. He was amazed at the even stranger circumstances he had observed which were woven into the life fabric that dominated the lives of these hoi polloi. He hadn't been here two minutes, it seemed, before he had been screeched and hollered at, money had been demanded of him from all sides, and he had been accused of degusting abominations, and now — here he was under a wagon for protection from the night sky. It was almost as if he had fallen off it. He reached for the jug of distilled grain that the two men had used earlier as a sleep inducer that now lay on the cool ground between them. It seemed to him that the social tapestry here was pure burlesque complicated with slapstick. Get a load of that innkeeper, would you, he bemused incredulously. Whew-wee! — and what will today bring? he wondered looking up, as if something somewhere up there had the answer. And then there was his new friend Smitty. He was something of a puzzle. A strange man, he thought (as he lived and breathed) that at that moment was lying beside him under the wagon that at this very moment was probably trying to listen to his thoughts.

As Dyfed had insisted on calling him Smitty, the man had then formally introduced himself as Festus. But Festus the harmonious blacksmith then added with a wink that he was also known by the name Maelgwyn. Could Dyfed remember that, he asked him. Dyfed wasn't certain why he didn't believe the man but he stored the information nonetheless. So, who the devil knows what his name is, he thought. For that matter, who cares? In hindsight he decided that to rely on anything that this man put forward (apart from his skill at the anvil) was preposterous. It was almost as if he had been intentionally sent, or at least had come to meet him on his arrival — god Zeus! — as they say here in this dimension in reference to the devil. But, then again, where would he be now without the blacksmith? Dyfed had hoped he might turn out to be one of the Hyperborean Masters of the little known universe contacts that Manandan assured him would get in touch with him over time. That was a good thing for it seemed likely to him now that this world, the world which he had willingly happened upon and not by chance, might be full of bizarre and complex idiosyncrasies that was continually ready and poised to inflict disaster onto the unwary.

Dyfed then reminded himself of the trolls that Manandan had warned him about that populated this world as well. And on top of that, he needed to be on the lookout for Haploids, too. He didn't think that the harmonius blacksmith, or the magistrate, or even the innkeeper, never mind the common churls at large, fitted the description of either of these. So far (he believed) all that he had done was to have gotten a glimpse of the banality of a few half-baked characters experimenting with insanity.

His one game saver in all of this was to get to the centre of the Amoran Empire as fast as he could so as to settle in and begin his commissioned mission. He resolved then and there not to dilly-dally any longer, but to get on with it and get to Amor where (naively) he had no doubt that assistance and logistical help would be waiting and made available to him.

In the early light which Radiance cast forth, and amid the kit and caboodle — common to a blacksmith and forger — that was piled all around them, he and Smitty (Festus or Maelgwyn) sat on the floor of the wagon facing each other eating a breakfast of hard boiled eggs and sipping the distilled beverage all of which they washed down by beer as they bumped along a pitched and rocky track. The workhorse, left unattended, obviously knew its routine. Meanwhile (beneath them), the wagon jerked and rattled from end to end as it was being slowly dragged behind the heavy plodding, large hoofed locomotion force. Then after dawdling for some time along the twisty track between the tall grass growing among the hilly country, Dyfed saw what from a distance looked like a pleasant little cenedl (township) nestled in a dip between two close by hills. This cenedl was perched partially on the side of one of the hills. It was toward this cenedl now that the rather impertinent Smitty pointed and suggested that since Dyfed took a shine to it, that this was as good a place as any to reside for a season or two. In any case, the man informed Dyfed that he couldn't take him any further, not toward Amor for sure, nor could Dyfed accompany him further than this to anywhere else, either. He was (he said) about to strike out in the opposite direction and into oncoming danger. He advised Dyfed to orient him self further, grab a hold of some current reality common to the hoi polloi before stepping out onto the great expanse that was to be Dyfed's life's journey. There will be those to assist you, and he added that their paths were sure to cross again. Later he advised, 'if you take my advice you will make for the city of Legion first then on to Nova Troia before you take on Amor. There is trouble brewing, Dyvie my man. Legion is out of its way for now, Nova Troia is not.'

Dyfed looked aghast at this shambles of a village that close up comprised of conical stone huts. It resembled a troubadour's fair or a carnival exhibition site on the morning after camp had been struck — all finished, packed up, their money counted, and their horses standing at the wait — although that, he thought, might have had more vibrancy, profile (never mind dignity) as a community than this burgh (berg) ahead.

What did this blacksmith know about the likes of him and his journey, anyway? thought Dyfed. But in the end (and since there wasn't a better one at the moment) he decided to take him up on the suggestion for a long as it took to get his bearings, but certainly no longer. The cart did not leave the main track but stopped adjacent to the village. Smitty spoke quickly to a shepherd child that was by the roadside as Dyfed untangled his large satchel from around the forge and unloaded it. He then watched as the young boy ran off toward the cenedl.

"More invasions from the Amoran establishment are coming this way,' the blacksmith said, 'despite the prospect of a general revolt against Amoran occupation. 'Anyway, by the first weekend of next month — in all likelihood — yonder cenedl from yesterday will be attacked, sacked and burned to the ground and that fat magistrate stuck like a pig and barbequed for the crabs to feast upon on the beach. The harbour, no doubt, will be saved. You got out in time, with my help. Wake up! Dyvie me boy. But, don't you worry; help's always nearby for the likes of you. But stay tuned in,' he said, 'and teach yourself to learn the reality common to the hoi polloi of this world.' With that he promptly left.

This backwoods community that Dyfed had arrived at was centred around a man named Owen MacShee. It was he, who upon being notified of Dyfed's presence by the young shepherd, that immediately appeared out of a large, round, windowless stone hive and was at that moment seen approaching Dyfed. He had alert, greyish eyes that were slightly red rimmed which fixed themselves on Dyfed as he drew up to him. Blocking Dyfed's way into the cenedl he demanded of the youthful lad: "Where is King Maelgwyn?' which was immediately followed by, 'and who the fuck are you?' all spoken in the same Brythonic language. Then — 'what do you want, here, anyway?'

It was this tough mountain dweller, Dyfed knew, whom he now had the ominous job of setting about to strike up an arrangement for accommodation. Allowed to approach inside the cenedl at this time only as far as one of Owen's bee hive shaped stone huts, Dyfed now sat here among the squalor to begin his negotiations for terms as to his residence here. Initially, he presented himself for employment, whereupon Owen MacShee snatched up the young man's right hand and quickly examined his palm. Then letting his hand drop unceremoniously, he carefully scrutinizing Dyfed's entire person in the gloaming of the building. Dyfed tried to read Owen's mind, but it wouldn't have brought much encouragement had he been able. Owen was deeply suspicious and not receptive to him or any other alltud (foreigner) being there. But Dyfed realized one thing. Having been delivered here (by the blacksmith Maelgwyn or Festus who he dubbed Smitty) was (somehow) a card up his sleeve on his road to Amor, though he didn't quite know yet if it was an ace.

"Maelgwyn dropped you off, you say.' The man's piercing eyes bore into Dyfed but he came up with nothing. 'Did Maelgwyn say when he was returning here? Where was he going and why were you with him? Was he alone?' These appeared to be the only questions that Owen MacShee seemed interested in and quite desperate to have Dyfed answer.

Unfortunately, the interrogation of Dyfed had not been drawn to a satisfying conclusion for the former. So, in exchange for a small sum of silver denarii, Dyfed bought the right to inhabit the environs around this cenedl and receive board and lodgings under one or the other of Owen's roofs until the vernal equinox. At that point, Owen MacShee told him, the festival of rebirth would arrive to begin a New Year cycle and Dyfed could set out afresh or be turfed out. Dyfed agreed but was set on leaving in only a few weeks hence. He would rest here just to get his breath and his bearings, was all. He wasn't planning to wait around in this far-flung back eddy until the vernal equinox that was for sure. It was now, accordingly to the old calendar by which Dyfed reckoned the year's cycle, only the middle of the sixth month, August. So that meant that under the contract agreement he was in need of having to pay up a sum of denarii until the following spring when March would bring in the New Year. Owen (Dyfed thought) could keep the change, for

Dyfed wasn't expecting to receive any kind of refund on account of his early departure by September's end at the latest. But plans made by mice and men — let's just say a beautiful woman changed Dyfed's mind quickly enough.

Dyfed had been prepared to pledge himself to Owen for the remaining months left in the year and act as his bard and adviser in matters of which he had expertise. The lord of the cenedl hadn't appeared to put much credence in that, however. Dyfed told Owen that besides acting as a personal assistant to him in every way that he would also take on students and tradesmen to help promote and educate them. Owen only laughed and told Dyfed that he had no need for such services from him, but if the enterprising young transient had something in the way of a trade himself he might be of some use around the place. This astounded Dyfed, for on the Isle of Peace his calling was a profession above all others. After all, one man's passion might be to collect valuable rocks while another's adeptness may be in pulverizing them into dust. A third might fashion the bellows that fan the fires to melt the ore dust into molten metal as Smitty might. Still, others applying the trade of his recent companion may be expert in building the moulds or be proficient in separating the slag and pouring the hot liquid metal and then pounding it into one shape or another. But, be-it a sturdy plough or a valiant sword its owner generally gives no thought to its genealogy. For who can read the earth and know its treasures? Who has familiarity with the elements and knows what composites and proportions to apply to properly forge this thing or that and who ponders and compiles the physical in all its many aspects and deduces by calculated reason, observation and experienced discernment the secrets dislodged by fellow minds throughout time? What trade confers with the celestial heartbeat or sniffs the galactic winds that blow in from the outer edges of the universe, or the depth of conscience, in order to make ready and be competent in the anticipation of the morrow? Who is it that in an unbroken chain draws his power from man's prime feast, the great conference, the universal assembly of disembarkation and migration and is the keeper of the laws, if not that of his own profession which is above all others?

These, in truth, were not fully Dyfed's qualifications as yet, but Owen in seeing him to be gifted and bright, and not completely understanding the lad's connection to Maelgwyn or anybody else, and knowing that he needed to be careful and not tread heavily in matters in which he was unsure, offered Dyfed an agreement. He would provide a limited friendship toward the stranger free of charge, but remarked that his goodwill in every other aspect that would be needed to feed him and keep him alive would cost (in exchange) as stated a monthly piece of silver. Take it or leave, was the final implication.

Owen MacShee most certainly did not know what to make of Dyfed. He was a sturdy young man, this Dyfed, but there was not much of a warrior sense about him. Yet… there was something else about the lad, thought Owen. He appeared to be a complex youth who may have some important benefactor watching over him. There was even an outside chance that he may be a spy working for the Amoran cause. Owen knew that the Amoran establishment had long ears and constantly struggled to keep abreast of local sentiment and petty feuds. In addition, not all of the Cymri were faithful to the old ways. It occurred to Owen, then, that perhaps the young man had fooled Maelgwyn and managed to connive that ambitious man in order to have him deliver him safely into the heart of Gwyneth in order to both spy and to solicit partisans on behalf of Amor. The lad was educated well enough, unlike himself, Owen thought. He might even be a spy sent to feel him out. But sent to spy on him by whom? Surely not by King Maelgwyn, his liege. It had crossed Owen's mind to quickly put this youth to sudden death and deny knowledge of his very existence, but he reminded himself that it might backfire. Best then to inform King Maelgwyn and King Cadwallopir to the south immediately as to the lad's presence here, he decided. After all, he didn't really know what those two kings actually might know, so it was best to be up front and report. This, too, could earn him merits in the long run. On the other hand, he considered that Dyfed might just be some displaced, hard up, down on his luck young prince from somewhere or another who was simply on the move or on the run during these dangerous times and happened to be befriended (or maybe rescued) by Maelgwyn. He may even be on the lam from the Amoran Empire, seeking the wilderness of Albion's west. He wouldn't be the first. Even the high King Caradog (Karatakos) had done the very same not too long ago after the incredibly complex events of his capture, his sentence to an excruciatingly cruel death which somehow was suddenly commuted without explanation and the extraordinary circumstances of his release from his prison dungeon. The other thing was that the lad was attired more as a Cymri lord, Owen thought, and that his manner was like that of an inspiring young acolyte working to become an adept. A man initiated into the mysteries of the priesthood, perhaps something which Owen MacShee was him self whimsically aspiring towards but so far struggling with failure. And then there was an outside chance that this lad was a renegade Druid from the Isle of Mona Major just to the west. This was far more likely.

Through funnelled intelligence (which Owen received sporadically from King Maelgwyn's and King Cadwallopir's agents) he knew that Gwynethian and Decanglian partisan fighters (guerrillas) were set to spring an ambush attack on any Amoran establishment occupying Gwyneth. And there was a rumour that the new Amoran governor of Albion (General Gaius S. Paulinius) was about to follow Scapula's footsteps of conquer to cover himself in glory. Further news was that even as Queen Boodikka was rearming and lashing out to the occupying Amoran establishment in the east, Paulinius' invasion of these lands here was imminent. So obviously King was seeking youthful and careless men for his army. Did the king have Dyfed deposited here, in order to be collected later along with others from this cenedl? There had been no note attached to mystery man's coat. But if he did, did the king have a care or any idea of just what kind of fighting prospect he had in nabbing Dyfed? Dyfed certainly wasn't a dandy or a klutz, but was hardly soldier material for he obviously thought for himself. For that matter, Owen wondered if he might not be a scouting agent for one of the Amoran financiers, a man named Seneca, who was forcing loans called donations through imperial channels on landowners in and around this newly forged province.

Owen remained deep in thought as he wondered and pondered the curious goings on around him in these trying times. So he settled on keeping Dyfed close to him but isolated from the others of the Tud, especially the ones earmarked as soldiers to use as his allegiance payment to King Maelgwyn which were needed to help swell the ranks of that king's army in the up-coming fight.

King Maelgwyn (Owen's lord and liege) was (as it turned out) only a semi high king who smarting under the aforementioned recent defeat by Scabby Pubes (the common name hereabouts for Scapula) had become the latest self appointed protector and custodian of the Cymri law and culture of ancient order in Albion's western lands. There were others, of course, they being King Cadot and King Cadwallopir to the south. Owen knew that Maelgwyn was still bent on ordering up an allied front to challenge Amoran total rule. And what with the rumour that Queen Boodikka of the Ikeni (who was known here in Gwyneth as Buddug) was planning to initiate a general revolt against the Amoran occupation sometime soon, Maelgwyn was probably planning to act in concert with her. None of this was information that Maelgwyn actually shared with Owen. The latter was kept guessing. But Owen did know that Maelgwyn was intent on settling internal differences within the local Cymric sphere for reasons of his own personal survival. And in this endeavour two other contenders for high king were supporting him; a certain King Ryan and a much more powerful and devious man named Macsen Wledig of Demetia who also went by the Amoran name of Bricus. Owen had thought that Queen Boodikka's challenge would be expedient enough on its own to draw Amoran attention away from the Tegeing (Decangli) who are the people hereabouts, and their close relations, the other Gangani folk on the Pen Lyn in Gwyneth.

Owen was fearful of attracting more attention here. For there was a very good chance, he thought, that Maelgwyn's interference would only complicate matters. Owen, however, dared not convert that thought into speech for fear of his own life. And the thought that somehow in some way this lad Dyfed could be involved in this somehow, along with those other possibilities, now began to dominate Owen's mind.

Owen was much beholden to King Maelgwyn of the Tegeing (also Decangli) upon whose southern border his cenedl was located. This local cenedl's community was not especially large and Owen partially relied on Maelgwyn for sustenance and protection. As stated, it had been King Maelgwyn's unprofessional soldiers that had unsuccessfully flailed against (then under the feet of) Publius Scapula's invasion that had crossed the river Dee to begin their Amoran assault here. That was about a decade before the present. At that time, General Publius Scapula, a statesman, and the successor to Aulus Plautius as the Amoran governor of Albion, was set to plummet the Decangli (also Deceangli) into the ground. Faced with imminent defeat, Maelgwyn quickly retreated to Cyngreawdr Fynydd. General Scapula' (or as already stated, Scabby Pubes) campaign had already run roughshod (successfully but indecisively) against two other western tribes, namely the Silures and Ordovices that were led at that time by the brilliant and brave Caradog (also Karatakos), a prince of the Catuvellauni people of eastern Albion. But Scabby Pubes, apparently, had recently died of some disease (that maybe had its origin in his nomenclature) and now the current threat of invasion across this area today was by a certain General Gaius S. Paulinius who as stated had become the new governor (or legate) of Albion.

Apart from leaving out Maelgwyn's name as being part of the fray, all of this was according to what Smitty the harmonious blacksmith had told Dyfed yesterday. But in addition to that he had also told Dyfed that Queen Boodikka of the Ikeni (who were neighbours of the Catuvellauni) were not only threatening to simply isolate Paulinius and his soldiers here in the west when they did arrive, and then to assist the Decangli the best they could, but also to spark a general revolt against the Amoran occupation of Albion. To accomplish this, Boodikka (also Boudicca) planned to strike the cites of Camulod and Nova Troia in an effort to annihilate the Amoran population. This was the news. So, "stay tuned-in and keep an eye out, and get with our program," he told Dyfed. These had been Festus the smithy's parting words to Dyfed.

Owen's cenedl consisted of a handful of permanent dwellings built of stone. The largest housed Owen's immediate family and contained grain, dried meat and preserved food-stuffs and an assemblage of equipment such as chariots and wagons. Besides his wife Ceredwyn, his family were comprised of five boys and a beautiful daughter (also named Ceredwyn but usually called Rhondda) who was the second eldest. Dyfed learned that Owen's eldest son (also named Owen) and his sister Rhondda were both away from the cenedl at this time. They were reposing in the kingdom of the Decangli near Cyngreawdr Fyntdd at King Maelgwyn's pleasure. Possibly they were hostages, Dyfed thought. He had learned of such diplomacy among these people. Along with important members of the community, Owen's family ate together in the largest white stoned hive. This main oval structure was also used as a communal venue when the cenedl needed to be addressed or if important community members arrived. It was also used as a lodge for gathering the people together to worship Io, the first priestess of Hera under the name Callithyia and the daughter of Inachus the Argonian river god and the Oceanid Melia. Homage here was being done because the domesticated cattle in Owen's cenedl were a great boon that this goddess had bestowed to them. How this came to be, Dyfed noted, was not exactly explained rationally. One thing for certain, though was that the domes-ticating of animals had had a revolutionary effect here that had been the cutting edge technology of the day that was equalled later by the process of fashioning iron.

Beyond the concentration of Owen's central domicile there was an array of wooden shelters and granaries, stables, and pens. And around these pens and stables were the mud hut premises that the subject population inhabited. Dyfed was greatly taken back by limited parameters of the new world that was all around him. But taking an interest in how the Tud are employed in the rudiments of daily survival, Dyfed watched them scratch at the earth and dig up peat and move rocks. They hauled water, gathered food, and herded domestic beasts, milked cows, and tended an array of gardens that were scat-tered about. This was the industry in the land hereabouts as elsewhere. Dyfed noted that for each day that creation allotted to this miserable existence, it was continually shy of precious hours and chores were left unfinished. But it was not on account of laxity and laziness that this was so. It was the overwhelming enormity of energy that it took every minute of the day to stay well and to stay alive since death from starvation was their more common enemy than marauding attackers or warriors. As food stock here were always at a high premium, and hunger and want was a companion to both the poor and the rich, society on the whole wasn't on the most even of keels. Like their dead, that lived in the shade just a stone throw from the living the living, folks too never drifted far from the graveyard.

O course, these folks were a long way from the gold and the gods that lay in Amor at the heart of the empire where the environment of entitlement and supremacy ruled. But as such, and under the circumstances, these folks of this cenedl were (in a sense) probably as susceptible to these Amoran vices as were anyone else. In the logical context of current advancement (and at the level which Amoran-type vice was currently being celebrated) Amoran-type behaviour would be this local cenedl's next port of call in a couple of thousand years, perhaps, given that no disrupting external influences occurred. Ignorance was sin and sin created ignorance in its own image. For it was as such here (at this lonely back-eddy in the sticks) just as much as in Amor (where the false prissiness of unnatural elements had been born and nurtured of late) where unjustness rose to absolute rule at some awkward moment of the crystallization of civilization. Yet at the same time it was a fact (Dyfed knew) that Amor was a lot more capable then this grimy cenedl of embracing a widely diverse culture which was testimony to the actual success of their fake reality and the remoteness and separation from which their denizens had become somewhat estranged from the natural world. For on the skids of civilization, humanity tends to move away from the natural world. But Dyfed also knew that though empire builders they may be, the Amorans were not adept at conjoining, conflating, and assimilating within the natural phenomena of the universe as the Masters of the Unknown Universe were: quite the contrary, and this was their sin. Probably the culprit being that they hadn't fully investigated this potential properly. For them nature and natural things were only props for their empire, a commodity to exploit. Losing their natural ability as the seer, the hearer, and the perceiver of the phenomenon of the universe around them cut them off from the true reality of themselves, which becomes the nature of their signature atrophy. It is their great pit. It was relatively the same type of nature that also took place with these churls within Owen's cenedl, and others like it. Atrophy is just another material phase (dimension) of entropy accelerating each moment (past present) of the universe into the nothingness of its own ego or reflection to begin all over, again and again. This isn't some characteristic blight which only the new age was spreading out into the world via Amor, it is the specific blight of entropy and the ever return that's happening everywhere at all times. This was the common lot of the hoi polloi of the third dimension, it seemed.

 Here in this community of the cenedl, dominated by a rough kind of leader and living in harsh times, a certain law and order prevailed, nevertheless. A serf whose chickens or goats (along with their own inspirations) managed to help them to dog the challenges well and rise in 'status' may incur a certain amount of envy. But it did not mean that they would automatically have it taken from them upon becoming aged and decrepit by the hot younger bloods that had passion and want. Though generally thought of as being contrary to the laws of Mother Nature (certainly at the relatively primitive level where the humankind of the hoi polio were) they were at least at the level where such barbarous social action was considered untenable for maintaining a decorum of order which fortified the wellbeing of the whole for the future of the clan. So certain refinements were necessary even for a stable back-eddy camp like this. That any display of youth strength over the wisdom of the more fragile elderly would be taken here as being disrespectful to elders. For them and commonality for betterment this was useful and it had been this way for thousands of years. There was also jovial companionship here among the locals. This, along with friendship, Dyfed thought, was universally important for all humans.

 In the grand scheme of things it was just a minor tool (mind you) to fashion civilization, and was little more than that; but it was a nice touch. And as far as the idea and notion of primitive mother nature always positioning Herself on the side of strength and youth to naturally usurped the weaker, and that eat or be eaten and survival of the fittest dogma being without question the indelible program at large, is not altogether true. The animal kingdom was full of random acts of amazing and unbelievable mercy and compassion. And this all comes down to the intricate play between two vitals which aren't the same but are closely linked; consciousness and self-awareness in juxtaposition with self preservation and the finesse thereof. Tempting fate (like those who attempt to trump mother nature by living apart or beyond her) needs a lot of consciousness and self-awareness, never mind an advanced and democratic sociology. It's a matter of folks getting along. Had Dyfed (as he paid attention and looked around him) seen much of that here so far? No, he didn't think he had. But neither was he and full-fledged adept, he reminded himself.

(Ceredwyn the Beautiful)

'Each man shall have what's due to him by fate. Such was the bargain. How praiseworthy he who shall have persevered even to the end!'

FRANCOIS RABELAIS

Rumour had it that the return of Owen's daughter to the cenedl (sans accompaniment by her brother) was once again imminent. Though his own hands were now calloused and rough from working alongside the Tud and his neck burnt from the sun and wind, Dyfed felt very much alive in his present lot, and as he glanced at those others around him it warmed him to know that he had a greater mastery than they over destiny. Dyfed felt very much alive now in his present situation, and sometimes he shook with ecstasy in anticipation of the great unknown that lay ahead on that vast barren plain that stretched before him: That barren plain which was his life. He knew it was the same with all men and women of a certain age whose barren plains also lay before them waiting to be altered, trodden upon, dug up, tilled under, built upon, enhanced, disguised, cut down, flooded or set fire to. But few of them truly realize their potential. And if these plains were not attacked with vigour they must at least be ventured out upon and altered in some way, or at the very least, discerned, if not closely inspected. 'Those who fail to vary in any way that great blank destiny of their lives that is spread before us all, they will have failed life's first and most compulsory of tests and will become a resounding dud in the explosion of life.' Mandan had said.

Among the Tud here, Dyfed noticed that any happy distractions were few and far between. Dyfed had been a distraction. He was an Alltud, a foreigner, which was a status somewhat higher (and less frightening) than being a troll. He felt his singularity immediately in the absence of any real familiarity at first with the people among whom he had come to dwell, and they constantly watched him. Dyfed remembered that Smitty had warned him about being an Alltud. They were considered dangerous foreigners, he had said. But Dyfed's amiable nature soon changed that in the eyes of the folks who took to him as they noticed his interest in them. He was also a great storyteller and when there is a story being told there will always be folks wanting to listen.

So, Dyfed found his element in story telling, for he was able to conjure forth a mish-mash of remarkable mysteries and histories drawn from countless sources he had learned from his mother and from Manandan. And since these yarns and wonderfully woven tales amazed everyone, he quickly capitalized on this. In this way he began to teach the Tud ancient history which was, in a sense, theirs and of their people, too, as he knew it to be. Owen (who considered himself well versed) quickly became aware of these noticeable attributes that Dyfed had and was the most amazed by Dyfed's stories.

Owen and his family would often sit together, after their supper, fanning the smoky air in front of their faces while the servants cleared the table and set upon the hearth a pail of mead to warm. The air was usually thick as the grey, blue smoke came off the newly fuelled peat fire and filled the circular stone dwelling where they reclined on the hard benches placed there for their comfort. Nothing much had changed for these people in a thousand years. The high doorway and a few strategically placed chinks in the otherwise solid stone structure allowed only a little of the fumigated air to seep out into the bleak afternoons and this caused Dyfed's eyes to smart and his tongue to grow thick in his throat. Later in the evening, as the rain which fell on the cattle and the mist that hung in the bare treetops disappeared into the darkness of night, other members of the Tud (with their day's work stalled by the encroaching darkness) would sally forth, tired and sore, and file into this communal abode and take their place around the walls to listen to the eloquence of this high spirited youth and to wonder at his stories and songs.

Dyfed told them of Bel who had become the raven and of Manandan and the Lord of Huge the many skilled, and how Manandan had once succeeded Pwyll in marrying Rhiannon Queen of Annwn who was the mother of Care. He recounted to them the story of Care called Pryderi, who had once given his name to these isles (Prydain), and of Angus mac Oc, son of the Dagda or third dimensional Creator god, who cast his arms around the lovely Caer and how they fell asleep in the form of two swans and circled loch Bel Dragon three times. He told them of Tir Na N Oc, a place beyond the present dimension, where no one grew old or sick or ever dies and where flowers bloom, where young lambs frolic and where peace and goodwill reign perpetually.

During those dark, autumn evenings the company of Owen's household never tired of listening to these wonderful stories that flowed from Dyfed's now swollen but eloquent tongue.

Dyfed had never seen such cold and dreary days as that autumn and winter he spent in Gwyneth. Fresh snow had fallen nearby on the great White Mountain only days after the warm winds and hot sun ceased to fan and beat down upon them; and later when the leaves had fallen with the weight of rain and mist upon them, the sky had cleared and a cold white sunlight shone through leafless branches. He delighted in the familiarity of the Tud but he abhorred their squalor that he shared and their stink that he continually washed off from himself. Everybody here stank, especially the fat magistrate who fancied himself as being Amoran, he recalled. Only Smitty, for some unseen reason, didn't stink, he recalled.

One evening as cold miserable showers of rain fell beneath a new-mooned sky, Dyfed watched as the Tud stumbled through the hard mud, herding the cattle into their pens for the night. He was now reflecting upon the approach of the Tud's magical and most holy of seasons. This was Sow-ain (also sham-an or Shamhain) whose symbol was the water reed. He noted that this festival would soon be upon them for it was due by the half moon, at which point the rain might even have turned colder and started to fall from the sky as sleet or snow. Everybody always hoped for a clear sunny day leading up to a starry sky, for the celebration of Sow-ain lasted from sunset to dawn and was an outdoor activity gathered around the big fires which were lit for ceremony.

Then one evening sudden distraction visited him. It was something else he could focus on and think about, surely. But it was a mischievous distraction nevertheless. Owen's daughter Ceredwyn Rhondda had (apparently) arrived that very day from Cyngreawdr Fynydd. And according to what the younger men had told him, she was indeed a beauty. Exited, the young men had smirked and made rude gestations that aligned with things that occupy young men's minds the most. This, of course, was to engage in carnal relations and to make passionate, unprotected sex with warm, beautiful young women. The latter were usually if not always in the plural. At this time (anyway) they were apparently unaware that their female counterparts were dreamily engaged with attracting the attention of a single handsome and strong man with faithful fealty who would love them to bits, want them to be quickly married so as to live happily ever after and long into life with many children requiring huge expenditures of gold.

As Dyfed (accompanied by the little dog he had adopted) having returned from a ride alone upon a horse named Trum (gifted from Owen) was putting the old sway-back mare up for the night, he realized he had been joyously anticipating meeting Owen's daughter and nothing much else had occupied his thoughts the whole long-lasting day. The first rumour of her arrival (and that of her description which had tantalized him) had not panned out and her arrival had been delayed and prolonged. This went on for months. Solstice was only now just around the corner. Finally she was here. He could impress her, he knew that much, and only needed the opportunity. He thought, too, that he might approach Owen on the preparations of the festival of Sow-ain for none had been started that he knew about. And there was just so much to do if it was to be the joyous and successful celebration to which certainly he was accustomed. A three-month preparation for Sow-ain could go hand in hand with a courtship with Ceredwyn, he thought, if she was as beautiful as the local yokels all said she was.

This festival of Sow-ain was a momentous occasion for all the Cymri and he wanted to do something to make it extra special this year. It would be his gift to keep on giving to Owen and the cenedl, he thought. Sow-ain was a time for the people of past and present to come together, and with the help of a shaman (with his help) and with the knowledge that his tutor Manandan and Violet-Eye had taught him, he thought he would be more proficient than enough to act as master of ceremonies. So, in putting this knowledge to practice he would strive to bring the Tud of this rustic community into companionship with their spirits of the past and even closure to some who had recently lost loved ones, which was a continuous and common occurrence.

He did not see Owen's daughter that evening as he had greatly anticipated, for she was absent from the evening meal where Owen and Dyfed ate alone. She would have been a good distraction, for Dyfed loathed and even feared mealtimes here with Owen. They revolted him. Instead Owen jovially approached Dyfed on what he called a delicate matter, one that Dyfed immediately thought might be an invitation to woo his beautiful daughter. But that was not to be the case.

"You have been with me now for almost a season,' he said, trailing the sentence. He reached over, and lifting a large cup of beer with his greasy fingers, he drained it. While he drank his eyes sought out, through the smoky, darkness of the stone, tomb-like hive, another lump of cooked flesh that lay on the bare boards of the table. His reddening eyes lifted again and locked with Dyfed's. 'Before you came to this lonely cenedl,' he asked, 'did your path ever cross with one who is known as Macsen Wledig of Demetia? Though he sometimes goes by Bricus.'

The two sat in silence, Owen waiting for an answer. Dyfed sat solemnly, his appetite gone but his mind was furiously working out to where Owen's conversation was leading and how he could get there ahead of him. The interior of the stone dome surface was a dark, mottled film of soot, and as usual the air (or what passed for air) was a haze of smoke that was highlighted by lighter blue-grey shafts that shone down in separate beams along identical angles from the open chinks in the curved structure's ceiling that were meant to let light in and exhaust the choking smoke. Whoever built this structure,

Dyfed thought, letting his mind relax a moment, certainly hadn't graduated from any architectural-engineering standard he had been exposed to. The man must have been a moron, he thought. Owen was still watching Dyfed intently. Then not having seen the telltale response he sought in Dyfed's runny eyes at the mention of this name, he tried another approach.

"He is a very clever individual, highly educated and equally highly regarded by the chiefs of Albion who have promoted him excessively, even making him king of Demetia, while Cadot was thrown a bone and holds the hollow title of 'Protector' or 'Imperator'." Still seeing no response in Dyfed's eyes he continued. 'Lucius Bricus is the name he has taken up with the intention to appear Amoran. I believe he may have other full names, the devil only knows.'

Finally Dyfed's eyes moved over to regard Owen. "I've heard of him,' he replied, 'don't know him, though.'

"You have?' answered Owen. What about Rigotamus? Surely you have heard of Rigotamus as well?'

"You mean Tamus?' asked Dyfed suggestively. 'He is not yet a high king, barely a low one. Some say he is not a king at all. But it's probably what he tells everybody below his status. In fact he is nothing more than a general like Bricus and not nearly as proficient a one as Castus the Admiral who's as good a soldier as he is a seaman, or so I've heard. I have been led to believe, however, that Ambrosius Tamus, as he calls himself when not employing the fanciful Rigotamus, is an intelligent young man of Dunmonii birth, about my age. He is slightly junior to Bricus to whom he is currently subservient and a child compared to Castus. These men are Amorans at heart, I know little of them, only what my tutor has told me.'

"Your tutor?' said Owen. 'Who, may I enquire, was he?' But as Dyfed only smiled and shook his head, Owen added…'Might you know then of King Verika, or King Karatakos, son of Kunobelin, king of the Catuvellauni? What about Publius Ostorius Scapula? Did your tutor talk to you about any of them?'

"Scapula. I say, isn't he the beastly Amoran commander who ransacked the Deceangli? His slight grimace followed by a thoughtful look as he fanned the dirty air in front of his face told Owen that even if he did have pertinent information about any them he wasn't prepared to comment in detail. Both were aware (of course) at the time that Paulinius' campaign was about to begin, though none knew it would be scratched temporarily then finally deep-sixed due to the outrage of Boodikka.

So Owen returned to the two men he thought Dyfed might know something more about. He needed to do something, anything that might help him manage his own affairs of state. For, at this very moment outside politics threatened to overtake Owen and come crashing down upon him here in his lonely pasture.

From the moment Dyfed had entered the stone dwelling, having been summoned for an earlier than usual evening meal, he had had a feeling that although there was no one in sight anywhere, he and Owen were not sharing this hovel alone. It occurred to him now that maybe his daughter was present after all, but reflected that the conversation wasn't going anywhere near her. Nor was it going in the direction of the upcoming and important festival of Sow-ain.

"I hear Queen Boodikka is soon to press Albion's cause against the might of Amor,' Dyfed said. 'Who around here is with her?'

Startled by the comment, Owen asked, "Who told you that, your tutor?'

"Oh, I thought this was common knowledge,' Dyfed responded, 'and it was certainly among the topics which Maelgwyn the smithy and I discussed on my way here.'

"Smithy? asked Owen urgently.

"The blacksmith I dubbed Smitty who you, I think you know him as Maelgwyn.'

"What else did you and King Maelgwyn discuss, Dyfed?'

"King Maelgwyn? Never mind what he told me, it's what I told him is what you want to hear. I told him that I serve nobody,' replied Dyfed. 'Neither Albion nor Amoran, but I will promote both for our own benefit.'

"What?'

"Yes, I told him that because I am a prince of the grove from the Isle of Peace, which apparently you call Mona Minor. Also, what I haven't told you is this. I am son of Queen Chloris Violet-Eye, high priestess and queen of Dardan, and I am the student of the mighty Manandan himself, my tutor.'

"What?'

"Oh, yes. Couldn't you have guessed as much? Your King Maelgwyn certainly did.' There, Dyfed thought, I've told him now. Perhaps I should have spoken sooner, he thought, but Manandan always said to keep my own council.

"You are?' Owen said, pausing and looking incredulous.

"Yes,' replied Dyfed. 'I am an adept. I'm a master.'

Owen whistled through his teeth and said, "So, you are a shaman who can travel to the other world and convene with spirits?'

"Absolutely,' responded Dyfed with a straight face, speaking in a straightforward manner without a hint of arrogance or even playfulness. 'Remember, I offered you my services once that you declined. And that brings me to the festival of Sow-ain. If you haven't organized it, then appoint me. And there is one other thing,' Dyfed said. I would like you to introduce me to your beautiful daughter.'

"You stay the distance of at least a horse cock away from my daughter. Listen to me Dyfed.' Owen's voice began to elevate and Dyfed instantly knew he had suddenly got the better of him.

"You told me that it was Maelgwyn that dropped you off here, or perhaps an agent of his.' He laughed slightly in an appeasing manner as if to enhance his reluctance to call Dyfed a liar where Maelgwyn is concerned. A misunderstanding, a slip; how would Dyfed know who King Maelgwyn was? he reasoned. 'And you have spoken just now about confidential discussions that may involve King Maelgwyn's business. But you see, I too am something of an agent of the king,' he stated solemnly and loudly.

There was a stirring then in the smoky shadows off to one side. Then as Dyfed watched he saw a youngish man emerge and come forward, fanning the dirty air in front of his face. I knew it, Dyfed thought to himself, wondering how the man didn't give himself up before now by coming down with a fit of uncontrollable coughing or simply die an agonizing death of affixation somewhere in the shadows and cause a loud bump when his body fell over. At least there was a little air movement here by the high table.

The man, not much older than Dyfed himself, slowly sat down next to Owen, his gaze never leaving Dyfed's cautious and attentive eyes. Dyfed returned the gaze in his bold and unapologetic manner.

"This is one of Maelgwyn's chief agents,' stated Owen, in a matter of fact way. 'But he doesn't remember hearing anything about you.'

"This is not Festus the harmonious blacksmith who I dubbed Smitty,' Dyfed said matter-of-factly, taking some pains now to look the man up and down in a demonstrative way.

"No, replied Owen, 'he is an agent of Maelgwyn's, and he would know about you and even recognise you by description if you had had any association with his liege.' Soon these two men were closely scrutinising Dyfed about this and about that and about the other thing in regards to the harmonious blacksmith named Smitty who had brought Dyfed hither. Dyfed responded in the most part in monosyllables. For a while a furious discussion took place only between Owen and the agent, leaving Dyfed alone out of the conversation and quickly becoming distracted. Dyfed then rose from the table and walked around. He was still hungry and his eyes hurt. Then caught up in coughing fit himself, and reeling from lack of oxygen, he quickly exited the stone dome into the glooming light of the evening and the cool freshness of a wintery autumn day. He exhaled smudge and smoke and then breathed in deeply.

The chill sun was beginning to set low in the distance and its cool rays shone sideways through a light snow squall sprinkling large white flakes that were floating directly down from a darkening, ragged and unseen sky. The unusual scene added a strange dimension to the landscape. He glanced at the cenedl's graveyard in the distance. After a few gasps of cool, fresh air, Dyfed returned to the interior of the stone abode and found the two men still feverishly discussing possibilities. So he decided to say goodbye, as he had now become bored with the situation and because neither Ceredwyn nor the matter of organising Sow-ain appeared to be on the roster for a topic of discussion. But they politely refused to let him disengage and immediately began asking him to describe the blacksmith one more time. In so doing Dyfed recalled that the man was possibly of middle age, or appeared as such, but he was not infirm, indeed, he was quite strong. Was he lame? they wanted to know. Well, no, he was slower on foot than other men, yes, but he was older, too. Wait… lame you say. Why… yes, god Azeus! The man was somewhat lame, perhaps. A slight limp as if tired at the end of a long day's walk, let's say. This condition can come with age…or because of a strained tendon…or maybe even a pebble in one's shoe.

"Of course,' Dyfed said out loud, more for his own benefit than for Owen's, as he slapped himself on the forehead, 'Since you now have a grasp of the situation, I will say this. He also called himself Festus. That would be Phaestus, or more properly, Hephaestus; the lame blacksmith, son of Hera, adopted and nurtured by Thetis, half brother to Athena, and by extension through Thetis, the adopted brother of Achilles.'

Suddenly Dyfed burst out laughing, primarily at himself. But the other two men had probably not heard him exclaim the last part for they had huddled together again, making references that only they, or any who may have been kept abreast or conversant in their discussion could understand. Suddenly, they agreed on something, whereupon Owen promptly, and loudly exclaimed:

"It's Caradog, son of King Kunobelin who calls him self Karatakos. Once he was a high king of Albion. He was caught a few years back and delivered to Amor for execution. He somehow survived, miraculously. Apparently the wily and talkative Caradog impressed Kysar Claudius Augustus and talked his way out of being executed and returned to Albion to fight on, hiding and taking refuge in the environs of these very hills, though few have seen him. His father, Kunobelin, is currently back once more upon the high king throne in the city of Camulod. At the moment he is frantically trying to control Boodikka from initiating revolt. This is who delivered you here, Dyfed, not anybody else.'

Apparently, this Caradog (also known to the eastern folks as Karatakos) had once been injured on the leg, either during his recent capture or during his escape from Amor, no one knew which.

Well, well, thought Dyfed. So the man wasn't just any radical dissenter lighting fires all over the Cuneddan Gwyneddian (Gwynethian) countryside — today a friend, tomorrow a foe — after all! Like his father King Kunobelin before him, this was a man about whom Manandan had once spoken to Dyfed.

(The hag in the half-moon light)

'To the brave belong all things'
KELTIC PROVERB

There had been a sudden and unspoken change of authority between Owen and Dyfed since that day when Karatakos' name had come up. It was Owen's show, we can't lose sight of that, but Dyfed was the uncontested shaman here. At this point of our narrative and in history (for what it's worth) shamans were still a powerful catalyst in society, in these parts. This profession was a closed shop and only a licensed Druid was allowed to fill the position of shaman. And to impersonate a Druid without credentials, the traditional penalty was death by fire. Not so much in Amoran society where they were referred to as high priests of witchcraft, did this happen, though. Certainly, the Amorans were keen on putting the run on Druids of any kind throughout the Empire for in truth they feared their which craft. But Dyfed wasn't in Amoran society, here. And he still needed to successfully prove that he could rise to the challenge; not only for Owen but more importantly now for himself and his demonstration before Ceredwyn the Beautiful that was what he now had in mind. He still hadn't yet set eyes on her, though. However, he had become extremely enamoured with the notion of her nonetheless. This camp (as Dyfed called Owen's settled commune) had (as already stated) been abuzz for weeks about the minor lord's daughter Ceredwyn finally coming home. She was more beautiful they said than any queen. They marvelled at her hair the colour of the sunset and her skin that was rosy and smooth like cream. She was tall and shapely, and athletic, Dyfed was told. She was beautiful and she smells wonderful. How they could know that was beyond credibility, Dyfed thought. The man that marries her, they said, will be a king. On an idle moment Dyfed did casually wonder where their bar for defining beautiful actually lay, never mind the 'smelling wonderful' part! At this point he was most inquisitive as to her legendary lure rather than being smitten with it like all the other men had been. But so far (as stated) he had seen neither hide nor hair of her. Furthermore, he thought that nobody else outside of Owen's family had seen her either. Already, now, he had talked himself into having lost any interest in her altogether.

    He first set eyes on Ceredwyn at one of Owen's communal gatherings. She was graceful and sensual with rusty red hair adorning a tawny long-legged body that reminded Dyfed of a tomboy. Her greying, cloudy blue eyes affected modesty but were not demure, but rather dreamy and veiled in a way that made them hard to read. He could see that she was full of mirth and temperament that she kept under strict control. He courted her in silence almost from afar and she reciprocated. By Solstice she was *his*. By Solstice he was hers. Although Owen kept Ceredwyn more secluded from anyone outside the immediate family, Dyfed had contact with her more than others due to his new status alongside Owen who looked on with interest. Dyfed was quite smitten with love and Owen could see that. What with her full lips, her rusty red hair that fell to her hips, an alluring figure and the most tantalising green-blue grey eyes that a woman could have, Ceredwyn's presence couldn't have effected Dyfed more had he been hit square in the face with a heavy cudgel. It was his first love. However, being young and inexperienced in matters of love, no matter how his outward performances appeared, Dyfed felt shy and awkward around her. Now, Owen thought, he had some control over the lad at last.

It seemed to Dyfed that there was much to do in preparation for Sow-ain. Sheep needed to be shorn and their throats cut and carcasses butchered and hung. Cattle and goats also suffered the same fate as the Tud readied themselves for the long, cold months that led up to the festival of the Dead Sun, the winter equinox. Many of the younger animals which would be spared would give birth in the spring after Fortuna and Trickster had had their day, when the Fairy Queen Mauve of the Pleiades blossoms. This is the time of the willow (saille) and the festival of Beltane, or the fire of Bel Disc the Relentless, the great solar deity that brings renewal so that the cycle can begin all over again. But now was the time for blood, the time of year when many of the animals are, shorn, harvested, smoked, cooked in salt or dried for later consumption. Some of the carcasses would be set aside for consumption during Shamhain that was about to take place. They would be cooked over the bonfires that would be lit as the sun went down for the start of that hallowed Day of the Dead and would fuel and feed the Tud from sundown until the next sundown when the festival of the dead would come to a close. But it wasn't just the animals to be harvested and laid aside for the winter; it was the processing and storing of wool, the tanning of hides that was part of their livelihood. There was also the autumn fruits and vegetables that needed attending to. They needed to be set up on racks (that were still waiting either construction or last minute maintenance) to allow air circulation to prevent mould and rot. And then there was adequate enclosures that were needed — which required similar attention — to prevent the groceries from freezing and kept safe from outside weather and sustaining damage as well as protecting them from becoming fair game to foraging critters.

And there was the festival of Sow-ain itself that needed immediate attending to, as it was to occur now in only two weeks time. There were mummers to select, skits to be arranged, actors to be chosen, singers and criers and banners that still needed to be painted, masks to be constructed or repaired and a whole lot more of human participation to be choreographed. Many of these were repetitive from previous solar cycles where props such as fluttering wind socks, flags and other banners would simply need to be located, unpacked, cleaned up and repaired, and trotted out; while actors and mummers would be returned to their well-practised and comfortable roles and organizers resuming their conduct of orchestration.

For his part, Dyfed set about getting a large drum constructed from two hides stretched tightly over a sturdy frame fashioned from alder. He also needed to get his hands on a sizable source of a powerful fermented libation, something this cenedl was drastically short of. This could be any highly intoxicating substance — entirely for his personal consumption. This was a tradition within this select shamanic brother/sisterhood; one he didn't feel qualified to change, either. Over a few months he had carefully observed the young men of the Tud's routine and discovered their stash of inebriants. It wasn't just the fermentation of berries and grain into wine and beer that they were practising here for he even found that they were distilling the beer and wine as well into a clear and highly inebriating intoxicant. This was quite a haul, he thought, for he had no time to distil anything himself, and distilled liquor was a faster track to inebriation than fermentation. He had brought with him, in his satchel, an ample amount of hallucinogenic in the form of dried mushrooms such as the Amanita muscaria, along with plants like Henbane and Datura, and the Mandrake root. Shortly before sundown on the eve of Sow-ain he proceeded to devour these substances washing them down by those other potent distilments that he doctored with berry wine to dilute the bitter taste. The lads in the cenedl were all eagerly with him now.

When the same local lads who Dyfed had stumbled upon in the process of refining their art of distillery had finally located him in the early evening of Sow-ain, he was naked and on all fours puking with all his might on the straw strewn floor of his workhouse beneath his old sway backed mare — Trum. His mind was like a white flash of light and as it paused between hallucinations he was plummeted back momentarily into his ego-enhanced being that was being racked by body spasms as pure white-lightning alcohol raced through his veins straight to his brain. This caused the semi consciousness that rattled around inside his head to spin violently. This, once again, induced more vomiting. When that ended there was an enormous vibration of his being, though physically he didn't shake or tremble as –once again — he was rocketed outward in a blinding light into the vast curvature of the universe that was neither beyond or separate from his third dimensional being.

"Honour, before all', the young men feverishly attending to him heard him say as he spoke to some fearsome and glowing apparition that was beckoning him into backsliding demeaningness. 'That is my motto. To be moral,' he shouted out loudly again, 'is always to feel a connected compassion, not a greedy opportunity for cavitation — you piece of shit,' he shouted over and over. His attendants eyed him with alarm. 'Compassion,' he continued, 'to all living things around you and to protect all life and cherish it. And staying connected with all that is living and has lived, in the Web of Fates, is what Sow-ain and the day of the dead and all hallows is all about,' he told them, slurring his words as the boys began to relax again. 'This celebration is hand and glove with rebirth that follows the dead sun. Rebirth or Beltane (also Abel, Abaal, Abelenos) on the going down of the sun to the rising up of May Day, which, as you know, is the celebration of the solar fire deity and Beltane,' he slurred again, 'that gives licence to the young men (each symbolic of the male sky god) to cavort sexually with the young women of the earth and among the Tud in the game of hide and seek in the forested area beyond the community.'

In respect to this, recently Owen (like other rulers) had struck down this practice fearing that young Amoran men infiltrating their communities might take advantage of their women.

'Stick with me, fellows,' Dyfed shouted again, 'we'll help each other out and get through this.'

That was all Dyfed had had to say. And each and every one of the young lads there were with him — all the way.

With great merriment and even awe at his demeanour, the youths quickly dressed Dyfed in his beautifully woven, woollen smock; they pulled his soft deer leather boots onto his feet, and then after struggling extensively in order to get him to sit squarely astride Trum, they donned him with his tall, wide brimmed hat by pulling it down hard towards his eye brows so it would stay on and not fly off or be blown away by the cool evening breeze. Then with pride and expectation in and of their achievement they led him forth toward the ceremony that was already in progression. They eagerly watched out for the crowd's reaction to them and the mounted Dyfed as they approached. When the younger people saw them coming they ran gleefully forward toward their newly appointed shaman. Soon, along with the former youths (those purveyors of inebriation), many spectators now were accompanying Dyfed toward the enclave where Owen, his family, and the rest of the Tud were camped for the pageant. Just as Dyfed was about to lose grip and tumble off, or (in reality) be thrown due to the discomfort of the bony mare, Trum came to a halt more or less in the right spot near Owen and his family and Dyfed slid off her with a nonchalant and disconcerted air about him as he adjusted his hat that was meant to give the impression that everything was quite as it should be.

Owen opened the festival with great fanfare with the two Ceredwyns close by his side as the young men of the cenedl whooped and hollered in exuberance. There were more people present than normally so, for folks from outside the cenedl from miles (an Amoran linear measurement) around had come to take part in this important celebration. By the time the fires were lit and song in its everlasting state of communion had risen up to fan those bonfires, a great commotion stirred among the people as the mummers emerged from the fringe of forest nearby that surrounded the sacred spring and its acre (another Amoran measurement of area) of cleared land that was the venue for the festival. These mummers were frightfully attired, some as human skeletons, or appearing savagely mutilated with grotesque wounds painted upon them, or arrows appearing to have been thrust through their heads and hearts. Almost all were wearing monstrous masks that displayed some form of strong emotion or another. Some even were farcical, others comical, yet frightening in their familiarity. Three people cavorted together costumed as a worm like creature that they wore over their heads while they danced. Other groups were dressed as ugly old hags — a popular theme — dressed in rags and decorated in tree lichen called old man's beard. They screeched out hideous laughter while they made appearance to solicit and harass youngsters who, flushed from the cool night air as well as from excitement, ran around screaming in bunches and groups, tumbling, pushing each other and laughing while they often rolled around on the cold, hard grassy ground. There were ghoulies and ghosties and long legged beasties, there were large black cats fabricated out of dyed goat hides dressed over willow frames which had small lanterns flaming in their head cavities that made their eyes glow in the dark to frighten the children. These contraptions were pulled around on small wooden platforms with wheels. It was a treat festival of trick macabre design. There were placards and banners with ghoulish pictures painted on them and everybody wore a hat or headdress of some fashion and the whole melee looked as if it were something from a Francisco José de Goya y Lucientes painting.

Musicians played fine airs, selected singers accompanied them or sang separately while the general melee either sang, shouted, kissed, talked, all the while drinking from large tin mugs or dried gourds. Revelry was abundant and formed a human mass as the fires flicked its flames into the windy air while the bare branches of the trees, now lit up from the fires' flickering light, scratched frantically at the darkened sky.

Then, suddenly, and just as rehearsed, the opening skit of the evening began to assemble around them while the Tud, maintaining their riotous mood, crowded closer. The dirty, sweaty bodies — covered with their grimy clothes now thankfully cooled with the windy night air — pushed and jousted about Dyfed. He closed his eyes from time to time to prevent his drunken third dimensional self from flying off the plane in a topsy-turvy curve in opposite directions out of each eye, that tended to bring upon him that foul condition again of projectile vomiting. And though the close proximity of the crushing bodies on every side may have been the sole reason that prevented him from falling to the ground, due to Dyfed's sensitive smell they were the prime reason behind his sudden involuntary urge for that aforementioned participation of puke. Nor did any of those crushing bodies belong to Owen's beautiful greyish green eyed, rusty red haired daughter Ceredwyn called Rhondda, for Owen himself stood firmly between Dyfed and her at all times during the ceremony. Owen was straining on tippy-toes at this point and breathing furtively over his left shoulder. What he didn't know wouldn't hurt him, thought Dyfed. What he didn't know was that there was no point in shutting the barn gate once the mare had bolted after the stallion. And bolted she had straight into his arms and they had made a little nest.

It was during the rhythmic emitting of frequencies during the pageant that Dyfed entered a trance. At first he was astounded at what he perceived for it seemed he was on the floor of an ocean or sea and all about him swam a school of blue finned tuna fish. Their movements were deliberate and methodical as if choreographed in slow motion. The as he gaped in amazement he noticed an ancient human, that is, a human from ancient times, heavily clad complete with headdress and holding a spear. Apparently he was either fishing or had found himself in the same conundrum of circumstance in which Dyfed was finding himself in at the moment, for he looked either confused or heavily absorbed in contemplation on how to bring in his quarry. Suddenly, it seemed, he caught sight of Dyfed looking at him, and although there was no demonstrative action that passed between them like a wave, they did share some kind of strange momentary communication. It was to him and to here that the forgotten ceremonial drum was brought and placed before him. It was all finished before the event had time to register and the apparition had disappeared and Dyfed and his drum were alone with other strange spirits breathing through hollowed out corpses that swayed like seaweed in a tidal lagoon.

There were some changes in protocol, the main one being that he not Owen was the target for jubilant festival going merrymakers and their goodwill this year. Furthermore, he was surprised to note that even though Owen was the master of ceremonies, it was to him — the one time Alltud — which the entire Tud looked toward for guidance in successfully experiencing Sow-ain. Although none were the wiser, the biggest change in truth was Dyfed's performance which would have either brought peals of blasting laughter or bitter scorn from Violet's and Manandan's lips had they been in attendance. Dyfed embraced individuals, some on stilts in their condition of ampliation brought about by his drunken and hallucinating exuberance that amounted to half nonsense and part theatre. But about him there was a small vein of authenticity in his quiet, slightly off-standing demeanour, now that his vomiting was under control along with his balance. Despite all this, the people, including Owen and the Ceredwyn, were much taken in by his manner and were somewhat in awe of it. Certainly the local youngsters that were in cahoots with Dyfed and who had helped pick him up off the floor earlier were impressed, that was for sure. On Dyfed's part, he was slightly confused, for having never experienced this category of out of body presence in quite the same way he subsequently chalked it up to either a loss of memory or a dream that was likely induced by the hallucinogens he had consumed.

Among the pantomimes, the singing — that lasted for hours — the pranks and ghoulish interpretations of normality that peppered the event, eating and drinking had been continuous. Dyfed now found his appetite. It was starting to grow light in the forest where they had gathered and the lower eastern sky was a pale silver-blue broken with long black logs of parallel clouds just visible through the thick grove of deciduous oak trees. The air was much colder now and the fresh spring nearby seemed to draw any warmth around — either from the fires (now burning lower and deep into the hard earth) or the sweet lingering aroma of cooked meat — towards and into it. People moved around in happy fellowship and had long trampled the acre's thin skin of crispy snow under foot into a sea of freezing mud as they finished stripping away the quieting feast of burning pig, calf and lamb flesh and quaffed back with kumis, beer, and other more gentler fermented liquids that were now laying as dregs in the bottom of the now almost empty barrels. Torches that had burned most of the night, throwing odd shapes of dancing light among the moving mass, were now smouldering in the tired, dim morning light.

Like the others among Owen's family, including his servants, Dyfed had eaten and drunk well. After his performance he kept close to Owen. Then at a certain point the folks of the cenedl humbly began to approach their head clansman who greeted them and bestowed blessings upon them. They also seemed to acknowledge Dyfed's contribution as shaman and in his ability of bringing them close to their loved ones who had now passed. As already stated, a great deal of singing had gone on during the night which was traditional with these occupiers of ancient Gwyneth but now with food and the spirits inside them, the singing had become spontaneous and uproarious. As Dyfed now applied a faster yet rhythmic vibration to his drum beat, they sang in groups, male, female and children together. One group or family would start and then another would follow and then another and so on. A strong powerful voice would suddenly rise above the throng and be joined by others of another family until everyone present was singing together. It was very melodious and rhythmic and seemed to move around the groups in waves. The cheery ring of the children's voices would suddenly be overtaken by the lusty voices of the mature and then complemented by the pure clear sound of the adolescent boys as back and forth and across it would go like a whirlwind of song. Owen, who had no singing voice, sang with gusto and Dyfed's drum rhythm increased to a furious crescendo.

Momentarily there was a lull in the singing followed by some casual banter as people looked to fill their cups or examined the now lean carcasses that lay to one side of the fire. Then suddenly, Dyfed began to sing. His voice rose clear, pure and intensely powerful into the cold morning air just as the sunlight began to flicker its first direct rays through the oak thicket and down upon them. The murmur and bustle of the crowd ceased as his notes rang clear and sharp into the encroaching morning light. The song that he sang was unknown to those around him, for long ago it had been a secret and sacred ballad sung only by the high priests of the Hyperboreans and later among those who had been initiated into the Lodge of Huge. It was the song of trinity of opposite poles that he sang and it told among other things of fire, water and earth and of the journey of the great raven who set the sun in the heavens to divide the night, and who later ventured over the troubled waters before the dove. It was Hosanna in the highest for all mankind, today and forever. It was the song of Azeus that was taken from the Muse hymn, that one hundred and eight paragraph prayer (seven lines to a paragraph) that Hyperborean masters once recited by memory in its entirety at their ceremony of confirmation.

    The ballad continued for some time and the people of the cenedl moved silently closer toward young Dyfed until they crowded around him in a mass, listening. To those appreciative of the youth's talent — and there were only a few deaf mutes among them — when his final note went up it seemed to hang above them for a moment in a pure state of resonance. Briefly, an awe-full silence followed, when suddenly, a great shout went up and the people were all pressing in patting and offering Dyfed all sorts of plaudit. He was the centre of a seething mass that smelled of body odour, wood smoke, human hair oil, pig and cattle grease, unwashed cloaks, coats, and hats and the freshness of the morning air. In a blurred collage, faces appeared strangely disjointed before him and then suddenly, seemingly without causation, faded involuntarily; their voices trailed out of their mouths like smoke or like passing ghosts disappearing down a long tunnel. Colours of human clothing blended with the flickering shafts that had earlier glanced all around from off the leaping flames of the fires. People seemed disjointed as they moved, as though most were on stilts, covered in broad bands of cloth, many appearing to wear inanely grinning masks with dishevelled, theatrical hair all askew, some curly, some straight, lumbering upon wooden straight legs and laughing hysterically, bumping into one another, embracing, gesticulating, kissing. Owen turned with tears streaming down his cheeks and hugged Dyfed like he was his own son. Then, with a cool sun having now ascended well into the sky, arm in arm and with jubilant laughter and joyous shouts, the congregation began to leave the sacred spot deep in the forest by the spring and return to their meagre abodes in preparation for the daylight events which were yet to come.

(NARRATOR'S PRIVILEGE)

We say that each civilization moves away from Mother Nature in order to blossom in its unique way, and that each one fails miserably in the end. Only Mother Nature doesn't evolve quite that way even while entropy (from order to disorder) is apparent in Mother Nature. That's because order and disorder are pivotal poles which is the nature of Mother Nature to begin with; like yes and no, male and female, good and bad, up and down, negative and positive, electron and proton and the like. Anyway, nothing is more persistent and unmovable than Mother Nature, and nothing is more desirous than Mother Nature, too. Mother Nature is a friend to all, but due to ignorance, selfishness and greed (and maybe even fear), humans undertake to disrespect and even despise Mother Nature and all which she entails, and for no good reason. We fully depend on Mother Nature. Mother Nature loves us because we are part of Mother Nature and there is no part of us that is not part of her. So, the greater the void between an individual's (paramatman-mind/heart) or a civilization's Idea and Mother Nature — the more it will lack those balanced and tempered values that operate with a progressive, constructive and natural discipline. So, instead of being in harmony with the universe (even if only in this neck of the woods), the result of this disharmony causes men and civilization to withdraw from its true (humanly) essence and crash and burn like Captain Crunch. The more one disrespects Mother Nature the more that individual or the civilization will fall afoul of Mother Nature and the more likelihood they will create, some unworthy paraclete or avatar to improvise with some phoney cultural-religious-ideological distraction (along with all its accompanying disharmony and sundry accessories) instead. Disharmonious man and his society and civilization will suffer because eventually Mother Nature will respond with a will and force of equilibrium well beyond anything humanity could curtail, surmount or even survive. Aside from the towering ignorance of hubris-ridden humans (or disconcerting dinosaurs) — who display a willingness toward assuring themselves that they have a universal will that has strength and actually matters — is the equally insignificance and puniness of their apprehension and appreciation of the phenomenon at large. It is false that human endeavours are of any universal importance, apart from witnessing the unfolding of themselves within the universe that they understand to such an insignificant amount, as yet. And also because they do this in an attempt to create the fact those golden and silver units for exchange, the privilege of ownership, or esteemed authority over others will do all that's needed to provide the ideal artificial environment. This is the alter ego of a puny entity that becomes a replacement of Mother Nature. It seems mind-boggling that anyone could even begin to believe in that farce, but surprisingly most humans do.

In the lead up to this narrative there was talk of its end time: a possibility of some future conflagration. If such imagined events were in the cards, it would (would it not?) be supremely important beforehand for an enduring number of adepts, philosophers, or supermen to attain a high level of universal awareness so that a cadre of professional friendship among companions midst the folly of this epoch of the current hoi polloi to become capable to forge themselves into a weapon of light and knowledge (to vanquish the current Haploidic mutant masters) and stepping forward pierce the ram that's needed to transcend at least the few to the next level. Also during this narrative we will uncover patches of time shifting, even though we don't know what time really is and our definition of it (although it suffices for now) is rather meagre.

But for the act of imagining an event (or in seeing, or otherwise being aware of it exactly during the only moment it takes place) to be a preview which is casually outside of the event's allotted multiples that's required for its manifested presence in a specified moment, is an act of transcending time which (seemingly by third dimensional rules) is not at all possible, other than in this tale of events. That's not withstanding the seer's ability to imagine some fearsomeness from a distance and being willingly prepared through genuine big-brained foresight to plan accordingly. Other than that uncommon attribute, any event would only be something capable of being witnessed when the seer is existent and present along (and together with) the same time frame of presence with all the sums that compile the event itself. And that frame of presence always coincides with all other frames of moments of presence interlinked together in a commonality to make the event function as it's witnessed. But being a witness seeing an event unfolding from different point, no matter how miniscule the difference may be, will obviously project a different order of undertaking of the event itself by the seer who observes it from that different point. The trick is being at the different point than everybody else who is seeing a train wreck. You might not want to see disappointment but rather something up lifting and wholesome and beautiful. That means you need to see the unfolding phenomenon from a different standpoint. And it may not be that tricky after all. I suppose some addition to and subtraction from these conjoining moments must be possible without being witnessed, too. And it must actually be that they are being witnessed from a different perspective if you can't see them. That's good, because otherwise the universe would then depend on a single witness, which just doesn't happen. **Parasolo**

(Appropriately undressed before the shimmering horns of Artemis-Diana)

'Men's natures are alike, it is their habits that carry them far apart.'
CONFUCIUS

In accordance to Dyfed's adherence to nature and the natural — the key to maintaining his self's equilibrium — he sought out the quiet spots of the pretty countryside around Owen's cenedl. One such place that he visited often was a dark and shaded pool not far from the cool, sweet water spring. In the early morning of the vernal equinox (four hours before the sun was up) he visited this place for the last time. Here his mind wandered into that other realm of his psyche and to the curious events that manifested parallel to it. At the dark sacred pond the reflection of sweet Artemis/Diana — whose heavenly light captured from Radiance/Apollo, her twin (whose location at this hour was still beneath the brim of the world) — shimmered and flickered ever so gently as Dyfed prepared his spirit. On this morning, he recalled his first visit six months before during the winter solstice. Then the ice that had covered its surface during the previous day was gone, along with the skiff of snow that lay over it. That day there was a sudden mildness of the air that had melted the snow into the pond over night. Only a thin crusty film of the frozen water had remained. It was as wide as the span of a woman's hand that ringed the pond's circumference against the shallow banks of the shore. It had been quite dark. The silver horned goddess peeped down upon the sallow pyre (lit in her holy name) and skittered across the flat, calm surface from a cool but mellowing breeze that fanned across her murky and mysterious alter. It was then that the creatures of the forest began to materialize and finally emerge from the canopy of night into her light.

First after Dyfed came Fenrir the wolf, sly and thoughtful. He appeared moody and said nothing. It was if his presence was circumstantial to Dyfed's presence that essentially allowed him to remain uninvolved in the goings on that was about to take place in this spot. It was as though he was acting as a guardian of some kind to the lone human but not necessarily to protect him from the creatures that were about to join them. After Fenrir came the small, five toed frisky mare. Her ears were back between her creamy coloured mane and the golden poitel around her neck glistened in the moonlight as she reigned herself in at the edge of the crusty marshy shore. Next came the hound of Culane masquerading as Tobit's dog for the occasion. And although he timidly trotted crisply along the pond's shore on tippy-toes with his nose to the ground and giving Fenrir a wide berth, he was, in truth, as bold as a bull. Nearby, Erod, a radiantly coloured serpent uncoiled himself and crawled forth on his belly from the roots of a hazel tree. As his long slender head sank forward and slithered across the slippery laced edge of the water to drink, his eyes — sparkling like rubies — cast a reflection upon the pond's murky surface. Suddenly, this lower set of small glistening coals gyrated and bobbed as they were washed by the wake of Fintan the fish that nosed to the surface. No one knew how he managed to be there, but reclining on his back — his head and shimmering belly partly out of the water — he welcomed the robin as it alighted onto an overhanging oak branch above. Raven, the colour of ink, suddenly spoke. He had been quietly listening to the chatter of the others as they had gathered together, but now his hoarse, raspy voice betrayed his location among the night shadows of the willow. The Billy goat, who arrived silently, without a word, was the least gregarious of them all, preferring instead to chew on succulent reeds that grew by the water's edge. He crunched the thin film of ice along the immediate shore with his sharp hoofs as he munched. As he spoke little, no one knew how much he listened, but he was a stoic creature who often bore the sins of others. Last to emerge was a seven tined, snow-white stag. This beautiful buck boldly stepped from the forest and waded into the pond to drink. Once more (Dyfed noticed) Diana's reflected light rocked upon the black surface of the pool like a boat at anchor, or like the dip and diving tips of some sacrificial flame. As the stag shook his tall rack of antlers he greeted the other nine and regarded Dyfed neither silently without comment nor with a commitment toward the need to utter one. Suddenly the serpent spoke up:

"Greetings brethren. Raven, as the guardian lookout you will protect our sanctuary from above against the approach of any eavesdropper and allow none to come near or enter unless qualified and welcome. Are all those present initiated and accounted for?'

"There is one present who is of the lower life and whose initiation is incomplete,' said Tyler the raven. Dyfed then felt all eyes turn toward him. But the dog interjected.

"He is appropriately undressed,' he said. 'That is, he is naked and unarmed. His material initiation may be incomplete, but he has come out of the night, he has emerged from darkness into the light of Artemis-Diana, contrary to those who come forth by day, whose lies, subsequently, are revealed to all as abominations. This human comes from a distinguished and certain line among the humans in general. As such, he shares the psyche of the earth in a similar manner as we do, according to his substratum, his sphere, his plane, his dimension. It is against the Great Law not to include the likes of him when they come forth via the nights of the spirits' which is our world and on their own accord.'

"Is there then a consensus to allow the admittance of this partial initiate?' said Tyler the raven. The hound of Kulane spoke again:

"It is well known that we dogs made a beneficial agreement with humbler humans long ago when we agreed to exchange companionship and devotion for food, warmth, and kindness.' Kulane glanced over at Fenrir whose slitty yellow eyes watched the proceedings without comment. 'Any integration that increases awareness between the creatures of Mother/Father Creation Being will,' Kulane continued, 'reward all those involved. I say let him stay.'

"Nothing less than a pandering pet is what you acknowledge yourself to be,' said the stag, also glancing over toward Fenrir. 'Its no wonder that humans think you a dumb animal which they can skewer around a spit of Rowan and roasted over their fires to conjure forth warrior spirits and summon death.'

"You have more horn then head and have got the story wrong,' said the hound of Kulane from his now curled up posture among the cold, stiff grass. 'They were hags not men whose incantations caused me discomfort. Furthermore, it was not my death which they sought, nor is this human one of their race. And it is venison of the likes of you that they roast over their fires, not dog.'

"Is there any other contention?' said the radiant reptile.

"Let the undressed one who is normally dressed adorn himself with the feathers of a crane and take up the pen,' said the mare. 'Then with the alphabet that is unique to his species let him record our compliances and contentions if only for the sake of posterity among his fellow humans.'

"Then with there being no opposition to the human's presence and with the pen being taken up, let us begin,' said the beautiful serpent, his red tongue darting forth beneath his burning, coal red eyes.

"As we are gathered together here in the name of the holy Sow and the Hare,' said this magnificent worm, 'we remember our brethren the quail, the owl, the eagle, and the hawk. We remember, too, the lion, the ass, and the ox, and all those afflicted by misguided, inequitable, and nonpareil oppression. We remember the coyote and the fox, and the lizard and the butterfly, the earthworm, the hummingbird, and the maggot. We remember each and every one of us, and in the going down of the sun and in the morning, we will now remember them.'

"We will remember them,' the others repeated in unison.

"Who is it then — brethren — who complete our triad?' said the serpent.

"It is we, the brethren, who are one before the eternal moment of Creation and meet here upon the single plane of consciousness,' shouted the animals once again in unison.

Dyfed, too shouted this out from the lotus of his heart in Shamskar[10], his mother tongue and the language of his ancestors who at one time were people of a special tribe of Hyperborean priest kings (magicians), a race who roamed the world. One such priest king was Shirkah, Dyfed's ancestor.

---

10 A sacred dialect (but not the written language itself) whose name meant — *to put together, make ready, or compose.*

(Battering her maidenhead
with coitus collision)

> *"He's a muddled fool, full of lucid intervals."*
> MIGUEL DE CERVANTES

The people had been mightily impressed with Dyfed's performance during Sow-ain that raised his station here in Owen's cenedl. But of all those within the cenedl it was Owen MacShee himself who had been impressed most of all. But for Dyfed it was still all about those beautiful green eyes of Owen's beautiful red headed daughter Ceredwyn that antagonised him the most during those few days before Sow-ain. But almost up to that day he had not set eyes on her, nor much afterwards, either. When he did it was very infrequently, at first, and always in the company of her father. Only a trace of a smile appeared on her soft full lips when they encountered. And despite him paying her close attention, she remained aloof and cool. All in all she had offered no plaudit in his direction at any time other than that tantalizing look she gave him from time to time with her beautiful green eyes. Indeed, it was perplexing to the young man. In the evenings while he lay alone on his lumpy couch, tossing this way and that (his mind and body all aflame) it occurred to him that he might have discovered something rather wonderful, maybe unique. At least wonderful in the hopefully short interim until he could fuse more closely with the object of his lust and possibly his love, although he wasn't in any position to discern the difference between them at this point. It was an enhancement of feeling that lay within a flight of fantasy which led to a pinnacle of exhilaration produced from the strangest yet most natural combination of stimulation resulting in sweet emission. It left him wondering why he had not come across it before. Of course he could only imagine at this stage, but for the moment that was rewarding enough. Then, for the next three lunar cycles, things changed dramatically between the two of them.

Then on the day of Alder the Green (the tree of resurrection sacred to Bran, Kronos, and Saturn), which is the day following the vernal equinox and John Barleycorn, he had sung Ceredwyn a short ballad, and before Beltane they had entered into full consensual union; the first for both of them. The mare was out of the stable and Owen was none the wiser. On that day, and ignorant of their union, Owen was busy plotting plans and making decisions that would have an ill effect on Dyfed and Ceredwyn for a very long time. Owen had to admit, if only to himself for now, that in Dyfed he could hardly have arranged for anyone more suited for Ceredwyn to marry, especially one that would have also remained as appealing and attractive to her, as well. Dyfed was a high-spirited, vigorous young man. That much Owen knew. Though still young he was taller then any man Owen had ever seen, and strong, with good looks. But it was his shamanistic qualities and his fierce intelligence that would bode well for Owen, especially if Dyfed passed this on to Owen's grandchildren through Ceredwyn. How could he lose?

So he now angled for an outcome that would see that she bore his son (daughters begetting a son was what every leader — who leaned toward the illusion of progeny wealth — hoped for). But, for her husband (on the other hand) he wanted a real political player with the savvy of a socially delinquent fighting churl who could find misplaced manners when needed. For this he had somebody in mind, and that somebody wasn't Dyfed. But all this Owen kept to himself for now. But towards the start of May as Beltane approached, the problem now was how to handle his daughter. Owen's timing in the steps toward becoming the grandfather of at least her first son by Dyfed (which he hoped to be quickly in the making) was quickly running out of time, at least by his reckoning. There was much to be done, still. How little Owen knew.

That Owen had earlier reversed his practice of kyboshing the breaching of maidenheads at Beltane had been his first machination towards the successful end he envisioned. But successful or not, Owen never had any intention of relinquishing full control over Ceredwyn's and his own future when it came to who fathered her first son any more than who he allowed her to marry. Of course he always had the intention of manipulating the chance meeting between Ceredwyn and the protagonist who was to batter down her maidenhead. He had never foreseen this to be a problem. The issue now was to tacitly set his daughter and Dyfed on a course for coitus collision during the newly revived free for all in the forest around about over the Beltane festival for which (on account) he had renewed its age old custom. The problem was that he needed to be able to manipulate the king he wanted her married to very shortly after she had conceived so as to fool the man he had in mind. He couldn't have his daughter ballooned out with child as she declared her vows to her husband who had only just made her acquaintance; not without a hugh bribe, one which he couldn't afford, anyway. Oh, but the irony of it all that was yet to come.

(The great game that's afoot)

"Oh, what a tangled web we weave…'
SIR WALTER SCOTT

One fine day well after the solstice Owen discussed with Dyfed to some extent the matter regarding individuals at play in the great game that was afoot in Albion. Here in the glorious Isle of Albion the blue-blooded folks were furiously playing catch-up where the cult of politics was involved. For whether folks here liked it or not, Albion was now very much part of the Amoran empire. Owen now talked once more about the man Bricus of Demetia. The name, however, Owen informed Dyfed, was always mentioned in conjunction with another, Blazingwolf. Dyfed was familiar with this name too, and through Manandan he had learned something of the man. Blazingwolf was a learned and capable scribe and a Druid from Armorica. Although this Druid had been educated in the old ways, he had read literature at Skander City (Xanderia) in the ancient Land of Khem during the time it was being translated into the Hellenic language. He had also converted (in a quasi type of way) to the doctrine outlined in the Septuagint and was radically anti pagan. He was also a master of many languages and had used those tongues to speak out as a strong and vocal adversary of many of the ancient pagan cults here in Albion. Dyfed remembered, however, that it was Manandan's opinion that Blazingwolf — before his conversion from paganism, as well as distancing himself from the classical precepts of Western Philosophy — had failed miserably in the end to pierce the secret of the Ram, the goal of every accomplished Druid, for what its worth.

Macsen Wledig of Demetia, commonly now being referred to as Bricus of Demetia, on the other hand was a precocious individual whose power (Dyfed thought) was Kasdeemean (Urian) in origin. Therefore, Bricus was a magician. But Dyfed had no idea where Bricus managed to pick up that ideological and cultural information. Perhaps through Asian influences, he thought, such as those mysteries of Mithra and Zoroaster being brought back to Amor and refashioned into Amoran acceptability as the Mithraic mysteries and so forth. It was also well to remember that this Macsen Wledig (Bricus) as the younger brother to Prince Aldroneus of Armorica and cousin to Prince Custennin Gorneu of Dumnonii was of a family who were hardly local for originally they were Amorans. Somewhere around 570 (as calculated from the year of the Olympiad), at the same time as Publius Scipio Cornelius Africanus' defeat of Hannibal at the Battle of Zama that took place during the Amoran Republic (roughly 200 years before the beginning of the current Amoran principate: ie in 200BCE), the family had set themselves up in Hispania as wheat farmers. From here they got rich helping provide for Amor's large demand for cereal. The family was exceedingly large and its young and boisterous soon sailed north from Hispania to greener hills in Armorica. There they ingratiated themselves first as wheat merchants and then slid comfortably into positions of influence. Using the useful tool of marriage as a means, they began to climb the social ladder. From Armorica they soon spread to that land's natural trade partner and royal gene-pool companion, Dumnonii. All this had pretty much been completed by Dyfed's birth. And it was through Bricus' influence as a Druid, as well as his wits, that were administered by Blazingwolf, that he became Protector of Demetia, even over King Cadot. This was due to him having been appointed by the Amoran governor.

But it was Bricus' companion, the aforementioned Blazingwolf, in whom Dyfed had begun to develop an interest, for in his own mind a great mystery had formed around this strange Armorican. Manandan's own underlying tone of resentment toward this man (who briefly, once had been his pupil) stemmed from Blazingwolf's incapacity to correctly administer certain rites involving the Keltic Trinity, a relic from the more ancient Hyperborean culture that was unused by Druids. This path, or way, however, was thought to be an anathema to the new world order direction that was being conferred by the might of Amor. So, in the long run the Keltic Trinity wasn't to be. The trinity (incidentally) was also the symbol for the Isle of peace, Dyfed reflected. This was not a coincidence, apparently. The Hyperborean Trinity was an independent concept of birth, death and re-birth and Dyfed's opinion was that Manandan might have regarded Blazingwolf's cavalier (if not a downright maverick) interpretation of the Trinity as being a cheap imitation. Perhaps, then the man's intentions were mainly for usurping authority. But he was certainly a sorcerer.

If a usurper of the likes Blazingwolf could become a usurper of the highest order, albeit. For not only was he initiated into the highest rung of the Druidic order, the thirty-second degree, but he claimed later to have ascended, finally, to the thirty-third degree, as well. To Manandan, Dyfed knew, such an affirmation would be meaningless, for that degree embodied Ram by piercing it thoroughly, and no adept would dare assert to having achieved that for fear he would lose everything, immediately. Embodying Ram by a penetrating piercing event over time wasn't like Prince Siddhartha's awakening gig or others who have claimed similar achievements. Piercing was actually beyond that which was humanly possible. A pronouncement as such was only meant as an understatement to acknowledge failure or to display extreme poverty of the soul (the wandering mind) in an attempt to open ones' heart and shun ego and all its distractions. But aside from that, Blazingwolf had been one of the first, Manandan had told him once, to champion the ceasing of human sacrifices that many of his Druid brothers so relished. But this had not come from the knowledge of the ancient rhythm from which Dyfed and his ancestors had been nurtured, but rather it came to Blazingwolf from a very recent and sensible Amoran edict that banned such barbaric practices. Though Manandan had told Dyfed that the authority of Amor solely to usurp more power and lessen the Druid influence had initiated the edict, the Amorans themselves were relatively civilized in their own way.

Nevertheless, this strange man's independence and force of character had caused him in addition to being a Druid, to become a respected priest in the new Amoran cult doctrine of Mithra as well. It was by way of this vehicle that Blazingwolf had risen to become a Pater and the guardian and then the mentor of the young Bricus of Demetia. So, despite Bricus' young age, Blazingwolf had managed to advance him to pater in the temple of Mithra at Venta Belga, the grand temple of western Albion. Apparently, Blazingwolf was also an acknowledged authority on salvation from an unlikely bedevilment called Original Sin[11]. This dressed-up peculiarity was part of a newly re-emerged

---

11 Original sin is a hot topic we will disregard in this discourse. It has, unfortunately, a number of definitions.

theory promoted by theosophical dreamers and architects of mythos that was being bantered about in certain circles. Although no one knew from where Blazingwolf had attained such knowledge or even from where that rejuvenated concept of original sin derived, it had become the liturgical language of the philosophy of a recent Abramist sect among the worshippers of Jehovah (JHVH/Jehweh) called Jehuanism. This breakaway unit had been toying around with reusing and re-interpreting this theory that they mixed with Hellenic logic from the likes of Plato.

Dyfed let Owen know that Kings Cadot, Maelgwryn and Cadwallopir's concerns should be that Pater Bricus and Pater Blazingwolf were two candidates all for causing subversion here in western Albion. This, he said, made it Owen's concern, too. The aforementioned duo was certainly two choices for an emerging role for unofficial Amoran officials working behind enemy lines against native Albionians such as Maelgwyn and Codwallopir. Maelgwyn and Codwallopir also thought that Bricus was in line to be mandated by Amoran officials to control Gwyneth, Demetia, and Dumnonii for the empire. In Nova Troia, on the other hand, the Amoran governing authority of Albion would tolerate Blazingwolf's anti-establishment and nonconformist attitude, maybe. This was because of his intelligence as well as Bricus' obvious dependency on him. This despite the sever eccentricity which the Amorican displayed.

Meanwhile, Maelgwyn's visiting agent to Owen's cenedl had apparently brought news of these two men's possible treachery to him. Owen's patchy and pasty face looked at Dyfed. He said to him, 'now that my daughter is expecting your child, tell me of your plans.' Owen had reason to show interest in Dyfed's plans for the future, of course, for had he not an invested interest in him and his daughter's future and their fortune?

Regarding Owen carefully Dyfed thought about his future life with Ceredwyn and the baby. Although this promised to be a big change it didn't alter his commitments for the future. He would share his life with her and that was something he badly wanted. He actually realized now for the first time that he hadn't thought through this particularly clearly, but that didn't matter now. In any case, he was entertaining the idea that the city of Legion would be their future only for a very limited time. He now realized that the city of Nova Troia would be his first real stepping stone to Amor.

"Now Dyvie,' Owen said, 'listen here. I have a proposition for you. Because we have lost so many cattle this winter through starvation and having to feed our people, I am preparing now to embark on a late summer hunt. This is to tide the cenedl over until the new calves, ewes, and lambs recently born have grown. Soon after that the game at large will have fattened up some more. Anyway, when the hunt is finished I will make for Hardlech. I have arranged for Ceredwyn to meet us there. And from Hardlech we will travel together by sea to the city of Legion to facilitate some important political business at hand that has come up. Here, arrangements have already been made. And there, after the business at hand is concluded and the festivities are finished, I will see you Ceredwyn wed in style.' Owen was once again filling his face and now leaned forward and wiped his greasy fingers on his clothes while he concentrated on Dyfed's reaction to his suggestion.

Owen was not going all that way and to all that trouble just to draw him away for reasons of his own or on the promise of matrimony, Dyfed thought. Something was about to happen, some very important matter of state was perhaps about to take place which concerned those other antagonists such as Blazingwolf, Bricus, Maelgwyn,

Cadot, Cadwallopir and Ryan, the new king of Mona. And there was something else in it for Owen, Dyfed knew. Owen was lying about something.

"You have the itinerary worked out well in advance I see,' said Dyfed regarding Owen with his winning and good natured smile. He held up his little puppy that smiled at Owen, too. 'How could I refuse such an offer as that,' he responded. 'A hunt; well I never!' he said as he rubbed his beardless chin. 'That is something to look forward to and to prepare for. I have grown slovenly in my dallying here and have fallen out of practice in shooting and correctly placing my arrows,' he said blandly tongue in cheek. Dyfed of course, had no formal training at all in correctly placing arrows anywhere.

(The Hare of the Wolf)

*'It is not those who inflict the most,
but those that can suffer the most who will conquer.'*
TERRENCE MACSWINEY (PLAYWRIGHT)

The morning ground was hard and the air was strangely cool. Dyfed recollected that it had not rained in a long while. The hillsides were faintly brushed with a hint of g green and the thick wads of puffy clouds had about them more the suggestion of spring. The three carts (one used as a store that was partially filled with their meagre rations and hunting supplies) rattled along behind the hunters, their wheels jarring roughly through the ruts that in the morning sunrise were still frozen hard. In their excitement, the dogs — accompanying the hunters — were hesitant to heel and each hound panted a cloud of steam from its mouth as the pack darted every which way with their noses to the ground. Puppy, who was not a hunter, kept close to Dyfed who was usually mounted upon Trum. But Puppy was continually under Trum's hooves.

In the frosty air Dyfed heard the voices of the men ring out sharply as they shouted commands to these canine companions — the sleuths of the hunt — as well as calling out in raucous jest to each other. Dyfed struggled under the circumstances to maintain his habits of hygiene. Twice a day he washed his genital area as well as his underarms and face. He washed his face with cold water followed by warm water he heated over the fire in the morning, according to his custom. Then before retiring to sleep, he washed his face with warm water along with his hands. His hands were washed 12 times a day, in the morning after he arose and before going to sleep, as stated, and approximately another nine or ten times during the day; before eating, after touching people and animals, and generally for cleanliness at all times. This habit and custom had now become a problem. But in spite of these unique hardships, he was in great spirits as he sat astride his Trum his swayback mare. For this, the first leg of his destiny was the start of the journey that was to lead him to Hardlech. Soon he would be married to Ceredwyn and climbing those lofty steps that would take him to the pinnacles of achievement and greatness before others. Such were Dyfed's joyful thoughts; thoughts which optimistic youths of every generation employ to expunge the pessimisms, which, if allowed to gain a foothold, erode the weak and the disillusioned as their years, advance.

The party of hunters under Owen's supervision wended their way through meadow and copse, over hills and by dell. Each man kept his senses alert for animal droppings, a trampled weed, or a chewed branch, and even a distinct smell would alert them to the presence of game. With eyes peeled and ears strained they moved stealthily through the forest. Dyfed more often now walked, leading Trum and carrying his beautiful, monogramed horn tipped bow unstrung in his hand and a quiver slung over his shoulder. Tied to his belt was a sling and occasionally to wile the time he would place a fine round stone in its leather cradle and rock it back and forth as he went along. If his eye caught a squirrel which could be roasted over a hasty fire, then he would swing the stone around in one rapid revolution and letting one strap loose, send the missile whirling through the air with a loud snap. He aimed none of his stones or arrows at little birds or hares, although the startled hens that flew up among the trees beating their wings in fright were fair game. Once when he had been lagging behind closely observing the new regions of this kingdom, Dyfed was surprised when suddenly (overtaking Owen and the hunters) he saw them gathered together and fallen to their knees like praying suppliants. Looking in the direction that they postured towards he saw only a young yearling deer standing starkly still and nervously watching back at them with one eye as its head was turned to the profile and one ear twitching in unison with its tiny tail. Bewildered by this custom Dyfed discreetly enquired after it and was told by Owen that the first stag to be seen on the hunt was considered good-luck. But it must never be harmed, Owen told him. Indeed, he said, the deer was often feared for the creature was the materialization of Faunus, the revered god of the forests. Faunus, indeed, thought Dyfed, seeing the two little velvet bumps on the side of its head. A stag it was not.

    The party kept up a brisk pace and the clip of the horse's hooves and rumble of the wagon wheels alerted many of the cleverer animals to their presence. The lead tracker dogs seldom barked as they scurried back and forth among the underbrush snapping twigs and shattering through the morning thin ice in their search for scent. But this uproar warned many in the wild kingdom away, though, not all animals were so smart. Believing they could elude the gang of men, some of the duller creatures stood their ground as others wisely rushed off to safety. Once the heaving of the hounds' hot breath, and the noise of their gnashing jaws became audible to some unfortunate creature, it was (by far) way too late for evasive manoeuvres. Those cold-nosed creatures of the humans were onto them by this time, and then (only at the last moment — and in panic) did the prey decide to bolt. Gripped in mortal fear as the raucous of the dog pack crept closer to its heels, the hunted creature searched desperately for escape. Quickly, Owen's hunting party spread out and advanced towards their quarry. Pain surged through the animal as the first set of fangs pierced its flesh. With its mouth a-froth and its eyes bulging with fear, it whirled around searching for defence. Flicking its head in hopes that a horn or tusk would discourage this first assailant, it felt instead the pain from a second and a third attacker as the pack closed in. As its senses focused, the doomed creature heard the strange rhythmic babble of the humans as they began to surround him. The dogs then retreated as the men whistled them back. Suddenly the animal felt its frame lurch and heard the rent of flesh as an arrow pierced its hide. The path of pain was swift and the animal's heaving body slowly warmed the deadly wooden shaft. Soon it tasted the warm trickle of its own blood and began to lose its sense of sight. The creature's instincts were to up and flee, but movement was beyond its capability now. And as its heart started to pound in irregular beats and its breath came in gasps and puffs of white condensate particles as it entered into the cool air, the life spirit drained out and fled.

    The hunters worked out of camps whose job it was for Dyfed, under the guidance of Owen's elderly quartermaster, to set up in predetermined sites. Owen MacShee would send them on ahead in one of the wagons loaded with the materials they needed to their next destination to prepare camp. Their camps, in any case, were sparse. There the two would wait for the main body of hunters to catch up, or they may return to the former camp if the latter weren't going to break camp for a day or two. The camps would be gathered up as they and the wagons of game returned to Owen's cenedl, later. In the meantime, the hunters would move in a progressive direction toward Hardlech. Around each camp snares would be set and nets strung between trees to catch birds while the hunting party scoured the countryside flushing all furred fauna and feathered fowl before them. Dyfed often amused his fellow hunters with his dexterity. With a show of great production to attract attention a couple of the hunters would tie a piece of bait attached to the end of a throng to a tree branch then withdraw to a place some distance away. Standing motionless beside the bait Dyfed would patiently wait for a magpie or even a raven, the hardest bird of all for Dyfed to catch alive and impossible for anyone else even to approach. Then while the bird was in mid flight and distracted by the lure of dangling bait Dyfed's hand would dart out and snatch hold of the bird by its legs and tail. Then calming the fluttered creature with a soothing sound he made between his lips Dyfed would gently release his quarry.

After the evening meal the company would sit around the fire and spin yarns of adventure. Some were of love while others were of battle and it was here that the men looked to Dyfed, the master storyteller among them.

"Once upon a time,' Dyfed would begin, 'during the division of the first and second world, the stars fell like rain and the night became inflamed like day so that the passage of time ceased. The gods left their paths and warred and the seasons became topsy-turvy; thunderstorms broke in mid winter and when Radiance-Apollo flew into the upper latitudes and the oak leaves shimmered and gleamed from his rays, snow fell. Oh, I must tell you! Echo first broke the silence and was heard before others and all the states perished as order returned to chaos. Even Jupiter and Juno were on the out and out in an un-comely spat. This is the time of which I speak. It was when the jackal and the serpent were brought together in battle, when Odin donned his eagle helmet and sat astride his eight-legged steed to converge on the Middle Earth. It was when Nergal imposed himself on Astarte and Tuesday laid claim to Friday in a lawsuit to end all lawsuits. Mars waded through blood until routed by Minerva, and when Radiance-Apollo rubbed cheek to Zenith's jowl, and the pathway to the palace of Heaven overlooked Annwn — that fearful underworld that lay opposite — the earth continued to shake and blood fell from the sky like rain. It was a time of general confusion when the gods waged war and Consensus was in revolt. Indeed, it was from these same occurrences that Amor was born and the jackal, belligerent and bold, slew the dragon and confined Hekate to the underworld to bide her time. But the thoughts of these rural men from Gwynedd were closer to home.

"Tell us, Dyfed, about Pryderi and of Angus mac Oc, son of the Dagda, and about Caer the beautiful who Elcmar deceived. We want to hear more about them,' they cried. Dyfed raised his hands in mock capitulation, his young beardless face smiling and glowing from the light of the fire. When he recalled Coaire Mor, the king from Hybernia who, it was said, was born of a bird and whose sword could sing, the men cheered. The men listened intently as time and again Dyfed conjured forth into their mind's eye the birds of Rhiannon that waken the dead and lull the living; of the cup of Llwyr, son of Llwyrinon; of the great and bottomless meat hamper of Gwyddnen and of the cauldron of Diwrnach, the man from the Emerald Isle. They also wanted to hear of the magic bottles of Gwyddolwyn the Dwarf, and of Rhynnon Stiffbeard, then about the harp of Teirtu that would play of itself when it pleased a man and be silent when one wished it to be.

The evenings were cool but the fires were hot and the wine strong, which was heated in a copper pot by the blaze. As the evening drew to a close the men sang ballads about life and love and Dyfed soon learned many a ditty of lechery and lust to add to his repertoire. They lived on the meat that they hunted and on the fish that they caught in nets flung from their flimsy shell shaped coracles that they launched on the ponds and meandering rivers of this land. The abundant honey from the swarms that nested hereabouts was mixed with their porridge or melted into bowls of hot goat milk that was used to float the hard pan of baked berry cakes. The men wasted nothing and ate the organs of the animals they killed, the heart, liver and even the intestines. The larger animals were butchered into quarters and hung, and after each camp had been struck (and the main party had moved on), one or two attendants remained behind. These men built racks fashioned out of young saplings that they positioned around strategically placed fires. Then they cut the meat into strips and filleted the fish. The strips of meat and fish were then placed on these racks to dry and cure from the permeation of heat and wood smoke. High conical walls of sticks and animal skins were erected around the fires and racks of game with a small opening left at the top. This helped trap and increase the density of smoke wafting around the stands of stripped flesh. Slowly the meat dried and was later bundled for storage. Only the fowl was not dried in this way. Instead it was hung un-gutted for five or ten days before being eaten. This was a delicacy that the men relished, although one which Dyfed found he was not partial to.

The men would rise early and push off the skins that lay over them in a heap. As the mask of Artemis-Diana shone crisply in a morning sky all a twinkle with slowly fading stars, deep down in the fire pits the embers glowed red under a thick layer of grey ash. A cool morning wind often blew through the treetops, but because there was no mist or rain the tents had remained bundled up in one of the wagons and the men continued to live under the stars. With the first sounds of activity in the morning, the dogs would begin to stir. First it was the younger hounds that became excited, and after stretching their limbs — with their tongues curled slightly upwards out of their open snouts — they stared intently toward the hunters. The older dogs, however, remained still and lay curled in tight balls close to the fires with watchful eyes wide open. Nearby, the very few horses that accompanied them — to pull the wagons and to mount only Owen and Dyfed — stamped their feet, snorted and shook their manes as their long noses scanned the ground for feed. Every day Owen hunted and they left camp well before the day got light. After an animal had been captured in a net or had been cornered and had thrashed out the last moments of its life, Owen gave thanks to the creature's spirit and to the goddess of the hunt as well as to Faunus, god of the forest. Then attendants cut the animal's throat and lashed its legs to a long stave. In this fashion they carried it back to camp to be skinned and butchered. Although steadily growing longer the days were still short, so when the Radiance-Apollo slipped beyond Zenith's high station and slid slowly into the cool rosy haze on the western horizon, the hunting party retraced their long weary strides back toward camp. As they trudged along, the last rays of the chilly sun would slant through the forest and throw out long shadows behind the rocks while the sky south of the big mountain folded into a puzzle of pale yellow and grey hues. At the end of the day the tired men sang roundelays as they trudged homeward to camp. Like the others Dyfed sang his heart out, their breath forming puffs of white vapour in the clean forest air as they sang. In the pale light they traipsed through thick wooded areas and followed cold rushing streams cascading down from lofty heights. After they were back in camp and the meal and chores completed, great roots and broken stumps of trees were flung onto the fire. This caused explosions of yellow sparks that flew up into the dusk and the men readied themselves for an evening of stories, song and grog.

(A day on the hump with a bolt of energy and a dash of thunderclap at his back)

'There is no light in souls in which there is no warmth.'
JOSEPH JOUBERT

Early one morning Owen called the men around him and ordered one of the carts to be filled with some of the spoils from the hunt as well as tents along with the meagre possessions of all those who would be accompanying him and Dyfed to the coastal town of Hardlech by the Sea. These folks would be his retinue. The remainder of the game would be loaded into the two remaining carts and they would all retrace to the junction where the previous camp was located. From there, he and Owen on horseback and four or five of his men on foot, would set out southwest for Hardlech while the remainder retraced their steps back to Owen's cenedl, picking up the butchered and smoked cured game along with the attendants waiting at each camp on their way. This hunt's kill now lay hanging in a long line strung out along the hunting route and guarded from predators by the handful of attendants who kept the fires fuelled.

The town of Hardlech, according to Owen, was a day or so distance away. Owen told Dyfed that there would be some festivities there for them upon their arrival. Owen indicated that these festivities would be attended by a number of notables from the surrounding kingdoms. Men like Duke Howel (he wasn't a real duke but rather that was his name) would be there along with King Cadwallopir and King Cadot, petty kings both. These men would be making their way to the city of Legion as well. And petty king Maelgryn, Dyfed was told, would be hoofing it to Legion from Cyngreawdr Fynydd. As for themselves, they would leave on the morrow.

So, with no further camps to expedite, and finding himself at loose ends that morning, Dyfed decided to explore the local countryside on the last day of the hunt. As the valley that they were in was flanked with steep slopes on either side he chose to climb above the camp to take in the lie of the land. Then arming himself with his sling and bow he set out on foot leaving Puppy behind to be minded by the other hounds. Halfway up the slope to the mountain shoulder Dyfed stopped to catch sight of a blue haze that hung above the camp and tapered off down the valley. As he watched it the haze collided with the treetops and the rocks that jutted up along the hillside. The air was fresh and besides the smell of rocks and moss a faint whiff of smoke wafted up and reached his nostrils. Like the environment around him there was a spring to Dyfed's step and no cares troubled his thoughts that morning as he clambered along grasping at rocks and roots as he ascended. Scrambling quickly up and over a steep knoll he climbed into a thicket of bush and struggled through it. As he made his way through this and up toward a barren crag that loomed above him, tiny chirping birds hopped along bare branches and flew about nervously fluttering from bush to bush. Besides these little creatures, squirrels wheeled and darted in short sudden spurts all around him. This action was accompanied by a burst of noise as they warned their fellow-kind of impending danger. To Dyfed it sounded like little squeaky wheels warming on their axles. Beyond the crag, which he scaled easily, Dyfed followed a ridge that rose abruptly like the back of a dragon. Along this dinosauric like ridge whose spine was comprised of sharp boulders that protruded out of the shale, he climbed upward with ease despite the uneven ground.

After awhile he stopped and propped himself up against a large protruding rock to gaze around. The valley bottom was way below him now and he could not see any smoke as he had done earlier. He could not see the knoll either for it was beyond a shoulder of the ridge that curved at that point to coincide with the contours of the valley. On the other side of the valley the topography was much the same. There the earth was thrust upward toward the sky, and in the distance a large mountain white with snow towered above all the land and glistened in the morning sunlight. Dyfed walked for a while then flopped down onto a large slab of rock to rest. He thought that the sky seemed very clear and blue and the only clouds that he could see were on the northern horizon which accumulated around the aforementioned big snowy mountain the way floating debris in a pond will gather around a motionless snag that protrudes up through the water's surface. Laying his head back on the rock and feeling the warm sun on his face he dozed for a while then fell fast to sleep.

Dyfed jerked awake and sat up. The sun had disappeared behind a white film that had spread across the entire sky and his skin had turned to goose flesh and the air was very cold. Clasping himself with his arms and slapping his sides once or twice he looked around him. The great White Mountain that had shone brightly in the distance was now barely visible. Picking up his bow Dyfed strung and unstrung it in a nervous reaction while he contemplated the elements around him. He had decided almost instantly that he had better get off the mountain and back into the valley without delay when suddenly there was a clap of thunder and a sudden fall of mist. This phenomenon now prevented him from seeing his own hand before his face, never mind the route ahead to lead him down. Dyfed had been startled by the sharp report and with the mist thick like fleece floating all around him he felt severely chilled. His vision had become so impaired that he was disoriented and unsure of what direction to take. On either side of the ridge the slope plunged sharply downward and he knew that he must follow the ridge along its crest in order to retrace his steps. Dyfed now crouched down as he felt his way along the rocky surface like a spider. Since he could barely see, surface pitches had become increasingly less obvious. After a short time Dyfed's hands became very cold and he rubbed them together and held them up to his mouth and blew his warm breath on to them while feeling his knees and shins ache from dashing them onto the sharp points of rocks as he had scrambled over them in his arachnid type crawl. The mist was so thick that once when his bow had escaped his grasp and clattered out of sight into the murky white fog, it had taken him some time to recover it. In this manner he slowly struggled and stumbled back along the ridge as he picked up bruises from the rocks the way one might pick up the furry heads of couch grass (Elymus repens; aka Dog grass, Devil grass, Witch grass, Quack grass) while wading through open fields in heavy socks.

Becoming quite still at one point, Dyfed extended forth his antennas of awareness and noticed the tremendous silence everywhere around him. Somewhere off in the distance he heard movement as small rocks or shale broke loose which then tumbled down the steep slope in a trickle of magnified vibrations on account of the sea of fog. Staying on course was difficult but he forged on. After veering off in the wrong direction a number of times, and then trying to compensate for his error, he became hopelessly disoriented. Dyfed was a lad of the forest; fog on a mountain slope (on the other hand) was (apparently) a cat of a different colour altogether. He cried out a few times in hopes that an echo would bounce back from off something, but since this was to no avail he continued to blunder on downwards until suddenly he heard the sound of running water.

Soon the going became more difficult and he got caught and tangled up in the terrain. Then, just as he was climbing over a rock, he slipped and plunged into a cold and unseen stream, twisting his ankle while severely knocking the funny bone of one elbow. Writhing to the aching jar upon his arm he responded quickly, nevertheless, and picked himself out of the chilled mountain brook as fast as he could. He limped lamely through the shin deep water as frustration began to take hold. Sitting down he nursed his elbow in the palm of his other hand. The fresh mountain water had flowed all the way up one sleeve and down the back of his heavy shirt and one numb leg was entirely soaked. Shivering, he retrieved his bow from the creek — re-soaking his feet and arms to the elbow in the bargain — and slowly picked his way downstream by using his bow as a crutch. He was cold and stiff, he limped and was sore all over, but the major factor contributing to his delay was the thick white bank of fog that continued to press in upon him, forcing him to feel his way gently forward. Due to his injuries he stopped and rested quite frequently, and before it began to get dark he found a sheltered place and resigned himself in having to spend the night upon the mountain. Although there was very little in the way of fuel and no dry tinder about, Dyfed soon had a small fire burning, its thick smoke billowing invisibly into the misty dusk. For the next while he was kept rigorously employed scrounging around naked in the murky blackness for fuel. All the while his boots and garments, propped up against rocks close to the fire, lay slowly drying. When he got too cold he would sit by the little flame for a while to absorb its meagre warmth then strike out again in search of more burnable material such as roots and the underside of mosses. He dressed himself as each article of clothing had somewhat dried, then finally in exhaustion he fell back into an uneasy slumber. It was then that he was visited by a strange vision.

He dreamed that he was walking in the clouds with gigantic blackbird that was really Blazingwolf, that strange yet powerful man he had never met. Suddenly as they walked arm in arm, Dyfed had tripped upon a protruding mountain peak and painfully stubbed his toe. Pausing for a moment to nurse his bloody appendage he noticed that his companion had continued on and was swiftly treading the cumulus fantastic some paces ahead leaving him behind upon the island mountain tip. Dyfed then called out in a loud voice begging his companion to wait, but the ventriloquial response that floated back to his ears was the warning that…"time waits for no man with honour, you piece of shit. One moment you are present here, the next moment you are present elsewhere.' As the apparition drifted further and further away, Dyfed grew angry and frantically continued in vain to climb back onto the fleecy carpet of cloud. Soon his shouts and pleas were met by maniacal laughter whereupon he realized that the underlining essence of this loathsome spectre was nothing short of demonical. This quickly led him into a state where he became convinced that he had been wilfully tricked, and with resentfulness rising within him like sour bile he became hateful toward the character of the apparition. Quickly, he un-strapped his bow and strung it while keeping his eye on the incubus that moved up and away from him among the swirling celestial nebula. He reached for an arrow. But what further trickery is this? That was no arrow drawn up alongside his bow, for it was warm and supple and he felt its life pulsating in his hand. It was a shaft of life plasma that he had plucked from his quiver for although tipped with a keen edged metal point, budding green leaves sprouted out at the end where the fleches should have been placed. Nevertheless, he placed the bowstring within the crook at the end of the living branch. Then using the thumb-draw (with that digit locked by his forefinger of his right hand) he held it close to his face and quickly thrust out his left bow arm to its full length before releasing the shaft at the demon's vanishing back. Then to his utter amazement the lively shaft floated softly from the bow and struck a fixed position in mid air only a short distance hence with the sharp tip pointing downward. There it gyrated and vibrated while emitting a terrific noise that caused the elements around it to stir and bombard him like the wind. Suddenly there was a loud crack and the arrow (that now resembled a dash of thunderbolt) became alive with burning energy. He watched in utter wonderment for nothing matched this thing's richness, a richness that resembled liquid gold. And he could more than feel its presence about him that seemed to engulf him like heat from a fire. Suddenly it began to speak. Although he heard no voice it spoke inwardly to him saying: "Cast down your aspirations, oh miserable mortal. Go forth to affect only what has been."

The arrow then spun on a central axis until the sharply pointed tip of the shaft pointed directly back at him. Then the gyrating and vibrating of the richly coloured fragment of energy increased — and with a loud report — it shot straight through him. Horrified, Dyfed screamed and waited for the agony of his death.

Dyfed lay on his back and clutched at the cold ground with his eyes wide open and his heart pounding. A moment or two lapsed and he could still feel where the thing had mentally passed through his body. He blinked at the white void that was all around him and stiffly sat up. When he got his hands and face down close to the fireplace among the stone, he found it was cold and dank and covered in heavy dew: And through the fog the blackened charcoaled tips of the burned out stubs of twigs appeared grey. Dyfed shivered more from the memory of the dream than from the cold itself and then slowly stretched his aching body. He then thought for a moment about the curious apparition that had come to him while he lay tossing and turning in the damp fog on his bed of sharp, uneven rocks. Quickly he put these thoughts from his mind for he realized that he must get off the mountain and catch up to Owen's party that would be leaving early that very morning.

Groping his way along in the bright whiteness, he discerned a change in the sound of the brook that he was following and noticed too a change in the nature of the ravine's terrain. He felt his way to the edge of a precipice and found himself standing on the brink of a chute where the water flowed out into the air and dropped a great distance before continuing to snake down the mountainside a long way below. Now he had to traverse a steep rock face and he reasoned that this might be the abutment to the crag that lay above the thicket of bush he had struggled through the day before. Descending across the rock face was strenuous for Dyfed as his hands were continually cold and this made grasping the tiny cracks and minute crevices difficult. In addition, his twisted ankle continued to give him a great deal of pain and very little support. The mist now was comforting, however, as it did not allow him to see to any extent the enormous height from which he was precariously perched above the sloping abutments below; but as time went by it became a hindrance as well for not only was he unable to see what progress he was making, but it also hampered his ability to plan his descending route. Because of this, a number of times he had to back-track from dead-end approaches that led him clinging to the mountain's face and sprawling dangerously above space. Finally, out of the grey starkness of the fog, a branch appeared and brushed against his sore ankle, then a few moments later he was standing on the upper reaches of the steeply sloped thicket. His thrashing through the thick underbrush broke the eerie silence, and then groping blindly he limped his way toward the lip of the valley. This time — as he made his way through the bush that continually snagged the bow that he had strapped to his back — no birds or squirrels chirped and squeaked around him. After a while the thicket ended and the ground fell away even more sharply and he descended slowly into the valley steadying himself with his hand against the slope. About halfway down the embankment the mist thinned and then suddenly disappeared altogether and the valley floor with its yellow pasture came into view.

As Dyfed walked with an infirm step across the meadow the recent nightmare that had occurred on the mountain was impinging on his mind like a shadow. Surely it had been a dream, hadn't it? he thought. It couldn't have been real. Yet, it had been unsuspecting. He had been startled when the thing called him a piece of shit, he recalled vividly. He had been greatly taken aback; and since he had been surprised by that remark how could his own mind, which was solely responsible for conjuring, composing and doing the whole single entity dream thing, deliver (at the same time) surprise itself. It is one thing maybe to be surprised at finding what you are thinking compared with being exposed to ones thinking process and be taken by surprise within the content. But it happened. This was very puzzling. Had it not been a dream, then? he thought.

Dyfed noted that there was no noise in the valley on this morning as there had been the morning before and there was no lingering smell of smoke either. Also as he approached the area of the camp no dogs barked. He called out for Owen, half expecting to be answered by an attendant who might have been left behind, but no one responded, only Puppy, who he had left behind, came running up. Then Dyfed spied old Trum standing patiently with pricked up ears and her long docile face regarding him intently. Puppy and Trum had been keeping each other company, he could see. In fact they had been tied together and were now tangled and Puppy was short leashed among the swayback's large hooves. Dyfed walked over and fondly stroked the gentle mare as he untangled them. The animal nudged Dyfed under the armpit with her soft nose while Puppy, jumping up with his front paws scratching at Dyfed's trousers, whined excessively. In a nearby tree an affronted raven tilted his black head and looked down at the trio with one beady eye. Then in an effort to either shoo away the human intruder or mock him, he let loose a throaty cry that pierced the cool air. He then looked back down at Dyfed again. Dyfed cawed back in perfect mock imitation before breaking into an ancient and rhythmic (not reproducible here) song that, though unable to imitate musically like a human, the Crow Clan had once taught his mother. Here is Dyfed's lyrical revised version:

> "Discern the rhyme, and claim the shrine,
> I am Saturn Apollo, and Diana's twin.
> I am Kronos in his prime,
> Thunder and lightning are my sign.
> As *Ammon-Zeus* I strove, and cleaved to Jove,

I honoured the mountain goddess.
A lion skin she me betroved,
I am, Hera's glory grove.
To draw my bow are twelve in a row,
The ram am I, as well as bull.
The priests of Thebes once called me Sho,
The serpent, acorn and mistletoe.
But in mid-summer colonnade
I am now hung displayed,
My horse and hound forgotten.
Then crucified upon the palisade,
I am beaten, castrated, and finally flayed.
Retrieved from oaken trunk, my blood is drunk,
High priest of orgiastic rites am I.
The rain ejaculates from my spunk,
And before the alter…t'was I, who slunk.
On an August dour, attendants devour,
My roasted flesh and butchered thigh.
My cured head sings, my genitalia flower,
By holy Communion, I empower.
And Poeas now wed, has inherited my bed,
As with sacred flame, he lit my pyre.
I limp to Hekate's realm of dread,
While mortals await my severed head.'

(A real live hermit named Morgant)

'I did not know whether I was Chuang Tzu dreaming I was a butterfly, or a butterfly dreaming I was Chuang Tzu.'

CHUANG TZU

Dyfed quickly built a fire and dried off while the mist against the mountain slope descended and evaporated in the warmth. As he scouted around and read the ground in order to interpret the camp's latest activity, the irritated raven flew about from tree to tree chattering away to himself. In their mannerism, Dyfed thought, raven was not much different from himself, although to avoid stares he (at least) had learned to chatter away to himself with his mouth firmly closed.

As Owen's tracks showed Dyfed that the company's departure had been earlier that morning, the lad knew that his party was not beyond easy reach. But as they tracked through the valley toward the direction of Hardlech it began to snow quite heavily and soon the signs became difficult to follow. There was no wind so the snow fell softly, silently landing upon branches and all about the ground. By the time he came out of the valley and arrived at a junction of two small streams, Dyfed was holding onto Trum's tail for guidance for the condition of the elements were as impossible as they had been on the mountain the day before. The white flakes were so large that they rubbed against each other as they fell; the falling snow was almost as thick above and around him in the air as it was upon the ground. Puppy had trouble wading through this environment as the snow balled up under his belly and between the toes of his padded little feet. Dyfed placed Puppy onto Trum's back. It was only by the direction in which the mountain streams flowed that Dyfed was able to orient himself at all.

He had remembered this spot from when they had passed this way a few days earlier, when Owen had pointed south to a valley and called it the way to Hardlech. It would have been at this junction he thought that Owen's group would have split up into two parties, Owen and his retainers going south west while the remainder would their game and head north and home. But the only markings to be seen on the surface of the snow were the fresh, shallow grooves from the abundant hares that bounded about in profusion with wide strides. Dyfed now realized that he was alone in the forest, not a particularly daunting thought he mused; he turned and brushed the wet sticky snow off the mare's back and gently whispered encouraging sounds to her. She answered by stamping one of her hind legs and swishing her tail in appreciation to Dyfed's caressing words. Except for the softy splashing of the two creeks, the snow had brought quietness upon the land. Dyfed stooped to drink a mouthful of the cold water then having crossed one of the streams, he led the old mare into the forest in a southerly direction.

Later as the evening drew quickly upon them Dyfed halted for the night. When he awoke early the following morning the snow had stopped falling and Trum motioned for him to get a move on by flinging her head around towards her rump. Although the morning sky was still a black fuzzy mass, Dyfed noticed a twinkle or two that had begun to shine down from the heavens through the broken cloud. Later the sky over the eastern horizon turned blue like a robin's egg and the dark scattering clouds lightened to a rosy hue that were rimmed with a rich tinge that reminded Dyfed of autumn leaves. Sunlight struck first at the upper reaches of the White Mountain and moved slowly down its slopes towards the dark forest now covered in a blanket of snow. Then all of a sudden the sun peeped over the horizon and its light burst across the white land in sharp blinding rays. Dyfed welcomed its warmth, for he had shivered with cold for most of the long, dreamless night with Puppy tucked into his coat to keep each other warm.

Radiance climbed into the high heavens and created a beautiful new day. With that great mountain shining brightly halfway up to the clear blue sky, Dyfed was able to navigate more accurately; so crossing the tracks of hares (which hopped madly all around him) he continued in a south west direction while Trum and Puppy trailed behind. The sun which shone down and sparkled in the snow also reflected off the shiny waters of the little brooks where the smooth, white crystals curved down to the water's burnished edge; and the rocks that emerged midstream lay hidden beneath their tall, white hats of snow. At length the sun raised quite high and the air warmed. Soon the snow began to melt and fall from the trees and the white hats on the tops of rocks began to shrink and slide over to one side and be worn like hats worn by cocky young men, or a drunk later trying to find his way home.

At length Dyfed came out of the forest and before him lay a meadow where a flock of geese had settled. He stopped and quietly strung his bow and reached for an arrow in his quiver. Suddenly a great cackling went up and a multitude of wings began to beat the air as a falcon swooped down among the geese. There was an explosion of feathers close to the ground and Dyfed ran forward shouting in an effort to frighten the hawk away. The bird of prey was startled by his approach and quickly left the ground and flew up among the rising geese in an erratic fashion. Suddenly it made a sharp, sudden dip and struck another bird in graceful flight. Immediately the stricken creature tumbled earthward and landed in the snow on the far side of the meadow. There was a great din of honking while the flock disappeared from sight over the low tree tops, and as Dyfed looked up he saw the falcon alight upon the upper most branch of a tall, sentinel-like elm situated on the far side of the meadow. Here he kept close vigil on Dyfed's movements.

Noticing that the goose at his feet was still alive Dyfed quickly rung its neck then ploughed a path through the even snow to the second bird that had fallen close to the meadow's edge. Puppy followed closely in his tracks. This bird was dead, killed outright by the hit, and as he picked up the still warm carcass Dyfed noticed three drops of bright red blood soaking into the dazzling white snow. He gazed down at the red spots for a moment, and then carrying the two birds by the neck he strode a few paces to the meadow's edge. With a side-sliding motion of his foot he cleared a spot free of snow and with his flint set a spark against a small pile of brown grass. Quickly he fanned the flames and refuelled it with dead twigs and some dry bark that he quickly bunched together to create a sturdy, bright yellow blaze. Above, with its head cocked, the sleek bird of prey sat upon its perch all the while keeping one or the other of his beady eyes on the two geese lying side by side in the snow. As the licks of yellow flame flared up and caught the sturdier branches and strips of bark, Dyfed tore the feathers from one of the dead birds leaving the other as it was. A plucked bird soon emerged from his quick hands all lumpy, white and naked. Then he broke open its carcass and scooped out its wormy-warm innards with his fingers and cleaned the cavity with wet snow. He roasted it on the spot and slowly ate it. With a sudden movement the falcon extended its rakish wings and circled once to gain height above the trees before delivering a screech that sent shivers through the rodent kingdom burrowing beneath the snow before it disappeared from view. Later, the youth with his puppy and the horse passed out of the meadow and started into a shallow and narrow gorge.

The afternoon sun dropped behind the dark green hills dusted with snow, and the white land now languished in a hollow light: this, the gloaming, was Dyfed's favourite time of day. Suddenly before him he saw wispy, bluish smoke rising above a few tall, dark green conifers towards which he cautiously led Trum. At length he commanded the mare to approach no further, and tied Puppy to a tree while he continued to advance; his trim and youthful form flitting among the rocks and tree trunks silently and unseen. Presently he came to a very fast flowing, fairly wide but extremely shallow stream that (with numerous ripples, foam and white water) scrambled noiselessly over and around the protruding rocks and water smoothed pebbles passed his feet. Looking up above him in the distance he saw the ramparts of a large rocky hillock that was capped with a hat of scrub trees. It was all green with moss that was also brushed with snow. Part of the monticule was comprised of an overhanging cliff, and above a bald rock face where bushes and small trees had managed to take root was a cleft from which the smoke (he had seen earlier) ushered forth in feint wisps. Though much higher than his own position, he noticed that at the bottom of the rock face and nestled in under the overhang was a tiny abode made of vertical sticks and plastered together with mud. As he stood motionless beside the rushing, silent and non-babbling brook, Dyfed exercised caution for it now occurred to him that the inhabitants of this place might be desperate folk indeed who lived here just beyond the fringe of the world of men for freedom's sake. Though on the lookout for Owen's tracks of a single horse and four or five men, he had seen none whatsoever or of anybody else, so far. But vagabonds, desperate men along with outcasts, would (surely) live together, he thought. But the little stick hut yonder that was crouched under the lee of the cliff could barely have room enough for one, surely. Then he saw an old spindly man come from around the cliff carrying a bundle of sticks for the fire he was stoking and Dyfed noticed that the man walked the steep and rocky path with great agility. With Dyfed's keen insight into the nature of the forest, his knowledge of its tricky patterns of light upon the forest floor and the way the shafts of sunbeams dance among the foliage and accentuate the shadows, this allowed him a broad sweep of movement within the parameters of invisibility in this environment. Like a chameleon, aided by the approaching darkness, Dyfed stood motionless and invisible as he watched the old man. Then as the old white haired sparsely dressed forest dweller reached the door of the hovel he suddenly but slowly turned and looked down from afar and straight into Dyfed's silvery eyes. Their eyes locked and the old man held Dyfed a moment before turning into the door and letting him go. At that moment Dyfed cheerfully shouted out his greeting and waved. For a few moments more, Dyfed continued to stand motionless in the forest gloaming by the banks of the rushing but noiseless creek. A wind descended and moved the treetops then licked at Dyfed's long hair. Above, the pale sky began to shade and darken; bulky clouds began to shed their orange and pink tinge as they raced toward the horizon.

While mulling over the image of the face that continued to fix itself in his mind's eye, Dyfed retraced his steps through the darkening forest to retrieve Puppy and Trum.

He was not frightened by what he had seen written upon the hermit's face. On the contrary, it was a friendly face, a welcoming face, and in a strange way it seemed personally familiar to the youth. As Dyfed lead Trum toward the old man's hovel he had the happy feeling that he had happened upon some kin who was of the same people as himself. This old man, he thought, was a fellow forest dweller and one with whom (unlike Owen) he would be able to converse in a princely manner. And then for a moment Dyfed's thoughts drifted back to the placid waters of the River Dhu and the lurching rollers that crashed against that shore that was most loved by Heaven.

Leaving the old mare to graze in a lush patch of grass close to the edge of the silent stream, he made his way with Puppy up to the rocky ledged hut that hung beneath the overhanging rock. It was here the hermit greeted him with a kindly smile. He then motioned Dyfed inside. Once through the door Dyfed saw that the wattle and stick abode was really a form of porch and that the main chamber of the dwelling was a dimly lit cave that had been hewed out of the rock face that expanded the natural cleft in the rock face. And this area lay concealed behind an inner curtain of woven reeds. At the far end of the dwelling and away from the door a small fire burned and provided the only heat. A draught that sucked any smoke up and out from the liveable quarters of the cave, was caused by the inner extremity portion of the original fissure of the vertical crevice that acted as a chimney. Dyfed observed that the hermit's aesthetic face regarded him carefully with intelligent, pale blue eyes and that the man's incredible countenance was accentuated all the more by tufts of white beard and receding hair that stuck out from his head. He reminded Dyfed of an elongated, giant gnome.

"I'm Prince Dyfed from the Isle of Peace,' he said in greeting, 'and I'm traveling to Hardlech for the festival with Owen MacShee, vassal of King Cadwallopir.' When the old man made no response but continued to regard him solemnly, Dyfed slowly repeated what he had said in a louder voice. When the hermit (with a quizzical look that suddenly crossed his face) still remained silent, Dyfed wondered if the man spoke a language or dialect unknown to him. So he began again, this time in the Amoran tongue, but very quickly the hermit put his palms together and speaking easily in the ancient tongue of Shamskara politely interrupted Dyfed.

"It is not necessary to repeat yourself over and over, young man, for though I am old, I am not hard of hearing. You say you are Prince Dyfed from the Isle of Peace? Of course you are.' He studied Dyfed carefully before continuing. 'You are traveling to Hardlech, you say, with Owen MacShee? I know well who he is, yet I think you are mistaken in stating that King Cadwallopir is his regent. But if my hearing fails me not perhaps my eyesight does for I see no such companion with you save an old sway back nag and this little puppy here.' The old hermit bent down and stroked the little dog that was acting rambunctious. 'But let me introduce myself. They call me Morgant Carreg, the farsighted,' he said, suddenly switching to the Hellenic tongue in order to test the lad's linguistic abilities. He smiled a crooked little smile while his discerning eyes searched Dyfed thoroughly. 'And I see you have brought our supper, by Jove. Ah me! How thoughtful of you.'

The belt around Dyfed's middle that bunched together his outer cloak had been tightened around the neck of the other goose that flapped against his thigh as he walked. Grasping it now by the legs Dyfed snapped the bird free from his belt and handed it to his host in the feet up position and returning to the Hellenic tongue replied; "My compliments to you, fellow Morgant, for your hospitality.'

They dined not on goose that night which the hermit had hung in the porch, but on a salad of asphodel, sprinkled by a handful of withered berries. A dessert of two or three sun-dried crab apples followed this meagre main course. Gluttony peered not from the throat of this spare hermit, and however accustomed Dyfed was to frugality of diet, his hunger on this evening was not to be abated. Soon, Dyfed and the old hermit were chatting away as an adoring child might converse with a doting grandfather. Morgant had no difficulty in discerning Dyfed's uniqueness from beyond this world's common dimension, and he wasted no time in questioning the lad in order to ascertain his acquired degree.

Although Dyfed had been anxious to continue on with his journey in order to arrive in Hardlech for the festivities, the old hermit was successful in detaining him awhile longer. On the first morning after his arrival Dyfed and the hermit rose early, as was the custom for each, and observed Radiance as he dawned upon the current wheel. As Pisces faded into the brilliance of the lit up sky in the east, the two men sat under the cliff wall outside the cave and moved in and out of Kundalini as others try on clothes. As they flexed and limbered themselves in the rays of the morning sun they challenged each other to riddles and thereby pried deeper into the other's mind. Below the cave, in the shade of the forest by the far bank of the stream, the snow still sparkled among the branches, but against the cliff where Dyfed and Morgant sat it had melted from the heat of the sun that warmed them now.

"Like Marsyas you are flayed, from water you are saved. Your green tops that we stave, produce what we crave, in that delicate octave. What are you?' queried Dyfed.

"I am the alder,' replied Morgant smiling broadly. 'Yet you are the spot, where the flute was forgot, that for seven wheels long, resounded in song.'

"Ha,' laughed Dyfed. 'I must be Hardlech where the head of Bran sang, and my immediate destiny to whose gates I should now be wending my way if I were not so loathe to depart such an embracing company as yours.' This time he answered in the tongue of his foremothers and fathers, the forerunner of Sanskrit, Shamskara.

Dyfed studied Morgant who now sat in a beautifully contorted yet preposterously impossible position opposite him in the bright sunlight. Like Manandan he was a tall man and very thin, whose brown weathered skin was stretched tautly over his large boned frame. He had a large forehead that towered above his bushy white brows and his limbs were very lineal. But unlike his old master, this man had a long forked beard the colour of snow. Dyfed further noticed that his large hands were comprised of rough and calloused fingers that were thick, long and artistic. He deemed the man to be very old, but noted that his blue eyes were clear and watchful like a youngster's. Those eyes now twinkled as he regarded Dyfed, even more closely.

"Ah, me oh my,' he answered slowly, also in that same ancient tongue. 'What have we here in Prince Dyfed, then? Could this really be possible?' His eyebrows shot up as he relaxed his body and reclined onto the rock. 'So, you Dyfed, would be the prince of the grove, son on Queen Violet-Eye and student of the venerable Manandan, it would seem.' Morgant stated this fact. It was not a question. 'I know both of them well,' he continued, still speaking this ancient language. 'They will be anxious to hear news of your endeavours. But what, oh what, should I tell them? pray tell! That you are traipsing around the countryside in the land of Arfon, in an unseasonal snow, following this or that king around, or one of their lackeys who's not likely to make a dent in the world?'

"You are gravely mistaken, Morgant, about Queen Violet and my master, Manandan. They are both gone, now.'

"Gone?' queried Morgant. 'Gone where?'

"They are gone from me forever,' Dyfed said, 'and I don't wish to be reminded anymore about it.'

"Heavens, boy,' answered Morgant. 'They aren't gone, as you say. They are anything but gone. They have pulled the veil across, yes. They have bowed out of this current environment, but they were only here, as of late, to introduce you. Now that has been done and now that you are trained up and grown up, and on you're own, well then, there is a life after child rearing, you know. Their life went on hold about the time you came along, I suspect, and now that your eyes are opened and you have found your wobbly legs, your still weak mind has relegated them to Hekate and destruction? Am I to believe that you have planted a marker above their graves? No, no, Dyfed. Ha. Graves aside, they will laugh when I tell them that. You are their extension here, yes, but still they are a lot more than that. They remain, Dyfed. Mark my words. You will meet again, but now and here is not the time. You still have a lot to learn, but rest assured, I will help you as time goes by. There are others, too, which will make themselves available. I am sure Manandan has told you as much. But if my nemesis who was Virus — the scourge of humanity — what could one say is (or will be) the Nemesis of Dyfed, Prince of the Grove?'

Dyfed thought about that for a moment or two before answering. An easy answer was difficult to cage but then he remembered that a one word name would do. "Zeus,' Dyfed answered at last.

"Ah, so then in the name of Azeus (that is the true spirit) who (then) is holding you back from transcending from the third to the fifth dimension?' Morgant asked, speaking inquisitively, yet already knowing the answer.

Dyfed then fell silent, not knowing what else to say on the subject. Morgant, too, dismissed the story telling for now and said it could be kept for the evening.

Dyfed quickly discovered that he had met his match in the art of being sparse, for not only did this ascetic hermit practice frugality in sustenance, neither did he have a table upon which to set his half empty bowl nor any chair on which to sit. Nor at any time did they lounge on a couch or on any other contraption of comfort other than the cold, hard stone floor. Of course comfort, Dyfed had noticed, was not exactly all the rage in Gwynedd, but in the living hemisphere of this hermit, comfort was scarcer than the proverbial hen's tooth. Even though the rock floor was uncomfortably cold and hard to sit on, Morgant had either declined or neglected to invest in simple creature comforts like cushions. What bliss then had overcome the hardy youth that first night when Morgant produced a plank of hard wood to sleep on in place of a cot, or more precisely, in place of no cot at all. It was as long as a tall man and as wide a two spread hands put together thumb to thumb. Then, as it had become apparent that Morgant owned only one such luxury Dyfed gallantly, albeit reluctantly, declined its offer. But the older man flatly refused to have his guest be put out in any way and had made it ready for the youth before taking up his position on the cold rock floor for the night.

(A Fate named Chance
and a roost called Ruck's)

'The man who has been of his own time has really been of all times.'
J.W. VON GOETHE

That first morning after they had exercised, plied riddles, and breakfasted lightly on chives, whole grains and roots, and relaxed together in the common language of their foremothers and forefathers, Morgant showed Dyfed his garden by the stream. The harvest here, he told Dyfed, when consumed in small portions would not only be able to satisfy ravenous hunger, but like Panacea herself were able to cure a host of evil inflictions such as the swelling of the joints, rotting gums, constipation, warts, arthritis, obesity, acne, stress, menopause, water retention, weight loss and haemorrhoids.' Morgant told him that with proper administration certain medicines that were extracted from these plants could even enhance the meter and rhythm of a patient's rhetoric and therefore was an important potion in which to be in possession. Although Manandan had taught Dyfed the rudiments of botany, as he and Morgant roamed the near side shore of yesterday's curiously silent rushing mountain creek, he listened with interest as the hermit explained their various uses. As they skirted the stream that kept the garden moist Dyfed cast his glance this way and that. Here, in this garden of Kirkee, as Morgant called it, he saw before him not a giant salad dish for the picking, but a pharmacy which harboured many a medicinal salve, lotion and liniment: A restorative of ready remedies from the scarlet petal poppy to the black hellebore, along with wild hyacinth, saffron, and milfoil. This was only a miniscule sample of what grew here.

   Later that afternoon, before the Radiance-Apollo had dipped too low, they climbed up above the cliff onto the bluff and looking west Dyfed saw a marvellous sight. From there toward the top of a valley, that sloped gently up toward a pass that bridged two mountain peaks, loomed a prehistoric forest. Its structure was so tall and commanding that he thought it the most majestic living creature he had ever seen. Even though its growth reached a greater height than that of the newer trees that hemmed other slopes of the valleys around, it was the enormous girth of each tree that captivated Dyfed's attention. He then noticed that a straight path led away from the hermit's cave and shot like an arrow directly through the gigantic woodland to the centre of the treeless, rock strewn pass above. From where he stood Dyfed could see that the soundless stream flowed out from this grand forest and meandered beneath them past the cave entrance. He also saw that the rock bluff from which Morgant's cave was carved was the south rampart or pylon to this valley while its northern counterpart across the stream was a spiked obelisk that protruded into the air from the uneven ground and glistened in the sun. These ramparts guarded the eastern entrance to the giant, prehistoric outgrowth that slumbered here in old age like the vestige of a glacier slowly melting in the warming shade of a hollow.

Dyfed now began to understand the presence of this strange and solitary man in this sacred place. He knew, or thought he knew, that in ancient times certain spiritually endowed tracts of land used to be attended and cultivated by the faithful followers who protected, nurtured, and watched over them as though they were children. These were the special forested areas as well as the cultural breadbaskets of the earth. Many other outlets also acknowledged this reverence of the life giving force. Such was the case with mammals that walked the earth and swam in the sea; along with many other children of the good-Earth. Ayr the shepherd, or priest, who protected the tropical lands around the northern shore of the Isle of Peace was one such individual. But Ayr was a provincial and was subservient to Manandan the high priest who as chief guardian assumed responsibility for all of the Isle of Peace and the waters around her that comprised its resort. In later days, although still before the Amoran intervention, this concept fell into disuse. Dyfed had learned that ancient civilizations, that had come after the transcendental shift unique to the Hyperboreans, such as the civilization of the Sindhu (now Indus) River Valley, the Valley Lands between the Euphrates and the Tigris rivers, and the narrow strip and broad delta watered by the Great River whose sacred god was the androgynous Happy (also Happi or Hapi), had mostly failed in their responsibility for custodianship and their duties as acting sentinels over the prosperousness of the land and its sacred life-force. Happy Land and the Land of Sindh had fared better than the eastern regions of the Fertile Crescent. And here in Keltic Albion (that part which was outside of Dyfed's anciently intact island home) it appeared that this task had been briefly resurrected by a certain sect of knowledgeable Druids known as the Lodge of the Blue Druids on account of their deep sapphire cloaks. Preferring a rustic existence and wishing to extract themselves from the rigors of society and remain alone in order to meditate and further develop their intuitive skills, these Blue Druids had taken over the responsibility of being guardians to principle *ley* tracts and sacred groves that the ancient folks that inhabited these isles had fashioned and cherished. But Dyfed had been of the opinion (until now) that the few remaining Druids or Neo-Druids (generally quasi-Druids) who practiced this work had disappeared long, long ago leaving the sacred sites abandoned.

"You'll be wanting to leave for Hardlech tomorrow,' said Morgant, interrupting the lad's thoughts. It will be a good day to finish your journey.'

"It will also be the full moon,' said Dyfed, 'allowing me easy travel after dark.

That evening, at dusk, Dyfed and Morgant climbed up the straight path to the ancient forest from where Dyfed gazed upon the grey mantle of snow that still blanketed the distant hills to the east. At the forest edge Dyfed noticed a large pit lined with charred oak wood and a thick layer of ash. While Morgant quickly lit a fire in the pit Dyfed walked under the forest canopy into the darkness where he came to paused for a time of meditation. Close by, the noiseless stream weaved its way among the thick beds of moss and over and around the thick, twisted and gnarled roots of the giant tree trunks. Dyfed breathed in the atmosphere of the ancient forest then turned and started back towards Morgant's fire. Here, this crackling engine of energy cast a net like shafts of light from a jack-o-lantern upon those giant gnarled tree trunks that lurked behind them: while in front, the natural light opened up onto the giant stone sentinels and Morgant's bivouac in the niche of the tree hatted southern rocky rampart. Unaffected by the fire's light, beyond lay a darkening forest below them that stretched away to the distant night in the east. To the west, above and beyond that enchanted forest, Dyfed noticed that golden tinged Radiance-Apollo was about to set himself down immediately onto the pass that bridged the two mountain peaks there in the distance. Then, as the two men watched, the sun slowly climbed down the other side beyond the ridge and out of sight. Then it grew very dark and the sparks from the crackling fire shot into the cool air and jumped among the stars. Dyfed was suddenly overcome by a powerful emotion, an emotion of infinite fellowship that he put down to presence of Morgant and the ever-present Apollo, and his aid (some say side-kick) Herakles. It was a wonderful thing that he had met a man who had known Violet and Manandan. Indeed, he may still know them, according to him anyway. This enveloping emotion of fellowship made Dyfed feel more at home with himself than he had since he left the Isle of Peace and on an impulse he began to loudly sing an old song as the shadows he cast danced a ferocious jig around the pit.

> "I am the breeze, laden with sea spray.
> I am the foam that breaks upon the shore.
> I am the roar of the tempest.
> I am the powerful pull of the flood tide.
> I am the graceful stallion at a gallop.
> I am the owl searching the evening dusk.
> I am the fragrance in a summer garden.
> I am the blossom of a flower fair.
> I am a sunbeam and a moon shadow.
> I am the salmon in a river pool.
> I am the jet-black raven who caws.
> I am the word of encouragement and advice.
> I am a lake hidden deep in the forest.
> Who is it that can reason with the wind?
> Who is it that speaks with the prophets?
> Who discerns the stellar movements
> And predicts the eclipse of the mother earth?
> If not I?'

Morgant, who had been standing like a sentinel himself marvelling at Dyfed's voice, suddenly called forth Baraka and commenced to dance an eerie and unearthly contortion about the fire. His old body twisted and turned with fluidity unknown even to children, for their muscles have not yet reached a point of development enabling them capable of such marvellous movement. Later, crouching down on their haunches by the fire, Morgant talked of his life while Dyfed, listening intently, kicked and poked at the embers.

It turned out that Morgant, a descendant of Llanfih, was extremely old and had cut a wide swathe across his life's plain. A long time ago and just after his initiation into the thirty-second degree of the Druid profession of priests that was presided over at that time by a Hyperborean magi named Abartos, Morgant had been called upon by the northern council to rid the world of a terrible scourge known as Virus. This scourge had been steadily increasing since the great deluge and although it had been widely spread in the warmer climates for as many as sixty degrees in the celestial time — or two zodiacal segments, during that period of which Morgant spoke — Virus was fast encroaching upon the northern latitudes. Alarmed by having to dispense with a valuable and prospective youth, the council however were under the sword to appear to be doing something about the threat, and because of that necessity Morgant had been chosen. Morgant was aware of the hopelessness of his predicament and his slim chance of success. All the same, he tackled the project with the tenacity he applied to all the challenges that faced him while remaining unaffected by the honour that the request (the council never entertained refusal) bequeathed. In truth the honour was somewhat hollow and was intended by the bestowals to be short lived. Being young and (one might think, dispensable) he was nothing more than a Billy-scapegoat, he thought. For failure meant death and the odds of success in wrestling Virus to the ground were incalculably small if even at all perceivable. After some long reflection, Morgant had quickly approached both Abartos and Dyfed's own mentor Manandan from whom he solicited advise. The former, he told the eagerly listening youth, provided him with the golden arrow which had delivered him into the Mysteries of Pythagoras while the latter, the much younger Manandan, had counselled him from his own expertise to pay close attention to his dreams, for through them, Manandan had said, the past and the future can be awakened. Then, on his part, Manandan summoned the help of the Lords of oracles — Dionysius and Apollo themselves — to aid Morgant through prophecy.

Respectively, each of these oracles of Dionysius and Apollo had been well established in the southern tail of the Rhodope mountains of Thrax (about seventy Amoran miles beyond the Aegean Sea's north shore) while the other had been established at Klaros some distance from Dionysius to the south on the Aegean coast of Anatolia near Colophon and just a few miles north of Ephesos and near the island of Samos. Adamantly and without dissent, most of the Furies who were later solicited refused to lend support to the endeavour, but one Fate by the name of Chance agreed to help and accompany Morgant in his pursuit.

"She was a plump little thing,' said Morgant. 'I called her 'Fat' Chance. Chloe, a sister Fate, also known as Marg, volunteered the service of her wheel that unravels the fortunes of life's thread. She also agreed to act as a witness to the event but declined further participation.'

It turned out, Dyfed learned, that this daughter of Night cautioned Morgant by exclaiming that even the gods could never successfully realize the enterprise that he sought. Somewhat consoled, the resigned, Morgant was then guided by fat Chance into the filth and cesspools in their search with only Raging Conflagration, reluctant to keep his distance from them, as their greatest and most horrific distraction. Eventually, through trickery and then by Chance, Morgant happened to captured Virus (of the genus ebola) and having collected and sealed it in an urn made of miraculous metal which the gods had provided, and on advice from an adept, he buried the thing deep into the ground in a far away spot called Khashm el-Qirba along the north-western fringes of Ethiopia.

Unfortunately the friendly Fate had not advised Morgant further in regards to precautions in matters of safety either regarding the transportation or the storage and proper containment of such hazardous material as Virus. And acting unaware of this peril, Morgant's advised chose of a tomb too close to the well from which Nile drank, and into whom Virus would one day slowly leach, thereby having access once again to the world. So, despite all the attempts, to which Morgant had gone, it remained, even in exile, a seasoned scourge and a threat, which no amount of courage could withstand, nor any weapon of the time overcome.

Save for the watchful movement of Dyfed's eyes, the lad remained still as he listened to Morgant relate this adventure. He concluded finally that dimmed by Time's lapse, perhaps it was only the hermit's memory that was responsible for the tale's fanciful flare.

Then in answer to Dyfed's question to him about Lord Huge's enclave within the forest of Ida, and specifically about a portion of regarding his mother (which had been told him on his last day at home), Morgant then called upon the two ever-illusive ones, Empirical Justice and Good Faith, to bare witness to his truth. Morgant saw that it was here at this summoned place within a certain space/time that the shining Vesta had reposed along with Violet who was the most beautiful of all nymph maidens on Earth. He then told this to Dyfed. The lad now swelled momentarily with a dangerous pride before involuntarily checking himself. He then quickly reined this emotion of ego in. This spot, Morgant continued to tell him, was also one of the last places in the world where one could nosh on ambrosia and swill nectar to one's heart's content. But the nymph Violet-Eye he was able to see, when not accompanying Artemis-Diana into the forests or carrying that goddess' gilded quiver upon her smooth white shoulder, would simply grace the sacred spot solely by her presence alone. She could often be seen, Morgant realized, just sitting by the shimmering rainbow, idly drying herself in the sun. And it was here that Apollo courted her, he noted. These words made Dyfed very happy.

"Do you attribute your success to any other being?' asked Dyfed.

"Hope,' replied Morgant. 'Hope and all her accompanying angels: After all it is she who defines the aspirations of the human race. But tell me now. What is your hope, Dyfed?' Morgant asked.

"To be a man in true harmony,' replied Dyfed, 'who with a true and accurate eye be the registrar, chronicler, notary, scribe, biographer, reporting journalist who records the commonality of the succession of each of the current presents within this phenomenon that I inhabit. This is to help to insure proper education for future generations to this end and to effect an implementation for change so that the hoi polloi will manage to merge into the truth of self being so as to assemble a civilization as a cocoon around them whose method and principles of rule is by law that provides equal opportunity and equality before that law where no one has special privilege. There is no other god but this,' he answered. Furthermore, this law must be their god, with no other likeness or graven image to impede them. And it must be owned and controlled by the people, this god, not by the priestly governing factors and their agents. This is the mistake that other hoi polloi civilizations have made. They have given up control over their individuality, which is their will, too easily. It is they who must drive the chariot of society and the civilization at large, and nothing less. This law, the staff of Rule, must crystalize into governing the people solely by suave equitably where no one is above the law; a law expedited to serve that civilization that is in its entirety is totally congruent to each stratum and division within society of civilization (reaching from the rich to the poor, from the genius to the imbecile. It's meant to function over a society (since strata will always exist within a civilization's society) where initiative and wherewithal will always rise to riches but where the poor will not be unduly margined on any account. This law, only a civilized society can make and maintain. It is one which (as already stated) has no reliance whatsoever on privilege, where no privilege exists whatsoever and where (again) all citizens are equal before the law and exist solely by the rule of that law. This and such a said state is called Democratic by its Hellenic name. And it rests within the pursuit of happiness and of individual freedoms of not necessarily being expected to, or having to conform to the status quo. The only alternative (assuming that the state in question is continually battling onward and upward) is democracy in progress. The remainder (which will be the majority will tell us, will only be quasi democracies or fledging democracies or oligarchies run by tyrants.'

"Of the latter, so Manandan taught me, they will provide the barrage of useless information to suffocate any civilization and will go on to adopt and worship Zeus. So, you can see, my humble task of recording the volitions and actions around and within the matrix of humanity is intrinsic to the innate nature of a free humanity where our tools of foresight and hindsight can be expedited efficiently in helping to undertake what steps are necessary for the sake of the hoi polloi and their future happiness: And to undertake the gaining of truth. For that, after all, is greater than any ideology or cult, including religion,' Dyfed said. 'My ambition is to skilfully document that which men say and what they do within the epoch of my life knowing full well that talk is cheap and actions speak louder than words. But most of all it is to guard the goddess Truth and see that she is not disposed and another set up in her stead. That is all.'

"That is all?' said Morgant, laughingly. 'So your reason d'etre, Dyfed,' he said, 'is to record the mechanisms which have factored together in order construct humanity in this coming epoch in general and to protect its guardian goddess. Is that it? This, and to compose a schematic, shall we say, a chart that at some future time would aid someone to understand the nature of the phenomenon of this creature and or be able to effect changes to the as-built of the prototype, or improve on changes already affected? Well, you have your work cut out for you; a rather ambitious goal, I should say. However, this of course, is over due and you, I have to assume, are the chosen one! Well, fancy that. Well I never!' said Morgant, again with a little laugh and becoming somewhat distracted now by another thought. 'Then the next thing is to take notice then of what your first responsibility is. Don't waste yourself in the incidentals. Don't sweat the small stuff, Dyvie me boy! Tackle the big questions and I suggest you too entertain and invite Hope to your council.'

Morgant's shiny face glowed as it caught the radiant light of the fire. 'This is your day, Dyfed. Take the initiative, find where lurks the beast Zeus and slay it in the manner that best suits you. Don't be just a foolish and juvenile coitus shooting blanks for very much longer in your life. Wake up Dyvie! Arouse yourself just a little bit more each time you advance. But what you seek you will not find here with me. No, no, Dyfed,' Morgant breathed out with a little sigh. 'You need to get where squalor of virtue and veracity reign and gain the most and where contention slacks and lacks. This is if you want to address the greatest concern to the existence of the hoi polloi. This is where you are needed. Zeus and the rule of Oligarchy are one. They are anathema to the Democratic epistles written and proscribed by the apostles of Lady Democracy who worships only Azeus.

"I am leaving you my old mare Trum and Puppy,' Dyfed said early the next morning as he ate hearty of the goose which he had brought with him. While Dyfed had slept the old Druid had risen and stuffed the animal with roots of ginger and tubers marinated in parsley sauce and had roasted it slowly over a low fire. As a breakfast side course he served up barley biscuits spread with a pâté of lamb bone marrow topped with rhubarb chutney. 'The mare hasn't many days left in her so it is better that she stay here with you and feed freely on the clover and drink the sweet water then be abandoned at Hardlech. Puppy will keep you good company, too,' he added.

"Return to the fire pit of last night,' said Morgant, 'and follow the path that leads into the ancient forest alongside the silent stream. Do not follow any paths which branch away from the water, and as you penetrate the primeval grove you will gradually climb to that pass you saw in the distance above the forest. From there you will clearly see the great White Mountain to the north and get a glimpse of Madoc Bay to the west. The trail of which I speak will lead you there and is a sacred and ancient track, one that I know you will respect. Once you come to the bay follow the shoreline south and you will see a large rock island rising out of the tidal sands that is called Rucks' Roost by the locals and close by you will see a river that empties into the bay. Ahead, you will see a rocky promontory composed of dark stone, which is Hardlech. Good speed, Dyfed.'

The two embraced, and seeing the tears in the old man's eyes, Dyfed enquired as to what would become of the old man when he became enfeebled? To this Morgant replied:

"You have not heard me, Dyfed. But you will learn. Perhaps — if it is easier to comprehend — I will just say this. One day I'll be away to Tartessus whose people will show me great respect: But not yet. You have not seen the last of me, Dyvie. Good-by Dyfed. Fare well until we meet again as we shall, and wake up, for god's sake.'

At the edge of the forest Dyfed turned and looked back. Though the sun was still below the eastern horizon it had now grown quite light and Dyfed could make out the two figures of horse and man below him with Puppy who he tied up so he wouldn't follow Dyfed. Trum, who had nudged him gently and watched him depart, had gone back to grazing, but Dyfed could clearly see Morgant standing on top of the bald rampart across from his hermitage, still watching him. Dyfed stood a moment and felt the hermit's presence slowly dissolving from his own. Suddenly he felt sad. He waved once then turning strode into the forest.

Although it was still dark in the forest Dyfed hurried on his way guided by the path that cut its way through the gigantic wooden columns that towered up towards the heavens. Soon the sun shot bright shafts of light through the forest as Dawn gave way to a brilliant day; and looking up into the sunlight streaming past, Dyfed saw that the oaks were turning green as the leaves were beginning to open.

Soon, as he gained height, the trees began to thin out and become stunted before shrinking into shrubs, and under the sunshine he brushed passed mosses and lichens and jumped from rock to rock before stopping at the pass to rest. Before him in the distance the sun glistening off an ocean that looked like a pool of quicksilver. Behind and off to the north was the big White Mountain and directly behind him he could just see the ramparts where Morgant dwelled and felt him watching still.

(Arrival at the outskirts of the empire #1)

'Do ut des.' (I give this to you if you give that to me)
LATIN PROVERB

The caravan Dyfed rode in from the port to the actual city-fort of Legion comprised of one medium and two large wagons, accompanied by a handful of light and heavy chariots that soon left them behind. As soon as they had passed by the sea-barns and out through the fortified main gates of the harbour-yard and set out across a marshy expanse toward the town of Legion, John of Munster took up his informative dialogue that had become a running commentary for Dyfed's benefit. The young man had recently become his companion during his passage from Hardlech to the port of Legion. Having been awakened earlier that morning before the sun was up, Dyfed watched their vessel pull close to the small harbour of Witerna coming up on their port side. He could just make out a tender that was been pulled out by a single oarsman accompanied by a small companion to meet their vessel. Then he heard the loud splash of the dropping anchor. A few of sailors soon gathered along the port side of the vessel and lowered a boarding rope ladder down in order to fetch the boy from the tender. This new arrival aboard ship, a well dressed adolescent, told Dyfed upon setting foot upon deck that he was John of Munster.

From this point they tacked east toward the rising sun, all the time following well within sight of the shoreline that glided by the port side of the vessel. As the day soon lightened into a fine, sunny morning, cries from the flocks of nesting birds carried out across the watery space. Apparently, this John of Munster had been in Witerna to celebrate the coming of the goddess of spring. He had, however (he told Dyfed) been born in the kingdom of Munster in the Emerald Isle and was returning to the City of Legion where he lived and attended school. Meanwhile, they, along with three other accompanying vessels, continued their journey east along the Seaway until it began to narrow and close together. There, the ships pulled up — each still in sight of one another — while the sailors buckled down to their business of steering toward the southern bank of the widening and more shallow inlet.

As they approached their intended port, Dyfed pumped Owen for information of what was afoot. Owen was somewhat evasive, saying only that some of the chiefs along with their advisors had met on Mona Major while Dyfed had been delirious and bedridden aboard ship. On Mona, he told Dyfed, they had discussed the situation of Amoran rule whose spreading influence into the traditional lands of the western Brythonic and Goidelic peoples was causing concern. There was much ado about Governor Gaius S. Paulinius' invasion of the West Country in his effort to conquer Mona Minor and the Gangani people. This was a new development, the one hinted to Dyfed by Smitty who, according to Owen, was a certain King Karatakos, Dyfed now recalled. But no sooner was Paulinius preparing to engage when news was received of Queen Boodikka's timely revolt which required of him to quit his campaign fold up his tents and return to the east to deal with Boodikka. The other thing Dyfed learned was that King Ryan from the Emerald Isle had been the host of the convocation on Mona Major (the old Isle of Peace) where he was now the regent and proprietor. Dyfed remembered him being a minor chieftain from Hybernia who had roused up certain elements of the riff-raff, undomesticated help that dwelled in the outskirts of the resort on the Isle of Peace. It had been from there that Queen Violet-Eye had banned this Ryan for breaking its peace. Presumably, with the masters' recent absence, he and colleagues had quickly returned. Owen mentioned another attendee at the convocation named Bade. Dyfed remembered him as an occasional welcomed visitor to Manandan's palace. From what Owen was now telling him it became apparent to him that this man's present duty on Mona was now that of governor. In every likelihood, Bade would be the brains behind any plenipotentiary powers King Ryan could boast of, he thought,

The situation at hand was such that Dyfed had hardly been aware of anything since shortly after he left Morgant. This was due to illness. As he now remembered, time had passed swiftly as he walked deep in thought among the scrub oak and ash trees on the path to Hardlech. He passed Llwyd Ffrwd where men were digging slate out of the mountainside and splitting them into slabs. Then keeping Maen Tyriawg to his right Dyfed remembered picking his way along an oak ridge that led him down into the flat meadows along the Dwyryd River. Here the season was advanced due to the sweet sea breezes of spring, and the burgeoning, green buds among the thickly wooded slopes were already opening. Suspended momentarily above him some gulls shrieked then glided away on a damp, salty wind that blew onto his face and rippled the tall coarse grass that brushed against his chest.

Suddenly there was a quick movement to one side and before he could react Dyfed felt himself being struck down by a terrific blow to the head. He lay stunned for a moment on the cold wet ground where the smells of the damp grass mingled with that of his blood. His skull felt numb as he lay on his side over his bow. Rough hands then quickly hauled him to his feet and he encountered two ugly and tough individuals who were scrutinizing him closely. They smelled revolting and were such an appalling affront to all of Dyfed's acute senses that his first impulse was to recoil from them and vomit. However, quietly composing himself, he addressed them in his usual eloquent fashion.

Because they were potentially dangerous, Dyfed handled them carefully. He disarmed them by showing no aggression and impressed them at the same time by demonstrating his superior conscious level and his willingness to share fellowship with lowly louts incapable of any expression of commiseration. He then skilfully conducted a non-condescending though somewhat one-sided conversation with the two churls. He told them that Owen MacShee who was resting in Hardlech where they were guests of the absent King Cadwallopir at his provincial home there accompanied him, but being young, he had decided today to hike the countryside. Dyfed told the churls that he, Owen, and the king were leaving Hardlech together by sailing vessel. Dyfed then said to them that he thought they may have seen the vessels at anchor and that he needed their assistance in directing him to the harbour as he had become lost. Of course, there would be a reward in it for them. The churls glanced at each other in a way that Dyfed took to be alarm.

"Don't let the derwydd jinx my god,' one of then exclaimed after a long thoughtful pause.

"You don't have to worry. I am not your god but you, apparently, are my jinx,' Dyfed said. He then put his palm to the side of his sore head and laughed in a successful effort to neutralize the two men. Once he felt that the men had been comfortably appeased and made comfortable in his presence, he stooped down and picked up his bow. The sea wind blew Dyfed's long hair across his face as he stood looking along the shore. It was starting to get dark and a smudge of smoke was visible on the Rucks' Roost. The beach that he was on were tidal sands and although the island was some distance from the shore one could walk there with ease while the tide was out but would need a boat when the tide was in. Dyfed communicated his intention of making for the island to the other two and started out. His boots squelched at each step as they moved away from the shore in a beeline for the island. Looking in its direction he could see the sea washing along the north side of the rocky mound as the tide began to move swiftly across the sands with each little wave. Here the waves did not break and roll back but spilled continually forward and flowed increasingly over more and more sand on its headlong dash to shore. The three men began to hurry and their feet made a flat splashing sound as they ran through the little pools and canals of seawater that lay upon the flat sands. Soon they were crossing shallow sheets of water that covered large surfaces of the sand which soon became one moving flood, and Dyfed could hear the hiss of the tide as new water began building up and lapping over top of the old. The water here was only ankle deep but as they ran it splashed up into each other's faces.

Soon it got deeper and it became necessary for them to lift their feet higher and even to angle the calves of their legs outward as they ran. They were being slowed down now by the deep water that swirled about their waists. And as the cold sea rushed in, they were heaved gently all around as they waded with their arms raised. The yellow sun dropped quite low and as they moved into the shadow of the island Dyfed shivered. Just when the water got so deep that he felt that he would have to swim the remaining distance, he stumbled onto a bank of sand that almost pitched him face forward into the water. These sands were the submerged feet of the island and from here he waded easily to shore. Once he was at the top of the island hill a more self-possessed young man approached him. He identified himself as Trachmyr and began questioning Dyfed. Dyfed's responses quickly impressed Trachmyr. This young red haired man told Dyfed that he had been to the festival in Hardlech but had had preparations to attend to and had returned to the island that very evening. He also confirmed that there was indeed a fleet of sailing vessels in the harbour and told Dyfed that he himself would be leaving this youth colony in the morning and returning to Hardlech for he was destined for a training camp close to the city of Legion run by an Amoran general named Flavius Cornelius. It was a pre-try out camp for the Amoran army who were looking for strong young men they could fashion into soldiers of their making, he told him. Dyfed surmised that that was the prime purpose for the presence there of a renegade general dangerously stationed in the north west where he was extremely isolated from any other Amoran legion in Albion. He was wrong in his estimation.

After the sun had set on the horizon over Hybernia (the Emerald Isle) and the Evening Star shone down to put the day to sleep, the young company ate some fish and barley boiled in rancid mutton grease. Meanwhile, Dyfed watched as some people (who it was now too dark to see) left the island and poled themselves to the far shore in some light sea-craft decorated with swinging lanterns which recorded their presence in the dark. As they bobbed and flickered out across the black water, Dyfed sat close to the fire on Ruck's Roost on the hill shivering in his wet clothes and surveyed the dark wilderness around him. Shortly thereafter, a deadly illness fell upon him. Lying down in the crude little abode which the leader of Ruck's Roost, Trachmyr, offered him, Dyfed's stomach soon began to heave. Keeping his eyes shut he strained his neck away from his body as far as he could and retched continuously for most of the night. Stretching out his sore and aching body upon the ground he had tired himself out by swallowing in rapid succession in a continually failed attempt to keep Bile, which Nausea beckoned within, down. Then shivering from cold and weakness he drifted back and forth between jarring and disturbing themes within sleep while listening aloud to the soothing sound of the waves lapping gently against the island's shore.

 Dyfed awoke suddenly with somebody rolling him gently with their foot. He opened his eyes and saw Trachmyr silhouetted by the bright golden rays of the sun that were just then peeping over the hills of Ardudwy and streaming through the entrance way of the stone hut. Dyfed rose to his feet, his head was frozen in hurt that tore at his skull and his neck mostly caused from yesterday's blow, but his throat was sore as well and his limbs and muscles ached from a shivering fever that was in full bloom and seemed to be seeping into his bones. Nausea was overwhelming.

 Dyfed was able to remember little of anything after that until he was aboard the vessel with Owen and Ceredwyn and well out to sea; and they were patchy. As it happened Trachmyr had managed to manhandle Dyfed back down the path that wound its way along the side of the rock island. During the night the water had receded back as far as the island's inland shore again and was still receding. All around lay the tidal sands of the barren sea bottom that were dotted here and there with glassy pools of water that rippled slightly in the morning breeze and shone silver in the sharp early light of the sun. Upon leaving the path at the beach, with Trachmyr half carrying half dragging Dyfed, they first traipsed through some shallow water that ringed the island even when the tide was fully out and headed in a south-easterly direction. The strong young man who was destined to join the Amoran army in the city of Legion helped Dyfed across the hard rippled fine sand and waded through the shallow sheets of landlocked seawater until he came to a fast flowing river that — in its passage to the receding sea — had cut a deep channel into the sandy muck of the tidal sands. The swift river was invisible until one was upon it where Trachmyr's progress was delayed for only a few moments while he floated Dyfed across this fresh water stream. Then, as the current sent him back toward the sea (with Trachmyr pushing against him — guiding him to the far shore of the river as hard as he could) they had to retrace their path away from the wet sands again back toward land. The swim had managed to successfully diminish much of the smell of sweat and vomit of which Dyfed had reeked. Ahead, the black bluff of Hardlech loomed closer. Dyfed's only memory at this point was that due to the retching combined together with the fever had brought upon him an extreme drought. Now his mouth and throat were of such a stale condition that it reminded him of the foul ground beneath his mother's aviary. With fresh water at hand, however, Trachmyr scooped some up in the cup of his hands to help slake Dyfed's thirst.

 Soon Trachmyr had delivered Dyfed to a makeshift festival venue just outside of town with its brightly coloured tents made of finely woven cloth and a multitude of pennants fluttering in the wind. Sometime later Trachmyr discovered Owen MacShee in

Hardlech down in Madoc Bay. He was in a state quite fit to be tied. Scouts that Owen had sent back into the northern hills to search for Dyfed had returned empty handed. It was an anxiously moment for Owen believing he had lost Dyfed and he was greatly relieved to hear the news which Trachmyr bore. Immediately he sent a chariot and a servant back with Trachmyr to retrieve the sick lad from the suburb and quite soon he had him comfortably installed in the building that he and Ceredwyn were temporarily occupying with King Cadwallopir. Upon seeing the state that Dyfed was in, Owen summoned a physician and ordered Dyfed to be stripped and washed. Then still in a state of delirium the next day, Dyfed was loaded unconscious aboard one of the vessels at anchor. As the tide turned and followed the moon in the early hours of the following morning, Dyfed still lay unconscious as he sailed out of Madoc Bay bound for the Gadhelic shore.

(Journey to the City of Legion... and Master John of Munster)

'Will you come into my parlour, said the spider to the fly'
MARY HOWITT

The two vessels sailed west from Hardlech and passed through the gap between Bardsey Island and the mainland then headed north. The first leg of the journey was slow going for there was hardly any wind and the ships were not equipped with proper rowers. But the following morning as they were drifting into the main channel between the Keltic and Hybernian seas, the wind picked up and they were swept up thereby making good time to Holy Island. This isle lay just off the southwest coast of Mona Minor (now Anglesey) and the two vessels made their way to her northern shore and docked at a small fishing village called Gybi, a port town dominated by fortifications intended to keep any would-be authority, including a coven of Druids, at bay.

Owen was looking in on Dyfed who lay on his night mat still severely under the weather from his ordeal. As for the latter, so far it had been a rough ride. Carried on board ship at Hardlech in an unconscious state by Owen's retinue, Dyfed would remember virtually nothing of his first important sea voyage. His memory of it became a jumbled contraption of confusion and flights of fantasy. Plagued by strange reoccurring spin-offs (that were derived from psyche oriented archetypes within) that were reacting to his physically detrained state causing him to sail through a storm of nightmares. Occasionally, when his mind was calmed, he caught glimpses of phenomena at large passing him as though he was swinging by his feet around a maypole.

They moored briefly at Gybi alongside two others vessels (their bows pulled up onto the beach shore). These were the vessels of King Cadwallopir (derived from the antiquated Kunulopur, and rendered with poetic license into 'the Good Hound of Gwynedd — or simply Cadwallopir the Good Hound) and King Cadot, the chieftain of the Dunmonii now surrogated by Macsen Wledig. There was a fourth vessel of which Dyfed had had no recollection. This vessel, an Amoran styled galleon man-o'-war, was to accompany these three transporters from Gybi to Legion. This man-o'-war was considerably larger than the other three and had many oars and a higher mast and contained sixteen heavily armed warriors beside the captain and his commander. She remained alert and lay waiting at anchor just off shore and had been supplied by Macsen Wledig (also know as Bricus) to insure that the two Albionian kings, Good Hound from Gwyneth and Cadot from Dunmonii, would have a timely and safe arrival at the city of Legion. This fact had only succeeded in raising Owen's suspicions about Bricus. And that man, Owen knew, was aboard this armed galleon. This caused Owen to wonder again if war council proceedings by the Aryan Brythonic and Goidelic speaking peoples against the might of Amor, which Bricus himself had initiated, was truly about to arise? Or was this simply a trap planned by Bricus, a potential traitor, along with his adviser and assistant chief executor, Blazingwolf? And somewhere in this mix was King Verika, a man from Sax and a servant of Amor who was under wraps and living somewhere in Albion.

Before the morning had drawn to a close, all had been made ready. Peering through delirious eye sockets from time to time, Dyfed saw Artemis-Diana and Neptune smiling blessings of good fortune. Meanwhile, the seafarers in an agreeable mood fashioned a leash onto prowling currents that Tide manipulated if not Neptune himself, and quickly they pushed off from the Gybian shore. As they rowed out into the harbour and unfurled their sails with a loud accompaniment of shouting, the man-o'-war weighed anchor, too, idly guarding their flank if need be. Then, with their wooden beams gleaming in the bright sun and still half naked under partial canvas, the three vessels swung their bows around in the choppy blue brine and sailed north past Carmelide and into the Hybernia Sea.

Once Dyfed woke briefly from his troubled sleep to the pitching and tossing all around as the small ship ploughed before a brisk south wind. From his mat positioned midships on deck he saw the green swells rise beyond the gunwales and heard the gulls and the vigour in the voice of the sailors' songs. In his mental restlessness, the patter of the mariners feet drumming upon the deck as they went about their duties, brought forth visions of a multitude of servants carrying him in a conch shaped litter, while the snapping and rustling of the canvas in the wind overhead lent a spectre of some battle that raged around him with men defending themselves against strange gods. Clearly, he had become a wounded casualty on this account, speared through by an improvised, man-killing thunderbolt by some incubus resembling Mars. None of this was actually a soothing diversion of a rested sea cruise that was likely better needed to still his fevered mind.

Beyond, out through the opening of the tent-like structure that covered this portion of the ship, Dyfed caught shapes that moved in and out of focus. They might have been Owen bracing himself against a gunwale while he looked out at the heaving seas, while beside him, all bound up in a colourful woollen cloak, was Ceredwyn reposed and tightly gripping hold of the ship's side rail. Voices and other natural sounds were not transposed correctly for his discernment. Now, he still felt terribly weak and his limbs harboured a painful ache. Once he made an effort to move, but as he attempted to struggle to his feet the deck dropped suddenly beneath his feet and he pitched forward. Catching hold of a slack guy rope (or it having caught him), he swung freely for a moment until the deck slammed back up under his feet again. This brutal jarring that knocking him back down only managed to compound the pain which throbbed in his head and pounded in his hot, aching eye sockets.

At one point as he gazed out into the motion picture that tossed around him, the vessel slid down into a sea hollow and either the slack body of Owen or the incubus that had shot him sagged away from him as the man or creature hung tightly onto the guy supporting the deck tent wall. Dyfed, even in his illness, somehow clung tightly to the deck under his mat. A moment later the rising seas thrust the craft upward again, and as they bobbed lopsidedly on a wave crest, Dyfed caught a glimpse of the man-o'-war escort as it toppled into a watery trough not far off their starboard bow. He knew at once that it was a sea battle in which he found himself, and the gods — having commandeered Amoran war-ships — were suddenly at hand and moving in for the kill. Everywhere the air was filled with spray and as the gulls rode alongside the sails like seafaring scouts they shrieked back and forth loudly to one another to enable them to be heard above the wind. Although not heard, Dyfed cried out in his mind and warned the sailors to listen to the gulls whose cry was a warning or an anxious exchange about what lay ahead. But he could tell, even in his state, that they would not listen.

Giddy, he fell back into a shallow breathed swoon, his mind resting among the background turbulence that his senses recorded. He could feel the turbulent waters all around him, and he remembered how much he loved the sea, and never tired of her smells, her sounds, and the relaxing motion of her body. No matter if he was on top of her, reposed and relaxed as he was now, or if he was inside her, struggling and anxious, she managed to sooth him, he imagined, only like a lover, or a mother, could. When he had played by her on the beach in front of his mother's palace, or as an awakening adolescent lying alert in bed during the still hours of the night, Dyfed had often felt his mistress's heaving breath and heard her gentle sighs. Whenever he was close to her and lying alone, Dyfed imagined her beckoning to him and caressing him the way a woman with a gentle love will do who is not yet fully enflamed and lustful.

He forced his eyes open for only a moment. There, with her beautiful green eyes, Ceredwyn was looking out to sea and he saw her rich, red locks streaming out off to one side of her head. Trying to focus on Ceredwyn Dyfed found that the strange reality beyond his eyes conjured a moving, topsy-turvy vision where there was a shamble set upon the deck beyond which was a broken wall of rainbow fog into which the vessel's bow was about to plough. As the vessel dipped into another sea hollow and careened downwards there was an explosion of spray and sea water spilled in before the craft righted itself again and then shot upwards on to the top of a swelling sea mound. As they rose and came level with the seas mean surface again, the wind then began tearing again both at Ceredwyn and Owen's hair with a raging howl. Even the gentler sound of Ceredwyn's distant voice was been torn from her lips by the wind. Just then as this wind was blowing the white sea-caps off the waves and flinging them into the air, a colourful fog lingered strangely and un-naturally in stillness just a stone's throw off the port bow. Then suddenly both the ship and its crew quietly plunged headlong into a cold, eerie vapour that engulfed them and where they seemed to fade into a dimensional oblivion.

Even before the doors of Dawn had been thrown back to allow its rosy light to play among the starry lights of night, restless Tide had wandered in and out, and as the anchor still lay wet upon the deck the little vessel began to move slowly as it put back out to sea for the third time this voyage. The crew worked quietly as its passengers were preparing to sleep. The still fat crescent of a waning moon darted ahead among the clumps of cloud, and as the shore fell astern, the dark outline of the Gadhelic shore arose before the prow.

"How are you feeling, Dyvie m' boy," Owen said who having seen him stir came over to have a closer look. He reached his hand out in the pale light of early morning and touched the lad's brow while he steadied himself with the other. He slid his big hand down the side of the young man's face and with his thumb he pulled away the tight, youthful flesh from under Dyfed's eye.

'You're much better, Dyvie,' he said. 'I think you'll pull through in time,' he said with a smile, while giving the youth a friendly slap to his pale cheek.

"Where are we, Owen?' Dyfed asked, his rasping voice eking out of him slowly and struggling.

"We passed the promontory of Carmelide a few days ago,' Owen answered, 'and we pulled away from the Isle of Mona Major in the dark hours just after sunset. With the sea running the way it is and the wind blowing at our backs, I'd say that we'll be ashore and in the City of Legion at the close of today'

Dyfed, having wakened now was feeling somewhat recovered from his attack of illness. After a time, the vessel dropped anchor in the moonlit sea by a promontory beneath a white stone house in the land of Witerna. That was when Dyfed saw a boat being rowed out to them carrying the youngster Jack who came aboard in the early morning light.

Then later, standing forward of the mast, Dyfed, still feeling woozy and groggy, gazed in anticipation as the fortified port of the city of Legion loomed closer and rose up out of the estuary. The two other accompanying ships were now crowding in quite close, at this point, and the galleon man-o'-war being commanded by Bricus was not so dangerous looking now as it had been when under the guidance of the gods. There were a dozen other small vessels tied up around the newly fashioned wooden quays of this port while a multitude of others lay fully beached close by. Dyfed had quickly noticed three very large Amoran liburnians that were dragging anchor just off shore. Rumours had been bandied about, he recalled, that the IXth legion Hispana under the command of a certain General Flavius Cornelius had been commissioned with cartographical duties of mapping Prydain's (Albion's) western coast. Clearly this fictitious tale was a cover for the IXth legion to be here unofficially. These liburnians were almost twice as large as Bricus' galleon escort vessel. The port itself was entirely walled with a wooden balustrade and fully fortified with soldiers. It also housed the imperial Amoran port authority.

Then with a cry of 'ship ores' and a loud splash, their accompanying escort galleon dropped anchor in shallow water as the other two vessels pulled slowly away from it toward the beach where they were to rest. The galleon tugged at its anchor and swung around in the tide, appearing now to be nothing more than a merchant craft, bringing in copper ingots or animal hides for trade. This was Dyfed's first hand observation of the local Keltic people's careful and measured actions as displayed before the watchful eyes of Amoran might (albeit limited) which was everywhere — watching and saying little, other than to bark out a harsh order when a local erred against some unknown Amoran bylaw. Only a fool, it appeared, would act rashly or cause a confrontation with a show of arms before the authority of Amor. Indeed, the escort's captain, upon registering, did in fact produce a manifest that listed a ton of wheat. It was here also that Dyfed caught sight for the first time of Bricus, the owner of many of the port's vessels. Dyfed quickly cast his glance around looking for one who was the latter's loyal companion, the incomparable Blazingwolf, the Armorican Druid. But he saw none that his imagination allowed him to accept. He noted, too, that the aforementioned Bricus tended toward an Amoran trend of presentation in his outward expression. He was treated by utmost respect by the Amoran staff at the port of authority.

Disembarkation was a big to-do and Dyfed watched in amazement as heavily armed officials controlled the landing process. Dyfed himself had little to account for. The money belt and pouch, which was filled with Amoran gold pieces, he wore around his waist. The accompanying satchel of brightly woven canvas, that had accompanied him from the Isle of Peace to Gwyneth, and had travelled to Hardlech with Owen in his supply wagon, was equipped with straps, allowing him to sling it over his shoulders and be carried on his back to free his arms and hands. It was all the wealth that he had. His horn tipped bow and quiver were dispensable for it was with his mind and his talent for the pen and numbers that qualified him to provide valuable service to a potential employer. 'Literacy and numeracy is my trade,' he now claimed. Cached, also, in his large satchel, Dyfed carried a short sword and some bolts of finely woven cloth that Queen Violet had given him before he had left the isle. They were a remarkable garment material that had come from a land beyond this world and from a time that lay outside the chronology of the day. Aside from his torc that he referred to as his parachute that was securely hidden beneath his shirt, the only other item of value Dyfed had was a single piece of ornamental jewellery that was a parting gift from his mother. It was a beautiful Amethyst ring cut in the shape of a Platonic solid that he wore on his left forefinger. This unique item had imbedded in it a broad lined design of shining quicksilver fashioned in the shape of a pentangle. Contrasting amazingly with the flashing glint of violet that the stone threw out, the quicksilver shimmered in its light.

For the second time he didn't bother with the dry route via the quay close alongside, and from which wide planks had been extended to the gunwales of the boat, Dyfed had clambered over the side of the vessel and up to his knees in cold water. There, he heaved his trunk up and onto his back with the shoulder strap and waded ashore. Although the ship's bow was beached, it had run ashore amidst a bevy of fully beached boats that barred his way, and it was with some difficulty that he struggled past them and up to the paved square in front of the Port of Authority where he set his load down again and looked around. It was then he noticed a large plague on the side of the wooden building with the letters S. P. Q. A., which although not having come across the acronym before, he reasoned stood for: Senatus Populas Que Amoranus, which was pushing it since he knew Amor had no legal authority here. This was entirely General Cornelius' show.

There were many around who were promoting themselves as procurers of this or that but Dyfed disarmed them with a quick remark that he spoke in eloquent Amoran and kept his own council. Just then he spotted one of the servants from his own ship that was standing watch over a pile of a minor official's belongings that lay in a heap in the open square. Dyfed had not seen any of the others while keeping a sharp eye out for Ceredwyn who he hadn't yet spotted and must have remained below deck. He carefully regarded the short middle-aged man who alone about his business had adopted a false air of importance. He had dirty blond hair, a stocky statue and a small piggish nose set above a full mouth that was pulled back and finalized in down turned lips. Distain for those who overlooked his petty importance and perhaps contempt for his own ineffectual and in-nominate sense was the only character etched on his silly, officious face. He strutted around like a little mastiff, leering in what he thought was a menacing and protective way toward people who showed no interest in him or the belongings he guarded. Casting his glances around him with unfounded confidence, the man — who Dyfed had heard addressed as Octha — beheld young Dyfed watching him. So he called out to him with effected authority.

"Ha, illustrious young friend of master Owen,' he said as Dyfed approached, 'you are wise for you travel lightly, I see. You should oversee this load of baggage while I go and arrange for our transference into the city.'

"I could easily do that,' replied Dyfed, nonchalantly, looking as though he felt compelled to suddenly set aside his own plans and comply, then of a sudden made a calculated and abrupt attitude turn as he closed in and looked down on the little man. 'But their responsibility are yours, not mine,' he said with a non-committing smile. 'However, while I secure transportation arrangements to the city of Legion for myself, I suppose I could see to the availability of wagons for the prince as well. Why don't you run and inform the others. Your chores, however, are a matter between you and your master. They are nothing to do with me'

"Ah, yes,' Octha replied in a condescending manner as Dyfed began to wander away. 'You are a man of the world, anyone can see that,' he said to Dyfed's back, secretly envying him but hating him now even more. He had hoped that his sarcastic remark would be overheard.

Dyfed pushed his way through the hustle and bustle towards the teamster depot, while he continued to search for the whereabouts of Ceredwyn. He had almost asked Octha about her whereabouts, but was now congratulating himself for having bit his lip in time thereby denying the man any thought that he gave him any credibility.

The fort of Legion had formerly been named after the Keltic god Lugus, or Lugh, as Jack — who, having caught up with him — was now telling him in his Brythonic tongue as he continued delivering a running commentary for Dyfed's benefit. This was the only language in which Jack had so far spoken, although it became apparent in time that he conversed in the Amoran tongue quite well. King Cadwallopir, King Cadot, Owen and some petty official or another also talked incessantly in that same language among themselves as they bounced forward along the main track in the front wagon. This forward cart, and one of three needed for their group, contained the aforementioned along with Dyfed and Jack, and the finally found Ceredwyn, to whom Dyfed's eyes constantly returned to. But she, on her part, remained curiously silent and glum much of the journey. The others, the servants of both King Cadwallopir and King Cadot's households, headed by their man-servants in chief — including Octha, chief of security for Cadot's chattels — rode in the two rear and larger wagons, along with the luggage. King Maelgwyn, who had sailed from Cyngreawdr Fynudd, presumably had already arrived. There was no sign of Bricus on the road into Legion.

There was a network of soldier camps in the outlying area around the north and western reaches of the city and as they proceeded Dyfed gaped ahead in excitement. As they progressed along the road's dead straight course which ran between the seaport and the town, their wagons rolled passed some of these encampments and Dyfed gawked every which way.

This was the turf of the newly arrived IXth legion Hispana now under the command of legate Flavius Cornelius. He was camped here, and among them (under the latter's watchful eye) were the Equites, the light infantry, the heavy infantry and the hastati class warrior. Dyfed suddenly remembered Trachmyr. That stalwart leader of the youth warrior training camp on Ruck's Roost had indicated to Dyfed that he had taken advantage of a local decree pronounced by the new Governor (Dux) imperium, Gaius Paulinius (stationed in Camulod but whose administration was centred in Nova Troia) to reintroduce a fighting class of front liners known as the 'hastati resurrection into the army here. To fill this improvised army rank encouragement was made to local young men like Trachmyr to join the IXth Legion Hispana while it was in Gwynedd. Unknown to Dyfed (due to his illness), following his departure from Hardlech Trachmyr and the IX Legion had also sailed out of Hardlech for Legion Caer. They had arrived here just before Dyfed and Owen on account of the latter's stop at Mona Major. In fact, it was quite an unknown fact here (or anywhere else) that governor Paulinius actually had no idea of the current whereabouts now of his and the empire's IXth Legion at this time. Paulinius was only aware that it had been employed, along with the XXth Legion (called Valeria Victrix) at Caer Victrix. This relatively new Amoran outpost on the river Dee was about sixty Amoran miles north east of Hardlech and little over one hundred Amoran miles south of Caer Legion as the crow flies. Paulinius had expected that after the IXth Hispana's successful campaign against Druids in and around Mona Minor in the far west to avenge the murdered magistrate there and then used to put the run on the Gangani in northern Gwynedd, that it would avail him in his defence back in Albion's east against that wretched Ikeni queen Boodikka who was on the war path at this time. But neither Cornelius nor the IXth Hispana turned up, and Queen Boodikka dealt a debilitating blow to Camulod and the Amoran occupied villages around, killing many Amorans. Just where the hell and the devil are Cornelius and the IX Legion, anyway? Paulinius wondered to himself in alarm. However, he was careful not to make his ignorance in this or even of Cornelius truancy publically known, especially to Emperor Claudius Augustus, at least not just yet. He would get even later, he plotted. It would turn out that he had not been fully aware that Flavius Cornelius had ventured this far north on his own recognizance and was now playing politics for his own sake by attempting to convert Luge and its port into an established local centre that was smack dab in the middle of the Carvetii tribe territory. In order to place himself in control here, Cornelius had quickly struck a deal with the local regent, a certain Queen Carmen (Carmanda) who had joined up with other local Kelts such as King Ryan and Bade of Mona Major.

After they had rattled passed these encampments, this inter-port-to-urban thoroughfare continued across the marshlands that lay all around. From the wagon Dyfed looked out over the bleak expanse toward the outline of the town-fort in the distance. Soon they would arrive at the ferry terminal where the wagons would roll out on to a wagon ferry, one wagon and team at a time. Beyond the river lay the town of Legion. And Jack told Dyfed that the Amorans were there at Queen Carmen's pleasure. It turned out, Dyfed soon learned, that the Amorans had an important Albion ally in Queen Carmen who was of the Carvetii tribe and the Carvetii were fiercely independent of the Keltic Brigantes. Dyfed said nothing in way of scepticism regarding Jack's remark and then learned moments later that Queen Carmen was the surrogate mother-protector of John of Munster himself. The younger man's open face and slightly toothy smile looked so proud as he looked up at Dyfed during the telling. Dyfed was learning all this from his bright and talkative companion who was surprisingly well informed, he thought: The situation very puzzling all around. According to Jack the purpose given for the Amoran bivouac here in Cael Legion was to protect the locals (along with the empire) from the people like the Ordovices and Decangli tribes. Yet Caer Legion was set just then to host convocation of western alliances that included Kings Cadwallopir and Maelgwyn who were kings of the Ordovices and Decangli respectably. So, this explanation didn't make sense either. However, when he suggested to John of Munster that maybe Amoran interest in this northern town of Legion was to be their northwestern defence against local expansion, such as by the Brigantes, he may have been right.

Since the village of Luge (changed to the Amoran Lugus and now being proffered as Legion, or Caer Legion) it was in the process of being rebuilt by the Kelts with Amoran army engineers' help, it was not surprising that it was a rustic station, indeed. It was also the spot where a few roads and a few rivers converged. Flanked by two of the rivers that meandered here across the marshes toward the estuary, Caer (fort-town) Legion (so, Jack continued to attest) would eventually be comprised of seventy-four Amoran acres. Sturdy, high wooden walls whose construction, it was rumoured, were planned were to eventually enclose the fort entirely. Later, he supposed, they would be built of high stone upon which one could walk and from where a person could look out to a great distance beyond the town like men in the preverbal watch-towers that graced great cities abroad. Caer Legion also had planned seven gates, two to the north, two to the east, and two to the south and one that opened toward the west. Two of those gates already existed, one to the north and the other to the west across the Caldew River. It was this west gate that opened into the city from the seaport road that was used for this route. And once the wagons were ferried across the river it was through this gate that Dyfed entered the city.

As they drew closer to the great wooden fortress, the late afternoon sun shone softly upon its reddish rampart which was in the process of encircling the hubbub of activity where the dust rose up and caught the light. A staggered row of new roof slate even glinted somewhere from the sun's failing rays and the dull absorbing hues of some of the building's rising wooden walls shone with a rosy glow. The clean-shaven uniformed officials stood at the gate and watched the three wagons pass. They were not the sons of Romulus and Remus, the founders of Amor, Dyfed noted. They were barbarians, all cleaned and dressed up and taking on the edict of the civilized Amoran ways.

As they pulled up in front of a large, well kept building, the wagon stopped and Jack climbed down. Turning around to around to address the boy Dyfed was immediately taken by an imposing image that loomed behind John of Munster.

"And to what terminal is this that you have found fit to take your leave, master Jack?' asked Dyfed. 'How shall I manage to get by without you by my side?'

"This is Queen Carmen's home here in the city of Legion,' replied the young student. 'It is also my home and maybe you too would like to take up residence here? I might say; you have been very closed mouthed during our journey together. Of course it is none of my business. You are staying on looking for employment, you managed somehow to indicate that much.'

Dyfed smiled at Jack's sarcasm.

"So,' the lad continued, 'we could billet here together if you like and become friends. Oh! I would so much like that. You seem to be such a nice fellow, though not much of a talker, and you know there is really no one of my age and status here to whom I'm particularly close.'

Amid the grins and smirks that Owen and his company shared, Dyfed's face and aura transformed as he concentrated now on this young fellow.

He said, "I'm awfully sorry to have neglected your company on this fine day's journey. In fact I've had a jolly time and am most impressed by your company. We will surely become friends; you and I, Jack, and I may just take you up on your offer to reside here, later, and with the host's permission if not invitation. As for whom I am; well Master John of Munster — I am a bard with additional literacy and numeracy skills, traveling for the first time in these parts. So I have been concentrating and composing. I'm afraid that I've left you out a bit, haven't I? However, I've been much taken by your interesting commentaries. Yes Jack, I am most certainly staying on, at least for a while for I am to be married shortly and…and since I have no best man to stand beside me I hereby ask you, Jack, to fulfil that role.'

At this point Dyfed shot a glance at Owen. At that very moment music was heard and a chorus of song rose from within the building. Jack smiled upon seeing the effect of the singing on Dyfed's face and said.

"Congratulation Dyfed. I would be honoured to be your best man. Now, please call me Muns. You can call me Jack on formal occasions or if you are cross. And this behind me is Queen Carmen's home. It is a place for singing my friend, and a place for bards. It is also a seat of great knowledge and teaching and a supplement for the order and legality of Amor. Surely it is to be here, at this place and no other that you have now come from so far away to find? But now tell me Dyfed, who are you really and from where do you come?'

"I am Dyfed who brings the Light, Prince of the Grove,' he replied. 'You see I was born at dawn in a sacred place on an ancient and holy isle which is no more, although Heaven once favoured it above all isles.'

"Dyfed who Brings the Light, Prince of the Grove who was born at the dawn,' repeated Jack watching Dyfed smile.

"I am Dyfed Lucifer,' Dyfed then said in the tongue of Amor. Since meeting the blacksmith Dyfed had decided to add Lucifer — the bearer of light — that Smitty had dubbed him to his name. At that precise moment the great door that was behind Jack opened up and a smallish, middle aged woman stepped out and stood looking aghast at all the commotion that was going on outside her house.

"Jack,' she called out and the young man swung around.

"Mama Carmen,' he said smiling, and then walking up to her he hugged the lady who was the same height as himself. He then turned and standing beside her and pointing to Dyfed said. 'This is Dyfed Lucifer, Mama. He is well educated and a noble person and I have asked that he reside with us. But I fear he wants an invitation from you. I had further hoped that I might have the opportunity to study under him as well. Dyfed Lucifer, Prince of the grove who was born at the Dawn light, this is Queen Carmanda.'

The woman, wearing a fine embroidered full-length shift, squinted at Dyfed.

"You may come and stay for now,' she said. She seemed about to say something else but remained silent. 'Come then,' she said, beckoning Dyfed.

(Caer Legion)

'It is no measure of health to be well adjusted to a profoundly sick society.'
J. KRISHNAMURTI

It was still night but the sky had begun to lighten and the low thatched roofs stuck out in dark relief. Dyfed was up before dawn, rising from the night mat where beside him was Jack still becalmed with sleep and breathing smoothly. Nobody else stirred in the great house that was the residence of Queen Carmen of the Carvetii. There were other youngsters here as well who had made up the choir that he had heard singing upon his arrival. They were orphans that the queen had taken in. While Dyfed conducted his morning exercises he could hear loud snoring in the lower apartments where the servants slept. He crept downstairs where an old dog lifted his head and wagged his tail. The tail made a thumping noise against the floor in the dark and this caught the attention of a puppy that had been lying on the outside doorstep fast asleep. Immediately aroused, the pup whined and scratched at he door. Quietly feeling his way, Dyfed stepped over the old animal and out through the door. Not far away the vague outline of the wooden embattlements (still under construction) of the fort jutted up into the sky and Dyfed walked in that direction through the narrow deserted streets.

To Dyfed, peering down from the shaky parapet atop the high wall which he had climbed up upon, the small fortified town at his feet appeared to be like a black, silent pool while against the horizon to the east the sky began to take on a rosy complexion. With the slow spin of Mother Good Earth, Dawn awakened and the still and murky pool below crept slowly toward that brilliant star that brought the day. A waning crescent moon above was struck against the pale southeastern sky, and as a breeze stirred Dyfed felt the meagre warmth of the Radiance Helios Apollo's bright gaze. He could smell the earth and the blossoms in the fresh morning air, but the breeze also carried an acrid tang that came from the marshlands and blew inland across the sluggish river into the town. And the town, too, smelled of human activity and stale effluence. As tiny streams of light coloured smoke began to rise slowly from the chimneys, the dark pool below began to lighten and he picked out shapes of buildings and streets as he breathed in the slightly caustic air. Cocks began to crow and dogs stretched: candle lights began to glow and their (barely discernable) diluted pale yellow beams hugged their internal environment, barely spilling out over the small window sills to the outside. Dyfed could hear the movements of stabled horses and smelled their odour as they urinated and stamped their feet. Below, the city had now lightened considerably as the slow morning sounds crept into existence and the small town of Legion awoke to a new day. The land, too, began to brighten and Dyfed could make out the barracks and other support encampments that were sprawled out toward the west. He could now almost make out the port with its multitude of freshly built sea barns that lined the shore.

Dyfed climbed down the steep ladders from his perch above the stables then quickly found his way back toward Queen Carmen's huge square three story home built of timbers and mud that positioned itself like a giant old growth tree stump in the centre of town. Mentally he summed up his prospects. Within the next while he needed to get an interview with the recruiting division. There he could quickly undergo an evaluation and have a review of his qualifications for employment at the chief civil servant's office at the partially built basilica. This was necessary, he had already learned, in order to get himself before their administrative board whose job it would be to specifically evaluate his proficiencies and level of attainment. He could easily manage their fee and if he was successful with the evaluation process — a prospect about which Dyfed felt quite confident — his application would be filed and it would be a matter of a short time before he could begin some kind of work within the Amoran administration. What work would be offered, he didn't know, but guessed it would be associated with the ordnance and legal offices of the basilica, probably drafting letters of communication, at first, then graduating to accounts. Maybe in time he could wangle a position in the local Treasury department, he thought, or become affiliated with the local legate's quartermaster general and be an assistant in overseeing the military's provisional and financial well being. This was his most probable stepping stone for advancement to the City of Amor, he reasoned at the time. He could arrive at the latter, he supposed, unemployed; but it made better sense to arrive there while being placed into an official position. As he walked back to the residence he passed a large inn called Juno's Peacock and through its open door, the fading lamp light (that had been momentarily thrown out into the street by the opening of its door) kept creeping back inside, withdrawing quickly away from the waxing sunlight. And just then, seemingly to counter balance the receding lamplight, out came the unmistakable sound of Owen MacShee's raspy voice, his tongue twisting around the consonants of his language.

When Dyfed walked in Owen was negotiating with the proprietor for room and board for Ceredwyn and himself for the next seven days, and the two men were seated opposite each other at a small table. Behind them a newly lit fire blazed in a large hearth, its flame tips drawn upward by the chimney's exhaust draught that helped suck out the stale smell of yesterday as well and whatever was underway in preparation for this morning's breaking of the fast. Somewhere upstairs a baby cried and Dyfed (shivering) heard the restless scratching of rats. Owen, whose attention was on the proprietor, glanced up as Dyfed walked in.

"Top of the morning to you, Dyvie,' he said, carelessly cutting in on the other's rehearsed haggling. 'Up bright and early as usual, are we? Your recent illness and the journey didn't set you back any then, I see.'

The proprietor turned around in his chair and looked directly at Dyfed without any change of emotion upon his bland face. After a moment he turned back to Owen and asked, "And who is this then,' indicating Dyfed with a back jerk of his thumb. 'Another one? Well I never!' he said, briefly looking back at Dyfed. 'He's a corker. Truly the most ravenous creature that ever walked,' he quipped, turning once again and giving Dyfed another quick glance. 'I dare say that the insatiable appetite I plainly see lurking within — despite his lean form — could…I reckon, put away half a calf at least by midday without even trying.'

"If yester-evening's victuals,' interjected Owen, butting in again, 'was the finest sampling which this establishment has to bestow upon its patrons, there shouldn't be a scrap of a calf to be found hereabouts and I would settle for the cooked marrow between the cracked bones of a dog. But not for the price you want for room and board. Substantial and wholesome groceries were quite conspicuous by their absence at supper last. That is my humble opinion. I hope, though, to be proved wrong in the near future.'

"I have immediate need of a tailor to attend to me here,' interrupted Dyfed before the proprietor could counter. Ignoring the rhetoric that was winding up between the two men. 'He can,' Dyfed continued, 'bill this inn for his time and his skill that's needed to measure and cut the cloth which I will supply. The cut of my garb shall be presentable to wear at any court in the land for first it will be for my wedding garment. But, mind that you don't throw care to the wind and summon some apprentice to outfit me at a king's ransom. Or you sir,' he said in what Owen thought was an uncharacteristically menacing tone, 'shall buy up the expensive and wasted cloth and pay off the novice yourself. So, summon an adept for my satisfaction. I would suggest you consider one of the tailors that are servicing the Amoran sector. Furthermore,' Dyfed continued without allowing any time for the distracted proprietor to respond, 'I will be dining here off and on with my two companions, Owen and his pretty daughter, who is shortly to be my bride. And don't think for one moment that you will be out of expense for board and for payment to the tailor on my account,' he added. Dyfed leaned forward and then threw down a heavy gold coin onto the little table. This is my share, you have yet to get Owen's.'

The two men were much taken back by Dyfed's sudden exclamation as well as by the sound of the heavy coin as it struck the table's hard surface.

"By Heaven's light from the loins of Lugus it's an Amoran aureus gold piece,' exclaimed the proprietor as he scratched at the table with his claw-like hands to quickly snatch it up, holding it then close to his face to examine it.

"Weigh that coin,' shouted the red faced Owen to the pale and bland looking innkeeper as he suddenly jumped to his feet. Then turning to Dyfed he said, 'There will be some change, Dyvie my boy, I'll see to it.'

I bet you will, Dyfed thought. Although unlike the squalid cenedl that Owen lorded over back along the fringes of Arfon and Gwyneth, the fabric of natural social order here was so much different still. Among his own people, Dyfed reminisced, it was taught that it was love and compassion that were expedient to properly maintain and understand the needs and desires of society's constituents, not gold. Gold had nothing to do with real value and is craved only by the shallow and the vain; two telltale traits that expose the ubiquity of greed and the presence of avarice, at least so Violet used to tell him. But he wasn't fool enough to believe that avarice and greed differed in poor villages and towns less that at the centre of Amor. Certainly, those gentle folk's otherworldly haven around Queen Violet-Eye's household was assured, and no gold was needed for that. Gold was cheap payment, his mother had said in answer to Dyfed's queries about it: Merely a false compliment that the Amorans, like other established machines of social disorder, dole out to irreplaceable servants. But his generosity today was a lot more than was normally prised out from the hands of the miserly Amorans as they trespassed into this proprietor's hovel to eat and sleep — never mind other lands in their attempt to increase their slave count and to broaden their market through plunder.

"It is cheap payment enough,' replied Dyfed to Owen's remark. 'I don't want change, but what I do want are two suits of expertly tailored clothes and a pair of fine leather boots, as well. So, you must consult a cobbler, besides. And mark you this.' He shifted his brilliant silver eyes back to the innkeeper, 'Jump to and get on with it quickly, for I am in haste to have them at hand. When I will return here for supper this evening I will bring the bolts of cloth, and if tailors were present then it would afford an opportune time to take the needed measurements.'

Owen stared at the tall, handsome and beardless youth he had come to know. He gazed upon Dyfed's shiny hair which (so different from the men of Amor) was wavy down to the nap of his neck from where it hung in curls past his shoulders and tumbled down his back. But there was something else about him that set him apart from others even of high birth. Dyfed had an electric awareness about him, and Owen noticed his commanding presence especially now as the youth cast his gaze around with those curiously bright, silvery eyes of his. Owen then had cause to reflect on his own youthful form, once lithe and graceful like the one before him. But he recollected that he had seen in this young man a tough resilience, a mettle that he had seen in few other young men, including himself or of men like Cadot and Maelgwyn. It was no wonder, he thought, that Dyfed had caught his daughter's eye. For a second he wondered if the gods had not shown favour to him in sending him such a talented and likable young man. For sure, Dyfed was expecting to be betrothed to his daughter, as he himself had originally promised. However (as intimated earlier), he had come to believe that he could pick up a bigger prize in King Ryan for a son in law. Indeed, he had already made the bargain with him on the Isle of Mona Minor two days before. The bargain had been struck and even Ceredwyn hadn't been informed about it as yet. These affairs were beyond those of young women, he reasoned, even if she was his daughter. With the child (that he believed she may now be carrying) — or not with child — a month won't make a difference. He had made up his mind, but he knew that her marriage to Ryan would have to go forward as soon as possible. And as far as Dyvie here is concerned, he thought…well, for the moment he doesn't have to know anything.

Owen looked at Dyfed as the young man explained to him that he would be residing at Queen Carmanda's residence where he intended to tutor young Jack, for a time. He didn't say anything about his intension of making an application for acceptance into the Amoran civil service or with the military's quartermaster general. Even though Owen would have been expecting him to seek some prospect or another in order for him to be able to support his daughter Ceredwyn and raise a family. In the meantime, he thought, he would play his cards close to his chest. Then speaking out loud he repeated his intention to dine at the Juno's Peacock with him and darling Ceredwyn for a few more days to come, but pressed Owen to set the date and make arrangements for their wedding.

Then, having settled the business at hand, Dyfed ordered breakfast. All around him now the inn had slowly been filling up with folks whose voices began to drown each other out. Owen soon left the table and tramped upstairs to somewhere or another. Dyfed, who assumed he was about to fetch Ceredwyn, had listened to the sound of his feet thumping up and along the wooden planks that then faded off where they muffled into the distance. Now Dyfed was alone again. Dirty and smelly patrons (free men) employed to labour for the Empire, crushed in all around him before starting work. They talked in loud, hoarse and emotional tones. And they kept on coming in to the abode from the street. Dyfed imagined that there must be a stinking, motley mob of mostly men who — loosely fanning out into the narrow street in front of the doorway — who filtered and filed in shuffling, short movement toward the entrance. They were naturally knotted and spliced together at the threshold of the narrow door like a true Gordian knot (Phrygian Gordium) where they were now squeezed in tightly together (finally) to a single man. Then, once through the door they expanded instantly like released matter under pressure whereupon they were forced into every crevasse and nick and cranny of the darkish and grimy room. In turn, this condition then set to by squeezing and crushing him in their hot and stinky human swamp. Already a dozen beady secret eyes below low brows, matted with greasy hair, cast furtive looks in his direction and bombarded his privacy. Then, with his fast still unbroken (and as Ceredwyn had not make an appearance for her breakfast) he quickly rose in an effort to leave the inn. Hurt and slightly disturbed, he twisted himself adeptly through the human high-pressure knot and moved quickly out into the street. Here he felt a sensation that he likened to having just broken the surface of the sea or from a spring pool after a deep dive within. Here he paused for a moment as he gulped in long breaths of air. It was broad daylight outside now, so he set out to explore the city.

The Queen's residence was an eerily quiet, cavernous hall ringed by a second floor wide balcony that was divided into rooms and then topped by the third floor apartments. When Dyfed returned there, Jack was waiting. Dyfed concluded a brief encounter concerning his eating and sleeping arrangements with the queen's chief of staff.

Jack was a robust youth with alert blue eyes, sandy hair and a mildly ruddy complexion. Although not as tall as Dyfed, or nearly as muscular, his build was heavier than Dyfed's, though not his over all weight. He had a square jaw with a wide mouth whose ends curled downward giving his face a casual air and he had about his presence a sense of humour. He was a good-natured young man and like Dyfed was quick to smile, and when he did so the tips of his upper front teeth became more than faintly visible beneath his top lip. He had been born in the west region of Connacht, he told Dyfed, but his family seat was at Munster and hence his name, John Galway of Munster, or Muns, he said, if Dyfed preferred. His close friends had always called him that he told him. Dyfed, as always the polite and likable fellow that he was soon found an agreeable friend in the boy who was quick and strong willed. Dyfed's immediate interest at this point was Caer Legion's current activity so he Muns asked many questions about it.

"What about the subterranean Lodge of Mithra?' Dyfed asked as Jack showed him around the stables of the house regiment's cavalry belonging to the queen and the ironsmith with its adjoining foundry. 'Does Legion have a temple dedicated to the rites of Mithra?' Looking surprised Jack replied that the Amoran soldiers had just begun cleaning out a cellar that was used once as a cold cellar. They were planning on turning it into a lodge but he knew little about that. A low cliff upon which the effigy of Lugus had been placed sheltered the smallish building in question. Lugus, of course, was comparable with Nodens, and equated with Mercury. It was near the newly constructed Amoran foundry and the chariot and coach manufacturing shop that had recently opened for business.

"Are you interested in joining the Lodge of Mithra?' Jack asked.

Dyfed was interested in all things that dealt with how functions were peopled and imported, and how important people functioned, most especially within the client and ruling states that he now inhabited. But he was committed about remaining un-affiliated with any cult, and that even extended to the cult of Orpheus, and of course Apollo, so closely entwined as he was with them. After all, they were simply a state of symbolic being in one shape or another that were usually quite quickly provided with an agenda in an environment where all agendas were not equal.

Later as he and Jack sat silently looking out at the distant hills wagons came into view, from time to time, and crossed both their field of vision, the noise of their progression coming to them as a hollow rumbling from a distance. Jack told him that most of the Amoran work force was done by slaves. But collecting slaves here was dangerous for the legate Cornelius the Un-Felix[12].

Due to his precarious position Cornelius needed tranquillity, which was one of the things he was working towards. Taking slaves from Carmanda's people, the Carvetii, would not enable legate Cornelius for very long, so he needed to go further afield to collect slaves. This was in the direction of the Brigantes that peopled the east. In this respect, Jack told him, Queen Carmen walked on egg shells to manage diplomacy between the Carvetii and the Brigantes, for any disruption that that might ensue which would certainly effect Cornelius and her own position. Dyfed's next question suddenly interrupted Jack's thoughts.

"What do you know of King Ryan?'

"Hardly anything,' Jack replied. 'His name comes up from time to time for discussion in the Queen's residence, but that is all I can tell you. He is now the king of Mona Major, but he has no input or meaningful intercourse with the Carvetii or the Brigantes, or any human affairs hereabouts. And he plays no part in the organization of the empire, as far as I know. That responsibility is taken up by military authority of the IXth legion which is precariously stationed here at the pleasure of Queen Carmen alone.'

"You mean the legate Cornelius' presence here is not due to orders from the empire's centre at Amor, or at least from Governor Paulinius?'

"No. The empire does not extend this far. Queen Carmen doesn't think Paulinius even knows the whereabouts exactly of the IXth legion, other than it out marauding somewhere or another. But it does provides some security for Queen Carmen under the circumstances, and she knows too that the legions of Amor are fickle.'

"And Macsen Wledig also known as Bricus? Does he show his face around here?'

"Never heard of him,' said Jack.

Later, before the star of evening shone and set the day to sleep, Dyfed gathered an arm full of garment material from his trunk and made his way back to the hopefully less congested Juno's Peacock for supper and the fitting appointment with his tailor.

---

12   This suffix was to distinguish him from his infamous brother Lucius Cornelius-*Felix* (*that means Cornelius the Lucky*)

(Naked, he railed on while swilling grog that sometimes made it to his mouth but usually it didn't)

"I can't go on. I'll go on."
SAMUEL BECKETT

"Well it's the damnedest thing that's ever happened! To me, anyway,' Dyfed exclaimed with a slurred speech. Dyfed was slumped somewhat over the end of the big table in the great hall of Queen Carmanda's residence. Earlier that morning, a messenger had delivered a letter addressed to him to the residence. It had informed him that Ceredwyn had being formally engaged to King Ryan of Mona Major with approval by Owen MacShee (claimant) and that the aforementioned King Ryan and Ceredwyn, daughter of Owen MacShee, would presently be joined together in marriage. 'Any falsely perceived privileges,' it went on to say, 'and rumoured promises that were thought to now need honouring; or rights or ownership on, over, or about the person of Ceredwyn, daughter of Owen MacShee, or any undeserved and unjust intercourse thought to have been conducted between Owen MacShee or his daughter Ceredwyn and Dyfed Lucifer (respondent) son of Violet-eye and receiver of this letter; are hereby considered and declared to be closed by the claimant; and any and all other business between Owen MacShee and his chattels, and Dyfed, son of Queen Violet are hereby considered and declared to be null and void. Furthermore, that any suit to be considered and filed against Owen MacShee or his daughter Ceredwyn by Dyfed himself, or representing Dyfed Lucifer towards a commensuration expedient only to the latter, will be considered by the claimant as an act of confrontation and aggression toward which grave steps will be taken either via a law suit or by direct intervening action by the claimant and his son-in-law King Ryan (co claimant). Finally, Ceredwyn, daughter of Owen, hereby releases Dyfed, son of Queen Violet, from the promise of love and any responsibility concerning sundry misunderstandings that he, Dyfed, son of Queen Violet, may have harboured or continue to hold and entertain.' The signatory name that appeared at the top left of the document, Dyfed noted, was Owen's shaky chicken scratch.

"Well, the devil can take him and Ryan,' exclaimed Dyfed in a thickening voice. From the moment he had received the letter, he had sat down in the great hall in Queen Carmen's palace and began to ladle, from her collection of intoxicating spirits, huge quantities of it into his body through his mouth. This was done for medicinal purposes, mind you, for it helped contain him and his wounded and tortured young soul (possibly ego). It was his soul that needed attending to, so he kept telling himself, let his body and its pain be damned! That course of convalescence (upon which he had embarked) had begun early that morning. Now the servants were bustling around the table catering lunch to Queen Carmen, Muns (her surrogate son) and some visiting members and associates of the queen's family. These guests were passing through Legion on their way back to the Gad-Hel and had dropped in for lunch and a visit. Their arrival, indeed, even their departure had gone unperceived by Dyfed, who (now well into his cups) had stripped down into nakedness to expire the heat generated by the spirits.

If the truth were only known, the visiting group of relations had made a point of dropping in on Queen Carmen mostly on account of hearing of this curious and notable man's presence here. However, they were not overly impressed, as it happened, although the pretty Princess Marg had been the exception. Used to commanding presence among young men of the hoi polloi who slobbered after her, she was faintly amused at this attractive young man who, all because of a lost love, was totally oblivious to her presence while completely naked as he railed on in a general slur, swilling grog that sometimes made it to his mouth and often it did not and having made the floor instead even splashed onto those sitting close by. In his less than unctuous and increasingly slurring state they thought it best to excuse him from any amiable conversation, as he ladled and flailed away, spiralling into an auto-tirade that sometimes drowned out the other's genteel conversation. The general contention was that it put quite a damper on their luncheon. Obviously, they would be forgoing any after-luncheon merriment with Dyfed that had been planned. As these Keltic togethers and nosh-ups often ended in a jolly good old knees-up and other forms of amusement, those plans intended by Carmen for such an occasion came to nought.

This situation concerning Dyfed continued throughout the day and long after the guests left earlier than planned that afternoon. When the day had expired and it was past sun down and the household gathered here once again for a late supper, finding him unmoved from the spot they began to implement his removal. With his head resting on his ear upon the table, the 'dear Dyfed' letter — that was responsible for his condition — floating in a puddle of spilled grog and his empty supper plate set gingerly out of reach of his flaying arms, the queen demanded that the staff remove him and take him up to bed. Dyfed maintained a low profile the entire next day and did not show his face until supper the following evening.

(Flav the Finger, Res Gestae, and Carmen the queen's guest rest)

> 'Force is always on the side of the governed…governors have nothing to support them but opinion…tis therefore, on opinion only that government is founded; and this maxim extends to the most despotic… military governments…and most free and most popular.'
>
> **DAVID HUME** *(FROM CHOMSKY'S PAPER 'FORCE AND OPINION' AS PUBLISHED BY Z MAGAZINE)*

"Feeling better, are we?' inquired Queen Carmanda with just a trace of sarcasm. Dyfed's letter now lay folded neatly as could be beside his empty supper plate as half starved he sat down to eat for the first time in almost two days. Perhaps it was meant as a subtle reminder to him of the events of the day passed, he thought. This caused a feeling not just a little embarrassment.

"Well, it's the damnedest thing that's ever happened,' he said in a low tone, running his hand through his hair. 'At least to me it is.'

"Well, you said that yesterday morning,' replied Queen Carmanda, 'and where did that get you? So, don't knock yourself out over Ryan,' said the queen, 'he's not worth it. I take it the girl's a beauty, though.' The queen's eyebrows rose as she looked up from her plate and contemplated Dyfed. 'However, if you plan on taking Ryan on you may be well advised to consider soliciting some help.'

"And from whom would you suggest I solicit that help?' Dyfed inquired, as he began to fill his plate.

"Why me, of course,' answered the queen. 'If I never see Ryan again, it will be too soon,' she uttered. 'He wasn't a problem before I invited those gorgeous Amoran sailors of General Cornelius' aboard his two triremes to drop anchor and stay awhile. I said stay awhile, not over stay awhile. And to think he blundered in here in a fog. Now it has become a tricky business to be rid of them.' As she said this she eyed Dyfed slyly.

"Would that be because Cornelius, and any lackeys like Ryan he pulls over to his side among a divided war-like people hereabouts, which is all beefed up by his IXth Legion, isn't the ideal situation anymore for you?' ventured Dyfed, picking slowly at his food and not looking up at first.

"Why, yes!' said the queen. 'How astute of you.' Although the queen could speak the Amoran tongue capably enough, the language common to her household was the tongue of Brythonic Albionians. Although Dyfed, who in all aspects (except his hairdo) resembled an Amoran merchant or bureaucrat in his dress and general presentation (especially since his new duds and boots had been acquired), he spoke the native language here (as well as Amoran) with ease and with o accent at all. Many of the queen's learned contemporaries thought she had been shrewd to side with the might of Amor, for it was a wise course opposed to the alternative. As she contemplated Dyfed who had come from the devil only knows where, she reflected (yesterday's childish antic aside) favourably upon this stalwart young man. Queen Carmen's renewed impression was that he was as sharp as they come. For she saw in Dyfed something of herself and consequently an interesting ally. If only he had some material resources. However, there was another quality that puzzled, indeed, worried her. Despite his calculations to arrive where he wanted, there appeared to be an unusual tendency toward the inability to compromise. She couldn't see him allying with just any ideological factor or trend just to be on the winning side unless it was compatible and able to be swooped up with his own current trend: that, plus the strength of will which supported and furthered his concept of what specifically was needed to win the day, and none other. And furthermore, she noted, confusingly, his focus wasn't about him, nothing was. His persona was such that he wasn't the prize, the winner to be, despite the fact that in most matters (except the matter over Ceredwyn, but the verdict was still out on that) he probably would be the winner, anyway. She, on the other hand, was more about everything being about her and that attitude had paid off in spades. Dyfed's strategy intrigued her. So, if not about himself, he was all about some acquired ideal he had taken a fancy to, or something or another he wanted to embody. And that was something that was very hard to read in people who weren't morons.

This is what the queen had gathered so far in her long, late night discussions with him. If Dyfed was going to mentor Jack Galway of Munster, she needed to know what made him tick. So, what's he all about? she thought. What's the deal here? Who is he really and what are his motives? This is why she had invited Princess Marg, a wizard in her own right, over the day before to help her assess him. But that had been an effort of futility, if there ever was one. At least Marg had had a good laugh, and perhaps at her expense.

And coupled with this unsavoury behaviour, the lad seemed not to give a royal damn about a lot of important things that were unfolding around him in the reality at large. Is he somehow secretly attached to King Cadwallopir, she thought, or even Macsen Wledig in the land of the Dunmonii? There was something odd about that Macsen Wledig, she thought, and his brother, or was it his cousin, over in Armorica. She knew they were foreigners, Amoran aliens first transplanted into Hispania (during the Hispanic/Amoran wars back in the days when Amor was a Republic). Originally they were folks of the House of Theodosios (Theodossius or God-given) who had genealogical connections with a scion that was derived from another intruder into Hispania. This was a certain House of Masensen (also Massena or Massinissa). Masensen had once been the Berber king of the Massylii. He was Masesen the Great. Could Dyfed be an agent of this ilk? she wondered. Or maybe he was affiliated with the western Demetae, or the Ordovice and the Decangli (and their cousins the Gangani)? These were (after all), the very leaders with whom Dyfed had recently rolled in to her kingdom, and on the same tide. This conference here in Legion wasn't just a meet of the Prydain folk on how to deal with a powerful empire whose strength was their aptitude for the science of authority. Perhaps its meant to be a congress, she wondered, where each of the attendees will be trying to work out where their place will be, relative to the others. They will be looking for what the Amorans call socii or foederati (allies), every one of them. Where did Dyfed fit, she wondered again.

This conference, and seemingly without legal Amoran approval (at that), may be the course for one like Cornelius to scale the cursus honorum (the bureaucratic ladder, sometimes called the roll [role] or run of honour): but at whose expense? What chance did the tribes have against Amor? And Amor (or at least Cornelius) would be clever to ally first with others early, certainly the likes of Bricus Macsen Wledig. Carmanda didn't want any of it to be at hers or her client tribes' expense. She did know with whom she was allied with but not whether Dyfed was worth being allied to.

This conference, called and headed up by the (somewhat illegal) sub legate Cornelius, and those attending such as herself, King Ryan of Mona Major, the aforementioned Macsen Wledig and consul of Dunmonii, Cadwolliper, Cadot and Maelgryn (all just south west of her), was the one and only chance they'd probably have to a secure future, she reckoned. King Cadwallopir, she knew, had his eye on the land of the Brigantes and the Carvetii. It was for that reason why she had allied with the Brigantes and the wild men of Albany (now called Caledonia) back long before legate Cornelius and his IXth Legion Hispana showed up. But since Cornelius and the superb Amoran military machine that accompanied him did show up, Carmen wondered what chance the rest of them that opposed Amoran rule actually had. She suspected that despite, or maybe because, the troupe of Cadot, Cadwallipor and Maelgryn had parleyed on Mona Major just prior to arriving in Legion, that already (aside from Bricus of Dunmonii, as he preferred to be called now) there may already be division between them. Owen having immediately cancelled Ceredwyn's marriage to Dyfed, assuming that Ryan isn't playing Owen (whose position compared to Owen makes it highly possible), may possibly indicate that King Ryan has Owen and maybe Cadwallipir who was Owen's king as well. And what about Ryan? He could be bought by Cornelius or Bricus, especially armed as they were. So, with Cornelius and King Ryan of Mona Major with Dyfed not thrown in, these would be enemies of considerable strength and of paramount danger to Dyfed. And since he'd hardly be a third wheel in the arrangement, she thought (if he was even valued at all), the long and short of it might put him into a fifth column against Cornelius and Ryan to make Owen suffer for his trespasses. And if he is fifth column, whose side was he on before and where does he stand now? As it stood he would probably stand against Cornelius, Bricus and Ryan, she thought. The queen had noticed Dyfed's torc, an unusual ornament to wear for the later generation of her own people, never mind for sympathizers of the Amoran way. Other than the wizards, for whom it was not a common adornment, nobody wore them anymore. Anyway, it was now rumoured that it was all show by rote. And as far as the technology of the ancients was concerned, it had long, long been lost. So now she seemed certain he wasn't part of Amor and maybe not the Prydains to the west, either. She would have to test him. And anyway, if any of this were the case, he wouldn't be stewing over having lost his girl. No sir! He would know just how to get her back, and promptly so. He would be up and out of his bath to become the Knight of the Bath, and she — the lucky girl Ceredwyn — back again and in the bath with him as fast as possible. If only, she thought.

She consciously had to remind herself that in her pact with Cornelius she was relying on him to protect her interests from the Dunmonii under Bricus along with Cadwallipor and Cadot. That may have changed now. But Bricus and now Ryan as well may not succumb to such a thing. They won't like her siding with Dyfed, either, assuming they cared more than a pinch of koon-kaka. Having brought the convocation congress to mind she noted Ryan was among the organizers, not Dyfed, and the king was weaselling in wherever he could and under any banner that he thought could stay the course. Dyfed wasn't a contender here, a no-show, if he was even expected which was unlikely. So, in the end, how would he actually fare against Ryan? she thought. With Ryan it didn't have to be something he believed in. He only believed in himself, anyway.

But in respect to this rash young man who was sitting at her table, the contrast between the two she thought was like night and day. What was he thinking? she wondered. You can't just decide what you want or think as you please unless you are a king or, better still, an emperor. Who do you think you are? You can't affiliate with the Amoran establishment, as she knew he was attempting to do, or have truck or association with specific individuals in the system and expect to successfully impinge your notions upon the stamp or disposition of a people, never mind on the character of the empire. They won't be changing for you. But she was beginning to see that with a man like Dyfed there couldn't be any other alternative. So, once again, what's his angle? In truth, aside from Marg's advice that he was a keeper, Carmanda was still trying to figure the answer as to how she could test him. And her indecision was really why she had tolerated Dyfed at all and allowed him o hang around as long as he had. He certainly didn't have mentor material for inducing kingship qualities into Jack. Well, in truth, there was more to it than that, though. He was likable, and charming, and good-looking, never mind quite special in his own way. But he is riding full out at a gallop and without a saddle, and it looks like the horse is leading the way, is what she thought. Yet, no, that's not it, either. There was more, much more than that. She could see it in his eyes and in how easily he manoeuvred through the troubled world at large, day-by-day, albeit with the occasional boozy binge and a torrent of temper over a trifling setback like love, of all things. His deportment was regal and exquisite, she had noted that from the start, and she had no doubt that he was a genuine prince. He had also befriended Muns, and it was a genuine friendship, she noted. He was well behaved, normally, and he was at all times considerate to her and even the servants, who liked him immensely.

"I know how to get her back,' Dyfed said after awhile. 'I think I know the route to weakening Ryan's position, not so much with Owen MacShee, but with the empire.

"Well then, that should do it,' she answered sarcastically. 'So, what do you have in mind?' Here, now was an opportunity to further assess this man. This could be the test.

"The empire is being assailed on all sides, at the moment, by rebellious Albionians,' said Dyfed. 'When it comes to information and leads that quells unrest and any opposition to their authority, the Amorans are able to wrestle this beast to the ground standing on their head. The chance for unrest and opposition to rear this head is what the Amoran governor and his legates were craving for. Somehow they slept better afterwards. In fact, judging by what you told me of the Amoran presence here, Paulinius may be wondering where in thundering tarnation Cornelius was when he needed him. Gaius Paulinius who keeps himself well protected and would not be seen around here, needs victory to ingratiate himself with the emperor which in turn will further his career. That was why he had undertaken the invasion of Maelgyn and the Degangli in the west. He also has Queen Boodikka's aggression on his hands. This fight is still raging with or without her. Certainly Kunobelin in the citadel of Camulod, the grand king of Llogia and of all Albion, who was a re-appointed successor to King Karatakos, appears to be playing his cards with dexterity as he sits at the high table facing Paulinius during their pow-wows.

All the while, what with those rebellious tribesmen Kunobelin represented who had his back, he was a stalwart symbol for the Prydains of these Isles no matter what tribe you were.'

"And what about Ryan?' she asked.

"Now Ryan, theoretically — through any alleged impropriety that I may be able to bring forward — can be the key to me winning the approval of certain factors within the system here, along with the demise of this upstart's rising star. Two birds with one stone, you see. As he is now currently in the process of ingratiating himself to the imperial might, at your Majesty's expense, by the way, won't matter a wit.'

"Won't it indeed!' said Queen Carmen a little acidly, possibly not understanding his implication to the full extent. 'Are you prepared to betray me for imperial favours, then? Furthermore, since you are not up to times, the Ikeni queen we call Boodikka is now dead, don't you know! And she was not a queen, as the empire has insisted in calling her, she was the daughter of a king, that's all: that arrangement does not make her a queen. But she was a stalwart individual herself, who I loved and supported. And now with her death the empire has even more of an upper hand.'

"But you,' replied Dyfed, 'have sided with this empire yourself, and all the while Boodikka was endeavouring to secure her independence for her people, is that it?'

"Not true,' Carmen responded. 'Her father, the king, sided with the empire, as I have done, and for the same reasons, to secure liberation through embracing new and advanced ideas, not to further servitude. There is a big difference between bending and influencing than resisting and breaking. You must encompass the over all and all in good time attitude for eventually These people will be absorbed by us in the end, you'll see.' The queen looked sharp and cross, Dyfed thought. 'You, on the other hand,' she continued, 'intend to trade favours and sell off other's advantages to further your own ends, it seems.'

"I intend,' replied Dyfed rather firmly, 'to do no such thing. I intend to be rid of Ryan, collect my sweetheart — at some point — and betray or sell off nobody. I know a thing or two; a thing or two that the Amorans likely know as well. I will suggest to the Amorans that Ryan is implicated in something of a situation, which in fact he is. They will believe me, because I will be very believable. And that will be the end of it, and you will be rid of Ryan as well. So if you could find the time, your Majesty, as soon as possible that is, to promote my usefulness to the furtherance of the empire to the local legate Cornelius, I would be much obliged and you well served, said Dyfed.'

"You may know some things about the comings and goings of our people here among the western Kelts,' pronounced the queen, 'I dare say. But are you aware that at this very moment the talks are on between our people and the Amoran representatives here, I mean right here, in the town of Legion?'

"Yes,' replied Dyfed. 'And likely without the permission of Amor, as well!'

"Cornelius doesn't need Amor's permission to advance the empire, I dare say,' responded the queen.

"That surprises me to hear you say that, your Majesty,' replied Dyfed. 'I believe you to be wrong. This legate cannot represent the empire without permission from the emperor in Amor. And although he could make that application directly to that emperor, it would be unwise of him to do so and thereby circumvent (by-pass) and go over the head of Paulinius the high legate and the seat of authority here. A blatant disregard of protocol, procedure, and due process, wouldn't you say? No, Cornelius must apply directly to Paulinius for permission to enter into talks with the like of you and yours, the savage enemy. And if Paulinius knows, which I'm sure he does not, then Amor would know. But I'm willing to bet that the emperor doesn't know just because Cornelius hasn't told Paulinius about the talks anymore than he has updated the IXth Legion's current position to him. In fact, I believe that this meet of yours is solely on account of Bricus, not Cornelius. It was he who secretly organized it with Cornelius on condition of a code of concealment and silence, at least until an agreement had been reached. And I believe it was initiated on behalf of Bricus' own grand scheme and personal agenda to dominate the western Kelts and eventually make himself ruler in place of Kunobelin and subject all the chieftains, including you, to him under the protection of either Paulinius or Cornelius. He may even have Cadwallopir on his side but possibly not King Maelwyn. Cornelius too may have found those terms expedient but for a different reason: in order to expand his own influence, right into the emperor's heart. This renegade Bricus, though, is likely your biggest enemy. And he is using Ryan to help soften the ground in preparation to sowing his seeds; seeds which will affect you even long before it deals with and effects Cornelius, if ever. You see, in all likelihood, once Bricus can set Cornelius aside one way or another, Paulinius will then emerge as his archenemy. Either that, or failing that, King Kunobelin will be runner up target for Bricus. At the very most the position of consul is Bricus' ambitious goal. Although that is unlikely for it would depend on the emperor. Why would it not be so? If Bricus allies the western Kelts under his command, manages to trick Cornelius into a compromise in which the latter would lose face and credibility in the event that he were to initiate a reverse of heart at the last moment, that would force Cornelius — either into committing suicide or by contributing the resources of the IXth Legion — into assisting Bricus in becoming overlord of western Albion in one way or another. Then, even if Bricus doesn't attack Paulinius in an attempt to seize the Amoran governorship — for in Amor's eyes it would need some evidence towards any type of betrayal against them by Paulinius — Bricus is still well on his way to becoming an Amoran sympathizing Albionian overlord. And either way he would be miles ahead of Cornelius and probably be eligible by a proclamation issued by Amor to receive taxes in order to contain his authority over the state.'

The queen eyed Dyfed for quite some time before continuing. "Do you know Bricus?' she asked at length.

"No,' replied Dyfed, 'although I witnessed the commotion around him when he was receiving the royal welcome at Legion's Port of Authority from the soldiers of Amor. I can tell you that much. And as we both know, soldiers don't think, not one iota, unless ordered to. In this case, that display of welcoming and pandering would be Cornelius' order, don't you think? He seems quite taken by Bricus.'

Queen Carmen considered what Dyfed had just said for a moment then she responded. "Since you haven't met Bricus, I can tell you that he is a young man much the same age as you, as you undoubtedly know, but who isn't nearly as capable in the thinking department, especially with the abilities toward shrewdness and cunning as I discern you to have. So how is it he is able to effect anything near to what you claim his actions and aims are?'

Dyfed now contemplated Queen Carmen. Aging, but quick of eye and action, she normally wore a bonnet or scarf over her head, but now at table and alone with Dyfed, she was bareheaded, the greying strands of her hair tied up over her head while a designated quantity of them were brushed down and hung around the side of her face.

"Well, he's got this far, hasn't he?' retorted Dyfed. 'But not by himself, that's for sure,' he added. 'You see, Bricus doesn't have to think; he doesn't have to be cunning or shrewd. For Bricus, you see, has someone who does all those things for him, and who does them very well. And that someone is an Armorican Druid whose name is Blazingwolf. Let me ask you this, your Majesty: Bricus, by any chance, doesn't happen to have a man accompany him in these on-going talks you speak of, does he? This would be a man who probably sits directly behind him and is constantly whispering sweet nothings into his ear.' Carmen stared at Dyfed with disbelief for a moment then looked down. 'You see, your Majesty, it's the mastermind Blazingwolf who's wearing the pants under the toga (or the Amoran kilt) here. It is he who is the real danger. Although it is Bricus who is pursuing this on-going agenda for positioning himself to be a high king, Blazingwolf is the chief threat. Now,' Dyfed rubbed his hands together as if they were cold on this warm day as Carmen shifted her full attention to this young man, 'the players, we can safely say — on this little northern stage — aren't so much Paulinius or Kunobelin (who may be unaware of their own secondary involvement at this time) but rather Cornelius who probably thinks he is on top of the game with an empire's might behind him if he begins to lose his footing. Next is Bricus who doesn't have to think because Blazingwolf is the pinch hitter in his act and a heavy weight that mustn't be discounted or underestimated at all costs. And finally, there is you, your majesty. Rule of thumb in my books: don't judge anyone, for in the event that you misjudge them they may very easily take the advantage and hold it over you. Now, what would happen if, let's say, someone around this table of talks as you call them, were to take Cornelius aside on their own and say that a spy has brought in information that all is not what it seems with the intentions of Bricus? And what would happen if they were also to say to him that Bricus, who, incidentally, is actually using Ryan against Cornelius himself, not to mention that he is about to play Cornelius off with Paulinius who may very well wake up one morning and discover that he has a major rebellion on his hands? Hmm? One might suggest at that point that Paulinius will be wanting to blame somebody for the inconvenient interruption of his otherwise semi orderly life here on the lam from the dog eat dog world in Amor until he can get a better leg-up; at least, that would be the case after he has had to take sudden, decisive action in assuming total command of the serious situation and begrudgingly, and reluctantly having to assume his position at the head of his troops in the shape of the empire's XXth Legion Valeria Victrix that would now be forced on the march despite the province's dwindling means stored away in their coffers along with a marked slump in bills receivable. The empire, after all, is being brilliantly run on the cheap, which is why it is successful and exists at all. And don't forget, when Amor called in Boodikka's loans after the death of her husband and father, they received only revolution and the expense that goes with it. Anyway — all the while Paulinius will be wondering if Cornelius is still asleep at his post?'

"Then,' continued Dyfed, 'that informing person Dyfed might then want to further inform Cornelius that the people here, and even those on Mona Major — with the timely impeachment of Ryan — may very well support and side with Cornelius against Bricus, if the opportunity were to emerge. And if the sub legate Cornelius would sign a separate treaty with Queen Carmanda, an extended treaty that's over and above their current understanding — which opinion thinks she would be willing to do — then a tighter and more expedient agreement between you and him could ensue. This would be to both to your advantages and under your directorship would give the Albion people, and of Albany, elevated civil rights. Why, would this not be a good thing? And, in addition,' Dyfed added, 'while allowing Cornelius mastery over greater integration of Amoran concepts of state and governance here it would be very likely that King Cadwallopir would be most anxious to support the agreement while bringing King Cadot along with him.'

Dyfed paused, running his fingers through his long and unruly hair. 'So with King Cadwallopir, Cadot and Maelgwn (who in these circumstances will follow Cadwallopir), Cornelius and you, all that is left is King Kunobelin, the regent of Llogia and overlord of all Albion. I hear that he is a good man and already a potential ally. What do you say to that? your Majesty. Of course it wouldn't hurt if this person discussing these matters with Cornelius in private (just prior to when their turn came to address the convocation) were to inadvertently drop the name of that spy in question; just in passing, of course — you understand?'

(Operation Giganticus)

Dura lex, sed lex (The law is harsh, but it is the law)
'A LATIN BROCARD'

Time had now passed somewhat and Dyfed had had no communication from the empire's official or unofficial (he wasn't sure which) civil representative here in Caer Legion. Queen Carmen, now a staunch supporter of Dyfed, had written the letter of introduction for him that had been delivered to Publius Servilius Maximus, chief civil servant representing proconsul Paulinius, whether the latter knew it or not. The letter had also included certain recommendations. Although Dyfed was quite assured that Manandan had instilled in him the ultimate letter of introduction, he accepted Carmen's help out of politeness more than gratitude. Then one morning a letter arrived inviting Dyfed to the makeshift basilica for a review of his accomplishments. The man he was directed to see was none other named Maximus himself. Maximus told him, however, that although he did answered to the sub legate Cornelius who commanded the IXth Legion officially, civil authority would normally be the responsibility not of Cornelius but the proconsul Paulinius who had the emperor's blessing and didn't need Cornelius'. After all, no one was at war here in Caer Legion and it was peace talks that had been opened up here. He probably said this to emphasize the division here of Amoran authority and to suggest that his branch under Cornelius' command was of greater status than just a regimental treasurer. But when Dyfed hinted that he knew more than he should by asking him about Cornelius' presence here at Legion that was thought by the tribe's chief (Queen Carmanda) to be officially unofficial, Maximus glared at Dyfed and said nothing in return on the subject.

During the course of fulfilling his duties Dyfed quickly learned that any imperial overall power invested into the proconsul Paulinius (who was either at his palace office in Nova Trioa or Camulod wasn't about to have any effect whatsoever here in Legion. There were no envoys nor were there any correspondence whatsoever between them. Cornelius was it. At present the situation appeared to Dyfed to be one more like moonlighting.

The interview had gone well and Dyfed could tell that his credentials that were quickly supported by demonstration during the second and practical stage of his interview impressed the young man, not much older than he. The audience was conducted in sombre chambers within Maximus' office and the interview dragged on for quite some time. In addition, it was made even lengthier by a further spate of idle chitchat done in a less formal atmosphere after the business of the formal procedure was completed. Although seemingly casual, this friendly post mortem (complete with refreshments of libations), Dyfed knew, was done to extend the investigation. In order to find out more about him, it wouldn't be uncommon to re-examine with the gloves off and the guard dropped; indeed, something of a mandatory practice, he supposed. But it also gave him more opportunity to impress, and in this he was very successful. In short, it very quickly opened a door for Dyfed. Then another door opened during this interpolation. It was a certain Gaius Lucius Julius, a colleague of Publius Maximus who was Maximus' chief pencil pushing paper-piler. He dropped by on the pretence of some after hours business or other of the empire for which he needed Maximus' signature. But the empire part Dyfed knew was a lie. But then shortly after a few jovial comments had passed between the three men, instead of leaving, Julius fell back into a comfortable couch and also partook of libations. Setting his business portfolio aside he very rapidly relaxed into the general conversation and the good fellowship at large. At this stage the wine began to flow a little more profusely and Gaius Lucius Julius hurried to catch up.

So with the addition of Julius, an administrative inferior and subordinate to Maximus, the conversation took a turn towards even more complicated congeniality, but one that maintained an even keel. Before long Julius managed to let slip quickly enough the pseudonym by which Maximus was known. The nickname was Publius the Purse.

It was a few days hence before Dyfed was able to estimate his status among these men. All of this meet and greet stuff was important to him (as much as for them) for he had never before been exposed to intelligent, educated young Amorans. He did not push or flatter, nor did he become a know-it-all, for he knew the likes of those types were quickly shown the step outside the door by the likes of these alpha males. But he concentrated on impressing his two new friends and gently commended them both on all sorts, as well as reflects or highlight their intelligence that he easily complimented. This pleased them so therefore he pleased them. He also let slip casually that he spoke many other languages quite well and many dialects, too. This impressed them immensely. Careful not to blunt his blade in the light of the full moon (as they say), he didn't delve too deeply into things or let on (for example) that he knew that orange-red light waves that were emitted from Krypton-86 gas amounted to approximately forty-two thousand of an Amoran inch. However, abled by his knowledge of old doctrine (archaic science now lost to Amor) he spoke of the marvels of science and applied mechanics on which he could ruminate intelligently and in a way that was within their understanding of practicability. His sense of humour and sense of adventure, not withstanding his recently lost love upon which he ruminated to some length (much to their glee mingled with sympathy), and the heart strings that were pulled on that occasion, endeared him to these other two young men who were egged on as well by his incredible capacity to scoff back the frothy red wine ladled up from the IXth Legion's own private store room. Wine, he discovered, along with other morally questionable luxuries, was a kind of stipend that was extended to the military white-collar bureaucrats who were tasked and responsible for oiling the gears and pulling the levers of the machine of state that kept the empire's legions of soldiers in business, let alone happy. And almost all of them were young men.

"Listen,' Maximus said to Dyfed after the three of them had consumed a dinner Maximus had ordered in impromptu, 'maybe we can help each other, who knows! You don't want to stay here in Legion any more than we do,' he said, indicating Julius and himself, 'and I don't have to know you any better than I do now in order to see that. We don't want to be here either. We didn't sign up for this. In fact Flav the Finger, as we call Cornelius when he can't hear us, is endangering our lives being here. This outpost is not even in the empire as you have already demonstrated to know; we are beyond even the fringe. We are a forward outpost at best and wouldn't be even that if it weren't for Queen Carmanda. Oh yes, Dyfed Lucifer,' the man stated 'I know! Our position here is solely to provide plaudit to Cornelius. He hopes to endear himself to the higher-ups, if not the emperor himself, and the boldness which he believes he is displaying here in furthering the empire beyond it's current reach is his ticket back to Amor and the devil knows what vices he'll entertain there. You see, Dyfed Lucifer, he might be a legate of sorts under Paulinius but he is not a real soldier. His merchant family are wealthy and entwined with the House of Theodosius. His position was bought. Furthermore, he walks in the shadow of his older self made brother Lucius Cornelius-*Felix* (the lucky) the famous, or infamous, if you like. And so here we are. This place? Well, it's a latrine, a shit-hole, beyond the farthest fringes of the empire by all that Jove covets and loves! The women here…you saw today even when we dress them up…are so vile that one would suspect that coitus contigo canis would be all the rage. Certainly, neither Gaius nor I would dip our dick into that. No, Dyfed. So, give me a little time and I'll get you enrolled in some civil schooling down in Nova Troia or Camulod with Flav the Finger's official seal upon the application. Nova Troia is not Isis (a city on the Sen River in Gaul, east of Armorica) nor is it Massalia with the warm clime of the White Sea coast. But at least it will be out of here,' he said accompanying it with a winning smile.

Dyfed then asked Maximus for more news about the empire, for he had earlier explained to him that he had been away for some time on a scientific expedition to the far north examining the Aurora Borealis. Unfortunately, his arrival here as a sole survivor on the western shores, he told him, was due to shipwreck.

"Mos maiorum (the custom of the ancestors),' Maximus said, 'is still the agenda for the day.' Maximus patiently explained to him that the empire was still like a colossal operation through co-operation, albeit an often-enforced co-operation termed, as Dyfed would know, Amoran Pax (the peace of Amor). Nothing had changed there, he told him.

"And this was still accomplished by the eradication of any and all opposition to Amoran interests leaving only the peace of Amor. Again, nothing has changed, nor would it ever change. The internal gears of the empire were as oiled and smooth as they had ever been, maybe even more so. They, the financiers of the intrinsic industry (soldiering) that kept Amor humming along, were indeed a marvellous mechanism which still remained at the core of this operation. To be sure, however, the further the empire stretched into the northwest the more obstinate the people were becoming. And as for Amor herself, that Eternal City: Well, as always was still a business in business. She was a consortium,' Maximus said, 'albeit with layered political overtones of greater depth which made everything more interesting. It was still the head of an idea. It was the top general, the chief basilica; it was the head office! And that is why it was known as the Eternal City because whatever successful city or empire in the western world that followed her would always only be her clone in more than one way.'

"But a word of caution Maximus continued to say, 'slurs against any of the methodologies applying Amor's interests, or against the emperor, or against powerful, stand alone Amorans themselves, whether they were proconsuls, generals or rich Amoran publicani (merchants) whose investments were the life blood or strength of Amor, were subject to immediate action with extreme punitive results, no matter who you were.'

"Shades of Socrates,' said Dyfed. He said that the true hierarchy of authority was in fact in reverse order to the status quo. Furthermore, a misstep or action by a self-important emperor or important official was often inversely proportional to its result that negatively effected the entire population at large. Instead of the great Cloud of the Spirit being passed down to king and high priest, redemption, acceptance and responsibility came first from inside each and every individual. In truth the flow of life force passed officially from the lone survivor through the king and the high priests to god that is where the denarius stopped. It wasn't the other way around. Man's ego and lust invented god, so man has to keep feeding that incubus he has created or lose it all. Others who march to a different tune need not heed or bother with it at all. The old philosopher was against what he called the fake sky gods to whom folks were sacrificing. Then in addition he claimed that these gods were smoke and mirrors anyway through which (and by connivance) were only fabricated in order to afford the power elite at large their (rather less than credible) authority. This authority enjoyed by the great king on his horse (and all the king's men) also (naturally) provided them the right to kill whomever questioned or opposed this idea. This was not Stoicism.

"Yes and no,' Maximus responded. 'It was just another door used by the strong and powerful to be able to legally inherit everything you own and sell you into slavery that was all beyond appeal. *Dura lex, sed lex*, as they say. This is Amor's legacy and one which will be forever copied down the generations.'

"But hardly the sentiments of the Gracchi who were also of Amor,' Dyfed stated, 'and a difficult and sticky wicket, what! And a really raggedy row to hoe (or rally behind) for any future revisionists.'

(Regretfully, Turnkeys & the Nightwatchmen were licenced to pilot the chariot of civilization driven that's driven by finance)

'Wise men argue cases, fools decide them.'
ANACHARSIS

Time had passed and Dyfed had settled comfortably into his employment status at the basilica. Ever on the lookout for Zeus, the despoiler of human tranquillity that was the sunderer in the pursuit of human happiness, all that was needed was for him to locate any disruption of the natural attraction for the good vibrations of congeniality, warmth and selfless love and find where that had been replaced instead by the lure and popularity (if any) for that preverbal turd in the equally preverbal punch bowl. Not surprising he didn't have to look very hard to find broken and disassociated of human sentient beings who were generally close to the bone of the establishment and its agents.

Dyfed began now for the first time in his life to take up the practice of a type of enhanced, existentialistic existence utilized by the ancient Hyperboreans. This format had been taught him by the two closest Hyperborean sentient beings he'd ever known, his mother (Queen Chloris Violet-Eye) and the local champion of wizardry, her adopted vizier. And there were more than a few who had this trait in common, but they weren't obvious. The adherents of Zeus, on the other hand were at least obvious to him as they literally pushed people away with their vile vibrations.

In his alertness Dyfed had already discovered the fingerprints of that aforementioned incubus of Zeus in the details etched into the volition that caused how Amor ruled and contained its empire. In respect to imperial law and order, which may or may not include good governing of and by (and in the interests of all or even the majority of) the people who make up and contribute to the empire, it was at least divided into two obvious portions of authority. The first of the two portions was the greater importance of the two. These were the Turnkeys, Dyfed discovered. These Turnkeys were not generally viewed by the general public as being potentially an insidious coven who could take away their freedom through imprisonment or sell them into slavery that they should have been. These Turnkeys were often seen as the purveyors of cruel and un-acceptable treatment and unusual punishment. They ranged from those who occupied magisterial positions of the courts which included judges as well as officers of the courts, and lawyers of the prosecution (once called the Crown [later the Imperial] attorney, and stretched right down to the actual blue collared prison officials such as the jailers who turned the stiff key of the dank and sooty embittered dungeon door. From this they get their name.

The Turnkeys had functioned relatively fairly for the common good while Amor was at its height as a kingdom. But later it adopted a greater accent for accountability as it morphed into The Republic. But instead of crystalizing and maturing as Amor expanded into an empire, it turned skunky as the Turnkeys' main function was designed to security-clad the apparatus of imperial palace power over both justice and the rights of the citizens in general as well as to gather into its fold the offices of the imperial treasury. This opened the way for imperial authority to manage the population as they saw fit. It was accomplished by tweaking and adding laws which made the business of Turn-keying easier all around for all concerned in that capacity and less chancy for any undesired outcome which was always now to be measured alongside what was most expedient for Amor and its capitalist beneficiaries, the Amoran oligarchs. These latter were a couple of rungs up from the aforementioned Publicani.

Complimentary to the glorified Turnkeys in this power share was the glorified Nightwatchmen. The Nightwatchmen were also known as the cavalry of all the king's (emperor's) men. They ranged from the top policemen of the land along with the top guard and descended from there down the ranks of the imperial police, special agents of joint chiefs of police operations division, the provincial police and the municipal police, along with sundry security officers, the basilica's or the agora's local Nightwatchman armed with a decidedly un-Diogenesian torch, and even down to the imperially sanctioned gangs of the uniformed neighbourhood watch. The machinations of the Nightwatchmen followed suit to the Turnkeys, as their duty was to uphold the authority of the law more than the law itself, which was securely in the hands of the magistrates and not the people. The Nightwatchmen drew their directives straight from the magistrates and crown (state) attorneys. So if the latter had an agenda, that agenda blossomed via the Nightwatchmen. The Nightwatchmen needed to be resourceful and full of savvy but not questioning or highly educated or even particularly knowledgeable of affairs outside of their careers or even the law itself. An imbecile will do, so long as he can follow orders unquestioningly. All these horses of the king (emperor) were bent on marshalling civil law which could easily ran rough shod over decency and human rights: in addition they cudgelled and imprisoned any and all who tried to initiate any civic duty beyond submission or institute interest in any civic authority whatsoever. But Maximus has already explained that it was this way.

All the king's horses could be given free rein (or reined in) by the Turnkeys as it suited them; but never the other way around, not in a perfect world of oligarchy. And the tools for the majority to turn the light around were disappearing quickly under the current Amoran rule. When more and more under the watch of imperial totalitarian authority than of their earlier the Nightwatchmen did move to petition for change so as to make more expedient their own work and reputation (as did happen on occasion) trouble brewed in Tinsel-Town. And it was to be seen that this happened Kingdom and the latter Republic.

Then, as now, the idea behind the concept of both the Nightwatchmen and the Turn-keys was to advocate a move forward toward a subdued, a submissive and divided and (most especially) an individually isolated society which they hoped would one day acknowledge and be open to a rigid, authoritarian program of duty and responsibility to Jupiter, emperor, and empire in that order. This, under the advice of certain and selected representatives of the state or crown which in way of a covenant and surety for the former's indemnity, had been once (and remains still) sealed with a social contract under the proffered authority of an unknown and mysterious ethereal being (Jupiter) before any civil liberties could be entertained and then only according to the sacred scriptures of the aforementioned god-incubus. It was undesirability common knowledge to the cultured ruling class that this was where any and all other proffered acts that challenged authority was held in abeyance without exception. Treason abounded at high levels within the oligarchy in their acts taken toward misappropriating the fortunes of the common hoi polloi.

The Turnkeys and Nightwatchmen, like the emperor and his cronies, believed that they drove the chariot of civilization; that it was they and not the people who made the decision on what was the common volition behind the society which the majority wanted and just how the people in it were to function and what exactly it was they all really needed. The establishment of Amor's attitude was that the people were to be at the pleasure of the emperor and all his horses and all his men even if it led to their detriment. This, of course, was a recipe for eventual revolution and was far from the psychological archetype that had been originally carefully fashioned as to morph into a culture according to Plato, et al.

By this time, not just a few springs and autumns had come and gone, and returned again. Muns and he had become the greatest of friends. Meanwhile, Queen Carmanda had proved herself to be an able intriguer and as shrewd and sharp witted as ever a queen could be. Back during the talks — when Bricus, Kings Cadwallopir and Cadot, King Maelgwyn, Duke Howel, an assistant to Bade, and the unofficial imperial sub legate, that master of misinformation, General Cornelius. These went hand in hand with the likes of King Ryan of Mona Major who were all jockeying for an advantageous position. Carmen, bless her soul, once again pulled Flav the Finger Cornelius aside one day and told him in confidence much what Dyfed had suggested. But it didn't end there. Carmen had already pulled King Ryan aside as well and suggested that his betrothal to Ceredwyn was not only foolish but down right tragic if not idiotic. Ceredwyn, beautiful as she was, and close as she was to King Cadwallopir who looked upon her as a surrogate niece was nobody! How could she be anything else? After all, her father Owen MacShee — a good man, a nice and dependable man, even a ruggedly handsome man — was, after the last beast was broken, only a nobody governing a lonely cenedl in the middle of nowhere. No, no! Better to marry someone attached to a proper clan of note behind her, not a cenedl. Better to marry a princess of a tribe, or better still, of a kingdom, and a kingdom that was essentially at her feet. Not Ceredwyn, she had nothing. Hello! What was he thinking? she had said to him sarcastically. So, therefore, the circumstance specific to the conversation (being as it was) quickly led to the following.

"So…who did the queen have in mind, then?' That's what Ryan wanted to know.

And Queen Carmanda wasn't bashful or backward either in coming forward and telling him outright, immediately, much in the manner that Johnny on the spot would have:

"Princess Marg, of course'.

"Princess Marg? What in the world has she got?' queried King Ryan.

"She is my heir, don't you know! She will inherit my kingdom,' responded Carmen.

"Oh yes, yes,' answered King Ryan almost mockingly, as Carmen's experienced eyes ran over this young warrior king's masculine and athletic physic. She noted with a warm flush that rushed to parts of her body as she took in up close his ruggedly handsome face, already slightly scarred. As Carmen began to mentally undress the vigorous young man before her, while searching for more scars and wondering at the muscular hardness of his body, incredulously, she suddenly envied Marg in that moment of dreamy projection.

Quickly, she wished for all the world that she could trade places (body-wise) with the bitch, if only for an hour or so, every day: but, anyway, at least Princess Marg was one of her bitches (so she thought, anyway). In this she found a way to comfort herself. And when she had offered the kingdom to this her most precious bitch of all, well, there was no question of her refusing it, and who knows where it could end for her, too. Of course, Marg's eventual coronation aside, she, Carmanda, would remain in charge, she wasn't that stupid. She was the brains of the unit, after all: but the child (Marg, only marginally older than Dyfed) could queen it up and lust at her heart's content. Who knows, Carmen reflected (customary to women her age and disposition) as she continued to closely watch King Ryan and fascinated by the sweat that penetrated through his clothes. Oh yes…she may yet have some opportunities with him of her own. She remembered then how Marg had closely scrutinized Prince Dyfed's stunning physical assemblage despite him having been face down on the table in a drunken stupor for the most part of that day. And she recalled having then noticed Marg surveying his lower parts as he was hoisted up and carried naked to his bed, having shed his clothes over the course of the hot day and in the heat of his drunken glow. Of course, she remembered. Her own eyes had followed suit and done the same, and she had wished after that she had removed all her clothes too and followed him up. At least there is always the morning after. Young men like him are always aroused, especially in the mornings, especially if nothing much had happened the evening before. It had crossing her mind to arrange something with Marg and Dyfed. But after she had discerned the frightening extent of Dyfed's towering awareness and his intellect possibly even over her own, she had thought better of it.

But in bringing Ryan and Marg together opened up possibilities for her in many ways, not least of all was the fact that she would be doing him a favour with a flavour, and that, perhaps, could be viewed as an investment: Or maybe not.

'So,' continued Ryan, 'when is this heir apparent of yours to be endowed as such?' he had asked. 'At some undefined time, a long way hence in the distant future, when your Majesty has frail and old, with me not far behind, or already dead?' he said in answer to his own question. Hearing his flattery towards her caused a shiver inside her. It was the uncontrollable effect of a directly applied adulating pander, pleasurable enough, indeed, but she knew it to be only a potential and nothing more. He words were not the more favourable circumstance of that of a strange, fascinating, and throbbing member upon one's clitoris, for an example. And she quickly reminded herself of this fact. No, she wasn't taken in, not just yet. She wasn't going to be flattered until he, or any other target for that matter, lay entwined and sweating beside her upon their soaking wet love bed, their genitals swollen, glistening and red and his testicles drained. That state of affairs, that delicious finale, was her normal prerequisite toward any thought of accepting flattery. And then she was fond of quickly withdrawing it and leaving her suitor drained and naked with a post coitus depression looming by his shrunken member.

She was flattering herself here, of course, for she certainly didn't know men as well as she thought.

"The devil can take my place on my thrown now, for all I care,' she answered Ryan, lying through sensually swollen lips and still attractively teeth. 'The rigors of ruling and all the forethought and planning which an expedient and secure regency entails these days has become tiresome for me now,' she lied again. 'I want to retire while I still have energy and able to enjoy the pleasures of life,' she added, batting her eyes in his direction.

Apparently Ryan had been taken in by Queen Carmanda where Dyfed had not been. Indeed, she had helped him but only after he had got the best of her. But none of this had got him any closer to getting Ceredwyn back. He was hoping upon hope that she would have seen fit to run away from her father and find her way back to him by now. At any rate, apparently, whatever one's reality is, it certainly has nothing to do with the common reality at large. Manandan had told him that nobody has any idea what conception another person has of anything, not one bit. 'If you did', he told Dyfed, 'you'd be very surprised. It is better that you don't know until you know how to handle the knowing which it is quite obvious the third dimensional hoi polloi don't know, and neither do you, Dyvie. All your other perceptions about this thing which you gather from your focus point as a third dimensional being will fail you unless you are very careful and thorough,' he said. Perception is everything for it produces a conception of what is,' he said, 'and you are subjected to the perceptions of everybody around you, and their resulting conceptions of you and everything else. And you can never really change that. Never forget that, Dyvie. And never forget the wise words of one of our own that said... 'Wise men argue cases, fools decide them.'' So, would he have to go to her? he wondered.

Needless to say, Dyfed knew nothing of Carmen's chat to convince Ryan to drop Ceredwyn and marry Marg. She hadn't bothered to inform Dyfed that Ceredwyn had a free hand again. So he remained in the dark about this. And if Ceredwyn couldn't make it back to him on her own then he would have to delay their nuptials now and renew his attempts later anyway. He loved her, he wanted her near him and he wanted her to accompany him as they walked through life together, as they say. She was also his first love and the first woman with which he had blissfully entered into carnal relations. He ached for her and he knew she ached for him and he just couldn't understand these people around him, people like her own father who intentionally kept them apart, and for what? What kind of man was Owen anyway? he wondered. It had been almost two years and he still ached for her.

Then Dyfed discovered that Ceredwyn had returned home under Owen's guard about a half moon after the talks when Ryan had his big show on the small political stage. It had been then that the latter had announced his candidacy to form and lead a confederation of Prydain states to secure their western lands from Amoran domination. But this description did not accurately describe the talks, either, for Blazingwolf and his sidekick and platform, King Bricus, together with Cornelius had seemed to support Ryan's bid. And this, Dyfed knew, was contrary to what each of the aforementioned wanted to achieve.

And it was this tentative agreed decision at the talks which had later spurred Carmen on to have a word in Ryan's ear and propose he not marry Ceredwyn after all while dangling the promise of her kingdom before him. Furthermore, Carmen was suspicious of the Amorans and would sooner see them float away for good down the tidal estuary that flowed out towards the western sea.

And now the prospect of being enrolled in an advanced civil instruction class in Nova Troia for imperial procedure 101, along with policy and due process had come open and was looming large on his horizon. It bore Cornelius' seal of approval but the assistant to the Quartermaster General of the IXth Legion had come to personally inform him. He then advised Dyfed for the sake of his future to be on the next imperial coach-train to Nova Troia. But that wouldn't be until after Marg's coronation and her wedding to King Ryan who, of course, we now know had dumped Ceredwyn.

(The Coronation of Convenience)

'We hang the petty thieves and appoint the great ones to public office.'
AESOP

The morning of the day of the wedding was a fine one. Dyfed awoke early and after his usual exercises, he then slipped noiselessly through the quiet streets and down to the river for the goodly ritual of cleanliness. As he returned into the town a local tribesman (manning the western gate) accosted him and enquired as to just what he was getting up to at this time of the morning by the river alone?

"It is the ritual of cleanliness, and generally pandering to the God of Clean,' Dyfed answered. 'You should worship there some time!' he added, as he slipped through the small inner door and past the guard.

Then he made ready for the big day. He had been personally invited to the reception by Carmen and intended to wear his finest attire that he had set aside for his own wedding. But he had also invited himself into the processional, the parade which promised to be the major attraction that preceded the main invitation-only event of the nuptials' union that was to take place within Queen Carmanda's residence. So, on this fine day, after carefully stashing his expensive attire in the royal stables (where he had paid a young friend of Muns' to watch over), Dyfed wearing only a purple cape, his family house ring and virtually naked otherwise down to his goat leather boots (a fitting attire for this fine warm May day), stood astride his two beautiful Andalusia mounts; his right foot upon the back of the white mare and his left foot on the back of the black stallion. He rode with grace, and standing proudly erect he received great and thundering applause from the thronging crowds. It should be mentioned that Proconsul Paulinius had earlier put in an order for three hundred fine horses from Further Hispania, some of which had a pedigree that were from Arabia, to be sent to him to refurbish, replenish and fortify his XXth Legion Valeria Victrix's cavalry. These had been off loaded on the right bank of the river Dee and left to free-run and graze on the Wirral Peninsula that stretched out west from the new fort of Deva which Paulinius had ordered build on the upper Dee in preparation for new troops (Sarmatians being among them) that had yet to arrive. Cornelius, who had sent a trireme from Legion down to the river Dee to learn news about Paulinius' campaign against the western peoples there, purchased twenty of them since the proconsul had returned to Camulod to deal with Queen Boodikka. When the horses arrived in Legion, Dyfed had denarii at the ready to purchase two Andalusians for himself.

The triumphal procession that midday was a grand affair. Indeed, nothing like it had ever been seen in these parts. As the sun rose to the zenith above the town and the level of excitement grew in ratio with the increasing murmur of the swelling crowds sweating under a burning sun, a few fat twists of dough-like clouds moved in from the sea and hovered above in stark contrast to the broad backdrop of a boundless blue sky. All around, the two stations of life — the elite (divided into Amoran and high born Kelts) and commoner alike — were united in feasting and merriment as they moved about the streets in good fellowship and drinking up the kegs of wines which the IXth Legion's quartermaster had imported before leaving civilization for just such an occasion along with other local spirits that were provided by John Barleycorn and his many admirers.

Because of the throng of milling townsfolk which had swollen in numbers, the ravens had moved to higher ground among the wooden ledges and turrets where they watched incessantly for unguarded and forgotten scraps (sometime dropped by the hands of children) to snatch up and eat. Seeing such a morsel discarded they would swoop down and pluck it up and take it back to their perch. While working in teams they vied with the dogs for these titbits. Ranting loudly, one or two of the big inky, black birds would torment an unsuspecting canine under a flurry of raucous abuse and the beating of wings in hopes that the cur might momentarily drop its prize to snap at them or give chase. If this happened, suddenly a third raven (waiting on the side lines, hopping jauntily just out of reach) would pounce. Then, with black wing feathers sticking out askew like fingers, the creature would quickly snatch the acquisition up in its beak. After that all three black birds would fly to their roost, and peering down upon the bewildered mutt, they would caw saucily with the marked gaiety combined with cheek and impudence for which these birds were well known.

Without Dyfed's company, the scholarly Muns — along with one or two of his younger friends — mingled with the crowd and fared on hot sweet buns sold by enterprising vendors while they quaffed back cups of wine. Musicians were everywhere and the strains of their instruments seeped up through the loud din, which permeated the whole environment. The lyre seemed to be the most popular instrument of choice but Dyfed had always favoured the kithara[13], another stringed instrument.

As the processionals made their preparations to begin, Dyfed, standing astride his mounts while desperately trying to settle down their rambunctious behaviour (caused by the riotous disturbances on all sides), sang soothingly to the two beasts beneath him. Snorting as they breathed, their hides swiftly shrugging off accumulating flies by affecting a rapid skin movement that made their hides shimmer with rapid ripples, each horse had both their ears turned up back towards him, listening, and waiting for his instructions. Suddenly, a great blare and fanfare occurred as trumpets blasted and bells rang. Then with a general uproar, people clamoured toward the northeast gate of the city where they congregated in a tight and untidy knot. The procession entered the city through what became known thereafter as the Triumphal Gate and preceded along Legionnaires Way.

First came Cornelius who rode a handsome and agile pony. Two of his generals rode beside him but slightly behind while the standard bearer clasped the IXth Legion's eagle. Directly behind him came the chief magistrates on foot, including Publius the Purse (Dyfed's new civil servant friend Maximus), followed by eleven mounted soldiers in armour. Next came a body of trumpeters each blowing on a copper carnyx that was only for show and behind these came a wagon train comprised of twelve large carts, each vehicle loaded down with an assortment of visiting personages that few people recognized. Next came body of musicians and golden voiced singers followed by acrobats and fire breathers. After this lot came a parade of slaves that carried blue cushions upon which were placed gifts for the bride and groom.

---

13   The kithara gave its name a thousand years later to an instrument of similar design, the guitar.

Then came a heavy Amoran chariot. It was drawn by four white, clodhopper hoofed horses and in it rode Bricus standing behind his driver and waving at the crowds with one hand that he oddly swivelled at the wrist. He hadn't even been officially invited to this occasion; but as he chased his rising star — which was certainly no Saturn — Bricus (that is to say his manager Blazingwolf) meant to push his presence on to the kingdoms hereabouts anyway, and especially on those attending this ceremony that had been official invited. And on this day (rumour had it) Bricus arrived with a communiqué he had received previous to departing Dumnonii that appointed him to take up the command of the XXth Legion Valeria Victrix that was temporarily camped at Fort Victrix and to discover the whereabouts of the IXth Legion Hispana and ordered for it to attend the aforementioned Deva on the river Dee. Despite the very hot day Bricus was attired in a richly embroidered long green coat over which was worn a harness with a number of silver Conchos on it. Beneath his overcoat he wore a light tunic that was belted at the waist and which fell to his knees that were bare. Armoured leggings or greaves further covered his shins and each area of skin that was left exposed, such as his face, hands and legs, were dyed blue. Here, Dyfed thought to himself, is a man out to prove something. Bricus cast his gaze from side to side as he passed between the cheering crowds that looked up at his beardless, blue, and unsmiling face. He did not appear to be armed but held some sort of short staff in his right hand. He was crowned with a silvery, short domed helmet wreathed with fake laurel and his hair was cropped fairly short for the occasion. Closely behind him trailed his sword bearer, bard, piper, porter, equerry, henchmen, chief stonemason and chief metallurgist, all part of his retinue that was meant to impress.

Next came Marg in a three horse drawn wicker chariot dressed in a richly embroidered tunic that was gathered at the waist with a rope type belt that was made of braided silver. She had on leggings that were stuffed into high boots and she wore a long scarlet cape that was clasped together over her right collarbone with a large broach. Dyfed thought that as the bride and queen to be, which (after all, was the occasion at hand), she should have preceded Bricus for certain, but probably Cornelius as well. Apparently, the coronation march had now become a joust that (it was soon to be seen) would leave more than one of them unceremoniously dismounted with flailing arms and broken spirit upon the ground.

Marg's coronation was to take place first as soon as she and her family were all assembled in the residence. Ryan and his suite, which obviously wanted his bride to be coroneted before he married her, would be admitted in order to witness the ceremony performed by an officiating witness who was a local tribal priest, and former lover of Carmen. A magistrate from the basilica would also be present, although this was unofficial as the local basilica hardly represented Amoran might at its height here in Caer Legion. This was to be followed by a mid day meal in which the queen's family and invitees were to gather along with King Ryan's suite. Muns, of course, was considered part of the family and he had been successful in soliciting an invitation for Dyfed. The wedding, which would harbour quite a few more guests, would occur directly after that. And it was for this reason, therefore, that Marg was not wearing the circular headdress of a regent during this the midday processional.

Following Marg came King Ryan. Dressed in his finest, Ryan drove his own wicker chariot with many Keltic soldiers following behind him carrying gifts for their liege's bride to be. Then after him came Dyfed. He, as already suggested, was virtually naked with his purple cape fluttering behind him in the wind while his gorgeous and snorting Andalusians set to and pranced a jaunty concerted jig in two part harmony dance style as Dyfed boldly balanced a foot on each of their slick, sleek and shiny backs. He had held back a little while Trachmyr (who he had hooked up with recently and the two had become friends) and a couple of his colleagues, who acting as seconds, were keeping the more enthusiastic revellers away from his mounts and the pathway clear for him to spur his horses on in spurts for the maximum resulting impression. This display and exhibit was done to demonstrate his prowess with horsemanship; and the horses' manes swished madly as they pranced forward with their more than impressing rider standing one foot upon each of their backs gripping the reins in one hand and gesticulating in a 'here I am, I told you I was wonderful' mimicking-type manner to the uproarious and cheering crowd. His attempt to outdo the half-hearted spontaneous applause caused by that of Bricus' presence was to be more than just successful. It was spectacular. This was partly due to his performance finale. Once Dyfed was certain that his Andalusians were calmed and used to the noise, he signalled Muns who handed up to him the kithara that he had painstakingly had built himself. From his stance upon the beautiful horses, this naked man with a violet cape streaming behind him as he strummed the kithara caused almost panic and a madding uproar among the youngsters in the crowd. Nobody had seen such a thing before, never mind doing it almost as naked as a J-bird.

The procession ended with the IXth Legion's personal guard who marched completely armed in full battle dress. As the triumphal march dragged on up Legionnaires Way toward the Queen's residence, Muns and his friends had kept abreast of Dyfed and assisted Trachmyr and his boys. Many of the young local men followed alongside Bricus whose money had placed them there. As Bricus rode he remained statuesque, appearing almost inanimate upon his chariot. The crowd on the whole seemed distant, however, toward the strange blue figure as he stood sternly erect in the chariot rumbling past them like some decked out and painted icon amid the clip clop of the horses hoofs. The crowd reacted most riotous toward Marg and that made Dyfed feel happy for her, but for some strange reason the queen was not in the procession.

Now cape-less and fully clothed, Dyfed entered the residence which he had once called home and joined the guests at their midday meal around the central table. Later, drinking beer and other intoxicating substances, and mingling with the wedding guests and casual friends, he and Muns surveyed the crowd outside which had spilled right across the huge central square dedicated to Lugus. From the interior they watched that enlivened and groaning mass outside through the residence's large main entrance that had been thrown fully open. To Dyfed it appeared to be some strange multi-faceted monster that heaved and roared and (as he watched it grow) both parties inside and out gained momentum, as jugglers, musicians and actors performed. It was these that seemed to orchestrate the rhythm as they beat the wild gatherings into a raving, drunken, tumultuous mass that continued through the short wedding ceremony and well into the night. It was then that many bonfires were lit outside, right on the streets. Each fire was sending an upward tornado of swirling, volcanic like sparks into the starry, summery sky where earlier a moon had risen bright and full. The interior crowd appeared to have become almost as raucous as their counterpart outside as musicians and drunken patrons reeled about and competed with their outdoor rivals. The wedding dinner table became the centre of attraction for those not dancing to the vibrant tunes or taking time out to recoup, as it was revisited time after time to sit at, and discuss around, or to refill and swill. As the evening wore on guests passed out and lay sprawled around the periphery of the dance circle. Others were pushed off tables, chairs, and benches into a no-man's land between the dancers and the animated talkers and drinkers that were still going strong. Dyfed was doing all three; dancing, drinking and dickering for whatever comes what may. He and Muns, with help from some others, had even set their labours aside at one point and cleared a path through the revelry induced carnage on the floor between the table and the dance circle. They dragged unresponsive bodies back and away so people could get back and forth without tripping over and slipping around the drunken discards: The servants, most of whom were drunk, mopped up spillage and puke. It was a happy time for all, it seemed, and the newly wed couple, Dyfed noticed, did not retire customarily early as polite society were wont to do. This state of affairs of staying the course, apparently, rather than being of King Ryan's doing (who wanted to duck out early in the direction of the boudoir), it was at her highness Queen Marg's insistence. She, apparently, was bent on maintaining a performance of revelry that set her ahead of the best of them. And she continued at that speed after most of the elite patrons were either passed out or fornicating off to one side. Marg, it seemed, was heading in the direction of doing neither. Dyfed danced with her and filled her cups for the duration. But still the wine and beer kept flowing, but now more in the direction of outside the palace where it was sopped up by the earthy and revelling crude; those hoi polloi who were in the mother of all party moods on this night.

(Descending from the sticks into the provincial arena)

"There is an infinite amount of hope in the universe, but not for us."
FRANZ KAFKA

Dyfed left Legion for Nova Troia full of hope and anticipation. His personal gear was loaded onto a ship that was designed eventually for Nova Troia. He carried a day bag that he flung over the back of the Anadalusa that tailed behind the other he rode. Full of hope and anticipation he decided to accompany the stagecoach that left Legion for Nova Troia. If he wished to stop longer than scheduled, he could easily accompany the next scheduled run (or ride alone) to the next fort or town where he would catch his baggage up. His first stop would be Deva Victrix then on to Camulod taking turns to ride one horse then the other to exercise them equally.

Occasionally he saw members of local tribesmen, the poorer, rural, and more rustic cousins, watching them as they journeyed passed, and although he didn't think the soldiers had discerned their presence, he thought it best to say nothing of his observations. Not all of these dark people native to Albion of late lived in proximity or even in subjection to the Amorans. Many preferred their own bucolic existence with its total freedom and individualism. Indeed, it was from this stock that some of those strange and insular shamans emerged. These folk, who generally remained alone and remote from their town dwelling cousins, were reluctantly to share their domain. The folks he saw without coming into contact were timid yet intelligent: They were a separate and dark breed that remained aloof even from others, though they seemed in touch with each other. The women, like the men were somewhat squat but excelled in knowledge of potions and a science similar to that of auguring who knew that certain cries of the morning cock, the cry of raven in the evening, and the death of a white hare on a Sunday could cast spells and warn of portents to come. Meanwhile, seemingly gifted with wisdom, these men silently watched on as the general populace around them stumbled and bumbled along committing outrageous acts of stupidity. Because the men had abnormally more hair on their body than other men, they appeared, he noticed, to have long, pointed ears. Yet strangely, these specific folks would continue to exist amidst the cauldrons of society without ever being influenced and affected by what noise and bustle passed them by. These folks were (or at least their unworldly culture of fortitude was) the catalyst that, once it was infused into any amalgamating, immigrating neighbouring new comers at large, it would help crystalize and one day (five hundred years hence) would fashion an empire that, if not of their own, at least one that they would recognize and approve of. This would be done by sorting, coding and filing momentous human attributes and sensibilities that contributed to their culture, especially language structure, that would become capable of forging and impinging itself in parallel with any incoming foreign data that, accordingly, would in turn be traced out upon any new ideas. In that way the certain aspects of language and custom of these ancient folks would eventually be retained Prydain (Albion's) heritage.

This dark, highly intelligent stoic minded folks he saw as he rode on were more like the animals of the earth and consequently their spirit was purer and they displayed more natural grace, Dyfed thought. They were more reserved and aloof, and certainly insular, and he didn't for a moment think that they had any phobia of fear for the big dark wolves that crawled over this land like lice. They did not fear the wild creatures of the land as the Amorans and the men of cities certainly did. They feared god. These folks feared the white lightening of conscious that produced phenomena around them out of nothing but their minds[14]. For it was their minds (psyche or soul) that produced their third dimensional senses, and contributed to their joy and their pain. The power that made this is what they feared. It could lead them all to madness or to nirvana. These folks who were considered to have been indigenous for some thousands of years worshipped Wodan.[15] He knew of others, or at least their descendants who had transcended; Abaris for one, and Antisthenes for another, even the recluse Diogenes who lived and breathed still, and Shirkuh, his own ancestor who was no longer of this third density world, were of these people who once lived across all of Europa. They were all the spirit and embodiment of Arete, the stature which he himself had set about to achieve; and having been helped by his upbringing and tutoring, he continued to aspire toward: Arete in the sense that nobody could achieve perfection but excellence was in the attempt to do so and was the first step toward transcending. It was the Druids (Dyfed had been told) that had imposed an aberration of the originally established order of Arete upon the Earth. Yet these Druids were the ones who had first forgotten the truths that had manifested not only during the time of the Hyperborean race before them, but even before that, during the time of the supreme god concept, or Saturn, the golden age of the ancients. So, these elf-like folks he saw flitting in the shadows were also closely related to those ancients pre-transcending ones in some special articulated way. And whose colourful jongleurs (bards) that lived among them still, balanced their equilibrium that was their defence for change that they knew was ever coming. And Manandan, he remembered, spoke of a genuine default race or clan who knew more secrets about the phenomena of the present around them in the third density than others did, and it wasn't the modern Druid. Finally, Dyfed would soon discover that many of these darker people, who now faced a gigantic variation in the world around them to come, would provide a bridge, though they were not destined to survive. But their legacy (which their jongleurs would leave us in the magic words of their language) would. And that would be enough.

Then on that same evening which was born from a sky of fiery red with a yellow land unfolding in shadows below upon the path he rode, Dyfed slipped into a strange consciousness. Here he subsequently discovered deep in his psyche something he had never experienced before. With a first hand reflection to guide him he saw how terrible a thing man could be. For terrible it is when humanoids look into the eyes of other humans (or even just any old creature such as a wolf or a horse, or the family dog) and see fear in their eyes as they look back at us constantly word-game-babbling Homo sapiens. For millions of years we have been brothers who have developed form side by side within

---

14 Fear in this instance is akin to reverence or respect.
15 Wodan is the wolf rider who is the ancient equivalent of the Norse Odin. Anciently, these gods were symbols only.

and alongside the vibration that makes up all that live on this earth. Together we are an intrinsic part of our animal/mammal life-cycle-sharing force created in the image of the Eternal Being of the Divine Ground that Good Mother Nature represents and symbolizes. But, to realize the great pitiless that there are certain humans who feel no tenderness and empathy for other forms of life when they see and realize the fear in their eyes is to finally see the forest for the trees. And it come down to just how clearly one sees how other species of life sees you is to know and recognize the sacrilege to life itself by failing to attempt any rescue towards these lesser and gentler beings. Discrepancy in this is the antithesis of life. For truly Dyfed saw that these creature hereabouts of the forest clearly saw that the moderns had no wish to share with them and that the modern man also considered that all there is and will be was theirs and not the folks of the forest. Nor do we even accredit them any value towards life's worth, or value what they represent in their own uniqueness. This is a bad thing; but when we ourselves bring about a condition within an environment into which Good Mother Nature has placed us both, but in which we have manipulated an advantage, and for them to witness at that point our plan now for their senseless destruction, even to see that recognition in their lesser sense of awareness of them looking into us and see in our minds that they do not even deserve life, that is something else: it is a great crime against unforgiving Nature itself.

What a pity how it alienates the modern wo/man (the perpetrator) into a singularity that rotates around an attitude of egotistical singular presence where the life (and love of life) that animates the vibration of the universe becomes absent and we experience, through our own deceptive, causational cycle that we are (and have long being) unable to control; that is, an eternal and ever lasting spiral into death with is nothingness. What pangs of guilt/fear/horror to which we have become oblivious when we lack in not even seeing in those creatures searching eyes — eyes that must look up to us but see only — that we give them no inherited right to exist?

With no spirit of love for (or desired companionship with) other life forms, that is when the will of creatures gives out. If they are dependant on our vibration, and we are their future, yet we are pathetic and not sympathetic in any way, then there is no future for them. Nor, perhaps, do we have a future beyond this state ourselves. The others no longer look to us for acknowledgement and acceptance as companions who walk this phenomenon of the present together. So it is at this point they wish only to dis-continue their existence here. This is what we have caused. For in sensing they are not wanted... their only desire, their only defence, their only dignity is to escape our reality and us by dying to this world.

This is the condition that was about to overtake these dark people of Albion, albeit with extenuating circumstances that bring dire consequences not only to them but all men. Dyfed saw this now. He was to learn during his life that certain slick, greedy humans — people Manandan referred to as the Haploids – who always seem to win the day, would be watched by many life forces which (knowing finally that it was unwanted) gasped its last breath in a final submission of futility. This was why an alternate system to those who seemingly controlled the present was so badly needed.

At this juncture the wagon train (its journeying companions and Dyfed, its lone rider) passed out of Albany and into the ancient kingdom of Lloegia, a part of mystical Albion on the fringe of habitation. Its northern border here was the river Trent and the Humber estuary that did not include most of the low range of mountains that ran from here to the north. Here (slightly away from the forested, undulating land that was infested with dark savages and the innumerable packs of large, grey, ferocious wolves who howled and roamed, unchecked), Publius Maximus the civil servant came back into his own. Here he found again his quickly accusing falsetto voice and his fast and flitting feet, so to speak. Quickly, and in a lavish tongue, as they pulled into Caer Victrix for the night, he called out from his wagon-carriage to Dyfed, who had arrived much earlier and was watching them pull in, and invited him to accompany he and Gaius Julius over the duration of their stop. These two, so it appeared, were set to submerge themselves in the bathes, the taverns with the finest foods and wine found in the area, and in the establishments at large which house the fanciest and most beautiful of whores. But in this they were to be quickly stopped fast in their tracks. Victrix was still a provincial military fort with muddy streets: it was a soldier facility (for goodness sake) on the empire's northern most frontier that lay cheek to jowl with wretched forests, savage natives and was the epitome of all what raw un-sophistication entails. The waterfront of the town was the river Dee that until recently had been a dangerous march (border-land) between ancient Albion and its wild, western inhabitants, the Degangli, the Ordivices and others. And still it was a dangerous place after dark. Where in the world did Maximus think he was that it could produce such a glamorous brothel? Military brothels were anything but glamorous. But rather than a stark decline, Dyfed hinted that he might catch them up later; he didn't elaborate.

Victrix was a fort town full of soldiers; many of them by this time were Sarmatian.[16] And as soldiers needed to be kept happy a tiny section of Deva (known as the amusement centre) was a popular hot spot. It was here that Dyfed encountered an acquaintance from the past before avoiding Publius and Gaius. It was at one of the few wine, beer and spirit houses complete with live entertainment that were available to men with a denarius or two in his pocket and for any military service-book carrying soldier to patronize. Entering one of the taverns Dyfed immediately spotted the familiar figure sitting with his back to the wall quaffing back grog. It was Festus the Harmonious blacksmith, of all people.

"Ay-op!' said Dyfed upon approaching. He immediately sat down opposite him. 'Well, if it isn't Festus the blacksmith. Or is it Caradog also known as Karatakos? Yes, yes; of course, that's it. King Karatakos. Dear me. You mistakenly gave me the wrong name last we met, old chap. How jolly forgetful of you. I say!'

Dyfed had not cracked a smile as he spoke and immediately proceeded on to another topic. It was as if they hadn't finished the last one they were discussing before they parted a number of years earlier. The blacksmith stared at Dyfed with incredulousness and alarm that prompted Dyfed to laugh out loud.

Immediately the two men then caught up on news; Dyfed's story of his sojourn to Caer Legion (formerly Caer Lugus) spilled effortlessly out and included Ceredwyn while Karatakos (who told him with a Cheshire grin of the cat that ate the canary) that it was a shame about his first love but added nothing else of why and how he came to be there. This led to a discussion about whether or not the XXth Legion Valeria Victrix was being pulled out of its make-shift home here in Deva Victrix and whether or not Macsen

---

16 Ethnically Persian: [Sarmatians were a people of Iran or Aryan origin] and similar to and culturally much like the folks of the Indus (or Inja) River Valley that may also include certain Slavic peoples and even modern day Farsi.

Wledig's (who was now calling himself Pater Bricus) next move would be against Cornelius or Paulinius now that he was going to be in command of that the IXth Legion?

"And, as I'm sure you know,' Dyfed said, 'Cornelius (*the unfelix*) is still holed up there with his IXth Legion Hispana stirring the pot while adding (from time to time) a wing of bat and eye of newt to the broth. This, even while Marg now has full charge of King Ryan?'

"Dyvie, me boy. How did you come to acquire any of this information?' Karatakos asked him in astonishment. He had (of course) recognized the impetuous juvenile immediately. 'My understanding is,' he said, 'that Pater Bricus has taken himself off to Legion with half of the XXth Legion in an attempt to usurp King Ryan's bid to form an extended federation. Of course I have no way of knowing if it's happened or whether it will happen. And I've just learned about this only since I've been back.' He winked at Dyfed who felt slightly affronted by the gesture.

"How could you learn that?' Dyfed asked.

"From the high king, of course. From King Kunobelin. He knows everything, you know. Nothing escapes him. Unfortunately, I forgot to ask him what Bricus was going to do with the XXth Legion.'

"As far as Pater Bricus is concerned,' Dyfed volunteered, 'there is no news that any of this was going to be attempted, never mind accomplished. King Ryan however did marry Queen Marg after she received her coronation to replace Queen Carmanda. And this after Ryan broke up my marriage plans with Ceredwyn. But whether this has stymied Pater Bricus, it's probably too early to tell. If that is the case with Bricus, however, his plans to thwart a federation with the western tribes certainly hadn't been successful up to a few days ago. But with the XXth Legion at his side, and maybe Cornelius' IXth as well, this will give him a leg-up.'

"Under Ryan's leadership this federation, along with the might of the Brigantes (whose allegiance he has married into) may fair pretty good,' said Karatakos. Here he scratched his head and one eye seemed extraordinary bright and sharp, the other glazed over, as he briefly stared into space. 'But if Cornelius isn't by his side then we will have a new front on our ever expanding occupation and either two civil wars happening at once will ensue or both the XXth and the IXth Legions will be at our throats. Yes, Dyvie. I know all about Carmen, and you may be very wrong about her puppet Marg.' Karatakos was now smiling to himself and appeared to be remembering something. Dyfed waited for more.

'If Bricus commands the XXth, and I'm not so sure he does or will, he would begin to look south and west for land gains but mostly south in an effort to consolidate a vast kingdom with or without the Amoran IXth Legion on board. And you can bet your bottom denarius that this would be a kingdom that Ryan would immediately want to take away from him, I can tell you that! And pending where Cornelius stood, the resulting turmoil would benefit Paulinius and even help the renegade Cornelius' out. It would also fit in well with the empire's policy of westward advance into Gwynedd (Gwyneth) again, which is their agenda. And where would that leave Bricus? Eh? Yes, it looks local, but this may be all Amor's doing' he said.'

"Then I think Bricus is toast' Dyfed added, laughing. 'He's hooped — finished. Finished if he doesn't ally with Amoran interests now. But he will never get his foot in the door up north or have a good night's sleep down south again without looking furtively over his shoulder. Rumour has it though that his manager Blazingwolf has sent away to Europa for a Saxen king to aid them. On top of that, King Ryan is going to have his hands full with Queen Marg, his new wife and partner in regency. He won't have time to organize anything while she's on board.

"If what you say is true,' answered Karatakos, 'I agree with your estimation, there. Unless Cornelius has sided with Pater Bricus at the convocation last year, then there's fat change of success. Rumour has it too that the Saxen king whom Bricus is soliciting is a certain King Verika, but Verika's dance card is full. Apparently, Bricus is not the only one trying to entice him over. At the moment he's fighting for Bricus' cousin Ateula in Armorica against our ally King Ban. Ban's only son and heir, a boy named Galhad, is being evacuated from Armorica, as we speak, and is headed for Queen Marg. You could call it Fate,' he said.

"So now Ryan will have a teenage step-son to contend with as well,' said Dyfed. 'Won't that be fun!

"Well,' answered Karatakos, 'my understanding is that young step-son will remain with Marg under her charge until further notice, or at such time he is deemed an adult. And that could be years, if ever. However, my further understanding is that the marriage between Marg and Ryan was a hoax. That is they were married, you were there, Dyfed, but she will have nothing whatsoever to do with him, at all. Apparently, he did not know about those terms. Ha! And one other thing,' he said. 'Ryan may be Carmen's creature, Dyvie, but I doubt Marg is. And I'm more certain than I am of anything that Marg is no fit to be Ryan's wife other than on some flimsy scrap of paper. Oh yes, Dyvie, she's a quick one that one and documents mean nothing to her. And yes, she is exactly what any intelligent king wouldn't want in a queenly wife, or Carmen as an influential surrogate mother-in-law, especially if she was still above ground.' But she has no sway over Marg, that's fo' sho!' Karatakos slurred in his customary way.

"Furthermore,' stated Karatakos, 'I can't imagine any reason why she would want to tie herself up in a queen ship, never mind be married to a rogue like Ryan, unless there is another and more important ploy afoot. Believe me, I know Marg,' he said. 'Now, I think I know just the person to help you. Once you get to Camulod you must look up King Kunobelin. You can't miss him for he lives in a big palace in the centre of town. Ask anyone. Tell him I, Karatakos sent you.' Reaching into his pocket he gave Dyfed a gold token. He then told Dyfed that he was happy to see that he was underway, and that he would relay that information that back (as he had put it) to our people. 'What do you call them, eh Dyvie, the Lodge of Huge? I'll be in touch,' he told him as they parted, 'so stay the course, Dyvie, and keep your wits about you.'

(Tasciovanus the defeated king and Boodikka the defeated queen)

'To recognize untruth as a condition of life: that is certainly to impugn the traditional ideas of value in a dangerous manner, and a a philosophy which ventures to do so, has thereby alone placed itself beyond good and evil.'
FRIEDRICH NIETZSCHE

The following morning before dawn Dyfed left on the next leg of his journey that was to take him from *Deva* Victrix to Viroconium. Again, he was accompanying the coach train that was destined ultimately for Nova Troia. However, there had now been two new carriages added to the caravan and one of them was turning off for Camulod. So Dyfed then stored his luggage on the top of that particular carriage; 'the carriage to Camulod' was what his luggage ticket receipt said. As they set out Dyfed recalled that Karatakos had been very keen to find out how he was getting along. Although he had not introduced Dyfed to anybody nor had Dyfed seen him in anybody else's company during their two day stop-over, which like their last meeting he thought was odd, still he felt through a sixth sense that the man had not been there alone.

After Viroconium the weather became overcast with a light rain falling. Dyfed headed south on an old and worn commercial artery that had originally been built about three centuries before. The initial architect of this turnpike had been King Belinus who (long ago) had once besieged the city of Amor itself. On that occasion Belinus had left his brother Brennus behind to rule over Amor for a time as a tyrant while he returned to Albion. Amor had never forgotten that, which was why they were wrecking havoc now, he thought. It was pay back time for the Kelts of the northwest. But on this occasion, if the Prydains of Albion and the Isles in general were receptive, the Amorans brought something with them that could benefit Prydain. This was a new mechanized organization. These Albionians (also Prydains) could receive something now from Amor that (in the fairly near future) would give them a leg up and cast the die that would catapult the folks of these isles into their own glory ride toward supremacy in the future.

Currently, though, the track leaving Deva Victrix for Viroconium was sketchy and rough, but there were plans for an upgrading to extend Watling Street further from Viroconium into the heart of the Cornovii peoples. But if the new and recent replacement emperor wanted to achieve this, then for that to happen Paulinius needed Cornelius to return the IXth Legion back into the fold. So, at this time the high street of Watling essentially ran from Durovernum by the Swale on the south shores of the Tems Estuary in the south eastern section of Albion, then crossed the bridge over the River Tems at Nova Troia and continued in a north western route to Fort Viroconium which now housed the XIVth Legion that had been sent there from Lindum Colonia. From Viroconium the next Amoran centres on the road south were Leto and then Venonis. Venonis was commonly called High Cross because it was at this point that Watling Street crossed the only other large military artery in Albion, the Fosse Way. The Fosse linked

Isca in the southwest to Lindum Colony in the northeast. That road, too, had also been originally built by that former mentioned olden day Prydainian king, Belinus. Between Durovernum to High Cross (Venonis), a few hard dirt tracks spider-webbed out every which way mostly to rural communities or mining and logging projects. The Amorans had been amazed to discover the well maintained remnants of a number of ancient roads (old straight tracks) that still criss-crossed the country straight as a die. These were the same roads that Amoran engineers were currently re-surveying and incorporating into their own road-grid system.

From Venonis Dyfed continued south east (keeping well west of the fens) and on to Verulamium where he turned left onto the last stretch of road that would eventually take him to Camulod. It was an arduous journey but easier on horseback than riding in a coach. The area of Albion through which he was now travelling was the home of the Catu-Wellauni people — the battle chieftains — and their defeated king, Tasciovanus. Verulamium had once been their chief tribal village. They called it Verulam. This village site had much changed since the Amoran occupation. Recently it was converted into a municipium and made into a regular town by the Amorans: But recently its battlements had been destroyed by the Ikeni queen Boodikka (also known as Queen Buddug in these parts). Verulam was still in a ruinous state at this time though now under repair on standing orders from the new Amoran emperor, a certain Nero Claudius Kysar Augustus Germanicus. It was he (though more likely suggested by his chief engineer of Public Works here in the Province of Britainnia — formerly Prydain) who decreed that important junctions, along with infrastructure in general, be maintained in a good state of repair.

Verulamium was a real, bona fide, organized Amoran town in the process of being tidied up and was the first Amoran town of its kind that Dyfed had ever seen. He wondered how change of this sort was affecting the locals who were witnessing major disruptions within their lives and their culture that was taking place before their very own eyes. After all, they hadn't been exposed to anything like the palatial abodes of the power elite along with the men that inhabited those palatial abodes and organized and controlled Pax Amoran's civil order and construction: And this order was controlled by men not unlike Maximus (Publius the Purse). Like Maximus they were ego driven and their natures tended toward a life of ease and luxury before turning their attention toward simplified greed, sloth and occasionally the art of highly organized and thought-out debauchery. They were Amoran alpha males of the empire, after all! Already, apparently, the vision of continuity that underpinned any noble ideal that could have been intrinsic to the people of this land had faded from memory.

Generally, the hoi polloi, whether they were Albionian, Amoran or Gaulish, were modest, honest and hard working. But with the Amoran arrival there was bound to be a big change. As Dyfed saw it (though the Amorans thought differently, if they thought about it at all) in time the locals would absorb the Amorans and much of their culture could commingle and be entangled. In the meantime, despite the psychological maturity of the crimes being brought to bear upon them, crimes against humanity, the flip side of what Amor was apparently bringing them now would ultimately be deemed a default indemnify. Such compensation, though, would be caused and brought about by the innate cultural resolve of the native folk of these isles. Therefore, rather than remaining strangely unperturbed at the abuse and marginalization which they suffered throughout their whole lives, outnumbering the Amorans allowed them (with their resolve for liberty to effect their own Idea) to correct, change and gradually and quietly restore much of their own culture, yet in an Amoran sort of way. So even though the former appeared to be puerile and socially childlike compared at least to the Amoran aristocrat, it wasn't quite like that. Interestingly, in their civilized culture all men (other than the Amorans, of course) parted their hair, even though their hair was sometimes greasy and matted and their appearance was somewhat shabby. To be sure, a civil order had also existed here for millennium for them too. And like Amorans they had been marred by plagues and starvation that was not unusual for anybody in this world, outside of pockets of Hyperborean resorts that were once camouflaged and secretly hidden away. In any case they were a contrast to the not so sweet-smelling and coiffured Amorans themselves whose traditional hair-do affected no part whatsoever, and if not shaved clean and bald, their 'do' was the combed down in every direction from the crown.

From Verulamium the wagon train took a left turn and headed northeast. Then at Braughing the coaches he was shadowing turned right and headed east for Camulod while he, anxious to explore some more, struck off on his lonesome own. He continued straight on northeast toward the Icknield Way. This tract led to the Metaris Estuary (The Great Wash) and Branodunum. He was instructed to continue until he came upon the River Cam where he must take a right turn and follow a miserable track south east that would lead him on a round about journey to Camulod. As the Prince of the Grove (who was never lonely or alone in the forests and the wilds) neared the River Cam he came to some ruined and nameless remnants of a vast and ancient civilized city that at first he took to be an abandoned fifth dimension resort. This artefact was nestled in the Gog Magog hills around whose feet skirted the River Ouse.

The residue of this ancient citified domesticity (though virtually destroyed as it was) had an appearance similar to the one where this Earth born Son had originated on the Isle of Peace. But today this spot was nothing more than an elaborately decorated crossroads that had been converted into a large caravansary with a spring fed watering hole that probably contributed to its popularity. Once this resort had been glorious, now, it was blown to seed. From here he turned right and followed one of the heavily worn ancient spokes (embedded deeply into the landscape) that radiated out from here in four directions. He followed the track leading southeast that had a pointer marked *Camulos*, the name of an islander god.

The Amorans had altered the Keltic name Camulos into Camulod which was what they called this colonia he was heading for. It had once been build on top of a Trinonantes' sacred mound honouring the god Camulos. Currently (as Dyfed was about to find) upon a holy and sacred spot in the centre of this colonia town was the building site for a monumental temple intending to be dedicated to the recently demised Emperor Claudius who had pioneered the Amoran settling here in Albion. This building promised to be much more grandeur which for the Amorans guaranteed greater permanence. Camulod (often mispronounced as Camelot in the annals of romantic fables of charismatic nonsense which subsequently arose) was the first major habitation that the Amorans had coveted and settled into upon their permanent arrival in Prydain. It was here that the terra sigillata pottery-ware industry was stationed as well as where huge, newly erected Amoran brick making factories were concentrated.

Dyfed's ultimate destination was Nova Troia, the more recent capital of the Trinovantes. But as Karatakos had extended to him an invitation to visit Kunobelin and because Queen Carmanda had provided him with a letter of introduction to this unlikely of allies, he had resolved to detour and make his way here first. This venerable man known as Kunobelin Rex had been a great king who, long before the Amoran occupation, had opened trade with Amor. Dyfed learned that the king had imported fine wines and olive oil from Italia, glassware, tableware and jewellery from the Trinovantes' Belgaeic cousins across the channel, and vessels of paste and sauces made from fish and spiced legumes from Hispania. He also exported to Amor certain goods that were in high demand such as grain, gold, silver, iron, hides, and slaves. The latter were almost always local criminals or unwanted immigrants. Almost all of this commerce passed through the port approximate to Camulod. Nova Troia and the broad sea-lane that led to it (the Tems river) was somewhat secondary but gaining favour now that that city was finally being fortified. Indeed, its fortification was what had stalled the rebuilding of Camulod after the Boodikka revolt.

So, upon arriving at colonia Camulod and clearing customs (validating that his presence there wouldn't pose a risk to the military post), it was directly then to the palace of Kunobelin that Dyfed rode up and halted before on his prancing Andalusians. Here he looked around him at the burnt cinder under the rebuild being hastily conducted by civic works that was in process. However, it was a delayed process still stuck between planning and excavating the second stage. Just like at the tiny town of Legion, Camulod's walls were still being re-constructed which were meant to replace the earlier earthen embankments. And even though the town had been the official provincial military capital for some time, once again, it was abuzz under the hew and draw of labour (if not the cry and clang-racket of general construction) and of some limited commerce.

He arrived at the palace that appeared empty. Kunobelin was a private man. The king answered the door himself, then accepting and inspecting Dyfed's letter from Carmen, he invited this tall, silver-eyed lad in. He immediately informed Dyfed (who he thought would be interested to know) that he had recently sent an embassy to Amor complaining of Paulinius' inefficiencies which resulted in Queen Boodikka's revolt that killed a lot of people including Amorans right here in Camulod. He himself, he told Dyfed, had even had to evacuate the town. And no, he had not been aware of the arrival recently of a wagon train containing the luggage Dyfed was asking about which was supposed to have been dropped off here.

Nobody had dropped anything off here at the palace, the king told Dyfed. Dyfed was never to see his belongings again. What he owned was what he was wearing along with his two beautiful Andalusians.

Anyway, it appeared that Dyfed's arrival had interrupted the king who was preparing to ship a pack of hunting dogs to be presented to Nero the newly appointed emperor in Amor. Their arrival, he thought (he informed Dyfed), might persuade Nero to favour Kunobelin's petition to sack Paulinius and replace him by appointing Karatakos as a legate here instead. After all, he told Dyfed, convention is only a guideline and is useful when nobody has a better idea. Not only that, he added, when King Karatakos was captured during an earlier Kelt /Amoran skirmish. He had then been taken to Amor in chains to face Emperor Claudius. He was sentenced to death by strangulation after having his legs and arms broken, but his demeanour so impressed Claudius that he pardoned him. Claudius and Karatakos got on so famously well that after he was released the emperor invited him to stay in Amor and keep him company for the rest of his life. Wisely, once freed Karatakos left the City of Amor immediately returned to Albion. However, that is another story. Before Dyfed had even been invited to sit down and have a beverage to slake his dry throat, King Kunobelin launched into the story of the recent uprising and told Dyfed that Queen Boodikka (though it wasn't common knowledge) remained at house arrest where she is currently under suicide prevention watch. Again, apparently (according to the establishment's version of the story) this was due to extreme depression she incurred following the Amoran failure to honour their agreed peace terms. Kunobelin, however, said he thought it was because Amoran officials had repeatedly raped her.

"So then,' said King Kunobelin, raising his arms and then slapping them down together with a loud smack onto his top thighs, 'as to encourage Nero to favour this plan, I've instructed my envoys to make the plea to replace Paulinius name for Karatakos' name, putting mine down as a second.'

He then informed Dyfed that the hunting dogs he was intending to send the emperor, as presents were his way of sweetening the pot and was also sent courtesy of Karatakos. Kunobelin was not such a fool that he couldn't feel the power of Amor, complicated with the idiosyncrasies of the new psychopath in the Imperial Palace, as well as the cool weather in the wind which blew towards his island home from there. A renewed revolt at this time, he thought, was dangerous, possibly almost as dangerous as the emperor himself. Boodikka was proof of that. And as far as his erstwhile stepson Karatakos (who had been poking around in the west country recently stirring up god knows what), the king had to find something worthwhile for him soon so as to keep him out of trouble. As far as taking on the job as legate, Kunobelin told Dyfed that the man could do it standing on his head. Then with a troubling trend that snaked across his face for a moment, Kunobelin (in a manner to reinforce his conviction) stated that before his arrest Karatakos had taken on the task of attempting to repel the IInd Legion Augusta; the IXth Legion Hispana; the XIVnth Legion Gemina; and the XXth Legion Valeria Victrix from conducting incursions onto his sovereign territory. But on the bright side he had added that even if he hadn't put the run on the Amoran incursions exactly, at least the legions had ultimately failed in that endeavour when the revolt ensued.

And the king continued to inform Dyfed that at the start of this turmoil it had been the jealous client legate Pater Bricus that had initially sold Kunobelin out to Paulinius to ingratiate himself to the proconsul. And Paulinius was still there, but it was time for new blood.

Then, Dyfed reflected, much of this had taken place since he had set out for Legion from Hardlech.

As Dyfed's stay lengthened from an extended weekend into months, King Kunobelin (who warming to him) had willingly taken him in and offered him many things in addition to valuable information. There were other reasons too that Kunobelin took to Dyfed, but the latter had not been cognizant of them. Kunobelin continued on to tell Dyfed that upon the Amoran's arrival and their firm purchase upon their land, his son had to flee Nova Troia for his life. And as Camulod was also swarming with Amorans, he took himself west. Kunobelin soon joined Karatakos there in the western wilds, he told Dyfed. Later, at the head of the Silures and the Decangli armies fighting against

Publius Scapula who was making incursions into the west, the former King Karatakos led the initial attack. Scapula's campaign there was successful but indecisive. In trying to keep one step ahead of the Amoran law that he publicly defied, and in trying to stay out of the clutches of Bricus in particular, Karatakos (Kunobelin told Dyfed) finally fled the west country and wended his way north toward Queen Carmen's domain and the land of the Carvetii. This had taken place some time before Dyfed had made Karatakos' acquaintance in his disguise as a blacksmith. When their two paths had finally crossed at the little cenedl called Bangor (the place of the Gangani people alongside Karatakos' hot, choking furnace and anvil), it was during his second flight there to warn the western kings along with the Druids, who Karatakos was hoping to enlist as well. He wanted the latter to help cast spells before the armies of the Amorans and their invasion to the West Country that was just about to happen. It wasn't so much a plan to help the Druids as frighten off the Amorans who feared the Druid spells. The casting of evil spells is best done to their face, he informed Dyfed.

"Of course,' Kunobelin explained, 'Karatakos, along with the rest of us know that casting spells and such is all hocus pocus mumbo-jumbo. However,' he said, 'the Amorans believed it and feared the Druids for it. It helped. Not much but a little,' he said. Then for a second time he had tried to flee north to Queen Carmanda where a convocation was about to unfold between Cornelius and some local kings. But unfortunately Karatakos was captured crossing the Dee River. So, as is generally thought, it had not been Queen Carmanda who had betrayed him, Kunobelin told Dyfed, it was Bricus who had finally caught him up. Then once the bound and wretched Karatakos reached Nova Troia he was handed over this time to Paulinius. Then (so he informed Dyfed, in the absence of his step-son, Kunobelin then took up the title of Rex for himself, once more, and returned to Nova Troia to make peace with the Amorans in which he was quite successful in doing. There were concessions, of course, but he did managed to retain his palace here in Camulod. He was also able to maintain another well-appointed townhouse mansion in Nova Troia that had been recently built. His governing palace by the river embankment, however, had been destroyed during the invasion and revolt and the land confiscated by Amor for the proconsul's newly built palace in Nova Troia. His new palace (the king told Dyfed) was situated just south of the city's north boundary wall (earthen bank) and adjacent to the temple of Harmony and Concordance. An amphitheatre and some baths were also close by, he told the young prince. It's decent but not up to your standards, the king had said to him. The king then told Dyfed that he wanted the lad to take up these premises as his own home.

"Now,' said Kunobelin, 'tell me your story, Dyfed.'

(Haploid versus the troll within)

"For children are innocent and love justice while most of us are wicked, and naturally prefer mercy."

G. K. CHESTERTON

At the moment of his birth, Dyfed told Kunobelin (the re-appointed High king of Albion), it was said that a vast wedge of migrating White Fronted geese (Anser albifrons) — nesting on a nearby sea marsh — lifted off to catch the first rays of Dawn. This was immediately after Lord Huge the magician who, in fulfilling his agreed upon condition for his residency status at the resort of the Isle of Peace with Manandan, had just successfully completed fabricating the magical veil (that misty curtain) which he conjured forth and wrapped around Dyfed's Isle in order to cordon it off from any prying and intrusive eyes of alien foreigners at large. This furthered to protect Queen Violet-Eye and he himself, her newborn prince.

Those alien foreigners, it was known, were strange folks who despite Aristoteles, Socrates and other prophets of wisdom, were without a meaningful system of law and justice and whose prejudice was raw and closer to the fire of fear that stemmed from the days of long ago. Thus the ensuing psychological fear followed well-worn tracks for it was ancient and historical among big-brained animals of the earth. Manandan had taught Dyfed about this, the latter explained, and said that it was ingrained into the original archetypical psyche of these alien foreigners' (both Kelt and Amoran) current prejudice, their judge-mentalist and condescending attitude combined with hatred which manifested towards others. Abaris the Hyperborean medical scientist called it the kunderbuffer syndrome. He borrowed this term from another member of the third dimensional-dwelling society of Hyperboreans (subsequently to be called the *pack*). This flamboyant individual was a certain Urartian (Chaldean) of the city of Kumayri (Gyumri) that was named after the Cimmerians and was situated in the northern part of Urartu (Ararat). This man's name was Beelzebub Gurdjiev, but he took other names as time went on. This city, where the aforementioned Gurdjiev set out to fulfil his duties and obligations to the *pack*, was where the home fires later burned in the summer palace residence of the Achaemenid emperor, the largest empire in ancient history.

In any case, Manandan and the masters on the Isle of Peace were not deluded into thinking that if the foreigners did manage to pierce the misty rainbow veil, that these frightful visitors at large from outside could be convinced to leave their nasty habits and ridiculous tales and hyperbole at the door. And the result for their quiet yet luxurious resort (set aside for the dimension travelling Masters of the Little Known Universe) would be disastrous.

"This resort,' said Dyfed to King Kunobelin, 'that was run by Manandan, verily thrived around the Queen Violet-Eye come-lately, my mother. Manandan was her vizier and chief functionary. He didn't inherit this functionary affiliation with her, though, not until after Lord Huge (as already stated) had fled the Isle of Peace when his craftsmanship as a magician had failed. For this failure had voided his perpetually ensuing contract that was needed to meet the condition for his residency upon the isle. But Master Manandan, Sage and Adept were really more than just a vizier or a functionary for my mother. But let me set that aside for now and relate that story later.'

It was also said, he continued, that the earlier mentioned geese had had to circle the isle five times counter clockwise before piercing the newly fabricated veil of fog that Lord Huge had so expertly placed there, at least for the time being. Anyway, Dyfed told him, that on the day of his birth, Queen Violet (carrying him in a sling close to her bared breasts) was puttering and wandering through her beloved garden basking in the sun when all of a sudden King Pel, a fellow ruling over his clients, the Kornovi folks, along with his nephew, Prince Penrhyn (a long time administrator of the tin mines in the land of the Dunmonii), suddenly arrived unannounced on the Isle of Peace. These two men (as probably already mentioned) were not rough ashlars with nasty tales and frightful habits such as what the hoi polloi usually embodied. Indeed, Dyfed told the king, they had even helped him in his education.

Its important to remember that the events which are taking place here at this time all happened during the beginning of the last quarter of the hoi polloi's fifth and final age which existed on the bountiful good Earth (of the world of our narrative) only in the third dimension. And it is now important to state that it was at this time that Dyfed Lucifer had been born at the Isle of Peace resort in that third dimension, just as the rough and archetypical hoi polloi had. But unlike them, he had the advantage of a Hyperborean nurture that included its education. By Dyfed's reckoning, the hoi polloi — the failures of transcendence and transformation — had been left out in the cold and the dark without the Masters of the Little Known Universe's close scrutiny and general guidance for well over nine thousand solar cycles by this time. That was back in what was called the Young Dryas period.

After the sciences, Manandan ventured to teach the child Dyfed about the world of men outside the enclave of the Isle of Peace. Now that he had graduated beyond the world of his benefactors, our young hero had been quick to discern that there was quite a disconnect between his own awareness of the Ideas which helped him sketch out the phenomena at large compared to that of the hoi polloi. It was obvious to him now that those unlucky fellows had been easily fooled and taken in to the fold of ideological, historical and religious confidence men. As a result they were ignorant of their true non-self's self and lived most (if not all) of their life in a state of waking sleep. The non-self was also called the projected self or reflection self. Love and compassion for fellow life forms was a way of life for the Hyperboreans. Love and compassion germinates knowledge of the great wheel. This wheel (chakra) is the universal levelling agent for all living creatures. This wheel (cakra in *Sanskrit*) is the powerful agent of energy for the psycho-spiritual constituents (or subtle, non physical body) of living beings and corresponds to a subtle plane of existence in a vast chain of being that culminates in the physical form of the sentient being. The knowledge thereof behoved the masters to reach out to certain tame, calm and seemingly rational hoi polloi who after being vetted and orientated, were given employment and were pulled into the fold of the masters where they were well treated.

Outside of this latter environment (despite its advantage) and in the world to which Dyfed was reaching out now and moving toward, he was subject to the nothingness of that world of those of common atrophied types as well as with the nightmares of their waking sleep, nonetheless. It was all around him, despite the fact that the hoi polloi were descended from those of he and his mother's own ancient race. They had simply not been able to transcend beyond this dimension and become masters. He marvelled that having been born himself in the third dimension he was really one of them. How different, though, he thought he was from them. That difference was his nurturing which placed him into contact with knowledge of the wheel. .

'And since we, the Masters of the Little Known Universe,' Dyfed then told King Kunobelin what Manandan had told him on their last parting. That was about the 'desire of the Masters of the Unknown Universe to rectify the disgraceful and disastrous state of affairs among humans here in this dimension. Furthermore, Dyfed had learned, that this had become his *reason d'etre*. You, Dyvie, Manandan had told him, were given birth here in this condition for that purpose. But mark you this is a dangerous mission that has been chosen for you to undertake, if in fact you choose to comply. You aren't the first hybrid, but others have recently failed and were destroyed. And you must also know that you are going to be constantly in danger in a similar manner to those of the hoi polloi whose lives are filled with remorse, suffering and misery. That is danger enough, but there is more. There are trolls at large, too. In this murky environment.'

"Now Manandan also talked to me about the Haploids of whom I must quickly become aware,' Dyfed said to Kunobelin.

To reiterate, they were ancient humanoid Homo-sapiens (hoi polloi) but who are different from the Masters in that they did not graduate into advanced awareness to meld with the Master Mind, as did the Masters of the Little Know Universe. However, they do have a unique advantage over the hoi polloi. Somehow, so Manandan explained, a small faction of these under graduates — freaks actually — did transcend (somewhat) due to some flaw or other. This gave them some limited capabilities of a higher order but they were degenerate and, for want of a better term, barren, or futile. These are the Haploids. However, due to the aforementioned on-going incompetence of the gullible and illogical little mind provided by the material brain in the hoi polloi, the Haploids (when in the same phenomena as the hoi polloi) could stump or pull the wool over the eyes of the latter with little effort. So now the hoi polloi not only had their own ill-equipped mind which generally ran the show for them in this current phenomena, they also had the Master Mind (which exists outside the subtle being and can be confused with the ego which it resembles but is not part of) downloading data from its probe mind and causing it some confusion. There was also the fantasy of phenomenon to deal with. This made the hoi polloi's life here in this particular world uncomfortable and untenable in the long run. They should never let their guard down too long or be inattentive to the phenomenon around them lest trolls materialise out of thin air that's part and parcel of this phenomena. For in that case dangerous apparitions would quickly blend into their existence and make them suffer even more.

"Trolls,' Dyfed said, 'were a kind of material shadow, an unrealised potential which — having failed to graduate — existed only in the psyche of the subject and had become grafted or appendage somehow to the subtle being. This is what my tutor taught me. So, when a subject encounters a troll, it is actually themselves partially outside their dimension. But the hoi polloi don't know that. In fact the troll is a potential that is a spin off from the Master Mind. Each and every one of these hoi polloi sentient beings is a failed transcendent, hence the troll itself, which is a failed transformation. For every hoi polloi these trolls are a form of failed genius that, if things had panned out differently, could have had a Master Mind (chakra) connection that paid out in dividends to the former's condition. Aside from trolls there are those other aforementioned entities or beings similar to these trolls. They had been given the name Haploid, and are actually psychopaths on steroids. These entities are separate sentient beings who are destructive,' said Dyfed.

For his benefit, Dyfed told the king, Manandan told him that the Haploids are freaks of natural that somehow, in some way managed to effect a transcendence, as stated, without a proper transformation way. This was way back when. And this prevented them from properly accessing that higher awareness as the rest of them (the masters) had to achieve in order to achieve the Master Mind of their newly acquired level. The Haploids would always be a danger to him here in this dimension as they were to everybody. This, Dyfed had been warned, was to be un-fortuitous for him in his present state, for as of yet he had no proficiency to transcend into the security of the fifth dimension when danger approached as his mother and all the other masters were able to do. But on his behalf the masters would help him work on that, although, under the circumstances, it would not be easy, they said.

As it turned out there were still Haploids in the fifth dimension, Dyfed learned, but being somewhat fixed and compromised they posed no danger that the masters knew of. They are only dangerous here in this world where (once returned here) they are eternally fixed and cannot return to the fifth dimension or advance anywhere else. This is the end for them.

And already Dyfed was beginning to understand what Manandan meant when he explained to him that the masters enjoy this third dimension because of its heightened sensitivity to forms and frictions. For this reason they favour its distraction for rest and recreation. "In essence,' he told him, Dyfed said to Kunobelin, 'the habitants or enclaves for the masters who live here are basically pleasing pleasure-able palaces which is why we call them resorts.'

But long ago the masters noticed all the hoi polloi were dejected, disgruntled and miserable beyond their ignorant state while in the same dimension. But the masters knew that somehow it was a bubble. Soon they traced the reason to the hoi polloi's individual trolls; but more importantly they saw it to be the complication and co-existence of the Haploid presence in their midst, as well. The Haploids had used ingenious inventions that have proved successful and were the culprits who had indoctrinated the hoi polloi with what they call mythos and who heavily edited and distorted history. The masters now wanted to amend this condition in favour of those poor fellow sentient beings and to make them happy again. But that wouldn't happen they knew in a society plagued with sore anxiety and where the rolling thunders of war, the rainy skies of cultural/religious lies, and where heaps of hunger, debt, and scores of others miseries visit daily upon the human condition. "We would right that at all costs,' Manandan used to say, he told Kunobelin. 'And that's where you come in. So, here I am,' said Dyfed.'

(Camulod and the Troad)

'The realm of knowledge knows no boundaries.
ISLAMIC PROVERB

Dyfed had felt compelled (somehow) to tell the king his story for reasons he could not explain. Perhaps, he thought, it was the steady gaze of Kunobelin's hypnotic eyes. He noticed, however, that in the telling the old king's demeanour softened. His mask of wear and tear that etched across the old man's face was due (he thought) to the trials and trouble at hand that the old king needed to address. Maybe he was just then recalling his own childhood and the early days of manhood, Dyfed thought. Surely, there can be nothing more sweet to an old man as these. But there was something of a Master about him, too, he thought. Once, as the king embraced him, Dyfed sensed that the torc he wore (though covered by his shirt) seemed suddenly, he thought, to have momentarily lit up brightly as if in communication with something. This was in the manner of which the masters conducted their unseen magic. Dyfed could remember their torcs had somehow sprung into life. Having forgotten Manandan's promise that he would be watched over and that members of the *pack* of Hyperborean Masters would remain in communication for his duration in the third dimension, it had not dawned on him that they would communicate thus. In fact, Manandan as a parting gift gave him the torc that Dyfed wore. But like the ancestral ring he received from Violet-Eye, also as a parting gift (which, incidentally, she told him had been worn by his ancestors, and possibly even by Herakles or Apollo), he considered them to like mementos and worn more like bling. And while he was taking stock, he thought, other than the rich cloth from the Isle of Peace from which the clothes he stood in were tailored, that was all he had left of his former life. What he had gained since were encouraging words from three persons: Festus (or Hephaestus) the blacksmith he now knew as Karatakos, and a former high king of Albion, Morgant the Gnome and High King Kunobelin, along with advise, hospitality and encouragement. Reflection made Dyfed more attentive of his host after that.

Dyfed remained a guest of the king for almost two months. He felt comfortable in Camulod, and Kunobelin doted on him like Master Manandan had done. As already stated he also learned a great deal from the king about Amoran and Albionian confrontational politics (another peculiarity of these folks in the third density) which had a long and ancient history, and one which may get them all killed in the end. And he learned about the city of Camulod's involvement with this history.

Long before it had been called Camulod or Colonia Claudia (colony of Claudia) by the Amorans after their now deceased emperor Claudius, the city had once been an old centre and an ancient commercial hub (albeit a secondary one, if not even a tertiary hub) once known as Forty-Mile. This was because Camulod had once been a satellite town forty miles distant from the ancient and revered original (but now long destroyed) site of the first city of Troia. This is what Kunobelin told Dyfed. And in its hay day, Troia (nestled in the shadows of the Gog Magog hills near the flow of the River Cam and the River Ouse) was the commercial and military hub of the golden age of Albion then known as the Troad, controlled by the House of Troia. The city of Troad (Troia) as Dyfed now knew was that ancient and sophisticated remnant of advanced civilization that he had stumbled upon on his journey to Camulod that he had mistaken it for a Masters' of the Unknown Universe resort that now lay prostrate as a decayed roundel. It was the southeastern track of the cross roads located there at Troia that he had been directed to follow so as to bring him to Camulod. The Nova (New) Troia that now exists on the River Tems (he knew) came about much later. This new city, he was told, was about fifty Amoran miles distance from Camulod.

The story that Kunobelin relayed to Dyfed about the ancient and original city of Troia was familiar to Dyfed who had been taught all things of importance by his tutor. Apparently, Ilum, a descendant of Aeneas of the House of Troia, was the man who founded the ancient trade city of Troia. This was back in the early portion of the fifth age whose symbol of enlightenment was Bronze. The city existed for the sole purpose of facilitating the important tin trade to the then high-density population that was spread from the Seuvic Sea (now Baltic) in the north all the way south to Mount Calpe, which (being located in more modern day named Further Hispania by the Amorans) is also known as the northern Pillar of Herakles. And it was (and still is) the Straits of Herakles which merchant sailors transporting tin from Albion pass through in order to access the White Sea and her corresponding lands such as Nearer Hispania, Gallia Narbonenis, Sardinia, the now Province of Africa (Tunisia), the Island of Sicilia, the Italia Peninsula, the Land of Hellas, the Province of Asia, ancient Phoeniki in the Land of Canaan, and finally the Land of Khem. Tin was brought here to these places from the Dumnonii mines in order to wrought the valuable metal bronze. But at that time, long, long ago, the northern part of the continent of Europa was much more populated than the south. And this was the deal: the overland tin-shipping route from Albion was a shorter version of the much later Asian Silken Road. In this case its originating terminal was at Troia with access via the river Cam and Ouse to the Metaris Aestuary (the Wash Estuary). With a quick ferry transport across the strait to Gaul, wagon trains of both refined tin and tin ore bulk could spoke off in every direction except west from there. Once Troia was in place, then even the lesser-desired Phoeniki merchant marine trade could be controlled by the owners of these tin mines in Dumnonii. Through their limited port there at Dumnonii and their main terminal controlled by the House of Troia (including their overflow plant at Forty-Mile — now Camulod), the mine owners and the folks of the House of Troia had their fingers on the pulse of the rising Western Civilization of their time, much the way the Amorans have today. This time is known to the third dimensional world as the Age of Tin, for tin was the intrinsic ingredient for bronze.

Back in the early days during the Age of Bronze, the first city of Troia had grown to be the biggest hub of all. From the Troad, as the ancient kingdom there was called (whose capital was the main city of the Land of Troia, even before it was known as Albion) the House of Troia shipped their product throughout the known world. Aside from being shipped to the White Sea it travelled north to the Saxens and the Goths of Gotland and the Baltic shores. Although tin was mined in many parts, the bulk of which Europa consumed originated in the mines of Dunmonii (once owned and operated by the masters of the resort there). And the export head-office (that managed the commercial end of it) was at Troia, two hundred and fifty Amoran miles (as the crow flies) east of the mines. Here, in the capital of the Troad, the Island Cassiterite Company of Dunmonii (known also as Big Tin) controlled everything. But they also had other strategically placed warehouses other than at Troia. These were positioned closer to lucrative markets around the coast of Europa. But there was only one head office and that was at Troia.

Loaded onto barges at the Troad's port on the tidal River Ouse from which they were able to gain the enormous Wash estuary (whose tidal waters at that time travelled thirty or forty Amoran miles further inland than in centuries later) they then (as already stated) plied the shipping-lanes of the Helle Sea (Oceanus) to the ancient Danaan (Danish) people who inhabited those lands to the north east. These folks were some of the known world's largest consumers of tin at that time, along with the Goths who inhabited the coast of the Suevic (Baltic) Sea. Another large consumer was the folk who lived around the vast delta of the River Rine (Keltic Rene) and the River Skeid. Using an alternate route via the river Camulos (Colne) which ran through Camulod on its short journey to the sea, allowed Camulod to become an alternate clearing house and staging ground for big tin's shorter and south easterly commercial traffic route across the channel between Albion and the sea lands of Phthia. And this was where Kunobelin came in, so the man himself told Dyfed. From here it was on to the Phthian island of Valkyren (meaning dead warriors: later Walcheren), where important rituals symbolic of the samsara-like cycle of birth, death and rebirth took place that Big Tin managed to get a foothold and build large sea barns where their product was stored prior to sale and where it waited to be dispatched to all parts around. This outer island was a plum site, for its position to Oceanus made it tidal friendly for heavy sea traffic to come and go from its busy port.

Furthermore, this outer Phthian Island was awash in bovines. Bull sacrifice was a large part of their cult and by this time the island of Valkyren had become a leading breeder that exported Druidic for-profit beef for household use both at home and abroad. But being a sacred island to the Druids and the Phthian culture in general, Big Tin got its foot in the door here with great difficulty. It was accomplished by its wealth and by offering to share a percentile of their profits of the tin trade that passed through this port with Phthia's royal house bureaucrats and the Druid cult, and to facilitate the latter in marketing and transporting their beef free of charge using their fleet of tin carriers on the back-haul in exchange for a donation of suitable ports and adjacent lands. Big Tin also built large silos and warehouses on the banks of the river Skeid (Schelde) at Antron (Antwerp). All this King Kunobelin told him had happened when he himself was still quite young.

This island of Valkyren, along with all the other delta islands, was constructed from the sediment flowing out of three rivers since the receding of the last ice age. The southern most (or lower) river was the Skeid (Schelde), a local word that means to part or separate (pass away or de-part). The middle river was the Moza (Meuse) and the most northerly was the Rine (Rene in the local tongue, which means re-birth). The delta and marshlands of Phthia then was a compatible location for a cult centre who brandished a strain of Druidism celebrating death (dead warriors) in preparation for re-birth (rene) that was purer and less diluted than that of the later and current cult and the likes of Blazingwolf. The cult of this earlier time showed itself to be more attuned to the Mithra cult of a Vedic nature which itself had come down (albeit inaccurately) from almost ancient Hyperborean times. Beside Mithra, the land of Phthia honoured Nehalennia (Persephony), Athena and Zeus among others. All of these pagan puppets to provide affiliated curiosity to the hoi polloi: Apparently, Western philosophy had yet to be born here.

In time they came under the attention of the Phoeniki people who were the world's most powerful commercial investors and shipping enterprisers. This sea going concern quickly took an interest in the product but wouldn't allow other enterprisers from the lands around the White Sea to trade with them. They monopolized the tin business in that part of the world. But they allowed the Island Cassiterite Company of Dunmonii a free hand to trade with the northern lands. That was their big mistake.

This situation continued, Kunobelin told him, until greed complicated with corruption got the better of certain entitled Europaeans (who as a civilization were undergoing climate change at the time, as well as being in a financial depression with soaring inflation). So they wanted to take full control over the tin trade and take the Dunmonii mines themselves away from Prydains and the folks of the Troad. But it wasn't going to happen, at least not without a battle: And what a battle it was, for it has been remembered from that time until now. It also turned out that a number of Europaean wealthier houses were in contention over who was the greediest of them all. So with the exception of the House of Phthia, the remaining royal houses of the coast of western Europa from the fifty-seventh latitude north to the thirty-sixth south formed an alliance. This alliance became a body of Soldiers of Fortune to which they gave legal rights as accorded those citizens of the kingdoms represented. The chief executive officers of the executive division of the Soldier of Fortune Incorporated offered more than they could afford or even had to offer. It didn't matter. Troia turned them down every time anyway. Tin was urgently needed for their Bronze Age culture, you see, and for the civilization (run by industry) to remain on a steady keel and footing they needed bronze. The Europaeans' Soldier of Fortune tried all sorts of alternative methods to gain control of the product, such as issuing bonds which they controlled and which were marked to the product so as to entice an increase of the product flow thereby lowering demand. This was meant as a negotiating lever to lower the mining and expediting company's profits. Of course it didn't work. How could it? The tin kings in the Troad (Albion and Prydain) knew that the Europaeans's insane methods would worsen everything — for everybody. Furthermore, Kunobelin told him, they saw that the vulgarity of accumulating wealth was merely an unconscionable greed and a insult toward the compassion of Mother Earth who continues to give us life and sustain us even through tin and a whole lot more to come. It was sacrilegious to the point of downright blasphemy. So the mine owners at Dunmonii and the executive sales management of the House of Troia (that included their branch at Camulod) suddenly initiated a cap and trade policy instead, thereby creating a market price for tin's replacement: namely arsenic. This element (which is chemically related to tin) was a toxic poison that was harmful to Bronze Age copper and ironworkers and forgers of metal who used it. This was not good for these workers, and as their body of compensating and safety union of workers were useless, they died of poisoning in droves. But the House of Troia thought if they put their mind to it at least it was something the belligerents abroad could manage safely and profit on. They thought they were helping them out, but at the same time they also believed that these Europaean peoples needed to own their own short comings,' Kunobelin told him. But they thought wrong.

The Soldier of Fortune co-operation headed by the royal houses of western Europa (but for Phthia) in no time had adopted the attitude of the entitled power elite and it quickly shape-shifted into its true form of being a coercive monopolist who set their own interests over all free market competition, never mind common sense. But now the Co-operation (as it was called), run by capitalists and the fascist minded entitled rich (supported by representatives made up of bureaucrats and Nightwatchmen of the kingdoms involved) had added an army of un-parallel size and formidability to their ranks and was the largest army so far ever amassed in the history of the world. By this time the Royal House of Daanan seized all of Big Tin's investments in their land. Their modus operanti was followed by copycat infringements against Big Tin by other kingdoms up and down the coast until all of the investments abroad had been pirated. Following that there were efforts of a forced entry into the Troad's sovereignty by the belligerent antagonists' royal houses that had allied under the Soldier of Fortune Co-operation and were being assisted by hundreds of ships. Here came then the rallying tide of anarchy and fraud as the Troad made preparation for war. Only the royal house of Phthia initially held back at this time.

However, today, the arriving Amorans sought to use the mighty Tems River to facilitate their control over the island through commerce. Six major bends on the river in from the sea was where the Amorans had found an ideal spot to ford that river more easily. As the river Tems was narrower here it was expedient for building a permanent bridge across the current and soon utility buildings were being constructed at the bridge terminals. It was the north bank huddle of river barns and domestic dwellings that soon became garrisoned that was called Nova Troia. It was here, some fifty odd Amoran miles from Camulod on the river Tems that the Amorans actually re-founded Nova Troia; for it was first founded by a man named Prydus (also known as Pruit or Brutus). Prydus was a descendant Ilum who had been a descendant of Aeneas of the House of Troia. Prydus having either fled Albion or (being born after Troia fell) then returned and began to rebuilt Troia's namesake. The name of the isles, Prydain, came from Prydus. This took place at the beginning of the later Iron Age that came after the Tin Age (sometimes known as the Bronze Age). Apparently, during their excavations to secure the river crossing and the trade that flowed in and out of Prydain on it, the Amoran builders struck old remains and remnants of an ancient city which, being the ideal spot, they reasoned was the one which Pythéas the Hellene had recorded long ago that had been built by Prydus.

Shortly after Dyfed had arrived in Camulod, Governor Paulinius arrived from Nova Troia. Kunobelin graciously received him tongue in cheek. The governor's mission among other things was to have construction crews select what he needed to be transferred to Nova Troia on the river Tems to help with finishing the new construction there. Also, as Amoran cement was backlogged and very expensive, Paulinius had searched for new material. So, in order to accomplish the building of Nova Troia by Amoran standards he needed to divert the signature Amoran red brick, which was currently being produced here in the Camulod brickery yards, to Nova Troia. Already the project was behind schedule and over budget. But they were in short supply in Camulod too, Kunobelin had told him, for that town was shipping them elsewhere, such as to Viroconium and Fort Victrix as well. And then there was the matter of the new tax increase that Paulinius needed to bring up. And so it went.

It was Paulinius' intention to elevate Nova Troia's stature and enable it to become the main shipping terminal of Albion via the Tems River. This was in an attempt to concentrate wealth in his prefecture that he wanted to become Albion's capital, rather than have it scattered around the province. Although customs and excise officials would be needed at every port, it was better to consolidate, thereby minimizing the transporting of large sums of gold over long distances. But at the end of the day, however much control Nero, the emperor in Amor thought he had over the tin mines themselves — as his predecessor, Emperor Tiberius Claudius Kysar Augustus Germanicus the First — found, little good it did them by gaining acquisition over the actual trade itself. It wasn't as if tin was no longer being traded, it was, but to a lesser degree. Entrenched in its contractual customs, renewed mine development and production phases were tricky and difficult to change, even for Amor. To be sure, Bricus, too, had been remarkably unsuccessful in his attempt to usurp the longstanding stakeholders' grip upon that commodity at home among the Dunmonii where he lived and ruled. And to his credit, it wasn't for a lack of trying. However, stakeholders of the empire, on the other hand, were not so understanding.

"Mark up another failure there to Bricus,' Nero had written Paulinius. 'And if high standing members of the empire are going to fail, even in the face of a fully success-guaranteed-clad shoo-in, well…we'll just have to pull out some arms (next time) and boil testicles!' That was his reply. 'You'll have get the wheels turning a little bit faster on that one, Pauli old chum,' he said, closing off.

This new friendship Dyfed had with Kunobelin immensely pleased the old king and gave him new life. He took no delay in passing his druthers about all kinds of things onto Dyfed. He even informed the silver-eyed young prince that they were like two peas in a pod, Dyfed and he…'members of the same *pack*'…as he was fond of saying. Dyfed listened to him intently. As Kunobelin talked Dyfed usually lap stroking one of the many puppies from any number of the king's highly strung hunting dogs that (swarming the king's sumptuous palace) obviously had the run of the place.

"Karatakos has informed me of the details he knows for sure about you, Dyvie, me boy,' Kunobelin blurted out once. 'We are of a like kind, you and I, as I have said. My concern, as well, is for my son Karatakos. He's a good man, I think, but prone to not always taking care of business that can be the difference between life and death.

Kunobelin told Dyfed that although the might of Amor ran counter to the Albion culture as a whole, just as it did across the channel as well, strangely a certain strata of the status quo among the tribes here supported it. Among those tribes, be they the local Keltic with their overlords and their client kings along with their bureaucrats, or the continental Kelts, and the early, but fairly newly arrived, western migrating Gutans, known as Germanic Gauls who had adopted the Keltic culture (folks best described as go getters, those boisterous birds who awaken early and plan on getting a giant slice of the pie, never mind the morning worm), he said, many warmed to the mechanics of Amor.

"Or such an organization which *empire* (any empire, for that matter) could offer,' Dyfed suggested. Legion had been full of them, including Carmen. And then there was himself: wasn't he about to study their program at length at the gymnasium of education in Nova Troia?

Dyfed then spoke to the king of his observations concerning this, and of the guiding force external to the Idea: namely the two pillared hand of authority, the Turnkeys and the Nightwatchmen whose iron hands brought the Pax Amoran to bear on all its citizens — conquered or native Amorans alike. The purpose of this two-pillared hand was essentially to part the raging seas of descent against Amoranism so as to cement the masses in the framework of the law. This would then be buttressed by a bureaucracy of bookkeeping, record-keeping and accounting. But such mechanisms could be applied to any ideology, Dyfed noted.

(Asterion and the merchants of beastliness)

'Imagination rules the world'
NAPOLEONE DI BUONAPARTE

Ideas are reliant on imagination, he suggested to Kunobelin. This determines what today is all about and has some influence (not much) on detailed imperial historistics on the morrow or the day after. Ideas make or break an empire…a civilization. You can fool the people or you can scare the bejesus out of them. You don't need a reason but reasoning paves a better path for your Idea. Take what others have done, for an example.

Asterion, the first king of Kreta — descendant of Dorus (the son of Hellen and founder of the Dorians who were of the House of the Herakalae) — was the consort of Europa. According to legend Asterion assumed the form of a white bull in order to properly stepfather Europa's sons that had been fathered by Zeus. One of those sons, Minos, was a most just king of the Isle of Kreta who judged the Underworld and was the keeper of the Minotaur at the centre of the labyrinth. This had come about because Poseidon had once sent Minos a beautiful white bull. In gifting King Minos in this way, Poseidon had been intending the former to sacrifice the bull in his honour. He waited and waited but no sacrifice dedicated to him came his way. Minos had been procrastinating because of the bull's nobility of disposition. Besides, as it was an honourable object of praise, Minos took pride in men's jealousy of him having it. The bull was a prize the king now coveted, so in having ownership of it, it became too valuable an item to slay. In the interim, Passive, who was Minos' amorous wife, had first fallen in love, then into lust with the beautiful bull. Craving for an unnatural sexual union with the beautiful, horny, and well endowed beast, and having nothing applicable left over from her hope-chest or bottom-drawer to facilitate this miraculous fantasy, she commissioned Daedalus, forger of metal, fabricator of all-sorts and inventor, to fashion a contraption resembling a cow to attract the beautiful bull to her advantage and sexual satisfaction.

So, Daedalus contrived to lay a layer of cow hide over a wooden frame and shaped it exactly like a cow with an orifice at the front resembling a cowlick feature of a cow's mouth from which Passive could draw air as she hunched over in a tight and squeezed-in position inside the contraption. Another orifice he placed at the rear of the contraption from which she could receive the bull's erect pizzle. After this he applied cow scent used for breeding. As the beast (successfully tricked into an artificial rut) mounted the fake cow frame, in essence he began copulating with Queen Passive, the Kretan king's wife who was wedged inside. Later, having then conceived, she gave birth to a creature that was half man-child and half bull-calf which grew up to become a ferocious half man half bull monster that terrorized the isle of Kreta, frightening the women, children and all the domestic animals, though probably no more than Passive managed to frighten folks herself by that time. Adult men ridiculed her and gave her a wide berth. 'One wide berth for another,' was the standing joke among them. This then, apparently, was god's plan for Queen Passive (also spelled Pasife or Pasiphae).

The folks of Kreta quickly named Queen Passive's freak child, Prince Minos-Taurus the Terrible, or Minotaur for short. So, King Minos then had to commission Daedalus himself, this time to fashion another kind of miraculous contraption. This one was needed, however, to contain the beast Minotaur and protect the folks of the countryside, especially modest women, from the fruit that had been wrought from Daedalus' last ingenious invented contraption. So, in reparation Daedalus invented a labyrinth from which Minotaur was unable to escape. The riddle of the labyrinth also confounded everybody else, except for one, a certain Theseus who slew Minotaur and with help from Ariadne — the half sister of Minotaur who was quite smitten by the daring and dashing Theseus — retraced his steps and found his way out. All the others who, managing to get in — then coming face to face with Minotaur — quickly wanted out in order (inevitably) to avert sudden death. Of course, with Theseus' success of averting his lot from simply becoming another mere sacrificial victim of tribute, he quickly returned to the City of Attika (Athena) where he took up kingship and prowled around adventuring with the incomparable Herakles. That's another story.

King Minos blamed Daedalus for revealing the secret of the labyrinth and had him quickly jailed. Daedalus, though, made good his escape from captivity by fashioning wings for flight so to flee jail and Kreta for the island of Sicilia, along with is son Icarus. Due to the lad's youthful vigour, though, and his careless barnstorming near the sun, Icarus didn't make it and crashed short of their destination into the sea which was later named after him.

All this had (indeed) stepped up the tone to jar the imagination of men and women from pillar to post already jarred and suffering delusions now in the Amoran world which only further complicated and confounded their fantasy about themselves and each other among their common confinement amidst the grand-phenomena at large here in the third dimension.

(Druids and a small clique of Amoran Capital asset seekers)

*"The greatest shortcoming of the human race is
our inability to understand the exponential function.'*
ALBERT A BARTLETT *(PHYSICIST)*

Now briefly: Druids had been around forever, and once they had been revered, and rightly so. Amor put a stop to that. But what Amor didn't put a stop to was the Druids' miraculous power. However the wizardry that they brandished about as seen from an adept was not of equal quality. This was because this wizardry had long before fallen into decay and disrepute. They didn't have any powers anymore, only the power of suggestion through superbly orchestrated demonstrations of brilliant sham propped up with smoke and mirrors. The Druids now were all ado with fakery. Dyfed had begun to wonder at one point if they were not all actually created equal. These once great practitioners of magic and sorcery, these seducers of the men of the earth became to be drawn into two categories; on one side were the Posidonius camp and on the other was what was called the Xanderian tradition. He considered that it was a possibility that certain important Haploids maybe still masquerading among them. In any case, according to Amoran law these priests must be under constant imperial supervision. That meant a sort of house arrest. But all wasn't as it seemed nor were imperial laws equal. Druidry in Albion had long since descended into fakery and witchcraft, as stated: not that there had actually ever been any genuine Druids — anywhere. Arising from the lore of the Masters of the Unknown Universe, the Druids had affected only a garnish of Hyperborean wizardry: But it was dispensed by rote and subsequently it was fake.

Although the Druids' fare was no longer tolerated within the sphere of the Amoran Empire, they had found a niche again among the Kelts in Western Gaul and in Albion's wild west. The former were the cultists that Amor had put under license and strict rules that then blended into Armorica, the latter were simply kept away from cleared land where they might settle. They were usually shooed back into the forested hills of Gwynedd. In fact, it had been a certain cadre of sleeper Druids among the hills of Gwynedd who had opened the back door of Albion for those latter day Druids of Gaul. These were the Gangani and the Decangi) Kelts, a Druid priest clan, a quiet and resourceful people who had come to Gwynedd (as well as the eastern Emerald Isle) only in relatively recent times. No one knows for sure from where they originate, but unlike the provincials from Gauls who just wouldn't shut up, they were quiet and not boastful or full of fakery. So the Gangani soon discouraged these Gauls from hanging around and blocked further emigration. Not wanted by the Gangani or the Decangi people, the former then slipped like a bunch of fuss-budgets all gather together in a huff into the townships of Albion proper where they were soon masquerading from anything from fortune-tellers, carnie-callers at the circuit circuses that travelled around the country-side. They even masqueraded as skilled Amoran magistrates (possibly the magistrate with the tall hat at Bangor on Dyfed's arrival upon Albion was one of them) or as regular strong-as-a-bull Amoran soldiers, if you please. Not only that but priests with strange ideas were also doing their rounds here. Having been schooled abroad and well learned in Amoran ways, half the time they got away with it.

Dyfed had suspected that this clique were Druids. Not only were the Keltic priests now being kept under close watch, Kunobelin now informed Dyfed, but the jongleurs (bards) and court jesters, too, were being subject to current Amoran domination. They had to operate under a licence according to strict rules. These were the hodgepodge and rag tag tacky columns that now sailed from Gaul and entered Albion on the south coast on the sly. Dyfed was of the opinion that Bricus was one of these cultists, along with his guiding light (that wizard Blazingwolf geezer) upon whose right shoulder he was firmly perched.

Essentially they were supposedly ordained by Amor to hold to the imperial story, or else. They were not as popular as the Cynics were. As for cynics, they too were now being outlawed outright and their adherents were being hunted down and crucified (after having had their arms broken and pulled out of their bodies and their beards shaved off and then left tied or nailed to a tree). This despite the earlier Amoran interest in cynicism, especially Emperor Marcus.

"The Amorans were here and they were there, and everywhere in between,' Kunobelin suddenly asserted, and in his opinion he stated that the laws and the guiding hand of Amor over any and all cultures which she encountered was to expedite nothing but for their own interests: to keep the ship of Amor, not that of Albion or anybody else, upright and afloat at all costs, for their own gain.

Listening attentively to Kunobelin, Dyfed concurred with a nod, for he now fell upon the notion that the definition of Amor was simply that of a small clique of Capital asset seekers. They, Amor, were a kind of coven of high priests or cult mongers, as Kunobelin had labelled them. After all, what truly were the Res Gestae, the deeds of Divine Augustus, if not something of a creed? (This document that had been duplicated in stone all over the empire from the time of the first emperor and the start of the current era, was in fact a Deed. It wasn't duplicated in Albion as yet.) And in a sense it was the legal rights that constituted the new empire as opposed to the recent republic. It was conveying the transfer of Amor from the Republican order to the Imperial order. The Res Gestae, are the things that were necessarily done that legally bind the relationship of Amor to the *hoi polloi* who it refers to as Amorans or loyal slaves thereof, and the responsibilities thereof runs both ways. That would also be the case for slavery, as well. Dyfed suggested this to Kunobelin.

"Unfortunately,' replied the king, 'all this would contribute to Albion's detriment, for the Amoran intention was to mould the Kelts into becoming Amoral clones with the immediate purpose of preventing us from proceeding to hold the seal of any meaningful high office. We would be left without the potential of having any plenipotentiary powers of our own until we had become an approved Amoran province within their state, and then only a whisper of any real chance of it. This, inherently, was the Amoran Empire's signature trademark. For the time being they simply needed somebody like me to organise the great, seething, unwashed multitude along their policy (Idea) lines and to culturally control our people into doing their bidding with slavish intent and to ask no questions. The Amoran elite wished the great unwashed to be beasts of burden, their hewers of wood and haulers of water, but always legally Amoran in style and by their legal standards. They mean to fix a place where slavery populates the empire (and one day the world); they mean to enable a monopoly over all Capital assets, as you have said, for the benefit of a few. Anyway, they know that few, if any, of us will climb up upon the world stage alongside them. But if that happens and someone does climb up, the Amorans, apparently, hope to have by then managed to persuade him or her into the fold of the Amoran Deed rather than for them to contribute any power of opposing persuasion on our own terms.

"I concur to a point,' said Dyfed. 'But surely the Idea of empire is bigger than that and so is the resolve of our people. I foresee us in time taking all the goodness of empire and manipulating it into our own language and custom. It came to me in a vision on my way here, as a matter of fact. Furthermore, remember the Idea. We won't get far without one. Surely *empire* per sé has a potential to have life that is separate and apart from that which fashions the current mould today. The current mould is simply Amor's Idea. And as its mould is influenced and fashioned from that Idea (though subject to constant change, as Emperor Marcus has told us) it stands to reason that any Idea can take any shape and have the potential to create a goodly and constructive empire of universality as much as that of a tyrannical one. Empires, after all, have inclusiveness about them. They bring folks together — millions of them — and give them a common identity. As you have said, it will aid to keep the cash-cow ship of Albion upright but for the current purpose and not of another. Can it not do more, not just for Albion but also for all of Europa? Empires, it seems to me, have the manpower to consolidate methodologies (agriculture and trade) and interpretations (ideologies and philosophy). They concentrate skills, talent and even wisdom. This, it seems to me is a good thing,' said Dyfed. 'Only the Idea is the variable in this equation; so the empire in question is dependant on its founding, or at least its guiding impetus. Nightwatchmen and Turnkeys aside, the Empire of Amor inspires me,' said Dyfed. We need to influence it, if possible, that's all, and contribute in fashioning it into a universal, sacred Idea, not an Amoran Idea per sé; or conversely, we need to fashion Amor into a universal sacred Idea; a benevolent, constructive world Idea.'

Aghast, King Kunobelin silently contemplated Dyfed for a long while before he spoke.

"Instead we have a small clique of Capital Asseters as the idea. I admire your spunk, Dyvie,' he said. 'But you are still young. A chance, you say, to re-direct the Amoran Empire…hmmm. You are still so young. You note that I do not laugh, but it is a stretch, I have to say that much. It's a stretch. I mean, just how easy do you suppose that task to be?' He smiled kindly at Dyfed.

"That will depend,' answered Dyfed,' on how easy it will be to financially and physically extend to Amor's quartermaster and the department of bills receivable at the office of the Privy Treasury, as many kings, queens, consuls, advisers, consultants, kingdoms, provinces, cultures, the unwashed masses of slaves for labour, and every ounce of all the silver and gold in all the lands (not taken, but given in a loan and a labour of love for the cause), as well as the volition and material for every aspect of the very infrastructure itself which holds Amor together — to well beyond their limit and means — and then, at the ideal moment, to call in their loan, I would say,' Dyfed answered smiling back.

Kunobelin suddenly burst out laughing. 'More wine, Dyvie? he asked.

(NARRATOR'S PRIVILEGE)

We must state at this point that Parasolo, the original narrator, is ultimately responsible for summoning the muse to provide for this tale. 'I did not meet the antagonistic hero Dyfed Lucifer (who was slightly older than me) in person until almost fourteen degrees in celestial time (or nine hundred and twenty-three solar cycles) after his birth. According to the reckoning of the Hellenic people, we met in the year 1690; while according to the reckoning of the Scythian monk Dionysius Exiguus, the abbas of the City of Amor from Dobruja who founded the modern calendar of today in the first half of the sixth century C.E., it was the year 914 C.E. that we first met. Incidentally, the Venerable Bede, of course, assured the universal use of this calendar two hundred solar cycles later in the beginning of the eight-century. I know about, and now speak of these early anecdotes only on account of Dyfed's writings and of the stories he told me first hand. Many of his works, in fact, remain unpublished or kept private while other works of his were banned and prohibited by law from being made public. But I had access to them due to my long association with Dyfed. This attests to their authority. I had access as well to anecdotes about him through his eldest son, Talsin Davie. This man, a poet and chronologist who will barely feature in this narrative, gleaned knowledge of his father through stories his mother told him.'

'All of this I pass on to you, children of my visions. Anyway, by the time 914 C.E. came along, Anlaf, a youngster still under his father's roof in Bruges that was where Anlaf first met Dyfed. He had come to Bruges accompanied by his son Talsin Davie. Anlaf's father (a former Angle/Saxen/Dane adventurer from the extended Flenburg tribe north of the river Elv (Elbe) had years before gone a-viking and had become an usurper of land and other riches along the banks of the river Rine) and was already a successful importer merchant and tribal chieftain, hence the later appellation and name — Konge (King). Initially he had settled his folks at Metz on the banks of the Moselle River but ran his shipping from a trading dock downstream on the Acheron. After that investment had been attacked and burned a few times he wanted safer and more protected shipping yards but also wanted close access to the northern Helle Sea (the sea of Hell). So he built our grand summer home which he called 'the slumbering Nehalennia' beside the Dijver canal a short distance from his newly constructed sea barns and boat pens that were one of the first shipping yards in Bruges.'

'Then, one day in 914 C. E., Dyfed arrived in Bruges and proposed a buy-out plan with this king. It was summer and Anlaf was in Bruges at his father's house. He was the same age as Dyfed's son but as Anlaf's language was lower Franconian and Talsin Davie's was Anglish, Anlaf took an interest in learning his language. The enterprise of the House of Lucifer, as Dyfed called his privateering business, was a merchant-trader. It was extent and by this time he was very rich. In the end Dyfed and the House of Lucifer had magnanimously settled for a merger with Anlaf's father although he actually controlled everything. His father had been mightily flattered that the House of Lucifer (that was much bigger and richer than the former's) had come knocking. Back in the day Anlaf (who became a trusted employee of Dyfed's) told me that if the roles had been reversed his father would have taken the House of Lucifer by force. But the House of Lucifer had a capable standing army and a few floating man of wars waiting off Bruges so Dyfed had been more than capable of usurping the former's wealth, had he wished. But he was always one who played fairly. Anlaf's father taught him many things about possession and ownership, but Dyfed Lucifer taught Anlaf that they were really worth nothing unless one had applied honour in the manner with which one acquired the said riches. It was good, though (he implied), to always apply a cunning respect when it came to business and the ability to keep one's eye on the prize at all times. But that is another story for later. So let me summon the muse so as to continue this tale.' (**Parasolo**)

(Meeting with a Remarkable Friend at the Bore and Bridge Inn)

> 'Sovereignty is the…ultimate location of power which legally commands and is not commanded.'
>
> **JEAN BODIN** (*SIX LIVRES DE LA REPUBLIQUÉ*)

Dyfed had made a big impression on Kunobelin who had then strong-armed him into accepting his invitation to take up residence in his townhouse in Nova Troia. This Prydain high king whose personal hygiene and cleanliness, Dyfed had noted, was not in any way substandard as were the other hoi polloi, including the Amorans. Furthermore, Kunobelin, he noted, parted his coiffured and stylish hair as well. He was also bound to his principles of duty to his fellow man like a centaur was bound to its hooves: He flatly refused to accept anything from Dyfed while managing to bestow upon the young prince much in return for nothing. That was the nature of this man toward Dyfed. One of the least of things he bestowed upon him was the decoration as an official Keeper of the Royal Palace in Nova Troia. It was intended to provide him with some authority at the king's palace there. This now rendered him into Prince Dyfed Lucifer of the Grove, Keeper of the Royal Palace. Superfluous as it might sound to folks today, it not only had a ring to it, it also gave him some wiggle room that would come in handy among the protocol indoctrinated strait-laced bureaucrats of Amoran's officialdom once he got to the big smoke on the river Tems: For this would enabled Dyfed to act (alongside the king's chamberlain) with some of the king's authority, such as his property manager within all matters concerning the royal palace at Nova Troia. This was a big deal.

King Kunobelin also cautioned Dyfed against Cornelius' earlier advice of being enrolled into the Amoran Civil Service Procedures and Due Process Studies offered at the Amoran Polytech housed in the gymnasium, an annex beside the old basilica.

"That will avail you not,' he told Dyfed plainly. 'I will try and interest my stepson Karatakos in keeping you company there at my townhouse palace. He has the ability to attract and be attractive to by all sorts whatever their nature and stripe.'

"Oh yes, he is a master of disguise,' replied Dyfed, his silver eyes smiling boldly as they locked onto the king's gaze. 'We met under such pretence, as I recall.'

"You can keep an eye on him for me,' Kunobelin laughed, 'for he's an impetuous fellow, at times. The two of you will get along well and he can lend a hand in tutoring you (better than anyone else) as to the Albionian and Amoran ways, complete with all our failings and called in loans, besides.'

When the summer came to a close Dyfed saddled up and rode out: Though not in any rush (rushing was not Dyfed's way), he departed early in the morning of September 12th, bid the old king good-bye and moseyed on down the road; destination, Nova Troia. Finally! he thought.

Sometime around noon of that same day Dyfed arrived at a river-ford called Kysar - O - Mangus (the recently renamed tribal capital of the Trinovantes), on the banks of the Chelm River. It so happened that he fell upon a merry acquaintance here. Actually, the acquaintance fell under him, or at least his white Andalusian stallion his was riding. Then a moment later the man narrowly missed being thoroughly trampled upon again and dragged by the black mare he had in tow. This all happened immediately after Dyfed clambered from the deck of the horse and coach ferry that fetched them across the river. Confronting the staging area in front of the Edgewater Inn that was situated right on the banks of the river, he had to pull up sharply in order to avoid an old gnome-like pedestrian who inadvertently (perhaps due to drink) had lurched himself into Dyfed's path as he drew up. The man was intending to climb into a large, waiting four-wheeled chariot (carriage). The man had actually miscalculated the step up the chariot at the same time its four horses had suddenly come under siege due to the sudden dusty arrival of Dyfed and his two Andalusians. The horses attached to the chariot quickly lurched sideways while the chariot pivoted to one side. This caused the little gnome to miss his step and tumble under Dyfed's horse. By some strange coincidence the merry gnome-like acquaintance was the same cliff hanging cave dweller of a hermit gnome from Gwynedd named Morgant, the would be exterminator of Virus (by his own admission).

The outraged innkeeper, who had been bowing and scraping and plying the plaudit to the departing spend-thrift Morgant, quickly changed on a denarii to face Dyfed and scream out angrily in a thick voice;

'The devil take you stranger, and your fiendish horses.'

But then with contamination and the defilement of dust having settled, Morgant and Dyfed suddenly recognised each other. So, waving the chariot away, Morgant turned back to the hotel leading Dyfed into a smallish room where with wine cups at the ready each used the handy excuse to wash away the dirt that had collected in their throats and set to and began to apply a heavy hand to slake their thirst.

Morgant listened while Dyfed told him his news and was over-joyed upon hearing from Dyfed of King Kunobelin's good health, and of the latter's recommendations and plans for him to reside at the palatial abode of the king's refurnished townhouse in Nova Troia. They chatted and drank for the rest of the day. Dyfed learned that Morgant had himself visited Legion. He then asked about Carmen and Ryan. It turned out that Marg had not shared nuptials with Ryan. As for Queen Carmanda, she was back on her perch fanning the rebellion against Amor while Marg, Dyfed learned, had been nowhere in sight.

Dyfed had the distinct feeling that Mogant knew more.

"So,' said Dyfed. 'What?' His eyes searched Morgant's face that took on a shrewd countenance as he studied Dyfed back.

"Karatakos,' Morgant suddenly answered, 'has told me she is gone from there, that's all.'

"But why be crowned with a lavish coronation, marry Ryan, and all for nothing?' Dyfed asked him. Morgant's gnome-like countenance dropped its shrewdness and took on a sly look.

"Maybe it wasn't all about Queen Carmanda, Dyvie,' he said. Maybe Marg's intention was to learn something about both Ryan and Carmanda's intentions and enlist Carmanda's unwitting help to do so by seemingly appearing to side with her. Perhaps, this petty little skirmish — this tempest in a teapot which could magnify effects elsewhere was to further help set Carmen squarely (for the incriminating record) right where she intended to be all along, in the middle of a rebellion. But it was not necessarily to her advantage.'

In other words, he told Dyfed, she did it to sabotage Queen Carmanda's ambitions and maybe those of General Cornelius as well. Anyway, he had heard through Karatakos that Queen Marg (so rumour had it) hadn't even so much as visited Ryan's bed after they were wed, and continued immediately after to live apart from him. She had also been on the out and outs with her surrogate aunt Carmanda who had (in her own fashion) come up with an excuse to annul Marg's coronation but not her marriage to Ryan. She was of the opinion (totally incorrect, as it turned out) that Marg would be compelled to obey Ryan. It appeared that the regency, never mind being Ryan's spouse, meant nothing to Marg and she paid no attention to either him or Carmanda. It wasn't a complicated trap even if you were hoi polloi, Morgant told Dyfed, but Marg was faster and cleverer than Carmanda or Ryan put together. That much, he said, was all he knew. But he had long known of Marg's superiority, he said. Furthermore, he told Dyfed that he had learned from Karatakos that someone had urged Ryan on to join with Pater Bricus and oppose both King Kunobelin, and Paulinius. It was commonly believed that that person was Carmanda, but maybe not. Karatakos, he said, thought it was Cornelius.

The old gnome-like sage and jongleur promised Dyfed to keep in closer touch with him in the future. It was a merry reunion that to Dyfed seemed like an odd coincidence all around.

(Nova Troia on the banks of the river that leads to Hell)

> *'In so far as the mind sees things in their eternal aspect it participates in eternity.'*
> **BARUCH SPINOZA**

Fording the Rhodius River, as Dyfed approached this city of Nova Troia he discovered that it was ringed with farmland. There was many a mud farmhouse and barn and mud and stick fence to divide the land and keep the multitudes of stock contained. The houses looked well kept and each had a mud-straw and stick fence out front that was all whitewashed and prettied up with roses growing along them. Plentiful, too, were the fields of produce and many an ox could be seen pulling heavily leaden wagons along narrow straight tracts between these fields while others were laden with cattle headed for market. And all around from each farm to the city, wooden wheels set off an infectious rumble upon those straight tracts (tracks): straight here and away, to and fro, back and forth they went, between the countryside and the city and back again, as farmers and tradesmen plied their occupation and commerce. Dyfed inhaled the sweet smell of country air mixed with soft, white, aromatic smoke that wafted across the highways and byways from small fires burning in the fields and along the roadsides. Soon the road skirted a large tract of sodden swam land. No dwellings or farms were visible from the path here. Once he had drawn closer to Nova Troia he noticed that earthen walls had once surrounded the actual city itself. However, now its fortifications appeared new and as the swampish pond had narrowed into a slow moving stream, channelled between levies, he could see that it entered the city through a protective wall guarded by a portcullis. Nearby he saw a guarded gate toward which the worn path led. As Dyfed entered into the city through her north-eastern gate, the sweet smell of the countryside disappeared to be replaced by an acrid and pungent odour of burnt fire log and dead burning donkey which quickly attacked his nostrils while the city smoke in general and the grime of industry made his eyes burn.

    At the gate, where officers of the empire were applying their duty of security, he was delayed, and questioned. Also Dyfed was asked to produce his permit for travel, just as along the way he had become used to road, ferry and bridge taxes which were as common as death at the end of a given life. At this time the traditional Moel-myd Laws (handed down from centuries before by King Dyfnal) which had once been deified by the local folks and were now being defied by the men who did not part their hair but wore it shaved or combed forward around their face. These were the men in charge here now. But it had been the former — that kind and well-loved Keltic king of long ago — who had once granted the right of public use to certain roads (without any necessary licence) just as he had granted sanctuary to temples and even some towns. All this he had done and more. He struck laws that governed punitive measures according to felonies committed as well as for weights and measures and even currency values. He did this besides having cognizance of matters that intrigued even Aristoteles. Much had changed, though, with Amoran occupation along with the devaluing denarii.

The city gate guards tactfully expedited this well dressed young man with a princely manner of etiquette whose language of the empire rolled easily off his tongue. And, it just so happened he was in the possession of two beautiful Andalusians thoroughbreds under expert control. Also in his possession were prestigious letters of recommendation from the chief king of Albion addressed to Paulinius the governor and another from General Cornelius. Furthermore, his permits were in place. Any delay here was caused more by their interest in this prince. After asking them the way to the temple of Harmony and Concordance, so that he might give thanks to the gods for his safe arrival at his journey's end, Dyfed was easily able to follow their directions to the temple so as to find Kunobelin's townhouse palace instead. Indeed, all was just as Kunobelin had told him it would be.

This growing city on the River Tems was fast emerging on top of its ancient forerunner. Besides the temple of Harmony and Concordance that had been built over half a millennium before by King Dyfnal Moel-myd (the re-known king of old), there were two other temples within the city, too. The first was a temple to Diana which was reputed to have been the first building constructed by Prydus in these environs and from around which the town grew. Others thought its inauguration preceded the present era of iron; therefore, they said, it was Bronzonian. Another theory was that Prydus originally placed the old town beside it and not around it to enclose it. No one truly knew how old it was. In any case it was apparent that the temple (along with the city) had been reconstructed more than once. The temple to Diana was the foremost and most popular place of worship in Nova Troia and was just a short walk of a few minutes west through the squalid streets from Kunobelin's palace (townhouse). One whose name today nobody could recall had also erected the second temple of similar origins nearby. Some said Prydus probably built it, as well, though others pointed to King Blaiddyd, a Dunmonii Kelt who reigned about seven centuries before the present. This was the temple of Apollo. However, this temple was not within the city, but had been constructed about two miles outside of Nova Troia's western gate. It lay just passed the south bend in the river. Indeed, since an early king, possibly Prydus or King Blaiddyd, had commissioned the erection of this outlying temple of Apollo, and that the much later Dyfnal Moel-myd had been responsible for the temple of Harmony and Concordance within, and what with the venerable temple to Diana almost alongside it, it was apparent, then, that worship and sacrifice was a hereditary impulse to the city's early denizens. This was a concept of action completely unknown to Dyfed until recently.

So it was also apparent to an alert observer that worship and sacrifice towards having a personal and social well being and a torch to light the way for one and all through the fog of phenomena was a hereditary impulse among the city's earliest denizens down to today. This showed that they were searching, and somehow they knew that the volition taken toward knowledge and in understand their own conscious presence, was the sacred path — the way to that sacred spot or the divine Ground. But the hoi polloi, Dyfed realized, were a long way behind the enlightened Hyperboreans at the time of their transcendence and that the former still had a long row to hoe before they even got anywhere near the point of desperation. That was the point when an adjustment and change was most likely (and desperately needed) to take place. For without new rules and attitudes towards the thing (an immediate necessity for the continuance of a viable future due to the realization that neither the old school nor anything else was working out for them now in the new reality), the social status quo (maybe their civilization) was destined to plunge headlong into an abyss of no return.

Philosophical ideology he knew did not include spiritualism but did include Hinduism/Jainism; Buddhism/Taoism (early grafts that came from closer to the bone and ancient roots when the eternal moment was at hand) had had better results both for social and political development in this confusing world. Spiritualism had its place and cynicism had also been part of this. But unlike the republic, the empire had been against Cynicism. And even there their aptitude and performance level was dismal. It crawled along at a snail's pace. Indeed, almost everything the hoi polloi had achieved had been done through a process of re-invention or renewal of the ancient understanding but without expanding and growing very far in the right direction. Usually when it did happen it was done on the backs of those few Hyperborean resorters who over the last few thousands of years had eagerly returned again and again to this dimension for rest and recreation where they were encouraged to provide a few moments of conscientious civil duty to contribute something helpful to the poor natives — those savage beasts of the third density world.

While living (to some extent) among them disguised as hoi polloi, these master resorters successfully salted the hoi polloi's paths of knowledge all the while urging them to pick this or that up and examine it, and to look closer at the other in a different way and see it thus. Through a myriad of methods these masters had (over the last thousand years) introduced a form of proto-science that started sprinkling analytical thinking into this slovenly civilization. This was achieved by the so called eccentrics, those master alchemists, philosophers, physicians, mathematicians, artists, astronomers, and logicians (all natural philosophers); while social philosophers — those other unassuming sages who lectured against beguiling flamboyant prophets and natural nonsense, those quick witted and contentious critics and cynics at large, and those intense and helpful poets of the people who ridiculed the status quo and threw their pearls before swine — had managed to drop a few gems of wisdom among them by this time. Druids were not included. But Druids, Dyfed was to discover, were not all created equal, after all.

The list of the names of these masters is long…from Alcmaeon who was of the ancient enclave resort of Croton, from Eukleides (Euclid) of Alexandria and Thales of the resort of Miletus, to Zeno of the enclave of Ely (Elea) and Xenophanes of the ancient west Anatolian resort of Colophon. It also included Anacharsis a Scythian from the Taman Peninsula on the shores of the Cimmerian Bosporus, and Antisthenes the Athenian, Diogenes the Cynic of Sinope, another Cynic known as Crates of Thebes, the Phoeniki Stoic, Zeno of Citium, and the Hellenic mathematician Eratosthenes of Cyrene just to mention a few. Some of the masters and sages who worked and played here among the hoi polloi were even once referred to as gods. En (also An or Anu) comes to mind first. This is followed by En.ki (who was known too as Eh) and Eh's brother, En.lil. Those are three Masters right there who the folks of the Ubaid and Sumer cultures (later by the time of the Akkad Empire) were described as gods. Another was Nin.gir.su. When you look at it that way, he thought, what the devil was he, Dyfed of the enclave of the Isle of Peace (even with his new honoured title, Keeper of the Royal palace) actually doing here and just what in the devil and the name of hell was he going to contribute? Obviously a rapid page-turner consisting of nothing for reader value. But everything is relative, as they say.

Miraculously, this aforementioned work that the dimension travelling masters accomplished for these somewhat dull and stupid people was all managed through the medium of the third dimensional phenomena's cause and effect. It was this latter condition, of course (along with false mythos proffered by the high priests of the third dimension's cults and other mesmerizers) that were responsible in the first place for playing havoc with the hoi polloi's reasoning which further kept them from the eternal truth. And now Dyfed could see that this roundabout method was going to be a slow one, possibly for the next couple of thousand years anyway. However, today's empire, he thought, was in some ways a breath of air (if not always fresh) for it was surprisingly advanced for its time, all things being considered. These Amorans were no slouches, put it that way. It was apparent that they had advanced in social engineering, though it appeared to Dyfed that as the empire had become bigger it had become more unmanageable. So to counter this he noticed that the Amorans had an historic tendency to quickly resort to brutal violence in order, not so much to curb disorder (for violence begets violence), but rather as a method to arrange for the power elite to maintain their elite superiority throughout. This was Pax Amor (the love of peace) where hate was love, war was peace and ignorance was correct knowledge. This was what his master called the Orwellian Syndrome (apparently after some unknown person who was obviously another inter-dimensional master). That whoever it was that went by the name Orwell hadn't even yet been born was never a problem for the Masters of the Unknown Universe because they taught that time wasn't lineal and that whatever was to occur at some point in space/time had already occurred since the space/time of the eternal place/moment had already occurred. Therefore at one level it was continuing to occur and in another was occurring continuingly in the eternal moment. But each of the latter two conditions was separate (kind of) and most definitely apart.

Furthermore, because the Amorans weren't sufficiently advanced enough in social engineering, they didn't understand that democracy (a social philosophy for governance having been proffered for many hundreds of years by this time, though it was much older than that) and socialism (a philosophy usually attempted for achieving some form of social harmony that was as old as mankind itself, even long before hunter-gatherers), both being the great champions of human history (and no greater champions has human history ever had). And this condition needed to be fully understood and implemented. Once that was achieved, it needed to be maintained at all costs in order to curb disorder without the use of brutal violence and to be able to just put one foot in front of the other and get on without violent reaction that stems from ignorance (or was it knowledge that was un-knowledge?). And each champion (whether it was a strain of democracy or a form of socialism), in order for one to be viable and strong it needed the other to be just as viable and strong. Without both together the other would fail in the end. You can't have democracy without a viable, and agreed upon social order. You can't have a workable and acceptable social order without a strong democratic platform of methodology; its love and marriage. Other than lacking this, they had so much else going for them that at first Dyfed thought that the effort to push them along and shoo them into the magic and sacred circle of the eternal moment might be just a leisurely walk (as they say) in the park.

Of course, he was to be quickly proven wrong. Unfortunately, it would turn out to be a walk leading him down the garden path. So, what was wrong? What was the cause… despite his hard earned logos of clear Hyperborean thinking towards the matter of benefiting the hoi polloi…of him being wrong in the first place? The question wasn't what. He knew what; for what (in effect) was the hoi polloi's ignorance of the calm centre that lay beyond desire, the eternal moment that was only accessible through the true self's non self, the soul, the stilled mind. No, the question that remained here wasn't what but whom? Who were those responsible for enticing the hoi polloi (especially their society's cultural, social and political anatomy) whose construct of ignorance at present and whose attitude toward adjustment (projectology) was utterly deficient? Apparently, they weren't capable of even avoiding and well flagged pitfalls that lay in their path which with wide open lion's jaws waited patiently to utterly destroy their civilization and their species, if not even the entire planet, in time? So, to quote the Hyperborean Dr Abaros, 'just who in the name of unholy fuck were they, these manipulators of culture and protocol?' That's what Dyfed, with an air of forced incredulousness, was now asking himself, too.

But in all these ways the ancient (and likewise the new) folks were not unlike the middling Amorans nor were they any different from other pagans elsewhere. Dyfed thought, however, that it was obvious — and it aught to be well known — that the current presentation of these religious mysteries had devolved to the point where none, not even their high priests of the temple, knew about the real events that lay behind their traditions along with its ancient message. The same had happened with the Druids. It wasn't that it was a lie. Rather, theirs was a mis-understood or forgotten truth, one might say, which had been re-packaged, fancied up and served up and was something now that was embodied by rote rather than understanding. This was common with most things within the phenomenon wherein the humans dwell, whether they part their hair or not or which side they do. Dyfed had made that observation quite easily. And after all, these sanctuaries of the pagan gods were once truly real repositories of ancient knowledge, even if today and yesterday, they were simply its reflection on a cave wall. It was just that the consecrated that laboured unceasingly to acquaint the muddling mass to the mystery had now become forgetful and un-skilled in their presentation. Dyfed wondered aloud if the people's gods of third dimension wear out, die off, or if they need re-electing from time to time? He ultimately came to the conclusion that the latter scenario seemed to be the case. They need to look facts in the face about the integrity of their vitality and make the call…what phrase was it Marg had once used? Yes…the shit of Taurus. That was it.

Although, when it came to losing the truth, the Druids — those old curators of the department of science — had done some of the most damage to themselves. To be fair, the pagan department of history had run parallel with Druidical concepts for a long time, though it had operated separately. Albeit, there were others, such as the cults of Orpheus, Lord Krishna and the awakened Buddha whose mysteries still managed to float rather sensibly. Yes, it was the Haploids doing, all right. He knew that much now. But the Haploids could be anybody attached to anything. Apparently they were dictators along with ruling tyrants, including past emperors. Or were the high priests of the Druids and their bloodthirsty demonism for human sacrifices ultimately to blame for this anthropological standstill, this peculiar quiescence, this stagnate fixity? Or was it the Flamen Dialis, those high priests of Jupiter and their wives (the flamines maiores) whose flashing of the knife into the bull and ram's neck (respectfully) to appease — what (who) Jupiter, Mithra or Dumuzid? Or was it something other than priests altogether?

Albeit, there were other paths besides Jain/Hindu/Buddha-isms, and Tao/Confucius-isms, and there were the aforementioned cults of Orpheus and Lord Krishna. The awakened Buddha whose mysteries, as stated, still managed to float rather sensibly and who had had little need for adjustment (projectology) over the centuries. In fact it seemed that most of these folks had never actually been dashed upon the point of desperation at any time during their long tenure. Furthermore, these latter cults had also left jewels for the easily muddled to contemplate in order to help themselves back onto the path of righteousness which is truth. Not so with the Druids and their Jehovah-like Dis. The latter mentioned Jehovah was the deity of a Middle East cult that the Abramists worshipped. This cult had certain Indo-Europa origins (the lands of Afghan and Inja) or influences as well, from whom a facsimile was emerging at this very moment in our tale as we read. It is called Jeshuanism. This religion was not based on the eternal moment where the Paraclete and avatar Jeshua the teacher of righteousness/messiah/prophet was forever and always coming each and every moment to all sentient beings throughout their eternity, but rather it was a stationary event in linear time. That moment in fact had been only a few years back at about the time when our protagonist/antagonist Dyfed had been born. Anyway, this recipe for a single (birth/resurrection) event is badly flawed, unfortunately, and no good can come of it. And it had already reared its head in conversation among mostly the Amorans here in Nova Troia who had arrived here recently from Amor and her eastern provinces. Dis, incidentally, was also a god in the Amoran Pantheon.

This is all relevant here due to the fact that near King Kunobelin's palace Dyfed noticed a hall that was just finishing being built. It was on the harbour that was the mouth of the brook that flowed into the river Tems and was adjacent to the governor's palace. Timbers still lay everywhere amid pools of drying wattle mud and tipped over wheel barrels. One crisp Autumn day in October a group of men who were obviously not labouring builders themselves, but appeared perhaps to be the well dressed owners who had commissioned the well appointed and expensive building, were watching others (who were the workmen) place and unveil a stone plaque with large Amoran letters chiselled into its surface. It was being inserted into an equivalently sized recess over the front entrance of the building that faced away from the harbour (and the stream that flowed into it) and was elaborately decorated and brightly painted. This shingle or sign read: Mistletoe Hall. The mistletoe (*Viscum album* — distinct from the related *Phoradendron flavescens*) was (Dyfed knew) a symbol of the Amorans, among others. He realized that this secular looking construction was actually a temple lodge dedicated to Mitra combined with utility facilities for user groups and such, as well. Curious, Dyfed drew near and over heard the chatter of the men who were within ear-shot. He noted that aside from Amoran they spoke Keltic, but with a continental accent. And he noted that it was the same dialect that had been spoken by the provincial Amoran magistrate — the man who reprieved him from blame by his nasty accuser from the inn back at the miserable little cenedl under the shadow of the mountain on the western shores of Gwyneth. That such a place was materializing here, now, wasn't out of time and place. After all the Temple of the Lodge of Mithra was related to the Gaulic Kelts who, like Albion Kelts, claimed to be descended from Dis and continued to worship this deity even over all the others within the Amoran pantheon: an act (incidentally) which was prohibited by Amoran law. And the collective symbol for their Druidic work was the mistletoe. And in this gloomy underworld cult of Dis one must discern them to be a direct descendant of the cult of the early ancestor to the Franken[17] (the Phthians) on the island of Valkyren.

Dis was a transcendent god, related to the Amoran Crow-god who had blood ties in Amor with Aesculapius (Asklepiós). But unlike the gloomy underworld of the Amoran Dis, these Gauls (like their cousins in Albion whose pew had once been the high seat of Druidism) pass on after this life to a long life somewhere else. And Dis was very much alive and well here in Albion, too. Having been suppressed it went underground. But Dyfed had seen evidence of it in the cenedls, in the City of Legion and in in Camulod.

Back near the beginning of this era, according to myth, Zeus killed (what he called that no-good son of a bitch) Aesculapius with a thunderbolt for bringing Hippolytus (son of Theseus) back alive from the dead for profit. Apparently, if it had been for kindness or compassion and not profit it might have been a different matter. To the Norse, Dis was a lady deity or ghost spirit associated with fate. For the Goth peoples Dis, like raven (crow), was a black ghost of the dead (murdered warriors included) who were associated somehow with carrion. In some legends the raven was thought to have once been white. Though the Amoran Dis was unique, to them there were virtually no differences between the Albion Druids' arrival at the worship of Dis via their death defying cults and that of this Franken whose Druidic priests sacrificed humans in lieu of Mithraic bulls during important high masses when bulls didn't have the power/strength of spirit to pierce the ram. At such times, therefore, bulls simply wouldn't do and human sacrifices had to suffice instead. And like the Kelts in the land of Gaul, the Albion Druids had worshipped Dis like no other, and the symbol of their religious work was none other than the mistletoe.

Kunobelin had told him that the Druids, those high priests of the lower river Rine (that were currently usurping Albion's local priesthood) were another matter altogether compared to the problem of Amoran occupation. He told Dyfed that even though these Druids and worshippers of Dis were in a wastrel state today and merely a shadow of what they had once been, they were now at their point of desperation and were looking for another avenue to explore in order to maintain power and control in the great game of organizing and controlling the masses. And this avenue, he said, appeared to be the new cult of Jeshuanism that was spreading out from Palesteen. It was Kunobeli's opinion that the Amorans themselves may be the lesser of evils here.

Dyfed had learned from his master's history lessons that Druids were a fourth generation of magicians that came out of the ancient Sumerian/Ubaid cultural centre at Uruk and had spread over the world. And that the Druids were not bonafide, failed transcendites in quite the same manner as the Haploids were for their failed attempts to transcend that had turned them into a curious form of Troll. Nonetheless, as such they were still failed contenders that lacked transformation. And as Trolls here in the third dimension, they sloughed back into a rote waking sleep that was much dazed and corrupted, even more so now than when they were the leading cult of Phthia and western Europa during the Age of Bronze. The myths of their powers (intellectual truths they

---

17 Franken (Franks) are a people still unnamed yet. Their kingdom to be will soon become the feminine noun, Francia (France).

had gained somehow about the universe) with the influence of some of the early aforementioned masters (which by the Age of Bronze were bonafide knock-offs) were now reduced to being just genuine fakes.

Incidentally, it had been at Uruk where Dumuzid — the shepherd, the great storm god, the deity of life-death-rebirth (the god of death and resurrection), lord of the sky who governs rain, the protector of life whose absence causes death and chaos on earth, as the next generations of the current age are about to find out in the coming Age of Aquarius — which reoccurs every twenty-five thousand, nine hundred or so earth years which embodies the rhythm of the earth's vibration and the reason for its name. For at that time the whole world will be praying for (and to the god of) water because all the frozen fresh water deposits of each of the polar ice caps, the extent of continental glaciers, the vast mountain snowfields and ice sheets, the many cool and deep lakes, the reservoirs of the cities of the world along with their iceboxes, their water-coolers and the source of water streaming from taps and hose bibs sticking out of the walls on every house-hold throughout the world will have all melted, dried up, evaporated or been flushed away by river, stream and sewer into salty briny Oceanus. And Big Tin, Big Oil, Big Pharm, and Big Food will become the Big Desalinate — though to no avail — in the absence of Big fresh Water!

Furthermore, it was at Uruk that Dumuzid (Adonis, the god of vegetation (especially corn), the tree of life and the son of the abyss whose animal is the Bull — came into being. This mythos descended from the Shamskar speaking peoples who (as luck would have it) had not yet transformed.

In addition, the Druidic Trolls coerced Dumuzid to cause into being the likes of Indra (an ancient leftover), Tammizi, Osirus, Teshub, Hadad, Ba'al, Zeus, Attis, Adonis, and Jupiter more or less in that order. The Minotaur impersonates Dumuzid, which is the rider of the cloudy storms. And since he's depicted carrying the sound barrier breaking thunderbolt we can in some way attach Thor to his identity too. So imagine if you can, when after a six day orgy of sex, drugs and very loud obtuse vibrations having been imitated from the lyre or the kithara (also cithara), as you stagger and rock and roll forward (even more obtusely) seeking a clear head, prepared at all costs to do penance, maybe light the candles upon your alter of faith at sun-down or sun-up (your preference) and turn over a new leaf in life, only to come face to face with a thunderbolt wielding, horny horned bovine smelling minotaur in an ugly mood with sharp-edged, filthy dung encrusted hooves (if you will) that's standing in the way between you and righteous salvation? To what avenue of hope, revenge or total distractions will the nature of your mind take you then?

Yes, there are folks who do wonder about such things.

It has been said that Dumuzid's consort was In.anna (the goddess of love, war, fertility and sex that can make it all right again for you). Her identity mythos eventually came to spawn Nintinugga, Isis, Ishtar, Demeter (again, also Dameter), Aphrodite, Venus, Persephone, Herecura, and Nehalennia. As the consort of Zeus (towards whom we gravitate in this narrative) she is Hera and Leda (Leto). In,anna (also En.anna) went down into the underworld, and in all certainty down on Zeus, too. She is associated with lions — (of course she is) — and her symbol is the eight-pointed star, and her holy city was Uruk (also known as Erech by the Hellenes and Warka by the so-called Sumerians, or whatever it was they called themselves) where all of this dates back to.

And when we bring up the latter mentioned Keltic goddess Nehalennia, it brings us back to the mouth of the river Skeid (Schelde pronounced Skeld) whose name essentially means death and whose fellow companion is the river Rine (Rene) whose name means re-birth, all of which empties here into the Sea of Hell. But it doesn't end there, either. Here the mythos takes on a new dimension upon which light can be shed. For so far, all of this seems good, Dyfed thought. But he also realised that it brought us back to bull sacrifice and Mithraic rituals of the dead which entails egregious abomination of human sacrifices whose euphoric high (that happy and hazy daze of delirium) is sweeter (they say) than wine or the exquisiteness of the male's sweet emission. The latter, of course, being in the throes of a hot and sweaty finale of passionately abandoned and unprotected sex, preferably with (In)Anna.

This all brings to mind a lost, ancient Bronze Age civilization (that is dead and mostly forgotten today) whose rituals (similar to Dis the Crow) are reminiscent of Valkyren and Phthia and the rivers Skeid and the Rine. And from their combined delta of ancient Phthia it is only a hundred Amoran miles as the Amoran Crow of Dis flies directly across the Strait of Helle to the river Tems estuary. And the location of this estuary is just a short hop skip and a dory ride downstream from Nova Troia and the Mistletoe Hall.

(The big stink)

'Where blessings can accomplish nothing, blows may avail.'
DOMINGO FÉLIX DE GUZMÁN (ST. DOMINIC):

Besides being the big smoke, Nova Troia was the big stink. At one square Amoran mile in size it was huge. Situated at a crucial point on the river Tems (that up to this point was used as a thoroughfare for sea trade), the city was a semi-walled stronghold defended by the ninth Legion. From here the city was able to control inland river traffic as well as the foreign trade navigating the widening Tems estuary. Nova Troia, therefore, was the natural spot for governor Plautius to be stationed so to have his finger (so to speak) on the pulse of the province. Since then all the governors have been stationed here, as was Paulinius.

Due to Amoran know-how and their advanced skills and sophistication, Nova Troia was also quite unlike the other settlements of Albion. For by this time it had turned into one that resembled those other capitals representing the authority of the empire from which provincial bureaucracy emanated by the might of imperial authority. However, the old custom and practice within the city of butchering animals on one's doorstep and leaving carcasses in the middle of the road to rot with other unusable remains — such as accumulated filth in general where they were burned or pushed off to one side — still happened to continue here in Nova Troia where bad habits die slowly.

Since the neighbourhood dogs and the maggots of the earth continued to fight over the offal and decay that lay around, and sewage was permitted to stagnate at a standstill while the responsibility of civic duty was disregarded and ignored by both civil bureaucrats and military duty, it sent up a big stink, especially around the harbour port. As a result of this lack of orderly cleanliness the environment had had a noticeably greater negative impact on the health and wellbeing of citizens here than in smaller centres. People were often sick and children were pale and had perpetually runny noses and sores on their lips.

What had been needed were rules to keep the filth at a minimum. The job of enforcing those rules had fallen upon Nova Troia's commission of newly appointed by-law officers, most of them locals. This regiment of guards operated under the authority of the politia (civil administration). It had been their responsibility to keep the city scoured clean of broken-down junk, such as carts and old furniture and to discourage such things as abandoning the carcasses of dogs, cattle, oxen, horses and portions thereof in the narrow streets which only served to block traffic and stink the place up. But the daily manure from the beasts of burden soon amounted to virtual mountains. So in a necessity to at least keep the traffic moving, manure was shovelled aside which found it ways into a central brook (fed by equally polluted streams) that passed directly through the centre of Nova Troia. The remainder of the upkeep fell to the wayside and was often left undone. In order to meet their responsibility of keeping the city in running order the politia's job was to tender out the work. So far, it seemed to him, they had failed miserably to come up with a budget or come up with employees who'll work for nothing. Furthermore, the politics of the palace where Dyfed now lived had it own convulsions. Dyfed's initial arrival in Nova Troia had caused a stir among the staff at Kunobelin's palace. But Kunobelin's staff soon warmed to Dyfed. However, Kunobelin's chamberlain (a nice but fussy little man named Togo Waugh) was frustrated to the point of distraction by pulling out portions of his parted hair when it came to negotiating and manoeuvring the running of an unofficial palace through the red tape and hoops of the Amoran bureaucracy at large. In his words: 'the situation here is bird shit. I look forward to help from you,' he said.

King Kunobelin's palace where Dyfed took up residence was inside the city's perimeter walls close to a brook that dumped out into the river Tems. Kunobelin's palace was a little better than halfway down this brook in the direction of the river. At a spot not far from the gate where Dyfed had first entered the city, the brook (flowing out from the marshy land to the north of the city) passed through a stationary portcullis, which channelled it under the city's northern wall, hence, its name — the Wall Brook. In effect, as this brook idled (not wanting to be rushed) to the river Tems it cut the city in two. King Kunobelin's palace was located on the city's western section or right bank of this brook.

In its journey to the river Tems, the Wall-brook passed close by the Temple of Harmony and Concordance which was just to the rear behind Kunobelin's palace with the city's amphitheatre back a little behind them both. A little further downstream on the brook's left stood the Mistletoe Hall (the new Temple of the Lodge of Mithras) where the brook flowed into the harbour. This harbour port had once been dredged out and artificially widened at this point. The port was also the mouth of the stream and its confluence with the Tems. At this point the effluence and refuge from much of the city flowed into the excavated harbour. The harbour was more tidal than stream and the dredging caused the movement of the generally placid water to rise and ebb during the day rather than rush and flow. Further down guarding the left bank of the widened port where the brook emptied into the river Tems was the governor's palace.

As it turned out, the smell of the harbour stink was somewhat absent alongside Kunobelin's abode that was not the case in or near the governor's palace. Here the atmosphere was befouled with all kinds of nauseating purifications. Paulinius was not amused. Dyfed often bumped into him at Kunobelin's palace where he even kept a bedroom now and an office. But he now began legislation to have the politia take a position to clean up the city and the Wall brook in particular, as well as keeping the harbour bottom dredged.

The governor's palace and the Lodge of Mithras both overlooked the harbour port that was, as already stated, navigable to sailing vessels. A short distance upstream from the governor's palace on the west bank was a poultry market, then further west yet a pig market that ran up to the Temple dedicated to Diana (Artemis). This shrine was chuck full of golden statutes and many other treasures and was the depository for the local Amoran establishment's wealth. In essence this temple was one big, well-guarded safe: It was one of many hundreds across the empire. In essence it was the Bank of Amor. It was also rumoured that the temple to Diana-cum-treasury's wealth that was inside her stalwart walls also contained a gold box wherein was placed a tiny bone from the little finger of the goddess Artemis. But in the meantime, from Poultry Street just outside her vestibule all the offal and manure from that particular market flowed down hill to the Wall brook.

Dyfed quickly discovered that all around Kunobelin's palace there was an assortment of activity which played havoc with Dyfed's sense of privacy and quietude, what with the amphitheatre where the roar and the wave of the crowd could go on for hours. And it, too, could smell on a warm day if the wind was blowing the wrong way. Almost directly beside was the Temple of Harmony and Concordance on his right flank (with all of its goings on day and late into the night). Dyfed saw irony in the name, but hoped for the best. The problem was that bulls and rams were slaughtered in ritual sacrifices in that vicinity, and in the warm weather (if the makeshift abattoirs weren't been constantly hosed down, which they never were) the lingering gore not only smelled to high heaven but drew flies by the billions that filled the air like a dirty, disease carrying thick dark mist. Aside from being constantly armed with fly-swatters, Kunobelin's staff had long been trained in a superior doctrine of housekeeping and domestic management which included waste management, never mind a weekly laundry schedule and general personal hygiene maintenance program for all the hired help. Dyfed vastly appreciated Kunobelin's observance in this. Indeed, any oversight of these rules by the domestic help resulted in dismissal. It was harsh, but he must have felt it to be an expedient recourse, as did Dyfed. I mean, he thought, who wants filthy cooks who scratch themselves or handle parts of their body then dive their fingers into the food they are preparing for you without a thought of ever washing their hands and under their fingernails? Either that or filthy body odour coming off the staff that wait on you hand and foot and serve you your dinner at the table with stinky armpits and loose hair dangling over your plate of food? In fact, he became to realise, the king was a lot more like his family than he had realised at first. Not even the waiters and servants of the Amoran rich and elite, who Dyfed had been introduced to by now, observed such standards quite as well as Kunobelin's staff did. Certainly Paulinius seemed to appreciate this environment, as had his predecessor, Governor Aulus Plautius. For during those hot summer months when the atmosphere around the official Amoran palace was befouled with all kinds of nauseating purifications, Gaius Paulinius (having been not amused) had taken to leaving his palace to move in with Dyfed where the air was that much rarer and the smell hovered just above the living limit of a rotting sulphuric hell. This helped, however, to eventually bring Dyfed into closer contact with the governor in a friendly and happy environment.

At one point shortly after his arrival, Dyfed introduced a policy of providing the young urchins of the city who were left unattended, left over foodstuffs from the palace table.

Even though the household had introduced him to Paulinus with great fanfare upon his arrival here in Nova Troia, the Amoran governor had had little time for him until now. However, during one late summer evening the following year on a particularly hot evening when an unusually great stink had floated up and around the harbour, the governor had retired to King Kunobelin's palace despite the monotonous roar from the fans over some sporting competition event happening behind Kunobelin's palace at the amphitheatre. At one point as the governor traipsed through the great hall going from one room to another, Dyfed looked up from his work and speaking out loudly reminded the governor of his obligation to Mitra. The busy and important man stopped and suddenly becoming motionless just stared at him with a long, deadpan face. Apart from its duty to pay its taxes how could the upstart cult housed in the Lodge of Mithras have anything to do with him? the governor wondered. It also appeared that he was wondering why it never occurred to this precocious upstart — who it seemed was always in his face while dragging the title of 'Keeper of the King's Palace' behind him wherever he went: a strange and affected young man with still stranger habits who (recently from somewhere or other in the sticks) was like a baby in bliss cooing under the Aurora Borealis, perhaps — that an Amoran governor might think him impetuous and ignorant of his place in addressing him (of all people) just any old time it pleased him. Truthfully on his part, Dyfed thought the governor was dumb and thick as a bag of sticks. Apparently, he didn't understand Dyfed's pointedly directed reference to Mithra (in his capacity — that is — of being the god of covenant, the god of contract and of oath) which those parishioners of strong minded brothers over at the Mistletoe Hall just another short hop, skip and a jump along the stinking harbour from his highness' equally high corridors of power in his now stink to high heaven palace might be holding him responsible (and their breath) to meet his long overdue obligation to cleanse the city and keep it free of collective stink.

"Mitra?' said Dyfed his arms rising on either side of him with the palms up and his fine physic suddenly looking like a large top-heavy double-U (W). 'The name itself,' he said smiling expectantly, eyebrows raised, 'is, after all, derived from the word to bind… as in bound to one's word or promise.' He held himself there for a moment then dropped his crooked arms quickly. With a humorously composed smile of frozen incredulousness on his face his silver eyes darted momentarily here and there as if he were trying to reclaim his persona of the moment or two earlier; either that or compose himself from an unexpected attack of forgetfulness of presence. Then appearing distracted he suddenly ignored Paulinus. He quickly looked away and became engaged again in monkeying with a strange looking gadget he had devised (and was in the process of fine-tuning).

This item was placed on a highly polished, exquisitely crafted wooden table. To have his work nearer to the light that was coming in through a window, he had dragged the table across the floor along with a small now skewered carpet that was still hooked to one table leg. Then out of the side of his vision he saw an extended but crooked finger shakily pointing as if struck by palsy.

"What's that you are playing at there?' said the governor's flat voice which had no sing-song elasticity in it whatsoever. But Dyfed (nevertheless) detected that it was full of curiosity. 'What's that contraption?'

After the Mistletoe Hall had been given one of the tenders to apply an organization for the clearing and cleaning of the city, Dyfed had been toying with the idea of a self generating mechanical pump so as to shift shallow stinking water lying around the streets toward the big river. The problem was he was having trouble keeping the machine running for more than a short period of time and always needed to replenish the raw substance that provided the power source. This substance he used for energy was expanding vapour-gas produced from boiling water. He knew that he needed to design a condenser so that after the energy was exhausted from its expansion, the still hot and expanded steam could be contracted and liquefied more quickly then usual so as to be quickly and easily pumped back into the boiler and expanded again. This provided a continuum of work that was needed to shift the shallow brackish and stinking substances somewhere else away from the noses of polite people. As yet, however, Dyfed was still having some problems with the condenser.

"This is what we call a machine,' replied Dyfed nonchalantly without looking up. The manner in which he answered obviously angered this important man.

"What do you mean a machine? he asked. 'What does it do, where did it come from and how on earth did you get hold of it, of all things?'

"It's a machine which I designed and built myself and have been fussing over the last few months to strike up a correct method for its operation and for easy fabrication. It's a proto-type machine for pumping out sour, stinky brackish water which is lying around your city collecting nasty little worms and incubating the eggs of flies and other horrible little insects,' he said. 'I'm looking to get a contract with the boys over at Mistletoe Hall to provide them service to pump this disgusting water out and away from the city's low lying areas. Apparently, nobody else they've approached to get it done as panned out. This will please everybody who lives here or visits the city, I'm told. Anyway, I've nothing else to do other than to improve myself with advance skills, not since I was turned down from attending the civil service graduate course that my endorser, General 'Flav the Finger' Cornelius had directed me towards, even providing me with an app...'

"What do you mean by calling General Cornelius, Flav the Finger?' interrupted the governor. With his high pitched voice the governor almost shouted this out, but managed to quietly tone it down to end it in a low bark and a measly growl. He liked the young man who had taken over the title of keeper of the royal palace, but didn't want to show his hand too easily. 'Is this any...' he quickly trailed off and then suddenly started to laugh which turned into a howl complete with tears washing down the side of his shiny face.

"As Jove lives, well, I never!' he said finally when he had composed himself, and dried the tears away with the inside of his elbows. 'Flav the Finger. Now tell me how much of a loan you need to contrive a machine gizmo to pump the slack and stale vile breeding grounds of water from the low-lying areas of my city. Please, I beg you.' he smiled at Dyfed now. 'And what's this about this civil service graduate course? It was General Cornelius who endorsed you? You don't say. There was something, I remember now, in your dossier about you being competent at accounts and I've had good reports about you from, what's his name, Gaius Julius. Even from Clemens or Publius…or whatever his name is, Maximus.' At this point the governor turned his nose up. 'You held down that position without incident under the quartermaster general for the vanished or truant ninth Legion, I think. Jolly good, then.'

Paulinus' face took on a different countenance at that moment. His dark eyes blinked rapidly while nodding his head slowly up and down and his lips moved as though he were either tasting something for the first time or spitting out tiny seeds.

"Ah…good evening to you, sire, and a happy next year's ground hog day…thank you, your worship, thank you,' said Dyfed, his sarcasm not quite penetrating his target.

(How much you pay, eh?)

*'Necessity is the plea for every infringement of human freedom.
It is the cry of tyrants; it is the creed of slaves.'*
WILLIAM PITT (AMONG OTHERS, APPARENTLY)

Karatakos had now left Nova Troia again. He would be back as soon as he could, he said. He hinted to Dyfed that he was working for the betterment of Albion and the Prydain folks in particular. It was all hush hush (as business such his usually was) but he did say he had some business in the City of Legion with Marg. However, up to then he had been helping Dyfed get settled and introduced him to one or two nice high born families who he thought would be the least irritating to him. Karatakos, unfortunately, had been wrong. Dyfed had his own mind about things. Karatakos had also helped him expedite articles and gizmos lying around wholesale (or from the city dump) which Dyfed thought would be useful for machine gadgetry, something with which he had taken to tinkering. And as a blacksmith, Karatakos knew his way around Nova Troia's tin-pan alleys along with colleagues of his who knew as much if not more.

Just across the Wall brook that flowed passed the front of the palace was a wholesale district. From Mistletoe Hall to the river was the well-heeled district of the governor's palace, but the northern extremity of the walled in yard of the Hall with its sea barn and utility sheds was the point where the shops of industry and wholesale started. From here it worked upstream to almost directly across the river from Kunobelin's palace. It also encroached somewhat onto the west bank of the Wall brook but stopped short just in front of the temple of Harmony and Concordance. Karatakos and Dyfed made good use of this district.

Of all the districts in this city this one was filled with the most useful and enterprising of activities. Here one could find metallurgists, forgers and blacksmiths and ironworkers down at the southern end and next to them were fullers, weavers and cloth makers, tanners and dyers. One could always know what colour would soon be in fashion in town in the coming season when the Wall brook and the harbour water changed colour from green to red or blue to a yellowy gold.

The industrial factories of this district were backed up beside each other and clumped together along a street where garment factory houses (that bought the dyed cloth which the fullers, weavers and other cloth makers fashioned) laboured to tailor into fashionable clothing for the denizens of Nova Troia. There were needle-threaders, seam-sewers, milliners and cobblers here, brass workers along with silversmiths, goldsmiths and jewellers each sitting cheek to jowl. And to and fro along this narrow street ran horse and oxen drawn wagons shuttling wares out to retail. Potters and glassmakers were in another part of town.

Recently one of the brothers of the House of Catulus from Amor had opened it doors as an advocate to represent folks charged with felonies. The wealthy House of Catulus were also experimenting with the holding and lending of silver and gold and they set up a store a few paces east of the corn-exchange in the central area. This instantly opened up the market for Nightwatchmen to undertake security for privately owned property, such as folks like Catulus, and industrialists and rich retailers. This was something never seen here before.

Once again, it was Mistletoe Hall that had soon secured pleas of protection from many businesses in the central area. This area extended from the basilica in the east that was situated directly behind the brick and mortar location of the House of Catulus, to the temple of Diana in the west, and a corridor encompassing a widened stretch of the Wall brook. This ran from the city's north gate (situated near the marshy moor that extended to the north of the city) to the harbour by the river in the south. The shadow of the brothers of the worshippers of Dis fell over much of the city at this time by their very act of forming a private brigade of Nightwatchmen. The governor, on the other hand, had his own security to guard his person, along with what the empire claimed as its own. And that guard was the recently re-covered ninth Legion Hispana: the military contingent of which General Cornelius has been unceremoniously striped. Relieved of his command Cornelius had been ordered back to Nova Troia and was currently in limbo. Meanwhile, his old regiment that now guarded the governor were composed of super-Nightwatchmen on steroids that didn't give a hang about any civil disobedience that didn't in any way involve the safety of Paulinius. Sometimes they were even the perpetrators.

On the sixteenth of May (the day after Merx day) of that year, Dyfed began work at the basilica (stoa). As stated, when Dyfed had first arrived in the city, his pre-registered application for a civil service graduate course was denied for reasons he hadn't bothered to follow up. Through Kunobelin's close association with the palace and Paulinius, Dyfed skipped the academy and with the governor's recommendation he secured a position within the basilica's chambers of bureaucracy. Quite some time later it came to pass that the same aforementioned curriculum — namely a freshman course on Amoran policy, and civil due process preparatory tuition — had finally become available for him. Upon the receipt of the letter (he was duly informed that) he was invited to sit through a screening competition. Although Dyfed had now dropped any interest in pursuing this, his curiosity was peaked. His appearance was to be before a panel of interviewers who were to evaluate his potential that was a prerequisite of entrance to the school. In other words, before starting classes he was to sit for an aptitude test so they could measure out how much un-noticeable, behind the scenes, subconscious intelligence potential he had so they could match him against previously scaled intelligence charts and accord him a level. This was the case with all unknown Amorans and all known non-Amorans.

Dyfed wasn't overly interested in letting people know just how smart he in fact was, that was the problem. He did advertise his potential, though, which he saw being different, at least to those scouring the countryside and on the lookout for something or someone to help give them the edge. But in this case his prankish nature didn't allow him to miss the opportunity to not only suss out the characteristics and abilities of other branches of the Amoran establishment but to shock senior members of the bureaucratic establishment itself, mostly for fun. So he attended the institute's screening process for examination in order to come to some measure where he stood alongside this seemingly infallible machine.

It was explained to him at the start of the competence examination that certain questions would be asked him and his answers would be evaluated. It was to decide, they told him, where his talents lay, and just how much potential he had. Even to see if he had any, they added. Many people had contributed to this science, they explained at length; indeed, countless solar cycles of labour had been employed in order to produce the system. It was a formula, they said, put in place in order to pigeonhole potentials and weed out the unruly imaginative and the sky gazing dreamer. Dyfed, of course, had no doubt about his capabilities. As a sky gazing dreamer himself (what else could he be, under the circumstances that found him here?) he even had a sense of superiority because of it (and in face of what he was up against), so he removed his casual aspect and put on his disdainful look that he wore to the interview.

He constantly interrupted them in intervals while he impatiently listened to their introductory orientation and rules of play. During these interruptions he managed to state emphatically and rather well that the time which these so-called experts had spent attempting to measure the unknown quantities that dwelled inside the heads and hearts of young human beings coming up through their own generation — bright young minds who the examiners didn't (in any way) know, in addition to the crude and inadequate measuring tools they had at hand for their disposal — that it might have been better to have spent all that energy and tax money in trying instead to inspire and challenge these students, not hack away at their fragile self esteem.

"These young, inquisitive, growing and supple minds…your students…the potential leaders of the future need encouragement,' Dyfed said, 'to develop, not criticism to stifle.' That was followed with an incredulous and condescending little laugh that was shot out in their direction. Oh, he thought at the time, I can be such an insulting jerk in my demonstrative way, and loving every minute of it. 'These youngsters don't need criticism,' he continued, 'certainly for a lack of something in which they haven't had any reason to commit towards. They don't need their feelings or their intellect assaulted, insulted or assassinated for a lack of something to which they haven't had a call to arms about, or even been challenged to address. You can't possibly know what they lack until you truly know what they will be up against. It is apparent to me, however, what you lack. As Quintus Septimius Florens Tertullianus has just recently stated…'*You can't teach by persuading but you can persuade by teaching.*' 'No, no! It is encouragement and aspiration that is needed here. It is needed in order to ascertain what gifts each and every human (in this case applicant) has in order that such and such can be applied to each according to their interests and abilities. It is needed in order to allow them to aspire and blossom into unique and gifted thinkers. Only then will their self-esteem and self-confidence provide the lift to facilitate their ability to explore areas of notion and fancy even you or others that have gone before have not yet understood. If it is your intention for them to further your shortcomings, then…by Saturn…by Jove…god of god…light of light…very god of very god…inspire them to believe in themselves so that before they know what it is you are asking of them (about which you know nothing and are desperately in need of an answer, while currently worried that it can't be answered) these ordinary, seemingly ungifted, run of the mill and distracted heaven gazers will figure out the absurd and the unimaginable before you can say Jiminy Cricket. And the world will have made another leap forward. This has been the case in the past, but thanks to your methods you have broken the circle and you, and now we, will remain in fixity on your account.'

It seemed to him, so his next interruption told them all, that taking his advise would be a way more productive course in order to manage and harness the student's fertile minds. Certainly better than trying to figure out what the students lacked, what their inadequacies were. Did they not think it was a strange concept to proceed that way without even knowing what gifts and talents and other mechanisms these students would actually have to have and need in the future in order to do what you will bid them do, which at this moment you don't know what that will be? 'How can you know,' he asked incredulously of them as he stood up to leave, 'how can you know what will be needed by them to answer the problems that lie ahead when you most certainly don't only not have the answer, you don't even know (at this time) what those problems might be? You have little inkling — perhaps not even one iota or one jot of knowing — what the new generation will want to invent, or in what direction of discovery they will be planning to strike out and explore for the good of the empire as you drool from the mouth staring into space facing a wall.

"Although,' he continued much to their annoyance (some already trying to drown him out) 'it is expedient to have standards as well as strict rules, such as experimentation and observation, something you lack, by the way. You can't possibly know what will come to pass. What! — have the plans been prematurely drawn up based on future knowledge that hasn't even yet been discovered yet conundrums thereof are already evident? Give me a break. You're a gaggle of foolish morons all set to fight the next generation war with weapons from the last war, as always,' Dyfed told them before thanking the civil servant examiners in a pleasant manner for giving him their time. He finished by telling them they would shorty receive his advisory consultation bill and that he hoped it would be promptly paid.

There had been no fall-out following his contrived interview with civil service graduate course interviewers. So, as it stood now, his new position at the palace (albeit at a starting level) was to rifle through the mountain of receipts of the department of bills payable. Besides aiding and abetting Amoran interests in a straightforward fashion, this also entailed helping foreign businesses to help Amor profit from the people and the wealth of the province at hand. The job was also to apply, update and enforce Amoran treasury and commerce laws and to collect fees, among other dues and fees for the emperor. The problem was that slim, quick-witted customers among the merchant class and the fertile and furtive minds of clever privateers tended — when dealing with the establishment of the emperor — to seek the path of least resistance in achieving the most profit for themselves and not for the empire. To these folks the empire was a means to an end, an avenue for capital gains, and little more.

By now Dyfed was beginning to understand human nature of the hoi polloi's business class and saw their point. However, he knew that any successful culture had to be built on trust, loyalty and respect. Cheating wasn't complimentary to any of those. But then again, where would the emperor and all his trappings be without the entrepreneur, the risk-taker, and the man and woman eager to enter into competition. This was where wealth was made and although the trickle down wealth effect was vastly overrated and was really something of a bare-faced lie, the denizens of the state won't have any common wealth without some form of trickle down and neither will the state itself other than through unabashed tyranny. The problem was, he knew, that this kind of talent works best in a free market. And a free market isn't one that is dominated by any form of coercive monopoly such as any entity (of Amoran imperialism or foreign or local capitalism) whose interests are to interfere with and maintain a monopoly over free market competition for the purpose of their own advantage and advancement.

This is what was happening now. The House of Catulus bullied the local market in their attempt to monopolize, as did the rich who were patrons of imperialism. Even the brothers down at the Mistletoe Hall managed to secure advantages of gathering in tenders over other eager tender seekers as the aforementioned were doing their level best to teach them all to whistle Dixie.

And really! what was the purpose of an empire anyway if it wasn't collective? Otherwise it was a shell game played over a long duration of time with a fight to the finish to own it all. So what the empire begged for was what the folks from Hellas called democracy, that illusive and flighty thing that's been around a long time in different guises but was absent here. It, along with the free market, also begged social order and equivalency. That is the work put in must equal wealth drawn out, but drawn out along a common standard. This is social order and it is what you make it. Once again, democracy and its relative humanist socialism, which goes hand in hand together, are the two champions of humanity. Furthermore, as previously said, one supports the other. And the Amoran Empire did not have this despite all the kudos one could give them for other things. And they didn't even have a middle class either, Dyfed mused.

Taxes (like Nightwatchmen) are necessary so long as there is mutual trust, loyalty and respect. If that isn't the case then taxes and Nightwatchmen becomes the people's enemy. That was the current case within the empire as far as he could see from his limited position here. However, he became pie eyed when he investigated property taxes. Folks had struggled and saved their hard earned earnings to purchase property and the emperor then taxed them every year after that for owning their property. If they sell it they are taxed for gaining income. Nobody owns property anyway. No body owns anything, Dyfed thought, its all only an illusion. Only the rich and the fools think they own anything. What a sham. For in the established Amoran Empire, every denarii in the pocket of Joe Citizen of Amor that was left over after providing under paid, back-breaking labour (or wily, uniquely skilled and talented tenacity) to an employer, and not before heavy unavoidable income taxes had taken its toll on a distinct portion of those pocketed denarii that somehow were left over, each and every spending transaction thereafter for each and every remaining denarii could not (under Amoran law without penalty) be conducted or fulfilled without having to pay a spending-transaction tax. That's because every item sold legally in the market had its own buying transaction tax attached. It is called a sales tax but really it's a spending (your already heavily taxed denarii in the pocket) tax. And don't thing for a moment that for Joe Citizen it might be the last of it.

Seeing an opportunity here in the palace, and wanting to impress Paulinus who had provided him a shoo-in, Dyfed was more than diligent when it came to catching cheaters and in discerning loopholes that smart minds had finagled out from the mountain (or was it the cave) which constituted the labyrinth of bureaucracy. He wasn't going to be a paper tiger, or shy away from the shadowy timber wolves prowling out from the cave's entrance in the growing dusk, either. But he needed long horns with sharp pointy ends if he was going to be the Minotaurish bull in their china shop. It was a Heraklean-type feat that lay ahead, but the job also entailed a lot of what he called information gathering by the Amoran society of census.

The Amoran bureaucrats wanted to know what folks had and where it was they kept what they had. The census wanted to know what the people wanted and where they got it from and how much they paid and how much they would pay. Pax Amor and the Amoran status quo, according to census, deemed the peoples' forced transparency as a necessary condition for them to stay in business. Somehow this spelled out a different definition of empire that Dyfed had of as being a healthy, safe, and happy environment for all denizens that embodied an equal opportunity for all before the law: In other words, a comfortable human social state of being. Furthermore, the diligence and energy he put into working didn't sit well with his brother bureaucrats, especially with Publius Servilius Maximus, although his junior colleague, Gaius Lucius Julius was more accommodating.

(Sire, the multitudes of peasants were revolting, and without a by-your-leave)

'In all confrontations, as in war, truth is the first casualty.'
ANONYMOUS

It just so happened that during this time and for the past few years, due to empire wide overt unrest and rebellion, intrigue and equally unsubtle unrest that had begun to rattle the seat of the imperial palace in Amor, sudden shocking trends in the behaviour of so-called polite society quickly began to change. It had been at this time that Cornelius had decided to come clean and throw himself at the mercy of Paulinius. The preferred trend that was overtaking Amor involved intrigue, dissension and murder such as by stabbing and brutal beating (though poison was preferential especially among women perpetrators). This became rampant among the royal and not so royal self-appointed contenders vying for anything from the top position and other offices of power in reverse from the emperor himself down — ladies in waiting…the emperor's house boy in lolly-land at his summer residence…and further down the gravy train to consul in waiting, chief magistrate, chief of police, chief sergeant at arms, head Turn-key, head Nightwatchman, special interest chiefs and advisors along with senatorial positions. The result of this constant reshuffling was a mixture of homicides complicated with suicides, divorces and law suits that dragged out contenders from their mansions into the streets of poverty. During this time emperors came and went in quick succession so that further incursions by Amor into Albion was all but ignored for a time by the executive elite. But it was in a swift and continuous response to those circumstances that were taking place abroad that the tribal chiefs in Albion used as an opportunity to revolt once again.

It was at this juncture that Flav the Finger's alliance with Bricus, the man who was now being credited by the Prydains with leading the rebellion (a quint-essential false flag event no matter how you looked at it) was out the window. And this didn't place Cornelius' current position with Paulinius in a better position, either. For no one at any given moment could tell for sure if the rebellion was for the tribes against Amoran occupancy or was pro occupancy against rebellious tribes. It was like a circus arena filled with gaudy painted Druids accompanied by an on-going loud fuss while (with standing room only) the fans in the stands on either side of the fray were on their feet staring in silence not knowing what the hell the score was and not even knowing which side was the home team. So nobody was rooting for anybody and apart from the Druid's barking banter, silence fell upon the arena. It didn't hurt either that the powerful union of tin helpers' and mine workers whose negotiations for better pay had failed in Dumnonia. Suddenly the whole works went out in a general strike. This started walkouts all over Albion and soon the availability a journeyman forger or a tinsmith willing to work were as scarce as hen teeth. Togo Waugh (Kunobelin's palace administer) thought and verbalized loudly that it was all bird shit: a cluster-fuck, Dyfed had even overheard someone say in the local language, for the Amoran tongue wasn't quite as vulgarly refined as the tongue of the Prydains here in this province of Brytain.

Realizing Bricus' betrayal in his eager grab for imperial recognition, the maverick Flavius Cornelius (who himself had been playing a dangerous illegal game outside of imperial authority), along with some of his men, hastily fled south in their superior but small fleet of triremes from the region of Legion while Maelgwyn, Cadot and Cadwallopir studied the unfolding events with some amusement in quietude from their hill-top forts in the far west. Now the Brigantes had been joined by the Pixies to the north, rumour had it, and the latter were giving the Amoran fleet chase along the shore until they tired and their footwear were worn out. Meanwhile, as that crew journeyed south, the XXth legion had moved west under the command of Esuprastus Prasutagus and was sacking and burning villages in the west in and around Gwynedd. Sub-legate Esuprastus Prasutagus was leaning on Gwynedd and demanding allegiance to Amor. From the standpoint of folks like the Decangi who were not known for their subservience, especially before a behavioural factor such as that which the entitled Amoran Legions displayed. So this was never going to be a gently enacted demand and sundry cenedles were being attacked and destroyed.

As far as copper was concerned, once General Cornelius arrived back in Nova Troia he reported seeing copper showings on Mona Major while on his voyage up the western coast a number of years earlier. Come to think of it, Dyfed thought, he had overheard somewhere that the Mistletoe Lodge Hall (as it was now called) was investing in copper mining somewhere out west, too. Ceredwyn, though, was still on his mind, for as far as he knew she was back somewhere in those west kingdoms and this worried him.

Meanwhile, consensus was that Cornelius would probably be accompanied out of Prydain (Albion) in disgrace at least as far as Amor in order to stand trial for insubordination if not for treason. It was also known that the emperor had decided to shore up his investment in this northern province whose isolated position bode them well. Historically, outside of Albion the upshot of any on-going dissention and outbreak of war had always been met with swift reaction from the emperors of Amor. Emperor Nero was no exception, but he was facing a greater challenge than had gone on before. As we will see he became the emperor that moved to swiftly check the revolting tribes ruling the roost in Gaul which also threatened Amor's authority in Armorica which itself had strong ties with Albion. So with the empire in a general revolt he elected to send two generals to sort out the situation in Prydain province and recall Paulinius. The man he chose as field marshal and legate was General Titus Flavius Vespasianus to be aided by his deputy General Gnaeus Julius Dietcola.

Under the new shuffle Paulinius was to shortly give up the title of governor. General Cornelius the maverick, on the other hand had the weight of his brother's reputation on his side to have any treasonous act momentarily set aside. So Nero simply recalled Cornelius in disgrace and ordered him home to Amor where he would deal with him. But Paulinius interjected and told him he should retain his command of the IXth Legion until Vespasianus and Dietcola replaced him. Vespasianus, however failed to show up and in lieu of him Nero decided on Sea Admiral (and competent soldier) Lucius Aelius Castus.

By this time Dyfed had been coaxed over into another department of the basilica that reported directly to the palace. The position was as a Magister Commercii in training. He was told that he was to study under a Carthaginian named Potamus Purplebal who was an outstanding Capital Gains entrepreneur. Apparently, he was to arrive with General Vespasianus. Of course, the latter never turned up and neither did Purplebal. Purplebal ultimately referred to himself as the House of Purblebal. But he had a younger married sibling with the distinctive name of Hipparchia Philostropodousalouspolousadous whose rich Amoran husband had recently died of poison. Initially Hipparchia had accompanied Potamus from Carthage to Amor after becoming a widow and was to have accompanied Potamus from Amor to Nova Troia, but obviously she arrived alone. Other than her hard eyes, gossip had it that she was an outwardly beautiful woman. Rumour had it that Potamus Purplebal was breaking into the empire's trading and banking sector. He was attempting to take advantage (the rumour mills said) of Emperor Nero's mandate to turn the ship of the Amoran state around. Meanwhile, Markus Catulus employed Philostropodousalouspolousadous. He took her up as a social receptionist who dressed up Catulus' boardrooms (some said the boudoir) during business and after hours.

Meanwhile, Dyfed set out and went it alone, as they say. He got what he needed straight out of the books he was given special access to from the palace library. They were extended to him for this purpose on account of Purplebal's absence that at that time was still thought to be his delay. And Dyfed's aptitude was such that he was able to master the science and comprehend the applicable theories and logistics in no time without any preparatory schooling at all. And no one (other than Servilius Publius Maximus and his junior colleague Gaius Lucius Julius who had learned of Dyfed's promotion) thought that the books alone would (or could) do much good to anybody without proper verbal tutoring. They were wrong, of course, and it was a rare and unique opportunity for Dyfed indeed. It was not something (this opportunity to exercise skill) which (generally speaking) would or could have taken place anywhere else in the empire, say in Massala or Mediolan, never mind in Amor which was still Dyfed's destination.

The new governor, Aulus Didius Gallus, who replaced Paulinius arrived on the ship on which Scapula and Paulinius sailed out on and home. It was at this last moment the emperor had instructed Flav the Finger to remain in Albion until Vespasianus arrived, which was delayed again as he was finally to await the arrival of Lucius Aelius Castus.

Meanwhile Dietcola officiated as sergeant of arms along with the IX Legion Hispana in the ceremony installing Gallus as governor who then took up his place in the Amoran imperial palace. Now as the acting Chamberlain and the Keeper of the Royal Palace of the Prydainian high king Kunobelin, Dyfed quickly responded with an invitation for Aulus Gallus to dine at the royal palace. This, then, was his own introduction to the governor, an introduction that did not go unnoticed.

In short order Gallus became quite intimate with the wise and ferociously intelligent and competent young aid in the basilica that had close ties with the imperial palace, as did the desk of the Magister Commercii in general. They soon came to rely heavily on Dyfed and on some occasions he was even on loan to the military. This situation brought him to the attention of Dietcola who apparently was still in communication with Vespasianus who was still expected to arrive, maybe even before Lucius Aelius Castus did. The former's workload had become overpowering due to the growing numbers of soldiers arriving every month and the logistics that went with it. It was common knowledge that unrest was all the rage in hot spots across the empire and now Gaul was flaring up badly too. This was the plight of empire that could threaten Albion as it burned out of control from Gaul (long prostrated and converted into the Amoran ways). It was well known that the Germanics on the right bank of the river Rone were poised for rebellion, too. In fact, if they weren't, something would have to be seriously wrong. For such a condition as peace in that region had seldom (actually never) happened before.

Even in the land of Armorika across the water to the south of Albion disturbances were still unfolding at an alarming rate as stated earlier. And any emperor worth his salt was likely as ever to continue down the path of Pax Amor as before to always make capital gains for the imperial coffers his approbated goal. He would do this in spite of overall monetary inflation (including the inflation of suffering among the hoi polloi). He would continue the motivation of empire no matter what, just as before while eschewing any change whatsoever. But things don't stand still: nothing but nothing stands still, anywhere. Even the eternal moment doesn't stand still from any one stationary spot, but revolves around itself. True, the Tao abides in non-action, yet nothing here is left undone. This is the doctrine of the mean. Standing still is to vacate life. To stand still is to deny life, death and rebirth. So, the empire (whether anyone liked it or not) would change despite the spirit of eschewal and despite the policy of non-change that the empire continued to adopt at this time: The question was, when would that happen?

Meanwhile, Emperor Nero moved to apply the Admiral Aelius Castus Syndrome. This seafarer's normal busy day (what with his tactical expertize and fleet of ships) had until recently been pirating, harrying, and keeping the superior seafarers from the north at bay from the Amoran plums along the lower river Rine and Tems. This is what had kept him from taking up his position in Albion. But once rebellion had broken out in Illyricum as well, the emperor had then sent Castus to protect the shipping lanes out from the Adriatic coast and the province of Illyrium that was providing a product that was in high demand: namely iron-ore. But then Emperor Nero reversed his strategy and decided to return Castus to safeguard Albion by appointing him as admiral over a combination of fleets under the banner of a naval expeditionary force to dampen down piracy and rebellion and unrest in and around Gaul and Armorika. So, there we have it, Dyfed thought. Apparently, it was the stability of Albion that worried the emperor the most, not so much the unrest raging out of control in Illyricum or Palesteen. So what gives?

This got Dyfed thinking. Maybe the reason for safeguarding Albion (the son of Poseidon) which included Alba to the north, was part of a plan to gain and vouchsafe a defendable fortress (for those power elites who meant to keep on ruling an empire that ruled Europa and the world after the power shift and imperial crash) and to safeguard it and put it aside for the (their) future. This then would become their home-patch in preparation for the might of a revived Amor to strike out one day in the future and control the whole world in time. They must know the empire will eventually run out of fuel at some point as things are now so that would be why Castus' fleet was once again being ordered to shift from the southern iron-ore shipping lanes he was guarding into mobilization for relocation back here where he would fill Vespasianus' still vacated position at last, after all, even if it was so far from the heart of Amor. In short, Armorica and the area around the river Rine was like a shield, a parapet and was meant to act in Albion's defence and help stiffen her abutment. This hinted toward the fact that the power elite of the Amoran Empire was planning to (at some distant time) relocate the heart of Amor to Nova Troia in Albion instead.

Due to his diligent work at the governor's palace, one of the riches jeweller, goldsmith, pawnshop and safe-vault chains in the empire then suddenly took an interest in Dyfed. This was the aforementioned House of Catulus that had recently set up a branch of their combined businesses here in Albion situated in Nova Troia. This new prospect that appeared to be (and stated that they were) backing Amoran advancement into Albion was controlled by a prominent equestrian family of Amorans from the part of Keltic Gaul that stretched south of the central Alpine mountains. These people were very wealthy and despite their short time in Albion, they already had a few houses out of which they were working. It was honest enterprise (so long as it was kept above board) and aside from being pawn shopkeepers, jewellers and goldsmiths they were also (what was termed) argentarii. As agents in this trade they kept strict books (tabulae) and owned very safe vaults. As such they kept deposits and acted in auctions and folks banked their jewels and gold with the House of Catulus for safekeeping. And often too their customers would draw on their gold and silver being kept there. They did this by having a merchant with whom they wished to do business accompany them to the House of Catulus so he could open an account (if he didn't already have one) so the latter could accumulate credit there (with that house) or retain a gold account.

Each house operated under its own name and mark that was brandished outside its door. This misleading dissection of their investment on their part quelled suspicion by others of any intention they may have had for establishing a monopoly, a situation that was normally expedient for bankers (or greedy types who believe they are more entitled than others) to strive for. Of course! the House of Catulus had intention toward monopoly. That's what capital gainers do, besides striving for being authoritarian in manner and positioning themselves to be able to call the rules of the game. This situation gave the house of Catulus, like any other practitioner, the distinct advantage of manipulating and maintaining control over competitive practices. In essence this manipulation is called capitalism, as opposed to free, and above board marketeering. It is the top of a very slippery slope. In the case of the wily House of Catulus, their false show of genuine competitive practices dispelled suspicion and lured other banking businesses to be drawn into a casino environment which they fashioned and where their House had all the advantages. This is what sophisticated Houses from Amor and other commercial centres do when they go to the sticks: They take advantage.

One advantage they didn't have (yet) was the use of a worthless token that could be lent out in lieu of gold or silver. Such an exponent or marker would have allowed the House of Catulus pawnshops — the jewellers and goldsmiths — to keep that precious metal owned by other folks and stored safely under locks and chains in the comfort of their own vaults to be available and therefore lendable again (maybe a few times over) to other borrowers behind the owners' backs without ever actually having to withdraw any of the precious gold. Dyfed saw the answer for such a method but kept it to himself. Nor at any time did he make an attempt to introduce this method that in any case would have needed a successful trust build-up and a trial run past the merchants at the marketplace.

At about this time King Kunobelin announced that he was stepping down as high king. He then propped up another of his 'sons' (Togo Waugh) under the weight of the high crown and rewarded him with an elaborate coronation. This professional arrangement was actually a ruse that allowed Kunobelin to still retain control while providing him the luxury (at least for a while) of easier movement and more personal privacy along with a modicum of well earned, semi-retirement and recreation.

Having already been warned by Dyfed about the shenanigans which the House of Catulus was getting up to, yet out of curiosity about their modus operandi and end game intentions that would affect the folks at the centre of Albion's commerce, Kunobelin (in wanting to investigate deeper) suddenly placed some of his large accounts into their hands. With Togo Waugh now as high king, Kunobelin bestowed on Dyfed the permanent title of Chamberlain (Treasurer) in his capacity to serve King Togo. This now compounded Dyfed's official title as Prince Dyfed Lucifer: Keeper of the Royal Palace and Chamberlain of the High King of Albion. This then placed Dyfed legally in charge of those accounts. Now it was his job to watch and if necessary, parry with the House of Catulus. Dyfed was up to this but was not left on his own.

Dyfed then took up a request of his own and asked Kunobelin for his support. It was an idea Dyfed had had and was now being given the go-ahead. This brainchild of Dyfed's was to form a single financial institution that he intended to call the Albion Union Bank and enter into a partnership with Marcus Lucius Catulus. After all, the House of Catulus had other irons in the fire with other banking outlets. But in the end Marcus Lucius Catulus, the patriarch of the Albion branch of the House of Catulus, kept stalling and finally refused to act, despite the advantage at hand and its potential prospects. Dyfed had proposed to share ten per cent ownership between the Regency (the Crown) and the House of Catulus. This was a condition which Kunobelin and Dyfed had negotiated between them, and which he had then proposed to Marcus Catulus.

Dyfed thought that every merchant, fleet-owner, landowner, industrialist, farmer, butcher, miller, greengrocer, tanner, general, soldier, sailor, rich man, poor woman or thief in the street with a spare denarii in his or her pocket to save would be willing to share in the remaining ninety per cent ownership of the company that would inflate each of the innovators five per cent into something beautiful. Never mind what the shareholders would reap on top of that as every man and woman rushed to cash in with this gold mine. And as for them, after all, five per cent of ten thousand or even just five thousand was better than five per cent of nothing.

So he petitioned Marcus to kingdomize at least one branch of his argentarii company and create a peoples' bank. It was a new innovation. In this, it must be said immediately, he wasn't very successful either; however, Dyfed held out some hope and later proposed to form a steering committee in order to help coax this brilliant situation along. But Marcus Lucius Catulus still stalled for time. It was always the same old concern; people cashing out, and this is what the Catulus committee harped on. It was a fear that grew on greed.

The problem for Dyfed was that even as the Chamberlain of the Palace he couldn't get enough money that was needed at the time to seed the venture and to push the issue with the Catulus family who weren't prepared to put up the funds in order to underwrite a business proposal where, as they saw it, other folks prospered more than they did. In their mind the net profits to them would be less than it's potential, they said. And Marcus' biggest competitor would be that foreign Phoeniki, Johnny come lately, no show here in Nova Troia — Potamus Purplebal — who was gaining wealth hand over fist in Amor and (so rumour and Marcus Catulus had it) all over the empire. Despite his monopoly Dyfed could see that Marcus Catalus didn't give a rat's ass or a round of sheep shit about anybody but himself, so the deal snagged on his hesitancy alone in the face of the kingdom's short-fall of funds. This was now being employed by the palace in an attempt to fight inflation. But Dyfed knew that this would only destroy securities that wealthy people invested in over the years. Soon the lazy, old-moneyed, very pissed off rich would be selling their chateaus. Here was a lesson to be learned.

It should be pointed out here that with empty pockets the rebellion began slowing down, and even if political intrigue continued, espionage of and around expeditionary forces, battle lines and combats tapered off too. But the piracy did not. It was around the time of Togo's coronation for high king that Karatakos had arrived back at the palace.

Having seen in Dyfed a potential interest for themselves, and by realizing the truth of, and value in Dyfed's connections to the House of the high King as well as to the basilica, Marcus Catulus took up an initiative of wooing Dyfed. Although he only offered him a limited knowledge of the House of Catulus' investments and overall concerns, he did open a window for him as to the genius of the former's success. Marcus tutored Dyfed himself, or at least oversaw his lessons. Most importantly, he told Dyfed, for a bank to succeed, it needed to learn the art and means of being able to avoid allowing one's investors of glimpsing any form of tenuity on the part of the bank's ability to remain as a thorough stronghold that's able to guard their money and prosper. This, and all the while allowing the bank to gain quick profits for themselves first and foremost from their customers' gold deposits that weren't just sitting safely in their safe but instead were being either lent out to good risk borrowers to purchase brick and mortar or used by the bank itself to invest in commodities such as farming or food transportation and distribution, or investing in necessities such as wine, beer and in horse breeding and raising. This then was a coveted secret that Dyfed quickly picked up. In addition to public trust, Dyfed eventually learned of other frequent vulnerabilities in financing, along with certain subtleties that was intrinsic to the wizardry of financial capital gains. Dyfed held his tongue and played the role of simple Simeon while his learning curve became exponential to his effort. This only took a matter of weeks. Both parties were successful in this endeavour, and it was about this time when it came to their attention that not only was Dyfed's understanding of finance impeccable, but that he also harboured ingenious insights. Quickly they promoted him with the hope that they could own him. But fortunately it provided him instead with a vision to found a People's Union Bank under his own control. Then with Togo's influence and support, aside from doing the math, Dyfed also began to set into motion the gathering up of necessities that were needed to satisfy all aspects for its successful logistics. This included the potential for a sufficient number of well-heeled businessmen whose successful business needed constant cash flow for maintaining the business (farm, industry or service occupation) and for investment in order to grow. Dyfed was determined, and he envisioned, that doing business with him he would guarantee that every member who had an invested interest in his banking firm, no matter how much or how little, would be able (theoretically) to profit according to each individual's percentile of investment. This was not, and never had been, the House of Catulus' mode d' employ towards their strictly defined purpose for promoting capital gains. Mind you, in respect to a People's Union Bank (which was to remain in name only for some time) the concept of its mode of operation was only in the foundation stage. No business practices as such were in place anywhere that he knew. Even the Amoran mensarii (state banks) or the governor's palace somewhat illegal ghost banks weren't taking a farsighted approach build up capital wealth into account. Dyfed reasoned that based on the idea of financing a large influx of borrowers whose businesses were not just financed but also advised and prodded into achieving as large a profit as possible with more investment promises later to expand their profits even more (always under an advisory of hawk-eyed well paid professionals), then with a careful application of juxtaposed interest rates according to development and success, bank profit could skyrocket and the bell chart curve for investor dividends would follow. In a short time this would cause a loyalty based both on greed and satisfaction as well as draw multitudes of others over to the bank. With a set low percentile for bank net profits so as to encourage investor euphoria, its profits would also remain low, at first, he reasoned. At least until such a time when so much money was at stake, the bank's percentile profit (though remaining the same) would logically have the numbers that represented each percentile, start to climb. And as investor loyalty to the bank was solidified even more through generosity, this bank's profit would climb higher and higher. Spend money to make money was something that Catulus taught him. It made a lot of cents on the denarii as well.

Anyway, as such, the system of the status quo which was in place at that moment remained in place which only insured that the rich got richer in a too obvious a manner until deflation took everything. This situation, which his system (he thought) could cure, also insured that no vast middle strata of consumers could ever materialise in order to hold the balance which could be applied like a flywheel and defray the shock of market expansion and contraction (as was currently happening, as always) so as to be in a position to assist in propelling this or any other empire onwards and upwards and dragging the populace up by their boot straps with it. But in the real world it was a finite game that the Amorans were playing here, Dyfed believed, where the establishment versus hoi polloi's end game would either be a win/lose, or lose/lose, loss. How the denarius system was played was on a slanted playing field. Here, only the most intelligent (if that was their volition) or the rich actually prospered, though it was the depths of the detail, something that didn't always affect the rich too drastically but always affected the poor, who suffered. In a loss, say, of ten thousand denarii it comes down to how much a single denarii means for you and your family. And guess what would happen if the Capital-Gains seekers of Amor's program nose-dived? So, that made his own concept of a union bank progressively invaluable to everybody when Amor eventually ran out of fuel and the energy of slaves. As far as the Catulus Bank was concerned they had closed the corral (kraal) gate too late. In letting Dyfed come close to the hearth and the warmth of the fire, the Catulus family had made a fatal error.

Dyfed's idea was hot; it cut the mustard and could eat like acid through the sham of Amoran banking system and take all their business and share it with the people while preventing the market from crashing, to boot. And crashing, he reckoned, would be the end game of the Amoran system and the grande-finale, one day. That was the most troubling. Dyfed had plotted it out using the logic of mathematics combined with the Web of Fates which Manandan had taught him, and he saw that a very few indeed would be left solvent under the current system if the bottom dropped out. In this scenario, these folks who presently controlled the world of finance would own everything only until they, too, owned nothing. For this euphoric environment, this garden of Eden that remained for those few rich and famous Capital-Gain Seekers that were left standing, it would only last, he saw, for a fleeting moment in the end. And that end would come, he knew: and then the grapes would be gone and nobody would have anything because there had been no investment for the future and no proficient and knowledgeable labourer would be able to be found anywhere that would be willing to keep the machine running, the water flowing, and the sewer flushing for a raisin or a peanut in pay. At least not a live one, and dead men don't work. And the machine wouldn't be working either; it will have run out of energy slaves and will have stopped dead. So there would be no fresh food in the larder, no cold beer and sweet wine in the cellar, nor would there be anybody ambitious enough to keep the barbarians who would then at the gate, at bay; at least not during the first few weeks, anyway. After that, the shoplifters and those who pillage in general wouldn't even bother to come around anymore to pick through the spoils. In fact they would be quickly joined on the road leading out of town by the only local yokels left who themselves would be itching to leave home, presumably looking for a new scene and a new start. Then, even the graves of the rich would become overgrown with weeds and their glorious headstones chewed away into oblivion by Kronus' grinding his old teeth. Kunobelin might have laughed at his idea, he thought, but his way could prevent that down turn and moreover it could create a new Idea of empire for the hoi polloi.

(No census on consensus)

'I love those who do not know how to live except in perishing, for they are those going beyond.'
FRIEDRICH NIETZSCHE

Despite the Empire changing horses in Albion mid stream (that is from building a provincial hen house to designing the nest for the eagle's golden egg), the Amoran machine was ever diligent in its mechanized movement forward to control. Census had begun in ancient times, long before the Amorans first arrived on the scene; but now it was widely sweeping, leaving no stone unturned. And it wasn't just a matter of gathering a record of numbers; it was also about keeping tabs of names and data attached to those names such as professions, positions and status' within their communities. It was about where and when folks were born, who their parents were, and where everybody connected to them now lived?...Did the person under consideration have a spouse?...Did they have more than one spouse?...Did they have any children? If so, how many, and when was each of them born and what were their names.

Also, with whom did they have these children; with which spouse, or was it with somebody else's spouse? The census was unrelenting, even down to notations on solicited remarks on people made by others who were not even necessarily credible, never mind professionally versed. Under these circumstances it didn't take too much for a caring, considerate person to be vile and abusive, or an intelligent individual to be insane and dangerous. The Amoran machine was also interested in what the activities of each person were and who they chiefly worshipped. Most especially, the empire wanted to know what each possessed. Articles itemized under this heading could be land, buildings, horses, cattle, pigs, and storehouses containing such goods as wheat, or hides, or maybe ingots of some precious metal and chattels, such as women and slaves. They also wanted to ascertain what interests and investments folks had, as well as the innate character of each yokel; specifically if they were interested in abiding by the law or not, for an example. Also, whether or not they referred to official decrees and statements as lies and more damned lies. When it came to full disclosure the census was unrelenting, and failure to comply brought the heavy hand of the Amoran law down upon the culprits.

Many, at this time, chose to live and operate outside the law. These sorts then quickly fell into the category which previously only harboured Cynics, and others critical of the status quo which also included unlicensed poets, unlicensed priests and even unlicensed historians; namely outlaws. The term outlaw, under the established Amoran definition, quickly became those persons who willingly chose and actively sought not to be endorsed or recognized under Amoran law. This was immediately broadened to include any person who chose not to seek endorsement or be recognized under any law by any established order or recognize Amoran authority. This, of course, was borrowed from the establishment's view of cynics and their followers who refused to recognize a system where any self established authority unilaterally strove to impose patronage over unbelievers in order to govern and restrict those said unbelievers' movements and beliefs. This was a totalitarian system where only a few per cent were protected by the law and the rest could expect no protection whatsoever from any accuser, including the established order.

That this included compiling them into a census initially created for taxing them became a separate bonus, a valuable tool that wasn't a friend of the hoi polloi. As far as the local Poets, Philosophers, Scientists (artificers all) and even Historians within this official Cynic enclosure, all of them unlicensed by laws beyond their own authority, all of them recognized only by the strict tradition of their own guild or humanitarian cult. And to those folks, this current state of the empire had become anathema.

Occasionally the palace threw a banquet for it bureaucrats. These were often grand signatures of imperial affairs. Dyfed seldom attended. On one occasion at about this time he did. As sizzling mounds of plated meats arrived onto the tables Dyfed thought of these poor penned animals being marched out and slaughtered in order to provide this feast and he gave thanks to them, in his own way. This thanksgiving at the table was on behalf of those stuffing their faces and gorging their guts with the flesh of the poor animal's carcasses, for no meat at this meal passed Dyfed's lips. He thought of his spiritual home and of his mother's banquets. On those occasions when live game ritually hunted and then served in the resort of the Isle of Peace, it was only to commemorate some natural phenomena or another, be it celestial or as earthy and lowly as a birthday. After all, it was common knowledge that animals needed to be culled otherwise they became diseased. As custodians of the earth (whose responsibilities fell upon that ilk that were akin to Dyfed) they were taught that big brained animals who had a higher intelligence had a commitment — and obligation — to tend to the lower life forms and maintain joy and happiness for them, too. At Queen Violet's table meat was provided from the library-quiet laboratories. Here, in large test-tube-like beds, the genetic engineering of the sages fashioned edible beef, pig, venison, and even chicken meat from seemingly in-animate nature by manipulating the chemistry composites of free carbon so as to provide an array of manageably sized (and shaped) morsels of protein packed victuals without having to slaughter a single living creature.

Unfortunately, on this occasion, though, the Amoran palace's head chef either failed to attend, failed to pass, or did not bother to enforce the necessary food safety course rules very seriously. By early evening, before the do was finished, everything had become a wretched and retching shambles. Guests were vomiting and excreting the vilest and the most disgusting substances from their bodies through their clothes all over the place. Even some of the musicians were sick. A great stink went up throughout the hallway and the floor was slippery with puke and slimy shit. It was agreed later that the banquet was not a success.

Meanwhile, Kunobelin continued to work behind the scenes in retirement but mostly he worked openly to secure fairness for his people. It came to pass that one-day that he decided to name a lance after himself. He didn't steal the design; quite the contrary, it was presented to him as a gift from an admiring subject who had designed it. Normally, in a sane world, that would provide honour for the designer. But to the Amoran bureaucracy this turned out to be a mortal sin. From the Amoran stand point, upon referencing their code of applicable laws they were able to demonstrate beyond any reasonable doubt that such an honour must only be bestowed upon the emperor, or else be bestowed by him! Aside from being past high king, just who the fuck did he think he was, anyway, was the general gist of what the established order was trying to achieve here. It was quite clear (in a case like this) that there was no avoiding the slight he had made to the emperor. And it didn't matter either if the people of Prydain didn't do it that way here in Albion. Laws, the Amorans claimed, were the will of the gods. And magistrates and emperors alike drew their authority from these gods, for as such they each ruled by divine right. So it was unwise to meddle in what the gods or emperors and magistrates wanted. What the magistrates wanted, it also turned out, was denarii. So the whole matter was settled with a fine.

(Queen Marg)

'Whenever justice is uncertain and police spying and terror are at work, human beings fall into isolation, which of course, is the aim and purpose of the dictator state, since it is based on the greatest accumulation of depotentiated social units.'

CARL JUNG

At this hour of the morning this large chamber of the basilica's library (where he was browsing) was normally vacated. Dyfed was in his usual happy spirits as he leafed through some manuscripts and began singing softly to himself when he found the one he was searching for.

"Who are you who sings like a summer bird at this hour of a cold spring morning?' said a soft voice.

Startled, Dyfed turned his head to see who had spoken. Barely discernable on the other side of the room was a lady with her back to him sitting in the faint light of a small low window. She had not been there a few moments before. Dyfed was as certain about that as he was about anything. Her beautiful jet black hair was tightly curled and long and had been combed as straight as possible and braided into three separate pieces that in turn were braided together and folded forward onto the top of her head. The ends of each braid then hung down, one on either side of her head and the third one down her back. She wore a beautiful sable coloured smock made from finely woven material and on the back was displayed a silver embroidered swan. Dyfed turned and stared at her. Was she in mourning, he wondered whimsically? Then he recognized her, almost immediately.

"I am Dyfed Lucifer,' he replied after a moment.

"Ah, Dyfed Lucifer,' said the soft voice speaking again. 'Jack has told me of you, among others. I am Marg, Queen Marg actually, but please, my lord, just call me Marg.'

The woman put down a small manuscript that she had been holding and turned toward Dyfed. Peering through the stale light he quickly glimpsed the beauty of the woman sitting there and noticing her wide sensitive black eyes and sensuous full mouth he thought her prettier than Purusha herself. Prettier than he had remembered her, though Ceredwyn had been fresh on his mind then. Generally not stuck for words, he found himself struggling to say something pertinent and meaningful.

"Queen of all you survey, I suspect,' he replied. 'Or at least of any — I'm sure — who survey you.'

"But you speak too kindly, my lord,' she answered, keeping up the polite façade which he suspected she could drop at any time. He was now remembering her iron will she let slip during the raucous which occurred after her wedding to Ryan. 'I have just relocated here for now but I reside far, far away most times.'

"Yes, I know,' he said. 'In Legion, I dare say.'

"Oh, heavens no,' she laughed a little as she answered. 'Hardly there, I should say: Maybe at Klaros the oracle by the sea or at the temple of Dionysus, high in the holy Rhodopes. And even farther still, don't you know?'

"Ah, yes,' answered Dyfed. 'The prophecy centre of Colophon and the temple of Apollo on the Aegean coast, being the first mentioned, and the temple dedicated to Zagreus, the Hellenized Dionysus in the mountains of Thraki just inland from the Aegean's northern shore.' Marg's face momentarily assumed an air of puzzlement. 'But I haven't seen you there before, Dyfed Lucifer,' she said.

"No,' replied Dyfed, 'I've never been outside of Albion. My mentor, my teacher has informed me well, however.'

"Ah, yes! Manandan, I believe.'

"You have heard of Manandan?' Beyond saying that, Dyfed was speechless "I have done more than just hear of him,' she replied. 'And Morgant, too,' she said. 'He was the one who told me to expect you in the town of Legion.'

"You have visited Morgant in the mountains of Gwyneth?' Dyfed asked, astounded.

"Great god Saturn in the heavens, no!' she answered. 'By Jove and Saturn most high, why would I want to go into the mountains of Gwynedd? Besides, Morgant does not live there, he resides and hides out there from time to time, and that's all. In any case, the Amorans have nearly completed their occupation of Gwynedd and all of western Albion.'

"Which is why they will soon be concentrating on Kaladonia in the north,' added Dyfed. 'Legion is just an outpost,' he added. 'So, why are you here, he asked, slightly perplexed, for though the fairer sex was not forbidden access to knowledge, he was unused to non Amoran women entering the basilica in general, although he was unsure whether or not that applied to queens as well. She laughed. It was a soft and genuine laugh not calculated or postured.

"Bricus requested my presence here at this city,' she said, 'and as it was my pleasure to come, I complied to meet him, briefly.'

Dyfed walked nearer to the young lady in order to converse in a polite and congenial manner and this gave him the opportunity to cast a happy and closer eye on this beautiful and demure creature. On her part she had been struck by Dyfed's uncommon civility and old world manners, something she had not remembered from before. So, in her customary capricious manner she praised him for it as well as for his beauty of face and limb but spoke not a word of it out loud. She had not failed to notice as well that Dyfed had about him the rich glow of vigorous youth. Instinctively she felt that the characteristics with which he was so well endowed was a denotation of his high and excellent breeding and she quickly lusted after him without guilt.

"You do not make a move to take me,' she said slowly, looking at him with her dark eyes in a demurred fashion. 'Should I then question your habits when it comes to lovemaking?'

"What on earth can you ever mean by that,' Dyfed replied, blinking once very pronouncedly. He then lifting himself up to his full height he stared down at her.

"Well, you know,' she answered, 'your little friend Jack. Were you and he conjoined in the pederastic roles of eromenos? Eh? Was little Munzie your catamite…your Ganymede, your Kyparissos?'

Dyfed suddenly grew angry, despite himself and the immediate fascination he had with this openly raw and sensual young woman. None of any of this was her business, anyway, he thought. Who the hell was she to cross-examine him? Who was she to try and put him on the spot, even if there was no spot to be put on? Muns was his little friend, yes. That's all. What's up with this woman, anyway? She's a man hater, he thought. But anyway, he was his own man and he did what he liked, and he certainly didn't answer to her. He couldn't remember much about her from before other than he remembered attending the celebration of her betrothal to King Ryan: and that man was nothing more than a second rate usurper of the Isle of Mona Major, for a start. Indeed, Dyfed was now considering, Ryan was a probable cuckold besides. Moreover, Dyfed himself was now seriously considering making him into one if he wasn't already; but this little bitch, whoever the hell she thought she was, could be damn annoying, that's for sure.

"Well, I'm certainly not your Iphis,' he said, 'if that is what you mean, my Cretan queen.' The alluring defiance in her eyes quietened a moment while she connected the insinuation. To his growing amusement she laughed, soundlessly. He contemplated her more carefully. It became suddenly apparent to Dyfed that Marg may not have been so much of a gift by Queen Carmanda to Ryan, after all. It was overwhelmingly more likely, he thought, that she was a bait bride that drew a small island kingdom and an ambitious young king into Carmen's domain and possibly her bed as well. As far as that vigorous young warrior's ability to stiffen things up in Carmen's kingdom (never mind her bed), and to offset Flav the Finger's dominance and authority, it was probably Queen Carmanda's hope that her bed would be where Ryan started. And now that he had the opportunity to consider her more closely, Marg (he thought to himself) would have been totally a most willing and cognizant participant so long as it was conducted solely on her terms. Either that or she wouldn't have been on the bill at all. Dyfed was certain about that now and he was even beginning to think that this little pixie queen — as he now began to think of Marg (who he had once believed was from the land of the Picts) — was every bit as conniving and smart-like-a-fox as Queen Carmanda was; maybe even more so. He then remembered what Karatakos had said in regard to her. He wondered then how she had come to know about Manandan and Morgant. Carmen had said she was her niece, but that could mean anything and usually did. Especially coming from her. That most likely meant she wasn't.

"Oh yes, that's right,' continued Marg, 'I had forgotten. You were jilted by a fiancé once that drove you to drink because you couldn't handle your loss; your loss of esteem, your loss of pride because someone else didn't consider you as important as you possibly consider yourself to be. That's right, now I remember. I remember how I listened to your senseless tirade, your lovesick drivel over lunch at Aunt Carmen's, one day, even though you spilled more spirits on the floor and sprayed it out onto everybody else around you than down your own throat. Oh, it's coming back to me now, yes. Then I watched while the servants carried you naked upstairs while, otherwise helpless, you flailed away and hollered out in a drunken stupor.'

Dyfed's face didn't crimson as one would think it might. It lit up and then he suddenly smiled.

"Alas, you are the charmer of my dreams,' he said, 'and so I have found you at last.' Swiftly, he snatched her into a strong embrace and kissed her, just ever so gently, though. He was not surprised, either when she didn't strike him around the head or on the back with both fists. He hadn't expected her to. Instead she moved in, pulling herself up against him while she wrapped her arms tightly around him. Suddenly she broke from him almost apologetically.

"Not here,' she said sweetly, leaning forward and kissing him again, gently this time. 'Come, we will go to my chambers within the palace where I'm staying.'

"Will your husband be at home?' asked Dyfed sarcastically, immediately wishing he hadn't said that. But instead Marg laughed out loud and smiled at him.

"I have no idea what you are talking about,' she answered. 'Why? Do you want to make love to Ryan instead of me?' By reaching up and holding two of her delicate fingers to his lips she didn't let him respond. 'I am Marg…Queen Marg, if you wish,' she continued, 'but I put no great significance…no import on something that is a somewhat unimportant title to me. That is who I am. And as far as Ryan, is concerned; well, Ryan is somebody else and I don't even share Ryan with myself, never mind sharing you with him. I will share you together with another young man if it would please you, as long as he is as handsome as you; but not with Ryan I won't. Ryan is not now and never has been my lover, much to his chagrin, I can assure you.'

Queen ship is unimportant to her? Dyfed was mulling over Marg's words in his mind. By Chronus, he thought, never mind Jove. Unlike Chronus-Saturna, to this woman, Jove's isn't much more than a backslider.

"Queen Carmanda, or Carmen as you call her,' Marg responded, 'defines marriage as others of this place do; that is, they define it as something to their advantage and for their material profit. I helped Carmen out, which is all. She now owes me, although she has nothing that I want. Not at the moment, anyway. Actually, I placed myself into the position intentionally in order for Queen Carmanda to solicit my help. It was my pleasure, you see, although you don't see, for I keep my own council. Furthermore, not only am I not Ryan's lover, I am not anyone else's lover, either, at least for the time being. But I will be your pixie queen, if you like, and your lover, Dyfed.'

"Pixie queen?' Dyfed said aloud.

"Yes,' she replied, 'I can read your thoughts…and (by the way); yes, Queen Carmanda's title is of no importance to me, unlike your mother's whose title is and remains real. Not like Queen Carmanda. Now come, Dyfed, despite the earliness of the morning, and that I have only been dressed an hour, not more, my bedchamber awaits us.'

The palace was adjacent to the basilica along the river embankment and they walked there on this clear, cold autumn morning through the white light of the sun that was shining happily down on the city. Chatting away and laughing, she holding his arm in the fashion of polite company, they picked their way through breezy streets thronged with people as well as being obstructed with building material galore. She told him that Paulinius had immediately extended an offer get Gallus' permission to put her up at the palace where she would have her own suites. They weren't close, Paulinius and her, or Gallus either for that matter. But she had certain information of politics about Ryan, along with Count Bricus and that strange Druid who acted as his attorney and shadowed him everywhere, a certain Blazingwolf. This is what interested both Paulinius and the new governor. In fact, she told Dyfed, she had been a go-between the governor and the rebels chief executive officers, namely Bricus, Ryan, and Maelgwyn who was a double agent and had joined them at the last minute. She told Dyfed that the rebels had been sorry to lose Flavius Cornelius, but he wasn't so stupid as to allow himself to be trapped and quickly coming to his senses had fled to support Paulinius. Marg told Dyfed that there was another fifth columnist that she knew about, a certain Bade who was an expert on tapping in on Ryan. Dyfed learned that Marg was about to leaving Albion. He asked her where she was going and she answered that she was sailing to the ancient Hellene port of Massalia where she would remain over winter until the following spring.

As they walked they hardly noticed the few folks on foot who curtsied and applied other plaudits of salutations. The highborn occasionally may have signalled from the security of their carriages to the two young (but obvious also highborn) persons on foot as they passed. It was unusual, however, for folks such as her and Dyfed not to be travelling by carriage. Other than a general congeniality and politeness toward their right of way, and an occasional 'good morning, my lord and lady,' the citizens in their turn paid them little attention. The legionnaires paid them less attention. Only the Nightwatchmen's greedy eyes for information followed them.

The people around them were a varied selection of the different tribes, the Trinovantes being the most common as were the Katuvellauni. But the Reprobates and the Kantii were also represented as were the Ikeni, who since their own revolt had become less ferocious towards Amor. The men of these tribes wore their hair both short and long. If worn short it was often combed or brushed straight up, back and out in a spiky effect that retained its permanent form with the aid of grease. This, coupled also with being dyed bright colours, certainly gave them a fierce look. Many had natural dark hair but an equal amount of others had brown or red hair. The dyed hair, however, was bright and brilliant, and often an Egyptian or Persian blue was chosen, or else a Scarlet or Crimson red. Otherwise (if worn naturally), the men's hair styles almost resembled those worn by the Amorans themselves, although the Albionian's hair were generally worn much longer, as was the hair of other, off-shore, barbarians who the Amorans had imported as serfs. Women's hairstyles now generally followed the fashions from Amor. Dyfed took notice that some of the men around him wore beards that were often dyed as well, and also noticed with interest that — unlike the Amorans — their skin was heavily covered in tattoos of swirling shapes. In this manner they were comparable to him, although none of them wore the pentangle, the mark of his heritage. This all made for a colourful pageant through which this couple wended on their way from the basilica to the governor's palace.

Once they were inside the governor's wooden palace Marg led him to her chambers and boudoir where they quickly embraced. It was nigh on lunch time, a time when the palace tables were laden with food, but neither party wanted to be bothered with the triviality of that formal ritual when greater pleasures awaited their first encounter with love. Love at first opportunity and gilded with a burning lust was the only menu they were attracted to at this moment. They would dine at Eros' banquet instead, and drink of the sweet nectar of love to quench their thirst and slake their dry throats in order to replenish their bodies of the fluids that flowed out with sweet emission. She lay on top of him, the soft, dark hair under her arms brushing against his biceps as he held her tightly, his hands clasped around her back. Her dark ringlet hair, now loosened from her coiffure, were tinged with faint glints of auburn in the cool, whitish rays of the Fall sun that shone through the tall windows. Those dark, curly strands of hers fell all around his head and shoulders as her tongue slipped gently into and out of his mouth, taking turns with his into hers. Her body was masculine hard, but her feminine skin was softer than chamois and was pearly white like fresh semen. Her dark luminous eyes smiled a dreamy cadence into his heart while he suddenly was confounded by a strange and powerful vibration all around, a kind of magical dance — a pixie dance, he thought — not completely unlike Kunobelin's strange divination, either. Marg writhed ever so slowly as she lay on him, belly to belly, and his manhood, swollen and gorged, released under the pressure and excitement of her slowly moving body. The warm, sweet emission spewed out and lay between their two bodies in the area of their belly buttons, now providing lubrication. Communicating without words, she immediately slid up further and over top of his sex crown, then eased slowly back down until he felt his gladius partially enter her hot and slippery scabbard. He flexed himself and felt his still swollen gland being encompassed and wonderfully compressed as she squeezed him there with her vulva. Then softly uttering the words, "Oh happy gladius,' she sighed faintly and then quickly forced a downward, sliding thrust as he pushed up, their mouths and warm saliva intermingling intimately as they pushed and squirmed and panted to a sexual crescendo which caused him another delicious release, and then another again after that. They continued this way into a far away oblivion where night had fallen, and then they crept to a place to replenish their stomachs and fend off the fiendishly fickle fingers of hunger from the most fantastic palace larder that Dyfed had ever seen; then back to the happy task at hand.

 They slept for awhile and awoke before dawn and Dyfed was amazed to see a multitude of lights spreading across the tops of the town right down to the river that appeared as a black ribbon wending its way among a feverish light of many pinpoints. He was delirious with happiness and sexual gratification as he submitted to Marg who fondled him lovingly and gently. At one point as they were about to fall asleep again, she got up and brought him a draught of the coldest and purest of beverages he had ever tasted. "It's a nectar,' she said in answer to his surprise, 'with a distilled substance that will make you sleep and strong for me again tomorrow.' "It is delicious,' he said, 'and the lights of the town? I don't remember this celebration.' "There are many things, Dyfed, you don't yet know,' she answered. They slept some more and awakened yet again a little later. It was the first light of day when they awoke refreshed and he had just come out of a familiar dream he had often had while a young boy.

This particular dream was a descending procession from a great height overlooking a wide valley. Generally he was ascending or descending a narrow track on a steep and dangerous slope, it seemed, with either a wide valley or a sharply pinched gulley below. It was usually a dangerous and monotonous journey, and sometimes he was one of many, a mere cog within humanity, a portion or a cell of the whole, snaking its way along a path quarried from the sheer stone cliff with the smell of rock dust and humanity in the air. The dream, as stated, was re-occurring but so it was within the dream, as well. As he trudged along in single file he was conscious that he had 'returned'. It was the wheel of the ever return, so it was. That is what he felt. He was there by himself, although accompanied by a multitude. On some occasions he felt he had been ascending like a convict in a chain gang, unable to break from his monotonous and enslaved uniqueness, but upon this last night he had been descending, carefree and happy in the life of Riley, foot loose and fancy free. That is how he felt now. His mother called it a magical staircase when as a boy he had told her of it along with others nightly adventures. Manandan referred to it as the golden chains of Dyfed's soul that were exposed to the winds of time in the vast see of immortality, like delicate chimes breathing music through nature's sighs. It was one port to our connection of who we are, both our past and our future. 'Read your inner thoughts, Dyfed, and take control over them. For they are our essence, and in the end, they are all which we really only have,' he often told him. 'Take care to never be able to not awaken from your ever return, for that is the lot of the Haploids,' he had said. Dyfed recalled that in his dream Marg had accompanied him this time and they had descended gently from a vast and lofty plateau in a soft, warm morning light — amid the hum of insects and the song of birds. Then, suddenly, they were alone moving toward the promise of a valley of music and friendliness below which led to a ultra blue and salty sea that hung low in the vibration of the distance. He smiled, then, at the thought of telling his mother about this adventure. At this point Marg embraced him and he opened his eyes and kissed her before they rose.

Just then the door to the boudoir opened and an aide entered. She was part of the palace's help and stopped in her tracks the moment she saw the two of them together. "Don't be shy. What is it? Marg asked. "It is your charge, my queen,' the woman said. 'He is here, in the hallway.' "Put him in my living chamber and take him some breakfast. I will be there shortly.' The woman made a funny face and fanning her hand in front of her nose made for a window that she opened. Dyfed, who by now was quickly dressing, presumed that the room smelled of passionate, un-adulterated and un-protected sex at its steaming best, and smiled to himself at the woman's overly demonstrative behaviour, albeit with a twinkle in her eye.

"Join us,' Marg said to Dyfed, as she opened the door that led from her living chamber to her boudoir. When Dyfed walked into the living room he saw an attractive young man sitting in an Amoran settee. "This is Prince Galhad,' she said as an introduction. 'And this is Prince Dyfed Lucifer.' The young man's eyebrows rose upon seeing Dyfed and he glanced at Marg before getting up and politely greeting Dyfed. 'Galhad (also, occasionally Galahad) is from Armorika and intends to return one day and regain ownership over his father's kingdom which has recently been lost to him.' Marg was speaking directly to Dyfed and not looking at the other man. 'His mother and father are now gone and he was lucky to survive.'

"But only with your help, my queen,' the man said behind her back.

Dyfed studied the man for a moment. He was tall and very slim as young men generally are. He, too, had very white skin, almost the same colour as sweet Marg's, and he had very dark, curly hair like her as well. Having taken note of Dyfed's actions Marg turned slightly in order to watch both men very carefully as they greeted one another and exchanged a few words. She seemed pleased after a few minutes and suggested that they all sit down to breakfast that was just being brought in.

"Beg to interrupt,' Dyfed heard a raspy voice behind him suddenly say. Dyfed had heard a slight noise just a moment before, but having been distracted by the enticing prospect of a new day with Marg and perhaps her young man for whom she had taken on responsibility, he suspected that it was only the chamber maid or one of the puppies he had seen earlier following the breakfast tray into the chamber. Marg gently broke away and turning her face gazed over Dyfed's shoulder. Dyfed saw her disappointed and irritated look. As he was stooping over and just about to sit, Dyfed changed course and straightened up and turned around instead. Standing just inside the doorway that led into the interior hall were two individuals who Dyfed had not previously seen in Nova Troia. One he knew for sure; it was Count (also Pater) Bricus. This man had patched things up with General Vespasian, though it was likely, Dyfed thought, that Governor Paulinius would remain leery of him. Count Bricus the Tyrant was beardless and was about Dyfed's own age. He had dark auburn hair and large unsmiling blue eyes that were placed midway upon a disproportionate but intelligent face. He had a large head and Dyfed noticed that his limbs were equally large and sinewy. His face was cross and there was an abrasive air about the young man that showed no sign of lifting even when greeted by the gentle voice of Marg. The other man he didn't recognize and knew he had never set eyes on before. Dyfed knew he was looking at a man whose face and bearing nobody would have forgotten. He was a very imposing figure of unknown age, swarthy of skin with very coarse black hair that fell from a high balding forehead past his shoulders. In addition, hair covered most of his face as well and plunged to his waist in a forked beard. He was about Dyfed's height, which (six Amoran feet and eight additional Amoran inches to boot) is to say quite tall, and he was very thin, though rugged in a bucolic way. Dressed simply like a peasant, he had about him a curious illumination that denoted a powerful intellect that was matched by his fierce, watchful eyes. Instinctively Dyfed knew that this was the man who had spoken a moment before and he felt drawn toward him by a strange magnetism. While their eyes were locked together as each mentally searched the other, his sense's told him that this man could be none other than Blazingwolf himself. His tip off, of course was the presence of Bricus.

"My lords,' Queen Marg said, and they acknowledged her politely. She paused and smiled a disconcerting but lovely smile nevertheless. 'My lords,' she commanded softly again, 'come here and kiss me.' When the salutations were completed, Blazingwolf turned again to Dyfed.

"Prince Dyfed,' said the raspy voice. Dyfed noted that the man was not using his question voice but rather a statement retort.

"Indeed, it is I,' replied Dyfed politely. 'Prince Dyfed Lucifer at your service.'

"But just who the coitus are you,' interjected the unpleasant Bricus, 'and where have you come from and why are you here?'

"Noble dearest,' insisted Marg. 'Is that not an unfitting welcome for a high born, such as Prince Dyfed Lucifer?'

Under this retort a sudden flush crimsoned the young man's unwilling cheeks and neck. But apart from that the youth ignored Marg and continued to look condescendingly upon Dyfed as his crimson flush shyly withdrew — frightened away now (no doubt) by the man's growing anger that was brought on by his sense of self importance.

"Where is Morgant?' asked Bricus in a menacing manner, or at least so he believed it to be.

"Morgant? You mean Morgant Carreg the Seaborne?' Dyfed casually answered. 'Coitus the canine, if I would know,' he added nonchalantly. 'Why you ask?' He glanced momentarily at Marg. It was funny thing, he thought. She too had mentioned Morgant's name only yesterday. Did this mean something? He now became even more guarded. Bricus's eyes shifted in some way without moving away from Dyfed while an immense hatred for the latter seemed to be whelming up inside of him.

"You are mistaken, I think, or you lie. How could you have really known him?' The Count's dark eyes narrowed and his voice echoed the uncertainty of his thoughts. Before Dyfed could answer, the thoroughly Amoranized Count Bricus continued to speak while carefully watching Dyfed's eyes.

"What's important is that you actually claim to know Morgant,' Bricus stated, his voice rising. 'Morgant has been dead, me thinks, these many degrees in the chart of celestial time and you, like myself, are young. Even Blazingwolf here never met Morgant, though he remembers the antics that that magician pulled long ago in Armorica. That was before the Amorans came and even before the Hellenes, men of Hellas, settled in Massalia. Morgant has long since become a myth, after he was a legend, and nothing more. And the only realm he frequents nowadays is that of Annwn or Hecate. And it is a long and arduous journey from that shady domain to here with (or without) a Eurydice to comfort or grieve for.'

"In that case, why then would you ask me the question you did?' said Dyfed, accompanying his remark with a condescending little laugh that was half flung into the Count's face. 'In that case,' he continued, 'I know not of whom you speak, but the man I knew as Morgant Carreg the Seaborne — the far sighted — was indeed very old, but very much alive on this side of Hades and very much a legend in his spare time, when I talked to him last.'

Dyfed suddenly noted that Blazingwolf's eyes shifted unexpectedly to a momentary only lasting expression. Then quickly the man's eyes returned back into concealment again. That was revealing, Dyfed thought, and tucked the notation safely away.

"Perhaps, after all, Lord Bricus, ' said Dyfed, 'it is not I but you, who are mistaken.'

"I?' said the Count pointing to Blazingwolf, his mainstay. 'This man here predicted Morgant's death without even knowing him, as he has accurately predicted the deaths of others.

"Be careful that he doesn't predict yours,' said Dyfed.

"Oh there must be many that go by that name. I know of at least two,' interjected Queen Marg. Suddenly, outside the role of Marg the sensual lover, she had become Marg the shrewd — formerly Marg the sweet — who for now (for some unseen reason) was most anxious to avoid a quarrel. She quickly threw a look toward Dyfed. But Count Bricus was still regarding Dyfed intently.

"Where did you live in Gwyneth?' asked the Count.

At this point Dyfed noticed that Blazingwolf hadn't uttered a word since he initiated the present conversation. But the man's eyes roamed about, and his ears (which were quite hairy along the upper lobe giving them a pointed look) took in every word spoken.

"I lived in Owen MacShee's cenedl,' Dyfed replied, politely smiling at the Count. 'Do you know him?'

The latter sneered, and then said…"No! Of him, yes,' he added. The area is now under Amoran control from Fort…what's it, at Bryn-y-Gefeiliau that's now newly named. It's called Fort Vespasianus. The cenedl was thoroughly destroyed by orders of that great General. Wanting to make amends — due to an earlier misunderstanding between Paulinius and myself over Albion's future — I quickly saw to that destruction myself. Owen is dead. I tricked Maelgwyn into believing I was supporting him and managed to capture him alive, so as to torture him to death later.'

"Dead?' repeated Dyfed almost nonchalantly in an effort to hide his emotions from the former. 'And what of his family?' he asked. 'He had a daughter…'

"Don't know!' answered the Count, as Marg's eyes suddenly alighted onto Dyfed with concern visibly apparent in them. 'He's probably dead, too. So, you are now employed here in Nova Troia,' he said then hesitated in a matter of fact way. 'You're employed in some capacity or other with the Magister Commercii? Is that so?' He then waited for Dyfed to answer.

"I don't answer to you,' said Dyfed softly, speaking an impeccable Amoran to which he had suddenly switched to from the Brythonic tongue. He eyed Bricus with an unintimidated look that cast scorn and slight in full spectrum upon him as only he could.

"Don't you know who I am?' Bricus quickly responded. 'Tell him, Blazingwolf. Tell him who I am.'

"Oh, I know who you are,' Dyfed said suddenly, before Blazingwolf could spit out a word. 'I don't need anyone to tell me that. You are nothing, is who you are. That's what you are to me, anyway. You are a little cock in the shadow of a big rooster, that's all.'

The youthful Count Bricus grew very red in the face with sudden and immense anger.

"Well then, let me tell you something, Prince smarty-pants. Gallus your friend and governor is finished. He was assassinated last night and I am investigating his death on orders dictated from the folio of general protocol that's outlined in the emperor's manifesto of governorship. So don't toy with me! Do you follow?' His voice had now risen to a shout. 'So, where were you last night, Sir Prince Dyfed Lucifer?' Bricus spit that part of the last retort that contained Dyfed's name like a slug of yellow phlegm onto the carpet.

"Oh, leave off!' said Marg as she stepped forward. Bricus could see she had suddenly turned into her angry bitch posture, and that it wasn't just a warning growl she had shot off, either.

"Calm yourself, your Majesty, I beg you,' Bricus said in a sudden mid sentence change of manner to one of almost snivelling plaudit. 'I represent the local establishment and I'm here to help.'

"You are so full of the shit of Taurus,' said Marg, flinging the remark back into his face in a levelling voice. 'You have no authority coming to my chambers without invitation or without notice. Now, get out of my sight, both of you; now.'

"Your Majesty,' interjected Blazingwolf with careful pronouncement, 'we were concerned first and foremost for your well being, nothing more, I assure you, your highness. But it is true; Governor Gallus is dead from treacherous assassination. Furthermore, we have just received information from out spies and informants that dangerous sea going pirates from across the Strait of Helle are currently successful in prompting niggling shore raids along the coastlines of the continent as they work their way south to pick the plums of Amoran Gaul. They are now predicted to visit the shores adjacent to the Ikeni and Trinovantes kingdoms here in Albion, as well. Soon they will be entering the Tems estuary to sail straight for Nova Troia. And I need not remind you, your Majesty, that there are but one or two warships at anchor here this morning. Nor will there be any more tomorrow morning, either, other than those in which the Peoples of the Sea sail and pull up in to tie alongside our docks. Also, at present, the Second Legion Augusta — which having helped put down the clan revolt — has recently again returned to be employed in the construction of the land wall around our town, have (unfortunately) some key factors of their legion absent and away from Nova Troia at the moment. This leaves us …'

"Get out!' Marg shouted. 'And as far as Dyfed is concerned he was here with me all last night and most of the day before. And just where were the two of you? That's the next logical question that needs to be asked.' Marg then turned and strode quickly to the door and shouted out for the attendance of a guard. And at that very moment the rumbling of footsteps of palace guards could be heard scurrying towards them on the wooden floor. Moments later those thumping noises of feet were joined by the pounding of the fleeing feet of Pater Bricus the Tyrant and his Druid attorney Blazingwolf, who it seemed had become something now of a wonky wizard, as they stumbled angrily out through the chamber door and beat a fast retreat.

(NARRATOR'S PRIVILEGE)

'Here we have the introduction of a new people, the People of the Sea. These folks are referred to also as trading merchants or sea dwellers who row, row, rowed their boat gently across the sea, and then as pirates they would ram other boats, board them, liberate any booty aboard. Then, after enlisting a few strong backs and arms among the captured to replenish their back up and rowing slave pool, they would kill the remaining alien occupants. The prospective occupants or wealth holders on sea or land, and targets in general, included monasteries that the new Abramic Jeshuans were constructing everywhere around western Europa in these days. In fact this situation of history involved the father of a certain Anlaf Konge. The latter will become a trusted employee of Dyfed's about a thousand earth years hence due to Dyfed's take-over/merger of his father's sea-merchant business. This man was a Harald the Fork-Beard, later Harald Konge (or King Harald). Having heard the story relative to our narration's present moment from his own father, Anlaf relayed the story to Dyfed nineteen hundred years later. The story King Harald told his son was that once upon a time King Haraldsson Ragnor — one of the chieftains — who led the amalgamated clans (his countrymen or tribes) a-viking at this time (before, during and after the current time of our narration) and who was active for a number of centuries, had once led his company of adventurous entrepreneurs on divers endeavours upon the ocean's far shores to secure booty. But it was also designed to deliver freedom and harmony all 'round' from Amoran tyranny, or so they saw it at the time. And that (he told Anlaf) brought a new meaning to the savage and/or the misdirected lives of their victims' abroad that were victims of Amor. In a sense it was politics: Therefore, it was about the money, stupid, and you can't lose sight of that and feel comfortable in this current third dimensional world, unless you are a monk, a mystic or spiritual. An of course one such adventurous entrepreneur under the aforementioned Haraldsson Ragnor was (as stated) Anlaf's own father, Harald Konge. Anlaf told Dyfed later that his family were of this race and the fitting name of Anlaf Rijk-Konge was given to him by his father, now the local king.'

'However, back to those sea-going merchant traders: So, those talented and intelligent sea-going violators and shoplifters also trained as efficient assault artists (if need be) and who wouldn't take no for an answer eventually managed successfully to scourge many of the pockets ripe for picking along coastal Europa. Later, these merchants of enterprise would expand hugely. The eastern Scandians (as they were sometimes called) progressed further east into the hinterland of western Asia and then followed river ways south to the Kara Sea and to the city of Byzas, later called Constantinople after an Amoran emperor Constantine the Great.[18] Byzas was a great plum to pick for it was receiving a glut of booty from the Far East along what was called the Silk Road. At this time these particular Scandians out a-viking were called 'the Rus' (the ones who row, row, row their boats gentle down the streams) by the civilization of the White Sea that

---

18 This young man was already politicking and beginning a calculated and circumspect campaign to unseat Emperor Nero behind his back. But, in the end Nero killed himself so Constantine needn't have bothered.

included the Amoran Empire. One of the largest sovereignties of the world that eventually encompassed part of Asia and northeastern Europa adopted their name. This was the Mother-Land of Rus.'

'These merchants (who bent on shop-lifting and such) later turned their attention to Albion where, known for their ferocity, were referred to as the Herd of Heathen Hordes.' **Parasolo**

(The People of the Sea)

'Man is the measure of all things.'
(translation: in this world of man there are no absolute truths,
but only that which individuals deem to be the truth)
PROTAGORAS

In ancient times past, long before Castus had been employed maintaining a shield against them, pirate raids (from beyond the river Elbe and along the Helle Strait and stretches of the Suebi Sea) had not been an entirely unknown occurrence around the coasts of the Rine River (as previously discussed). Seeking warmer climes during a sudden climate change a couple of thousand years before (2200 BCE), these ancestors to the current Dana (also Danaio, Danaan or Danae) and (now referred to as Norsemen or sea people in general, but better known to history as the descendants of the ancient ancestors to the Dorians) had designed and built the fastest and the most manageable of sea going ships seen anywhere in the world at this time. These vessel designs were even ahead of the ancient Phoeniki design, another engaging sea peoples, some of whose ancestors had once invaded the land of Tilmun (Dilmun, now known as Bahrain) sometime in and around 2200 BCE before blossoming back in Canaan and around the shores of the White Sea. From Tyre (Sur) the Phoeniki set out to encompass this entire western sea by building ports and trade-cities around its coast. These included Krotone, Siracusa, Carthage along with Gades (also Gadir, now Cadiz) and Tarshish (Tartessos) in the far west. Some of these cities were later revamped and newly outfitted by other traders such as the Dorians themselves and also by the Hellenes. And it was during this time that these mercantile mariners (the Phoeniki) and the ancient Dorians (those ancestors once or twice removed from the current-day Norse, Dane, Angle and Saxen marauders who while out a-viking also at that time) eventually came upon one another in the vicinity of the White Sea.

 The Phoeniki were comparatively advanced competitors, but (despite that) the Dorian Norsemen having maundered their way south set about to populate and enrich themselves first around the eastern bank of the Adriatic coast at a place called Palasa where they had settled. Here they mined iron-ore that was in the area and they may have been known as the Chaonian people after Chaon their king or chief. But later these Chaonians or Dorians sailed to the Isle of Kreta and had also occupied the Isle of Rhodes in addition to laying claim to land between ancient Lykia and parts of western Karia. They were adventurers with the long genes.

 Indeed, the earlier Kretan, the aforementioned King Minos — a Minoan (which is a made-up demonym, and not an historical one) — who may have been either a Phoeniki (Canaanite) or Hurrian aristocrat (soldier/priest-lord) being heavily influence by (or directly controlled by) either the Phoeniki rulers of Sur (Tyre) or Hurrian and a mixture of Asiatic nomads (multi-layered pseudo-Scythians) from the city of Avaris in the land of Khem — had (back in the day) fought a war of attrition on his isle with Dorian invaders. As already stated the Dorians eventually gained a foothold on this so-called Minoan island where they partially supplanted the Canaanite culture that had taken root there. This latter Canaanite culture that included the Phoeniki (possibly dominated by Hurrian folks as well as being heavily influenced by the Land of Khem) had earlier infused itself with the people of Khem in the land of the pharaohs. This had caused anguish and suffering for the aforementioned Hemetic speaking folks of Khem. This had opened the door for the Mitanni and the Hittites (part of the multi layered Hurrian/pseudo-Scythians) that helped cause an Asiatic Canaanite mix. The Dorians were contempory and somewhat kindred spirits to the Phoeniki, but due to their start at a-viking in the eastern White Sea and being subjugated by posterity, they were a slightly later addition into this mix although they may have also been among the inhabitants of the city of Avaris on the Nile Crocodile Delta and may have even helped to populate the land close by that was being called Palaistina, whence stemmed their name later known to history — the Philisteens.

But today, thirteen centuries later, the descendants of the forerunners of these sea wolves were now sacking the coast of Gaul and taking advantage for profit of the anxious and hard times of others. These north men were anxious for more locally commercially profitable entrepreneurial contact without having to go too far afield. And while they had opportunities there they left Albion alone, for now. From certain reports, many of these depredators (marauders out and about and merrily a-viking) were not destroying as they might have. It seemed, then, that their policy here at this time might be an early attempt at 'seeding'. This was a policy that was emerging with a mind to give plunder the opportunity to grow anew so that profitable return raids could be regularly scheduled in the future. Their tactic was economically as well as ecologically expedient. It was Europa's earliest foraging into the science of conscious commercial ecology (CCE). This practise was for the prevention of depletion, and they even used selective harvesting programmed- pillage for local long-term maximum output. Here everybody wins; here there were no losers. Contrary to the current popular beliefs, barbarians a-viking at large (scrounging) today (like in almost prehistoric ancient times) were intelligent and talented. Besides implementing ecological plundering guidelines that went hand in hand with commercial planning, they showed themselves to be away ahead of their rivals, including (in some instances) even those non-ecological minded Amorans who were pillaging to exhaustion not only the riches of the land everywhere but the races too that peopled mother earth.

These modern Sea-type Peoples, like those to follow in greater numbers in the next centuries, were remnants of those same old Dorian Sea-type Peoples who (unlike their snow-bird brothers, at the time, a-viking on the White Sea) had remained put in the north during the last geological shift and kept warm by keeping the blazing home-fires burning. These folks (too) worshipped Zeus/Jupiter who they called Thor (also Tor, a word derived from the same root as Jupi**ter**) who with the assistance of [W]Odin, the perpetually reborn. By these items of primitive superstition these folks realised their modern aspirations.

Meanwhile, those earlier Dorian folks (who in antiquity settled along the Adriatic at Palasa) had become avid iron-ore traders and mine operators. And it was this product that they shipped abroad across to Italia, Hellas and around the White Sea from their Adriatic port to help bring to a close once and for all the old and backward Bronze age and help usher in the Iron Age for many who had been left behind so they could have a fighting chance in the new world. The descendants of these folks today, whose land (that was subsequently conquered by the Amorans just under two hundred solar cycles before the present) was now an Amoran governed province called Illyricum, continue to produce iron-ore to this day which they supply to the needy markets and the greedy Amoran capitalists hungry for gain and fame. And it was to protect those same ancient shipping lanes that Admiral Castus had been summoned of late from guarding the northwest coast to this vicinity. But now, of course, he had been summoned to return to the defence of Albion and its protectorate Armorica.

So, in a way this invasion that was a continuum they eventually spilled over onto Albion was the wave that was to provide the ingredients needed to begin that fine tuning of the folks that in the end were to people Albion. There was even one brief invasion five hundred years after that which tweaked that growing trend. It was known as the Invasion of William the Bastard. And inevitably when that travelling troupe the Norse, Dane, Angle, and Sax did finally show up and took up residency in the town of Nova Troia's high-end quarters (free of charge, we might add) and took over to deal themselves into the prerogatives at hand (and a free hand) to legislate a comprehensive general tax collection system, besides. Then after playing the city off and on for some time, and even traipsing around the mud of the countryside a bit, putting on the sundry dog and pony shows here and there, these alchemistic, self applying vessels of magic ingredients for eugenic transmutation ultimately brought indelible change here to Albion. And the folks who resulted from this chemical mixture devised a culture on top of the Amoran foundational one that was subsequently to affect not only just the Albionian Isles as a whole, or even all of Europa, but ultimately the whole and entire world.

(The Word Game & the eclipse of the Kunobelin)

> *"Where was the expert who could magically transfer his sojourn in the Atman from the sleeping to the waking state...?'*
> **HERMANN HESSE**

Anyway, for the time being it seemed to Dyfed that the Amoran establishment, who were constantly on border guard duty and forever improving imperial security here in Albion (while over conscious about their failure in Gaul province), were miffed at what they considered grandstanding by Bricus, probably at the behest of his guiding wizard Blazingwolf. But it was so obviously an attempt by Bricus (who in the big kiss and make up treaty between him and the Amoran establishment that initially had him promoted to count [also consul]) which successfully made (along with the wonky wizard) themselves look more instrumental in programming and indoctrinating the western natives and in preparing their local establishment towards Amoranism than they actually had been. This, of course, was all in preparing for the future of the Province of Albion in the off chance that the wheels didn't fall off the cart of state in the next while, but hopefully kept on rolling along the twisty track and over the next hill, at least for now on their watch.

And in regards to that aforementioned indoctrination of Amor over Albion, this took affect it in such a way that the provincial image of its established order soon almost replicated Amor. This was certainly the case in respect to its definition of Capital (not Capitol) Asseters whose chief influence (behind that of the palace) was still Marcus Catulus. But Hipparchia Philostropodousalouspolousadous, it should be noted, had branched out on her own and had become a queen-like bee at the centre of a vast villa on the Isle of Thanet. And it should also be pointed out that the palace in Nova Troia remained the provincial palace, the governor's house that took orders from Amor, not the house of the high king of Albion. Though (as we shall see) on that front (in years ahead) Nova Troia and Albion out-matched Amor by far if one overlooks the fact that different eras are actually difficult to compare and most certainly should not be. For the time being, however, and in so far as the presence of these marauding, sea faring Danaean sea wolves were concerned, the bows of their short-drafted longboats as they struck the shores of Albion were not so much like gathering sea-foam and flotsam in and about the shores of Albion, but rather contained to short, sharp incursions that took place few and far between. Most often they occurred along the northeastern coast and far from Nova Troia. More often, it was still the Rine lowlands of the Belgae that that these Norse speaking Danae invaded, as well as along the banks of the river Tranquility and the (larger) River Sen that led the marauders to the City of Isis and beyond. It was at this time that Harald Konge had (along with other ships) arrived off this coast and settled on a river island among the Batavians. Later he moved his show to a port town later called Brugge (also Bruges) that had closer access to the sea. Here his marauding companions plied the rivers and sloughs, rowing and fighting their way inland: But more on that much later.

Once again (although presently outside the chronological progress of this narrative) it's suffices to say that of the occasion when the first serious wave of battle-ax waving merchants having come a-viking who eventually did tie up neatly alongside the river docks on the waterfront of Nova Troia (in their preparation for moving into Nova Troia's high-end digs), that event actually did manage to act as the impetus for the city's guardians of the time to finally construct (after the fact) the first defence wall along the river side of the city, including the harbour. Better late than never, they say. To this end the first real meaningful sacking of Nova Troia served the town well in the days and years to come. And, in view of protecting this province as a valuable enclave for Amoran posterity (if not yet on it own sovereignty), this state of affairs helped to show the incredible disconnect (or laxity) that was somehow hardwired into the greedy Amoran power elite at the time who were at the helm of the provincial government in Albion as in Amor, too. But this was to be the nature of the new Amoran Empire that was now being ruled by an emperor as opposed to the republic that was conducted by the rule of law. It will be seen in the future that even democratic republics, themselves emerging out of kingdoms, once they set their course for empire and imperium rule and authority over that of democratic rule (rule of the people) and authority, this becomes the tolling of the bell of the disruption of their order and their ultimate demise, if they weren't careful.

Obviously, this was true for the province of Gaul, as well, where Amor had really dropped the ball. And these certain men, often backed by certain women, were at the pinnacle of their power-achieving journey of career success because of one reason and one reason only. That is that each and every one of them had either made a wish while sitting on the knee of a rich uncle, or some other pervert, or a commission had been bought for them that maybe had jumped the queue, or resorted to deadly foul play. And its purpose was solely to gain wealth. Wealth that led to higher power and power that led to unfathomable, soul-destroying indulgences. Some were violent and unmentionable while others involved such an exercise of ego inflation that included the worshipping of oneself and the ever present and corresponding false supposition that others worshipped you, too. However, along with this, each one of them (almost without exception), with tenacity, intelligence, and cunning to blind them of honest to goodness reality, managed (as already mentioned) to drop the ball on their foot in an effort to achieve a false immortality. After all, were they not really just the descendants of the (previously failed-at-the-art-of-transcending) hoi polloi that were everywhere at large? Of course they were losers every last one of them! Sometimes they even cut off their nose, not so much to spite their face, but so their face would more comfortably fit in to the place where they assumed it would do them the most good. Good was in getting rich. So they must have assumed that they couldn't climb the ladder of power and wealth if their faces, distorted by the projections of others, didn't fit in somewhere: A commonly believed fallacy, to be sure. It seemed that being rich and powerful suppressed their fears; the fear of loneliness, the fear of being unloved and the fear of starvation and death. But, unfortunately, being rich and thinking people love or fear you is a false sense of security, for what they should fear more than anything else is their own self-desire. Sometimes they even cosmetically altered their faces to resemble others who already had power and wealth. If someone was born looking like some very important person (VIP) this was taken as a good omen.

Apparently, this can often mean putting on an ugly face of dissipation or of desperation and ridden with psychopathy. This then (at least at this time) was the Ackilles (also Achilles) heel of those psychopaths who made up the lion's share of the greedy power elites — those Capital Asseters — who worshipped atop Capitol Hill where they made their location for their object of desire, which was also the Bank of their material fortune first and of the temple of Jupiter (Jove) second. And as true history will show here in these pages, they have (in all the years since) maintained a perverted and twisted control over empires and civilizations while endeavouring to place the descent folks (like us) into their eternal debt.

And as Dyfed's endeavour was to break this mould, what needed to be done was to somehow clearly draw the program's carefully designed flaw to the attention of the hoi polloi. But he needed to do more than just draw their attention to this disadvantaging defect. He had to impress via some inflammatory measure in order for them to mark and take careful cognizance towards this pitfall, and to heed the adage of 'forewarned means forearmed'. He maintained that if he could cause the penny to drop, then the people could easily control the relatively few resident psychopaths ensconced within the establishment. But it didn't work out that way, as we all know. The detox wasn't as strong or as effective as the poisonous program they blindly gulped down disguised under many cloaks. Dyfed soon realised he still remained a great distance from his goals.

Eventually, a warrant for Karatakos' arrest was suddenly issued by the Governor's palace. He was, they stated, as a person of interest in connection with Gallus' murder. This was not explained by any disclosure of evidence, but rumour was spread that he had been intending to usurp the authority of governor of Albion so to become the head of something — anything — since he no longer had a kingdom of his own. But the conspiracy of trumped up charges to validate the issuing of a warrant for the arrest of Karatakos was the quintessential Bricus Syndrome, and sadly it was a predominate pattern which, in time, Dyfed was to see occur at all levels of the establishment throughout the remake of civilizations yet to come. This disease manifested (seemingly) with dexterity and ease within the oligarchic empires and plutocratic states that eventually even extended to parliamentary kingdoms and the senate of republics of the future. The appointees or dictators of any established order, no matter who they were and in whatever era they might operate, played a Word Game to position themselves beyond approach. In almost all cases they used understatements such as –'we were constantly misled…being continually subjected to unfortunate occurrences…due to extraordinary circumstances and unforeseen events…regretfully… not having received all the appropriate information… somewhat unfortunate…youthful shenanigans…in this instance only…and…rambunctious, inconsequential good fun.' Other proclivities and personal excuses ensued… 'and I would just like to say how terribly sorry we are…I wish we'd paid closer attention to the situation… we're now looking into how it happened…without it having being brought immediately to my attention…I'm currently seeking treatment for any unexplainable distraction caused by hard work, complicated by short term memory loss… again, obviously, I'm very, very sorry'…we know you will understand. All of these and more are utilised by predictable pundits in order to describe themselves and minimize any of their grievous acts which may have caused people misery and suffering.

But when it came to those good people themselves, those captive among squalid misery and suffering over whose necks the establishment continues to cause the sword of Damocles to swing, the former tend to condemn those same actions by others in a much more final and vile pronouncement. Now they take up certain aforementioned bumptious proclivities most contrary — 'those most unconscionable…the wilful destruction…'heinous behaviour…abject deceit…lies, lies and more lies…calculated provocation…the reckless…the un-provoked act…the villainous of this…the disgusting deeds done without remorse…a nasty and irresponsible affair…clemency will not be entertained…we are here to help'. This was when phrases of this calibre (and spoken by this ilk) were being improved, upgraded and modernized to help perfect the Word Game.

(Governance, the weekend, Divers arts, smoke and mirrors on the Cutting Edge of Disaster)

'God is pro war.'
JERRY FALWELL (CHRISTIAN EVANGELICAL FUNDAMENTALIST)

It was true, Dyfed thought, that in a real sense the people (the hoi polloi) were potentially generally more dangerous and unruly than any aspect that governance was able to make the ruling class into. Despite its array of impotent and self-important little men with their shiny badge of authority backed up by the Turnkeys and Nightwatchmen, governance simply doesn't have that volatile spontaneity of incensement against injustice as the real human masses have. And that is important to remember, by both government and the people. Government doesn't have in abundance that gift of independent thought, either, not the way free willed individuals working together outside the box do: That pure creativity that in greater or lesser measure is part of each of our lives. Especially if governors or emperors and their class cronies start to push, thereby taking away the former's identities and safety zones while backing them into a corner. That is when the free thinking and free willed individuals will not rise to power, but rise to power over and above the power of the cult and the state authority, if only for their country and its citizen's well being. Unless, of course, they are thoroughly beaten through control programs that leave them without will for survival. But then all is lost, lost for everybody and everything, including the power elite.

So, since almost any opposition to the ruling class elitist wish list wasn't an option to be tolerated at any time, the Amoran establishment in Albion felt it necessary to keep a big cudgel at hand at all times. Here, as throughout the empire, this cudgel was the legions of thousands of highly trained and heavily equipped soldier-slaves under the command of highly paid generals who in turn were at the beck and call of the over privileged, the entitled elite who controlled the market place and its temple/bank head office to an infinitely greater degree than the average run of the mill dirt rich or any crony-of-the-people were able to. In addition, the aristocracy of the established order of governance kept a finger on the pulse of the militia, as well as a firm grip on the professional spies and the palace guards and police. These were the good servants of the enshrined status quo, and in the course of this story the nature of these plutocrats never changes, or ever will. Of course, nobody could exactly remember who enshrined this so called 'status quo' that was enforced upon the hoi polloi and revered by the few who benefited from its celebrity. Nor could anyone remember the individual or special interests cult head that had originally suggested the pantheon of pantomiming pagans under its present manifestation. That they were different but the same should come to nobody's surprise. But their culture and mode d' emploi remained the twisted and perverted interpretation of the pantheon that remained financed by the unwilling masses that headed up and made ready to lead the cultural parade forthwith thereafter for the sake of the few not for the well-being of the many. Unfortunately, when weak or stupid tyrants instinctively reach for and wield these dangerously designed cudgels in order to maintain that which they want enshrined forever, it creates an irreversible situation that becomes historically hereditary and systematically prevents humanity from moving forward. Conflict then becomes a permanent state. This is the state of affairs now favoured which has become the status quo in the Empire of Amor. In time, Dyfed came to realize that the confounding of progressive wills and the disruption of constructive action (to which end caused the said inability of humanity to move forward socially in a meaningful and encompassing sense) was the desired methodology or tool of that enigma about which his master tutor, Manandan, spoke. However, that enigma, which Manandan called Zeus (actually, more accurately, the virtual Zeus), was still utterly unclear to Dyfed, as yet.

Although the term weekend was not yet in vogue at this time, during the week's ends — that is the last day of the week which is sacred to the true and great god Saturn (also the Angle-Sax Saetere) or Saturn-day, and the next day which was the first day of the following week. That day was sacred to the sun or the god Helios/Apollo, or Sun-day that had also just been adopted by the Cult of Jeshua Adon — Dyfed would go into the land of the Dunmonii for the weekend. This was where Kunobelin now secretly camouflaged himself and where his stepson Karatakos (called Caradog in those parts) had now joined him. Dyfed would journey up on the day of the earth mother known by the Norse as Friga, then journey back in the early hours of Moon day morning. It was during one of these visits when Kunobelin revealed something of himself to Dyfed — but not in the eastern metaphysical sense. During one of these events with Kunobelin's help, Dyfed — without divulging in an excess of alcohol and drugs as he was used to in his capacity a shaman back in Gwynedd (also Gwyneth) — entered another world in which the now revealed sage, Kunobelin Master of the Unknown Universe, led the way as his guide. There he awoke to find his old master and sage Manandan and his mother Violet-Eye bending over him, both tickled pink and happier than Comus. Although it must be stressed that dimensional travel is never routine, it became the only aborted venture into the world of his ancestors that he was ever to undertake during the early years of his life. He would have some success here when it came to this as will be later seen, but Dyfed was limited in expertize here. And this may have been due to Dyfed's uniqueness that lay in the fact that almost exclusive to his race; he alone remained here in the third dimension, throughout his life. But while they waited and smiled at him, trying gently to coax him into a casual conversation, they could see that he was terribly awkward and confused. This condition descended him quickly into a panic stricken funk. He found it hard to maintain the breath in his earth bound third dimensional body and that threatened to bring expiration upon him. This was usually unnecessary for transcended adepts that didn't have a third dimension ground anymore. This frightened him greatly (he admitted later to himself) along with those hosts he was attempting to visit. They became very concerned for his safety and shooing him away quickly waved him goodbye. All the while Kunobelin was encouraging Dyfed to catch his breath and calm down. It was the last time Dyfed ever saw Kunobelin, either in this world or that.

(Zintacus of the Aryan dialect)

'…if everybody fought only for their convictions, there would be no wars.'
LEV (LYOV) NIKOLAYVICH TOLSTOI

Previously there has been mention of the Amoran need for a constant supply of slaves that obviously arrived by sea to Albion via transport vessels. One such fleet of transport ships arrived at Nova Troia carrying a few thousand Sarms. These Sarms were nomads from the eastern steppes who were fine fighters and even finer horsemen. They were not a society of slaves but rather an ethnic group of nomadic fighting men who were related to the Alans (also Wu-Soon in the Land of Ch'in) and were part and parcel of the Scythian Indo-Europaean sub-group that were being pushed out of the Tarim basin by the Huns (Turks) as well as the Mongols at this time. On a cool, clear winter's day on the Danu river ice (that was flowing in the direction of the Kara Sea), the legions of Amor came into contact with these Sarms on their eastward migration in search of profitable aggression to keep the wolf from the door, sort of speak, and to pay the bills and keep the empire up and running. The Sarms had indeed impressed the Amoran fighting men with their horsemanship, their weaponry and their bravery. They then quickly sought to secure a contract with them to fight for Amor.

"If you must fight,' said the commander of the Amoran expeditionary force who had come across them on frozen Danu that day, 'please fight. But you don't need to fight us whose fight (in the end) you cannot win. But we will employ you to fight. So fight if you must but fight for us and we will pay you in gold.' The Sarms secured a contract for just that, on the spot. Due to the current circumstances many of these marvellous fighting steppe nomads were destined for the marches of Albion where a potential for the shakiest and most porous of borders of the empire existed at the time.

One day, with a chilly sun peeping around clumps of grey cloud that lay over the cold river as it swept past the city, Dyfed noticed that the harbour a barge was ferrying horses ashore from a large transport barge. Already about half a dozen of these fine looking creatures were waiting patiently by the dock not far from Dyfed who noticed a couple of attendants keeping close eye on them. Also at that moment some men were coming ashore in a tender from one of the towering Amoran war trireme that was precariously anchored on the river Tems. This was part of the still absent Aelius Castus' advanced fleet. They were all waiting for the admiral who was aboard his flagship with the remainder of the fleet that was still being outfitted at Carthage.

Most of the men here were obviously Amoran soldiers and they were smartly dressed in their easily identifiable garb of the legionnaire. This consisted of the segmented plate armour, the advanced and practical helmet, the trademark shield, and the short, sharp gladius and the dangerous javelin. But then Dyfed noticed another who was attending to the horses where single-handedly he was controlling about forty of those beautiful beasts with ease. This man was different and was dressed differently too. It was his armour that set him apart which shimmered even in the dull sunlight in a way that resembled a suit of snake's skin or maybe a fish. Then others dressed like him disembarked from the ferry.

Then this man who he had first sighted did something that any other cavalry officers could not do. This armoured clad man strode directly with ease to one of the horses which he took hold of and upon which he effortlessly mounted. Armoured clad men don't usually move or hop onto their mount as easily as he did. And the curious horse he climbed upon was a Tarpani and it had a grullo colour to its body. Long extinct in these parts (and throughout western Europa in general) Dyfed knew that it must have come from the eastern steppes.

A junior magister militum under him at the Basilica was standing quite near Dyfed at this moment waiting for instructions. He was an odd-jobber for Servilius Publius Maximus and Gais Lucius Julius. Dyfed asked him about this foreigner. Then reading from a list the young and energetic odd-jobber had he told him that the man was a Sarm general and that he was from the eastern steppe via the land of the Thraki. He told Dyfed his Amoran name was Zintacus. Apparently he had been singled out by the emperor himself who had put him in charge finally of aiding General Dietcola in the quelling of rebellious barbarians around Albion. A few thousand of this foreigner's countrymen were accompanying him into this province, he told Dyfed, and they would be stationed in Victrix. Dyfed thought that the arrival of these Sarms wouldn't hurt the Amoran prospects or their plans of keeping an abundant amount of reserve troops here at hand, either. These eastern men disembarking from the ferry tender were tough and intelligent folks, he was to discover. As stated earlier, in most cases their families accompanied them. This, he thought, could even bode well beyond Amor's Idea for an Albion identity tincture supplement with the stalwart Kelts and Amoran mix.

Instinctively Dyfed knew that these scaly looking horsemen were true nomads from the east, men to be reckon with. Then he then overheard Zintacus giving orders to his horsemen. The man's voice as it travelled through the cool, crisp air, Dyfed was surprised (indeed, shocked) to discover, was a vulgar and extensively more primitive dialect of Shamskar, the language of his own forefathers.

(Admiral Aelius Castus)

'The greatest obstacle to discovery is not ignorance,
it is the illusion of knowledge.'
DANIEL J. BOORSTIN

Dyfed watched as time and again the towering war vessels of Amor sailed up the Tems River and disgorged their contents of men at arms. But these were not the promised Goths that the discredited (in Dyfed's eyes) Pater Bricus and Blazingwolf the Armorican (also Armorikan) Druid had threatened would come. Dyfed knew that their arrival was due to rushed orders now being dispatched from the Eternal City. It was true, perhaps, that on account of the Goth threat to Germanika (also Germanica) and the Daanans out a-viking and swarming into the straits of Helle, the emperor was pulling out all the stops to aid the security of Amor's power elite here in Albion and the assets of the capital gains men in order to prevent any further haemorrhaging of wealth and power from this apparently important island province. His endeavour was to tighten the noose along with the restraining bracelets he was attempting to fasten onto the barbarians.

What was to become of Albion? Although semi-isolated, as earlier stated she was central to what one-day might become a central location of the Amoran Empire. It would be a newly aligned Europa but one in which Albion could become a central player. But would Amor take her there; would the empire actually succeed intact and be able to open an opportunity for Albion to influence Europa for her own commercial benefit? That was the sixty-four denarii question. After all, during certain seasonal intervals Albion was a pleasant enough place that was populated with pleasant enough folks of the Tud. It was also a land that was somewhat advanced and civilized from the time of antiquity. It was also conducive to Amoran living and well being for vineyards were already starting to be cultivated around select villas. Not only that, but with their tentative foothold already in the process of being secured and the far sightedness of certain power wielding Amorans, this slightly remote island of Albion could indeed act as a safehouse or fortress for future idealism along Amoran lines. If Albion really was to become the imperial successor of Amor — Dyfed thought — and failing any act of the dreaded architect of change that might materialize in the form of the 'hand of Mother Nature' and that of the god Saturn, if not Jupiter himself) from intervening, there certainly was a lot of work yet to do: If that was to be the case.

Directly to the south was the rather unruly land of Armorica. And at this moment she was undergoing rebellion concurrently with Albion's unrest as Goths were pressing against Gaul's eastern border. In any case, in an attempt to save themselves many of the Armorican chiefs were spreading canvass to the wind and sailing north to the land of the Dunmonii on the south west coast of Albion. The Armorican uprising was a civil rebellion not much different than the rebellion here in Albion with outside and inside forces at work. The main outside force was Amor, once again which had spared no expense to smote the rebel's towns and villages along with their means to exist all the while putting thousands to the sword which turned the rivers and their land red with blood. Marg's charge, the child (now lad) Galahad, had been previously sent to Albion from Armorica for just the same reason that others had fled, safety.

Initially Amorica had been subdued by the great Amoran psychopath, Julius Kysar the Butcher himself. That was at the time of Dyfed's birth on the Isle of Peace. Later the Kelts of Armorica had not only overturned the localized status quo as of late, but now these troubling tribes were attempting to thwart the over all Amoran established authority. This was the case with the father of Marg's charge, a certain Prince Galhad whose name was Ban. Ban had lost his tiny clan kingdom of Armorcan Kelts to a dominant Kelt (an alpha male) whose name was Ateula but who called himself Arviragus. He was of a separate clan to Ban. Some had said that Ateula was in fact a horseman from the east, an early migrant of the soon to come Lan folk (also known as Alan or Wu sun in the Land of Ch'in, remember? from whose approximation they derived). Ateula along with a few of his cousins and their families were a hundred years in advance of this aforementioned migration. Here they and their family clan had settled in and among the Kelts of Armorica just north of the Liger river valley in a secure and unsettled area. Migrating here they built on to a village that went by the name of Joscelyn. This village retained its uniqueness due to the character of its builders and later was a magnet for the Alan peoples who gravitated toward it four hundred years later, and where they made it their preferred centre in all of Europa. By that time, though, Joscelyn (Joslin) had grown into a large, tight, and fortified city. That was not the case today.

These Armorican folks, mostly Kelt, had not suspended their reverence to their own gods (which was more of an expression of their lives) simply on account of Julius Kysar's request. Nor did they bow to the edicts and rules dictated to them by Amor. For many of the folks were kindred and their cult world was as they liked it, simple. Ateula's cult world was somewhat different but it intrigued the Kelts and was not at all adverse to their customs. The two were compatible. Furthermore, nomads like Ateula anticipated that when their central Asian relatives arrived here out west (as they would in good time), he wanted them to feel welcomed by familiar customs. And as far as the home grown Kelts were concerned, they had made careers out of fighting other pushy Kelts and their Amoran cousins for generations and weren't about to say uncle just yet, nor turn against the newcomers.

Unlike the Amoran provinces of Albion and Gaul — who having been inundated with the Amoran program and were (by and large) becoming good little clones — the Armoricans were quite independent. In retaliation after retaliation by the Amorans against them, the Armoricans suddenly suspended delivering up taxes to Amor and sent their Amoran tax collectors and legal advisors packing and racing off into the night. Furthermore, they let it be known too that they didn't want the swinging screen door on their territory's back porch slapping these shyster solicitors across the ass on their way out, either. So, in response to that and to quell the rebellion is why Emperor Nero had ordered the recently appointed proconsul Pater Bricus to send the Sixth and the Twentieth Legions there, selecting Admiral Castus to act as Field Marshal General to be accompanied by a Sarm general. This lieutenant (pronounced lef-ten'ant) to Castus was a certain Zintacus.

Castus was a good choice for this job. This man had earlier earned his roll of medals by being an old sea-watchdog that kept the old Prydain coast clear of undesirables to the best of his ability. At this point (with the threat of marauding seafaring Daanans, Saxen, Angles and Norse who were all out and about a-viking and reversing Amoran fortunes around the river Rine, including the uprising in Armorica) the choice of Castus was an easy one for Nero. So, after having been employed this past while defending shipping lanes of iron-ore in the Adriatic Sea of late, he set out in a small boat from Massalia (where he owned a vacationing villa) and set out on a journey to Gadir (on the southern tip of Hispana) where his flagship the Victoria was harboured. By that time the refitted fleet (he was to command) should have been anchored off Gadir (also Gades) where Castus had only to board his quinquereme flagship there, spread his canvas to the wind, and lead his fleet north. However, due to delay, his fleet (as already stated) that was being refitted and made ready at Carthage was (at this time) still undergoing the repairs of hull scrapping and replacing the zinc anodes along with the electrolyzing copper strips. This delayed their grand spectacle of spreading their collective canvases to the wind, on the appointed morning of the ebb tide, and sailing forth from Gadir's shining and grand harbour in plain view of its citizens that were expected to congregate in admiration upon the waterfront promenade that graced that ancient city. But, in any case, they must have been a wondrous sight — those quadriremes, triremes and liburnians — when finally (one day) just after they had slipped out through the strait and passed through the western gates that guarded the White Sea, they — having then moved into formation behind the Victoria — ploughed forth, out of the Gulf of Gades and into the Atlas Sea.

But as for this foray into Armorica, it was Castus' view that the preparations for it had become slightly complicated, what with the recent disappearance of Gallus and the equally recent presumed lacuna regarding the results of responsibility following Bricus' newly appointment to proconsul (governor). It wasn't so much that he anticipated Bricus' interference as to the actual military job at hand, but rather it was the likelihood of his interference through the allocation of vital funds that was intrinsic to his campaign's outcome. That is what concerned him. War (like anything else), Castus knew, was all about the LSD (the Libra, the Solidus, and the Denarius) factor, as he called it. That was the bread of commerce, trade and war along with every other human endeavour. High on the list of Castus' preparation in advance of moving the Sixth and Twentieth Legions across the channel into Armorica was this tricky war budget that was needed there once he had entered into the hostilities. It was vital in order to finance the military action that he needed in order to win. But Bricus the new governor, he knew, would keep a tight grasping hold onto the purse strings. That's how it always was.

Prior to the Admiral's arrival in Nova Troia, he had sent communication prompting Zintacus (who he had already been informed would be his lieutenant general) to act on his behalf during his absence at the war budget table. Bricus (at the emperor's urging) had already given orders to start the budget proceedings so that by the time Castus arrived at Nova Troia they could get on with their invasion without delay. But Castus concern was still about being able to commensurate tactfully and expediently with the Albion office of the Magister Commercii. This, after all, in lieu of a proper war cabinet was the de facto Provincial Department of Finance of the time that would secure his funds in the end. And, as stated, governor Bricus held considerable sway here. Castus had hoped Vespasianus would show up for work in person soon and help assemble a war cabinet in order to provide military advise. But he had learned now that this soldier general had just been sent to the Illyrian front just at the time his own fleet had been pulled out of there to be refitted at Carthage in preparation for sailing to Albion.

(Marg relocates to Massilia)

'The men of intelligence must combine, must conspire, and seize power from the imbeciles and maniacs who now direct us.'

ALDOUS HUXLEY (CHROME YELLOW)

Then one cold day just before the solstice with snow in the air, Dyfed sorrowfully watched Marg sail away down a smooth and frosty Tems River that was specked with ice. But before leaving Marg had bothered to pin a certain responsibility on him. She had lumbered him with her fine young protégé, Guillium Galhad Raymonde de Joscelyn (Joslin), the expatriate from Armorica. Dyfed's responsibility was to the boy's well-being and all that that entailed, Morgant would help, of course. This situation, she had told him, would only be until such time when she was settled. Then she would send for the lad. Over protests from Dyfed she provided both he and Galhad with enough denarii, a stipend to Dyfed, (a gift for the latter) to cover expenses. She would settle up, she told Dyfed with brimming mirth in her large, beautiful eyes, with the House of Lucifer (as Dyfed was beginning to refer to himself) later, if need be.

Dyfed might have been distracted by Marg's absence, had he time to waste thinking about it; but the fact was he didn't have any. For now Dyfed had begun to form an important plan. That plan was to stop dilly-dallying and lollygagging about and build up some serious collateral. The plan after that was just get to the heart of the empire as fast as he could, all the while soliciting Morgant for advice. But he urgently needed backing and it wasn't to Messrs Catulus and their House that he turned. Indeed, it had been Morgant who had stepped forward initially and offered him unlimited gold pieces to seed and begin the work in putting together a people's bank which Dyfed had set his heart on, preferably in the grand old eternal city of the seven hills itself. But finances all around the empire cast a poll over his ideas. Like elsewhere, it seemed that the people of Albion were currently witnessing the result of heavy deficit spending by the Amoran imperial governing factor. It was the same in Gaul but more advanced with the result of the uprising and unrest there. The effect of heavy deficit spending was financial inflation which led ultimately to wage-price spiral. Amoran officials quickly blamed the stupid Gaul Kelts and the Germanics for their foolishness in causing this condition. But the stupid Europaean hoi polloi themselves apparently weren't quite that stupid after all, for they knew both the physics and the economics of the situation and were angry at being blamed for that which the Amoran bureaucracy was responsible for. The ensuing incensement by the stupid hoi polloi was what pushed them over the top into a rebellious attitude where push came to shove.

Dyfed formed a pact with Morgant (though, actually it was visa versa). The pact was that business between them would remain between them, and them only. It was solely at Morgant's discretion to bring someone else in if, and when, he felt it necessary. And at this same time he also approached Dyfed with an offer to help him realise his goal of laying the foundations for his own bank: the House of Lucifer. Meanwhile, Dyfed continued at his duties and responsibilities at the Magister Commercii office in the basilica. Marcus Catulus was also encouraging him to apply himself at this job, but for his own selfish reasons. From the standpoint of Marcus' private for profit enterprise (with Dyfed remaining employed at the Magister of Commercii office) this provided the former an opportunity. He believed it would enable the House of Catulus to gain foreknowledge of what and when Blazingwolf (through Bricus' seal of government) had in mind next for the province and how it was to be implemented (even when cast alongside imperial for profit notions and their sundry foibles). Knowledge of just what infrastructure they were going to tackle next and what kind of a loan the imperial palace (the palace of the high king of Albion was forbidden to access loans other than through the imperial palace) would need were pertinent questions for maintaining the House of Catulus of Albion, and to keep its breathing apparatus above water. This was a feat that their besieged House of Gaul was even managing to maintain for the moment amidst financial inflation and rebellion there, Dyfed had learned. From Dyfed's perspective this arrangement was kept in line with his integrity under the adage that so long as it was accurate and truthful (no matter how negative or disruptive) any knowledge gained was good knowledge.

Meanwhile, General Zintacus the Sarm had been posted to the end of the road at Valeria Victrix Fort, accompanied by the Twentieth Legion Valeria Victrix. This was in the land of the Cornovii and quite near the Gangani and the Decangi people. Here, on behalf of his Sarm cohorts, he had petitioned to rename the fort Deva Valeria Victrix, or Deva Victrix for short. The name, deva was the word for settlement or city in their central Asian language as well as throughout Dakia. Even parts of Thraki (in the area that lay just west of the Kara Sea) devas were the common name for settlements. The ordnance to make the name Deva official had been done with the emperor's consent as a tribute to these tenacious nomadic horse warriors from whom great things were being expected.

Further orders permitted Governor Bricus to gather up the Twentieth and the Sixth Legions (now beefed up with thousands of Zintacus' armoured Sarm horsemen) and hand them over to Castus. A compliancy from General Dietcola was needed and received, of course. This, along with orders for Bricus to facilitate the preparations for the two legions to make ready to sail south to Armorica at the earliest possible time to facilitate the empire's interest that was under challenge there. These demands emerged as a clear directorate from the emperor that eased Castus' concerns over the usual bureaucratic dilly-dallying.

(The war room)

'War's a banker, flesh his gold.'
AESCHYLUS (*AGAMEMNON*)

When the meeting got underway at the appointed time at the basilica, for the purpose to identify the funds that was needed for the Armorica campaign, and from where and what project (probably already underway) those funds would be solicited and diverted, Bricus was more than mildly hostile toward Dyfed's presence. Publius Servilius Maximus (the Purse) and his sidekick Gaius Julius (or Julius the Jerk) who were on hand had gained a huge regard for Dyfed's capabilities and both were slightly intimidated by him and by Bricus. They were also aware, however, that Dyfed was not intimidated in the slightest by anybody. The Jerk who often sat at the table in lieu of The Purse was actually relying heavily on Dyfed to circumvent any kind of brow beating that the governor may wish to dish out, or any consequential financial or military disaster that could arise out of an inadequate budget that would quickly reflect on his and The Purse's magister-ship. Julius the Jerk hoped that Dyfed's ability would spell success for his career as well as reward and stability for his future. That, rather than doom, which was where it looked to be heading at the moment. In any event — so he was able to reminisce later — Dyfed rose to the occasion and covered them both all over with glory.

From day one, Zintacus the Sarm quickly became a slight problem for Julius the Jerk. This was Zintacus' lack of ability to speak and understand Amoran very well. His ability here actually left a lot to be desired unless you were content with the usual category of a proficiency bracket common among the novice travelling-types…'hello…I love you…won't you tell me your name…you got nothing to sell I want…hey asshole — go to hell.'

Bricus, for his part, couldn't have given a tinker's damn one way or the other, for as far as he was concerned anything that Zintacus said or didn't say — or didn't know how to say — was irrelevant. And furthermore, he (Bricus) was better off for it. It was his opinion that Zintacus had no authority over Amoran money not matter what Castus wanted; and as he, being the colonial proconsul (on the other hand), did. In Bricus's mind Zintacus was no problem, it was the other two; Dyfed Lucifer the so-called Prince of the Grove, Keeper and Chamberlain of the Royal Palace of the High King of Albion and his sidekick the Jerk (who'd been too long in the sticks). That's who bothered and annoyed him. And the latter (who he mentally referred to as the doubling jerk, the jerk of exponential qualities), he highly distrusted and absolutely hated that son-of-a-bitch. Furthermore, he had wanted General Flavius Cornelius (Flav the Finger) to be at the table instead, since Flav had been reluctantly re-appointed legate to the Ninth Legion at the last moment. Even though the Ninth Legion wasn't mobilizing in preparation for campaigning abroad, this brilliant general who actually did think outside the box, even if protocol dictated that he shouldn't, was a proper Amoran legate and not just some miserable little wog dressed in snake skin scales from the east trying to make good in Amoran Albion: Nor was he a smart-aleck upstart prince of some sort from some or other wog's world being showered from above by the northern borealis, which (according to his self incipient rumour) was where Dyfed came from.

To Bricus' mind, this was what Zintacus and Dyfed ably embodied. But that was just fine if Castus sooner preferred to be represented at the table by a couple of morons (and maybe even jeopardise the entire war initiative) than give someone else who was a real soldier's quartermaster (like himself) an opportunity to claw himself ahead. And who knows, maybe, in the end, he may even outshine the great general Castus himself before the emperor and all of Amor, Bricus thought.

On the first day of the meeting around the war table, Dyfed had suddenly caught Zintacus off guard, never mind the others around that table. Just about on cue all of their jaws dropped open almost down on to table in astonishment. The occasion was when Zintacus (after attentively listening to a bumptious, posturing and lengthy discourse that Bricus had just delivered; and despite Zintacus' own intelligently postured expression accompanied by the nodding of his head throughout at what he hoped was at the right moment) had had to admit secretly to himself that he had no idea what Bricus had been talking about, not really. Then, all of a sudden Dyfed (who had been carefully watching Zintacus and had surmised as much) began speaking in an Indo-Europaean dialect that was exceedingly close to the other man's own native tongue. From Dyfed's professional point of view, he had done this for the very reason that the Sarm was hardly able to understand the level of Amoran being spoken here, and the man spoke no Brythonic at all, either. Dyfed knew that (under these circumstances) this would not bode well for Castus' success. So, it became expedient, he thought (as well as providing a psychological advantage for himself on behalf of the future of the House of Lucifer's treasury, never mind the treasury of the province of Prydain, to switch to a mode of speaking with which Zintacus was comfortable, namely his very own native speech. Zintacus, as it happened, was only too happy to have Dyfed, in turn; express his own desired words back to Bricus. For it was necessary for him to convey important particulars intrinsic to warfare that could not be pared back or have some or another chintzy makeover applied. These were costly particulars that he would need expedited properly if this campaign in the name of the emperor was going to be successfully pulled off. On top of it all, Zintacus also wanted and needed to impress the still absent Castus upon his arrival and to do the right thing by him. And on his own part, the Sarm could also see that despite Magister Maximus and Magister Julius (the former's sidekick) seniority at the table that the men looked to Dyfed for assistance in all but a few instances.

From Dyfed's view it was an advantage for him, too, to interpret even if he had to improvise and dumb down his own advanced dialect of Shamskar from time to time in order to facsimile words into those of the common or vulgar hand-me-down dialect which Zintacus was accustomed to speaking. Often, though, Dyfed corrected Zintacus' own grammar and pronunciation, as though he were the latter's grammar teacher. Zintacus, an intelligent, bearded man with long blondish hair, was not insulted by the former's manner for he was well aware that Dyfed was speaking the long lost classical and educated dialect of his own language which truly amazed him. He was further amazed by the young prince himself and he was beside himself with happiness that the gods had seen fit to provide him with such a valuable ally. And it all worked out well in giving Dyfed a lot of control with negotiating the budget toward Zintacus' and ultimately Castus' end. And so it went.

And as this was the provinces, not Amor, so there was no need for superficies such as a third readings of the budget, and so forth, in order for it to be passed by what took the place of a makeshift senate here in Albion. Bricus finally, simply, and grudgingly affixed his seal to the proposed expense sheet that they had agreed upon, and that was that. And then while talking directly to Julius the Jerk and ignoring Dyfed completely, Bricus further took this opportunity to inform Magister Gaius Julius that under the authority invested in him as governor, he was replacing Dyfed with a better placed assistant for the future. Anyway, he said that Dyfed had two masters and that wouldn't do. Dyfed's responsibilities would therefore now be transferred to Publius Servilius Maximus, The Purse. This horrified Gaius and you could see it in his face.

Dyfed (who was sitting as usual at the table alongside the three other participants and their aids) then nonchalantly stated that there was no need for that as now that all here was signed and sealed, he thereby tended his resignation that was effective as of that moment. Smiling broadly and speaking directly to no one in particular, Dyfed continued to say that he had done this because Zintacus had kindly offered him a position within the general logistics division of his Twentieth Legion's legation authority. Bricus had no idea what that meant and kept his mouth shut. Dyfed turned and nodded to Zintacus who, not keeping properly abreast of the conversation between the other men that was being spoken in Amoran, broke out in a big, wide smile and nodded back.

"Therefore,' Dyfed continued, 'I will be employed by Zintacus, and ultimately by Castus from now on. And along with the Sixth and Twentieth Legions, I will accompany the former to Armorica for the duration of the campaign. And as such,' Dyfed reasoned out loud (for he was well within earshot of the governor), 'one wouldn't need a special dispensation from the provincial authority, and nor would one need a permit, for example, in order to leave the province and travel abroad: not since one was now in the employ of the war machine of Amor — at war — would one?'

(Karatakos gets to Work on his Tan)

*'Search back to your own vision —
think back to the mind that thinks. Who is it?'*
WU–MEN HUI– K'AI (CH'AN [ZEN] MASTER)

Dyfed laid his cards on the table before Castus as well when the latter did arrive. Castus had already had glowing reports of Dyfed from Zintacus moments before. Then, in his capacity as an advisory clerk at the war room's financial and budgeting conference, Dyfed explained to Castus the whys and wherefores of his role in having achieved an adequate war budget and his intention of working the campaign alongside Zintacus, king of the Sarms. He also took this opportunity to ask Castus for a favour. That was for the Ninth Legion Hispana, to give up a certain Trachmyr of Gwyneth (Gwynedd) and cause him to have that man transferred to the Twentieth Legion and then given leave to attend to Dyfed as his personal batman. This would, after all, be in accordance with Dyfed's new position. General Gnaeus Julius Dietcola, he said, could easily be coerced in affecting this request. Dyfed also explained to Castus that he also needed to be accompanied by a youngster who was in his charge and under his responsibility. This was Guillium Galhad Raymonde de Joslin, better known now as Galahad. Castus complied with Dyfed's requests.

King Karatakos (who had finally turned up to defend himself against charges of homicide and had made bail) accompanied Dyfed to his audience before Admiral Castus. It was not surprising then that he too had a request of his own. In light of the fact that he had already ingratiated himself to Claudius, the last emperor, he asked Castus to request a pardon for him as well as permission to join the emperor's illustrious legions to Armorica in order to help put down the barbarian revolt there and to help strengthen Albion's southern shield. Why he was doing this was something for which Dyfed had no answer. But it made possible (it crossed Dyfed's mind) an opportunity for Karatakos to dodge the Albionian rain and chase down some warmer weather in the south where he can get an early start on his tan. And Karatakos was clear to Castus about wanting to be a free agent; he didn't want to be tied down, he told him, he wanted an open arrangement within the jurisdiction under the magister of war. Castus, who knew the story of this gregarious and complicated king, complied immediately, knowing full well that if he ever bothered to put his mind to it Karatakos would be a huge asset.

Early that spring, Dyfed, Trachmyr, Karatakos and Galahad (who as his charge had been legally entrusted to Dyfed) clamoured aboard ship. This vessel was one of eleven, including six triremes and two quadriremes that made up the fleet that had anchored along the south bank opposite Nova Troia. Here they made ready to ship the two legions to Armorica. That afternoon with an ebbing tide they rowed and drifted down the river Tems where, spreading their canvases to the wind and their multiple levels of neatly rowed oars now dipping into the dark, grape-wine-blue salty sea (accompanied with little white splashes and splotches) they rounded the Isle of Thanet to its seaside (not navigating the shallow inner channel that separated Thanet from the land of the Cantii). Then they rushed headlong into Helle's Strait they then turning to starboard they glided westward alongside and below the chalk white cliffs that lined the south coast of Albion. The land here was considered unfriendly, indeed, it had been marked out to be soon subdued and conquered by the II Legion Augusta that was supposed to have been under the command of General Vespasianus' when he arrived, whenever that would be. As such the fleet avoided making landfall and even bypassed an attractive Isle on Albion's south coast which some of the Germanic folks aboard called Wextiz (little one) or Vectis (lever) in the language of the Amorans. From here they then sailed southwest into the Atlas Oceanus as Dyfed glanced astern and whispered goodbye to his old life.

After a time they turned directly south and later, fighting to keep the ships off the dangerous rocks that formed the westernmost shores of Armorica, sailed south then east again toward the great salty mouth of the River Liger which poured out here into the sea bay.

At first the plan had been for the fleet to sail up river to Portus Nat, a walled Armorican city under Amor's control, and to reconnoitre. But shortly after entering the muddy waters of the flow they encountered other Amoran vessels being swept seaward, coasting along with an alert helmsman and the occasional oar to keep them from running the banks. So heading back out to sea, the ships of the fleet now joined those from Portus Nat and made north for Dariotum in the land of the dead Veneti, a people who the tyrant Julius Kysar had butchered during the initial Amoran expansion.

Indeed, it was the Kysar's manifest destiny program for the expansion of Amor under his tyranny that drove him to slaughter more than half of the poor Keltic souls that had once inhabited Europa. This travesty of human justice, this unjust brutal bullying and unrelenting thuggery, catapulted Kysar into the seat of the tyrant's easy-chair at the old republican palace (formerly the roost of the likes of Quintus Fufius and Publius Vaticanus, now currently replaced by the corridors of imperial hegemony and oligarchy) that was located back in that biggest of smoke among the seven hills. But by Julius Kysar's time the Republic was finished, the dictator saw to that: exclaiming in a long refrain to feel the cold rain on the plain of the old dead republic. Dictator Gaius Julius Kysar the Tyrant had been followed in fast succession by Generals Markus Antonius, Atropa Belladonna, and Cornelius Dolabellae (Cicero's son-in-law), followed by Imperator Filius Augustus Gaius Octavius Augustus, then by Tiberius Claudius Nero Kysar Filius Augustus, to be followed by Gaius Julius Kysar Augustus Germanicus called Nero. The present emperor Nero Claudius Kysar Augustus Germanicus was the grandnephew and adopted son of Tiberius Claudius Kysar.[19]

The fighting, once the Twentieth and Sixth Legions engaged the Armoricans, was fast and furious. It was also sporadic as the Legions had to hunt the truant and rebellious Armoricans down that was far from easy and extremely time consuming. Many of the Armoricans fled to the rugged lands to the Armorican north and west where as horsemen without chariots they were able to throw up a temporary good defence before fleeing quickly again. Often, without warning, they would appear on the south coast or on the eastern marches to wreak havoc among any and all who were either simply asleep

---

19 For convenience we will be referring on the most part to each of these men who followed Julius Kysar as Emperor, rather than Augustus. Maybe it should be pointed out for the reader's information that the advent of Imperator Filius Deus Augustus Gaius Octavius' tenure occurred in the year 777 of the Olympian standard calendar and essentially was year one of the current age.

or out to lunch. This seldom was the case with the wary. From Dariotum (headquarters of the Amoran Twentieth and Sixth Legions) the military advanced to a village called Josselyn (also Joscelyn or Joslin). It was decided that Castus, along with Dyfed and Trachmyr and their suite of support staff, would remain there and erect a main command post and supply depot. Meanwhile, the two legions along with King Zintacus and his Sarm horsemen from the east would scour the land from top to bottom, and east to west, raking in any dangerous dissenters and addressing the lax tax remit problem. In this they were quite successful and after only two favourable seasons of campaigning Castus was sitting back satisfied and awaiting new orders from Amor. It was just by chance that the small city of Josselyn (Joslin), where they had located their command base, was also the capital of the kingdom at this time. And it had been here that Ban, the father of Galhad (Marg's ward), had ruled before being usurped. Ban had been well liked by his people so it didn't come as a surprise that the locals were happy that the Amoran legions from Prydain had liberated them from an eastern steppe interloper who had put the run on Ban and killed him. This new interloping chief they called Ateula, the servant of Mars, but he called himself Arviragus.

Then, in the late Fall of the following solar cycle; Castus got a communiqué from Nova Troia. The communiqué was from Vespasianus of all people. He conveyed to Castus his many thanks and appreciations for his hard work in the field. Dyfed learned that the message was strangely contrite while at the same time it was confusing. Apparently, Vespasianus took pains to inform Castus that Publicus Servicicus [Serviceicus] Nemesis Maximus Augustus Usurperus[20] was dead, or disposed somehow. But he provided no proof and Castus himself was unsure and told Dyfed so. Vespasianus further insisted in his communication with Castus that he was preparing to return to Amor so as to take over control of the empire and make a bid for the official emperorship itself. Furthermore, he informed Castus that due an outbreak of starvation in Amor, he was arranging for vital shipments of grain to be dispatched to there from the Land of Khem to fend off this scourge. There had been no word about starvation in Amor, but starvation was something that happened all over, all the time. So this at least was possible. Therefore, Vespasianus continued, he now had immediate need of the Sixth and Twentieth Legions to assist him in providing relief for Amor.

But it was apparent that Vespasianus' only real anxiety was to express care and concern for and about Castus' compliance to help him secure his bid for the emperor's crown. Vespasianus made it quite clear that to be successful in this he needed a signed confirmation by him — including his generals' signatures as well — at the earliest possible moment. Vespasianus had already taken the liberty to draw up the document of confirmation ('please find original document enclosed,' he stated in his communiqué) that now only needed Castus' and the other's signatures prior to being returned and handed over to a statesman and a retired general named Mucianus in the city of Amor. Mucianus had been Vespasianus' trusted deputy and governor of Assyria who, Vespasianus wrote, would be waiting for the signed confirmation document on the outskirts of Amor's main western gate on every Saturn's day at noon.

Apparently the late incumbent had already agreed (rumoured to be in Vespasianius' favour) to the terms of his resignation or his death (whatever and whenever it was),

---

20   Publicus Servicicus Nemesis Maximus Augustus Usurperus' was Vespasianius' name for every nemesis he ever confronted.

but Vespasianus wasn't leaving anything to chance. He had also taken the precaution to send Hadrianus (another contender and obvious potential Publicus Servicicus Nemesis Maximus Augustus Usurperus) to Thrax, he said. This implied, Castus and Dyfed agreed, was where Hadrianus would be well out of the way and less of a contender for now.

So anyway, to that end Vespasianus ordered Castus to forward to the aforementioned Mucianus the completed and signed confirmation by a favoured and trusted messenger immediately, if not sooner.

He also informed Castus that the Ninth Legion Hispana that remained behind to guard Albion were on board and standing at the ready to proclaim Vespasianus as emperor. Vespasianus also ordered Castus to stand at the ready and be prepared to move south into Hispana at a moments notice, if need be, or north so as to guard the approaches to Albion. He also cautioned Castus to keep his soldiers in training and to secure the roads and granaries as well as the more important towns surrounding their present location. He made it clear, however, that this arrangement didn't necessarily interfere with the thriving campaign-after-market of shoplifting and pillaging, the backbone, it seemed, of the army's, existence.

Since Dyfed had no real need of a servant to feed or dress him, from the moment of their arrival in Armorica he relegated Trachmyr to pull duty on many of the minor tasks that had become Dyfed's responsibility. These included checking manifest lists and conducting inventory. Dyfed felt that his immediate responsibility was to clearly understand the entire situation around how Amorans campaigned and record it. This, he thought, may be to his advantage at later date. Although Dyfed was against war of any kind, other than those for purely defence reasons, he thought that even if war was unstoppable (under the current phenomenon at large and circumstances at present) at least he could figure out how to make a towering profit with which to help the families of the dead and to rebuild their destroyed villages through a commonwealth of ownership within each of the tribes. It was also a viable way to increase the strength of the victorious tribe or clan who were fighting off aggression, surely! Again, Dyfed's naïveté and galloping gullibility was running headstrong ahead of the pack, for learning is sometimes an accumulative experience.

Quickly he noted that money making and business in general was immediately attracted to the theatre of war, especially here in Joslin where the headquarters and the military quartermaster resided. It turned out that the banks and the Amoran aristocracy in general had figured out how to make a towering profit while war remained unchecked. In regards to the latter, communicating with and assisting Catulus and other major moneylenders who were far from the theatre of war was, in part, also among some of the responsibilities that were passed down to him.

And although no magister mensarii or negotiators were actually present here, Dyfed saw the quick arrival of another class of businessmen, the mercatores. They were a sub set of negotiators who generally acted as agents in auctions and private sales and also kept deposits of money for individuals as well as providing cheque cashing services and availing themselves as moneylenders. Dyfed also noted that their books were accepted by the Amoran justices of the court as proof legal in most cases. And what with the vast looting and pillaging that accompanied the campaigns of Amor at war, soldiers and privateers could exchange stolen and liberated goods for quick cash with these plebeian and freedmen folks in a hurry. These businessmen had quickly set up their places of business along a quiet street in Joslin shortly after hostilities began. At once Dyfed saw that the market in Joslin that was run by these mercatores were asset short and vulnerable. This meant that they could easily be open to being garnisheed and placed under the umbrella of any enterprising mensarii. These latter were those public bankers that were appointed by the Amoran establishment: the House of Catulus, for example. And this consolidating banking firm, he thought, couldn't be far from hard on the heels of the legions.

Acting on his own initiative as an argentari, while communicating with the House of Catalus in Nova Troia for legal documented support, Dyfed met with these mercatores and promised to personally back them in lieu of any mercenary mensarii who were likely to pop up momentarily from the devil only knows where. With the boy Galahad's help he had earlier located a sympathetic rich local. This rich local's name was Egidius (and known afar as Egidius of Jocelyn), and he was the brother of Galahad's own dead father. And it was from this man that Dyfed rented property that included a stone building (unusual for here) in the centre of the village of Jocelyn (Joslin). The building came with sheds and corrals that backed the building and extended in pasture land beyond to the outskirts of the village. Here he set up the incorporated (in the sense of a legal entity in itself of commencing upon matters of business, with association with others, and capable of acting as an individual represented by Dyfed himself) House of Lucifer for the very first time. Suddenly, Dyfed found himself in business. In addition to being notarized as a mensari, a certified title that Castus was able to provide him, Dyfed also immediately applied for, and received, the title of Publican, which he knew would allow him to be provided funds from the empire in order to buy supplies for the troops and collect local taxes. And since he enjoyed a close proximity to Castus, this placed him in a lucrative position all around.

By the time he had received the papers for consignment, he had made so much money he didn't need the Albion branch of the House of Catulus any more, or any other mensarii either. He was on his own. However, as he had not closed down his account with the former House, he retained that credit, though only a pittance of it now languished somewhere in the bottom of the account left to be exploited by the House of Catulus. As he did not feel good about earning a prince's wages on the losses and suffering of others, being able still (if he so wished) to deposit blood lolly into his account with the House of Catulus instead of the House of Lucifer, was simply a fake, demographic structured relief that actually amounted to nothing in the end, he discovered. It was true, though, that he was more likely to draw it out and spend it assisting others; at least more than those other run of the mill financiers or banking magnates would. Anyway, that was how the game was set up, to make quick money off suffering. Indeed, so he had quickly discovered, suffering for another's' gain was often why the game was set up.

Dyfed kept profits neatly accounted for, less expenses, so as to be able to put them forward one day to the construction of the Union of People's Commonwealth Bank that he was still envisioning, as well as toward a compensation fund he planned to put into the hands of boy Galahad one day for the despoiled Armorica. The lad was still an uneducated adolescent and needed a start in life. Where better than to provide for those people of Armorica who were his fellow denizens that had once looked up to, and looked for help from, his father and his uncle Egidius of the town of Joslin?

For convenience to their prospective clients (like negotiators or mercatores), folks like himself in the argentari business utilized the banking businesses of holding deposits, cashing cheques, serving as moneychangers and acting as agents in public and private auctions. But Dyfed also provided highly armed mobile services as well as the customary stationary corner bank and vault. This entailed heavily armoured and guarded four wheeled wagons full of gold and silver leading trains of empty carts to the front in the field of battle in order to firmly establish themselves in being first to be positioned to finance purchases from those mercenary folks who pick through the still bloodied hands of the loot leaden fighters. And it was here in the death zone of the front line where the battle seasoned, early birds managed to secure the best and richest of the lolly, generally coveting more than they could carry in one trip back to Joslin's quiet streets with its corner bank of well dressed, neat and tidy employees, in order to sell there or ship to bigger markets. So Dyfed provided transport as well as silver and gold *denarii* (which what the Amoran currency was called).

This was convenience banking at its best and the House of Catulus had pioneered the way (so Dyfed had been informed by the proud Marcus Lucius). Now Dyfed was putting this method into practise on his own and by the time the Lugdunum branch of the House of Catulus actually did show up to open shop, hostilities had dwindled and the loot had all been bought up. This, of course, had been to Dyfed's credit.

Soon, Trachmyr (under Dyfed's direction) didn't even have to unload the gold to pay the first line mercenary scavengers. Before long, all he needed to do was send Trachmyr out with the wagons and a receipt book, while the gold never left the vault. Now he just simply gave out receipts and then trucked the booty back to Joslin where the net value of each business transaction was deposited into his secured vault under the name of the customer's account along with an inventory of the purchase with a duplicate that was attached to the goods of booty which were then stored in equally secure and guarded stone warehouses that once had housed horses out back. This booty became Dyfed's gross profit along with storage rental space Dyfed provided for the booty-goods of other traders. Though the House of Catulus hadn't actually practised it quite in this way, Dyfed had learned from Marcus Lucius Catulus' own motto: keep other peoples' money in your bank vault. Don't let it out of your sight, even if you lend it to someone else. Pay a little interest for keeping it but charge more for lending it out in promissory notes.

Once the booty was retrieved and sorted out as to who among the mercatores bought what up and what mercenaries needed to be paid out, and how and when, and all the paper work clean off the desk, then the booty was trucked by wagon train to a central market depot in Lugdunum to be sold for profit. Dyfed was in the market, too. Armoured transportation was needed here, and since carrying around large sums of gold or valuable goods was a dangerous habit for individuals Dyfed expedited this transport on other's behalf. Expeditors like him provided this service to and fro Lugdunum and were credited up at a registered state bank in that city. This gave further substance for validating his accumulating wealth and in a small way acted as a laundry for the masses of coin that tumbled into his coffers from Morgant's private and mysterious mint. His silver and gold came from the mountainous regions of northern Italia.

Dyfed made a mental note that this business of laundering loot through an exchange of gold (or better still, a promissory note) worth only a fraction of the goods value, was a prominent and intrinsic element to the event of war itself. To be sure, this quick sketch of the hows and wheres of the average shoplifting financial sheet wasn't quite what took place here in Joscylin (Joslin), he noted. Armorica was not a land so leaden with riches and other wealth, and there were no giant markets with throngs of potential buyers purchasing goods here either. This is where the mensarii came in with their established branches of banks that fanned out across the empire. As such, Dyfed's association with the House of Catulus came in handy here too. With his registered promissory notes which his credentials helped validate, along with Catulus' letter of recommendation, this allowed him to take part in the great exchange, and his customers' gold (that he kept in his vault) could stay in his vault yet be easily exchanged via a promissory note for gold in a branch of the House of Catulus a hundred or a thousand Amoran miles away. This loan, however, was able to be easily paid off simply by him accepting another's debt back which occurred somewhere close to his own vicinity which he could pay off on the other's behalf: tit for tat; you scratch my back and I'll scratch yours. It was like a game, Dyfed thought.

Sometimes the heavily guarded and laden down wagon trains of booty filing away from the fields of battle, or even from the jolly town of Joslin towards distant markets such as Lugdunum, clogged the highways and byways to the degree that even the military got bogged down waiting for them to pass. It seemed that the wagons of commerce were a priority, even to the point where they took precedence over all other traffic including the military, unless the latter were undergoing an operation on high alert. And all the while the already chaotic transport situation was further confused and befuddled by those other wagon trains that came rattling back for more. Even Dyfed took to parking his chariot while on military business on this account and rode instead upon the backs of his two Andalusians while standing tall and shouting out loudly to those causing congestion to make way. He did this to provide punch to his profile as he dashed about.

And now as hostilities shrank, and Dyfed's duties were no longer of any utmost military importance, Field marshal Castus (who had been casting around for a candidate to deliver that important message to Amor on behalf of Vespasianus' dangerous and chancy venture) immediately chose Dyfed for the job.

Once all the signatures were affixed, the affidavit was to be immediately dispatched by sealed pouch to his man in Amor, a certain agent Mucianus, who would be waiting for them. Trachmyr, Karatakos, and the boy Galahad under his charge were to accompany him, along with twelve centurions to guard the packet's safety. Trachmyr, despite being a barbarian, had already achieved a sufficient rank proficiency to act as batman to a senior centurion named Germanos who took command over the dispatch alongside Prince Dyfed who carried the pouch.

Dyfed needed to transport his goods' profit along with the contents of his bank safe from Joslin to Lugdunum. And as this city was on their way, as they wended their way toward Massalia then Amor while being accompanied by Amoran guards commissioned by Vespasianus to guard his delicate bid for emperorship (namely the signed paper consignment with support of the XXth and the XIth Legions), worked out well for Dyfed. Once in Lugdunum Dyfed was able to sell his booty quickly at market as well as utilized his little used account he had opened years ago at the House of Catulus Bank in the name of the House of Lucifer. Into this languishing account, then, he deposited (therein) all of his worldly denarii. This added much to the big smile from Markus Catulus' brother-in-law who was managing that bank branch at the time. This sum of denarii (cashed in gold and silver) included the funds from the profit of the market sale of war-booty he had purchased from mercenary soldiers. It also included Morgant's allotment to Dyfed of thousands of silver denarii back in Albion prior to leaving Nova Troia. Later, once he had arrived and was settled in Amor he would arrange for his account to be transferred there.

Gaul, especially in the south toward Massalia, was no back-eddy like the environs around the town of Legion had been, or even Joslin. The paved Amoran high roads that had been laid down right over top of the ancient Keltic tracks were well maintained and now were made arrow-straight to the point of destination. They were built in such a way that the water poured off them and into a parallel running ditch, and debris rolled toward the side keeping the road clear. And the closer one got to Amor, the better maintained they became, often with uniformed servicemen of the state labouring in their upkeep alongside and among the artery's growing traffic of chariots and commercial wagons. So it was under these conditions that the party, dispatched to Mucianus in Amor, from the town of Joscylin (Joslin) in Armorica arrived at Massalia quite quickly and without incident, with the exception of a business layover at Lugdunum, which was also a military protocol. Time was of the essence. That had been instilled into Dyfed's orders as well as his scheduled route, so he was to make for Massalia from where the party of twelve — along with their sixteen mounts and eight heavy, but high speed, chariots — would set sail to Ostia. This was Amor's official port and fastest access to the city.

Dyfed was beside himself. He was somewhere in the midst of Massalia and Marg, at last (he thought). Soon he'd be rid of the irritating adolescent Galahad. Very soon he could pawn him back onto Marg along with a dowry of sorts that Dyfed had founded in the lad's name to help the poor disgruntled folks of Armorica. But he never did quite understand why she took him on in the first place.

At Massalia a peculiar serendipity overcame him, for it was from this very port four hundred years earlier that the ancient mariner Pytheas had set sail looking for a new source for tin, only to arrive upon the ancient shores of the northern isles. There, Pytheas had chanced to set eyes upon the Isle of Peace as he explored greater Albion. And always the good mariner-scientist, he consulted with his instruments and continually noted in the ship's periplus[21] the angle of the sun's rays as they struck the deck of his vessel. He also marked down the descriptions of noticeable observations about his geographical surroundings. He collected these readings and descriptions in an effort to correlate corresponding readings relative to times and dates so as to correctly place his ship's position in the proper latitude and longitude position for each station of observation. Ultimately, these readings helped him to print and indent marks consisting of crooked and wavy lines upon the blank white open spaces on his global charts that would intelligently conform to the coastlines of lands he had come to explore.

But pulling into the harbour beneath Manandan and Violet's palaces, Pytheas and his Hellenic colleagues of trespassers hunting for tin had been utterly astonished at what they saw. Told by the local tongue that he had arrived in Prydain he incorrectly wrote down Brytain. So it was initially upon the event of Pytheas' visit — that history misnamed Prydain and called it another — and what initially spurred that sage Manandan to think about scouting around so as to acquire some modern day Daedalus to fabricate

---

21   A manuscript document listing ports and coastal landmarks along with intervening distances and a general attestment of local geographic. Also: a type of ship's log.

for him some form of magical device to shield the Isle of Peace from the prying little eyes of any old tin-digging, rubber-necking merchant on the make here in the future. Although he had procrastinated for about four hundred years, and although he had been unsuccessful in his endeavour at the time, ultimately this had led Manandan on an unexpected journey with an unexpected outcome. The upshot, which was to consign the task to Lord Huge who had been currently (at that time) stationed in the Anatolian Dardan along with Queen Violet, to permanently conceal the Isle of Peace with a miraculous cloud.

As for Dyfed, he had been inspired by hearing Manandan's account of Pytheas' quick stop-in at the Isle of Peace on his journey back to Massalia and the man's long winded account about the wonders he discovered on an even more northerly isle (later called Thule, also Iceland) in the land of the midnight sun. Speaking tours in the lands around the White Sea weren't organised in those days quite the same manner as they were in more recent times, so Pytheas' tales became hear-say, and eventually they became heresy. But from being told of this encounter, much later Dyfed was (in order to explain his presence among the hoi polloi, at that point) able to imagine (then intelligently spin) his own tale of having been shipwrecked while on a scientific excursion to the northern regions where he was investigating the causes for the displays of the Aura Borealis. But that wasn't necessary now here.

So, the moment Dyfed and his entourage arrived at this ancient Hellas port on the White Sea coast, he quickly sought out Queen Marg by inquiring after her whereabouts from the local gentry. It turned out that they only had rumour of her, and very little more. She was a recluse, one man said, and seldom attended the social circle's festivities and their invitation-only amusement venues.

"Being an attractive, even seductive, high born made her an automatic qualified attendee and various invitations to her had been sent out,' said a rich landowner.

"But she had constantly been a no-show,' said the pale, dark haired lord of another manor where Dyfed had enquired. 'But you will find her,' the latter man told him in accented Amoran, 'just south and east of the port. Her mansion is high up on the headlands over by the slope looking west out over the bay toward the islands.'

In the offices of the port authority of Massalia Dyfed quickly tried to make reservations for their party to sail on the first tide after the following day's dawn. But the sallow faced little man with wispy hair only shook his head, implying that it wasn't going to happen. Dyfed then produced the written orders from Vespasianus, Emperor Augustus that was addressed to Castus and only then was he slowly and methodically referred to the Amoran customs officer who took a long time looking over the correspond-dance. But before he could mount his white Andalusian and set out to find Marg, which is what he wanted most of all to do most of all, he was delayed with further protocol and administrative observances.

Booking a passage of some few days duration that included twelve men and sixteen horses and eight chariots was not going to be a cheap excursion, Dyfed was told repeatedly from a small crowd of official onlookers who had gathered round to watch and offer opinions. As yet, the customs man had not yet mentioned the fare involved, not at all. After Dyfed had refused to show him the signed and sealed affidavit — had even refused to withdraw the envelope that contained the affidavit from his pouch — the man had not spoken another word. His fingers caressed his pursed lips as he kept re-reading the written orders.

"By Saturn, the authority above and beyond the great god Zeus!' exclaimed Dyfed as the time ticked away here in this cramped office. Here he was, trapped in a dingy donjon (dungeon) while just outside — only a stone's throw away — the bright White Sea sun danced off the yellow ripples and turquoise coloured waves like shimmering diamonds. Nearby, a tethered Andalusian restlessly pawed the ground with a left hoof, its skin trembling along its shoulders and sides the way wind stirs ripples in a pond. All this was taking up his time as the charms of Marg's were waiting, and while her longed for embrace lapsed, idle and unfulfilled. And the office smelled of men, of dirty, old, boring men who scratched their itchy crotches and picked their noses. This arrangement that joined the two separate links to their journey from Lugdunum to Amor was at least to have given Dyfed a few precious hours with Marg that was now quickly melting away. It was causing a mounting frustration within him. Furthermore, he felt he didn't need to be delayed at all in any way in carrying out his mission. One night with her, was all he wanted, not two. Not now, anyway. Dyfed glanced at the timepiece that was on a mantle and for a moment watched the fine sand lightly trickle through the narrow neck.

When the customs man finally stamped the clearance for his entire party, Dyfed was suddenly overjoyed. But when the grungy looking cashier (down the hall with a dirty working toga) asked for his payment, price was so high that Dyfed wanted to hit the roof with his fists. Either that or punch the smelly, boring apparition with the lack of imagination written all over his ignorant stupid face that was carefully watching him with a sneer that was directly in front to him.

"Menstruating Leda, by Jove,' Dyfed managed to say politely without showing any outward anger whatsoever. But he paid up. Upon that exclamation, the office crowd that had been idly standing by to take in the excitement of their version of someone running the gauntlet, the crowd who had now followed him to here, hemmed in even closer, choking off Dyfed's air. 'This is banditry,' he responded gently with a growing smile as he counted out the denarii that fell onto the desk. Then looking around at the stupid faces surrounding him he uttered, 'you are all pirates, by Jove. Wait until I tell the new emperor.'

After all, he thought, am I not on the empire's business, here? Castus had certainly weighed him down with some of the Empire's gold coinage — most of it all spent — and the fare for their last leg to Amor was so outlandish that Dyfed had to put in from his own pocket, only in the end to be denied a receipt? Enough is enough, he thought. Trachmyr and the ten centurions had all remained outside with the horses and were a short distance from the approaches to the port of authority offices. Now he hollered out for assistance at which Trachmyr and five centurions including the centurion Germanos quickly arrived to see what all the fuss was about. As it was they had grown sleepy and bored and most of them had laid down in the shade while wondering about the delay. Suddenly the crowd around Dyfed drew back with an audible 'ooh, ah'; some of them were even rudely pushed aside and thrust back, as the centurions formed a ring around their captain, to which Dyfed was now referred. Germanos and Trachmyr who now stood beside Dyfed, both took pains to inform the cashier (and the now whimpering and suddenly silent crowd) that they had more centurions outside who on their command will fetch the guard from the garrison. They were told they would place many of them under arrest and he would need to confiscate the cashier's cash box and receipt books as evidence. Dyfed wasn't sure whether Trachmyr and Germanos were bluffing or not. It didn't matter, though — for as they put on such a fine performance — compliance was immediate. Then as the cashier quickly began to write out Dyfed's receipt, the latter commanded the slovenly little nerd to clearly itemize their discount, as well, then mentioned pointedly that their imperial rebate due to their being on business of the Empire must be subtracted from the total.

"We are on business of the state,' he said loudly and clearly toward the crowd that was now slinking away to their grubby, little, sunshine starved, pigeonholes. 'We are on business of the office of the emperor.'

Finally, at long last, Dyfed was outside in the warm sun astride his white Andalusian, and in no time had located Marg who resided atop a hill nearby that overlooked the bay, just as the lord of the last manor he had consulted had said. But it was a most pleasant surprise for Dyfed to find Morgant, that old bandy legged gnome residing there, too, and comfortably lodged in one of Marg's guest rooms. But what followed their reunion was remarkable.

Shortly after being welcomed to her palatial apartments on the hill, folks from all over came to visit. They were well known to Morgant and Marg, apparently, but in some way they made Dyfed feel as though they had come especially to see him that he thought unlikely. Anyway, it became obvious that they knew a lot about him. Dyfed (too) knew one or two of them, but only by reputation. Many were men and women of Hellene origin and all were quite famous like Klaudios Ptolemy for one, and Paredros of Phigaleia, the cortegé chief of staff to Poteidaon and Demeter who was accompanied by a most attractive young woman named Despoina. Democritus of Abdera had been the first to arrive. Pausanius from either Lydia or Sparta (pending upon when, or sometimes, how you asked him about his origins) was there, along with Heraclitus of Ephesus accompanied by the ever-present Logos. Timon of Phlius, a sceptic and writer of satirical poems, turned up but immediately upon being introduced stated that he was unable (or didn't want) to maintain his social visit here for the duration. Apparently, he had better things to do with himself, though he didn't stipulate what. Stilpo of Megara showed up with his student Zeno of Kition (a Kypriot) and the founder of Stoicism. Finally, a local scientist whose records and writings about the arctic had once enthralled a young Dyfed showed up. This, of course, was Pytheas himself. This gnarled old man told Dyfed that his door was always open. Whatever that meant, thought Dyfed (aside from the door never being closed, of course, he guessed).

A banquet ensued followed by lively talk bordering on debates. Stilpo espoused on the differences and similarities between the Eleusinian mysteries and the Orphic mysteries, both of which promised advantages in the after-life. This interested Dyfed a little but seemed to bore Timon of Phlius silly. Klaudios Ptolemy was quite keen to espouse mathematical theorems about the cosmos. But due to Democritus' scoffing laughter and heckling, he did not finish nor did he remain at Marg's palace much longer. He left immediately after dinner. Each of these folks had their idiosyncrasies, Dyfed noted. But Democritus (after he had eaten) had wiped his hands on the under-lining linen of the crocheted tablecloth.

(The House of Lucifer comes to Amor)

'If you'll just come with me and see the beauty of…
Tuesday afternoon…I'm just beginning to see, Now I'm on my way,
It doesn't matter to me, Chasing the clouds away.'
JUSTIN HAYWARD (*MOODY BLUES BAND*)

After a short sea journey, Dyfed, his companions of centurions (led by Germanos), along with Karatakos, Trachmyr and Morgant (who had now joined them as well) finally arrived up river at Amor. Dyfed's two fine Andalusians and a puppy (which Marg had given him as a leaving present) had accompanied them. He had, on the other hand, unloaded Galhad onto Marg in Massalia. The purpose was to advance his education. It came to pass, however, that that hadn't worked out very well, either. Earlier, before they had left Joslin and the Vilaine and Oust rivers district (a back-eddy west of Nantes where most of the battles had taken place), Galhad the Young had begged Dyfed to let him stay in Armorica with families he had known as a youngster; either that, he said, or be returned to his people in the land of the Dumnonii who lived west of the Dowr Tamar in south western Prydain.

"As for the prospect of me becoming a part of the regimented life among foreigners in the Amoran capital,' he had told everybody, stamping one foot in frustration, 'I don't wanna!... and I won't go.'

Galhad was at an awkward age; something Dyfed was quite eager to concur on this point. At any rate, Dyfed had baulked at all of Galhad's alternative suggestions and instead he dragged him along to Massalia and Marg. But once the ugly reality of living with Galhad the Young (Adolescent) was plainly stuck straight into her face (this took all of half a day), Marg quickly began to carefully rethink the situation over. She came immediately to the ultimate conclusion that the lad was programed for high maintenance. Upon discovering this, she immediately convinced Germanos that on his return to Massalia from accompanying Dyfed to Amor, to take and to drop Galhad off in Lugdunum as they made their way back to Armorica. Marg's gold, after all would be used pay for his attendance at boarding school there and Morgant had recommended and provided Galhad with a tutor to accompany him.

As for the people waiting in Amor for Dyfed, Morgant, Karatakos, Trachmyr (and company) at Amor's main western gate of entry on the river embankment at noon hour on this fine Saturn's day noon (as agreed upon and expected), Mucianus was conspicuous by his absence. For aside from the cluster of hard-eyed Guards there were only a single set of civilian eyes on them that had paid any attention to their arrival. At one point, after they had cleared customs, the man who wore those eyes stepped forward out of the cool shadows of a plane tree and embraced Morgant with a warm welcome. It was a happy reunion, Dyfed could see, but Morgant's eagerness to introduce this old friend (a senator named Cato) to him had (at the time) interrupted Dyfed's pensive thoughts.

It was dawning on Dyfed just then that either everybody took it for granted that the emperor was a lame duck, or were totally unaware of Vespasianus' plot to overthrow

Nero Germanicus Augustus. For (he now recalled) they hadn't been long on the road to Massalia through Gaul before they had been perplexed that nobody but themselves seemed to know that the emperor had died in some manner, or had been usurped (or was in the process thereof, also in some manner). Their reaction was that the emperor was alive and well; hip…hip…hurray! long live Nero. "I mean what the devil? Dyfed had overheard Germanos the centurion mutter at one point while looking quite perplexed. Karatakos, on the other hand, smiled but said nothing. Certainly the people's reaction was that Nero wasn't dead. He was on the throne last they heard, anyway. It could be (Dyfed thought) that they had no inkling and were totally unaware that the process by which Vespasianus was to advance to emperorship was even afoot. Although it is true that often most folks one meets are abjectly indisposed of (and about) any information beyond their own shadow cast by the sun. They are ignorant of the great game of life that is going on around them. Apparently, according to people Dyfed and company encountered on this journey of theirs (which included senior military staff folks at the two large Amoran centres of Lugdunum and Massalia), Nero was still firmly seated on his throne and was expected to remain there for some time yet, despite Vespasianius or for that matter — Constantine.

Now, standing there before the city of Amor, whatever hidden doubts he had had about Vespasianus' own version of history that was unfolding before his fantasy, it suddenly melted away like snow under the April sun that shone down on this fine Saturn's day. If arriving here in itself was humbling, a sudden cognizance that (though not actively relative on a one to one basis, and certainly not similar to something like Radiance rising in the east to take charge of the new day) flooded over him was. It was like a new Saturn's day morning in June. Indeed, the sudden gathering around him at Massalia during the meet with great men (and ladies) at Marg's rented palace last week was something of a precursor to this. It had been a gob-smacker that had left him in a daze. There must have been something in his wine, his heavy head told him that next morning. For Marg and Morgant went on with their day as though nothing had happened. Dyfed had even sought out Karatakos, enquiring as to whether he had taken notice of the company that had been noisily hanging around the previous evening drinking and supping. But, having remained and dined in his apartments alone before accompanying the centurion soldiers to a local bar and grill pub that same day, Karatakos replied that he had not seen anyone, and looked with concern at Dyfed. Unfortunately too, Trachmyr (an alert and up and coming stalwart soldier of the Empire) had also been absent that evening from the goings-on that were levelled (it seemed to Dyfed now) directly at himself. Trachmyr had told him that he and Galhad had taken the company's horses back down into the city earlier on that day to be shoed. Since they billeted there over night, neither of them could be of any help to Dyfed about the last night's mystery. Oh well, Dyfed thought as stood on Amor's embankment rubbing his eyes with the crook of his forefingers.

Cato, the name of the man who had greeted them at the riverbank customs gate, was looking at Dyfed. His smile was restless when they finally exchanged greetings. Dyfed quickly learned that Cato was concerned that the Guards as participants of a contrived event were viewing the arrivals. He thought they were bait and their arrest was imminent. When that didn't appear to be the case as they entered the city, then he cautioned that their arrest by the Nightwatchmen was to follow perhaps that evening: perhaps with an added advantage of enabling the imperial establishment to net even more traitors and dissidents in one fell swoop. That, too, proved not to be the case.

So, Dyfed, Morgant, Trachmyr, and Karatakos settled down into a roomy town villa, a walled-in settlement of buildings in the area of Amor called Esquiline Hill. Dyfed thought it was Cato's home but it turned out to be Morgant's. Apparently, Morgant (that bucolic hermit he had first found nestled in the mountains of Gwyneth and living in a starving cave and sleeping on a hard plank where there was hardly room for a puppy to lie) had a dual inhabiting capacity. It quickly dawned on Dyfed that it was he who was accompanying Morgant back to the big grape, not the other way around. Nor were they on an equal footing here. It seemed that Dyfed who was encountering the capital of the empire for the first time was being chaperoned (in some way) by Morgant who leading the way here. It appeared to have all been arranged, but surely (he concluded), it must have been coincidental.

Indeed, the sprawling complex of the Esquiline residence was certainly Morgant's, and there was nothing skint about it. It was vast, compounded and lavishly appointed. It was bleakly monumental from the outside and a shining palace from within. This was the flexibility of the man. And while Cato had a home in another part of the city (or a hole under a rock — no one seemed to know where the man lived), he also had digs buried somewhere among the many suits of Morgant's Esquiline Hill Palace residence where the former Cato often stayed for weeks on end. It was obvious that he and Morgant were comfortable with each other. And for the first few months after their arrival in Amor this is where Cato made his home so as to help with his old friend's safe assimilation again and in bringing him up to speed, which in those days was called 'bringing him the news'. And the local news here was all that mattered anywhere in the Empire and there wasn't a whisper lurking anywhere about Nero's immanent death.

Cato was also indispensable for helping Dyfed orientate onto the axis with the highest level of vibration anywhere on Earth today. It was he (more than Morgant) who paved Dyfed's s way in the beginning to the foyer (foy-yay) or vestibule just outside the corridors of power here in Amor, and even unto the vestry before the imperial chamber whose rarefied atmosphere embodied the temple of the Empire itself, the Imperial Ledger containing the balance of its financial accounts.

As for the occasion of the recent death of Claudius Kysar Augustus there was still much ado about it within the city. Although the wailing had stopped, after all this time folks were still talking about it to no end. The occasion of the poor old emperor's death had been sudden and untimely. He and his tenure had expired with not so much (I might add) as a by your leave. Of course, Amoran emperors don't have to beg leave, and more to the point, were seldom given the chance (that is to say, opportunity). Tiberius Claudius Kysar Augustus Germanicus Britannicus was dead: poisoned, it was said, by his not so loving wife. At least that was the official rumour. Anyway, this emperor had hung around for quite some time. He had made a go of it, and certainly his tenure had outlived and amounted to much more then just a few of all of the emperors so far who had preceded him. It turned out, too, that the choice to appoint the aforementioned Nero as his successor (by the way) had been the real cause for all of the earlier mentioned lamination and moaning that had been heard going on. It also brought into vogue the expression *'qui bono?'*

Yet still no sign of Vespasianus. Dyfed, however, now turned his attention to matters at hand — the House of Lucifer. And while he did so Karatakos milled around at large doing what he does best. As a prisoner imprisoned by the very man who himself had been intrigued by this Albionian (Britainicus) king and who had once spared his life, Karatakos still had some kind of status among the old guard here and connections to some of Claudius' powerful former yes-men from the senate who now, on one hand were still crying into their beer while keeping a sober eye out for any future opportunities with the other. Trachmyr who felt and acted as if he were on holiday sometimes accompanied Karatakos. Together they jousted elbow to elbow with a strange mixture of the scrubbed aristocrats and the scrubby rubbie-dubs among the multitude as they jostled among folks through the streets or sat guzzling down wine, beer and sundry products of distilled beverages at local public houses. And these quaff-backs were not all just stand-around and munch, dine and dash affairs. Some provided and served up the most delicious and agreeable victuals to be had anywhere accompanied by entertainment. These were real, hearty, sit-down nosh-up affairs with all the finery that attracted an attendance of well-heeled folks who talked shop on current flying rumours about this senator and that consul-general almost as much as the loose tongued rabble did who congregated and frolicked around at the sidewalk tables of finger-food.

Aside from the prestige of Cato's company, Karatakos-the exRex and Trachmyr — the waif from the woolly hills of Gwyneth and anti-establishment and dissident community leader for wayward boys (gangsters) who (horseless and penniless) prowled on foot around the Gwynedd 'hood' doing whatever it took to remain alive — were themselves now afoot mingling with the Amoran populace. Between the ousted exRex[22] (the former king of Albion) and Trachmyr who was the graduate and superintendent of Ruck's Roost, the college of hard-knocks, the would be soldier of fortune and now soldier of Amor, it was they more than anything else who were acting as the eyes and ears for the others back at the Esquiline Hill Palace residence. This residence became known as the headquarters of the *pack*, and the aforementioned (along with Cato) kept Morgant and a host of unseen associates in the know of just how it was that the politics were unfolding in the capitol. In turn, so Dyfed believed, Morgant kept the Hyperborean Masters informed of who was lining up behind whom and for what result. Spying, after all, was one of Karatakos' successful proficiencies. It was his forte that included a lot of luck that he kept up his sleeve and always had at the ready. Trachmyr, on the other hand, was a rough and tumble lad and in some ways like Dyfed. But Trachmyr's urchin background had provided him with attributes to make it up as he made his own way up and collect what luck came his way as he goes. His form combined with his attitude easily cut through the Scotch mist and morning fog of the moving phenomena at hand that had not dealt him many other useful cards.

Throughout the City of Amor beautiful and talented singers were forever taking to the stages around the public courtyards and piazzas singing gloriously to the people of Amor accompanied by professional musicians. Inspired by the likes of celebrates such as the great baritone singer Giaus Markus Cuzo, or that darling of the musical theatre, Julia Livia Fuvio, the people danced and sang along too. The latter was a shrill and demonstrative fandango singer and performer from Hispania who was beloved by all of Amor.

---

22 Rex or rics (riks) and reiks: from a proto-Indo-European word meaning ruler: Sanskrit *rajan* and old Irish *ri*.

Every day (it seemed to Dyfed) the hoi polloi had ample opportunity to ratchet themselves up into a higher height of arousal during the noon hour and later into the evenings through music, song and political gesturing which were both organized and impromptu stage acts, the latter which materialized briefly then just as suddenly melted into the crowd and disappeared from sight until reoccurring elsewhere, later. Amor was a city of music, commotion and other hubbub pivoting around its people and their daily focus. But behind this façade were battalions of slaves and other poor and downtrodden folks.

During this time, with Morgant and Cato's help, Dyfed began to search around for a method of securing a licence to hold an argentari seal within the City of Amor. He also made an application to be appointed as a licenced public banker (a mensari). The chance of achieving this position was certainly iffy at best at this point. This was Dyfed wasn't known within the city by those who needed to know him. At least as an argentari he could run a number of businesses out of the House of Lucifer in order to get started. But Cato summoned a man named Philostephanos of Corinth who just happened to be on some secular pilgrimage and was in the vicinity. This man was able to bend the ear of some of the Amoran Pooh-Bahs who were intrinsically linked to the imperial bureaucracy. Surprisingly, this Hellene was made quite welcome at the Esquiline Palace residence where he, too, stayed for about a year. But having now seen the lie of the land, Dyfed now became most interested in becoming an advocate. After all, advocacy was really what he was about. There were very few good advocates in Amor, so Morgant's friend Cato quickly advised him. Certainly, considering Dyfed's manner, his education and upbringing under his master Manandan (specifically his ability to divine the probabilities of how events might unfold and how to prematurely tweak designs and stratagems to avoid catastrophe, also his incredible memory along with his well learned proficiency in rhetoric), there were opportunities for Dyfed to aid the cause, here.

Although there had been a three hundred year old law of upholding the tradition of prohibiting an advocate from charging an assistance fee to argue the case for an accused, the stuttering stumble-bum of the old emperor who had recently bellied up amid his gilded pond that flowed up from the big muddy where he ululated and chirped his last croak only just a decade or so before, had recently put an end to that practice. For reasons known only to himself, Claudius had recklessly abolished and made illegal and subject to punishment any person or persons who defended or attempted to defend an accused[23] through rhetoric and cunning before an imperial court who in addition received or did not receive any traditional advocacy fee for services rendered unless that advocate was a registered professional who was especially consigned through permit and privilege that specifically allowed him or her to approach the bench so as to take on the case at hand before the court. And further, it was well known that any such advocate capable and licensed to argue the case for any defendant was by law now expected to swear their allegiance firstly to the emperor and the emperor's courts of justice before all else. Furthermore, such a professional advocate was held to maintain imperial and senatorial standards by being highly scrutinized and constantly under review to ascertain and ensure that they were beholden first and foremost to how the emperor and the senate wanted to proceed in any given case. That contributed to giving the court an interest in

---

23   Traditionally the accused must defend themselves but were allowed a 'friend' to assist and advocate on their behalf.

the case beyond that of the duty of proof and equality before the law. This amounted to something akin to poly-potential powers that the imperial seat and the house of the senate had over the system of justice to which each and every member of the general population were bound to. In other words, it was no longer a just system. As such (so certain philosophical thought had it), Claudius had gone ahead and flung wide open the door for legalizing judicial advocacy as a professional advocate for the emperor's and the senator's wishes, by which they let truth, the equal rights of the hoi polloi and justice itself be damned. Fortunately, the senate was usually divided.

But imagine, rhetoric that was professionally paid for, or, if you like — fees demanded. Now here we have it. Plainly, this was just how injustice was being institutionalized nowadays here in Amor. Not un expectantly, this development (so it was thought among the aforementioned ranks of philosophers who have come in and out of our tale so far) was a page-turner, a bookmark for a game changer; and that sly old stuttering Claudius nimble-wits knew it. As it was, Dyfed's first design (a natural emanating desire which he had, and one that was closest to his heart) had been to secure an appointment by imperial authority to found a public bank as a foundation for the House of Lucifer. The concept of advocating (to advocate) — the true volition behind that aforementioned vocation as well as the attitude of his entire being — was a not-for-self-profit side-line which cleanly fit into his associates' (the *pack's*) cause and raison d'etre, anyway. The plan of the Masters of the Hyperborean civilization (a condition, not a race) to infiltrate that infantile and twisted Idea, which the Amorans still held on to, was becoming more complicated.

It was equally burdened and hampered by its primitive and superstitious culture of sacrificing to the gods (or even in their primitive belief of those gods, itself), especially the two hoaxes, *Jupiter* and *Juno*; and now possibly (and more recently) *Jehovah*. This was the divine father of the new messiah Jeshua Adon. Though not fully established around Europa as yet, it was arriving in Amor in droves in the minds of migrants. These aforementioned gods were the three 'J's, soon to become just the one and only 'J', or the one hoax event shared by a monotheist poly-cult that was soon (the all-seeing Masters of the Unknown Universe knew) would later be smashed again into three pieces; creating a condition where each would be set upon by each of the others to no end. Divide and conquer being the rule of the day then, and today. At this rate (so the all-seeing Masters thought), how could this atrocious and depraved state of being become transformed by anybody into a caring and considerate Empire whose Idea is to help out in any way they could in an altruistic way to aid and abet the fledging hoi polloi at this point and not suffocate and stifle them?

So, as Dyfed saw the situation at hand, in the current state, advocacy would benefit if the advocate were not only proficient in rhetoric but also most learned in all the law of the land besides. Therefore, the upshot of Dyfed's hubris (as Dyfed himself exclaimed to Morgant and Cato) was that he would become a specialist in the law. He would become a jurisconsult, a licenced and gold-sealed public responder which, aside from contributing toward the *pack's* general cause of inserting a balanced idealism into Amoran culture, it would further the cause of the House of Lucifer.

With this in mind Dyfed set about to compile a library of Amoran law in order to separate what was legal and what was not in the affairs between folks and the ever-changing laws of the land. But just as importantly, his endeavour was not just to compile and list those definitions and decisions made in the high courts, nor just to have those historistics so much at his finger tips, but rather at the tip of his tongue. This contributed in developing and registering the House of Lucifer for certain tax exemptions on the front burner as well. This now drew attention to him and his House. But to do all this, Dyfed knew he had to work like O'Billio by throwing himself into his tasks. So, it was a good thing that he and Marg were as good as separated from each other on a regular basis. He would have no time for her, anyway.

As Dyfed went about his day busily sniffing around and purchasing law manuscripts and applying for licenses and generally getting the feel of the lie of the land, Cato quickly and quietly advised him. Industrious that he was, Dyfed still remained intent on drawing as little attention to himself as possible, though some attention was assured, some necessary and some unwanted. Dyfed was happy in his new surroundings and his face showed it, but just as long as the able Morgant, Cato and Karatakos remained by his side as his confidants, it seemed. Dyfed didn't do well with set backs and failure. Morgant and Cato (and their associates) helped open doors and provide access for him. Trachmyr and sometimes the Ex-Rex were his companions of the evening as they sought out the customs and the pleasantries of what Amor, the kernel of the Empire and the centre of the world could offer by the thrills of its nightlife to intelligent and enquiring men like them. Much could be gleaned, and important and useful associations and acquaintances could be made where the rich and powerful aristocrats played, gambled and reconnoitred. And this took more than just a pocket full of those precious golden coins of the realm. At this game one needed to carry along a safety box of gold to cover expenses, something Dyfed was not short of.

NARRATOR'S PRIVILEGE

Talking about safety deposit boxes, with the nuisance of getting just a little ahead of ourselves in the chronology of this tale: events such as looming catastrophes of bankruptcy are always on the agenda to suddenly (and inconveniently) materialize any day. This is according to what Manandan had told Dyfed many times. And such catastrophes were even beyond the capability of the Amoran aristocratic dons to avert. Beyond the scope of provincial locality, and in the bigger picture, it had been prophesied that one day to come, disease and disaster would descend upon the entire extent of wretched humanity. On that day the one per cent of humanity (those filthy rich aristocrats) could kiss their portfolios and their glossy profit-sheets goodbye. Dyfed referenced this prediction and inserted it into his (as yet un-named) magus opus. This was his personal soliloquy in script to the general Idea that featured impoverishmentlessness. This was that once untouchable and usually untenable condition and situation of the joyous and happy safety deposit box extraordinaire that belonged to fellow *pack* member, Brother Morgant, which was never, empty.

Obviously, Morgant's arrangements were better than just a vault lodged in the corner bank or stashed away somewhere unanimously in the middle of a block of unoriginal corresponding-looking houses of business. According to ancient sources he received from Manandan and other tamer and somewhat lamer lore, no businesses were ultimately to survive that aforementioned event that (just as it has already happened in the past) was about to come about again in the future and reduce every man's fortune to rubble. No businesses (per sé) with the historic exception of prostitution and salvation, that is. But the life duration of both prostitution and salvation (which have something strongly in common) only trail in age duration somewhere just behind the existence of Cyanobacteria and the half a billion year old Horseshoe Crab (which is quite different from the common body crab, or crabs in general (which do have something strongly in common with prostitution and possibly even salvation). However, bacteria, mesmerisers, whores, and crabs aside, the tenacity and shrewdness common to the two aforementioned professions has a commonality with the street smarts needed to stay chowing down at the head of the food chain. It was not an ideal manner of existing in a not so ideal world, but there it was. In any case, in an already not so ideal situation, banking houses apparently shared a reputation (along with the concurrent legacy of damage to the general psyche) with those of current cult shamans of salvation and the pimps of individual gratification for the immediate want of self-satisfaction.

Dyfed had come to notice that Morgant was beginning to sound a lot like any of the multitude of brave new cult preachers and mesmerizers attached to the doctrine of Jeshua Adon that one saw hanging around the market squares who (rumour had it) lived outside of Amor in some bedroom community suburb of caves. Morgant, it seemed to him, had that same sanctimonious tone of insurance to any and all when he told them that he had a far securer place to keep riches safely laid away. He even told Dyfed once that the place of his own safety deposit box could secure all what he had and needed for all of time; it was indemnified (apparently) to the erosion of one civilization after another if need be and was even invulnerable to the passage of begginingless time itself. But he said this with a funny little laugh whose meaning of which Dyfed remained ignorant. Anyway, it was followed by "That's where I bank. And I know that in some small way you do too. But I'm here only to help.'

But was this spending value he was talking about, or what? Dyfed hadn't been quite clear about that. However, Morgant always delivered. 'Its not just about money, remember!' Morgant had stated many times. Dyfed thought that that was certainly the case, here, especially with him. Indeed, at any given time it didn't seem to Dyfed that Morgant had need of a safety box of any kind, never mind a vault at the corner bank. The man was unable to jingle any two silver denarii in his pocket at any given time; that is, until he needed to come up with half a million or more gold aureus pieces either to facilitate something or other for the *pack* (and for the cause), or specifically on behalf of Dyfed and his ventures, which hopefully (Dyfed thought) everyone thought were one and the same in the long run. Then suddenly when somebody needed a lot of money, presto! Actually Morgant always insisted on a fourteen-day notice and another fourteen days for a timely delivery with a full turn around of twenty-eight days. The lolly would materialized early one morning before the mist had lifted as Morgant would arrive home accompanying a heavily guarded wagon whose rumbling, and the clip-clop of the hooves (probably golden shod) of many horses would awaken Dyfed as they came through the heavy gates of their Esquiline Hill Palace Estate residence and enter the courtyard on that the twenty-eight day. And not just any dung wagon, either. This wagon would be loaded with over half a million freshly minted gold and silver coins. You could set your watch by it. To put it another way: Morgant (in order to fill the order) was actually capable of seeing a mound of golden aureus coins materialize straight out of thin air for every single second that made up the duration of a week. And what he did during the remaining twenty-one days was a mystery to Dyfed. He might as well have saved time down the road and asked Morgant for just a couple of hundred million aureus. At this rate he could save time (and maybe space), he used to think.

Life with these folks was so much like that stretch from reality into the dreamy world of make-believe and pretend which (he had long noted) made up so much of the fabric of this world on the outside of Peace. Dyfed liked the outside, but it seemed he couldn't escape it, even when among his own. The real reality, however, was the question of just what treasure it was that one needed to guard. And it certainly wasn't gold or silver. That much he knew.

What was it again that Morgant had said about security and invulnerability to the passage of beginningless time itself, or even to the erosion of civilizations when it came to guarding his treasure? Apparently, it wasn't money when it came to Morgant, or other Masters, either. Whatever gold and silver mining operation Morgant could plug into at will was something operated and controlled somehow by Hyperboreans ingenuity that was right here under the noses of the hoi polloi and their civilization of the third dimension. It had to be, since it has no use anywhere else. (**Parasolo**)

(The true throne and temple of the empire remains free of the trampling and the roar of the herd)

> *'What is troubling us is the tendency to believe that the mind is like a little man within.'*
>
> **LUDWIG WITTGENSTEIN**

Cato and Morgant brought another strange man named Gregorios Agricola into the circle to provide something, although Dyfed never truly understood what. An alchemist, Gregorios Agricola was a resident of Alba Longa just outside of Amor. He was a man who in all seriousness and with no trace of pulling your leg (meaning taking the piss or the mickey) claimed publically face to face with the hoi polloi (which in Agricola's case included many dons of the equestrian class) that he was the brother of Rhea Silvia. Although he made no such imposition to the members of the Esquiline Hill Palace Estate residents themselves about this (who in turn, in no way made any similar assumptions or even remarked upon it thereof, and ignored the implication completely), to be (in fact) the brother of Rhea Silvia was an important status to have (heh, heh, ha) especially with gullible folk like the hoi polloi. For as the brother (an older one at that) to sister Rhea Silvia, he was, therefore, the uncle of Romulus and Remus, the legendary (some say mythical) founders of Amor. But otherwise, the man was a recluse even compared to Morgant.

At some point Dyfed felt compunction to look in on the Amoran branch of the House of Catulus whose head office was here in Amor. This was aside from assuring that his account had been successfully transferred from Lugdunum to Amor, as had been his wish, much the same as he had it transferred earlier from Nova Troai to Lugdunum on the bank's suggestion. Surprisingly, they had no idea whatsoever of his personal situation, but they had been expecting him, they told him upon his appearance. He told them, of course, that he was pursuing legal education here in Amor at his own expense. This was to better learn to how to conduct the business of making money. He did not elaborated, however. Immediately upon congratulating him on the outcome of his successful ventures in Armorica, which they knew all about, they provided him an offer for a position of client auditor. This, they told him was in their money investment and lending department here at the Amoran branch of the Bank of Catulus. It was obvious to Dyfed that the nooks and crannies of late into which he had stuck his head (and his neck out into) was nowhere yet near to where he was sowing and cultivating towards in preparation to advance the House of Lucifer.

Dyfed's provincial mensari licence he had acquired had expired. It was no good in the City of Amor anyway and the House of Catulus would have known that. Further to that, his licence to run a mensari in Amor had not yet been granted, though Cato and Philostephanos of Corinth were working toward that end for him. So, in accepting the position at the Bank of Catulus in the interim, he thought, it would enable him even more to enrich his knowledge of the huge and entangled Amoran moneylending system and gain him more insight into where money lay and in being able to not only network that family's connections, but to put the information to use for the advantage of the House of Lucifer once that business was finally up and running. He wasn't about to ignore the fact that these bankers were the powerful equestrian class of Amoran aristocrats. War and make-merry was their agenda. This was something Dyfed had learned in Armorica. Maybe this city-folk crowd of equestrians happened to be a little less adventurous when it came to getting saddle sores on their thighs or their faces splattered with blood, but they were often more astute in social survival and better educated in superficially organized life than their country brother equestrian men sari in the field were. However, he took the position with conditions: he would work only part time as his studies came first.

As Dyfed had learned to keep his cards close to his chest when it came to others outside the *pack* who were the only ones he trusted, the House of Catulus remained unaware of Dyfed's enterprising plans all told. Meanwhile, juggling the interests of the House of Lucifer on one hand, he rubbed shoulders, ledgers, and account books in general with street moneychangers and small loans arrangers that were attached through some loan or other with the Catulus bank: that, or else rifling through the deposit boxes of mercatores and their lines of credit for wholesalers doing business in the shops and the uncovered markets throughout the city which he was required to look over in his capacity of auditor. When he wasn't doing that he was excepting invitations from a few of the aristocratic houses who were dangling daughters in front of him across heavily laden banquet tables amid the sweet sounds springing from the strings of lyres and sundry merry-making schemes done with a back-biting panache that would be a credit to the gods.

Soon the House of Lucifer, now working pretty much full time (in one capacity or another) out of an office among some of the not too shabby wooden town buildings that made up the Esquiline Hill Palace Estate residence, began to prosper most affluently. Meanwhile, Dyfed still put in a few hours of work each week regarding audits in the interests of the Bank of Catulus. Meanwhile, Cato had secured (as well) a suite of beautiful apartments for Dyfed in the ritzy Palatine Hill neighbourhood. This was a well-heeled district of the city whose neighbours included former emperors and such. This Palatine Hill mansion that Cato got his hands on was meant to eventually act as a show house statement for Dyfed. It was a front for his social status and that of the House of Lucifer. Both Morgant (who was to personate himself there as Dyfed's butler and chief servant) and Cato thought this was quite necessary and fitting for a rich man (who without having historically earned any fortune that was on the local books, or having attracted any forthcoming kudos from the aristocracy up to this point) needed this residence to be taken seriously. Obviously, the average aristocrat could surmise that he had brought his money to Amor from accumulating it abroad in the Empire. That could mean that he didn't owe any of it to anybody else, at least not here. It gave him a certain credential note. "Why, that's mighty Amoran of him' the locals might exclaim upon hearing of a certain magnanimity proffered by Dyfed that had floated up within earshot of these ever ears-to-the-ground posturers.

These high end, swanky digs where Dyfed now called his part-time home, sprawled along the south crest of the Palatine Hill. Through the picture windows, on one side of the apartments within the palace, the view faced southwest toward the river Tibur, and on the other it looked over the northeastern terrace down towards the Forum. One of the imperial palaces and a few of the homes of the Amoran thoroughbreds who were the crème de la crème of the alpha males among the Amoran entitled (aristocrats and other dons of lesser families than the current royal blood) hemmed him in all around at this location. Though much 'too close for comfort' to the ratio-active one per cent (the extreme haves) for Dyfed's liking, but it was a modified coup d'état in political/financial terms which were always subject to the financial outcome anyway and therefore closer to Dyfed's heart. Such a cliché and condition of being too close for comfort (we suspect) was quite uncommon for any other Amoran man or woman around. But this push and squeeze to cramp one's style was old hat to Cato's natural alacrity, and that ever nerve wrenching proximity (if not the familiarity) didn't phase him in the least, nor offend him either. But that was Cato's personality. Folks, including the republic's consuls of late and the last few emperors (and a troublesome lot they were), had tendency to leave Cato to his own devices and not involve him in their intrigues. And the one time they had maligned and bore false witness against him back in the day during the reign of Gaius Octavius when this era began, Gregorios Agricola had come to Cato's defence and decimated the antagonists with a very selective pathogen he cultured into a raging plague of virus (or some such infection of bacteria) that struck down and killed the plotters at once. Curiously, it had been Cato's divining predication that after Claudius, the next emperor would be Nero.

The costs for purchase and upkeep of Dyfed's padded palace on the hill, along with the daily social responsibilities toward the 'hood' in general which went with it, were only to be measured in crates of gold. Fortunately, procuring gold wasn't a problem for Dyfed while Morgant was at hand. Not only that, Dyfed was now becoming financially successful in his own right.

This palatial abode that Dyfed had purchased had formerly been the family home of Lucius Cornelius-*Felix* (as opposed to his brother *unFelix* or unlucky, the legate of the XX Legion), who was a former dictator of Amor. Wedged in between consuls during the republic this man was the famous (some say infamous) older brother of Flavius Cornelius or Flav the Finger, whose path Dyfed had crossed at the City of Legion many solar cycles before. In time, with the former tyrant retiring into a recluse of drunken perversion who wanted nothing more to do with responsibility and public life, this palatial mansion had in turn been passed down to his brother Flavius Cornelius.

But what with Flav the finger's setback after his shoddy and even treacherous behaviour in Albion, and the unwillingness of the new emperor Nero Claudius Kysar Augustus Germanicus to promote him in any capacity now within the Empire, Flav Cornelius had languished unemployed and under flattered there in that very mansion and most miserably so. Meanwhile, his branch of the House of Cornelius haemorrhaged gold bars by the day. And the dictator (big brother Cornelius-Felix) who (as already stated) was now retired from imperial service and living somewhere away from the city of Amor wasn't one to be burdened by sentiment and apt to jump in and provide his brother with help, neither that nor any other random act of kindness, for that matter.

Cato had had a long, close, and cordial relationship with the House of Cornelius since way back when. He had confided in Dyfed by telling him how Flavius had told him (Cato) of his dire straits at being recalled to Amor by an emperor who was now a dead pigeon (presumably of the passenger carrier species), so with Morgant's urging, Cato then re-approached Flav the Finger to act as an agent offering to relieve him of this unnecessary expense by having a rich young friend purchase his real-estate upon the hill. The upshot was that the owner's deed for the old Cornelius place was put under the name of the House of Lucifer. But since Dyfed had no overriding desire to live there full-time, he magnanimously offered to allow the Cornelius family to continue to reside there and occupy at least most of the apartments. There was an understanding, however, that there would be (at times) certain events when Dyfed, accompanied by Morgant as his butler and perhaps one or two other members from the Esquitine Hill Palace Estate residence would need the main palatial rooms to entertain important folks. During these occasions Morgant — now impeccably, although simply and unostentatiously dressed for the occasion — acted as his private concierge. Also in public, as in private, the curiously gnome-like butler performed the duties of a chief expeditor and appeared to live in the Palatine Hill residence with Dyfed and acted as his chief servant. As the mansion was vast and spacious, Dyfed also took to visiting there a few days each week in order to be seen coming and going. And then there was the matter of Camelia Lisabet, one of Flav's beautiful teenage daughters who had taken a liking to Dyfed. They could be seen often walking the hill together and Dyfed often assisted her with her studies or helped to shoo away her bothersome older brother.

Between relaxation and fellowship at any one of the trendy, up-beat thermae spas which the aristocratic members of society (along with crème de la crème of the business class) frequented, as mentioned, Dyfed organized business meetings with potential customers and associates and invited them back to the hood on the hill in an effort to suppress any doubts or misgivings they might have about him. Being in the imperial neighbourhood boded well for most things in this topsy-turvy world where position and wealth accounted for much, and certainly a lot more than the strength of one's character with qualities of honesty and propriety and filial piety. However, Dyfed was careful never to forward a change of address to his official employer, the House of Catulus.

As earlier mentioned, the palatial mansions that were clustered around about Dyfed housed some very highly strung, highly entitled psychopathic city-folk who worried immensely about their riches and their station in life. And at this present time of electrified transition when Nero Augustus wielded the power of the crown, it worried entitled capitalists to no end. But Dyfed wasn't one of them. Indeed, he took Nero to be an intuitive man, gentle and pensive, which was not the normal character of an emperor, at least not one that survived the first week of his emperorship.

These neighbours also took excessive steps to guard against all their worst fears. This fear they had was to loose everything they believed they were entitled to or even to lose just one little thing. It didn't matter how trivial, the wrenching fact was they had lost it. Poisonings and brutal clubbing were now on the rise again for the first time in a long time. 'Enemies abounded' were the buzzwords that catered to the hue and cry-crowd. Very good at confronting competitors of every shape and form, these neighbours who lived above and around Dyfed were antagonists extraordinaire of the first order. And each and every one of these dangerous creatures around him were a worry to him. And each of their postured relationships with Dyfed were characteristically different from each of the others according to the vibration and Idea which each in turn had of the picture in their mind's eye of their own invention of just exactly who they were. This created an invisible shit storm environment that hung over the hoods like a black pall. It was a veritable artillery barrage twenty-four seven where invisible barbed missiles thickened the air all around and where the social atmosphere was so strained and complicated that if it were to become unexpectedly rent or ruptured in any way as to appear to leave one of the antagonists vulnerable, a calamity (laced with false witnessing followed by blood shed or poison) could quickly unfold upon everyone with an unbelievable viciousness at a speed to take one's breath away. As least on a high note, Dyfed knew where he stood with the boys. Although Dyfed might have been left with the high note, Emperor Nero had the high ground, though he chose not to live here but over at Quirinal Hill in the 'valleys' district, instead.

But the Esquiline Hill Palace Estate town-villa-residence still provided Dyfed with more comfortable living. Besides being spacious it also had a large courtyard, a few warehouses and other outdoor storage enclosures and corrals. The entire area of just over an acre and a half was completely private and securely walled in. Two Nightwatchmen-dressed-alike guards (who were confidants of the family of Masters) that lived on the premise, along with a few work-a-day attendants who were employed at different jobs, all helped out to keep the estate safe. There were metal forge facilities on hand, a carpentry shop and an alchemist laboratory that Gregorios (often spelled Gregorius) Agricola utilized for it was better stocked than his own over at Alban Longa. This, after all, was Amor, not some lazy forgotten back eddy. Though, Alban Longa was no slouch either when it came to capitals, the Esquiline Hill Palace Estate town-villa-residence where Dyfed lived, miraculously retained some rural bucolic atmosphere. As far as Alban Longa was concerned, she had once been the capital of all the early local tribes hereabouts, but that was a long time ago, and as we know, the nature of phenomena is to continually change.

There were even a few rental properties among the Esquitine Hill Palace Estate town-villa-residence that were being used as hardware and construction shops, mostly for providing and refurbishing chariots, four wheeled wagons and for the manufacturing of leather goods such as horse trappings. These shops fronted onto an artery road that came directly into Amor from the east and passed directly by the estate where the road angled in the direction toward a thriving forum nearby. And this set of fora contained many goodly markets.

The rentals contained in the estate, along with their narrow enclosed alley-ways, and their large common courtyard (to which each had access) that lay between them, were sealed off from the larger portion of the compound which contained the House of Lucifer's business office, an old well (in addition to newer plumbing that brought water from a local spill off from a eastern viaduct), a bakery, warehouses and a multitude of apartments alongside Morgant's private area surrounding a gated courtyard. Morgant's apartments, and the House of Lucifer's office and its adjoining private apartments for Dyfed and Marg (when she bothered to stop by) were on the upper portion of the property that scaled a rocky hillock that was on the lower reaches of Esquitine Hill. It could have easily been a hilltop bastion. Guarding the extremity of the buildings was a solid wall (which in many cases incorporated the buildings themselves). And although the upper apartments (which Morgant, Dyfed, and others used) could look down onto the courtyard, the whole area was screened from outside viewing, including most of the rentals except their roofs. It was a mass of grey stone and red brick, but the apartments inside the master's main living area were sumptuous and lavishly appointed as earlier mentioned.

As stated, the Palatine Hill residence was a front so when not entertaining or making an appearance there for personal reasons, Dyfed would mostly be at his more comfortable digs at the Esquiline Hill. It was also near the aforementioned centre of the commercial district of Amoran life. Otherwise (by this time), he was either forging forward and upward for the House of Lucifer or at work at the Catulus bank in the forum or wherever Dyfed needed to be. He had by this time long since released Trachmyr from his servitude as batman (servant). At first Dyfed was concerned, for Trachmyr was very valuable to him. But the man from Gwyneth had received orders now to re-join his regiment among the Twentieth Legion Valeria Victrix that at that time were still in Gaul. This was something that Trachmyr had wanted, however. So re-join he did.

At the same time, what with the reign of Nero now having settled into his niche and found its comfort levels, an increase of investments were now being made not only by the wealthy but by the very ambitious who more occasionally were plebs. These were hoi polloi who were quickly attracted to the tinsel provided by certain opportunistic varieties of (so-called) free enterprise. Free was the pivotal word, but free from whom was the question. These particular folks had done well to achieve success in this field where (in this case) success was based on the accumulation of wealth and nothing more. That they may have given anything, or nothing, back to their community (apart from employing a thousand or more workers at slave wages, or provided free room and board (with a minimum amount of free specifically defined adult amusement) in lieu of pay, was neither here nor there, other than to the worker's families, that is. Also, they were folks to which the natural legerdemain and its accompanying cohort, obfuscation (that were almost its universal rules) of the aggressive extravert alpha male type, were second nature to them. Their turnout form and brand of capitalism favoured them well. This was something the system allowed for, despite the upper crust attitude that there were only dons and plebs who walked the face of the earth. This, of course, allowed no flexible buffer cushion in-between for ideas and growth, nor any spacious grey collage in-between these folks' starkly limited reality that generally consisted of saturated black stuck smack-dab against scant white. And since nobody in truth wanted this either, capitalism got its way despite the fact the Amoran society never came to grips with (or ever actually understood) the benefit of the middle class that helped to lessen and to cushion the pot holes and the broken axles in the Empire's journey from rags to riches, or more importantly, the journey back. That journey was always trod in anguish. Under these circumstances, inflation flared up constantly at any given moment. And that route is renowned primarily for its heavy jar, the one caused by the sudden stop at the bottom of the fast fall from riches to rags. This co-called free-fall is known in the trade as the quick-change artist trick. It can also provide a quick change of wealth ownership. Under any circumstances, exponentially regulated inflation can flare up constantly and at any given moment, but these were just gentle trembles compared to the big one.

But certain ambition beyond just wanting to be envied for ones riches which stirred here and there and rose above the heads of the crowd, this individuality of unconformity which, believe it or not, is innate to human character in general, was the crack in the armour of Amor's signature Idea. Dyfed now saw this. Strike now, he thought while this iron was hot. A move of correction to set the Empire on a more benevolent path was needed now when it mattered more than anything. Dyfed was also coming to the conclusion that the Empire's law and order, including the its punitive leanings, cult temperance, and its financial structure which revolved around the marketplace, were the lightning rods to provide the elixir needed to pull the track switches in order to shunt the train of state to another track and nudge it in a slightly different direction. Too big a change, he knew, would be disastrous. Dyfed was planning to specialize and bring some heavy weights in with him.

The aforementioned condition of Amor's Idea, in light of progressive human character, effected the Empire's karma (here at this time) much in the same way that sappers who with unobtrusive and incessant excavating and burrowing will dig down the wall and gate that surrounds and guards the ivory tower of their own safety. It's a double-edged blade, of course, for if business and finance fail it becomes very difficult for the general populace all 'round' to survive, never mine thrive. Always it the plebs who are rung out, dried, and starved to death first before the wolf draws anywhere near the door of the dons. That's a given. But to overwhelm ingenuity and let the dons (aristocrats) profit to some extent because of it, especially those businesses that are the lifeline of the city of Amor, not forgetting the City of Amor's infrastructure itself, was good business. This included the businesses along the docks beside the Tibur River and also at its seaport of Ostia twenty or so Amoran miles away. The developed industry along the river's edge that was closest to the city markets was the first real money arena Dyfed descended into. It was here along the embankment in those precious idle moments that Dyfed watched the barges bringing staples and other goods from all over the empire up from the capitol's main seaport at tidewater and into the city. It was near here that he had disembarked that first day. It was especially important that this area is functioning. But barges were almost always excluded from hauling goods here during the wet and stormy months of the year. This was around the time just before the winter solstice and right into the first month of the New Year when March flooding occurred to the time of the vernal equinox. This coincided with the beating of the skin clad Mamurius Veturius. Known as Mars Silvanus[24], this poor Scapegoat was beaten by rods by the earlier (than today) folks of the city as they drove him out of town to make room for the new incoming god. The flooding was due, of course, to the swelling of the Tibur as snow melt and thousands of rain run-offs were channelled past the water viaducts and into the blood stream of the god Tibur, causing dangerous currents as it's water flow churned white and choppy and caused the level to rise and rush with increased velocity. Soon its level rose until it widened and flattened out over the soggy embankment flooding the Field of Mars.

One day Dyfed approached a don and his crew of pleb employees who were in charge of the division of Pubic Works responsible for the city's embankment. Accompanied by Cato, who the don recognized as an astute and once revered senator, and the gnomish but studious looking Morgant as his assistant and secretary, the don listened intently as Dyfed explained that in shoring up the embankment and installing winch machines on

---

24 This old Mars (replaced each year) was a god of vegetation (not war), and as Mars Silvanus he was the god of the wooded land.

the river container barges that were (after all) the lifeline of the city, could assist these heavy and awkward vessels to be managed more safely and easily in swollen current conditions than the currently used teams of horses could. During the Spring before, as it happened, more than just a few teams of these animals, while hard at work and driven even harder, had thrashed helplessly around on the soggy ground that lined the river in their attempt to pull the barges up for mooring. But then the floundering and too-heavily loaded barges had been dragged by back down stream pulling the horse teams that were braying loudly and frothing at the mouth with fear and fury into the turbulent river to die without anyone being able to do anything to stop it from happening.

Furthermore, the handful of teamsters who owned the horses that had perished had sued for damages. Most of them had lost their case which caused hard-feelings and job loses, increased drunkenness and wife-beating, accompanied by costly arrests and imprisonments; all of which caused, as well, an even more expensive glitch in the life-line of the city at the centre of the empire that no more needs a glitch of any kind whatsoever if it can help it, anymore than it needs a raging and contagious outbreak of fire. In fact, the first lawsuit that had been lost cost many folks their livelihood. But by luck, and with Cato's help of introduction, Dyfed (now a succeeding advocate) had been successful in a second bid to represent a half a dozen other teamsters out of pocket (and out of horses) in his capacity of jurisconsult and public responder. He amalgamated their lawsuits together in a class action suit against the city's council that exposed a Public Works that was bankrupt in efficiency and impoverished in ideas towards modernization. Dyfed had championed and won their case for them. He now told the Magister of Public Works that it was remiss of them, indeed, incompetent to the point of malpractice of duty, not to remedy this situation as proficiently and as fast as could be. Furthermore, he told him that he was the man who could help do it. And that would make the Magister of Public Works, look good. And it wasn't just a matter of the city losing business, either. What with vital supplies being delayed because of their mismanagement a lot was at stake here, he said. Not only did people lose business, prices skyrocketed (good for wealthy businessmen), pricing out the majority of folks who (where as staples were concerned) quickly starved. It would appear, Dyfed gently told the alarmed Magister of Public Works, that there were opportunities for people like himself who not only as a jurisconsult and public responder who could act as an advocate to redress wrongs brought on by incompetence, but also as an engineer to rectify the situation by designing anew.

Shortly after that, he presented a design for a system of winching heavily leaden barges through the turbulent currents of the Tibur during rain run-off-seasons, along with a prototype he had King Karatakos fabricate in their Esquitine Hill Palace Estate town-villa-residence workshop's forge. This was where Karatokos could be found most often anyway (along with the resident carpenter) when if they weren't commiserating on rare and arcane arts and crafts (or whatever) and drinking flasks of expensive wine or smoking hashish[25]. Dyfed then set to and organized a public demonstration to be held which was to winch two heavily laden barges up the growing rapids at the same time, one towing the other. Now it was the morning of November the 17th and the rains were upon them again. It just so happened that general Vaspasianus had been summoned by

---

25   Medicinal hashish arrived along the silken road from Persia and Inja and into the homes of both the wealthy and the poor.

Nero to attend the palace on that chosen day for commiseration regarding the security of the empire. This was the first Dyfed had heard anything about Vespasianus since his arrival. Anyway, it just so happened that the day was Vespasianus' birthday as well, so in an ad hoc fashion, and what with the public interest (all of whom would be out in droves despite the inclement weather) it was an opportune moment for Nero, along with General Vaspasianus the hopeful, to wave at the crowds and be seen by them to take an interest in modern mechanisms that also aided/abetted and paid off the hoi polloi for a change. At the same time the happy crowds could flatter Nero and him, so long as everything went according to plan. Dyfed had already come to Nero's attention, as well as having been advised of his competency, and had been assured that it would come off successfully. So, what with the emperor, his wife, and their entourage of maids and yes-men who all came out to observe the event, it turned a dreary November day into a bright and happy gala. It was a great success, naturally, and so was Dyfed. Shortly after that, the senate quietly approved (and he received) his appointment to act as a mensari. At last the House of Lucifer was free to make money by creating debt, preferably to rich Amorans. At least that is how Dyfed saw it. That was something he could take to the bank, his bank. And it had been because of Nero that Dyfed got this licence.

(A day in the life)

'Know myself? If I knew myself, I'd run away.'
VON GOETHE

To Dyfed (a businessman of the busy streets here in the capital of the empire; though still longing to become once again the prince of the grove) all around him the men and women of the city were attired in their usual costumes of dress according to their station in life. In the hundreds and thousands they were like a current of swirling eddies rushing swiftly away and towards each other while on the move. Usually their journeys were short lived. They walked, rode and carriage purposefully here and there and everywhere around the city…to the markets, the local temples, the schools, the banks, to music lessons, to the government run toilets and latrines, to the Colossal, the Hippodrome, and the barber shops, and always the baths. Often each enterprise or cultural expression had marked out a distinct district for itself.

There was many a back eddy, a virtual pool-cum-cess-pond of culture (no pun intended) that lingered in these narrow streets. Many of these streets were cordoned off to wheeled traffic. And in these, with the rumbling of wheels sounding far off and away, men visited and squabbled, vendored and purchased, while lovers met and touched, and tenements were crowded with people and cooking pots a-cooking, all hovering over and around them — steaming, laughing, drinking fighting, over-flowing. For hundreds of years, and hundreds of years hence, nothing much changed or would change here. Here, aside from commerce, war, and athletics, some men plotted to change the world, only to failure find long before their hair grew grey, which it surely did unless they died young which many did. Here in Amor new ideologies were springing forth with ease, their seeds — their meagre and puny spunk — cooling not in the warm womb of practicality but on the cold pavement stones trodden by the sandaled feet of a million or more.

This hubbub of life all swirled around and beneath the ancient local's mythical Mound of Creation (Capitolus Hill) and designated burgh (fort) against which had first been built the Temple to Saturn at its feet, but upon which now (at it summit) sat Juno by Jove at whose own feet (only a hop-skip and a jump away) were the embankments of this mighty river Tibur that fertilized and keep his people alive. And it was here (still been watched over by Jove and his consort Juno from the top of the Capitoline Hill as already stated) was where the tents and the first lean-tos and wharves had come together long ago. And nothing much had changed here on the river's bank. This same place was now still strewn with commerce and industry. The city relied on it. Wharves, warehouses, and workmen; masts and rigging fulminating against the wind and with the river's current abounded here on both sides of the Tibur's banks. The river himself, the god Tibur, sometimes brought these floods to the city but conscientiously compensated for its disasters. It provided water in abundance and was a highway eager to truck food from the far reaches of the Empire to every table in Amor. This embankment was a landmark that wound through the city of Amor as if it was the fertilizing power over the people, that in a way it was. It was as though the god Tibur's semen flowed here into Amor, the womb of the empire. Here (in precious idle moments) Dyfed would watch the barges bringing staples and goods from all over this empire and up from the capital's main seaport into the city. He took it all in. He took in the established houses that (engaging together in business co-operation) were (thus authorized as a single entity) and were considered 'incorporated'; soon to one day have a soul for themselves and certainly the right of a human being. Generally they were founded and operated by aristocratic owners of the richest of houses who owned and had controlling shares in banks. And on any given sundown just as the river traffic began to thin out, the dark yellow dusk (like gossamers of golden smoke spreading like sepia through the cooling air on a autumn's evening) cast a dank blanket over the brightness of day. Then as the chilled air would stir around the water's edge and mix the smells of staple and spice — adrift — to waft up into the lazy breeze, a string of widely spaced, empty hay-boats could be seen — the last traffic of the day — following the sunset, downstream, gently, and picking up speed as they went, wending, and then suddenly being swallowed up in the gloaming of the evening.

Aside from staples the river brought immigrants, as did every road, track and thoroughfare that led to Amor — for all roads, everywhere, led here. And with the immigrants came innovation and freshness, and foreign mythos that were often eagerly embraced. But it also brought virus and disease, both of the body and mind, along with foreign manners and foreign ways (not all of which were welcomed), and crime. And there had been no check point Augustus, Cornelius or Hadrianus erected in time to obstruct or slow down their flow into the city. And when control came, it was after the fact not very affective with respect to it initial idea but subsequently very affective general persecution of the settled home-bodies. And in the sky above the city where now once the blackened rooks and golden eagles that had once flown with abandon in abundance, Dyfed now noted there were very few eagles that remained among the city's smoggy hills. Less often now one could glimpse birds of prey like the griffon vulture searching above the haze over the hills of the city for carrion below. The pigeons conglomerated where corn and board were provided them. Spillage of any kind, though able to get a man fired from his job and a slave badly beaten her in a world where being well beaten was worse than a bad beating, were evident around the docks. Garbage, too, was evident throughout the city beyond the window-sills of kitchens and outside the back doors of restaurants that provided three squares for the proverbial ever straying cat and packs of affable dogs and the hordes of rats and the lords of Amor that were fattening up at home.

So the first thing he did now with his new found celebrity was establish the House of Lucifer Banking Company to finance and fund his well-being (the principal House of Lucifer in person). As the patriarch and chief oligarch of the House of Lucifer, Dyfed retained the position of chief overseer of its general account. But along with this he obviously remained the lord and holder of the House of Lucifer Bank's title of chief ledger, or (as Morgant funningly called it) the Temple of Lucifer. This arrangement endured with Morgant as his second. But although Morgant was his beneficiary and visa versa in regards to the Lucifer Bank, it was Morgant who remained his chief benefactor in so many other ways.

Quickly, the House of Lucifer began loaning capital to industrious men who were attracted to do business with industrious men like Dyfed himself. Before long, Dyfed found himself in business with shipbuilders, harbour dredgers, and merchants who in the end made up much of the House of Lucifer's fixed assets while also becoming something of a mercantile agency of its own well before its time.

Meanwhile, the House of Catulus couldn't understand why so many clients of theirs — who, they noticed were constantly schmoozing Dyfed…inviting him and sometimes that beautiful woman he was on occasion seen with, out to galas, the circus, and sports events at the hippodrome…(half the time just to be seen with him) — were not following it up with huge loans being drawn on the Catulus' bank. Just whom were these trendy aristocrats dealing with then anyway? Catulus didn't understand until word finally got loose and came within earshot of the Catulus family. The word was that the House of Lucifer was to have mensari status, no less. It was the moment that the Catulus Banking firm fired Dyfed Lucifer. But Catulus initiated a civil law suit of misrepresentation against Dyfed that quickly followed. It was unsuccessful, but none of that mattered now for he was rolling in lolly; and lolly is king and power.

In the more down at the heel sectors of town where the majority of folks lived, Dyfed began shoring up respect and trust in view of the *pack's* big push to gently replace major components of the Amoran Idea and to refurbish it into a new Amoran Idea to be based on liberty, equality and a general, all round sense of propriety. It was to be a self-mending system built on sustainability whose purpose was for the benefit of all. And it was the multitude of folks that was needed to sway the balance for this new Idea and those who understood the big picture were needed. These were folks who wanted common abundance and common grandeur over the individual kind: and neither one over the other. These were folks whose good works and their dedication to the spirit of humanity in whatever form of proficiency they could provide would prevail. These were folks, who didn't want the machine of *the temple* from displacing their right and their place in improving society, or in dominating and influencing the Idea (the overriding dominance of their culture) on its own. And these types were not scarce or even in the minority over all. In fact, these folks (at all times) dominated even the tiny percentile of aristocrats and dons who owned and controlled history and its societies never mind the majority of remaining per cent. People had power, they just didn't have the comprehension of what that meant and what they could do against the Haploids that were bent on enslaving them. But the desires of the former being naturally sated by an indigenous wisdom made them pliable toward this end in the end. Furthermore, the city of Amor was filled with them. Here then was the *pact's* medium to aright the course. But Dyfed knew that aside from moral pull they also needed to have influence over the temple finance, the supreme ledger, in order for them to sway Amor and eventually over the Empire's entire public opinion.

Along with some of the company he kept, this single concession by the emperor to allow him a banking commission gave reason for certain folks to perceive that Dyfed was on the same footing as the aristocracy as a whole. What the general host who were paying attention still didn't realize was that Dyfed's social life with the rich and infamous…the aristocratic and the famous…was superficial at best, but in a different way than they the former were between themselves. As richly smooth and smartly powerful that they were, this crowd that tried with all their hearts in their flush but prevaricating way to penetrate Prince Dyfed Lucifer, met with virtually no success. Dyfed's hated of suffocation and the notion of belonging to a set of normality, rules or a specific grouping, protected him. In fact he often said (sometimes even out loud around outsiders) that he was…'an outside the box as possible free thinker; and one whose intention, as such, is to remain free of the trampling and the roar of the herd.'

So, with such as opinion of oneself as that, any investment of pandering (and so forth) toward him from the side of the aristocracy and their cohorts was bound to (and did) fail and fall on barren soil. Yet, he saw to it that it did so with accumulated advantages to him. The score after the first few decades was… Dyfed, the lion — fifty… Amorans, the pathetic believers in primitive pagan superstition — zero, at least according to his tally. Others saw it differently. Indeed, articles about Prince Dyfed the gorgeous, Dyfed the likeable and the unlikely barbarian, who really wasn't a barbarian at all and spoke Amoran without a hint of an accent and fulfilled a civilized existence; seen everywhere and surrounded by interesting young-turk-type dons of the aristocracy and with beautiful aristocratic women on each arm, were soon to be seen posted to heralding billboards that decorated the walls of buildings and even pillars and columns topped with Doric capitals throughout the city. The billboards in this case, of course, were walking, talking heralds with loud and commanding voices, for few among the hoi polloi could read or write during these times, apart from the educated one per cent. So these heralds would frequent the markets and the concession stands around the hippodrome, or stand hawking their news beneath the Doric capped columns of this or that building of administration or commerce, or in front (or approximate to) one cult centre-temple or another during the days of the week to speak the news whatever it was. And that news now included Dyfed Lucifer. But whatever else it was, it also included juicy gossip to help draw the crowds, and the herald's loud, carnival-type verbal launch was always additionally slaked with commercial advertising to help with their commission. In this way the ignorant multitude could kind of keep abreast of what was going on among the rich and famous, or what the emperor expected of and from them as well as news from elsewhere in the Empire. But it was a ways and means for the hoi polloi to feel apart of the bigger picture too, and it informed them of this gala or that, such as Dyfed's winching demo, for example. It also helped vendors advertise as to where the hoi polloi should spend their denarii.

(The Merchant of Amor)

'Come, wake; wake you too; wake each other; come, wake all!
Shake off your sleep, stand up. What could that warning mean?'
AESCHYLUS (THE EUMENIDES)

So, aside from his own flourishing business of funding fleet merchants and the buyers of everything labelled with a price from each and every curve and corner of the Empire, the House of Catulus had proved useful in providing many a prospective contact (generally of the foreign persuasion) for Dyfed. These were often merchants who came from all over the Empire selling everything from grain to goo-gaws, with a gnawing and heavy want to connect with rich markets in Amor or around the Empire. Two obvious types of folks (Dyfed noticed) were arriving in Amor these days. It didn't matter if the mob just off the boat consisted of refugees fleeing chaos at home, dead-beat n'er-do-wells, loners and alcoholics just wandering around aimlessly or on the run from creditors in another kingdom, side-tracked and lost remittance folk who were often easily pleased at every turn, young men looking to expand their education, or those sharp witted business types and con-artists on the make and take, where one type was thankful for what they had and the other type were ungrateful for what they didn't have. And it didn't matter how coin golden and credit gratified the latter type had been upon their arrival, these smarmy, slippery and often younger men were out for all they were worth in order to gain an awful lot more at any cost (no matter how high) to some poor unsuspecting group of fools who could be easily (or with difficulty) parted with their money. Dyfed found friends among the former category and had a hearty dislike for the latter. However, the latter were interested in borrowing money while the former invited him into their kitchens to break bread and meet their family and coddle and kiss the children.

Meanwhile, the greedy dons of capitalism continued to invite Dyfed into their lusciously crisp salons to mix with a rich company of predators, all of whom had their eye on the market and were looking for an opportunity to get in under detection and on top of the deal of a lifetime. And the first (of many) that Dyfed met was to throw an entirely new slant on his life. But we are again getting ahead of ourselves.

In the more down at the heel sectors of town where the majority of folks lived, Dyfed began shoring up respect and trust in view of the *pack's* big push to gently replace major components of the Amoran Idea to refurbish it into a new Amoran Idea to be based on liberty, equality and a general, all round sense of propriety. It was to be a self-mending system built on sustainability whose purpose was for the benefit of all. And the multitude of folks needed to sway the balance for this new Idea were those who understood and big picture; folks who wanted common abundance and common grandeur over the individual kind: folks, and only folks, neither one over the other — other than in their good works and their dedication to the spirit of humanity in whatever form of proficiency they could provide. Folks who didn't want the machine of *the temple* from displacing their right and their place in improving society, or in dominating and influencing the Idea (the overriding dominance of their culture) on its own, were not scarce or even in the minority over all. In fact, these folks (at all times) dominated the tiny percentile of aristocrats and dons who owned and controlled history and its societies. And the desires of the former being naturally sated by an indigenous wisdom made them pliable toward this end.

But it was on the threshing floor of the industriously rich, that Dyfed was able to quickly find another avenue to mass riches galore in his effort to funnel them to where it would do the most good for the cause. This was the old standby, the goldbricked avenue of IOUs. Dyfed turned to investing in people he discovered wanting to build and provide anything from new docks on the river, more anchorages on the seaside harbour port, to a fleet of sailing vessels, all of which were more and more needed to transport live cattle, corn, grain and oil, and other necessities that Amor desperately needed. Some of these merchant vessels were capable of five hundred tons.

Other ventures included the forest cutting industry to provide the wood needed for shipbuilding, building factories for making oakum, or tarred wool used for caulking, as well as other factories for sail making and sundry fabrics including the garment industry. He also lent seed money to merchants who were willing to drum up business by going abroad to buy up precious goods and wares to sell at market in Amor. Like all intelligent financiers, Dyfed funded business investments that were mainly employed in accessing and providing the necessities which Amor needed available every single day. Dyfed reckoned that if the import of essential goods were somehow, for whatever reason, interrupted, the city's stockpile of sustainable staples had a shelf life of about four days before there were only bare shelves left and nothing coming in with which to replenish them. At that point folks would start to die and chaos would erupt. Dyfed also funded mortgages.

On top of Dyfed's specialized business in profits via investments through loans, mortgages and industrial and military insurances, he employed other measures such as the lucrative IOU' trade. There were also special currencies or imperial warrants available (if one knew where to look and who to ask) to which — though issued judiciously, and often secretly, by the emperor or his treasurer to powerful associates and dangerous opponents alike — only the very privileged had access. These imperial warrants were a sure bet and even if in tough times the emperor were to dishonour them, the next emperor — predictably close on his heels — along with other privileged families on the climb, would. In one aspect, life in Amor was a lottery. Dyfed could sense that the richer and more knowledgeable you were immersed in the rules of the game that encompassed its perversity, and the more one's mindful attention strayed away from the everyday process of breathing, drinking the morning beverage, or folding one's clothes in preparation for sleep, or in quietening the mind for prayer, or meditation, the greater were the odds of coming out less scathed financially but cheapened or de-spirited and exiled into an indescribable loneliness and estrangement from one's own self in an equally perverse and unexplainable way. It was, if you like, the accounts department of the universe balancing the budget: The budget here being the shit that happens (noun). And shit happens (verb — perfect participle) always at the interaction of the Being with that fundamental apparition of all apparitions — the Phenomena. Outside of this, there exists absolutely nothing. Life encapsulated in perception and idea is the interface between the observant being and the phenomenon at large. It is the life as it is known here in the third dimension. But, of course it is. Who doesn't know that? It's a page-turner for one who can't read.

Dyfed assumed that as it was with every empire, so it was with every life, and that this disturbing trend of greed established itself under the illusionary precepts of individual entitlement whose affects were mental dysfunction, disorder, and chaos at both the civilizational and the personal level. Although there is currently no proper algorithm to flesh this out there is certainly a correlation. And judging how the Empire at present was panning out, it was the over-lying culture of pagan creator/destroyer gods and such which — more or less being the world theme here in the third dimension — that necessitated the status quo and contributed and aggravated humanity's ethereal disorder by influencing the hoi polloi's neglect ion to abide by certain laws of their realized universe. It is not the universe that is to blame for humanity's inability to rise to the level needed for being able to have a competent and comprehensive interface within it, however. It certainly hadn't been this way in his Lodge, his resort on the Isle of Peace which functioned under the Masters: there, they employed the essential practise of maintaining in sync with both the natural ethereal/mind/spirit laws of the cosmos along with the natural non-ethereal or substantial slash objective laws of the Universe.

As such, and with the understanding that was factored into his reasoning, Dyfed soon discovered that the trading values of the aforementioned imperial warrants could easily become enormous when cast against natural market cycles with the applied dash of human greed. Their trading values were often in access of the market value of a gold Libra. There were also promissory notes and special no name warrants whose holders were bonded to a percentage (according to their made out value) of specified riches that the emperor held and owned on behalf of the Empire. They were tiny, microscopic pieces of the Empire and its Temple of treasure, but they were extremely valuable.

A lot of the financial stability enjoyed at this time was due to Nero, Dyfed admitted to himself. Nero encouraged trade and business. As stated earlier, Nero fancied himself as being gifted. He implied that he was an artist and certainly his interest in playing music on the lyre and in writing poems, instead of historically undertaking what his imperial predecessor did, showed him to be imaginative, perhaps even intuitive. And like anything else, interests are not solely dependent upon an individual and his or her interaction with the phenomenon, but also upon the character and energy level of the culture and time in which an individual resides. Generally, so it is thought, when it comes to personality types the human race is neatly divided in half with little or no over-lapping. As this theory goes, one side is made up of artists and dreamers while the other side consist of scientists and engineers. But the lion's-share of people in either trait fails miserably within their category and diminishes into nothing. So, those who succeed among the first set are folks overly concerned with the enhancement of aesthetics and in providing ambiance and decorum. These are the intuitive types who are considered romantics. The other half who succeed are mechanics and are often, and erroneously, regarded as being dry and un-romantic.

This model, of course, is highly inaccurate. The two do over-lap and produce philosophers and ideologists with a bent toward either the artistic or the mechanic, and often toward both sets. A successful person is a little of both, anyway. A very successful person is quite good at being both, and so on. Real and genuine geniuses are extremely good and highly skilled at aestheticism on one hand and romanticism on the other in single or various categories. Whether or not Nero was simply nothing of an artist or of a scientist, he certainly ran the empire as good a captain as any who runs a successful ship. Nero was good for business but unfortunately his high strung nature caused him to be too critical about himself, both towards his art and also with his lack of confidence that prevented him from wrestling with mechanics in an effort to open the blinds and let in some deserved, and well needed light. Continued, this unimproved inability sorely affected him as it does millions upon millions of folks the world over.

But Nero unfortunately was no Kleisthenes. In addition, he was a high energy (with little result) man with one or two major exceptions. He was an obsessive compulsive who mimicked being a schizoid during one half of any given day of his average life while during the remainder he kept to himself. To the common observer he was about as riveting as chariot race where the slowest and last cross the line wins. All hail fellow well met one moment and an entitled alpha male grasping for unattainable satisfaction on a tsunami whirlwind of ego the next, Nero spoke to nobody, other than on rare occasions. Nero thought folks were laughing at him. Nobody in their right mind laughed at an Amoran emperor, least of all one who suffered from psychopathy and other personality disorders. The only ones who laughed out loud were mad. Remember over half the Kelts of Gaul who were minding their own business were massacred because Julius Kysar the Psychopath didn't have time to train them as to how he wanted them to behave in or out of his presence and thought that those people were laughing behind his back... 'putting him on'... 'taking the piss'... 'the Mickey Bliss' — the old tease, mock and scoff routine.

I say that Nero was no Kleisthenes, and he certainly didn't enhance democracy. But, to his credit, he did focus on Amoran diplomacy and trade and also tried to leave a building legacy. If only he had been better understood, perhaps his shyness and shortcomings would have fallen away and the brilliant light of ingenuity and success would have shone out brighter then the brilliant flames of his blazing city. Interestingly, the noun *nero* means water in the language of the Hellenes.

In addition to his own empire that he was struggling to place onto sound foundations, Dyfed also invested in that meagre mensarii that had been owned and operated by Egidius of Joslin in Gaul. Once (if you recall) he had single-handedly rescued this business from destruction. In appreciation, Egidius quickly, and wisely, had requested a merger with the House of Lucifer. Dyfed had complied, but, renaming the Armorikan mensarii the House of Joslin (in honour of Egidius), he kept it as a client company of which he owned ninety-nine per cent and was operated by the two of them rather than merged proper. At the time Dyfed had appointed Egidius as his managing director of the House of Joslin in his absence. Though hampered by law to name a company after Amor, he now created a branch of the House of Joslin here in Amor and began to convert and re-model this business into the Union of the People's Commonwealth Bank. It was called the Commonwealth Bank of Gaul, not Albion, as he had always wished. Anyway, this was Dyfed living his dream. For common wealth among the majority of hoi polloi within the civilization, never mind just the Empire, had always been his dream (his Idea) since Nova Troia. And this Idea was in line with the Idea of the ancient Hyperboreans And to this end Dyfed set out to re-invent money sharing and in trying to pull innovations into the system that would facilitate such a commonwealth among the majority of citizens making them well heeled, well housed, and their families secure and safe as could possibly be. This, Dyfed knew, was the road to humanity's salvation. And its only opponents, he knew from observation, were those same clingers-on to the cult of the temple (which provided the laws and standards for the whole system run by the rich) who is protected by the cult of the temple and who had fixed their position with little chance of being ousted. The temple, of course, had been the brainchild of the Haploids. They were the game fixers. These were generally alpha-male folks who wore the same colour jersey with the same badges and medals attached…had the same attitude and level of entitlement and expectation of others to glorify them while the former stumbled about to fall in behind and provide support and make the latter more whole and richer and connubially identifiable with the dominant cult which has the say-so and the what's-for. All the while the out-classed ninety-nine per cent of the hoi polloi were constantly kept poor and in debt by design and continually subject to changing laws and standards that favoured the former power and wealthy elite.

The direction in which Dyfed now moved had specifically to do with creating a central banking system. The system would be empire wide and not just in the eternal city of Amor. He was certain Nero had his back for Nero would benefit as no other, at least the way Dyfed explained it. Dyfed did not want to involve his bank in the general way with queues of citizens lined up outside its doors. Rather it would initially be involved exclusively with imperial loans needed to fund and run the Empire as the emperor and the treasury saw fit. Aside from Dyfed maintaining the status of full owner and chief executive officer and chair of the Imperial Central Bank (as it was to be called), Nero had agreed, promised and swore that once ratified and implemented he would provide the mountain of gold that would be enough for this purpose. Dyfed wanted a signed promise from the emperor, endorsed by the senate, stating that while at the business of empire building itself, the emperor and agents of the Empire would borrow exclusively from him (Prince Dyfed Lucifer: Keeper of the Royal Palace and Chamberlain of the High King of Albion now the Emperor of Amor) and from no other. This borrowing condition not only included loans for expenditures towards Amoran infrastructure, but also (if need be) included large loans to other states and statesmen. The real costs for running the Empire (Dyfed knew) would go however towards expenditures incurred by the imperial armies whose purpose, aside from fighting other armies, putting down unrest and enforcing Amoran law and order (Pax Amor) was to capture and domesticate thousands of foreigners every year that were enslaved. And as the latter were literally building the Empire, the military legions needed to continuously maintain this work in progress along with the emperor's slaves throughout the empire.

But there was one other condition which Dyfed needed from Nero, a condition which so far had held up the emperor's and the senator's signature. That condition was that the emperor must also promise and swear to allow Dyfed to introduce promissory notes in lieu of gold used to pay off the army and agents of the Empire. This was also to be an advantage to the emperor who would not have to provide mounds of gold, he told him. And this was why the delay. It wasn't yet known if the soldiers would accept paper denarii in exchange of silver or gold. After all, they needed to spend their pay in the marketplace of wherever they were, so others needed to accept the idea of promissory notes too. Would this be acceptable to folks around the Empire? This was the sixty-four billion denarii question. Dyfed, of course, would also provide gold and silver for the Imperial mint to coin, and there would be enormous hills made from bars of gold and silver all secreted and stashed away neatly throughout the Empire in vaults (House of Lucifer's safe houses) securely defended by imperial guards to back up the fiat currency if a problem developed. As the imperial financier he had promised Nero that he would provide him with more than enough gold backing for all the promissory notes he printed up for the purpose of funding his armies and agents throughout and beyond the borders of the Empire in case redemptions were needed in some extraordinary cases. But Nero and the Imperial treasury would have to provide the rest. This, he told Nero, would protect them both.

In his attempt to be credible he told the imperial palace that his profit was his return from reasonable interest rates that would be set by his central bank and by nobody else. He didn't breathe a word about inflationary values nor did they ask him. Nor was he asking (he said) or expecting the imperial treasurer to personally pay him interest. But they would have to collect all interest on loaned gold (or rather on the representational promissory notes of that gold) on his behalf every time any of the notes changed hands. And only the imperial palace could enact that service toward the purpose of providing him with a rather more than slight capital gains profit. If anyone handled his promissory notes as receipts for any kind of payment or for any gain, they needed to be taxed. That tax along with certain interests, was the central bank's fee for providing the service and the Palace was to monthly reimburse the central bank's bills receivable account department with gold and silver coined metal (not paper gold) to the total monthly interest value that was owed to the bank.

What service was that, again? That was the question with which Dyfed was always at the ready to tactfully counter. 'Why, the service of providing promissory notes in circulation for vast, daily and continuous loans of gold to the emperor in order to keep the wheels and the lights on and the Empire running, and in having mountains of gold on hand to back all the circulating notes up so the Empire wouldn't have a financial melt-down,' was his standard answer. For this was the service he would be providing. Otherwise, all would fail, he told them. Once implemented, he said, failure was not an option, for remember (he continually reminded them) the health of the imperial economy paralleled the health of the emperor's suite.

And obviously, Dyfed had to retain the sole right to print these said promissory notes at all costs and any and all other copies must be considered forgeries. And forgery was punishable by the strictest of Amoran laws. However, it was all a pipe dream in the end.

At least one element of Dyfed's idea was well received by Nero, though. That was the idea of his design for the promissory notes. Dyfed was a competent artist and put in time and effort to create a mock-up. Only the number of the note's value (either a one, a two, a five, a ten, a twenty, a twenty-five, a fifty or one hundred) would make them different in appearance. And in order to tell these notes apart from other bills of commerce that were floating around the Empire like flakes in a snow storm (even some legal imitations would undoubtedly surface in time, he thought), Dyfed placed an image of Nero Augustus in the centre of his palm sized note directly beside the numerical domination value on one side of his template note. On the reverse side he placed the bold likeness of Jupiter Capitolus holding a thunderbolt in one hand and a serpent in the other. The ratification by the emperor (which never came) was also to include a copyright for the note's design. Anybody copying the note would lose their shirt, their life's savings in their bank and, in every likelihood, their life. That was the truth behind Dura lex sed lex.

He was well aware that the financing he was proposing here through a central banking system would primarily maintain and keep alive the very nasty idea of debt control and the power of the elite over the denizens at large. This, ironically, was the very idea with which Dyfed vehemently disagreed, and even loathed. But it pushed important buttons and it could get the wheels rolling beneath this monolith. Either way he had his benign finger on the pulse even if he was not able to gain sufficient influence for a game change. But he may be in line though to adjust (even fix) the system once it crashed which he knew it would whether the senate went with his proposal or not. Mostly, his initiation of it was that if he got in first nobody could get the jump on him and run in different directions with this idea (sic).

But central banking aside, after the trick that Nero pulled, Dyfed was especially careful with his mortgage loans to clients wishing to buy real estate property and brick and mortar. But this did not prevent Dyfed Lucifer from very tactically presenting his brilliant idea of becoming the sole financier for the crown.

(Nero Claudius Kysar Augustus Germanicus)

Eroticism is dependent not just upon an individual's sexual morality, but also upon the culture and time in which an individual resides.'
HONORÉ DE BALZAC

The alleged, aforementioned trick, which the blue eyed blond haired Nero Claudius Kysar Augustus Germanicus was said to have pulled, was a fantasy. It never happened. But in regards to an imperial central banking and treasury concept, Dyfed had to be careful that the fantasy ploy here wasn't going to be copied by others. The Haploids were the first to come to his mind. Once you rig or fix a common event, even in rumour, you have to come up with new rules to cover and protect your assets. This, Dyfed said, is what the establishment call history. In a sense it's all a crock, of course, but there it is. What it meant was that now the *pack* had to somehow come up with a method to jerry rig the imperial financial infrastructure. Although all this had some bearing on the aforementioned trick that Nero was blamed for, it was only part of the story.

Emperor Nero was the last of the House of Julio-Claudio, and he had been showing signs of strain for some time. A sensitive man, in some ways, with artistic traits, he was imaginative and composed music and wrote poems (all now lost to history). He tried and failed to understand many things in which he took an avid interest, such as technology. Apparently, this strain (called the imperial strain) which may have been caused by a general misinterpretation of who and what he actually was in relation to other members of his species who lived and breathed around him, this was aggravated by those other conditions with which he had struggled from youth; such as the aura of emperorship that he embodied. These conditions caused symptoms that altered his state of being. They were: acute egotism (for a starter) complicated with hatred (especially toward his benefactors such as Claudius, his predecessor, who was responsible for placing him on the throne). And though he was not psychotic, Nero did suffer from dissociation (a detachment from reality) rather than a loss of reality. It was said, too, that he had a strong, unpleasant body odour. Although Dyfed never got closer than within ear shot of the emperor during his life, this personal malady of his would hardly have been remarkable, for Dyfed was offended by the smell of people in general, and had been since coming out into the full fledged third dimensional world.

But Dyfed was never offended by anything Nero did in regards his duty to the empire. More despots were yet to come; pathetic, psychopathic interlopers like Publicus Servicicus Nemesis Maximus Augustus Usurperus the Ist, the IInd, the IIIrd, the IVth, the Vth, the VIth, the VIIth, the VIIIth and the IXth, ect. But Nero wasn't one of them. Anyway, though Nero the prankster was fond of levitating himself up and setting out to pull his same old tricks (excuse the boring cliché) — a custom of his was to try folks' patience — this particular little imperial trick we are concerned with here was to set fire (so it was said) to a large part of the Palatine Hill area that quickly spread. In the end the fire burned up a big chunk of the city of Amor while Nero (again, so it was said) retired to the conservatory to practice his lesson on the lyre, or was the Kithara (later guitar)?[26]

Anyway, this deadly fire spread north and east away from the river across the city. Human life and property loss were horrific. The rumour that the ferocious furnace of fire that raged through the city was initiated by the sadism and irresponsibility of Nero was pure hooey, pork-slap and bull-chutney. In fact, Nero worked diligently and tirelessly to bring the fire under control, even getting himself into the fray and shouting out demanding orders in every direction to (presumably) competent men by his side to help control the infernal blaze.

Then failing in that, he helped the victims of the fire. He even temporarily housed victims in his palace. He also provided and distributed food subsidises and other emergency relief items to tens of thousands of people who were in dire straits and needed immediate assistance and sustenance. He did not (as a beneficiary) collect on a huge fire insurance held by the state Imperial Insurance Company, that (it was said) in his contrivance he had dastardly arranged beforehand. No such company actually existed to Dyfed's knowledge. What he did do (after the fire was finally put out) was to buy up the entire Palatine Hill neighbourhood (that included Dyfed's mansion on the hill that was left unburned). Furthermore, from the Palatine Hill he purchased a big chunk of burnt city that lay to the immediate east-north-east of it which included part of the Esquiline Hill and the so called 'valleys' district' that stretched to the north from that hill. The 'valleys' district' was defined as that being the area encompassed within a north eastern hilly finger (within the walled city) which was called Quirinal Hill (and where Nero chose for his personal palace), and the south eastern most hilly finger of that area called the Esquiline Hill hood where the *pack's* Palace Estate town-villa-residence and work-shops were located. Between these two hills were three valleys with Vimi Ridge (also Viminal Hill) somewhat in the centre. The appropriated land bought up by Nero (that was to constitute Nero's new estate) only contained the southern part of the valleys and the land stretching west to include the Palatine Hill. Immediately to the south of here within the city but outside of his appropriated estate, was the Caelian Hill. (Now we have learned the names of at least five of Amor's seven hills) Nero then demolished every existing edifice, the partially burned palaces, as well as the perfectly good and unburned mansions in order to converted these lands into his golden palace and its surrounding grounds encompassed by gigantic walls. This estate (that sprawled across the city) would come to dominate Amor as its glittering structure proudly shone brilliantly in the sun. Directly in front and west of this golden house Nero had caused a one hundred Amoran foot statues to be erected of him emblematically undergoing a metamorphic transformation into the sun god Sol[27]. Nero called it his party house, for as stated already he resided on the Quirinal Hill nearby.

The remaining folks of the hoi polloi called it the golden house (Domus Aurea or Oro), and not too shabby a domus it was, at that. Dyfed was invited there many times, as was half of Amor. But it must be stated that Nero also provided ample compensation for these properties, and the central portion (the low lands) had once been where most of the poor had lived. A new and better facility was found for them. But the rich folks like

26 According to historic rumour it was said the instrument he played was a fiddle. But again, that couldn't have been since the fiddle hadn't yet been invented and was not available to emperors or the paying public for another 1400 years.

27 Also Ba'al. Bel, Helios, Beltane, Adonis, Apollo Radiance etc.

Dyfed and the professional company he kept, along with other aristocrats, all of whom had owned the higher ground on the Palatine, Quirinal, and Esquiline Hills, along with Vimi Ridge, never stopped whining about being shorted. Dyfed, on the other hand, had no need to whine, and wouldn't have anyway — what is, is what it is! Anyway, Morgant's Esquiline Hill Palace Estate town-villa where Dyfed actually lived was on the extreme south-eastern slope of the Esquiline Hill and as its repo status was over-turned, it was left untouched. The estate was quite near the fine old Servian city wall that had been built of tuff rock[28] centuries earlier during the reign of King Servius Tillius. To Dyfed Tillius was just another shadowy character from the past in this strange world that embodies our story. The wall which he built, though (that still hemmed in and protected the city), as well as Morgant's estate were (as earlier stated) just north of one of the city's eastern guarded gates that punctured that wall.

It ought to be noted that with the compensation Dyfed received from the imperial treasury for the appropriation of his Palatine Hill apartment that formerly belonged to the Cornelius family, he used to purchase for himself a well-heeled new suite on the southwestern slope of the Capitoline Hill. This (now the sixth named hill of Amor) was the site where the earliest (and maybe the most historically important) religious ceremonies were held, and around which the City of Amor gathered and grew. Called the Capitolus, it was where the ancient bonfires had been lit and where ancient folks here had sacrificed expectantly to the most important and supreme deity Saturnus, the generation and fertility god that are equated with the deity Cronus, father of Zeus. It was also here on the summit of the Capitolus Hill that the later forefathers of the current folks had also first built the Temple Optimus Maximus (Iovis Optimi Maximi Capitolini; or Temple of Jupiter Capitolinus) to glorify Jupiter (Jove)[29] the Amoranized Zeus. Today, it remained the site of the temple to that god where two more important deities of Amor had been added to him. All together they were: Jupiter Optimus Maximus Capitolus' (Jove) and his consort Juno Regina (to rhyme with vagina, not rejeena). The other was Minerva. Minerva (not surprisingly) was the goddess of poetry, medicine, wisdom, commerce, weaving, crafts, and magic who the Amorans equated with Athena. Each of these deities had their own cella. Athena was the supreme goddess of neighbouring Hellenic peoples whose former civilization was now overrun by the Amoran Empire at this time. In any case, Minerva had similar attributes and inspirations to the former mentioned latter-day Athena. These attributes included courage, civilization, law and justice, mathematics, and (perhaps most importantly) — olive oil. These cultural entities, namely Jupiter, Juno and Minerva, were the underlying form of the Amoran establishment's make-believe and pretend. They cemented mythos and demanded of the citizen's obedience and worship, at least until Nero, along with Publicus Serviccicus Nemesis Maximus Augustus Usurperus and company, came along and demanded that they themselves be worshipped by the people as gods. This too became an important part of the Amoran mythos. Consequently, the temple atop the Capitolus Hill (acropolis) at the moment was a constant scene of sacrificing the thighs of white bulls wrapped in fat to Jove, Juno and, usually on Tuesdays, to the emperor. It was on the scale such, as Dyfed had never seen.

---

28   A mass known as tufa; or Earth's incubating semen that often lies dormant for ages and is made from volcanic rock and ash that's ejected during volcanic eruptions.

29   This pagan god was brought to Amor by the first Latinos from Alba Longa located in the Alban Hills.

The new bachelor digs that became something like weekend cabin near the river, was made available for purchase to Dyfed (with Cato's and Gregorius Agricola's help). It was located upon this esteemed Capitolus (Capitoline) Hill and was located on its southwestern slope. Its position was approximate and close to a landmark called the rock of Tarpeia. Tarpeia was one of the vestal virgins who betrayed the ancient citadel (acropolis) of Capitolus to the Sabines during the war between Romulus (the first king of Amor) and Titus, a king of a rival tribe called the Sabini. According to the Amorans who used to utilize the Olympiad calendar, this event took place on/about the year zero, or at the time of the first Olympiad.

That latter event occurred seven hundred and seventy-six solar cycles before this yarn's present era which began with Augustus Divi Filius. Obviously, such a location as this could fetch top denarii, and just as obvious it was a location that the rich would fight over. As it was, the pretty price the seller wanted was in the neighbourhood of the cost of an enormous mansion apartment fit for the well heeled on the Palatine Hill, if not fit for an emperor himself. The Palatine, after all (as already stated) was where members of the imperial families frequently settled. And although his Capitolus Hill digs were considered to be elaborate suites, it was considerably smaller than any Palatine Hill palace, never mind his permanent residence at their Palace Estate town-villa in the Esquiline Hill hood.

The palatial mini-pad Dyfed purchased was out of the way somewhat from the general activity of the city that suited Dyfed just fine. It hugged the cliff and was positioned as a penthouse. Beneath was another structure that was partially chiselled out of the lower portion of the steep cliff. Part of this solid abode was like a street entrance lobby that provided access via a stairway to the penthouse suite above. This suite, Dyfed was told, had once been owned by Quintus Catulus (no relation to Dyfed's former employer Marcus Catulus). This character had been a man of great wealth. He had been a general, a poet, historian, and a builder of Amor and was a consul of the Republic over a hundred and sixty years before.

Quintus Catulus had sided with Cornelius-Felix during the latter's civil war with Marius, another consul of the Republic. Quintus' son of the same name inherited his father's property that included the Capitolus' residence. Quintus Catulus the Deuse had also been a consul and statesmen who like Cato was a people's man who worked to improve their lot in life. As a wily politician he had been in charge of the rebuilding of the Jupiter Optimus Maximus temple after it had burned to the ground about a hundred earth years or so before, in the year 707 according to the year of the Olympiad, or about seventy years before the current era began (as later construed). The Capitolus residence that Dyfed purchased had been one of Catulus the Deuse's many shops and working office residences he used while he was under contract to build the second temple to Jupiter.

Obviously, to purchase such a property was something of an honour. At the time prior to purchase the property in question belonged to a certain Servius Sulpicius Galba, a grandson of the Deuse. Cato had known both the Catuluses (Catulus uno and Catulus duo) and Gregorius Agricola was a close friend of the Deuse and his grandson Servius Galba, the vendor. This elderly, long and sharp-nosed man had a tight and dry appearance that was bold and haughty. His stark and heavy presence was presented as a slim and wily customer who was cleanly shaven of any hair whatsoever when Dyfed met him. As Dyfed stood before Servius Galba at the man's palatial apartments on the Palatine hill in preparation for the business of purchasing the Capitoline Hill residence (that was called *the Capitolus Tarpeia* written in large Amoran lettering on a plaque on its rock wall by the entrance) the latter's equally sharp eyes cut and slashed backwards and forwards across Dyfed's friendly presentation before he further attempted to peel away Dyfed's exterior accompanied with a surprising alacrity. This alerted Dyfed to beware of this man and he quickly urged Morgant to pay him whatever he wanted.

Just about the same time that all this was taking place change came suddenly to Amor. Right after Nero's vast Domus Oro warming party (that lasted for months), Nero had a change of heart about everything that should have been dear to him, but apparently wasn't. Just as the emperor and his same-sex spouse[30] could afford to kick back and relax sumptuously in his new palace, and romp and rub shoulders with common artists and win over his nay-sayers and whiners who made up their guest list, all the while taking pride and enjoyment in the works which he had initiated, Nero, the appraised emperor of the Amoran Empire, Nero the misunderstood who under momentary duress suddenly decided to commit suicide, without a bye your leave which, by the way, was his privilege. And in this effort (unlike others he took on) he was quite successful, indeed. As it happened, Nero's suicide took place on the day that the sale of the Capitoline Hill residence to Dyfed came through.

The house warming party Dyfed planned was over-shadowed by a momentous bash held instead by Servius Galba at his Palatine Hill mansion. The whole city of those who were (or wanted to be among) the *who's who* was there. Dyfed did not attend. The celebration wasn't so much for Nero's life, but rather that his life was over and finished with and that nobody had to put up with him anymore. His same-sex partner wasn't in attendance, either: rumour had it that he had been caught within hours of Nero's death of trying to leave town. He was then publically dragged before Nero's gargantuan effigy statue and strangled. As for other news of Galba's celebration, everybody who wanted to be somebody needed to be there for Galba announced at that moment that he was grabbing the imperial title for himself and needed support. He had already refused such an invitation and (at least for awhile) had loyally served Nero who had been promoted at that time instead. Apparently, Nero's death occurred just prior to Galba's intention to return to his governorship of Hispania that Nero had earlier bestowed on him.

On account of the Emperor Nero's untimely death, Dyfed's central bank design to finance the empire in order make managing and controlling the integrity of the Imperial finances more expedient, and to increase the House of Lucifer's profits, was shelved for good. The fiat currency concept was (of course) never officially adopted so none were ever put into circulation. However, templates were produced for only two of the eight denominations of denarii proposed. These were for the one and the five denarius notes. And as a one-off trial for exploratory circulation had been planned as well, a limited printing took place that produced two bales of this money, one bale for each denomination. Both fiat currency notes (bills) were identical (as earlier stated) except for their

---

30 Named Pythagoras, this man was Nero's fifth spouse. Nero's first three spouses were women and the next was the boy Sporus who was castrated for the occasion. For his fifth and second same-sex wedding, Nero fulfilled his duty as a veiled bride who took Pythagoras as her husband in a public ceremony during the Saturnalia Tigellinus' banquets. Nero was the son of consul Domitius and Agrippina Minor who later married Emperor Claudius who she poisoned, thereby affecting Nero's successful emperorship.

allocated denomination. One printing was for a one Denarius bill and the other was for a fiver. Dyfed retained one of each specimen as a personal keep sake (and ultimately as artefacts) that was eventually turned into two very valuable objects d'art after the plates were destroyed. Centuries later, he framed and hung the one and five denarii promissory notes from a nail on his study wall in Couver City. The other notes had been promptly burned and no other templates were ever fabricated.

Dyfed had learned earlier through information that filtered into the precinct of the *pack* that earlier Nero had intended to put Galba to death. This was the reason the latter had returned to Amor when he did. It was a decision to negotiate putting a hold on his own death while he organized Nero's instead. In this, apparently, Galba was successful beyond his expectation. Another man, Julius Windex (of noble family) who was governor of much of Gaul (that now included Armorica whose rule would have extended over the village of Joslin), had sided with Galba and the latter's intention of usurping Nero as soon as possible. But Windex, who had openly rebelled against Nero (in an effort to bolster Galba), was defeated by Nero in battle as a result of this treachery. And though he survived the battle, he too had committed suicide in disgrace of failure. Galba was disgusted at this and wandered off wondering if life was worth living.

Anyway, Galba's Emperorship (according to the rebute doctrine of Vespasianus) morphed quickly into another Publicus Servicicus Nemesis Maximus Augustus Usuperus which was followed in quick succession by increasingly greater numbers of the same that all occurred within one single revolution of the earth's journey around the sun. When the next grouping of Publicus Servicicus (pronouncement reminder is Ser-viss-i-cus) Nemesis Maximus Augustus Usurperus that rose up and championed the throne in the final hours of that revolution, the die was finally (by some intentional streak of irony) cast by Vespasianus Imperator himself. So, it now came down to Titus (or General Titus as he preferred), the son of this current Publicus Servicicus Nemesis Maximus Augustus Usurperus the umpteenth whose commanded him to sack and demolish the Abramist's temple to Jehovah (Yehwah) at Al Quds (also phonetically pronounced Qadesh), which is now known by the epithet Jeru-Salem (the keeper of the peace), in the Land of Judah. This turned out to be a stick in the hornet's nest and also in the craw in many of the adhering Abramists' throats; according to some.

(The Perfidious Direction)

'And here I stand with all my lore, a fool no wiser than before.'
GOETHE (FAUST)

However, it didn't take long before the House of Catulus, the House of Purplebal and the House of Florentius got wind of Dyfed's application to print money. Fortunately, aside from having no design of their own for a central banking system blueprint as yet to work from, it needed a lot (and I mean a lot) of gold up front even to float such an idea). And (since) there was no chance whatsoever that the three amigos-amicus — those aforementioned houses of Catulus, Purplebal and Florentius, and there may have been other Capital Gainers too who had learned of Dyfed's intention — could ever have agreed (once the cat was out of the bag) to share the central bank concept between them responsibly, the idea was like a still-born centaur bound to his hooves but stopped dead instead in its tracks. So the concept remained shelved for fifteen hundred more years. By that time the House of Florentius, which was controlled by Gregorius of Turones (Kysarodunum), finally came out way ahead of the others. But by that time the Empire had dissolved into multiple kingdoms therefore the sovereign's responsibility toward its people, and the central banking system by which the subjects were being exploited, had no interests in common.

It appeared that the perfidious direction upon which the Empire had been historically fixed, and was to remain fixed, with a ineffective tweak here and a negligible tweak there, always to the advantage of the rich, was (in fact) not historical but the result of a earlier axiology called for by imperial proclamation. And this proclamation had been decided upon by the rich and powerful under the authority of those housed in a number of curae scattered around Amor. But most importantly it was in the Curia Julia (once an Etruscan temple) that was nowadays the meetinghouse of the senate. That proclamation was the Idea by which the Empire identified itself within the heart and soul of it's every expression; this included Capitalist Amor and Pax Amor. However, similarity of imperial traits aside, unlike yesterday's empires, today's Amor ruled the relevant world. So, in that case the implications of Amor's mores would, by logistics and necessity, become subject to vast exponents. This condition would also be subject to the passage of time, hence (voila!) — entropy, or at the very least, a change within certain aspects of the Empire's nature. The attempt by Amor to over come the civilizations that circled the White Sea and of Hellas in particular was one thing. Today, first and foremost, Amor's concerns were the barbarians. These shoplifting folks extraordinaire — over-lapped as well as pulled alongside and then ahead of the deteriorated sophistication of the degeneracy of the Hellenes. These latter were long in decline while the barbarians (if not in their prime) were in their infancy in their attempt to become a world power. Furthermore, the barbarians came in two separate parts from two opposite directions at the same time. And if that wasn't confusing enough, and challenging, one set were the physical barbarians relying on warrior brawn and adroit slyness who came from the north-western provinces (yet were being replenished and even pushed by another horde of a like-kind that came from the far east) while the other set were a cultural infestation of religious zealots who surged up from the direction of the south east and the land in and around Canaan.

It is here at this juncture — in information theory — that the certainty and precision of a thing enters into an equation which by happen chance becomes a further light of hope for optimistic philosophers; these were the likes of Dyfed and his companions who were also called idealists. For by the definition of the established order, entropy is the logical thought behind the probability of the irreversible tendency of the said system (like any other) toward increasing disorder. Hence the great hope of optimists, for it may provide a chance to overthrow a tyrannical condition within an order (in order) to gain some freedom, or in this particular case, a pervasive equality of opportunity to billions of people each and every one of whom will remain unequal to each other. And so goes the global reduction of personal debt: So, a tipping for sure; if not an outright overthrow.

This thinking, of course, is nonsense. The inference here is that historically it was incumbent upon emperors, kings, chieftains, high priests, pashas, sultans, archdukes, caliphs, emirs, rajas, potentates, sahibs, first ministers, presidents and even an unremarkable cadre of political and cultural shamans right down to the common garden variety house psychopath that was suffering from cerebral epilepsy and an aggravated case of short man syndrome (each graced with the divine mantle of established authority bestowed on them by the gods, of all people!...or non-people…or down right nonsense concept compounded by hocus-pocus and mumbo-jumbo) to strive for a determination towards an attitude of thorough submissiveness by the seething and revolting mass of the multitudes who (if the truth were really known) scared the living bejesus out of the aforementioned kings and priests.

Furthermore, they were to achieve the general acceptance among the entire public for this pacified state and temper, globally. Since they were incapable of introducing and administering lithium globally, one might think that this was a tall order. But by the tenets of its own nature, this system will be seen to replicate itself into just a position without virtually anybody acknowledging that it was happening. And this is why the thinking of the optimists is nonsense. Much more has to be done than what (apparently) they think: Because that stinks.

As will also be seen, this entitled cadre (of the divinely privileged) will certainly remained true to this notion of entitlement and superiority no matter whose porch or back yard their empires influence, or how much opposition there is to it — or how out numbered they were.

Nero (among others) was no Kleisthenes. For he and the others did not enhance or in any other way further democratic law. But, to his credit, he did focus on Amoran diplomacy and trade as Galba focussed on financial responsibility and expedient restraint. If only they had been better understood, perhaps their shortcomings would have fallen away and the brilliant light of ingenuity and success would have shone brighter then Nero's burning city the night she became all a flaming blaze.

Winter solstice was in the air by the time Vespasianus Augustus (emperor) had finally stepped up into the cool limelight. Dyfed wondered at the time if the man was not in a different time zone than most folks. It was certainly a different time zone from Dyfed. Alongside his number one yes man and state fixer, Mucianus, Vespasianus never once appeared in the least embarrassed to engage Castus in conversation, according to what Castus himself told Dyfed. On one such occasion (with Dyfed by his side in attendance at a gala at the hippodrome), Castus casually, but pointedly, introduced Dyfed as the man who had brought the signed and sealed affidavits from the XXth and VIth Legions in Armorica all the way to Amor to secure Vespasianus' chanced to climb onto the throne (thrown) chair. And if his majesty remembered, this was all for fantasy imaginings of (securing for himself) a throne for his not so royal ass to sit comfortably in. In other words, my noble and gracious majesty (he seemed to have said), has it never crossed your callous and nimble-wit to acknowledge the service which Prince Dyfed expedited in a most efficient manner for you, the moment you wanted it? Never mind how gullible or misinformed you'd been as to the reality of your chances at taking the helm of imperial ship in the first place. Which, as it turned out, was not at large and ready for your taking. Vespasianus (at the time) merely stared hard at Dyfed with a rather far-away look without showing any emotion whatsoever. Perhaps the emperor to be was just testing the waters back then, thought Dyfed. He was hardly an incompetent emperor. In fact, even if his tactic for the renovation and modernization of the inner city space of al Quds' didn't pan out, he was greatly successful of other things, under the circumstances, and did initiate the beginning of the royal dynasty of the Flatuant Flavians before Hadrianus Antonius Markus Verus Commodus tripped out a new page of history that ate up another century.

During those earlier days Dyfed was most eager and keen to paste chunks of surrealism that passed for reality here into his mental exercise scrapbook in order to have them handy (mentally) so as to study and memorize them in his spare time. He desperately needed to understand how the ruling power elite had put this world together. In time he would also advance business acquaintances that stretched plum across the entire section of Amor's society. His success here was on the premise of what he patched together from those chunks of reality. The good thing about empires, especially being at the very centre of them, was that they attracted intelligent and very ambitious folks from all around the world. As a mensari (banker) and especially as an advocati (defence attorney) he met complicated and interesting folks. And through these folks he met another kind of interesting sector. These were men such as Claudius Ptolemy (Klaudios Ptolemaios), a Hellenic poet, astrologer, geographer and mathematician who had come up from Xandria. He also became friends with Gaius Plinius Secundus, an Amoran author and natural philosopher, and he even picked up a trick or two from a clever chap called Strabo. Strabo, a Hellene who was born in Anatolia in the kingdom of Pontus, was an historian, a philosopher and a geographer who had come to Amor to take account of the place. Ironically, this man once had had a legal association and relationship with one of the greatest opponents of Amor, and was himself once an opponent of the dictator tyrant Cornelius-Felix in particular. The man in question was a certain Mithradates, king of Pontus. This highly intelligent polyglot (who had eventually been brought low by Pompey) used to ingest poisons so as to build up an immunity to guard against assassination.

It was Strabo who told Dyfed that history (unlike Manandan's version) was comprised of a quasi-knowable para-virtual reality substance that is fifteen per cent within the realm of truth and eighty-five percept that is comprised of lies, hoaxes, flighty sketches of imagination and the stinking shit of Taurus the bull. Dyfed reasoned (then) that Strabo must have been referring to third dimensional history. Strabo added that of that first fifteen per cent that's in the realm of truth, ninety per cent of that is actually quasi truth exaggerated beyond reason, five per cent more is convoluted truth, and of the remaining five per cent, four per cent of that is a relative and unreliable truth combined with a *gossip* of honest to goodness hearsay; and that's the truth! What you have in the realm of truth when you contemplate its stand-alone historic value of any kind is a whopping one per cent. You had a better chance; he said, of gaining reliable insight about history through augury, the horoscope, or the divination by a *drove* of asses, a *clutch* of chickens, a *murder* of crows or even a *trip* of goats. 'So, there you have it,' Strabo told him.

Through Cato, of course, he met many inquiring men including Publius Cornelius Tacitus, an historian and contentious Amoran senator. Tacitus was one of the first men of repute who spoke to Dyfed of and about the new-age cult that folks throughout the Empire had recently become exposed to and subsequently interested in; along with its presumed founder and initiator, an individual named Joshua. Apparently, Rabboni Joshua's personalized shtick had just recently even arrived (and been received) right here in the City of Amor, having come initially from the provinces.

P.C. Tacitus told Dyfed that the cult appeared to have originated as a schism (if not a downright recantation) and discontinuation initiative of the old Abramist school of thought while holding on to the precepts contained in the first five sacred books and verse of the old school (called the Torah, or the Pentateuch in the tongue of the Hellene). It was a break-away Abramist cult, he told Dyfed, and amazingly much research and individual homework had gone into achieving such credibility from such dubious resources in order to launch its acclaimed new covenant, he said. It may have come from the provinces but it had a lot more than your run of the mill provincial quality when it came to propaganda, that's for sure. As to the origin of the new covenant and its people, Tacitus told Dyfed that nobody knew for sure. Certainly, the Abramic Nazarenes (Nazareans or Nazarites), an antagonistic sect among the mainstream breakaway cult known generally as the Essenes, along with the Chasidim (fellow zealot, like-minded religious-cult extremists), have adamantly stated their claim to the franchise over the new covenant of righteousness. Furthermore, they maintained that the divine atonement and forgiveness for all humanity before the end of times ante ceded (by far) those current rabbinical Abramists' who still followed tenuous tenants and interpretations derived from the Torah of the old school whose purpose was for sensationalism that was old hat and weren't properly thought out. And that wasn't all. Aside from giving short shrift to any current relevance to the ideals of the old school, along with its adherents, these messianic, new covenant Nasrani (Essenes, Nasarenes or Nazarites, and Chasidim combined) who worshipped the righteous teacher Joshua, whose name was generally shortened (sic) to Jeshua or Yeshua, also vehemently accused the old school's wicked priesthood of intentionally killing their messianic saviour Joshua (Jeshua).

But the question remained, however, as to what came first; Joshua the egg, or the undisclosed chicken; the latter being some disgruntled sector of the Abramist society looking for a folk hero and a cause? Tacitus (either Tacky-tus said fast or its modern pronunciation being Ta-sight-us) favoured the latter. It seemed that due to the hard-nosed and relentless attitude of the Hellenistic King Seleucus Nicator (and his dynasty in general), the resultant effect from this disruptive attitude caused vast disharmony within the Abramic culture at that time. Wanton destruction then ensued. This annihilation included not only the Abramist's scrolls of testament and sacred verse that backed up their cult, but it was also an annihilation of their morals and ideals. Then under a succession of wicked priests (at least three, sometimes referred to as Phinhais, Pinhas and Panhasy, or Jubula, Jubulo and Jubulum and sometimes tweedle-dee, tweedle-doe and tweedle dum) which followed this disaster, this situation caused the integrity of the temple to wither and disappear into the scorched sands of Judah that was later renamed Judea or Judaea by the Hellenes and the Amorans. If one was old school and wanted to remain and live, one denied the old covenant. This was not the case with the old school die-hards and the messianic leaning zealots who morphed into the bulk of the Nasrani. These die-hards and extremists that remained resistant to change quickly fled the temple and its environs while the remainder old-school recanters, those weak old covenant cult adherents, either converted or were scattered to the winds. Either way, all of them were now scrambling for all they were worth.

In the meantime, the breakaway Abramists had had a head start. In their effort to stay clear of Seleucus' establishment (which a couple of centuries later was followed by the occupation of these same lands by the Amoran Empire and it's established Pax Amor) they had flocked mostly to the region of the Hauran and the Land of Uz (or Oz) to its south. These Messianic Abramist (that division of the New Covenant known now as Nasrani) had also by now been spurred on to display an extreme tenacity of zeal and conviction for their teacher of righteousness who had now become an atoning saviour who was preparing for the end of times. The end of times, apparently, was the lasting and indelible impression (some say gift) that both the Seleucid and Amoran states of establishments had had on these people. So, in response to this new covenant, the Essenes (and their satellite persuasions) got busy collecting, redacting, cataloguing, editing old relicts and even compiling sacred verses into sacred history like O Billio! The insertion into the LXX manuscript (also called the Septuagint) of a redacted script from another older scroll took place at or about this time. This important book was placed immediately following the first five books. This inserted scroll, therefore, became the sixth book in the new compilation of sacred verse that took place in and around this time; it was called the Book of Joshua. One telling aspect of this sixth book is that it has a lists of nations marked for extermination!

Furthermore, the followers of this cult now claimed that their teacher Joshua (Rabboni) was the Saviour of humankind in his preparation for the End Times (sic). Incidentally, aside from the name Joshua or Jeshua, Josephus and Asaph, he was sometimes also referred to as Issa or Isa, ben Pandera or ben Josephus (and later in the future, Joey Virgo), and furthermore, it was stipulated that he was their founder (and even their ancestor) who was responsible for the new covenant on and by the authority of god (sic). This theme quickly got woven in betwixt the lines of the five books of the old Torah (or Pentateuch) during redactions and other editing. But more importantly, the bibliographic testament of the five most important books was capped by the book of Joshua who (it was said by the new messianic Nasrani Abramists) was god's son and saviour of man-and presumably women-kind. And at their insistence, only god's people had immortal souls. And only they, in the end, were worth a pinch of coon-ka ka that needed to be (and would be) saved. Salvation of the soul only applied to humans for no other creature had souls of any kind, anyway, at least any that were subject to becoming perishable through sin. The new Abramists now claimed that their Rabboni had been sent by god (sic) to save souls thereby circumventing the responsibility of the soul owner having to transform him or herself. They called this paraclete Master and they placed him among the old works (now shuffled and rebound) where one can now find him referenced (among others) in the updated edition of the book according to Isaiah. This heavily redacted (and historically questionable) scroll is dated at about the time of the first Hellenic Olympiad itself, namely the eight century prior to Imperator Divi Filius Augustus, the first emperor of the empire.

"Do you know Andronicus?' Tacitus had asked Dyfed. But Dyfed had been unsure of the name and had given off merely a shadow of a shrug in response.

'Simon Judas Andronicus MacAbbey? No? I'll introduce you to him some day. He knows a great deal more than I do on that subject,' Tacitus once said.

Morgant, who was on hand and was closely milling and puttering around doing something or another, cast the two men a glance.

(House of Purplebal)

'Once nature starts to foreclose — with erosion, crop failure, famine, disease — the social contract breaks down.'
RONALD WRIGHT

There were a number of rising houses of the merchant class. One such house was the House of Purplebal. The patriarchal head of this house was a youngish man originally from Carthago.[31] His name was Potamus Purblebal the First who claimed to be the thirteenth bastard son of King Jugurtha of Numidia. Dyfed thought that it went without saying that if there was no previous family member of the same name then it stood to chance that the individual was the first that didn't need numbering. Ostensibly then, this was the same man who had earlier talked himself out of being forced by another emperor to repair to Nova Troia at the fringe of the world if he desired the junior position offered him there within Amoran legitimacy. He was the same man to whom the younger Dyfed would have answered had he arrived. Apparently, there was a god after all. Now it may be the other way around. Either way, at least Dyfed will keep his independence.

By this time it had a few hundreds of years since the city state kingdom of Carthago — located on the tip of north Africa a short distance due west of Sicilia — had been something of a rival to Amor. By a succession of wars the extent and privileges of Carthago had been broken and it was now subservient to Amor.

Purblebal was the proprietor of the White Sea Bank that he had recently founded in Tarsus in Anatolia. It turned out that this individual, an intense man just a little older than Dyfed, had once been a wily employee of the House of Apuleius. There, his intent had been to ruthlessly overthrow the hierarchy of that house. In his success of doing just that he also robbed the House of Apuleius' family heirs of their inheritance and fortune. Purblebal used this wealth to form the White Sea bank in order to fund his up and coming House of Purplebal. Dyfed discovered this after the fact. Strangely, it was through a meeting with some a certain remarkably man from the Kushan court named Rama from Nananda that Purplebal's mysteriousness evaporated. But his character was always obvious to Dyfed.

Potamus Purplebal was a tall, sinewy man, although shorter than Dyfed, who had a grim countenance with large olive black eyes, one of which was lazy and gave him a slightly crossed-eyed look. This made it difficult to tell whether he was actually looking at you or not. Indeed, keeping other humans disconcerted and at bay at all times by shielding his thoughts and his lack of emotion behind an un-penetrable wall was his most obvious characteristic. But after meeting the man, this one affectation about his eye was the one folks came away remembering the most.

In spite of Purplebal's flawed character of being morose about all things which negatively affected him, and long tirades about who were to blame for his misfortunes, and how everything was grossly unfair and deliberately set against him (including the

---

31 Carthago or Qart-ḥadašt in the Phoenicio-Punic tongue (which means New City) is derived from the Kanaanite language whose name eventually devolved into Carthage and subsequently, Cartagena.

Amoran establishment), a man who neither complimented anyone, or had a pleasant word to say and a manner to match, and who generally was one who is not sought out by others, but avoided by decent folks at all costs, Potamus Purplebal was extraordinarily successful at accumulating wealth. His one weakness, however, was in having a certain phobia. This was fear of risk and a foregoing to extreme lengths to eliminate unforeseen loses, usually indirectly at a considerable cost. So he tended to borrow heavily on behalf of others with their gold in order to create a booming business for them which, to the best of his considerable abilities, he planned on milking and stealing away from them once the risks were over and it was successfully up and running. To do this he often needed to heavily borrow and mortgage. Dyfed took advantage of this situation and safeguarded himself by being able to quickly conduct inexhaustible and painstaking research so as to place his bets as correctly as possible. When doing business with Purplebal, and others of high risk, Dyfed decision was of course to aim always for profit but restricted profits to being small profits that minimized any loss. In other words, take large investment gambles but break them up into little tiny-wee bits and scatter them as much as possible throughout the minefield of lucrative investment.

If asked, he would even assist Purplebal to invest in the smoky air that floated over the city of Amor if need be, so long as Purplebal was additionally prepared to put up something for collateral, something he actually owned and had value that Dyfed could hold for security. From the Carthaginian's point of view, purchasing seemingly ridiculous concepts was something he was prone to doing, so long as he was convinced there was some profit and prestige in its acquisition. But you can never overestimate the bizarre imagination of the greedy, even if their greed is simply to look trendier and sexually alluring than others: and generally that turned out to be the case. This should never be mistaken for the very human wish to be noticed, accepted and loved by our fellow humans and the very great disappointment to us when we aren't. To be shunned because you're not sexy or not feared or envied doesn't cause disappointment, it causes anger and hatred. It will only do this if you place the props of your self-esteem there.

Of course Dyfed initial fee for the trouble of convincing the silly borrower that nasty stale air was a sound investment was a hefty one at that. And if convinced that they would be hailed as an innovator extraordinaire — perhaps even a gifted *artiste* — if they coveted and bought up all the foul smells and slimy, stinking sludge which the City of Amor produced, that hefty fee and it complimentary profit would always come right off the top and into his own bills receivable and general account pocket.

Most of Dyfed's business, though, was large and elaborate investment loans that had a lot of forethought based on fifth column information; again, thanks to info sussed out by Morgant or Cato. In this game, commercial properties changed hands regularly, and ships and their commodities were being bought and sold in the boardrooms of the market place banks while still on the high seas. When it came running this enterprise Dyfed ran it directly through his private House of Lucifer Banking Company which was where he kept his general ledger and his profit account and not through his up and coming Union of the People's Commonwealth Bank of Gaul.

As already stated, the Union of the People's Commonwealth Bank of Gaul, was a banking system in which folks' accounts were considered to be shares in the bank, thereby sharing profits and losses. This bank had expanded and Egidius of Joslin was now managing its head office that Dyfed had recently opened at Lugdunum. It was here that the former developed his sir-name 'of Joslin' for good reason: since he wasn't of Lugdunum. Dyfed held fifty-one per cent ownership of that bank's shares at all times, along with all of its capital assets. However, as a form of casino where one gambles their money it was a winner, and was almost a sure thing for the shareholders (those who kept an account with the bank). And the more people who invested in the bank's affairs, and the greater amount they deposited, the greater was the bank's purchase power so the greater became the value of the bank's over all worth over time. And all this was reflected in the account holders' savings accounts. It was becoming a great success. Soon he introduced it in Amor. The trick was not to be greedy and want to make money at any cost. It was about helping everybody make a little money constantly, day in and day out.

Dyfed also re-invented what he called the penny-ante-up market. The idea had come to him while dealing with Purplebal. Apparently, it was a type of market gambling used by the ancient Phoeniki and their descendants, both the Cypriots of Cypress (Kypros)[32], and the Cretans from Kreta (Crete) and others.

This kind of investment used a system where one quickly bought into an established valued market, thereby providing the pool of collateral with more capital. This swelled the stock value of those particular market shares. The common shares in this market were called the copper stock, or here in the Amoran Empire, they were known as the assarius. These were aimed at smaller businesses such as shops, small industries, and even small co-operative market centres. Sometimes these enterprises were clumped together under a single investment that then sold shares that represented their best guess-timated total value of their assets. Other times the business that had received an injection of cash flow or gained capital assets were repackaged under a new name and promoted accordingly. It could easily be a win-win situation so long as there were no sudden downturns in the market. Downturns happen when folks get begins to increase in value. The talent here was to be fast on the mark, patient in the long run, and not to be greedy. If everything went well according to an honest market, one could make a little profit here then hop over to make a little profit there — nothing excessive (mind-you) but profit nonetheless. In slower times, the worst-case scenario would be a standstill with no profit to speak of, yet no losses, either. Big banks generally didn't have the stomach for it. Dyfed did, and he used the shareholders hard-earned savings from the Union bank to do it. His strategy in using the copper stock seldom failed to increase little by little the investment value of those shareholders of the Union of the People's Commonwealth Bank of Gaul who, by and large, were poor, hardworking common folk. Naturally these folks stood steadfast by Dyfed because he wasn't fleecing them. Later, he used his connections he had with the House of Theodosus and started up the Union of the People's Commonwealth Bank of Hispania where the aforementioned family had huge agricultural land interests.

Generally folks get nervous when strife and shaky politics run rife. On these occasions they quickly file up outside the bank to withdraw their gold and silver from the bank's big safe. Though usually the folks withdrawing were offered a promissory note with the solemn 'I promise to pay' slogan attached. And if they were very foolish they accepted it. For the well-armed man in the street, or the field, along with his household, to withdraw his gold was good business sense. For the unarmed it was dangerous. But

---

32 Cypress (Kypros) has been settled since 10,000BCE. During the last few thousand years it was populated by the Phoenician peoples, the Assyrian, the Egyptian and the Persian empires. Its name is the origin of the word copper that has been mined there since forever. The Sumerian word for Bronze/copper was kuber.

this was not bank talk for good business, however. As the head of the House of Lucifer Banking Company, aside from Morgant's and Cato's invaluable contributions, he could use this Temple of Lucifer (as he funningly referred to it) as collateral and as a means to bolster the Union bank's assets on the occasion when the bank's investments were shorted due to market slumps or to unfortunate investments that crashed usually attributed to some other rich capitalist aristocrat's scamming or lying. Dyfed reasoned that bailing out shallow drops in bank stock value by dumping in his own gold to replenish the pot when profits dipped was nowhere near as costly as a run on his bank, something that was common with all banks.

And run on banks happen because the banks aren't powerful enough yet (at this time) to demand imperial legislature that insures them that they can't lose. That is to say, they were not yet in control of the almost full-blown all powering, socially imposing Imperial Ledger. The scenario here would be that it might be the peoples gold that the bank is holding safely for them but (should a shaky situation arise) ultimately the people would be prevented from withdrawing any of their gold or silver other than on the bank's say so. And that won't be any time soon until the situation that was causing the shakedown came to an amiable conclusion in the bank's favour. This may not happen if the imperial authority has no loans with the bank in question. But emperors and their suite are greedy too and want more than they've got. So, the only situation which could affect this decision to open the doors and allow folks to withdraw from the bank again and have access to hold their own gold (their tool or life-line for survival and personal security) in their nervous little fingers, would be the happy conclusion of some market recession or bank default (generally caused by the bank itself) and not something else. Ordinary folks and their actions can't and don't cause (on their own) market fluctuations, crashes, or bank defaults any more than ordinary folks can serve up wars and be the cause of major conflicts. If such a thing happens, it will soon be seen that the party on one side or the other are essentially barbarian without civilized principles and prone to act in the most puerile of manner. Usually it is the mis-expenditure or over extension of the emperors at large or the banks themselves. Occasionally it's ideological. That's a hopeless situation where if not immediately corrected all will lose, eventually.

So, withdrawals are the hoi polloi's only recourse from a failing bank or banking system. It may be short lived if the market actually (hoaxes here are not unknown) does crash and burn anyway, or not. And in such a climate, frenzied withdrawals lead directly to the run on the bank. It was immediately obvious to Dyfed that the people, or representatives of the people, needed to have control over the imperial ledger. Attaining this was obviously the ultimate struggle and one that could affect the market in general, and how it ought to be run.

Dyfed's newly formed Union of the People's Commonwealth Bank of Amor was situated by a fora near the Esquiline Hill district. It was a busy neighbourhood of (cheek to jowl) fruit sellers, viand vendors (selling sides of pig, sheep and oxen), dairy merchants (that often specialized in skin enhancing goat milk), vegetable markets, fish mongers, and garment markets, alongside goldsmiths, musical instrument makers, and jewellers which kept the market bustling throughout the day and into the evening. In the centre of the fora was a fountain in the middle of which a statue of Hermes (who the Amorans called Mercury) had been erected that looked down onto the fora. This is also where a great many people gathered under temporary canvas pavilions, to shield them from the burning sun in summer, to visit and do business. The majority of the folks in this 'hood' were poor to middle class.

Dyfed's private House of Lucifer's Banking Company (his fourth banking interest) had a new storefront on the forum, but the mechanics of his enterprise for each and every bank he had resided securely inside his brain. And anyway, if money weren't being made today it would be tomorrow. After all, it was only gold, not food and water. Indeed, food and clean drinking water were historically the measure that the market was based upon in practice, anyway, though this idea was now being challenged by the recent and aforementioned axiology ordered up by the senators of the curia. It was (as they say) business as usual today and tomorrow; the playing field starts up hill here on our side and ends in your end, down there somewhere in that-there bog. The first portion of the last sentence (business as usual today and tomorrow) was the Union of the People's Commonwealth Bank's slogan; the second portion (the playing field starts up hill on our side and ends in yours, down in your bog) was the motto and the attitude of the rich business-o-crat of which there was no shortage of in Amor.

These aristocratic businesses were generally flagged as the House of such and such. The House of Cornelius-Felix (headed by a former Amoran dictator) was one such entity, as was the famous House of Theodosus. Another up and coming individual with a *House* attached with a flourish to his name was a certain Giorgius Florentius from Colonia Lugdunum. This man was a well-born Amoran aristocrat of Etruscan origin. Born in his ancestral home of Florentia in the Olympiad year of 717 (59BCE) during the Amoran Republic, his father was an architect who helped design certain functionalities, such as a bridge and civic domus for the city of Florentia. Later, Giorgius accompanied his father, along with consul Lucius Plancus, to Gaul where his father began the design of Lugdunum after Plancus founded that city so as to benefit the great Amoran Republic's influence. In recent years Giorgius Florentius had become a convert to the Jeshuan cult. The lord of the House of Florentius, however, was to change names many times over the centuries and end up as Giorgi Posh, the most influential and most powerful man in the world at more than one point.

Anyway, it came to pass that the glorious House of Theodosus ran the rocks in a tempest around this point in time and needed to jettison some of their hardware to stay afloat. This wealthy and highly placed family's Amoran office for their consolidated business was right next door to Dyfed's own House of Lucifer Bank business front. The House of Theodosus's bank was called the Consolidated Amoran Bank. The Theodosus family's financial ability to undercut by far their competition proved to be a powerful tool for them. A tenacious lot (although they didn't show it) the Theodosus family had the moxy to grin and bear social and financial discomfort through skint times with haughty fortitude. And although they thrived during the reign of Nero, by the time Emperor Hadrianus at toppled from the roost, the Theodosus family bank was hurting due to having over extended themselves in recent lean times. Emperor Augustus Publicus Superior Nemesis Usurperus III further hit them with bankruptcy and a run on their bank in Hispania. This state of their affairs was accompanied by sudden foreclosures of vast loans they had out which caused rebellion among their clientele, along with other charges of inappropriate behaviour and business practices which with further investigation ushered in embarrassing disclosures of fraud, embezzlement, and corruption: Hard times, indeed.

Even now after all this time that Potamus Purplebal had been in Amor, he was still struggling from the suburbs of credence and power to get a foothold within the inner circle of the Amoran business sector. Now here was his opportunity and like lightening, such a stroke of luck would only hit in the same place once. Here, then, was an opportunity for him to merge himself with a branch of the House of Theodosus, that prominent family from Hispania Tarraconensis who had once exported large quantities of gold, tin, timber, marble, wine and olive oil, some of which Dyfed had provided insurance and help mortgage a service industry around which to accompany the House of Theodosus' adventure.

Although the first proposition toward the Theodosius' family had initially been a private offer from Purplebal's established White Sea Bank, the House of Theodosius thought they could benefit by having an open house affair to invite other potential buyers into the fray. The House of Theododus was intending, therefore, to get the word out that they were willing to sell shares in their bank and in some of their producing businesses. Towards this end they approached Dyfed at the House of Lucifer. Along with his expertize in Amoran law, they wanted him to act on their behalf as an argentari and conductor of private auctions, which he agreed to. Dyfed was also concerned about conducting an audit on the bank. He asked Varus Antonius Catulus, head of the Amoran branch of the House of Catulus to arrange it but that man refused. It seemed that he too wanted in with the chance of a merger. So, Varus Antonius, who didn't trust Purplebal and had made a point of never lending him money, at least not directly, now also interested in Theodosus' sell-off he too bellied up to the same table to bargain for a merger and mix. It was the talk of the town. Everybody wanted to keep abreast of this newsy item. Varus Antonius Catulus, head of the Amoran branch of the House of Catulus who didn't trust Purplebal and had made a point of never lending him money (at least not directly) bellied up with other aristocrats to the same table for a merger and mix among the House of Theodosus' forced fire-sale. Meanwhile the well known happy go-lucky entrepreneur, Furius Claudius, immediately invented the Merger and Mix as his house drink for all his high end and popular dance hall bars and restaurants. He even featured it as his happy-hour specialty.

Dyfed then turned to Cato for implementing the audit and his choice was favourable to the senators involved. Meanwhile, he made a fortune after that and was probably able to out bid against the Houses of Catulus and Purplebal.

After the preliminaries were conducted (which was done to outline the House of Theodosus' conditions of sale and to answer questions and make available to serious buyers the books of the businesses), Georgius Gregorius Florentius, having been prompted by Dyfed and Cato with all the aforementioned vital information, took his place at the table along with the latter's childhood friend and accountant, a man by the name of Flavius Claudius of Richelieu. That strange aristocrat and man of strategy then showed a great deal of adeptness as he thrashed it out with the House of Catulus and two or three other up and coming investment firms that were hungry and on the climb. Gregorius' mission was to drive up the price that subsequently bumped up Dyfed's commission. Aside from the House of Purplebal, one of those houses was the House of Altan-Uruk whose representative was a man named Khinglia Ephthalites, the white Hun. The whereabouts of their head office or palace (more likely a felt covered wagon constantly on the move pulled by some brutish animal or a horse cavalcade such as a team of Przewalski's[33]) was unknown to them. Talking together privately, Morgant and Gregorius thought it might be at Antioch in Anatolia that was the western terminus (at this time) of the so-called Silken Road and the springboard port by sea to the Amoran west and its capital here in Amor. It was either there or at Turko-Mongol Karakorum or one of its northeastern end trails on the last leg toward Chang'an and Luoyang, the Silken Road's eastern starting terminal. It was quickly noticed that Purplebal didn't actively compete against the white Hun, showing that they were in collusion.

The other, interested party here was represented by a suite headed by a light skinned, brown haired man dressed casually in a loose fitting robe adorned with appendages of fabric that wound around him somehow, all made of silk, but only still partially covered his beautiful body. He said his name was Rama and that he was a courier with the House of Kanishka from the Kushan Empire. His eyes shone brightly and his light brown-reddish hair was long and coiled up upon and around his head and held together by golden objects that were encrusted with rubies and sapphires. A golden emulate embossed with a depiction of Demeter was visible upon him and to a remarkable degree of beauty and emphasis he spoke the tongue of the Hellas.

Although Amoran emperors and members of the Patricians were generally still heard sputtering out the Hellenic language in some lesser degree of grammatical competence, in the business and intellectual high society circles it was still the language of the academics. But not so for the common folks of Amor such as the merchant class, it was all Greek to them and they understood none of it, except for Rama the man from Nananda who's Amoran was still poor. Dyfed was subsequently to discover that originally this man was from Nananda. So it was in the Hellenene language then that he and Dyfed used when they spoke before the others. In private they spoke a Sanskritized Prakrit language called Pali. It was similar and proximate to Dyfed's language of Shamskar.

Dyfed was not greedy, he only wanted an in with the House of Theodosus on some of their fine vineyards and cattle ranches in Hispania. In the end Potamus Purplebal got the lion's share of the remainder, with Varus Catulus picking up a few congenial partnerships with the House Theodosus.

---

33   The Equus caballus przewalskii: the Asian steppe horse.

(The winding Tibur and memories of the Land of Gwyneth)

'Dio mi la dona, quai a chi la tocca'
(God has given it to me, beware of touching it)
IN THE NOVEL WAR AND PEACE **LEV TOLSTOY** ATTRIBUTED
THIS QUOTE TO **NAPOLEANE DI BUONAPARTE**

On quiet days, while usually watching the river Tibur winding (not venting) away like a yellow ribbon in the sunset before the glooming, Dyfed thought of Ceredwyn and the Land of Gwyneth. Then one fine afternoon shortly after this while walking on the Capitoline Hill Dyfed saw Seutonius Paulinius who was probably taking his daily constitutional. This was the same Paulinius who had once spent a stint as governor of Albion. Dyfed had known that Paulinius had invaded and squashed the sacred Druid settlement of Mona Minor, this island which lay across the channel or strait from the little cenedl of Bangor in Gwyneth (Gwynedd) beneath the mountain. It was here many years ago that he had stepped ashore from the Isle of Peace. The decimation of Druids and Prydain freedom fighters on Mona Minor had unfolded (Dyfed recalled) just as Blacksmith Karatakos had predicted. Then as he recalled the Amoran-like magistrate who spoke in a Frankish accent, and from whose pronouncement he had once benefited against the accusation by that nasty little innkeeper. Dyfed enquired after him. Paulinius a bearded and almost savage looking man (compared to the clean shaven Amoran generals one was used to) answered that indeed he had once had a Druid arrested who locals told him had been impersonating an Amoran official. He told Dyfed that the man had been strangled to death after his arms were pulled out of their sockets and his legs were broken. Paulinius knew nothing of Owen's cenedl in that land, of course, and so there was no news of Ceredwyn.

These memories of folks and fond friends of Dyfed's from back then were now old and worn. He still visited them often, though. He cherished them and nobody could take them from him or impinged upon them in any way to alter their value they were to his heart. At least not yet. These thoughts and recollections were given to him by his involvement in the great give and take exchange that was the phenomenon in which he was immersed. It was the source from which uplifting heart-warming moments originated but they were not attachments in the true sense.

(The world around us only materializes from our senses)

> 'One's own culturation...the thing that guides or attaches itself to your attention which may dominate your idea is called 'Shining Forth' by the phenomenologists...'
>
> JORDAN PETERSON

Amor was the centre of the known world. Of the unknown world (as everybody knows), there is much that was not known to any given person. But even Amor, the microcosm of the world, was — logically speaking — just as unknown in the greater sense while appearing not to be so. This is so with everything. One normally doesn't think that the panorama of the great city if (somehow) scoped up close would be outside one's individual, and comfortable cognizance. And as such, for the city to realistically be any different (intrinsically or not from that comprehended by one's own sphere of reality) is nigh impossible: that is — outside of surprises and unknown titillations that's acceptable or not to one's own mores, which if discerned would be sensed and viewed, anyway, from one's own mean level. This vision...this, the sum of peering out into the world around, then depends on one's achieved comfort level among the phenomena of life (in itself) which tints the lens of every potentiality of cognizance through which ones scopes and surveys anything. It goes without saying then that the more broad the concept one has of what reality is, a greater acceptance one will have of further flung notions, apprehensions, and sentiment which amounts to the more accurate a picture over all.

But what Dyfed did know was that the one thing that didn't change, here or anywhere else is constant change, a thing in and unto itself. So, aside from Amor — the centre of the known world that mattered — into which Dyfed had by this time burrowed like a sapper undermining a kremlin (citadel) by digging down its hard and impenetrable wall in order to ascertain and analyse the soft and tasty ideological infrastructure and its archetypical prime causes of its insides which acted to fashion its idea, he had also updated his school boy visions of those other splendid and glorious cities which his tutor Manandan had once described for him. Where once his mind's eye to had recreate a type of hologram, now he fashioned a holograph instead from experience and logical reasoning. These splendid cities were the great human centres of Athena, Xanderia, and Chang'an (Xi'an rendered She'an) the city of Perpetual Peace (sic) in the land of Ch'in. These all existed in the third dimension only, whose images in the present were moot and of little value to Dyfed: whether he knew that or not (which he did) for that, too, was part of the holograph signature of Manandan's gifted teachings.

And if the Isle of Peace was the blessed timelessness of cosmic harmony and concordance whose technology was far and away beyond Amor, Amor was the city of sparkle. But it had none of the fineries of harmony or concordance as the former had had and even though her technologies were advanced sufficiently ahead of other empires, including Hellas, and Khem (along with their idea of government and law) it paled compared to the former Hyperborean outpost villa resort once stationed in the third dimension. To the people of the Empire (and beyond) Amor was called the Big Grape, which Dyfed fashioned by the concord (no pun intended) of consent among members of the *pack* into the Big Gripe.

Amor — the city of explosion, the city of ideas, of architecture, of vision and of fulfilling its foray into whatever arena it chose and at all costs. Amor, a law unto itself but not any more immune as to the plight of the hoi polloi who in calling themselves Amoran destined their self image into lawlessness. Dyfed saw the emperors stray from the mean too far and consequently a city invincible in the eyes of its inhabitants was affected accordingly. Maybe this was where it all started, Dyfed thought. It is always thought, it seems, that the city's invincibility (or the invincibility which is associated with it) was to turn away any attack towards it by the whole world, if it came to that. Such attempts would, it was thought, be inexpedient and ineffective. The idea was a dangerous myth. But we already know that these folks have squandered their entire inheritance on myths. In any case, this out-of-control bluster of miscomprehension which Dyfed knew was of the past, he had seen for himself to be the future, he could see every minute in the bold gaze of Amor's citizens in the cities that were to lie beyond the setting sun. Even the marble statues that lined the broad thoroughfares and squares displayed this arrogance of entitlement and prestige. They each shouted out that they were the entitled rulers of the empire. They stared out, these icons of hero-gods, as bold as brass not directly at, but over, above, and passed the by-passer at hand. But arrogance is sly and shifty and sometimes it hid alongside the fear that lingered in the corners of the people's eyes. He heard it more boldly in their words, for fears are often words that are spoken more loudly than others. Dyfed doubted the Imperial dream that Amor would become the new city of friends as the executive members of the pack had always hoped for. He certainly did not see Amor becoming the place of comfort for either the Masters or their helpers and expeditors (the *pack*) to inhabit without care. Not here, now, at this rate at any rate, though the rumour would linger for some time yet like a bad smell and rust away in a stilted jaded reality that would impinge itself in one negative fashion or another into the final result; its ideological effect of hand-me-downs.

The empire had become something of a formulated society and its formula was a regulated convention with its sticky sidekick etiquette and its wincing side winder-mince. To this was added a lavish dash of postured proclivity. Amor went a long way in attempting taste versus compulsion, perhaps not equalled until the end of the Second Empire in the eighteenth and nineteenth centuries current era. The point of its rise seemed to be a metaphor while its history only entertained three situations, wars, negotiations, and seductions. The rest was only make-believe.

(Masked buffoonery)

'Purple-robed and pauper-clad, Raving, rotting, money-mad;'
BYRON RUFUS NEWTON

Daily, wagons of refuge could be seen crossing the Tibur via cabled ferry so as not to cause traffic jams on the pontus Aemilius and the old wooden pontus Sublicius. Pontus Fabricius and pontus Cestius were now off limits to all commercial traffic, anyway. Refuge dump sites had first been organized by concerned citizens back in the days of the kingdom, before the republic. Amor may not have minimized all obstacles in order to efficiently rule over an empire, but it wasn't wanting when it came to providing running water and sewage disposal, street cleaning. The manure removal from tens of thousands of horses alone ate greedily into Amor's city budget. And never mind imperial general order of house-cleaning where chaos once ruled beyond the empire's boarders — such as in Germanika, Nordcum, Dacia, and other eastern fly-blown stations which were now making inroads towards Amor. Why, it was the Amorans who showed the world how to provide cities with fresh water right where they are without having to move the city to the source, which was what others were more apt to do when the water ran out. They engineered conduits and viaducts that transported large volumes of fresh water over hill and dale and across many, many miles from the snowy mountains and wooded lakes to the valley cities for their daily use. Engineers of this fashion, who were capable of such deeds in this otherwise squalid and disorganized world of the hoi polloi, were a denarii a dozen here in Amor.

At the north side of the city were large charcoal plants. This industry had reduced wood into this favourable substance for cooking. And in every house and every tenement building throughout the city people cooked on open fires that burned wood, rubbish, offal filth, and charcoal. This all caused a great deal of smoke, ash and acrid smell. And men lived here and walked the streets. They breathed in the air and dreamed their dreams, generation after generation. They greeted each other on the street and shared their ideas. Termed the Big Smoke, to Dyfed it was the Big Stink.

During the day crowds swirled around Dyfed as he went about his eight hours of work. Normally, his remaining eight hours that one needs to devote towards family and/or recreation before the allotted eight hours of rest and sleep, he kept privately to himself. His family was the tight circle of he and Marg, Cato, Karatakos and Morgant. This also include Galhad when he came home on holidays from school. They all lived at the large and rambling estate on the south slope of the Equitine hill. Nowadays, thought, it seemed Marg was absent a great deal and that Galhad's visits were becoming extended causing him to be idly under foot here in the city of Amor for longer and longer spells (probably up to no good in the dens of iniquity that festered throughout the city for young men such as he) while spending lesser and lesser time at boarding school in Lugdunum.

Dyfed would dine early with Marg and Galhad (when they were around), then just before the evening he set out for his nightly prowl so as to fix even more vivid images into his head which inspired his old desire to high-jack Amor's Idea and fashion it into the ideal for maintaining the golden mean. Here he met and meandered mean streets that remained as crowded as before but the genre of networking and human exchange had become something of a masked, costume-open-aired festival. Here propriety was sometimes replaced with baboonery that sometimes replicated or even out matched the baboonery of the establishment. It was a strange microcosm wherein plots were hatched with jesters, fools, and even puppets acting as though they were philosophising orators of note who should be listened to. At first, sometimes-even Dyfed got confused, but owing to his impeccable computation of logic, he certainly faired better with his judgement in this than the multitudes did. At first he thought the people at play with this were funning…putting the dons on…taking the piss, so to speak. Some were, but these dangerous folks often quickly disappeared, sometimes on their own accord, but mostly not. These theatrical people were different than the average, run-of-the-mill Julius, or whomever. And there were two kinds of theatrical folks; one sort were strictly for amusing entertainment while the others were pointedly dead serious about pulling out the stitches of the social fabric. Pending ones' intellect and sense of awareness, these were either dangerous or desirably supporting and favourable. It was these latter who happened to be capable of providing a different form of comic relief.

However, all these complicated and hard to understand tones of third density vibrations buzzing around, this caused natural vibrational effects that affected the captive audience at large. Unbeknown to the establishment's guards and Nightwatchmen, their knee-jerk reactions generally compounded the confusion that caused an abrupt questioning among the citizens of Amor. Evil was often anthropomorphized here, and not just spoofed as one might think. One time, a man replicating a figure straight from an Alexei von Jawlensky painting furtively appeared suddenly out of a the darkening and delirious crowd waving a purple hand. To Dyfed's great distaste the man cupped his mouth to Dyfed's ear with that same brandy-wine coloured logo hand and rasped the name of Moloch into his consciousness a nano-second before he and his voice were snatched away into a void of nothingness by the disgustingly smelly whirlwind around him. To Dyfed's mind this was a lot more than carnival that was happening here. It was akin to the Hispania fandango on microdot and the wild side of super nova Livia Octavia the street dancer extraordinaire high on over proof. It was as unlikely a body of entertainment that could be glimpsed virtually nowhere else on earth but here. The euphoria of stimulation that was had by all reminded Dyfed of a blessed Diana wine festival overflowing with the juice of distilled moonshine which (when spiked with the combination of the poisonous effects of Datura and the nightshade-like stupor of Atropa belladonna) was the House of Dionysus' signature drink. This was adult entertainment at it best. The prerequisite, however, was not adultness of age but adultness of virtue and of propriety, never mind filial piety, of which very little was evident at this phase of Dyfed's on-going freak show.

Dyfed worked hard and generally retired early. He also rose very early, allowing him enough hours of alertness to attend to those things that allowed him to grow spiritually toward the ultimate conclusion of every life. This was first. The second was duty. His duty was to excel at his profession. Generally his relationship with the hoi polloi was strictly professional, and nothing more, though he did devote time in managing to aid and abet many of the latter and nudge them in directions he knew to be favourable to them and their society as a whole.

According to imperial standing orders for the regular day, two hours after sundown, just before the city's official Nightwatchmen were set free to slip their leash, the denizens of the fanciful frock and crock would dry off from the baths, finish up sucking on the pipe of Morpheus and to slip home to their dinners and beds. Apparently, this semi-slumber at the pillow until dawn was to add pretention towards any pedological discovery or disclosure: It was the part where you awaken, that they appeared to have failed to grasp or at least lost the understanding thereof. The state of being awake is of utmost importance here.

Dyfed's mentors were quite against his participation in Amor's spontaneous and unlicensed nightlife, but they recognised that though a light-year older and mature than Galhad, he was still young and boisterous. Anyway, the need to know about anything that was afoot here at the heart of the empire was needier. To know (after all) was Dyfed's career.

The Nightwatchmen worked twenty-four seven under the authority of the guards who were protected by the imperial seal of authority. The Turn-keys on the other hand who included justices of the peace, were the triumviri capitals who oversaw prisons and executions, but did not include police whose superintendents who were considered officers of the Nightwatchmen. The chiefs over both the Turnkeys and the Nightwatchmen was (of course) the empire's top man, the emperor himself. He was in charge of everything and although he needed to delegate to certain magistrates and senators he trusted, he had to be very careful. Wise and strong emperors kept the guards close by. In his case they were like family to the emperor. Each one served the other. There had been many an emperor unseated because the guards had switched their allegiance to support another imperial contender, often a nephew or cousin of the failing or insane emperor who needed to be toppled from his perch for one reason or another. Reasons were not hard to find. This was often for someone's gain that promised a trickle down effect to grease the palms of the guards. The contenders to the throne and other high postings were always within the highest of the higher echelon of Amoran society. This condition or state of affairs and status quo, Dyfed was to learn, was not to change greatly, even over the millennia. The establishments ever present Royal Guards were nothing more than glorified Nightwatchmen.

Where the guards' duty stopped, the legions of Amor took over. But the legions were not permitted by law to enter the City of Amor unless invited by the emperor. This rarely happened other than to celebrate the death of an emperor or a great victory that had occurred somewhere within the empire. Furthermore, this latter event centred around the emperor who invited all the citizens of the city to celebrate with him while he decorated and promoted brilliant generals and sundry soldiers for their out-standing performances. And the accent here was on great victories, for victories were expected and thought (at least at the civvie-street level) to be the norm. In effect, the invitation for a legion to march into the city with its spoils of victory (along with a subdued king or chieftain) to the spirited cheers of the gladdened people was based on sound a public relations that was meant to guarantee the army and the citizens' glorification of the system and the emperor in particular. It was a form of indemnity on the emperor's behalf toward his people for allowing him plenipotentiary privilege and power over the people and that of the legions: it was power he meant to hold on to with all his might. This protocol was also to continue for millennia.

But other than for treachery, such as when a legion backed a popular and famous general who they wished to place on the throne by scrapping the incumbent, the legions kept their distance; even when popular generals came to confer with the emperor and his magistrates or perhaps to visit with their family. Most of the generals, and even emperors (these days) were not local, whose families were often elsewhere. Many were from the provinces such as Gaul, as was Emperor Claudius, or from Hispania or Serbia, as was the present emperor. In any case, the Guards ruled the roost under the emperor in Amor. Although they didn't interfere very often at the aforementioned civvie-street level, the Guards (an elite and senior cadré made up of Nightwatchmen officers) who outranked the run of the mill Nightwatchmen per sé, controlled the rackets lavished on the populace. Their job description was to keep their eyes and ears on the people night and day and report all comings and goings to their senior officers or liaison officer. In reality they sometimes baited unrest through fights and strikes, even runs on banks, and were known to have caused market shortages in the past. The volition followed by action to undertake this form of manipulation did not originate with the Nightwatchmen themselves. For these types of men were not that smart or resourceful, all of which needed intelligence and imagination. Nightwatchmen were exceedingly short of this. It was instituted, of course, by the rare variety of intelligent aristocrats or by the intelligent and ruthless outlaws vying for position and acceptance. These were no pranks by men drunk on wine or authority. They were well laid plans of rich and powerful schemers. Normally, the Nightwatchmen were employed to have a profile and to be seen, but also they were to break up fights in the street, compromise and put the run on illicit sexual behaviour, gaming entertainment, and any black market sales by organized amateur entrepreneurs without licence and initiate false flag disruptions in an effort to separate the bills receivable accounts of these outlaws and find the opportunities to place them instead into the hands of their established competition. This was the establishment per sé, those who ran all of the above with Nightwatchmen protection. They were folks such as Furius Claudius. After all, these were the folks who could be trusted to contribute the most to the Nightwatchmen's annual pension fund and paid for the march of the marriage of Mars and Venus parade every new year's eve on the vernal equinox. Anyway, when all was said and done, the evening of an abused day of shenanigans would end with claw-back, such as a steep fines, or dungeons to culprits charged with breaking the emperor's peace and arrested, while other folks underwent a thorough fleecing before being sent home to their dinners and beds before midnight. If serious enough, such as perversion of a sexual nature or a gruesome murder, the targeted culprit would be killed by strangulation, after his arms and legs were broken then pulled and wrenched free from his body. This punitive result was (again) only at the civvie-street level, mind you such as the common hoi polloi. Those just beneath the imperial family and their ilk roamed at will like a current in the river or the gusts in the wind performing atrocious crimes often without any punitive result and kept living in their comfortable palaces with their arms and legs intact and a head on their shoulders.

(Zhongyong the unwobbling pivot)

> *"If there were no debts in our money system,
> there wouldn't be any money."*
>
> **MARRINER STODDARD ECCLES**
>
> (BANKER, ECONOMIST CHAIRMAN OF THE FEDERAL RESERVE BOARD)

With time marching on, Amor, now the great light of the western civilization, was, as always, in a provocative state of being. To Dyfed it was a material galaxy firmly grounded in the third dimension which had only a veneer of sophistication and technical know-how compared to the ancient Hyperborean masters and (as it now has turned out) like-mined transcending migrationists from other parts of the world. Who knows where they all may have originated? However, it still provided him with great amusement. The city had fountains overflowing with fresh water tunnelled in by underground pipes. These lead pipes also provided domestic running water to communal stations in town squares. Also there were the lavish public baths in the well-heeled, scaled up town addresses to which the rich gravitated that were so loved, along with the squalid neighbourhood baths in the down at heel postal districts. Then there were goldfish and lily-pad ponds, the domestic garden streams and fake waterfalls to keep replenished.

Half a million working horses were at large in and around the city. Each one had to be housed in stables and needed to be watered and fed. Warehouses full of hay that was barged in from the distant fields abounded everywhere. There was no grazing facility here. The earthy smell of the creatures of this species (Equus ferus caballus) quite gently, and not obnoxiously, constantly permeated the city. Yet the streets were kept clean and manure from these animals was quickly removed and used for fertilizer. The scent of that distinct animal under pinned the smell of Amor's streets along with that of the attending men caught in this time-frame reality. What with the stinking scent of fish mongers' gutters, the abattoir's acrid effluence that belched from their chimneys and spewed from their waste drainage pipes as swarms of flies blanketed the raw and filthy offal awaiting to fuel the charcoal ovens used to fervour the bakers' dozen, the covered and open markets with their pens of pigs and chickens mixing in gerrymandering deception with the brilliant waterfall of fragrance from the millions of bright and tender flowers that grew in the soil that lay under the hot sun; all of these were abreast of the impish and flitting image one got of the spirit of Amor herself. But if you looked for it or directly at it, you could never even have a hope of seeing it.

Folks walked everywhere when not riding in a chariot, wagon, or carriage along the thoroughfares of the city. Apart from the imperial grounds that were off limits to just about everybody, guarded along the perimeters by day and night watchmen, the hoi polloi moved hither and yon in and around the city at will. They were headed for, or returning from, the public baths, the libraries, and a relaxing hour in the public parks. They visited the fora and the forum; they walked the embankment and rushed to the horse and chariot racetrack. This was called Hippodrome (hippo being the word for horse in the tongue of the ancient Hellas who controlled the civilization preceding

Amor, and dromos meaning course). They flocked to the Colossal (that gigantic, semi covered arena, that not so peace loving gargantuan that dominated the skyline of Amor) for some of the greatest depictions of high definition reaction of motion theatre produced and wonderfully choreographed that was ever performed by man.

Though technically out of his true element as a prince of the grove, Dyfed had managed well for himself here. Steeped in the mysteries about fixed connections that each and every one of us have with cosmic vibrations which permeate the endless universe throughout beginningless time, he felt for the stupid and ignorant who through fear (mainly) grasped at desire and want. Being ensconced in the sedentary life of Amor had no negative effect upon his attributes. Dyfed was cognizant to universal immortality the way others were to hunger. For this reason he applied himself with calculated attention to every detail that washed over him. Dyfed was a man who paid close attention to every seemingly miniscule and insignificant event that over took him via one form or another throughout each of the days of his life when others ignored them at their own peril. He loved life. He loved all the living things and their personalities that he encountered in this phenomenon. This was his path. He shone by example and, as such, unknowingly became a teacher by example. Folks like him who follow this path, the path of duty, are a superior type of person who are cautious indeed. Not all of them are Hyperborean masters. Some are folks who have attracted the attention of these masters who then influence them. And those that walk this mean show no contempt for their inferiors. Such a man or woman always does what is natural according to her or his status in the world and never exceeds their natural order. This path is called the doctrine of the un- fluctuating pivot, the don't-think-twice axis, or zhongyong[34].

The goal of the mean is to maintain balance and harmony and direct the mind to a state of constant equilibrium. The mean is relative to us. As Aristotle explains it, the mean is equally distant from either extreme, which is one and the same for everyone. But the mean that is relative to us is neither too much nor too little, and this is not the same for everyone. In the same way one with understanding in any matter will avoid excess and deficiency, and search out and choose the mean that is relative to us.

This was the path of the most honourable. It is the mean upon which his people, Violet in particular, had set him on. The most honourable were those who must possess tangible and intangible wisdom, great knowledge and esteemed virtue. To have this means understanding the mean. The only problem was that the other large brained, upright walking mammals who hadn't the benefit of the Hyperborean masters' enlightenment were far from being honourable. This latter majority had hugely complicated multi egos with attitudes that were busy constantly constructing fantasy universes of their own around themselves that impinged upon others and not paying a jot of attention to what really is. This was what caused the biggest headaches, not only for Dyfed and the *pack*, but also for the entirety of humankind in general who were just trying to get on and through their lives. Collectively (for the record), the former were the cause for all the misery and suffering that manifested on the face of the earth. This condition has been innate in humanity from sometime since the beginning of the Age of Ages, and most especially during the last and fourth Age of man. This situation was untenable for a fully conducive continuation of fifth dimension beings remaining here in the third dimension. It made the situation dangerous for them and frightening. It was the reason

---

34 Zhong: meaning bent neither one way nor another. Yong: represents the unchanging.

that the Hyperborean masters, along with all of their families and friends who had transcended, had pulled out of the third dimension holiday venture mode here, destroying the evidence of their resort villas such as the one on the Isle of Peace among many others. Logical ideals had so far failed to deactivate the situation among the hoi polloi due, in all evidence, to the mentality of the Haploids. You can talk logic until you are blue in the face but until you have a grasp of reality based on theorems tried by observation, reality will escape you. Buddha, Confucius, Lao Tzu and Bodhidharma made a life of riddling the reasoning of reality for the benefit of those gifted enough to comprehend: so had Antisthenes, Anacharsis, Socrates and Diogenes, in their own way. Despite all their disadvantages Dyfed knew that the restless dis concordance stirring in the spirit of the hoi polloi could be moulded and trained to mirror the universe. Indeed, it must be moulded and trained. It was what he was trying to do here in Amor, along with Morgant and Cato and some others who were known as the *pack*. Long ago (within the present age) the hoi polloi had not fully grasped the doctrine of the unwobbling pivot[35] without some help, but with that help they certainly managed to expand on it. That is to say simply observe and not interfere even for their benefit. For from early days the hoi polloi have strived forward while living in social units of some form or other in order to fill their Idea. Gradually (as they prospered) they had expanded.

Then they over extended and depleted their resources only to wither away into the dust. Then they had to move and find fresh resources to exploit and cause to wither. This was accomplished to a Tee in the great river valley civilizations such as the Indus, the Euphrates, and to some lesser extent the Nile. Only the Yellow River civilization seemed to dodge the bullet due to its rich glacial sediment.

Traditionally, the cultural makeup of any given society is provided by and influenced of mythos. Mythos is the elixir of the source of authority, it deals with the traditional gods of the people, the history from where the people originated, their language, their imaginations, their art, their inventions, their industry, their practices, their hopes their dreams, their mores and the stories of the clan (tribe or racial groupings) and the ruling elements thereof which defines their social culture — the society. It is who we are. As the civilization's societies continue to advance, some of the elements within the mythos crystalize and form the beginnings of logos. The meaning of logos here is a reasoning that sets off an evolution within the society. This is meant to stabilize the society within the overriding culture itself. Unfortunately, it has failed with us. It is mostly the product of itself which set out in turn to seek out greater expedience and in weeding out superfluous primitive superstitions and lancing useless carbuncles by evolving methods, mores and morals into a science which is a method of trial and proof whose authority, unlike that of mythos, is based on positive and effective results which enhance the social element for the benefit of continuing the process for the betterment of the human society. Soon, this logos begins (or is supposed to begin) to take on a rather different identity than the exuberance of the social culture per sé. One of the more important factors within the social element is governance; how a society is run and controlled. Many methods of governance are available but to select a tried and proven method that is socially acceptable and most expedient over all, is one for all and all for one, a collective mean. It lifts society up to the highest form. It produces over all the greatest happiness and promotes

---

35 Thank you Mr Ezra Pound, and you too Master Confucius.

the highest form of social security. It is totally inclusive and shuns any exclusiveness. Its logos are called Beneficial Social Order for the Common Good (BSOCG).

Hyperborean Masters mathematically proved this concept long ago. Almost all of the other methods of governance have socially failed our societies miserably. They did this by promoting only a tiny percentile of the entire populace into a class known as *the power elite* whose actions are always to ensure that they themselves remain in place and retain their positions as lords of authority and due process over all the hoi polloi who they see as being beneath them in every way. These hoi polloi are then placed and kept away from the elite. When it came to any form of privileges to do with law and life-styles, never mind equal pay and benefits, these entitlements were scaled down. Even the hoi polloi themselves could be divided up into separate classes based not on their happiness or their compassion, their talent or even their intelligence, but on their meagre material worth. Furthermore, they too were encouraged to look down upon those others who had less wealth than they. Although nobody had heard the starting gun or had shown up at the same time for the meet, somehow it was all a competition. But it was a competition that brought out the worst in everybody. Called Social Order, it was Social Disorder.

This was a poignant problem when it came to administering and according equitable justice. The laws of the land define Justice and in practice the law has always found it difficult to cross class lines. For the easiest method here is to out price the cost of justice beyond the reach of the majority of the working classes. Few societies have shown promise, for the easiest method is not to have class divisions at all. This is where the aforementioned logos of a good common social order come in. Unfortunately, the debilitations with which the hoi polloi have been programmed now makes this almost impossible. But it was the former materialistic, class conscious, out pricing justice for the poor, with varied totalitarian methodology of governance that, in the end, was what Amor had invested in here. And this is what Dyfed and company were up against. But there were good examples for a decent society at large despite this, and examples that were in living memory. The one that stood out of course was the Athenian politics of democracy. Athens democratizes their social culture to prevent it from running rampant. Democracy was seen to be the natural logos of governance that was attracted to the rising logos factions of rising socialism within their social mythos. It was a natural fit. This flavour of socialism briefly flourished here with democracy. Democracy itself was (and is) only able to flourish with a beneficial social order for the common good. This is true socialism. It was a no brainer. So what happened to Amor? At least the Hellenic folks gave it the good old college try. It ultimately failed, of course, yet it perseveres still in the collective Idea of people who believe in having free will and the opportunity to learn from the mistakes they will make. All this as best they can in the hope that one day they will learn how to free will correctly for the benefit of all.

It should be pointed out, however, that it wasn't the Hellene folks of Athena who initially invented this form of democratic governance nor were they the first to promoted it. And as far as free will was concerned, very little of that was going around then. Anyway, the Trmmli people more than half a millennium earlier than the current era first developed democratic governance. The concept of their Federal League, as it was called, was a marriage between the Trmmli's mythos and the natural result of logos creeping into their culture and governance as a necessity for their happiness and security. It grew from a wish for secure commonality. The League included a number of city-states within their land. We know this because of information provided by Strabo and Livy, and more recently from Gaius Plinius Secundus[36].

The League consisted of twenty-three member cities that elected representatives to the Assembly (Synedrion). The largest six cities — the river and bay city Yellow, the Aegean coastal cities of Patara and Pinara, the mountain top city of Tlos, the White Sea coastal city Myra and the city Olympos — each held the maximum of 3 votes. The Assembly elected the chief representative (Lyciarch) and other federal officers. Minor magistrates and jurors in the federal courts were elected from each city proportional to its voting power. The Assembly building (Bouleuterion or Synedrion) for the league was housed at the important port of Patara in present day Anatolia at the mouth the Yellow river (near west), renamed by the folks of Hellas as river Xanthros (their name for Yellow). The port of Patara lay about five Amoran miles downstream of Leda, the chief cult centre (mythos) of the Trmmli. This site was set upon a rampart on the east bank close to Leda (Latoon) and was the Trmmli's most ancient and prominent city-state named Yellow (renamed Xanthros). The name came from the colour of the water and not from their name of some river god. It is unknown whether the Trmmli folks even had a god for their river, as most people who were contemporaneous to them seemed to have had. Their most important god (actually goddess) was Leto (pronounced lay-to) or maybe Leda (lay-da) from lada[37], and was the Trmmli word for woman. However, one thing is certain. What those other people who were contemporaneous to the Trmmli's folks didn't have and the Trmmli did, was an ideal and long lasting social democratic order with common privileges and equality before the law and equal opportunity. Maybe the other folks had no ideal real ladies, either. The Trmmli did, or at least the beginnings of one of each. They passed both concepts on to the Hellenic peoples (Doric in particular) who introduced what we now call Western Philosophy into Europa.

Anyway, this League of the Trmmli held extensive rights over all the cities of the their people. We know the land of these folks as Lukka (Lycia) whose language was of the Luwian family. In the late Bronze Age the empire of the Hittites and the empire of Khem described the Trmmli as rebels, pirates and raiders. But what they didn't note in their record was the Trmmli's enlightenment and inclination toward social democratic organization. This was something that neither ancient, the modern Khem, nor even the Trmmli's relatively close neighbours, the Hittites, ever stumbled on. Ancient Khem records describe the Trmmli and their ancient land of Lycia as allies of the Hittites, and Lukka may as well have been a member state of the Assuwa league circa 1250 BCE. The League, Dyfed knew, was the first known democratic union in modern history, and existed long before the light of Athena and the Hellenic civilization. It wasn't clear, though, just how advanced their socialism was. It appeared to Dyfed that historically a certain composition of uniformity seems to eventually become a major root of all social evils that advances the kingdom or state in question into fascism. Creating a society rigidly environment controlled by uniformly narrow-minded conservatives and other very stupid and dangerous people was a well-trodden trend, it seemed. A point in question was the once optimistic and carefree Amor as an example, he thought. Anyway,

---

36   Known commonly as Pliny the Elder, this man had recently died trying unsuccessfully to flee Stabiae by ship that became enveloped by the wind and fury of a pyroclastic surge from the erupting Mt. Vesuvius (year 855 of the Olympiad or 79 CE).

37   The resemblance to our word *lady* is obvious.

later, the Argivian Dorians among others came to this neck of Anatolia and made it their home.

In any case, this was the template Dyfed wanted in order to act to ensure the durability of the fifth age: but with much more developed social democratic aspect. Indeed, one may ask: What (in the end) will the fifth age brings for this race of human hoi polloi if democratic socialism doesn't become advanced? Social democracy, therefore, is the mean and the preverbal end is coming towards us at a ferocious speed.

In the course of his discussion about aretê (virtue or excellence) Aristotle developed the doctrine of the mean in Book II of the Nicomachean Ethics. All excellence, he stated, has what makes it good, and enables it to perform its function well. If this is true in all cases, then, the excellence of a human being will be that disposition which makes him a good human being and which enables him to perform his function well, perhaps with or without the guidance of law but especially without having uniformity control him; and that's the thing that separates him from the beasts of the wild. Such functions or characteristic activity, he argued, is a way of living consistently with the exercise of the psyche's capacities in accordance with reason. Excellence, he then said, is that condition which best suits us to perform those activities which are distinctively human. Hence an active exercise of one's psyche's capacities in accordance with excellence that will involve the best life for a human being. And where does the mean come in here? Aristotle tells us that excellence is a settled disposition determining choice, involving the observance of the mean relative to us, this being determined by reason.

His own race had taught Dyfed that the fifth age is the last age before the dawn of the ever return: The latter being the non-Age of reception and total flexibility. This non-Age is where the hourglass of endless eternity is turned over and beginingless eternity replicates itself once more all over again. People of the dharma who still hold this to be true, call this last phase of eternity — k'un (khwan) (…not to be confused with kun, the third hexagram of the I Ching [Yi jing — pronounced ee-dgeng]). K'un can also refer to that same phase of eternity in the individual life of a man or woman as it can to the human race in general. And directly before K'un comes the hexagram Po while directly after K'un come Fu, the return of the light. But we don't know what or where that will be; we only know it is next.

From his showroom suite on the heights of the Capitoline Hill Dyfed looked out over top of the Marcus theatre that was directly below him and out across the Tibur River towards the south. Almost directly before him was Superbus Island that lay centre stream. On this side of the embankment were what was once the docks of the old market that ran along its water's edge downstream toward the temple of Portunus in the distance. Above that and beside him (at his same height to his left) were the buildings of the imperial palace while over and behind him on Capitoline Hill was the much-revered Jovian Temple.

With the Empire in full swing and galloping along on fast steeds, emperors came and went now at an even more furious rate than fashions did. The last was Emperor Vespasianius. Some like Vespasianius were bold and full of vim and vigour while others were frail and defensively pious. Most were greedy, egotistical psychopaths who were exceedingly dangerous. Their normal agenda as emperor was to maintain the establishment's current system of privilege and support of the wealthiest citizens' business strategy at all costs. This — so they believed — maintained the emperor' power. There was the occasional emperor that was marked with scruples. These hopefuls — emperors like Markus Aelius Aurelius Verus Kysar or Flavius Claudius Julianus the Apostate — never truly panned out. As each new emperor assumed command over the tax wealth of Amor, each tried their hand at something in order to leave their pitiful mark upon the Empire's history and the world. Like Vespasianus and Hadrianus, most built something for the enjoyment of all — some solid object to take up space and impress in some way — rather than some encompassing policy of legislated largess for all citizens to enjoy. And it wasn't just emperors who caused these developments to happen, even rich family houses got into the act as well. An exquisite great hall for elaborate public and private banquets was built on one side of the Palatine by the House of Apuleius: it was named — not astonishingly — the Apuleius Grand Banquet Hall. Not to be outdone, the House of Theodosius Music Stadium was soon completed in the Field of Mars, as was the Catulus Bath House Spa. Other enterprises took shape in the form of theatres, brothels, and amusement parks in the city sections of Aventinus, Caelis and Velia. Sometimes these houses formed a consortium to compete with the emperor and the senate's ability to raise the huge funds needed to complete these vast projects.

Of course many temples were being dedicated to gods and goddesses, and these were quickly thrown up, along with cheap and measly copies of the city of Amor's Coliseum that began to spring up all over the Empire. But the greatest of the Amoran jewels remained here in the city of Amor. This was the mythos of Jupiter enshrined atop the Capitoline Hill. In truth, unlike the Parthenon in the City of Athena, most of Amor's lolly was housed in the private banks in the Forum.

There was another such venture called the Brotherhood of Industry and Commerce Union Hall that began to take shape on the eastern end of the Palatine, not too far from Dyfed's once ritzy Hill residence. And though quite modest in spatial area compared to others around about, the BICUH daily haemorrhaged silver denarii by the wagonload. Obviously, this was Dyfed's venture although he was careful not to mark or imprint the House of Lucifer anywhere on its edifice as he had done so on his bank and business offices. The purpose of this aforementioned organization was to bring in codes for standards of expedience and simplicity, safety and fair wage, along with equality and recourse to complaint and redress in all matters concerning industry and commerce which also included labour in general. But under Dyfed's orders it also threw money — as earlier stated, by the wagonload — not only at the model of its own advocacy (fine construction standards in addition to a high minimum wage — continually pushed the construction costs skywards), but also to influence and bring contractors who employ tradesmen and labourers and businessmen who hire scribes, accountants and other professionals, into the fold. It was a brotherhood because women in general, apart from powerful, rich and important women, had no status whatsoever to speak of within or without the Empire, generally: Especially if they weren't married and didn't have a husband to protect and support them.

Of course, the women of the emperor's family along with the families of powerful and rich senators were above the people of the hoi polloi. The same could be said for Marg, too, and even for Dyfed and Morgant, along with Cato his friend, but their volitions led to a different karma than of the majority of the Amoran high society. Many of the old established families were morally conservative, indeed, prudish to some extent, like the populace at large was. These folks took great care of their womenfolk. They also distained ostentatious displays of vulgarity and of sexual licentiousness, and they often strove to keep the actions of a truant family member under close wraps. The socially accepted mores of sexuality of the time were not an issue with Dyfed, or with Marg, but they certainly were for the majority of the Amoran folks. In the end, folks are folks, though, who have only one common enemy, the vulgar rich, the entitled greedy, and the Ideas of the psychopathic destroyers of all that is happy to others. These then are purveyors of suffering. The trick under their program is not to be a consumer.

The establishment cult of Pax Amor remained in its semi permanent state of flux during these early years. Nor did it seem to anyone (certainly not to Dyfed) that the Ideas, which embodied the capitalistic and psychopathic expressions of its nature, could be easily altered even by geological game-changers that shifted the stars, the sun and the moon, and cast the world of men under the feet of all of their creator/destroyer gods of paganism. Nor was there any likelihood of them warming toward the proclivity of Jain dharma or even Buddha dharma's stratagem. However, momentarily anyway, the move in that direction was being thwarted by the environmental might of the new finagled and latter-day definition of the god Saturn (Kronus) — son of Sky — all conjured up allegorically, of course. This cult's deity was referred to as the god of the House or Lodge of Abram, the same god (apparently) who Jeshua Adon called father. Although it must be said that the soldiers of the Empire had a tendency toward the Lodge of Mithra while some of its philosopher types leaned towards the Lodge of Stoism. Others sought out the Lodge of Samothrace, the Lodge of the Mysteries of Orpheus and even the Lodge of Freemasons. Meanwhile many in the Empire began to suddenly take note of this aforementioned devotion to the Lodge of Abram while all the while the aristocrats struggled to put the kybosh on any and everything that wasn't pagan.

But four-eyed Argos (Panoptes or all-seeing) hadn't fallen sleep after all, it turned out. For the chief priestess of Mother Earth, entreated by her mistress, was (as we will see) eventually to summon Poseidon, Thor, and Zeus (along with their consorts) to a vigorous ceremony which included a light show along with a whole lot of shake, rattle and roll down at the kingdom hall for one and all. But now we are ahead of ourselves again. And that brings us to one of a number of phenomena which were unfolding at this time.

(The streets of mean: by Parasolo)

'In the police you will see the dirty work of empire at close quarters.'
GEORGE ORWELL

Why should excellence or virtue involve the observance of a mean? The notion of the mean, and that of the observance of the mean, would have been familiar to those who attended Aristotles' lectures. They were at the conceptual centre of the most advanced and sophisticated science of the day, medicine. Aristotle's father was a physician, and medical concepts and examples played an important and widely recognized role in the philosophizing of Aristotle's day. Health was believed to lie in a balance of powers, in a mixture so constituted that none of its constituent elements eclipsed the others. The author of the Hippocratic treatise On Breaths Aristotles writes; "opposites are cures for opposites. Medicine is in fact addition and subtraction, subtraction of what is in excess, addition of what is wanting." Aristotle himself expresses this view, e.g. in the Topics. Of course it does for unity, the emergence of a living existence or God, is always comprised of opposites that are equally balanced while the motion toward equilibrium is the flux of life. Therefore, proper balance or proportion makes for health, lack of it for disease just as it makes something from being non-existent into becoming existent, or the quickened dead, as they say.

Aristotle imports this way of thinking into his account of ethical excellence or excellence of character. Bodily strength and health are destroyed by excess and deficiency. Too much food, or too much exercise, are bad for health, just as too little food or exercise are. The same holds in ethical matters: Here too excellence is so constituted as to be destroyed by excess and deficiency.

Bodily health is a matter of observing a mean between extremes of excess and deficiency. Further, Aristotle says, this provides an apt visible illustration of an invisible truth about ethical health. Excellence of any kind, Aristotle says, aims at the mean. Excellence of character is concerned with emotions and acts, in which there can be excess or deficiency or a mean. For example, one can be frightened or bold, feel desire or anger or pity, and experience pleasure and pain generally, either more or less than is right, and in both cases wrongly; while to have these feelings at the right time, on the right occasion, toward the right people, for the right purpose and in the right manner, is to feel the best amount of them, which is the mean amount -- and the best amount is of course the mark of excellence. Likewise, in acts there can be excess, deficiency and a mean.... Hence excellence is a mean state in the sense that it aims at the mean.

A person aiming at a target can miss to the right, to the left, above, below; a crooked shot can glance off the target, etc. To hit the mark one must land a shot within a relatively small, more or less precisely defined, area. Just so, Aristotle suggests, what is excellent and commendable to do is definite and limited. There is a correspondingly vast, relatively unlimited area for wrongs and shots that miss the mark:

Missing the mark is possible in many ways while success can be had only one way (which is why it is easy to err and hard to succeed -- easy to miss the mark and hard to hit it). This in the sense that badness is a form of the indefinite (to use Pythagorean terms) and goodness being a form of the definite Now while hitting the mark is in this sense a much more precise matter than missing it, there is still room for variation within the shots that hit the mark. More than one shot can hit the bulls-eye of a good-sized target, and all such hits are scored the same. And a shot need not hit the exact centre of the bulls-eye to be an excellent one. In the same way, Aristotle's simile suggests, virtue rarely demands a single precisely determined act, or an emotional reaction of a particular intensity, duration, frequency, etc. It rather demands that one's acts or emotions fall somewhere within a more or less precisely delineated range.

For example, the person who flees from every danger is cowardly; the person who does not flee from anything is rash. What is courageous, then, falls somewhere between these extremes; courage is "preserved by the observance of the mean". The same is true of temperance; what is temperate lies in a mean between the extremes of excessive enjoyment of sensual pleasures and deficient enjoyment of such pleasures. Similar things can be said for each virtue, so Aristotles believed. There are important differences among the dispositions which Aristotles calls virtues; but each virtue involves the observance of a mean between extremes. One extreme consists in some sort of excess while another in some sort of deficiency. Our task in trying to be good is to find these means and avoid these opposed extremes.

(Flavius Valerius Constantius Macaronius)

'There is never a democracy that did not commit suicide.'
JOHN ADAMS

And the clear morning light shone upon Amor. Her facades and marble columns fastened together by the empolion and polas method learned from the men of Mycenae and the Dorians (early men of Hellas) glistened in the sparkling air. Statues were raised above the colourful canopies, gardens all brightly shining and the tread of feet stamping this way and that. All roads, it seemed, did lead here to Amor. Her empire now stretched from Judah in the east, Khem to the south, and all the way to the Albionian/Alban border in the north whose demarcation in part was the gated barricade known today as Hadrianus' fence. And with the advent of the wise men from the east, trade even flowed from strange and mysterious kingdoms and other dominions that wended their way towards the empire's borders. The usual conveyance by choice (or not) was by camel and ass then by merchant ships, some of whom Dyfed owned or financed their construction. And along those roads came merchandise from Persia, Inja, and even from the far off land of Ch'in in the Far East. Along with them came Nastika Sidd Sambahatti, the man from New Nanda. As a religious prophet of some kind he supported the Amoran soldier's attraction to the religion of Mithra. By way of a rant he elaborated upon this by suggesting that moral rewards were not the work of a divine creator/destroyer but the result of an innate moral order in the cosmos, a self-regulating mechanism of karma. He was quite popular for a time but he had an honourable competitor that eventually put Sambahatti asunder. Surprisingly, the competitor was long deceased leaving only his followers to fan the flames of his revolution of interpretation. His name had been Jeshua ben Joseph, though he was now referred to as the messiah and the saviour of humanity from some or another not quite understood original sin aspect that apparently had been recently invented by the priests proscribing the Jeshuan cult. Formerly Abramists, these folks had flooded into Amor primarily from Anatolia and the land of the Hellas.

And now Amor had a new emperor. He was Flavius Valerius Constantius Macaronius. He fell in line behind Hadrianus, Vespasianus and was a form of Vice Emperor to Eastern Emperor Diokles (Aurelius Valerius Diocletianus Augustus also known as Diocles) whose palace was in Byzas not Amor. Macaronius was a pompous, ambitious man. He was born in Dardania in the province of Moesia whose tongue was related to both the Illyrians and the Thraki-Dacians. He was unique in that he was one of now two emperors who ruled the Amoran Empire. Macaronius who had earlier been made governor of Dalmatia (an Amoran province just north of his birthplace) was then promoted to Amoran Emperor-West. It was here at Amor from which Macaronius Augustus ruled the western portion of the Empire only. Meanwhile, the dominant Amoran emperor (Diokles Augustus) ruled the remainder of the Empire from Byzas on the Bosphorus. This is because this powerful and clever emperor had earlier divided the Empire into halves and had taken the eastern portion for himself where he still remained fully in control. Although the latter competently ruled the eastern Empire, he also maintained certain influence here in the west while keeping any western emperor he placed there at arm's length from his own piece of the pie. Diokles was an intelligent man who hired and maintained two other intelligent men as advisors and minders who were often in attendance in Amor on official snooping and minding other people's business. These two were Saturday Borgia (now Sir Saturday Borgia) a former Olympic winner of the Stadium race who was a rich mercenary, formerly an Abramist, who had been taken prisoner by the Amorans from a Hellenic galley upon which he had been earlier imprisoned. Due to his skills the Amoran establishment quickly promoted him. The other man was Count Agenbite of Inwit, a recovering advocate and attorney at law now working part-time as an advisor to the curia in Amor. He was also advising Diokles.

As for Emperor Macaronius of the West, his primary objective now was to retain the Amoran status quo, as it was in order to profit thereby and keep many a senator in his pocket for good measure and for a rainy day. As well, he needed to find ways and means to be seen by the public at large as a moderator on behalf of the plebeian poor. For from his vantage point on high (as he saw it) the two antagonists whom he needed to placate were the privately privileged and the publicised plebeians. Naturally he was eventually to turn to Dyfed for help.

These aforementioned aristocrats and plebs were what caused the warp and woof in Emperor Macaronius' dilemmas in proficiently administering his own profit and most importantly his legacy. For reasons we don't have time to explore here, Macaronius (who as we have said was not indigenous to Italia) quickly became both suspicious and curiously impressed by Dyfed the more he heard of him and saw him over the fence and in places where business and high finances took place. The latter (it seemed to the emperor) had an exceedingly sharp intelligence that the emperor defined as alarming. In any case Diokles acknowledged that ability enabled Dyfed to profit easily within the system while maintaining an aura that attracted and commended Amoran aristocratic loyalty to him yet manage at the same time to retain a relatively low and unassuming profile which was (according to Macaronius) completely contradictory. The first condition was generally Dyfed's ability for divining: that is…to read the waters and win in matters of the choice that he subsequently made as a result. This benefited him financially. And it was here — in the latter named arena — where recently many of the pivotal rich were on a lamentable streak of loosing their toga. And in this even the emperor's fortune could be made or lost. And although Dyfed was from the province of Albion (a far flung region off among the cold sea fogs — and then some), there was about him — and those of his close companions — an aristocratic air that was subtle, even mysterious. And it was the mysteriousness about him that had spawned many a rumour that he was some kind of a wizard; or at least was an apprentice to one, maybe that gnome-like character that he follows around?

But a much greater chagrin to our hero, however, was that he quickly realized that Macaronius wanted to know more about him than Dyfed cared for him to know, or wanted to share with him. Soon, it came to the point where the emperor was forcing himself on the former with what seemed to be way too much Bon-Amie that was ungenuine and certainly more than Dyfed wanted.

Then one day the planets appeared in their most unfavourable position to each other. This calamity resulted in a breakout of runaway inflation within the Empire. It had started, if you recall, during the tenure of Vespasianus who had begun to water down the silver denarius. It had been the second watering down, the first had happened during the Social War during the Republic. A multitude of emperors that followed Vespasianius in succession continued to take the path of least resistance by not checking the rising market costs on which the poor masses depended. Emperor Macaronius made no expedient adjustment to that. And in addition, at the same time he introduced an increasingly heavy escalation of taxes. On top of that, the ranks of slaves labouring for the state (along with those other retched souls who were labouring for the private aristocratic houses) had by now ballooned to ridiculous proportions. And they weren't fairing well under the current economy. Neither were the farmers or the help throughout all the professions and trades. There was no intermediate class, or middleclass — as Dyfed was apt to call it — and this (he thought) was an economic oversight. The Plebs had few tools to fight the establishment but they could withhold their service of labour.

There was also the matter of repeated disobedience regarding matters of expedience among successive aristocrats who wore the toga of the Chamberlain of Amor. It was the job description of these men, along with their underlings, to be responsible for balancing the books for each province of the Amoran State; and this, combined with greed and corruption, compounded by a single entry bookkeeping system was how Dyfed (who predicted the situation) knew the Empire was sunk. It was not as though it hadn't been listing for quite some while, either. Macaronius, having a lavish and unhealthy over-respect for his own authority urged the Guards who were the elite of the Nightwatchmen to clamp down hard upon the citizens. This was just a few weeks before the popular *Gods of the Week* festival was to take place.

Suddenly, the latter reacted. Riots broke out which could easily be heard from Dyfed's suite at his Esquiline Hill residence. As it so happened, earlier on that same day while walking from his bachelor pad to his business in the Forum, Dyfed was intercepted by Imperial agents who quickly whisked him into an audience with the waiting emperor not far away on the steps of the building that housed the curia and close to the statue of Victoria. Macaronius then attempted to strong arm Dyfed to open his suites on the lower slope of Esquiline Hill on a scheduled day to receive an imperial visit from him and his imperial suite during the upcoming *festival of the gods of the week*. This was according to the tradition of hosting (sponsoring) a day of this week by imperial request. To be a host of the emperor who comes to the sponsor's palace on that day was supposed to be an honour. Many a rich man bribed officials and suck-holed whomever they could from here to a week from Thursday to be granted such an opportunity to host the emperor at their home. The day the emperor chose for him to sponsor was Mercury's Day. Dyfed, as courteous and engaging as could be, agreed wholeheartedly, even feigning an affable slight upon his person (accompanied by a brimming smile) that it took so long for his majesty the emperor to ask. He did, however, manage to change the venue from his secure Esquiline Hill home to his Capitoline Hill bachelor's residence, citing renovation at the former made it expediently impossible.

Dyfed sat pondering his tactic to counter the emperor's over familiarity towards him. He disliked the imposition of being forced to fund a day during this festival. So what that the emperor would personally pay him a visit at his suite on the day of the week he agreed to sponsor. Was this supposed to be some kind of reward? It was an imposition!

As he sat at his windowsill, below him the din from the swollen crowd strolling the river promenade on this evening after a working day of no work and an empty purse, he noticed that the crowd was like a swollen creek cascading down the slopes of a wooded mountain. On this evening the hoi polloi had finally boy-coted the theatre in protest of the Emperor's callous actions. This had brought out the actors and the cruel jesters who had more psychological pull upon the people nowadays than the monotonous stupor that prevailed from the senatorial curia or the pretorian ranks of the elite guards.

Morgant and Cato, who had been absent for some time, flew into town especially to help plan the strategy to be employed during the upcoming crisis that loomed high on Amor's horizon. They weren't much for third density festivals like the *Gods of the Week*, either. Marg had been back home with him for some time, though she too took her long absences. Upon her last return she had informed Dyfed that she had given birth to a son and that he, Dyfed, was the father. Dyfed, ecstatic over the news, bade her to send for the child for he wanted the child to be with the both of them here in Amor. But that goodly and still beautiful woman said that for now the child would remain beyond this world where he would be safe from the psychopathic tyrants that people out the political stage here at the present. Morgant, upon his arrival, brought the latest images of the child on his torc for Dyfed to behold and pressed upon Dyfed to learn the art of transcendence so as to visit that world, the home of his people and his new son, while on leave from his duties here.

Meanwhile, the emperor's attempt to pacify the populace against their increasing poverty, rising costs and high unemployment along with a devalued denarius, had soon morphed into that week of festivities. It was to begin on next Sol day, the day of the sun or Sunday. It would begin with prayers and sacrifices to Apollo who would be the patron for the day. Apollo or Sol Invictus…also commonly referred to as Helius (Helios)… Hyperion or Titan, was the sun. As he was the son of Leda, Apollo (once cherished by the ancient Trmmli) was one of the most important and complex gods among the Amoran religion. He appeared as a beardless, athletic youth (son of Zeus/Jupiter) and variously recognised as the god of light, sun, truth, prophecy, poetry, music, and healing that often lent himself as the patron of Sunday. It wasn't lost on Dyfed that Jeshua Adon of the Nazareans (who referred to god as his father), the new and most recent messiah who was being championed by the new Jeshuan cult as their saviour, resembled Apollo somewhat in representation at least. Also, the Jeshuans had chosen Sol day as their holy day. Free medical attention was to be provided that day (along with free festivities of frivolity) to all who needed it by fine Hellenic doctors. The remaining days of the weeklong festival would each be dedicated to the remaining gods of the Amoran religion according to their place in the week.

Also something from one or other of their honoured associations would be the theme for the day, to be paid for by the day's sponsor. So the following day — Moonday (Monday) — it was Diana (Vesta) who was revered along with free apple cider that was abundant and flowed ceaselessly…followed by Mars the following day. On this day war battles dominated the stages of the open air theatres matinées accompanied by musicians providing robust, imperial songs. In the afternoon of the same day at the Colossus there was even a naval battle re-enacted. Everybody who attended was admitted without charge no matter what class you were or your lot in life. Mercury (the god of commerce and financial gain) came next and was the only day where criers were busy exclaiming that donations toward venders and performances would be gratefully accepted. Mercuryday was the day allotted to Dyfed. This was the day when the emperor would visit him at his Capitoline Hill residence. Dyfed was the sponsor for Mercuryday whose Albion and northern Goth equivalent was the god Woden (Oden). For this reason it was subsequently called Woden's day or Wednesday in the northern Albionian tongue, whereas it came to be referred to as Mercoledi and Mercredi in the Amoran influenced tongue. It turned out that Mercury day's sponsor paid the heaviest toll of all, which was why the emperor chose him. This was not a profitable day; it seemed, at least not for Dyfed. He came to call every Wednesday after that Lostleaderday. And its impact was felt on him and the *pack's* purse. Dyfed was not able to avert the unmovable that was impending, so with Morgant's help (along with Cato's panache) he decided to splurge. Although he knew it would increase Macaronius' greed and envy towards him, the happy surprise would give him a slight respite and time for them to move their own knights and rooks across the board. The game was afoot. After all, the Empire was beginning to flounder, even if ever so slightly. There would be a new morning, yet. It was a gamble though.

Mercury day was followed by Joveday when Jupiter lent his personage to become patron of that day. It was also the emperor's sponsor day. That meant that everything was free per usual for the hoi polloi on the emperor's bill. Of course, even if Emperor Claudius may have once owned up and footed the bill on Jupiter's day, Emperor Macaronius was certainly not about to do it. It was the jovial day, when the most merriment was meant to be gotten out of life and to Macaronius jovial didn't mean spending his own money. It meant spending other peoples' money, something he did very well. Slapstick puppetry and stand-up comics would crowd the stalls and the stage theatres on this day. Presumably this would take place only if strikebreakers could convince the actors' guild to wobble, or preferably totter. It fell to those talented people's performances that got everybody up and into a jovial mood. Throughout the day white bulls would be sacrificed upon the Capitoline Hill in front of Jupiter's alter, at great expense.

Jupiter (Jove), of course, is the Amoran name for the Hellas god Zeus. (A triviality to note: the equivalent to Zeus and Jove among the Goths and other northern tribes was the god Thor — in truth the god's other name — which subsequently transposed Joveday into Thor'sday among northern cultures instead) After Jove/Thor's day came Venusday, named after the noun for sexual love and desire. Venus, unsurprisingly, is also the mother of Aineías (Aeneas) who as every Amoran knew was a Trojan hero. He was a hellion and the legendary father of Romulus and Remus who were mystical founders of Amor. This was adult day so there would be many more supervised gardens for children on this day so that their elders could let their hair down, if they so desired or were inclined, and indulge in anything their little hearts desired from ribald sexual humour to downright pornographic participation and group sex.

Finally we come to the last day and most important god of all, Saturn. Saturn is the pagan god of gods, the very god of very god who was self begotten, not made. Saturn the Hellenic god Kronus, the keeper and watcher of all time: but he is not the god of redemption or confession. The name Saturn transposed into Sabato, Samedi, Saturday, Sabbath, and Shabbat. This is the Abramist's first and true god's real name as it was for many others in histories past. This god is the originator of the god of Abram, Allah, the Father, and by association, Yahweh and Elohim who (once upon a time, directly after the mother goddess was overthrown and the Hyperboreans had fled the earth) all humans worshipped and acknowledged on this day. This aforementioned status quo was prior to any latter day religious irresponsibility.

All (it seemed) had been arranged now in the emperor's attempt to pacify the masses that burgeoned the city. Thronging the streets, denarius-less…maybe…but as Aurora (Dawn) dawned on the first day of this festive occasion, everyone seemed genuinely happy. Everybody, that is, except seven of the rich Houses currently out of favour with the emperor who he had in turn challenged…made them an offer they couldn't refuse… to chip in together and foot a sizable piece of the bill for the gods of the week gala's projected budget. The budget was in the hundreds of millions of denarii. In addition to Dyfed, some of these out and outs who were approached by Sir Saturday Borgia (who had now permanently moved to Amor) was Gaius Grouchus, Dyfed's neighbour from the old Palatine hood whose elder brother (some years earlier) had been murdered by the Republican establishment while he was attempting to legislate an order in council to transfer land from the rich to aid the poor. Gaius himself had followed down a similar route as that taken by his brother. This was a route that was a narrow and dangerous tract to take, one that was normally occasioned only by mountain goats and was definitely a high aerial act for any politician to embark on. And like his brother, he too had been set upon and was forced to flee Amor.

Having not been seen again in these environs for some time, it was rumoured and presumed that Gaius had committed suicide. Only recently, after a couple of centuries had passed, he returned. But the shrewd Macaronius (who was continually on the lookout for easy prey from whom to solicit and cajole for favours and funds) plotted to mine him dry before declaring him a traitor come lately and then demand his suicide. This too was eventually sidestepped. Another was Asinius Scopalius whose inherited wealth was much diminished, and Julian Agrippa the industrialist who owned mines in Albion and Gaul.

Amor was transformed on this first day of the festival of the gods of the week for everywhere you looked stalls were set up for dispensing free food and drink, along with makeshift stages for impromptu puppet shows for children and adults alike; and other platforms were built to accommodate theatre actors to strut their stuff, or for musicians to perform melodies. Each of these venues had ample room cleared away in front for an audience of a hundred or more. This festival — with its decidedly carnival flavour — stretched from the Circus Flaminius alongside the Tibur river at the Field of Mars right over the Capitoline, right through the Forum to the Colossal (Colossus or Coliseum). In addition to the aforementioned distractions there were, as stated, the aforementioned open houses of the rich and famous. These, generally, were the same homes of those rich Houses whose hierarchal head had been cajoled into participating in this placating scheme by the emperor: either that or they were the nouveau riche who wished to become hosts out of false pride and haughty magnanimity, or simply to show off their luxury. The nouveau riche were generally susceptible to the emperor's honey-tongued enticement. Most foreign lords upon taking up residence in Amor were heavily fleeced.

We have the annual festival of Good Deeds; the festival of Good Intentions; the carnival of Happiness; of Politeness; of Sleeping, followed closely by the festival of

Awakening; the carnival of Fellowship. We even have the festival of the Week of the gods and the Urban Vinalia Festival Day. But this year was the eight thousand year anniversary of the solemn promulgation of the chronicles of the past that had been surreptitiously filed at the Universal Repository of Lists under the heading of 'the World's Chronological and Sacred past, and it was also the three hundred and forty-seventh anniversary of the Res Gestae. The first mentioned would now go completely unnoticed, but as for the latter, this year was a rejuvenation and a re-attachment of the aforementioned Res Gestae in an effort to re-instil the legal terms and conditions into the populace by a solemn renewing of their vows of acceptance. And as it befit them, despite the cult of Jeshua of Nazareth that was gaining steam and the accruements heaped onto Mithra by Nastika Sidd Sambahatti, the hoi polloi continued to worship Io. And Dyfed wavered. It was getting to be all too much.

(The festival of the week gods)

> *'The capitalist system is a Darwinian struggle where power, rather than morality, was the primary factor determining the eventual outcome.'*
> **FARREL DOBBS**

As previously arranged, the appointed day for Emperor Flavius Valerius Constantius Macaronius' swing-by visit, along with his suite, to Dyfed's digs on the south slope of the Capitoline Hill was suddenly on them. In addition to his pick-up and pay suite, the Emperor was accompanied by one or two handpicked senators along with a cenuria of Amoran soldiers armed accordingly and on guard commanded by a senior centurion. It was on Mercury's Day that this took place. Dyfed greeted the emperor by handing over a million denarii worth of gold bars secured in a heavy carrying case. The emperor's cold, steady blue eyes took in everything with unreadable glances. He was obviously surprised at all the loot Dyfed was handing him without strings, but he said nothing as his four personal guards quickly moved it outside and into the imperial chariot and kept it under guard. If he was waiting for Dyfed's wish list to be sung off along with praises about the emperor as a return favour for his generosity, he would have waited in vain. Quickly he introduced Markus Grouchus to Dyfed along with another senator who either lagged or somehow got lost behind somewhere in the portico whose name doesn't matter anyway. Dyfed was pleased to meet Grouchus who he had heard a great deal about. Apparently, the feeling was mutual for Markus Grouchus smiled and seemed genuinely pleased to be introduced to Dyfed by the emperor, no less. Marg, Morgant and Cato were present so when the introductions took place Dyfed sensed that Grouchus somehow knew Morgant though he greeted him as though he did not. It was much different when a moment later Dyfed introduced his guest Cato, first to the emperor then to Grouchus, for Grouchus and Cato threw their arms around each other in a tearful greeting while the emperor stood by with a stony face and said nothing. Dyfed caught Morgant's subtle smile that their reunion brought but which he cleverly turned into a polite invitation for Macaronius to demand of him anything that an emperor might desire. But Macaronius ignored Dyfed's polite gentility. Instead he began to pace around Dyfed's apartments breathlessly and talking excessively…mostly patronisingly to his suite…and not to Dyfed. Despite the fact that a great deal of trouble had been done to provide victuals of great taste and beverages galore, the emperor never sat down and declined to eat or drink anything during his whole visit that somehow seemed truncated and which, before very long, he abruptly brought up short. At one point, with a bland condescending smile carelessly pasted onto his long, thin and tight skinned and wrinkled face, he announced to Dyfed that he wanted him to accompany him and other guests to his villa at Tibur — some few hours by chariot outside of Amor. It had actually been Emperor Hadrianus' villa that Macaronius had purchased with a mortgage secured by a loan of imperial (public) funds.

"Today is Mercury's Day — April 20th,' said Macaronius. 'And Saturn's Day, the last day of the week, will also end our wonderful week's festival of the gods. That will be

April 23rd. This date, as it so happens, is also the Urban Vinalia Festival Day.' Emperor Macaronius had set out to plan his own festival of the gods of the city of Amor week (held at least once during an emperor's reign) to precede the six days before and then end on this traditional Wine Festival Day which was held everywhere on this date in honour of Jupiter and Venus each year. And now this celebration of Jove and Venus would overlay on top of (and be celebrated together with) the god Saturn. This was fitting for it allowed the god Jupiter to be celebrated twice and Saturn only once within the same week. The first celebration of Jupiter was to be tomorrow, which the emperor will host, and then again three days from now at his villa for Urban Vinalia Festival Day on Saturn's only day. 'It would please me,' he added, 'if you would bring your suite.' This, Dyfed knew, would certainly mean Morgant his chief domestic and possibly Marg, who the emperor thought was either his wife or his mistress. He watched her carefully, and she him back. She considers the emperor not to be intelligent enough for her, however, while he thought she was too intelligent to mess with. She was beautiful but he disliked her immediately. Macaronius' spies like Saturday Borgia that had been provided him by Diokles, hadn't figured out the House of Lucifer's arrangement as of yet. Cato, however, taken to be nothing more than a friend of the family was not welcome. That was made clear by the emperor who upon bidding Dyfed's House adieux said, "We leave in the morning on the day after tomorrow. Happy Mercury's Day and enjoy. Please accompany me to Jove's temple to sacrifice tomorrow, I am providing the white bulls.' Then ignoring Morgant he turned to Cato. 'I don't suppose I will have any reason to see you again,' he said without any other salutation. Then he left.

Being Mercury's Day, the patron god of gain and profit, and possibly even usury, and since Macaronius wasn't likely to be confused over what day it was, Dyfed had stationed a large donation box that was flagged 'large donations gratefully received... thank you very much' by the left of two stately columns that framed the main entrance of his residence through which Macaronius and his accompanying suite of twenty-six well heeled Amoran citizens and patrons by design passed through on their exit to re-join the centuria of armed guards outside. These men were still standing ceremoniously on the sloped street by the squad of chariots watching the goings on over down by the river. They had remained stationed to escort the emperor on to the cheering crowds of his next venue of the day. Meanwhile, after leaving Dyfed's, the emperor's suite dispersed, most likely to return home and cry into their beer on their bad luck and the emptying of their bank accounts over this week's occasion of excess extravaganza for Macaronius' glorification. As his guests left (those desperate and soon to be ruined suck-holing yes-men who as the emperor's suite had been literally forced onto Dyfed and his House on this day), the host awarded, as a gift with a smile from his House of Lucifer to them, a large, fat, gold ring to each of them. Each ring also contained a voucher allowing the ring to be engraved at Ebreo ben Jamin's goldsmithing, jewel-forger and engraving shop on the high street by Esquiline Hill at Dyfed's expense. This was customary for Dyfed as he appeared always as a man bearing gifts. But, too, he was also fully aware that here in Amor only folks of a certain status (which had to be acknowledged by the emperor) were allowed to wear a gold ring at all, at least in public. This was a small and irritating mechanism of authority and control, a throw back to olden days when only they of high status (priests and kings) were permitted, for instance, to wear hats on their heads in public. It was similar to Dyfed's altered reality memory of the future where hoi polloi men were not permitted to wear beards. And if would-be dissidents however did grow beards, argue against or speak out in contrary terms about any official policy, criticize the governing factor or the culture of its power elite in any way and attempt to radicalize or even sway the people's trust and loyalty away from *the regime* simply by not conforming socially, then their Security Credit[38] vital for every aspect of each hour of their lives would be quickly frozen and the culprits (since they had nowhere to run and no resolve or fight left in them) were quickly hunted down and their arms and legs were broken, water poured into their lungs before being strangled in any one of the many Home-Land security offices that dotted the cities and the countryside.

Anyway, back to these irritating suck-holes the emperor had chosen as his suite that he had already roped in to pay for his week of the gods festival, certainly none of these folks were among those the emperor would have deemed it within their right to don a gold ring on their finger. Dyfed's expensive gift therefore, could also (perhaps) act as an insult to both the receiver as well as towards Macaronius himself. And as for the emperor, Dyfed had gifted him an elaborate gold ring that was set with a giant ruby (the emperor's birthstone) garnished around with diamonds which Pliny, once in his capacity as the leading Amoran naturist of the day, had said were the most valuable things on earth. But somehow when Macaronius carefully examined the beautiful ring afterwards, he couldn't find any suck-hole type pandering script already written to him anywhere on it. Because of that he didn't send it in to Ebreo the jeweller for an imperial embossing, but discarded it instead. Some said he threw it away.

For Dyfed, it was a win, win situation. The insult cost him nothing, for — ye Gods, he thought — Morgant could conjure up wagons full of money like nobody's business. Even Ebreo the Ebonite forger, manufacturer and goldsmith was to make a killing. Not only did he provide all of the rings for Dyfed's guests that fetched him a pretty sum, but he also benefitted by the engraving bill that he would send to Dyfed as well. Ebreo had come out ahead on this one.

So, Venus' Day duly arrived and the litters and carriages of the twenty or so families chosen to accompany the emperor to his villa gathered around the column of Titus. These families were not his suite during the previous six days that he had chosen to plunder and bleed money from in order to pay for the week long festival. The folks that he included now were the engines of the western empire. As the point arranged to depart the city, Titus' column wasn't chosen so as not to interfere with the crowded Forum and the goings-on there. After all, even if daytime traffic was banned in Amor, as it had been since the days of the Republic, the emperor could do whatever he wanted, within reason: And that included arriving in a two or four horse drawn chariot or carriage into a crowed square or the Forum, or even through the doorway of the Senate House itself, if he wanted. No, the purpose was for expedience towards an unhindered and easy exit of a train of vehicles from the centre of Amor to the nearest city gate. Dyfed and Morgant were alone, accompanied by no one else. Marg was absent. They were riding in Dyfed's

---

38   A mandatory account in future days. It was meant for every citizen and it fully identified him or her along with all information pertinent about him or her. Aside from providing authorized agencies to peer and rifle through any citizen's personal profile, it also provided the citizen with the only means to be protected under its citizenship status. Without this account an individual was not a citizen of any kind and were unable to purchase anything and were actually prohibited from living. Related apparatus of identification were *rfi* implant chips that succeeded plastic cards that in turn succeeded tattooed numbers on the hand or wrist.

newly delivered, custom built chariot, complete with an innovative, modern carriage suspension system with an anti-sway mechanism along with narrower wheel rims with a lower profile that acted as an anti-skid adaptation which made for easier handling all round. These were important safety features which Dyfed had innovated himself in view of his intention of innovating a chariot, litter and carriage manufacturing business for general consumption, though initially for the well heeled. That is, to those whose habitat were the Palatine, the Capitoline, the Esquiline and even the Caelian Hills area of town, the latter being where immigrants from the besieged city-state of Alba Longa had been settled over seven centuries before. The remaining districts were generally too poor to contain potential clients for an expensive, fine crafted item such as advanced, custom built chariots. This late-modelled chariot prototype was not a cheap construction for this was no ordinary model. What with new fabrication materials — such as bend and crease resisting bamboo from the land of Ch'in — for its body parts, and the tough and durable Mesua ferrea from Ceylon that was used for the moving parts of the chariot's undercarriage — such as the axel, wheel rims — its reduced weight over all — plus its added torsion and tensile strengths in sundry metals and those areas that sustain acute stress and wear, such as where the wheel meets the road — this chariot was compact and as swift as the wind. Add to this Dyfed's dual horsepower (the two Andalusians, one black the other white), and the problem became road conditions during inclement weather along with cornering at high speeds. It was high time then that steps that needed to be taken were taken to minimise accidents due to the poor handling of most high-speed chariots. Dyfed had published his mechanical innovations in the hope that it would be taken up generally and that vehicular improvement would thereby save the lives of operators, pedestrians, and horses. Instead, although cart wrights and chariot carriage-makers showed interest many (who were part of Dyfed's Brotherhood of Industry, Commerce and Labour Guild [BICL-G] were committed to standardization). Senator Flaccidius Fellacio — who headed up the Imperial Department for Science and Innovation — quickly slapped Dyfed with a hefty registration-for-innovation fee. This created something of an Imperial patent, which in turn allowed the Imperial Tax and Excise Department to levy heavier taxes on manufactures. Since it was against the law for a non-Amoran to enter into a licensing agreement with Imperial Amor (although not the other way around), Dyfed wasn't to receive any royalties. And enterprising chariot builders — due to sudden requirement changes made by the Imperial Standards Department and their rushed in Health and Safety ordinance (something which the aforementioned Brotherhood of Industry, Commerce and Labour Guild had been pushing for) — were now forced to comply with Dyfed's design and be taxed accordingly.

Those who had arrived at the Arch of Titus had mostly come from the Palatine and the Capitoline. None, of course, came from the Trans-Tibur district beneath the Hill of Janus that lay west of the Tibur and the city of Amor. This is where residences and businesses were carved up into smaller sections that had names like Little Khem, Little Syria, and Little Hispania. There was (to Dyfed's keen amusement) even a Little Albion. Donning a disguise, Dyfed often roamed this colourful area to try out his palate on ethnic food and drink. The Abramis, though, were allowed to live and do business throughout the city, but mostly they were poor. They all had to pay a tax to the sanctuary of Jupiter that sat upon the Capitoline — above Dyfed's bachelor pad — just like they once had to pay the Curia of the high priests of their Temple back in Jebus. Even the

Jeshuans now had license to move around the city and prosper if they could. Few had managed to achieve that yet, however. And many of the latter, either Abramis or Jeshuan (the new Abramis) often fled back into that aforementioned ghetto of the Trans-Tibur or further afield to the catacombs for protection obscurity, especially if they found themselves under any suspicion and were being sought by the Nightwatchmen or any other guards of the establishment.

Once the Imperial entourage — including the Imperial guard — arrived with Macaronius dressed in brilliant purple, they all proceeded together to the Aurelian Wall where they exited Amor through the Tiburtina Gate. Policing guards had this route temporarily cleared of pedestrians so the Imperial chariot-cade could safely pass. Shortly after exiting the city, they stopped, whereupon the emperor changed into his travelling outfit and tucked his expensive (for the eyes of the crowds viewing the emperor from a distance clothes only) back into its trunk. It was dark when they arrived at Tibur (no need for the quick-change performance here) and the blessings of Aurora's favours upon the land were not yet forthcoming. But the town was brilliantly lit with torches that were mounted in front of large round, shiny discs of polished metal that were attached to walls so as to amplify the torchlight.

The wind had suddenly blustered up upon them as they had drawn near the town; so as the trailing travellers — those who were the codicil of the Imperial suite — now bunched up and tight-reined their charges to steer the chariots into the steep approaches and narrow lanes as (still climbing) they entered the village. Here, the clattering of the horses' hooves and trailing jangle of the chariot wheels on the stone and mortar road rankled even the genius of the suburbs hereabouts. This dryad, naiad, or aura (the latter so named after the dawn goddess) who single handed (or all together) gyrated with annoyance at this rude intrusion even now before the birds were due to rise, that it caused the long shadows of the arriving company to twist and swivel as the train of horse drawn vehicles manoeuvred their way to the emperor's villa set here into the Tiburtine Hills. It goes without saying that the digs — even if its just the home away from home… being the villa of an Amoran emperor — is going to be just a little sumptuous, grand, and brilliantly magnificent to its full and glorious extent! So there is no need to delay this tiresome tale any further to state the obvious here.

There was to be no sleep for soon, after they had been settled into their rooms, the rosy hue of Dawn shined forth and a lavish breakfast served on silver ensued in one of many great halls. It was April 23 and the day of Urban Vinalia. This was the conclusion of the wine festival held in the honour of Jupiter and Venus. Once it had been only for one day but a succession of emperors had lengthened it out to a week of frolic and fun. Its original purpose had been to sample and bless last year's wine crop and to pray to the god and goddess for their blessings on the next harvest. Later, other festivities unfolded with all the village people joining in whether they wanted to or not. Fortunately for the upper crust of the establishment, most folks were intoxicated by power and wealth and for those that have it. Any dark and scurrilous looking suspicious types who would be caught lurking around paying no notice to the Imperial court as they postured and posed for their audience — all the while done up in their dandified dress of gilded togas — would quickly be hauled by the scruff of their necks and made to grovel before some petty imperial ordinance enforcer before being heavily fined, maimed, or cruelly put to death on charges of sedition. Most of the villagers were vassals of the state, anyway. They were poor, they were in debt, and owned nothing. Everything they received, even the right to live and breathe was at the magnanimous whim of the emperor. They could certainly be counted on to follow the imperial orders. So, to this end, lots of singing ensued from the moment the fast was broken at the break of day, where wine…that beautiful, luscious, full-bodied, and heavenly nectar of Dionysus…was served up. On this day, although not from the imperial tables or from the same amphorae, even the village churls, the masses of the hoi polloi dressed in their finest were served up wine, tid-bits and even rare-bits in tradition with any Imperial Festival. And from early morning and throughout the day everywhere could be seen elbows flapping up and down as wine was greedily swilled by all sorts. Only the very elderly, the physically infirm, and the raving lunatics were kept shut-in, pacified and calmed, tied up, or simply chained to a post. Soon, at this rate — Dyfed thought — they would all be raving lunatics at large, anyway, and all needing to be securely bound. For he knew that folks (such as these) who unlike him couldn't handle the gallons of wine allotted to each and every one of them, even if it was an April and not a July sun beating down on their fuzzy heads from overhead. Later in the afternoon, after down time to capture some quietude or a short nap, a huge feast was brought out. It was to be a court picnic. These victuals were set out on laden down tables that had been erected both in under the porticos and out upon the neatly cut lawns. The fare wasn't in the category of cucumber sandwiches, either, but fresh trout, sea bass and pheasant with plum sauce, vegetables of every colour and size, along with pasties, fruit, jams, chutneys and baklava sticky with honey and nuts. The emperor and his family, along with the superciliously hand picked guests who were favoured senators or other aristocrats invited to add colour and content, all ate together. It was the first time that Dyfed and Morgant were able to survey the entire gathering barefaced and eager to be seen along with the dark horses among them. Macaronius was some distance from them and Dyfed was pleased of the breathing room.

"I tried to encourage Marg to accompany us,' said Dyfed suddenly. But she wouldn't come.' Morgant glanced at him briefly then looked away. Although the day was warm it was changeable and he was dressed in a tall hat and wore a light cape thrown over him like a toga. Dyfed was traditionally dressed except that he wore a wide brimmed hat that cast a broad shadow. But instead of a tall upper portion as in Morgant's case his hat had a shallow, flat upper portion that virtually cast no profile. It closely resembled headgear depicted on some early red figure vases from Hellas, though perhaps more utilitarian and less elaborate as the former. Unlike Morgant who had a very long beard, Dyfed was clean-shaven, still a popular trend here among the younger men.

"I cautioned her about attending,' Morgant said simply in way of reply. 'Anyway, I've had an unsettling feeling about all of these recent goings on; this hobnobbing with the emperor, no less, along with the ruthless senators and rich hail fellow well met Capitalists on every side. Something has been telling me that all is not right, and now I think I know what it is. You see that man sitting beside the emperor's wife, over there?' Morgant didn't look their way and neither did Dyfed.

"There is a man over there,' replied Dyfed, 'who reminds me a little of Cato in some way, though unlike Cato he is brutish looking and dissipated. In fact he is much bigger of stature than our friend. Do you mean him?'

"Yes,' replied Morgant. 'That is Cornelius-Felix. He is an exceptionally dangerous man and a former emperor, as I'm sure you have heard. He is rarely seen, if never, at least in public gatherings. So why is he here? one might ask themselves,' he continued.

"Urban Vinalia Festival Day and the emperor's Week of the gods Festival aside, what's happening here at Macaronius' villa is not a public gathering,' said Dyfed.

'You can bet on one thing, though, Dyvie,' Morgant said. 'Since he is here, it is Cornelius and Cornelius alone who is in charge here, not Macaronius. And whatever is taking place at this festival tucked away from prying eyes in Macaronius' villa, is very important, indeed.'

"Okay,' said Dyfed, a little irritably, 'but it was you who encouraged me to get close the corridors of power: both with the senate and with the governing factor in general, including the ruling aristocracy from whose base the former derive. It was I who saw the wisdom in concentrating on the bankers and financiers.'

"Absolutely,' replied Morgant who provided him with a type of smile that hinted to Dyfed of a kind and patient instructor who was trying not to lose his patience. 'Learn to keep your distance, that's all,' declared Morgant flatly. 'Anyway,' he continued to say, 'keep your distance as well from these luscious desserts who are romping around allowing us to feast our eyes and fuel our desires upon them. Many of them — you know — even under normal circumstances, are not just bathed, powdered, and dressed up whores from the hoi polloi class…all doused with perfume and done up with coifed hair-dos and pretty dresses which are rented. As it goes, that would be just fine if that's whom these devilish delights really are. But at an emperor's shindig like this? I don't think so. I think,' continued Morgant, 'that if I were to reach out and grab this gorgeous treat who is conveniently at hand, just here by you at this moment,' he nodded his head toward one quite close, 'very quickly a tough servant or obedient slave of Lord Puke the Bed with the bald head, over there — or whomever — would suddenly be on hand to quickly intervene and whisk her off and away from me, of all people.' Morgant made a comical face, the tough and tanned skin of his forehead and cheeks — so much different than Dyfed's smooth skin and pale complexion — rolled up in furrows. Dyfed laughed involuntarily. 'For all intents and purposes I'm just your slave, albeit with a title of chief servant,'. Continued Morgant. 'But that would probably not happen if you were to reach out… don't you dare, Dyvie. And yet she remains coyly engaged otherwise so as not to appear to be propositioning, much like even a high-end professional prostitute would do. But in truth these beautiful young, unattached (as far as we know) and eligible ladies are actually the scions of lords and ladies who either live in mansions on the Palatine Hill hood and are engaged in the senate, or fill in as the crowned heads of some client city state who is a slave to Amor's whims. These girls we have here, Dyfed, are actually very much like the flashy lures imitating fat insects which the fisherman use in the stream nearby to catch this morning's trout we've been feasting on. Just like those lures, these daughters of the rich and powerful are simply doing what they have been fashioned and bid to do; trawling back and forth in the same way so as to attract your attention, spark your lust, and then catch your seed For most of these are daughters of the aristocracy who are being proffered here by the Houses of influence for that very purpose of receiving your seed for the benefit of the great House to which they belong. You see how they mill around and flutter. It is quite obvious that they mean to attract you, along with some others here of similar stature to whom they aren't related in any way. The problem is that normally it is hard to tell the whores from the daughters of the noble class: But not here, Dyfed, not here. Here we only have the whores of the noble class. Are they buzzing around you Dyfed because you are young, dashing, and handsome? Never mind announcing yourself to the majestic and the mighty by having boldly stepped forward with a strong foot in the most competitive of arenas of the empire. By that I mean, by Georgius,' said Morgant, 'to stake a claim in that domain of material wealth! Now that! — Dyvie — is something the establishment recognises. Otherwise, unless you were a senator, you would not be here today keeping the emperor company. Or is it, do you think, because you are also a handsome, rich, flesh-bag of new, healthy blood? New blood to invigorate old blood, old established blood. Bloodlines are everything to the Haploids, Dyfed. Everything' Morgant said. 'Not that it isn't in the interest of any family — no matter how low their class or how poor — to guard their family blood lines in order to keep them strong, healthy and free of the diseases of the body and mind and in the prevention of adopting unbecoming or repugnant traits. But it is especially important to old established blood tainted from the breeding in of unsavoury characteristics, some accumulated when carefully selected inbreeding has gone awry. Although one would think that the Haploids themselves should know better, since they achieved their transcendence and transmutation by flaw, they simply don't have the expertise to comprehend human technology or even humanity to any extent. That's why they desperately need the hoi polloi. They need them to focus where they can't, to ponder what they don't understand, and invent what they can't imagine. New folks are seldom welcomed into their tightly closed circle of hierarchal establishment, but an opportunity for new blood with spirit and spunk to be injected into old established blood is seldom sneezed at. It's ironic, since the Haploids are themselves freaks of nature. Anyway, it's in our mission's interest here to dirty the gene pool of the Haploid's as best we can yet not add our genes to theirs in any way. As well, any attempt to strengthen those bloodlines of the hoi polloi and help them get it through their thick skulls that they serve only as food and energy for the Haploids will be of enormous assistance which is why we do what we do to improve their lot, and ultimately our lot here in our own vacation and recreational land of the third dimension. But surely, Manandan has taught you all that, although maybe in not so direct a manner. But look here, now. A man is approaching over there, Dyfed. Do you see him?' Dyfed glanced up.

"He looks like a Gaul,' said Dyfed.

"Yes,' replied Morgant, 'and I've seen him in Amor before. 'I'm sure that he might be another top Haploid, although I don't know who he is or the importance of his station. So I will pass that mission on to you.'

"That he is here at all tells us something,' said Dyfed, still watching the tall man chat casually with the emperor's most prominent guests who closely surrounded the former. The man then slowly strolled over to take his place beside the emperor's wife, but sat on the further side to where Cornelius Felix sat. The two men embraced and Dyfed and Morgant made note of just how comfortable they were with each other.

As stated, the day was sunny and warm but changeable. Here, in the emperor's villa, spring was blooming in the neat laurel hedges around about while summer was already establishing itself as a sprinkling of budding baby-green among the dark cypress trees. Jonquils sprouted like weeds and hyacinths — sprung from the spilled blood of the slain and adorable youth which Apollo so loved — thrust forth their heavenly fragrance to such as degree as to create the impression here of that of an outdoor boudoir. After lunch a short rain shower was sent to freshen up the new flowers and unearthed the fragrant smell of the dark soil. Dyfed breathed in the salubrious air. With the fall of the first drops of rain he noted that slaves appeared suddenly, and with an ardour that far exceeded moderation set to and hastily put up parasols over the tables of food and beverages where servants attended. They also erected colourful canopies to cover the guests who were lounging or at play in order to shelter them from the momentary inclemency of the weather. Routinely informed of their duties, nobody spoke to the slaves and they spoke to nobody in return; and apart from the servants, no one even noticed them. Dyfed noticed however that Cornelius Felix and the tall Gaul had been joined by Emperor Macaronius while the latter's wife had been trotted off (probably to the baths), accompanied by a small group of wives and consorts belonging to the alpha Male rank and file. The eunuchs, well armed and muscular, who were in attendance with the wives and consorts, were a new introduction at court from the east. One couldn't tell what language they spoke for they never did. The general rank and file of men in attendance who were closest to the emperor were engrossed now in discussion, but their attention span was easily broken for laughter sometimes broke out and their body language changed with their voices, as was even the languages in which it was expressed. Amoran was the official language, but the native languages of the empire were numerous and occasionally during moments of relaxed and joyous chatter these languages emerged: sometimes it was Hispanic, while at others it was Gaul or Thrako-Illyrian. And of late, even multiples of Germanikan. Dyfed wrongly assumed that the men who were more remote from the cordiality of Macaronius' inner core here in attendance and not having to endure the Emperor's close inspection of them, would quickly gravitate toward the sumptuous baths which the villa contained This was generally the early afternoon custom at such gatherings. But, to his surprise, close by some senators who, obviously far from the loop of the inner circle who were mostly industrialists and financiers, were playing at a game of bocce. They stood around in groups egging each other on, shouting out encouragement and whooping in almost childish delight at someone's success or drooped in satirical moaning and groaning at another's' failure. Their purpose, Dyfed now correctly assumed, was to add some kind of dimension or depth to the sought after cordiality.

The grit of the sauce being served up for inspection and review at this gathering had little to do with these latter folks, however, and more to do with the powerful engines that drove the empire. Morgant and Dyfed both agreed on this point. Dyfed noted that men such as Postumus Cornelius Felix; Drusus Gallus; Julian Agrippa, Furius Claudius, Pollux Scipio were conspicuous by their very presence together. The scholar Flavius Philostratus was also here (possibly it was an annoying coincidence on his part), as was the very extraordinary and the fabulously rich Julia Domna of Emesa (currently Homs), descended from Arab priest/kings who was the mother of Marcus Aurelius Severus Antoninus Augustus (aka Caracalla). Apollonius Tyanaeus showed up later and out of sorts. Apparently, he and Flavius Philostratus did not see eye to eye on things. Julia Domna loved and hated them both equally.

These were all people, Morgant pointed out to Dyfed, who controlled the empire in a more pertinent way than Macaronius or any other currently in-office-emperor was able to. For these latter controlled the very essence that bound and moved the empire forward; or moved it in any other ways such as backwards and sideways. By being more basically alert to the perceptions of pleasure and happiness along with pain and fear that were functional to foster behavioural supervision and direction away or toward costs and benefits, certain types of folks on this earth who had this perception gravitated toward getting their hands on the master levers of the mechanisms that controlled the multitudes. And the lion's share of this type of folk who were present in the empire was, he pointed out, gathered here at this place today. The results for these folks with this aforementioned perception as well as the results for the multitude at large were obvious, he advised Dyfed. For these former were the pivotal people who controlled the vast agricultural lands throughout the empire, as well as being in control of the empire's means and network of communication and supply and demand of trade. They were also, in essence, in charge of where and for what the Amoran army campaigned, along with their ranks dominating the positions of high finances and money lending which were able to capture and harness operation productivity and mete it out to those whom they preferred and when they preferred it. They did this primarily by not losing sight of the fact that as the power elite they were the privileged entitled. Of course another genus of this animal that was included here courted a short cut to the inner circle. They were usually highly successful soldiers, like Cornelius Silly and Julius Kyzar, or were advocators of law like Gaius Anteius Capito and Marcus Antistius Labeo who were also here today. That there may be others equal to this rank and file was also a factor, of course. But, if there were protagonists, and if there were more than just a few of them all told, then the power elite needed (from time to time) some form of intellectual, cultural, and ideological (even ethnic) cleansing to whittle them down to a manageable size so the slices of pie that was needed to go around wouldn't become too small to fight over, thereby crippling the empire and their wealth.

The other problem is in expertizing. Every empire needs intelligent men and women and a certain amount of expertize to go along with them. But as empires grow more sophisticated in every way, its advancement becomes too much for a single individual to have a handle on the whole. Therefore, specialization is needed. However, at some point the more any given individual knows about almost everything relevant, the more productive is the whole that is not beyond a quantum-type system of organization which we may find to be decidedly un-human. The problem here, the sages have told us, is that once an empire's needs require individuals in greater numbers to specialize more and more, it moves toward a point where more and more valuable and intelligent folks are wasted in knowing almost everything about absolutely nothing that is relevant which in itself is virtually worthless: hence — two empires beyond the first and current one — the up and coming worthless empire, or the Turd Empire as it was fondly called. Stay tuned.

Back to the present: It was in this way, then, that the power elite here and now and elsewhere in this climate was like the barracuda (*Sphyraena: and only genus in the family Sphyraenidae*). And it mattered here that information processing was functionally organized into systems of justification. Information on and about the empire was paramount when it came to the purveyors and reapers of Amoran culture; and it was, after all, the three hundred and forty-seventh anniversary of the Res Gestae Divi Augusti (as has already been mentioned) that also mattered very much. Where would the empire be without it? For it's about information, everything is. And here is where the elixir of the gods as preached by their high priests kick in as well. Not that it had to be that way:

which is what Dyfed and *the pack* were all about. After all, the empire's elite should never have been about entitlement and privilege in the first place, but rather about responsibility and duty where fear and pain are minimized through love and compassion, not utilized for their benefit. And the problem (as Morgant told Dyfed, which has been discussed previously) was that this state of affairs had been the Idea of the dominant minds of the empire and was a creation of the human mind (the unfolding of their imaginative universe) that occurred to them at another previous moment in space/time for which no one had any further control over and which was now subject to third dimensional cause and effect. The masters, Morgant told Dyfed, had warned that this bode ill for the future here in the third density for already the Amoran power elite had produced the most socially conservative empire in the western world to date which was headed (with no reverse yet installed) for the centre of a non-ethereal labyrinth dreamt up in a far away moment now beyond anyone's influence that was located amid an ethereal nightmare. By nature (Morgant reiterated to Dyfed) plenipotential control over multitudes squeezes the people into tight conservative conformities bereft of imagination. And this rather un-idealistic situation and state affairs leaves them without a future. And it would have repercussions which was why it was so important for the power elite of the present, those advocates and lawyers for justice, judges and other law makers, Nightwatchmen and turnkeys — makers and shakers of the social/cultural and financial element for any society — to fashion and create nothing that was anywhere outside of the present moment yet was flexible to remain inside every moment now and for all time.

"Such a thing does actually exist,' Morgant told Dyfed. 'Its called the moment of truth.'

(Dictator Cornelius-Felix)

*'No friend ever served me, and no enemy ever wronged me,
who I have not paid in full.'*

LUCIUS CORNELIUS SULLA FELIX

Later that afternoon, Dyfed received the dreaded invitation (without option to decline) to accompany the emperor and his tightly knit suite of about twenty persons, all male, to partake in the ritual of lounging in his private baths where they would be attended to by beautiful young creatures of both sexes. Dyfed loved bathing but generally stayed away from public baths, a pastime that was popular here in the Amoran Empire. Of course, it was somewhat customary to visit the toilet facilities prior to entering the baths. In the great public baths in Amor, for instance, attendants were even employed in the capacity to assist in this and to screen certain classes of Amorans and direct them to wash the first couple of layers of filth off themselves before entering the public bath area proper. All of the bath patrons filed past the toilets on the way to the thermae. Dyfed never lost his habit of treating public toilets and public baths as he would the ravishing plague. Here, however, he was obliged. The baths here at the villa were not public, anyway, and were called balnea. The emperor's toilets that facilitated his villa's balnea were located just outside its entrance and were like any other. Dyfed fancied that they might be cleaner by far, though in after thought he put that down to hopeful thinking.

Entering the premise, on one side of the interior of the building he noticed a long raised bench (made of marble in this case), rather than plain stone or concrete. Cut into the bench's flat top slab were holes spaced about three Amoran feet apart from one another upon which patrons visiting the toilet sat. A few Amoran feet beneath the toilets ran cold water, channelled here from the rushing stream that provided the famous cataracts. This water flushed out the affluence that was deposited below. As the patrons sat on '*the thrown*', sometimes all in a row, they also faced a conduit channelled along the floor by their feet filled with running water. This narrow trench was within easy reach of '*thrown*' sitting patrons who with a rag on the end of a stick could reach forward and dip it into the cold fresh running water. The toilet holes in the marble slap were round except for a slot missing that was closest to the front edge of the bench and between the patrons' thighs. In addition, the marble front that enclosed the area between the toilet seats (directly back of the patrons' leg calves) and the floor had a slot cut out directly beneath and matching the slot of each of the toilet holes tops. So, after dipping the rag stick in the clean flowing water near their feet, the patron was then able to insert the stick cloth end first between their legs and then through the vertical slot at the front of the toilet so the rag is directly underneath them. From here they are then able to scrub brush around where needed. In this way a patron was able to wash away any un-cleanliness and tidy up the area of his or her body after the business was done. As stated it wasn't Dyfed's cup of wine, but since he was here, attending the emperor in his private baths, he chose the cleanest of holes and the least nasty smelling of all the mops.

After the men had succumbed to the leisure of the heated waters which had also been redirected from the cold stream, the Emperor Macaronius directed what were obviously carefully thought out questions to Dyfed about his business practices, his interest in support guilds for professions and labourers along with his concern over Amoran standards. This, after all, was the authority of the emperor, and after him the senate, not Dyfed's. Why was he interfering? What right did he have and by whose permission? After all, he wasn't even an Amoran. Finally, just who the hell did he think he was? and was he interested in purchasing a citizenship for a very large sum of denarii? He certainly had the money. Dyfed's reply was also well thought out. His delivery to that end was not only an exceedingly polite and minutely detailed exposition of his position and ability to stiffen up Amor's already accomplished strengths, but he demonstrated in an astounding fashion his own unique abilities to contribute intrinsically to heap glory upon the emperor and cause him to shine even more brilliantly than at present. As we will soon see, that may not have been the most favourable offers he could have made under the circumstances, but Dyfed's proficiencies in dialectics allowed him to articulate in a rhetoric that amazed the emperor, but more importantly made a marked impression on Cornelius-Felix whose eyes never once left the young man. Dyfed took notice of this as he contemplated that although Macaronius might exert himself to be the success of the empire, he may yet become instead the victim of its weakness. Emperor Macaronius may not be the first victim here. As for himself, Dyfed — simply a junior banker and businessman (as far as Macaronius was concerned...nothing more, as far as Dyfed knew) who overnight had become one of Amor's richest men. And he had attained it with an astonishingly little ado and a reputation for these successes as well. On top of which, he had no family to connect him to the nobility of Amor. In truth and under the circumstances, these realities now forced the realization of their disadvantages upon Dyfed and he now began to feel uneasy of the situation at hand. He was without doubt cloistered at this moment — and guards without — not only by the most powerful men in the entire world, but also men whose duplicity was unparalleled along with their brutality. It was nerve racking — he thought — in an exhilarating sort of way. At one point Cornelius-Felix threw Dyfed a question.

"Tell me about your gods,' he said in a steady and authoritative voice. Such a question could just as easily reflect on one's politics and morals, Dyfed thought as he absorbed this powerfully influential man before him. 'Who is it that is close to your heart? Do you know Mars? Do you know Bacchus? Have you heard of the name Abris? What of today's celebration and where do you stand with it? And since you are not an Amoran, what are you really, Dyfed Lucifer?'

It was an insolent, cruel, and hungry face that contemplated him, thought Dyfed. His eyes were blue and his blond, curly hair was combed forward with no hair parting in sight. But the lower half of his face was weak, Dyfed decided after a moment of contemplation. Possibly he had lost some upper teeth...he was unable to decide...for the man's lower cheeks hollowed under his prominent cheekbones. His brow was creased and did not slope back. He wasn't just nominally intelligent, Dyfed finally decided, he was decidedly clever like a fox. There was a momentary silence as Dyfed, who had not as yet been formally introduced to Cornelius-Felix, did not reply but continued to regard him with an intense appreciation with those silver eyes of his. This strange glance seemed to act as a cocoon that served Dyfed by retaining remoteness about him almost to the point of him becoming something of an apparition. Dyfed's gaze then instantly shut Felix out with a blink of both eyes: a nano-second later (and without so much as a slight turn of his head) Dyfed's eyes snapped open again and his gaze bored off instead into those furtive eyes of Emperor Macaronius. After that awkward moment the emperor, with sudden apology to Cornelius-Felix, introduced Dyfed to the latter. Tactfully ignoring Cornelius' question about Abris, in a blink Dyfed re-fixed his gaze upon Cornelius Felix the former emperor-tyrant and kingmaker again as he stated that Mars was a red planet in the heavens, and therefore far beyond his reach to know anything else about it. Apollo, on the other hand, he told Cornelius, is beloved.

"And as for the Vinalia,' continued Dyfed, 'that is today's festival — it is set apart from the excesses of Bacchus and is more favourable to Vesta or the Penates. And who, then, would dare,' he continued, 'to entice the wrath of the Maenads or the scorn of pretty Dionysus by denying him his due, and his love? As for myself,' Dyfed stated, gathering an air of momentum about him, 'I am obviously a descendant in some way of the Heracleidai and an enemy of Lysander.'

The truth of the matter was that Dyfed was not descended as such, for the Heracleidai were descended from the remnants of the Hyperboreans who — for elaborated reasons is beyond the scope of this narrative — had no transcending skills and had been forced to remain behind in the third dimension. The fact that Dyfed was intentionally reinserted at his birth into the third dimension was something that he discussed with nobody.

"Have you ever come across the name of Eonnurzazagesibababal?' asked the dictator, his eyes boring into Dyfed's but not into his thoughts and mind. This man was a powerful cog among the entitled but he was no Mencius. Dyfed knew Eonnurzazagesibababal to be an ancient Hyperborean-type name only, so only a Haploid troll would have a name like Eonnurzazagesibababal here. He shrugged, and looked directly into the dictator's cold but surprisingly expressive eyes.

"What's that, exactly? he answered, 'an extinct species of some kind of crustacean?' Cornelius-Felix's eyes narrowed but continued to search and swim all over Dyfed as he looked for a telltale emotion that he could not find or make out.

"Have you brought me greetings from abroad?' Cornelius-Felix then asked.

"Anyone in particular?' asked Dyfed, his silver eyes steady and fixed on Cornelius-Felix. The dictator momentarily looked away before regarding Dyfed again. Now his bright eyes bore down onto (but not into) Dyfed once more while the man's body language quickly adopted an animated, supercilious mien.

"Get rid of him,' Cornelius-Felix demanded of the emperor, and spoke no more within earshot of Dyfed. He hadn't got anywhere with Dyfed, but the latter hadn't learned much about Lucius Cornelius-Felix, either.

(Dionysus Temple and the Cave)

'It is easy to go down into Hell; night and day, the gates of dark Death stand wide; but to climb back again, to retrace one's steps to the upper air — there's the rub, the task.'

PUBLIUS VIRGILIUS MARO (THE AENEID)

Later still, about an hour before sunset on this celebrated day of Urban Vinalia, the emperor's suite took to shank's mare and to traipse (staggered would be more accurate) over to the circular temple of Saturnus. It didn't really matter to whom this temple was dedicated, for whether it was Saturnus or Dionysus, it was just as easily Thor's, Zeus', or Jupiter's as well. And, if it came to that, Jupiter would be sharing it with Venus on this occasion, anyway. Some folks, especially of the village, worshipped Herakles (Hercules) here along with the local sibyl. But aside from Jupiter and Venus being honoured on this the day of the Vinalia, the Penates — originally associated with the source of food — would be remembered here today too, as in fact they were each and every day and at every meal. The rituals invoked toward the Penates, such as delivering a tiny portion of the meal's victuals into the hearth fire or a drop of wine onto the rich earth, was the origin of grace before a meal. The Penates or Penetrales were not only the tutelary deities guarding the storeroom of the family home's food, wine, oil and salt, they were also the guardians of the domestic household all told and had become a symbol of the continuance of the family itself. In giving thanks to the Penates as their home guardian, the homey folks thus associated the Penates with Vesta, the Lares and the Genius. These, respectively, were the goddess of the hearth, the guardian deities, and the individual instance of the divine nature of things in general. Temples, Dyfed thought, were for all and any gods, after all. It was even rumoured that in some places the now up and coming Jeshuans, the novo-Abramis, had even adopted abandoned pagan temples and converted them for their own use in which to worship. It gave the location credence, after all, and with any luck maybe credence to the new cult, too. This temple here by Hadrianus' old villa, now Macaronius' newly mortgaged one — and the one in which the men were presently gathering — was set upon an acropolis which in turn was placed precariously on a precipice overlooking the plain below the village. It consisted of a cella in the centre of a circle of eighteen Corinthian columns. And it was a colourful spectacle besides, for no drab abode in dull greys and rock browns was this. In keeping with the culture of Hellas that Amor had adopted independently, as had those earlier cultures that preceded the latter back into the dimness of time (quite contrary to the present, I should add) this temple's marble sparkled in bright blues and whites with elaborate trims in yellows and reds. This was the case for religious and secular buildings all across the empire and the greatness of the cities was dependant on its colourfulness, in addition to its size and its noted inhabitants of elevated importance. The spot chosen for the site of this Saturnus temple was quite unique in that it had a river which — flowing ever downward — swirled in currents around one side the temple in a wide curve and then flew off the precipice in four distinct cataracts. It plunged over the edge to the plain below from where it snaked down toward the Tibur River in the distance. The village townsfolk — although they were virtually the servants that in the most part managed and maintained the emperor's slaves that were posted here to the imperial villa, were able to come and go as they wished unless the emperor was in attendance. They were not permitted, for instance, to bathe in the villa's private baths or to accompany the emperor's suite to pray to Jupiter and Venus unless called to do so. They were not to associate themselves or be identified with the emperor other than to be his subjects or his slaves. Certain handpicked slaves — men and women who had no identity whatsoever — were more likely (apart from the elite) to associate in closer approximation to the aristocrats, including the emperor, than any of the free citizens of the empire could. So, the aristocratic women and their servants now lined the way that launched the emperor's suite as the men began to mosey toward the temple. These noble women would follow at a slight distance but they halted before the temple and entered another square, stone building that was adjacent to it. Behind them many of the villagers followed suit, but only the more affluent managers from good families that were among them entered the square stone structure with the aforementioned. There was no mixing of the different classes of folks in Amoran society unless these underlings were simply there to serve. Many of the lords and other aristocrats in the suite had servants in attendance. Dyfed had Morgant. And for his own amusement, and for Morgant's cover, he often found some call or another to command the latter to some menial enterprise or chore in full view of onlookers. As it contributed to complete Morgan's cover it didn't seem to irk the latter whatsoever.

The men gathered within the columns of the temple facing the cella. Dyfed and Morgant were on the peripheral edge of this temple. Inside the cella some priests were doing incantations that to Morgan sounded to have been dedicated to Vesta. Morgant could feel a cool breeze against his back here, and the incantations made by the priests were difficult to catch because the noise of the river as it raged round about the rocks and spilled over the edge in a cascade of rushing water that continually crashed below. He noticed now that Dyfed was acting peculiar, not that he didn't normally. But now, having first rested back against the nearest column (Morgant thought it might have been to shield himself from the chilled air and the mist rising from the cataracts), it seemed to him that Dyfed had lost consciousness for the most part and had slumped forward now partially leaning on him. He had then uttered something about the blackbirds contrasting against the grey clouds above that were catching the slanted rays of the sinking sun and how they had brought Marg (whose real name, he had recently learned from Morgant, was Sibyl). Morgant poked his head around to glance at the sky and saw there were no clouds. In fact it was still a beautiful afternoon and the birds about were robins and wrens and certainly Marg-Sibyl was nowhere in sight. Then, much to Morgant's surprise, he lost sight of Dyfed: He had vanished. When the light did begin to finally fade, a single torch was lit and passed to a priest. This priest made a noisy incantation of some kind and afterwards handed Macaronius a small clay figurine that could fit in one's palm. It was a symbolic figure of the emperor's personal household Penate — which was Vesta — which he was meant to carry throughout the ceremony. The chief priest had a similar figure that was Jupiter while the secondary priest carried a small effigy of Venus. By certain standards figures or depictions of Saturn were taboo. Not all abided by that, but in polite company, such as here, one complied so as not to offend anyone.

Dyfed now perceived that the troupe proceeded to follow the head priest along a precarious path that circumnavigated the rock cliff among the mist from the cataracts. This literal goat trail that crept along high above the churning water below, was the narrowest of tracts imaginable that sloped dangerously away to the precipice below and was paved with loose stones that continually plummeted over the edge. It led finally to a cleft in the rock face. Here the priest stopped. Cloaked in condensate from the mist of the plunging cataracts, this wretched and shivering ensemble waited here on a more comfortable ledge for all to be amassed together. Each person carrying an unlit torch now had them lit off the torch that the chief priest held as they filed past him and through the cleft in the rock face and into a cave behind. All except the emperor, that is, who went before all of them. He had his two personal guards/servants carry his torch. Once inside Dyfed saw that he was in a large hewed out room. Then much to his amazement he saw Marg-Sibyl standing by. She stood elegantly though haggard looking behind the two other priests and the emperor. Dyfed noticed that her eyes looked wild as she assumed her role as the subterranean Maid. Soon, all the participants were together inside and the priest once again led the way with Marg-Sibyl leading, followed by the chief priest. After a moment they passed through another hole in the cave-room wall where Dyfed found himself descending some shallow steps that had been chiselled out of the rock under his feet. Down they went. At first the ramp was straight then after awhile it began to curve then tighten up into a spiral that suddenly descended straight down. Down and down they went into the bowels of the rock fleshed Earth. It was exhausting, and soon grunts and groans began to rebound through the spiralling corkscrew shaft in an eerie sort of way that matched the jogging and jabbing of the torch light and shadows effect that streaked along the perpetually curved outer wall. Finally they arrived from the tiresome vertical onto a horizontal and level tunnel that after a few moments of walking led them into a gigantic room. Here, the secondary and tertiary priests busied themselves with lighting torches and chandeliers that were fashioned and made ready. Some were attached to the walls while others hung from the cavernous back of the magnificent and marvellously hewed out cave. Soon, the blackness with its multiple spheres of light merged into a dim gloaming where the flames' rays glinted off objects that sparsely filled the room and off the faces of the men whose expressions now were hauntingly strange and satanic like those seen in a later period painting by Goya.

Incantations to Saturn, Jupiter, Venus and Vesta ensued as they all stood though seats were available. But Marg-Sibyl had turned into some kind of incubus that alluded to the characterised by the demonic nature that gods possess from time to time. Dyfed was not able to discern which nature and of what god or goddess she was possessed by, as she whirled and danced in a strange trance. He then beheld that she possessed and held high above her head a fairly long, slim and ornately decorated golden bow. He saw no quiver of arrows slung from her back. He realised at once that there were only two gods, indeed, a goddess and her brother; which that could represent and both were closely associated with him. Suddenly Dyfed felt someone push by him moving toward the front where the priests and the emperor were standing. Marg-Sibyl seemed at this point to be suspended in the air above them, flapping as though she was some giant bat on the wing after having been disturbed by this procession. He watched in a dreamlike manner when suddenly a man bumped past him and approached the emperor and whispered something that none could hear. Dyfed, in his acute state, fancied he heard…

mumbo jumbo…hocus-pocus…taxi dispatcher, which was immediately followed by a loud crack as though a bolt of lightning had just struck the Earth's surface. Having penetrated here to the very bowels of the Earth it had somehow retained its sharp crack that had not decayed into a dull thud. Surely, Dyfed thought, it had been but a laughing bat-like shriek that had escaped the now gigantic, teeth laden mouth of the subterranean Maid as she fluttered and disappeared into the corner shades. But it was the taxi out of this subterranean and encroaching hell that Dyfed was silently contemplating on, just then. Meanwhile, he was further ruminating on a terrible familiarity that was like falling asleep and plunging into a nightmare that was waiting to settle on him like a waking conscious. He heard a rattling kind of whistling sound and felt something crawling across the entire surface of his body. That phenomena manifested into a cocoon that smothered him like he was encased in jelly or cotton batten wool. Suddenly he heard the Sibyl shriek again and saw her throw the golden bow up which glinted as it caught the light from the torches. That was when that terrible thing forced its way into his consciousness once again. Encased in an invisible cocoon-like tomb, Dyfed grew frantic as he suddenly concluded that shank's mare would be have to be called upon at this very moment to assist him again in his hastily retreat from this place at once if he was to survive. But he found it difficult to move never mind run. Then all of a sudden that quasi-realistic state of mind that had overtaken his dreaminess exploded into a harsh, frightening and earthly reality. Dream! This was no dream he remembered thinking. Suddenly the reality of the mountain crag in the Land of the Great White Mountain came back to him, and that arrow of living plasma that was a thick, deep, lush, golden incorporation of every visible colour on the spectrum that somehow — in some fantastic way — even included the wavelengths that were not even visible. Now here, once again, it miraculously materialised with all its attributes gyrating and vibrating and announcing themselves in this shadowy gloaming populated by what looked like a gang of outcast, gnarled old gnomes that glistened occasionally as the torches flickered from the light-waves cast off from this vibrating golden arrow. It was either that or else from the seemingly inexhaustible waves of incantations that flowed from the priest's mouth. This drivel and mumbo-jumbo flowed seemingly without end like a cold morning fog over a swiftly moving river.

But Dyfed wasn't paying them any attention anymore. He had forgotten what was happening up front and all around him except for a spot in time and space beneath the glum, soot-grimy and blackened back (roof) of this subterranean cave deep in the bowels of the earth. Then that incessant vibration which the miraculous arrow-thing gave off grew stronger and then with bony elbows it had forced itself front and centre into his consciousness of multiple dimensions, once again. Dyfed felt a vague premonition, a strange remembrance of some unknown previous death accompanied by an old familiar knell. It was a distant recognition having been long buried and forgotten under the moments of life until the present. And now there it was, and apparently nothing had changed and all had been a dream. This was reality. It was that living, golden arrow which — unlike men — having un-questionably been endowed with a free will could materialise without any solicitation whatsoever. Dyfed, noticing that the priest wasn't even aware of it (along with everyone else), reasoned that the man's incantations most certainly had nothing to do with the thing that had grabbed his attention. He was sure of that more than of anything. He knew instinctively that the priest wouldn't invoke such a thing to begin with. Yet, there it was. Its vibration which affected everything around it within Dyfed's perception began to whine and then to spin — slowly — as though it was searching for a certain victim whose presence was the very purpose for its dispatch: That was the reason for its presence here where it was searching in its hunt to pinpoint towards that moral man/woman to whom it must aim.

In this way the golden arrow was like some beyond-this-world compass, a south pointing lodestone aligning with the Earth's magnetic lines even here, deep in the earth that guided humanity's nature in some unworldly way. Dyfed — now frantic with fear — was trembling terribly as he tried in vain to shrink from out of that thing's terrible presence. His body began to expire sweat so fast that his clothes almost immediately became soaked to the skin, even though he noticed that his sweat was cold. As he shivered his teeth rattled and chattered and soon he became aware that Marg the Sibyl was beside him, and others were beginning to take notice too and start to gawk, peering at him through the shadows that became a multitude of rapidly flapping raven wings. At last, and with his eyes tightly shut, Dyfed heard the expectant sharp report. It was ear shattering. It burst with frightful fury upon his present state of awareness.

In quietude rained upon him there while his entire body jolted as though struck by lightning. He let out a loud agonised groan that quickly stirred up everyone around him. And they, so he perceived, immediately began to murmur together at once like one gigantic beast. Dyfed was looking down at his body and trying to feel where the lightning bolt had painlessly pierced him and was just about to say…"look to yourselves, my fellow mortals, for I'm unhurt'…when looking up he suddenly saw what the others were exclaiming over. The emperor, who just a moment or two earlier had suddenly pushed the late arrival aside (that same man who had shoved Dyfed aside in his urgency to speak to the emperor) was seen to rise sharply and step forward toward the chief of priests. He was apparently unaware of the danger in their midst, Dyfed thought, and presumably the emperor was rising to bathe in the glory of what ever god (or ghoul) — either that of Rebus or Maloch — which the chief of priest's incantations was just then bringing down into this subterranean depth for unholy communion. Then, quite unannounced, the emperor screamed as the aforesaid bolt at large apparently struck him through the heart, or some such place not necessarily as intrinsic to his having love and compassion for his people. Dyfed sensed its approach and even heard the impact that it made upon striking the man's body; it was, however, more in the higher awareness broadband wave realm than in the world of ratcheted sound itself. It began with a PWOOSH…followed by a most terminating…HUH-THWAAAP!! The gnarled gnomes that surrounded Dyfed suddenly all rushed forward like beetles scurrying over and past the unmoved and immovable. Dyfed felt as though his flesh was on fire when moments ago it was freezing, but then he became aware that Morgant was holding him tightly and supporting him. His kindly friend and mentor then quickly took out a flask of distilled fermented grape elixir from the inside pocket of Dyfed's garment. Uncorking it with difficulty and struggling to prop up Dyfed's large, lanky and solid build, he managed to pour a large quantity of its contents down the latter's throat before pouring the remainder down his own.

"What happened?' Dyfed whispered to Morgant in a rough voice. The babble of flushed and agitated voices inside this subterranean tomb suddenly seemed like voices above water as one sank beneath its surface: It sounded like a passing gust of wind, or an animated conversation at its height between a group of people while they passed by on galloping steeds, their voices strained as in a vortex or a vacuum. He then noticed that he and Morgan were almost alone and back on the peripheral edge of the temple of brightly painted marble again. He then recognised that the high notes he had heard weren't shrieks but were the women folk's exited voices that were now mixing with exasperation in the tones of the men. It was coming from the whole procession, both the emperor's suite along with their wives and families that had come to mingle together on the pathway a short distance from the temple as they now all wended their way back to the villa. And as they went they began to softly sing an apopemptic.

"Moments ago a messenger had arrived,' said Morgant softly to Dyfed in explanation, 'to inform the emperor that Amor is burning again and the people are in full revolt. I'm afraid that the emperor took it badly, as we have seen. What can you remember, for sometime after slumping into a delirium where I became sorely afraid for your health, you suddenly disappeared from sight, as it were,' Morgant said to Dyfed. Morgant keenly looked over the latter with concern. Dyfed, who was sitting on the temple's cold, hard floor and leaning back against one of the glistening Corinthian columns, was still shaking, but now his arms were crossed and he was rapidly rubbing his hands up and down over his upper arms to bring warmth back into himself. Briefly and quickly he related his subterranean adventure to Morgant.

"We must now get away from here as fast as we can,' Morgant said to him, looking astonished yet concerned. There is nothing keeping us. The emperor could be dead from cardiac arrest, possibly due to the news from Amor, I'm not sure. The ceremony quickly came to and end and he was rushed back to the villa ahead of everybody who is now following, as you can see.'

Dyfed was just then squinting in their direction in the twilight, peering through the gloaming that girds the Earth just before complete darkness falls. A long moment passed as Dyfed increased the size of his breath. High above, and just beyond the cupola of the temple — now girded in the shades of night — the partially dilated moon appeared to rest upon a shelf of luminous cloud.

'Macaronius,' said Morgant suddenly, startling Dyfed for a moment, 'was accompanied by his son, Fulvius Officius Constantius who is here on furlong from Imperial wars at large to visit and get advice from his father. I now realise that he was the big man sitting next to the emperor at lunch. He sat on his other side from *Felix* — staring out at everyone — and for all the world looked like large a king fish that are caught in the White Sea. Aside from him and the paramedics, plus their guards, only two other men accompanied the emperor and his son. They were Cornelius-*Felix* and that tall Gaul we saw earlier. And as far as Macaronius is concerned, he may or may not be dead or dying,' Morgant ended, looking thoughtful.

"Long may the emperor remain dead,' Dyfed hoarsely whispered in answer, clearly still in a fit of languish and a retarded stage of normal awareness that caused him to not quite be able to keep up to Morgant's dialogue. Morgant shrugged.

"Its not the emperor we need to worry about,' he said, 'emperors come and go. It's Cornelius-*Felix* — the quasi emperor-maker himself — that concerns me. You are still a little fuzzy-minded and woozy from your ordeal. You haven't grasped the severity of the situation, Dyvie. There may or may not be a people's revolution in the streets of Amor as was announced earlier. That may be a ruse. But there surely is a marked change of direction here at the leadership level at the top of the food chain. Its not a coincidence, either — I don't think — that Fulvius Officius Constantius, son of Flavius Valerius

Constantius Macaronius, is visiting just when Cornelius-Felix unexplainably turns up and is seen in public…at the same party…and for the first and only time in almost four centuries. No! Something's up Dyvie me boy. We need to get far away from here to think and seek other news. And we need to leave now.'

"If what you say is true,' said Dyfed still in his hoarse and rasping voice, 'we won't be any safer in Amor.'

"We're not going to Amor,' Morgant quickly replied, glancing down at Dyfed. 'We will go to Tusculum where Cato's villa is. It's his only home here in Italia. Also I advised Marg not to accompany us! I also advised her not to remain in Amor but to accompany Cato and stay close to him and return to the Hyperborean fifth dimension for now where she will be safe. You really need to bone up on transcendence Hyperborean style. You definitely need to knuckle down and Master of the Little Known Universe up. Do you hear me? You are after all a prince of our race. Remember, Dyvie. You are a player here.'

(Fleeing Tibur)

'The bible teaches us how to go to heaven, not how the heavens go.'
CAESAR BARONIUS

It was with heavy heart that Morgant found he couldn't entice Dyfed to immediately accompany him to Tusculum. The latter was most set and thoroughly bent on returning to Amor to try and safeguard the future of his servants and staff there, while attempting to salvage what might be left of the House of Lucifer along with its extent banking and commerce enterprises. Dyfed felt he had an obligation and a responsibility to those who trusted him and relied on him. This, of course, was finally the argument that Morgant could not counter. Dyfed was to steal away that evening on his black Andalusian while offering the white one to Morgant. Morgant recalled that it wasn't the first horse Dyfed had offered him, though the white Andalusian was a darn sight better than the last old nag he had tied up to his garden fence a couple of centuries ago. Dyfed's journey back to Amor was relatively uneventful, apart from nearly getting himself captured by the emperor's troops who were sent out from the villa at Tibur to find and arrest him and bring him back to answer for the rudeness and the suddenness, hence suspicious and unanswered questions, about the reason for his sudden departure: That, and his callous attitude towards the emperor's health despite the fact that Dyfed did register such an enquiry before he left. But the only thing that got captured that night was his black Andalusian. However, the discovery of this animal grazing and rider-less prompted a concentrated search that was focussed in that immediate area of the Alban Hills where Dyfed had in fact dismounted and where he sought refuge among some rocky cliffs set in a thickly wooded area. This rustic and bucolic world was the Prince of the Groves' natural terrain, and even though there were many shiny stars twinkling up in the blackened sky, Dyfed was further aided by that pervading darkness that had cast an even more amazing obscurity over the land. Diana had become his ally tonight and took to hiding herself beneath the dark horizon. For Dyfed, this is the spot where 'relatively uneventful' ends, and where *an* event becomes *the* event; like the first kiss, the first sexual union, and one's first born child. So, here — now and in this state — he began to spin his new found magic, hoping for an outcome somewhat as before. The problem was that his was a type of magic with approximate proportions that had a tendency to be more digital than analog. He needed analog and since the soldiers were closing in and around him, he needed it fast.

It was then that the strange semblance of reality he had suffered back at Saturn's temple so recently occurred again, this time with Dyfed being a little more in its driver's seat and his competency level being a teensy-weensy greater. Morgant's words of advice to Master up, now returned to his ears. Fortunately, as well, it had been the civic holiday Vinalia — which like other days of holy celebrations in the empire — had been a restful one without any pressing disruption beyond the pleasures of recreational drinking and rest: Never mind that it had ballooned into six days of rest. Dyfed's normal day allowed (for the most part) for disruption and interruption for business and personal affairs beginning at six in the morning that lasted until eleven-thirty later that same morning. From then until two-thirty in the afternoon was his personal time with no impersonal disturbances. He utilised this noontide non-interruption break for his midday dinner, perhaps a bath afterwards (instead of later in the afternoon like other Amorans), as well as for reading. He certainly saw to it that it ended with a short siesta and a wake up call at two-thirty in the afternoon. As stated, this was his personal time and he did whatever he wanted with it. His secretary and his servants were specifically instructed that he would not take any solicitation or conduct any business during this time. After two-thirty in the afternoon he then continued with his interruption and disturbance time again and worked until eleven-thirty at night, although, hardly anybody contacted him after four o'clock for business. A lot of his business time was free for him to pursue personal activities as well, all of which can be tiring, if not exhausting. But because the last six days had been one of festival, Dyfed was more than rested up despite his ordeal earlier on. So he was quite refreshed at this juncture — when his freedom, if not his life, was on the line here — and he was not suffering any debilitation from a deprivation of sleep. This helped him immensely to concentrate in order to conjure up his magic the best he could: And he certainly needed that concentration, believe you me! It was now or never and he needed that concentration in order — like a baby bird's first push out of its nest high up in a tree — to flit between the dimensions beyond his third density — that common medium at large — and what could be, if not Nirvana, a sudden-stop density of the ground floor below.

Once again the Golden Bow (Bough) presented itself in the steady hand of Marg the Fate who now resembled Sibyl. The two of them seemed to be alone this time and were not being perturbed by any violent tempered god.

"It's just you and me, baby,' she said, with her come-hither smile on her pretty face. 'Come and get it.' Once again, Dyfed felt the disassociation of physical orientation. But this time he was not confused. Marg was a big help this time; unlike Morgant, she had a woman's touch. Dyfed suddenly remembered the first time they had lain together, and then immediately there was a shift in a space without time that resulted in a transcendence fully completed.

It suffices to say at this point that our hero Dyfed eluded the Amoran soldiers who had been sent to capture him, much to the chagrin of Cornelius-Felix, apparently. But, fortunately, the latter had bigger troubles to attend to just now. The biggest of them was in the presence of a man named Diokles of Dalmatia. Known as Aurelius Valerius Diocletianus Augustus, he had earlier become the all-powerful ruler over the entire Amoran Empire that he ruled from Byzas. It should be pointed out that the empire had now grown and had overreached itself to such an extent just like a big tree with huge overhanging limbs, unless these limbs were propped up and supported, they would break off. It had been Diokles who after effecting circumstances which promoted him to emperor, sought first to divide the empire and its governing into halves and then quarters (the tetrarch). Each section — first two, then later four — were headed up by an emperor de facto which Diokles appointed. He chose well, usually soldiers who he had commanded and had worked well under him. As the supreme authority of Amor it was he who had appointed Macaronius to the position of ruler of the Western Empire. Diokles had been a prickly thorn in Cornelius-Felix's side. The latter rued the day when he had perilously overlooked not weeding him out back in the day when he had had the opportunity. Now it was causing a case of mild alarm in the boardroom of the Haploid camp — I can tell you. Everyone has a boss; even the powerful and seemingly indestructible C. F. had a boss to answer to. But at this time Dyfed, or anyone else in the *pack* (Masters of the Little Known Universe in residence), hadn't managed to figure out who that individual was. The *pack's* ace in their pocket and their ticket toward manipulating the culture of the empire toward glorious Utopia for a big part of the world, at least for starters, was in the person of Diokles, the supreme emperor. And Diokles or Aurelius Valerius Diocletianus Augustus — as he renamed himself when he became emperor — was himself one of the *pack*. This was no small thing, but it wasn't to be the end all, either. But just as Diocletianus knew that no one man can run a huge empire alone, he also knew that no matter what, that an empire as big as the Amoran Empire, it was vulnerable in many other ways including time; although that inevitable sapping and breaching that needed to take place would be painstaking in detail and heavily time delayed. But it was all about time, wasn't it? For at some time the *pack* and their associates wanted a Utopia, not an empire. And they wanted Utopia to be world encompassing, not imperial. Amor wasn't built in a day and Utopia couldn't be either. It had to start somewhere…sometime, and its progress needed to be constructive.

Ironically, despite the political machine's progressive governing factors of managing to generate good law and order, combined with mounting capital that cast protection over Amoran society on the whole, it had sudden backsliding tendencies that were like earthquakes and landslides. Along with its process of organization it had corruption, and the world's intelligentsia that flocked to Amoran corridors of power in droves, though diverse and exceptionally unique, lacked the stamina in the end to resist the empire's protocol of exorcising individuality to fit the Idea of Amor. The empire could also (from time to time) display other protocols that promoted diminished wisdom that attained only chaotic repercussions from which good order, or economics, seldom ensued. Here, in this furious fusion of empire, even the most powerful among the elite were not able to retain security and sensibility for long. But what they did have was technology of system that stemmed in part from their flare for organizational skills. But for those with eyes to see, within the engine of the empire there was more in the way of third dimensional gratification whose seeds of destiny were replete with suffering and misery of the heart. Dyfed preferred the other, the outside the empire, short on sparkle and bumptious posture, long on quality of character. But this wish was not to be. For it was to the machinations of responsible and natural control that he had been schooled, not for what only passes for a control centre of empires. It now seemed possible to him that he and the world around were incompatible.

Not surprisingly the *pack* was eternally concerned for Diokles health and especially his safety. Diocletianus was heavily protected, sometimes with wizardry, according to contemporary standards, and he lived in Byzas not Amor. The *pack* however had long identified Cornelius-Felix as Diokles' arch enemy and chief villain of the good fight in their holy quest to fully emancipate the hoi polloi and indelibly steer them toward the culture of freedom from suffering. But Cornelius-Felix never let down his guard or lifted his plan of attack against Diokles. When Dyfed and Morgant, along with the hand-picked senators who accompanied Emperor Macaronius to his villa, there may have been three or four hundred soldiers around the emperor and his son at the time. When Morgant identified Cornelius-Felix presence at the villa the following day, Dyfed had reported to him that he estimated there to be at least four thousand troops now in the surrounding environs and immediate vicinity. These, then, were Cornelius-Felix's troops, as well as a veritable host of fifth-column agents that with the entire empire was crawling. Oh yeah — Cornelius-Felix was a problem for the *pack*, all right. That was something they are agreed on. How to get to him with their somewhat paltry third dimensional resources at hand? was the question. After all these years that wily old dictator retained his remarkable property of being assassination proof.

When Dyfed eventually arrived before the walls of Amor, all the gates were closed for the night. It was now the third day after the close of the Vinalia festival. Well disguised, he awaited the ritual of the morning gate opening in a tavern of a small village set beyond the shadow of Amor's walls. And whom should he find there? but his old new acquaintance Markus Grouchus. Of course, the latter did not recognise Dyfed and looked quite distracted by the goings on immediately around him in particular. When he saw Dyfed approaching he began to look even more nervous, and at one point rested his right hand on his gladius. Just as Dyfed was about to speak and put him at his ease, Markus Grouchus' face suddenly lighted up and quickly rising to his feet he rushed forward. But it wasn't to Dyfed that he showered his greetings. Instead, he threw his arms around a sickly looking man about his own age that had just gruffly brushed past Dyfed. The latter stopped in his tracks in a swamp of incredulous surprise. It was this action (and his close proximity to the two others) that only then attracted the attention of Grouchus and his friend more closely. Now they were both suspiciously regarding him.

"It's me,' Dyfed said softly, looking directly at Grouchus. 'You know me, we met at the House of Lucifer only last week.'

"This is P.V. Maro,' said Markus to Dyfed in introduction to the other man. 'We can trust him. 'In fact, he was solicited to help find you.'

"Aye, but solicited by whom? said Dyfed playfully joking in his good-natured way.' The other two men laughed.

"Solicited by Cato and the other man…that gnome-like creature who pretends to be your servant,' answered Markus.

"That's right,' exclaimed Dyfed, now remembering. 'At my home I noticed that you and Cato had once been well acquainted. And of you…?'

"Ah,' injected Markus quickly, 'P.V. is a poet, in fact he is one of Amor's finest.

"I know,' said P.V. to Dyfed, 'from speaking to Cato that your intentions to salvage your empire. That is the reason for your return.'

"Not really,' answered Dyfed. 'It was initially to fend for my staff and servants.'

"Don't worry,' replied Markus. 'You see, P. V. has that in hand and I am here to help him. We need pertinent information, however, from you in order to carry out your wishes, and we will need denarii.'

Dyfed debriefed the two men in order for them to sufficiently expedite his desires. He then informed them that he would lead them to money on the morrow. Then remembering something Morgant had said to him about Marg retiring at Alba Longa got him wondering.

"What is Alba Longa's claim to fame?' he asked.

'Alba Longa,' said Markus, 'was the founder and leader city state of the Latinius League until the 7th century BCE, when it was defeated by Amor.'

"Alba Longa is a beautiful village of whitewashed buildings placed high up on a hill crest over looking Lake Albano,' interjected the poet in a soft voice. 'It is a cool and tranquil place under a big sky from where snowdrifts of clouds reflect up from off the waters of the lake below that match the bright canopy above. It is just south of here and I recommend it. However, on the off-chance that we come across you, Cato has expressly informed us to direct you to his villa in Tusculum which will be much more safe. We heard about the soldiers you eluded and how you are now hunted like the dangerous criminal that they have made you out to be. Though you are not an Amoran citizen as such, you benefit greatly from the empire at large and they (the oligarchs) want to conscript you into the military where you will probably be killed. So, they hate you. They hate you all the more because of who you are and what you represent within their prejudiced, narrow conservative minds,' the poet added, sympathetically.

"Ha, welcome to the club, Dyfed,' said Markus, who — compared to the poet — was much more robust of nature and who gave the latter a wink and clenched his fist in a sign of brotherly solidarity. 'Oh, and one other thing. Rumour has it that Macaronius has set his sights on some inconsequential unrest among the Pixies in far away Albion and that his son Fulvius Officius Constantius is to accompany him there. Apparently, that is why Macaronius summoned his son for the Vinalia festival. Meanwhile, the big news is that Diocletianus (Diokles), the senior Amoran emperor and ruler of Byzas, has taken over the full reigns of imperial power again, temporarily we can assume. This is a good thing, Dyfed, but it has infuriated Cornelius -Felix. And this sojourn of Constantius' into Albion may have its roots in Cornelius-Felix. It's hard to say but he is planning something. He has become a rampage on the warpath which presently clouds Amoran issues of state and plays havoc with our economy but may provide the murky waters which can aid and abet the *pack*.' At the mention of this, Dyfed's head shot up and he scrutinized the two of them closely.

"What do you know about that?' Dyfed asked.

"Not as much as you do,' replied the poet this time, with a nod of acknowledgement to Dyfed's superiority in that. 'But both Markus here and I are contributing as much as we can toward the cause. We share the vision and appreciate what you and Cato are capable of doing.'

There now occurred a moment of serious reflection for Dyfed. He wandered among archetypical relics of the past with a sense of bewilderment and bereavement over the recent events. Menstruating mother of Jeshua! he thought. Just how the devil had he got himself into all this? He was a Watcher; that what he was. He wasn't truly a programmer after all. If they bothered to ask, it was he who contributed by watching and reporting to the Masters of the Little Known Universe of what it was that unfolded here, as seen by him. His Idea, nothing more, or less, was what he contributed. It is what it is. And this is what he had always done. And so it went.

(A White Sea Cruise through the looking lens at the temple of the Sabaens)

(Whoo-eee baby: Won'chu take me on a sea cruise?)
HUEY 'PIANO' SMITH/FRANKIE FORD

There had been a lapse of time since Morgant had shown his face around the place, but Dyfed knew from experience that once in the fifth dimension folks seem to lose track of time (third dimensional time, that is) whatever it is. Immediately upon his arrival (though) Morgant took Dyfed aside and told him that he wanted to send him on a mission. This mission was a journey to the largest man-made structure in the world and the oldest of the Seven Wonders of the World. This particular venue, as it so happened, was the largest and the oldest pyramid at Giza. He informed Dyfed that he was to have a special rendezvous with a man named Akasa who was a priest from Luwnuw (LWNW), the City of the Sun. He let Dyfed know that more would be explained later.

Then to bring Dyfed up to speed in other important matters he told him that among other things the *pack*, along with affiliates from the pool of Masters of the Unknown Universe, had finally identified the tall, mysterious Gaul, that curious attendee they had wondered about at Macaronius' villa during the festival of Urban Vinalia. His name, apparently, was Georgius Gregorius Florentius, who Dyfed immediately dubbed, Gorgeous Georgius Gregorius.

The man was about the same age as Dyfed himself and was actually referred to as Bishop Gregorius of Cenabum (later Orleans). Apparently, he had been (and still was) a priest of the Jeshuan cult, though at the time they had come across him he had been disguised (that is to say, not been decked out in the order's usual habit). This familiar get-up and gear that priests habitually wore consisted of a scapular and a cowl with the liberal use of either black or white for its sole colour coordination. Dyfed remembered that the mysterious Gorgeous Georgius Gregorius had been dressed as an Amoran aristocrat. Little did he realize at that time how often this man Gorgeous Georgius would cross his path (literally) in the centuries ahead. Nor was he aware of the power this man would wield. If Cornelius-Felix of the House of Felix-Cornelius was a high king of the third dimension, then Pastor Gorgeous Georgius Gregorius Florentius would become its high priest in the world that was shaping up to be. He and Morgant agreed at this point that this man definitely had Haploid material written all over him, for sure.

Meanwhile Dyfed prepared for his journey to the Land of Khem. Then out of the blue came another blast from the past. Marg arrived back in Amor and somehow seamlessly into step again with Dyfed's hurly-burly life-style. Furthermore, she debuted in the here and now in a most flamboyant manner (that was peculiar to her) with a sharp whiff of jasmine perfume floating around her in the air accompanied by an incessant, yet alluring, melodic whine which she affected that subtlety had the capability of being categorized as… "whoo-eee baby, take me on a White Sea cruise, wee-you?"…in tune with the vibration that emitted from her full and sensuously moist, motionless lips. This provided Dyfed with an excuse to be distracted. It allowed him (he realized) to kill two birds with one stone. So, he then quickly set about in preparation to embark on a White Sea cruise where (on one hand) he could estimate whether there was any point (any longer) in trying to patch things up with Marg. He doubted it from the start but set out to make the best of what may become a bad thing in the long run. On the other hand, he now had the perfect cover and a burning interest to visit Khem, that ancient light of the previous world along with the old Ka'nite lands and parts of Anatolia and the Aegean Sea. And it could all be accomplished on account of his orders from the Masters of the Unknown Universe, relayed to him through Morgant.

Trachmyr was next to join them. This stalwart individual (if you remember) had himself been a sailor since childhood like all men of the Cardagan coast. Having secured temporary leave from the Amoran army to return to Dyfed's domicile for a well-deserved rest and recreational respite, Dyfed was to facilitate this soldier in his time of need. It was a furlough really that — like the former's many commissions within the legions of the Amoran military might — had been bought by Dyfed. Dyfed had spared no expense over the years in order to promote and safeguard his old acquaintance. However, recently Trachmyr had been severely injured while fighting to protect the empire in Moesia and the latter had solicited Dyfed's help in order to recoup and recover back in Amor. It had come at an opportune time for Dyfed needed a first lieutenant to act under him and to keep discipline among the personnel accompanying their vessel. This vessel was the *Aura Maré*, Dyfed's recently commissioned private large lug rigged sailing yacht. Her crew, which he employed along with an ancient Hellenic mariner to pilot her, were mostly Illyrians.

The couple, along with Trachmyr posing as Dyfed's batman, set out on, the *Aura Maré*. There was no need to apply the prefix S.V. (sailing vessel) to her name for like all acre-eating sea vessels at this time she either moved by that very breath of life in its bodiless state of freedom over the waters or was oared like a graceful winged seawater creature that cut through those cold briny seas by the muscle and sweat of tough oarsmen. But the rigging of the *Aura Maré* was different than the normal Europaean lug rigging, for Morgant had provided him with engineered prints of a concept that was a lot more efficient. Dyfed learned many years later that the men of the land of Ch'in (the Amorans called these men Seres) had similar riggings that were termed junk rigged.

The old city of Xandria was their primary destination and in putting out for there they made only one stop. This first haven had been at Matala on the Isle of Kreta. The incredibly fast passage from the time that the Doric columns of Poseidon's temple at Taras (currently Tarentum, the future Taranto) fell astern behind the *Aura Maré* until the hour they had entered into the gulf of Mesara, was only three days. Now, as they sailed and pulled themselves toward the harbour at Matala, they skirted by the Paximadia islands (the birth place of the twins Apollo and Artemis) that passed just off their port gunnel. From there they made anchor in the shadow below the harbour hill that sloped steeply up from the water on their starboard to the south. Here was the dock and main loading and off-loading structures of the port of Matala that facilitated the ancient centres of Phaistos and Gortys. Beyond their bow (facing an easterly direction) were the thick olive groves that climbed up into the stony hills around the ruins of the old palace at Phaistos; and further on from that lay the alluvial plains of Messara.

When they came alongside, Dyfed noticed a little stream beyond the ship's bow that cut through the land beach-sands and flowed here into the sea from the direction of the olive hills. At Matala they took on water and some fresh produce. Matala at this time was in the final process of being rebuilt after having been struck by a succession of horrific waves that were caused by a large underwater earthquake. This event utterly destroyed the harbour facilities with Matala's domicile structures that were devastated along with the countryside around. As such, lodgings were slim pickings and wanting to sleep apart from the bunk aboard the *Aura Maré*, Dyfed choose one of the resident caves that were carved into the large rock cliff at the north end of the beach for his shelter. Some of the elaborate caves were already in use but most had not been cleared out from the debris deposited by the sea flood. So it was there, under the crooked Matalan quarter moon on their first night ashore, Marg slipped into Dyfed's bed and the two lovers officially made up.

Xandria, on the other hand was an enormously vibrant and beautiful city on the great river delta in the ancient land of Khem. Here were harboured many temptations. The moment the two re-united lovers washed up upon its shores they lavished forth and lapped it up. Quickly they planned their stay and their visitations out to take in its sights. As their stay would be extended due to Dyfed's side trip into the interior, he rented a lavish room in the beautiful Chateau Cleopatra across the street from the Antony Hotel and the famous Hellene pavilion with the city's even more famous bibliotheca just up the street. This bibliotheca was the famous Royal Library of Xanderia that was dedicated to the nine goddesses (Muses) of the arts and was part of and in the service of the grand Musaeum (institution of the Muses) that was founded by Ptolemaîos Philádelphos. Ptolemy, the king of Ptolemaic Khem, had fashioned it after Plato's own school of philosophy that was located at Akademia in an olive grove sanctuary sacred to Athena which once lay just outside the walls of her city. The academy in Xanderia (now quite old and showing signs of affliction by fire) had once been capable of provided the most significant and extent information in the world, but no longer.

During the evenings Dyfed and Marg indulged themselves at caféterias and restaurants in Xandria which offered them the finest dining that could be found anywhere along the entire coast-line of the White Sea, which, of course, included Italia, Hellas and the ports of ancient Phoeniki. In dance halls they twirled and swooped as they enjoyed fine music brought in from Ethiopia and Arabia, and they visited the Hellene theatre with their captivating performances written by some of most famous playwrights of all time.

Often along a quiet snye of the Black (Ar) River (called Neilos or Valley river by the Helenes, from which emanated the name Nile), Dyfed and Marg would often stroll hand in hand and arm in arm at dusk and again late in the evening. Many birds were to be seen here but wading birds especially were plentiful like the giant Grey heron, the Great egret, the Northern Red Bishop, the osprey and of course the gigantic Sacred ibis that was every bit as tall as a tall man's leg. It was an intriguing sight shortly after the sun had set, with the silky sky still a pale, pale bluey bright, the water channels demarked by ribbons of yellow light but the dusky land all bulky in heavy shadow. Here, with a heaving and husky voiced breathing, the city was crouched now into strange bulky shapes, quite darkened but noisy in a distant way and alive. Here and there thousands of tiny points of fire blazed. Suddenly, a shaky movement of dark and twisted angles would occur like sails being rapidly dropped from a ship's mast. But what appeared were the haphazardly broken and bent out of shape image of either a heron, a pelican or an ibis. With wings cockeyed at right angles and feathers and legs splayed out sharply, it looked for all the world like some prehistoric creature with giant broken canvas-like wings cartwheeling and tumbling out of control and was about to crash into somebody and injure them seriously or break the spar on the mast of a river barge before plunging backwards into the yellow surface of the river with a giant splash. But then suddenly again, this creature would transform before your eyes into a graceful shape that swoops sharply again and then like a ballerina and softly letting up with the genius of an aerial pro, it would glide down to make the smoothest and the quietest landing imaginable with barely a ripple upon the glancing yellow sheen of the river's calm surface.

Dyfed even made an appointment and had a short and challenging interview with Theophilus, thus giving the latter the opportunity to defend some of his outrageous claims; though Dyfed recorded that the man had failed quite miserably at that with him when it came to his art of defence.

A month or two into their stay and after Dyfed had struck into the interior for Giza; Marg had struck up a friendship with a brilliant mathematician, engineer and scientist. This woman's name was Cynthia of Hypatia. Both Dyfed and Marg had already become acquainted as well with Catherine Pergamius who was the daughter of the prefect of Khem, a certain Marcellinus Pergamius. Catherine was a most compassionate young woman who was a well-read academic and was a recent convert to the Jeshuan cult. She was a particular beautiful woman, Dyfed thought, and this made him happy along with making his blood run faster when he was in her company. At this point Dyfed made plans to travel up river to the old city of Memphis. Dyfed relieved Trachmyr of his duties as his manservant and placed him in charge of the Aura Maré (that was dragging anchor in the harbour of Xandria), with the added responsibilities of keeping her fit and tidy and her crew of sailors out of jail. That, and an eye on Marg, though he knew the latter would be way too much for Trachmyr to manage. Furthermore, Trachmyr, as trusted servant to Dyfed who was his lord and liege, was also to act as his secretary in all things to do with wages and expenses in Dyfed's absence.

Following Morgant's instructions he travelled up river through the Nile Crocodile delta by felucca to Peru-nefer, the main port of the ancient city of Men-nefer (the enduring and the beautiful) that was also known as Aneb-Hetch (White Walls, also White Fortress). Here at Men-nefer Dyfed found the ruined great temple of Hut-ka-Ptah (also translated and transcribed by Manetho in his Hellene tongue as Ai-gy-ptos or Aigypt). This translation for the great temple ultimately led to an alternate misleading name for all of Khem in general, in the long term.

Being ahead of schedule Dyfed placed a wide board on an easel and then took pains to paint a rendition of Hut-ka-Ptah's (Aigyptos') faded glory. This site was among many other ruined archaeological sites of which Dyfed created effigies that he composed from sketches and paint — edifices such as the Pillared Hall of Ra-mose (progeny or re-birth [also son of] the god Ra). It should be remembered that Ra-mose (Ramses) who ruled from this ancient city over fifteen centuries before Dyfed's current visit was nineteen centuries after Narmer who was Khem's first king that ruled here over thirty-five centuries before this time of Dyfed's depute. Then as the assigned time approached, and as instructed by Morgant, Dyfed hired a small craft to take him from the river port of Peru-nefer on up the river Ar to Helwan. There, at the appointed time of the first new moon after the vernal equinox, he was to make contact with a priest from Luwnuw (LWNW), the City of the Sun. There (in a clanstine manner) the meeting was to take place in an ancient cemetery once used by the citizens of Aneb-Hetch or Men-nefer city. This having been successfully completed, the strange cowled man that materialized suddenly before him out of a nearby darkened tomb…this man whose raven black eyes that glowed in the dark of night like hot coals, appeared irritated (rather than happy to be at Dyfed's service) over the bother of having been summoned hither. Indeed, he loudly claimed to be otherwise currently engaged on his own errand in Heliopolis that was of much more importance. He said that this engagement at Giza for reasons unknown and even unknowable (he emphasised the latter) was one he had been roped into and had taken him away from his work and detracted from the precious time allotted him, now lost. So, in an irritated manner he accompanied Dyfed back to Men-nefer. There he instructed Dyfed to go to a nearby river warehouse to collect a party of workmen who by former appointment would be waiting for him there. Then from Men-nefer Dyfed rented another felucca and he, the scowling and cowled cleric along with their small party of workmen returned north again, sailing downstream to a spot on the river close to Giza with its ancient structures that included, among other things, a colossal human faced lion and three large pyramids. Just prior to leaving the port of Peru-nefer Dyfed sent mail via a state run felluca back to Xanderia. In that packet Dyfed informed Marg that he desired contact with Morgant at once.

Once they arrived at the village on the banks of the Ar adjacent to Giza they made their way toward the largest of the three pyramids that was attributed to the royally entitled King Kufu which was situated close to the lion shaped creature called the sphinx with its human face. Here they stopped making camp along the pyramid's northern flank.

While he was still a boy Manandan had told Dyfed about this particular pyramid. Indeed, it was Manandan who had coined it as one of the wonders of the known world. Close by their camp the pyramid's external skin of shining marble had been breached, its scar a blemish on this mega structure's once shiny white facing. However, many of the white facing-stones had been long removed by this time. They had been mined to decorate other structures in the ensuing centuries following the ancient dynasties. But the location of the scar was had been the place of forced entry dating back to antiquity when ancient robbers had tried to access the interior of the pyramid believing that there was treasure hidden within. Remarkably, they had broken through at a point where with only a minimal amount of floundering around about through the rubble they had managed to gain access to an inner shaft. But the moment of 'Eureka!' would have faded quickly for them. For the inner shaft that the robbers had stumbled upon due to a certain acumen applied by those sappers of long ago simply descended in a depressing downward decline into the bedrock beneath the great pyramid and to no avail for erstwhile robbers of treasure. It would not have been a happy moment, other than for the long gone builders who may be smiling from the shades.

The next morning, a Thursday (Thor's day) as it happened, the workmen that had been hired climbed up, clambered through the breach, and entered into the long ago discovered passage way. Under orders from the strange cowled priest, whose name he told Dyfed was Akasa (Akasha), they were to locate a secondary portal which when followed would take one away from the direction of the bedrock and into the heights of the thing.

Having arrived on site first, and under an order of silence, the workmen quickly began busying themselves tap, tap, tapping the large stones that lined the descending shaft with their hammers. Dyfed having waited for the priest then accompanied the latter into the shaft. Laughing, the old gnarled fiery-eyed man then told Dyfed to strike his little hammer at a certain spot above his head. This produced an unusual sound. Dyfed had struck one of the large and heavy stone blocks along the back (ceiling) of the descending shaft and the sound that emitted from it was hollow compared to the sound which the others made as the workmen tapped away. Smiling the priest point at it and then calling out, motioned for the workmen to carefully remove this plug that would expose the start of an ascending shaft. This shaft, he told Dyfed in a low voice so the workmen wouldn't hear, would ascend up toward the middle of the pyramid wherein lay two chambers, an upper and lower chamber. Their destination, Akasha said, was the upper one that was located approximate to and directly above this giant stone mega structure's centre of mass. The priest instructed the workmen to build an apparatus with the heavy timbers that they had brought with them. He was very particular, Dyfed noticed, imploring them to perform their work exactly to his instructions and not to be in any haste when manipulating the stone itself. Apparently, so Dyfed noted, the stone needed to be partially pressed up and in then carefully (with one side securely propped up with timbers) the other side could be gently shifted to one side through carefully but strenuous lever actions. At no time or in any way could the stone fall through and into the shaft below. Accordingly, he cautioned the workers to be careful not to lose control of the large stone plug which he wanted to move temporarily clear of the portal so he and Dyfed could climb up and enter through thereby. He was most concerned that the huge stone should remain balanced on his specifically designed framework made of timbers so as to allow the heavy stone to be easily manoeuvrable and equally easy to lever back exactly into place using points of pressure and methods of mechanical advantage. Proper replacement was imperative he warned them. It was obvious he didn't want to dislodge the rock plug in such a way that replacing it again would leave room for mistakes that potentially could alert others to the hidden shaft. Once they had it moved Dyfed noticed that the plug stone was irregularly shaped so when it was in place its weight tipped it to one side that caused the opening to remain perfectly sealed and unnoticeable from below. Then he and the priest Akasha (which amused Dyfed for that word meant 'sky' in Shamskara, his traditional language) explored part of the vast anatomical-like mechanism at hand.

At first Dyfed was wary of being entombed within the megalith by having the plug replaced by the workmen out of malice once he and Akasha had journeyed up into the ascending shaft. But Akasha pacified him, telling him that not only being handsomely paid for their work meant more to these crude hoi polloi then anything else, the stone (he said) even when replaced could be opened with ease from up top and inside.

Ascending at about thirty degrees they climbed until they entered a marvellous gallery that led to an equally marvellous chamber that had a hollowed out, empty red stone structure that resembled a sarcophagus placed within. This sarcophagus-thing, he reasoned, would have had to be placed here before anything above it had been built for the object was bigger than any of the openings leading to this chamber. The chamber itself which, as stated, was more or less located in the centre of the giant pyramid, was topped, Akasha told him, with massive stone blocks that created relieving chambers so as to defuse the tremendous weight of thousands of tons of stone above and around it by glancing that weight away toward the slanted side-base of the pyramid which pushed in and down to secure the centre of mass below them. In order to be effective the largest of these weight shifting monoliths, he was told, weighed two or three hundred Amoran tons. He was amazed and his mind quickly turned from how was this stone machine built and who (in fact) had such technology that was capable of building it in the first place, to what purpose did it serve? For that purpose, whatever it was, would necessary need to come first before anybody would (or actually could) build it in the first place, never mind wanting to and then being bothered to actually doing so — surely? The answer there (in this manner of thinking) made one thing obvious. The pyramid was meant to radiate knowledge (once individuals were past an attainable threshold thereof), of course. And aside from that it probably had a function in spite of itself. Why waste energy? What the pyramid was not; was a tomb. Nor was it meant to hold, stifle or conceal anything other than from the uninitiated. To Dyfed that meant it was a pointer for the folks who could move toward spiritual transformation and transmigration within the current phenomenon. So, it seemed to him, it was intended as a storehouse for ancient wisdom and the accumulation of vast (perhaps ethereal) energy that could serve as a blueprint or as a map for any future enlightened folks and be culpable for helping them move forward. Even though Dyfed was often confused and even experienced strange dizzy spells during the ordeal, he wrote the experience of the adventure of the giant pyramid up in his log as best he could and eventually passed the recorded information on to both Morgant and (at a latter date) another man named Theoderic the Great for them to ponder over and formulate expedient conclusions. One thing was for certain, that apart from rest and recreation he was beginning to wonder why he had been dragged into this.

History and those who fabricate it will eventually embellish and even cloud the discovery of this ascending shaft that Dyfed had climbed. It has become the custom to do this. According to the usually reliable al-Mas'udi (the famous father of the equally famous Caliph Ma'mum), Haroun al-Rashid was the one who discovered the ascending shaft about five hundred years after Dyfed's debut. The truth is that one of these bandied legged, aforementioned characters may well have dislodged the plug (which Akasha had pointed out to Dyfed) and thereby re-discovered it while they were violently boring into a structure they knew nothing about nor had they any possibility of understanding it, let along getting anywhere close to explaining its purpose. So it became a tomb, what else?

The colossal human faced lion with the headdress on and the three large pyramids were too tempting for Dyfed to ignore recording pictorially. Wanting to sketch and paint them so as to take their images back home and show and impress his friends, Dyfed had come prepared with sketching and colouring materials as already stated. With the workmen paid off and the priest having vanished somehow suddenly and quite strangely, he now settled down to some wholesome and therapeutic recreation. He set up his makeshift easel and began to paint and sketch.

But time was beginning to run out on this leg of his adventure. Marg would be waiting impatiently back in Xandria, he thought. On his return Dyfed caught an early morning sailing on a non-stop inter-urban felucca back from Men-nefer (rendered once again into Memphis via the Hellene tongue) to Xandria the very next day. The idle, sleepy hours of its relatively lengthy journey allowed him to fish along the way. To the gasps and surprise and even scolding from his fellow travellers he managed to net the large channel catfish. Once, many years ago, the priests of On or Atum (who insisted on the literal worshiping of the sun, while they the priesthood acted in capacity of Treasurer of Bills Receivable) had declared these same fish sacred for which no fishing licenses were available, ever. Furthermore, it was adamantly prohibited to fish for them at all or of anyone being in possession of, or simply of being caught consuming these fish in any way. All felons were to be prosecuted. All prosecution ended in being flayed alive and buried in the burning sands of the desert far from any aquifer. Catfish consumption was licenced for special religious festivals by law that was administered only by the priesthood. These priests of On were both scribes and magistrates who controlled and administered their formulated justice over all men of this land. The sun had no say any of in it and neither did the king. "What is and how it is…is as we say it is.' So said those noble priests of Heliopolis, formerly Lunu, then later called On by west-Semitic speaking peoples.

As far as catfish were concerned, they were a special species that breathed air beneath and above the waves. They gave live birth and it was rumoured that they suckled their young. Obviously they had confused catfish with seals, or some such mammals. It was even said that these catfish had once walked upon land with the dolphins to whom they were related and who in turn were related to men who walked on the land before them, but after them with killing instruments. This may have been true, but the verdict was still out. Anyway, that was why the dolphins, the seals and the catfish returned to the sea and the men who remained above it still managed, though, to catch and kill them. Catfish were unique as they had the skin of a mammal and not flaky scales like the sea bass or the tuna, and they were sacred to the priests of On who were the only men who were allowed to eat them during sacred ceremony. And it was a female catfish that swallowed Osiris' penis, though queer as it may sound some say it was a male. In the event that you may be wondering how it came to be that a lowly catfish swallowed a god's penis, this took place after that god had succumbed to blows from his brother-god Set during a foolish argument over nothing that couldn't have been resolved affably in a more congruous manner. Though (apparently) being indifferent to the passion of his sister Isis, who was Osiris' lover (and sister — which was common among the families of the royal House of Pharaoh) and Set being indifferent to his brother Osiris' own rights for self-assertion, never mind the mournful family circumstances all around and his brother's violent demise at his hand, Set then dismembered the god Osiris and in no particular order threw the pieces left of him into one of the channels of the Nile-Crocodile River (known at that time as the river Ar) or the valley river which gave life. Certainly (Dyfed thought), the catfish were indeed sacred, for there were no fish as tasty.

Dyfed knew from Manandan that the priesthood of On (also An) was the oldest fake religion of all that was still in practice in the Land of Khem, though it may have devolved into such a religion from an ancient time that had a real understanding of the workings of our common phenomenon like Hinduism once had. An (On) was oldest and most supreme god in Sumer/Akkad and Babylonia (Mesopotamia), Uratta, Hurrian, Hititian and Kizzuwatna et al. It (he) dated back before time. An's centre was Heliopolis or Sun City which was located at the apex of the vast Nile-Crocodile delta on the banks of what once became the river Ar's eastern water course. Here stood the chief temple of the ancient realm of Khem, the great House of (A)men, or (O)mun, also Amun Ra, but also Atum (then later Aten along with Bel [Ba'al also El] before becoming Aden and finally developing into Adon [Adonai]). This became the era's greatest and highest sky god play-thing (think fake torc) of them all, who of course descended from Enlil (Bel) that was second only to the aforementioned An, or On, Anan, Anannan, Amun, etc, etc...ad nauseam.

In the frame of primitive superstition that supports and promotes religion, no matter when or where its worship is undertaken, the human element confuses and fools itself into believing any old load of cods-wallop and clap-trap — obviously. Such was the case (Dyfed knew) with the new Amoran cult god. This was the deity Mono: hence, monotheists, the worshipers of Mono, which of course was nothing new as the Hindus had believed in the one God of Unity and the source of all things since the beginning of time. And in its simplistic form, the Sun god is the symbol of the Grandest Kahuna of the biggest and the best and most sacred of all the kahunas, ever; and our prime cause for being, whatever the hell that is (you choose), depended on it. No material symbol can take the Suns' place without imbibing and infringing upon duplication. Shining in Its glory, we may still amount to nothing, but without it we would be much less than nothing! And in a jolly, damn good sense we are intricately a part of this shining, wondrous life-giving object even if it is far, far away. Still, even at that we are not separated from it in any way. There is nothing to fear from it, it never holds a grudge, it seeks no redress of any kind for any action and takes no revenge whatsoever. So, it was from this holy edifice (the House of the Sun god Amen-Ra) that Sun City got its native and original name that was Luwnuw (LWNW) or Lunu (luna). This word Luwnuw is translated as The Pillars. Naturally, its priests (who in the grand scheme of things were Its weakest link) were, therefore, called the priests of Luwnuw. As such (naturally once) they were (in turn) the Pillars of Life who were bent on perverting the Idea in the end; for many things wrought by the will of God can be perverted by the hand of man. It was the west Semitic speaking Canaanites that translated the city of the Sun into On (that, as we know, was a variation of An from their origins among Mesopotamia. Later the Hellenes translated it into Heliopolis (also meaning Sun city).

And these priests of On often repeated, as they prayed out loud:

> 'Oh living Atum (Aten, Adon, Aden),
> Inspiration of the Grand Master of Wisdom,
> Beginner of life.
> Remote thou art,
> Yet thy rays of life are upon the earth.
> In plain sight of man thou art,
> Yet thy ways are unknown.
> Thy shining ray-beams nourish every field
> which are known to men.
> These fields live for thee, rising — they shine forth.'[39]

The Canaanite people (who initially worshiped Ba'al, the rider of the *storm* clouds) went on to adopt a pseudo Sun god they called Shalim (among others) and referred to it finally as Adon while other cults picked and chose their own Adon or Adonai. One cult, the cult of Abram, which may not have been so much the forerunner of the current Jeshuan cult as it first seemed (though continues to appear as such for the time being), claimed to take up a religion with an enhanced monotheism (single deity like the Sun)

---

39 A truncated composite (by the author) taken from the original translation by Finders Petrie. (*History of Egypt*)

approach. Having first partially ditched certain storm and mountain gods from the past who were trendy in their day but probably didn't answer their prayers fast enough (such as on the double), one such god these same folks picked up in lieu of (everybody needs at least one pet god to temper their fears) was Bel Sadé (also rendered as El Shade) once a weather god who may have (in sympathy for the region) dropped the storm part (of his act, at least). But no matter: patriarch Abram still had to climb the bloody hill (if that wasn't a high enough climb in itself — and at his age) to the threshing floor above Urusalem (Qadesh) to commiserate with Shade (Sade). But that god didn't pan out in the end too well either, apparently. And then under the advise of an un-named somebody who went by (or is remembered only) as '*Mosis*' (the word meaning 'the son of' or 'the embodiment of...such as Thoth-mosis (son of Thoth), or Ra-mosis (son of Ra: also Ramses), who (after talking his tribal folks into it) settled for a god he called Yahu. 'Yahu!' is what he must have called out, at some point. Anyway, Yahu (Yhwh or Jehovah) was strictly another mountain-storm god where this man named Mosis, 'the son of (whomever?)', needed all of his mountain-climbing skills that he could summon in order ascend toward the clouds and commiserate and converse with this Yahu. But by 150 BCE - 50 CE, the Nasrani (also Nazarean, a sect of the new Abramists) were prone to revere Yahu-mosis (son of Yahu) [sic] who was referred to simply as Adon (also Adonia).

(Horus)

> *"Anyone who believes exponential growth can go on forever in a finite world is either a madman or an economist.'*
> **KENNETH EWART BOULDING** *(ECONOMIST)*

In the interim the people of Khem seemed to lose interest in Amen Ra. They resurrected one of the oldest pagan deities that reached back into primitive (though not necessarily always the case) prehistoric times. The god was Horus the Great, a far cry from the glorious Sun god and more along the lines of a pagan demi-god: And what a great tradition Horus is. He was the son of Isis (the lady who longed for Osiris' penis which the catfish swallowed) that was a widow not only when her son Horus was born, but before he was conceived. But more importantly for religion-ites, but what is a monstrous anathema for truth- encrusted wisdom-ites, is the tradition that she was also a virgin when Horus was born. A virgin mother! How unoriginal is that nowadays. But the myth of Isis, Osiris and Horus was at a circa of about six thousand solar cycles BCE, or about sixty-five centuries before the present chronology of Dyfed's life.

Horus, so we are told, was born of a virgin by miraculous birth (i.e.: immaculate ejaculation). That's all pure pork slap and bull chutney like all virgin births, given that virgin means without any reproduction activity. Like, lesson number one: observe the goings on around you and total up all the virgin births and keep these observations separate from your favourite fairy-tales and nursery-rhymes: Either that, or its time now to put away childish things now that we are (at least) six, never mind sixteen or sixty. Ho hum! But it still begs the question (so Dyfed now mused) as to why a man with a Shamskara sounding name of Akasha was a priest from Sun City and what the devil was he doing there? Why wasn't he from Mehrgarh or Harappa? But then again, Manandan had once been here too, it seemed.

It seemed astonishing to Dyfed that Manandan (his singular and private tutor) had also resided in Luwnuw and therefore had materialized (perhaps into the flesh) via the essence of the Great House of Amen. For it was there, Dyfed recalled, that Manandan had laboured in the courts of heaven. And it was from there that certain sentient beings enter into matter, he was told. In its earliest days, when its mythos of being a solitary (monotheistic) god, the Sun's persona had derived from the celestial body Saturn which shone in the logos amid the dusky day and night sky and influenced life on earth. Later this was literally transferred to the sun. Saturn was and remains the titan of time, agriculture, wealth and liberation. Mandanan once told him, that Saturn had been the earth's fixed companion long before it had been captured by the current sun and placed within its inner solar system. Besides, the violent injection of the Saturn and earth infusion into the Sun's system that resulted from space/time/caused much havoc to the gods of light that were then (as now) circling all around. All except for beautiful Apollo the stationary, that is he that is reminiscent of Horus, also Ba'al, Beltane, Belyn, Belinos, Helios and Adonis. In one sense he was the obligatory transgender, the fiery warrior with the alter ego of the supreme mother goddess. The Sun of fierce and burning life that sustaining rays was the bull and the cow in one that brings us back to unity. That titan, however, the luminously glowing spheroid ball of plasma of hydrogen and helium that was seen charging across the sky was illusionary. It wasn't a god but merely an atom of god and anyway it was only passing across the face of the void relevant to the earth as it milled daily, churning fully around its hinge. And this star, this deity-godhead image of Amun-ra-marduk-apollo, along with the accompanying gas titan Cronus, that semi-vector/scalar clad moment that was equally incapable of dictating dietary laws or had a care to enforce its rules on earth beyond the imagination of the earthlings. It remained a large, whirling, twirling gassy giant with an electron magnetic moment to match that continues to dissipate reduced radiation (infra-red rays) out towards its close planetary companions within the solar system to this day; but how easily we digress.

So, lying back on deck under the canvas in the shade of a hot and heavy sun as they drifted downstream, his crafty artwork spread around him and his fellow travellers comingling in fellowship or sleeping off the excesses of earlier hours, Dyfed pondered this land's ancient taboos with a curious cynicism. No, they've got it wrong; specifically there were no sacred fish here, or anywhere else on earth, he said to himself. Fish, all fish, like all stationary and animated life everywhere, were sacred. Even Folks just didn't seem to get that it simply wasn't what it was about. What it was about, apparently, was Haploids feeling entitled about telling the hoi polloi what to do, what not to do, what to think, what to not think, what to eat, what not to eat, and what they should or should not want and how and how not to act. It was a primitive concept of indoctrination for curbing the fears of phenomenon about which the hoi polloi were ever afflicted. Even the priests of Jeshuanism, with all of its new-fangled order and modern trendiness, hadn't managed yet to fall too far from the tree or think outside the box there, either, Dyfed had noticed. Pish-posh to it all, he thought as he trailed his fishing net from the stern of the commuter felucca while he sat sorting through his many sketches and coloured drawings he had fastidiously composed.

(Sarapis of the Quick and the Dead who Rose Again and Again and Again)

'...are you ignorant, O Asclepius, that Aigyptos is the image of heaven?'
HERMES TRISMEGISTUS

Back in Xandria Dyfed took to seeking out any and all individuals of note who resided or were visiting the city. There were many, Callimachus of Cyrene a scholar at the city's library, for one. And aside from the library, another place the place to meet and mingle and fall into discussion was at the Serapeum. The Serapeum of Xandria had been built only about six hundred years earlier by Ptolemy the Benefactor and dedicated to Serapis, the protector of Xandria, who it was named after. It was situated in the neighbourhood called the Rhakotis (Ra-Kedet) in the western portion of Xandria and was situated on a rocky plateau that over looked the city and the sea. And within this temple's precinct, and almost beside the image of the god Serapis (also Sarapis) itself, was an offshoot or adjunct of the Great Library of Xanderia that acted as a spill over from the library and was referred to as its daughter. The Serapeum was the largest and most magnificent temple within the current Hellenic quarter and was located close to Pompey's pillar and the Heptastadium causeway. This latter mentioned dyke had been built over six hundred years earlier and linked the city with the island of Pharos. To the right of the dyke was the great harbour where ships at anchor were guarded by the Pharos lighthouse. This was where the Aura Maré now swung at anchor. To the causeway's left was the Old Port guarded by the gate of the moon.

The institution of the great library had been founded by Ptolemy the Saviour whose career had been as a brilliant Macedonian military general under the Great Xander of Macadonia, the Argivian (of Argos) king and son of Philip of Macedonia. Now (at this time) on Dyfed's search for information that could shake the world's foundation, he met an amazing woman. This was Ms. Hypatia. Though all in all there were actually two new and unusual women that he came to know at this time, Hypatia was amazing while the other one was sensually attractive enough to put him on his guard.

Marg had earlier met Hypatia when Dyfed was away. Hypathia was a scientist of the Western Civilization persuasion. Beautiful and totalling alluring, Hypatia wowed the other scholars around her not only with her looks but also by her books and her brains. To suggest that her stand-outishness as a woman (at this time) reflected others (especially male scholars) that frequented the Sarapeum in any negative way was to grossly underestimate Hypathia. She reflected people's light back at them and made them shine.

The second woman was another one of Marg's acquaintances. Her name was Catherine Lisabet Pergamius. She was the daughter of the local Prefect, an Amoran named Marcellinus Pergamius. Aside from her being a kind and gentle sort with an affable nature, she was a beauty as well. These observations took place while he was attending workshops of various interests at the Sarapeum.

The Great Library had by now long since been destroyed and the capacity of its collection of material for inspiration and knowledge vandalized and scattered to the far winds, just as tension between the new Jeshuan faith and the increasing power of its bishops were being fanned to the point of becoming a raging inferno, the ecumenical minded user groups that sought the path toward truth and understanding were now beginning to centre around the Sarapeum. Here the historic ideology of Sarapis that was of enquiry and tolerance had not yet faltered and yielded to Jeshuanism. Paganism was certainly under stiff assault, too, but in a general way Western philosophy was not under any real assault whatsoever. It was under transformation. Sarapis had been part of that but now the influence of Abramism was having its natural effect. In the melting pots of the flesh and flash-thoughts, such as the city of Antioch, and also here in this very city of Xanderia, an ideological tincture was coming about due to the blend and merger of some ancient pagan concepts along with Abramism that was being confused by and conflated with western styled ideology that was based on science and philosophy. The result: a new Ideal was immerging. Either way, no matter what shape or form it or they took, they were still the mortal enemy of a certain minority extremist cadre of raboniism and its embryo, the rapidly expanding new and organized Jeshaun cult. And it now was becoming formulated specifically under the logo of the Church of Amor. In any case, it was here, in the low-key environment of this annex, Sarapeum, that Dyfed first met Hypathia.

The Great Xander (who as an adolescent) went out of Macedonia to rule almost the entire known world at this time accomplished something that is a vastly different thing (and a far more valiant) then just going out to almost rule the entire known world. After all, we've all pretty much done that, almost! Ptolemy the Saviour, and one of the Diadochi (successors) to the great Xander of Macedonia, had come by this time to rule over the valley of the Nile and the Land of Khem (Aigyptos) as a satrap (governor). Then after forty years of warring against his fellow Diadochi, and with a well-ordered realm still intact, he went on to found a dynasty. And aside from the great library, it had been this same Ptolemy the Saviour who sponsored a mathematician named Euclid. Not only that, he was equally responsible for introducing and instituting (by his order) the cult of Serapis. As already stated, Ptolemy the successor then commissioned a temple (the Sarapeum) to be constructed at Xanderia where the protocol of the ideals of Serapis (Latin), or more properly spelled, *Sarapis* (Doric)[40], would be taught. *Sarapis* was a syncretistic deity derived originally from the worship of Osiris and Apis. In the ancient Land of Khem, Osiris is a god of the afterlife, the underworld and the dead, but equally the god of resurrection and regeneration and a god of transition. Apis (also Hapis) was the son of the Ar (Neilos) or Valley goddess Hathor (meaning house or mansion of Horus). She is usually depicted with a sun disk and Uraeus on her head while holding a sceptre (rod) or staff in her right hand and an ankh in her left. The *genius* of all this of course is pure *hoc es pocus*. It was exactly with what ancient folks had been targeted en mass and to which they ignorantly fell for and gleefully lapped up. Within the Hathor worship protocol, Hapis (son of Hathor) was assigned the significant role of being sacrificed and reborn. He also served as an intermediary with god for any and all human beings who wished it. This mumbo jumbo may sound similar, and familiar to certain worshipers of Jeshua (Joshua) Adon.

40 As Argives themselves, the Ptolemys were descendants from the Doric folk, not the Attic.

So, when it came to amalgamating cults of a foreign origin to create a commonality to control the masses so as not to weaken the kingdom, the great Xander of Macedonia was not to be bettered. He created a uniformity from the god Apis and Osirus whose image looked decidedly like a Hellene. Anyway, once this Ptolemy dynasty-instigated-cult of *Sarapis* was up and running, along with other formulas (such as the amalgamation between Thoth and Hermes, to name just one), this format could be found all over the place from one sacred temenos, say at Telmessos, to another sacred temenos at Tunisia and everywhere in between. In the vicinity of the City of Amor's main port at Ostia, for instance, even a Jupiter/*Sarapis* entanglement managed to issue forth (a stepping stone or a rung up for primitive pagan locals there). And now there were other concept gods being entangled with *Sarapis*, such as in far off Anatolia within the temple of Pergamon (also called Pergamum) and also at Ephesus. At this particular temple in Ephesus there lies directly behind it the ancient library of Celsus (for which Ephesus is famous). Here, also the two institutions are almost adjoined. In this it has a close similarity to that of the Sarapeum's relationship with the once great library of Xanderia whose annex was conjoined to it. Furthermore, it would appear that this cult leaned more toward recorded logic and inquiry, and the search for truth, rather than toward the perplexing magic and mumbo-jumbo that's for muggins and morons who can't concentrate for long, absorb very much or really make sense of anything.

And it should be recalled that the cult of *Sarapis* (with its interests in the arts and the occult) wasn't in fact something of a new school: Not at all. Dyfed realized that with the temple of the big pyramid that was the pilgrimage destination for the ancient Sabians, for instance, logic that had gone into it's construction wasn't built by daydreamers on mythical imagination. That there was an attempt within the worship of *Sarapis*, especially by certain enlightened Xanderian pagans as well as Jeshuans (like Cynthia Hypathia) to shift the paradigm within the *Sarapis* worship from Atum/Amen and Amun Ra to the beliefs of those of the likes of the Teacher of Righteousness, is evident. That this took place during the first few centuries after the Amoran occupation of Philisteen is assured, if un-acknowledged.

But not all Jeshuans, apparently, were pushing in this same direction. It so happened that through the activity and will of the Church of Amor being bent on a detailed agenda of orthodoxy in regards to the gospels — things went awry. They were so unlike Origen of Xandria the so-called self-castrator, vegetarian and teetotaller who fasted for months on end, or of Clement of Xanderia, or Pantaenus, and Philo of Xanderia who used philosophical allegory to meld and harmonize for the sake of commonality. Even still, these latter, too, were also indoctrinated into the Haploid program of default conversion with their special cross to bear. As such they harkened back to the worship of Ba'al, An, and Absu, et al. However, by this time *Sarapis* was beginning to be denied and was ultimately destroyed by the unrelentingly narrow-minded sect of mythmakers within the wide and (at one time) diverse scope of the cult of Jeshua Adon, along with its vision. Even the scholarship contained within millions of manuscripts in the Great Library (that had been meticulously gathered from past civilizations) had disappeared long since: many of them were observations of the phenomenon at large that remained accurate after exquisite investigation and many a trial. The research that was once conducted at the Mouseion (Musaeum) had become contracted by this time and finally its activity ceased and initiation desisted.

Here then was the continued struggle between the Haploids (aided by big brained programed hoi polloi priestly puppeteers) and the fledging truth-seeking giants of Western Philosophy. Amazingly, these few men and women (Pythagoras, Thales of Miletus, Anaximander of Miletus and Anaximenes of Miletus, Socrates of Athena, Heraclitus of Ephesus, Democritus of Abdera, Hermippus of Smyrna, Plato of Athena, Callimachus of Cyrene, Aristoteles and the afore-mentioned Ms. Hypathia of Xanderia; just to name a few) had managed to miraculously pick up the scent that those stalwart members of the regiment of fifth columns, such as the *pack* (among others) dangled in front of them or placed squarely in their path for them to trip over. Still (over all), the reasoning propended by the latter went clear over the heads of the majority of the hoi polloi. Consequently (on the most part), wise government and peace and good order to aid and abet the hoi polloi in general was avoided at all costs. And instead in its place remained the progenitors of mythos that had been installed many millennium before who propounded the great lie.

The true path toward righteousness and nobility was avoided at all costs because that was the Zeus program that was the order of Haploid design. Azeus still remains concealed as much as possible and those that preach about Azeus are marginalized, attacked and (if need be) destroyed. And it would appear that our old acquaintance Constantine Augustus followed by Emperor Theodosus who contributed immensely (as did Pope Theophilus of Xanderia) to the old program of mythos dressed up in new clothes, were puppets of the Haploid psychopaths. For it's such people as these who (despite their immaturity and their cult's fakery) were inspired to attack the cult of Sarapis, along with every other cult that didn't adopt the guise of the specific persuasion of the Jeshuan cult according to those very few who propounded specifically the Amoran variety. As it turned out, Sarapis may have been the last of the esoteric cults of all time, at least (that is) until modern times when Capitalism and Communalism prospered. But aside from knowledge, Sarapis unified humanity, and anything like it wasn't to be seen until the spirit of Azeus broke out many centuries later during the age of enlightenment. This was to be short lived. But we are getting ahead of ourselves.

(The Calm before the Storm)

With stupidity even the gods struggle in vain.'
FRIEDRICH SCHILLER

Meanwhile, Dyfed noticed, Marg hadn't been quite herself these days. He was coming to think that he wasn't quite as dear to her as she continued to be for him. Things had looked up while cruising beneath the Matala moon on their way to Xandria as well as their first months here in this city. But since his return from up river, she appeared to have slumped back into her old funk. Marg was like a bird, he thought, resting tentatively on the wire and was about ready, without warning, to suddenly up and fly quickly away. Then suddenly without warning or notice or explanation she moved out from their suite at the Cleopatra Chateau. For four worrying days she hadn't come home, while Dyfed and Trachmyr searched the city far and wide looking for her.

Then suddenly, Cato magically materialized. It was he who informed Dyfed where Marg could be found. Apparently she had relocated to a sumptuous mansion somewhere beyond the outskirts of the city. Dyfed had been surprized at Cato's sudden appearance. The latter told Dyfed that he had been appointed to keep an eye on him while he was here in the Land of Khem. He was here, he said, just to ensure that if anything untoward should unfold and threaten to collapse in on him, he would be here to help. Meanwhile, he told Dyfed that if his report on his recent sojourn into the interior and the visit, enquiry and discovery in and about Giza and Xandria was finished, that he had been commissioned by the Masters to receive it from him so as to convey the text back to them via the secret and sacred portal. That portal was the familiarly known bunny hole hop, the so-called rent that existed in the physical phenomenon that the Masters had located. Apparently, these noble Sages of the Unknown Universe were rather timid at this juncture (even if Dyfed was altogether virtually unaware of such juncture) at venturing out and about and exposed to the third dimension at large. Anyway, soon after this, Dyfed relocated to the Delta Hotel with Trachmyr in tow. There he rented the whole top floor with a large living room that had a roof access for those hot sultry nights. Here, after a day of satisfying his curiosity and thirst for arcane knowledge at the Sarapeum, he often entertained musicians when (after all the bars had closed) they and intellectuals from the Sarapeum welcomed the morning from the roof of the Delta Hotel with allsorts, including hashish, wine and strange (intelligent and sometime somewhat lewd) women with the ever present song delivered with instruments, such as the Kithara and the human voice.

At this time, Dyfed had taken up playing that ingenious string instrument himself and he welcomed the input from professional musicians. Also, the large room within his top floor suite stood in for a studio where he set up his easels and composed paintings of the magnificent buildings, the choppy harbour waters bobbing with boats at anchor, and the pastoral scenes beyond the fringe of the busy city centre. And now that Marg was absent, when he wasn't reclined in comfort and engrossed in discussion at the Sarapeum with the likes of Philo Judaeus, Clement of Xanderia, Origen, St. Antony the Copt, Bishop Cyril who was Theophilus' nephew, Diodorus Siculus and Manetho, he would recline on his roof-top garden surrounded by his bonsai palms and date trees with Trachmyr comforting him and standing guard. He soon came to appreciate the situation. But as always, it seemed to him, there was a dangerous moon rising. Then one day Dyfed saw a face from the past that he recognized only after seeing the man refuse some finger food offered to him at a gala at the Sarapeum. It was Ebreo ben Jamin the Yuhu Abramist.

Although it had not become obvious at first, and even though the Jeshuan cult's charter and creed had been struck and founded within Emperor Diocletianus' (Diokles) own backyard, and not in western Europa, the latter proved to be a much wiser man than either Constantinius or Theododius who had been the ones to drop their guard and drop the ball on this pivotal crossroads event. Neither had done their homework. If they had they would have discovered that it was Cornelius-Felix who had managed to snatch up a big piece of the Jeshuan cult's say-so and in doing that had secured the latter's future and cemented his policies for world dominance in the bargain. Of course, what wasn't known at the time, the real infallible dark horse potente at the centre of the Amoran web who lurked in the background standing stock-still, was Gorgeous Giorgius Gregorious Florentius.

One can understand Constantinius' position here, though. The Amoran culture at this time had appeared to have been brutalising the Jeshuans as they had brutalised everybody and everything else that was — or seemed — an unnecessarily foreign implement affecting how they governed and kept order via the laws of the land; or with anything they couldn't see to use as an asset such as different aspects of cultural beliefs, as they often did. If this wasn't the case they had no reason to accept it. A point in favour is that the Amorans never adopted Dionysus — the twice born of two mothers — who was either regarded as a foreigner or else as one returning from afar who was still cloaked in the mysteries of the unknown. Yet Dionysus was a beloved god of the ancient pagans long before Amor was ever famous. The irony here, of course, is that this god of Epiphany — the God who comes — besides being the patron of copious wine swilling, also acted as a divine communicant between the living and the dead, and as such, is both divine and chthonic. This immediately reminded Dyfed of none other than the Jeshuan messiah/saviour himself, Jeshua Adon: He was a divine being (according to those proponents in his favour) who died and was buried in the earth before ascending (for a short time) back into the midst of men. But one can feel the humanity in Constantinius' tendency to cast aspersions on his approach until you see the situation more clearly and of Cornelius-Felix's' involvement. The former (being unaware of the famous Cornelius-Felix duplicity) helped to promote the latter's agenda that (also) in the end was itself furthered by the Jeshuan cult.

Contrary to Constantinius' inability to read the signs, the pragmatic Diocletianus was aware that the Jeshuan cult which at that pivotal time was waving in the turbulence of great winds brought on by the continental shift of human climate. And among what he saw as the virtuous proclivities of Jeshua the Nasrani, that declension of authentic integrity, was blowing up a turbulence that picked up the seeds of all kinds of languor and crumble with the wind-strewn debris it created. He was also suspicious of the fact that organized Jeshuanism (i.e. the Church of Amor) remained somewhat entirely unconnected to the Amoran military and bureaucracy, and as such, how could the Jeshuan cult contribute to the Amor they all knew and loved? There were no observable Idea of logos within the Church of Amor, only the passion and mythos of messianic end-times.

All of this Diocletianus observed while being fully aware that one of Amor's strengths was in the Amoran's willingness to adopt and embrace many cults so long as they made them truly Amoran: That, and bureaucracy. At this time, Jeshaunism was not prepared to go that far, though they didn't mind creating their own red tape and utilizing the Amoran iron will of ruthlessness themselves when to their advantage. These turned out to be a splendid example for controlling social and political elements ay large. In any case the new cult was hell bent to be part a controlling element of the Amoran equation in a way that their older founding cult, the old Abramists, were not. But like the old Abramists they too were adamantly hesitant to adopt or even acknowledge the logos of the pagan gods that would have, could have, should of have been handy and helpful as a social bridge. As for Dyfed, his inquiries and studies had shown him that Jehovah was simply descended from (or in the guise of) any of the Mesopotamian, Hurrian and Canaanite (Ka'anite) mountain, storm and fertility gods such as Bel Sadé, El Shaddai, Ba'al or even Saturn, a corn god whose name Satur means gorged (or sator that means sower and obviously related to the word sate) all of which certainly relied on the rider of the clouds that created the storm and the rain and was equal to Jupiter and not lesser than. But this, of course, was something which, at that time, all the orthodox brothers (and other cults too) refused to acknowledge.

(My name is humanity, master of all I survey. Look upon my works and despair)

'Sudden enlightenment followed by gradual cultivation.'
CHINUL (1158 – 1210 CE)

At the dusk of the fading day, aboard the *Aura Maré*, reunited again for their departure from Xanderia, Dyfed and Marg breathed in the sea-air, slaked with (along with the pungent odours of cooking-fire smoke) spicy foodstuffs being prepared and the drifting scent of all and sundry that floated by on top of the oily water alongside the lateen rigged feluccas, the rafts, and other floating debris. This, along with bobs and dobs and particles that were in the process of breaking off from this coastal fringe; this rind of the stifling hubbub of humanity that spilled here out off the shore and out over the quietude of the shore waters.

The *Aura Maré* lay just on the cusp of this seething mass of smocked-dressed, perfumed and sweaty citizens whose patch-work of smells now drifted out to them along with the knocks and clangs and gongs, that uproar of material friction and the movement of people in the course of each moment. It was the hack of each cough, the bark of each dog, the cluck of each hen and the sizzle of each cooking pot that drifted on the breeze all comingling together. And that atmosphere was glued to the ambience framed within the low Xanderian wooden and clay skyline that (composed of ancient edifices that harboured new Amoran sects along with their brick and mortar structures posturing to pagan gods) settled down among and themselves, struck up the band, and competed with brass and bronze where incense smothered crowds that gravitated to murals depicting horned gods while others were giant fists of human-like gods holding lightening bolts all arranged in and among the temples of the Abramists, the Zoroastrian cedar fire-pits and the Buddhist's domes and spires. Each and every one of these emitted noises commingled together so that they sounded here like the fullness of a gusty wind of air rising into a dull tattoo that rose into a crescendo of sharp and pointed sounding jabs.

By nightfall it had all disappeared to stern for now the good ship *Aura Maré* was outward bound from the land of Khem as she heaved to by the oar; her sail was trimmed so she could tack soon against the wind as she came about and began the next roundabout journey home. In a perfect world — with Trachmyr, Dyfed's trusty batman-manservant and first lieutenant (pronounced — lef-ten-ant), who stood to one side a step behind him watching carefully, Marg, dressed in luxurious silks and smelling of a summer rose in the heat of a June evening, who shuffled back and forth anxiously, it seemed as it they were poised to leave Xanderia the very moment when the gods would smile upon them and ultimately return them back safely toward Taras (Taranto) or Ostia by Amor to live happily ever after. But instead of setting their bearings on the points of the compass at three hundred degrees west-north-west that would retrace their course and take them back to Matala on the south western coast of Kreta again, Dyfed plotted to the north east towards the coast of the Divine Land not far off the inland city of Heliopolis in the land of the cedars that was not to be confused with the city of Luwnuw, just north of Giza at the apex of the river Ar's (Neilos or Nile) delta. Dyfed had never been happier. In fact until Marg had returned singing plaintively about a sea cruise, Dyfed had thought that she was drifting away from him. This had triggered the summoning of Melancholy, that most wretched and dead-beat of companions, to say the least. But now she seemed lifted. It wasn't to last and a couple of days battering against the sea might have done it.

Anyway, they anchored at Berytus (present-day Beirut) where they went ashore and checked into a lavish hotel. In the harbour, at that same time, they noticed a young Amoran aristocrat disembarking with her tiny suite. This was Catherine Lisabet Pergamius and the second most important woman Dyfed met at this time. Marg had got to know her in Xanderia.

Much sooner than later, Marg had invited her join her and Dyfed for refreshments. It turned out, she told them, that she was here on a mission. Her poor brother had become ill, it seemed, and he desperately needed assistance in returning to their father's home in Xandria. However, on the very next day a swiftly moving, shallow keeled escort that the navy used caught up with them at Berytus. The captain of this escort vessel had a message for Ms Pergamius. The message was that the new Imperial Regent, Emperor Flavius Honourless Augustus, had sacked their father from his position of diplomat and he and the family were being recalled to Raven (Ravenna). This was where the Pergamius' family home was located. So, once she had scooped up her brother, they were to return to Italia. Apparently, Dyfed later discovered, her brother was a certain Albus Agrippa Pergamius, a well known dandy who fancied himself as an Amoran explorer when in fact he was more of a drifter, a loner and an alcoholic who got under people's feet and under their skin. Needless to say, he soon irritated the piss out of people to an unnerved distraction. In any case, the erstwhile explorer/adventurer was stranded, Lisabet told Dyfed on that first day at Heliopolis. Since Dyfed, who was bent upon exercising his new found artistic urges, had planned on visiting the site which was his reason for swinging into Berytus in the first place, offered to accompany her there to collect her brother. The next day he and Lisabet journeyed inland together to Heliopolis in the old land of Phoenikia by carriage. Meanwhile, Marg (once again back in a funk) and pulling the silent act, stayed at Berytus.

It didn't take too long to locate Lisabet's brother Albus Agrippa but a lot longer for her to organise staff to dry him out, get him dressed and presentable before the three of them took the coach back to the coast. Meanwhile, Dyfed set out to explore.

An old well dressed man upon seeing him sketching the temple of Jupiter the next morning told him that this ancient hill site had existed for ages and that the present temple to Jupiter had been built on the foundations of the temple of Ba'al which had occupied the site for almost a thousand years. Anciently, a raised court had been constructed, he said, and successive ages had provided improvements. The man had thought and told Dyfed that the previous construction had been completed by the Kn'ny peoples (the Canaanites). But none, the old man assured him, had been as meticulous and as scientific as we, the Amorans, had been in raising the temple to Jupiter.

"Well its being kept in the family, then,' replied Dyfed. The man stared at him a moment. 'The temple sanctuary,' Dyfed replied again, nodding towards it with his forehead. 'The apple didn't fall far from the tree here. After all, preceding the aforementioned

Ba'al who had been none other than the incomparable Adad (Hadad) and who had emerged more or less out of the concept of the great storm god Teshub. And the blossoming of Teshub had originated and probably been caused by An, or Anu, the ancient Mesopotamia god of decisions and effects. And according to those Mesopotamian folks, An had brought them there from Aratta whose name may be related to long ago kingdoms such as Urartu and landmarks like Ararat. Jupiter, just like the genius of his forefather, Zeus, who's a far cry from Azeus, are just extensions, nothing more. Storm gods they are, each and every one, just take your pick. Even Absu, the spirit (god) of sweet (fresh) water must be represented here in some way. I'll bet'ch they'll be constructing a Jeshuan baptismal font here anytime soon,' Dyfed said in order to stir a response from the man.

The old man wasn't having any of it. He shook his head violently. As an Amoran engineer himself, he told Dyfed, his career in part had been (in fact) to rebuild this former Hellenic hilltop of Heliopolis — named after the sun (mind you) not an electrical storm complete with high winds and lightning. He then told Dyfed in specific and certain terms that the apple had indeed fallen far from the tree, and that he (Dyfed) didn't know what he was talking about. 'Come, I'll show you,' he said.

Dyfed hadn't bother to point out that Helios the sun — which bore the lion's share of responsible for the earth's magnetic field and therefore its storms (and probably had a hand to some degree as well in every other disturbance on the face of the earth) — was for sure the dominate storm/sky god.

The old man then almost took Dyfed by the hand and showed him up close some of Heliopolis' wonders that had been wrought by the men of Amor. Below the Corinthian columns at the base of the site he pointed out ancient foundations. Dyfed thought they may have been built by the Kn'n/Phoinike folks, those fascinating seafarers and avid tradespersons and trading merchants who originally — according to Herodotus and Strabo (Dyfed knew) — were from Tilmun (or Dilmun also Tylos) in the Persian Gulf and had migrated here to the eastern White Sea coast close to a thousand solar cycles ago (at least), if not longer ago. These folks, it seemed, had a close resemblance to the folks of Inja around the Indus River valley as well as to the Aryans of Persia. But like Sargon the Great, these Phoinike folks (who were non-monotheistic worshippers) spoke with the Semitic tongue.

Anyway, by this time the old Amoran engineer, a keener of physical and mechanical strategies and science who had introduced himself as Vitruvi, had begun to point out to Dyfed the great works that his Amoran institute and regiment had done to rebuild and improve on this site. One of the works he was proud to show him were some vast monolithic stones weighing possibly up to five or six hundred Amoran tons each. These had been placed at the western end of the site below the upper platform whose edge here came to the side of the down-sloping hill upon which the structure had been built. The reason they were placed at that spot on the side of the slope, old man Vitruvi pointed out, was because they were needed in order to anchor the foundation stones and shore up the site and protect it from soil erosion. Vitruvi then asked Dyfed to note that no lewis-holes or notches were visible on the large rock slabs that had been moved into place from the ground level. The latest project had been completed by Amoran engineers, he said with pride, and was a little over two hundred years in the making, compared to those other rock slabs placed by earlier engineers who used the lewis notches and took forever to construct. But Dyfed didn't know how he knew that. Vitruvi told Dyfed that the placing of these megaliths had being part of his doing and it was done in order to strengthen and shore up the large retaining wall which having been built many years earlier by the Kn'n/Phoinike (though it was improved upon later by Hellenic construction workers) that had been inadequate for the ambitions which the modern Amoran builders had had for the site. In any case Dyfed produced three well-constructed paintings of it and six sketches in all.

Upon returning to Beryus, Lisabet said her good-byes to Marg and Dyfed as she and her brother made ready to board an Amoran trireme for their journey home to Revenna. Their ship lay against the quay at Beryus among a fleet of vessels plying the waters that connected the empire. Each one of them was coming from and going to different locations in different directions. And their vessel was no different, other than it was returning Lisabet and her sickly and diseased young brother home. Dyfed then noted a heavy stone obelisk strapped to the deck of a large barge at anchor. In every likelihood that obelisk had come from somewhere in Khem even beyond Giza (where Dyfed had just come from) and had been shipped down the Brook of Khem (the river Ar) to the City of Xandria on its first leg to Europa following the coast with Berylus being its first stop. This giant two mast-rowing barge was resting for the moment in the shelter of the bay with its sails tightly rolled up on deck. But it appeared as if at any moment it was about to return to the savage wind and waves of the White Sea and continue its journey of transporting the obelisk either to Byzas or Amor.

"Call on us soon at Raven,' were Lisabet's last words that Dyfed heard.

After a number of rough and slow-going days of crossing over the white-capped sea, the *Aura Maré* swung into the harbour beneath the acropolis of Lindos located on the south eastern shore of the Island of Rhodes. From there they hopped over and anchored in the sheltered little bay in front of Knidos in the land of Karia to wait for the wind to turn. Knidos, like Lindos, was part of the ancient Dorian Hexapolis. Here, though, they noticed that it was windier and less hot as Lindos. At Knidos Dyfed and Marg lived ashore for a few days. They were invited as guests to the beautiful home of a rich merchant who lived on the island that adjoined the peninsula and formed the western shore of the harbour. The abodes here were very civilized with toilets and running water. Back across the bridge and to the north of the harbour lay the agora, the Ōideion (Odeon) or theatre and three temples: one to the god Dionysus, another to the nine Muses, and finally one to Aphrodite. Here, at this last temple stood the nude statue of Aphrodite by the famous Athenian sculptor Praxiteles. Looking at it Dyfed was mind struck and remained speechless for hours. Here, at this place Dyfed saw first hand how transformation into a type of materialism of exquisite value was conducted and formed here by people through organized ethereal thought and reason. Nothing he had ever seen, apart from similar creations at his ancestral home that once existed on the Isle Peace, matched what the Dorians had once fabricated here on the western shores of Anatolia. The ancient land of Khem with its finished-product pyramids and numerous other dusty antiquities were quaint compared to the created logos summoned by the philosophy, art and science that composed Amoran/Hellene style Western Philosophy that he saw here.

It was precisely this contrast before him now (in this fuzzy reel of the world that passed before his eyes) which acted as fertilizer to the pejorative thoughts of Dyfed's mind. Western philosophy, and all which that entailed, had arisen long ago during a period when the mythos of men (presumably) had been pagan and superstitious to the core. Yet somehow it hadn't deterred or dissuaded the culture of classical logos and learning to proceed and go forth through the generations and multiply. And where would the (until very recently) pagan-steeped culture of the Amoran Empire be today without Western philosophy's classical culture at its beck and call? This was a philosophy, we must add, which (from the start) denigrated and minimized the very same primitive superstitious mythos which paganism and Abramism was grounded in? So why the difference elsewhere, and today? Why is mythos once again returning with a vengeance? Dyfed asked himself. Interestingly, there was something he had learned while visiting the land of Khem that was populated by Hamitic and Semitic speaking peoples, some of who were A-rabs that were surrounded there by classical philosophy, paganism and Abramism. Though at this time they hadn't yet emulated the later of the other two existing Abramists (Jeshuanism) by fashioning for themselves (or having had fashioned for them by someone or something else) their own personalized — hardly unique — messiah or saviour type prophet, still at this time they certainly excelled in the sciences of mathematics, astronomy, medicine, and philosophy. And they were also able to produce glorious works of architecture, art, poetry and literature. So, what with the mixing cauldron of Abramism, paganism, Hinduism, Jainism, Buddhism, Taoism and Zoroasterism overflowing the think tanks of Antioch and Xandria, what the fuck? Dyfed thought. Why weren't the hoi polloi doing better? Why the failing grade, the flunk, the big goose egg?

At Apasa (later Ephesus) in ancient Ionia that lay to the north of Karia, they needed to take on more fresh drinking water and restock their grocery larder. In those days the sea washed the shores of Ionia quite close to that ancient city. Visible from the Aura Maré at anchor was the Temenos dedicated to Augustus Augustus. The magic circle that was sacred to the gods which (in Ephesus' case) Diana — formerly Artemis — was cast forth from the epi-centre of her temple, the Artemision. Solemnly, Dyfed (accompanied by Marg) made the short pilgrimage there to that ancient temple once known to be one of the Seven Wonders of the World. Having been rebuilt about three times at this stage, it now lay in ruins again having been laid waste more recently by Goth marauders. The city's gymnasium, the stadium and Celsus' old library beyond the agora were still in use. The theatre sat squat, bleaching under the hot sun while the gates of Herakles and of Mithraidates stood like lonely sentinels, open and abandoned.

Their next stop was the oracle of Klaros near Colophon. Here, at Klaros, the Doric temple of Apollo welcomed Dyfed but in a way that the ritual of the countless hecatombs preformed here in the ancient past never did. During the few days in which Dyfed sketched the oracle and mapped its layout, he and Marg stayed in the ancient yet still usable guest houses just to the west of the temple that had become something of a beach resort. They gently declined an invitation for dinner from the king of nearby Colophon, for Dyfed was running low on gold and most of their trading supplies were now gone. Once back out at sea again, they swept to the west around Χίος (Chios) and ancient Smyrna and ducked in beneath the isle of Lesbos to the small port at Atarneus that was now deserted of any inhabitants. According to villagers nearby it had been struck by plague and never repopulated. From Atarneus they rode by rented horse and chariot to the hilltop of Pergamum that had just undergone an unsuccessful siege by a tribe of Kelts.

It was here, at this time, that news reached this Anatolian Amoran hilltop city (that once boasted of having the most extensive library in the world after Xandria) of two catastrophes that had befallen two of their friends (both women) from Xandria. One was regarding Catherine Lisbet Pergamius who had allegedly rebuked the new emperor of Amor. Her rebuke to him was in the manner in which he the emperor allowed brutality throughout the empire, especially towards the new cult of Jeshua Adon. As she herself was a convert to this cult she had felt insulted by the emperor, she told him by letter that had been sent on forward in one of the merchant ships bee-lining for Amor's harbour at Ostia. He was understandingly extremely angry with her but on account of her beauty and family position he hid it and tried to woe her family over. He failed. She insulted him a second time by turning down his hand in marriage, all done by correspondence. Rumour had it that the emperor then had her strangled and her father, whose prefecture was then impeached, was himself banished off to somewhere like Tomis on the western shores of the Kara Sea. This turned out not to be exactly all true.

The other catastrophe was that the prominent Jeshuan Theophilus had burned the great Xandrian library to the ground once and for all. But more importantly that Cynthia of Hypatia, the Hellene philosopher and mathematician who had earlier befriended them, had been horribly murdered as well. She had been dragged from her carriage into the street and beaten to death and then skinned. This had greatly distressed Marg who, having sought this fine and intelligent woman out, had told Dyfed that she was of their own race and more highly placed than any master wandering the world in this dimension that she knew of. Besides, the woman had also been a friend and mentor of the people of the earth, the hoi polloi.

Although there was no evidence that Theophilus was responsible for the woman's death as was rumoured, his professed and loud denial, along with those of his partisans, did more (historically) to hold them fully accountable than anything. After all, the Jeshuans claimed that she was an evil magician. This in itself was verbal transcendence. It was overkill because to the cults of the god of Abram the word magician was tantamount to the devil. This, of course, was another intentional misinterpretation and part of the word game. In this case the poor woman who was the victim of this gross, outrageous, and unconscionable assault upon her person, an assault that caused such a violent and painful death and shock to others had been (to Dyfed and Marg's mind) not a devil at all but merely a brilliant philosopher, scientist, and mathematician, and nothing more egregious than that. Indeed, she was something of a priestess in her own right who was working to repatriate Pythagoras reputation into the current world and was something of a stoic herself. It was the Abram cultists who didn't recognise her as such because she didn't and couldn't, in her learned pronouncements, be bothered to employ the trappings of the great lie of the god of Abram simply for the sake of social posturing. For this reason not only could they not acknowledge her, they didn't want others to fully understand the science she had mastered and had sought to teach to the world.

Dyfed's growing awareness of some secret and powerful king with all his horses and all his men that, indiscriminate of where civilization and it citizens were aching to go, was an entity that was always there to prevent it from happening. He was growing tired of it all but he sensed that Marg was well advanced than him in this condition. He had known for a long time that something or some entity *was* standing in the path of human development. After all, Morgant and even Manandan had said as much, albeit in their own words. Even the revered prophet and cult leader Jeshua Adon the Nazrani seemed to have intimated as much.

They then sailed north toward Lemnos that lies off the Thrakian Chersonese (Gallipoli Peninsula). At this spot they passed by the narrow entrance into the western strait called the Hellespont (Dardanelles) that flows into the Marble Sea. This sea passage (if followed upstream, sort of speak) leads to Byzas on the Golden Horn (the capitol of the Eastern Amoran Empire) that's situated on Bosphorus that is the second strait before entering the Kara Sea. Byzas had just recently appropriated the authority over Lemnos from Amor so they continued past it still sailing north. Coming onto Samothraki (once referred to as the sanctuary of the gods: nobody knows what its ancient name was) they anchored on the northern shore off the old city of the ancient Pelasgians that was reminiscent of Mycenaean architecture of antiquity. Here (accept for Marg who was still depressed over the news of the horrible death of her friend Cynthia) Dyfed, Trachmyr and a few of the sailors went ashore. Dyfed delayed their departure from here for two full days, as he was interested in exploring the site where the mysterious rites of Samothraki took place, which were similar to the Eleusinian mysteries. Then leaving Samothraki they approached the city of Maroneia on the south coast of Thraki proper. This city was world renown for its nectar-like wine and its worship of Dionysus.

The sun had sunk low in the heavens; the wind, which had accompanied them north and brought them here to the Thraki shore, now dwindled; its fury (presumably) having been agitated by the presence and the power of Radiance, now had the presence of mind to acquiescence to the power of Mars whose youthful shadow had long been cast over this land. From Maroneia Dyfed and Trachmyr trekked the sixty Amoran miles into the east Rhodope Mountains (hills) to another ancient oracle. Once again they were unaccompanied by a still saddened Marg who stayed behind. This oracle (set upon a mountain of shiny white rock) upon which they had arrived was dedicated to Zagreus, unlike the one at Klaros that was dedicated to Apollo. Zagreus was a god worshipped once in long ago Orphic ritual and was often identified with Dionysus. This site had been here for thousands of solar cycles and was the location where Philip of Macedonia had brought his young son Skander to enquire after the priestess who at that time held sway over Zagreus' oracle. The enquiry was as to that of his son's future. Gaius Octavius did likewise bringing his son Gaius Octavius II for the same reason. Both oracles proved prophetic. We know Gaius Octavius II as Augustus Augustus, the first Emperor of Amor.

Zagreus' oracle, that lofty platform of prediction anciently carved out of the living rock, contained (at this time) a multi-storied palace that was girded by a fortress that cemented the upper portions of the hilltop together. It had a series of out-lying walls beneath the girded the ramparts of the hill which gave it the look of a hemi-spherical labyrinth. From the top of the oracle Dyfed and Trachmyr could look down upon the beautiful lands that lay all around. The famous temple of Dionysus which sat atop the acropolis, whose purpose here was to martial sweet drunken abandon, accompanied by oodles of passionate, multi-partnered and unprotected sex, was now a mere footprint of ruins scraped clean and hard upon the granite. Then having passed through a magical forest of crooked and stunted trees they arrived back at Maroneia almost three weeks from the time they started. Marg was in a huge snit by this time and remained out of sorts from that time forward.

Before Dyfed had set off, Marg had told him privately that in times past (especially in the ancient days), she had often vacationed at both Klaros and Zagreus, and that it was at Zagreus that she had lost her virginity to Froberic, a Keltic king. With this admission, for what it was worth, Dyfed knew that something was up with Marg's psyche and peace of mind. This troubled him even though the confession may or may not have been truthful. Due to Marg's extended current sadness over the vulgar violence which was escalating around them and his suspicion of the truthfulness of her comment, upon hearing her confession Dyfed bit his tongue and squashed the jest which alighted immediately upon the tip thereof; and (by way of that thoughtfulness) he managed to omit telling her in fun that he may yet be able to assist another shimmering, rose smelling delight — just like her — who was burdened with such an affliction as that which she herself had once gladly been assisted to be relieved of. But despite the former abuse by this Froberic geezer, he noted to himself that the puerile attempts of that Keltic king's (alleged) puny penetration had, however, never been evident, at least not to him. However, he kept quiet on the subject. On his return he now told her instead that he had turned away a multitude of virgins in his lengthy celibacy and that the only company he had kept to warm his back at night was Trachmyr.

From here they sailed and rowed west along the Thrakian coast stopping briefly at Abdera, which was founded by Herakles and was the birth place of both Anaxarchus and Democritus. Here Dyfed explored the Nestos River, but due to the current muddy conditions there he had to follow the coast further and took on fresh water from the Strymon River near Eion instead. This was the traditional border between the Thraki and the Paeonians to the west. By this time Marg had become quite pale and had no appetite. Once they were anchored off Eion she took to locking herself in her stateroom refusing any audience. Dyfed was exceedingly frustrated. So leaving her there anchored in the mouth of the Strymon (sru is an Indo-European word for stream) he explored that river which flowed down from the north and passed beneath the hill fort of the City of Amphipolis before it dumped into the Aegean Sea. Once they were past Amphipolis, Dyfed (accompanied by Trachmyr) paddled up lake Prasias and then followed a succession of shady gorges into the Rila Mountains. Resting a few days at the hot springs at Scaptopara they summoned a well-needed time of forced relaxation before returning to the Aura Maré where they found Marg still locked in her room.

Turning south they took turns rowing and then sailing past Mt. Athos due to the sporadic wind conditions and then finally made their way into the inside channel by Euboea. After they rounded the promontory of Sounion the wind died down altogether so they had to literally pull themselves into the port of Piraeus that served the City of Athena. Here they laid up the Aura Maré at the local neosoiki (ship sheds) to have her hull cleaned and any waterlogged planks replaced. At this point Marg was forced to show herself and behave as though she was part of the team. She quickly took up digs, however, at a convenient hotel in Piraeus where she intermittently slept, ate seafood and slept some more, all the while refusing to budge from there.

Piraeus was once one of the world's most important harbours (three in total) and back in its day could accommodate a couple of hundred triremes. That was just the military port. The commercial ports could accommodate another two hundred commercial vessels or so, bringing the total capacity of Piraeus' harbour to four hundred ships, maybe more. It was also a shipbuilding centre. But it was much less important today and most of it was decrepit and consigned to rack and ruin. Its decrepitude, Dyfed noted, was in the realm of virtual rubble. The ports were rubble and although cleaned out and tidied up a bit, the Aura Maré was on a waiting list to be serviced as facilities here were now acutely limited. And the one time opulence of the Hippodamus of Miletus Agora built five hundred or more years before the present, with its magnificent public buildings, such as the Temple of Hestia, the Scolarcheio, and the Bouleuterion, along with the Agoranomeion, were now all rubble. Once a hub of trade and commerce it was now all but deserted except for that ever present rubble. Even Marg's hotel, the fanciest to be had hereabouts, was at best a one and a half star, with no pool, no pets, and no hot water and where she had to come up with her eight weeks stay in advance. Dyfed dubbed it the Hotel Rubble for Rubbies.

And although, too, the area of the Agora was being cleaned out, all the marvellous statues and columns that decorated Piraeus had vanished and the gilt scrapped down to the bedrock. And this had nothing whatsoever to do whatsoever either with any pillaging Kelts who had last swung by this neck of the woods about three or four and a half centuries earlier. No: this had all been the work of Cornelius-Felix before he had made it to *Felix-Dictator* (Lucky Dictator) where he had been in charge of running the show. The ruins that were Piraeus today was his version of scorched earth defence. General Cornelius-Felix had over re-acted, which was his acclaimed modus operandi. Having become infuriated by the willingness of the Athenian folks to side with Mithrid (Mithridates) the king of Pontus who had fashioned himself and his empire after the people of Hellene, Cornelius-Felix had smashed Piraeus to smithereens in a temper tantrum.

Piraeus had never been an island in living memory by anyone's standards, but it was in a sense an opposite land in that it had once been somewhat separated from the adjacent coast by marshy mud flats. And to cross over to it one may have had to wear floating wooden shoes or needed a scow pulled behind an ox or a dolphin. The Hellene verb *peraio* that leads to *peran reo* or *diaperan* means to ferry across. In this case it would mean across the so-called alipedon, that aforementioned marshy area that was here in the olden days. As folks needed to be 'ferried' back and forth across the marsh and mud flats, perhaps, Dyfed thought, this contributed to the origin for the area's name being Piraeus. However, Dyfed was too well aware that if it wasn't barefaced fantasy, then the world he lived in was built on a polyglot of mistranslated conjectures that were usually illogically supported by rumours and *qui bono* agendas.

The person responsible for designing the urban planning of Piraeus about seven and a half centuries earlier (once some semblance of a causeway or an all-out fill-in job had been successfully completed) was Ippodamos the architect. But the six or seven Amoran miles of inter-urban access highway connecting the City of Athena to its valuable commercial and military port at Piraeus at this time was more than a little vulnerable during times of siege. So about six centuries before the present, Themistocles concocted a plan to stiffen up its defences, thereby allowing manpower and goods, such as food and materials coming into the city, to flow unimpeded and secure while between both the commercial and naval harbours and the City of Athena. This was good thinking. It shows that not everybody at that time were killing brains cells by swilling back pithoi (plural of pithos) of wine on a regular basis for the sake of Dionysus. Themistocles managed this feat by walling in the entire road on both sides; in other words, by joining fortified

Piraeus to the battlements of the City of Athena with a fortified access road (or corridor) that ran between them.

Not being able to lift Marg's cloud of depression, he hired local women to keep her company. With a heavy heart Dyfed and Trachmyr left her be and took the street of 'the long wall' (as it's called) from Piraeus into town. Town was Athena's agora district. Here they visited the amusements such as the city's patron goddess' initial temple, the so-called Erechtheion. This edifice was perched on the north side of the acropolis. Built about six and a half centuries previously it was a replacement of the earlier temple of the goddess Athena Polias that had been destroyed by Aryan aggressors from the east (known by the Hellenes as Persian pirates). Although the Erechtheion mainly housed Athena's *xoanon* (cult image), this new and improved building had been built with an extension that was dedicated to the cult of gods and three local heroes, namely Erechtheus (sometimes pronounced Derechtheus), Hephaistos and Boutes: hence the temple's name. And in its basement it continued to house the briny spring that flowed from a cleft in the bedrock said to have been caused by Poseidon's trident in his lost battle with Athena for status-hood over the people of the city.

Above and adjacent to this temple was another fine and much larger temple called the Parthenon. Located atop the cliff on the south side of the acropolis it was erected by Perikles and dedicated to Athena Parthenos. The superintendent over all the chief foremen and masters (journeymen) of trade-skills during its construction was the sculptor Pheidias (also Phidias). Unlike the current time, accomplished artists, dreamers, along with philosophers and poets were considered valuable in those days and were often the first to be appointed to construct into being monumental things fashioned out of stone and imagination that actually mattered to the masses of the hoi polloi at large. Some examples of these are just laws along with equal rights for all in a show cause environment. They were also big on social and financial harmonies that are needed to effect acceptable mores and conduct along with correct and democratic avenues of political sciences combined with the studies for the current necessity for cherishing the historical relevance for the people's past. And finally, architectural (along with technological) phenomenon is of the utmost importance, too. And these aforementioned artists demanded, and were given, a necessary and sufficient budget so as to successfully accomplish their task be it in stone and brick, or on paper fashioned into codices for govern-mentation. And because of this, the artefacts of the infrastructure of all that which was good during the historical past continues to shine brightly today — partly physically and mostly in history books — even if the new-comers who've just moved in and taken over the joint don't shine much at all and are rather dull. Ordinarily, they would be called poor custodian, not modern gods.

Once more, as happened back in Knidos, Dyfed's thoughts were about (among others) the Dorian created logos that went into providing for a sound Western philosophy and its contrast to the mythos of paganism and the primitive superstition of any number of false paracletes that flourished profitably amid the chaos caused by the greed of entitlement and exclusion. This latter arena was where the ever-present fragility of the state of logos could be caused to shrivel up and die, for it was the place and space of Zeus (not to be confused with *Azeus* (without Zeus).

In any case, the centrepiece of the Parthenon (if there was one) was the magnificent gold and ivory statue of the dangerously armed goddess herself that once (long ago) adorned the interior cella. Today, as he placed his easel, and chatted with the crowds, Dyfed noted that the place was a virtual tourist trap. Also it was mostly well heeled Amorans from the northern provinces that were here on business or vacation with their families that kept the property values up along the high street. And the booty of the Parthenon, including the statue of Athena Parthenos that was once its heart and soul along with the sparkling golden stash that overflowed the coffers here, had been long ago looted from this noble temple's sanctuary. Traditionally, apparently, Athena's cult priests had never failed to falsely assure the local hoi polloi that the wealth stashed here was common wealth, and not the treasury of just the high priests of the cult. For this was not the case. What was true was that the priests had more of a say in where the treasure was to be spent than anyone else.

Dyfed noted the relationship and connection here between the technical logos of the material existence [built by artisans] of the magnificent temple compared to the cult mythos proffered by the priests which effected and determined the material existence of the hoi polloi within the floundering levels of their society. This, Dyfed knew, indicated that a powerful force of totalitarianism had always been at large (and still was). *Furthermore, he suspected that when this social and economic regimentation was not able to be kept in tune with the leash and tight collar by the usual daily pap provided by cult controlled mythos, the helping hand of a healthy dose of fascism and police order were not far away.*

However, out of sympathy for the curiosity of thousands of modern Amoran tourists who visited here each year now, once again — this time on account of the hidden and secret congress of the otherwise transparent Amoran governorship here provided that — the cella was filled to the brim with bling, at least. At first Dyfed sat back disgusted at the sight of it all. Taking up his brush and dabbing it into his pot of gold pigment he quickly filled his rendition of the cella of the Parthenon on his paint board with gobs of shining gold. Tourists were naturally attracted to him and gathered around. But then something struck him and it made him laugh so hard that folks then just stared at him. Alarmed, Trachmyr stood over him protectively. Probably they were thinking that he was some wealthy hashish trader which was why Dyfed wasn't interfered with and arrested for breaking the peace by any of the scads of Nightwatchmen that crawled all over the place. Wearing the uniform of Amor, and heavily armed, these aforementioned nosey and intrusive bureaucrats kept their steely eyes alert and on visitors at all times who they suspected without exception to be casing the joint for valuable artefacts or in profiting from information services to tourists without a licence.

Weeks (and a bundle of finished paintings) later, and just as they began to head back through Long Wall St., the crowds suddenly swelled into a crush. Rumour had brought word that the Goths (Geats) were on the warpath and were about to descend on Athena from the sea. This implied that they were almost within sight of Piraeus, and were at that very moment rushing forward in their slick fleet of sleek and shallow boats which even at low and ebbing tide (rumour had it) could beach and deliver their payload of axe wielding berserkers almost to the high water mark just for emphasis and assertion. Of course, contrary to popular belief, many of the young women (not all) inhabiting the lands targeted by these Goths (and others gone a-viking abroad) weren't at all actually bound and determined toward a frightful flight in the opposite direction from these current marauding pirates presently predisposed for Piraeus, but were (in fact) on the beach waiting for them with a sharp and plaintiff, 'well, it's about time, boys!' on their smiling and welcoming lips. They were the Viking-Velcoming crew and were once dubbed the mascots of menace and the progenitors of providence and strength. 'So much water under the bridge (it was being said under the breath of certain folks) that one can no longer recognize the place today!'

Anyway, in consequence to this rumour, the hotels were fast emptying, along with the bars, brothels and sidewalk cafés all over Athena. While nothing once emptied Athena's popular venues such as the agora, the acropolis and the theatres in the old days faster than the cry: 'time gentlemen please, our entertainment has come to an end for this evening', and 'attention; Theseus son of Aegeus has left the stadium', today it was a simple; 'attention! We interrupt your day with breaking news that the hated Goths are descending upon us in haste. Quickly, now; flee for your lives.'

Having jostled with sharp elbows to clear Long Wall St. they entered Piraeus again. The hull repairs and inspection of the *Aura Maré* having now being completed and the vessel newly commissioned, Dyfed assigned Trachmyr to gather up and wrench Marg away from the seemingly welcomed discomfort of her shabby hotel. Then the crew then rowed them out of the harbour at a one/two beat of the drum leaving behind the single and last great lion that was still intact and precariously guarding the port of Piraeus against the northern Goths. Of course, they were not yet in sight and may have even taken a turn toward somewhere else before they got anywhere in sight. Who knows? You know what tough mariners at sea for lengthy spells — where the labour of rowing under a hot sun is strenuous and thirsty work — are like.

The *Aura Maré* sailed directly to Korinth where, fortunately for her shallow draft, they managed to pass into a partially flooded channel that was cut into the land bridge through which they rowed into the gulf beyond. From there they sailed along the north coast of the Pelopes. Once they were to the west of the land of Pelopes they veered north of Ithika then (due to a drop in wind had to row) into the Ionian Sea and later passed Actium (under sail). After this they rowed into the gulf of Ambracia in Thesprotia in the land of Epirus.

At this point they came across two Amoran triremes one of which Catherine Lisabet, their friend from Beryus and her brother Albus Agrippa, were aboard. Here Marg continued to be aloof with Dyfed but made a great fuss over seeing Lisabet again which increased Dyfed's suspicions that she may have fallen in love with the beautiful young lady herself. Certainly Marg had fallen out of love with him. And though Marg was anxious to get on to the oracle of Dodona she wasted a few days on board the trireme with Lisabet. The latter had the good manners, though — he noted, to invite he and Trachmyr as well each evening to dine on aboard the trireme in Amoran style with them at a most sumptuous board. The drawback, Dyfed found, was her brother who grated on everyone's nerves but most especially on his. As far as jealousy was concerned, he was plagued only a little by this affliction due to Marg's monopolising of Lisabet's time. For Dyfed had first been intrigued with this beautiful young woman then he had become smitten, probably on account of Marg's cold fish attitude which mostly was blocking his way to her. And he could tell, too, just in how often the beautiful lady gazed past Marg to encounter him with a whimsical and alluring smile, that this wealthy daughter of an Amoran oligarch was intrigued with him as well.

Despite that, Dyfed showed no emotion while around this bothersome Albus Aggripa. All of this, of course, proved at least that the new emperor of Amor hadn't had Lisabet strangled.

From here he and Marg embarked on a somewhat conversation-less journey together, accompanied by Trachmyr. They stopped briefly for the night at the abandoned and ancient city of Ambracia. Arriving at the temple of Dodona that was dedicated to Zeus, Marg perked up a bit, but Dyfed by now thought her none too talkative either way. Once they got there Marg quickly set to and sought out a man who she called Pherecrates. This strange man, who apparently had been previously known to Marg, was intimate with the attendants at the Dodona shrine. But only when she told him that he had once been an intimate friend of Lysander did he became concerned.

And as far as this man Pherecrates and friend of Lysander the Spartan that Marg was intending to commiserate with was concerned, Dyfed thought that he might still be an old lackey of Lysander's who having lost his way was still at large and too foolish to get himself back on track so as to get on with something constructive for a change. Dyfed knew that Lysander had been a great enemy of the Amoran establishment who once had thwarted its emperors and had connived to put an end to the kingship of the Herakleides. Furthermore, Lysander had been anxious that the priestesses of the oracle at Dodona didn't favour the Herakleides as kings. He had been quite confident of this outcome. This confidence, apparently, came about through Lysander's further friendship with Pherecrates.

It was true, Dyfed knew, that the Herakleides were (as earlier stated) also the untranscended ones who were left behind in the third dimension when the sages of the Hyperborean race departed for the fifth dimension. But at that time the Herakleides (who had managed to retain Hyperborean ethics) were the closest prospects to being capable of shortly following their masters through transcendence into the fifth dimension (which some later did), but also of being able to lead the hoi polloi through pagan example to individual spiritual salvation. They did this in a way that only they knew how. This was through the tree of knowledge of good and evil so as to comprehend the tree of life and thereby enter into communion with their individual souls, their original universal essence of being. This was the true self for all humans.

Dyfed also knew that those Masters of the Little Known Universe (the Hyperboreans) had made themselves known to the Herakleides who they aided and abetted in their struggle here. The Herakleides were the first of the hoi polloi in the third dimension to come into contact and act alongside the Hyperborean Masters in an effort to improve their lot. Some of these Masters on the move who way back when (eight centuries or so before the story's current present) that had collided with the Heraklaides had come from the land of Canaan, Manandan had once told him. Their teachings were gnostic; they had been the magicians who as the children of Thoth (long before it had degenerated into Horus) had influenced the worship of Adon through Atum (Amun or Amen) and others that had been impinged upon the imagination of King Amen-hotep IV. In a sense these Herakleides were an earlier version of the current *pack* with who Dyfed was associated and who moved quietly and furtively through the third dimension at that time, long ago. But they were not exactly an equivalent value, for most of today's *pack* is comprised of masters and very few hoi polloi. For example, Trachmyr (you will remember) was an associated member of *the pack*, through his close connections to Dyfed. There were a few others in similar positions. And Dyfed himself identified with the Herakleides because although technically a (small M) master himself, he was more closely associated with the third dimension than with the fifth, just like the Herakleides had been. Not so Marg who (although he had long realised that she) was a full-blown Hyperborean Mistress (Mistress), she was a Master Mistress with an attitude.

Unlike third dimensional emotions (where often there can be no conditions to being in love or to love, or of having huge emotional responsibilities) fifth - D conditions per sé did exist as such; though they were conditions that Dyfed didn't quite understand because his mother never had any conditions when it came to loving him. Nor did Manandan, though he may have had an agenda. And now due to Dyfed's greenhorn status among the Masters, he felt the brunt of that difference when he should not have had to. It came down in the end, he later supposed, to Marg's ignorance rather than her callousness. And it turned out that Marg sought Pherecrates not for any emotional connections but rather to access the higher sanctity of Azeus (or Odin, and for that matter any other super-Saturnian entity) through the god of wisdom, which (always mindful of others) was compassionate and loving. Dyfed, then, found that out in a hurry. He found that out right then, at that very moment.

For it was at this point that she now informed him that she was breaking off all contact with their third dimension relationship until further notice. It sounded permanent, though she did add, "at least until the problem of the Haploids had been settled and the hoi polloi were beyond the former's influence and control.' She added on top of that, 'the actions and general behaviour of the hoi polloi, as well as their conditions of life, were simply just the very limit.' She couldn't go on, she said.

"You must go on,' Dyfed told her, pleadingly.

"No, I cannot go on,' she said adamantly. 'After all, here in the third density, humanity wasn't able to comprehend much of anything which takes place within its phenomenon,' she stated in a very matter of fact way. 'Humanity certainly wasn't intelligent enough yet to experiment with religious cults and their ponderings thereof, *that's foe' sho'*, she exclaimed, emphasizing the last two words in a funny way. 'My proof? she added, as she extended her right arm out that encompassed a wide sweep. 'Look upon its works, oh mortal man, and despair!' She suddenly laughed almost bitterly. It was a denigrating type of laugh, he noted. 'Humanity, isn't even fit to live with,' she said. The next morning she was gone.

Dyfed had earlier arranged for Trachmyr to retrace his steps and bring the *Aura Maré* around to the port of Tintani on the Ionian Sea at an appointed time. The plan had been that from the oracle of Dodona he and Marg were to make their way west to meet him and the ship there. Now, as he left Dodona alone heading due west, Dyfed was concerned for Marg.

What was she up to and what was going to happen to her? Was she actually going to perform her magic here among what were already Dodona's ruins and in some mysterious way return to the fifth dimension unattended? Why not? Maybe, he thought, she was already transformed. She was a dyed in the wool Master (Mistress) who could shift dimensions at will. Or would she too retrace her steps to the trireme in the Gulf of Ambracia and hitch a ride in comfort to somewhere or another in the arms of Lisabet with her drunken older brother tagging on for the ride looking distantly and aghast at the world around him before passing-out below deck? He wondered on these possibilities as he suddenly became aware that his body shivered and his mind was growing clouded.

When Dyfed arrived stumbling alongside the banks of the Thyamis River he knew he was finally approaching the Ionian Sea coast at last: and not a moment too soon. He was obviously approaching a mental funk as well that was now complicated by the physical sickness that had just recently set upon him. While this low ebb that had somewhat reduced Dyfed's bodily resistance, a passing miscreant pathogen (finding him vulnerable) entered his throat and lungs like a hard headed, hard rock miner or collier burrowing underground into the rock beneath the earth's surface to set up shop to scope out the potential — the abundance, the ore-bodies' (or the colliery's) wealth, the pay dirt — the lolly. No wonder he had such a headache. His imagination then began to rage as he raved on to himself while his contagion ravished his mind and body.

Finally, having reached the Ionian Sea port town of Tintani off the coast of Theprokia, Dyfed (at this point) languished feverishly on a hard bench beside a greasy spoon kitchen beneath an awning of a hotel he had stumbled into. Here he waited and watched while in the faded and small distance on the edge of the windless horizon Trachmyr had set about commanding the crew to row the *Aura Maré* into the harbour to fetch him. But to Dyfed, his ship appeared to be stationary and it appeared to him that he waited for days for it to draw near. Sometimes it looked even like it was rowing away from him. At any rate he noted that it moved at a glacial speed no matter which way it was going. Meanwhile, as he too remained (apparently) immovably stationary, his cold and patiently waiting plate of fish n' tripe cooked in garlic and leeks, served with tomatoes (a strange occurrence at this time for the tomato plant was unknown here), along with rough bread spread thinly with fish liver pate. He was hungry but his stomach churned unpleasantly and that ring of fire was constantly present at the toilet. Occasionally he puked onto the floor. These incidents, he blurrily noticed, fetched a kitchen hand to mop up. Still his lunch lay dormant and touched in front of him as he sat there shivering. He noticed, too, that a large and broad shouldered man (conspicuous with his reddish, light brown beard which almost touched his slim waist) was casting concerned looks in his direction. By the way he wore his manner as he milled around comfortably, even ignoring other clientele, Dyfed thought him the proprietor of the hotel or possibly the chef.

"Eat up, young man,' he even said to Dyfed at one point.

He repeatedly spoke those words to Dyfed on the three or four occasions and it was all that Dyfed heard spill from the man's lips in the course of the long hours and days it seemed to take for the *Aura Maré* to approach the shore. Dyfed didn't find the strength to answer him. At least the man in the long beard had made an attempt. Dyfed spoke to no other as he contemplated this man before something else took hold of him and casting his mind this way and that, pulled his thoughts to some far away place. Fortitude was quickly draining out of Dyfed and the other man clearly saw that. As for Marg — though her dwindling sense of presence prevailed, her looming image continually dogged Dyfed's fevered brain. But somehow he had the fortitude to realize that he had fantasized long enough over her. She didn't care about him as he had cared about her. That was obvious to him now. He needed to move on. But it was going to be difficult.

(The yellow cucumber-shaped machine)

'All poets are mad.'
ROBERT BURTON

From the Ionian Sea port town of Tintani that was governed by the district of Thesprotia in Epirus, a sick and lonely Dyfed set sail for Italia. The skipper (following Captain Trachmyr's commands) headed due north and passed through the narrow channel that separated Kerkira (Corfu) from the mainland. Then continuing northwest the vessel brushed passed the Acroceraunian promontory or peninsula that jutted out from northern Epirus almost opposite Otranto in Messapia (modern Salento) located on the heel peninsula of Italia. Otranto is not to be confused with Taranto (Taras, Tarantas or Tarentum) located on the inside or western shore of the same heel peninsula. Dyfed had been trying for some time to get a message to Morgant without success of receiving any return communication. His last entry, when he was still hail and hearty had been posted aboard an Amoran outgoing trireme from Athena's port of Piraeus destined for Amor non-stop. That communication had been the last of many since Men-nefer (the enduring and the beautiful) known also as Aneb-Hetch (White Walls or White Fortress) sent from Peru-nefer to Marg in Xandria for her to expedite. That had been years ago. Obviously, the important message was the one he was looking to receive back from Morgant, a message that wasn't very forthcoming and forthwith, he felt. And he didn't mind saying so in just those words with his persistent follow-up entreats. But there had still been no word. And still he waited for some sign or another…some miraculous materialization of Morgant or Cato, or for that matter, some other master…some toothless vagabond even…the avatar of a Master of the Little Known Universe in disguise or a willing and indoctrinated hoi polloi. Who cares? Somebody care, anybody at least.

Quailing continually from the sudden emotional change of status between he and Marg, combined with the inevitable remembrance of the agony over Ceredwyn as well, both brought on and magnified by his fever, as well the sudden awareness of his raging passion he now had over Lizabet, all this suddenly acted further to complicate his already failing physical state and cast him into a terrible funk.

As sad as he was over he and Marg's breakup, he was determined to keep a bold chin-up and not become too discouraged, for Europa was reshaping and undergoing ferocious change. And no matter what the change was, there were (after all) many fish (or mermaids) in the sea. But — oh! he could hardly bare the thought of recollection, for even if his heart was torn over Marg, the memory of Ceredwyn still managed now to cause a second lump in his already clogged up throat. And then there was Lizabet. Others, too, paid their visit to him at this point. There was Cassandra (Cassy) and Clemintine, too. And one mustn't forget Thecla (not her real name), a sweet girl, who easily got her way with men and was jealously and cruelly called Sappho's Lesbos. Compared to her (so Dyfed's troubled mind reflected), Lizabet was a bitch. Thecla wasn't a Sappho's Lesbos, and furthermore she had an inordinate interest in theology, he remembered.

Anyway, these visions displayed a turpitude within which a nightmare of horrors unfolded where there was no sands left in the time jar with which to sort it out, never mind to quell or slay the dragon (a false metaphor to begin with) like some fanciful Archangel Michael or Buffy the slayer of vampires. And all the while Dyfed continued his tossing and turning on his sick bed in the thick atmosphere of his stateroom below deck. He turned from hot to cool, from one side to the other and then back again twenty-four seven. And if that wasn't enough, soon Lizabet joined Marg in his bed. Good gracious! He could hardly contain himself but hadn't the energy or the inclination to do anything about it to relieve the tension. This infliction affected him by sorely constricting his breathing that affected his heart rate and his pallor and so forth. Now he lay in his blanketed hammock bed aboard the *Aure Maré* bleeding from the heart as well as from the nose and his teeth.

Life without Marg was going to be like life without Ceredwyn who he still loved (he now realized, again) and whose place had not been quite filled by Marg. Yet despite the passage of time it was with a feverish clarity that he recalled Marg's remarkable golden hair that encircled her beautiful ears and fair skinned face (even as he tried to push it out of his troubled mind's eye and focus now on Lizabet). This unfolded even now though these recollections vividly contrasted with his memory of Ceredwyn's winning visage that had never really faded from the tenderness of his heart, either. Yet when thinking of Ceredwyn, time and time again he involuntarily conjured up Marg's image instead. He saw her in that wide-brimmed, flaxen coloured hat she wore of late on the back of her head to shield her browned neck and shoulders from the exposure under the fierce sun. Meanwhile, her green and red tunic — the one he had bought her in Xandria — that she often wore over a bright yellow smock which fell to her ankles and matched her coloured sandals were what now suddenly clothed Ceredwyn, in his confused mind. And with her fashionable, trendy Amoran vestments of impeccable finery sculpted in shining silks, and dolled up hair-do in rolls of curls that emphasized her beautiful face, these suddenly in his infatuation for Lizabet turned nightmarish. For it seemed to him now that this latter woman's wardrobe stood apart from the other two in a superficial way that grounded her to the material present and in his fever induced hallucinations it made Dyfed uncomfortable in recalling that he had once even coveted her. Spikes of hot guilt penetrated him to his very heart. But these depths of envisioned delirium were somehow enclosed in a singular memory chamber that also contained his fond memories of Ceredwyn and Marg that was newly mixed with Lizabet. Somehow, his grip on the vector quantity of organized singular emotional continuities were now being dragged along as easily and effortlessly as the *Aura Maré's* dangling anchor and short chain in a very deep moorage raked with high storm swells of a stiff wind at high tide. The result was a scalar quality where the three women were all wrapped up into one value, and the unique commonality between the three of them merged in juxtaposition and lowered the common mean of Dyfed's once loving enthusiasm. Now the contrasting silver sea blue, green and daub eyes of Ceredwyn and Marg with the red, straw and brunette hair done up in rolls, buns and blowing across their faces soon became a blur from somewhere deep within his depths of despair and loathing abhorrence for himself. Here, Ceredwyn, Marg and just as easily pretty but fake Lizabet (with that languished longing in her dark eye-lashed gaze that seemed to look at him over the shoulders of the aforementioned two women) now materialized like the dark soil beneath the fade of the melting snow. And whether he was asleep or awake didn't seem to matter. A garish and fixed dance with a promenade here and a do-si-do there that was lock-stepped in a ménage et trio began to be replicated like the verbal rolling of r's in his feverish mind that sounded like a rapid Mephistopheles' drum roll. Whew! he thought; did that ever act to help complicate his state of being in a strangely disjointed way! Then soon his mind began to resemble a cobweb in a fire storm and his body was like the flopping of a beached whale or a wrecked ship torn open upon a dangerous reef, its retched and split sides spilling out and taking in volumes of water.

As his fever flared his flamed imagination raged. Confined exclusively below deck, flailing from one side to the other in his hot and sweaty bed, Dyfed twisted and turned desperately seeking out the cooler portions of his bedding. Furthermore, he sought out every psychological sanctuary of refuge which came to mind as well and solicited immunity common to all states of remembered bliss while in love, as well as being spurned in the course thereof. He did this as he waited for an upturn (and return) to his normal state, whatever (and if ever) that may be. But, of course, it was futile in this state to defy illusion. It was also all a mistake to think one could rethink and change the past and alter its effect which brought one (and all) up to date and speed and into the present. It was too late now to go back and recourse anew…it was too late to once again set foot onto one's own pure and unaltered plain of destiny that once lay bare and untilled before us all and be able to set to now and reform one's life of the past. There is no going back. What is done is done. It can't be undone or redone. What on-going ploughing, tilling, hoeing and sowing or poisoning, burning and general destruction that has been done there on that undulating plain of one's life is done for. It's all for good and for ill (read bad). Of course, this state was only a remembrance and therefore Dyfed's remedy was of little help in the end. But (in any case) his rising sickness and dis-ease may (somehow) have helped to quell his psychological sorrow; for in struggling to breathe and quell the choke of death that snuffs out lasting hope, his physical suffocation and oxygen deprivation to his brain may even have helped dull his mind from perceiving the cascading pain in his heart caused by all his failed hopes that manifested not so much as broken dreams, but rather as failed initiatives concerning his true self. Here then was his endeavour to move on. And at this moment came the difficulty with which moving on entailed. For having so long sought the solace within Marg's protective comfort sheaf that helped to fence off and shield him from those perceived dangers with which this peculiar world reality was fraught, was the source of his suffering. If it came to it, might it be the same with regard to Manandan, Karatakos and Cato, as well? Dyfed shuddered and moaned and his attendant rushed quickly to his side.

Meanwhile, at the start of this, his last leg of their journey home to Italia, Trachmyr had had to round up a new crew for the *Aura Maré* as the old hands from the last shift had quickly deserted ship at Tintana the moment they were paid. As stated earlier, before his illness had struck in full force Dyfed had initially ordered Trachmyr to sail on toward the city of Raven. Anyway, after only a short time at sea and having come abreast of the promontory of Acroceraunian, Trachmyr — having become worried that Dyfed's state of earthly being was deteriorating so rapidly that he was on the threshold of entering the realm of mortal peril — changed course to find him a doctor at once. So, he needed to set the bow for Taras (Tarentium or Taranto) instead and have Dyfed consulted by a reliable man of medicine. So, as they were currently abreast of the Acroceraunian promontory of northern Epirus at that time, in order to do this they needed to change their northern course for one that took them south west and around the southern tip of the Messapian (Salento) peninsula (sometimes referred to as the heel of Italia).

Shortly after Trachmyr gave this command, he was confronted by one of the newly hired help. This man was a surprise to Trachmyr in the shape and form of a strong, tall, slim-waist man with a long beard. After having set out for Italia, it had never crossed Trachmyr's mind that among his new crew that he had hastily hired to help man the *Aura Maré* that there might be specifically a competent that he could rely on to help him in any way to find a way out of this particular conundrum. So it came as a stunning surprise to find two new developments aboard that led to one and the same result. This long bearded man said his name was Pyrrhus Molosos Pentadaktylos. He told Trachmyr that he was the man labouring below decks as the bull-cook changing Dyfed's bed sheets and clothes and what-not, while keeping him as comfortable as possible. Why he was coming forward, he told Trachmyr was because friends of Dyfed had told him that they needed to set their bow to Hydrus, not Taras. Anyway, to sail all the way around Messapia to Taras was folly, the man added. Hydrus (Hydruntum, also modern Otranto), on the other hand, was close at hand. It was just across the narrow strait to the west. Trachmyr replied that he needed a highly skilled physician, not an army doctor that was probably all that Hydrus boasted and could rise to find.

As stated, it had come to Trachmyr's attention that this man had taken on the duties of ringing out Dyfed's sweat drenched clothes and bed sheets and had a gentle bedside manner despite his appearances and seemed kindly toward Dyfed.

"I remember you from the start at Tintani,' said Trachmyr, 'Your intention for service on the *Aura Maré* was to pay your way to Brindisium, or Brentesion, as the Helenes say.'

"True,' replied the other man, speaking Amoran in a halting accent. 'It was a ruse to get on board. I had orders to see that Master Dyfed would proceed there and I was ready to make any excuse needed to succeed.'

"So, what's at Brindisium?'

"A rendezvous, that's all"

"You are an Elir, aren't you? Who gave you such orders? And rendezvous with whom?' asked Trachmyr.

At this point the bull-cook was quick to correct him. He told Trachmyr that his real name was Pyrrhus (Pyyros) Pentadaktylos and that he was an ancestor of the Argeads and was more properly a Danaan or Danios. He then told Trachmyr that he had been told such things by a Master friend of Dyfed and was doing his bidding.

"And who would that be? asked Trachmyr automatically. His interest now peaked.

"The man in question is a master named Morgant, and he tasked me with intercepting Dyfed and delivering him to a regiment of the *pack* for safe keeping. I was told not to speak with anyone about this other than with Dyfed's batman. Morgant told me that a ship under the control of a Professor (or doctor) Torsionfield was to pick Dyfed up at sea off Brindisium and he gave me co-ordinates according to the stars of this season. And since it developed that Dyfed was unwell, I was to inform you to get him there as quickly as possible.'

"A Doctor Torsionfield will attend to him, then?' asked Trachmyr.

"I don't know,' Pyrrhus Pentadaktylos answered. 'I was under the impression that he was in some way in charge of the rescue ship. However, he is a Master of the Little

Known Universe, he told me that much, although I didn't need to be told. From the witness of Herakles, himself a demi-god, I have known others among the Shining ones who are the descendants of An. Strange folk they are. Anyway, you see, what's important to know is that this ship that Morgant is sending to pick him up does not float upon the seas as others do, apparently. It travels through the water beneath the seas' surface.'

"For lands' sake! What are you talking about?' demanded Trachmyr, regarding the man as if he were a lunatic.

But that was what Pyrrhus had been told. He had the coordinates and they needed to rendezvous at sea at night with nobody to observe the goings on of a transfer of personnel from marine-vessel to sub-marine vessel. And if Dyfed's condition worsened, alternative orders were to rendezvous just off Hydrus (Otranto) instead. This is because it is closer: And because it is smaller and currently ship-less.

(Philip Fairface of the House of the Bear)

'Nothing of political importance happens by chance.'
FRANKLIN DELANO ROOSEVELT

Aside from the individual referred to as Pyrrhus Molosos Pentadaktylos, Trachmyr quickly discovered his second surprise for the day. This was that the natural tongue of one of the men he had hired to help row and sail the *Aura Maré* was a Cymraeg (Brythonic) speaking Kelt. This language was spoken in Gwyneth and throughout Britannia secunda only. And the man who spoke it had a story to tell which now causes our story to turn a corner.

The ladies and the lads, apparently, called this personable Cymraeg speaking sailor Philip the Fair that emanated from his Amoran name, Philippus Cinaed. Philippus combines philos — lover or friend — and hippos (horses). Cinaed, on the other hand means fair, handsome or good looking. This translated Philippus Cinaed into the handsome lover of horses.

It turned out that Philip the Fair of Face (and later Philip Fairface) was from the land of the Decangli people to the west of the Dee River. He said that originally he was a son of the nomadic Sarm folk who Emperor Marcus Aurelius had introduced into Albion. Later, after his family were killed, the Decangli people had adopted Philip. The Sarms were traditionally horse people from the steppe lands and he plied his trade of horsemanship. Philip had a tattoo of a bear (or actually a hairy bore) on his forearm. Always when asked why it wasn't the tattoo of a horse he would say that the hairy bear (or bore) was the totem of his family's clan. Furthermore, Philip told Trachmyr that he had once been in the employ of Eudaf Octavius Hen ab Einydd, or simply, Octavius, king of Prydain. On the crossover toward Hydrus, Philip Fairface filled Trachmyr in on the gaps and absence of news about the recent goings on in the offices of both the eastern and western emperors, their deaths and the details of appointment, and their replacements in succession and so forth. The empire now had a new and wily emperor. His name was Flavius Theodosius, and Pilippus told Trachmyr that he now ruled over both the eastern and western halves of the Amoran Empire. Theodosius had succeeded Emperor Valentinianus (another follower of the Jeshuan faith) who had succeeded Jovian Flavius Iovianus Augustus Emperor, also an avid follower of Jeshua. The latter had succeeded Julian the Apostate. This last named emperor had attempted once more (during his stint) to fan the flames of paganism and blow smoke in a manner most annoyingly into the Jeshuan cult's face when attempts to blow it directly up their ass had failed. The late last ruler, Emperor Valentinianus, had been the first Jeshuan emperor of the Nicene function variety. This (aforementioned) was a recent council (organized and attended by Jeshuan bishops) that was named after the host city by Lake Askania (Hellenic, or Lake Ascanius in the Amoran language) in Anatolia.

Philip told Trachmyr that this bishopric convocation had taken place within the last few decades. It had been Valentinianus who appointed his brother Valens to rule from Byzas and help him out. But Valens was killed in battle with the Goths at Adrianople that, as it turned out, was to become a turning point for the Amoran Empire. The new emperor, Flavius Theodosius was the son of Comes (Count) Theodorius a well-known Hispanian. Recently, Theodosius who was battling vandals and shoplifters around his western provinces had appointed his son Honourless as his western co-ruler while he took up the chair (throne) in Byzas. For the Eastern Empire also was under duress from the Visigoths spilling over their borders without permit and the ominous rumour of the approaching Huns from the east.

Anyway, there was another vying at the time for the kingship of Prydain (Albion) who went by many names. Locally in Albion he was called Macsen Wledig and Bricus of Demetia, as he was known back in the day. Currently his more recent nomenclature was General Flavius Claudius Maximus Constantine (W. E. Constantine III). He was, of course, the son of an Amoran-Prydain named Linus (Llewelyn) who was himself descended from Emperor Constantius Chlorus (the Pale) of Illyrian stock who had been born in the province of Hispana. In addition, Linus was related by marriage to Comes Theodosius who somehow had wangled a legacy of having saved Britannia (the Amoran name for Prydain, also Albion) from the great conspiring revolt in Albion's north. That was back in the winter of three hundred and sixty-seven C.E. Like Chlorus, Comes Theodosius also issued from Hispana. These convoluted relationships made Maximus Constantine (otherwise Macsen Wledig or Bricus of Dementia) an in law of the Comes Theodosius family clan. But more than anything this Bricus (aka Constantine) wanted more than anything to become emperor himself, and to that end he had been working on getting himself promoted in that direction with the help of the men who filled the Amoran legions that were installed in Albion. And this led to him being called Constantine.

"How it all came to a head, happened this way,' Philip Fairface told Trachmyr. It transpired that Macsen Wledig Constantine) had successfully wooed and married the daughter of Eudaf Octavius Hen ab Einydd who was Prydain's high king at the time. Eventually he filled his father-in-law's shoes and then with the help of two early freedom fighters from Cunedda named Maelgwy and Tamus, Constantine became Constantine the high king of Prydain himself. Immediately, with Tamus and Maelgwy's continued support, he took charge over all missions in Prydain under the Amoran Expeditionary Forces Command. Now he was RigoMaximus (high king) of Prydain but he had ambitions of gaining more than just Amoran provincial rule under his belt. As already stated, what he wanted was to at least become a western emperor. And this promotion was not without precedent. Just before Emperor Chlorus died at Eboracum (of the Yew tree, later called Eyoric or York) after campaigning with his son in northern Albion against the Pixies from Caledonia without much success, he encouraged his son Constantinus to up and magnify their campaign hardships into glorious victories substantially enough to up and ride on them now to proclaim himself Western Emperor Constantine I. His father's troops supported him. That was in the Olympiad year 1082 or year 306 of the current era.

Intrigue, such as vying for the takeover of the highest office in Amor was not for the feint of heart. It was also a highly skilled and dangerous game. It was better sometimes to hold back and let others pave the way for you. One might even avidly support the advancement of other aggressive and intelligent types before ultimately allying with their enemies and plotting their downfall after the fact. Letting these folks lead the way and run ahead of you was the best tactic. Later, you can support and exploit their exorcism. Once the most likely to succeed have failed, your chances are much better. The wise who reach for such glory trophies want those with lesser competence and skill (than their own) to remain behind and beneath them (which is in the correct and logical order), and for them remain there for as long as possible after you have succeeded. Bricus of Demetia who eventually became Constantine III did not follow Constantinus I's example, for the latter remained in Albion after succeeding to emperor. Constantine III and his companion, the Druid mast Blazingwolf, sought out that achievement. They had to for no other option was open to them.

Our old acquaintance and manager/agent, the guiding light and force of Bricus of Demetia, the now Jeshuanized Pater Blazingwolf, anxiously counselled Constantine to hold back and bide his time, even if the Western Empire's remaining soldiers in Gaul were prepared to support him. Having become aware that Theodosius was casting around for a potential ruler to help his son Honourless to rule the Western Empire, Constantine became furious over the wait and what he referred to as Theodosius' tyranny in placing his own son Honourless to this position and not seeking him out first. Meanwhile Pater Blazingwolf sought out and sent Philippus Cinaed on a recognisance tour of northern Italia, Nordicum and Dalmatia. He wanted to know the full lie of the land to better serve Constantine's chances of success.

Philippus advanced across Gaul and was set for the Italian city of Mediolanum (Medio) to where Emperor Diocletian had some years earlier moved the Western Empire's capital. He noted that Medio, a fortress, would be a valuable position to own. Then he set out east. However, upon reaching the Thrakian city of Serdica near the Moesian border, he learned that Theodosius had just arrived at his western capital of Medio where he was taking charge of his campaign against the Foederati uprising. These folks included those Goths who stretching from Nordicum through Pannonia to Moesia had been receiving Amoran military assistance that included prominent Amoran Goth generals who had been trained at the Amoran academy. Philippus then turned south hoping to reach Epirus. It was at this point that this agent of Blazingwolf met a fellow Kelt in Trachmyr who was looking to hire help aboard ship bound for Raven. And, as he told Trachmyr, without a by your leave, he left the service of Blazingwolf for that of a deck hand.

What with news of Vandals, Shoplifters, mercenary thugs, West and East Goths, even Swabians breaking through the border from time to time, one moment allied with the Western Empire, the next either claiming neutrality or running an out and out fighting battle against the Empire, this meant something much more to Trachmyr. It meant that his brothers and comrades in arms would be back in the business of being in the thick of fighting for the Empire. This meant that he was needed back, and now all that Trachmyr wanted out of life was to take leave of Dyfed and return to the sort of action that he knew something about. He had had enough of baby-sitting.

It appeared to Dyfed that at some point the *Aura Maré* seemed to stop rolling and dipping upon the waves of the Adriatic Sea as she had done on every sea she had crossed. He felt a change of deployment and thought he may have been carried from his stateroom and had been relocated into another. Perhaps he had even change ships. It had been a strange place to which he had been brought. It had nothing in common with the *Aura Maré*, that's for sure, for he had felt entombed where noises had a hollow sound to them now (and there were a lot of them, scrapping, scratching, thumping and banging), and all the smells that should have been familiar were foreign. Even the taste in his mouth was foul. Something was intrinsically different all round. And still there was that constant and infernal noise and its accompanying vibration. What was that about?

Remembering it later, he assumed he had slipped into a coma. He may have even been drugged because he now recalled some strange and vivid dreams. It had been explained to him by Morgant (who had strangely materialized at this point) that he couldn't be helped up on deck to breathe the therapeutic airs of the salty winds that blew over the water, or even broaden his horizon from inside by gazing out the window through the wooden hull. And the reason, he was told, was because they were in fact inside a metal tank that was being propelled by means other than oarsmen and quaffs of wind to get them across the Adriatic Sea. This vessel, he was told, burrowed through the water a hundred Amoran feet below its white-capped surface. He'd have to wait until Ra-diance slipped over the western lip and the stars shone out from a dark sky in a supernatural brilliance before going above decks. Shortly after Dyfed slumped into an uncomfortable dream.

Later, during one of the starry nights aboard, they did surface and he was helped up and out onto a cramped platform where he saw the sparkling stars and the brilliant smudge of the Milky Way as it twisted its way around like a giant sparkling worm through the black sky. And all around him in every direction he felt the dark choppy sea while a ribbon of moonlight skipped before and aft across the slightly shimmering waves tossed up now by a brisk and rising wind. Only then did he feel the natural rocking movement of a ship at sea. All was quiet and they must have been quite some distance from shore for no dark headlands rose upon the horizon. After an hour or two, during which the others, including Philip Fairface and Pyrros Molosos Pentadaktylos who had also been transferred to the submarine, forced some food down their throats while standing on their feet or leaning slightly against a metal railing, there was suddenly some minor commotion and a buzz of low whispering started up among the sailors. Now an air of concern seemed to descend onto the deck. When he asked what was taking place Morgant informed him that another sea vessel was approaching. A lookout had caught the sight of its sails in the moonlight and Morgant coaxed him to keep his voice down and be ready to be assisted back down into this fantastic sea craft that had no oars (or sails) and was fashioned out of a hollow metal cylinder. Twice they surfaced during the voyage. Each time it was at night and they took precautions not to be seen by other sailors. For whatever reason, the people on this boat (even when surfaced to breathe the medicinally rejuvenating fresh air) didn't want anybody to detect them, it seemed. Was it that the empire's western and eastern factions were at war? he had wondered. Or were there some other unseen factions confronting each other. He didn't understand. Every time upon leaving the wind-swept deck and entering back into the claustrophobic metallic cylinder which defined the vessel he was assigned to he could feel that strange oily and tarry smell oozing out of the stuffy internal metallic air that permeated his skin, hair and his scant clothes that smelled now like everything else that was contained within the iron hull of this sub-marine vessel. Later he referred to this episode as his Aura sub-Maré-vision dream.

When Dyfed next opened his slightly less gritty and grainy eyes, he was once again on deck of this peculiar craft. This time (the fourth time) it was not in the middle of the night but at a very early start to a generous morning. Although they weren't (exactly) standing out to sea, they were still about an Amoran mile off shore. It didn't appear, either, that there was a problem in coming to dock or anchor in shallower water. Instinctively he knew that even if he were the least of their concern, the vessel and the crew were particularly concerned about remaining wrapped up in a cloud of secrecy and obscurity.

In a manner to collect his stabilizing mind Dyfed's thoughts returned to the riveting sea journey that had taken him out to Kreta, the land of Khem, and then on his return he visited coastal Anatolia, Thraki, Hellas and Epirus. And for the last leg, he's been sealed in a hot, smelly, riveted-together cylinder-shaped iron-can vessel that in a magical sort of way somehow hadn't immediately sunk to the bottom of the Adriatic Sea. That was a miracle. Then with the miraculously loving care of the eccentric Dr Quizzi Gizmo's wonton wizard's magic wand (and the tender urgings and promptings of Dr Torsionfield) — accompanied by lots of smoke, oily grime and a heavy application of tricky mirrors — the iron fish breast-stroked the journey to completion and resurfaced him here close to Amor's new capital at Raven. It had been on the last leg of the journey that Dyfed had been mostly consumed by a form of torpidity in a stupor, constantly being visited by the illusive child of Turpitude that had caused the acute sense of disconnect and apprehension which induced a spurious type of turmoil into his strained, maimed and brained out mental equilibrium whose effects from which he was trying to recover at this time.

It was still quite dark but he could see what looked like a lug rigged sailing craft obviously operating here as a tender a short distance away. Apparently it had been standing out at sea waiting for this moment. It was meant, he was told, to take those going ashore quietly on their way (pronto) while still under the cover of the fading darkness that was quickly turning into a murky grey and grainy dawn which is often seen to emerge before the clear morning light here at this time of year. But anyway, at this point providence intervened on his behalf. Cato suddenly showed up out of nowhere upon the small carrack that came out to pick him up. He greeted Dyfed and Morgant warmly. But his attention seemed to be concentrating on the ship that Dyfed was aching to leave. Then two other men who had appeared to be officers of this strange submarine vessel came forward to speak to Cato and introduce themselves to Dyfed more formerly. One was Captain Doctor Torsionfield. He was dressed in a strange navy-blue jump suit and identified himself as the engineer of the Aura sub-Maré. Much to Dyfed's amazement and confusion he referred to himself in a demurring but at the same time humorous manner as the skipper of *"your* (meaning Dyfed's) *alter-ego marine machine'*. The other man was a relaxed looking nonconformist with startlingly alert eyes who wore a broad brimmed, short-flat topped straw hat and was dressed extremely casually. His name was Quizzi Gizmo and he described himself as a theoretical and experimental scientist, whatever that all meant. After some quickly exchanged but warm words and accompanying body language, the two men said good-bye to Cato, Morgant and Dyfed then returned into the yellow cucumber shaped metal sub-marine machine which (once the carrack had pulled away from it) quickly sunk out of sight with an explosion of gurgling bubbles.

Dyfed, Morgant, Cato, Trachmyr and the bull cook Pyrrhus Molosos Pentadaktylos were left standing together. They waved goodbye once again to the submarine vessel that had disappeared already out of sight and then they waved to Philippus Cinaed, alias Philip Fairface, as he wended his way back to Albion, after he first checked out the lagoon city of Raven.

(Gorgeous Giorgius Gregorius Florentius)

'The illusion of freedom will continue as long as its profitable to continue the illusion of freedom. At the point where the illusion becomes too expensive to maintain, they will just take down the scenery, they will pull back the curtains, they will move the tables and chairs out of the way, and you will see the brick wall at the back of the theatre.'

FRANK ZAPPA

In the meantime, Cato and Morgant accompanied Dyfed, Trachmyr, Philip Fairface and Pyrros Molosos Pentadaktylos back to his old modest digs in Amor that were close to the Tarpeian Rock on the south western slope of the Capitoline Hill. Then after tucking him in for a long, well deserved rest, Cato and the two other men disappeared for into the noisy city's precincts. Awakening much later, Dyfed discovered his bachelor suite still intact just as (and where) he left it beneath the temple of Jupiter the usurper.[41] Here he hunkered down to lick his wounds and to consolidate what he'd learned and accomplished from his past experiences and gains while waiting for Cato to return. His larder needed stocking, too, and his collection of alcohol bottled in leaded glass decanters on his shiny oak liquor cupboard had all been licked dry and sat collecting dust with their cork stoppers (along with some of the broken decanters) lying across the floor.

Dyfed was now anxious about his regiment. These were those military trained officers, agents and soldiers he managed to maintain for the benefit of the House of Lucifer. Still intact, Dyfed wanted Trachmyr to recoup his position with them. But first, before he and Dyfed's regiment could legally join in on the fray that was unfolding on the world theatre, they would have to consult with Stilicho, the Western Empire's most prominent and powerful general and military leader at this time.

One day shortly after his return a knock came to his bachelor suite door. Upon opening the door Dyfed saw that Cato was back, along with Morgant. They were carefully appraising him with concern.

"Everything is kind of intact,' said Cato, 'although the House of Lucifer's business was currently stalled and the general account was bankrupt and its bills receivable account remained penniless.' Furthermore, they told him that his bills payable records were missing and presumed lost to all and sundry. Nevertheless, he told him that his bank and business accounts (on the other hand) were holding up on their own and his infrastructure was still somewhat in place. But markets were down, of course, and inflation was soaring.

"Then define that 'everything is kind of intact', demanded Dyfed curiously.

"You bank and business connections are all still there,' he answered.

"Get out of here!' said Dyfed. 'Are you kidding me? He jumped up and kissed the smiling Cato. 'That calls for celebration,' he said. 'Morgant,' he called out, 'let's take up the dithyrambs and summon the god of wine, me hearties. Oh, and break out the Injun

---

41 The Capitoline hill had once been dedicated in ancient times to the god Saturn.

hashish. And you, Pentadaktyros, or whatever your name is — to the market with you. We need fresh wine and fish.'

What Dyfed had arrived back to was vastly different to what Europa had been when he had first arrived in Amor. Theodosius was now emperor in waiting and ready to be to be co-ruled in the west at Medio by his son Horatius Honourless and co-ruled yet as well in the east at Byzas by another son Arcadius. But at this moment Emperor Theo was still holding court in Medio. It was his last days. Europa having descended into an imperial/capitalist induced turmoil, Theo the Thug had installed a part Vandal Amoran (nephew by marriage) named General Stilicho as magister militum and sent for his daughter Placidia to join him in Medio. Dissatisfaction and unrest, however, were on the increase and with many of the empire's generals and troops being foreign Goths, fear and panic was spreading among the intelligentsia. Aside from the promotion of Jeshuanism, these were the hallmarks of the era of Flavius Theodosius, sometimes called the Great or the Thug. He was the last emperor to rule over both west and east. But mostly it was the growing distance between the present and the glory days of the grand old republic (GOR) that made the difference here.

The empire wasn't a patch on the republic that had had strict morals and sound ethics that soothed their souls. There had been a short period of time nearer the beginning of the empire (almost two hundred years earlier) that was considered to be the most glorious and most peaceful and rewarding days of all time on Good Earth. The great Emperor Marcus Aurelius Philosopher took up part of that era. But compared to that, the present cadets of the empire were slovenly, greedy, vain and ignoble. They cared only for their own skin and what it amounted to (specifically their ego, their stomach and their genitals); they respected no obligation and had no accountability or integrity and neither virtuosity nor righteousness were words with which they were in the least familiar. Also, contributing to the general unrest there was a severe contagion that was causing many to die. And as Dyfed's condition had deteriorated in the interim of the short voyage to Raven, this similarity of condition seemed to be replicated, and then fanned by the winds of change it played out via some strange perverted harmony across Europa. Disease (as it happened) was rampant here today due to this contagion that was thought to have arrived with the siroccos that blew here from across the White Sea from the deserts of Libya in Africa every Autumn. Although this was strictly not so, rumour had it that this plague (peste) had floated across from Greater Maghreb (the land of the Berber) to southern Europa during the last full moon close to all hallows eve[42], an old pagan holy day. This, after all, was a time when the normal attitude that existed around the White Sea was measly, meagre and miserly. The attitude was one where sickos and cripples were just losers and if one were found stumbling around in your way, it was acceptable that it was roughly pushed aside just as you boxed up and shipped your affable next-door neighbour leper to some colonized rocky crag on some distant island on a one way ticket to a no-frills sodomizers' haven to rot and suffer out the remainder of their miserable lives. And a percentile of young children of the poor were constantly being bought up and used as objects for sexual gratification to seriously ill scions of

---

42 Traditionally in ancient times each day began and ended at sun down. This is why all Hallows Eve (even today) doesn't begin until sundown on the last day of October and ends at sundown on the first day of (once the ninth, but now) the eleventh month, November. What follows that is the Day of the Dead that ends on the following evening of November 2nd, not November 1st.

the entitled wealthy as were (sex) slaves in general throughout the household society. It was even common rumour that the late Augustus Augustus had regularly performed self-gratifying perverted sex with infants only days or weeks old who never outlived the encounter.

How different Dyfed found it to be back here this Fall compared to those happy, lazy, hazy, crazy, days of summer in Xandria where the warm but fresh winds passed through the tall planted date palms growing in a row, and the ambience of those nectar perfumed and butterfly impinged breezes that rippled the smooth sky-reflected waters of the drab and dirty-sandy dug channel that redirected a piece of the big muddy waters of the Ar (Nile) that led part of that river across parched sand and shale to the drying and greedy lips of the City of Xandria. What was that great son of the Houses of Argead/Aeacid thinking, anyway, to set up a corner store of civilization far from anywhere along this nasty and dusty, barren coastline? The audacity of the young man, however, was graced with such spontaneity that it turned a derelict corner store into an oasis of civilization. But not, of course, without the help of the Ptolemys (i.e.: Claudius and the Soter [the saviour]).

What had been a somewhat watertight empire that had floated quite well on its own without listing too much and had managed to remain centrally controlled (more or less), was something of the past. For reasons of expedience towards better management and rule, the empire had earlier been divided into western and eastern portions. Then its divisiveness was further expanded into quarters by a Dalmatian born emperor (Diocletian). This caused certain administration awkwardness with the addition of many co-emperors. So to aid the Empire, Diocletian established new administrative centres. One of them was at Medio. As Jeshuanism (the breakaway Abramistic cult) had already spread throughout the Amoran Empire, and its bishoprics were assuming secular power and were well on their way to take over the reins of the official conscience of Amor's trimmed down pantheon, Medio developed into a key centre for Western Jeshuanism. By this time the Jeshuan cult, although something of a breath of fresh air due to its initial gnostic character, combined with its glorious infusion of Ahura Mazda/Zoroasterism, Jain/Hindu/Buddhism, tempered with the Hellenic philosophies of Plato and Aristotles and the rural, bucolic, aesthetic mysticism mixed with orthodox Abramism and Injin fakirism. The latter had become shackled and bogged down with the complications that historically come with materialization of hierarchy and organizational power politics that was further complicated with superfluous competition, greed, and an over abundance of passionate, do-gooding adherents who suffer acutely from cerebral epilepsy and third stage exaggerated short-man (and penis) syndrome.

Needless to say, despite all of this, the temple of Jupiter still sat at the top of the Capitoline Hill. But now, after all this time, it sat towering and vacant, keeping to itself. To keep it company it only had the wind, an occasional visiting poet and evening lovers; those few who sought its darkened inside façade (from which to gaze out through) to grasp the beauty of its gaping columns as they looked out into the past and the silver streaks of the western evening sky. At least it remained. The gold statue of Victoria (Victory[43]) had already been removed from her outdoor alter beside the Curia Julia. More than a statue, she had been an empire-wide psychological goddess. The Emperor Constantius Chlorus (the White) had been legally responsible for the latter's removal but a Jeshuan

---

43   From the word vincere, 'to conquer'. (re: Sabine goddess Vacuna)

Bishop named Aurelius Ambrosius (mentored by a certain Flavius Richeau) of the newly instituted diocese of Medio was at the seat of getting her physically removed. This event was an important benchmark and an ill omen.

By this time Ambrosius, the bishop of Medio, had become a notable influence upon another churchman, a certain Aurelius Augustinus of Hippo by name. This intelligent and grasping control-freak had just formulated his frightfully fallacious doctrine of original sin in readiness for its grand launch upon an unsuspecting public at large. But since he was still only just beyond the puerility of youth, one can forgive him, I suppose. At that moment he was just then in the act of setting his Idea afloat like a battleship upon the Jeshuan See. It was to be billed a clincher for tolling the bell that would inevitably summon a countless multitude of frightened and innocent souls across the empire who (having succumbed to mesmerism would now, necessarily out of duty) would find their way past a row of empty silver collection plates in any of a number of churches near them. The prerequisite here was for filling those omnipresent yawning alms bowls. It was the parishioner's life-long duty. It was a *Jacob's*[44] (Yaakov) *ladder* that was meant to lead the people to the door of heaven. Perhaps Augustus of Hippo didn't get it after all!

It should be noted that at this point in time, irrespective of the conundrums of the age and the trials that have befallen Amor and the foibles of Dyfed, the philosophical focus here happens to frame a goodly number of individuals (Masters, Sages, Teachers) cogitating with considerable cognizable abilities. And the names that have come down to us turn out to be mostly men like Yeshua/Joshua (also Jesus Isa, and Yesu and sometimes Yeshu[45]), as well as Philo of Xandria, Titus Flavius Josephus of Qadesh (also Jebus, Jerusalem), Ignatius of Antioch, Papias of Hierapolis, Bishop Polycarp of Smyrna, Irenaeus bishop of Lugdunum (Lyon), Titus Flavius Clemens of Xandria, the Berber Quintus Septimus Florens Tertullianus, Origen Anamanthius of Xandria, the Berber Thaschus Caecillius Cyprianus of Carthage), Eusebius Pamphili of Alexandria, Hippolytus of Amor, Athanasius of Alexander, Jerome (Eusebius), Epiphanius of Salamis and back again to Augustinus of Hippo, just to name a few. But we can fairly assume that almost all of the above essentially contributed toward change, but not in the same direction and in the philosophy of the original teachings of Jeshua the Nazrani, Philo Judaeus of Xandria and others of eastern mysticism, paganism and of western philosophical persuasions that coupled at this time with the cult of the Abramists. Some may add the likes of Clemens and Origen, too, but that still needed a worthy second opinion.

Neglecting the God within and forging blindly ahead, the aforementioned young Augustinus (as stated: a Berber from the Tyrian colony of Hippo Regius, hence his title) was poised at this point to become the most uncompromising quasi mystic towards all the Jeshuan non-mystic hypocrites proffering false hope. In the end it earned him a saint hood from the Church of Amor. Better them than I, one should think. So, with the early and eager philosophical environments happening in the cities of Antioch and Xandria

44 The name Jacob (Yaakov) means 'held by the heel': but in what sense, 'feet to the fire' or the heel of Achilles'?

45 Yeshu (et al's) true nature is a single identity common to the true self of all humans and is an internal Messiah as such. Its concept was prominent and was initially conceived in its current form around 200BCE. Most likely it became known as an intrinsic Nazarene (Nazri) concept born in or near the land of Hauran (known also as Horan and ancient Bashan). This concept certainly visited Antioch and Xandria's intelligentsia. In one way or another its conceptual entity was a major contributor to Western Philosophy and Perennial Philosophy in its role as the Righteous Teacher within and ultimately is the kernel for certain aspects of Western Civilization.

where overtones of a Zoroastrianism, Jainism, Buddhism, Taoism (combined with the Torah [Five Books or Pentateuch]) had suddenly come together to mix, this hub-bub now morphed into the Hellenistic Mystery Religion whose adherents were known as Gnostics. And this appeared to provide gris (usually pronounced *gree*) or for that which is defined as the Perennial Philosophy. And this added substance to the concept surrounding a certain cadre of the aforementioned ancient mystic sect of Nazrani (Nazri or Nazrean) that existing as the kernel within the machinations being currently formed by the Cult of Jeshuanism and whose primary direction was grounded in Particularism (only about the individual in this dimension and not concerning itself so much about God the Eternal). It was this upon which the concept of Jeshua was always fixed, right from the beginning and what was stressed more than anything else. Jeshua didn't die so mankind can live. Instead this Paraclete exists for all time within every advanced life form in order to bring information that phenomenon is individual and that only the self-enlightened could progress through a volition of self-faith reliant, not on one's outer self, but on the natural and true self within that's common, perhaps, to all creatures and things. Furthermore, there is no trickery or programming involved here, only a self-volition of faith that's also related to self-gnosis in its relationship to the phenomenon.

Unfortunately, for those potential enlightened ones (just like all those other organized religions of the world that appeared to win out in the end on the big screen with fanfare) the non-proto pro-orthodox Jeshuanist programmed religion at large compiled as it was by the likes of Ambrosius and Augustinus, along with Epiphanius the Amoranite Juhuda, rules to this day. But it, too, in the end will be seen to be a dead end.

In a sense, though, Jeshuanism was a stabilizing element among the furore that was beginning to flare up more and more around the Western Empire's northern borders. But in the corridors of Amor's power per sé, it wasn't having that affect at all. Shortly after the death of Emperor Thedosus, one of his sons and future heir to the Western Empire, Emperor Honourless, moved from Medio to Raven. Once a back-eddy or isolated sny, after the Adriatic coastal city of Raven had been incorporated into the Amoran sphere it prospered greatly, especially during the empire. This was in no short of consequence due to Emperor Trajan having provided it with its own aqueduct. Previously the town of Raven had been encompassed within the older (pre-Amoran) Etruscan[46] state of long ago. In the early days of the Empire Raven grew mouldy and somehow that stigma was slow to recede. But that had all changed. And now that it housed the palace of the western emperor it needed a wily and intelligent cleric of the Church of Amor to be in attendance there. The newly arrived bishop who had come to the Amoran Empire's capital was one of those men who stood shoulder to shoulder and marched in lockstep with other powerful elite clerics of the Church of Amor. He was none other than Gorgeous Giorgius Gregorius Florentius, now also the name of his vast estate in Gaul. He was, of course, from the province of Gaul that was now being referred to as Frankia. Although the lion's share of this Jeshuan's work was being catalogued, filed and passed into ecclesiastical law in the Eternal City of Amor, the circle elite around his Holy Immanence, the vicar of Jeshua Adon, a certain 'bow your head' Anastasius, relied on hundreds of other clerics to spread the pro-orthodox word through daily practise out

---

46   By 750 BCE Etruria had expended itself into the Etruscan civilization. As the Etruscans had been heavily influence by the Hellenic and Phoeniki peoples, their belief systems were immanently polytheistic. By the 4th century BCE, the Amoran Kingdom had assimilated much of the Etruscan culture into their own. Amoran paganism was in the most part an Etruscan loan culture.

from the Eternal City and to all the church parishes throughout the empire. All told, these were the men who were refabricating and reworking the newly formed Jeshuan cult into the indomitable machine that it was to become. They had become the contender for the fading empire's new power-elite that was intending to right matters and put the horse before the cart and the collection plate before the masses. They were bent on creating a Holy Amoran Empire.

(Polyglots and oligarchs)

"History would be something extraordinary, if only it were true.'
LEV TOLSTOI

The submerged and secret power-elite that controlled Amor's governing factor now raised its ugly head to a new level. First it needed to control the cultural myth and establish its authority. This same old, same old was virtually completed as such. Then it needed authority to tax and control the many avenues of hauling in money. Money was power. Next, it needed to beautify itself in the eyes of the hoi polloi. This actually meant staining and soiling the image of others so that they themselves appeared to shine. As to the first instance, turning avenues of trickling pocket change into rivers of gold and silver was an on-going feat, helped along by steely thugs of Nightwatchmen and the threat of Turnkeys who manned the courts and gloomy citadels of torture (languishing unto the pain of death) at the end of the stinking tunnel. The second instance of beautifying itself was (un-ironically) superficially easier. Like the emperors and royalty in general, his holy immanence, along with his many bishops and a cadré of deeply submerged social savvy polyglot-type clerics silently dispersed themselves among the royal families of the Empire. This provided the powerful families with valuable assets such as lawyers, accountants and sometimes, such as by marriage, spouses. In this way, once again, the Haploids managed to surrounded themselves with extremely attractive types along with beautifully painted woman and men dressed in the Empires' finest apparel, who spoke eloquently on the finer points of life that entailed their culture of belief, behaviour and matters that mattered in and about the society which publically displayed the emperor (king/rex/consul) and members of the royal family being in lock-step (of course) with the Church of Amor and vis-versa.

Dyfed of course knew that unlike the mystic movement, one of the most dangerous manifestations which challenged the proto-orthodox members of the currently rising Jeshuan cult were the Gnostic movement and the conservative right. The folks in these movements were strong and dedicated groups of the Jeshuan order 'of their own definition' and there wasn't just one or two strains of them, either, there were many thousands of strains. And since the ever present polyglot mystic arm of the originating order utilized some form of logic with a heavy tincture of Neo-Platonism that they put into play here, the religious oligarchs with an agenda that led the myriad of other persuasions of opinionated, proto-orthodox Jeshuans had their hatred for the mystics broaden beyond measure. Only the few quasi orthodox that maintained a Neo-Platonic base such as Augustinus of Hippo and an assortment of others over the next centuries, managed in the end to comfortably fit in without attracting attention. One such mystic who slipped into the mainstream of the oligarchic mainstream of ideological catholic apostolic church conservatives unnoticed was Valentinius who Dyfed had befriended in Xandria. Valantinius, Dyfed recalled, had told him that the material world is ignorant of the Father. In conversation, and over time, Dyfed realized (or thought he realized) that by *Father*, Valentinius had meant the True Self that was being conducted, animated and sustained by Azeus rather than being the god of Abraham per sé: The two actually only being one that constituted a human unity. This, in a sense, was the Logos of Heraclitus. This, then, was the Father, or the Monad, the circled dot, sometimes mistakenly associated with the Euclidean circled square (which is actually descended from an 1850 BCE old papyrus whose approximation was to the value of 3.1605 rather than the more recent 3.1416). Nor was it related to the philosopher's stone, either. But in a philosophical, and even spiritual, sense it did mean for a sentient being to be aware of, and in fully appreciating what was around itself in every direction in as far a distance as was humanly possible. In other words, this was a certain knowledge or gnosis, from which the Gnostics were named without actually being labelled as one. Not all Gnostics were incredulous or incredibly stingy of love, empathy and heightened awareness. Anyway, but since the material world is ignorant of the *Father*, the physical world is (now and always will be) in error. This, in turn, causes deficiency in abundance that causes continual error that therefore becomes dominant instead of Truth, the paramount of ideals intrinsic to natural life, as is love, that is — true love, not lust. Otherwise truth, and subsequently natural life (evidently), is eventually left out of the picture entirely by the process (and its end game) utilized by the material universal that is currently and inescapably at large. Then, in the fullness of time, as the material world sets about in preparation for creation (of any kind), it worked (and continues to work) in error (of course) and therefore Truth was either being unintentionally or intentionally substituted instead with Power and Beauty (whose true definitions have been also substituted) which are poor substitutes indeed. This, in turn, leads to a further and continuous causation of an error-inflicted deficiency over all. This state will continue until it is so remote from the actual truth of natural reality to enable it totally functionless and sterile. And since Power and Beauty are its hallmark it should be readily obvious to all who are alert (throughout the civilizations) and thereby help serve as a sign of warning to them. Hence, the world of yesterday, today and tomorrow in which we live: Full stop.

It was almost like theatre to Dyfed and even though he was a banker and owner of large shipping companies, he seemed strangely detracted from it all as he watched it unfold.

(The cult of Jeshua and the case of the burning mirrors)

'Have you ever seen a beautiful, transparent stone at the druggists' with which you may kindle fire?'
ARISTOPHANES (SPOKEN BY STREPSIADES A CHARACTER IN 'THE CLOUDS')

On the heels of the earlier Macaronius debacle regarding the metropolitan lock down of Amor City (and the revolt that never was), word had come that Emperor Macaronius was dead in that far off land of Albion. But with it also came news that his son Officius Constantius had quickly replaced the dead emperor by having the allegiance of his legions promote him by arranging to have him sworn in there and then. As things stood now Officius was returning at a furious pace back to Amor. Quite suddenly the political climate changed, and not just for Dyfed.

One cool, bright spring day not that long after he had returned from the Land of Khem but with a sufficient time lapse for the march of time to debut a string of make-shift emperors to strut across the world's stage, it soon became clear to Dyfed that paganism, having once been so merged into the secular infrastructure of Amor, then having undergone a decline under Constantius, then returning for the last time again under Flavius Claudius (J)Iulianus Augustus (known as Julian the Apostate), was now finishing its final decline into oblivion. This, of course, is the common route of all ideologies at some time or another no matter how good they are, though most of them aren't good at all. This brought in the clouds of worry over the unknown if truth failed in its attempt to exalt social and democratic envisioned justice as originated by a religion of Western Philosophy. Would it take a back seat to that new Abramist's Messianic Cult of Jeshua Adon which was the upshot of the earlier Seleucid debacle in Canaan? Or would they join forces?

The Capitoline Hill temple was then quickly sacked, although its goodies and lolly had all been misspent long ago. After that it simply sat as a naked outline against the evening sky in a semi state of ruin. Constantius' attraction (against Diokles' advice) to favour and promote the Cult of Jeshua now (already having been struck from being status non gratis to becoming decreed as the legal religion) under (another new emperor) Theodosius' recent tenure had become the empire's official cult in favour over Jupiter. Now Jeshuanism had begun to bloom. It was the beginning of the era of the Vicar of the messiah and the bishops of Jeshua Adon. Those days (when what passed for imperial jubilation and when the entertainment score board read: Lions 6, Jeshuans 0) were now long passed. Although that aspect was mostly just sensational hype and untrue for the most part, organised cult lore of Jeshuanism wasn't far behind it in regards to such sensationalism itself. And even if the wheels of propriety hadn't yet quite fallen off Vespasianus' oval amphitheatre the Colossus (also Colosseum, though it wasn't called that then), there certainly had been a paradigm-shift of late.

As for the aforementioned amphitheatre, it was named the colossus after (and because of) the hundred Amoran-foot bronze statue dubbed Colossus Neronis, designed and built by Zenodorus the Hellene and was originally placed in the vestibule of Emperor Nero's beautiful Domus Aurea (Oro) before being altered somewhat by Vespasianus Augustus, and then moved to its location proximate to the oval amphitheatre by Hadrianus Augustus, where before long it was even converted by Publicus Servicicus Nemesis Maximus Augustus Usurperus VI into a statue of himself. There it now reposed.

Meanwhile, though he had taken up residence immediately after returning from the Land of Khem, Dyfed had solicited Gouchus' help to legally re-claim his Capitoline Hill suite that was positioned beneath Jupiter's ransacked temple that Macaronius had confiscated along with everything else. All in all Dyfed's sentiments were that the situation was nothing less than a son of a bitch. Now if there was anything he wanted that he had once owned, he had to buy it all back again.

These digs had been Dyfed's secondary residence to their Palace Estate town-villa-residence in the Esquiline Hill hood since back in the day when a swath of Amor had gone up in smoke during the Great fire. And even if his Palatine front or their Esquiline Hill neighbourhood residence hadn't burned to the ground, as was the case, it was on account of Nero's tenacity (or luck) to eventually curb this great historic fire that this wasn't the case. Dyfed had been sorry that the artistic and nervous Nero had become so distressed at the realization of being trapped in his physical sentient state that let him to commit suicide. He had liked Nero. Obviously the condition that brought that on was of not being in touch with his true self or not knowing exactly who he actually and really was. This is the condition of not being in touch with one's own soul which could often (so Dyfed had found) be activated by one's muse which acted as the conduit or the sphere of vibration which the creator of all life (the universal soul) cast out around Itself so as to accompany and even be capable of guiding the ethereal incarnation of Itself and its everlasting Spirit through the phenomenon of the ephemeral.

Dyfed poured out pity for Nero and thought that his tenure at emperorship may have been in the right direction. Nevertheless, although the flaky and somewhat scatter-brained emperor had once confiscated his Palatine property, he had compensated him well for it. Upon having his Capitoline Hill property confiscated by the deceased Macaronius, he hadn't been compensated at all, not a sausage! Now he had to buy it back. The reason for reclaiming it legally and the rushed commotion to get it done was because Cato had recently been given notice that their town villa by the Esquiline Hill had been appropriated by the state in order to facilitate a new highway that would be going through. That meant that new residences for *the pack to congregate and accomplish their business, was badly needed.*

Only supreme plenipotential authority can truly claim to dabble in ownership. But this only refers to personal material, whereas authoritative administrations that are made up of assemblies that in turn utilize agents and a myriad of advisers where tyrannical leadership is absent and cannot make any ownership claim. Administrations of authority (labelled governments which were not yet known of) can only possess. This is because 'to own' actually means belonging to oneself, and assemblies (which make up governments) are not a singular self and no one person specifically can claim any ownership there; apart from the aristocrats of seedy virtue and reigning oligarchs of any and every generation and era who are always lurking and poised into the pouncing position so as to be able to take possession (and in every sense the ownership) of the fruit of the people's hard work at a moments' notice.

But still, they can never actual take ownership themselves; this is because nobody can. Nobody owns anything other than their own true (or false) self; those attributes and vices are part of everyone's makeup. In any case, the matter of metropolis (civic) infrastructure organization and property management or mismanagement (then) was not easily absolved with Macaronius' death. It was all part of a new city planning management project coming to a residential area of Amor near you: Though some, such as the socially responsible Julius Iacobus and Sons, a community-based urban engineering company, thought the plan of cutting the city by pushing through a highway would isolate the citizens of Amor rather than bring them together. From the social element point of view, it was a step backward, they said.

Finally, Cato and Gouchus were successful in achieving the repatriation of Dyfed's Capitoline residence, as well as locating another site in lieu of the Esquiline Hill estate loss. By the time of Morgant's arrival back in Amor there had been a lapse of a few years since he had shown his face around the place. But Dyfed knew from experience that once in the fifth dimension folks seem to lose track of time, anyway. As for the positioning of this dimension or any other dimension in conjunction with each other, well, that was the most puzzling of things to Dyfed. However, he thought, perhaps it was true because Morgant often told him that theoretically (at least according to a Hyperborean Master Dr Torsionfield) if a particle could be in two places at the same time, so could he. Dyfed never understood any of this philosophy-speak, though.

As earlier stated, that these Jeshuans were quickly on the rise throughout the empire was what concerned that other antagonist, Diocletianus Augustus (known as the cissoid kid), mathematician and founder of the Amoran tetrarchy. Diokles (as he was called) — who finally became affiliated with the intransitive verb to grind that turned into a gerund complicated with the superlative adverb *most* — was tactfully toying at that time of hid coronation with a reinvention of Archimedes' version of his burning mirrors (grounded lenses) as the curve ball to bat out the two arcs of Abramism in order to create a reflection or inversion and fashion a symmetry of an Amoran social/cultural order instead of a Jeshuan one. Unless someone had the time and the inclination to indoctrinate this wayward cult toward Western Philosophy, or discourage them altogether, Diokles and the Master's of the Little Known Universe's vision of Utopia was on hold, and nobody knew anymore what would come of it, never mind when. And had the hoi polloi's own manner of questioning and coming to grips with the quasi reality that the idea of the universe could have been altered for the better, then many of the multitude could have been spared the ravaging that this social typhoon had spawned.

(Dread Portents of Descending Fire and Rising Parthenogenesis)

'And if you hear vague traces of skippin' reels of rhyme,
To your tambourine in time, it's just a ragged clown behind
I wouldn't pay it any mind, It's just a shadow you're seein' that he's chasing.'

BOB DYLAN

The family of: Morgant, Master and Sage; Markus Cato, Master, stoic, and political fifth columnist; Karatakos, Master, adventurer, and former king of Albion; Pepsicola Celsus, Master, and alchemist; and Dyfed Lucifer, Prince, Hyperborean cadet initiate, third dimensional central committee lieutenant (currently on probation), and honorary Master according to Hyperborean custom; had all continued uninterrupted with their social intercourse here in Amor just as before. But now they realized their idea for the future would be interrupted one again and put on hold. Dyfed, if you recall, was also the chamberlain to a former high king of Albion as well as his palace chief executive officer and had since become the recipient of the Order of the Gladius from Emperor Hadrian. These folks were capable of taking care of themselves, along with senators and distinguished friends of Morgant and Cato (Celsus had no other friends), but their hoi polloi friends were less equipped so were given a heads-up and a word to the wise. Of course, Marg, Hyperborean Mistress and former queen of the Carvetii (now abdicated), was absent and probably wasn't even in the third dimension as she had threatened to leave and not return. And as Trachmyr was now back serving in the Western Army, he too was also still absent at this time and was somewhere fighting under Stilicho, the western Field Commander.

But for aware and responsible citizens it was going to be tough going. As usual the majority of others were drunk on ego, and being susceptible to a controlled and induced fantasy of grandeur, apparently they remained oblivious to the milestones (and headstones) concomitant with the countdown to final obliteration.

At this time there were many Gothic armies of amalgamated tribes under leaders with names like Fritz and Herman, Alaric, and Radical Gaius that were amassing on provincial borders. And at this rate they may soon be before the gates of City of Amor. These barbarians were called the Goths and they weren't concerned over any entrance fees needed to enter the city of Amor or (with one exception, to be expounded on later) of any welcoming intonations of invitation from its friendly people therein. They didn't need it. They had a free pass and it was called tactical militia with the biggest and bloodiest of professional killing-men wielding the biggest and bloodiest of swords. And Dyfed thought that the folks of Amor all knew that. So why were their heads in the sand? Dyfed reckoned they had no other choice.

Behind the Goths came other wild peoples, the Lans or Alans (also Wu sun in the language of the orient). The Lans were an Indo Europaean speaking people from the northern fringes of the Tarim Basin and Taklimakan desert. They lived under and between the Mountains of Heaven (Tien Shan) and the Altai and these folks were part of the Saka Sarmatians whose umbrella (some say) were the Scythian peoples. Many of these folks were already here, such as the Sarms who had come early to find a good seat and a warm valley to wait for the onslaught before settling in permanently without having to contribute too much. And the Huns (also from the region of the Altai mountains) were not far behind them, and so forth. The latter were truly deadly. So, aside from a persistent change in climate that was the real reason for this migration, in a way the Huns were root to the whole problem that caused it to lurch forward in domino fashion that in the end brought the Eternal city of Amor a thorough sacking. But the sacking didn't come from the Huns.

Most of these folks were nomads who moved constantly on horse back or riding the axle of a horse (or oxen) driven wagon as they followed the game at their feet and the blue skies that stretched above. They were used to dwelling permanently in this manner. Even at that moment on a dreary day in February as Dyfed walked to his reclaimed business in the Forum, hoards of them were thundering across the ice of the upper Dana River without resistance. All hell bent for leather in attacking and plundering Amor itself, soon they would be clambering down the Julian Alpine mountainsides and into north eastern Italia. But more had to happen before then.

But apparently, it was all to come as a surprise to the sleeping white-collar sentinels whose job was to stand on guard for Amor and provide for the legions in every way. Yes, it had come to that. It was, in one way, unfortunate that at this juncture that the empire was as sophisticated as it was. It had come to be that the hierarchy of authority were to make decisions affecting the warrior class, not the generals and their boss of bosses. A soldier's soldier calling the shots and being able to do so correctly is a good characteristic for a military man to have, mind you, but it was also dangerous. It was bad enough when emperors made decisions. And it had been the likes of emperors such as Flavius Claudius Iulianus (Julianus) Augustus (known a Julian the Apostate), a capable emperor and student of Western philosophy (even if he leaned a little toward paganism) who was followed by Jovian, and then finally Valentinian who had had (in the end) to finally deal face to face with these unwelcomed gate-crashers who were following any and all paths of least resistance to arrive safely upon the borders of the empire. In turn, the Western Amoran Emperor Valentinian had worked competently with his brother the Eastern Emperor Valliant, also called Valens, who he had appointed there. Both were committed to employing their legions toward the defence of the vulnerable pieces of the empire for fear that the Goths would attack and become absorbed into them. This in fact had already been the case with folks they called the foederati.

And so it went; and with coordination between their armies, Valentinianus and Valliant somehow had managed to stand their ground, so far. But the mechanics of empire were meant to assist, and without competent assistance it wouldn't have happened, and ultimately didn't. So, when incompetence rears its ugly head, beware. Incompetence at this level is usually the companion of alarming social state entropy.

And as related earlier, via our friendly Philip Fairface, it happened that the Albionian, Macsen Wledig, also known as Bricus of Demetia (now the high king and calling himself Constantine) was also on the brink of spearheading himself into this swamp of imperial problems. However, before this took place, a few other things needed to have happened. The first of these was that Emperor Valentinianus who co-ruled with his son Grathian, had to die. That was a common and easy enough thing to happen to emperors, anyway. Further to that, co-ruler Grantian would probably have to die too. And any successful contender would not want any past (or future) contenders around if he could help it. Furthermore, it was also likely that the eastern emperor, Valliant (Valens), would also have to come to some kind of grief.

So, let's start with Valentinianus and his son Gratian. For some time now a barbarian (who was probably from Ancyra [Ankara] in the Amoran province of Galatia located in central Anatolia) had, in a personal maelstrom of greed-lust and personal destiny, up and moseyed in the direction of Gaul. Here he took on the identity of an individual of Franken habit (if not origin) and sought employment with the Amoran military. The name of this man was General Flavius Arbogastric (himself a foederati and since his induction into service for the Amoran Empire he had been exceedingly successful in aiding it against the barbarians (his own peoples) coming from the north and east. He was a man with powerful ambitions. The Amoran military service at that time was under the command of Emperor Gratian. Arbogastric quickly rose through the ranks due to personal attributes. Then, western co-emperor Valentinianus was discovered hanged close to where Arbogastric was stationed. There was an inquest and many fingers pointed to Arbogastric, but the latter endured. Actually Valentinianus suffered an apoplectic attack caused by a belief that he had that the said Arbogastric was usurping his authority. He was not hanged, though maybe he should have been, long before. Anyway, this left Valentinianus' brother (Emperor Valiant) in the east still co-ruling and his son Gratian ruling in the west. At the time of his father's death Valentinianus the deuce then became a co-ruling emperor. He was Gratian's brother, according to his father, although that was no recommendation.

Then something else happened: the eastern ruling emperor (Valiant) was still at his post and campaigning in northern Thraki when his life changed forever. Having been alerted to trouble brewing, Emperor Valiant raced down from Serdica (the capital of the province Dacia Mediterranea, now called Sophia) to confront gatecrashers, shoplifters and aggressive vandals in general who were breaking through the line. All of a sudden everything went sour and south. The clash he conducted in his battle with this ilk of dangerous vagabonds took place just north east of the Rhodope Mountains where lay the city of Hadrianopolis. Formerly known as Orestias (Hadrianopolis is now called Edirne), it had been built by a certain Orestes, son of King Agamemnon. Many don't believe that, though. Anyway, Emperor Valiant had set up his campaign headquarters alongside the riverbank close to where the rivers Marica and the Ardas converged. Coincidently, at the time of Valiant's fall Dyfed was visiting the Oracle of Dionysis that was barely fifty Amoran miles away to the west. Anyway, Valiant had fallen from his horse here in this battle and onto the rough and dusty steppe and (to use a metaphor), he never got up. Emperorship was a risky business.

A combined army of Lans and Goths that had been led by the barbarian Fritz felled Emperor Valiant. Fritz's armies may have been lost and by mistake had swarmed south of the Dana River. After the Cibalae (Croatian) born Emperor Valiant had been killed in battle on the outskirts of Edirne he needed to be replaced quickly before more disaster unfolded. The replacement chosen was a general who had served the empire well in Albion (the Province of Britannia), and had been used against the Sarms and Gothi that had recently been foraging close to the Provinces of Pannonia Secunda, Moesia Superior and Dacia in their aim to access the Aegean sea via the Dinaric Alpine mountains. The general in question was Flavius Theodosius born in Hispania. Historically he eventually became Theodosius I (also known as Theodosius the Great). Incidentally, many of the previous Amoran emperors were Pannonian Illyrians after the empire had provincialized them back in the days under Emperor Octavius Augustus Divi Filius (the son of god) and his successors. Theodosius wasn't one of them. He was born a Hispanian and he returned to his homeland where he founded the House of Theodosius. Theodosius the Great was especially responsible for furthering the authority of the church of the Jeshuan Adon Cult throughout the empire that led to the authority of the Church of Amor to eventually gain control of the empire. He did this by making this cult the legal official Amoran religion in the year of the Olympiad 1156, or in 380 of the current era. This was fifty-five years after the convocation at Nicea (essentially the foundation of western Jeshuanism and the Church of Amor) and sixty-seven years after Constantinus the Great made Jeshuanism a legal religion in the empire with the Edict of Medio.

In any case, Western Emperor Gratian, who proceeded Valentinianus and was the nephew of Emperor Valliant, had once been a capable ruler but he had been left holding the bag (alone), and with the cat suddenly outside that bag (and at large, just once too often), his status had been changed in the flick of an eye, as we will see. At this point in time Gratian reversed from being the toast of the empire to becoming just plain toast (such as that wheat edible which is covered in that preverbal flat black carbon molecule). He was finished; it would be all over for Gratian. And with that in mind, it happened this way.

One evening Gratian left his cold, unfriendly bed (and colder consort that lay in it, and all that despite the fact that she was still breathing) and visited the barracks to cajole with the boys and drink and play cards and engage in the rough talk of fond exploits long past. As they cajoled and drank in their officers' mess there was one of them present who was the upstart Constantine, the former Pater Bricus of Demetia and his handler, Blazingwolf the Druid (now Pater Blazingwolf who had even converted from Pelagian Jeshuanism over to the flavour preferred by the empire, the Church of Amor).

Not too long after, apparently, the replacement co-emperor Valentine II (Gratian's half brother) was suddenly murdered. Arbogastic said it was suicide. Quickly Arbogastric rounded up a few unfortunates who were failing miserably on their soldiering exams and their physicals, and after breaking their arms and legs he had boiling water poured over them. Then he had a few others flogged for good measure. By this he meant that these soldiers must have known beforehand or assisted in the suicide. But it acted to dumb them down instantly and prevent them from ever being able to speak again or either tell any tales or truths. Everything was all very convenient. He then sent a letter of apology to Theodosius who by now had been officially promoted (with ceremony) to emperor of the east. Adroitly, Emperor Theodosius made a note to keep a close eye on Arbogastric. However, with Valentine II dead Arbogastric, with his authority as magister militum, then quite suddenly promoted one of his own senior civil servants into the position of Western Emperor. This man was a certain Eugenius who was something of a scholar. As the emperor was about to place his own son Honourless onto the throne of the Western Empire, Arbogastric's act of usurpation set Theodosius into motion. He set out from Byzas with an army to strike the side of Medio (if need be) where Eugenius had been instated as Western Emperor and where Arbogastric's Western Army were being fed and rested. Medio was the city where Constantinus the Great passed that Edict to legalized the Jeshuan cult faith, followed much later by Theodosius' own edit at Thessalonica to make that cult the official religion in lieu of the old pagan one. The battle that was to take place shortly resulted in Arbogastric and his Western Army (along with is pet Eugenius the Western Emperor) being totally decimated and expunged. This battle took place in the Julian Alps and was not merely an army contingent revolt, or the actions of a commander usurping the command of another. It was the face of how it was in the Western Empire at this time. It was a matter of the barbarians within, for the Imperial armies were rife with the foederati being paid by Amoran loyalists that now even included the Church of Amor.

The aforementioned church practised by royals and high nobility and honed down into something resembling a single entity, was now in full swing as a contender to seal their domination over most of the multiple Jeshuan sects at large. It was the culmination of about four hundred years of their big push by the likes of Ignatius, Tertullian (and their fellow pro-orthodox descendants) to succeed. Certainly, within the Western Empire (centred in Amor), this initiative had now been accomplished, as had certain demarcation lines that (drawn in the sand) had been centred on definitions about aspects of the Jeshuanism. It was also one of the first historic moments (if not the first) that barfed up the insidious hatred and minimization against the main core cult (religion) of the Abramists. It was incorrectly termed anti-Semitism: being a Semite or a Semitic, of course, meant the tongue, the language used (spoken) by a vast array of folks, including the A-rab[47] along with the ancient Phoeniki and Canaanites, the people from Judah, and the Amorites in general. It had nothing to do with what primitive superstitious religion any of these people subscribed to; at least that is how Dyfed saw it. Anyway, that's why it is now called the Church of Amor and not the Church of Byzas that in turn coveted the Eastern Empire.

The City of Byzas in fact had two doumos (cathedrals) for cult exercises to take place and to worship in. The oldest one was the Sancta Irene. It was build by Emperor Constantinus the Great. But Constantine had also built a House of God here in the city of Amor, was well. This last mentioned Jeshuan temple was one that he built over top of the more ancient temple of Magna Mater (the Great Mother) dedicated to the goddess Cybele. It was located north west of the Capitoline Hill (located passed the Field of Mars and across the Tibur River) and situated on top of Vaticanus Hill.

It should be stated that the second mentioned duomo[48] or cattedrale of Byzas (the Magna Ecclesia called the Holy Wisdom) in the eastern empire had been consigned and completed by the more recent Emperor Theodosius. That eastern section of the empire would soon find a variant denomination of Jeshuanism other than Church of Amor to last them over a thousand years from the present into the future. It would last until such time when a new Abramic monotheistic religion not yet born cult[49] would bring it to a close, though not necessarily for the better, or even for the worse. And the ideological, historical and tweaking, fabricating re-interpreting would all continue for both at least until the end of its days. But there was also a clash between these empire's two religions,

---

47 Also: Arab from an Akkadian word (9th C. BCE) referring to people of Aram (or Aramea), specifically Bedouins.
48 Derives from the Latin *domus* (house)
49 Mo'mhadism (of the people of the third-wheel of the monotheistic Abramic cults) would, at least at first, become surprisingly more permissive and obliging toward other cults and faiths than the other Abramites (especially Jeshuans) were towards them.

that is, polytheistic paganism and Jeshuanism. This was a battle between the Imperial and noble followers of the Jeshuan cult and Amor's many senators, lawyers and scientists who wanted at this time to revert back to the good old pagan one.

Incidentally, the Jeshuan chronicles of the time recording the battle between Emperor Theodosius and Arbogastric and his usurped Emperor Eugenius, wrote how omens came to feature during this conflict and how a solar eclipse and a Bora wind sent by God attributed to Theodosius' victory.

When Theodosius' eldest son Honourless took over the Imperial western seat, their capital at that time was at Medio. And this was where Theodosius eventually died the following year in 395 of the current era. As stated already, another newly self-nominated Western Imperial candidate was about to arrive on the stage. He was the aforementioned Macsen Wledig, also known as Bricus Maximus who had earlier become Constantine the high king in the Province of Prydain (also Prytainia). His Amoran legions there elected him into that position which was further supported by the Amorans in the Province of Gaul as well. And it was there, in Gaul, where this Constantine had recently arrived now to take up his position of pomp and glory. But this meant more than resting on his past laurels. It meant that he must move to convince Western Emperor Honourless to accept him. This was not going to be easy by a long chalk. His road to glory meant the road through gory. Constantine the Albionian and would be emperor now moved on Medio (or at least intended on it). Consequently, he did not get there, and even with the assistance of others he was not able to even enter Italia. Even so, no one including General Stilicho was able to put Constantine on the run. It was at this point that Trachmyr arrived back at his post taking charge of his regiment.

The truth was that at this time, as he never got as far as Medio, Constantine was only the ruler of Lugdun. The city of Lugdun was still an important fortress and he had taken it away from the western emperor. It was situated at the river bend of the big muddy mid way its course as it rushed towards the south and drained the glaciers and lakes of the Alpine mountains into the White Sea. Lugdun had once been an ancient Keltic city before being commandeered by the Amorans. But, unfortunately, Constantine didn't want to stop there in Lugdun. But it was to Lugdun that he returned to regroup and form a new strategy against mounting armies. Then the following spring he suddenly made a rapid move towards Italia and the road to Amor. The established Amorans here worried that this situation may entice the barbarians east of the river Rine to move west and settle illegally. Already the Sicambri tribe had established themselves in the lowlands at the mouth of that river where they had accumulated a mountain of unpaid taxes to Amor. More like brigands they posed a problem to organized Amoran authority. These Sicambri people were henceforth to be called Frankens. And it was through the land of these people that Constantine would pass through on his way to Italia. At this point Honourless (with the help of General Stilicho) took charge in repealing Constantine.

In the eastern empire the Dana River was the border and the frontier while in the west around Nordicum it was the Rine River. It was from here that Honourless' own senior statesman advisor and armchair general, Gorgeous Giorgius Gregorius Florentius of Richelieu (now recently joined by Trachmyr) were pulled to concentrate their forces in the south where Constantine was being confounded in his advance and finally halted by the tribe of Allobroges before reaching the Cottian Alps.

Still, Western Emperor Honourless did not recognized Constantine as his western co-ruler. At this time barbarian invaders such as the Vandals, Burgundars, and Lans were casting a blizzard of bother and turmoil on the northern edge of the empire in Nordicum that spilled across the river Rine from time to time at this point as the marauding invaders went to and fro somewhat freely. It was at this time that Emperor Honourless evacuated his court from Medio and moved the capital to the city of Raven by the lagoon. Constantine, however, was actually successful in winning a few confrontations with the Vandals. But this did not gain him any endearment from Western co-ruler Emperor Honourless, quite the contrary. Nevertheless, under direction from his chief general Geronimoius, Constantine left the border defences to concentrate on Honourless. Honourless then ordered his Magister militum General Stilicho to expel Constantine. He failed to do so leaving Constantine free to control all of Gaul Province. Stilicho's troops were barely holding their own, meanwhile Italia was still devoid of Constantine's authority. Constantine was nervous because Hispania was securely in the hands of the House of Theodosius as ever and loyal to Emperor Honourless. Constantine now feared encirclement and a pincher invasion from both sides. That spring Constantine made Arles his capital. He then suddenly attacked Hispania and defeated Honourless' generals in charge there and their forces. After the House of Theodosius' defeat in Hispania, and while Constantine's chief general Geronimoius remained there to organize the new authority under Constantine, Geronimoius switched allegiance to support another candidate, rather than Constantine for the title of Western co-ruler. He had been paid, of course. In addition the great soldier and leader of men, Alari, had returned to Raven to collect land and gold as was promised him by Stilicho for his help in driving out the unwanted from the empire. Constantine may have bribed Alaric; anyway, Honourless was incensed by the situation and refused to pander to Alaric. All this potential around these events should have soothed Honourless a tad and opened up possibilities for him. It did not. Instead the worthless Honourless took revenge for that earlier defeat by ordering that the decorated General Stilicho (part Vandal himself) be executed for treason. Italia, meanwhile, along with the provinces of Noricum and Pannonia especially, underwent pandemonium as the horrified loyalist Amoran army suddenly mutinied. Also, enormous social disturbance ensued on top of the current social environment when Honourless ordered the massacre of thousands of foreign hoi polloi throughout that part of the empire (especially in Noricum and Pannonia) who received benefits from Amor in exchange for military services. They were considered barbarian mercenaries who were permitted to settle within the Western Empire and were called foederati. The foederati had looked up to Stilicho who himself was a foederati. With law and order in a free-fall, and abandoned by his western army, now left Emperor Honourless defenceless in his capital at Raven. Scrambling, Honourless then summoned Constantine to a parley where he agreed for the two of them to become joint consuls of the Western Empire. Un-curtailed on his journey to Raven, Constantine had finally succeeded in achieving some sort of credence to his longed for imperial title. His vizier (and life-long companion) the wizard Blazingwolf must have been very contented at this. Alaric later would return to Italia and sacked the city of Amor.

Finally, now known officially as Constantine III, the man from Albion made his excuses (to a relieved Honourless) that he had to vacate Italia and rush back to Gaul to fix fences. In his two year absence from keeping an eye on Amor's defences along the river Rine in order take on Honourless' armies, Vandals, Lans and other western Goths (having been pushed by encroaching Huns behind them) had in the interim broken through Constantine III's Rine defences and burned and plundered a swathe through the province of Gaul. Later they over powered his garrisons in the Pyrenees Mountains from where they made their way into the province of Hispania. Alaric, who had an imperial pass, could come and go (it seemed) as he wished.

Constantine III status didn't last long after that. General Geronimoius' deputy general (the candidate of co-emperor), the aforementioned Constantius, somehow managed to become an imperial contender with the backing of unnamed elite, including Honourless. Then with Geronimoius leading the way north with troops from the House of Theododius (who were additionally supported by many of the recently arrived barbarian allies), they advanced on Constatine III who was back at Arles.

Also, there was trouble brewing for Constantine III back in Albion, as well. Saxen pirates were now looting and pillaging large tracts of this land. Nova Troia was often under siege. Discouraged by Constantine's failure to keep them secure from this vulnerability, the civilized Amoran inhabitants of both Albion and Armorica immediately expelled his officials from those lands. Then that certain Flavius Constantius, one of Honourless' generals working alongside the treacherous Geronimoius, managed to corner Constantine III in Arles and kill him. As for Constantine's sidekick Pater Blazingwolf, he was recorded missing but later pronounced dead, at least according to unreliable rumours at the time. This was in the year of 411 of the current era.

At this same time Honourless (still hold holding out), had found his new co-ruler. This, of course, was the aforementioned Flavius Constantius, the future Western Emperor Constantius III.

But a lot of other things had been going on in and around this part of the empire as well. And it was all happening in a parallel time zone. For instance, the goings on of an extraordinary leader named Alaric (Ala ric or King of All) for one. He was a Visigoth and after having his earlier attempts to invade the empire confounded by the skilful General Stilicho, this man (who was full of alacrity and intelligence) hired on with the empire bringing many of his armies with him. But this was after he had pillaged Corinth, Megara, Argos, Sparta and even Piraeus, the port of Athena and put fear into the hearts of one and all throughout the empire.

Jumping a wee moment backwards in time, in the year 410 CE, Alaric sacked Amor and had been the first to do so; and at a time, at that, when he was supposed to be on Amor's side. Perhaps that is true, Dyfed thought; Cato certainly did.

Although Amor was still Amor, Raven was where Honourless was stationed. Ravan remained the capital after Medio had been abandoned by him a few years before due to a threatening turbulence of barbarians (whose re-located hood) had become too close for comfort. It was a case of there goes the neighbour-hood. These days Honourless was panning out to be a contender for longevity when it came to holding imperial office it seemed. Honourless' brother Arcadius, who had joined their father as co-ruler at Byzas in the east, was dead. Arcadius' son and Honourless' nephew Theodosius II was to last another forty years before being killed on a routine horse and chariot commute. But Honourless would last another twelve years from today. As in all good stories, just like the general orthodoxy of make-believe history itself, the plans of mice and men fail and the ineffectual Honourless himself was soon killed. And we still haven't come to the one exception of non-welcoming intonations of invitation to enter the City of Amor. For that invitation went to Atla the Hun, not King Alaric, or other notables. But we are ahead of ourselves.

Meanwhile, Senator Priscus Attalus of Hellenic origin became emperor by Visigoth consent in 409CE and was supported by King Alaric.

(General Aetius & Aelie Galla Plecentia Paradiso)

> *'The vengeance of history is more terrible than the vengeance of the most powerful General Secretary. I venture to think that this is consoling.'*
> **LEV DAVIDOVICH BRONSCHTEIN (AKA LEON TROTSKY)**

Among the numerous scions (including the blood relations) of Emperor Theodosus the Great, was his strange and deranged daughter Aelie Galla Placentia Paradisio (392-450 CE). She was born in Thessaloniki, married Western Emperor Constantius III. It should be *remembered that this man was a Serbian who served under Aelie Galla Placentia's half brother, Western Emperor Honourless. And under this emperor he achieved the rank of Magister militum before becoming emperor himself for only seven months, because then he was found dead. Honourless then took up the reins [reign] again and* was a major force for most of her life in Amoran politics. She was also the daughter of another Galla who in turn was the daughter of Valentinianus the Great. Dyfed despised the direction in, and the impetus by, which she grappled hold of the levers (mostly of an anthropomorphise category and tenure) of state control to steer this wheel-less chariot into the ground or this Amoran-state trireme into the depths of the deep blue sea. Aelia Galla, as she was called, was a patrician. She was the younger sibling of Emperor Gratian, and Arcadius and Honourless (as already stated) were her half brothers. In Medio she had presided somewhat at court until her father died there in the year 395 CE. She has once resided and remained close to General Stilicho the Vandal and his wife Serena whose grandfather was Theodosius the Great's brother that made her Aelie Galla's cousin once removed (or something like that). Aelie Galla was also betrothed and entered in union with Stilicho's only son Eucherius. Then her husband was killed by two of Emperor Honourless' eunuchs. Shortly after that the emperor had ordered General Stilicho murdered. Aelie Galla then left Raven and fled to Amor for safety.

At some point before she arrived there she was captured by King Alaric (if your steel trap like mind will recall) was the first king of the Visigoths who initiated an unsuccessful invasion of Italia in the year 401 CE, prior to being hired on as help to defend Italia and the western provinces. In capture, Aelie Galla easily conspired with Alaricus (as he liked to be called) to undermine the resolve of Amor for the not-so-Eternal city-any-more's own good so that he could rule along side the Jeshuan Papal authority of Innocent I, Vicar of Amor, which he would observe and comply with. For her it was a no-brainer, so she took up residence on the Palatine Hill in Dyfed's old home. Here she resided with his old tenants the Cornelius family, sans *Felix* (the lucky).

So to continue; Aelie Galla also became wife to Atta-Wulf (Father-Wolf), commonly reduced to Ata-ulf which was pronounced and spelled *Athaulf* in the Amoran tongue and script, and later Adolf in the language of the Visigoth. If Alaric was their first Vizigoth king, Adolf was the king who transformed their quasi, lost, tribal kingdom into an imperial contender. Athaulf (as he was known at the time) was the brother-in-law of King

Alaric (the all-king) who later conducted the first thorough sacking of Amor. Aelie Galla and Adolf had at least one son together named Theodosius who was born in the city of Colonia Julia Augusta Barcino (now Barcelona) right after Adolf soundly defeated and executed the new two rival western emperors located in Gaul, Emperors Jovinus and Sebastianus. Anyway, these two men's heads were quickly forwarded by special delivery to Honourless where they arrived at his court at Raven on a hot sunny day in August. Subsequently, the heads were further forwarded on in dilapidated state to the walls of Carthage for some now forgotten reason. Adolf fabricated a successful rumour of a Marat-style death in the bath. He then disappeared for a few centuries to no one knows where. Later, her half brother, Emperor Honourless, forced the fake-widower into marrying Western Emperor Constantius III, the same man who convinced Constantine III to surrender himself up with a promise for a pensionable retirement but then murdered him instead. Aelie Galla and Constantius III had a son. His name was Valentinianus. Aelie Galla became the boy's regent until he became Emperor Valentunianus III. Later, after the death of his Holiness the Pope Zosimus, during a papal succession crisis where two factions of the clergy each elected one of their own that acted as rival popes, Aelie Galla intervened here and petitioned Emperor Honourless to favour a certain Eulalius over a candidate named Bony-face which he confirmed. But to little avail for a couple of synods later as well as the intervention by imperial troops, the rival, Bony-face (also Bonnyface) won out.

 Meanwhile, when the Western Empire underwent total social disintegration, it was at this point that King Alaric stepped in and led the thirty thousand fighting mercenary foederati (who flocked to him) out of Pannonia, across the Julian Alps thereby initiating his second invasion at this time. Then after he had performed his capture and release trick on Aelie Galla, on the twelfth day of a sunny September morning he suddenly stood before the Aurelian walls of Amor with tens of thousands of cheering armed barbarians at his back. Here, at this time, a great and giant chant went up. Dyfed and Cato (lying on their couches in Dyfed's digs by the Capitoline Hill, along with their three side-kicks and handymen, Markus, Philip and Pyrrhus) heard the uproar and jumped to their feet. It signalled the beginning of a two-year siege that was followed by a resounding, no nonsense jolly good sack. Somehow, Dyfed thought, although Aelie Galla may not have been the architect of such a trouncing that the imperial city had never before received, certainly her name was written all over it in some way. Yet despite their differences at hand (in their day to day lives), Dyfed came to realize that Aelie Galla's derangement and disconnect with the phenomenon around her was either very much like his own, or completely opposite. In other words, she lived in another universe that somehow was colliding with his. He wasn't sure which it was.

 Certainly she quickly became suspect when she arrived in and behind the walls of the city of Amor after being released by King Alaricus. She already had had a long history of having certain volatile domestic secrets escape the walls of the imperial household. These rumours, after floating out and being grabbed out of the air by sundry folks, then made malleable in the hands of petty enemies, were fashioned with sharp, hurtful barbs designed to be easily flung back at her by the common hoi polloi at large. For a patrician such as her this was most disconcerting. She was adroit enough (normally) to dodge most of them, but one niggling, long standing rumour was of her incestuous, carnal love with her brother Emperor Honourless which had a resolve for persistence all of its own. Even with the hoi polloi aside, this was something that the clerics of the Church of Amor could use against her, especially his Highness the Vicar of Jeshua Adon Bony-face himself who she had vehemently opposed in the great ecclesiastical pissing match during the Pasqua (Easter) of 419CE.

With Amor sacked and incestuous implications waving in the wind in full view, a papal order supported by the Eastern Amoran Emperor, Theodosius II (Aelie Galla's nephew through her dead half brother, the former Eastern Emperor Arcadius, brother of Honourless who was responsible for murdering her first husband), materialized one fine day at the palace. Also a letter of disparagement on the situation (viz; the lack of decorum that was being conducted at this time in the Western Empire) had even arrived from the Benevolent Berber, Aurelius Augustinus along with a copy of his *apology* 'On the Holiness of the Catholic (organizational) Church' and his latest work 'The City of God Against the Pagans' that was written to console his fellow Jeshuans after the sacking of Amor by Alaric and his roaming vandals of Visigoths. It also turned out that Augustinus had also written to Theodosius II recommending that he demand of his uncle, Western Emperor Honourless, that the patrician Aelie Galla be immediately expelled from the Western Empire and be sent east to him in Byzas. And to help persuade Honourless to comply, Augustinus recommended that he (Theodosius II) turn the large Prefecture of Illyricum back into the hands of the Western Empire, which he did. That way Theodosius could deal with the woman, and not the clergy. Eventually Theodosius II followed through with this, but he took his sweet old time (about fifty years).

 This brave and religious Berber Augustinus (who by all accounts was a man to be reckoned with) had once engaged to be married to a ten year old (girl). While waiting the two years for her to attain the legal marriageable age of twelve, he fell in love instead with the idea of becoming a celibate priest: Although, in the end, the celibate part didn't quite take hold as he had once envisioned. In any case Aelie Galla got word of what was a foot in respect to her immediate destiny. At this time the root of all evil disruptions that were coming to bear upon the empire was a scourge named Attala. This Attala was the name of a Hunnic nomad genius warrior from the east. He was no ordinary leader for his followers were not only Huns but consisted also of Lans and east Goths. After crossing the Volga Attala rapidly advanced. He was over efficient at engineering successful battles and sieges; he was over ambitious, over equipped, overly manned, over powerful and now he was over here on the marches of western Europa at the time when its Empire was the least, and its last few vestiges of what it had been were fading fast. And it was at this point that Aelie Galla took up her pen and putting it to paper penned a sweet love letter to that mighty destroyer promising herself to him in a marriage that towed a huge dowry (called the Western Empire) behind her. Oh yeah! She could deliver all right, she promised him, and even provided a few details. All he had to do was come to the city of Amor, starve thousands of folks the death, batter down the walls and rescue her before it was too late; nothing less than what he does best, and all in a days work. She signed her name Justina Honoria. Here then (as promised) is that one exception against Amor refusing to proffer any welcoming intonations of invitation to dangerous foreigners to enter the Eternal city.

 Now both Aelie Galla and Attala had an odd trump card up their preverbal sleeves. The first was that Justine Honoria was Aelie Galla's somewhat disobedient but reliable daughter and sister of Galla's son Valentinianus III. The latter had recently succeeded

Emperor Honourless who had died in a drunken rage of apoplexy, although the official report claimed that terrorists and enemies of the empire and its established authority had assassinated him. So, not only was her son now the Emperor Valentinianus III, but he had also recently granted Attala the honorary title of Magister militum. That would be the card up Attala's sleeve.

But Attala had one rival. That was Aetius, the great General Aetius.

(A round the table with Rama from Nananda)

> *'A bad artist copies; a good artist steals.'*
> PABLO PICASSO

At this point in the story, having met and become working partners with the likes of entitled aristocrats and strategy-type entrepreneurs (who were often base and mean and certainly not noble), it now came time for Dyfed to meet another and noble[50] new species of man. The person in question was a curious individual from Zhu named Meng Zhu. It was also curious how Dyfed met him. One day, shortly after the conclusion of the House of Theodosius merger affair, a Kushan courier and representative of the House of Kanishka named Rama who was visiting Amor approached Dyfed at his office in the forum early one morning at the first light. Apparently, Rama (by chance) had earlier witnessed Dyfed speak as an advocate for an Amoran senator being sued for having being drastically in arrears of debt repayment. He was also aware of the Dyfed's successful handling and outcome with the Theodosius file affair. Rama told Dyfed that he was among a few men who had come from the east encouraged by the tales they'd heard back home of the City of Amor. Rama explained that he was originally from Nananda that (he told him) was actually a presence of mind more than a place, and one he could attain wherever and anywhere he happened to be. His pink tongue contrasted with his shaded skin as he laughed. More truthfully, he continued, he was actually from Uttarakuru.[51] This place was an ancient land (he told him in his smooth voice) that once cut across the current lands of Afghan, Kuchan and Bactria.

He informed Dyfed that other merchants, all of whom wanted to open up massive trading contracts with Amor, were accompanying him. This included a noble oriental man named Meng who was originated from Zhu (Zhao) in the Far East. This man, he told Dyfed, once served the goddess Queen Mother of the West and much later had been an advisor to his own kin, Qin Xi Huang (the first emperor of the unified seven states[52]). Dyfed later came to realize that Meng (whose Amoran name became Mencius) was their wise man. His job was to rivet the Amorans toward the companions' cause. He would do this through the genius of his fascinating abilities once he had their full attention. Dyfed was soon to realize just how good the man was at doing just that.

And in turn, so Rama told him, he and Mencius were accompanied by a small troop made up of merchant men who were vying for position among the lucrative eastern trade business via the old silken road which (at this time) was being upgraded. This upgrading was being paid for with the toll-tax profits of its renewed heavy use. This road

---

50 Noble being the result of the achievement of the personal obligations one assigns to oneself, and not gained through inheritance.
51 Lalita-Vistara describes the Uttarakuru as Pratyanta-dvipa, or a frontier island among other kingdoms.
52 The seven warring states were Qi, Yan, Han, Wei, Zhu (Zhao), Chu and Qin. The latter was destined to be what the unified state ultimately called itself that (even unto the present day) is the Land of Qin (Ch'in).

was being extended and now ran from Qin all the way to Amor. He and the other men wanted to solicit business (Rama from Nananda explained) and they wanted Dyfed to act on as solicitor on their behalf. They preferred to meet in the evening, he said, in private, adding; 'how convenient would tomorrow evening at his place be?'

When Dyfed's guests had arrived as planned he ushered them toward a large circular table in the high hall portion within his suites. Although there were eight of them all told around the table (he and seven guests), Dyfed had only officially met Rama. Once they were each seated upon individual cushioned couches and provided tea by Dyfed, Rama looked at each of his companions individually before turning his eyes to focus and concentrate on Dyfed.

"I'm aptly named,' he said. 'More correctly I am descended from father Ram.' The brown haired Rama was almost ancient looking Dyfed noted. His beard was long and thick.

"Your father was named Ram,' Dyfed said, trying not to appear too bored or patronizing as his gaze swept across the others' faces.

"No,' replied Rama, 'as a sixth son himself my father had a different name. But often the eldest son was named after Ram, an ancient deity (who we once called Mesa). This Godliness vibration gazed down at the lesser vibration of our people. The power of Mesa/Ram began to influence us over two thousand years ago, but is much, much older than that.'

"I see,' said Dyfed. 'So what. Let me guess. The name he used before that was Tavros the Bull.'

"Vrsabha,' Rama corrected him, smiling at Dyfed in a pretence to compliment him at his apparent astuteness. 'Vrsabha is what we call Tavros the Bull, yes. And before him,' Rama continued, 'the buzz- words were Castor and Pollux, known as the twins. Essentially they were an older representation of Uranus (Uh-ran-us) the sky, and Gaia (Gay-ah) the earth. Of course she descended from our Earth Mother Mahimata, or previously Méh-ter[53] who was the consort of Dyēus Phater[54] who was the Sky god. Dyeus Phater who is our father god (or literally god father) was later shortened by the Hellenic people to just plain Dyeus that they pronounced *Zeus*. And the Bull Tavros or Taraus,' Rama stated, 'is traditionally the supreme god of Kreta (Crete), the birthplace of the aforementioned Zeus. And this island and its early flux (the so-called Minoan civilization) is the founding preparation plinth (or the providing fixture of Europa). It is the root and substructure of Eurys (Europa) herself. The reference here to Eurys, of course, is no accident. For Eurys is derived from the original Akkadian word *erebu*: that is meant to be the going down of the sun (the occident). It was from Kanaan (also Canaan, also Phoinikoi) that lay across the White Sea in the east over to the shores of his beloved Kreta in the west that Zeus (disguised as a white bull) carried Eurys (Europa) on his back.'

"Leto (he continued) was an important Earth mother and the daughter of Phoebe the Shining and Koios (Coeus). She is said to have given birth to twins (the children of Zeus) on an island off the southern coast of Kreta which folks then called Letoai. These twins were Artemis and Apollo. From the island Leto and her twins managed the

---

53 Obviously the root of our word *mother*.
54 In Sanskrit (dyēus or dzeus) is the word for god. Phater (obviously) is father. Hence: dyeu-phater or dyēu-piter (Jupiter).

short distance to the quite visible port of Gortys (so called as it was later occupied by the Gortyns) and is now called Matalum (Matala). At this place she founded a Mother Earth commune. As Earth Mother, Leto also founded the olive industry among the southern hills there which semi-circled the ancient hill city state of Phaestos, just as she promoted the cultivation of produce that grew in abundance upon Messara. Messara is the alluvial plain that stretches out beneath the original commune of Phaistos of abundance that clung to the sides of a rocky hilltop. This helped Kreta blossom into the first Europaean civilization. From this ancient polis of Phaestos (whose ruins still lie on the southern skirt of Messara) one is able to see the high blue hills and the snow capped summit of Mt. Ida (the birth place of Zeus) shimmering in the distance to the north,' said the obviously well informed Rama.

"And all this western folklore talk from a man from central Asia,' interjected Dyfed, warming to the conversation. 'But of course you are aware too, and have demonstrated as much, that the source of the genius of Western Philosophy (that is the foundation of the Western Civilization) was initiated by the flux of the ancient civilization of Indo-Aryans (Indian-Iranians). Then later we have the men from Kreta who sailed north and settled upon the Hellenic lands and brought a reform that had been the mainstay in Kreta.

So, Khem, Kanaan and Kreta (the KKK — with an injection of wisdom from Central Asia) seemed to have served hand in hand as stepping-stones that helped found the foundation stones for the people of Europa who named themselves (and their first city) after their goddess Athena. She, it is said, sprung from the mind (forehead) of Zeus,' he said. Was she then *the injection* of genius from Central Asia or was it Apollo and Artemis, the twin brother and sister children of Zeus and Leto? Will we ever know?'

"Yes, Athena of course, but,' replied Rama, 'it was thanks to Leto in her attempt to assist this new shoot of civilization, that from her commune at Phaestos she caused a tree whose branch was the symbol of victory for peace to be grafted and transplanted into the garden of Athena. And after that, in the land of the Hellas, the Acheans and the Dorians for the benefit of all the hoi polloi, there (now) grew the olive.'

"But now it is Jupiter (a male Athena) who is atop the Capitoline Hill,' replied Dyfed.

"Fancy that. How things change — eh? Said Rama

"Or not,' responded Dyfed. 'But, look here. We are (supposedly) in the beginning of the Piscian age, and you still have the name of a god from another age before. You have some catching up to do,' Dyfed said as his eyebrows shot up and he then surveyed Rama the man from Nananda, a place that was everywhere while he was from somewhere else.

"Yes,' said Rama, 'the last such god was known as Mesa in our old Sanskrit, but as you see, I've adopted its western name now. Anyway, whether he is known as Mesa (Ram) or Mina (Pisces) it's the same god now as was before. That's the way it is with gods and these things. As a word of caution, let me say that nothing really changes, as you have just noted. After all, we are dealing with beginningless time.'

(Master Meng-Zhu)

"The feeling of commiseration is the beginning of humanity;
the feeling of shame and dislike is the beginning of righteousness;
the feeling of deference and compliance is the beginning of propriety;
and the feeling of right or wrong is the beginning of wisdom."

MENCIUS

At that point Rama, the man from everywhere explained that his original home was actually the City of Kukuta in New Uttarakuru. Now he turned and introduced another, a certain Ab Ram (Father Ram) who he said was stationed in Mesopotamia at the port of Eridu. Long ago Ab Ram had adopted the Mesopotamian tongue, he told Dyfed. Then he added that originally this man had been from Bactria, and was his grandfather.

"He is your grandfather?' Dyfed asked in surprise.

"He is still Ab Ram, Rama added quickly. He then added that his grandfather's wife and mother were both from Uttarakuru.

Dyfed believed that this might mean that this New Uttarakuru and Uttarahuru in itself were two different places during two different ages. Dyfed scrutinized Ab Ram. He was obviously of ancient age. Dressed in beautiful coloured garments, and wearing a cap of some kind, he was also fairly light skinned with old white hair that ran down into his long beard. Dyfed found that they were searching into each other's eyes when all of a sudden he realized that their two minds were interfaced and the other was searching literally into his mind.

Oh my dear old soul, Dyfed murmured to himself defensively. He panicked momentarily for he knew full well that in some mysterious way his thoughts were being scanned if not somehow indelibly recorded or downloaded by Ab Ram. Dyfed now instantly broke out in a light sweat and felt his skin flush. He cleared his throat. Suddenly he wished that he had paid more attention to what his old Master tutor had taught him, along with his mother's advice about such onslaughts and trespassing of others against one's person.

But Manandan the Master of Hyperborean origins (who were of the Little Known Universe) had indeed taught him well. Dyfed automatically began to secure himself outside and within the realms of present thought in order to prevent himself from losing control and becoming merely a conduit for his mind to be easily accessed and debriefed. A moment or two later he regained his composure. But the aged man had felt the sentient power of Dyfed's own unseen self and changed tactic. He then spoke to Dyfed directly via that existing conduit that had been maintained and which connected them without any apparent vibration caused by physical sounding words being spoken between them. Instead he used the Universal Vibration, the cycle that indelibly transmits and records all things. He then told Dyfed that he knew that he was the son of Violet-Eye, and as such he must recognize his host as a prince of the Hyperborean people. This caused a small but visible reaction among all but one of the others. This indicated that he had read Dyfed up to that point and apparently all the other men (but one) had also received the communication at the same time.

The man told Dyfed that Uttarakuru, with its numerous northern kingdoms, was essentially the north- western region of their prevailing civilization of the time that was in parallel, and also that Pratyanta-dvipa (a frontier island) was the kingdom of the Hyperboreans that was also divided into portions: One such parcel was inhabited by the ancient Pryderi who monopolized the island of Prydein (Prydain). Indeed, as we know, many of the Kelts still retained that name.' He continued to tell Dyfed that he and his wife had once made their home in the southern part of the civilization, in Janapada that overlooked the Asian subcontinent. But, unfortunately, their beloved Janapada had already preceded New Uttarakuru and its kingdom of Hyperborea peoples into the abyss of ideological and social decay a long time earlier. It was then they relocated to Port Eridu via the Isle of Dilman. Ultimately it was their Mythos that brought the people their ultimate down fall, he said, for their society was a disconnect to the true Idea of Mother Earth. But, as Dyfed himself must know, he added, the end came and the civilization was finally broken into fragments. Men make their own reality, and it was no coincidence that with the slide of society into the abyss was solely due to their toxic and obnoxious Idea and Mythos complex. It was as if their material reality cavitated at the same time bringing upon them geological catastrophic and destruction. One of his own sons and one of Rama's uncles — he communicated to Dyfed — had fought in the great Trojan battle against Troia. But what could he do, he said. Like Dyfed, that son too had been born into life apparent in the third dimension. As it was, the great age of Tin (Bronze as it is known now) was coming to a close at that time and the Masters knew that what with the demise of tin, the civilization would collapse unless the hoi polloi made a quick and calculable change to their world Idea, which they failed to do. But to those hoi polloi at the time it was the glorious city of Troia that stood in the way of easy access to the vast tin deposits in its western region of Dumnonii. And here, with this remark, Ab Ram let it be known that the glorious city of Troia and its trade in tin was the capital of those aforementioned, long ago isles that were once called Pratyanta-dvipa before they were called Prydain.

Dyfed knew that his own second cousin Prince Penrhyn had had control of those same tin mines, but he never thought that thought. In this way he intentionally did not divulge that information to Ab Ram who silently waited, his mind listening.

According to Ab Ram they saw this tin deposit as a lifeline for the debased third dimensional remnants of the Hyperborean civilization as a whole that was still steeped in a bronze age. This should alert anyone, he said, who has penetrated Ram, that this Idea was atrophied and sick. But they didn't see that. They saw no alternatives within their decomposing society other then to make internal war against Pratyanta-dvipa in their need for desperate grab and greed, caused by fear. Other kingdoms of third dimensional Hyperboreans from the continent also attacked Troia, and were successful in defeating that ancient capital in the end. But in the end it did them no good because they hadn't adjusted their Idea to be one with Mother Earth, a prerequisite for transcending to transmigration, at best, and pulling up your socks with what you had, at worst. Ab Ram's mind went silent for a moment while he watched Dyfed.

When he continued he said that they (the hoi polloi) were the unfortunates. And then, what with economical sliding and ecological disaster, accompanied with a cooling of the northern hemisphere, chaos ensued. The ancient kingdom of the southern-west portion of greater Uttarakuru that is now known as Hispania (another antagonist toward Troia, and contender among the kingdoms) suddenly dried up. Survival in this region became a hostile battle to its benefactors. Many folks who fled Hyperborea and greater Uttarakuru migrated south and east into the northeastern region of the White Sea where they sometimes they renamed their homes after the old world. Remember, he reminded Dyfed; "the ancient men of Hellas told you that it was the Hyperboreans who brought them the art of medicine, astronomy, and mathematics. This migration took place about fifteen hundred years ago from the present,' he stated, 'with the toppling of Troia another few hundreds years before that.'

Dyfed had stopped sweating at this point and felt a modicum of comfort. Without taking his eyes off Ab Ram he communicated in return, wondering if the others were keeping up.

So (responded Dyfed's mind as it took up communicating with Ab Ram once again), in consequence we now have a city in our own time called Nova Troia. Ab Ram answered that the modern city of Nova Troia wasn't build on the same site as Troia. That older city he said had lain atop a hilly area further to the north east of that present day city. Beyond the old city was a broad lowland that gradually reached out toward a vast but shallow fjord, the basin of an inland sea that was able to accommodate one of the largest armadas ever gathered along these or any other shores by the ancients. Their permanent camp complete with horse breeding, dairy and agricultural farms, a grid of connecting roads, administration buildings, along with parade and field practice ranges had been spread out for miles. This was needed to accommodate a hundred thousand permanently stationed soldiers for a decade dig-in. In the miles that lay between these semi urban villages of the protagonists and the Pryderi defenders at the City of Troia lay the protagonists' heavily fortified earthen defences. Behind them (with their backs to the sea) was another mile of ample room for industry such as warehousing and ship building that stretched for miles along the beach. It was considered one of the most organized offensives and the greatest and most momentous battles of the ancient world, he said.

Ab Ram dropped his eyes and let Dyfed go. It was a courtesy. Dyfed was capable of such disengagement himself, if need be. Anyway, he knew the story that Ab Ram had been so patient in telling, but gave no reply. Rama then spoke up by continuing to introduce the others. Oh my dear rotten soul, thought Dyfed momentarily again, now what? What have I got myself into?

"Paredros of Phigaleia, and Democritus of Abdera I think you have met before,' he said, hesitating. They are middlemen. Then, getting no reply, he continued. 'And over there is Ebreo ben Jamin.'

This man, Dyfed remembered. He was the youngest of all the visitors that evening that was different from the others in many ways, Dyfed thought. Apparently he was an Edomite who had spent the last couple of centuries denying his blood relationship with King Herod. In comparison to the companions with whom he accompanied here tonight, Ebreo wasn't actually one of them at all. It appeared that he was a metallurgist and an alchemist of some sorts. And if the yet to be introduced Mencius was the wise man, this Ebreo, by the nature of his body language, was the resident wise guy of the group, Dyfed thought. The others, no doubt, were wise trading men from the east. Their trade was two fold, Dyfed now realized. Yes, they meant to set up a chain of souqs or markets stretching all the way from the east in the land of Ch'in, via a route which could accommodate wagons for merchants to actually be able to peddle goods as they go, with an eye to establish Amor (at least the Amoran Empire as such) as its western terminal. They were soliciting help in implementing this and in over-coming hurdles of Amoran law and policy and it was to this end why they singled Dyfed out. Possibly it was why Ebreo was among them as well. But Dyfed also sensed that they sought something else.

'And then over here is Stilpo of Megara,' Rama was saying. Stilpo was gnome looking with a thick, heavy, forked beard.

"None of my works have survived,' the latter hastily told Dyfed rather nastily, waving his large stubby hands around his head as though he was trying to signal that he was hallucinating. 'The new age,' he said, 'has twisted my intent to favour dialectic, accompanied, of course, by logic and they now claim that I argued that the universal is fundamentally separated from the individual. This is untrue, and let all the goddamning gods damn it and let it go to hell. In fact, I argued the exact opposite. I said that Mother Earth and her biosphere and her connections to grand Radiance and its system, and the universe beyond is concrete and part of us. Nothing is separated, that's what I said. Nothing is separated! The newbie's, that is the proponents of the new cults immerging now have a different agenda, it seems. And I'm afraid for us because of it.'

He spoke as though he didn't care about whether anybody else thought along those lines or not. That's all there was to it.

"So,' said Dyfed, 'you were misquoted. As you said yourself, none of your work survives to this day. Dyfed glanced back toward Democritus, marvelling how he and Morgant resembled one another.

Rama then turned to finally introduce Mencius (Meng-zhu), the man from the province of Zhu in the Land of Ch'in (Qin). This man was relatively tall and stout and was covered in layers of beautiful cloth garments that made him more rotund than ever. He had a sparsely whiskered, long forked beard though his upper head appeared to be shaved except for a knot of hair somewhere behind his head with something stuck through it in the shape of a wing nut or the miniature handle of a simple reciprocating pump. From it hung a pigtail that was so long it rested behind him on his cushion. Then on top of his shaved head in the manner of a hat he wore what Dyfed thought was a fantastic pi-bald coloured contraption. It had a partial brim that was quite wide and stuck out on either side of the man's head but not over the front or back. And from this brim down to about the length of one's middle finger dangled weighted Ping-Pong-type balls that remained motionless until he moved his head. Then these balls would gyrate all about just managing to come short of hitting each other or him in the cheeks or ears.

Dyfed was fascinated. The man was an inventor, and here in Amor after a hot summer day like today, the markets, and the abattoirs were attracting over a billions flies. Here was this man's remedy. He had managed to figure out how to keep them off his face and head without having to raise a finger to swat at them.

It turned out that Meng-zhu was from the area of the Hwang-He river valley that bordered Qin. Surely, Dyfed thought, this man's raison d'etre for being here was different from the others. But Dyfed was surprised when the man spoke in person. Though the tongue of his countrymen was unintelligible to Dyfed, Mencius spoke Shamskara fairly clearly. He exclaimed his fervour toward Dyfed's liberal approach to banking that was as natural as nature itself. He was a big supporter of his cause, he said. He liked how Dyfed did business and his overtures of invention when it came to simple and easy to run rackets used to create wealth without inflation.

Dyfed, speaking in his mother's tongue answered that his methods were intended for the purpose of altering the Amoran Idea. Slavery and masses of downtrodden were not acceptable standards for a civilization to grow in a healthy way that could otherwise enhance the people. Honourable standards needed to be attained for folks to be able to aspire towards a higher authority of their own volition through self-discipline in order to achieve nobility. This is what he was about, he told Mencius. All the men nodded in agreement with this.

"So, you are of the way of the Tao then, as well as Confucius,' said Meng, referring to that philosophy which extends the maintenance of compassion, help, and support, along with universal well being for all fellow men (and women) on earth in the natural way.

Dyfed answered in the affirmative. Then feeling the cool eyes of Rama's grandfather still on him, he shifted an eye to see what old Ab may be contemplating. But his mind seemed to be asleep with his eyes open. Turning back to Meng he replied that, in respect to the here and now and that which he viewed as his moral authority in such matters, he favoured the dharma of Buddha and the latter's influence from those sages of Jainism as a life philosophy, again, in the present of the here and now. So long, he added, that it was kept simple.

"Ah-so,' replied Mencius, leaning acutely forward and bowing his head from his seated position with the garment knots now bouncing all around his head. As he began to raise himself again to the perpendicular, he uttered these words — 'the simplicity of the vibration of the universe encompassing beginning-less time…'

At that point Dyfed heard no more of what Mencius had to say.

(N'ha-a-i-'tk and the land of Giants)

'Never let it be said that I am deaf to persuasion.'
ANONYMOUS

Mencius raised his eyes. They were eyes, Dyfed noted, that had the slitty appearance of the silver sliver of the horizontal hugging moon. The eyes of both men came into a fixed contact for the first time as Dyfed peered into these two crescent moons and noticed they had a silver translucent sheen across them that seemed to glitter in the candlelight. But Dyfed couldn't penetrate them any more than he could hear sound vibrations around him. Then he suddenly felt a vibration that caused a dizziness to suddenly come over him. It was more pronounced than his experience with Ab Ram. He began to sweat profusely.

All of a sudden Dyfed realized that he was sprawled awkwardly upon a familiar looking comfy chair in front of a big and equally familiar desk in an elaborately appointed and familiar room. He didn't know or understand why they or anything else around him should be as familiar as they were; like deja vu they just were. In a manner of routine habit he adjusted his glasses that he hadn't realized he was wearing as he leaned back and looked around in amazement. Where the devil had he been just now? he thought. He then remembered some scraps of his ancient past. Something wasn't right. They had strange and personal memories sewn into them...personal memories…memories he had forgotten about or hadn't thought about in a long time. He searched backwards again. In comparison to where he was or should be, he was reminded of his old home library and his study back in Couver City. From his desk there he remembered gazing through the tall windows in the direction of the sea. Somehow he knew that currently he was now fifty miles from that old home and the sea, the Peaceful Ocean. With rising ocean levels now, he thought, that may all quickly change pretty soon too. In no time he might be able to rent out some of his western pastures to pleasure seekers as a beach getaway if things didn't improve.

These thoughts amazed him, but only momentarily. Dyfed had become immediately cognizant of the fact that it was from inside his present reality that other fantasies and pretend, along with memories of his past, no matter how much he may favour them, were outside of space/time present. And the retention ability of being aware of this, he noticed, was easily retainable. That calmed him for a panic had been rising inside of him. There were, after all, supposed to be only the present with past presents in tow. Now it might appear that there were future presents quite relative as well, pending on where your present is. That was the key to reality, supposedly. It was apparent that the present wasn't as fixed as folks thought. This was contrary to the cosmology about which Aristotle and other recent ancients had often ruminated. However, what they had said and what most folks believed hadn't been what he was taught. Here was proof to him, anyway, that the theories of the Hellenes were wonky. They may have been a baby step during a despotic age but observation now proved them wrong, in many ways. The past was supposed to be manageable; the future, it seemed, was supposed to be a mystery. But Manandan had never said that, exactly. What he did say was that the folks in the third dimension anticipate the future with fervour but in truth they don't understand the past or (for that matter) even the present any better.

Dyfed looked around him as he gathered up cognizance and memories. He now further recalled how this minor world metropolis of Couver City that he was presently remembering had grown up around his and Ceredwyn's old homestead. Now he was aware that he was reaching back even further. This homestead, he recalled, he had built for her and this had happened shortly after their refreshing layover and rest with Flying Sturgeon and his wife Flowering Daisy. This now brought back other things to mind.

Then he remembered Walks on Clouds who was of the B'otuck people and there was somebody else…he strained his memory. Silent White Sitting Bull…that was it. Furthermore, he recalled now that Walks on Clouds was his son from a gentle noble woman who once had lived on the western shores of the Atlas Sea. That is, on the east coast of the Merikan continent. He remembered his son bidding he and Ceredwyn a temporary farewell on the bald prairie of the western plains as a warm wind blew, and how the younger man had given her a long parting glance. She in return smiled back at her stepson lovingly. Ceredwyn and Dyfed then left their winter shelter among the prairie hills that (scattered across the grassy plains) were like a green archipelago of jade jewels. They had descended again upon the steppe land on foot with their little four-legged, freeloading friend Wolflet that tailed furtively behind them.

Suddenly, it was all coming back.

Shortly afterwards, purple mountains had risen upon the horizon directly in front of them. It was just as Born in a Tepee at the Foot of a Rainbow had said they would see. This chief was a plains man and a friend of Silent White Sitting Bull. In his language of the Cree nation these mountains were called *as-sin-wati*. This mountain range shot as far as the eye could see to the northern and southern rims and were later to be discovered as the spine and the backbone of the Merikan continent. There were two continents, actually, but nobody knew that then. It became quite obvious to Dyfed and Ceredwyn that this mountainous barrier was far greater and loftier than any they had ever encountered. For Dyfed, who had seen more of the world than Ceredwyn, they seemed even as great in height as the Alpes Mountains that topped the Adriaticum Sea and the Italia peninsula where ancient Mt Olympus (now White Mountain) cast its shadow far and wide over the land. Evidently these mountains here were a sentinel, a gigantic, foreboding silent guardian that defended the far west from the harshness of the steppe and kept the far west green-housed-in by trapping most of the clouds of moisture and with its high mountain peaks prevented them from blowing any further east. This made the far west a luscious hothouse of fertility. As they marched forward for many days, walking at a furious pace, even before the foothills came into view these mountains continued to grow and loom up. The foothills, Dyfed and Ceredwyn found (when finally they were under foot), were a beautiful rolling land covered in spruce, aspen, and a mess of roses and berries where game was plentiful and Wolflet, their wild canine pet pup, bounded about barking and yapping and snapping with a happy smile on his sharp toothy face. So it was not surprising that other blackened feet tribes such as the Siksika people of the Niitsitapi confederacy were gathering here from all directions to camp in preparation for the summer. It was these people who were the cousins to Born in a Tee pee at the Foot of a Rainbow who now directed their white brother and sister towards a pass that led through what had risen before them into a formidable sight. With its great white-capped peaks scraping the sky, it was like a vertical sea wave, a motionless tsunami, they thought.

The local people were helpful and cautioned Dyfed that the journey ahead into the highest levels of the earth was fraught with unseen dangers for many spirits of the land lived there as well as the spirit of the great white headed eagle. Standing on a rough granite rock covered in lichen as he talked, the council's chief stood in a bent and crooked stance with one eye closed, his short stature covered with a hide smock. He pointed at the mountains. They were told that they would have to ask the great spirit of the mountain for its blessing in order to pass through the enfolds of its accumulated amassment and miscellanea safely enough without incident. Born in a Tee pee at the Foot of a Rainbow had earlier told them that from time to time they would need to bestow upon it numerous concessions and much caution, and pause before drinking the fresh cascading waters to slake their thirst. And as for any animals they needed to kill for sustenance, he told them that they must have their entrails laid out with theirs heads or sculls, intact, facing the direction of the western winds. However, in order to reach the shores of the western ocean (according to the people of the blackened-feet) they needed to cross not one but two mountain ranges. And in between these two-fold western topographical occurrences lived a race of hybrid giants who (legend has it) sometimes tried to come inland by climbing over the mountains. Before the chief stepped off the flat granite stone he told Dyfed and Ceredwyn that it was fortunate that this mighty wall, which was the spirit of their mightiest of gods, remained steadfast for it provided the plains people with greater protection from these dangerous giants whose smoking fires could sometimes be seen from the tee-pees around their own fires here on the plains. Apparently, they couldn't for the life of them understand why anyone, especially two ignorant and vulnerable pale-skins, would willingly go there.

Abiding by the natural laws of the land Dyfed the prince of the grove broke trail as he and Ceredwyn toiled up and down steep gorges being flushed with rushing torrents, and wound their way through forests of spruce, balsam, and fir while ever hemmed in by the steep, majestic land that unnervingly tipped up and up, grinding and heaving, folding and climbing over and on top of itself, while pieces and corners broke off and (being attracted by the acceleration due to the earth's gravity) slid, tumbling violently back down at dangerous speeds. Being strictly subjected to the nature of the environment, hunting in the traditional fashion was awkward. So Dyfed then resorted to trapping with snares that he make from sticks of branches and strips of supple bark that grew on young deciduous trees. Fish, it seemed, were unknown in the streams at this altitude and they saw no deer. But large game trails were plentiful and helpful in their progress through the thick underbrush. Occasionally they blundered into the presence of ferocious beasts like the large humped bear whose sleek, silver tipped fur glistened and rippled as he ran (usually toward them in anger), displaying tremendous strength and speed. Dyfed learned to lead them downhill where he had an advantage of descent control over them.

One evening, after a day of descending a treacherous scree slope, they sighted a lion. This was just as they were approaching (and recognized by description) a spot that Born in a Tee pee at the Foot of a Rainbow had told them about and given directions as how to locate it. It was a hot spring where they could sweat out the poisons of their body and the wretchedness of their spirit if they approached it correctly. So after baiting a trap for the lion at large he and Ceredwyn retired to that steaming natural pool to submerge their naked bodies in its hot mineral waters whose heat were allowed to diminish in a series of cooling pools located at different descending levels. The following morning he and Ceredwyn were awakened early by the howling screams of this poor mountain creature. Dyfed hurried to the site in dread of the inevitable sight that he knew awaited him. The animal had been well caught and in thrashing and twisting around in his endeavour to escape, he had hopelessly tightened the snare around his neck and Dyfed looked upon the trapped animal with pity and admiration as it lay contorted and panting. It reminded him of the little bird he had once senselessly killed in the forest of Arfon. He also recalled the geese that the eagle had killed for its survival in the forest near Morgant's cave. In response to that debt of remorse for that first incident which once again welled up again inside him, Dyfed quickly put an end to the poor creature's struggling while honourably praising the animal for its courage. Then in a posturing and penitent fashion before the spirit of the mountain that watched on, he intentionally failed miserably to compare himself to the killed mountain lion. Over the next few days, and in its honour, he meticulously skinned and cured the beast's hide. Then he vigorously rubbed it in an effort to make a soft, pliable and loose fitting vest. He had seen the women of the plains chew similar pelts to make them soft and pliable, but he wasn't about to do it himself or ask Ceredwyn to take up the cause. Once he had asked Born in a Tee pee at the Foot of a Rainbow for a pair of moccasins, he recalled, now with a laugh. The chief had quickly replied — 'what, you got no woman?' he laughed, crinkling up his eyes and glancing over at Ceredwyn. He then winked at Dyfed.

They set out then to take up their journey west once again. Only after a labour of many evenings at the end of each rigorous day was his mountain lion hide fitted and ready for comfortable wear. The creature's hind legs, complete with claws (along with its tail) he let hang down his back around his upper thighs and between his own legs, while the flattened head (he had removed the skull as he had been instructed by plains folk) with the front paws dangling down the front. These floppy appendages flapped gently against Dyfed's front and rear thighs as he walked.

By the time they were descending the mountains and moving toward a pretty land that was warm with fresh, breezy winds that moved the heat around, the small plums were already forming but still green and the moon was rising full and late over the mountains behind them as they descended into a series of many beautiful valleys whose bottom lands were filled by long, serpent like, shimmering blue lakes. The summer sun was excessively hot here and the pine forests, radiating a strong aroma, twittered and hummed with an array of birds and the latter's daily diet of winged insects. And although it was arid in the high country, the valleys were lush and humid and smelled of yarrow and earth. Here they found a friendly, non-nomadic people living quietly in abundance on a profusion of vegetation and game. Apparently the people whose land they had descended into, had been recently embroiled in conflict with their neighbours to the north who had plundered and burned one of their villages. In response, they had posted lookouts, and it was these who first detected our friends approaching them. Being amazed, however, at their shining appearance and recognizing them to be of a race unknown to them, the people of this valley allowed the two foreigners safe entry, believing them to be either strange spirits or unknown gods that had ushered forth from the towering domains to the east where only gods reside. But occasionally the gods would allow certain vagabonds cloaked in derision to travel through the mountains that scraped the sky, as well. But that did not describe these strange brilliant beings, one of whom they marvelled, wore the skin of a lion, something that their people would be very careful to carry out and use only in ceremony.

In due course the lookouts anxiously reported to their people that one of the creatures was in fact a lion god who had for the most part assumed the characteristics of a man but retained the long hair of his mane which also grew from his face; the other, they said, was an admirable goddess whose head was an un extinguishable flame. Both of these beings, they reported, shone brightly. When the others heard this it caused a great commotion and they busied themselves in preparation to welcome them.

Despite the tremendous heat, Dyfed noted that the men and women who at this point confronted them were heavily dressed, sporting, among other items, colourfully dyed hides, feathers and stiff leather leggings. All of them wore sturdy moccasins and many of them carried brightly coloured carousels made of long dyed grass or reeds. Suddenly, while effecting appeasing gestures, three men ran up close to them and offered colourful trinkets that they lay down in Ceredwyn and Dyfed's path before quickly retreating. Standing before the tribes-people, Dyfed and Ceredwyn both held out their arms in front on them with their palms facing down. Then they reversed their palms and stood motionless for a few moments more before clasping hands and kissing each other on the lips. This had a marked effect upon three or four of the alert tribesmen who Dyfed recognized as being councillors or advisory chieftains. This included Chief Radiant Springs, a large and jovial man. Having consoled the tribesmen in this manner, the company drew near and surrounded them. Their spokesman told them that they were the people of N'ha-a-i-'tk, and that they welcomed the lion man and his flaming consort; and that if it pleased them a feast of venison and fresh land locked fish along with dried river salmon awaited them at their nearby village.

Even though it was just mid summer, Dyfed and Ceredwyn decided to remain in this place until the following spring, and while the women fussed over Ceredwyn, Dyfed set out to discover the land and its people. The people of the N'ha-a-i-'tk, as all people of the earth do, took their name from their god or from some other strong influencing spirit. After awhile it dawned on Dyfed that N'ha-a-i-'tk was more than a morphological spirit, but rather it was an actual creature, or creatures, towards whom these people showed both reverence and fear. As their young chief, Radiant Springs, explained to him; it was a fearsome animal that lived deep down in the waters of the lake although he breathed air like a man. Once, in the time of their grandfathers, the N'ha-a-i-'tk, he told him, was numerous and they gave live birth on land. But now, he said, they had dwindled and no one was sure just how many remained.

Normally sceptical about notions that people from the altered state profess (such as the descendants in the third dimension of his own race who relied on institutions of will and intention), Dyfed was less inclined to do so in respect to these people of the earth who repose naturally in mysterious design. He had some sound reasons for this. People of mysterious design and of the earth, which anciently encompassed all peoples and though now vanished at this time throughout Albion and Europa, they appears to survive only in very small pockets anyway here the new world (as well as a few other unknown places). They each have something very powerful in common; namely their perceptions and their visions. These perceptions are timeless and reoccurring but are automatically suppressed by the so-called modern and sophisticated people in the altered state of will and intention due to their hugely incurring spiritual debt caused by their growing and unnatural ego. These timeless perceptions are also the origins for all valid religious thought as opposed to the compensatory and false pseudo religious thought brought on by the aforementioned and cursed debt which is born out of greed and grasping. If only the weakened souls of will and intention would let go their desires and to own and control and awaken to enlightenment, they too would be able to perceive the same images and visions common to ancient man. Dyfed thought that these flashbacks that occurred among those contemporary to his age were really the psyche repairing unto its origins in an attempt to correct its path and make reparations towards its debt and redirect itself towards harmony, its natural equilibrium. In the material sense, the vision is immaterial.

So, upon hearing of this creature N'ha-a-i-'tk, it awakened the memory of a familiar being deep within himself. This memory was one which often came from a dream like state, so when Radiant Springs told him that the remnants of these creatures were the tribes sacred relics, Dyfed requested the honour to behold them. He was led to a cave where to his immense surprise he saw some very large bones. There were only three of them, each one having a vast diameter, and upon closer inspection Dyfed pronounced them to be the vertebrae of a behemoth, but he knew the creature had been a giant mammal and not a fish. Apparently, then, these were the remains of one of the hybrid giants.

As the summer heat was intense, Dyfed shed his lion skin and covered his skin only with his lightest cloth. Seeing it cast aside, one of the talented women that had been assigned to their domestic abode had picked it up and after meticulously lining the leather she then beautifully decorated it with an assortment of turquois beads and polished black basalt and bone. She also rubbed the animal's claws into a high gloss. On the first full moon after the equinox and the time of the changing seasons, the air grew cold and Dyfed looked for it again. It was then that he discovered the servant's handiwork with great surprise and pleasure.

Shortly after this Dyfed and Ceredwyn said their goodbyes and departed the N'ha-a-i-'tk. Radiant Springs had told him that a great river would lead them to the womb of mother Earth and that a great smoking giant would alert them in their approach to the land by the sea. This titanic creature, he said, resided peacefully for the most part on the shores of the great ocean. But, when she mourned for her dead mother who lay partially submerged in the waters offshore, her sobs often quaked the whole earth and her fits of sorrow caused even the happy countenance of the sun to darken.

Having passed the jagged peaks at the summit of the second mountain range, Dyfed and Ceredwyn quickly descended steep gullies again, and then with hands sticky with pitch, they beat their way down through dense underbrush out onto a flat river valley. Here at their side was a rushing river that poured out of the mountains through cataracts, and swooped around in a wide bend spreading its muddy surface out into the valley floor where it flowed lazily toward the ocean. This was their first glimpse of the Sto:lo River.

As they wended their way west they walked in the shadows of rounded, bluish coloured mountains that were spread open wide by the broad river valley. Unseasonably warm, the air was humid and fresh and any patches of mountain snow had long disappeared. As they continued, the valley widened even more and although the mountains to the north remained abrupt, those to the south melted into hills and Dyfed and Ceredwyn noticed that beyond them, glistening in the blue sky, lay a shining, white mountain whose summit was perpetually covered in snow. This, they reasoned, was the smoking titan. And its fire and smoke was what the Siksika people witnessed back inland on the plains, far from this place.

Despite the enormity of the land, the industry of the population was quite evident for it invariably hinged around this river whose south bank the two travellers followed in a westerly direction. The land was pristine and the only evidence of any un-natural fabrication to mar its gentle and child-like face was the fishnets that they frequently passed. These nets were intricately woven from pliable cedar strips and other vines. Often they were anchored or at least weighed down by heavy stones in order to spread the net through the water's depth. The upper part of the nets had been fastened onto long poles that stuck out from the surface of the moving waters. After some hours the nets were hauled in to reap the fish that were caught with their gills and fins in the net. Aside from this, other fishermen were seen standing stalk still on the riverbanks holding long spears at the ready. Close by, there would be a clearing in the thick forest of green vibrating leaves where the fisher people's houses stood altogether, not individually apart. These were built of split cedar. Whitish blue smoke wafted up from under the edges of the roof of the buildings permeating the smoke-drying fish inside while the fresh, clear air outside smelled of land, smoke and a hint of the sea. Narrow paths wound down from the huts through the tall grass amidst the clusters of dense brambles toward the marshy shore of the river where the fish traps were anchored and the river canoes moored.

As they drew closer to the sea the climate became even more humid and a little cooler, and the villages of the local people became more numerous. The people here spoke an up-river dialect of the Salish Halkomenelem language, and generally ignored the travellers. They were the Sto:lo and the Chehalis people. Although they often stared at Ceredwyn's red hair they also displayed aggressive behaviour by shooing the two away whenever Dyfed and Ceredwyn passed too close to their possessions. As time passed they came upon others such as the Katzie people, the Kwantlen, and nearing the coast the Musqueam.

(Xats'alanexw and the potlatch mask)

> 'We live under a system by which the many are exploited by the few, and war is the ultimate sanction of that exploitation.'
>
> HAROLD LASKI

Finally they entered a huge delta where the smell of the sea attacked their nostrils. The going was harder here due to a network of natural canals and slow moving snys that swept inland from the course of the main flow. Finally they came to a spot just upstream from a three-way fork where the river narrowed. It was here that they had learned that the river was referred to as Sto:lo. Across the river to the north, rose a gentle rise of heavily wooded land, and beyond that, through the shimmering haze of heat, a ridge of blue, snow capped mountains climbed abruptly toward the sky. To the south still lay the great fuming giant with her glistening white sides and curious circular hat resting just above her head like a crown. After a few unsuccessful attempts to find a crossing, Dyfed and Ceredwyn came upon a kindly Musqueam couple that lived with their grown family. Flying Sturgeon the elder was a boat builder as well as a fisherman like all other men. And scattered everywhere around his yard was a thick carpet of wood chips and long fuzzy straps of cedar bark. All around were potential canoes still in the shape of huge trunks of cedar in varying stages of completion. With a crinkly smile this man offered to ferry them across, but Dyfed, whose interest in the man's technique of dugout building had peaked, first offered his assistance for a number of days as payment for the ferry service. Although Flying Sturgeon selected the trees he would carve, younger men cut them and floated them downstream to the man's camp. Once he had roughly hewed their hulls he returned them to the water where he then marked their buoyant positions. Shaving each log flat he burrowed a succession of wide holes into the top of the trunk where he lit fires to burn and soften the wood. Then standing with his feet apart on a wood plank that was balanced across the top of the smoking log, he attacked it with a stone scoop and other gouging-out tools. In this way he slowly hollowed out each of the cedar logs into dugout canoes. The bow and stern of these large vessels were not curved but straight, slanting outward, and peaked, and sometimes he carved ornate designs of animals along them.

While they remained there at this riverside spot, Dyfed and Ceredwyn resided with Flying Sturgeon and his sweet wife, Blackberry. Ceredwyn helped her at her duties while Dyfed lit and dosed fires, and hauled logs much to the local's amusement. Besides ingesting the vegetation that was at hand, their diet consisted mostly of fish, small mammals, berries, foliage and roots, and occasionally some big game. One day, when the man broke off from his work to catch fish from the river, Dyfed discovered how he came by his name. Using a long handled baited gaff instead of a spear, the boat builder stood quietly poised over his bait with the head of the gaff submerged beneath the surface of the moving river. When a large sturgeon came to investigate, he gave a sudden pull, and jerking the fish up and out of the water, he wielded the gaff in a wide circular motion. When the flapping and contorting fish was high in the air above his head, he gave a slight twist with his wrists and the sturgeon came loose from the gaff but continued to fly a great distance through the air and land on the shore where it flopped around but unable to get back into the river. By that time some children managed to pounce on it. Silently, Flying Sturgeon dipped his gaff back into the water and resumed his motionless stance to wait for another fish to visit. After their refreshing layover and rest, Flying Sturgeon ferried Ceredwyn and Dyfed across to the north shore of the river.

Here they came upon the Skwxwu-mesh (Skwaumesh) people and their close kin, the Tsleil-Waututh (Sleel-whoa-tooth). Both of these latter mentioned folks were radically coastal folk. For them this land was a commitment. Rather than using the smaller, but versatile river going vessels which the Musqueam, the Kwantlen, and the Chehalis most often used, these former mentioned serious coastal folks generally always employed the larger sea going cedar dugout boats with their tall platform prow and stern. They used these not only to cross the choppy inlets and the navigate the sounds, but also to plough through the dangerously ferocious rip tides that flowed between the archipelago of islands that dotted the coast and the eastern shore of the big island to the west, the submerged mother of the smoking god that guarded the Sto:lo River. Aside from shuttling folks back and forth from one village to another safely, and in navigating up and down and around their dangerous, marine world fishing, communicating, and employing commerce, these large sturdy vessels were ideal for handling the many rip-tides (actually they are rip-currents) and the turbulent waters in the perilous flow of the wide mouth of the Sto:lo River which flowed here into the sea from the Backbone Mountains. These were the sea going vessels that they would paddle many days to the south and equally many days to the north to communicate and convey important messages throughout the extended settlements of their people. The Skwxwu-mesh were a people who wore fur hats and outlandish cloths, some of which were even woven with strips of bark from trees such as the cedar, while others were fashioned with skins of animals such as sea lions and the woven hairs of mountain goats. Sometimes their garments were a combination of the above. They thought nothing of paddling away out to sea before the light of day to harpoon large humpback whales to feed their people. One day Dyfed watched as the young men paddled out to sea singing and chanting, then returned later that morning with two or three of their big canoes lashed to a harpooned whale. Nothing from any animal they killed was wasted for that would be an insult to the animal and wasteful. In Dyfed's terminology wastefulness, like greed and envy, was the process of attaching oneself to bad karma. The folks were brave and innovating, Dyfed decided, and he had not seen or met men quite like them anywhere during his life, but they reminded him a little of the early Prydains. And they were friendly to Ceredwyn and Dyfed. The Kwantlen folks, however, had earlier warned them to be wary of this twinned clan, along with the Musqueam, claiming that they were nefarious liars and unprincipled, but Dyfed did not find this so. In any event, it was more of a good-natured rivalry than anything else, he decided.

Dyfed was much taken by the place that he and Ceredwyn had stumbled upon. Here the living was easy and the marine grasses were as high as a Great Blue Heron's eye, and the people, if not always even-tempered, were calm. Amid the geophysical calm on sultry and radiant evenings, the purple mountains of the big island to the west would momentarily prop up the golden, blood red sun. It lay long and gentle on the near horizon and blended together from here with the islets that surrounded it and on the whole it visibly appeared like a continuous pod of Orca sea gods.

Here was paradise, we thought and so unlike the great steppe, those broad and brutal plains that he and Ceredwyn had earlier crossed, where the nomads there were so unlike the sedentary folks here. For the Skwxwu-mesh (Skwaumesh) people and the Tsleil-Waututh (Sleel-whoa-tooth), breakfast, lunch and supper were only a short and lazy walk away (in one way or another) from the tidal sands and nothing like attempting to approach a trampling herd of thousands of bison amid the disorientating fear and thunderous noise all stirred in a storm of dust and debris where the aim was to nudge and arduously try and coerce the separation of a handful of bison therefrom and drive these racing enraged animals over a so-called *buffalo-jump* to their deaths. This was how the plains folks put meat on the table. Their existence was base and less advanced than here Dyfed, remembered thinking.

The siyam (chief) of these two clans (the Skwaumesh and the Tsleil-Waututh) was a man named Xats'alanexw. Khat-sah-lano was the best pronouncement of his name that Dyfed was able to muster with his tongue that was tied a little differently. This tall, handsome and larger than life man lived simultaneously in the villages of Xwayxway and Senakw. And according to Xats'alanexw his people and the general population hereabouts were among the southern portion of an ancient civilization that extended from a great river (guarded by three mountain gods, two of them male) that was many days south by sea-canoe to way up into the northern temperate regions where the jumble of coastal islands cease and where the landless sea and the foreboding headlands are guarded by the giant of all mountain gods. And according to the spirits that were the genius of the Totems throughout all the nations that developed out of this civilization this civilization, Xats'alanexw told Dyfed that this civilization had so far lasted for five hundred generations of their people. This civilization was divided into many nations up and down this coast. The nation that Xats'alanexw's people belonged to inhabited the lower (most southern) portion. There were other strong and heavy populated nations on the big island to the west.

This unheard of longevity may have had something to do with the temperate climate and because instead of bison and prairie-dogs to eat (along with deer and like creatures), the people here had the salmon, the seals, sea lions and many deer and moose, elk, and a myriad of fowl and fresh vegetation which could also be preserved for out of season. But they also had a fish called eulachon (ooligan) that is of the kingdom Animalia. These ooligans were a smelt that were here in abundance and provided an especially rich fat and fish oil that was called grease. This in itself was a valuable commodity and it was even used sometimes as a currency. As chief, Xats'alanexw had a head and primary residence in both his villages. But Dyfed soon discovered that this was primarily in order to divide up his two wives from each other, one from each village. Initially this dividing of his chief residences (which were run by his wives) was done for cultural reasons and for ceremonial expedience as well as for the sake of his own sanity. All these people spoke the Sa'lish tongue. The village of Senakw (Snauq) was about four or so Amoran miles as the crow flies south west of Xwayxway across the sea bay where it was located on its south shore. It should be noted that these people were interspersed and intermingled that were not divided by land but by bands which determined regenerative relationships and progeny rules. The division itself between the Skwaumesh and the Tsleil-Waututh together with the Musqueam comprised a loose fitting tribal band. But the Musqueam people, whose chief at this time was Flying Sturgeon, were also related through family ties to both former mentioned clans and lived primarily south of the river. The totem dear to the Skwaumesh was the orca whale, the raven was dear for the Tsleil-Waututh and the sturgeon was close to the heart of the Musqueam. Like all old world people throughout the continent (indeed, the world over, as far as anybody knew) they all revered the Thunderbird. This was a mystical bird that these people identified with the white headed and white tailed sea eagle of the region.

The people were a tough people, but a gentle people all the same who loved each other. They were respectful of the Earth along with the sun that gave them life; them and other elements and compounds, and they understood their place in this heaven (Nirvana) along with the other animals and many creatures that populated the earth by the grace of the Great Spirit. Although they believed in the Great Spirit they didn't have a tsaba, or in this case an assembly of gods such as the Hellenic or Amoran Empires had. Traditional agitators and raiding shop-lifters to Xats'alanexw's lower assemblage of peoples were the menacing Laich-kwil-tach (also Kwakwaka'wakw) whose traditional lands were extent throughout the area of the northern channel that pierced through the conglomeration of islands between the mainland and the big island at the top of the broad strait that separated Xats'alanexw's southern people from the big island. But in turn, these Kwakwaka'wakw kept the Xaayda (Haida) nation who inhabited the island of Xaayda gwaay that lay north of the big island at bay.

Central to the coastal land (where these peoples villages were placed) is the village of Xwayxway that means Place of the Mask. Out front and around Xwayxway were tall, thick, straight poles made from the trunk of a cedar-tree. On and out of these poles were carved and painted masks and spirit forms of stylized objects, mostly of animal index (tokens). These he was informed by Xats'alanexw represented the conjunction of the natural phenomenon and the human psyche. The mask was the symbol of transformation and the art of transformation was powerful medicine. This spiritual art was guarded and remained in the hands of the so-called medicine men, the shamans. The conjunction of these objects (which were represented in the spiritual world) with humanity also blended with their ancestral footprint. To these Skwaumesh and the Tsleil-Waututh peoples (along with all their fellow coastal nations) their ancestors were not dead. In fact nobody and nothing that was animated becomes dead, only changed and now placed in a different dimension. Dyfed immediately understood this. Dyfed noticed that the mask was a ceremonial object and had a place of reverence among all the people here, unlike the imperial masquerade balls (attended by the aristocrats and the decidedly un-noble nobility) that descended into drunken orgies he had witnessed in the City of Amor.

The mast was a sacred object, too. Carvers of masks were spiritual folks, and their art and their story and their ceremony were not mere secular entertainment, joyous though they may be. This was religion reduced (in many ways) to its common and natural denominator and was very carefully controlled. Symbols of the totem and the medicine of the mask were essential to help maintain the levels of their people's being and to remain in harmony with the Great Spirit's dissemination. It was very much part of their living genius. As for ceremonies, it was the potlatch that was the most important of all.

There were many types of minor ceremonies among these folks but the potlatch was of paramount importance. Although it had diplomatic and even certain confrontational aspects effecting power struggles among the more powerful players, the potlatch was first and foremost about transformation and its only transcending symbols were the Mask and the Idea of the natural impermanence of everything by the ever present bestowing and of the taking away. This cycle takes place for everything each in its own time. Potlatch represented this and was the grand ceremony of ceremonies. Its power was obvious to the intelligent white men who came later for potlatch was the first of many things they banned alongside its ceremonial drumming. In the hands of these indigenous peoples, according to the attitude then of the immigrants from Europa, the drum was a dangerous weapon; it was a terrorist weapon, a weapon of mass destruction.

Dyfed and Ceredwyn's homestead was located on a north westerly jutting peninsula. The peninsula is in the shape of duck's head that is turned with its bill turned to the right and facing east. The top of the duck's head along with its beak forms a narrows through which the sea flows into the large inner inlet. The duck is leaning back with its head turned and its bill twisted. The bottom of the duck's bill (from which hangs some bits of algae and weeds) and the front part of its neck demark a pointy sharp and narrow bay that ends in mud flats in the midst of the duck's throat. Dyfed made plans to build a dock and boat-building site just beyond the mud flats on the south shore of the inner inlet. The village of Xwayxway was located up top where the duck's beak begins and faced east toward the inner inlet. The big open bay and the sea-strait are to the west of this. Beyond this is the big island. A dead-end river-like tidal sny that penetrated for about two Amoran miles inland of this open bay may be considered the under belly of the floating duck which (as already stated) has its head turned to the right facing the east. On higher ground, somewhere just south of the Duck's throat and overlooking the mud flats lagoon area and his harbour, was where Dyfed began to clear timber. In time it was to become Couver City's west end. These thoughts were pure nostalgia for him as Dyfed now brought them to mind.

The location they chose was near the topside of a gentle hill was above and east of the muddy flats and tidal lagoon. The sturdy timbered structured house was eventually to become a two storied building and from its roof garden patio you could have seen the sea bay and the straits to the southwest. On the other side one could look down onto the lagoon to the west and from the front terrace you could survey the harbour and boat-building area to the north and watch the orcas[55] skim-surfacing the inlet water on the prowl for vulnerable seals and such. All around was a thick, tall-treed green forest which transmitted the howl of the wind in it branches while Xats'alanexw's Place of the Mask emitted its sounds of sing and chanting and drumming that clearly reached Dyfed's homestead. They camped here first while they selectively cleared a view of the horizons to the west and the east in order to gather enough large trunked timber. Before them on the horizon to the south beyond the tidal sny was the scented forest that teemed with game and beyond that was the tidal flats and the wide mouth of the Sto:lo River.

The summer sun was hot here in this climate, the sea air refreshing which slightly cooled the land and all around the natural beauty that surrounded them seemed boundless. But what occupied a greater part of Dyfed's attention were the trees. This was a land of dense, temperate semi-rain forest that consisted mainly of cedar, fir, and hemlock, interspersed with maple and alder, varieties common the world over. But never before had even Dyfed seen such enormous giants as what grew here, and it was with great

---

55 Also known as killer whales and more locally as black fish.

difficulty that he felled and split only the couple of cedars needed into the heavy timbered lumber for their dwelling.

During the following solar cycles, they finished constructing a sturdy home built of squared, adzed-faced cedar on top of a natural rock foundation with three large, flat-sided stone chimneys. By early summer of the next year Dyfed and Ceredwyn had settled into the first floor of the domus-abode. Dyfed selectively cleared a little more land around their domicile and burned slash and brush over the next few years to create an open, but shaded parkland surrounding their homestead. The locals were amazed at its construction and marvelled at its size until it dawned on them that the white man was building two communal long-houses of his own, one on top of the other that were big enough for both the communities to use jointly. Why else would it be so grand? Otherwise, it would all be needless labour. That is…unless this pale skinned chief of somewhere or another was expecting to be joined by his sizable clan who were somewhere hard on his heels. It was about then that he couldn't get any more help with the moving and lifting of heavy objects. It was then that he had to design and build mechanical advantages into his building and lifting techniques. After the big long-house was half completed and Chief Pale Face Mountain Lion's white tribe hadn't yet arrived and moved in with him, by the following Autumn many of the locals had. This was their way — *en to pan*: one for all and all for one — so Dyfed couldn't just throw them out on their ear and tell them it was private property. Private was in their person but did not exist on common ground per sé, or in property really of any kind. In fact the idea and the word for property (one's own; ownership) didn't exist for them, though bold men always knew when they had crossed the line and usually then someone lost their life. Personal meant extended family or more often the entire settlement.

Dyfed also fashioned his own first gigantic dugout complete with mast and lug rigged sail, all with local help and expertise. So, here at last, for the first time since he and Ceredwyn had fallen in love all those years ago, they were together in their very own home; a world away from the disquiet of will and intention and institutions along with life's other pollutants that existed in the world as a poor substitute in place of real and vibrant civilization. He recalled that pollution always had that particular smell of Amor about it. But not here at that time that he was remembering back to there wasn't. Not now, not yet. Also on quiet evenings Dyfed and Ceredwyn could easily discern the wispy smoke rising from Senakw (Snauq) across the bay from their new partially erected home.

(The visiting Visigoths and Vulcan's raspberry sundae)

'When you meet a master swordsman, show him your sword.
When you meet a man who is not a poet, do not show him your poem.'

LIN CHI *(LINJI YIXUAN) CH'AN MASTER*

Meantime, the noble Xats'alanexw was having trouble with one of his wives. She was the executive of the Senakw settlement. So, placing his eldest son in charge, Xats'alanexw took the opportunity one day to take his leave of absence and lead an excursion that Dyfed had organized to seek out and explore the big island. So one autumn day Dyfed, Ceredwyn and Xats'alanexw along with Dyfed's little bear dog he got from Xats'alanexw which he called Edward the Third, they and their small seafaring crew were paddling passed the smoking white god high over their left paddle arm and shoulder as they wended their way west toward the big island. It was mid morning and the air was fresh and the men were paddling like O'Billio and singing at the top of their voices as the porpoises skimmed alongside when suddenly there was an earth shaking, gigantic explosion. The sea slopped and sloshed and the earth rumbled and shook. As they all glued their eyes to the mountain god in surprise, a great mass of flaming debris erupted out from the top and passed through the middle of a smoke-ring shaped grey mist that clung close just above the mountain's summit: This was followed by a column of grey smoke that began to disperse and settle. Fortunately, the wind was coming from the northwest and blew the smudge away from them. Before evening, after encountering seven or eight giant sized waves, they wound their way through some small islands as they approached the big island and arrived at a little cove that was positioned just beneath a large round rocky hump that the locals told them was the left eye brow of a submerged giant creature. Dyfed thought that this was unlikely. The night before they left their inlet home, there was something else that was unlikely, too. Dyfed had noticed that the dogs and other animals about (that included birds) had for reasons unknown all gone quiet and were acting strangely. This should have been the people's warning signal for animals are exceedingly alert to seismic disruptions like earthquakes and volcanoes hours and sometime days before we are. Though the night was cloaked in silence as was the morning as they cut through the smooth waters towards the shore, here, where hardly any beach greeting them and the forest of fir and the peeling red arbutus extended well out from the shore and over the water, the evening birds here were now out and in the throes of their musical performance of the year as if it were a heavenly prayer to the mountain god across the water. This giant creature whose snow cap was tinged orange by the downing sun (having spewed out its mist and smoke) and the fiery red lava now running down its sides in streaks made Dyfed now think that it must have looked like a raspberry sundae.

As they waded ashore pulling the canoes in under a low canopy, Dyfed kept a keen eye out for mountain lions that (contrary to their name) don't always live in mountains but while on the hunt will often comb the beach shores for easy game and seek safety upon the boughs and branches of trees. It wasn't until then as they had entered into the shadow that the shoreline cast, that he realized there were a hundred people silently watching them from the heavy forest that grew along the shore's embankment here. Then all of a sudden a thunder bold came down from out of the sky (followed by a great crack) and reaching through the smoke, the mist and the fiery lava it struck deep inside the earth to the mountain's roots. Dyfed decided there and then that Vulcan (the Amoran god of fire) was announcing that he was present and in attendance; so pay attention. Suddenly the local big island people let out in unison a loud OOOHH…AAAHH! Xats'alanexw had told him that these big island folks also spoke the same Sa'lish language as their brothers and sisters on the mainland. Night fell quickly after that. The local people who had been monitoring the great explosion of fire and smoke that was taking place across the waters showed that they received an equal entertainment value upon setting eyes upon Ceredwyn and Dyfed who they saw as shining gods, possible connected to Vulcan and the pyrotechnic display of the decade that same day. None of these people present has actually ever seen Dyfed and Ceredwyn but word of their arrival years ago had got around. But only a few of the local chiefs and their suite had actually journeyed over to his homestead to look them over. They immediately dubbed him the lion man. But the other one was altogether quite remarkable. They thought she was a goddess or consort of the mountain itself whose head, like the other, was now all aflame, and it appeared that she was being transported by the lion-man to her waiting and accommodation suite on the big island with the help of slaves from among their own kind until the excitement blew over. In a sense Ceredwyn made a far greater impression on these people then Dyfed did, but they were both warmly welcomed. Dyfed, however, had made a contact and it was one that was to be very long lasting, even unto to the end of his days in this dimension.

He and Ceredwyn discovered that the people hereabouts were the Tsa't-lip and were the cousins of the Ma'la-hat who dwelled in the bluish ruffled higher ridges in the distance. Further to the northwest, in the eastern belly of the island, lived other cousins, such as the Kow-a-ch'n. In time, Dyfed would become a trusted brother to these people, but at the moment (as he now fondly remembered) he was just the ferryman and they ignored him while showing Ceredwyn the utmost courtesy and reverence.

The two Albions decided to remain on the island with the Tsa't-lip until late the following spring. Xats'alanexw and three canoes with a skeleton crew remained with them. The rest returned. That winter was colder than usual and by the time of the full moon that followed the autumn equinox, the head of the island was covered in a blanket of snow and the forest lake, near to where Dyfed and Ceredwyn camped in a oak forest, remained solidly frozen for over a month during that winter. It was almost two moons after the spring equinox before they struck out again and began island hopping along the east coast of the big island. As they enjoyed fishing behind the floating kelp beds for oolicans (also eulachon), and taking refuge among the crystal coves of the archipelago that nestled in the shelter of the island, Dyfed and Ceredwyn were enjoying a happy holiday.

The first sign that the world of mysterious design was about to change occurred while Dyfed and Ceredwyn were camped on a small island. Shortly after daybreak of the second day, however, Dyfed and Ceredwyn were astonished to see a large dugout swiftly approaching them through the mist and a drizzle of rain. Full of what appeared to be wild beasts of the forest, the craft came from the direction of the village towards them as they stood close to their fire that blazed up from the beach into the damp morning air. The sight of this crew was unusual enough, but most amazing of all was an enormous bird creature that was perched on the prow of the dugout. This animal, while prompting its companions on, bobbed its beaked head backwards and forward, and from side to side, and flapped its wings in order to keep its balance on the narrow bow as the dugout tossed and pitched among the choppy seas.

Suddenly, as the boat's prow struck the beach with the whoosh of a wave, the great bird lifted its beak and gave out a shriek and a squawk. Then stretching itself, as though it were about to lift off and fly away, it flapped its wings and fluttered off its perch only to alight heavily upon the loose pebbles with a sound that reminded Dyfed of clashing swords. The others followed. Dyfed felt rather tense as these strange animal men approached them, but when the bird creature whipped off his head dress and the man's dark eyes regarded Ceredwyn's magnificence with disbelief, his concern abated.

These people, like all the coastal residents, were adept at fishing for the giant creatures that swam in the ocean and in catching schools of oolicans with their nets which they made from strips of cedar bark. In fact, almost everything these people used was made from the cedar. Besides their dugouts, their longhouses, and the material used for their totems and other carvings, fishnets, rope, baskets, and even their apparel originated from this tree that was known as the provider of life. For was necessary that their fabric shed the dampness of the mist that whitened all but the lower legs of the trees, and protect them from the ocean spray that flew up from the rocks along the beach, as well as from the drizzle and the great down pours that fed the jungle of salal and ferns, and fattened the thick carpets of moss that grew up across the vertical face of rocky cliffs. Consequently, the men and women who populated this coast fashioned all their clothing from a tightly woven but flexible material made from fine strips of cedar bark that acted as an ideal water repellent.

An oddity, which Ceredwyn and Dyfed noticed right away, even among the Sa'lish, was these people's propensity to wear hats. The people of all the nations on this continent (at least those whom they had come across) wore headdresses during ceremonies, and fur muffs around their heads to keep their ears from freezing during extreme conditions, but otherwise, apart from a feather or two, they went about bareheaded. But these coastal people, on the other hand, all wore a peculiar, tall, wide brimmed hat for every day use, and the Kwa'ki-tol and the N'oot-ka constructed this covering from material made of the tightly woven cedar bark. As their cotton constructed clothing had become threadbare and worn through long ago, Dyfed and Ceredwyn had also adopted the dress of the local Sa'lish. Dyfed, of course, continued to wear his lion skin, but now with the dampness and continual rain, it sagged heavily upon his back. So the white folk traded some metal fish hooks for weaved cedar capes to wear over their hide clothing, and tall conical shaped hats to place upon their heads in an attempt to shed the ever present precipitation.

After continuing down the west coast of the island, Ceredwyn and Dyfed arrived at its southern head in early summer. Here they entered an inlet and passed the place which the locals called Kamo-soon. From here they canoed inland for about two and a half Amoran miles to an opened area that constituted a shallow lake. They were not able to make much headway past this point, so after beaching their craft, they walked for a few hours in the direction to the spot where they had previously camped upon first arriving on this big island. It was raised area forested with large oaks that was near the south end of a wooded lake. The oak forest lay on a slope facing south where a marshy bottomland ideal for gardening abutted up against it. Realising that a salt water bay just to the east of them was closer to access, and more direct to return to their home on the mainland, Dyfed sailed their craft around the south end of the island and beached it in plain view of the big white smoking mountain.

The weather was very warm at this point and one or two local children were swimming in the lake. One day, in the middle of the afternoon, Dyfed heard a bevy of exited voices go by, and seeing a group of Tsa't-lips hurrying passed their bivouac, he called out and asked them what the matter was. They answered that some Ma'la-hats had come to alert them of the arrival of strange men who sailed in a big canoe and worshipped a cross. Apparently these men had come ashore up island but were now sailing south, and should be within sight from the highland above the bivouac.

So Dyfed and Ceredwyn walked to the embankment that looked east over the islands of the archipelago and the strait. Before them, much to Dyfed's dismay, and lying at anchor in the very bay that he and Ceredwyn had paddled into on their first arrival, was a number of tall ships, one which whose name he was just able to read...'Buenos Noticias'. His eyes immediately sought out her insignia, hoping to see the grinning skull, but instead he saw at once that its only colours were those of the Visigoth established Empire of Hispania, and that they fluttered unaccompanied.

The locals now conjugated around Dyfed and Ceredwyn, and their chief, Little Beaver along with Xats'alanexw, anxiously inquired after Dyfed's opinion about the vessel. Suddenly, a puff of white smoke appeared off her starboard bow and began to drift astern, followed a moment or two later by a loud report. This startled these poor people and Dyfed explained that the sailors were firing cannon shot, probably to frighten them before coming ashore. Then, as they watched, a couple of launches set out from two of the boats, just as Dyfed had suspected, and were quickly rowed towards the beach. Dyfed did not climb down the embankment toward them but remained were he was. He would let the Visigoths from Hispania come to him, instead. Already he could see an officer, a priest, and four well armed men climb up from the beach onto a meadow that was directly below the highland.

Having instructed Ceredwyn to stay out of sight and remain upon the heights, when the sailors finally topped the rise Dyfed (accompanied by Xats'alanexw the six members of the Tsa't-lip tribe) approached the Visigoths who suddenly halted in their tracks. Little Beaver walked ahead, with Dyfed following behind with the other men. The priest made a sign of the cross in the air, and one of the sailors cautiously stepped forward displaying some shining trinkets. These were mirrors and useless metal trinkets that he dangled from his fingers. The Visigoths spoke among themselves, and Dyfed listened while they quickly passed judgement upon these children of the earth in a most derogatory manner. Suddenly, Dyfed stepped up beside Little Beaver with Xats'alanexw by his side and addressed the officer who he took to be the captain. Speaking in the tongue of the Visigoth Dyfed said.

"You aren't actually expecting to buy us up, along with this land, with just a hand full of baubles of bling and some cheap ornaments, are you, signor captain?' He glanced disdainfully down at the glittering litter. 'For if that is your intention,' he said, throwing a glance at the scrawny looking priest with bad skin, 'then you will need a thousand fleets, composed of a thousand ships full to the brim with gold. If not, then at least a promissory note in the name of your sovereign King Philip of Hispania, endorsed by the House of Hapsburg, guaranteeing the wealth of his entire empire (along with Duke Francisco Gomez as a hostage to guarantee and bind the abiding of the agreed terms) in return for only the land you can see from the spot where you now stand, and not an acre more, and then only after we give it further considerable thought.'

The Europaean men of Visigoth discordancy were startled to hear a bearded and strange looking savage speak their language so fluently, never mind what were stated with those words. Although they retained their distance of four or five paces, they closely scrutinized Dyfed. Meanwhile, their temperament went from one of arrogance to acute caution and their casual discourse, which until then had continued between them, ceased. Little Beaver, who had easily discerned the sudden change of mood among the visitors, laughed out loud in three sharp notes, while the other five of the others followed suit. This seemed to alarm the men from the galleons even more, and the priest crossed himself and took a step backward.

'And I can further inform you, *caballero*,' continued Dyfed, 'that if it is gold that you are seeking here instead, you will not live to find it. True, after the filth and squalor of Madrid we noble and golden, sun-burnt-red skinned men and our bountiful land must appear to you…'*alegre como su sol*'. However, it is only the bounty of our sunny land and the spiritual light of nobility that shines out of us, not gold, that dazzles you, for we have none of the yellow metal destined for your hands here. Furthermore, the Strait of Anian[56] that you also seek is not a passage in the real world that you think it is. Anyway, it is much further south of here (he fibbed) if it were. So go seek it there, or anywhere but here.'

Later when the Visigoths weighed anchor and drifted south a bit with the current and then turning, tacked west into another strait (eventually named after the Hellenic marine pilot Ioannis Phokas who navigated for the king of Hispania) that would flush them back into the open ocean to the west, Dyfed, Little Beaver, and a few of the younger men followed the vessels closely with their eyes. Ceredwyn remained and waited by their bivouac and Xats'alanexw and his men returned home immediately. Near the settlement of Kamo-soon (Camosun) atop a well-fortified point that overlooked the strait they watched the ships pass by. There were dangerous shoals and treacherous rocks off shore here which at high tide were mostly just barely submerged and many of those there that day hoped that these ships would all run aground and become wrecked and all the sailors drowned (pronounced drown not drowd-ded). However, the men of the 'Buenos Noticias'[57] that led the fleet, tacked their vessel far out from shore and beyond the rocks and shoals. Finally they disappeared beyond the western point towards the great Peaceful Ocean. Wishful thinking aside, Dyfed now knew that only preparation for change could deliver these earth people. When Dyfed and Ceredwyn returned home to their peninsula on the inlet, they found their home had been burned and its charred remains lay collapsed among the foundations. It was a heart wrenching sight which saddened them both and resulted in anguish and grief. At first Dyfed had suspected that the Sa'lish had been responsible, or irresponsible, as the case may be, but Flying Sturgeon who had crossed the Sto:lo River to observe, told him that strange white men had come ashore from a ship that was powered by billowing clouds and discovering the home, had utilized it for a few days while they made obscene gestures towards the people. Xats'alanexw, of course, had been with Dyfed and was not available to advise the tribe. Then, upon their departure, they had torched the building.

---

56 Anian is the northwest passage: or the northeast passage when searched from the west coast of Merika as it was by Capt. Drago (Dragon or Drake) of Albion in 1578CE, among other later seafarers).

57 Captain José Sebastian Ortega Fernandez's fleet flagship.

(Couver City)

'I am myself the matter of my book' but '...what do I know'
MICHEL EYQUEM DE MONTAIGNE

As Dyfed sat at his desk still absorbing the flood of so many reassuring memories, he then recalled that after twenty decades his homestead settlement that (aside from steady use) had begun to emit a slight and hollow echo of an incipient industry-hum. With a layer of pine sap floating upon salty breezes mixed with gear oil juxtaposed with the sting of horse manure and hemmed in with the constant chopping and sawing and hammering noises that reverberated alongside sounds and smells of the logging and timber industry mixed with sea air, the acrid environment of fishing boats and canneries and of mining equipment and warehousing and of horses and carts and shouts and laughter as the Europaeans started to arrive gave Couver City its unique atmosphere. So, what became of old Couver City? He remembered that soon the arriving newcomers, though often stand-offish, with the locals became fastened and cobbled together and controlled by the white collared, city slicker hat crowd that were housed no longer in tent and cabins but in the tall head offices. That's what had become of Couver City, of late. Alas! Progress, he thought.

Couver City by this time, though, had now arrived into the twenty-first century, as a vibrant show and was moving forward destined for the majors. It was still kept clean by the winds that either swept off the Peaceful Ocean or blew down off the snow-sprayed and fir covered peaks that loomed close by. Those salty fresh and evergreen sweet breezes seemed constantly to flush the straight sloping streets of the grid-developed city with breathable air as each avenue and lane stretched between tall buildings down to bays and inlets in every direction. And the coastal mountains — that jagged, rolling escarpment...that continental fault whose sentinels towered up into the blue sky to watch over the city — snagged most of the prevailing humidity that was sponged up from the sea's surface (the ocean-effect) into the atmosphere under a warm and sunny climate. And as the humidity level climbed, and as the puffy white clouds turned heavy then coagulated into a grey making them unable to summit the sky-high and blur the rangy horizon that blocked its way, then the moisture would suddenly sift through soft, porous rainbows and shower down onto the city. As such, its straight streets were washed and made clean at regular intervals.

This condition seemed to curtail those adverse ecological effects that plagued most large modern cities at that time. But by the time that this metropolis' original back forty with is stumps, axe blades and horses out to pasture were pushed another forty more Amoran miles further out that enclosed today's suburbs, the situation had changed drastically. And as time wore on, with urban sprawl expanding in all-important cities throughout the world, festering carbuncles began to attach themselves here as well. At first this festering was noticeable just on the outer industrial sections that sealed its circumference like a rind. But this rind grew thicker and thicker both inward and outward. It was this grimy rind of industry and manufacturing that pumped out toxic effluences and soon the showers that softened the parks and the city gardens contained high amounts of nitrogen and sulphur dioxide. Now a city worker would turn raw as the day wore on and the sulphuric sweat dripping from his eyebrows burned his eyes and soured his lips. Couver City was now becoming a major urban centre unfit for living in.

    Major urban centres were a premium now for the anxious and the restless schizophrenia fraught psyche of the sorely compensated yet entitled-all-the-same big brained human who needed to dwell in an all compensating, exclusive all inclusive, globally programmed security structure with additional bells and whistles designed for their own personal ear-marked fears that the trendy schizoid-maniac cult and crowd all had in common. From there, like the cocks atop their relative ammonia stinking dung heaps radiating particles of nitrogen and potassium, and what with the trail of cock-ups these turds of nerds left scattered in the debris trail of relations and connections of their life they left in their wake behind them. Along with comfortable shoes, a warm place to shit and the lion's share of all the fruits of labour from the countryside that robbed the clusters of domiciles and urban architecture that was light in the loafers and a spring in its step that now required a heavy carbon footprint tax and bill for transport costs to boot-freight it into the cosy corners of the community bedrooms. Here, each operational engineer, administrator, human resources personnel, maintenance and service crew at large, standing by with their colour-coded identity labels that read: '*Lasciate ogne speranza, voi ch'intrate*'[58] sewn onto their lapels so that they could mete-out the demands of society's inmates' for their lithium laced sweet-coated smiles with their medication ration licenses in hand to dish out sundaes of soma-sodas with a cherry on top that was provided by special delivery sugar-daddio-bureaucrats hardly at work on pensionable time far from the level and it crowd. This was their evening of the Sundowners that they never really earned. And in the morning, no one will remember them. Yet despite all this accompanying bravado, they didn't even understand, not one single one iota, about their life and their reality among the phenomenon in which they were all immersed, nor were they even able to competently comprehend themselves in the three-dimension in any realistic way.

    Like all the kings' horses and all the kings' footmen and emperors fantasies of old, they didn't know their head from a hole in the ground or how to raise and tend to cattle and crops, to forge or fashion this exquisite object or that blunt instrument into existence or even how to construct something meaningful with purpose such as a sunny disposition and personality or even personal integrity, never mind the imagination to construct a shrine such as a Versailles or an Alhambra or write a readable volume, or paint, draw, inscribe, mark or chisel some pleasing pictorial thing, to name just a few of many talents, and the infrastructure needed, for a goodly and well ordered society.

    Now the cities in the new world appeared to be constructed of shards of steel and glass set high on concrete pedestals. Once again the structures of shock and awe rose into the clouds while the masses at their feet pretended not to grovel, and aside from paying their taxes while they were at it, they filed in once again like drugged automatons and loaded up the shiny silver collection plates each day. Meanwhile, few understood that the high priests of every semi-civilized era known to the hoi polloi have always had to totally rely on expertize for which the high priests and their shining gods themselves

---

58 Abandon all hope, ye who enter here.

had no cognizance or skills for, whatsoever. This ingenuity, aptitude and felicity that the high priests of regiment and uniform of social order lacked were the talents of scholarly poets, free-thinkers, philosophers, inventors, artisans, engineers, teachers, medics/nurses, miners, forgers, fabricators, public service workers and jacks of all trades of imagination, intellectuals and academics that each marched to a different drummer, and supported all by the equal and fair wages for a safe workplace Brother and Sister-hoods, were the very people necessary for the high priests of the economy and finance branches of Capitalism's next meal, if not their next breath. Hopefully, it would stay that way. But Dyfed didn't think most people would buy into that, and so it seemed that a collapse into misery and suffering on a catastrophic level was immanent: But this happened only if it was in one's nature to think such a thing and pull such sensations into your own personal phenomenon. It's always up to the performer on the stage of life to be able to act just as they feel fit. But in this, of course, commonality across society is everything. We all make our own heavens and our own hells here, but we are also loyal subjects to the nature of the current vibrations as a whole. Therein lies the danger.

Up and at 'em one more time, was the call to arms; but it was just the echo of Dante's *basso loco* and the precincts of hell all over again. However, now the discarded apparatus that once represented their well being, that glorious fair and equal wages for job positions Brother and Sisterhood that seemed only to last for a day in the sun in this era before the machinations governing industrial clouds were drawn closed across the scope of the aforementioned's mercy-guilds, and where it soon followed that the motion to reintroduce the return of misery for a pittance that was seconded, and then all being in favour, found itself passed. And with the wringing of hands and the worry wrinkles of a mother's brow as if watching her sons march off to war, the wise looked out across the land knowing full well that its famine of despoil would start with the weak, the disposed, the ignorant, the poor and work its way up to the middle class and then the nouveau-riche until it ate like acid up into the soil roots of the high priestly one per cent cadre who now owned ninety-nine per cent of everything on the land but didn't have the wisdom nor the aptitude to turn their rig of despoil around even if they had a whole three thousand mile diameter continent to do it in. How now that so many degrees of entitlement and its franchises would reverberate. From the bottom right up to the top it would trouble even to the loftiest, and noble beggars; and even the saviour Virgil would soon be replaced by Joey Virgo, and Dyfed's old acquaintance Count Agenbite of Inwit, who had taken himself off to a far and distant spot in New Zeeland (New Sealand) amid the Peaceful Ocean, had refused to visit his old friends of any kind who didn't have clear breathing air, clear water and a clear conscious to share.

(House of Lucifer estate Sto:lo River, Bountiful Valley home)

'Home is the place where, when you have to go there, they have to take you in.'
ROBERT FROST

As stated earlier, this residence where he was currently sitting at his large office desk, was about fifty Amoran miles inland from his old Couver City home where presently the salt chuck and the tide lapped lazily against the shoreline. Opening up beach allotments covered in carrousels for rent here at the eastern end of the Bountiful Valley was, apparently, still premature. But the time may come. The property his estate was built on consisted of a number of farms, thirteen in all. They straddled some of the most beautiful agricultural land around. The initial problem had been, he recalled now, that the farms hadn't all been available for purchase, at least not at the same time. That they weren't all for sale wasn't a bad thing, though, for it allowed him to approach the farm owners individually at different times to offer them a lucrative price for their land rather than conducting a sudden attack blitz. He didn't approach them himself, either. Here *the pack* had helped out with more than one individual proposing as an eager land purchaser. This managed to defuse any suspicion of a mass take-over of land by some behemoth, greedy bad nasty with deep pockets such as an international corporate conglomerate would have and one that's on the capitalistic make. That method would only tactlessly draw attention from those governing factor agents that these days had virtually become the eyes and ears of the former, anyway. Indeed, this method of Dyfed's had cemented the impression, not only by word of mouth among the outlying farmers that stretched out all the way down the flat sprawling Sto:lo River valley to the west, but also with the lands title office and insurance companies that as far as these deep pocketed exploiters of the land were concerned, nothing of that sort was happening here. Which of course was correct.

This conglomerated land estate which Dyfed finally assembled, backed up into a hilly and heavily forested area on the easterly section of the land and extended west for miles from here. All told it consisted of thirteen separate land holdings totalling seventy-two sections. This was considerable, for this made up seventy-two square miles of eighteen thousand, seven hundred and twenty hectares, or a whopping forty-six thousand and eighty Amoran acres. All of it registered under the Dominion Land Survey (DLS). He now remembered he had even set up apparent leasing tenants for different properties under the auspices of an agricultural co-op so as to thoroughly stump and confound any bureaucratic compilation of his business's true structure and its ownership.

He had also made sure that any sections of his newly acquired land that was normally productive (whether for crops or for dairy farming) continued without any change while he devised his overall plan. Very slowly he tore down what was not needed or was below his standard. There were a number of buildings (such as those many beautifully architectured barns) that were now considered quite old. They were big and red, or white, and faded. They were often just left open now to the starlings and other wildlife that flocked and conglomerated in them in clandestine concordance. These hollow and vacated vertical spaces and their large, broad and vertical placed flat-boarded sides blandly blanked out chunks of the blue sky, the green swathes of surrounding corn fields, and areas of the thick, dark brown loam of the earth. They were markers — boundaries of perception. And like subtle beacons they shone out from almost any standpoint, whether from a distance while one was passing by in a motor chariot by road, or by barge on a canal adjoining and fed by the river Sto:lo. And in the evening these giant structures jutted up and out into pale, fading skies that could make one — while standing in its shadow — feel excited again with an intrigue and playfulness of youth within that moment — within that life. In one way or another these heavy built barns with their stone foundations shoring up the bank of any number of irrigation canals — skirted with tall grass — that crept slowly in straight lines across the flattened valley, managed to touch up the beauty of a pastoral scene and furnish the natural world of the meadowlark, the raven, the fox, and the coyote with the gentle blend of organised humanity. And from inside and out, the lonely interior of these giant outbuildings were re-enforced by Dyfed's crew who reconditioned the giant structures of their jilted architecture and imposed something of a yesterday's sheen and importance that could not be missed but was often left un perceived by the dimensionally shallow. Otherwise, and in other words, they were left to be perceived as they were and acted as quiet, standoffish sentinels outfitted with auto dial-up International Mobile Subscriber Identity (IMSI) devices and other advanced surveillance of wave and vibrational tones active in the ether, watching, protecting, blending, recording, and deciphering mobile subscription identification numbers. And that was just a fraction of their electronic intelligence. This was his responsible guard duty of home management that measured individual wavelengths and not the trendy mass surveillance that, Dyfed intuitively knew, was essentially a futile exercise of not seeing the forest for the trees.

Now Dyfed's memory shifted forward practically to his present. And the city that currently occupied his attention on this day was precisely one of those stinking, festering sores long skilled in killing the natural world around it, though, that's not to say that millions of hoi polloi tried to. It was one of the most famous and certainly the first well maintained urban centres throughout the world for producing a climate of normality for the scads (and growing) human schizoids and multiple stages of psychopaths. In the end the city was just called Megatropolis. And it was from this city that Dyfed had quite recently just managed to escape his weeklong incarceration from an asylum, and then escape capture and probable death by the skin of his teeth that same night from the rooftop of his high-rise in one of his a company's merchant dirigibles. And this was not a slight against any dental hygienic practice he might have, either. And that escape had only been last night. Indeed, it hadn't been until the early wee hours of that very morning that he had arrived back on the estate here of the House of Lucifer that was sprawled across the Bountiful Valley through which the Sto:lo River flowed. The memory was still a nightmare; one from which he may have awakened but was left rattled all the same and unlikely to forget any time soon.

It had only been this afternoon, eastern standard time when it had all begun. In any case his reason for vomiting had been troubling. It was the cause of his chain of mistakes he had made upon his arrival recently back from the fifth dimension into the third and its tangled aftermath that resulted. It was something of a blur as the stark impressions that accompanied the memory of the last few days burned like a contagion into his imagination. He recalled looking out from his elaborately appointed Manna-hata district sky-roof apartment that until the day before had been secure. Manna-hata and the huge city of Megatropolis sprawled out surrounding him one hundred floors below to street level. He even remarked to Trachmyr that it appeared to be under siege. This was the case, not only from the approaching hurricane's right hook that was coming from the south east off the Atlas Sea and colliding with the coast of Merika here at this point, but from a calculated abandonment toward chaos of what seemed like street fighting being enacted below due to the condition of human pain, of human misery and untold suffering that was unfolding there. Quite fitting, he had supposed, that it happened to be Halloween and the Day of the Dead was soon to follow. Throughout the day there had been rumblings and sharp reports of missile exchange and dangerously sounding explosions that he could hear far beneath him at the street level. And there were other ghastly noises that made it sound like there was a running riot rampaging below as though there was no tomorrow. Fire had broken out in many places. Where the city's poorest postal codes had encroached and taken over much of the city to date, the scene was straight out of a Caravaggio canvas. Furthermore, more than half of all the districts that comprised the brightest lit city in the world were in darkness. Earlier Dyfed had given orders to go black across the board, and that meant to darken his building too. Black meant that from any external visual and electronic view focussed on his building, the information would be flat-lined and silently still with no apparent life form within. But inside it was still a flood of brilliance for its occupants to carry on as though it was still early in the twentieth century.

But soon overhead, and well above the aerial navigational lights of his building and all the other buildings in and around Manna-hata, a great churning and chopping got underway as the hurricane hit. The sight reminded him of rounded boats as they used to bob about in those peculiarly choppy seas that encircled the ancient city of Byzas. On this night it was the sky and not the sea that was something of a bobbing lightshow. A multitude of brilliant Fresnel fitted lens-type searchlights with reflectors were continually sweeping their allotted portion of the dark sky that night, he remembered. They were a marvellous display of multiple glowing pencil shafts. Many of these powerful beams of light criss-crossed the night sky and cut each other at mid beam while they swung through their orbits — catching giant air machines that were at anchor or had broken anchor — in their brilliant columns of white light. They were like twisting projector lights as in a darkened olden day movie theatre where upon striking the screen they depicted a grainy old motion picture film of battered zeppelins against a swirling and murky sky full of flak and debris with sirens wailing.

Although the lion's share of the city's tethered zeppelins hung like a cluster of pulsating artificial clouds marked with logos that hung and quivered above the city, screaming with the clicking, flapping, and high pitched humming of a thousand lanyards, guy lines, and flags that one would hear in an immense and thickly berthed boat marina during a heavy wind, some of the giant ships above had already broken free and were either being sucked into the spiralling dark mass of the hurricane or were caught, entangled in the tethers of other air ships causing a twisted and tangled mess. The tether-sturdy airships that stood their ground (that is air) to the coarse blasting wind and for the moment seemed unhampered by the counter tugging forces caused by dragging anchors and other chaotic debris which the blowing flotsam of airships had collected, were vibrating furiously like a pennant on speeding race car. They gyrated and shook with a vengeance, their guy ropes and tethers rattling, straining, and groaning while the wind screamed through them like a thousand banshees. Dyfed half expected to see an entire roof ripped free and lift off. He imagined it cartwheeling away in the ferocious gusts and saw in his mind's eye the flying roof's attached airship rapidly revolving around it like a fast swirling satellite, its tether shortening at an alarming rate as the two spiralling and revolving objects quickly and fatefully moved towards collision and total disintegration while the debris tumbled killer-like down into the city streets below.

Though thankfully he had returned safely home here to the sanction of the House of Lucifer's central control at his Sto:lo Ranch (a code name for the House of Lucifer), the future was no less foreboding for ahead loomed the spectre of another city that epitomized his disquiet. This urban venue was called Cloud Nine City and there was an accompanying problem that always made him throw up and feel dizzy, like now. And the crux of that problem was his part that he was being expected to play at ground zero in Cloud Nine City at zero hour. And that was Sunday, December 20 of this year at 18:00 hrs. He had been briefed about the plan just before his truncated capture, incarceration and escape back in Megatropolis that managed to turn the palms of his hand sweaty and cold. But it was in the hour that he arrived home (not that many hours ago) that he got the coded instructions as to his part they expected him to execute in the upcoming Cloud Nine Affaire, and instructed him as to how to proceed and when. And when was tomorrow, already.

It was to be the worst of the worst whereby the records of other holocausts, infernos and the olden day lances of blinding brilliance where the ultimate power of Zeus/Jupiter and Poseidon the shaker of the earth, all paled in comparison. Tick tock, tick tock was what he now constantly heard in his head. Here, without proper authority (which would never have been granted by the gods or even the Masters) had they been in charge and control: tick tock, tick tock as misappropriated, newly gained nuclear technology (whose repercussions were still little understood) had been channelled and the count down now started and set to unleash its evil power for the sole purpose to evaporate Cloud Nine City and thereby to exterminate completely and forever the scourge of the human Haploids. And when the countdown ended and the finger of fate on the lever-trigger to close the circuit and unleash the power and by the might of the nuclear material-stir, fry all and every life form within sight of Cloud Nine City would fry in a Nano second and then evaporate. But even that wasn't the worst of it, at least not for him.

Suddenly he threw-up on the carpeted floor beside himself.

Those currents of emotion were devilish, he thought; then suddenly he heard…

"Ah-so, there's no bout adoubt dat den, dat's fo-show. No no: doan yu fak we me –– cah-sak cah.'

It was Fan Tan (actually Tan Fan) the housekeeper from the land of Ch'in who had come in to clean up his vomit with a shovel and a dustpan. She seemed quite aroused, as in angry while Dyfed knew she was more than mildly concerned over his uncommon condition. She'd been with the House of Lucifer quite some time now, Dyfed thought as he watched her fuss. He hadn't seen her like this before. She was Sun Tan's (actually Tan Sun) wife, or at least one of them. Sun Tan had worked for him ever since the days when Dyfed used to run his show up and down the Peaceful Ocean coast from Couver City north to the Klondike and south down to Caulifornicatia. Sun Tan was his front man who in Couver City had fourteen laundry businesses, twelve restaurants (two of them Italian and one Greek), three used chariots sale lots and an illegal money recovery from bad loans business. One thing Dyfed remembered about Sun Tan, he got out front of whatever business he ran and blazed the trail. Sun Tan had been he and Ceredwyns' gardener at first when they had built their second home Couver City back in the late nineteenth century. Then he promoted him to general foreman of his harbour-dock operations close to the lagoon that was surrounded by anchor buoys.

Later, alone and agitated with a dry throat, Dyfed sat silently on the patio couch outside watching the evening simmer into the darkness. It had been quite a day and he hadn't even packed yet for his journey to the Atacama Desert via Denver Color-rado tomorrow afternoon. He had come out onto his study patio with a cut lead-crystal glass decanter of Irish whisky in one hand and a matching goblet in the other with a lit Cuban cigar clenched between his teeth. Sitting down he then poured himself a full glass neat. It had grown dark now and quiet. In the distance he heard the deep rumbling engine groan as mass times acceleration multiplied the metred out distance as the big diesel engine climbed the long, slow many miles of gradual incline pulling an Amoran mile of heavily laden steel cars of cargo. He lifted his hand and gulped down half the whisky in his glass. Suddenly he felt dizzy again and everything seemed to move around him. Then as he realized he might have kicked over the decanter, he tried to stand but pitched forward with a terrible, raging noise in his ears. Quickly, earthquake came to mind. Using his elbow on his knee to rise himself up again and stand up straight, he felt lost, maybe even frightened. He saw Sun Tan's face in front of him the glint in his shiny, half-moon eye. Whipping the cigar out of his mouth angrily with one hand he quickly moved toward the door but couldn't turn the handle as he still had the half full glass of whisky in his other hand. He wanted to shout at someone, but it was like trying to run or punch someone in a dream. He stopped to calm himself and take a deep breath. He then looked back in the darkness toward the sound of the night train that he could still hear that kept grinding upward and onward.

"What in the devil was that, Fan Tan,' he said as his old friend's wife quickly came out through the patio-doors to his rescue.

"Ah-lert-quake, I guess,' she responded.

"You mean an earthquake?' said Dyfed.

"Well she sho doan mean a milkshake, Mistah Dyfed,' shot back Sun Tan, Fan Tan's husband, as he emerged just then from inside the house, his shiny round face full of laughter and earthy mirth.

"What the devil?' said Dyfed without thinking about it.

"Yas Mistah Dyfed. You know all 'bout de devil. Your name is Lucifer. Ha, ha, ha, ha....'

"Shut up! Dyfed said good-naturedly. 'What do you know. Your Sun Tan, and it's the start of November. Sun Tan only comes out when you're in summer, or abroad at a place like Kreta or Mozambique. Ha, ha, ha, ha! Maybe even the Hawaiian Islands. Ha, ha, ha, ha. But how would I know? I have never been there. Now, don't just laze around. Find out what's going on and get Rosy on the phone.'

"Remember,' he continued, 'we got a lot of dairy cows out there on them fat green fields; and each one of them fat dairy cows have fattening udders full of milk. Rosy is in our Couver City office and she's in charge of customer service, if you haven't forgotten. And a damn good customer service head of department she is too. Now, do we provide deliveries of curdled milk, buttermilk, sour cream or milkshakes to our distributor? No. That's all done by retail. You should know that, Sun Tan, even if you're only my head of timber division. And something else you need to know. Now listen up, here! Under the circumstances of what happened yesterday, and after all those nosey yuppie city morons this morning who wandered in and stomped around all over the flower beds in their city-slicker clod-hoppers with not a cow-pie in sight anywhere, certainly not near our manicured lawns, I think I need to get over to the office of our city suite, *tout-suite*, at least before business hours begin tomorrow. I got some hot irons in the fire and I need to take care of business before I leave for South Merika tomorrow evening. Are you second-guessing me here?

"No sah. No sah!' Sun Tan said in a posturing manner.

(The eight-second cowboy's Ticket to Ride & the corporate conglomerate's golden logo Idea)

'Money is a new form of slavery, and distinguishable from the old simply by the fact that it is impersonal — there is no human relation between master and slave.'

LYOV (LEV) NOKOLAYEVICH TOLSTOI

When his guests (bowing low and uttering Namaste) had politely (with poise, palms clasped together) backed out of his door that he then instantly shut behind them, it left Dyfed wobbly legged and feeling immediately very alone and insecure. He had no idea what stark and nasty spirit or incubus horribilis had just galloped in a roaring fire-blaze and passed roughshod through his conscious mind ripping out synapse controlling cerebral stability. Peeking through a narrow outside window he glanced around the courtyard to see if candles or lamps were burning the midnight oil over at Morgant's. Seeing none he sat down alone in his quiet apartment mulling over the event. He glanced over at the hourglass and noted that the duration of the meeting of the minds with the men from the east had been only an hour; it had seemed like a week or a month, or maybe two. What had he agreed to with these people? he wondered. Between cold sweat flashes he ached with disquiet and unsettlement as though he had either just awakened from the dead, or had awakened to find himself entombed in an environmental coffin for the living dead.

Suddenly, when a quiet knock came from somewhere he almost jumped out of his skin. Finding himself on his feet he cautiously (even nervously) checked to see who was at his door. He jumped back inside his skin again when he saw Morgant's gnome like figure and intelligent face smiling up at him.

"You've had some important clients visiting, haven't you,' Morgant said in matter of fact way. 'All is well, I hope? I knew they were going to approach you so I enrolled Paredros of Phigaleia, and Democritus of Abdera to watch over you as best they could. How did it go?'

Dyfed, pale and shivering ushered him in, sat him down, and after providing him with a hot honeyed fermented brew immediately told him everything that had transpired between he and the men from the east. He then blurted out that at least he knew that Ceredwyn was alive and that one day they would be man and wife.

" So, all is well?'

"No!' said Dyfed breathing with some difficulty. 'All is not well. Not at all.'

"I take it then that one or two of them channelled you into a quasi-form of transformation and transmigration.'

"Yeah. And without a mask,' answered Dyfed.

"Pardon?'

"You'd have had to have being there,' said Dyfed.

"As you know,' Morgant said to Dyfed, 'or should know, this transcendental materialism shuffle stuff is not any easy feat. Vary the cycles of vibration, then what? In two shakes of a lamb's tail it's presto, Bob's your uncle? I don't think so! You think you will enter a new reality? It's not that easy. In the end it all comes down to the mind: unlike the brain, the mind is a marvellous, matter-less creation without a lick of energy (electrical or otherwise), as we know it. Now, if somehow the vibration rate of its materialistic properties, which is already higher than any other visible matter at hand, is increased multiply times then the ability to artificially transform and transmigrate becomes apparent with or without your approval,' Morgant said. It's akin to involuntary work. Everything is subject to many conditions that have taken the Masters a long time to understand. This is the trick. Its not easy, as you well know, but on the other hand exposure to exceedingly high vibration can destroy your body like *O Billio*. However, on the other hand tiny base particles that make up everything in the universe can actually vibrate at trillions of times per second. When it comes to electromagnetic waves, such as heat and light, it is frequency (number of vibrations or cycles) relative to the objective matter that determines what the wave will be and how it will affect the targeted object. There are other electromagnetic waves too, which explains how the Hyperborean masters' torcs and other devices of theirs used for communication function. It's all the same type of energy. It's the frequency per second (maybe one per second, or a thousand trillion per second) that determines what that energy actually does. All waves come from some vibrating particle somewhere that does not move but sets up the wave action. Presumably, since they make up your body, too, observing certain conditions leads one to understand something of the process. You have had so little time, Dyfed, but remember the adage, 'seek liberation through knowledge. This then is freedom from ignorance, also called self- knowledge known as Moksha. The question is how did the Masters here tonight accelerate the overall frequency? And the answer to that is through the pyramid of mind built on knowledge, not mumbo-jumbo hocus pocus and sleight of hand.'

Morgant asked him more about their deliverance. It seemed to him that while they were apparently seeking assistance and succour they were probing Dyfed. Concerned about this he then encouraged Dyfed to speak further. The latter then told Morgant about their initiative to set up a trade route between the Far East across the world to Amor. He mentioned too that they had warned him about a disruptive individual who they told him they knew was already known to him in the business world here in Amor. That man was Potamus Purblebal, and they also asked about Gorgeous Giorgius Gregorius Florentius, Dyfed told Morgant. Also the committee from the east had told him that although the home address of Purplebal's House was Hipponensis Sinus, a hundred and fifty Amoran miles west of Carthāgō, this entrepreneur was first and foremost from the coastal city of Sur in the land of Khna (Kanaan). Furthermore, through probable incompetent actions, he had ruined the House of Apuleius for whom he had once worked. Perhaps, though, it had been intentionally after all, they had told him.

Potamus Purplebal was certainly known to Dyfed, all right, and he explained to Morgant that from what he already knew, and from what Rama had told him, Purplebal was anxious to secure contracts with Amor to expedite on behalf of the empire business from the Amoran provinces that were abroad, mainly from Khna and Aram. He told Morgant that his visitors indicated that they were in the process of setting up a caravan route from beyond Kashi in central Asia, through the Kuchan Kingdom to Inja, then across Mesopotamia and Anatolia, and into Europa to facilitate Amor's trade with the east. His Asian visitors told him, he said, that Purplebal was trying to set himself up as a middleman banker right at a pivotal point just before their envisioned caravan trade route took to the sea and spring boarded to the gates of Amor proper. And to that end Purplebal has entreated four other partner entrepreneurs. These were the likes of Furius Claudius, an entrepreneur and dance hall manager residing at Piraeus who was meant to anchor his control over that important section of the Silken Trail trade route; Pollox Scipio, a rich senator and investor was to sent envoys to set up operation at Tarsus; Asinius Scopalius, a rash and unreliable wheeler-dealer about town was to keep an eye on Knidos, and Constantino Asinine, a rich man's son who had already squandered his father's fortune was to be a go-between. Purplebal meant for these men to join him in forming a consolidated venture for inter-empire marketing. And that was why (Dyfed told Morgant) Rama had approached him to act as their advocate and help set them on towards a sound footing. The wise men from the east did not want this man Purplebal and his partners interfering, but knew there was little that they could do about it on their own. Could Dyfed help? Purplebal would get rich, they told him, at the expense of the Amoran consumers, otherwise, they said. So what's new? added Dyfed to Morgant.

It seemed to Dyfed this point that Morgant had felt satisfied that his enquiry had covered all the bases and aspects necessary for expedient conversation in polite company. Now he sought from Dyfed something else. Morgant now turned to inquire about the phenomenon that Dyfed had encountered while on sojourn abroad into that other time under Mencius and Ab Ram's influence. What reality was he aware of? he asked of Dyfed.

"Perish the thought,' Dyfed answered, 'but I've seen my own demise as clearly as if I looked down upon my own maggot corrupted corpse.' He shuddered again as he rose and walked to the cabinet where he kept his liquored potions of spirits along with a small box of laudanum.

His body, Morgant observed, moved like a sleepwalker. Grabbing a carafe of clear distilled grog and refilling his cup, he told Morgant that he didn't like it one bit. He'd become aware, he told him, of a cruelly ruled world much different again from the current cruelly ruled world. Albeit, he told Morgant, it was more pampered and a different but strange naivety existed there. There was intelligent and furtive enquiries, he continued to say, into the personal lives of folk by invisible agents with invisible surveillance methods that travelled unseen at the speed of light through the air lurking in abundance. He told him of great cities and wealthy corporate empires called nations populated by vast swaths of programmed, sub-organizing hoi polloi busy-bodies clambering officiously about this or that and operated fabulous land, air and underwater ships which they propelled by miraculous machines. The world was connected in ways impossible to explain or understand today,' he added. 'Like here, many folks there believed that the intrinsic condition to life was power and wealth, but more pronouncedly so. Sovereignty and its hallmark ideologies existed not in a superlative sense but were reduced instead to being superciliously superfluous and designed for an *I, my, me, mine* mentality that had global implications and repercussions. The division between the normally intelligent haves who were the movers and shakers and the have not's who were the unintelligent revolting masses was gravely blurred, he said. Consequently, global terrorism had been un-leashed to its full abundance. The former clique that composed the power elite who controlled the bus was not so much the wise and wonderful but strictly the wealthy like here. As for their minions, apart from being powerless they defied definition. But everyone was worse off from being self-possessed but materially even the downtrodden and destitute were richer by far. And this seemed to spring from something they called a democratic social politic combined by a free enterprise market. Another invention they called Laissez-faire that in a sense means anything goes, prevents the king's men or any such from interfering in private transactions. This I thought was a good thing, at first. But ultimately where discipline and authority along with good governance are lacking, Laissez-faire will incur greater problems in society and even overthrow institutions that protect the people.

The great conjuring trick here that these men and women of the future managed somehow to pull off with ease was that almost everybody believed they were better off than they had all been back in the olden days. It wasn't exactly true, though. Also, god, emperor, and kingdom had new definitions here in this future place, he said. Kingdoms moved to become privately owned by folks who wished to receive the benefits of the hard labour of the masses at large: Certainly a recipe for trouble. These were not done by plebiscites but by wily and often secretly contrived legerdemain. The premier representative of these nation states started out by being highly intelligent innovators and movers and shakers. But by the time that I exited to return here, when Mencius pulled the plug on me, I guess, these leaders were often just buffoons of some kind; usually of high profile that combined a trendy social talent with exceptional abilities to serve and service the elite. Seldom were these buffoons actually endowed with intelligence, for the actual leadership quality needed for leading the people had only become a slogan, and to appoint an individual with any character of non-conformity and a notion for free-thinking was deemed highly dangerous and far too insecure a thing to be undertaken seriously without strict control and guidance from the Haploids and their select minions from the hoi polloi class.

Dyfed then suddenly remembered something from his exposed projected outside of causational memory experience. It was a man who had achieved emperorship (actually he was referred to as President) who was intelligent and naturally did question the status quo. This questioning and its results, along with certain pangs of soul-searching that it brought forth, caused this president (on one fine, sunny, cool autumn day) to ride a cavalcade down between a city's two sidewalks lined with a huge throng of rubberneckers and well shysters and not so well wishers. It was the beginning of his next campaign to be re-elected, a political move that turned out to be a turkey shoot that got him self shot dead from unknown assassin(s) that formed a semi-circle of rifle toting killers at wait and on the ready. Of course, it had all been done for money, stupid. It was always the money. Greed created money and therefore money was begotten by greed. More importantly, he remembered that this man was his old friend Muns, John (of) Munster from Galaway who had once lived in Legion under the protection of Queen Carmanda. Thinking of him and how he was ignorant of what had lain ahead for him was very disconcerting for Dyfed, and Morgant was able to read the emotion on his face.

Currency, at this time, he told Morgant was essentially fiat currency. Fiat currency is part of the big hoax that the financial system actual is. And at this space/time it was actually only related to the symbol of wealth: i.e.: the denarius, or (as it was to be called) the Dollar. The dollar (and those who wielded it) controlled the people's god: of and by the people for the people. So, the Dollar people, Dyfed reasoned with Morgant, were the future Haploids and a select few of their minions. The rest of the hoi polloi were the potential followers. Unfortunately (for all), the ninety-nine per cent of the hoi polloi (including all of the Haploid minions) made up the rank and file of these followers. But that didn't mean that the remaining one per cent who were quasi dollar folks didn't happen to think that they were happier (meaning better off and had more money) under the new world plan as were the idiots that had been fooled into thinking they were, though they weren't. These "un-fooled" were the minions of the Masters of the Unknown Universe, or *pack* minions.

Of course, in a sense the hoi polloi's concept of being created in god's image was accurate. It was that they were too sophisticated to think simply and understand it in that way. God is life so of course humans are made in its image.

And another aspect of their religion was the concept that the ticket to ride untoppled the eight seconds of that ultimate condition for any cowboy was simply from the point of having the opportunity (come hell or high water) of being born or raised and schooled in one great sprawling urban centre of the world and being associated with, and affiliated specifically to, this or that giant corporate conglomerate's logo. It was this, and only this, that mattered, as opposed to remaining and being a rustic bumpkin hay-seed from nowhere's-ville (which was the entire remainder of the hoi polloi in the rest of the world at large) who were considered ignorant nobodies who didn't matter a lick. Here, he told Morgant, power and greatness was not based on morality or the retention of self gained knowledge. Nor was it attributed to the slow compilation of space/time anecdotes that help amass wisdom and where filial propriety (as existed in all truly human brothers and sisters environment) flourished. This seemed to have no importance whatsoever, he told Morgant, at this space/time he had found himself immersed in.

And there were no spiritual gods, either. None. No gods of rivers, not goddesses of mountains, no gods of compassion, or of love. Nothing. The only god he caught sight of was a blatantly fake, corrupted god they called Cash that is somehow (it was believed) closely related to wealth, at least in some way. Not even gold, silver or exquisite things had any real value to them anymore, not here anyway. These folks knew the price of everything but were incredibly ignorant of the value of anything, he told Morgant. People here were generally of the one-dimensional persuasion. And as such, in this space/time they were turning up cheap and shallow.

Anyway, this may have come about because folks were hardly valued at all anymore. The only thing of value was the grand medium for slavery. Its icon was the all valued promissory note. This was the ultimate IOU and the currency by decree known to one and all as Cash (dollar bill). Its purpose was for the purchase for any and all things that the heart desires, which to the wise happens to be the one and single most dangerous thing of all time. But such a pronouncement there would have only brought forth laughter, guffaws and then sharp, critical ridicule, he recalled. And like any happy god from the olden days that had (thighs of oxen, sheep or goats wrapped in fat and burnt in sacrifice to them) when this Cash God bought something for desire — in the cause and altered effect world which the third dimension had invented and which these folks had taken to a new level — it subsequently sold something else that caused exponentially more despair. Through a sense of indifference Cash magically distributed favours such as a reverence for and a fear of (along with a jealousy by the Cashless) toward those who the god Cash had rewarded. The Cashless were seen by the former to be those puny miserable folks who didn't have or didn't keep the faith. They were the unbelievers and the punishment being skint or bankrupt was their just rewards. And for those who cleaved and worshipped the holy semen of Cash — the lucky charm, this prophet of wealth and entitlement, the Son of God — was more than capable of dishing out grievous punitive gestures to unbelievers. It put the current Amoran display of the restricted (adults only) and more grisly murderous entertainment of post matinee, after-hours performance at the entertainment and sports Colossus in the centre of Amor to shame. Cash was King of the world and Prince of Darkness as well; but what's in a name? And what people clambered for and bought when they had Cash wasn't to solely supplement themselves and their families with proper nourishment and providing decorum for clean happiness and jolly good fun or even helping out the more unfortunates, but rather to buy people, buy power and receive delicious envy and be able to afford jealousy and revenge, never mind lewdness and vulgarity. These were things Dyfed had seen in his strange vision grounded by gravity.

And these wealth monsters threatened poor cashless folks too that (more often than not) caused poor folks to respect the rich monsters so as to minimize the monster's disrespect for them. Respect hinged only literally on a single accompaniment, wealth. If you didn't have wealth you didn't get respect: End of story. Morals, kindness, forethought, empathy, all the things that should attract respect elsewhere were absent here in that strange space/time frame which Rama and company had shown him, Dyfed told Morgant. And wealth's common denominator and bottom line (the dollar) was one's embodiment with the god Cash in whose image and with which the wealthy and the incredibly shallow feverously sought out constantly and with which they hoped upon hope to remain embodied. They prayed to cash day and night. They often played with Cash that in such instances they called lolly and even had physical sex with Cash; and their semen mingled with the semen of their god. They would kill anybody who stood in their way to worship, attain, have, and to hold Cash. In this way it was much like the current Amor, he told Morgant, except it was on steroids. It was about how much wealth you had that could buy you other people and wreck havoc at will. And it all came down to Cash as it did the denarii in circulation within the empire.

And the individuals of the future's greatest social skills orbited around the methods of the Cash accumulation game and didn't give a pinch of coon shit about gravity or any other useful knowledge. And another thing, Cash Accumulation was a first cousin of the word game. The more devious and the richer you were the better citizen you were. And many looked up to you and folks beat a path to your door for everybody wanted to hear your opinion that mattered and was obviously the most worthy of all. For this you didn't have to be wise, you had to be rich. This, in the future, was decidedly more one sided then the present. There was a certain amount of finesse about accumulation, too. Theft of Cash (and that included what could be sold and/or reduced to Cash) was one of the most punitively focussed endeavours and the most indictable felonies imaginable as well. It could (at the very least) put the felon into a dirty dungeon forever or cause their arms and legs to be twisted, broken and pulled off before being strangulated, especially if the theft was incurred from the system's mainframe such as the taxation department or from expenditures to improve the image of the power-elite and so forth.

Theft had many definitions that (understandably) were not very transparent and these definitions were highly un-pin-pointable. This was an advantage the more Cash one had and the greater need to discourage anybody getting their mitts on you denarii at any cost. Yet, it was a fact that the rich themselves were very creative when it came to them thieving from those who were not as rich. Here, the definition of theft was even looser. However, but then, even if you were rich (and sometimes just because you were rich) it could quickly and without warning reverse on you. You could become a target for others a lot greedier and richer than you. That is why the quasi-casino system of the future here was labelled the Alternate Currency-state Status-quo. And like Amor, the most dangerous of folks were the power-elite who were highly integrated with the state's governing-factor. Unlike Amor, however, the power-elite of the future realm which he got a glimpse of, Dyfed said, had huge advantages over the hoi polloi due to information technology and technology information as in accredited know how through science. They (being the power-elites) could watch, hear and know mountains of details about even unimportant individuals. Nobody it seemed was invisible to scans, not even Dyfed himself without taking huge precautions. This meant that they had oodles of powerful pools of ability tools. These tools were what they (the future people) called fuck-you-up power-tools. And they were relentless when it came to employing them. Or were. For like everything else of that later time element, Dyfed had the sense that it was all quickly disintegrating along with the seething masses of population by some unknown algorithmed-out exponential: But that was still unclear to him, he had to admit. This was something to admire and respect, too.

"And so you discovered something of yourself,' Morgant stated.

"Not really,' replied Dyfed. 'I discovered something of the phenomenon of the future, not me.'

"But of course you did,' countered Morgant. 'You discovered something of yourself that's not in the future for it doesn't yet exist, as such. You discovered yourself in an all-current space/time, and that is one that can be projected. What were those images of the future world of yours if they weren't perceptions? They weren't my perceptions, or Mencuis' either. They were yours. Projected perceptions to be sure but they were yours, not anybody else's. Like it or not, you own them, they are yours. Other people have their own, you know.'

"What do you mean?' asked Dyfed. 'What with Rama's or Mencius's interference or contribution (which ever way you want to look at it) I visited the future and saw things.'

"No Dyfed,' said Morgant, 'you actually witnessed yourself being projected into that place, nothing more. It was you and your place. It may have been due to Rama and Mencius' machinations, but the future place and space/time you went to wasn't their place of space/time or even mine or anybody else's. It was strictly yours, and even now (still) there maybe room for future adjustment and maybe improvement for you in your future 'current space/time' slots. Nothing is written in stone, anymore. But what you witnessed was your phenomenon, no one else's. And in seeing your individual freedom, as you perceive it, quickly threatened the manifestation of a social order or disorder that you fashioned into lock-down (not anyone else). And further to that, you finagled to have it subjected and influenced, by yourself, into a highly efficient system of control by methods of mind policing that you disapprove of. What all of this indicates is that you have an unshakable passion for individual freedom, at least for yourself, and all which that entails. That you fashioned such a thing as your Idea, which, through the sum Ideas projected by your majority (relative to you) that is also you, may (or may not) compromise you in the present of your future. But this depends on your awareness and the strength of your discipline and the quality of your integrity and your nobility. It is the same with everybody. Most have little or no noble qualities that are intrinsically parallel to the depth of their integrity. In your case the verdict is not yet out, Dyfed. You are one of us. This fact is that seeing by your concern for yourself and those relative to you who you favour as well as your resolve to correct that reality come hell or high water, you have exquisite qualities of nobility. But, you will not be correcting the world, or the people in it. Know that much, Dyvie. Whatever hell others devise for themselves will remain unaltered no matter what you do, though its been said that (these days) the star of influence is on the rise. But I don't know. And I don't believe it. But whether you may be able to influence others is very doubtful. Remember that. It seems that this is the mission of the prophets. Is that what you think you are, a prophet? Wake up and smell the new morning brew, Dyvie. Have any of the prophets been profitable in the end with their endeavours? Have they made any difference to the outcome of the world? No. The only difference that has ever been made here are to the persons themselves by themselves. And this is the particulate nature of the Jeshuan cult during it conception by the Nazareans about a hundred years or so BCE, now, sorrowfully, somewhat forgotten about. So you see, Dyfed Lucifer, Prince of the Grove, once the Chamberlain to the high king of Albion, and if I'm not mistaken, recipient of the Hadrianus Gladius award; and from now what you tell me of the future, you are also Chief Pale Face Mountain Lion of not anywhere in particular, and (to which I can add) an honourary Master of the Unknown Universe.

So, do not confuse the places of your mysterious design and those of will and intentions. These, as far as you are concerned (do not include anybody else here), are decidedly relative and interchangeable and have much (if not everything) in common with you and you alone. Otherwise, there can be no long effecting logical historistics that show influence, let alone change within the phenomenon at large.'

From what Dyfed had said (and even though it was Dyfed's collective world), Morgant was cognizant that there appeared to be a shift in the status quo in the future. It seemed that maybe the definition of slavery would change and put on a happier mask even if the condition was more entrenched than ever. In a strange way slavery was a condition with an even greater finality than in the past. But it was not a fixed condition, but neither was being twenty-one years of age, white, and free, as they used to say in the day. This was where any form of the emasculated could revert to become the un-emasculated again. It was becoming more personal in the future. It wasn't so much racial as individual, though the genre of steeply ingrained tribal archetypes were still a template to reckon with; only now definitions had become altered which muddied the gene pool allowing everybody to be slurred. Though more people had more amenities, such as owning their own homes, and everybody it seemed had motorized chariots at their disposal and service, ratio-wise there were far less free people in the future that Dyfed had gleaned, compared to today. This was certainly Dyfed's conclusion.

Dyfed had told Morgant that slavery in the future was a personal condition that many folks appeared to opt for under their own volition. Their excuse was that it was easier; less fuss and muss, with fewer headaches. Here — have a nice day, eh — actually meant 'shut the fuck up stupid and keep your turnip-head down'. The only side you want to be on is the winning side no matter how fast it uses up all the breathable air on the planet and contaminates all the fresh, domestic drinking water. Just let the power elites do it the way they want; that was the prevailing attitude here. Whatever you do just don't antagonize or resist them or they will fuck you up. Follow, don't lead and whatever you have, don't have an opinion. It was more like a glorified imprisonment with attitude independence being the go back to jail and never get out card while attitude dependence will keep you out and give you a rich salary all on pensionable time. That's the name of the game. But the penchant for futurists to acquire logo association somehow seemed to provide them a strange unexplained sense of security status.

But what is worse, a forced prison of confinement where you escalate within the counter forces that you face that actually face and confront you, or the freedom from being able to have any imagination or in having an independent volition along with all its other death-dealing drudgeries? Dyfed told him that he thought that in future times most folks will choose to be individually snuffed out and simply want to exist within a dull sensory of befuddled mediocrity within the herd. Morgan queried that now.

"But folks like us,' Dyfed answered, 'wouldn't be able to live with ourselves if we conform. The choice is to not live comfortably with yourself while been told you are free to live with, and under the same standards, conditions and styles equally with everybody else, and with standardized, non customized freedoms, achievement levels, intelligent requirements, personality and moral equability requirement along with an emphasis on standard regulation expectations not to excel or show any superiority of conduct or achievement in any way but be cut from the same cloth as everybody else and to live comfortably with yourself confined to a very small space with a conforming, non-individualistic attitude. Thus being the case…we will be alone. Do you hear me? We will be alone and possibly dead.

Dyfed had also expressed astonishment at the future gadgets that connect people (not necessarily a bad thing pending on how they are used) that seemed to make the world run at a peculiar gait. One such gadget of prominence was the aforementioned torc. This instrument (he had noticed) had taken on an entirely new image in the future as an instrument of necessity, and not one that was earned. Though it has to be said that the necessity was not so much for the individual but rather for the power-elite. For in their world the torc now monitored each and every non-individual-individual. No individual was to be without a torc. All individuals were to be non-individuals. Any individual who did not wear a torc at all times, or who saw themselves as an individual and in this way considered themselves, and others, unique (among others) in any way, were outlaws. And outlaws needed to be avoided by any and all law-abiding folks. Indeed, the public was instructed to avoid them on pain of sever punitive action to be taken against them. For all outlaws were a threat to national and international security whereby anyone foolish enough to aid and abet, harbour, turn a blind-eye to, aggrandize, promote, celebrate, or enter into fellowship with, counsel, or pray with or even pray for, were to be found guilty of maintaining and showing extreme, harsh and unnatural tendencies of callousness towards the well-being of humanity in general that was equal to (if not more serious than) treason and mass genocide. Furthermore, all of these accusations (or charges, however by chance they appear) are indictable offences that deserve and will result in pre-emptive convictions without appeal and without compassion wherein the normal punitive action such as torture followed by the breaking of arms and legs prior to strangulation will be the unalterable outcome. Outlaws were dangerous folk, indeed. They were felons without conviction.

Once no more than relics dug up from Keltic burial mounds, the new torcs of the future would be nothing more than a stylized objectivity imitating the ancient Hyperborean device while providing insane records of almost every action and syllable of an individual that could be publically (without sensor or appeal) disclosed but was certainly privately (without any consensus by the individual whatsoever) used to catalogue and to eventually provide a profile of the individual (that could also be tagged onto other presumed like-individuals without any psychological monitor) that was physically and legally unable to be disputed. That is to say, no magistrate in any court would support dispute.

"Violet and Manandan wore torcs,' Dyfed told Morgant. 'As a child I wanted one to wear too. But I was told that I was too young. But I received one from Uncle Penrhyn for my following birthday, anyway. But to my dismay it was a facsimile. It was a toy torc, a knock-off torc. A fake. Further to that, when a Keltic Cornovii chief who fleeing 'the Wirral' following an insurrection there washed up on the Isle of Peace when I was a boy, he too wore a torc. But what was remarkable was his was simply a shiny ornament he hung around his neck like a ring or an identity badge. His was so very different from mine, and the genuine Hyperborean ones that are worn by the Masters. At least mine was lightweight and had shiny colours of the spectrum on it just like the Masters' did. The Cornovii chief's torc was quite decoratively fancy and made of gold, silver plate over tin. I could tell that his torc was heavy. The masters' torcs were broader and shaped like a wide quarter moon, the wider portion to the front resting just above the chest. Like my toy torc, they were fabricated with an unnatural material that was very light in weight. The masters' torcs, as you and I know, were also shiny but unlike my toy one, yours displayed holographs and other marvellous objects within the material that spoke and communicated in one form or another with other genuine torc wearers. The torcs could also down-load specialized data such as information, instructions, philosophical wisdoms and could even convey transactions and capture both still and motion life into a visual-video record file. They were amazing. The future had these similar gizmos, Dyfed said.

"So be it,' said Morgant smiling at him. 'Good for you.'

"For what? I didn't do anything,' Dyfed protested. Morgant laughed at his denial that was uttered as if he didn't want to be caught out as having done something wrong.

"But you most certainly did,' replied Morgant. 'Tonight, in a matter of an hour, you managed to get a glimpse into the moments of centuries in the recorded minutes filed in your psyche's mainframe that can be a huge benefit for you. Your Idea reinvented the torc without permission from anybody on high. Never forget that. Now you need to work forward in producing them for personal use now, along with an algorithm for good government and good order to achieve a good society that's detached from privilege and entitlement. This will not be easy, but now anyway you have the advantage of foreknowledge. What you have to worry about now is your visions that may run counter-force and be compensatory to an Idea you founded that's being influenced by the sum of Ideas. You glimpsed what use a future torc may have. Because of that it may once again exist. You need, therefore, to come up with an antidote to trump all furtive torcs. Masters like Dr Torsionfield and Quizzy Gizmo (for instance) can provide for you the materials needed in doing this in order to produce a limited edition of real torcs. Well done, young feller, well done.'

PREFIX TO THE SECOND EMPIRE

(all along the watchtower)

*'The public must be put in its place (so we may live)
free of the trampling and the roar of the bewilded herd.'*
WALTER LIPPMANN

The *pilgrim* leaned back, his vision penetrating the darkness that had crept over the twisty road of tomorrow that wound down and around below him through the flattening foothills to Flathead. He knew that it was there at Flathead that Harvey Fulcher Brown, alias Johnny Rocco resided, waiting for him. The elderly *wayfarer* then winced regretfully as he recalled that it had already been thirteen days since starting out on this annual solo outing.

The *hombre* now recalled the past two weeks from the day before he set out. His daughter had phoned home to talk to her Mum and told her that she and her husband wanted to invite her out to visit them soon. She had heard, he remembered her saying, that he and Wanda had bought a new Mercedes chariot.

"The two of you please come out by chariot in comfort,' she had said, adding that 'Dad can find some new destination to sojourn later in the year and resume his annual trek next year.'

She then explained that their family annual summer's holiday that brought them west and out to the Big Island each year had to be cancelled this year due to financial hardships they were having, caused by the industry turn-down in general in Alberta.

Vacations and travel now-a-days meant doing it before the heat of summer burned down over them in a white fuzzy haze that as usual would be accompanied by cyclones of towering fire, and lightning storms all strung together like a string of pearls composed of a searing blizzard of blistering dust and heat to beat the band just like on a merry Santa Klaus Day down under. The floods of winter and spring had just subsided of late, and the annual collection of rotting bodies of people that had gone missing during the winter and collected from the riverbanks and mud flats had already begun. Here now was the narrow window before the frighteningly devilish summer weather that was fast beating its path towards them again would arrive. The weather (in its negative intonation) was a cyclic shape-shifter, and it may be absent now but it was always coming; it might have just left you in its dust and destruction, but never mind, it was soon about to return before you could say Jack Robinson a thousand times with a straight face.

For a hundred and eighty or more years the city of Cowton had held a rodeo every July. But for the past decade and a half it had been slowly moved ahead to the early June and recently now to mid May to be in advance of (and to avoid) the fierce and deadly summer storms that raged, seemingly earlier and earlier lasting longer and longer, across the entire continent now. This put the floods of spring and the ripping twister winds and burning fires of summer on an overlapped route of collision that was fenced in with fierce electrical storms. Caught unawares there was no chance for escape no matter who you were. But each season was treacherous in its own way. These violent warm weather disturbances of wind and fire that threatened each late spring tore across the land killing almost more thousands of folks this season than the receding floods of spring had already done. And this was now an annual all-seasonal event.

'Welcome to the Age of Aquarius,' the pilgrim's mind's ear heard someone whisper from the past. And the wind brought rain and electrical activity of such a magnitude that had never been seen before and caused billions in property damage not even counting crop destruction. Spring/summer season was the annual plague of flooding rain, avalanches and raging fires fanned by tornados and hurricanes, as much as autumn/winter indulged in hurricanes and tornados fanning raging fires followed by freezing rain and frozen floods. It was the sole culprit for the greatest net food produce loss the world had ever experienced in recorded times. And this now had been happening on an annual basis for years. Indeed, world food production had shrunk to one fifth of what it had been since the olden days of recent time. And the world population was plummeting along side it. And what with plagues and destruction complicated by super bugs decimating the population with contagion, it wasn't a matter of whether or not there was enough food to go around, because the world population was plummeting and commerce and transport was grinding down to a slow standstill, so it didn't much matter any more.

The condition that caused the greatest change was a result of the recent shift in climate environment that was an enormous global alteration that was still turning the corner but was well on its way to being a permanent game changer for the entire earth and all the creatures that inhabited it. It wasn't at its worst yet, either, but not to worry over dalliances, for worst was fast on its way.

Supposedly, the armchair and fake scientists and pseudo intellectuals who had pooh-poohed late into the final hour of any change coming had been to the point of riveting boredom. Now the same armchair fakers were predicting and warning that the worst was yet to come. Duh! The traveller thought that if public tax denarii were paying these guys, it was a good argument for tax revision: And reduction. As for insurance coverage (and the like) to steady the way, well, that was already so like yesterday. It was a thing of the past: Forget about it. And for at least the past few decades the venture called indemnity was a highly rigged lottery anyway, and only the extremely skilled (the capital rich and powerfully endowed) played in its league and generally only with other people's money. For hard working farmers and homeowners and people like the regular hoi polloi and the likes of those who are referred to as the salt of the earth, it wasn't their cup of tea, that's for sure. Not anymore it wasn't, they couldn't afford it. Now insurance policies had gone the way of the great auk, the hedge fund and the passenger pigeon.

As for the tornados and hurricanes, on the other hand, it was noticed that as each decade went by, they were growing into a dominate occurrence which came to attack the land and the cities of people with an even greater vengeance that came earlier and earlier into the world's growing seasons. It was at the point now, it seemed, that folks couldn't be bothered to rebuild and farmers just couldn't get on with their business anymore. And it wasn't just relevant to this quarter of the earth, either. This phenomenon was worldwide. Astonishingly, in the big-city states like Megatropolis, Byzas, Nova Troia, Sao Paulo, the imperial city of Edo in sight of Mt. Fuji and finally Yanjing (also known as Fanyang as well as Youzhou: the city of liberation of names), their fun-loving urban denizens took no notice. Here, worldwide ensuing chaos was not the most popular subject anyway, especially during the happy martini and candy-flavoured cocaine of choice hour crowd of the world corporate chains and the now not so jolly bar and grill lounges.

Nor were attitudes any different at the glitzy toys and Yuppie fashion shows whose well-heeled idle rich and the wastrel imaginative (though to be sure, many of these were short listed and destined to be idle and wastrel no more). This clientele would have done well to start boning and honing up on hunter gathering skills such as learning to replicate heat by rubbing two sticks together to take the chill off the environment and learn new ways of preparing culinary half-cooked (or fully burnt) porcupine friendly dishes over those kindled fires. The only alternative to a varied diet was to hunt high and low for their very own copy of the long out of print The Joy of Road-Kill Cook Book.

It was strange how every little thing was different now that Dyfed was gone, the old *pilgrim* thought. So far though he and Wanda and their family had survived. Now, sitting beside a small dyeing campfire looking out into the darkening gloaming of north-western Montana, he thought of his wife of many and happy years. Once long ago, in the shadow of *Haba Snow Mountain* in Yunnan province he had met wonderful Wanda along with two other young women, Delicious Doris and luscious Lucile Ophelia. It was there that the four of them became entwined in a romantic whirlwind that took them in a horseshoe curve from the Tiger Leaping Gorge of Yunnan north across Sichuan, Gansu and Qinghai in the western portions of the Land of Ch'in, across Tibet and the Himalayan Mts. to Inja, then a passage love-boat to Italy and finally to Ivisa in the Balearic cluster of islands stationed seventy-five Amoran miles off the Valencian coast of eastern Hispania.

In the end he had chosen Wanda. This was her Anglish or Angle-lander name and the name he always called her by. Her real name was Lianhua Shan Zhizi. This translated to *Child of the mountain Lotus whose mother was a daughter of the Land of Ch'in married to her father, a poet from Wrexham in Wales where both her parents, now deceased, had lived at that time.*

Then the wayfarer thought fondly of heir daughter Azalia and her husband Mac again. They lived on the edge of the prairie nestled in the foothills of the eastern slopes of a great white-topped mountain range with their family of two children, with another expected. And now that this year's trek and visit was over, he had said his goodbyes. The aforementioned annual ritual to mount his two-wheeled chariot to make this journey he was presently on, was centred on the Rodeo Stampede whose venue was the City of Cowton on the western prairie. This event, that is billed as 'the greatest outdoor show on earth' was a yearly attraction for him and only twenty Amoran miles south from his daughter Azalia and husband Mac's home at Cochrane. This year was to be the Stampede's two hundredth anniversary and the festive performance for the occasion was billed as a celebration on a grand scale, though not grand enough to entice the traveller's wife who had never been, never wanted to be able to say she had been (or be seen) there, ever. His family, though, knew how much he enjoyed the Cowton Rodeo Stampede. This passion probably originally stemmed from his years as a rancher in the southern Cariboo region of the Northern Dominion's western province to where (many years before) he had partially retired to manage a beef cattle ranch, a co-operative attached to the House of Lucifer.

So all in all that the whole two week vacation he was currently on was to chalk up some serious fun miles of adventurous motorcycling, cache in for a nice visit with family (daughter Azalea and son-in-law Mac, and grandchildren), take in the Rodeo Stampede, the greatest outdoor show on earth with its many carnival and side festivities, then a few fun days of fishing up at their Fish-Ghost Lake cabin to lounge around for much of the day in an open boat under an umbrella while guzzling cold beer before heading back to the coast. That this trek made it the ideal invitation for a holiday each year was a given. No matter what else Wanda and he might do during the remainder of the year, including having the kids and grandchildren come and visit them later in the summer, this was his summer-holiday ride. But there was an added attraction this year. For this year, he reminded himself as he set out on his venture, was the first time in almost twenty years that he was actually working with a deadline again. And this was to finalize an initiative that Dyfed Lucifer had put into place about years earlier. And for that he had to divert his return route to the coast via the road south into the Unified States to Montana and conduct his business with Johnny Rocco.

But first things first: So as this *companero* and *comrade of life* sat alone in a high altitude deserted Montana campground, he retraced his holiday in his mind.

After riding his motorcycle off the ferry between the Big Island and the mainland thirteen days ago, as the *wayfarer* made his way from the coast on this adventure, he had followed the Sto:lo River. Soon he was riding his motorcycle chariot passed the thousands of acres that had once made up the House of Lucifer's agricultural holdings that had been at the centre of Dyfed's international conglomerate. This journey took him past the mud flats that were once blanketed with herons and whose warm, flat and fertile over-burdened land was now crowned with raptors circling in the dark blue skies overhead. Once, there had even been migrating swans at hand here, first in April and then on their return in late September. He had rolled past fields and fields of tall leaning grass, and vast, flat lands dotted with dairy and produce farms of the western delta, most of them now lean and slim, derelict and bankrupt. He was approaching the point where in a few miles the huge delta would be squeezed together and finally hedged in by the sunny rock faced coastal mountains topped in green woolly fur (fir) that were glazed in the summer sun. He glanced off past his right handlebar across to the raised undulating bench of land that snuggled close to the rising forested bush land in the direction of where Dyfed's palace was located, and to where at journey's end he would return coming up from the south. From the road this palatial abode wasn't visible. Once he was further east he was quickly squeezed into the narrows of the Sto:lo River channel where the air was slightly chilled. In the cooler seasons here, he remembered, this area was shrouded in mists while the rain fell from the grey clouds that skimmed their summits. Next came the lazy, echo defying interior farming valleys more steeped with rushing streams and falling water and whose buildings (stiltedly erected) tilted alongside corals (kraals) now empty of horses and domestic livestock, all precariously cliff placed over-looking rounded valleys of pruned fruit orchards hedged in here and there by rock and tumble weed. Further on old, faded and deserted roadside produce stands yawned with crested chests now infested with rattle snakes whose crusty old semen-like sloughed skins got caught up in the cobwebs and blown against wire fencing entangled with chest high long stemmed grass.

Later, the semi desert climbed back again into granite rocky shelves and pine forests before another descent that opened up on to lower elevation lush black earthed, flat valley bottoms which produced crops of onions, tomato's, leeks, cabbage, lettuce, carrots and beets. The heat here also provided for the vineyards that were further up facing west on the eastern slopes of a series of plentiful valleys, now depopulated and mostly quiet. Here too the fast moving streams were being replaced with wide and slow moving rivers. Many rundown domesticities encircled by black-loamed earth had been abandoned. They were lying fallow, the livestock gone, either from starvation or gone to feral. Next came the hot energy of the cool, steady mountain climb. It was curious for apart from minor traffic (mostly giant motorised multi-wheeled wagons hauling produce) he saw little of other travellers and motorists. The ever present heavy girded wagons running on steel rails and pulled by a series of powerful diesel fuelled compression ignition engines also made of steel and composites were, surprisingly, constantly evident. One could hear their engines working and the rumbling of their mile long train of carriages from afar. However, now down from a train every hour to one every ten hours, these machines carried heavy cargos like parts for giant farming and construction equipment on flatbeds and mega tons of wheat along with other materials of industry. Oil and gas, he knew, were moved by pipeline and surrounded in places by swamps of devastated pollution from product leaks caused by ruptured pipes.

Other than that the only movement were drones silently criss-crossing the sky above and where congested shipping air lanes that were once filled with jet-propelled aircrafts, all was quiet. Extreme weather and the calamity it wrought, the expense and the fear of financial loss or death itself, had long since destroyed the air passenger and air cargo transport industry.

Cool ghosts of men, and their narrow meandering roads of the yesterdays' and long ago, criss-crossed the deserted wide new thoroughfare through the tunnels and passes of the majestic Backbone Mountains.

At one meandering crossing he had been stopped by two members of a highway patrol squadron stationed nearby eating breakfast had quickly run out to flag him down. Normally in and around the centres of civilization either the roads were now closed to moving traffic or shifts of guards were used to mind the checkpoints twenty-four seven. It was near a seemingly deserted mountain hamlet identified by a chapel that long ago had been built just off the side of the highway where he pulled over to park. Beyond it was a clearing where there was scattered the hamlet buildings now weather worn into dark brown and faded grey. They had been used long ago for domesticity then were abandoned. Now, with a few relics partially dressed in blotches of shiny new paint, they were back in business and being reused once again by refugees, a downtrodden refuge of humanity indeed. It was a commune of Bohemian minded folks who had left the strife and disease of Couver City on the coast or Cowton on the prairie and a few of them now gathered together here in the cooler air. They reasoned that the coolness and more rarefied air would help them remain germ and virus free. The traveller had stopped here and as there were only one or two folks about the hamlet, he shut off his two-wheeled chariot and dismounted and prepared a bivouac.

He looked up toward a steep hill covered in a misty cloud that hung low to the earth. From his location he couldn't see much but he knew what was there. It was a hot spring that poured water and steam out of a cleft in the cliff and he recalled the place from a long time long ago. He remembered one winter when returning there he Dyfed and Ceredwyn slipped and slid on the ice that had formed on the smooth rock makeshift patio. Dyfed had told him then that long, long ago before any other white persons had known about this hot spring, he and Ceredwyn had camped right on that very same spot; the spot where the plains people had directed them to. They were told they would find this hot spring on the path through the pass where the blood of the gods gushed forth. Be respectful they had been told unnecessarily. And it was here that he had spotted that first mountain lion whose hide he fashioned all those years ago into a vest. He remembered Dyfed's vest. It was fashioned from the entire body, complete with four legs and paws with claws: two hanging down in front and two behind. It was the prize, Dyfed had once told him, that the mountain lion had given up especially for him. He was still honouring that sacred creature even back then.

Once his he bivouac and motorcycle were secure he wandered toward the chapel. He then saw an air ambulance parked close to one of the local buildings nearby being used as a hostel. Then like a bad smell or a dangerous fear, out from the hostel a malicious rumour suddenly spread that a man was dying there from a super bug. Super bugs were mutated viruses that to some extent were initially caused by the World Pharmacy Corp. who for the last century and a half had been creating stronger and stronger vaccines and anti inflammatories and anti this and anti that to effectively fight deadly viruses and infections. This unfortunately had inadvertently resulted in the natural order of the virus community itself to take on new and improved properties and spawn a new super bug not capable of being so easily beaten. The result was that millions upon millions of people were now dying daily, worldwide, for which no affective vaccine was worth a pinch of coon kaka. This situation thoroughly affected the medical world's entire treatment procedure for the sick and ailing; anyone could tell you that. What had once been advanced medical technology had virtually become useless overnight. Common surgery procedures such as limb amputations, removal of diseased appendages and organs including transplant operations that were once all too common and ho-hum routine were now too dangerous to perform. For now they were susceptible to untreatable infection. Doctors found they had no viable tool to fight against any of these infections: This, along with tainted blood! And this situation thoroughly affected the *bon-amie* of the hostel and its surroundings.

The following morning wisps of mist were still clinging to the evergreens as he came back down from the hot springs. He then noticed that a group of young men were gathered around his motorcycle chariot talking enthusiastically. He smiled at them and excused himself as he gently pushed in and straddling his machine, fired it up and rode away to the next highway patrol check-in station that he knew would be at the summit which was not be too far away.

Then just past the summit pullover, a flit of cool mist and the rarefied air provided him with a dizzy rush before he plummeted down onto the prairie far below where in the distant haze he suddenly caught sight of jerky and vibrating branches of lightning hovering over the haze of Cowton.

All along as he made this journey he was experiencing the continuous exposure of the burning sun and the scent of the warm wet earth streaming into the reel-life motion spliced-picture-show of his space/time phenomenon where the wild spruce scented wind on high swiftly passed through the scented tree tops and the speedy squalls that splashed particles of misty condensate into his florid face and across his goggles and into his very being. These senses of material were there solely to lovingly buffet him and securely embraced him and comforted him by simply being there with him and accompanying him, as always. It was nirvana, or the next best thing under the circumstance.

The hombre was happy as he continued on with his errand minding his own business, so it was not surprising that his mind then wandered back to Wanda and their large comfortable home and farmlands that lay close alongside the Quw'utsun River over on Big Island. This Quw'utsun River was a life giver to the early peoples here as it was to him and his family when they were young. From a lake of the same name in the interior hills west of his homestead, it flowed east passed their estate to be flushed finally in and among the archipelago of the Salish Sea. This sheltered inland sea — gracefully engulfed by beautiful forested islands — shimmered in the distance from their Quw'utsun River home outdoor patio.

Days later, after the winner of the rodeo's last eight second bull ride competition had been handed down his first prize platter-sized shiny silver belt-buckle that featured a bull and rider in bas-relief glinting in the sun, along with a ringing chorus and a brace of fresh-faced and glowing cowgirl queens bent on kicking up the dust down to the mud, and after the fat lady's final Yee-Haw had been flung out from her like a song, just like her cowgirl hat that had floated up instead and over the heads of a row of seven rodeo cowboys that were stuck, twizzled and twisted onto the top rail of a nearby corral, fidgeting and looking inward like faded clothes-pegs with hats — the *wayfarering* holidayer and his son-in-law Mac had packed up the beer and tackle and headed out to their fishing hole at Fish-Ghost Lake as usual; leaving the rest of the whole damn-fam under Azalea's command to prepare and pack and come later.

It was here on the shores of this sacred fishing spot that their daughter and son-in-law had built their summer retreat cabin, situated among the coulees. Here the two men caught trout, bass, and pickerel (walleye) and catfish, all of them stocked. Meanwhile, as they fished and drank beer at the cabin, Azalea made preparation to follow with the whole family in tow later. Beside coming to the coast and the Big Island every late August, it was here and here alone that for the last two weeks of July and first two weeks of August that his daughter's family spent their annual six week vacation every year. No Disneyland or Pinocchio-world for them.

His son-in-law had been the son of an oilman but had studied to be an earth scientist. With the oil industry here and around the world having been scattered into the dust and thrown to the four strong winds some time back, this son of an oilman had managed to make a good living pretending, like the others, to nurture Mother Earth back from the ravages of rack and ruin. This coffin lined graveyard of nature with its oil field operations, the wide spread practice of fracking along with the tar sand-pits, open mining pits and unattended-to tailings ponds and other sour pits leaching out poison in which the foul mess they had left behind malignantly settled and lingered still. The son-in-law did not pretend with him though, and as they fished they filled their boots with silence on the topic of ecology. That got nowhere now, anyway. Even the last few remaining, still tacky, late night televised talk-show hosts avoided the subject.

One day with their bare feet against the ribs of the boat, the two of them filled up four coolers with fish for the fifth day in a row. They left just enough room under the lid to cover the fish sufficiently with ice from the cabin's kitchen icemaker. That was when the family arrived. All alone on a sturdy table covered with a red and white-chequered plastic tablecloth they feasted on walleye sandwich with for lunch while granddad absent-mindedly listened to his grandchildren nattering away, on the porch. The time had come, he decided, and after saying his good-byes the following morning, he left. Though they had begged him to stay, knowing full well that he wouldn't, as always, they waved as he noisily rode away.

But he wasn't all done in and ready to return home yet; not by a long shot. As stated earlier, having languished in forced retirement for almost the past two decades, it had come to pass, so it seemed, that the old professional game (once orchestrated by Dyfed and his pack) was afoot once again. In the way that the pilgrim saw it, that put him back working for his mentor once more, even if the later was missing in action. Of course he kept this all to himself, letting the family caution him about this and that '…say hi to mummy or granny…' while wishing him a safe ride home through the mountain passes back to the coast and Couver City. 'And don't forget to block your bike on the ferry,' they reminded him. 'Say, have you got your permits? What about your tickets? Do you need to make a reservation of any kind? How's your gas?'

Just how the hell did they think he got through a day of his life before they came along, he thought.

What they didn't know, what everybody didn't know, was so much the better for them, he reminded himself. That too had been Dyfed's policy all along. It was done, Dyfed told him, so Ceredwyn wouldn't worry, the *pilgrim* remembered. It was his policy now. So, when he revisited the junction just west of Cowton and the road he rode in on, it wasn't onto that road that he now turned on to ride out. No sir! It was the road south to Montana that he took instead, for — Yee-Haw — he was Flathead Lake bound.

This area called Flathead was once considered to be across the line and into the Unified States of Merika (USM). Before that, three hundred years ago and more, it was solely the land of the Flathead people. It was hard to put your finger with any exactness on to the spot where feelings changed to any degree from yesterday to today, but Montana was still the Unified States of Merika and Alberta on this side of the line was still the Northern Dominion. It just wasn't called the line anymore, that's all. It was called the National border, a no-man's land now strongly focused upon by the Department of Homeland Security and USM National Defence. Divisive and non-inclusive from the start, National borders were a growing reality of the fence mentality that was related to the mind-field mentality that was another matter altogether, especially (that is) from what used to be prevalent around this neck of stubble and grass. It wasn't like it used to be, anymore. Nothing was. Not since Dyfed disappeared, it wasn't.

Being proximate to (or in the vicinity of) National borders (never mind crossing them, like mine-fields) was not the most pleasant of pass-times one could choose in today's world. Especially, too, if the border led into (or out of) the Unified States that, as we now know, was the nation south of the line from the aforementioned Northern Dominion. The usage of that word Dominion (which comes from dominus or master, as in being dominate or 'to master') was something of an unfortunate anomaly here. It was a misnomer in the international sense for it had been the Unified States (USM) that had risen to world dominance about a century earlier, not the vastly larger lands of the Northern Dominion. This tiny little quirk of history managed to keep at least twenty-five per cent of the folks living on the northern side of the line a little more humble and polite while seventy-five per cent of those living on the southern side not exactly arrogant and haughty, but often ignorant that anything much actually went on here or anywhere else beyond their back yard. And it had been under the US's watch as a world power that the rather grungy new world order being enforced worldwide had taken root.

But the new world order phrase was also an anomaly. People talk about the new world order and such but they don't know what they're talking about, he thought. They must mean something to the effect of a new and improved old world order. The world order that has long lock-stepped its advantages for mastery of those entitled and privileged over those of the common man has been in place for thousands of years. Only now that technology has advanced (thanks to the swollen ranks of intelligent masses of hoi polloi) they are the controllers of world destiny that's now within reach of such a powerful mastery over all of the world's individuals that has never before been possible. What we have here is still the traditional and current world order of old, but now it has escalated and elevated itself into a much more ominous machine. Soon it will have a far more advanced artificial intelligence tool (developed by…you guessed it… intelligent hoi polloi) at its disposal that will stifle as much as possible, and as much as is needed, the volition of the common man and woman and the other intelligent folks that built it so as to prevent them all from exercising any minimal individual freedoms they may have or desire to have. It will also greatly complicate and confound the volitions and actions of the already reduced and very precious, free-willed folks who wish to function individually and be on top of (and maintain) their own errand (purpose of being). These latter categories of freedom are the most troubling for the controlling Haploids who wish to eliminate and expunge non-conformity and freethinking and freewill altogether and at any cost. And that is precisely what they are attempting to do. These actions, the hoi polloi are told, are necessary for helping and promoting the new established order to take effect and to become. And these actions that these Haploids are taking to successfully accomplish establishing this order of theirs is what they call 'defending freedom', believe it or not! Oh, yeah! And these are the same Haploids that went ahead and permitted the poisoning of over half the world's songbirds that only took a little more than a decade.

Obviously, the hombre thought, what was needed here was a beneficial crisis to arise and shift the world's narrative construct in order to form a new conversation and a new world order so the hoi polloi can benefit too and be lifted out from living within a domestic prison slavery environment they seem to be acutely unaware of.

Anyway, after the onset of the current global climate change crisis, this latter mentioned powerful elite have used their advanced facilities to shake the old order out of its tree completely now and super size and expand their new found power into an indomitable machine. With climate change happening and throwing a wrench and a wonk into the season's greetings that brought forth towering winds, rogue-sized waves, deluges of biblical proportions, and lightning and thunder bolts with the strength of Zeus a hundred million times over that were thoroughly on their game, change was no longer readily being seen as our friend and in being a good thing. Then with this entire catastrophe happening and underway, another catastrophe came on its heels to upstage it. This was an unexpected planetary electric charge increase that was followed by a sudden and violent decrease (occasioned by a close passing comet which had come into the sun's inner circle to swing around and fling itself back into deep space). But once the planet's voltage storm (that destroyed zillions of denarii of infrastructure) had sloughed down to an over all lower planetary mean charge and magnetic-field level, this situation suddenly played havoc with all things electrical and electronic. New order establishment had forced industry into a hastily configured re-build in its aftermath, but the agendas were all theirs. It had become obvious that Earth as we knew her and the phase in which she had spawned and nursed our life for an eon was finished and that that old world was truly dying all around us: To begin anew, perhaps, but no one knows. But for the time being, and for our eternity, knowing wouldn't do us any good because by that time we'd all be toast anyway.

Today was cross day. Crossing into the Unified States from the Northern Dominion or visa versa didn't used to be as treacherous and hostile as it currently was, the *traveller* noted. This was the result of fence building and divisive thought in general. But for his future to pan out as planned by financial planners entrusted by Dyfed Lucifer, the time had come for him to bare the cross of responsibility and honour. He was to cross today, get the job finished and then re-cross the border again. Any delay from here on it was not optional for otherwise he would run out of time in order to be back for the important appointment at the House of Lucifer's palatial home and world international headquarters in the Bountiful Valley of the Sto:lo River delta.

And one no longer took the border crossing experience lightly, either. The *pilgrim* had observed and learned from the best there was (and had ever been) when it came to the magician ship of being able to tactfully and deftly handle agents of the Establishment the world over. Furthermore, he was prepared. He put on a good face, as they say, though he wasn't sure who *they* were. Nor was anyone else sure, he realized. He knew he was going to make the most of it and that was the part he was most sure of.

He wasn't frightened or distracted in the least, even when he approached the border with its tall rows of barbed and razor wire fencing and the white blazing searchlights which were kept shining brightly down twenty-four seven from a very high white wall. He saw the dogs on the ground, the camera surveillance, and the heavily uniformed guards armed to the teeth with automatic rifles and their instant radio communication devices. All of these armed uniformed recruits were perched high up along the watchtowers of the tall white wall that shadowed the entrance/exit portal along with miles of white wall to either side. He saw guards peering at him through binoculars from the distant interior towers, but that's what guards did. Others were scanning the horizons. This they did day and night. They were trained to do this. They were good Nightwatchmen, and clever. For them promotions were always in the air. Above the portal itself and along stretches of the border (especially where no physical wall existed due to long distances and exorbitant costs) hovered armed, un-manned air drones being controlled day and night by Nightwatchmen who sat at desks in front of monitors in white shirts with rolled up sleeves. These strictly office Nightwatchmen worked these unmanned armed drones and spy-cams from afar. They did it from atop new government high-rise buildings of steel and glass in cities far away with names like Waco, Santa Fee, Flagstaff, Boise, Minneapolis, and Buffalo which housed military centres and installations. They peered through their monitors assisted by sensitive props, with bells and whistles, at close up situations from the comfort of their easy chair amid the workplace's social environment being peppered with casual office banal banter. Transmission was relayed to them either by coaxial running hundreds and even thousands of miles or fire-walled internet (only a narrow band of internet was available to the public now at this time that was almost fully limited for consumer purposes) from the focus points of interest on the borders and inside the country all the while keeping an eye on the weather charts. Drones which they also used for independent back up monitoring and surveillance were vulnerable to cyclones and fierce electrical storms which torn them apart and hurtled them to the earth. No one wanted that unreported on his or her watch.

This branch of elite white-collar workers (their uniforms were only for the parade ground and national holidays) took orders from a special branch of the Turnkey elites. The Nightwatchmen in turn dispensed orders through electronic pigeonholes to the necessary lower ranks of the Nightwatchmen. They also secured the necessary court injunctions and permits that the Nightwatchmen needed daily from the Turnkeys in order to retain the authority needed to do the job. They were also in contact with the military but only under the orders of magistrates. These latter Turnkeys were the higher elite folks who from time to time donned ritual costumes of authority of their own over their shiny, expensive and not so forthright uniforms that they purchased privately from Fifth Avenue and Savile Row for the occasion.

Entrance/exit portals along the US border were now much reduced in number from what they used to be, along with the number of folks passing through these checkpoints. That didn't affect the necessity of the border security industry, however. Border staff had increased. Our pilgrim in question had picked this entrance/exit portal for it was the closest one between Cowton and his destination of Flathead to the southwest. Though thoroughly checked and rechecked, his identity — along with his ownership of transportation, his licences, passes and his permits for being able to purchase necessities such as fuel and oil or even for purchasing food (for soon he would be a lone and unsupported alien in the US). And for that he needed to be capable of articulating everything exactly as it should be including being specific about where he was going, how he was going there and by what route and so on. They weren't dealing with any little old rinky-dink amateur, here, he could have told them. Not on your nelly! Who the devil did they think he was? Fortunately (for the *pilgrim*) they didn't know, exactly, just who the devil he actually was. That was a good thing. Anonymity was his friend this time. Not always is that the case. But they were going to do their utmost to find out what they could before the day was out and the last dog had died, that much he knew for sure. That they wouldn't find out was what he was counting on. It was just a game and you had to know the rules and how to play. That's all. But that was something they didn't understand, not one bit. Nor did they have to, of course. That wasn't their expertize. They didn't play games. What these Turnkeys and Nightwatchmen did was they destroyed game playing along with the players as well as with other people's rules. The only rules were their rules. And the rules changed as they saw fit and then they made up new rules to apply. They do this all the time, and it was with an insouciant manner of indifference that they changed rules and laws, provided certain privileges irrespective of personal nobility and character or lack thereof, and privatized justice to the highest bidder with the deepest pockets. Aristoteles the pseudo god wouldn't have been impressed. The *pilgrim* was sure of that.

It is he or she who is able to pay from the great vault of common wealth that controls justice and law, not who is unseen and is seen only to play the piper. This state of affairs was obviously an Aristotelian oversight. The only thing these bureaucrats among the echelon of the elite played well with was the system, their system, which was actually the Haploid (untouchable elite) system. And part of their obligation to everybody who had an identity (and a licence allowing them to have that identity and to remain alive and unfettered and outside the inside program) was to program them into the system for their own good and wellbeing. 'Apply to be programed today, do not delay', was the ingenious slogan that defined their attitude, along with their belief that 'the happiest occasion for non-conformers, malcontents and dissidents alike is their absorption (finally and gratefully received) into the security of the mainstream of conditional society.'

The Nightwatchmen at the watchtower certainly didn't delay, either, in contacting the party that the *hombre* had indicated to be his destination at Flathead on his application. He expected that. They had even enquired after and ascertained the nature of his business. This business was a reunion between a famous motion-picture photographer named Johnny Rocco and himself. But there was another matter between them and that was to settle a condition in the conveyance of Dyfed Lucifer's will for which he (the *pilgrim*) was the executor. Because it involved money, a special and financial forensic branch of the border agents poured over the paperwork like maggots on sheep guts. They dilly-dallied and lollygagged and found every reason under the sun to delay his departure from the dreaded sweatbox at this port of entry. Ultimately, everything was in order, at least from their slant and perspective (what he thought, believed, or wanted, or didn't want didn't matter to them), so finally, and suspiciously, they allowed him to continue on since they had exhausted all avenues to hold him. They could have done worse. Under a law of reverse onus they might have pre-emptively imprisoned him on suspicion of unnamed felonies. They could suggest, and be permitted to argue unreasonably that:

"In all likelihood, your honour, it's believed he is planning to commit such and such a felony."

For this being their assertion, they had a duty to bring charges against him pre-emptively.

The 'clash-rooms' used by border officials for interviews and shakedowns that were positioned between every entrance to and exit from the US were also stuffed full of uniformed no nonsense Nightwatchmen. They were about mature themes only where one would find that the use of a careless gesture or a flippant word, never mind an outright hearty or gently slipped expletive would not be an asset. It was all about posturing. He was surprised that they hadn't chanced on the carefully worded advertisement he had sent out in his effort to locate Johnny Rocco who had become a recluse and had artfully covered his tracks. But perhaps they had. The contact's real name was not, and never had been, Johnny Rocco, by the way. But Johnny Rocco was the most common name for Unified Statesian men during the last couple of centuries, so that was what he had chosen to use. His real name was Harvey Fulcher Brown, plain and simple.

This motorcycling *wayfarer*, in an endeavour to successfully complete his personal pilgrimage of responsibility, had conducted his search notice on a cleaned torc that was normally blacked out for protection anyway. But no longer were torcs capable of communicating via satellite anywhere in the world. As already stated, the band upon which folks could communicate today was very narrow with very defined purposes, mainly consumer oriented. The torc's original purpose was to be able to deliver and receive live conversational voice, voice messaging, text messaging, still and motion pictures transmission, and was able to access (where applicable) bank accounts, records, administrations, encyclopaedias, and vending houses in order to purchase any number and types of goods through any kind of mail-order system from anywhere in the world where service was offered. That couldn't happen now anyway with the drastic drop in the Earth's electro-magnetic field.

Fortunately for *the traveller* his torc had come from the laboratories of Dyfed's *pack* and were enhanced like no others on the market. He was even confident that all the blacked out data on his torc was comfortably invisible and hidden even when exposed to advanced scrutiny. Most weren't. Anyway, as for his electronic notice, he had written:

"Parasolo is looking for the Johnny Rocco who engineered the movie 'Fantasy City', staring Anlaf Rijk-Konge'. In finalizing his search notice he wrote…'Pls. contact Parasolo @ the House of Lucifer ASP.'

Four months later and one and a half months ago he received a contact answer informing him of Johnny Rocco's address. And as for today, all held out for his dangerous transference from The Northern Dominion to the Unified States and the state of Montana just as he knew it would.

PART TWO

HOODWINKED TO FUND THE HOLLY JOLLY, JUICY DEUCY EMPIRE

(The Pantomime)

'Tell me, where is the place that men call hell?'
CHRISTOPHER MARLOWE (*FAUSTUS*)

The house was raucous, loud, and brimming with people. It was difficult to tell whether the patrons were angry because of having to wait for the play to start, or whether they weren't angry at all, only jubilantly exited and over anxious. Also, because there were so many of them — all scrunched into this not overly large, oval playhouse — this scenario indubitably added an exponential factor to the appearance of their demonstrative animation. Before them was a circular stage dissected neatly in half by a tall, heavy, and elaborately adorned curtain that descended from behind a stout and gilded Roman ovolo whose length allowed it to extend slightly beyond the width of the opening. In this way the stage was divided into fore and aft. The curtain did not extend along the flat, front wall but was tucked in behind leaving the stage looking neat and clean with a well defined (albeit curtained) open centre stage. Goodness only knows what was in preparation and taking place on the semi circle behind that curtain the crowd must have thought. As for the stage in front, people had already thrown worthless objects onto the platform. Suddenly a skinny, raggedly dressed man climbed up onto the stage with help, or possibly (despite his resistance) was hoisted up and thereby tumbled upon it. Standing up, in order to look for a quick exit down, he suddenly became the object and target for more litter to be cast his way. A sandwich — no one except he could tell whether it was ham or beef — struck him in the face, accompanied by shrieks of applause. Stagehands came out from behind the curtain and dragged him backwards through the curtain and out of sight. The great arena that lay below and in front of the stage was configured into a crescent moon shape that was formed by the convex semi circular stage in front, and the circular outside walls of the playhouse behind. And fleshed out along that curved outside wall facing in towards the stage were three tiers of boxed-in seats where the better heeled sat above the smell. It is from this position that we observe the stage.

    Unfortunately, there was one draw back to this position that the well heeled coveted and reserved. For during the hot months the tight compression of those sweaty, hot, seething and heaving bodies below gave off a great stinking heat, and that revolting stink rose up into the tiers above. It didn't help either when the play was under way that fanners stood on the edge of the stage on either side and fanned the rising stink away from the stage and back toward the rear towards the classier seating arrangements above. Fortunately for the gentlemen and their whores this evening — for any woman accompanying a gentlemen to a theatre like this was not his wife as for gentlemen did not bring their wives to such outings as this to expose them to the vulgarity of political-religious and other scandalous behaviour with sexual innuendoes and overtones — it was the winter season where the stiff cold (both inside and out) diminished the stink somewhat. Indeed, outside the playhouse at this very moment in the shivering air were heavily wrapped-up citizens of the city of Nova Troia. They had walked here to the centre of town on the frozen mud of the streets gazing up toward a pale yellow evening sky. Some even walked across the frozen river Tems. But the shape-shifting sky quickly dropped into a brown-grey, leafless band of bare foliage that sharply defined the wide and frozen expanse of the Tems River that (blandly blanketed in snow) appeared on this evening as a dirty white band snaking among the splotchy riot of the brownish-grey movement of the city. And there, along the river's banks, now clouded in that magical light of dusk, pedestrians could see the bristling bare masts of ships that were held fast in the ice of the frozen river. They were able, too, to detect that each ship had a series of well worn, dirty brown paths distinguishable in the dusky light that lead to and from them from the brick and mortar sewn buildings that shored-up and hemmed-in the commercialised river-front. Other dirty brown paths criss-crossed the river.

Back at the playhouse a great rush of cheering rose up that could have been heard even as far away as the far side of the river. Then suddenly a thin man in a bright and gaudy frock and top hat stepped out from behind the curtain and onto the stage. He clasped a Venetian leather satchel in his hands and untwining its leather tie cords as he looked out over the crowd and began to address the audience below him in an ad lib fashion. He berated them for their poor taste, bad manners and foul breath that prompted him to call for the fanners to fan harder and more diligently. This only moved the cold air around. Needless to say, the common crowd in the arena, although less so from the hoity-toity in the tiered seating, began to applaud and show their appreciation by hurling food, such as rotting fruit and old vegetables at him. These latter mentioned delectable were sold by the pocket-full outside the main doors before the start of every performance. Even unmentionables, wrapped in filthy handkerchiefs were flung up at him; but even this did not deter the brave thin man in the gaudy frock. As soon as he had got most of the patrons riled up he then changed character and his top hat. Then — reading from his book bound in Venetian leather — he quickly outlined the play upon which the curtain behind was about to be raised. He then announced the name of the playwright, a certain Theoderic Horace Douglasson. That announcement was accompanied by a drab, half-hearted applause that was mostly drowned out by the background murmur and general chatter of exchanged gossip that was customary during this preamble. And it was also customary that if a silence were ever to occur it would be suddenly interrupted by a succession of loud and prolonged farts that would set up such laughter (and its ensuing din) that the rafters would begin shaking violently.

But up among the cushy box section on the third tier, at least two men acknowledged the playwright's name that was called out. This was the accustomed box of the Earl of Oxford who on this evening's performance was joined by two other male companions. The Earl by this time was well passed middle age while the other two were still fairly youngish. One of these was a certain Mr Kit Marlowe who was about the same age as the playwright but was already rather seedy and dissipated looking. He joined the Earl of Oxford in acknowledging the other beside them who was the playwright (play write or play right) Theoderic H. Douglasson himself. He was cradling a puppy in the crook of his arm. And while the three men talked animatedly he stroked the little puppy and kept the gentle, beautiful-eyed creature calm amid all the noise and terrifying shrieks of the crowd. Unlike the others below them in the theatre these men were each armed with a sword and dagger upon their bodies while beside them leaned a rod and staff, now commonly called a gentleman's walking stick. But in addition, and quite uncommon at that, was the fact that Mr Douglasson was decked out with a fully loaded gunpowder fuelled pistol. The weapon was well concealed beneath his clothing.

Although, Douglasson was unreadable he had a similar manner of body language to the other two. All three indicated some element of privilege coupled with non-egotistical pride of self-excellence (arête) along with some helpful wealth besides this. Unusually, they were decidedly devoid of the characteristic stamp of entitlement that many establishment men generally had about them. But there was something else about these three men. It was the wolfishness of their humour and the easy and casual self assured manner that wasn't a masked projection in a form of armour, on their part. They were casual fun-loving men of very serious nature who each resembled something of a wild animal that was certainly dangerous if provoked by the wrong person. Otherwise they were easy-going and forgiving. These marks of character stood out and separated them from the powerful oligarchs such as those that gathered and suck-holed around her Royal Highness Queen Beth who was the daughter of Henry Tudor, himself a descendant of Theoderic the Great (known in the west country as Teudur).

This character of nobility is what endeared these particular three men to others, especially to the poor folks and the dispossessed. The attraction may have been their softer under-wool and their rascally bushy-tail look that they had in their general appearance, compared to other men of status. They had broader chests, rounder (rather than elongated) heads with parted hair and longer ears. The mean-spirited oligarchy/establishment men, on the other hand, like their masters the Haploids who they served, would find them dangerous and frightening.

And there were two men who had close connections with the three men. Their names were Walt Ralay and Francis Draker (also Drago), who were also individualistic, free-thinking men of similar stamp. The first of these last mentioned, besides being a soldier, poet and spy, was an aristocratic entrepreneur who dabbled in exchangeable resources and goods that the new world of Merika provided. He brought these to the Europaean market for greater profits to reinvest back in Merika. This attitude eventually brought charges of treachery against him for which he was executed on orders from the Royal Crown. As for the latter, Drago, he was a sea captain and navigator by profession that was forced by circumstance into a promotion (and the obligatory higher pay category) that made him Her Majesty's Chief Royal Pirate. He was also the first Europaean sea captain to circumnavigate the world. These men all were of a similar character and stamp and were pivotal in helping to forge a new and immerging kingdom. Whereas, the establishment men (those aforementioned royal suck-holing, greedy minded capitalistic self providing entitled oligarchs who make out that their shit don't stink) fear surprises and all things unknown, unfamiliar and unorthodox when it comes to how others around them act and react. And they most certainly had reason to fear the fellowship of the former five, namely, the Earl of Oxford, Marlowe the spy, Douglasson the playwright, Ralay the entrepreneur and Draker, the pirate of the Hispanian Main most dreaded by King Felipe who was the most powerful emperor and king of the most powerful empire in the world and leader of the Holy Amoran Empire. And all five of these men were intimate with her Royal Highness, Queen Beth the Virgin: Relatively intimate, that is, except Ralay who was betrayed by this greedy queen, and the Earl of Oxford who was the queen's lover and close adviser and who may have been turned against Ralay as well.

These five weren't meek and mild men, but at the same time they weren't assertively rash or violent either. They tended toward reason and to apply logic rather than to suddenly react. Anyway, reacting wasn't something you wanted to be faced with when dealing with them. They were also in their own way quiet men. But their personality wasn't the problem. The problem was that there weren't enough men like them to make a difference in the end, not in a world with a burgeoning population, and not without super natural strength and will, there wasn't.

The current fellowship of these five (soon to be increased by Roger Bacon, Francis Bacon (no relation), William Gilbert and Isaac Newton) had interests that constituted the philosophy of Prydain. It was during this era, and over the next four centuries, when this tiny kingdom (now being called Angleland) fashioned itself into the most powerful empire on Earth. This was directly on the heels of Hispania who had a serious claim on all the Merikas except for the northern bulk of North Merika that had some Francia interests but was mostly claimed by modern Albion or Prydainia.

And the influence that these five men emitted and extoled was for fair and equitable governance across the land and the world under a democratic law of logos and of similar statutes that enforced individual participation. All the while the current suck-holers' on the continent that were more closely descended from Amor than Prydainia, kingdoms such as Hispania and Italia and in some aspects Francia that were now heavily immersed in the Holy Amoran Empire maintained that their best remedy was to stay the course and maintain the status quo. By and large, establishment men prefer a populace of will-less sheep, not wolves; definitely not wolves with a free will to range. On the other hand, these aforementioned five philosophical movers and shakers along with a few others sprinkled throughout gave evidence of a dimorphic occurrence of Amoran organization and strength within their society combined with a restless nomadic tendency to shuffle off down the road and go a-viking. Starting from the time od many millennium ago this dominant trait took the hominid out of the Great Riff of Africa and spread their species throughout the Earth. But in time the great majority quickly mellowed out and homogenised into a sedentary existence with no adventure or fight left in them. The result is often a placidity that's combined with abject senseless violence. And in this, the former resembled something even more voracious than the common forest wolf. They were what would become known as the timber wolves that guarded civilization as certain ones now guarded the *pack*. They were the type-two with the genetic allele DRD4-7R.

Anyway, at the mention of the said Mr Playwright by the master of ceremonies, the Earl of Oxford and Mr Marlowe shifted their eyes toward the other sitting beside them, each raising an eyebrow. Then they nodded their heads and smiled in a form of a recognition salute. Apparently, the Earl and his seedy looking guest also knew that the name of Mr T. H. Douglasson was a pseudonym that this man used as an alias as well as a penname. Apparently, he had often affected this name when writing his inflammatory prose and verse. In fact, at that moment only Mr Marlowe knew the other guest's real name; the Earl did not. In fact, the theatre tonight outing was an introductory meeting between Oxford and the playwright, for Marlowe was the common denominator here and he knew the three of them together wouldn't be a crowd, but get along like a house on fire.

It was now beginning to grow very dark inside the enclosed theatre and some candles were lit near the stage by the fanners just before the curtain rose. Up at his third tier box, the Earl and his companions were warmly and very expensively dressed. Mr playwright himself who was in transit through Nova Troia, was the most expensively dressed of any man there, probably the best dressed in the entire city which included the richest in the land and even the consorts of the amorously polygamous daughter of Plantagenet. At least, that is what the Earl had thought upon first seeing him. But he was certainly no dandy, either. Far from it, for he noted that the man's alert eyes and large hands helped to compose a body language which was confident and calm and possibly even threatening if provoked: this despite being told by his friend Marlowe that the playwright was a meditating pacifist but one who had never attended the Jeshuan cult centre at Westminster on the day of the sun or even to have ever entered the cathedral at Canterbury even though he had resided in that town many solar cycles ago. He was true to western philosophy, though he never belittled Abramists of any kind or other cults as well and supported the belief that knowledge and truth were greater than all religions and were what led to a manageable concept of universal law and order. So, being appropriately dressed, each in a fur hat that covered their ears, the men kept warm while most of the other patrons shivered in the chilly stink. Also, the Earl had ordered his well armed batman (who was his virtual shadow and was never counted separately from the Earl) to ensure that the small exterior window that poked outside from the second tier level directly beneath them was opened to allow the stink to seep out before it rose to this third level, if at all possible.

It had been the end of a long day for Mr Douglasson so far because earlier had visited the famous Virgin. Known for their indiscretion in everything, the current royal Teudur let herself be called the virgin queen. Soon to be dead of syphilis induced dementia or insanity she was bald and wild of eye, this daughter of Henry, when she summoned the playwright for an audience. Since they disliked each other it was their first and last meeting.

Then the curtain came up and the audience saw a great goat come onto the stage, walking on his hind two legs. His long, magnificent horns were spiralling up high over his head that was adorned with a warm, felt, pointed hat. The he-goat was dressed in a long black frock with his long white hair sticking out from beneath his hat and beyond his sleeves as well as from his lower legs below the hem of his frock. With a satchel slung over one shoulder the goat proceeded to walk around reading quietly to himself from a book. He was followed on stage by a troupe that morphed into a wolf pack. There was half a dozen of these darkly mottled, sleek canines, each with big yellow eyes and two large, white cuspids on either side of a long, pink tongue that dripped with saliva.

The clan chief, or king carnivore of these sleek yellow eyed canines, a certain Snarl Tamewulf, by name who was dressed as a courtly king, began complaining about the current conditions under which he was forced to conduct business in order fortify the livelihood and well being of his wolf clan. Indeed, other wolf clans were taking advantages of his disadvantaged state, he complained. Even the odd coy coyote and the occasional sly fox were encroaching on his territory. The other cast of wolves then set about sending up hurtful howls into the audience, and bayed woefully in their disgruntlement to the lights of the highly raised stage candles as if they were glowing stars.

"It is apprehension of the aggrandized state of our former quarry, the pigs and the sheep, who now risen — who summoning forth mighty vanguards woven from fantasy that have whipped up such forces — have unleashed havoc upon mine own comfy and settled horizon, me thinks,' said Tamewulf. 'Gadzooks! What say you, Grand Deputy and minister of the hunt and of defence, also of health and welfare, what say you?'

"I? Oh Grand Chief Executive, king of the Caucasian canines,' said a big grey, his mouth-full of sharp teeth cajoling his words that slid smoothly out around his salivating, pink tongue. 'Well, your majesty,' replied the deputy minister, 'me thinks you aught to appoint someone who you value over others to be your ambassador: One for the pigs and the other for the sheep while keeping them suspicious of each other. Best, too, to have separate programs for each. This is what I think, m'lord.'

"Ah, divide and conquer, is that it then? So, endowed with brains to convey my wants and desires,' said Snarl Tamewulf, 'and as my deputy minister, I deem you to be of said value. To wit: I appoint you as such, Slick Silvestre Grand Deputy, chief of ambassadors.'

"What, little ole me, m'lord?'

"I send you, Grand Deputy, to see that the pigs and the sheep are taught the necessity to reason as I do, and help them to clasp conclusions that only an alert and savvy canine can manage, and only if chanced to have apprenticed as such his whole life. Go forward, Slick, my Grand Deputy: go forward and purchase honour and grace from mine own eyes alone on behalf of our clan. And may Wotan be with you.'

As the play unfurled, the he-goat would oft times bridge the spoken lines by reading the background noise (as in the affaires of state) out aloud. Sometimes, though, his responsibility was simply in delivering a soliloquy or two in a timely fashion. This was conducted mostly in between those lines of the other wolven cast. But now he took centre stage, and set his legs apart to place himself securely in situation and to convey his immanent importance for import. Then in a much louder voice, he told how Slick Grand Deputy went forth to the tribe of Pigs and the tribe of sheep with a letter of introduction from the Crown with Snarl Tamewulf's personal seal upon it naming him ambassador in chief for the Wolven Clan. The cast then began to scurry around the stage in quick motion, the he-goat returned to his prominent position in the wings where he continued to read out loud of the ensuing events, and Slick Silvestre Grand Deputy of the Wolven Clan and ambassador in chief, approached centre stage. As the clan of Wolf left stage left, tribe of Pig entered stage right. It's cast (so the he-goat explained to the waiting-in-anticipation audience) included six members with its high executive being a certain Mr Fat Pig, who the tribe was named after. They were the Pig Fat Tribe, and although they didn't have a king or an emperor of their own, these cagey creatures were, nonetheless, extremely shrewd and sagacious with wit and tact enough to disarm even the most cautious, and those whose excellence was in vigilance and self-possession.

Then it was the tribe of sheep's turn. Its cast included ten members with its high executive being a certain Mr Sheepish Ram. The he-goat (extrapolating on what was maybe about to occur) stated the fact that: "Mr Fat Pig was also Mr Big Pig, who had worked and wormed his way into the position of 'he who was all high', or chief executive officer. This was due to those same earlier stated merits indigenous to the Pig Tribe in general, plus to the power of six. This made him very intelligent and important, or at least in their minds.' Mr He-Goat said he wasn't certain in what order the words intelligent and important should be placed: That is whether he was important because he was intelligent or intelligent because he was important. 'In any case,' he added, 'this mode of virtual intelligence was important. It was the intelligence of convincing people to believe what was most favourable to himself (the speaker) rather than themselves and of then taking advantage of the opportunity it opened up. Maybe this intelligence was simply ruthlessness and uncaring, devoid of charity, kindness or any love for others in his heart, as well as domineering, calculating, and full of enmity and outrageous ferocity to the power of six. Cunning wasn't so much second nature with Mr Big Fat Pig. Nor was it the second nature of any of the chief executive officers in general who graduated into that position, as it was with others of the greater tribe of Pig,' Mr He-Goat said in his raspy yet loud voice.

"Cunning, He-Goat said, 'was intrinsic to Mr Big Fat Pig's very state of being, itself: as opposed to that more common complexity of a psychopathic haploid being that was necessarily stripped to the raw and completely expunged of all feelings other than the wants and desires of his own ego. In any case, and apart from that, Mr Fat Pig's job as chief executive officer was to arrange for the kings, emperors, and the necessary established order that they represented which lorded it over the hordes and societies of other species, to be at all times and in all ways in Mr Big Fat Pig's pocket. Sometimes this also meant in his pay, but usually the emperors and kings could conduct lucrative business for themselves — often in the old established way by stealing — in so long as some way or another Mr Pig Fat Big had already arranged for it to happen and had given his puppet ruler the green light. In this way the Pig Tribe connived and manipulated in their attempt to dominate the Sheep species at large, and for their own profit and pleasure. And it was something that they were quite successful in achieving, as it turned out. But if a cheap king or a sheep emperor didn't play ball and wanted to do whatever he felt like doing, come what may, then that interfered (or was seen to be interfering) with the Pig Tribe's authenticity and elite status quo. In every single case this then necessitated him in having to take immediate steps such as defensive action and see to it that a real, live, honest to goodness war with its accompanying turmoil, pain and suffering to the people (even his own people but not so much him) be brought to break out among the Sheep.

But there was more to it than just that,' the He-Goat said. 'Hitting upon by accident, hearing of other practices by chance, and encouraging certain rumours and folk tales, and tall tales, and old wives' tales, the tribe of Pig managed, also, to conjure forth a virtual psychological society of Sheep amid an array of rules and beliefs, sacred cows and hallowed ground which acted like a big comfy cushion for the king or emperor of their choice, and all of his yes-men, which they then placed down into its big, soft centre completely surrounded with burning bushes that were never consumed.'

At this point the He-Goat finished speaking and returned to gaze at his book. The troupe of the tribe of Pig then quit their movement and the rustling and sabre rattling upon the stage were now instructing the Sheep clan (who were standing meekly by, waiting for directions as to what to do next) to encircle the lone member of the Wolven clan who had remained behind.

"What have we here?' said Mr Big Fat Pig to the deputy minister of the Wolven Clan with his eyes that were wide and fat which expressed mock surprise. Meanwhile, the fellow pigs were busy marshalling the Sheep clan.

'We have a species of the wolf among us, if I'm not mistaken. Who, then, might he be?' he said as he snatched the written communiqué from the wolf's claws and proceeded to read it out loud.

'A letter of introduction for his majesty's ambassadors from the Wolven Clan,' he stated loudly. 'But is this truly so, my fellow underlings?' he asked with a mocked tone of inquiry and in a punctuated manner. 'Is there really a wolf here among the pigs and sheep? No, of course not,' he exclaimed with glee jumping up and down, while the other five pigs squealed in delight as Slick Silvestre Grand Deputy wrenched off his fake wolven head to show a fat little pig's head beneath. It would seem that the ambassador's best before date had unexplainably expired.

"He is just another pig in wolf's clothing, a pig working for us,' Mr Big Fat Pig chimed in again. Then he addressed the ten members of the Sheep clan. 'We have saved you from the wolves,' he said, 'so you will continue as before, but with these corrections and adjustments. We will appoint auditors over you and we will now increase your taxes. It will be necessary for us to approve of all your clubs and associations as we approve your religions and all of the laws governing you. And this new ambassador to the Sheep clan will chose some of you to serve out the poison that we will feed the wolves over time.'

Then the He-Goat addressed the audience saying, 'And that poison will be the great lie that will be hurled against the true truth, as it be made to besmirch the real things of great importance to the Sheep clan about themselves, especially the truth about the state of their being and the state of their not being, or death. In essence, the poison will create or found a form of universal acceptance, a god, if you like, which they will fixate upon, so it will never occur to them to reason and discover the truth about the lying pig's big lie. Our Mr Slick Silvestre here will keep the wolven king on the straight and narrow while the king in turn will keep his loyal subjects on the same path. Ha, does it get any better than that? my fellow pigs. It is a triumph or the un-natural over the natural, is what we have here. Our collective job, of which I am chief executive officer, is to keep those un-natural-all-'round subjects loyal.' Mr Big Fat Pig deliberately said the last four words of that sentence slowly and individually to the accompaniment of first, the thumb of his left hand being stuck up and out at the first of the four words — 'keep' followed by the forefinger with — 'those', and so forth. He then added, 'and my specific responsibility is to keep the king loyal to me.'

Suddenly the pigs began a fast circular motion around the lone wolf as the He-Goat resumed his poetic role as interpreter…"And then the pigs all sang,' Mr He-Goat said. At that point the pigs, led by Mr Big Fat Pig himself, began to sing as they circled around and around the lone wolf.

"We watch and watch,' they sang, 'as the wolves go round and round in our circle game.'

At that point the chief ambassador re-donned his wolven head and stood solemn and still in the centre of the stage with an extended index finger to his wolven forehead as if in deep thought. The pigs while still continuing to sing louder and dance around the ambassador faster and faster began also to move out into a wider circle. Just then the Wolven Clan, led by King Snarl Tamewulf, began to re-emerge single-file back onto the stage from behind the curtain into the centre of the dancing and singing pigs where they crowded around the deputy, Slick Silvestre. Now they were all on stage together and the pigs suddenly produced before their faces the hand held comedy geek masks while the wolves produced their geek tragedy counterparts. Then with great fanfare, Mr Big Fat Pig, now bedecked with smiling mask before his fat, little piggy face, broke through the circle into the centre where he took up King Snarl Tamewulf's hand, the one which was not holding his unhappy mask before his hollow and harried wolf face. These two individuals then began to dance together as though it were a cross-dressing princess' coming out ball. In Snarl Tamewulf instance, it wasn't so much a case of a princess than that of a queen's coming out ball, for being one he was now the Fat Pig's bitch and gaudily dressed as such. The remaining cast members, which included the troubled but thoughtful Mr Grand Deputy, then coupled up as pig and wolf and they all began dancing together. Then suddenly the dancing and the singing abruptly stopped, and Mr He-Goat who, having moved to centre stage and taken up a kneeling and crouched-over position (while holding an entire clenched hand to his forehead as in advanced thought), stood up tall and straight, his horns towering above and catching the candlelight. He then faced the happy first couple.

"Wolven Snarl Tamewulf, do you take this pig to be your lawfully wedded husband, to hold and cherish for as long as you both may live?'

"I do,' he answered.

"And Mr Big Fat Pig, do you take this wolf to be your lawfully wedded wife?'

"I do,' he answered.

"Then by the power over the people's psyche which is necessarily invested in me, I pronounce you man and wife before the power of the illusion of god. You may kiss the bride, Mr Pig.' Then all the couples began dancing again and swirling around and around mimicking the circle game. The newly wedded couple danced together, more slowly and whirled around more or less in the same spot, centre stage. Mr He-Goat had a big, sly smile on his face and his eyes had turned into slits that gleamed red in the flickering light. Suddenly the He-Goat pulled a flute out of his vest, and as he, too, danced he began playing a rippling tune to which all the players took to one last lap of dancing before quickly embracing and moaning and groaning as they entwined on the floor. Then each wolf got passively onto their hands and knees while their pig partner mounted them from behind. Then, with the exception of the flute playing He-Goat, they all began to copulate and hump in pantomime. After a spell — with all the noises of having sex in a group inevitably drowning out the flute — they got up and somewhat embarrassed, cleaned themselves off as the audience went mad with delight and howled louder than the wolves could possibly howl.

Then some of the Pigs pulled out smoking pipes and a substance that had just started to arrive in Albion from a place in the newfound lands of Merika that had been named after the Plantagenet and the Teudur families. And this substance that the acting ensemble began to smoke was nothing short of being the most valuable payload that was returning with the ships sailing back from this new found, and newly named Virgin's-land (Virginia) after the queen. And as for the payload itself — tobacco was the name of the game. Smoking was quickly becoming the thing to do now, and to be seen doing, and they had none other than Walt Ralay to thank. At that point all the Pigs lit their pipes and smoked apace as the raucous audience, silenced for a change, gawked on. Then, with each couple holding hands again, they took turns running off stage, the first couple exiting off stage left, the next exiting off stage right, and so on until only the He-Goat was left playing his tune. Suddenly the flute delivered a calamity note that was both out of tune and not in sync with its musical piece. Then the lights were quickly blown out and all was virtually dark.

Silence and tobacco smoke hung in the air over the arena momentarily again until the curtain was quickly raised and the entire troupe came out each holding a lighted torch. Then the silence of the audience erupted again into a sudden and jubilant cacophony. Upstairs, in a box at the third level tier, the Earl of Oxford was slowly nodding his head. Mr Marlowe and Mr Douglasson carefully watched his reaction.

(Bulging eyed Mr Toad barks at the big man with the puppy)

> 'None are more hopelessly enslaved then those who falsely believe they are free.'
>
> **JOHANN VON GOETHE**

The carriage train slowly pulled out of Liverpool Street station just behind the old Bishop's Gate that these days butted up against a huge and complicated maze of stables. Its earthy scents and underlining hubbub of trembling and neighing animals gave each of the twenty-four horses of the four-carriage train a rousing send off. After circling around to the right, the carriages got onto the main road, lined up, and headed for East Sax county through a newly erected suburbia of factories that were forging parts for large iron machines used in different, newly constructed, never before seen industries that were sprouting up all over the place. Never since those days when Amor had failed and her light dimmed had such mechanisms and gadgets of contraption been manufactured at such a rate as it was now and here in Albion. The streets and roads they trundled along in this Nova Trojan suburbia were uneven and rough at the best of times as they were accustomed to serving large and heavy carts that were often pulled by teams of twelve horses or by oxen. But in this cold season, the frozen chunks of mud and dirty ice which got under the carriage's wheels heavily rocked the horse drawn carriages (cars for short) and jarred the passengers to no end.

Six large horses pulled each car that seated eighteen people. In each of the horse drawn contraptions five cushioned seats were placed at each end of each carriage while the two remaining rows of seats in between sat eight people in total and were back to back, the forward row facing to the front of the car while the reversed seating behind faced backward toward the rear row at the back of the car. Cutting each of the middle seating in half, with the two back to back sets of two seats on either side was an aisle or short passageway to walk from front to back. There wasn't much room either way. There were four doors that opened out, two on either side up front and the same at the back. There were three windows running down either side of the car with a window placed in each of the doors that left one central and larger window between the doors on either side of the carriage. For the two people that sat next to that window, one faced one way and the other faced the other. This was so for either side. The individuals who sat next to them had the centre aisle on one side of them or the other. There were no windows front or back. The roof of the car contained a highly fenced container and storage area called a luggage rack that was usually piled high with large leather cases and trunks. Sometimes the carriages (cars) pulled a two-wheeled cart behind if there was more luggage than normal.

But that was only on the high end and expensive transport lines, such as with this particular carriage train. As the first car to leave was also the only first class car among this high-end transit-coach company, it was more elaborate than the others. Unlike this car the three trailing cars did not have cushioned seats nor were there any jugs of drinking water for passengers to slake their often dry throats on warm dusty days, or hot chaw on colder days like the present. Chaw (chai) or tea had recently begun to turn up in the city's coffeehouses. This phenomenon resulted from Albion's recent freedom to travel more securely at sea. For with the help of Her Majesty's Chief Pirate Drago her the Angl-ish navy had sunk and put asunder the great lurking and dangerous Hispanian navel armada once maintained by King Felipe of Hispanian, who was also king of the Portuguese, king of Napoli and of the Sicilians (Si-chil-ians), and finally also by right of *jure uxoris*[59] he was the king 'in waiting' of the Angle-ish and the gentle people of the Emerald Isle (Hibernia) as well through his wife Maria (Mary or Mari) who had directly preceded the so-called virgin queen, daughter of Tuedur.

As the first car to leave the station was also the luxurious first class tender (the remainder all being economy), it was full of well heeled customers who wouldn't have to eat dust in the summer or put up with splashing and flying mud and wet the rest of the year. As such, everybody aboard that first car out was very well dressed and one could tell by the spoken words that the folks here were not only travelling in style and had money but were also well spoken and educated. Today this first class car carried only seventeen people, which included four women and a child. Two of the women were travelling together while the other two were accompanied (presumably) by husbands, one of which was the mother of the child. The rest of the passengers were male. A still young looking middle aged man, rather large and lengthy of arm ands leg had bought two travel seats. That made up the eighteen-seat capacity. But amazingly, it turned out, the man's second seat was reserved for his little puppy. The two of them sat in the back corner by the rear right-hand door.

Aside from the exasperation of the jarring caused by the road's uneven surface, passengers were further irritated by this man's absent minded left hand that was playing with the puppy he kept on his lap or on the seat beside him. The puppy growled its sweet and un-intimidating little throat noises and snapped and bit at the man's twisted handkerchief he kept wrapped around one hand. The puppy had earlier been content to lie on the man's lap for back at the station the first customers aboard had found the man had already settled in and was apparently asleep before the first wave of travellers (to beat the rush) had arrive and climbed aboard. The bumping and thumping of luggage being stowed may have awakened the little dog but the man's eyes had remained shut until they pulled out of the station. Immediately to the man's left was the puppy's vacant seat. Further to his left were three articulate older people, a man and wife and another man of the same age. These folks were irritated and annoyed by the man's little dog, but more likely at the man himself for bringing it along. 'After all, this was first class.

Dogs don't belong here at all', so folks on board overheard the older woman to his left snip.

"And maybe the man himself doesn't either,' the older man in the far corner said a little louder.

Although a few others' pointed remarks were said out loud, the man or the little puppy didn't respond or take any notice.

Others noticed. Across from the man with the dog were two well-dressed young professional men who were not talking and presumably didn't know each other. On

---

[59] *By right of his wife*

the other two seats — across the aisle from the two young professionals — were two women together, one being a little older than the other. They faced the three irritable travellers just left of the man and his dog, and both women, so the man with the dog thought, were very pretty. He also noticed that they were both eyeing him with a healthy appetite. The stern and conservative older folks might have noticed it too, for the man next to the window on the other side of the car kept poking his head out and around the others to glance toward the man with the dog even when the dog was quiet. He may have even heard what the ladies were whispering to each other about, as they glanced up and often caught the tall, big boned man's eye for a second or two before looking away. Then there would be a flurry of quickly delivered sentences said back and forth between them in bursts of low, hot breaths. By this time the man wondered if they weren't even two sisters. Apart from them, the man with the dog didn't seem all that interested in the people around him. Furthermore, there was an indication in his nonchalant manner that he probably didn't much care either, about them or what they might think of him and his little dog. After a time the man set the little dog down onto the car floor and it began to scramble around panting gruffly like a little dog. The man smiled as he watched it and reached into his heavy coat and pulled out a flask that he tipped to his mouth. Soon one of the women had attracted the little dog, and along with much gum-sucking and heavy sighing from the three older folks in a display of their disapproval, soon the dog had become a going concern with it wanting to play with the two women who were encouraging it while three other pairs of conservatively booted feet were shuffling and kicking to keep the little puppy at bay. Catching both of the women's eyes at the same time, the man smiled and politely offered the two women a dram of drink from his flask, wiping the lip with a clean handkerchief he pulled from a pocket and offering them the use of a small, handle less silver cup. The women politely declined, but thanked him and he noticed that they looked pleased that he had offered.

At that moment the little puppy piddled on the floor by his master's feet, accompanied by so much moaning and groaning from the three opposite the two ladies that the remaining passengers up the car (who wouldn't have been able to clearly see what was going on) all strained their necks to look. The four closest with their backs to them had twisted their necks around and craned to see what the fuss was about.

Just then the youngster that was aboard, whose voice had been made known to the travelling companions, rushed forward towards the only really interesting domestic event at hand. He landed on his hands and knees near the dog and the pool of piss.

"Whoa,' he shouted out loudly which only caused more cross and irritable folks to gum-suck with more tisk-tisking while catching each others' eye and shaking their heads in frustration.

"Oh my word,' the dog's master suddenly said more loudly than the others so that all in the car couldn't help hear. 'The dog has peed a little puddle on the floor, and people all around ask, good grief, what for?' The man sing-songed the obviously made up on the spot rhyme then chuckled to himself. 'Just what are we going to do? Oh my. For dullards, aghast and galore, the world is going to come to an end and, so I fear, be no more.'

As he spoke he dropped one of his handkerchiefs onto the small puddle of piss he looked wide eyed in mock amazement into the youngster's face. This unusually animated and entertaining grown-up man and his antics transfixed the youngster. Then he watched him slowly move his leg and set a large foot heavily onto the handkerchief that he kind of daubed and moved around a little with his boot. With a whimsical smile across his face, the man's eyes never once moved away from watching the little boy and the latter's amusement in all that was going on. On his part, the youngster was overly curious at this giant of a man who could safely indulge in something outside of grown-up behaviour that always amuses but is usually denied a little boy. Why didn't more grown-up people do more of this? he must have thought. But then the boy quickly remembered having been told that grown-up people that could amuse children by seeming to be children were insane, or at least descending into that direction. And this was all caused by some disease that was the result of the sin of fornication and what not that men indulged while defying god. Furthermore, these types of fellows were dangerous. One must avoid them at all costs.

The doors on the car opened out toward the front. As they were travelling at a good clip, the man pulled down the window so that if (or when) the door was opened it wouldn't act like a sail and snap wide open with the force of resistance wind pushing against it. This could cause unnecessary surprise or damage if manned incorrectly. Then keeping his left leg stretched out with the little boy and the little dog safely on his left side, this giant, insane and dangerous man moved the other foot over and quickly flicked the urine soaked handkerchief over toward the door. Then strong-arming the door with his large right hand gripping it at its window-ledge he unclipped the door catch and pushed it open against the rushing wind no more than the breadth of one of his hands so it wouldn't catch the passing stream of air and tug at his wrist. For the bare moment that it took, he steadily held the door and at the same time by using the outside of his right foot, he pushed the urine soaked handkerchief out the door and quickly slammed it shut then pushed the window up again. This motion, it seemed was done all in one fell-swoop in a matter of seconds.

"By Jove!' shouted out a loud voice.

"What the Deuce is going on back there?' another demanded, jumping to his feet and rushing forward through the aisle towards the man with a stupid facsimile of responsible concern written all over his pathetically fleshy and worried stupid little face. He bumped into someone directly in his way before stopping, which instantly knocked the postured alarm from the latter's face to be replaced by one of bewilderment. Other people were beginning to stand up, too.

"You — hold on there,' someone cried. 'What do you think you are doing?'

"Great god-Zeus, the man has gone crazy,' said another.

"He must be drunk, said another woman somewhere in the front, presumably not the mother of the child from whom no peep was heard. 'Hold on, you.'

"There's a child there in danger by the open door,' resonated a shrill intonation intending on injecting fake fear (or maybe not) in their hysterical voice; the same trend of fear that was also visible in the lines on some of the strained faces bobbing around about. It was the type of face that one gets from inevitable hopelessness, and that lonely sense of impotence and the feeling of being irrelevant and unimportant. Here now was a chance to shine. This may have been the thought that shot through their bored and boring brain on this occasion. But that's not assured.

"Yes, boot that pissing mutt out and close that damned door. Good heavens. What's the matter with the man?'

"The door is closed and nobody is in danger,' said one of the young professionals sitting beside the door and opposite the man with the puppy. He had cricked his neck around as he threw the words over his right shoulder with air of irritation and a hint of amusement besides. He and the other young professional sitting beside him then shared a word and a restrained laugh then immediately went back to minding their own business. An older man by the aisle, sitting directly behind and back to back with the younger of the two women, got to his feet and turned his body around in a manner that showed he had a permanent crick in his old chicken-roped neck and couldn't much turn his head around any which way. He had a rather top-heavy looking brimmed hat on his head, too, and his face was wide along with his eyes that were widely spaced apart and bulged out like a frog. He was sour looking and beneath those bulging, watery pink rimmed eyes was a wide lipless mouth that seemed to stretch from the bottom of his jaw under his left ear that slit along up in a rounded curve to just under his nose and plunged back down to the bottom of his right jaw like a big wide W.

"I have put up with just about enough of this…this irresponsible goings on and commotion,' he said, rather slowly in a loud but hoarse voice. 'A minute ago the fool was trying to solicit these women here, offering them alcohol, brandy, probably. I can smell him from here. His brandy breath is foul. He's a drunkard and a backslider, if I ever saw one. He's a bounder and he doesn't belong in this class of car.'

"Let's get this car stopped and get him off,' said one of the earlier mentioned older folks who was sitting in the back row on the other side of the car near the man with the dog.

"Let's get him off without stopping the car,' said an immature voice from the other end of the car that was accompanied by some dribbles of laughter.

"You, up there,' said the inflexible but persistent former complainant, 'rap on the hatch and inform the driver to stop at once.'

In the meantime, the man with the dog who had suddenly and unjustly been subjected to this unfair display of brutal abuse without a lick of any natural compassion from many of his companions, seemed, however, to be unperturbed by the assault. This, despite the fact that it now looked as though he might be rejected and turfed off the coach and he and his puppy left to fend for themselves on the side of the road in the snow and the cold. He had remained seated up to now but had slid down further into a low slouching position, and his long limbs (that took up too much room) made it look uncomfortable for him. But the man himself, who languishing in this slouching and casual posture (his chin almost on his chest), was very much characteristically set apart from the other men present who were rigid in comparison and sat upright and kept stern expressions on their sever and dull faces that always frightened children. But this large, exquisitely well dressed man who was obviously not a dandy, neither was he one of the young and privileged members of the current pampered generation, looked fully relaxed and appeared to be stifling an urge to break out into laughter. He seemed almost amused by the negative attention directed towards him by his fellow coach companions and did not appear to be slinking into some secure cocoon to hide. He had just picked up his little dog again and had placed it standing on his almost horizontal stomach and was actively getting the little creature worked up again with gentle pinches to its tail and pokes to its mouth which made the little mutt yap and jump with glee all around in circles on the man's tummy. Across from the two women, the austere face of the older (very verbal and nasty) gentleman was cocked and twisted as his face stared over at the obviously puerile and undisciplined man playing like a child that was destined to be a lunatic on account of his lack of disciple and his rejection of any respect for his responsible betters.

To the man with the little dog, that former's head and face appeared to be that of a scruffy wet feathered chick of some giant prehistoric bird of some kind. It was an enormous face with the visage resembling that of a shivering and vibrating vulture. The strangely reversed lids of its cold beady eyes that were fastened among the tight furrows and folds of his pink and wrinkled skin blinked each eye as it was aimed in the man's direction. Each eye took its turn to scrutinize him as he turned his head this way and then the other way, his plumage jiggling and shaking all the while. Other than the shaking and quivering and cocking of the head, these sideways bottom-blinking eyes continued to be fixed motionlessly upon him. And within them there was not so much as a modicum of human empathy or tenderness; but rather they were full of fear and the companion of that dangerous emotion's — hatred.

Then the two women noticed that their amusing man was smiling at them, this time with a certain twinkle in his eye, and it seemed as if he was just about to get up for some reason. Just then they all heard a loud voice cry out inquisitively.

"Dyfed Lucifer? Good heavens, man! Dyfed, it's you, isn't it? Surely…I'd know you anywhere, even after all these years.' At that point the people in the carriage saw the man with the dog wiggle around into an upright position and then stand up in order to look down the car at the man who was coming towards him through the aisle, pushing past the elbows of the people to get closer as he called out his name again. The former had finally got to his feet with a pleasant but slightly surprised look on his face. Unfortunately, his larger than average height wouldn't allow him to stand straight up as everyone else could, so his head was tilted to one side which, with a little dog cradled along one forearm, gave him a comical look.

"Well I never,' the tall man said pleasantly in a strong carrying voice and in a strange western Keltic tongue which few of the travellers present, if any, understood. 'If it's not my old friend Munzie coming to my rescue.' Suddenly, there were tears in this big and menacing looking man's silver eyes, which were immediately noticed by the two women.

"John Galway of Munster, by golly,' he said now in the Angle-ish tongue. Placing his little dog in the crook of one arm, and watching Jack Galway barge past the frog-man with the top heavy hat, he reached out then with the other arm and flung it around his old friend's neck, pulling him forward then so they clung to each other. Dyfed then kissed his old friend.

Most of the people had sat down by now and the car had quickly grown very quiet, though every single eye was still carefully watching the situation. All of them had seemed embarrassed and even offended at the display of emotion and intimacy. But John Galway of Munster, they could detect, was obviously a man of means and also of importance. He quickly sat in the vacant seat beside Dyfed. And even though the passenger travellers might have been all dressed up like a dog's dinner in their rich and fancy suits, once Dyfed stood (tried to stand) his height, they now saw that he was clothed in tailored garments the likes of which put all of theirs to shame, even those of his friend from the front of the car. For all of their outpouring of expenses to be clothed by their tailors, those tailors may as well have been clothing prisoners destined for the dungeon compared to the elegant garments this tall man wore. For they were richer than any they had ever seen up close before, what with his embroidered great coat, beneath which his trousers, shirt and cravat were fit for an emperor. They hadn't noticed this until now.

But the latter noticed that the man with the bulging eyes and the great swoop of his down-turned front part of his mouth that reminded Dyfed of a toad wearing a top hat that was the same man who had called him a drunkard and a backslider and said he didn't belong in this class of carriage, was still staring at him. In addition, his body language was such that it was meant to incur encouragement to the others to continue on and take up the fight and throw him off. Dyfed stood up again, this time his head was tilted to the other side. It appeared that somehow this obstinate bulging-eyed man hadn't yet caught up with events that had clearly moved on since the moments before. And he still had that appalling shit-eating snob-nob look on his wide, sour ridiculous face. Apparently, so everybody was told by him, he was a circuit magistrate on some last minute and unscheduled emergency, and he had quickly let this drop out of his mouth on the first chance he had on opening it, which seemed to be the only foundation and authority behind the criticism which he had flung in Dyfed's direction. Presumably, everything to this man was an emergency, and a serious one at that.

Holding his little dog in both of his big hands like it was a big, fat, writhing fish that was wagging its tail, Dyfed now stepped towards this man and leaned down quite close to look him over.

"Mr Toad? I presume,' he said unassumingly, followed by a loud *riibbit* sounding croak in his voice, accompanied by a disarming smile as he towered over the man. 'Well, your fun is over and finished now, Mr Toad. Please face the front and sit down, or you can fornicate right off this coach if you have a mind to; but I'll see that we get it stopped for you in order to facilitate your timely disembarkation without discomfort or embarrassing clumsiness on your part. There will be no more disturbances here. Eh? You've had your fun. Now, shut the fornicate up, will you? Menstruating mother! Let folks be. Travelling in these boxed cages is nuisance enough as it is without folks like you causing a ruckus and getting other folks all riled and worked up and smelling the car up with your farts and body odour, eh.' He then held the little dog (which might just as well been a wind-up toy for the gimmick he was about to pull) and held in front of the man's face. Then, placing his own face right behind the little dog's head, he suddenly imitated the sound of a vastly more nasty and dangerous dog as he shook and rocked the little dog in front of the man's silly face. Of course that caused a growling, squirming wiggling and puppy barking action of its own from the little dog just as suddenly it produced a fit of giggling from the two ladies close by and some snickering elsewhere around the carriage that suddenly now seemed to be on the up rise. The suddenly from out of the young boy's throat who was still standing wide-eyed beneath Dyfed watching him, a husky and hearty growling laugh suddenly erupted.

Dyfed produced his flask of whisky and poured a considerable amount of its contents down his throat, smacked his lips loudly once or twice, then looked around. Then he leaned forward again toward the bulging eyed Mr Toad (who still hadn't moved). He exhaled softly into the man's face followed by a broad smile.

"It's whisky, Mr Toad. Whisky. Can we say — whisky? Can we say — not brandy? Can we say — I can not tell the difference between whisky and brandy because I'm just a know nothing blow-hard idiot whose intent is first to impress the easily impressionable and not really know anything much at all about my fellow humanity besides. And even though I'm a magistrate in my own right I'm right out of my mind. How are we doing with that, Mr Toad?' Dyfed said with a nod accompanied by a guarded smile.

After that Dyfed tucked his pet under his arm again, ruffled the boy's hair with his free hand has he turned back to John of Munster whose stiff eyebrows had shot up high onto his forehead as he said half laughing…"Some things don't change after all, I see.'

The catching disposition and attraction of the large man who was now standing more or less in the centre of the car as well as at the centre of everything that was taking place in the car and attracting attention, was obviously that of a man who was well in control, not only of himself but also of the situation. His antics that had thrilled the youngster a few moments ago were now entertaining the adults and that quickly helped to change the mood of the onlookers in general. As he confronted Mr Toad, Dyfed's brightly lit silver alert eyes also sought out the other loud-mouthed aggressors. And his steady gaze now lingered upon them, as he looked these men thoroughly up and down. And it wasn't lost on too many that Dyfed's little heart to heart chat with Mr Toad was meant for the ears of all in the car, especially those who had been a little too eager to be a tad vocal. This was due to, and controlled by their weakness of character, he told them now, and their temperament along with their mealy and abusive mouths. They had been like a den of skittish and hungry little carnivore pups confronted by a strange, large and passing lone wolf. But apart from a few posturing nips and some high-pitched yappy barks in his general direction, they lacked (apparently) the guts to lead their pack onto the kill with any genuine intent until help of greater numbers arrived. And that didn't quite pan out.

The general melee in the car had reason now to quieten down and keep a low profile. Soon they all began to smile and nod to one another, which reminded Dyfed of the prostrations of the bitch who lies on her back among a strange dog pack and allows them to sniff her while she lays motionless, with the exception of her pink tongue flicking in and out licking the air in slow motion.

In this case, however (he thought with a sense of irony), he alone was the *pack* of one, and the lion's share of all of them, were just a bunch of squabbling little bitches. He turned back toward his old friend and his eye caught Mr Ugly-Duckling in the corner. With the little dog smiling and sticking his pink tongue out and around him from the crook of his master's arm, Dyfed poked a finger in the elderly gentleman's direction and said.

"I didn't catch your name, bub?' he exclaimed cupping his large, free hand to the back of one ear for added effect. Dyfed had now taken a step back and stood in front of the rear seating. Muns was immediately to his left. Still standing directly in front of him also to his right was Mr Toad.

It was the latter that motioned toward the face of the giant baby vulture, saying:

"This is Mr Raywald Friesie (Freezy). He too, like me, is a magistrate and an acclaimed barrister. Mr Friesie, attorney at law works for Mr Egidius Joslin of the financial House of Joslin. Anybody whose anybody knows who the House of Joslin is.' It was obvious to all that the man spoke with a genuine intent to impress the confronter, as he obviously was himself impressed with Mr Friesie's position and status.

"Ah, is that a fact' responded Dyfed. 'Everybody knows who the House of Joslin is, do they? An acclaimed barrister at that, is he? Then you must have made yourself into a valuable and useful tool for the powerful elite, eh, Mr Friesie?' he said turning back to the baby Lappet-faced vulture. Dyfed's eyes fixed again on the man in the far seat. 'A solicitor, and for Mr Egidius Joslin of the House of Joslin, at that — well I never!' Dyfed added after a pause, clipping the pronunciation of Joscylin to Joslin. 'Your ticket, please, Mr Ugly-Duckling, barrister at law for Egidius Joslin, if you wouldn't mind. Otherwise you will have to go along with Mr Toad over here. Paying passengers with honest earnings and clean money only on this carriage, I'm afraid; and that means Messieurs Top-Hatted-Toad and Ugly-Ducklings included.'

Dyfed (now feeling the matter well settled) turned and smiled at the two pretty women.

"I'm Dyfed Lucifer, chief executive officer of the House of Lucifer that I myself founded well over a thousand years ago,' he said, ignoring all the accredited accoutrements which had become attached to his name. A hush immediately followed by a hum of low voices that charged the air of the coach.

Certainly, Dyfed was an unknown to all but Jack Galway of Munster here, but the House of Lucifer decidedly was not, for this merchant and trading company were well known to all here and on the continent. And although his Tournay office had amalgamated with the one in Bruges, the one he founded along the River Tems' embankment at the end of the sixth century CE in the centre of Nova Troia was still in operation and was a going concern even to this day.

"I'm Rose Springfield,' said the older woman, 'and this is my friend Felicity Harcourt. We are…ah-hem, young widows,' she said, batting her eyes at Dyfed. She then told him that they had been up to Nova Troia making application to the queen's minister in charge of *veteran's affairs of foreign wars fought for queen and country*. They were seeking financial relief due to their calamitous position; that is, the loss of their husbands who were killed in Flanders and in Gaul, respectively. She pointed a finger to her friend and herself. To begin with, all of this had been against their wishes and beyond their control, she told him, as they were now in dire straits since their husband's deaths that had now left them pennilessness.'

"Indeed,' answered Dyfed, marvelling at the woman's ability to weave herself and her friend and their immediate plight so seamlessly and suddenly into the conversation at hand so as to instantly turn the situation onto its head. 'And how's that going for you — ladies?' said Dyfed.

(Uther and Vortigern's feet under Dyfed's table)

'Sleep, not… Awake, for you know not the hour.'
ANON

Dyfed neither took further notice nor sought to converse anymore with anyone other than Muns after that.
  "I can tell you that after the last few gasps of the empire while still dressed in its old and now dirty uniform, the city of Amor began to change rapidly,' Dyfed told Muns, and he began to bring his friend up to date about his past. He missed the force and the accoutrements of the Amoran Empire during its nadir power days, he told him, and how he preferred the stable routine, abundance of education for students, the availability of the rich and expensive goods of every kind from garments, gismos, victuals, wines and do forth that the empire was able to provide for millions of people empire wide, until the end. We couldn't and aren't able do that today, he said to Muns: "Look at the cities of Nova Troia and Isis, for an example. They are in chaos, worse than Amor.'
  He added that he had never touched the especially expensive highly sweetened wines that the Amorans often mixed with regular wines. The sweetener was brewed in lead cauldrons that emitted dangerous toxins that were absorbed by the wine that rich families drank. The lead emitting toxic particles paralysed and crystallized the brains of its drinkers over a period time and rate of consumption. For that reason, he said, he had never eaten or imbibed at social gatherings, either. He, along with Marg, Morgant, Karatakos, Trachmyr and the *pack* had also been very careful to select the few public water fountains or water mains to tap into that had the familiar red clay conduit running to them from the source at the viaduct. Viaducts were safe for they were made of stone and cement but many of the pipes that ran to fountains and public buildings and the private residences of many of the rich were made of malleable lead. The poison from lead debilitated the brains, the body and finally the mind of all mammals like us. And as many of the wealthy homes of the rich had a central domestic water system piped with raw lead, it behoved one to remain alert before accepting an invitation to a wine and boiled fish and cabbage soiree at the neighbour's. An observant person could detect the results of such exposure often just in the actions of the folks and neighbours as they became dizzy and confused with a complaint of constant buzzing in their ears, or were forgetful and were developing double vision and a general deportment about them easily described as living the dream in a happy daze with the bliss of the grinning idiot. And it wasn't just people who were toppling over and off their perches, either. Frozen and deadened with a paralysis of thought and movement also existed in the lives of these people's poor little dogs, cats, pet monkeys and donkeys and other mammals which ate and drank from their hand and not the field. All of Amor itself, including royal family members, magistrates and every other kind of officer of the state, along with the hoi

polloi it seemed, were going down the same destination road first to the homes for the bewildered and from there to the early grave.

At the point in time not long after the Amoran Church succeeded to power and ancient Amor was fast vanishing, Dyfed told John of Munster that he quickly liquidated his assets, gifting much of it away. What he kept was his banking house that was virtually an entity he contained in his head and was something he could activate anywhere when needed and hire help to facilitate the demand. After that the next biggest tool of which he was in procession was his personal army. Trachmyr had had a big hand in attaining that. Times were tight and lean and armies of every type and stripe not only fight but also live on their stomachs. And since his soldiers' pay was three generous squares of porridge, ham sandwiches, and boiled mutton with a fruit dessert a day, he had a good turn out. Dyfed told Muns that he had been hoping that with an expanded infrastructure, in time the Church of Amor would be capable of acting like a conduit for the people's well-needed and deserved sustenance. Whether or not they would do that, or indeed contrive not to, was yet to be seen. And although he had not given directly to the church, or to the pagan temples, he did give lavishly to flesh and blood that were close at hand and in need no matter what persuasion they were. His army were practical in helping out in this way as long as Dyfed could balance the financial sheet. It also kept his army oiled and productive when not battling antagonists. This prompted him to avail his banking interests with the use of his army, too.

Dyfed had at no time discouraged anybody from their convictions or beliefs, mysterious, religious or superstitious, if in fact there is a difference there and if that's what they wanted. He cautioned against it, that's all. He did encourage all of his close associates to become noble and to better themselves before their fellow humans who they should not demean or mistreat or dominate in any way. He encouraged them to always seek the truth and to continue the practice of never allowing themselves to sink into debt or be convinced that the search and struggle to understand life had somehow come to an end. That's because it never did.

Naturally, when the Goths came to town and attacked its citizens of Amor it hadn't been anticipated and was quite unexpected by the majority of the Amoran population, but that was mostly because they chose to not see it coming. The House of Lucifer's Army, through his commanding officer Trachmyr, had aside from thumping marauding vandals who stole the winged sandals and the candles, were always on the ready to defend and protect the House of Lucifer and further its cause. And among the rank and file of those shoplifters and wagon wheel cap heisters that were like a swarm of locusts tramping over Italia, there was also a little bit of an air of the travelling circus and a theatrical performance about it all; or would have been if it hadn't been for the depreciations of the status quo that had always well served Amor and the grave deprivation suffered by the Italian people. Even if the inner ring of that circus was Aelie Galla's Amoran household who managed to dine in sumptuous elegance and comfort in the midst of the general squalor, that wasn't a reason to believe that an up-turn in the economy was just around the corner. Later historians would suggest that the attack had been a betrayal by Aelie Galla Placentia Paradisio herself. But it was never anything of the sort, at least not from Dyfed's recollection. Nor was it the recollection too of others who, like Dyfed carefully chose their water sources, avoided certain substances for consumption and outfitted their cupboard with glass or china drinking vessels instead of lead goblets and had a bevy of healthy pets ruling over the family domus. By this time Dyfed certainly had been aware that hospitals (for want of a better word) were overflowing with masses of the bewildered that were all dying from the fried brain syndrome like flies that had no less a death rate than from starvation and those killed by dagger wounds or from a hefty dose of grudge poison.

Last heard, Trachmyr was somewhere out in the dangerous provinces fighting to keep the barbarian Goth at bay while their Hun reinforcements had slipped through and were now camped inside the gates of the capital of the once more civilized world. He had been heading northwest from Moesia to head off General Flavius Claudius Maximus Constantine III, formerly Pater Bricus also known as Macsen Wledig. After Constantine III's death Dyfed had received scant news about Trachmyr. Then suddenly the latter returned to a besieged Amor to join Dyfed, leaving his army at the coast close to Amor. This was just when news arrived that the rumour that Albion, which had being de-nude of it's Amoran guards or militia (as earlier stated), was facing another conundrum. This was that King Ryan (that pushy and unpleasant Kelt) was back in the news. The rumour was that Ryan (who in addition to having ruined Dyfed and Ceredwyn's engagement and marriage plans) who after promoting himself for the last four centuries had at last obtained the position of Overlord (Vortigern) of the Western Kelts and was asserting himself like *O'Billio* throughout western Prydain. Furthermore, this unrest was a continuing unrest that was the result of the diminishing availability and vacuum of imperial might by Bricus' (Constantine III's) absence and incompetence, or at least that of his Amoran stay-at-home administrators while he the cat was away trying to hang the head of the western emperor of Amor from his belt. And now Constantine III, of course, was dead, and there was an even bigger vacuum back home. At any rate, even the retired and business-minded legion men of Amor who had homesteaded and settled in Albion were now up and disappearing in droves.

At this rate, Dyfed told Muns, he thought it would be sooner than later before the folks of Albion would lack any professional Guard to keep order. And on top of that the Pixies were beginning to shake their spears. All of this, it appeared, was in preparation for a quick land grab. And then there was the Irish. They were turning up again on Mona major and minor as a precursor (apparently) to an all out full-blown invasion and occupation of western Albion (Prydain). But it was the men a-viking, those Germanic Angles and Saxen and the Northmen (Norse) whose name posed a greater and immediate danger at this moment than any other. An if that wasn't bad enough, Ryan, the grand overlord, was inviting these very folks to become his resistance guard against the Pixies, the Irish and other scallywags who were descending on Keltic Prydain and Albion in general. And when those Irish brutes arrived, the Kelts of Prydain would be caught in the middle between the latter and the more brutish inclined Danes and Norse who being on *a viking* (verb) were also already beginning to encircle Albion's northern waters and even settle in the Emerald Isle itself. And this would cause further migration of Irish (stiffened by new Dane blood) to spill out over the Wirral peninsula and into the heart of Prydain. And mark my word here: they wouldn't just be Scotch mist or leaping leprechauns on the lam, either: No sir: They would be a vicious and mechanized killing machine.

This invasion, it appeared, would be fought on two fronts: number one, via the Mersey and Dee rivers as just stated, and if rumours were anything to go by, soon they would be sacking the relatively newly constructed devas such as Chester (formerly called Victrix and Deva) and Viroconium. These aforementioned towns (or devas) had been populated by the Jazyges along with other nomadic (Sarmatian) tribes placed there years ago by the governing Amorans for security purposes against just such an infraction. And number two, the other confrontational front was the one already underway along the east coast beaches upon which Angles, Saxen and men with no names were already descending, but only in trickles at this point. And with their sleek, shallow drafted boats that skimmed across inland water shallows as slick as shit flowing from a cormorant, nothing (but nothing, it seemed) would stop their advances when the time came.

Furthermore, now that Amoran security was all but defunct here, the Vortigern who held the staff of authority here would have his hands full and much in need of certain miracle workers. And rumour had it that the Druid cult element had raised its ugly head again and were demanding human sacrifices to appease the gods. And nobody wanted a return to that. There was talk that Kelts abroad on the continent were longing to return home and instead of keeping the barbarians at bay from Amor, wanted to set to and start keeping them at bay from the blessed Isle of Albion. In fact, rumour has it that there has already been some talk of the Albionian Kelts hiring some of those blood thirsty savage Danes and Saxens who were trickling in of their own anyway to help shore up their defences before it was too late. This proposed defence design seemed to be quite trendy and was going global. It also confirmed those aforementioned rumours being grinded out from the mill of loose-talk. So, with Trachmyr now being back in Amor and the House of Lucifer's army close by, it was time for Dyfed to make a move.

"And since I had many men from the legions now under my command, I had more than just a little strength. And as the empire was now *kaput* (as they say here) I was frantically seeking plans for the future of the House of Lucifer with my consolidated army in tow to avail me success.

Furthermore, being under siege (or even seen to be so) was not Dyfed's thing, so he and three of his companions, he explained to Muns, bid Galla and the Jeshuan high priests good-bye and left the city of Amor together. This was accomplished with actually little stealth. These companions of his were Karatakos, Philip the Fair or Philip Fairman, as he now called himself, and Pyrrhus Pentadactyl. Manandan and Cato were in Albina at this season anyway. Dyfed was now determined to return to Albion to look over the situation there. News of unrest was peaking and a new Vortigern, or high-ranking king, was stirring the cauldron of Prydainic Albion that already contained a mixture of west Kelts, Amorans, Sarms along with a new wave of Saxen peoples who the Vortigern had recently special ordered in from across the narrow Helle Strait from the land of the Saxen, Frisian, and southern Flat-landers. Obviously trouble was brewing and something, Dyfed thought, might be gained in that. Dyfed was hoping that with Karatakos and Philip the Fair who he thought may know his way around the block there (as the politics in Albion had greatly changed since the olden days) and that between the three of them they would cross paths with the likes of the Armorican wizard Selwyn, who was reputed to be somewhere in Gwyneth, as well as with the Vortigern whose identity they were still unsure of but believed it was Ryan.

So, with the *Aura Maré* packed and ready to sail, they ventured forth with two other triremes in tow filled with Dyfed's army under Trachmyr's control. They set out from Italia for the river Deva that is also called Afon Dyfrdwy (currently the Dee or Eryri

River by the locals). They rowed the Aura Maré up that river and pulled it ashore on the muddy banks a stone's throw from the shops of Chester. There they enquired after identity of the Vortigern (overlord) and the whereabouts of Uther. Neither questions had a simple answer.

Uther was the son of Bricus (later Constantine III) and King Ban's sister, Rudumphel. Rudumphel who was Galhad's aunt was a player if not a contender. If only he had stayed in contact with Galhad, Dyfed thought, for Galhad and Uther were first cousins and the latter was likely to know where Uther was. The feeling was, you see, since Uther was Bricus' offspring he may be a chip off the old block and therefore a danger that was about to cause the happenstance of another catastrophe in Prydain. The other individual they were concerned about was Ateula (the servant of Mars) who called himself Arviragus. This man had recently fled Armorica for the west country of Prydain.

In due time they discovered that in fact it was Ryan who had grasped the situation early enough to ensconce himself on the throne as Western Albion's vortigern, or high king. This garrulous man had lost none of his savageness in the interim and upon learning that Uther, son of Macsen Wledig (Constantine III), was Ryan's only major opponent, Dyfed's heart sank. Just where else could it go from here than down, he thought.

Bye and bye Dyfed and Trachmyr got word that the war council that Trachmyr had been earlier attached to in the dying days of old Amor was now somewhere on the upper reaches of the Rine and Schelte Rivers fighting the invading armies of the Hun Attala. This war council was under the command of Theo, king of the Visigoths, and supported by the Salian Franken king Childeric (pronounced Khilderic, the Kh part with a back of the throat sound like you're going to hock up a spit). Attala's choice to battle his way into the land of the Texandri (Toxandria) for the final winner takes all confrontation against the Amoran Western armies forced the western commanders Aetius, Theo and Childeric into a last-ditch line of defence. Childeric, initially a barbarian ally to Amor, saw that such a win was crucial for any unhindered beginnings of a new and improved Amoran Empire North that he was intending to spearhead; even if the Vicar of Amor and his priests hadn't yet got around to signing up any of the leaders of these local northern Frankens, Gauls and Goths (men like Theo, Childeric and his son Chlodovechus) into a partnership of obedience with the fast growing authority of the Church of Amor Central, back at the Holy See in Vatican City, Amor.

The Texandri were a Belgica people comprised (among others) of Salian Franks. From the beginning, back when Amor was expanding into northern Europa, the Belgae Salian Franken proved to be a difficult people to rope and rassle to the ground. Amor failed miserably at this. But now that they'd been improved by a few hundred years of civilized Amoran culture and technology, men like Childeric were quickly forging their local culture of trade and education into becoming a powerful entity. If the fame of old Amor, despite now being commanded by barbarian commanders like General Flavius Aetius and comprised of a military conglomerate of barbarian soldiers, were able to stem the Huns, Childeric knew that taking part in the defeat of Attala the Hun would be a green light for the well ordered and organised Frankens to press on and forge a dominant Europaean dynasty.

Toxandria (whose etymology refers to the people of "the south" banks of either the Muse or Rine Rivers), is situated between the Shelte and Rine Rivers and was the area that produced the cereals that had once fed the legions of Amor's western army since the time of Julius Kysar and was now being maintained by the local Franken with administrative help from Childeric. He was the man that Trachmyr had earlier been backing before disengaging to aid and abet the well being of Dyfed and the House of Lucifer's assets in and around the City of Amor during those trying times of the early fifth century CE.

At this point Dyfed toyed with and then decided to send Trachmyr and his legion veterans away from Prydain and back to Childeric and Toxandria to work where they would get the House of Lucifer a bigger dollop for their denarii and a better return for its expenditure than Dyfed was getting here in western Prydain where nothing much was doing for him.

"It was a brilliant idea,' Dyfed told his friend as they jostled along the east Sax countryside. 'Move my armies into the watershed of the Schelte and Rine Rivers, I advised Trachmyr, and while waiting for orders from the designated Field Marshal, purchase or appropriate land and begin building fortifications for a House of Lucifer citadel on the riverbank adjacent to the town of Tournay. Chideric's citadel was also located here,' Dyfed told Jack.

Trachmyr's army set sail and Dyfed's orders were quickly begun. This hadn't been a hasty decision for earlier, upon leaving Amor, Dyfed had decided to bring his House of Lucifer north and closer to where the action and where a new spark of civilization was brewing. Dyfed still felt that the Amorans always had Albion in mind for a centre of the future world empire; and so in hoping to be innovative in doing just that, Dyfed now chose to establish his centre of operations at Tournay that currently, unlike Nova Troia, was fast becoming a hub of finance, business and authority. It was only a matter of time, he knew, before very serious priests would be showing up there too.

Dyfed's army was to be encamped at Tournay where they would wait for instructions. In the meantime the army could begin to construct the fortified House of Lucifer citadel. The man Trachmyr put in charge to undertake this was his military chamberlain, a certain Ebreo ben Jamin, vassal of Dyfed Lucifer.

"Our reconnaissance in Pydain lasted another two months,' Dyfed told Jack. 'Then when word of rumour arrived that Attala the Hun was on the prowl and moving north from Lyon, and with no King Ryan in sight and all relatively quiet here on the western Prydain front, I decided to join Trachmyr and my army.'

(No memorandum of the establishment moulded the Grail castle)

'Hell is other people.'
JEAN PAUL SARTRE *(AMONG OTHERS)*

Although Dyfed and Mun's conversation was not meant to be overheard, soon — after opening salvos of boring snippets of sordid privacy all covered in squalor that surfaced here and there among the carriage that, furthermore, were vacuumed clean of any redeeming qualities — their's (it turned out) was the only conversation that was actively sought out and listened for. And after awhile nobody wanted to miss out on one word of it. The two chatty widowed coughers and the one bored and restless child who were enroute were quickly hushed up with a deliberate clearing of someone's throat or a scowl flung their way if some of their noise got in the way of any eaves-droppers not being able to over-hear. The two young professionals across from Dyfed silently read. The topics discussed between Dyfed and his long-lost companion were of a catch-up nature and consisted of each other's comings and goings that was interlaced with well rounded discussions about the world's state of affairs and the politics of the power elite operating at that particular time from their virtual world and how it was affecting the hoi polio who kept the actual world turning so that the sun would come up on the following morning to a relative state of calm.

"How long have you been home, Dyfed?' Muns asked as soon as he was seated again

"Since when?' Dyfed responded. 'The first time I was home in Albion or the second time?

"Good gracious Heavenly Lord,' stated Muns, still incredulous over their chance meeting. 'I've tried to keep tabs on you. I've read some of the things you have written…'

"Ah,' interjected Dyfed. 'That would be the stuff which the Church of Amor either didn't fully comprehend and consequentially wasn't brutally redacted, or somehow it slipped through those grasping fingers on their grubby clutching little hands and (somehow again) managed not to fall into the book-burning fires of destruction,' he said, laughing. 'They must have been my satires, then.'

"So, when did you first return? Dyfed,' he asked.

"Oh, about a thousand years ago, more or less, I'd say,' he answered. 'About, or shortly after, the tremulous time of the war of the worlds whose battle ground being the expanse of the sky which clashed overhead, bringing forth earth shattering thunderbolts and fire of the gods that shook and burnt the whole world and toppled monuments and mountains, caused the earth to shake, volcanoes to belch and spew forth into the atmosphere that fell to the earth and paved the way for destruction, disease, deep-freeze and death. That was the onslaught of the age of darkness and cold, famine and intolerable suffering and mass death that no village or city surrounded by their corpses stacked and stinking to high heaven could escape. Nobody can forget those days, eh Muns? How did you make out, my little friend?

"Before the settling dust,' answered John of Munster, 'when the atmosphere was a giant field of magnetism and electricity that also caused cyclones to tear across the face of the earth as well as across the surfaces of the oceans which brought deluge and expunged many coastal cities here as well as to help and further a declining Amoran civilized order throughout, I was doing what everybody else was; just trying to survive.'

"Never before have any of us seen such astounding electrical phenomena at large as that. Not in our lifetime, said Dyfed. But, it was not the first time such a catastrophe has visited us here on earth nor will it be the last, I'm afraid. Unfortunately, most did not survive this natural holocaust from the heavens. And the ensuing plague that resulted caused most of the interfacing horror in Europa and elsewhere. Then the big chill came that froze to death so many of us. However, it was a big leg-up for the Church of Amor who at this opportune moment took up that welcomed opportunity to bravely boast of their badge of authority. Then brandishing quick action, it gifted pity and redemption (but no more) to the suffering along with a warning of god's rancour and retribution towards all things opposed and contrary to that which the Church of Amor and it priests represented. Have I got that right, Muns?' Dyfed asked. Then before Jack could answer, Dyfed continued.

"Perhaps, sadly and unfortunately, logos and reason are missing here. Anyway, for me, migration at that time would have been most opportune if only it had been possible. Few people were able to move anywhere, apart from locating some ideal situated shelter close by away from the stench and foulness of the rotting carcasses that were piled up like cord wood outside the cities to burn. These abodes that dotted the bleak pasturelands were divided by long failed croplands hemmed in by the blighted and leafless forests of trees that was caused by some beastly poisons that descended from the heavens to the Earth. Hanging grimly onto life by a thread, many sought to escape to better regions of easy proximity for scavenging food and securing a certain element of safety from dangerous, hollow spirited human beasts of prey. To the great misfortune of the House of Lucifer, I have to say that a certain few of my entourage remained with me while I remained in Chester on the river Dee, where I had recently arrived from Amor. It was the time of the west Prydainian uprising. My army and my commanding officer that I had sent back to the continent were now encamped just west of the Ardennes at Tournay in Flanders on the river Esco[60] (also Schelte or Schelde). I had sent them there to assist the allied armies facing the Hun. At Tournay the House of Lucifer found a new digs and was where we dug in and set up shop. It was also here where the uniting of the Franken tribes began and where together they created a Salian dominated Franken dynasty called the Merovingians.[61] Later the Salian Frankens under Chlodovechus (Chlodowig, Chlodio or Clovis) soon managed to get a healthy head start on the Second Amoran Empire by boldly breaking out of the chaos and carnage of the status quo, despite General Flavio Guiliani's efforts to contain them.'

"Second empire?' enquired Muns. 'What is this about?

"It's a form of rejuvenation of the Amoran Imperial system, if you like,' replied Dyfed. Anyway the aforementioned tenacious and ferocious Salian Frankens who were running with it were men who with an unwavering eye as to their goal, ventured out into the

---

60 This is the name of the rivers pronounced in the local Walloon tongue, a vulgar Amoran language.
61 Named after Merovech (Merovechus) who supported Amoran troops against Attala the Hun at the battle of Catal.

desolation at the time to establish an authoritarian hold on the land. With an Amoran-like presentation and the advantage of having Clever, Wit and Ambition as close allies these Salian Frankens concentrated on old Amoran type law and order to pull them all together. And it certainly didn't hurt either that through successful trade they were considerably wealthier than the other tribes. This put them into the driver's seat of what was becoming the Second Empire, as I said. However, they weren't the owners of the chariot they were driving; they were just the mechanics taking the chariot out for a test drive. The Church of Amor somehow got hold of and held their debt and soon the church had the Franken's IOU securely locked up in their strongbox at the Vatican Bank. That was around the same time when the suite of the Franken royal advisers began to let the authority of the Vicar of Jeshua and the Curia of Amor place the tribe's crown on their king's head instead of the local shamans and medicine men. Furthermore, that placing was done in the name of the church and their God, alone. Soon the crown itself became the property of the church, not that of the royal house or the tribes', and if the king or the tribe bucked the ecclesiastical system that the church forced them to adhere to, the curia could cancel any and all of the kingdom's favourable status and its important dispensations and have them clasped in excommunication. This last item alone showed the power of careful Church of Amor programming. Otherwise the words would be empty. Obviously by even this time the situation involving spiritual matters had already gone the way of the great auk and the passenger pigeon and had come a long way from being responsible for showering compassion and succour on humanity's suffering and dispossessed. And all that aside from the good news of just who Jeshua Adon really was; and how this revelation and its personal epiphany caused the early Jeshuans to choose death over rejection of their Father. Now there is something you don't see every day anymore.'

"So from the time of Clovis on,' Dyfed continued, 'the Salian Frankens were confined to the debt they somehow magically incurred to the Church of Amor. Yet they also used this to their advantage. In this they displayed the cunning and intellect that was not unlike the Lans, those Indo-Iranian-Eurasian pastoral nomads who (like the Jazyges that were related in some way to the Scythians) were a free people of the vast steppe lands. Arriving in the west (along with the Huns), the Lans' dispute with the Amoran armies was only momentary and came in the form of a battle at Hadrianopolis in Thracia where Emperor Valens was killed. From Hadrianopolis the Lans, under their King Respendial, pushed west— along with the Suevi (Suebi or Swabian) and Vandals, accompanied by the West Goths. They permanently crossed the Rine River approximately a century before the blitz of magnetic storms and other oddities (that featured witches riding broomsticks across the sky called comets, and the descent of poisonous fallout and its resultant devastation) had struck the earth in the sixth century CE.'

"What revealment do you mean, Dyfed?' John of Munster asked suddenly.

"But you are a Jeshuan convert, Muns. What are you telling me, that you don't even know why men and women would easily without hesitation choose death than defile themselves eternally by disclaiming and thereby abandoning that what Jeshua symbolizes for them? And that it is the only truth that could possibly matter for them in this world? Spit on you God, Muns, I say to you now or I will eviscerate you on the spot. What would you choose, Muns? You must realize that deny means deny, not clever concealment. You couldn't easily scoff off the gladiator or Pretorian guard that let you live on a sworn pronouncement that you meant to be false. And I can say to you that I would never deny myself and my faith in God who is my Father from whom I am descended who is the origin of all things known and unknown, Muns. And I'm not even of your religion, or any other religion, apparently!'

"You underwent an epiphany?' asked John of Munster.

"I remember a huge shooting star exploded at high noon high above Amor on that day. On that same day the Vicar of Jeshua and the curia of the Church of Amor brought in the Second Empire's most audacious and ridiculous dispensation decree to date, and perhaps of all time. It displayed irreversible proof that the Vicar of Jeshua and its curia had absolutely no notion or concept of what the Saviour concept of Jeshua really was. Since it was a dispensational decree, sort of like a wild card, that decree was not initially acted upon until many years later during time of Innocent III, about four hundred years ago. The penalty for not acknowledging the Holy See and for not converting to the Church of Amor was death. Pagans and backsliders were specifically defined and described as non-believers as to the ways of the new Abramists and the liturgy of the Church of Jeshua Adon that had now become the exclusive possession of the Church of Amor that was defined also by that same church. Therefore their authority came from their own creation and at this time any who denied or challenged this were labelled heretics. Later in the twelfth century CE heretics quickly became the walking dead. Anyway, shortly after this earlier turn of events I set sail from Amor for Prydain.'

"And that was a thousand years ago, you say?' said John of Munster. The tone in Jack's voice sounded incredulous. 'We heard that you were at the centre of the empire,' said Muns, smiling up at his old friend once again with admiration. 'We heard that you were even decorated with the medal of Fellowship of the Gladius, or some such thing: and by Emperor Hadrianus himself, no less.'

"Really, you heard that?'

"And more,' replied Jack.

"Most of it isn't true, of course. I'm here this time for different reasons, Muns. Albion has turned a corner and is about to join the club for the leadership status of the human race for the first time since King Knut or Forkbeard, or at least to join in the ranks with the likes of those ingenious folks of their time from the Land of Khem, the Land of the Hellenes and of Amor. Albion is now positioned, and with luck will within a century be in a circumstance favourable to begin creating, influencing and reaping the returns of a worldwide region of modern industrialization. But the fat lady hasn't finished her singing her song and we are not completely out of the woods yet. If we are successful in this, though, we will shape up to lead the world in a race not just in the direction of becoming a world power but towards the creation of a Western Philosophical Utopia. Unless the Haploids pull the wool over the eyes of the new age hoi polloi once again.

Up until now and because the Church of Amor reigns as our spiritual king and its progressively ingrained program to maintain itself is flourishing, the hoi-polloi simply fill the ranks of indoctrinated slaves and automatons used for running and maintaining the gears and wheels by pulling on certain levers that helps guide the kingdom-going and state-becoming power along its contrived tracks. Unfortunately these tracks follow a program that is only intrinsic to the Haploids well being. It is the golden vehicle for the oligarchs to continue and to complete the bidding of the Haploids and it is this that threatens to clone us to certain debilitating aspects the Amoran Empire that will rob humanity at large of the rewards in store.

But despite our necessary similarities, we do not want to be a clone of Amor. That's a dead end that has run its course. However, we have a window of opportunity to take charge of the second empire and fashion it into that aforementioned utopia of western philosophy. By that powerful reasoning alone we hold the key to the promises for elevating humanity and bringing equity through equality to the dispossessed and to the poor without infringement upon the witty, the competent and the more able: And this, Muns, is done by ensuring that the hoi polloi will achieve a status that gives them and everyone the right to live not by privilege but by the right of law. And to succeed, this right must remain irreversible, never to be over-turned. And where this status is not achieved or is over-turned in any way, the status quo at that time and place can not claim that western philosophy is their ideal.'

"First empires, second empires, Haploids and the fat lady who hasn't finished singing,' said Jack of Munster with a wide open look of incredulousness spreading across his wide, flushed face and shone like a gaping yawn.

"Listen, Muns. Let us pull ourselves away from the crowd choking us from all around (for the moment) by lowering our voice here. I sit here,' Dyfed said in a whisper, 'before you speaking as a stoic and cynic. All I really have is mine own existence to associate or compare anything to. I have nothing further to that. And in fact, it is from an empiric lot in general that I endeavour to cast mine own die that's legislated by an attitude leaning strongly towards veracity and one that's not moulded by some or other memorandum of the establishment or of any of their agencies and programs of primitive superstitions. Add to this my relationship to the Spirit of my Father and God and that, Muns, is how I make out. This, aside from the benefits I received at the hands of my benefactors as a child while growing up, I sit before you as a self educated man; and well proud I am of it, too, I might add. And I pass it on. You see, we have here the opportunity to indelibly and negatively affect the current program that's ramping up again and leading the hoi polloi down the same old garden path to failure of faith and comprehension. We have the opportunity to help these helpless minions from becoming something of a hallmark for the human machines that will labour for a new program for the old order, rather than it being the new order. And that will quickly and soon will be beyond all of our ability to control, altogether. Greed on behalf of the Haploids and their useful minions, and greed that will be needed by the psyche of the slaves to continue to drive themselves on expectantly, will become the program's necessity — that is; the cry of tyrants and the creed of slaves.'

"So, my present raison d'etre here is to try and plant a helpful anecdote or automatic defence mechanism into the hearts and minds of the people to prepare them for the future trials ahead so we can succeed.'

"Grounded on true western philosophy my purpose and mission is to enact some subterfuge that can be engrained or naturally passed down through the generations to help all people, everywhere, to ignore the path of least resistance in this world; to shun senseless wealth and egotistical ceremony and fight instead for the right to find and flex their own personal and natural expressions of their individuality. This must become their highest prize. In this way it is hoped that nothing will suppress the natural joy of humans. Furthermore, it is also hoped that through inner strength (gained through self-realization of the true self) the common hoi polloi will become immune from the will forced upon them through extraordinary influence by trashy mesmerisers and their dominant alpha males and their fake enactment of sermons on the mount and their ceremonies waist deep in the snys and back-eddies of pseudo sacred waters everywhere and of every flavour. Yet, ironically for the hoi polloi, the condition of not striving to desire must become their most efficient weapon, their anecdote, against want, and also against submission and control. I have taken up this challenge, with encouragement from mine own superiors, but woe is I, I'm afraid. How can I accomplish this, Muns, my old, faithful friend? I am at a loss and in great doubt about the success of my seemingly impossible mission. But the mission is, I believe, somehow attainable.'

After a long silence, and a cautious look at Dyfed, John of Munster spoke in a hushed voice.

"Fine,' he whispered, seemingly a little annoyed and looking down at the floorboards of the car. 'You have made it quite clear that you're not moulded by some or other memorandum of the establishment and that god is a hoax.'

"No, I did not say that; I said that religion as we know it is a hoax. Now listen,' Dyfed said. 'Do you remember Galhad, better known now as Galahad? You see, on the lad's maternal side he was the grandson of King Pelles who was of the House of Corbin. Pelles is believed to have been a Ka'nite (Canaanite) prince from Ugarit; although others say he hailed from Sur (also Tyre) or maybe even from that most ancient of kingdom city states thereabout, that of Ebla. An employee of mine named Ebreo ben Jamin told me this. In any case, desolation and destruction overtook his lands and family affairs there that prompted King Pelles into becoming a mercenary pirate. As such, he set out upon the White Sea and worked the circuit out of Carthage before relocating to Emporiae (Empuries or Emporium) in the lands of the Hiberi (also Iberes), later called Hispania whose locality is now known as Catalonia. From Emporiae (after accumulating a great wealth) he retired to the southwest to Montserrat, the multi-peaked and serrated edged mountain. It was here that he built the House of Corbin citadel, the so-called Grail Castle. Others have placed this castle in a multiple of locations all over northern Europa and even here in Albion, if you can believe it, Muns. But the curse of desolation and corruption and destruction followed the family even unto Armorica. This is the same danger we now face.'

"Ah, the Fisher king,' replied John of Munster.

"Exactly. Anyway,' continued Dyfed, 'as the desolation followed him to (and then from) Montserrat (also known as Munsalvasche or Monsalvat), once again he became afflicted. What I'm also getting at here is that Galahad, who is actually here in Albion as I speak, is the son of King Pelles' youngest daughter, Princess Helizabel sister to Runfendal. Incidentally, in Catalonia it was said that both Pelles and Helizabel were of an ancient royal bloodline. So, as it turns out, Queen Marg, whose wedding to the usurper Ryan from Mona that both you and I attended at the City of Legion long ago, had always been jealous of Helizabel's beauty. Again, it turned out that the two were close associates. How was I to know? One thing led to another and at one point Marg and I fell in love. That was back in Nova Troia about fifteen hundred years ago. Who would have thought it, eh, Muns? Nonetheless, before Marg and I had fallen in love, she had taken charge over young Galhad's well being after the disappearance of Helizabel; but more on that, later, Muns. Anyway, that is how the charge of Galhad's well being had been passed to me for a short spell. I rue the day. But the point here is that Galhad had reason to introduce me to his paternal uncle in the town of Joscelyn while we were in

Armorica attempting to put down the revolt there. That ran concurrently with having to liberate King Ban from an invasion by the interloper chief who they called Ateula, the servant of Mars, who called himself Arviragus. This took place during the first century of this current era (CE). And this paternal uncle (of whom I now speak) became a trusted employee of mine in the business of finance.

"But later, it was I who provided him help so he could achieve wealth and security. I thought I was doing the right thing. A few centuries later those Keltic sea-faring Veneti (the original Armorican inhabitants of the area around the village of Joscelyn had been overrun by the Lans. These folks had (in the interim) provided a similar service to the people there, namely sensible civility. And the name of this uncle of Galhad's, this younger brother of Lans-lot, was Mr Egidius Joslin (also Joscelyn). But I fear, Muns, Egidius may inherit the desolation and corruption that plagued the Fisher King. And that corruption is contagious if not carefully contained.'

"Eventually Egidius Joslin (Joscelyn) left Armorica and relocated to the land of the east Saxen here in Albion. And (in fact) that is where I am now headed. It is to a place called Newbigging I go. Then on to Hedingham Manor and the Earl of Oxford where I will remain as his guest for some time before arriving at my final destination which is Cambridge. I hope that is where we will meet up again soon, Muns.'

The three carriages stopped at horrible roadhouse at noon each day so the travellers could warm up and nosh on some rustic country food before the long, drawn out hours to the cold twilight when they would finally halt for the night. After a long, cold, cramped day with few rests and leg stretching, they reached the ford over a trickling stream called the River Hyle. This was their destination for their first night. Shortly before their arrival, darkness fell over the cold and snowy land. They bivouacked that night in a cold and draughty hotel-inn, and the next day was even longer as they got an early start but ended at the same time, just after dusk. The next morning they entered the great forest again and travelled almost non-stop at a fast rate. Brief stops were made to necessitate the women with regular pee breaks but they still didn't arrive at Burnt Wood (a vast clearing in the great forest) until after dark.

From Burnt Wood they travelled to Kysar-o-mangus where Dyfed had un-expectantly encountered Morgant Cerreg while travelling to Nova Troia long ago. Following the ribbon of dirty white snow that doubled for a road that wound through the darkened forest, it was well after dark when the six horses pulled up in front of an inn set upon the same foundations that supported the old inn beside the river and the coach ferry crossing.

On their arrived at Thaxted late in the cool evening of the next day, and having said their goodbyes, Dyfed set out on foot for the home of Egidius Joslin while John of Munster went on to Cambridge the next morning. Dyfed didn't fail to notice that his ugly duckling companion, the insulting magistrate, also sought accommodation for the night at the roadhouse inn. At the House of Joslin, much to his pleasant surprise, Dyfed found Guillium Galhad Raymonde de Joslin residing with his uncle. There was warmth between Egidius, Galhad and Dyfed that evening. The following morning Dyfed was working his pen over the pages of his apagoge while lounging out of his travelling clothes in a relaxed state, sipping warm honey-mead before Egidius' broad fireplace while the latter prepared for the arrival of Mr Friese — attorney at law. Dyfed blatantly ignored the latter, and then, after a few days, it was off to Hedingham Manor and the Earl of Oxford with Galhad (now Galahad) in tow.

"Anyway, so after sailing to the sea lands of the continent and up the River Schelde to Tournay (Turnacus) the city of King Childeric (the son of Merovech) Karatakos and I found Trachmyr and my army still encamped. I used this opportunity as a time to reconsider everything, including reviewing the plans for my new citadel and what lay ahead in Prydain. That being done my intention was for some basic house cleaning and to look over the lie of the land, politically speaking. Europa had heated up politically, what with sundry barbarians constantly at the gates and I knew that I hadn't heard the last of Ryan and his western Prydainian separatist movement. I expected it to turn into a full-blown Albion take-over attempt. When that happened I would need to take Trachmyr and the army back and influence Uthur if I can. Either way, since Ryan was a principal participant in the ruination of my relationship with Ceredwyn, I wasn't going to be lenient. I was going to crush him and banish him from Albion.'

(Allies Gather against Attala)

'An event has happened, upon which it is difficult to speak, and impossible to be silent.'

EDMUND BURKE

"At Tournay Childeric told me that the big show was being undertaken against Attala about a hundred Amoran miles south east of here. This is where Trachmyr and my army set out to ready themselves for the big push about a week after my arrival. I now accompanied them. Meanwhile Karatakos took charge of my new House of Lucifer office that was still going up in Tournay under Ebreo ben Jamin's supervision while we dashed off toward the Fields of Catal,' he told Jack.

It was an exhilarating scene that stretched before Dyfed's keen and observant eye, and to an inexperienced eye it would doubtlessly have appeared to be the centre of confusion. Once Dyfed saw the scope of the impending confrontation with the Huns that was to unfold on the morrow on the plains of Catal, he then asked Trachmyr to provide him with a detailed inventory, a list of the army's compulsory needs along with projected logistics. For as unlikely as it would come to pass, Dyfed wanted Trachmyr to draw up a comprehensive statement of operational battle requirements for their contingent. The company of troops were still under Dyfed and Trachmyr's control, at least for the moment, but ultimately the chief field marshals such as Flavius Aetius and King Theo would control them. And Dyfed knew that he needed to seek out these men within a few hours. Then with this statement of battle requirements in hand he would approach this command of the joint armies with General Trachmyr by his side. And with the latter's reputation throughout the empire as a competent general as leverage, he intended to make an effort to present their contingent army' statement to the joint chiefs of allied forces and their staff. Dyfed's hope was that he would be listened to and that its merits would be noted. From there it could be hoped that it would be adopted over all, and thereby — with any luck — minimise a higher than necessary death toll in the end. This manoeuvre was partly an effort on Dyfed's own part to gain insight as to how united these far flung yet allied factions actually were, and also how they planned and prepared for the inevitability of events that were soon to come to pass. Furthermore, and most especially, what and how fifth column agents of the allies were employed and what reliable information had been received from them so far. Karatakos had suggested to Dyfed and Trachmyr to address these questions pronto, before committing themselves. In truth, it was a requirement of the Masters, apparently. All of this was to achieve an expedient outcome of the upcoming battle for Europa. But also it helped to give Dyfed an insight as to how this governing factor that was here today operated. For it was obvious to him (and the Masters) that the northern Franken were positioning to succeed in ruling the empire in the future. And they would do it from Tournay, and hopefully, along side the House of Lucifer's citadel. But other great cities such as Isis, Divodurum Mediomatricum (Metz) and Aachen would be waiting in the wing and vying for power.

The zephyrs were active now and alive. Though spring was here the chill was late winter before the ides of March. Promise, however, was in the air. The first full moon after the equinox was nigh and the land beneath it and the sky was almost a month behind in growth. A bit of rain fell now and again but the clouds were airy and plump promising of fine weather. Even though it was afternoon, here, alongside the plains of Catal, it was like a new morning with an A.J. Casson sky looming high overhead. The sounds and smells of the horses, the voices of the different tribes of men, and the fury of preparation was every-where around them, as the gusty wind moved the hair upon men and beasts, and the mixtures of their scents were scattered to the four winds in a funnel of whirligigs (pronounced whirly-jig).

Later that evening the chiefs gathered. This were no meagre rag-tag commiseration of armed men at this the final council which was set to decide on the action needed for tomorrow's finale. As already mentioned Aetius had estimated their number at one hundred and fifty thousand all told. Many armies of Goths and Frankens were camped nearby, and all around was the stirring of anxiety mixed with excitement.

Later that day, as the eastern skyline darkened, he watched the sky in the west pale as long, log shaped clouds shunted slowly across its lower horizon like floating whales strung out snout to tailfin, or those giant air-machines arising from some scrap of Dyfed's fragmented memory of the future. With Dyfed leading the way he and Trachmyr wended their way toward a large but low profiled wattle and daub thatch roofed house that stood on the horizon of an adjacent hill backed by a dark forest. This was the requisitioned headquarters for the joint chiefs and their staff. Although Trachmyr didn't seem to notice, Dyfed found that the building's main cooking hearth, used as well for heating the abode in cold weather, was stuffed with disposable garbage and junk as the evenings now were fairly warm. This hearth area acted as a partition between two large rooms that shared a common low wooden beamed ceiling. In one room were many men, all staff and aids of one kind or another to powerful men, shouting and coughing, while in the other large room — although more subdued — were towering citadels of iron girded egos.

Although there were some tribal chiefs and twice as many dukes (also dux, though it was becoming fashionable now to call them kings) in attendance, most of the leaders were Amoran generals, the majority of who were either west or east Goths, Serbian, and Thracian. Nobody was sure of the difference anymore, anyway.

Besides Flavius Aetius and King Theo, Dyfed spotted Aelius Castus who happened to be a Sarm from the great steppe north of the Kara Sea. Zintacus, another Sarm was there along with Dux Chlodio the Sicambrian of Toxandria, and Merowe FitzMannus, Chideric's famous uncle, nephew or kin of some kind — nobody knew which. Another Franken calling himself General Van Richelieu who Dyfed recognized as Gorgeous Giorgius Gregorius Florentius was also present. Also present was Ateula, the Keltic chieftain from Armorica. Most importantly, though, was the presence of General Sy and the first mentioned, General Aetius. The latter was descended from the people of Scythland and was born on the banks of the Dana River in the land of the Thraki not far from the Kara Sea's western shore. The last two were the most brilliant Amoran generals ever since Cornelius-Felix the Amoran general, statesman, and dictator of the Republic who was conspicuous by his absence.

General Sy was an Amoran official and a Kelt who had made good and ruled his own inherited state, no longer as just a chieftain, but as a magister militum. And as the Amoran Empire began to fade, Sy was just beginning to bloom and blossom into a full-blown warlord and ally of the Salian (Salii) Franken. Dyfed was very interested in getting to know Sy, for he thought he would know and understand these Salii more than most. For now, Dyfed had his eye on them, especially since he planned on living among them.

King Geuric, Duke of central Gaul was there and took to being cavorted around on a throne-like chair by slaves for the purpose of pissing other egotists off. Geuric (who despite being a Westgoth king) was actually a Lan and a well-placed Italian puppet king. The Italians favoured Lans as fighting men and viewed them as people with leadership qualities. They often put them in charge of castles, fiefdoms, and kingdoms for the latter's safekeeping for many of them could write and had studied law, accounting and religion.

Also present at this high command was King Gundahar of the Burgundars along with Jovinus, his puppet emperor, but their fighting force numbers were smaller. Aetius didn't trust the Burgundars and once he himself had even employed a large contingent of Huns against Jovinus at the town of Vorms on the upper Rine when the latter had attacked Amoran controlled Gallia Belgica in the lowlands there. Indeed, in addition to that, and in spite of his entanglement with Gala, rumour had it that Attala had just got himself engaged to be married to a Burgundar princess named Iko. This was probable since there had now been sufficient time for the tenuous arrangement he had had with Gala to have fallen through.

King Goar of the Lans[62] was of course there in the command office, too. With his skilful cavalry, King Goar and his men were a weapon unto themselves. And finally there was Theuderix, the Westgoth king. King Theuderix was, therefore, the field commander in chief of joint-staff, and directly answerable to Augustus Byzantium that was taking precedence of authority over Amor.

These then were some of the men and players who were present here to lean their shoulders into helping move that first little pawn forward to start a whole new round — a new cycle if you like — or a new rubber of this great and inglorious game of bridging the un-bridgeable: the great game of empires and their resources versus personal power.

That afternoon in the entrance of this high officers' headquarters, Dyfed hastily inserted a well-delivered speech of introduction for himself. This, he hoped, would make him welcome and accepted. He spoke quickly, alternatively in educated Amoran and the more acceptable Goth dialect, as well as Keltic just to demonstrate that ability. Of course he could have spoken in Aramaic, Koine or Coptic, too, for that matter, never mind in the classic tongue of the Hellenes. He apologised for not being fluent in the Salian Franken tongue and promised in the few words he knew in their language that he would correct that oversight immediately. He then delivered a quick synopsis of his statement of operational battle requirements, suggesting that his should be immediately compared to their own.

---

62   Also Alans: from the Indo-european word *Arya*, meaning nobly respectable or civilized. First mentioned by the Amoran historian Josephus of the first century CE, the Alani, like their regional neighbours the Mannaeans, the Medians, and the Persians, were Europaean-type peoples of Indo-Iranian stock; they were specifically tribes of Sarmations (or Saka), as opposed to Scythian, and were synominous with the Massagetae, whose cousins (the Indo-Aryans) had ventured south and entered Inja around 1500 BCE.

Trachmyr's reputation as a strong general had been a trump card in allowing he and Dyfed to be accepted here among the big players at the Joint Chiefs of Staff office in the first place, but Aelius Castus supplied even more impetus. After listening carefully to Dyfed's outline of his statement of operational requirements, the Sarm general ratcheted this strange silver eyed aristocrat up a notch or two in the eyes of the others; others who for the most part looked upon this strange and unusual man for the first time. Remembering the young man's help and support on the eve of his invasion of Armorica years before, Castus politely welcomed Dyfed's contribution in rather glowing terms with approving murmurs from Zintacus, who was also present. Even Aetius showed his appreciation for Dyfed's organizational skills and grasp of logistics. And then Castus preceded to debate some of Dyfed's points, speaking to him like a brother in his native Sarm tongue, much to the amusement of the others. Later that night, with success in his first endeavour to contribute now behind him, and excitement tingling his body for adventure like a youth, Dyfed crept undetected through both the allies' and the enemies' lookout lines towards the Hun camp for a closer look-see. Dyfed had not lost any of his natural sense of camouflage that as a prince of the grove he had developed during his formative years on the Isle of Peace. He passed undetected through the Amoran watch-posts with ease. And as he carefully made his way closer and closer to the Huns position — quickly discerning their lookout posts and a series of hastily laid traps they had set out as a welcome — Dyfed soon felt the closeness of the Hun's presence. He could clearly hear their camp sounds and smells and easily make out the chatter of their voices amid the rattle-clash of their high-density music that was metered out into the cool night air by a fast and rhythmic array of drumbeats that was not unlike those among the people of Araby. He listened intently to their strange and unfamiliar voices as they cried out in thrill melodies full of forlorn. They may have been bloodthirsty enemies on the make or maybe on the run, in this case, but Dyfed knew that in a few hours time it would be the moment of truth that would tell the real story: That story he had received via a communiqué handed to him from a stranger a few hours before. He had read it wide-eyed and in disbelief and didn't realise at the time just how right the secret disclosure would be, and how shocking the truth was.

But at the present, these vain and energetic people — these eastern men and women — who were full of vim and vigour, jumping into the air amid their smoking fires and brandishing their weapons as they conducted contests of agility and prowess among themselves. Dyfed actually marvelled at the intense noise and vibration that this host emitted, so unlike the old worn-out Amoran armies of Goths and the Albionian, Franken, and Lan allies. The Burgundars, maybe — he thought — were a little livelier and musically inclined. But still, these allied armies were quiet compared to the Huns, though the former displayed considerably more bon-fires that dotted the countryside here and there and some strains of music could be heard now and again. Apparently, the lengthy and mandatory Jeshuan prayer sessions that the priests held every few hours were completed and the folks had now taken to drinking and dancing once again while the soldiers of rank continued their preparation.

Dyfed explained this entire goings on to Jack.

(Cleverly clogged magicians set the sting for the Battle of Catal)

'Truth, persuades by teaching, but does not teach by persuading.'
QUINTUS SEPTIMIUS TERTULLIANUS

As it became apparent to Dyfed that very little fifth column information would in fact trickle back into the Westgoth headquarters, Aetius as senior general or Magister militum (and second in command to Theuderix) who on Dyfed's behalf moved to push on with an immediate attack to see how the Huns would respond. Some of the Frankens disagreed, as did other independent Goth tribes. Nevertheless, the next morning as Dyfed looked on from the headquarters of the joint chief of staff he watched the two armies that lay slightly below them come together with a loud clash. Dyfed quickly identified Trachmyr and their company of privateers but they were only about a thousand strong among seventy thousand or more soldiers all told on the friendly side alone.

These soldiers, despite the blaring of musical pipes to call the battle to order and horns blaring to deliver commands — as well as a great deal of rushing back and forth and to and fro between headquarters and general's aids — mingled alongside tired and panting messengers with dust covering the furrows on their brows. Many others stood around with their hands in their pockets leaning on their weapons for most of the day. To the onlookers like Dyfed, it was the battle that wasn't. Then suddenly, with illustrious Radiance approaching the western horizon and the fighting hours of the day almost finished, Attala up and made a dash for it. But instead of rushing the Amoran allies, the Huns seized one side of the high ground of the playing field while Dyfed watched the Amorans and their allies (some of whom were uncertain in regards to their loyalty to begin with) seize the other side of Catal field leaving a crest of land or small peak that lay between them.

Then when some Hunnic soldiers attempted to seize the crest, Dyfed saw both Lans and Amorans foil the attempt by being faster on foot. In this situation the allies, that included the magnificent Burgundars, managed to repulse the Huns who then fled in poor military order back into their own forces where the chaos seemed to be contagious. Although Attala made some attempt to rally his forces in order to hold his position, the speed of the Westgoths' second attack was even faster than any of the nimble Lans, Frankens or Burgundars, and the former fell upon Attala and his personal guards so that the latter was forced to retreat the field in earnest.

For Attala, his Hunnic attempt to be victorious over Europa's armies and conquer this land had failed on this day and may well be finished altogether. Under the circumstances there would be no reprieve. At this point, somehow (nobody knows how or why, exactly), Theuderix was killed having sustained a mortal wound to his head, and Attala escaped in the resulting chaos and in the falling darkness of dusk that slowly poured in before the night took hold. Thus, Attala had, undoubtedly, at least accomplished what his plan B was designed to do.

During the mental post-mortem, Dyfed found it interesting that Attala's plan B wasn't a separate entity; it wasn't something whereby in switching over they would in essence leave off where they were and start from scratch, or nearly so. Like all great strategists Attala incorporated his plan B, as well as plan C and D if necessary, with plan A (his initial goal) along each and every inch of its duration until the unaccountable moment of failure in order to orchestrate a successful departure from the field. His end game was in staying alive along with as many of his troops as possible. In other words, all of his plans were intricately integrated to this end. Otherwise, alternate plans, no matter how many one had, would likely fall flat on their faces like dominoes of failure.

Attala's defeat was perhaps a lucky stroke for the allies. But his escape wasn't lucky; it was by design. Dyfed saluted Attala for that and an admiration for him took hold. Attala was the kind of man he wanted on his side, put it that way. He was no nonsense man who was tough and resilient, ploughing forward and finding his courses of action as they came up. Attala was the kind of man that made it up as he went along, yet was brilliant enough himself in having it all fit in perfectly with his plan A's and B's along with his ultimate plan to win, or lose but live to fight another day. And on top of that, he had been generally successful, for his planning was tactually abstract, even whimsical, and a class well above any others. He was a man, Dyfed thought, who would do well to be introduced to Sun Tzu, if he wasn't already. Even an introduction to Taoist founder Lao Tzu, or Confucius, or even the current blue-eyed monk and Dharma master, Bodhidharma (whose recent — the art of Zen along the path of Buddha — which was coming out of Luoyang via the Silken road and was all the rage in the land of Ch'in) wouldn't hurt either. For this would help to outfit Attala, or any other *type-two* ruthless thinking warrior, with a new makeover. At least provide a new cap, robe and sandals to give these types a friendlier face. But, he knew, this was wishful thinking because Attala was trying with all his heart to lay waste the glorious western civilization with its Western Philosophy along with its stoism. The day following Lucius Aelius Castus' victory Dyfed gleaned some valuable information now from a memo from Karatakos. This information was a window that looked into the sordid affairs that governed the machinations of how the reality of history that effected and subjugated the hoi polloi really unfolded. What Dyfed didn't learn, however, was whom the players were that made the decisions regarding this unfolding. Poor Attala, Dyfed thought, and then quickly came to realize that it was the latter that had been on the wrong side, nobody else. The Hun, no matter how brave and tenacious, and even intelligent he may have been simply hadn't realized certain facts and truths about fighting Amor. Or did he? Anyway, how god-awful those facts certainly were. And beside manipulating, or tricking the great game to the advantage of the more cleverly clogged magicians that had been pressed into service for this particular slight of hand, it also pushed the reset on trend. For what the mechanism was that kicked in here, fortunately on this occasion, Dyfed came to learn from loose talk that was to keep turning up over and over for the next two millennium and in almost exactly the same format. Attala had been set up and the Attalas of the future would not have his (albeit minimum) respect for humanity or his integrity. So for those with eyes to see, ears to hear and a brain to reason look and listen up and pay attention.

For the whole game had been a sting operation from the start. Attala was a dangerous marauder who, it was supposed, in time would turn toward the west. But under the circumstances the west may very well have become indefensible by that time so a plan was hatched to speed the process up and induce Attala's attack upon Europa while the latter still had a fighting chance to win. And of course the Salian Frankens had a reason to pony up and chip in too. The folks in charge of making these decisions, apparently, couldn't for-see the future clearly enough to be confident of success in this matter at a later date. Furthermore (and more troubling), there was meant to have been a turkey shoot that was meant to immediately follow the eastern horde's defeat in an effort to expunge and exterminate these Hunnic folks altogether, once and for all. And it was also meant to exterminate many other folks alongside them.

Only, in that the Hun had outsmarted the Amoran organizers in the end by disentangling themselves from the Amoran, Goth, and Franken host to make good their escape so as to live and maybe come back and fight another day, if need be. But that was not to be the case.

The planned extermination of the Hun was only the final objective of the grand scheme that had ingeniously been constructed and to the most part brought to fruition. Although considered necessary, or certainly desirable, extermination couldn't have been the kernel objective, for what could be any more base and disgusting than that? That must have been a sideshow, Dyfed thought. Indeed, he thought again, that question isn't asked enough. Anyway, in truth, although Dyfed hadn't fully realised it at the time, the persons behind the caper appeared in sensitised to this notion and felt no sense of shame or any undesirability in mass murder. Nor had they any conscience about it or about the terror and plight of others to whom they may cause suffering and misery.

However, their prime objective, it seemed, was not so much just to eradicate a potential enemy in days and years to come, but to create some form of elixir that would be a shot in the arm for imperial Amor. Something — anything, that might enable them to pack up their troubles in their old kitbag and swallow all their foreign and home-grown foes and nay-sayers whole without a tooth mark in them, and smile, smile, smile!

Besides that, this operation was meant to kick-start an aggressive economy. It was to be backed by a new generation of legionary troops that came from all over Europa which (obviously) were even already somewhat integrated. It was hoped that at first, like a drug inhaled, this new and improved mechanism would inflate the miserable and withered state of the collective and suggestible mind of the hard pressed Amoran hoi polloi taxpayer just enough to allow the wealthy to fool Europa's general populace once more. And fool them just long enough to call them on again to arms. This secondary plan would be a ruse to reinstate and rejuvenate a failed empire back into a brilliant economy, if only temporarily and only in the hoi polloi's imagination for the purpose of vast gain to so few. Either that or by seducing them with freshly printed fiat currency (worth way less the current currency) in the form of imperial promissory notes and imperial bonds with a promise to make every investor rich and the rich richer.

And under these circumstances, they would be able to make a last grab for such a fortune that was unprecedented to date and to then convert it into something of meaning with real value. Dyfed had become aware that Clemens Publius Maximus' old colleague, Gaius Lucius Julius who had remained in the employ of the lately deceased Augustus, had taken up an interest in his own earlier attempt of controlling the Amoran currency through monopoly. Then, in so doing — and before the ranks of the peasant masses and the ignorant multitude slumped back down once again into irreversible debt, failure, and oblivion — those few who controlled the empire and used it as their own tool or weapon of business in order to maintain personal prosperity, would manage to spin a false environment just long enough that would allow them this aforementioned window of opportunity. And under these circumstances, they would be able to make a last grab for such a fortune that was unprecedented to date.

That fortune was to own and control the entire known world that mattered along with its accompanying slaves while the rest went to hell with starvation and locally inspired brutality and its ensuing chaos. And any blame or outstanding bills would be laid at the feet of the dead for the next generation to inherit.

This scheme had been the brainchild of some very intelligent and very devious men and women, no doubt about that, Dyfed thought. But as he later learned — partly through information that Karatakos had relayed to him, as well as through a symposium or council that also occurred immediately following their victory that Karatakos had attended without Dyfed — Gala and the estranged Adaulf were being attributed credit in this. But Dyfed wasn't to believe that, not for a minute. But it certainly seemed as though Gala had pulled out all the stops to get Attala to overrun Italia, if not the eastern empire as well and direct them away from Gaul. It hadn't happened that way, though, but Dyfed knew that there were no coincidences in politics. Nor did that wily old emperor try and direct Attala to subdue the Salian Franks, either? Indeed, the Salian Franks had come out ahead and no doubt they wanted the Huns exterminated too.

But as everyone was eventually to witness, the grand scheme for Amor to reinvent itself suddenly out of the blue reversed and appeared to backfire big time with the ultimate rise of the Franken kingdom of King Chlodwig (Chlodio) the long-haired who being the son of Chlodovechus was soon to control the important cities, highways and byways that connected Albion to Amor and the White Sea to the Baltic trade routes.

But the inner clique of power elite within the Amoran establishment who one moment were thought to be looking on in horror and dismay at their ultimate demise and loss of empire, magically and quickly without any fuss made a quick comeback by offering King Chlodio everything he (or they) needed to regain an empire only a scant few seconds later. And the representatives of those powerful elite were there on hand, and johnny-on-the-spot (we might add) to make the offer and deliver the imperial promises. Nothing is written in stone, anyway, they say. So with Adaulf's presence here as well as that of Giorgius Florentius (Giorgi Posh) as well as the presence of Gaius Julius, it seemed in some way to indicate that this was the game.

Shortly after the battle at Catal, while Dyfed returned to Tournay, Trachmyr, along with five hundred of their surviving and willing soldiers, had pulled away from Catal and followed a series of rivers and roads south. Dyfed had ordered Trachmyr to relocate the lion's share of the wealth which the House of Lucifer's Guards had hidden (prior to the fall of the city of Amor) among the caves in the vicinity of the Allobroges people near Cularo recently named Gratianopolis after Emperor Gratian, now called Grenoble. Cularo was a town in the vicinity of the Alpens where the Burgundars extended their control. Trachmyr was to return to Tournay, a city just under a hundred Amoran miles south of the river Rine delta and the Phthian island of Valkyren (meaning dead warriors). Tournay, the city of Childerc who at the time was suspected to be one of the movers and shakers in the battle for succeeding to the authority of the fast waning western Amoran Empire which, having run its course, was now run down. As the successor to his father Childerc, Clodio's (Clovis) star was rising quickly.

Soon this man was to unite all the Franken under his singular rule, proclaiming himself king, as predicted. He followed Amor in converting his dominion (kingdom) known as Frankia (Francia) into the cult worship of Jeshua Adon. By crossing the river Somme to the south and renewing his ethnic cleansing against the Dominion of Syagrius, Clodio set out to consolidate the foundations of what was an initiation to form the second Amoran Empire. And when General (Duc) Syagrius fell, there was nothing to stop Clodio, whose victory signalled the tolling of the imperial bell for the First Empire of Amor. Soon he had most of Gaul under his thumb with the exception of Burgundy.

(Theoderic the Great strangled Ogre right there on the spot)

'Antisocial behaviour is a trait of intelligence in a world full of conformists.'
NIKOLA TESLA

Dyfed and John of Munster were comfortably seated together at a roadhouse called the Yeoman's Arms in Cambridge where they had hooked up again and were staying.

"Later, in those last days Muns, Cato and I discussed those times during the days when after Amor lay disintegrated and the Western Empire fell apart and was scattered around, with a few valuable articles able to be picked up here and placed somewhere else over there. That's how it was. At this point a struggle separate and alongside and in tuned with the Church of Amor ensued to inherit its power. As for the Merovingian kings, Mero may have been an instigator but his descendants Childeric and Clodio were culpable for providing a conduit for the Church of Amor to unnecessarily assume religious/philosophical control over all of Europa and influence it away from western philosophy and impinge it with primitive superstition no further advanced than paganism was. Jeshuanism, however, could have been presented differently to an even greater advantage to all of mankind. Georgius Florentius was another such arch villain who lent a sympathetic profile towards a truncated and false narration of the true Jeshuan philosophy. While my guards returned to Tournay to establish the physical House of Lucifer at Tournay, I returned to Amor to set about picking up and gathering together the virtual remnants of my business. This entailed tapping into a larger cross section and variety of society that Amor had for attitudes and knee-jerk responses around financial security as well as recipes for inhibiting the condition of awry that's becomes its effect. Morgant had just returned from the fifth dimension so I saw a fair bit of him as well as Cato who visited from time to time. I also hooked up with Mencius who was expanding his business distribution along the Silken Road while business was slow and prices were still cheap. Despite the war effort, along with Europa's tough soldiers in Amoran armour fighting like *O-Billio* and covering themselves from top to toe in glory with their solid defeat of the Huns, the Amoran economy continued to sink below the air breathing surface due to inflation and increased demand. Strangely, this did not seem to displease or perturb the oligarchs waiting on the sidelines rubbing their hands gleefully in anxious anticipation. Aside from being angry the hoi polloi were stymied, their livelihood, their families and their future were all hanging in the balance. This was because the spending value of the denarii for the ninety-nine per cent of the hoi polloi (among the population) continued dropping, as did their spending consumption. Not so with the likes of Purplebal. But with no middle-class cushion the aristocrats quickly stagnated and the poor disintegrated. Mencius, the entrepreneur and a charter member of the Silken Road was now looking for something beyond Ravenna or Amor."

"Mencius now approached me,' Dyfed said to Muns, 'about coupling his House of Mencius merchant goods distributing business with the House of Lucifer. I told

Mencius that I was relocating to Tournay and that once I was settled I would have easy access to Albion, Alba (Albany) and the Emerald Isle along with the ancestral lands of the Friesians, the Angles, the Saxen, the Dané. This would include,' Dyfed told Jack, 'the lands around the Mare Suebicum (Baltic). We both thought that the spending power of any copy of the Amoran denarii was about to continue to shift in the general direction of down in the near future. But with Mencius' connections and my financial know-how,' said Dyfed, 'this promised to be a fruitful union of houses.'

At this time Dyfed took up hobnobbing with many some of the sparks in the dying ashes of the old and fading empire. Potamus Purplebal was one of these as were Adaulf and Gala. As such, the folks in question happened to be fairly close business acquaintances of Dyfed's (in and around this time). In fact Cato was startled by these men's influence, especially Pater Cardinal van Richelieu, the alter ego of Giorgius Florentius. That suspicion had now elevated him into the Haploid elite's prime suspect bracket. Cato and his cohort Marcus Aurelius had voiced their concerns about him more than once, along with Cornelius Felix. They identified them as being potential dangerous Haploid kingpins. According to Morgant, Manandan had similar reservations and Morgant's own Master handler Thrax, who always remained in the fifth dimension, apparently had communicated orders for Cato to see to it that Purblebal and Georgius Florentius were killed without delay. But Manandan had been more cautious and — through his emissary Karatakos — told Cato (for the sake of the *pack*) to only observe them closely and to report back every fifty to a hundred years. Only in this way can we learn more about their organization, he said.

'I'm going to have to stop introducing you to folks I have befriended,' Dyfed reportedly said laughingly to Cato. 'But I did tell you that Giorgius was a dyed in the wool Jeshuan wolf on the lookout for himself.'

"Listen, Dyfed,' Cato responded. 'I'm not overly suspicious of most of the new Amoran nobles, or the hoi polloi, either. But there are some of these folks that just keep turning up all polished and shiny that keeps catching my eye. So, I convened with my old friend Antisthenes recently, while I was back in the fifth dimension for a stint of rest and recreation. I expressed my concerns about this with him. You can't talk to Thrax anymore; he lives in the past and thinks the Bronze Age still envelopes this world and is a masquerade party designed for fun and frolic primarily orientated towards tasty morsels to satisfy the tummy combined with passionate, unprotected sex. Anyway, one day I would like you to meet Antisthenes. He was the founder, you know, of the Cynic movement right here in this dimension. The purpose of which, by the way, was to try and coax humanity into sloughing their ego like a snake sheds its skin for rebirth. According to the book of lists this was crystalized here in this dimension by those immortals of the serpent race that were the first gods of the hoi polloi. However, although the tale is real, the reality itself is pure hocus pocus that was initiated long, long ago by the Haploids. Anyway, Antisthenes and I obviously support this. We feel that it could be the anecdote needed for humanity to become immune from the fantasies or whatever it is that madly drives them into becoming an object of derision: derision and this infernal substitution of reality, or whatever it is that makes them blind and stupid. If his attempts had been more successful, the failure of Pelagius wouldn't have set us back too far.'

But Dyfed then responded by saying that he agreed but there was more to it that that. Look at the goings on with both the doctrinal and political imaging and whatnot and who knows what else over the Hunnic invasion and remedies thereof. It's a narrative construct, only and nothing more. There was talk of obeisance, but talk is cheap. What transpired was evil: Evil machinations by cruel, weak and pathetic human beings. Only the dying emperor rose to the occasion. These were not the actions of men whose thoughts and actions are not tied to the material plane. They are sentient beings that have become literally inseparable from the material plane whose awareness has no meaningful intuition. Their hearts are not free of dust nor are they void of form for they live in the world of their own making. They dwell now in the world of the confused ego whose conditions are limited to the exponential effects of long ago causes that are now beyond their scope of reach to influence or repair. They know nothing of the mystery of heaven and earth, nor do they care. Nor do they tend (or care to tend) to the path of immortality. As my friend Mencius would say; they shirk and refrain from cultivating the Tao (pronounced Daow) and nor they could never recognize the place for contemplating peace and communion. They are dangerous ruffians who are responsible for the misery and the suffering of others.

In time there were other men like Constantine Augustus of Byzas, Julius the Apostate, and even that terrifying Goth, Theoderic the Great. This man had momentarily towered upon the world's stage and by re-positioning a no nonsense trend he re-established Amor's western imperial form. And even if he hadn't re-established her in line with Western Philosophy as its apex with Cynicism and Stoicism as its genre, at least it was with a decisive and cynical eye toward straightforwardness in honesty, fairness and integrity. Under him the western sector became a vital contender. But he, too, had been brought down, and those who were decidedly unsympathetic to Theoderic's tactics and were the cause of his fall were some of the names that Cato had suggested kept turning up polished and shiny but with distinct stink and odiousness about them. He wondered why these folks were being promoted when they should have been set on fire or drowned in the river. It was a matter of being where your enemy's enemies are your friends.

According to Cato, despite the uncharacteristic elongated skull caused from artificial cranial deformation, Theoderic the Great was a sturdy, self-possessed and intelligent East Goth and descendant of the Amal family of Goth rulers. It had been the eastern emperor himself who had taken a shine to and had pitted Theoderic against King Ogre. The emperor had earlier placed King Ogre in Ravenna as consul from where he ruled Italia. And rule King Ogre did, just like a tyrant amassing a personal fortune at the expense of the people. And from a distance he even challenged the emperor himself who remained in Byzas. And so a lengthy conflict broke out between the armies of the eastern emperor's appointed king of Italia and his newly appointed vice consul, Theoderic who the eastern emperor had sent for reconnaissance.

Cato, who was present when this Theoderic the East Goth arrived in Ravenna a victor to finally present the emperor's orders to Ogre to accept him a vice consul, told Dyfed how this rather tall, magnificent looking man with blondish hair and piercing but friendly blue eyes arrived at the capital. Rather then adopting a haughty manner and attitude over Ogre, he brought presents instead for King Ogre who he praised and flattered most eloquently despite having just fought and subdued his soldiers on the battlefield. He then produced the decree from the emperor in Byzas that instated him alongside Ogre as vice consul. But Theoderic most excellently and convincingly placated the tyrant to the effect that Ogre believed he was more interested in the city's women and its wine and that he was not interested in administration whatsoever: For he only waited, Theoderic had told him, for Ogre to point him in the direction in which he, Theoderic vice-consul, could best serve him and lead his victorious army to battle for Italia. Cato relayed, that the East Goth wanted to know the layout of the grand scheme so he could assist the king in any way and not be troublesome or make mistakes that could irk his majesty, King Ogre. And then only two days later Theoderic had managed to organise and pay for a grand banquet in order to celebrate the occasion of his ascension to the position as co-ruler in name only (it was becoming obvious Ogre wasn't going to mark the occasion on his own initiative) and then after distributing more gifts to the king and the attendees he encouraged Ogre to rise in order to hesitantly deliver an introduction for him which was customary. When the latter had finished his slow, confused and barely audible presentation, and had half heartedly welcomed Theoderic, he then sat down in front of his plate and waited for Theoderic the East Goth to deliver his address. It was an address which Theoderic was just itching to give, so Ogre believed…although, this new vice consul's bold strut out into the circle of power here in Italia would probably be to no avail in the end, Ogre thankfully thought to himself as he sat down. For Ogre had already made plans to keep Theoderic hamstrung and helpless thank god!

"Theoderic slowly rose from his chair smiling as he cast his eyes all around (Cato had continued obviously enjoying the retelling of the story for the umteeth time). Then he put a friendly hand on King Ogre's shoulder who was sitting immediately beside him. Suddenly, in a very rapid movement and with little or no fuss as if it was a normal procedure, Theoderic (in front of fifty dignitaries) immediately strangled Ogre right there on the spot with those large and strong hands of his. Those aforementioned honoured guests that were sitting around the table were suddenly left speechless and horrified. Yet they remained unmoved to react. All of this happened before Ogre could even get his first glass of wine lifted to his lips or an opportunity to taste a morsel of the food that had just been set in front of him. The entire banquette fell utterly silent. Cato told him this with a straight face,' Dyfed relayed to his friend Muns.

Once Theoderic released Ogre, the latter had slumped forward and crumpled banging his upper teeth on the table's edge as he slithered down collapsing dead onto the floor beneath it. There, he lay motionless amid a pool of his piss for the remainder of the banquet. Once King Ogre was put in his place, Theoderic calmly sat down again and broke the silence by calling for a priest to say the grace before the onset of food consumption. You see, although Theoderic claimed to be an Arian Jeshuan and not a devotee of the Church of Amor, grace by a priest or some such official of god, as you know, is the custom, protocol and the correct etiquette to follow before the start and consumption of a banquet here in Italia where the Church of Amor reigns supreme. It was something the Ogre should have already done. Cato gave a little laugh. *'When in Italia do what Italians do.'* This became Theoderic's motto. But he tried also to introduce respect for the religion of others that simply didn't fly later after the great man was ousted.

Cato reported, in his dry sense of humour, that the table chatter over dinner on that day of Theoderic's investiture was a very polite affair after that opening incident. And it wasn't until all the posturing and prematurely sated guests had most graciously thanked their host and pushed themselves away from the table and hastily beat a retreat and fled the palace and its grounds with furtive backward glances. Later Ogre's body was hauled out from under from under the table by two well-dressed servants who dragged the dead king unceremoniously across the marble floor and out a side door.

In any case, Theoderic kept Italia's indigenous customs maintained for all the years that he ruled there while vastly expanding their empire under East Goth secular and military customs at the same time. And he played nice with the Salian Frankens' new kingdom of Francia that misled the Vicar of Jeshua in the Vatican to believe he was a believer.

Theoderic the Great was an important player (arguably the most important) in the development of the second empire irrespective of Clodio (Clovis) and those others who our friends in the *pack* continued to search for. His was truly a positive influence while the former fugitives whose identities remains under wraps were positively negative. As already stated, Theoderic was an important player for the Frankonian empire in particular which was itself the kick-off for the Holy Amoran Empire which became the Second Amoran Empire of the western world, although the Church of Amor had a lot to do with that. Theoderic was a breath of fresh air for the good guys like all the Joe and Jane citizens of the main and mean streets of the world who needed and wanted a fair and predictable viceroy or first leader to protect and nurture them. And protect them Theoderic did, even from the emperor in Byzas — when necessary — from whom he quickly became quite independent.

Theoderic the Great was a champion of the common man and woman as well as the laws that protected them. And in some ways Dyfed thought that he was akin to Diocletes (Diocletian Augustus) in a similar sense that the Tyrant Cornelius-Felix was not. Theoderic protected and even enhanced these laws and saw that they were executed with justice and the people of Italia were not even his people or his tribe, but they certainly were his responsibility, and he met those responsibilities with all the integrity and energy that he threw into his everyday life. Theoderic, it was hoped at the time, would be a man before his time and not of his time that would shine a torch into the future, and hopefully find that hope was not a relic, an extinct life form that had surfaced as a fossil from some ancient eon during the early times. And Theoderic the Great was also the making of Frankia; for, as we shall see Clodio and even Karl the Magnificent could not have advanced their empire to what it eventually became without his cooperation.

Theoderic the Great wanted to expand his empire of the East Goths into Hispana that previously had been dominated by Adaulf and his West Goths. Chlodio (Clovis) who seeing an advantage in this sent his son Theuderic to Theoderic the Great to clinch a deal to become allies and back each other's interests. To this end Chlodio presented his daughter Autofelada to Theoderic the Great with an offer for marriage to seal their pact. This deal having being clinched helped put the run on folks that threatened Chlodio thereafter.

This tough and tenacious East Goth had been born in Pannonia south of the Dana (also Danu) River as a king's son and had been held in the eastern capital by the Byzasian emperor as ransom for security against his father's atrocities toward the empire. Theoderic's upbringing here at the centre of civilization in the great city of Byzas taught him the arts of governing. Later, while still a youngster, he also graduated from the military academy there. This upbringing allowed him access to valuable tools to be used when he got out on his own. Theoderic was an original thinker and a unique human who used the ruthlessness of his race combined with a sharp shrewdness he possessed in order to dispatch his enemies in short order and minimized the laying of waste to their fortunes by having most of them preserved and transferred instead, and without delay into his own account. But he was fair and he was loved as much as he was feared and loathed by those greedy exploiters of downtrodden humanity. These downtrodden, those ever-present hoi polloi, needed a friend to pick them up and protect them more than anything now and Theoderic saw the fortune in siding with this majority. It became obvious very quickly though that the axis of enemies which lined up in a row against Theoderic were the old and established moneylenders and political bureaucrats from Amor, and more recently from Ravenna, not to mention the commercially independent and self banked villas of those rich and big houses that were now scattered around Europa. Although this powerful East Goth had taken decisive control of the western empire, he had been slipped a Mickey Finn and in the end it hadn't worked out. But it mustn't be forgotten that he had set out to bring monumental change. Although he was championed by the people none of these actions warmed Theoderic to the old in-crowd.

Usury was one name for the crime in which this old in-crowd imbibed. These money cheaters and hoarders and debt makers employed every form of trickery for capital gains in their roughshod use and abuse of the less fortunate in order to attain wealth themselves. But of late, Dyfed had been racking his brains for a more specific handle to describe their sinister-ism, those sins committed against unsuspecting commoners, the hoi polloi. This practise, now being in excess of what went before wasn't just indigenous to Amor. It had reached out everywhere even into Lothar through the Church of Amor's presence. This psychological tick, this inhumanity they had was something like a phobia for materialism, although that wasn't specific enough. So Dyfed played with treasure-ism and affluent-ism, and even settled on opulent-ism for a while before stumbling on 'capitalizing' on the poor and downtrodden. So that was it. This form of capitalism[63] was their crime. But it was more than just the crime; it was the sin against their true self. And although it had always existed (as an ideal in some way), now this drive for wealth was a self-imposed veneer at the expense of others that had become even more enhanced and streamlined. That special veneer was one of entitlement. Entitlement in turn was even an urgent requirement for that special condition which went with it; it was a special aura, the aura of superiority that contributed to being escalated above others which was necessary for those belonging to a special elite that the religious sentinels helped make them into. This morphed into specialized privilege. Many continue to think as such even today.

"One such man is a certain Johanus Cauvin (Kalvin, also Calvin) who is quite prominent in this century, as you probably have heard, Muns,' said Dyfed to his friend Jack of Munster as they sat in the Yeoman's bar and grill in Cambridge.

Many still continue to think along these lines. This was the case especially in the organised echelon of the Church of Amor's application of secular Amoranism and their strictness for the law, a little something they had picked up from their antecedents. This stemmed from back in the day when they scratched and clawed their way out from the culverts and caves that carved out their rats' nest under the city of Amor. From there they had vied with anything that could come to hand — and whatever come what may — in order to own and control mean old main street; at least the one that went to and

---

63 A simple ideological tool that comes in many forms and flavours. Also, it can be used by a myriad of political ideologies.

fro from the market bank to the palace of the Vicar of Amor. And it seemed that that was all they needed or wanted.

Under the concept of the god of Abram, the Jeshuans set about to initiate a total lockdown of freedoms such as the freedom of movement once again, as well as freedom of choice for religious believe, freedom of profession, freedom of individuality, but not the unquestioned freedom and right to be rich on account of hard work and fair play. You could be rich, you were encouraged to be so if you could, but that road was an expensive road to haul down and was a shortcut away from hard work and fair play; that is if you had any chance and likelihood in succeeding. And you needed to be very good at making money in order to cover all the tolls, concessions, endowments, donations, gifts, obligations, tributes, gratuities, alms, offertories, tips, bribes and baksheesh needed to get you there. The dice were loaded and with the cards marked the odds were stacked against you. Few could hold out and run the full gauntlet unless blackmailers or brothers in crime securely backed them. This was what swept Theoderic away in the end and destroyed his chance to right all that had been wrong in the past. Theoderic had somehow managed to point the horses that pulled that carriage out into the clear only then to have them tripped up and the carriage dragged back into the slums of debt once more. Who then was responsible for stealing the light from the world? Who was the thief responsible for stealing Jeshua the Nazarean's true identity and fashioning it into the great caper, the ultimate scam for its official representative only to be able to program humanity to follow the rules of greedy con artists, liars, and unconscionable characters who warmed and fuzzied over their trespasses while engineering mass slavery of the people? Who were they? Once again Giorgius Florentius name came up.

At this time, Theoderic the Great, and another man, although of an entirely different nature, were two people who had peaked Dyfed's interest. The second man was a certain Julian the Apostate Augustus, a former genuine emperor of Amor in his own right.

Theoderic, on the other hand was way more available even if he was about to be on the run from the establishment that at one time he had championed. At that time Dyfed advised him to repair to the wilds of Prydain.

Although vastly different, the two aforementioned men had the Arian religion close to their heart that they each promoted, although that was probably about all they had in common. And it hadn't taken Julian too long to chuck that cult, either. Dyfed had already learned from Cato that Julian the Apostate had been raised as an Arian Jeshuan, but had fairly preferred and returned to the paganism that was of the persuasion associated with the former state of Hellas from whence Julian was descended through his mother. But Julian's real calling was not paganism per sé, anyway. In fact it was not paganism at all, as Dyfed saw it. Being monotheistic in nature Julian's beliefs were simply a segment of Western Philosophy where Helios was the representative of the godhead or Absolute. And since Western Philosophy had lived well enough side by side with paganism in the past, it was apparent, he thought, that Julian assumed that if simpler minds couldn't comprehend Western Philosophy's finer points they at least had Helios to turn to in lieu of. Theoderic, on the other hand had remained Arian. He, like Dyfed, also believed that people were not really equal but were only born equal. Then from that time forward each and every one decides just how equal they actually are in a slightly different sense, or how equal they want to be. Being equal was not about not putting oneself above others or by being brought up to another's level. Nor was it by manipulating a situation so as to get the advantage and appear to be above others. It was about being noble. Prosperity and being rich or feared did not necessarily place you above others in this context. But there was nothing wrong in being rich; and being rich can provide one with the opportunity and insight in how to help others. In fact richness can be an important challenge for oneself as well as a fountain of happiness. Dyfed had always been rich, in a sense, but he was a lot richer by being noble. But money can't buy nobility.

(Once upon a time in a far away land & the story of Dyfed)

'If you wish to serve and glorify god, serve humanity'
MOHUMUD THE PROPHET

Before taking Dyfed's advise and sailing away to the River Dee on the Isle of Prydain, Theoderic had become interested in that same man that now lounged on the couch before him.

"Jolly good work, my dear Lord Dyfed Lucifer,' he said to the Prince of the Grove in the Amoran tongue that was accompanied with a slight accent. 'Now Cato here has told me scant little about who it is that you are exactly; however he has spoken well of you. So, who is Dyfed Lucifer?'

"He's a Cynic by choice whose religion is Western Philosophy just like all the other greats, including myself, of course,' Cato quickly inserted without so much as taking his eyes off reading his book. 'Plato, Socrates, and Aristotle, for instance,' he added, 'along with the proponents of the unity theory of ancient Hinduism were just some of the early initiates to form the genesis of modern monotheistic religious thought, make no mistake about it, Theoderic. There is no longer any God per se or avatars thereof with personalities and judgements. For in respect to the discussion at hand there is only the human mind that perceives the phenomena. Many don't understand that Western Philosophy, along with earlier Hinduism, is essentially (from the metaphysical point of view) a form of Monotheism. If the olden day current Semitic speaking believers invented the single god of Abraham concept, as is suggested, then they must have been our Indo-Iranian forefathers and the fathers of all Europaeans in general. Unfortunately, it didn't all get sorted out by intellectuals battling this out between the first century BCE and the first century CE in the forums and think-tanks of the cities of Antioch and Xanderia.'

"Well that may be,' Dyfed said, 'but remember too that the ancient believers in the god On that was in and around the Nile Valley and the Land of Khem also believed in the one god concept. So it too was monotheistic. But for me, to change the subject and answer your question, Theoderic, it all began long ago,'

Dyfed then relayed this response in the third person and in storybook form:

"Our mother, Violet-Eye,' he said, 'had been born far away in a royal city called Dava in another land just about the time the fifth world began. She was the great-grandchild of the beautiful Lord Shirkuh the Lion-heart, born of Galatea. Her father had been King Skuza of Saka son of Thrax. Her mother was Queen Kimri of Gamir. Although referred to here as king, Skuza was a priest-king, a leader and shaman of his people while Violet's mother Kimri was a priestess-queen and also a shaman. It had been Kimri of Gamir who was the descendant of the beautiful lord Shirkuh, himself an overlord shaman priest who carried a staff and like his forefathers before him thought wise thoughts. This man originated in Hyrcania (the land of the wolves) commonly called Varkana. When as a young man with his education completed, Shirkuh (that means mountain lion) left Varkana and roamed the steppe beyond his doorstep. He quickly became a leader of men then an overlord because his ability as a warrior was as acute as his intellectual and shamanistic capabilities. He challenged the authority and supremacy of other tribes and married the chieftains' daughters who had fallen under his rule. Overlord Shirkuh was of the people of the horse. Attached to his standard was a large red and black windsock shaped in the form of a dragon-like creature whose head resembled a wolf, although its elongated body form represented a tusked boar and not a dragon. The horde displayed many exact totem-motifs as this. These large, fluttering, conical bags that were fastened on tall staves (staffs) were mounted on the stirrup of the many colour guards that accompanied Lord Shirkuh like a shadow wherever he rode. When the horses were at a gallop across the steppe, and as the wind that was being forced through the creature's mouth (where sound emitting reeds had been fashioned) ballooned out the boar shaped fluttering bag behind it, it was then accompanied by a shrill sound that shrieked from the totem-motif. This was meant to be a fearsome warning to un-nerve their enemies. Like all the other identical totem-motif windsocks of this horde, when Shirkuh was at feast or at sleep his own standard stirred silently in the breeze above and around his nomadic wagon wherein he resided with his family when on the move. Residing at seasonal layovers, their mobile conveyance living quarters were traded for easily assembled tents constructed of felt and animal hides stretched over wooden prefabricated frames that were lashed together and warmed with a hearth to ward off the bitter steppe winds and winters.'

'Lord Shirkuh, who had apprenticed with Vulcan and had become a gifted metallurgist, had as a personal family seal a design called the pentangle –the five pointed star — that had been passed down to him from Dogone (legend has it) who was a patriarch seldom glimpsed through the shimmering reflection from the other world. And the likes of this design appeared as tattoos on his and each member of his family's body; and it was branded on the family's many horses and other possessions as well as emblazoned on the sides of Lord Shirkuh's fiery red and black fluttering boar motif. When Lord Shirkuh left the district around the Hyrcanian Sea behind and journeyed west beyond the land of Subar, the world was still inclined towards the age of Bronze. From the time of his birth Shirkuh was shined on by Surya, his mentor. And Surya aligned Shirkuh with Vulcan. Vulcan in turn led Shirkuh to the huge treasure trove of iron ore, a necessity for the manufacture of the new age. That enriched body of metals happened to be embedded throughout the rich Taurus Mountains in the west, and it was to here he came. It was here also that Surya, his benefactor, brought Lord Shirkuh into a fabulous wealth of stimulation and enlightenment, and helped him fire his forge while forging his wisdom and zeal. Surya (also called Shuryash) was also known as Shamash by the Hurri people. These latter folks were a priest-king oriented people distantly related to Lord Shirkuh and had occupied this land since ancient times. Lord Shirkuh located himself in Karkem where he met Kubaba, the patron of that city whose name was changed to Cybebe. Originally pronounced Ki-be-be, through the function of simple etymology it eventually became Cybele (pronounced Si-bel-ee and Si-bel). Later, Shirkuh settled in Nesa Karum on the high steppe where he amassed great wealth and established a seat upon which he placed a Hittite ruler named Zipani. Lord Shirkuh then relocated to a great mountain that was nearby and visible from Nesa Karum where he lived in a palatial, lofty and well lit stone barrow with a pediment above the entrance. It was from here that he dispersed guidance to his people via shaman-priests. Only his extended family and kind were permitted to come within leagues of his residence that was surrounded by natural gardens that were prowled by wild creatures, mostly wolves that were tamed only by his mind and his voice. In this way the crude and simple people he ruled over and moulded toward enlightenment, but although well tended and cared for, they were kept at bay.'

'Queen Violet-Eye had been orphaned while still a little girl when her brother Daceneus, who suffering from a recently diagnosed condition of psychopathy (a condition then unknown among the people), committed the treacherous act of parricide against their honourable parents. A short time later shamans from abroad approached Daceneus' mountainous kingdom in the Karpates in order to exact justice by way of imposing death upon his earthly existence. So Daceneus rapidly vacated his usurped kingdom Dava that gazed east over the land of Dobruja and fled in terror to the north Atlas Sea for fear of his life. There, under a new identity, he was said to have sought refuge in the land that was part of ancient Hyperborea. By then, Violet Eye had been adopted and cared for first by an uncle named King Zalmox, and then by Lord Huge and his consort Belini the Shining.

'The previously mentioned Lord Huge, a magician from Armorica who long before had settled on Samothrace from where he had fled with Belini the Shining after it had undergone invasion, had set out for Frygia which was situated north of the ancient land of Arzawan. Here he had come under the influence of King Zalmox, a brother to King Dardanos whose kingdom was to the west. Both Dardanos and Zalmox were uncles to young Violet and it was they who placed the princess into Lord Huge's hands for safekeeping. Shortly afterwards Lord Huge and his consort, along with young Violet, set out for the kingdom of Cilic. They journeyed southeast across mountains and a rough and rocky steppe to Kappadochy that had suddenly, without warning, come under attack. Here they took shelter in a vast underground city that remained constantly under siege for many years by warring tribes of mixed Aryans. This name (of course) is an anomaly: Aryan means orderly and civilized, something these rough folks were not. Therefore, they could then be termed Turans, meaning chaotic and disorderly. These are words from the ancient Sanskrit tongue.

The language of these Aryans was somewhat different than that of Violet's and her two companions, whose tongue also differed from hers in subtle ways. Belini the Shining, however, had refused to remain there in an existence beneath the ground, so in the Autumn when the land was cooler by day and a lull in the attacks had provided an opportune time, they had vacated their subterranean dwellings (a vast complex of abodes that were chiselled out of the volcanic rock) and journeyed on south through the Gates of Tauri to the newly formed kingdom of Cilic. Cilic was situated in the ancient land of Kizzwatna where Belini the Shining was said to have been born and where Violet Eye's great-grandfather was said to have died quite a few degrees of time before from a red-hot metallurgic explosion during an experiment to create a stronger metal called super-iron. Belini was a daughter to the legendary King Kirtan of Mitann, himself descended from Shirkuh, and she quickly secured herself an important position as curator in the temple dedicated to Sin and Shamash. It was here under the tutorship of both Belini and Lord Huge that Violet Eye received much of her finishing school education. Later, during her adolescence, Belini had died of a mysterious and incurable sickness, and Violet Eye and Lord Huge had journeyed in sadness by vessel from Mallos to Paphos on the Isle of

Copper where King Aerius had deified Violet-Eye in a failed attempt to woo her into matrimony. Upon leaving the Isle of Copper they sailed to the western most reaches of Luwia, stopping at seaports in Lykia, Karia, Ioni before they passed through the Straits of Dardan into the Propontis from where they reached Frygia. Once there, Lord Huge turned and moved towards Dardanos' kingdom where amid a sacred grove deep in the forest of Ida he conjured forth a paradise. It consisted of a palatial labyrinth of polished stone that he had hewn out beneath a sheer rock face that remained hidden behind a constant rainbow formed by the holy waters of heaven. This shower cascaded down from the precipice above into a pool the colour of blue topaz whose cool ripples lapped at the palace steps. It was so concealed that Artemis and many other gods and goddesses of the pantheon had thereafter often come to repose, refreshing their white and naked limbs in the chill waters of the pool while watching the life of the forest come down to drink. Violet Eye had often stalked the neighbouring woodlands with that nimble huntress Artemis, and had just as often, she had later told Dyfed, made music with the goddess's twin brother Apollo who entertained her with compositions upon the very lyre that Mercury had fashioned for Orpheus. Meanwhile, she on the other hand was able to accompany him with her sweet sounds of natural song that radiated out through her slender and gifted throat. Here, among her polished repose deep in the Idian forest and under the protection of that crafty artisan Huge, Violet Eye had remained in the stillness of time.'

'Then one summer Lord Huge had a visitor. This guest was Manandan. To this northern sage, Lord Huge's retreat in the sanctity of Ida's grove was a welcomed respite from his travels, so he tarried here awhile on his journey homeward. It had been long before this (during former catastrophic times) that Manandan had cast off from the land of Hyperborea. And spreading his canvas to the wind he had voyaged south across the seas and up into the delta of that great river that fertilized Masr more often called the Land of Khem; the land of geometrical configurations and the sister seat of old doctrine. He had disembarked at Innu and at first had taken a position as a lunar priest in the temple of the sun where he taught for the duration of one degree in the chart of celestial time (approximately seventy-two Earth years). This was the duty required of all adepts wanting recognition and diploma from this land. Many degrees later, and with a successful promotion, and having completed his service and duty, Manandan retired to the House of Sokar at Rostau on the west bank where he found fellowship among others northerners like himself. Then one day he went up and journeyed out of Masr called Khem and travelled on the first leg homeward through the so-called divine land and its people. The first people in the land of Canaan that he came upon were the Pilaestini of Kaftor in the south while to the east and north were a collection of Semitic (pronounced Shemitic) speaking kingdoms peopled by a race known collectively (and inaccurately) as the Hapiru who in general term were Amorites. Many of these pious and industrious souls were labouring under the yoke of a wicked priesthood known as the Levis who forced the worshipping of Molloch while the few remaining dissenters (mostly dispossessed rebels, raiders, mercenaries, and migrant labourers) were struggling against suppression and debt. Most of the priesthood referred to themselves as god's people. One such priest at this time was a certain Ezra[64] who many centuries later turned up in

---

64   Not Ezra the descendant of Sraya (the last high priest of the first temple), but an earlier one.

the Land of Gwyneth as a Druid convert. Along with coercive persuasion and thought control experiments, the divine land was besieged with suffering and misery at this time primarily because these aforementioned priests were conducting such experiments on their captive congregation.

Manandan tarried a season in the Pilaestini city of Doggone before continuing towards the Tauri Mountains through Canaan and the Phoeniki people who were also Amorites. The Pilaestini (it should be pointed out) were a sea going merchant tribe. They spoke with an Aryan-Indo Iranian tongue. This Aryan speaking race was an early convert to the Iron Age who had settled here some time earlier from their motherland in the north. In Doggone (where for commercial expedience the Aryans had adopted the Semite tongue), Manandan had secured an armed escort from here to accompany him north along the coast of Canaan through the troubled zone to the Phoeniki kingdoms. These latter were a peaceful conglomeration of Semitic and Aryan-speaking city-states that spoke the Semitic and the Aryan Hittite tongues. Like the Pilaestini, the Phoeniki were a skilled sea going merchant people. The Semites here, unlike the warlike Hapiru (servers of the temple) who were influenced and controlled by the people of god, were calm and focussed as merchants but who, like all Semites generally had converted from bronze to iron much latter than the northern Aryans.'

'Many of the latter mentioned Aryans were descendants of the mythical Hyperborean red haired sea people who had fled their northern home during the last reoccurring catastrophic upheaval and climate change that had decimated the human race and who had then taken to the waves and sailed into the southern sea. The Phoeniki at this time were a tri combination of sea invaders from Hyperborea and other Aryans left over from the ancient kingdom of Mitanni and also from Dilmun in the Gulf of Persia.

It was these people who long ago controlled the environs hereabouts along with the above-mentioned Semites who benefited by the amalgamation of these races. From here, Manandan and his escort of Pilaestini warriors — all decked out in their finest of armour — arrived without incident in ancient Cilic, now under new management and name that lay at the foot of the Tauri Mountains. After passing through the gates of Tauri and crossing war torn Kappadochy, they paused briefly at the great mountain by Nesa Karum, where Lord Shirkuh had once lived, before journeying west through Galatia to Frygia. Having safely arrived here — and being sufficiently paid off by Manandan — the escort retreated back into Kappadochy in the southeast to continue their employ of mercenary for hire. Meanwhile, Manandan traversed Dardanos' kingdom to the west intending to set out for Samothrace by boat, but discovered Huge's magical enclave in the forest of Ida, instead. Here he found relaxation by collecting butterflies and once even managed to capture the swarm around a queen bee: And it was here that the aged Manandan caught his first glimpse of young Violet Eye to whom he brought sprigs of blooming Hawthorn, in memory of his own youth, it might seem.'

'It had happened one day that Lord Huge was busy adjusting the mixture of light and water needed to create the variegation in his obscuring curtain of coloured mist. That same day Manandan chose to lay back upon a comfortable poolside couch to quaff back nectar from an electrum cup that he replenished from time to time from a carafe hollowed out of solid amethyst. From his repose, he idly watched the tall and beautiful Violet Eye grace the landscape around the pool with a group of her handmaidens as she trilled like a summer meadowlark to the accompaniment of a hidden lyre. Manandan rubbed his eyes in disbelief, for surely, he thought, this must be the illusive huntress Artemis herself. Manandan was quick to take a fancy to this beautiful girl, who had remained in Lord Huge's care, and seeing in her the shape of nature's shifting beauty, he quickly extended to her an invitation to return with him to his isle resort upon the mist swept sea on the fringe of the inhabited world where here in the third dimension she could remain a Hyperborean queen more securely. The embarrassed Violet-Eye was taken aback by the unexpected proposal (just as she had earlier been by King Aerius' advances) and immediately refused the invitation. But Lord Huge (upon learning of the incident later) saw merit in such relocation and secretly kept the thought in mind. Some time after Manandan had left the Idian region and had returned to his home, Lord Huge saw the opportunity to appeal to the Hyperborean's invitation.'

'By this time the debt (wrought by powerful kings and tyrants wholly without piety and lacking any civil integrity whatsoever) had through the passage of time been lifted by natural and unnatural events. As well the suppression of social amenities and the control of the culture of day to day life by powerful oligarchs who held hard fought dominion over the common lot and administered the need for unnatural law and order, combined with heavy taxes always owing, had replaced equilibrium with lawlessness and social squalor. This was the state of being not just in Anatolia, Syr and Masr, but throughout the whole world as a most dread portent took effect, complicated by an ingenuousness' inflicted upon the common psyche of humanity. The sun that for more than a whole solar wheel gave forth a most dim light caused this condition. And each day during which no shadows were cast, this blue sun cast upon the earth a greenish twilight that shone at noontide dimmer than the full moon for only a sixth of a full rotation of the earth rather than the normal half-day. During this time the season failed to change and there was no rain and fruits and grains failed to ripen and all goods and services came quickly to a grinding halt. Starvation spread like grass-fire. Swift to follow was violence and chaos among the cities of men as daily order disappeared and fear gripped their hearts. What had been the accustomed became void and the frightful and the bizarre became the norm. To check the acceleration of suffering and misery a massive de-population ensued along with other catastrophes that came from the heavens. Such portents were these that are frequently drawn toward any manner of disorder and decay that lingers anywhere for too long. These, too, now visited the Earth to harry and plague the already beleaguered thus enhancing the remaining and struggling people's appalling conditions even more. This further setback was an attack upon the planet by a scourge of noxious and suffocating air that was not unlike the fire-breathing demon that descended from the heavens during a previous and similar event that caused the annihilation of well more than half the planet's population. Some said later that it was the dragon just like in the early days (many degrees in time before the present) that resulted in the great migration of humanity to flee south. But whatever it was and had been, the fifth world (still in infancy) was already struggling for survival. Even Violet Eye's adventitious suitor, the welcomed and noble brother and twin of the huntress, had become conspicuous by his absence. Instead, this shining master preferred to dally on Delian soil where dwelled (it was said) the charming daughter of a local miller. This caused in Violet Eye a debilitation towards natural labour of childbirth that Lord Huge did not think fitting or healthy for the young queen. With this (and the aforementioned situation) at hand, Lord Huge's concern for Violet's safety and wellbeing became most acute.'

'One day, during a new moon, Lord Huge, Violet Eye and the entire occupants in residence there, left the forest of Ida and fled in pursuit of Manandan and his island home. According to the legend which the event caused, thirty-six chariot pulling griffons were provided by Violet's faithless lover (at the behest of his twin sister, Artemis the huntress) to convey the enclave's one hundred and eight people to the aforementioned northern isle that had been made available by Manandan's invitation. Then with the passage of fourteen solar cycles, sympathetic Diana, bloodless and bold, beamed full and broad, and lit the Gaelic shore adjacent to Manandan's peaceful isle in time for their safe arrival. Here the general host encamped while Lord Huge and Violet Eye sailed across to Manandan's resort retreat where the crafty artisan presented the princess in distress. Although Manandan was happy to see the nymph of Ida again, he was perplexed at their arrival and listened attentively while Lord Huge asked him if it was within his heart to provide additional asylum, not just for himself, but for the remaining one hundred and six, as well. Understandably, Manandan was put out by this invasion upon his lonely retreat. But in the end he agreed to comply on terms. Since the Kreti magician from Armorica had easily arrived upon his blissful isle still at this moment in the security of the obscurity, Manandan reasoned that others with a mind to leave the turmoil behind could do the same. So Manandan's request was to have Lord Huge obscure the isle from prying eyes more permanently by any means possible so long as the result did not affect the isle itself.

'Without delay Lord Huge the artisan conjured forth with all his might the extent of his powers and resources. He created, as a crowning glory to an illustrious career, his most exquisite work in the form of a veil which he fashioned from the sodden mist, which matched in beauty even those miraculous achievements performed by the ancient Hyperborean builders whose echoes had long faded from the land.

"It was here, when all was made ready,' Dyfed said, finishing his tale, 'that I was born.' This then was the story told by Dyfed to Theoderic the great and late moderator of the western Amoran Empire.

(Two Houses: the red dragon & the white dragon)

*'…and yet the black raven…at the feast where he
and the wolf bared the bodies of the slain…'*
BEOWULF: *(LINE:3022-25)*

Dyfed and John of Munster (to remind the reader) had hooked up again and were staying together at a roadhouse called the Yeoman's Arms in Cambridge.

"So now I was to investigate the northern waters for the purpose of trading. Initially on my return to Albion soil back from the City of Amor my first port of call was at Thanet to plan it,' said Dyfed quietly to his friend Muns. From there I was drawn to the city of Kenterbury,' he told his companion. 'In the early days under Amoran rule, Salian Frankens had either been drawn to that same area from across the channel due to Amoran development or had been relocated there by force by the Amorans and other contingents during the first empire. You probably know this. Just before the greatest cataclysmic event of our lifetime, and shortly after economic collapse of the aforementioned empire, this area of southeastern Albion came under attack by the Angles, the Saxe, and other peoples from Juteland. At this time the armies of Uthur, son of Bricus, cousin of Galahad and leader of a combined kingdoms of Gwyneth and Powys, was finally in a struggle with King Ryan, the Vortigern. Ryan had hired mercenaries from Juteland to create order and maintain Keltic control over the area. The result was the rivalry over the House of the Red Dragon and the House of the White Dragon. This brought devastation to the land now called the kingdom of Kent, for the struggles may have been for Prydain in particular but the wash from that disturbance sloshed back and forth from Gwyneth to the Kingdom of Kent. Although it was Dyfed's opinion at first that it was Galahad (who inhabited Kent at this time) who may have been partly the cause of all this due to the Fisher-king syndrome, but in the end this turned out to be all hooey, pork slap and bull-chutney. As usual, Galahad had nothing to do with anything.

'It was precisely at this point when the priest Aurelius Ambrosius returned here from Gaul and tried to intervene between these two Amoranized locals. And it was Aurelius Ambrosius who actually took the name of the Red Dragon. Shortly after this the kingdom of Kent suddenly became the stomping grounds of Aurelius Ambrosius who finally quelled the dispute and brought order. From this singular act he developed forever more a feeling of entitlement for greatness and recognition as such. The people of Albion didn't always reciprocate this sentiment. However, Hengist the mighty Jute king and mercenary who disavowed Jehuanism still lived right here in Kent. Eventually he was brought low by other means, but not by Aurelius Ambrosius' army alone. I should point out, however, that it was the only army at the time, and the last Amoran trained army ever to campaign in Albion. All previous armies including the XXth and the IXth had already departed here long ago for good.'

'Albion, at this time was amid transition, for at that moment in time Angles were washing up upon the shores of northern Albion like the foamy white froth from a stormy sea. Quickly control of the lands of the Brigantes fell under Angle newcomers from across the sea of Hele, as it was once called. Initially founded by Ida the land of the Brigantes was succeeded by Ida's son AEthelric whose own son AEthelfrith eventually succeeded him. Now that AEthelfrith was king, the Brigantes were now being mispronounced as Bernics or the kingdom of Bernicia. This kingdom was established along the shores of the northeast coast of Albion and nestled under Alba. It was along the east coast line that these Angles had arrived after crossing the sea in their sleek little boats that their race had employed for thousands of years over the waters. (Indeed, they were part of the seagoing people like the Norse, the Dané (Dan, Danaan or Dorian) and the Jutes. They were the hoi polloi descended from the ancient northern people of the long faded Hyperborean civilization (minus their extreme nobility) in a similar way that the Pixies of the north portion of this isle and many of the so-called early Kelts of Albion were. But of late, AEthelfrith of Bernic and his armies were starting to dangerously penetrate the Rheged region all the way west to the Gadhelic shore. Moreover, he had stepped up his attempt to possess the remaining domain of the Wotadin that lay between him and the estuary of the River Forth to the north and the land of the Pixies. Soon, King AEthelfrith's domain became quite vast as he conquered more and more territory from the Albionians than anyone of the newly arrived invaders had done as yet. And he was in the process, also at that time, of replacing the Brythonic language with the Angle tongue that was configured into what was being now called the Angle-ish tongue.

'But now a new kingdom of sorts was forming to the south of AEthelfrith. This new kingdom, though, was a unique kind of clearing house, a composite or an amalgamation of peoples including the Brythonic speaking Albionians such as the Brigantes as well as the vestige that remained of those few Amorans who had stayed on in the north. Even strains of the relatively newly arrived Angles and their Saxen brothers who had struck out on their own and were not part of the other Goth-like settlements, were attracted to this newly emerging, centrally located kingdom that was called Mercia (also spelled Mersha and pronounced Marsha).

'And just at this particular time a man who called himself Sideric, and an entrepreneur of sorts, who was of unknown background had arrived in Mersha with letters of invitation signed by both Cadwallopir, king of Gwyneth and King Ryan. Apparently he was also on some kind of amiable terms with AEthelfrith, besides. And the task he seemed set on was that of a mediator between the western peoples around the Gadhelic shore and the Angles on the Helic shore to the east. In addition, he certainly had a degree of sympathy for the Albionian people at large. I should tell you that this cunning and capable man was in truth the viceroy of Italia acting on behalf of Emperor Zeno in Byzas. He was Theoderic or Feoderik the Blond as the eastern Germanics knew him by. He was also more commonly called Theoderic the Great.'

'He had only come to Albion upon my advice so as to ride out the storm that ravaged Europa and hide out from those dangerous elites whose agendas he had managed to block, confuse, side track, and delay; much to their resentment and rage. I should also say that Theoderic was an associate of *the pack,* that elite regiment to which we are now quite familiar, Muns. Those other so-called power elites that were currently engulfed in resentment and rage were much different, they were the game-changing-for-the-worst people like the gang chowing down at the House of Theodosus at feeding time, for instance; or the likes of Potamus Purplebal and his sister Hipparchia Philostropodousalouspolousadous.'

"How's that again…? said John Galway of Munster.'

'Aaah…skip it for now Muns; anyway, there were other dangerous hombres at large, men whose boots were under the family dinner table at the House of Catulus, or the House of Meroweh (Mero) currently occupied by Chlodio (Clovis) and of Ateula Arviragus the Resplendid. But most worrying of all, believe it or not, Muns, was the newly named and decorated Cardinal van Richelieu. This was the same Gorgeous Giorgius Gregorius Florentius who now called himself Giorgius AEduini (Edward) Sax Goth Burgfeld of Hunover. He's a man I formerly knew who mentored a certain Duke du Plessis who in turn took on the name Cardinal van Richelieu. He had arrived here in Albion to attend the upcoming Synod of Whitby. This convocation, that in the end favoured to go forward with Amoran Jeshuanism over the existing and thriving Keltic Jeshuanism, shattered Albion's cultural future right there in one fell swoop. This was thanks to Saint Hilda whose father later had killed AEthelfrith king of Bernicia.'

'Anyway, Theoderic had arrived here in Albion from Italia by sailing up the Severn river on a high tide bore and had briefly been associated with the governance of the old Amoran colony of Gleven which they had long ago abandoned but was still there on the banks of that river. It had been here at this spot that he had dipped a toe into its murky midst to test the waters for a tentative comeback into the fray of politics, state intrigue and war. He quickly allied with both Cadwallopir and the vortigern Ryan with a careful eye out as to how the southeastern kingdom of Cent (Kent, also Kant) was developing. He feared Kent he later told me, and for good reason. At this time Kent still had controlling monetary interest in King Keredic's kingdom of the west Saxen. It was the west Sax (Saxen for proper plural) who, slowly moving north and west (crippling those who stood their ground before them) and eventually overran most of southern Albion. However, these Saxen (no *s* needed) who so unlike the northern Angles at the time yet seemingly similar in other ways, were quickly integrating with the locals as they encroached the west. But when they finally did arrive in Gleven on the Severn, Theoderic (the newly invented alias Sideric) saw opportunity in the advancement. But, as already mentioned, this was especially the situation in the north where expediting a bloody displacement of the Kelts was every-where as well as along the south coast where the Jutes were advancing. But this was not the case in Albion's central region of old Llogia. This was the Elfed kingdom region now called Mersha that was just being formed. Here folks from all around were peacefully merging into the general population and were busy marking their territory. But this was no pissing match, to be sure. And as this kingdom had the potential to be an important buffer state to insulate Gwyneth and another recently formed kingdom called Powys, from the more dangerous Angles and especially the east Saxen. Those two aforementioned kingdoms of Gwyneth and Powys were heavily influencing Mersha and its cultural politics at this time. This natural and independently organised buffer zone of Mersha was an important and pivotal development for all of the Brythonic speaking folk, for Powys and Gwyneth had now become the backbone of the ancient Albionian Keltic people.'

'As you have told me, Muns, you were by this time in Nova Troia, so you may not have known of some of these events. One such people that Sideric noted who were currently under attack by the northern Angles were the residue of the Wotadin folk crammed in by the estuary of the River Forth in the south east of Alban (also Alba). The Pixies suffered from the same re-population that threatened to push them into extinction. For reasons Sideric well understood those Keltic Albionians who remained semi squashed toward the western part of the isle were feeling much pressure and quite under the gun so they naturally sought to minimise any further expansion of their traditional land by any means available. Consequently, they were quick to ally with others of the same tongue no matter how far flung they may be form them. These ancient people may have once had their differences and even fought like cats trying to escape a box on fire, but now they were fighting for their very survival and the survival of their ancient culture. So, as far as the people of Gwyneth were concerned a Brythonic speaking Wotadin was part of the folk and even the Goidelic speaking people among the isles further to the west were all the same people as well. This was also the case even with the Pixies of Alba, those dangerous and treacherous north-men who with their painted and tattooed bodies, sticky, spiky and bristled out hair-do that reminded some of the older folks of the early Trinovantes and Ikeni peoples from before the Amoran occupation. Certainly, like the Pixies of Alba and the remnants of the Trinovantes and Ikeni, the Wotadin were closer to being kin than were the Saxen or the Angle peoples.'

'For the moment, however, Sideric's conundrum was a matter of which side he could or should position himself to support: either the Albionians or the Angles and Saxen? Certainly the Angles had the advantage of strategy and accumulated wealth, although the Wotadin (the people of Wodan) had the backing of the folks of both Gwyneth and Powys. The Pixies, unfortunately, having been long semi isolated were technologically out of their league when it came to fighting these peoples, although their will was there. But the two kings of Gwyneth and Powys, especially King Cadwallopir, a former overlord of Albion during the Amoran occupation and someone who we have already been introduced to, were richer by far than many realised or expected.'

'Sideric had noticed that in Mersha the east Saxen (who were much in similarity both in looks, dress, and culture to the Angles) of this area considered themselves Mershan rather than having any strong attachment to the kingdom of the east Saxen. The same was for the Angles. Sideric, now identifying himself as an east Saxen that was corroborated by his blond hair and blue eyes, chose in the end to ally with Cadwallopir and the Brythonic folk rather than with the northern Angles. However, he didn't burn his bridges so fast that before becoming active in his alignment of choice — but certainly after he had secured a pact with Cadwallopir — he made a reconnaissance gathering journey north to reconnoitre the extent of Angle's collateral as well as with AEthelfrith the chief Angle himself. Sideric had done this in order to gain insight into the peculiarity of the character of the Angle, that incorrigible insubordinate, that flagrantly free-willed loose cannon, that grand disturber of the peace.

Introducing himself to the king, Sidric first listed his credentials that stemmed back into the Amoran Empire. He named names and places in an easy effort to impress this Angle king. He then pledged to apply his somewhat valued talents to spy for the Angle cause in the south or wherever he was needed, for that matter. Ultimately, of course, he told the king that he could command AEthelfrith's forces, too, for after all had he not fought alongside general Flavius Atius the greatest of all the Amoran generals, and alongside general Trachmyr the Albionian of the Brythonic tongue whose methods of warfare he knew like the back of his own hand? Surely, one could see the value in him? He then reminded the king that Trachmyr was still alive and active among his people and was commanding his own army under King Cadwallopir, a king of whom the Angle had some need to be cautious.

And it was during this reconnoitre that Dyfed himself had discovered that Sideric had come to meet Ceredwyn, his own former love.

Once Sideric had returned to the south west he immediately planned his campaign of extolling gold and information from AEthelfrith all the while aiding and abetting the Brythonic cause with his top priority of wooing that beautiful redhead into his arms and then into his bed. Unfortunately, Sideric had had to leave one or two other wives back in Europa and as yet had not found a suitable replacement, especially for Autofeleda, the sister of Chlodovechus (Clodio or Clovis) who he had married earlier.

'Hostilities soon opened up in the direction of Legion and even within Elfed for which Sideric had been handsomely paid by Cadwallopir to only report on, at least for the time being. So at this point in his new career Sideric hadn't got around to organizing campaigns as much as he had done in the old days, but through impartment he was able to deflect a horrible harm to certain Albionian peoples from the hands of the Angles on the most part. He was also successful in extracting Ceredwyn out of Legion and into Mersha by her own willing and desire.

'King AEthelfrith the Angle was also fixed upon uniting his kingdom to that of Dere, the other Angle kingdom on the east coast just south of Bernic, and as the cunning double agent all round that Sideric was he saw in that prospect another opportunity. Now Sideric was also in the pay of the new Mershan regent, King Searl. Searl, seeing opportunity in any level of conflict between the Angles, wanted Sideric to encourage Aethelfrith's hunger to swallow Dere. Cadwallopir agreed. So to effect that outcome, and with Cadwallopir's blessing, Searl quickly sent Sideric the friendly Goth (whose former emperorship of western Amor was unknown to them) to embrace the latter, accompanied by a mounted legion to aid him in that venture. At the same time Sideric suggested to King Searl that aid and advice be sent toward the king of Dere and his successor (the youth named AEduini or Edward) for this would not go amiss or un-rewarded in some way or another, either. So it was agreed between them that Sideric should get word to the king of Dere that his son and successor should be sent to Mersha and out of harm's way of AEthelfrith's broad sword. Finally, upon the completion of the rather bloody annex of Dere, AEthelfrith — now the sole king — had a hugely consolidated power at his disposal that threatened everyone, especially Raywald the east Angle whose kingdom of the East Angles was further south still. AEthelfrith also decided now to rename the lands of his new kingdom North of Umbria. That was because the Umber River was now directly on his southern border. This new kingdom extended from that river north to the estuary of the River Forth. It was during this exercise that Sideric showed his metal in fifth column work as well as in campaign organization, much to King AEthelfrith's surprise and gratefulness. However, in many ways AEthelfrith had misjudged the situation entirely. He had left that loose thread in the person of AEduini (prince of the swallowed up kingdom of Dere) unattended. AEduini (Edward or even sometimes Edwin, though he was mostly known as just plain Eddy) had fled Dere at the approach of AEthelfrith on the advice of Sideric's courier who possessed a letter of explanation from King Searl, the neighbouring Good Samaritan who offered to take him in at no cost as his own son.

In this intrigue the aforementioned King Raywald of the kingdom of the East Angles who were really south Angles living cheek to jowl with their cousins the east Saxen that bordered on the River Tems that (also having good relations with Mersha) played a part. Raywald was the go-between who took charge of the young man and eventually delivered him to the kingdom of Mersha.'

'Then Raywald the East Angle, who was no push over himself, didn't waste any time in hunting AEthelfrith down with his own considerable army where he cornered him just west of the lower Trent river, and killed him there in battle. This positioned Raywald as the overlord of the surrounding Angle-Saxen kingdoms, or would have if it hadn't been for King AEthelberht of Cent (Kant). Certainly Raywald quickly helped place Eddy on the throne of the Angle kingdom of Dere that was vacant with the death of Eddy's father, the old king. In this, the cagey old Raywald had effortlessly created a client king for himself, it seemed. Then Eddy the Client set to and with Raywald's help once again and quickly annexed the kingdom of Bernic to the north and began an ethnic cleansing of his own, namely the Wotadin and other Brythonic speaking peoples all over again. This string of recent events with its successful conclusion of AEthelfrith's death also pleased this aforementioned AEthelberht, the most powerful of all the integrated Angle and Saxen kings, as well as pleasing Cadwallopir and Searl, the kings of the newly incorporated kingdoms of Powys and Mersha respectably.'

'As you remember, Muns, AEthelberht was the king of Cent (Kent or Kant), the former lands of the Cantii tribe. He was known as the Prydain-ruler (or Bret-walda in the local tongue) who held imperium over surrounding Angle and Saxen kingdoms and was the first Jehuan convert king, on account of his wife, the queen who demanded it and wouldn't put out until he kneeled before the high priest. But this was Albion and the Vicar of Jeshua of the Church of Amor had no secure authority or following here yet and the free-wheeling Prince Ead, AEthelberht's pagan son, also ruled the roost in these parts. Upon hearing (with his especially long ears) of the plot between Mersha and the east Angle kingdom to trick the northern Angle AEthelfrith into conducting a rash and too eager a move against Dere, AEthelberht then sent his son Ead to Raywald the East Angle with gold enough to help them in the quashing of AEthelfrith. In truth, though, it wasn't either king who prompted the proposition to fund a multi offensive against King AEthelfrith, but rather AEthelberht's wife, Queen Bertha. This esteemed woman's father was King Cherryberht, one of those longhaired Salian Franks and the current Merovingian king of the burgeoning city of Isis that that lay on the Sen River a hundred and twenty-five Amoran miles south of Tourney. Cherryberht was related to Mero and Clovis (Meroweh and Chlodio). But then AEthelberht, without a by your leave, suddenly up and died leaving Ead to fend on his own against his mother. Ead was a rebellious man who had refused to give up that paganism of the good old Angle-Saxon variety that believed in Wodan. He also argued and fought tirelessly with his mother Queen Bertha who inevitably ruled him. Ead quickly sided up to the Angle king of Dere, Eddy the Client, for whom it seemed he had developed an unnatural attraction.'

'Meanwhile a new antagonist entered Albion. This was the arrival of Augustine the Monk of the Church of Amor. The fact that Bertha being the daughter of one of the most prominent of the Jeshuanized Franken kings had become the wife of AEthelberht should have posed a *shoo-in* for the cult. But Augustine should have arrived here on the heels of Bertha and AEthelberht's marriage and the latter's conversion to the cult of the Church of Amor, but instead he didn't. Possibly the Vicar of Jeshua at the head of the Church of Amor had been ignorant of the fact that there already existed a Jeshuan cult here in Albion. But that's unlikely so Augustine the Monk mustn't be held responsible for the clash between Keltdom and Amoran Jeshuanism here at this time. Keltic Jeshuanism had existed here since Amoran times; but the cult here was considerably different than the Church of Amor per sé. And because he had no authority over Keltic Jeshuanism, the Vicar of Jeshuan Adon had no way of controlling its variance and opposition to the Church of Amor. So, pursuant to the Church of Amor's so-called divine decree that it (and it only) had authority over the entire world in all that matters, he insisted now on sending the belated Augustine as his chief henchman to keep a sharp eye out for backsliders the Amoran Church. Therefore, the Vicar of the Church of Amor's action here amounted to being a direct action to have the Keltic Church destroyed and contradicted the essence and the spirit of Jeshua Adon's original teachings. This was to cause no end of problems, forever.'

'Anyway, once Eddy had taken command of the lands north of Umbria with Raywald's help, he too then hired Sideric who immediately decorated himself with the rank of Comes et Magister Militum; in essence he became the Commander in Chief of the Northumbrian army although King Aeduini wasn't capable of reading the insignia. However, illiterate that AEduini (Edward, Edwin or Eddy) the Client was he was nevertheless encouraged by Sideric's enthusiasm. However Sideric had been intelligent enough not to keep all his eggs in one basket and as an old fifth columnist himself, and one who relished the extra pay-bag of gold coins from time to time, his first duty had been to quickly misadvised AEduini (Edwin, Eddy) to forgo the destruction of the northern Wotadin and concentrate in finishing off any and all Brythonic resistance that remained closer to the Umber in the land of Elfed, instead. Sideric did this after first advising the new Mershan king Pendar that he (Sideric) would gladly except gold from the kingdom of Cant (Kent) on behalf of Pendar's sovereignty over Mersha and of King Cadwallopir of Gwyneth's troop along with logistic expenses to help this double-cross fly straight and true. Ead and Cadwallopir quickly agreed as they foresaw the expedience of this action. So, having been advised and nudged slightly with a false flag operation against one of his own outposts, Eddy did just that. He attacked the Elfed, another Brythonic speaking territory, by crossing the Trent River heading west. This was potentially a great shock to the Albionians, for this area was the beloved Trent River basin and despite their foreknowledge they made a big to-do about it. But more to the point, King Aeduini had now encroached upon the marches of Mersha and entered a trap. Waiting for him was King Cadwallopir and his armies from both Powys and Gwyneth, and they were not in an amused mood. As stated, Mersha being a confederacy of Amoran, Angle-Saxen, and native Albionian folks, it had become an important concept for Albion, but it was not yet a very powerful or a very influential concept. But there were many who didn't want it to stay that way. At the moment the only reason that any of the Albionian based kingdoms around about were looking in on Mersha out of sympathy (with an eye to help out) was that with Albion stripped of yet another partly Brythonic speaking area, its history and its ancient people got crunched into a smaller percentile bracket and became more insignificant. This was the case (if not as much for the mainly Angle dominate kingdoms) certainly it was for the Saxen kingdoms for here the Keltic or Albionian underlay was active and still strongly represented like the Cantii (Kentii) were down under in their kingdom of Cant (Kant or Kent). And there, too, was a new threat, what with its capital at the City of Kentbury having converted its cult centre over to becoming the diocese of the new Church of Amor.'

'Anyway, this move by Eddy the Client across the River Trent also suddenly brought him into direct proximity with the kingdoms of Powys and Gwyneth that was now the very heart of the last ditch of true Prydainian defence. This alone, and by itself, seriously contributed to Eddy's downfall in this short chapter of events that was to be his life. On an early morning with the sun low and shining in onto the green and forested hills beneath the clouds, Radiance had just climbed higher into the sky when all of a sudden the morning darkened some and the shadows swelled and blanketed most of the earth: And with the mist in the treetops and a steady rain beginning to fall, Cadwallopir attacked Aeduini the Angle through a rainbow and killed him while Sideric, who ironically was King Aeduini's top general, kept him and his armies pinned down along a small river. Because of this they were unable to respond effectively. It was a joint venture, it seemed to everyone, and the folks of Mersha and their neighbouring Albionians and Angle-Saxen all celebrated ferociously afterwards. This left most of the countryside hung-over and the inns fresh out of libations. This also halted Northumbria's encroachment to the south and south west, although that kingdom continued on without much change otherwise (apart from a new king), and it did this for quite a long time yet to come.'

"And it was at Cent (Kant or Kent),' said Dyfed to Jack Galway of Munster, 'and alongside Augustine the Monk and the cult of the Church of Amor that I made my home, although I often ventured north to visit the kingdom of the East Saxen, especially after Egidius of Joslin had moved to Thaxted in the early tenth century CE. But let me ruminate upon the incomparable Sedric, or Theoderic king of Italia, as I knew him.'

(Talsin Davie and Alley Oop)

'Sudden enlightenment followed by gradual cultivation.'
BUDDHIST SUBITISM

"So in 1276, according to the Olympiad calendar (or 500CE), having made a short stop at Thanet to plan it, once again I relocated into Kent. I had known nothing of Sedric and Ceredwyn's arrangements, you must understand,' Dyfed said to John Galway of Munster as the two of them were still seated in the Yeoman's Arms in Cambridge. 'This time I rented an old abandoned Amoran villa on the edge of the North Downs and the High Weald that was located close to the River Darent. The sprawling villa had once been very opulent and was situated not far off from that portion of Watling Street that ran from Nova Troia east to Durobrivae (currently Rochester). Rumour had it that back in the day Emperor Publius Aelius Hadrianus had resided here for a season or two.'

'So, shortly after Dyfed had settled into his new digs along the River Darent was the time when Augustine the Benedictine monk (or black monk, as they're called) arrived in Albion from the city of Amor. As stated, he was sent here by the Pontiff of Amor and became Augustine of Kent and its representative of the Church of Amor here in Albion. But at the same time a Keltic monk by the name of Gildas of Demetia (eventually to become Saint Gildas of Demetia) had already been employed in continuing the introduction of the indoctrination of Jeshuanism into Albion that had begun almost four centuries earlier, anyway. These two men were followed by another of the Keltic Jeshuan persuasion, a certain Cuthberht (also Cuthbert) from Lothia of the Otadini people. This was at the northern reaches of Aethelfrith's kingdom of Bernic that along with the kingdom of Dere to the south was all contained north of the Humber. Bishop Cuthbert was a hermit monk who became not only a saint like Gildas but also a patron saint of all of the northern section of Angle-land that was now called North Humber-land. Cuthbert settled down to hermit on at Holy Island whose community of likeminded men included Aidan of the Emerald Isle along with Eadberht and Eadfrith. Cuthbert was to eventually prompt a gravesite cult at Dun Holm alongside the River Wear. Furthermore, contrary to popular belief that has arisen since, there was no confrontation and violent conflict at this time between the two strains of Jeshuanism (i.e. the Keltic Church and the Amoran Church) any more than there were between the many different sects of the Church of Amor itself; such as between say its monastic and its mendicant orders. But it was certainly a bold, open faced bid by the Amoran church to reach new and greater audiences in order to extend their shiny, silver collection plates under the noses of a new flock of ignorant sinners. This was (by the way) an important mechanism for helping to fill their thirsty coffers with collateral and cash. For the organization and their logistics for programming millions of people so they could live out their miserable existence well enough under the guidance of the church until the church could get them into heaven, was not only a long row to hoe but a costly and thirsty work in progress, besides.'

'Then Dyfed had another visitor. He knew he was coming because folks around knew Dyfed and he heard tell from them of a young man who was searching for him.

But he didn't know who he was. When he did show up the tall young man flung his arms around Dyfed's neck sobbing and preceded to call him father. At first this was rather disconcerting. But soon the man (whose name was Talsin Davie) explained that Ceredwyn was his mother.'

'This had all come about at the time of his involvement with the goings on that were taking place then between King AEthelberht and the king of Mersha. Talsin Dyvie, apparently, was a poet and quite the grown up man that winter when they had first and finally met. This good-looking young man's white skin was very pale and complimented with dark reddish hair. Dyfed could see that he took after his mother Ceredwyn in his appearance but had Dyfed's build and mannerisms. So, that was that! The young man was also a frequent visitor at AEthelberht's court where it was known to all that he was working on an important poetic script called Bay-eh-wulf. Poetry at this time was not fanciful ditties of imaginative love and a hurting (pronounced hurtin') theme. Real poetry at this time was the story about the people, the clan. And Talsin Davie had been enamoured by the stories of the newly arrived Angles and Saxens whose language the boy had quickly learned. Here too, it seemed, is where he took after his father. The stories inspired Talsin Davie to write their history in an enthralling adventure he called Bay-eh-wulf.'

'Dyfed, who as a free-man, a noble, and a notable one at that who had a great deal of means and whose connections even linked him to influential Amoran emperors (from way back when) commanded respect wherever he went. It was no different in Kent than it had been in Amor, except that here he wasn't and outsider. And he was conciliatory and un-dictatorial which is why he was liked. Also he had an eye for the ladies and was considered not only attractive because of his substance at hand, but because of the physical pleasure that oozed from him and was much richer and more satisfying than that of the insidious flattering kind. As such, Dyfed was successfully able to recommended Talsin Davie as a reliable courier to Queen Bertha, for the handsome young man had more than enough talent to go around. It turned out that the queen already had her eye on the delicious youth and so had Prince Ead. But the latter had been whisked away and was no longer, anyway. And indeed, Dyfed also went out of his way to promote Talsin Davie as much as possible because he had missed out being the boy's father until this time. Talsin Davie achieved more than just being a delicious youth at the queen's court, he became the Kingdom of Kent's royal deputy and chief emissary acting between Bertha and Ead's replacement, King Eork, and later King Ecgberht (that extended to future reigns) and foreign courtiers that came a courting. Also, Dyfed's recommendation helped him become an important emissary between the ruling kings of Albion and the Franken kings for many a year to come: Eventually becoming a confident of a certain King Carolus (Karl) the Magnificent. This astute man was of the Franken clan and succeeded King Peppi who claimed descent from Carolus (Karl) Martel who succeeded to the throne after the last Merovingian Childeric had been roughly disposed. A Carolingian instead of a Merovingian, Karl the Great usurped the Amoran western Imperial crown out from under the authority of the Imperial House of Byzas who until that time had continued to control the western empire. This, apparently, pleased the East (Ostro) Goth known here as Sedric (the former King Theoderic of Italia) to no end. In doing what he did, Karl the Great brought about a new and invigoured western empire. Henceforth he became emperor of the Second Empire now called the Holy Amoran Empire. And it was due, in some part, to our old friend Gorgeous Giorgius Gregorius

Florentius that he managed to do this. The career of Florentius, now known as George Hunover Edward Sax-Goth Burgfeld, would now run parallel with (and in some strange way be somewhat responsible for) this second empire which he would help to keep relatively competent and exceedingly strong that would see it last for generations to come. But despite the not so goodly Cardinal Gorgeous, some good things did manage to come about during the duration of the second empire of the Holy Rollers.'

'At about that time Dyfed had begun to hanker after a new mission, a new adventure. This one would take him to the continent far to the west beyond the Atlas Sea. This was the land that the ancients called Merika. And it wasn't as if educated people of the day weren't aware of the place. Some were even beginning to go there. After all, the Basks had been fishing on the far side of the sea along Merika's eastern shores since Jeshua was still a cowboy knee-high to a grasshopper, or whatever bug (maybe locust) they have in his land. Even now Norse adventures a-viking were settling there now after visiting those shores with attractive and comfortable stopovers like Greenacres and sunny Iceland to visit on the way. Dyfed had now figured out that these Norse were to become his ticket to getting him there so he decided that he would take his own ship but have it manned by Norse sailors. Although we are slightly ahead of ourselves, by the time AEthelstan became the king of the Anglish that plan was finally to fall into place.'

(The Darkened Age of Enlightenment)

'Amidst the errors there shone forth men of genius; no less keen were their eyes, although they were surrounded by darkness and dense gloom.'
FRANCESCO PETRARCA

'The periodization referred to as the so-called Dark Ages (coined by Petrarch the Tuscan, a humanist and scholar of the fourteenth century CE) had coincided with the Amoran Empire's first descent into disintegration. This signalled the beginnings of the Middle Ages. And in the heated fury of abandonment to throw caution to the wind and a lust for change and for something new it also signalled the conception of the second empire. But it was hardly dark and hardly a time when the sun didn't shine forth from brilliant minds whose personal light flowed out upon the conundrums that had been intentionally created and earmarked for men. Nor (for that matter) was it a time of abject ignorance and superstition other than the residue from certain non-scientific influences, namely those controlling elements left over from the earlier empire and of the new control mechanisms being constructed and cleverly placed by the mesmerizing engineers of the new Abramists' cult of the Jeshuan Church of Amor. In fact, apart from the latter, the Dark Ages were a brilliant time since the philosophical think-tank days at Antioch and Xanderia for reintroducing free thinking western philosophy and applying it to the modern day and in advancing logos along with theories, experimentation and observation of the elements around us. It was a time for men and women of imagination. It was the time to enshrine ideas for enacting social change in view of universal wellbeing. Some folks even envisioned that the cult of Jeshua Adon would enable and assist such a social revolution. They were wrong, of course, but it could have been different. Probably because they underestimated the power of the Haploids and the latter's influence over hoi polloi weaknesses in general that included the antics of the clerics and curia of the Church of Amor itself. This was before psychotropic drugs were put into common use to mould, fashion and control the masses of society to remain docile and unquestioning as they do today. It was before lithium induced comas were capable of keeping the peace and the quiet so as to provided wiggle room for the secret and underground mechanisms so that a Haploidic envisioned utopia could be advanced whereby its programmable slaves would be semi-efficient and unable to organize even a piss-up in a brewery never mind begin a successful revolt against them. So it became necessary then to highjack free wheeling, free willed religion again (as always) and use that to program humanity into slavery.'

'At this point Dyfed's friend John of Muster who already fearing for his friend's soul asked him to state now his evaluation on the cult of Jeshuanism and: "of our Lord and Savior Jeshua Adon." '

'Dyfed responded: "Back in the day (150BCE to 150CE) the think tanks of Antioch and Xanderia brought the metaphysics of the known world together with most of their important cultures,' he said. 'This was Hinduism, Jainism, Buddhism, Taoism, Confucianism, Paganism, Abramism, Zoroasterism and a little known (and less understood) breakaway cult of Abramism known by its adherents, the Nazareans, as the true doctrine of the Teacher of Righteousness. This is why Jeshua is sometimes mistakenly (via an ancient typo-error by the Church of Amor) referred to as Jeshua of Nazareth. Anyway, these latter Nazareans who clung only to the Torah (Pentateuch) shunned the orthodox cult of the Abramists claiming that it was they who murdered their teacher of righteousness well over thirteen and a half centuries before the Amoran Titus brought destruction to Kadesh (now known as Jerusalem or the Peace of Judah). Their belief is similar to aspects of the ancient Hindu that states that the Spirit Father in unity with Mother Nature materializes in an advanced level as a presence only found in the human being. Lesser organisms may have lesser consciousness, though that has not been proved. In any case these ancient Nazareans appear to have believed in something similar to ancient Hinduism that Nature or the works of the field is only a temporal phenomenon within the everlasting and that the eternal Spirit and the knower of the field who is the true self can survive the death within this phenomenon by receiving and understanding and acknowledging the knower, the true self. These then were the teachings of the Teacher of Righteousness as well. What is still unclear is whether or not they believed the teacher of righteousness was a one-time prophet or whether, as I believe Muns, the Teacher of Righteousness is the Spirit Itself that is a continuous manifestation that continually unfolds for every single second for every human being throughout the entire duration of their lives: In other words a slightly advanced and enhanced consciousness over the everyday conscious level. As such, this Teacher of Righteousness didn't live once upon a time almost fourteen centuries before the Amoran occupation of the Holy land, but constantly lives every second of any individual's life. Jeshua Adon didn't die at the hands of Emperor Tiberius' establishment, because the Spirit can't die; Jeshua is eternal and is being activated every Nano second within phenomenon. Only the temporary dies. Jeshua Adon is alive, because you are alive. And it's all about you the individual, Muns.'

'Dyfed's friend Jack stared at the former for a long time but didn't respond.'

'So, it should also be pointed out that existentialism and phenomenology that existed since the time before Socrates now took root again throughout Europa just as Angleland was coalescing into a ferment. At this point the aims of those with a clear head was for social improvement. And the machinations of the Middle Ages were focussed on progressive innovations such as existentialism, just laws, sound cathedral-building and safe working standards and the strengthening of an array of worker's unions (guilds). All this is true, though of a miniscule scale compared to later times. But it occurred because it was a time when surveillance and rigid control by the power elite had loosened some which opened doors for the *pack* to produce some of their accomplishments as mentioned above through example and suggestion. These were meant to advance the hoi polloi toward a new light while being relatively undetected; and with the *pack's* help and their hints and their suggestions that this would cause the flashes of brilliance in grasping truths about the elements in the phenomenon around them that would help immensely to jump-start modern day Western Philosophy. And where would the world be without it today? It was Dyfed's finest hour, with a lot of help from his friends.'

'Stuff that was more like hen-pecking banter and quite dissimilar to the somewhat mis-guided vision of the Fourth Way that G.I. Gurdieff would eventually promote, the Church of Amor's Third Way (aka economic philosophy) was the notion for

Distributionism for Profit was what came into vogue at this time. As stated this was primarily based on principles of the Church of Amor's social teachings that they inherited from the Amoran Empire. But alarmingly an even greater undermining of social wellbeing was being laid that began to take hold and undermine all and any of the important precepts of Western Philosophy that embraced the ideals of free will and existentialism and individual autonomy. And this disturbing status quo would finally blossom after another thousand years and was perfected almost single-handedly by a certain Jehan Cauvin (aka Jean Calvin) and was aided and abetted by the conditioned gullibility and naivety that the Church of Amor's program of control had provided.'

'Cauvin even erroneously claimed that God inspired his idea and that God had insured him that when tightly combined with the cult of Jeshuanism in particular, Distributionism for Profit was the foundation of western philosophy. This Cauvin-ite piece of shit actually admonished free will and existentialism by pretending to create an algorithm that erroneously claimed to be founded on free will of the individual inherited from God but was really a fallacy of Pseudo economics and a branch of the Pseudo sciences. But, according to Cauvin and his sycophant followers this condition only kicked in and became applicable if the individual in question (apparently another prospective greedy, entitled piece of shit just like himself) enjoyed a certain social class that placed him (never her) among the top one per cent of the wealthiest folks on earth. It was from him that the adage '*cleanliness* (and financial so-called success) *is kin to godliness*' which emerged from the assumption that the rich bathe regularly and the poor never do. The truth is that all human species wipe their ass but certain ones have it done for them. It would seem that the acolytes among these greedy entitled folks know the price of everything and the value of nothing. And Cauvin taught them. He was not alone, though.'

'Later, it was recorded that the Dark Ages were a dismal moment for humanity that was plagued with sluggish and slothful thoughts until raised up in Gloria in excelsis Deo (Glorious Excess in Denarii) again by the Church of Amor. This is nonsense, of course, and only believed by folks who had their heads stuck up where (simply put) the sun don't shine. All the brightness of the so-called Dark Ages, however, resulted in the not so superstitious and decidedly less ignorant flux that was the matrix for the dissimulation at large and the flowering of the past into that periodization that has been called the Renaissance. So, it would appear that the ideological divide within the cult of Jeshua — that idea of Distributionism for Profit for registered business shareholders in the elite's bid to rise and become part of the gold-starred, solid-state one per-cent who were out to personally grasp hold of and control ninety-nine per cent of the world's wealth versus those of the true self, the adherents to Azeus (and apparently along with certain aspects unto those certain believers of Jeshua Adon as the Teacher of Righteousness as well) and those in pursuit of free will through existentialism — turned out to be the greatest conflict raging during our era.'

'And that belied much of what Gibbon — an obsequious flatterer vying to further himself, a toady for the establishment — had to say a number of centuries later. Superstition and ignorance, however, is a powerful tool that when well honed and maintained can be beyond value to a tyrannical Power Elite in order to further their own ends. Here the hoi polloi can be susceptible, but they have never been completely deluded and misinformed. If that were not the case, the likes of philosopher John Wyclef, philosopher/enlightenment writer Francois-Marie Arouet or philosopher/scientist Francis

Bacon who much later joined with Cato to convey his vision of a utopian New World for the Merikas across the Atlas Ocean would never have existed.'

'It was during those same so-called dark days that got Dyfed started off in the right direction as far as securing enough wealth to fund come what may in the future. Besides his heavily armed and defended fort at Tournay, he also now had (as already stated) a villa along the River Darent in the Kingdom of Kent as well as having harbour docks yards on the south bank of the Tems estuary. This, as well as a secure strong house with a quay along the north shore of that same river just outside inside the walls of Nova Troia that morphed into what became known as the Steelyards that were eventually taken over by the Hansa League's Albion branch. In the years to come it was to here that Dyfed's ships brought goods both for consumption and trade from the Rine River valley. This was at a time when over ninety per cent of hoi polloi men were bonded labourers who existed in a sever world of servitude or were outright slaves who hadn't even a name to themselves. Remember, this was shortly after the time of the ascensions of the Houses of Chlodio and Marwig and Carolus among the Frankens and around the same time for the differentiated clans of Saxen, Angles, Jutes and Frisii who descended from the tribe of the Ingvaevones, with their flexible intellect, had begun to flex their long dormant but equally flexible limbs. Mannus (according to Tacitus) was the source and progenitor of the confederation who made up these tribes.'

(High ho a derry-o a-viking we will go)

> *'If the ballot box was such a necessary and powerful tool for the hoi polloi to self rule, the governing factors of the power elite of all ages would have long withheld it from their grasp; which in fact they may have been doing all along.'*
> **PARASOLO** (APOLOGIES TO MARK TWAIN'S FEATURE OF SIMILARITY)

'Those fearless men of Scandia (like the gangers that they were) never turned down an opportunity to go walk-about (or in this case a-Viking) upon the seas. This system of the second empire (the Holy Amoran Empire that had now burgeoned forth at this time) went from being a slight but tentative authority for keeping the peace around Europa (with the Franken monarchy now in control) to becoming a plum of easy pickings as the former Scandians pilfered and plundered any and all booty at large that was not only nailed down but secreted away deep in a fortress' keep and heavily guarded besides. They had 'vays' — these men off on a-viking unto themselves. So if and when at any time the bottom fell out of the market that had been set up between Scandia and Franken peoples, then trade turned into war and pillage instead. It was here at this juncture that Dyfed's sporadic and casual acquaintance with his Jack of all trades employee and Trachmyr's accountant, Ebreo ben Jamin, suddenly came to the fore.'

'Prior to being employed by the House of Lucifer in any capacity, this man had been playing an important role as a weapons inventor and merchant. Because of his metallurgical skills he had quickly become a commodity in his own right by putting into play an arms race that involved a weapons' manufacturing technology that was capable of quickly attracting attention to him due to his equipment construction being vastly better and infinitely more reliable than any competitor. And so was born the Ulfberht sword. He did this by utilizing secret formulas he had obtained back in A-sham (Dimashq), that great and ancient city of the Middle East. The commodity that Ebreo lent to the agility in the mode d' employ for manufacturing and the marketing of modern weapons that more than suited the Norse's code of conduct. Whether it be trading or looting, with an admirable ability Ebreo increased an all round accessibility that took whatever it was you wanted straight to the heart of the matter and straight to Ebreo's purse. And the Ulfberht sword was such an item that could facilitate this: It was the precision instrument that was good at looting and good for selling. To most, his implements of war were magical and Ebreo was a wizard, and magician. He had a standing contract with the Holy Roller (Amoran) Empire Numero Duo to provide them with the finest steel available. But he also quickly expanded to include markets wherever the Frankish Empire did business of trade and even warred against, such as them who go a-viking. That only made good capitalistic sense in Cauvin-economics, anyway. Dyfed was amused but cautious. So be it if Ebreo was an enterprising capitalist, if anything he was the House of Lucifer's capitalist. But the two-sided sword of saving grace in the matter was that he also quickly attracted copycats who (unfortunately for their buyers) didn't have or use the right metallurgic formula and whose ingredients were inferior. In addition, these knock-offs that were sold under Ebreo's name had to be equally high priced so as not to warn the buyer to beware. Buying a cheap piece of shit and having it bent and broken after a short life of normal wear and tear was annoying enough to the buyer who generally kicked himself for being so cheap in the first place. But when such a let down occurred upon shelling out a princely sum for supposedly a quality item, well, that was another thing altogether.'

'Agility had always been the North-men's trump card, so to speak. For back before the start of the second empire these north-men had (as already stated) begun to sail their hardy little boats south to Albion, Belgea, the Frankens and so forth. These North-men (Norse) also sailed along the coast of the mainland and up her rivers where they spilled out of their boats and pillaged and plundered furiously, and at will. How easy was that, they must have asked themselves in astonishment at their success. Having not flexed their individuality since ancient times thousands of years before, riding the sea coasts, drinking, looting and having passionate unprotected sex with young women on the sea shore and river bank who were just waiting for them to come (and arrive) was like a drug of testosterone and adrenaline rolled into one. But as we shall see they didn't only limit themselves to Albion and Francia, as the kingdom of the Frankens was now called. Besides this they set out to explore the rivers flowing into the Baltic Sea and traversing adjoining rivers by which they crossed the Land of the Rus to the Kara Sea which took them finally to the gates of Byzas and even to Italia and Sichilia (Sicily) where they set up fiefdoms and dynasties made up of families and clans.'

'As stated, these North men (centuries in advance of those now going a-viking) had sailed south and penetrated Francia by river and settled here on a permanent basis. This identity of the North-men (that included Saxen settlers mostly, although Angles, Frisians, and Danes, along with Scandians in general who had accompanied their resettling of the coastal lowlands of Lower Lothar and Francia) had become quickly established in Europa's northwest. This included Brabant, a territory roughly placed between the Rine and the Sen Rivers. And they clearly put their stamp on the local populace there. As stated, these northerners had quick agility and adaptability and this expressed itself in their shrewd willingness toward piety and magnanimity to the folks of the villages they conquered. The North men were want to employ talented and learned local men to work their confiscated and liberated land. They also married into the local highborn families whose seat of power they had replaced. Although many of these new masters of the land were illiterate, with winning ways they were now seducing the literate clerics from the Church of Amor for the purpose of bookkeeping and interpreting due process of law such as legal ownership and matters requiring probate. The recently arrived Lans were quick to capitalize on this as well, and Egedius Joslin had once been one of these providers of legal security. The Lans, of course had been among the horde that had included West Goths and Vandals as well. These folks had poured across the Rine River in the beginning of the fifth century CE. From there some Lans had gone on to sack Amor while others gravitated to the cult of the Church of Amor in pastoral Armorica and Brabant where they achieved high clerical positions in this powerful and growing entity. Once again, Egedius Joslin had been part of that and then three centuries later had arrived in the land of the east Saxen as a magistrate and accountant with many other skills under his belt.'

'But currently, with the forming of the middle Medieval Ages still in vogue, these North men were restless and eager for adventure and fortune. So, many of these folks, and the children thereof, sallied forth as advanced fighting armies armed with Ebreo's finest steel for weapons. Referred to as North men they set out not so much as to pillage and conquer but to found and set up their own kingdoms and dynasties wherever a pleasing sight beckoned. And that site, be it flourishing that was already at the height of its productive power yet needing direction and assistance, or be it a warm and fertile valley facing the sea peopled with fine, hardworking men with gobs galore of expertise coupled with voluptuous women most pretty of face and limb was where a clan would put down stakes and set up shop. Centuries later the captains of these armies would have names such as Edmund, Bohemund, Aethelred, Tancred, and Rollo.'

'It was at this time too that the cousins of the aforementioned, those indomitable folks of the far north, began to go a viking and were regularly crossing the wide expanse of the Atlas Sea to the new-old world of Merika in the west that, perhaps, was the illusive and mythical Elysian Plains of the Hellenic peoples. And having heard no end of this place, Dyfed now told Muns, as they sat in the Yeoman's Arms in Cambridge swilling and guzzling down tankards of beer while Dyfed talked and talked, he told Jack that he had become most anxious than ever to see this land for himself. Apparently, he knew that in time (if the *pack* and the friends of the *pack* couldn't work their magic, as they were as yet unable) this new land would quickly become a haven for many a quack and pontificating lunatic suffering from cerebral epilepsy as well as daydreamers and dangerous predators alike. Furthermore, many of these would have taken a leaf out of Johann Calvin's book and swallowing that mesmerizing and charlatan's toxic swill — hook, line and sinker — the land would soon be all hell and gone and bent for emerging as early capitalists without inclination for restraint or reform towards commonwealth and the pursuit of happiness and equality before a just law. The latter would be looking to increase their number of slaves that they would have toiling to their death without respite in order for the landowners to amass power and strength through wealth and privilege. Soon this new land would mirror what we've achieved here, Dyfed thought. Then the masters of these slaves would form kingdoms there, or pseudo republics in name only. Banks would open, of course, and other purveyors of either loaning or selling something or other in an attempt put folks into debt so as to control the land in the future centuries and to idle away their time by making a quick zillion silver denarii in the bargain.'

'Dyfed (it turns out) had provided Talsin Davie — along with his own friends and employees who by now had joined him in the Kingdom of Kent in Albion from Tournay — a big home to share with him on the aforementioned Amoran villa estate he'd eventually purchased from King Aethelberht. Dyfed had then summoned Trachmyr leaving Karatakos in charge of Dyfed's business operation back at Tournay in Lower Lothar. Also his old companion Markus Cato from Amor visited occasionally as did Lucius Aelius Castus, the Belgic Gaul and former commander of the Albionian-Amoran fleet. Dyfed had set up the business operations in both the cities of Rochester and Nova Troia. He had done this after the same fashion as he had conducted his operations in Amor, except on a now much smaller scale. It was at this point that Dyfed had come into contact with the metallurgist Ebreo again, the gifted jeweller and forger. While scheming to build a fortune among the Salian Frankens by way of multi-tasking as jeweller, a smithy, weapons manufacturer, merchant and translator (as well as being a successful shylock-loan shark), he unaccountably took to employing a forged letter of credit from the House of Lucifer. This caused him to quickly ran afoul of the House of Lucifer and Karatakos had him arrested and charged with fraud. Dyfed advised Karatakos to swallow him up, financially speaking. They bought him out but employed him at the same time, paying him grand dividends on profits he made for the House. The man, being anxious and heedful to do what it takes to become secure in wealth, began once again to apply his valuable knowledge of metal compositions and a talent for smelting. As already stated, this was an art he had brought to Europa from Asham in the east over half a millennium before. So he, too, joined them in Kent from time to time. Ebreo had a sidekick who watched his personal store when he needed or chose to be absent. This man's name was Hodge. He too was a northerner but most folks knew him by his nickname, Aesop. He was a very rustic man who also had extensive expertise in blacksmithing. Opinion decreed that Ebreo the Elamite and Hodge the Gypsy (who tried to pass himself off as a Goth) were more than just a fit pair.'

'Another young lad — actually, a grown up and handsome man by this time — was Prince Guillium Galhad (Galahad) Raymonde de Joslin of Armorica. Looking back now it was a memorable time for all of them. Galahad became a close friend of Talsin Davie when the latter wasn't off doing what an emissary does. The two did what young men do best and consequently, along with the allure of Dyfed and his high born and gifted friends, the House of Lucifer in Kent was often full of attractive young women galore and other hangers on to boot. And it was there at this time that Talsin Davie began to write a spoof on the life and times of Uther and Aurelius Ambrosius. At that time Dyfed was not in favour of such a digression as writing imaginative fiction for entertainment purposes only. Dyfed had read his son's work called *Bay-eh-wulf* only when he saw how popular it was. Talsin Davie's version was not an original but another translation, one of many, it seemed. Then he became highly critical of it and chastised Talsin for what he said was a translation that needlessly injected the Haploidic religious/culture of organized and false notion of Jeshuanism, such as the Church of Amor's version, into the poem. Of course, in those days nobody wrote anything unless it was either one of two extremes; that is historic in nature, the lives of Kysars, Kings and the Kapitalists of their day, or about their young women the queens. And this would require an awful lot of flattery, fudging with a healthy heap of flowery poetic licence along with straight out and out lies. But fanciful (not necessarily historic in nature) writing (that was the other option) incorporated a mix of ecclesiastical olden day scrolls and fanciful rubbish, along with other programs to do with authority aimed at dumbing down the general populace and topping it up with misinformation for the benefit of the queen bee or those hoity-toity who stuck close by her and sucked up to (and whatever any other sucking may have occurred) where it was required.'

'But despite Dyfed's druthers on the matter, Talsin Davie went ahead anyway and wrote a titillating tale of fancy solely for frivolous' sake. Sons seldom listen to their fathers anyway, although Dyfed hadn't had much of an opportunity to take on such a role. In the end Talsin Davie had even created a fable around those rather peculiar men like Uther, Ryan and Ambrosius. This also included Talsin Davie's own close friend Galahad. There was another favourite character that rose into the public domain from his pen at this time. This character was Sir Gwalchmei (Gauvain or Gawwayn) and the Green Knight was inspired by Dyfed's discussions about archetypes of modern behavioural

Homo sapiens and Talsin's own advantages of learning about trolls from the North men. But trolls are a subject for later. So, after Talsin Davie had composed his piece, complete with quasi historic events as well as very much alive friends that often visited Dyfed's house and were dubbed into the literary work as fictitious knights sitting around Uther's oblong table much like Dyfed's, along with others, his books became overnight hit-wonders and big sellers even if marketing was slow due to illiteracy and a lack of a moving printing press. Furthermore, he filled that quasi novel with a writing style and form that was unmatched at this time. In any case, folks took it quite seriously, you see. Dyfed always associated illiteracy with smell, as in not so pleasant, but it occurred to him now that if illiteracy could be stamped out in this dimension then maybe so could bad smells. There was hope yet.'

'Talsin Davie's success even challenged the stories and quasi truths that had been written as scholeys in the margin of the olden day works as well as those fitted in between the lines from the relatively newly comprised addition to the Book of Sacred Law that were popular with the hierarchy of the Church of Amor and their disciplined devotees. Very soon Davie himself became quite famous and popular and all sorts were quickly beating a path to the door of their Albion branch of the House of Lucifer in order to make him their acquaintance. And all of them went away again with illusions of grandeur dancing in their heads. Many took to later writing down their own version of Talsin Davie's story in order to become famous themselves and have attractive women swooning at their feet. These literary inventions of Talsin Davie had no precedent at that time nor did they have any logic attached, either. What they did do was immediately set a trend. Of course, it should come as no surprise how easily people are influenced or manipulated. In no time there were many, I dare say even hundreds, who were trying their hand at this same composition while thousands of women swooned, many injuring themselves in the bargain when they were not caught in time before striking the floor with their head. And this at a time when the population was only a tiny fraction of what it is today. It goes without saying that almost everyone in Albion and in Europa was caught up in the fanfare and the trend of Uther and his round table. Some writers changed or varied the tale here and there, others wrote sequels. Why not? It was a good mould, why break it! Oh, they all had such jolly, great fun in those days. But it was just silliness.'

(The Chemical Wedding)

'We must all hang together or surely we will all hang apart.'
TOM PAINE

'Sleek, silent boats were skimming over grey turbulent seas toward Albion once more: This time it was Northmen on a viking that were grabbing everyone's attention. Soon these folks were terrorizing and plundering Albion's eastern shores at will, coming in to the Umber estuary (the coast north of that was considerably better secured by Angles) as well as into the Wash further south. Fortunately, these days the Angle and the Saxen folk had now more or less crystallized into the Angle-Saxen peoples. The man initially responsible for this was King Ecgberht of the monarchical House of West Saxen Folk. King Ecgberht was descended from a West Saxe king who ruled the Kingdom of Kent at the time of his birth, but when Ecgberht's time came he had to fight off King Offa of Mersha, the dominant kingdom of the south. In addition to that, he had to fight off Offa's West Saxe puppet before regaining a foothold there that was his steppingstone to finally ruling both the west Saxen and Mershan people directly. Power struggles ensued against him but ultimately the other kingdoms became his dependencies and King Ecgberht ruled as an overlord.'

'Meanwhile, Kent's functioning infrastructure, considered considerable older than that of the other kingdoms retained an air of semi independence mostly through its dominance now by the Church of Amor. Kent's hub was the large, diverse and multi-cultured urban civilian centre of Kentbury. This burh (or burgh; borough; meaning fort or defence) retained a close cultural and trade contact with Europa, especially with the Franken empire as it had done since the time of the Salian Long Haired kings.'

"Of course, Muns,' said Dyfed, 'I was mainly responsible for this as the House of Lucifer domineered here in this burgeoning and lucrative business. Even my son Davie had been drawn into its maze and was working out well.'

'But despite its flavour and heterogeneous aspects, Kentbury itself was a tightly conservative enclave due mostly to the abbots who owned the conscience of its people as well as those in the countryside around. During King Ecgberht's time Dyfed had expanded his business north to the old Amoran town of Eboracum, now called Eorwic (Jorvic) on the river Ouse, just as Ecgberht received the submission of the Northern Angles whose kingdom lay north of the Umber River and whose hub berh was Jorvic.'

'When those aforementioned sleek fleets of ships a-viking arrived, Ecgberht — dubbed the Ruler of Albion — had first lost Mersha to King Burgred but in retaining Kent he had then been replaced with a certain young and rather sickly king named AElfred. As a family relation and descendant of Ecgberht, AElfred was of the House of West Saxe. It became AElfred's job in history to defend the West Saxe folk from the onslaught of those a-vikings who had landed like waterborne locusts on the east coast among the south Angles. In the meantime, egged on and led by the House of Ivar, these Danes scoured the countryside in a northerly direction beyond the Great Wash where they took advantage of unrest among the North Angles. They took the fortress (burh) of Jorvic, only to pull back to the south a few years later when the Angles regrouped and retook it. These Norse/Danes were truly the barbarians of the barbarians. Their supreme Deity was Odin god of war and they were immediately termed the Great Heathen Army Horde. But the Angles and the Saxe, too, had worshipped such a god, a god they called Wodin who was directly related to Odin. But now the Angle-Saxen kingdoms mostly worshiped a cult that was essentially early Jeshuan as it was stemmed primarily from the much earlier Pelagius doctrine, and not the Amoran version: This, as opposed to the later Augustine tenet whose persuasion of cult the folks of Kent were more prone to accept, and had done so since the time of King AEthelberht of Kent, husband of Bertha a descendant of the Salian Franks.'

'But irrespective of their cult of persuasion, the fighting spirit had not altogether been lost upon these Angles and Saxe folks, quite the contrary. So Mersha fought back and had help from the House of West Saxe in doing so. Indeed, AElfred and AEthelred, the former's brother and interim king of the West Saxe, first came into prominence in helping the Mershan king defend his kingdom from Norse/Dane harassment (pronounced har-ass-ment) first through bribery then by partial defeat. The victory didn't last, and it became obvious that the Dane's newly acquired western front that bordered on the kingdom of Mersha would be a porous border at best and ultimately wouldn't hold.'

'In respect to the Danes a-viking, they permanently secured a big chunk of land between Mersha and the sea that stretched from the Umber to the Tems River. From here they planned for new and far-reaching raids to come. Along with constant warfare ensuing between them and Mersha, the Danes destroyed and dispersed settlements of Angle Saxen in the southeast while beyond the Umber river to the north the Northern Angles, Saxen and their Norse warrior kings lost ownership of north Albion to the Norse Danes. AElfred, son of AEthelwulf, brother of AEthelred, soon replaced the latter just at a time when they were frantically attempting to hold together the West Saxe Empire. Now those a-viking struck AElfred in his own kingdom while also overrunning southern Mersha. Having been bought off with payments of gold and silver for this campaign, the Norse/Danes returned to Nova Troia in south Mersha to regroup and plan for the next heist. All seemed lost for the West Saxe and the kingdom of Mersha while the East Angles and East Saxe were already doomed.'

'After this, the idea of a Saxen/Mershan/Angle merger presented opportunities for all sides. Soon after this marriage swapping began at an even greater rate. Saxen kings (primarily AElfred and his West Saxe folks) and their elite, and the Mershan king and his elite, gave over in marriage either sisters, daughters, cousins, or mistresses, and even perhaps a still young but widowed aunt to the other in an attempt to form long lasting blood ties. This became known as the time of the forging or the chemical wedding.'

'Meanwhile the Northern Angles and their Norse kings continually failed to turn back the Danes from overrunning their kingdom of Jorvic which the latter successfully managed to do. After awhile the urban principality of Jorvic (after which this Northern kingdom was named) rested securely in the hands of Danes. This kingdom was more properly called the Kingdom North of the Umber River. Despite the fact that this northern burh of Jorvic — a city that lay in the kingdom's southeastern portion north of the Umber River — was a heavily walled city by this time, it was destined to be the object and goal of other Norse descendants of the House of Ivar. And at its conclusion it will be where this present episode will end. In the meantime the city of Nova Troia in southern

Mersha along with her valuable mints, not to mention Dyfed's wharfs and warehouses, were now in the hands of the raiders out a-viking. Fortunately his ships had all been evacuated, some to Kent and others to the Rine delta.'

'The ships sailing down river to Kent carried away all the gold, silver, and copper — all raw items that the mints along the Tems River stockpiled — along with a fortune of minted coins as well. All the king's precious metals got away to safety, mostly to be spent bargaining with the thieves and shoplifters over some other matter later on. The monasteries in Kent, that were controlled by the abbots of the Church of Amor, were another depository for gold, silver and other wealth. So they, too, had to pay fees to the Great Heathen Horde for their protection. Indeed, those monasteries — the concept of which had originated during the early Jeshuan era in either Khem or Anatolia — were in an often unspoken though deadly struggle with the Saxen kings for authority over the folks as well.'

'Then directly following an unexpected Saxen comeback and minor victory which AElfred led against the retreating Danes at the end of their marauding season, he then made a sudden appearance at the high seat of government in Kentbury to commiserate with the kingdom's surrogate king and top officials. The purpose of the meet was to work out some kind of coordination between all the southern kingdoms against the common enemy, those who live for the love of a-viking. It was meant to put the run on them once and for all. AElfred, it became immediately clear, was frantically reorganising. Probably because of the kudos Dyfed received for his contribution towards evacuating Nova Troia before the onslaught of Norse/Danes, Koolwulf who was the interim king of Kent summoned Dyfed to attend this latest convocation. AElfred told the Kent surrogate king that in addition to total reorganization of the Saxen defences on land through a series of burhs (Angle-Saxen forts) that he intended to build, he was also intending to form a navy to keep as many of the Danes at bay and away from their shores when and however possible. As for those who landed on fair Albion, and for those who were already here, he meant to stymie them in the rivers and in the estuaries and in other shallow waterways to prevent them from any easy movement into the interior at will.'

'He told his allies that they will never cease fighting those marauders a-vikings and they will never surrender until they leave them or become one of them. But he wanted to do more than just throw rocks at their boats and fling arrows at their manpower from the shores. He wanted to confront them with an armed fleet of his own. Dyfed immediately recommended Lucius Aelius Castus (the Belgic Gaul) to take charge of whatever fleet was available to the Angle-Saxe.'

"Who knows, Castus might be able to round some Franken vessels up in the Rine delta,' Dyfed had told AElfred, carefully neglecting to mention his own fleet. 'In this way,' he said, 'we may have a fighting chance to ward away the marauding Dane pirates from Albion's shores.' Dyfed had noticed that AElfred was listening tentatively to him.'

"He accepted my suggestion to place Castus as admiral of the fleet if it amounted to that, Muns,' said Dyfed to his friend who was listening carefully. 'It turned out that the smaller and shallow hulled fighting troop carriers for river and tidal estuary manoeuvres turned out to be more successful in the end against the Danes than most of the open sea battles. Here, out to sea, the large high-sided Amoran styled vessels of war could easily overpower a Danish fleet whose boats only held about half the soldiers each compared to the Amoran design. Ostensively, the Albionian fleet were meant to simply frighten away the Danes from giving battle and hopefully from landing near populated areas. But if the Danes were caught on the high seas that was another matter and odds were not in their favour. Consequently, in the ensuing sea battles the enemy tended to give AElfred's sea going navy as wide a berth as possible that in turn pushed them in closer to the coast to take shelter among the shoals. Here those a-viking adepts found safety in crouching close to the shallows along the shoreline where the weight of the large Albionian war ships caused them difficulty to move among the tidal sands. But AElfred's had built other new and improved ships of lighter construction which had been designed for just that kind of application. They skimmed over ankle deep receding tides and easily bounced over mud flats and sand bars and they turned on a denarii in a narrow river or tree lined snye. They were easily and quickly launched as well as quickly and safely disembark able that just a few soldiers could portage them across a field or two to the next waterway without breaking a sweat. This latter feature made them even more flexible and useful than the Dane boats themselves from which AElfred had copied his design,' Dyfed told Jack.'

'As already stated, besides a navy AElfred commissioned a new defence system for the West Saxes. He built burhs that in the beginning were just defendable earthen banked fortifications, sometimes moated, nothing much more. He also incorporated older hill forts into this borough (burh) system of his and where applicable some of the old Amoran centres that still remained the hub of urban and commercial enterprise were incorporated as well. This provided a form of defendable, urban organization. It was best when they lay along side a river or were at the confluence of rivers, say, and especially border towns. In this way — along with new rules to keep up a standing army that he also used to repair the old Amoran roads and bridges needed to provide for a quickened movement of commerce and troops as well as for communications — AElfred quickly formed a finely honed organisation needed to protect his culture and allow it to forge ahead.'

'In this way it became easier to both attack the advancing warriors a-viking when they came as well as to be able to protect the army and the citizens behind defendable walls, if necessary. It also broke the army up into sectors, and if a Dane-besieged borough somewhere was swinging in the enemy's favour help could be summoned from fairly close by and be able to assist within a day with fresh troops. This plan of AElfred's also worked to the advantage of traders like Dyfed. One of Dyfed's concerns over the recent turn of events was that his trading ships and their cargo and the packets of gold and silver he carried — never mind his warehouses and his staff — were now in constant danger at all times of being raided, robbed, killed or confiscated.'

'He had been trading for hundreds of years with the walled borough of Jorvic. Originally it was with AEduini, the landlord of Jorvic, king of Bernica and Diera, son of AElle, brother-in-law to AEthelfrith, with whom he initiated business. This quickly extended to more lucrative trade with the House of Wuffingas and the East Angles to the south. Dyfed's traders were soon arriving or leaving the Umber estuary every week, sailing up the Umber River where Dyfed had constructed a dock with warehouses and where he maintained a boat construction facility. From there the House of Lucifer plied an old Amoran road to Jorvic, then a booming commercial town which lay just to the north of the estuary and one that readily consumed his goods.'

"It was here, Muns, I have to tell you,' said Dyfed, 'while on my initial exploratory venture to drum up business, I fell in with a bunch of your Jeshuan friars who were rich, educated and especially open to commercial enterprise. These men were educated by Pelagius styled monks from the Emerald Isle whose dogma was quite different from that of the Church of Amor. And men like Cuthbert and women like Hilde became my friends and with whom I have remained ever close, despite Hilde becoming a turn-coat.'

"The problem was when the Danes arrived. Not only did they pilferage everything they also burned down my docks and warehouses, something even they could have used. I could have used them by trading with them. They wouldn't have had to forage far and wide and all around and about for something I could have brought to them for a modest price. Menstruating Mother, Muns,' said Dyfed angrily, 'they could have even made a profit by selling it to the locals who made up eighty-five per cent of the population. The sales taxes alone would have filled coffers. After all, I didn't own the retailers. I am a banker and a trader, Muns, although I have managed to fall on hard times since, occasionally. But never have I had to recoup so much as since then,' he said.

"Also, as I stated, I also plied the Trent river and its watershed supplying both the East Angles to the south and even the Mershans to the west. Well, that all certainly came to a screeching, bloody halt pretty damn quickly when the lords of lamentation arrived; I can tell you. In a nutshell the arrival of those a-viking in extreme was bad for business that up to then had been helping to aid a strong economy that kept the hoi polloi happy, their pockets heavy with coin and the nasty creditors and chaos mongers at bay. It also made the local king look good. This a-viking as you go, this a malicious wandering or pirating was a different kind of chaos than what we had become used to. This variety was of a kind that even the power elite, those controllers of empires feared. This was no false flag conspiracy concocted by the filthy rich and greedy power elite in a further grab for power over minds and land, I tell you that, Muns. For the folks who subscribed, and were comfortable — and comforted — with this, the lifestyle of those who go a-viking we will go, didn't (and possibly couldn't) have given a good goddamn, cross-dressing Jeshuan messiah about any law and order that wasn't first of all a fist full of loaded dice that favoured them; or that didn't involve deranged and senseless cruelty to humans and animals of lesser order. They were all about blood and guts, rape and pillage — those a-viking folks were — with none of the niceties and refineries of life being employed on the battlefield, either,' Dyfed said.'

"In fact, it was a sign of the times to come, one could say. They brought real battle to us, these folks did,' said Dyfed to his attentive companion. 'This is why this migration of belligerent berserkers were known by the civilized Saxe folk — and by the Angles and the Kanti people as well — as the Great Heathen Horde from Hell. This heathen horde came from over the Sea of Hel or Helle and was most fierce-some indeed. We still use this word hell in a relative context today, don't we Muns.' said Dyfed.'

"I might add, too, that as a banker and trader who has profiteered I do not consider myself to be an empire controller, not by a long shot. But I can now tell you I know some who are. But I must also tell you now, under my breath, that I have friends: Yes I have friends. I have friends in high places that are levelling agents in league under a common cause of trying to pave the way for a happier and harmonised world society, Muns. This is something the world power elite is attempting to check and impede — not like the Great Heathen Horde from Hell — but in their own way. You are an intelligent man,

Muns, and an educated one at that. Anyway, this levelling agent of which I speak is all for the express purpose of opening up an opportunity for each and every folk right across all the kingdoms no matter who they might be. We need this levelling agent in order to create a situation where it doesn't matter that you aren't a king or an emperor or even a rich banker and property owner, or a rich man's son or daughter in order to have something worthwhile to say or in being someone worthwhile listening to. In the end, it won't be mumbo jumbo, hocus-pocus, and abracadabra dogma that will propel humanity into Utopia. Heavens to Betsy, no Muns, I say. This flavour of Utopia is the destruction of humanity. But what we aim for will not be a religion or political ideology, nor will it be some social timetable or trend. These are all subject to opinion. It will be knowledge of the truth as far as we can know it. It will be a journey to attain that knowledge. It will be the natural and truthful education of the masses and the universal, unchecked and uncensored, fully open and transparent communication of truthful knowledge throughout that will be available to any and everybody that wants it and seeks to find it. Mark my word on that. And mark something else; people who in any way and by any fashion attempt to confound, delay and pervert those attempts to achieve the truths about the phenomenon around us are our true enemies. And if it be your neighbour, your king, your brother, your mother who in some manner or other attempts to waylay you into other distractions then to seek the truth, so be it. They are your enemy. They are your closest enemy, your most influential enemy, but not your only enemy, Muns.'

'Now that AElfred was more prepared than before, he had managed to open talks with the Norse king of the Northern Angles with whom he had common concerns over the king's peace. Obviously, no Dane king, especially a Norse king from the House of Ivar wanted peace. That's exactly what they didn't want. There was no profit in that, and in an ironic way despite the absence of a conspiracy, these dangerous marauders had something in common with the Europaean world aspiring power elite. But it might have been a lesson learned by those pugnacious elite for it must be seen to be a foreshadowing of the future in many ways. There is nothing new under the sun, after all.'

'So, during the next campaign the Northerners directed a raid into the heart of Mersha, once again. One day a flotilla appeared on the Tems in an attempt to penetrate deep into Mersha from underneath. This was much to the amazement of the Saxen onlookers who watched as the flotilla slowly came upriver against the tide. This left the fleet quite vulnerable to the Saxen artillery that lined the banks. But the Mershan and their east/west Saxens didn't capitalise on the situation because they thought to wait until later when the Danes were entrapped by the Saxen blockade further up river.'

'At this time the city of Nova Troia had constructed a makeshift defence across the river comprising of flotation hulls loosely lashed together and fully manned. This naval equivalent of ditch or trench warfare was positioned just down stream of the main bridge crossing that — having been newly erected — was close to where the Amoran's had built their bridge back in the day many years ago. But there was an advanced fleet of warships that went before this flotilla that was also manned by those a-viking. And those warships of were carrying many hundreds of warriors. And this advanced unit successfully battled their bloody way into and finally through the manned blockade as the rest of the flotilla hung back. Then, as soon as the last of their advance boats had made it through the breaches (which they had wrought in the floating blockade), and as soon as they had gained just a little more river for the advantage of gaining speed, they quickly turned about in a well timed manoeuvre and spread out. Now, with bending oars, along with the running tide which produced a maximum velocity for them — and with their sails full of wind for added super strength — they rocketed downstream in the direction of their awaiting flotilla flinging grappling hooks where they could against the flimsy, floating, and broken up Saxen blockade that spanned the river. Some of the Saxe fighters quickly turned around to face upriver while other panicked and jumped over. The Saxens tried to fight back with fire but to no real avail. In any case the northerners managed to pull the pitiful blockade down and scatter it apart, driving it in pieces downstream toward each side of the river bank in an effort to keep the refuse and litter clear of the following flotilla that flowed past them down river in the direction of the sucking sea.'

'Now those men a-viking had total command of the waterway from where they could defend their ground (water) and land ashore in order to engage their entire fighting force at will on one side of the river or the other. They could raid Nova Troia, the hub of hubs, or continue west up the Tems River and its tributaries as they had planned. Eventually the Saxens prevailed with Mershan assistance in containing any compromising situation and in the end they successfully expunged the northerners only to wait for their return under a new king'.

'It had taken all of AElfred's stint at the helm to consolidate most of the Angle and Saxen territories, at least temporarily, against these bold and obstreperous men a-viking. AElfred had also had the foresight to marry off sisters, daughters, and even aunts and other young widows in his family to men who had kingdoms across the channel in Frankia, like the House of Carol (Karl) among others just as he had done with Mersha, Kent and the East Saxen. But the royal lineage of the two largest kingdoms here at home, Mersha and West Saxe who now dominated the south, had merged and overlapped their bloodlines so much that the frontier was in some ways invisible and flexible.'

'At least this was the case for kings and the noble gentry and did not apply to the hoi polloi in general. However, what the nobility of AElfred did was all about the hoi polloi, at least to the extent of consolidating them and forging them into one. It wasn't always as such for these were the folk who swelled the ranks of the king's armies and died with his name and that of God on their lips. They were folken (folks) who with cap in hand pleaded for audience with the king and his nobles where they begged for justice and mercy and for pardon of any unintentional transgressions they may have unwittingly committed while they tilled the former's land, hauled water, milked the cows, slaughtered the pigs and served them in their masters and lords' giant mansions. Yet, for all of this, they had little or no say whatsoever in the direction of their lives, no appeal for their lack of right to be educated or be able to choose their career and trade or indeed even in what village they could live. It seemed that only when the kings and the nobles themselves disagreed was when problems of state arose. And as for the men who with self-will ignored the hierarchy of the nobles, they became instant outlaws and were hunted down and killed without warrant or justice.'

'But Dyfed remembered AElfred as a pious young man who was more of a cleric and an intellectual than a warrior king. Indeed, he was a writer and chronicler much like Dyfed himself, and he was deeply religious and a devout member of the Keltic church according to Pelagius. But cunningly he also supported the Church of Amor. He was a reformer, which Dyfed admired, and he introduced a functioning type of administration and a fair taxation system for his day. There was also legal reform on which he worked very hard. He travelled abroad and visited his relatives as well as keeping up a close friendship with Karl the Magnificent who was now on the throne of the Holy Amoran Empire. In many ways AElfred wisely copied Karl the Magnificent. Dyfed liked him, but AElfred admonished Dyfed and eventually refused to have anything to do with him on account of the latter's ignorance of Pelagius and his beliefs as an adherent solely towards Western Philosophy. This, apparently in his mind, meant that that Dyfed rejected out of hand any concept that the Jeshuan cult embodied. Also, because of Dyfed's personal wealth and because the latter didn't walk around in rags or abandon his mansion in Kent and make the residence and abode of the House of Lucifer a barrel or a turned over tub to crawl into at night to sleep or get out of the rain (never mind from which to lend a denarii), he ridiculed Dyfed for what he called his hypocrisy in calling himself a Cynic. But mostly it was because Dyfed had no connection with the cult of the church that had coroneted AElfred. This was his worse crime of all for it was this cult that now gave him, the king, his authority in the eyes of the people, so he supposed.'

Dyfed thought that the man had done more to create his own authority, and had done a good job of it at that. Dyfed tried to explain that he had moved on from needing to live as a pauper to be a Cynic, anyway, as if he had ever lived like that. But let it not go unnoticed that he was still, after all, searching for an honest man. Cynicism of the day, Dyfed told the king was — aside from not being just about buying into ritualised cults about God, or secular ones about gaining power over governance in order (somehow) to promote humanity through some doctrine or worse still, some personal vision — what he was about and that it was simply about enabling humanity's well being as a whole. There was to be nothing fancy about it. It was about not joining or founding trends and adopting slogans and logos that simply attested to be about saving humanity. It wasn't about segregating societies nor about dividing them with the *us* versus *them* mentality, keeping the high born from the low born, the rich from the poor, and there was to be no exclusiveness or intolerance — whatsoever — in order to serve some elite crowd who saw things the right way. Rather, there was to be a universal atmosphere where a total, bar-none inclusiveness was to prevail. And its purpose was not to get rich or powerful but to expand the physical and mental horizons of our species to the outer most limits of our capabilities for each and every one of us. And this was something Dyfed didn't think the church that crowned him represented.'

"If you truly believe in a god, I told the king once, Muns,' said Dyfed, 'if you believe in a creator then you must grasp the simple fact that in a universe where creation exists, nothing — I mean nothing — is excluded for everything is part of the whole and is intrinsic to it in one way or another. If you believe in the love of creation you will know that there is no such living thing as hate, only lesser love due to some atrophic condition or other. If you believe in the good of creation then you will know that in living things there is no such thing as evil, only lesser good due to some other atrophic condition or decay. Many of the conditions of humanity that serve up these atrophic states of being are caused by human ignorance and the indiscipline of weak and fearful individuals. Western Philosophy is all about enlightenment and discipline towards nobility, a task that one puts to oneself in order to better oneself; something which I perceived the king had a great deal of, I told him,' said Dyfed, 'unlike the Jeshuans and other cults who claim that animals don't have souls. Their souls aren't as developed as ours but they aren't without one. The Western Philosophers are quite unlike the Abramites, including the newly arrived third wheel, the creed of the Ishlamites,' said Dyfed. 'These latter mentioned that had only just recently floundered into Europa have been known to be on a mission to shove their doctrine down the throats of those who don't want it. But, as it turns out, Muns, that wasn't the case either. Those poor bedraggled Hispanians were grateful and welcoming towards the Ishlamites whose attitude was more Western Philosophically oriented that were the current Jeshuans. And this was reaching the ears of other northerners who also wanted the Ishlamites (Moors) to come and help them produce viable farming and irrigation and build beautifully architected buildings that the Jeshuans seemed unable to do.'

"This, however, proposed a threat to the Salian Frankish Empire. So one day it just so happened that a kin to Karl the Magnificent had taken his Franken and Burgundian army out and with considerable force ungraciously turned the encroaching Ishlamites around and sent them packing and on their way back to Al Andalus (that was their quarter in Hispania) and told to remain there and wait for the Hispanic Inquisition when pitiless suffering would be doled out to them as well as to the folks from Judah.'

(AEthelstan the greatest of kings)

*'The men who try to do something and fail are
infinitely better than those who try to do nothing and succeed.'*
LLOYD JONES

'But when a new king succeeded the kingship of the West Saxe sometime after AElfred, suddenly the old world changed here forever. It happened that raids had begun again, this time they had arrived and were ravaging the land south of the Severn Sea in the old Kingdom of Dumonnia in the extreme west. Great bloodshed was being spilled there in a racial cleansing as a result of the fact that that kingdom hadn't been immunized from defencelessness by King AElfred's modernization. This was because it was not part of West Saxe kingdom at that time. And no one expected attack from that direction. But things were different now for a new type of marauder, a new threat was dangerously at large. They were the deadly combination of Gaelic Norse now coming out of retirement and back out a-viking. After they had swarmed over the Emerald Isle and become complacent and seemingly subdued, they now broke out again and attacked Albion from there. The new and uncontested king of the West Saxens knew full well that he could not leave himself open to dangerous intruders being left to themselves and piling up on his western flank. Furthermore, these raiders (usually referred to now as Gaelic Norse) hung over Albion like the sword of Damocles. The threat came from the Gaelic Norse House of Ivar and king of Dublin who after a hiatus was back up and running again. And he had allied himself with old friends, the Danes. It had become a tradition of late that the king of Dublin was also crowned the king of Jorvic, something that had stemmed from back in the days when the House of Ivar took Jorvic during the invasion of the Great Heathen Horde from Hell. In the meantime, Dane territories in overrun Mersha and in the land of the East Angles and East Saxe had been taken back by the stalwart men of the West Saxe folk. But the Dane king Sihtric still ruled the portion of lands around Jorvic (Yorvik) on the river Ouse. So with the aid of old friends the Danes and with some Norse Angle folk of Northumbria placated and bought off, the Gaelic Norse were now in a position to threaten the peace of Albion. And Mersha was once more in danger of falling first. Jorvic in itself wasn't much of a threat on its own but with the potential of that city allying with the Dane law to their south and an army from the Emerald Isle taking advantage of the Mersey estuary to the west as their port of entry, it could spell disaster not only for the kingdom of Mersha, but for the West Saxens. It was these West Saxens that the Gaelic Norse needed to defeat if they were to take all of Albion. This was the state of affairs then when a new Saxen king wrestled and snatched the throne of the West Saxens that still the dominated kingdom in the south. What lay before this new king was the greatest of trials, not only for himself but also for the Angle-Saxen folks in general. And pivoting on what he accomplished in his success would shape the face of Albion for the future and leave his stamp on this our western culture forever. This king's name was AEthelstan.'

'And that new king, so Dyfed reminded Jack Galoway of Munster, was to become one of the greatest king of his time, and not just among the Angle Saxens, either, nor just in Albion. But the fact that he outshone kings before and after his rule, does not alter the fact that little is known today of his fame. AEthelstan wasn't as young as he looked when a king's crown was placed upon his head. Due to the fact that that he was somehow descended from AElfred and that the Saxen House of West Saxe had inherited Mersha (the two kingdoms having become united), the Mershan nobility used the precedent in order to elect Aethelstan their king when their throne became available. Ostensibly, he was to be king of both Mersha and the West Saxe. But, as AEthelstan's Mershan orchestrated election stuck in the craw of the folks of the West Saxen kingdom, they wished to elect another as their own king instead. The two kingdoms suddenly and unrepentantly became disunited overnight. As luck or politics would have it the West Saxen elect didn't last two minutes in the running. This changed everything for AEthelstan. When the West Saxe candidate was put up a great and unexplainable fear suddenly took hold of him and he fled across the channel destined for the kingdom of Karl the Magnificent. But it didn't change the mind of the folks over in the West Saxen kingdom that were now left candidate less, for they still rejected AEthelstan. Nevertheless, AEthelstan was crowned king of Mersha at a Mershan and West Saxe border town on the Tems River just outside of Nova Troia subsequently called (not un expectantly) King's Town. The intent was to intimate that he was also the king of the West Saxen, too. In any case, he now referred to himself as King of the Angles. His were the southern Angles, you understand, as the northern ones were still aloof, although AEthelstan had designs to change that. When he said he was king of the Angles he meant all Angles, even though the southern ones had by now more or less become indistinguishable from the Saxens.'

"All strange circumstance, when you think of it, eh — Muns? I tell you this, Muns, because I had the good fortune to chronicle his reign from inside the king's circle, although I passed it over to my son Talsin Davie to publish.'

"One day I received a summons at my Kentbury home to attend the king's presence in Nova Troia. I was just setting in to rest from a recent return from a business mission back in Tournay and my nose was out of joint at the summons as I had some quick business decisions to make. When I arrived in Nova Troia the next day by boat I was whisked into the presence of the young king by his guard of noblemen. I saw a lean youngish looking man that nevertheless was sinewy and tough looking. He was tall and wore a long sleeved red tunic that fell slightly below his knees that was belted at the waist from which a sword hung. Over flax coloured socks and leggings he wore decretive greaves that were fastened loosely under the knee as well as to heavy soled and highly polished boots below. Over one arm and around his shoulders and down around his back was an embroidered cape the colour of a Spring sky that was fastened close to his right shoulder by a large silver and gold clasp. His rather cool, pale blue eyes searched me immediately as I came into his vision and I noticed his flaxen coloured hair and beard mostly covered an intelligent but slightly strained face. He did not smile upon my greeting him but informed me immediately instead that he was putting me in charge of the two mints he had recently confiscated in the city Nova Troia. My job was to oversee the minting of his coins, he told me. I was to follow his orders impeccably to the tee; orders that I would receive from him and him alone that were under seal. He then showed me his large signet ring and asked if I had any questions. I had many questions. The first one was why me? He answered that my reputation had preceded me. True, in my three hundred years here I had left some kind of legacy, I suppose. AElfred may have left some notes or documentation about both my aptitude and my attitude, I thought, but neither was likely to be very flattering. On the other hand I was in communication with some of AEthelstan's relatives in Lothar specifically and Frankia in general. It was possible but not likely that the information he had on me had come from them. I didn't take to AEthelstan at first and over the next few years we didn't seem to see eye to eye on matters that were important to me, such as my business, although he certainly was no slouch at his assumed vocation and interests. At this time his interests were primarily a matter of subduing invaders and in trying to amalgamate the Angles and the Saxens, along with the Kelts and whomever else, into one people and one kingdom from top to bottom. And that could include the Danes and whomever, as well. This worked for me. In fact, I'll say it now just for the record that this rough mannered and strange man opened my eyes, somewhat, and on the very questions and among topics which interested me and my friends, Muns.'

'Calling himself king of all the Angles was bold. But it turned out that besides controlling the elite of Mersha AEthelstan had the thorough backing at first of the early northern Jeshuan church. The early Jeshuans were influenced by the likes of Plato, the Buddha, and even Lord Krishna and was a gentler version than the later Amoran based one, the one which now holds sway. This earlier Jeshuanism became the Church of Albion. And unlike the Church of Albion which was organised by monastic orders from its centre out, the Church of Amor changed and began to organise itself from a bishopric standpoint and fought against the concept of the monastery which they labelled as cults. Such were the cult of St. Alban, for example, or the cult of St. Cuthbert which grew out of these individual monasteries, although monasteries were also established in Kent close to the Church of Amor's headquarters where Augustine became bishop.

"I know you to be of the Church of Albion, my old and dear friend, like my old acquaintance Pelagius. It is a wonder at all, Muns, that this church actually survived the Great Heathen Horde from Hell, but they did. But it did not survive the Church of Amor.'

'It was this organizational change that became the Church of Amor's method of disposing of the Church of Albion. However in a bizarre twist of irony that displays its genius of design the Church of Amor that was under the bishopric of Augustine in Kentbury here in southern Angle land had also been instrumental in providing AEthelstan with his initial crowning glory, that great awe inspiring ceremony that functioned as an invitational tip of the applicant's hat toward the church as to who it is that currently embodied the authority of God after all, as well as being a clear demonstration to the hoi polloi (those great unwashed masses) of just who was in charge here. So the last message also worked in favour of the church as it did to the applicant. Clearly, the monasteries took a back seat in this.'

"As far as Augustine who was once a monk and is now a bishop is concerned, I didn't know him, you know,' said Dyfed to Jack. This Augustine is not to be confused with St. Augustine either, by the way. The latter was a Berber from Africa and known as Augustine of Hippo. He was not an evil man but delusional perhaps and self centred; he was certainly vain and of the persuasion of a raving maniac in general, just like the rest of us, I suppose.'

'The monks of the Church of Albion wore a tonsure, a special haircut for clerics, and one day when Dyfed visited King AEthelstan in the city of Glevum he noticed that he too wore such a haircut. You see, it is unusual for kings to adopt such mannerisms. But this king was a fan and great supporter of Saint Cuthbert who was associated with monasteries in the kingdom of Northumbria where he was the patron saint. Dyfed saw a comparison between his adopted saint, Saint Niklaus, or SantaKlaas and Saint Cuthbert. One day Dyfed was in the City of Glevum to open up a People's Union Bank that he had just founded under AEthelstan's warrant and I was overseeing the delivery of a box of newly minted coins that he had purchased for the occasion from one of the mints in of which he was still in charge. The king happened to be in town when Dyfed arrived and it was a great surprise when the king invited him to join him. Noticing his tonsure Dyfed smiled. When asked if he disapproved and if so why Dyfed suggested that it may offend the Church of Amor, to which the King Aethelstan replied that he gave that church many concessions as it was. At the same time he reached over and picked up his light utility crown that he often wore when out and about and carelessly placed it on his head. Of course, the tonsure didn't show, then. Dyfed then asked him why he would give that church concessions at all, and the king replied that it was safer and altogether more expedient to include all these different cults and beliefs than to exclude them.'

'Now he was talking Dyfed's language. The latter agreed with him in that but cautioned him that encouraging a cult like the Church of Amor might prove disastrous. To which the king replied that managing the repercussions of certain necessary actions was a necessary concession. He then went on to say that he supported Dyfed's philosophy but the status quo was somewhat different. This meant, he said, the use of complex numbers and the Pythagorean theorem in order to transpose ideas so as to put them on the same line. Not only that, he added, he needed to deal with what is, not what might be or should be. He was the king, after all. Amor, he told Dyfed, went Jeshuan with ceremony of bell and smell instead of Western Philosophy and its metaphysical intonations. He then shrugged. He then told him that he favoured and curried favour of the Cult of Cuthbert. Although its tenets may not be a constant, for the moment it is a given calculation and the northern Angles and Saxen seemed fascinated by this saint. Even if, he continued to say, that he thought that humanity could presently manage Western Philosophy to the fullest responsibility in order to enhance itself, which he didn't think possible at this time, he still wouldn't sacrifice or exclude the remainder just because he thought they are following primitive superstitions. That isn't the way forward. We all have to go forward together for it to be meaningful and lasting, he said.'

'The Hyperboreans, Dyfed told him, might disagree with him. Dyfed said that haphazardly and half under his breath.'

"Oh, I don't think so," the king immediately replied, giving him a look-right-through you glance.'

'Dyfed felt a strangeness come over him. It was a pins and needles sensation under his armpits and on my forehead.

"What do you know about the Hyperboreans that I don't?" the king asked Dyfed, as his cold blue penetrating eyes continued to stare through the latter until he seemed to have seen enough. Then he looked away. 'I know you,' he added, 'and I know who you are and you will do as I say for I am king. I became king of the Angles, even though only the kingdom of Mersha recognised me at first, followed finally by those north of the Umber

River as well. I then followed that trick up by eventually establishing my authority over the West Saxe, and even the easterners. I managed this with my coronation that I had to talk the Church of Amor into and pay for with a king's ransom. Not long after I adopted the Rex Anglorum application. The West Saxe didn't take to me at first but that had to do with the fact that I hired the bishop of Kentbury of the Church of Amor to officiate. I needed Kent, you see. This pissed the West Saxens off. Not only that, the bishop (actually archbishop), following my request with payment, crowned me with an actual ordo that as a crown was my tangible and fully publicised order of service, you might say. This was a first. Do you hear? A first, even though similar goings on took place with Karl in Frankia. Of course the West Saxen officials didn't attend my coronation, did they? At least none other than a certain few nobles whose support I had. But I won them over in the end, but it took a few years and when it happened the bishop of Winton resigned on the spot, didn't he? The bastard.'

'Aethelstan then shook his fore finger in Dyfed's face as though he was pantomiming the past confrontation for his benefit. "And then there was Edwin,' he said. 'Edwin the upstart who didn't know shit about carving out a viable and solid authority to run a independent consolidated kingdom, at least not the kind of kingdom I envision. A kingdom needs to encroach all of Albion and civilise and absorb the ruffians or destroy them.'

"The king elect drowned,' Dyfed piped up. 'He drowned swimming to Frankia, as I recall.'

"He wouldn't have had to swim,' AEthelstan responded curtly, 'if he hadn't fallen out of the boat.' The king looked disgusted more than being effected by any other emotion. 'As far as the folks over at the city of Winton were concerned,' he added suddenly, 'the sun shone out of Edwin's ass. Anyway, after that the folks there, and in West Saxe territory in general, came over to my side. Now we are Mersha, the West Saxen, the East Saxen, and Kent that also includes the Jutes, and we have a regrouped the North Angles in the land north of the Umber. What I still don't have is the Kelts and sundry mixed blood Amorans of the west. And I need them. We need them. We need them because we are still facing grave danger from the Gaelic Norse who are poised to invade us in greater numbers than before. And once that happens, the Danes of the east will take courage again and retake Jorvic as their capital citadel. Then we will have both the Gaelic Norse and the Danes stomping all over Mersha with their muddy boots. That is where you come in Dyfed.'

"Me?' Dyfed asked. 'Why me?

"Because I need people that you know, that's why,' he told him.

"Like who and what for?' Dyfed asked him.

"Like Owen MacShee, for one', he answered, 'never mind King Cadot and also Count Bricus the former tyrant of Demetia. And last but certainly not least I need the host with the most, I want King Cadwallopir. We might want to include Rhodri who you don't know, but he is a constant companion to Aurelius Ambrosius and Ryan who you do. I want them, too, and I want them to be on my side.'

'Dyfed told AEthelstan that to the best of his knowledge Ambrosius had become a recluse and that he didn't know where he or King Ryan were. King AEthelstan shrugged, his left knee was doing short up and down bounces, stopping abruptly, then starting up again just as quickly again as he sat across from Dyfed in his high chair. It was a nervous tick that was uncharacteristic of him and this made Dyfed wonder if there was something else on his mind. Then drawing out his words slowly, he told Dyfed that that there was a man named Castus, his knee abruptly stopping its furious movement again. This sea general did not come to AElfred's summons for assistance, AEthelstan told Dyfed, presumably because the fish offered to him were too small to fry. I want to tell him this time that I need a mighty warrior to help me for I will be using an armada of ships to move men and fight on the seas, if necessary. And lets not forget that he has much to bring to the table here and will receive what he deserves, recognition and payment. And you also have over five thousand well trained and battle tested men in your personal army still stationed in Lothar. You are also rich so you can get those men over here and lend them to me at your own expense. I can give you something in return, if you want.'

'Dyfed didn't answer him right away as he was thinking of Owen again and this brought back memories of Ceredwyn who he must find soon as he knew through Mencius from long ago that they were destined to be bound together, eventually.'

"And what do you want?' AEthelstan suddenly said gruffly, bringing Dyfed's attention back into the moment. Dyfed told him that he wanted to know how the hell was going to deliver Owen to him when he didn't know where he was, and if he did he had a bone to pick with him first and also with Ryan who he heard had turned into a paranoid and was in reclusion somewhere on the continent. With that King AEthelstan replied that his will comes first and any bone picking will come later. Dyfed told him that he could send someone to search for him. AEthelstan agreed but said he wanted one of his own men to accompany his in that search, a certain Alick of Monmouth. The king added that what he just needed from Dyfed was to be ready to convince each one in turn that they must come over to his side and to bring over with them those others on his wish list.'

'Dyfed told AEthelstan that his man Trachmyr who can command an army and captain a ship and is in charge of the House of Lucifer's personal guard could be of help to him. Soldiers and ships Dyfed could loan out temporarily to AEthelstan until the battles the king wishes to fight have been won, and in this Dyfed's armies will assist him, he told the king. But without his army and ships of trade his business would fail, he said, and then he'd be of no use to the kingdom after that. Dyfed told the king that there was a temple in Winton dedicated to Epona the Keltic horse goddess. He then asked AEthelstan if he would gift him the site of this temple in exchange for his use of his ships and army. The king readily agreed. Finally, he asked him to be officially released from his duties as overseer of AEthelstan's mints.'

(The alchemistic trick)

'...the triumph of barbarism and religion.'
EDWARD GIBBON (DESCRIBING MEDIEVAL SOCIETY)

'Meanwhile, having assailed and assimilated the amalgamated Angle, Sax, Dane, and Amoran concoction to the north, south, east and even the west into relative compromise, AEthelstan then forged into them something of a singular identity with an accompanying vision. This was his alchemistic trick. Castus, of course, never turned up. Dyfed's soldier-spy who he had sent to find him managed to locate that old gum toothed reprobate living in Nijmegen on the Rine, but Alick of Monmouth (AEthelstan's man) promptly killed him by evisceration. Imagine that, and Castus suffering from thanatophobia and all! As it turned out they had had past history together. Alick had been his imperial treasurer back in the day, so perchance, the enmity Alick showed was deeply rooted and caused by an apparent slight of some kind. It was probably about authority over money or personal pay. Treasurers and the like are usually chrematomaniacs, anyway. That was another Amoran induced trait, and it goes to show that at least some of them are also psychopathic. They can also be dangerous killers who don't mind eviscerating you if they feel that you have somehow gotten in their way and between what they are entitled to. Either that, or aren't paying them the attention they believe they deserve. But on the other hand, it was certain and it was clear to Dyfed that this had been AEthelstan's call, not Alick's, although it was unlikely that the former had prescribed the actual manner of Castus' death. This angered him for Dyfed perceived that he was not being trusted by AEthelstan, although he wisely said nothing, deciding to keep his cards close to his chest in these dealings, as always. But he continued to admire AEthelstan, as he had also admired Castus, although always from a distance. Doing AEthelstan's bidding by applying effort in the field to bring the Norse and their Kelt allies together with the Angle Saxens also allowed Dyfed some breathing room away from AEthelstan where maybe he could come into his own. Anyway, aside from avoiding a disastrous battle clash between four or more massive armies — not the ideal get together — there was the matter of Dyfed's longing to search for adventure in the western lands of Merika beyond the Atlas Sea. What with his release from the responsibility of the Albionian mints, and as all his affairs and his house were in order and doing well despite the climate of unrest, more specifically there was the notion of the opportunity now to set off and slip away unnoticed in that un-retractable way.'

'Dyfed remained in Gleven to finish off setting up his bank that was to use AEthelstan's new currency, a currency which as overseer Dyfed had been responsible for minting. He sent a soldier back to Kentbury to fetch Ebreo, his lieutenant (pronounced lef-ten-ant) accountant that was due to arrive from Tournay, as well as documents pertinent to the bank's legitimacy which were to be kept under lock and key on site. Dyfed then set up the mint at Hereford and under Karatakos' eagle eye he trusted Ebreo to finalise the up and running of his bank there and in the land of the West Saxe. He also entrusted the overall running of his empire during my absence to his son from Kentbury, but under the direction of Cato and Karatakos who were also to keep a close eye on Ebreo. And once Trachmyr was clear of his civil war responsibilities under AEthelstan he was to oversee Talsin Davie and Karatakos and continue his responsibilities with the House of Lucifer and to follow Dyfed's orders. He also was to handle the management of certain capital assets Dyfed had including the upkeep of the Epona temple under his property management department and an employee directly under his authority was to conduct conveyance of any kind that was necessary and needed. Dyfed's staff would need to be diligent with AEthelstan's staff on most matters.

Dyfed then decided to accompany Trachmyr on the first leg of his adventure. Glad to be away once more from the confines of city life and free from his long stint at civil duties at the mint in Hereford, and especially the vast workload of running his empire during these difficult times, Dyfed rejoiced once again in the fellowship with the sea and the forested and rugged shores of western Albion. Aside from the commission AEthelstan had given him that he passed over to Trachmyr, Dyfed's first endeavour was to build up greater self-esteem. This stemmed from certain doubts that had crept into the corners of his mind about himself, of late that stemmed from the discovery that he had had a son he knew nothing about, and he him. It went down from there.'

(The doldrums)

'We are opposed around the world by a monolithic and ruthless conspiracy which relies primarily on covert means for expanding its sphere of influence.'
JOHN FITZGERALD KENNEDY

'Despite his successes, looking back at his life's path from different angles was not a particular comforting one when combined with his own tract record of failures. Apparently, he didn't have what it takes. Manandan had told him he had been given valuable tools not possessed by just anyone. Only now he wondered if King AEthelstan's obvious stellar performance and over all influence of events upon the world stage had somehow brought these doldrums upon him. And once again Dyfed considered focussing on his own successes. After all, had he himself in some way ever really enacted, or been engaged with anything that had had a positive even if minimum effect upon those who dwelled in phenomena at large? Was his promotion of a once obscure SinterKlaas the exception, and his only claim to fame? It seemed so at least from the standpoint that with the help provided by the fifth dimension's tech support SinterKlaas was fast becoming all the rage. But it wasn't fame Dyfed wanted. That much he did know. Maybe it was acceptance that he wanted? He considered this thoughtfully. Acceptance even of himself by himself, and of his place within this phenomenon that he called home. Clearly, he thought that somehow he lacked the acceptance of the who and the where of his own sense of presence. This was not good, but it probably had to do with division of his birth right here in the third dimension and of his upbringing by folks who lived in an entirely different world. Kind of like an extreme generation gap on steroids. Also at this time, during this his current mental voyage of discovery, Dyfed was poignantly reminded of the executive officers' decision — so it seemed to him — to constantly overlook him time and time again and choose others such as Pelagius, for instance, for the job of attempting to pierce the Ram (as they say in the trade) instead of him. Though it was those same officers (some who funnily enough referred to themselves as angels) that had chosen him to promote Nikolas of Anatolia to deliver that special message of love and endearment. And that was the point. It had been Nikolas, not him. No, no, they wouldn't choose him for that; they didn't have confidence in him. Despite Queen Violet being his mother and Manandan his master he wasn't accepted like other members of *the pack*. And he couldn't blame them, either, of course. After all, he had been much younger and inexperienced. But what nagged away in the back of his mind was that he hadn't even been brilliant as a back up component — for goodness sakes — either! And, as it turned out, even Theoderic the Great had been promoted by those same officers to advance the great agenda by highjacking the Amoran Empire from within before it was too late and to guide it down the straight and narrow. Dyfed now openly wept while wondering about King AEthelstan and how he might just as well bob up and down in that man's wake as well. Marvelling, though, at AEthestan's abilities, Dyfed instinctively knew he could also end up playing second banana to him, too, if he didn't get away from it all and away from him. Anyway, it wasn't lost on him that so far he wasn't just a consummate failure in most things during his life, he was a two-bit failure player in most things, at best. He had lost Ceredwyn and only through someone else's help in his destiny might he get her back. And it wasn't lost on him either that her father Owen MacShee had found someone he thought was better, and of course, Marg had spurned him of late. Love is an important factor in one's life and any happy matrimonial existence of his own was spotty. Decidedly, this was not a comfortable feeling within, not his moment of paramount contentment, for sure.'

'Earlier Dyfed had sent for his company's new flag ship the Aura Maré II that had been at anchor in Nova Troia. Trachmyr was aboard as her captain and Dyfed joined him aboard at Gleven when she arrived there. From Gleven the Aura Maré quickly sailed back down the Severn River again and into the Severn Sea. They caught a southern wind that blew them into the wide channel that lay between Gwyneth and the Emerald Isle. Aside from those two, Trachmyr had arranged for her to be manned by Keltic sea-dogs so that once he and the other Amoran civilized looking Dyfed were aboard and at sea in the western lands they wouldn't be portrayed as any unusual spectacle as they entered the realm of the western Kelts as petty traders, as they were designed to appear. Dyfed's other ships and his army that would be in them would join the fray later.'

'As far as the Kelts were concerned they were categorized into quite a few brands, but these western folks of Albion were mainly referred to as Welsh. This also included the Gangli people. Further to the north were the Pixies and the remnants of the Brigantes and so forth. They all had something in common with those Kelts on the Emerald Isle, now being called Irish. But there was one group of folks in these environs who were the Gaelic Norse. These were the Irish whose people had been overrun by the Norse that had taken possession of much of the Emerald Isle under their Gaelic Norse warrior king ensconced in Dublin and also at his winter home at Jorvik. One place in western Albion where this Gaelic Norse folks had gotten a quiet foothold and were not causing any unnecessary trouble was the Wirral Peninsula. This promontory of land was edged in between the Dee River that separated it from northern Gwyneth to its south and the Mersey River estuary to the north. Directly to the east was the Mershan border battlement of Fort Victrix and modern Chester. Dyfed and the Aura Maré II were headed for the River Dee and the spot there where the Gaelic Norse resided. And their purpose there was to put their ear to the ground and listen for news while talking to the locals in their funny accents about the goings and comings that was happening around them. The latter (having adopted the Keltic language) had to twist their Norse tongues around the Gaelic words they now spoke in their adopted tongue.'

'Dyfed needed to become alerted to any and all upcoming events, he wanted to know of any movements of armies or of any raids that were being conducted, in Mersha especially. But just before that they dropped harbour in Hardlech (their old stomping grounds) he and Trachmyr could get a glimpse the Ruck's Roost and momentarily immerse themselves in some soothing nostalgia. This cheered Dyfed up. That old ocean rock, like some treeless, giant chunk of dark shale or low grade jade that had been obliterated by millenniums of accumulation of white guano that like cement lay over its mossy green was to be the two men's touchstones to the past. They had met each other on its summit hundreds of years ago. And once ashore, it was their first destination in rejuvenated childishness of the past that can help keep one young if administered correctly. Now the two of them rushed there like little boys leaving their crew (along with sundry locals, watching aghast) to attend to the harbour authority. The crew, long faced and silent, were quarantined aboard ship until such time as Dyfed and Trachmyr decided to return. Then, as ship owner and master, Dyfed was forced to pay the harbour fees and complete the declarations required. This procedure — damned annoying red tape to most — was a newly instrumented Angle Saxen law that was being imposed by AEthelstan on coastal towns even here (especially here, under the circumstances) in western Albion. Before the town of Hardlech they saw that some fine sleek looking Keltic ships had been beached. Dyfed now took an interest in seeing the town and its harbour. Long ago, just out from Owen's cenedl and a day or so late, he, having been deathly ill, had missed the town for he had passed through it in delirium and oblivious to everything.'

'The players that were to gather in western Angle land, once called Prydain, and who were to spill out upon the Wirral included the so called welsh represented by Owen, the Welsh king of Strathclyde, the Pixie king of Alba (former Alban) with the decidedly Amoran name of Constantine, and the Norse House of Ivar represented by Olaf Gothfrithson king of Dublin. In addition there was the representation of the southern Welsh under King Cadot and some king of the Dane infringed territory of the East Angles south of Northumbria. Northumbria had been under the rule of Sigtryggr the One Eye king of Dublin and Jorvic, brother in law of AEthelstan. But he had died and his brother in law AEthelstan had assumed the title over Jorvic (latter spelled York) while Olaf had grabbed Dublin. But like any good descendant of the House of Ivar, Olaf wanted more. He wanted to be king of Jorvic which he believed was the property of the House of Ivar, and that was what this was all about. In the interim AEthelstan supposed that Gothfrithson would wait for the opportune moment in order to find the time to strike Mersha with the help from sympathetic kings like Owen (Owain) and Constantine for sure, and possibly King Cadot, the spokesman and overlord of the western Albionian Kelts, or the Welsh.'

'It occurred to Dyfed now that so far he had gone to considerable lengths to accommodate AEthelstan's dream. He had provided a competent, battle experienced fighting army of about a thousand of his best men of his own for the cause, plus another army twice that size made up of Germanic Frankens who had been presently at loose ends and hanging around the public houses of Tournay. The latter, hearing of the potential conflict abroad with at least one side flush enough to pay, who having a copasetic and cordial relationship with Dyfed's soldiers, begged to accompany his men. Armies willing to fight, of course, have no money of their own, so Dyfed ended up financing them in his endeavour to please AEthelstan and account for something in his mind. He needed to do business in Albion when all was said and done and the fighting was over. Also, it was in his interest to have Norse pirating and their ruling the wave minimised. In addition to that, although he had already planned to vacation away from his business and travel to the world across the ocean to have a look see, nevertheless he was running a risk of losing valuable fighting men in this affair which were needed to stiffen up any opposition to his business endeavours or defend his House of Lucifer's empire when necessary. Apparently, he had found himself somewhat urgently needed in helping an undermanned commission to reel and teeter through a deficit of AEthelstan's doing that ultimately covered the latter in glory and not him. So, he too had a vested interest now in this clash of kings and cultures.'

'In the weeks leading up to any notice of invasion, besides the arrival of the Icelanders, AEthelstan's army was divided mainly up among the burhs or forts that guarded the kingdom of the West Saxe. The Mershan army was also guarding their borders; especially the northwester border on the Mersey River and Fort Victrix itself was full of soldiers. It was here, too, on the Wirral peninsula between the Mersey and the Dee rivers where spies descended by the boatload. We were one among of them. Although there had once been a skirmish at Fort Victrix which the Saxens had had to hastily defend, no other incident had occurred and these Norse Gaelic newcomers got on well with their Welsh neighbours who continued to inhabit northern Gwyneth to their south and the west coastal regions to the north and into the land ruled by the Norse warrior king of Northumbria. Dyfed then began to wonder at one point if these rumours of a take over of York (Jorvik) by Olaf were in fact true or if there was some other agenda behind them. Certainly, as mentioned, Dyfed had an invested interest in expunging the dreaded men gone a-Viking once and for all who were bad for the trading business and a drug on the market all round. In addition, he believed AEthelstan's motives to secure his overlord status in order to bring organised and sophisticated governance to the land to be exemplary. But it wasn't just about the havoc the Viking curse impinged upon his northern trade, or anybody else's. If the Gaelic speaking Scandians or Norse Goth of the House of Ivar were involved in seducing the Welsh Gaelic and the Pixies in a revolt to disrupt AEthelstan's calming influence and effective standardization of the Albionian culture in order to be able to apply governance against that which was mostly raid and pillage based, then a face-off was necessary. Anyway, Dyfed's contribution was certainly more than a thinly veiled attempt to secure some all-round gratitude. In time he did, both from the established order as well as by IOUs (read UOMEs) for future perks in trade agreements and licensing. Dyfed didn't yet get to make up the rules but he did have to play by them. Either that or change them, and at the time Dyfed saw AEthelstan (not *the pack*) to be doing just that.'

'The Keltic/Nordic positions were easily detected as Dyfed's and his sailors and guards slowly moved up into the River Dee. Without a shred of camouflage or any attempt to hide, their posts were first indicated by the myriad of boats that were beached nearby their camps, along with Scandian sailors and soldiers alike staggering aimlessly about or passed out. Normally most of them were three sheets to the south wind anyway. They seldom posted sentries for nobody in their right mind would engage them under normal circumstances, and anyway Welsh scouts would warn them beforehand. Dyfed had already worked out that if there was to be a problem with his mission (any problem at all) it was to be the former who would be at the crux of it all. Menstruating mother of cross-dressing messiahs and other major religious cult heroes alike! These berserker sons of bitches operating under the likes of the House of Ivar, or for that matter any kinsman of Rognvaldr who was the most powerful Norse ruler that the Angles, Saxen, and Kelts had ever seen, were the most dangerous people on Earth. Yikes! And they were more than up to the job (hardly a task) that awaited them. And killing Angles and Saxen or anybody who looked liked them or wanted to look like them was their job. You can understand Dyfed's worries and concerns over his own commercial empire.'

"With the help and support of Cato, Karatakos, Morgant, and Cassius Quintus Paulinius, and more remotely with the likes of the now renamed Flavio Juiliano, and Pius Lucius Livius Theodosus, Lysander, Pyrrhus and Mithridates, along with a host of others, not to mention Manandan and Thrax, all of whom had a purpose that was to secure harmony in order to point our civilization in the right direction, I was a small cog in all wheel of immensity, as you can see, Muns,' Dyfed said.'

(The Battle of the Burgh)

> '…how dangerous is the acquirement of knowledge, and how much happier that man is who believes his native town to be the world, than he who aspires to become greater than his nature will allow.'
>
> **MARY SHELLY** (*VIKTOR FRANKENSTEIN*)

'Dyfed told Muns that he had come to this western campaign in support of AEthelstan, but papers showing that he had been commissioned by the Welsh king Owain (also Owen) of Strathclyde, and not by AEthelstan, had been prepared for him. AEthelstan had managed to obtain a copy of that latter king's seal that Dyfed reproduced on a charter purportedly giving him authority. He was to take in the situation regarding any prospective allies among the Gaelic Norse and the southern Kelts, and report back to AEthelstan. It was made clear by this forgery that King Owain of Strathclyde didn't want to commit his troops and journey south to help battle against the Angle Saxens all for nothing. The impression was that he didn't want to be on the side of losers: Now, there's a sure way to set yourself back a pace or two, maybe never to recover again. Better to stay home and watch if that was to be the case. Go big or go home, as they say. Obviously the former document that gave Dyfed an opportunity to scout and spy for favourable indications in view of AEthelstan's success under some cover was unknown to the Welsh King Owain. In addition to that, on the off chance that Dyfed may somehow be known to any of those examining his credentials, AEthelstan had printed a warrant for his arrest to help him not getting arrested by any of AEthelstan's enemies. Apparently (and erroneously), Dyfed was supposedly wanted for treacherous activities against the king and his west Saxen realm (according to this bogus warrant). Back in the day, it stated, Dyfed was wanted for illegally transporting war materiel and other restricted goods to Sigtryggr the one eyed king of Northumbria. Therefore (so the fake document informed), any person or persons knowing of his whereabouts or knowing of property belonging to him were encouraged with reward to report that information. And aside from being credited with his arrest, it went on to state that the informer would share in a portion of all Dyfed's assets that were seized and confiscated under the authority of the king. So, they were a believable party of adventurers looking for an opportunity, along with the fact that not only did they speak mostly Keltic — and always spoke it among themselves — what with the particular group of young men who were actually accompanying Dyfed and Trachmyr, they certainly all looked the part.'

'Dyfed told his friend, who (perhaps unlike the reader) so far had lost no interest in his tale, that they landed ashore on the Wirral peninsula alongside the River Dee amidst chaos all around. It turned out that Olaf Gothfrithson had conducted raids into Mersha by sailing up the Mersey River where a thousand soldiers disembarked. As the king of Dublin, Olaf was hoping to make quick contact with his scouts somewhere on the south shore of the Mersey in order to join forces with King Constantine of Alban and King Owain of Strathclyde. Together they believed they had the strength to invade the Anglish with success. Then, quickly overrunning any Mershan resistance they intended to strike out for Tamworth where scouts told them AEthelstan's armies were congregated. And somewhere there their intention was to take on AEthelstan's gathered forces head on. From there Olaf intended to march a hundred Amoran miles northeast to Jorvic which he would then claim for himself, having already bought the Danes off beforehand. So the king of Dublin foraged and raided easily with little resistance before being joined by the other kings. Then together they turned south in good spirits looking for the Anglish. But they didn't get very far when soldiers out from fort Victrix circled around behind them initially blocking their return to their fleet on the Mersey. At the same time AEthelstan and his armies suddenly appeared descending the highlands to the east and headed directly toward Forth Victrix. Quickly AEthelstan's northern arm beefed up the Fort Victrix boys who were holding any retreat Olaf and his allies could make back to their beached fleet in a tidal swampy area of the Mersey near the northern tip of the peninsula. Despite the large numbers of Olaf's combined armies, or maybe on account of it, this manoeuvre hemmed them in which threatened to cramp their fighting style. Olaf quickly broke out and fled northwest. But soon he had to defend himself again. He wheeled around to face the pursuing enemy in the vicinity of a burgh erected on slightly higher ground by a little river named Dibbin that flowed north into the Mersey. Once again they had to defend their position. The clash here between the kings of either side was intense and sent up such a noise that it was easily heard from the shores of the River Dee and far and wide.'

'It was a bloody affair this battle and soldiers skidded and slid on the red, slippery gore that greased the grass. King AEthelstan and his vast army now spread out like a giant advancing crab that crept toward the retreating Norsemen forcing them south. It was difficult for the Anglish, too, for their soldiers were tripping and stumbling over the fallen Norse as they pushed forward to keep them engaged. But here Olaf made a decision to cut his loses and get himself and his nobles out of harms reach. His soldiers — all experienced fighters to a man — would have to go it alone now, he reasoned. Most would die, he knew, but they were soldiers. Olaf and his nobles, of whom many were his top henchmen, turned and fled toward the tidal lagoon on the south shore of the river Mersey while their armies continued to block and hamper an Anglish rush forward. Meanwhile, this allowed the Norse/Keltic nobles to quickly escape inevitable death. The other kings such as Howel, a last minute sign up from Rheged, King Owain, King Constantine, Timir (commissioner of Mona), and King Cadot from Powys) were not as lucky and a great rout ensued.'

'It just so happened that this event (which Olaf and his nobles were embroiled in) was now playing out as Dyfed's reconnoitre party arrived at the very landing spot at that very moment when Olaf and his nobles having turned toward the Dee River to escape death were arriving in great haste. Dyfed could see and even smell the fear of these men amid the whirling axe blades that were severing through the flesh of humans and cutting into the bone as the AEthelstan's army caught them up. At that point Dyfed commanded Trachmyr to venture ashore with some men and steering clear of any Donny-brook that may break out while extending a hand of assistance. Dyfed thought that extracting Olaf and his nobles from immanent danger might win kudos for himself. Accordingly, Dyfed signed over and gave Trachmyr written orders that were addressed to AEthelstan explaining his wishes and also both the latter's warrant that embodied Dyfed to act on behalf of the king's interests, as well as the knockoff warrants which AEthelstan had contrived for their protection. He placed all of this into Trachmyr's hand. In the former written orders Dyfed had decreed that his army was to continue to serve under King AEthelstan, but only so long as it was commanded by Trachmyr. Immediately following a victory, however, they were to receive spoils as agreed and Trachmyr was to return them to Tournay in the land called Flanders.'

'Don't worry about me, Dyfed told Trachmyr as they parted. For this was Dyfed's opportunity now to proceed alone on his plan to seek out the new world for himself. He told his trusted batman, guard and friend that he had great confidence in him and that he would reward him more when he returned to Tournay on his journey's end. Dyfed immediately dismissed the other Kelts who had accompanied them, paying them in full. Meanwhile he had sent Trachmyr to offer King Olaf Gothfrithson and about twenty of his nobles a passage to safety on the *Aura Maré II*. His plan was to ferry them back to the Emerald Isle and safety. With twenty-two aboard, and with sixteen men at an ore, the *Aura Maré II* was almost at full capacity when they quickly rowed and drifted under sail in order to distance themselves from the destruction at hand.'

After a turbulent voyage across the waters Dyfed deposited King Olaf and his nobles back in Dublin from where they had originally set out to aid King Constantine of Alban and King Owain of Strathclyde. Olaf was very thankful for what Dyfed had done and much surprised when he was told the true nature of Dyfed's business with AEthelstan.

"After all,' Dyfed told Muns, 'AEthelstan, the greatest of kings, didn't want violence and death. He wanted to forge a new conglomerate kingdom of Kelt, Angle, Saxen, and Dane/Norse that was able to defend Albion from Holy Amoran Empire aggression and interests, if not from the Church of Amor per sé. And Dyfed wanted what King AEthelstan wanted, a strong and vigorous kingdom to come together as one people as soon as possible. That, of course did not happen quite as history and amendments to the book of lists have suggested. But it was soon to happen. And when it did come, and although the surrounding phenomenon wasn't torn or rent in any obvious way; something shifted.

Meanwhile, King Olaf offered to reward Dyfed for his services, but declining material gain, Dyfed asked instead for advice and directions from Norse sailors under his control to accompany and pilot the *Aura Maré* II and him to the new world and back. Olaf immediately recommended a Nordic Icelander at hand by the name of Eirik Camphaug (or Erik High Camp).

(The hauling of Hakon the Wanker's ashes)

> 'A man without force, is without the essential dignity of humanity. Human nature is so constituted, that it cannot honour a helpless man, although it can pity him; and even this it cannot do for long...'
>
> **FREDERICK DOUGLASS**

"I had fled from the Wirral and the Battle of the Burh,' Dyfed told Muns, 'with King Olaf Gothfrithson and about twenty of his nobles who I rescued despite them being on the opposite side of the ruckus to my candidate, King AEthelstan. We sailed to Dublin in my vessel the *Aura Maré II*. Then on advice from King Olaf I commissioned an adventurous Norse marauder named Eirik Camphaug to become my guide to the new world to which we set out from Dublin with one quick stop at a thickly forested fjord in Norland. I had learned that he had already on one occasion, after skirting a great ocean to the north in a flimsy craft, had visited many cold lands far to the west. Although he said they weren't so cold, and I have to agree. At least not then they weren't. In time he and his crew had come to a new continent where a strange race of people lived whose colour of their skin was truly remarkable for it was bright red. At that moment I focussed on taking the same voyage and getting Eirik to navigate my ship following his old route. So with a crew of fellow Norsemen that he had selected from the one stop fjord shop in Norland we finally we set out.'

'But how on Earth did could a pilot or navigator manage to plot a course, was what Jack Galway of Munster wanted to know. And although Eirik (also Erik) was the ship's pilot Dyfed had brought with him his navigational tools that he had been devising to better his shipping enterprise. This knowledge was partly based on ideas he had with a little un-common sense thrown in. Dyfed stated how one such device he had used to measure the degrees from the sea's horizon to a given star by which he was able to determine their position to latitude. Knowing where that star was placed above his island home for each month he was able (by this method) to estimate his position north or south of Mona, for example. And from that point he made adjustments accordingly. However, the Polar star that was the one on which he fixed, soon became less and less visible as the season progressed until it became altogether invisible and he had to focus upon recalculating according to the more visible wandering *gods* of the firmament. But it was also necessary to gauge their position east or west of the longitude relative to Mona. By using his ingenuity Dyfed was able to come up with a rather crude method for determining this as well. It utilized a series of hourglasses. One of them measured the full span of time from a point that demarking one full day to the next. For an example this hourglass would run out at sun-up while at harbour in Mona. Next, he needed to adjust according to his relocated position relative to the sun on the horizon each morning at a given point of the hourglass. If it was the same, he hadn't moved. This was not entirely accurate in that from mid December to mid June the sun rises slightly earlier each morning while from June to December its progress is retarded, never mind the adjustments needed for changes in latitude. But along with two additional glasses this method sufficed. One of these glasses was used to record the differences or increments (plus or minus) of any given day pending on the observer's position before or after the solstice. As for the third glass, it was used in the following way.

Dyfed knew that the sun could be seen to rise over the sea's eastern horizon earlier in a twenty-four hour period while moving east of a given point, or later moving west. If he voyaged west along a latitude from a given location for a full day he knew that when he saw the sun's morning rays begin to peep across the sea the hour glass running out of sand would indicate a time later than those previous, unless he hadn't moved at all. Inversely, the opposite would be true if he were travelling east instead of west. He also knew that the time difference between when the sun was first observed at each location would be proportional to the distance separating them. This being the case Dyfed would record from sunrise to sunrise on the hourglass as if the vessel were motionless and make his adjustments on the increment glass allowing for the sun's earlier entry according to the lengthening day. After a number of days (so as to make the differences more noticeable and therefore more calculable) he would record on the third glass the difference in time from when the sun would be coming up at the given point east of him until when it actually rose in his present position. That difference in time could be converted to distance and subsequent longitude. This could also provide him with the speed in which the Aura Maré II was moving. If he knew where he was going (which was not the case at hand) he could estimate a relative time of arrival. For an example, Dyfed had come to know that at this particular time of year the sun rose over the horizon at Kobenhavn just under an hour and a half before it did at the city of Legion on the same latitude. So if after a few days of fast travelling he discerned an hour and a half discrepancy in when the sun should have come up at any point at a similar latitude and when he actually saw it rise. It would seem then that the distance that he had travelled from that initial point to where he was at the moment would be equal to the distance from the Kattegat to the Solway Firth, for example. If he managed to keep up that speed (relative to tides and currents along with seasonal winds) he could estimate his arrival at a given location within a day or even within a few hours. Admittedly, this wasn't Arabian medical science (science in its true sense didn't exist among the western hoi polloi then), but he made it work for him.'

'Dyfed, as we know, knew folks who had infallible devices to ascertain such calculation in fine detail that were unfathomably small in size. But they were useless without an infrastructure of support. During the long, uneventful days at sea, Dyfed mulled over ideas for improvement. But sufficient knowledge to manufacture a precision instrument is one thing, and to have the tools and all the necessary materials and equipment to be able to do it is another.'

'In this manner, along with the Norseman's experience, Eirik and Dyfed led the crew in a large arc stretching northwest from Norland to a number of fascinating settlements. Many of these settlements were mere camps set among fields of mud nestled between the seashore and receding glaciers of dirty brown ice. The further they travelled north the more noticeable were the differences that occurred in the appearances of the people, not just in their dress and customs but also in their physical appearance. Dyfed noticed that the people who dwelled in these more westerly regions were broad faced, dark haired and were shorter and sturdier in physique. Mainly nomadic they lived off the migrating herds that they followed closely and from fish and larger sea mammals, including whales. In the partially ice locked lands to the west the people followed the herds along a great land mass that was boarded by ocean ice upon which they spent most of their lives hunting and fishing. According to Eirik, one tribe of people who he called the Skraellingar were surrounded by ice for ten months out of the year. And they permanently camp close to areas where small bodies of water exist that are called a Polynya. These remain open and ice free all year, even during the dark cold months of winter. These stories of the Polynya dwellers and their customs intrigued Dyfed who now pushed the little *Aura Mare II* further and further west. But as the tiny vessel continued on this course, manoeuvring among giant mountains of drifting ice, they encountered no signs of civilization and the only permanent shore they saw was the great white coast of grinding ice that was too dangerous to approach. And just as Dyfed feared they would, the crew soon grew restless and frightened.'

'Very early one morning about a month before summer, Dyfed had stood against the dragon carved prow of the *Aura Mare II*. His companion by his side was a stray dog, a Rottweiler he named Leto but called Leda, which he had gathered up from Norland and had brought aboard as the ship's mascot for the journey. Dyfed had been looking aft while listening to Venus and Father Zeus (Zeus-Pater or Jupiter) who were both singing just above the horizon before the sun. Leda the dog, of course, was accompanying them with melodic howls. Suddenly, he noticed Eirik talking furtively to the giant first mate that was stationed at the tiller. This man's name was Hakon the Wanker. Dyfed was aware that these two had had secretly exchanged communications already this morning with one other individual among the crew. This had been the ship's shaman, Svein Haraldsson. Under these circumstances this tete a tete alarmed Dyfed now. Leaving Leda to howl on and pushing past the crew minding their morning duties, Dyfed approached Eirik and the giant. Decidedly, Eirik was himself a distinctive looking man with a strong and lithe build who had dirty bond hair and one good eye the same colour as the frothing green sea. The other eye, the left one, was white and unseeing. Most prominent about his bearded face though, with its rugged and ruddy complexion, was the thick welt of a scar that ran from his left temple, across his white blind left eye that then ran down to cleave the left flare of his left nostril, and possibly even across from his upper lip to his lower, although the wicked welt had long since haired over and his mustachios concealed any wound there. It was a humdinger of a scar, and there could be no quarrel about that. Since this was the only prominent scar on his head and face, Dyfed surmised that in some axe fight from long ago he had just managed to dodge coming in second. That prize went instead to his now dead combatant opponent. This dangerous looking scar had in fact become a tribute to him and in turn made Eirik look as dangerous as he really was when it came to battles where the combatants wielded axes and broad swords in the immediate direction of each other. Dyfed had ribbed him a little about that and took to calling him Eirik Firstplace. In retrospect, Dyfed had thought the man may have misunderstood and had wondered if Dyfed called him that why the giant had been made first mate instead of him. But Dyfed had wanted he and Eirik to be on a fairly equal status aboard ship that he thought would encourage the man and help to encourage the crew as well. And the rather unfriendly giant certainly looked to Eirik, not Dyfed, for guidance and orders no matter how impressed they all were with Dyfed and his magical instruments.'

'As he approached Eirik, the latter stepped toward him and began to deliver a cautionary dialogue about the dangers for continuing along this westerly route. Instead, he encouraged Dyfed as commander to halt their progress and immediately make in an easterly direction back toward the Island of Ice or even the friendly Faeroes.'

"Today is a new morning,' Eirik said, 'and the time has come to halt and to return from whence we came before we become helplessly lost to the sea.' But rather than complying Dyfed answered instead.

"There must be peoples hereabouts with whom we can initiate trade,' baiting the Norseman who had remained strangely silent regarding any details about his earlier voyage and of the peoples they had discovered. 'So, we will continue,' he had told him adamantly, clapping his hands and thereby calling the attention of the rowers to his will and command. Then the latter that were working the oars in the brisk wind and were more likely just keeping themselves warm from the chilly air while they facilitated the progress of the *Aura Maré II* through the rising seas suddenly dropped their ores. Dyfed announced to them that they would continue until they discovered peoples of the new world where they would be able to stock up on provisions, so row on MacNordics. But Eirik soon became agitated.'

"You are a fool,' he had said in an attempt to appease the crew that now regarded Dyfed with menacing eyes. But Dyfed told them that they can get water from the floating islands of ice upon which rain water has frozen and that they had more than enough cured fish to stave off hunger for almost three weeks if they ate sparingly. Even without procuring food this would allow them to be able to return at least as far as Iceland. 'We must turn back,' said Eirik. 'What do you say men? The crew that had been oddly silent now murmured their approval to Eirik, the man who they looked to as their natural and even lawful leader.'

'It was true that Dyfed was the captain and owner of the vessel and something of a pilot, even a miraculous one, at that. And they had all gaped at the detail of his approach to commanding the natural forces around them and in taking on the mysteries such as being able to globally position the *Aura Maré II* to some theoretical spot on the high seas upon his map in progress. And they marvelled at the mechanisms that he artfully employed to do this, along with a great amount of finesse and proficiency, all of which was somewhat beyond their comprehension. But for them a glance at the sky and the condition of the water told each one of them as much, they thought. Never mind that, for every one of the northern seadogs aboard were all experienced, lodestone toting and consulting mariners. So seeking a consensus on the situation at hand, one of the sailors of higher rank, a man with large hands and intelligent eyes that were set in a small head, called out over his shoulder.'

"Camphaug says to retreat from these dangerous waters,' he called out as his voice, caught by the wind, was ripped from his mouth so only a few heard him speak. But it didn't fail in the endeavour to communicate to the others as it rushed quickly in a jumble of sounds over and past the ears of the crewmen.'

'There was probably a few reasons why Eirik commanded respect from his fellow Norsemen. Besides his impressive battle scar that he wore proudly as a badge of honour, and his tumultuous on and off affiliation with Olaf Gothfrithson — the feared king of the Emerald Isle stationed in Dublin, and sometimes king of Jorvik in the Dane quarter of Albion — Eirik commanded respect because of the sword he owned and wore with pride. It was a broad sword and on the letters read: +ULFBERH+T. And Eirik's sword was a weapon well used and therefore it was one of Ebreo's genuine models. Dyfed himself owned one and now had been forced to wear it constantly on account of Eirik who wore his as a symbol or seal of authority and denotation of class. Of course, like anything of value these swords may be won and could even be stolen. But even then only the most alpha of males among the ranks of soldiers — usually the king — managed to successfully covet the likes of an Ulfberht as no others can. This was accomplished through their enforced right as king or leader to confiscate anything of value that is won on the battlefield or acquired as booty. And just any old scallywag would not brandish a sword of this calibre for very long anyway before it was taken from him over his dead body if necessary. The Ulfberht sword had what many considered to be unique and magical features. For one, most swords could not flex and bend like a wooden longbow or strike or be struck hard without snapping into two pieces. Yet, when shear and tensile stresses were applied to an Ulfberht, either by challenging its elastic potential through excessive bending as in the aforementioned example, or through a deformation by exerting torque, such as inordinately twisting the blade to free it from remaining embedded in an opponent's sturdy shield, say, the steel did not break. Not only that, but once the stress and strain caused by these deformations were removed, the Ulfberht sword, unlike any other weapon of the day, would immediately return to its former true and straight form. And it would do so time and time again within a wide elastic limit of distortion. This was magic in itself, at least that was what contemporary sword owners thought. To Dyfed it was just a well-manufactured tool. It had no other personal association to him. Some named their swords like Ex-calibre that had been the late Ambrosius' sword, for example. And there were others; Karl the Great's Joyeuse, and Durandal, the sword of the greatly romanticised protagonist Hruodlandus.'

'This was the thing about crucible steel. So, here now was a sword which if stuck deep into an opponent's shield, or his femur, one could simply pry it free by twisting and flexing it without fear of breakage or damage by having it being bent all out of shape thereby rendering it useless to the operator. And on top of that, the sword's tough and versatile blade kept its sharp cutting edge through it all. Many a battlefield until Ebreo and the Ulfberht came along had been a comedy of errors (and horrors) whose close had come more by a melee of uselessly bent, twisted and broken and dulled swords discarded all over the place that left the combatants unarmed. This obviously impeded the soldiers' ability and brought on waves of distraction that ended in tears of frustration that called more for hugs and manly reassurance on both sides.'

'Eirik Camphaug the Norlander from Norseland, the owner of the only other Ulfberht aboard ship whose oath of subservience had been made to Dyfed his master, and who had thus far in his duties acted correctly — now suddenly changed tactics. He decided, apparently, to try his hand at mutiny. Standing stark still this tall Norse leader gazed coldly with his one eye at Dyfed who having picked his way aft along the deck came face to face with him. Suddenly the sun's rays shot out across the ocean as the Earth Star peeped over the terrestrial brim and the wind caught Eirik's long dirty blond hair and lashed it about his neck. The Norseman quickly looked around him and Dyfed noticed that the man's single angry grey-green eye that matched the cold filtered, ice-tossing sea saw everything he needed to that was around him at that moment. Eirik's other eye was like a ball of crystalized ice in his head. The smile that he flashed suddenly was sardonic and defiant as he now turned and regarded Dyfed, the lone Albion from Prydain who towering over the other men blocked his way forward toward the sailors and rowers. Dyfed was standing beneath a canopy of reindeer hides that sheltered the entire stern section and a third of the vessel. Dyfed and Eirik slowly exchanged positions and the sailors began to move aft and gather behind Eirik. Dyfed faced Eirik and the remaining crew looking down the ship to the prow while behind him, to one side, stood the menacing giant who gripped the rudder with giant shoulder blade sized hands. Littered all around them were the belongings of the men; their bedding and cooking utensils, an array of tools and Dyfed's own large sea chest containing his instruments, manuscripts and his on-going attempts to chart the voyage in sketchy maps, and other books and keepsakes he had brought along. In addition to these items that were scattered around the deck, were the now empty coops and other small cages where chickens, geese, piglets and other animals had been stowed before they'd been eaten, as well as boxes and sacks which had contained dried vegetables and fruits and vases for oil. Hanging from the frame that supported the canopy made of animal skins were the hourglasses, bowls, baskets, a couple of large seal oil lamps, weighted strings of bells and feathers, fair weather knots and other articles of Norse superstition. They all swung slowly back and forth and spun around and about just at Dyfed's shoulder level as the vessel heaved to and fro in the sea troughs or suddenly listed as the large sail caught the wind.'

'Dyfed sniffed that wind now, as it blew his golden blondish hair out from his head and whipped the ends while with his silver eyes he surveyed Eirik. The hanging and swaying articles were in the way of an assailant's striking path, and Dyfed used this to his advantage. The seventeen other men who had remained behind Erik now closed rank partially under the hide canopy where they were handier to close in on him. But they all remained behind the sailor with the intelligent eyes who stood directly behind Eirik. This sailor was Svein Haraldsson, and he wasn't just a sailor per sé, he was a Nordic shaman. It turned out that he was in the pay of Erling Pettykongerekke. As a contender vying for power among the kingdoms in the Norseland, Erling Pettykongerekke wanted information about the new world. This expedition was as much his, this political contender had thought, and he had seen to it that Svein Haraldsson was placed on board the Aura Maré II. It was the opening days of the North Sea Empire that was to eventually bring Albion, Norseland, Daneland and parts of Sweden together and for a while it was brought under one king, Knut the Great.'

'Swinging close to Dyfed's head, and partially blocking his view of the tiller man who stood back behind him to his left, was a full wrack of smoked fish that made three passes across the ships aft beam. In preparation for their primary and most important meal, breakfast, a small charcoal fire burned that was positioned between Dyfed, Leda his Rottweiler, and the motley crew that had now bunched up behind Svein Haraldsson and Eirik Camphaug. Then as the wind suddenly wafted the blackish smoke across the littered deck, Dyfed made his move. In a flash his own Ulfberht sword was out of its sheaf and in his right hand and while gripping the swinging wrack of fish with his left hand he swung his blade and cut the bundle loose. As it started to topple to the deck Dyfed began to jerk it back to yard it out over toward the stern where the dried fish would plunge back into the cold sea. At that moment Hakon, the giant first mate at the helm, let go of the tiller and plunged himself forward a step. He then erred in his decision to try and do two things at once; first to grab the last of the ship's viands with his right hand before they went over the side, and to strike down Dyfed with a blow from his broad axe that he wielded in his left. His mistake cost him his life as the axe only glanced off Dyfed's gloved left forearm and fist that caused bleeding wound. Dyfed, whose feet had not moved, was twisted slightly to his left as he had first pulled then pushed the weight of as much of the fish rack in the direction of overboard as he could. As the giant lunged and swung his axe, and as Leda in guard duty suddenly snarled and lunged forward at the giant's left arm, Dyfed quickly recovered from the strike. Uncoiling to the right with a swooping backhand motion, he delivered at lightening speed an upward cut that caught the man under his right arm that was raised to shoulder level and sliced up through the man's body just under his ball and socket joint that almost took off his right arm. Then wrenching his Ulfberht free with a twist, followed by a windmill motion, he brought his sword around in a wide swoop back down onto the left side of Hakon's neck cutting his jugular and throat through to the giant man's spine. As Hakon the Wanker immediately plummeted, falling directly beneath his own weight, Dyfed twisted his sword loose. The ship, the men, and even the dog took on becoming strange and eerie elements of an unreal atmosphere on deck as they tossed and bobbed about in sudden silence on a heaving and rising sea beyond sight of land.'

'Suddenly the present was like a collection of different moments compiled together in a hodgepodge fashion that was being unleashed in slow motion. Then Dyfed's dog Leda snapped out a shrill yet questioning bark that seemed to say, 'there, is it all settled now.' Dark red liquid more precious than gold quietly spurted out from the giant's throat onto the ship's aft deck until his heart stopped beating a minute or so later. The giant in his attempt to snatch hold of the fish wrack and cleave Dyfed's head in two, or cut off an arm with his broad axe, had startled Eirik who had almost been standing in the way and the quick ensuing fracas had set him off balance. Dyfed now glanced at Eirik who apart from having moved a leg and foot to one side had not moved since, and neither had Svein Haraldsson.'

"You are a fool,' the Norseman said in alarm. 'Our crew is now reduced to nineteen and now it will dwindle still to nothing on account of starvation until you alone are left languishing here with parched pallet and shrunken innards upon this windblown deck'

"Or murdered first by mutineers?' Dyfed answered questioningly. Then the wind caught the other man's deep throaty laugh that was immediately torn from his lips.

"You haven't a chance,' Eirik said. 'Put down your weapon for you are outnumbered, and the sea outnumbers us all.'

"We will continue west to a new land,' Dyfed replied immediately, now looking past Eirik to address and convince the other men and take advantage of Eirik's recent weak performance to take command. 'We will continue to where dwells the ancient brethren of another race of humans.' He turned back to the Norse leader. 'You cannot revoke my destiny, Eirik Camphaug, or you either Svein Haraldsson, for you are now part of it. Let this be an end to your mutiny and I will put it behind me, too. You cannot kill me for I come from the other world. What are you blind, man? Can you not see? he said tantalisingly. Threaten my life or my will again and I will kill you all. And I promise you that you will not dine with me afterwards, either, at least not in the hall of Valhalla you won't.'

'Having said that, Dyfed smiled at Eirik and let his eyes turn and sweep over the other Norsemen. He noticed then the flutter of fear that gripped them as each of the men contemplated — perhaps in some way for the first time — a new and frightening image of this tall, mysterious Albionian with the strange silver eyes. Was he, perhaps, the real spirit of Odin (he thought they might be wondering) or just his avatar? In any case he was adept and ruthless. Then as soon as his eyes came to rest into the gaze of Svein Haraldsson, the shaman suddenly screeched out some cry or another in his own attempt to trump Dyfed's bold and successful move to cast a psychological net over them all. At the same time the man (used to the practice of theatrics) adopted a certain pose that was meant to resemble some kind of incubus: Or maybe it resembled a troll now screeching or a vampire reacting to the early morning sun rays that were streaking across the top of the green sea, catching him out…exposed and indefensible as he had now become. Dyfed may not have fully succeeded in his attempt to shock and awe Svein, he thought, but Svein on his part was quite sure Dyfed had succeeded in shocking and awing the remainder of the crew all to hell, including Eirik. And the latter had still not moved a muscle and could not take his eyes off Dyfed, either, he noted. It was somewhat obvious too that the remainder of the crew all thought that Dyfed had the powers of a magician. Possibly, even Svein might be thinking that Dyfed, who towered above him, had powers more potent than his own. And with those strange silver eyes of his and the wide-brimmed felt hat that he wore strapped to his head with a leather thong around his chin and his remnant of the old fashioned Amoran over-his-shoulder mantle that fluttered briskly in the rough and restless morning wind, he certainly resembled none other than Odin himself. Immediately reading their thoughts as best he could, Dyfed then produced a small silver box from his clothing. He then shouted out loud, 'where the hell are you Manandan, damn it all to hell.' But he hollered these words in Shamskar, a tongue he knew nobody else here knew. He then let out a thick and hearty laugh. Then holding the ornate silver object in front of him so that all could see, he proceeded to flick the lid. It made a 'pop' (another rebus) sound as it opened. The tiny container was filled with a black powder he had purchased from an eastern caravan that had come into Amor many years ago during the empire. A tiny mechanism inside the box was immediately activated with the motion of the lifting of the lid that caused a struck flint to send a spark into the black powder. Dyfed had practiced the movements many times and just as the lid opened, he flung his arm up…and a sharp explosion emanated that showered bright, phosphorous sparks into the air followed by a heavily scented cloud of white smoke that was quickly caught by the wind and blew with a swirl of deep acrid scent across the deck and into the nostrils of the crew. Psychologically cowering in a unanimous fear the men became riveted to the deck with wide eyes that were fixed on Dyfed. Got'cha, Svein, Dyfed thought to himself. Better that one if you can, you lutefisk[65] feasting flat faced Laplander. At this point Svein even thought to himself that considering Dyfed's brand of magic (all 'round magic at that) that he might also have the talents of Loki.'

"Gather some of the ship's carpentry scrap materials and fashion a raft to float the giant Hakon the Wanker Snorrisen and attach it by a rope to the stern of the Aura Maré II. Then pile more wood scraps and disposables on top of Hakon the Wanker and light the raft on fire,' commanded Eiric, speaking at last. 'We will have a pyre for Snorrisen. You, Olaf, take the helm and set us a southerly west course.'

'No sooner had Hakon the Wanker Snorrisen's body, first blazing and fiery then smouldering like a smudge pot, been reduced to glowing ashes astern on his pyre, when

---

65 Lutefisk is usually cod, ling or burbot that is soaked in a preparation of cold water and lye before eating.

the men settled down from their earlier anxiety. A lean, raw-boned youth with reddish hair had been appointed by Olaf to step up and man the stern rudder.'

"Take up your duties men,' said Dyfed, 'and as for you Svein Haraldsson, this is my adventure, my ship and my enterprise. And it is my denarii that pays your way here, not Erling Pettykongerekke's. So from now on unless you want the attention Hakon is getting being hauled half a boat's length astern in a smouldering heap, do not cross me or disobey any of my orders'

'Just about an hour before the *Aura Maré II's* bows were about to over-run the sunset, and when all the while Hakon the Wanker Snorrisen's smouldering ashes were still being hauled astern, the pile of the dead giant's remains at the end of the day suddenly slid off the smouldering pyre board and scattered forth — bobbing up and down — on the surface of the sea. Almost at that same moment in the northern twilight land was sighted over the starboard (right) bulwark and the sailors went ashore. Though it was now quite late, according to Dyfed's chronological devices they were near the sixtieth parallel north and a little further west of the Emerald Isle than the Emerald Isle was west of the Land of Khem. Here the direct sunshine shone late into the evening and accompanying the lightened sky was a beautiful twilight upon the Earth that left the land features quite visible. They remained here for a few days. The coast here was quite rugged and although the weather turned warm, pack-ice drifted along the shore.'

'It's been said that like the woollen kilts, the bagpipes were left over from the Amorans who loved to play them. Suetonius said that Emperor Miro played them, though he was probably dressed in a comfortable loose fitting Tyrain purple toga and not a woollen kilt. But, hell, even the ancient Hittites played the bagpipes, and who knows what they wore to hide their private parts? Anybody who was anybody played the pipes, that much everybody knew for sure; and that's all there is to it! The pipes were an Aryan-Indo-Europaean culture touchstone that permeated the likes of all the Kelts, Pixies, and northern Goths as well. Pipes were the reason why these folks were all hot to trot to gather wind to squeeze out into some rudimentary tune; and though to some it sounded like loud irritating flatulence, to others it was music to their ears. So these Norse sailors who here under a bright northern sky with a faded Aurora Borealis flickering in a slippery-slide-show of sepia green and blanched red colouring that danced and slithered across the pale night sky, Dyfed waited patiently as his companions huffed and they puffed and blew their pipes from the deck of the *Aura Maré II* to the tippy-top of the bleak headlands ashore.'

(Norse West Passage to the New World)

> *'Let the wind blow high, let the wind blow low… across the waves in our kilts we go…and the Shawnamunks and B'otuks all say… Hallo!…Olaf…where's your trousers?'*
>
> **ANDY STEWART** (*APOLOGIES FOR THE AUTHOR'S VARIANT THEREOF*)

'While they went about collecting provisions from this land, the men from the Aura Maré came across some nomads who were hunting the summer seal, the skins of which they used as apparel to cover their bodies. They were a small friendly people who called themselves Inuit, and Dyfed noticed that they did resemble the Skraellingar who they had come upon weeks before on the coastal ice to the northeast. Like the Skraellingar they ate raw fish and whale fat and travelled together in small but efficient family bands. Their language was unintelligible to the Europaeans but like communication among all men they quickly grasped each other's meanings. One of the men who called himself Avit told Dyfed, who had enquired after the red men, that such a tribe of men lived on an island far to the south but that they were unfriendly and that it would be better to seek out the Shawnamunks first to act as peace makers.

Dyfed, Eirik and the remaining crew of the *Aura Maré* continued to sail south along the coast until they entered a strait that led south to west. Seeing a large camp that overlooked the mouth of the strait from atop the north bank, the crew anchored the vessel a little way off shore and watched cautiously as a few of the camps inhabitants paddled out to them in flimsy short canoes. Dyfed soon discovered that these were the Shawnamunks and although the Albionian had nothing much to trade he gave them an axe and a cheap sword in exchange for their hospitality. The chief of this branch of the Shawnamunks was very friendly but he adamantly disagreed with the Inuit who had told Dyfed that the red men were unfriendly and not to be trusted. The Red Men (or B'otuks, as he called them) were a highly advanced people who lived just across the strait on the island called the Land of Abundant Codfish. Many generations ago, he told Dyfed, the B'otuks had inhabited the area all around long before other tribes had arrived who had been drawn to the area as they themselves had been, to benefit from the B'otuk skills. Some of these people, however, like the Shonacks who lived further to the south were warlike and jealous of the B'otuks and the chief cautioned Dyfed to stay clear of them. However, the Alnanbai, another tribe to the south, were friendly and would be interested in trade, if that is why the white men had come.'

'The Shawnamunk leader then presented a woman who Dyfed took to be the chief's wife. She was startlingly beautiful and Dyfed was amazed at how light her skin was compared to the other Shawnamunks, or the Inuit who had different features still and were much darker. The chief told him that the woman was a B'otuk princess, and her easy manner and obvious position of high rank within the Shawnamunk tribe indicated to Dyfed that these people were on an easy tenure with the famous red men. But why was she white, not red? The chief discerned Dyfed's confusion and explained that the woman was now Shawnamunk and that it was not the Shawnamunk custom to be red.

Indeed, it was forbidden by the B'otuks for others to imitate them and was considered a great insult for which retribution often followed. Instantly, Dyfed understood. The B'otuks (the red men) were in fact white much like himself, although darker than the Norsemen who tended to be quite white. So these folks, called the B'otuks, practised the ancient art of body painting just as Dyfed's own ancestors had done in the mysterious past. Furthermore, he also was to find out that like the early peoples of Albion, the B'otuks dyed their skin red with bright ochre.'

(B'otuks Beware)

'Fear is the main source of superstition and cruelty.
To conquer fear is the beginning of wisdom.'
BERTRAND RUSSELL

'Upon their arrival to this western settlement Dyfed and his crew had been obliged to remain with the Shawnamuncks for some time, presumably while the chief enquired after the white man's reason for arriving upon their land and specifically in the manner in which that took place. He showed a huge interest in their sea-going vessel the Aura Maré II. As well, it provided the chief with time to send emissaries to warn the B'otuks of his approach. During his pleasant stay, Dyfed examined their customs through simple observance. And with the help of the B'otuk princess who dwelt there among the Shawnamucks, and whose name meant Gentle Rain, he slowly pieced together a crude working knowledge of her language. For the most part the Shawnamunks were sparsely dressed for it was warm weather but Dyfed noticed that the apparel they had at hand were mostly shawls made from deer hide. The inhabitants were simple and far removed from the vice and shrewdness that characterises the people of the old world. Dyfed thoroughly enjoyed his visit which reminded him a little of when he first left the Isle of Peace and chanced upon Owen's Cenedl in Gwyneth. But Eirik and the crew, however, were sullen and bad tempered during their stay and animosity between them and the Shawnamuncks soon became obvious.'

'One day, about two or three months after the solstice, the chief came to Dyfed and told him to go. He pointed out to sea where he said they would find an island and from there they were to sail and row directly in the direction of the noon sun in order to reach the Land of the B'otuks. The island that the chief mentioned was flat with a low profile but approaching in its direction, and once spotted by Dyfed, he veered sharply to starboard and headed toward the spot on the southern horizon directly below the noonday sun. That having been done, Dyfed and the crew of the *Aura Maré II* continued across the strait for the rest of the day and throughout the night and the next morning they drew near to the Land of Abundant Codfish.

'Since Dyfed had been exposed to the process of transcendental time manipulation through the genius of Mencius (also known as Mengzi), he had had about six hundred years now to remember that event, an event he often thought long and hard about. So it now occurred to him that he had proceeded here to this new found land that the B'otuks inhabited which is an island called the Land of Abundant Codfish; and that it would be along much the same sea lanes that he had just taken to get here that the Italian discoverer John Cabot (also Zuan Chabotto or Giovanni Caboto) would follow (while sailing for discovery for a new king of Angleland named Henry) in order to discover, and be the first Europaean in the Age of Discovery to set foot on the terra firma of the New World of Merika's northern continent (for that matter, either northern or the southern continent). That event would take place in the year 2273 (calculated also when divided by 4) according to the first Olympiad (one every four years thereafter); or 1497CE (see folio #70). And that, he quickly calculated, would be in about five and a half centuries from now.'

'Dyfed peered anxiously over the starboard bow bulwark toward the land that was now quite close. They had been slowly gliding past a rocky shore for two days and had seen no signs of humans though the place teemed with life of every other kind; cod, salmon, otter, deer, fox, caribou, lynx, bear, gulls, ravens, black hawks, ospreys, eagles and an array of water fowl including swans, geese and a huge flightless bird which the Norse called an auk (a flightless alcid of the genus Pinguinus). Dyfed had never seen such a bird.'

'But apart from fish and game no people were seen. They followed the coast for a few more days, the sailors bending the oars to keep them off the beach and away from shoals. Then they oared and sailed east to a group of islands where they found a small flock of auks, one of which Dyfed shot to provide for the crew's galley. Seeing that, the North men of Norland offered prayers to the holy might of thundering Thor who had, apparently, either indulged mortal man merely by being on hand or through this avatar of (W) Odin who had shot the thing. Upon investigation, Dyfed found only a few bird's nests and believing the creature to be threatened by extinction (similar to its' situation in Norland), issued orders that forbid any members of the crew from hunting the auk ever again.'

'They continued to sail aimlessly south, for Eirik, obviously, did not know his position in relation to the coast any more than Dyfed. Apparently, Dyfed now learned, on Eirik's once only previous visit he had not arrived here by choice at all but rather had been blown upon these shores by an easterly gale whipping up the sea while attempting to voyage east from Greenland back to the Faeroes from the western land of the Skraelingar. However, in time Dyfed and his companions came to a beautiful coast of islands, rivers and inland lakes. Here the shoreline was so dotted with islands and inlets that the experienced Norse crew grew wary of a sudden attack by the Red Men who they thought maybe waiting in ambush. With eyes and ears strained, Dyfed continued to look over the starboard bow at the unfolding land around him. It was the season of the salmon run and the swirling water beneath the *Aura Maré* II was a heaving, darting silver kaleidoscope mass of fish in the millions swarming around each river mouth that they passed. Above them, in the tree tops, eagles waited patiently, black hawks squawked and ravens chortled while the oarsmen pulled the *Aura Maré* II silently along with the sailors' each pair of eyes (with the exception of Eirik Camphaug) peeled for any sight of danger and with their axes at the ready.'

'Soon the bank pulled away from them and they rowed into an inlet. Looking down toward the end of the broad estuary Dyfed noticed that a waterfall leapt down from a crag and into the trees while below it a sandy beach reclined in the late summer sun beneath shady trees. By the beach a stream tumbled around large boulders and under fallen tree trunks as it rushed from an unseen pool beneath the falls to the sea. As the day was hot and there was no wind it looked to Dyfed like a good place to camp and give respite to the crew who were still pulling the vessel along with their long ores. Eirik leaned over the side and searched the inlet with his trained eye, but it was Dyfed who first spotted the ochre stained canoe buried among the foliage close to the mouth of the stream. With a quick motion of his hand Eirik signalled the crew and the ores dipped without a sound into the shallow inlet waters. As the bow of the *Aura Maré* II glided quietly onto the beach the men silently waded ashore with weapons drawn and Dyfed approached the canoe by skirting inside the trees that lined the beach. With him he carried his bow with a quiver of arrows slung by his side.'

'The birch bark canoe was laying slightly to one side and as he came up to it Dyfed saw that it was in poor condition and that the deer hide that was used to sew the bark together was coming apart. Inside the light craft beside two old paddles was a rudely constructed bow and some arrows that needed re-fletching and Dyfed thought for a moment that they were nothing more than old abandoned equipment left by some previous passer-by. Then he heard a shrill shout. A short distance away the waterfall splashed down into a pool with considerable noise and as he listened again he heard the sound of a youngster's voice come through the din of the falls that was followed by another young voice. Gingerly Dyfed made his way through the forest in the direction that the voices had come and soon came to a point where he could clearly see the stream and pool. There he saw two young deeply tanned white skinned boys who were completely naked. They were both pre-puberty and their faces looked almost pale against the shock of their black head of hair and dark eyebrows compared to the Shawnamuck boys of the same age. They had been catching the salmon that were jumping up into the falls, but like all youngsters their age, after a morning of work they had found their task tedious and by the early afternoon had taken up swimming and playing in the pool.'

'One of the boys came toward Dyfed from around the rocky pool and stooping down picked up a willow sapling by its root. Dyfed saw that the sapling was solidly packed with salmon. Inverting the twig the boy had taken each fish and thrust the sapling's root through one gill and out the fish's mouth. When the little tree had become laden with salmon, the branches at the other end (which had been left untrimmed) prevented the fish from slipping off onto the ground. The second boy, whose head, meanwhile, had been bobbing on the surface of the water, then came splashing out of the cold pool and Dyfed listened to their jubilant and excitable voices as they chattered back and forth. The one boy continued to examine the fish as the other looked around him while holding his hands up to his shivering mouth. The boys reminded Dyfed of himself when he had been that age playing on the beach on the Isle of Peace, and he could tell by the way they talked to each other that they were close and bonded friends as humans of this age are. And should be. Dyfed Lucifer could have remained in close proximity to the children without detection but he intentionally moved. Immediately he was seen by one of the boys who dropped one arm that swung and slapped the other on the elbow. As the two boys stared at him Dyfed turned and walked back toward their canoe. Now he understood why the canoe was in a dilapidated condition, it was the youngsters' canoe. Dyfed then un-strapped a knife and sheath he was carrying and laid it in the bark vessel beside the paddles and returned to Eirik and the crew who were waiting up the beach. After awhile they saw two young faces peer at them from over the lip of the canoe. Suddenly the boys jumped up and while one hauled the light birch bark craft toward the water's edge the other dragged the two seedlings loaded with salmon. Casting furtive glances in their direction, the boys quickly threw the two saplings loaded with fish into the canoe and rapidly paddled away toward the far side of the inlet. That night none of the Norsemen slept and although the air was warm a large fire was kept ablaze. With the fire close at hand it was difficult to see beyond into the dark night but Dyfed felt a presence and knew that they were being watched by the illusive Red Men. Early the next morning they came. Standing by the water's edge Dyfed counted fifty large canoes as they came from across the inlet, each stained red and with five men to a canoe. The men, too, were also stained red, as were their bows. Just before they got too close to the Europaean party they split into two fleets comprised of twenty-five vessels each and landed on the sandy beach on each side of the *Aura Maré* II. Then while one group stayed by their canoes the others walked toward them. As they got closer the main group halted and only five men continued to approach.'

'Dyfed intently watched the man leading the party. He thought that he looked quite a sight, and one who would have caused a stir at home among the Angle-Saxen and even the unruly Norlanders had he landed on their shores. He was completely naked, apart from his bow that he held in his left hand and a bunch of arrows that he clutched in the other. And along with the others with him he was dyed red. Only his hair was natural, Dyfed thought, as he gazed at the man's thick black mop that was bedecked with three large eagle feathers and some seashells that were also stained red. As strange as this man looked to the Europaeans, who fidgeted with their weapons, Dyfed quickly noticed the man's profound countenance and his alert eyes. Other notable features about him was his prominent nose beneath a noble brow.'

'Facing the man as he approached, Dyfed put his palms together in prayer fashion and bowing his head slightly spoke a B'otuk word of greeting. The man stopped in front of Dyfed and after making a sound like a bird he knelt briefly, placing the fists of both his hands (which continued to hold the bow and arrows) firmly onto the ground before standing upright again. He was a tall man, almost as tall as Dyfed and exceptionally muscular. Dyfed smiled and tried out a few words of B'otuk that translated roughly to 'take me to your king.' The tall chief smiled and then speaking rapidly shot a quick glance around while the four men who had kept close behind him laughed in a good natured manner.'

"Our king is busy,' he said. 'Can you come back much later?' It was Dyfed's turn to smile and his silver eyes gazed into the dark watchful eyes of the other.'

"Tell him an ancient brethren has journeyed across a vast ocean (Dyfed made a swooping motion with his arm out toward the sea) and that he wishes to pay his respects before continuing on.' The Red Man said something that Dyfed did not understand and the other red men laughed again. The tall chief then made a motion with his hand that first indicated the *Aura Maré* and then the direction toward the distant side of the inlet from whence the red men had paddled. Dyfed understood and asked the tall chief to accompany him in the *Aura Maré* II.'

'As Dyfed's slight, sleek but sea-worthy craft, accompanied by the fifty red canoes, rounded a point and entered a beautiful fjord, the tall chief, whose name translated to Stone Deer, shouted a command to his men. Suddenly two canoes shot ahead and Dyfed and the Norsemen marvelled at their speed. Even with the strong Norse crew pulling at the ores and with a favourable wind billowing out the sail, their ship was not able to keep up with the chief's vanguard that made a beeline for a smudge of smoke in the distance. It was not until they entered a cove that Dyfed saw their camp, or *mamatek* as it was called in the B'otuk language, nestled haphazardly along the shore. Everywhere, racks of salmon were drying in the hot sun or being cured by the smoke of numerous fires. This was not a permanent camp, Dyfed realized, but a summer fish camp and he doubted if their king would be present at this place. Dyfed and the Norsemen remained at this mamatek until chill autumn had begun to turn the leaves red. During that time

Dyfed occupied himself with learning the language and customs of the red men. He also noted that while Eirik looked longingly out to sea the other sailors dallied with the pretty young women who toiled around the camp and he became worried that the B'otuks would become incensed over this attention. However, the red men did not appear to become angry over the Norse behaviour and neither the tall chief called Stone Deer nor any of the other B'otuk men brought the matter up to Dyfed.'

'When the salmon run was over they broke camp. Large cargo canoes were filled with the dried fish as well as makeshift shelters of dyed caribou and deer skins: the *Aura Maré* hoisted sail once again, the Norse bent their oars, and the entire armada journeyed out of the fjord and south along the coast. After a week they came to a city, or chief mamatek, comprised of wooden buildings (painted red of course) set upon the gently sloping banks on either side of a brisk stream. Dyfed counted about a hundred structures but his vision was partly obscured by the cloud of thick blue smoke that rose into the air above the settlement and drifted out to sea. The small watercourse supplied the city with all its' water needs by rushing directly through the middle of the city. It had many short bridges spanning it. Where the stream flowed through the urban portion of this busy mamatek, it was hemmed in and channelled by a breakwater of large stones that defined its course. As the stream reached its mouth, it flowed through a large covered wooden building built around and over it where many canoes were kept. From here it emptied directly into the inlet.

'As Dyfed and Stone Deer came ashore a regal and distinguished looking man approached them from a large and ornate building that was positioned at the head of the small B'otuk city. This chieftain's body was painted red and his hair was grey. But instead of the ever-present bow that all the men carried he held a large staff in his hand that was carved into the shape of a serpent. The man also wore a shawl of red caribou skin that was draped over his shoulders and the polished black hoofs of the animal that were inlaid with colourful stones and bells dangled and jingled about the man's ankles. Dyfed noticed immediately that although many of the painted bodies of the villagers were naked, a number of them, especially the elderly, were clothed much the same way as the king was. This too was similar to the way he had seen the Shawnamunks dress. The fashion here was to have the flattened out and tanned skin of the caribou (in some cases a deer) head draped onto one's chest while the remainder of the animal skin covered the body like a cape or gown. The leg skin was always left intact and the hoofs provided some weight to the mantle so the garment would drape properly and not easily fly up in a wind. There were also bangles and heavy bracelets wrapped around the lower legs just above the hoofs that helped hold the mantle securely on the wearer's shoulders. The children and youths were not clothed and some of them were not painted. Sometimes the red ochre was washed away due to swimming or the rain. This enforced Dyfed's observation of how light skinned these people really were. In fact, they were no darker than he was and the adults were exceptionally handsome.'

'Dyfed greeted the B'otuk high chieftain in much the same manner as he had the tall chief Stone Deer, and showed him great respect while taking steps not to diminish his own person and appearance in the eyes of the great chief. Although reluctant, the Norlanders bowed in a subservient style as Dyfed had asked them to. This was to be enacted, Dyfed told Eirik, in order to give a good impression and nothing more, for Dyfed secretly admired the North men as well, despite all their domestic trouble for him so far, and thought they were folks who need not bow to any man. Indeed, he now contemplated, they may be useful as associated *pack* members.'

'Like Stone Deer, the supreme chief whose name was Weithidic, was tall and exceedingly noble looking.'

"My sister's son,' said the man, indicating Stone Deer, 'has sent word to me that you are an ancient brethren who is on a long journey, but has taken time out of politeness to me to stop here briefly in order that we become re acquainted.'

'Dyfed noted the charming smile and the man's dark alert eyes that sized up both him and his companions in a glance. The B'otuks had from the start showed an interest in the utensils and weapons as well as the clothes that their fellow white men from across the ocean wore, so Dyfed had Eirik present some of these items to Weithidic. The chief was also interested in Dyfed's scientific equipment and the Albionian quickly came to realize how knowledgeable the man was in respect to the affairs and movements in the night sky. There was something else which the old chief said that intrigued Dyfed. According to him neither the B'otuk princess or any of the Shawnamucks had in fact alerted him to their arrival in these lands. He knew of Dyfed's coming due to the fact that he frequently consulted an oracle that had for some months been foretelling the event. For some unknown reason this seemed quite logical to Dyfed because of something in the back of his mind that Manandan had taught him about the occurrence of mental and physical events that coalesce into a quasi genius with a friendly relation to any second dimensional substance that also can have cavitation affects from magnetic fields and electric potential differentials that under an array of conditions either acts to micro or macro its subtlety within the third dimension. Of course, he couldn't explain any of it, himself.'

'Shortly after their arrival to this chief mamatek of Weithidic's, which had a name that translated to Jellyfish Bay, great storms began to blow in from the south eastern regions of the Atlas Ocean that not only hampered the Autumn cod fishing that year, an important harvest for the B'otuks, but also prevented the *Aura Maré* II from being able to leave the shores of the Land of Abundant Codfish as had been scheduled. As the cold autumn descended, the B'otuks began to dress and by the time of the Equinox hunt, only the young and hardy remained unclothed. By this time Dyfed had deeply impressed Weithidic who had insisted that the Albionian, now a valued guest, take a young woman called Telquaejit (a pretty name meaning tender human) as a wife. This was meant as a great honour and as the youngster was very beautiful, Dyfed readily agreed.'

'The season's hunt commenced after a three day celebration feast which took place during the Equinox. This was the time when the B'otuk people gave thanks to the Great and Glorious Breath, the Splendid Spirit, the G'itchy Manitou, for what they had received from that Boundless-One during the first half of the year. It was also conducted in anticipation and faith for what the Omnipotent would bestow during the remaining months as well. To Dyfed the event was a solemnization that had a specific and valid practicability. Although in making ceremony in the way they did according to their custom, one that was quite unfamiliar to Dyfed, it was nevertheless in keeping with the Rites of Rhythm. And besides, Dyfed thought, with a an arduous journey safely completed as well as the recent endowment of a wife, he felt he had absorbed a great deal of the new unknown that now needed harmonizing and fine tuning in order to be properly assimilated into his Karma.'

'The celebration was a colourful ordeal of dancing and eating and during this jubilee these naturally frugal people sat before courses of dressed cormorants, partridge eggs, roasted bear, cured venison and seal and raw cod and salmon. But to the lone Albionian shaman, and the Lord of the Keltic Forest as well as being an adherent of other ancient rites, the most interesting aspect of the entire ceremony was the peculiar dances that Weithidic and the priests enacted that were reminiscent of those he remembered seeing his mother and Manandan performing when he was a child and later the movements of those adepts from Inja and the Land of Ch'in.'

'Dyfed had become truly aware of dance form after realizing its underlying importance that Morgant, Karatakos, and Kunobelin (Sun dog) had attached to such movements. From that time he had then paid close attention to subsequent interpretations by cult dancers throughout the White Sea areas that he had visited. Many of the people joined in as Weithidic and the magicians of Celestial Wisdom whirled frantically about to the sacred undulation which the musicians beat out with different sounding drums. These were made from animal hides, dyed red and stretched tightly over trunks of hollowed cottonwood. Dyfed, like all alert, sensitive and receptive people the world over, could flow with ease into union with Rhythm and its collective inspiration. He quickly jumped up, and to the astonishment of the Norse and even the B'otuks themselves, he gracefully began to accompany the dancers.'

(Red men, Spider Woman and the G'itchy Manitou called Parazoa)

> 'But natural foreclosures also take place thru other developments where climate fluctuations and changes are the greatest culprit. Surely it's the earth's complicated relationship with the sun (that rules over everything here) which has the first and the last word over that which affects our planet.'
>
> **PARASOLO**

'Dyfed was anxiously anticipating the coming hunt. The red B'otuk men wearing nothing more then bear skin mantles and moccasins of seal hide trekked into the forested interior of the Abundant Land of Codfish to hunt. Along with them, under guard, came the obligatory slaves. Apart from the occasional Alnanbai renegade that chanced to buzz too closely to the Red men's territory, mostly these slaves were from the hated Shonack tribe to the southwest on the Merikan continent. Dyfed personally accompanied Weithidic and Stone Deer who led the hunt and he became astonished at the B'otuk hunters dexterity. The men carried their bows that were rubbed with red ochre in their left hands, while their arrows that were also dyed red they clutched in the other. When they saw game they bent down on their right knee and placed the bow on their left foot. From this position, and using their right hand to draw the bowstring made of wolf or fox gut, they were able to release their arrows in quick succession. Dyfed, who by now in his own land had been once considered nimble and fairly proficient in this art appeared clumsy and slow compared to these children of the Old Forest, though he too held some surprises in store. But the method of hunting was what astonished the Albionian the most and awakened in him an emotion that was something akin to a far off voice calling, or a dream that was like some vague recollection just beyond his grasp. These men, he discovered hunted with their minds, or more precisely, certain disciplined thoughts that originated within their minds rather then aggressively tracking and hunting the animals down. This was done through accessing inner truths about themselves and once again utilized the aforementioned second dimensional genius that was capable to cross through the third density. It was for this reason that the hunters knew who they were and no other member of the mamatek could or would even consider accompanying the self-chosen hunters. It was their minds, their dreams that gave them hints of where to hunt and how to attract the animals they sought out with the use of certain magical songs and chants. And also specific animals within a species were sought, or actually called. And Dyfed learned that many of these animals had individual names. This specialty was accomplished, Dyfed learned, through identifying with the Great Spirit that is within oneself (as it is in all living things) although its domain is the entire cosmos and the Alpha Omega of Totality. This Great Being inside all men was what the B'otucs called Parazoa. It was also the spot on the horizon where the sun currently rose and was always in context to the three other spots or corners of the earth on adjacent horizons, Dyfed discovered.'

'There was, however, one other important aspect of this ritual which was conspicuous by its absence. The B'otuc did not employ sympathetic magic. What is meant here is that they did not net or spear a symbolic prey in the pre hunt ritual. Rather they dreamed, chanted and danced to become the spirit of the animal themselves. Dyfed had witnessed this during the equinoctial celebrations but he hadn't grasped its importance at the time. Sympathetic magic, the B'otucs believed, was considered blasphemous and could it destroy a man's dreams along with his soul.'

'Weithidic was very inquisitive and asked Dyfed many things about the civilization from which he had come. Was Dyfed a chief or a priest and why, Weithidic had wanted to know, were his fellow companions different from him in a strange way? Were they a subservient tribe of which Dyfed was in charge? What records, what stories (passed on by their people) had Dyfed's tribe kept which informed him and his generation of their place in the cosmos? He also wanted to know if tales survived in his land from the old western sea traders who once upon a time had contacted the Ongwano sionni, the People of the longhouse? Was it the Ongwano sionni who he really sought by coming here, not the B'otuks? And what about the Akochakanen? These latter, Dyfed learned were white men like him who long ago had mysteriously appeared amidst the Ongwano sionni nation from across the ocean. And the name Akochakanen was also the Ongwano sionni name for the B'otuks themselves. Were these strange people going to return again with many vessels filled with many more Akochakanen? About this, the oracle of theirs was silent, Weithidic said. But he also thought that the answer to that question would affect his tribe's future. On his part Dyfed wondered to himself if in fact the Akochakanen folks were contemporaneous to the Hyperborean folks, or were Hyperborean in nature. But Weithidic didn't know any more than he did about that. As for the story of the people from where he came and their place in the cosmos, Dyfed remained silent and the reminder of it disturbed him.'

'As for his companions, Dyfed told Weithidic that they were his expeditors. He was on a private mission and in a sense he was his fellow companions' benefactor, nothing more than that. He provided for them in return for them doing what he favoured and to expedite his will. Weithidic, however, could not understand the concept were a chief's will, never mind any man's will, could not be for the benefit of all the tribe or even a clan. What in kind did Dyfed provide them in order for these men to willingly take up another's spiritual image and slip outside the character of their own spiritual beneficiary? That's what he wanted to know.'

'Weithidic then spoke about the dark peoples which lived all around them and of their customs. There were the Alnanbai, who were intelligent and industrious, as well as the hated Shonack, the coveters, and the Ongwano sionni, a serene and ancient race who lived to the south and west. Also there were the Algonkin, who were Ojibwa, and further west the hardy Hatindia, while to the north were the Shawnamuncks who were their allies and further north still the Inuit. Of the latter, Weithidic said, that his people despised them. These, the chief said, were the darkest of all men and were uncivilized and filthy.'

"And who are the B'otuks,' Dyfed asked one evening as the two of them sat around a fire warming their feet? 'Who are the red men whose civilization is both coveted and praised by its peers here in the old world?' While the two men talked they ladled out a strong smelling liquid into their clay cups from a warm pot by the fire and relaxed, each slowly sipping the potent intoxicant. Weithidic was rolling something in the palm of his hand and while Dyfed asked Weithidic the question, the red man stuffed the substance from his hand into a hollow reddish clay tube. Dyfed watched him with rising curiosity. Suddenly the chief reached into the fire and pulled out a burning ember that he touched to the end of the pipe and puffed out a great billow of blue smoke. He did this a few times then gave the smouldering clay vessel to Dyfed motioning for him to follow suit. As he did that Dyfed regarded Weithidic who was watching him whimsically through the pungent cloud that floated around them. Then as Dyfed erupted into a sudden fit of coughing from the inhaled substance the chief began to talk again.'

"The words which B'otuk spoke are known by all here as 'the eclectic truths'," said Weithidic, 'and his teachings tell us that one day during the fourth manifestation, man will destroy himself through deceptions and irregularity and in his inability to bridge the state of dream and awake. Then the G'itchy Manitou will breathe a great breath of purification into the nostrils of the Spider Woman and under the sign of the Blue Star the white brothers to the ant clan will unite and usher in the dawn of the fifth world where harmony and collective atonement will reign. I see you, Dyfed, and your crew as forerunners of this state.'

"I know of your Spider Woman of which you speak,' said Dyfed. 'She is the immortal Aracne whose domain is also in the eternal Agarta. But what did B'otuk say on the subject of atonement?' asked Dyfed, inquisitively. 'And what fabric is it that can span the state of dream and the state of awake?'

"B'otuk,' Weithidic answered, 'once parablized it thus: 'If there were twenty five humans, each one believing that his or her path to righteousness is 'the' path which categorically differs and must differ from the others, then harmony between all twenty five persons will not occur, not now, nor at any time in the future. In fact,' Weithidic added, 'B'otuk himself said that historically the results show that such conditions are going to be disastrous for each one of the twenty-five. But if each of them labours to insure that their path resembles the others, which is to say a manner of forming common atonement, then the practicability of humanity will be more in accord and it's functions will become less abrasive with fewer opposite effects. Finally, that which will arise will be stable and cohesive. But stability and cohesiveness is maintained by extrication, not through coercion and compulsion. This is the simple but great secret,' said the chief, 'for behind love and all of which that word implies is the G'itchy Manitou called Parazoa. In this state everything can be in tune, and if it is orchestrated by ultimate profundity (which is aggregate yet absolute simplicity) it will breathe or manifest as a comprised singularity. This is the fifth world.'

'It is like that great life force, the ant, which man resembles. For the 'ant' is really its' sum which is the assemblage of millions of procreative entities or cells that is the life blood that moves freely without an exterior organ of skin, for which it has no need. For even without that encompassing organ it can move across the land and cause and divert effect. It consumes and provides and although it can reform and mass into a great living trunk for communion and warmth, or a limb for communal sustenance, its' functions remain dependant on the individuality of each separate unite, cell, body, that acts as tentacles, as vessels that relays in relevance to the colony. This skinless conveyance, this harmonious capacity then crawls forth to cause and effect. Certainly there is seldom strife between the bee and the ant and they constitute a similar type of abstract organ.'

The word Weithidic used for abstract was synonymous with the word he used for both spider and trick.'

"In respect to the fabric that spans the void, I can say little,' said Weithidic. 'Some claim it is a celestial song, some a tree, complete with roots and life sap that reaches up toward the sky. Meanwhile, others say it is only the bark of a sea canoe that can ferry the traveller across the abyss, from shore to distant shore.'

'Winter was cold in the old world of the B'otuks. The hunters arrived back from the hunt in a storm that blew the tops of the waves off the sea that then froze and descended onto the B'otuk villages in a blinding torrent of ice. One day Dyfed's young wife, Telquaejit, took the frozen bear skin down from the hide frame upon which it had been stretched and after washing it in a solution mixed with red ochre, sewed it into a garment mantle according to the local fashion. Previously, she had expertly crafted the creature's hind paws into warm moccasins for Dyfed's feet. Up until then he had continued to wear the clothes of his people (the long woollen kilt and cloak the colour of broom blossoms against a shining sea) but due to the extreme cold he now adopted the B'otuk winter dress of bearskin. In November the weather cleared although it remained cold and the Norse sailors battened down the *Aura Maré* II and winched her further up onto shore. Later a heavy snowfall froze to her deck and bleakened the world about them into a land of stark beauty. Then before the winter solstice occurred ice formed on the coastal shoals.'

'Dyfed spent many hours with Weithidic. He learned that the peoples of this continent had an extensive trade apparatus in place which was responsible for distributing the fine sugary syrups, nuts, dried fruits and distilled spirits that the people here consumed during that long winter in exchange for commodities in which the B'otuks were proficient in fashioning or that existed about them in abundance. Such items for export from the Land of Abundant Codfish included sea canoes and cured cod, bales of seal, bear and caribou pelts, mammal oils as well as stylised records of the antics of Spider Woman and the story of the ant clan during the first three worlds of life that were painted by B'otuk artists on stretched caribou hides and carved on fat round tree boles which every self respecting manetek up and down the coast and along the inland waters wanted to possess in order to decorate their longhouses. From Weithidic Dyfed learned a little about the complex history of the old world and its' peoples who were hunter gathers. The chief told him that when B'otuk first moved his tribe onto this continent and later, with his disciples, had crossed this ancient land whose surface had once been extensively covered in ice. But before that, the wise master and chief had first to discern (then woo) a partitive of the great unconscious, the G'itchy Manitou or Creator Being, which was the collective ancestral spirit of birds, beasts and man in this segment of the world. Even then, Dyfed learned, trade existed between the five hundred or so tribes who lived here (many were closely related), not because the people were bent on commerce for individual or tribal opulence, but because they believed that static material wealth was harmful to all the manifested denizens within the G'itchy Manitou's dream Idea and that because all men were brothers, each was responsible in some way for the others which were extensions of one's self. Therefore, wealth must be in continual motion and must be shared.'

'And like its' inhabitants, the land, too, was divided into tribal allotments whose frontiers, fixed by geographical expressions, were linked by spirit trails which were carefully observed by game as well as man. These were the migratory and trading routes that kept the land and the creatures that lived upon it in balance. Being new to the land, and in order to safely traverse its' expanse and to cross these frontiers, B'otuk had to learn the sacred songs and the holy dances that were necessary and indigenous to each area. For people thought that certain songs and body movements assimilated humans into the great rhythmic vibration that is part of the Breath, part of the G'itchy Manitou, while the trails and the footpaths of the animate (the tectonic frontiers), the psychic thoroughfares from the state of dream to awake, were the Shining Paths, the Sacred Ways that all who were initiated trod. Dyfed also learned that each of the individual nations, or tribes, continued a unique and separate tradition of identity in culture and motif that by and large, expressed the exact same concept or notion shared by the other nations. The major cause of disorder, Weithidic told him, was of a different source. That problem was with the legacy of the human being itself. And this was that most of their ideas, whether scientific or philosophical, were essentially all bullshit in the end. In turn, due to the human's idea having never come to realization (or ever will, under the current human condition) incurred cult radicalism and the subsequent inability in not being able to appreciate common atonement. Their idea and their individual lives became a hatred race for the top in absolute domination that will never happen or even materialize outside of phenomenon, either. And all it will accomplish is to make men ignorant and unhappy.'

"The Shonack were in this category,' said the chief. 'Their debasement of ancient ideals, their greed for riches, ownership and domination are threatening local stability that will have far reaching effects through the past, present and future of the land in which they live. For the great prophet, B'otuk, taught that the ultimate concept of G'itchy Manitou is It's unity into singleness to everything that exists, including the humble conceptions envisioned by each and every creature the world over.'

"I know some people in that category, too,' answered Dyfed. He contemplated Weithidic for a moment. There was no indication that the man lived in the past, thought Dyfed.'

The snow melted from the land first, and then under the warm spring sun the frozen bays and coastal shoals softened. Once again the sea air smelled different. As soon as it had thawed and had broken up into chunks of slush, the surface of the thick White Sea quickly dissolved and the Norse men dragged the *Aura Maré* II down and out upon the sea. Once again her prow sailed forth and broke the smooth glassy blue waters and rippled her reflections. Dyfed could no longer hold them back, so after the Nordic sailors had poured some local fermented spirits onto the waters along with the entrails of a seal and some ashes of incense while they entreated Vanir to guide them safely home. Promising to one day return Dyfed and Telquaejit said their teary and sad goodbyes throughout that last night. In the morning he said fare well to Weithidic, asking him to care for his wife until his return. Then they cast off and spread their canvass to the wind.

(Moor Moorings. Ahoy)

'A truth that's told with bad intent beats all the lies you can invent.'
WILLIAM BLAKE

'Dyfed plotted a course due east back across the Atlas Sea intending to make some minor adjustments upon nearing the longitude of their destination. On the sixth night out Dyfed stood watch while the *Aura Maré* II found favour with a gentle breeze that blew them towards the new day and a rising crescent moon that hung in a starlit sky that night. As the bow ploughed the sea throwing luminous foam to either side, in the murky ink (beyond Diana's yellow beams of light) ten thousand lights sparkled radiantly like diamonds.'

'By the following morning the wind howled around the mast whose sail had earlier been dragged down by fearful men; and where the sun would have risen, only dark clouds pressed down upon the sea. Just as he discerned that they were making very slow progress they were struck by a terrific storm that battered the little ship off course for days. The storm was so ferocious and the mountains of water all around were so high that in the hollowed out water valleys between the wavy crags Dyfed was able to discern the ocean's sandy shore covered in seashells that lay beneath them. He was not able to discern the position of his vessel, however. This was on account that no stars shone in the night sky and even the time of the sun's daily debut was shadowed under thunderously heavy storm clouds. All during the day and those following nights they lurched and tumbled on the sea. Then during the following week it got worse. Now the storm raged even more and the sea hollows were now so wide and the sea bottom so visible that the sailors claimed to have counted the crabs as they rushed along the sea bottom for cover from the wind. One sailor, a Swede who wasn't in his right mind anyway, climbed out of the boat at one point and walked on the sea bottom in order to stand on solid unmoving ground for a change. And it was not just the waters of the sea that sloshed all around them. The great storm god also caused the rain to pour down from above and join hands with those reaching up from the sea that tossed the little craft about like tinder-flotsam running white-water rapids. Expectantly looking in every direction while seeking for signs of shore and refuge, they lined the gunwales and searched through the blackened light of day from port to fore and starboard to stern.'

'Then early one morning the *Aura Maré* II struck something immovable. Having being subjected to a powerful battering from Ba'al (that great storm god and the rider of the clouds), Poseidon (Ba'al's infernal nemesis) now stepped up his anger and at this point Dyfed's ship began to break up. Fearful of being caught unawares and trapped or struck hard by one of the twisted splintering planks that were coming undone and popping out from their place along the entire length of his vessel, or to be struck and crushed by the falling mast, Dyfed called out loudly to abandon ship. Flung about by the wind upon the crazy and unnatural slant of the fore-deck they each tossed themselves off from the only life-craft within their possession and into the flying spray just as the watery peril seeped in through the rents in her hull and sucked the Aura Maré II under and tossed her over and over like a broken black and bleached amphora.'

"Whatever my thoughts at the time were, Muns,' said Dyfed, I must confess — I will never know. It is possible that I thought to save myself by swimming, and if that is true then I need not have bothered. For upon entering the brine I was sucked under and felt the tide move me very swiftly beneath the surf. I struggled desperately to reach the surface and remember swallowing mouthfuls of briny salt water as I was dragged under and swept along (perhaps by the rage of that upstart Neptune). I gazed out through salty eyelids through the murky brine to watch a spectre like none I had seen before. There, the pale, bloodless corpses of my shipmates swayed like bits of seaweed that you often see grow from the ocean floor and ripple in the sea current. I tried to laugh at their fate along with my own, but only bubbles burst from my compressed lungs as fish darted to and fro. The escaping air from my lungs floated quickly upward toward the silvery ceiling above me where they gathered like tiny beads of luminous pearls. Every so often a corpse, too, would belch a bubble forth and I would watch as a string of glistening air spiral aloft. Then — all of a sudden, with a crushing force — I was hurled by a surface wave chin first against the gritty edge of a continent. Apparently, I had found my way back.'

'From the place where Dyfed had beached he looked up and saw the tower of Herakes (Hercules) from whose light that shone through the night from its tippy-top that was supposed to warn mariners that they were now skirting the sea's marches and that here at hand (for sailors only) was the hard: Stay soft, sailor — stay soft and stay back. Of course, Dyfed no longer had the safety of a boat under him and he longed for the hard and it didn't matter if it was rocky and dangerous even to swimmers.'

'Upon seeing the old Amoran lighthouse he instantly knew he had touched down on terra firma on the shores of Keltic Gallaeci of northwestern Hispania. On account of this tower dedicated to Herakles he knew he was quite near an old Keltic settlement (modern day A Coruna), and not the Emerald Isle, say, or even the broad bend of the river Dee estuary, both of which were much closer to where he wanted to be. Dyfed realized now that he needed to make a change in his travel arrangements.'

'But now he cursed his wretched and useless body as it listed from side to side and often positioned itself in such a manner that Dyfed was un able to orient himself to the idea of the normal phenomenon he had known. This sensation embodied him as tightly as his own skin before it had fallen loosely away from the bone like boiled chicken. Then he had a strange sensation of internal/external perception. This (he knew) was a reoccurring sensation but this time it came from outside of him. Still, his sole sensation was only of perceiving this thought which he appeared not to will — yet it had the familiarity of himself. Then (as he was being guided by his perception from beyond and outside of himself) that same thought suddenly came from within and he was transformed.'

'In his newly conceived space/time, Dyfed perceived a being that was engaged in the discourse of thought. At first he assumed it was with Breogan son of Brath before he then he realized it was with himself. He smiled as he talked and talked and he saw that he stood amid a wilderness of beauty. He then noticed that he had become hot and that overhead the sun shone directly down: "Shall we stand over there in the shade beneath that tree, Dyfed,' his other self said, 'for I am feeling quite warm.' He felt tightness in their thighs and they agreed that the looseness of his flesh was uncomfortable as they moved toward the leafy tree and felt also the warm grass brush gently against them. The terrain around them, they noticed, was gently hilly and he glimpsed a shiny river nearby ((Rio Mero) which meandered between woolly mounds. Although rock was evident it was generally hidden under a thick growth of green moss and the surrounding forest and meadow were magical. Silence was everywhere and they noted, each to one another that no birds darted across the blue sky or chirped from the branches above their head.'

"It is too hot for them at this time of the day,' he said answering himself. 'Wait until the evening when it is cooler.'

"I am dead,' he said quite suddenly. He looked at himself in surprise.'

"You're not dead,' he said. 'You are alive, and although you believe in a death wherein lies life you do not fear it. So, what's your point? He contemplated himself much the way he often contemplated himself.'

"You say you are dead but did you not feel the heat from the sun upon your face a moment ago, and are you not cooler now that you are here in the shade?' He gazed upward into the canopy of the tree and saw sunlight filtering through the greenery and shine down golden shafts all around them.'

"I remember plunging into the depths,' he said. 'How is it that I am here?'

'The will and the power of thought,' he replied at once. 'Where would you be now without the power of thought?'

'Dyfed had been circling the tree as he talked, his mind deep in thought while his other self had been doing the same but in a counter direction to him. Often as they met face-to-face they would momentarily stop and one or the other would hold up a finger and expound (often in a single crowning word either on one's own account or as a commendation of appreciation to the other) before continuing again, around and around. Before it had grown dark a large pink moon rose casting shadows across our path as we paced.'

'Suddenly Dyfed grew weary and stopped his progress to lean against the tree. Then his other self drew near and they regarded each other in the glimmering of the soft darkness. Then each noticed a curious light shine from the other's eye. His other self assisted Dyfed to his bed there upon the ground and taking Dyfed's left hand in his he placed his right palm upon his forehead. Dyfed slept. There he evolved from the succession of discursive spheres and dreamed a strange dream embodying the realm of the intuitive. His tutor Manandan, and Queen Violet-Eye, were standing beside him as he gazed upon a gentle song bird that lay dead upon the ground from his own arrow a long time ago. Dyfed was sorely ashamed and wept for he knew that without reason he had altered the course of creation as surely as he had altered the existence of the little creature's that lay before him. The two of them then raised their arms into the air and began a dance accompanied by a chant which Dyfed instinctively knew was meant to absolve him of my sin against myself.'

'While he slumbered, Dyfed perceived that his other self had climbed into the tree to look out across the beautiful land that shone in the new morning light. He didn't know then but he was on the lookout for the dangerous, warlike Kelts that lived in the nearby cenedl comprised of castles. It was best to keep his voice down so as not to alert them that they (he) were there. But despite that he commenced to sing out loud a poem he knew. As he listened to its familiarity, he was filled with joy. Then as his eternal state of single dimension re entered the three dimensional moment a great flapping of wings occurred as some creature took flight from the boughs above him and disturbed his dream so that he became partially aware. As he lay on his back with my eyes closed he perceived a heavy weight that lay upon me. It was his para conscious and he then opened his third eye, the preverbal pineal orb and the entrance to the fifth dimension that must by-pass the fourth dimension because that state of time is voluntarily attached only to the third density. During the duration of seven dreams, exhausted he woke up and renewed himself.'

'Suddenly, he discerned a weight upon his belly as he lay upon his back. A large serpent had coiled itself there him to take comfort from Dyfed's warmth with its tail by his groin and its head alongside his own neck. Here light is warmth. Dyfed did not fear the serpent but took solace in its presence through which he glimpsed the stage of the Omniscient Totality. But at that moment the creature sensed Dyfed's wakefulness and uncoiling itself it slithered up across his chest and over his shoulder and into the tree.'

Then Dyfed saw a man about the same age as himself approaching, accompanied by a young girl. They helped him to his feet and with their assistance Dyfed returned to their comfortable dwelling in the forest shade. These people were the first he had seen since his ordeal and he was most anxious to converse; but the man put his finger to his lips and bade him to be still and rest. At length Dyfed fell asleep and when he awoke the man was gone. The girl, noticing that Dyfed was awake, came to him. She was a sweet thing, young and tender in age and after bathing Dyfed's face in warm water, she began to pick out the stones that were buried in his flesh from his unplanned beach landing. But, because of Dyfed's beard, this chore was difficult. Then she told him that her father had gone to check his traps and would not return for some time. She then set before him a dish of fruit, nuts, shell fish and berries along with a bowl of rich buttermilk. She then enticed Dyfed into thoughts of carnal seduction. But Dyfed's weakness came to confound him for being too weak he found his body would not respond to lust.'

'Now that you have been sustained and eaten your fill, go,' she told him, somewhat miffed, 'and complete the mission for which you strive upon this journey.' Thanking her, Dyfed kissed her on the forehead then not knowing under what skies he walked he asked her the name of the land in which he found myself. She told him that she and her father were Gallaecian. From here Dyfed journeyed due east away from the shore and ascending a mountain range he walked into the lands of Bizkaia and Gipuzkoa.'

'It was here that Dyfed had now come among a hardy race that was fiercely independent from those who inhabited their marches on all sides. Their language, which they called Euskara, was difficult for Dyfed to comprehend; although he did manage to make sense of it by the time he reached their most easterly border. This was in the region of Nafarra along the ridge of the Pyrenees Mountains. However, before reaching that region he was delayed in Benapara for some time. Apparently, it was a requirement (before proceeding further) that he be interrogated. The official who conducted this lengthy enquiry was a man named Euagoras, a holy man with a congenial disposition who invited Dyfed to reside with him during the debriefing. This old and interesting man who besides challenging Dyfed on all fronts found reason to entertain him about the story of his people which we will not be exploring here other than to say that these Euskara speaking peoples, so it seemed, were a conglomeration of sea peoples who came out of the regions of Ionia and Caria. But briefly, bye the bye Dyfed learned that long before the great migrations of Indo-Europaeans that the forefathers of Euagoras had sailed west past Atika, past the Isle of Pelops and the Dorians and Spartans, past Sichilia and Sardinia (where they mined silver) and through the western gates of the White Sea, the Pillars of Herackles, and into the Sea of Atlas called Ocean: In fact the ancient city of Gadir that's in the land (island) of Ithaca had been founded by them. Guided by ancient maps these folks crossed the vast Ocean of Atlas discovering of foreign lands in the west before returning to the eastern shores of Bizkaia Bay and in the mountains around the headwaters of the Ebro River. These folks were known as the people from Euzu (who though many generations removed from them) were incorporated into the former's kingdom. Euskara, the name of their language, is stemmed from this epoch. These were the people of which Weithidic had informed him.'

'Dyfed jumped up, refreshed, and looking around saw that — but for the memory of the serpent — he was alone in his garden by the tree which was now burning radiantly but was not being consumed by the fire. He watched it in amazement for a while. Then in the morning, as the sun rose, Dyfed set off for home.'

(The caliphates that stemmed from ibn Ayyub back to Umayyad and Alley Oop)

'My turban, my robe and my head — all three have been appraised for less than a dirham. Have you not heard of my universal fame? I am nobody, nobody, nobody.'

MOWLANA JELALUDDIN BALKI (ALSO KNOWN AS **MOULANA OR RUMI**)

'At the time of Dyfed's arrival onto the northern shore of Gallaeicia, the majority of the land encompassing the Iberian Peninsula was currently under the control of the Umayyad family dynasty, the House of Umayyad. The conquering Ethio-pia (burnt-face) peoples from Afrika had been here in this land before, back in antiquity. Now they were back again, led here from across the Ak (White) Sea by a Berber (Kelt) named Tariq ibn Ziyad. This follower of one of the false prophets that having been easily influenced while alone and away from his own people (some say his home was at the Siwa oasis, just west of the Qattra Depression) had gone native and adopted that new third wheel of the Abramist religious family — namely Ishlamatism. This new cult was flowing westward (as well as every other which way) at a furious speed. Ishlamatism was that belated desert flowering third petal of the cult of Yahweh (Jehovah the god of the Abramists).[66] Currently, these Ethio-pia peoples (burnt-faces) were being called Blackamoors. You can see the connection. And these Blackamoors had spring-boarded themselves from Africa in and around the Gallaeician sector of Hispania.'

'The main Blackamoor region-extent on the Iberian Peninsula (that was primarily to the south east of Gallaeci) was under the Umayyad family control. They called this land al Andalus. This burgeoning empire also included the Maghreb and all of coastal north Afrika as well as most of Khem, the Levant, Assyria, Armenia, the Caucasus, Mesopotamia, Arabia Central, Persia (Iran), Transoxiana (Central Asian modern Uzbekistan, Tajikistan, portions of Kygystan and parts of Kazakhstan), and the Sindh (north west Inja, now modern southern Pakistan). Ruled from Ash Sham (also Dimasq or modern Damascus) in old Assyria, this Umayyad Caliphate had become (virtually overnight) the largest empire the world had ever seen, even greater in size than Amor. The Ishlamite cult of this empire was also known as Mohamadism. Mohamadism had become the latest of the mono-theists cults that had been spawned from the ancient gods of the Mesopotamian and Amorite peoples, especially Ba'al, Bel Shadé (also El Shaddai), Teshub and Adad (Hadad). This Abramist cult was divided into two sects — Sunnie and Shite — much the same way that Jeshuanism was now divided between Pelagius and the Keltic Church and the Vicar of Jeshua Adon and the Church of Amor. The House of Umayyad was Sunnie. They believed that a certain Muhammad H. Mahdi

---

66 Abram actually hiked up Mt Moriah (also called the mountain of the lord) to commiserate with his almighty God and to offer up the burnt offerings of his only begotten and covenant ridden son Isaac. But at the time this god was not Jehovah, rather it (he) was called El Shadai [also *El Shaddai*]. Fortunately, El Shaddai stopped Abram from sacrificing his son just in time.

was to be sent by god (sic) to be the redeemer of Ishlamitism. Obviously, they hadn't thought this through very well. The rumour was that he would rule the world before Judgment Day (sic) came thereby ridding the world of evil. The House of Umayyad fully and completely believed that if they paved the way for Mahdi he would glorify their House. So it was all about them! Dyfed remembered from his Mencius' induced vision that a similar ingrained cult of hallelujah, praise the lord, hurrah for god, rah, rah, fricking rah that were called born again Jeshuan Adonites would take hold in parts of Merika (not quite as much in the Northern Dominion — thank you God) and even in the Unified States government heralded the beginning of the demise of the second empire. Anyway, the Mahdi (as he was commonly referred to) would no doubt favour them, so the caliph of Umayyad thought, along with all the Sunnie in general: And then (hopefully, so they thought, and in all likelihood) all those pathetic others who didn't meet with the Mahdi's approval here on earth would perhaps turn away from Sunnie to become Shite instead.'

'Dyfed, as mentioned, had heard this story before and was still mulling over this feeling of dejavu upon arriving at Tournay on the last wagon train of the evening of Wednesday, May twenty-third of the year 1742 according to the first Olympiad (or the year 966 CE). He had been gone for nine years.'

'Like little children they quarrelled. The two breakaways from the original Abramists (the Jeshuans and the Ishlamites) couldn't get along, and that was obvious from the start to all and sundry; those millions of innocent, miserable and suffering bystanders. At first this took the heat off the original Abramist cult whose centre remained at Kadesh (also Jebus or Jerusalem) but they weren't forgotten for long for soon a general distain for the original Abramists and its more modern third wheel Ishlamites became a hallmark of official Europa and the Church of Amor in particular. For this reason, and because both the people of the Yehud and Ishlamite religions spoke a Semitic tongue (Hebrew and A-rabic) which differed vastly from the languages of Europa, a certain acute discredit toward and a hatred against these two religions arose within the Europa establishment that was called by an anomaly; anti-Semitism. Apparently the hatred toward the Yuhudic original Abramists was due to how they spoke. Yet, this was not an issue in Europa's establishment's resentment toward the Ishlamite religion that spoke almost identically similar. They appear to be discredited because their Paraclete was considered just another false prophet. But of course the religion of the original Abramist and its potential Paraclete was just that, a religion, and one that wasn't being forced upon unreceptive denizens of Europa, either. On the other hand prophets of all time are relative and therefore essentially false in the long run: Semitic-ness didn't come into it one way or another so that word became nothing more than part of the world word game. Ultimately, of course, since there is a God and bad karma, the word game over anti-Semitism was soon to be erroneously played by both sides.'

> 'Don't pontificate to me, infidel: This is my God,' said the Ishlamite.
>
> 'Oh no he's not, heathen heretic: He's my God,' retorted the Jeshuan.
>
> 'No he's not.'
>
> 'Yes he is.'
>
> 'Just wait until my God comes a round; he will beat your god up.'

'Oh Yeah? My God is bigger than your god and he'll beat your god up, you mean.'

'No he's not…'

'Yes he is…

'My god's bigger…so, there…'

'It had been early in the eighth century when the A-rabs overran Spain and finally took almost complete possession of it. But although Arabia was the birthplace of Mohammed the Paraclete, the Arabians in general were less fanatical than any other followers of any of the False Prophets that were now lining the halls of new and growing empires around the world. For one thing they did not insist on a wholesale conversion of the conquered people: For they loved the gold the Jeshuans horded away more than his conversion. So on condition of paying a tax, Jeshuans were allowed to follow their own religion. In 1469 CE (calculated by the modern era and just over five hundred years in the future from the current time in this story) Isabella of Castile would come to marry her cousin Ferdinand of Aragon: thus, the two Hispanian crowns (oriented toward strict Jeshuanism) were united and then everything would change. This royal duo would have zero tolerance when it came to the brand and flavour of religious primitive superstition that they decreed everyone must practise. Generally, heavy fines were laid upon a first-time felony of un-observance of Jeshuanism followed by execution of any repeat infraction. The Abramists of the Jehovah persuasion would be given three choices; leave Hispania immediately, convert to Jeshuanism immediately, or be executed immediately. The converts to Jeshuanism from among the Jehovah Abramists would be called Marranes (subsequently, those who fled would eventually be known as Shephardic while those who did neither would be called dead. The converts to Jeshuanism from among the Blackamoors (also called Saracens) would be known as Moriscoes. There would be the same amount of choices for them, too. Any Hispanian Jeshuan or Atheist converts to Mohamadism would be called Mozarabes. They would have one choice — to flee undetected and live as far as they could that (unfortunately) wouldn't be far enough. And, as suggested, that choice won't pan-out very well. This state of being herein described that will come to pass in Hispania (in four or five hundred years hence) will be called the Hispania Inquisition. The Inquisition would be a tribunal (and the Love of Jeshua and its mission statement and chosen raison d'etre) that the Church of Amor will call into being at that time. It will be done in order to flush out and punish all heretics and divest these backsliders of all their lands, businesses and wealth in general, and finally of the very breath in their throats.'

'These aforementioned A-rabs, on the other hand, were a people that Dyfed had taken quite an interest in. They were dangerous, but they were marvellous at the same time, he thought. Dressed in the most fantastic and flamboyant gear from their wild, swirling turbans that were perched giddily on their heads to their attention-attracting flowing and colourful robes and their bearded faces that put other dress trends and personal appearances to shame (with the exception of the Tajiks and the Pashtuns), they were at the same time highly intelligent and (generally speaking) more advanced scientifically and philosophically (never-mind poetically) than the Europaean Jeshuans of the east or the west. And from their often shrill A-rabian speech with which they created a story world of fantasia that melded easily with their ever accompanying, fast percussion drum beat (that may have been a loan-influence from the Keltic Berbers), and the sorrowful and lonely laments that girded their lyrics for their music and their poetry, these A-rabian men quite nonchalantly traversed their dangerous empty stone world of blistering sand and burning heat riding atop their camels in strings of caravans that traipsed from one oasis of charged mirages to another. Here, with Bedouin beauties clothed in silk and riches and other varieties of a bevy of pretty effeminates, they languished by cool fountain waters in the deep shade of the date and palm trees that lined their route from east of the Red Sea to the Maghreb that lay hard by the Atlas Sea.'

'Though not in resemblance, but in a strange way, their theatrical but potentially baneful everyday aspect about them reminded Dyfed of another marvellous looking clan of men who on occasion were seen in Amor back in its hay-day. These were now long faded descendants of the Dorian folk who took up habitation from the Thraco-Illyriun Epirus to the Mani (Maina) peninsula on the island of Pelops. This was a time of resettlement of those who fled south from the great cataclysm of the last era and settled in the mountainous terrain here along the eastern shores of the Ionian Sea. And as for the A-rab man of the present who among them has somehow forgot — that there was once a spot (at least outside of Inja and the Land of Ch'in) — where in the tenth century men mapped and followed the courses of the stars in the heavens, even the unmovable stars that they claimed also moved, and why that was so, and who would have thought that these men of whom we speak here were the men of A-raby? These folks — of this spot — could even predict eclipses of the moon and of the sun, never mind the appearances of certain sky traversing witches on furry-ended broomsticks; those calamitous comets. All the while the Jeshuans of the time were fussing and then arguing over whom it was that figured out first how to predict the eclipse of the earth! But times have now changed, thanks to the true religion of Western Philosophy that thankfully changed the attitude of many Jeshuans, as well.'

'Anyway, way back when (and once upon a time on that stark and spicy spot called A-raby) that aforementioned land was inhabited by men who used mathematics like the Hellenes and the ancient Indo-Europaeans of old. Even your common A-rab (it seemed) could re-invent such tools as the numerical zero and divide the whole into numerical parts intelligently and be able to add and subtract and multiply these parts and even discern the important prime numbers. And it was also here where men understood many of the sicknesses of the human body and mind and were adept in performing surgery on the brain and the eye. They invented every kind of tool for this doctoring practice of which many designs are still being put to use in this our modern and present day. This was something that the highly indoctrinated, haughty — my shit don't stink — type-thinking Europaeans were unable to accomplish. This was because their own program — the one devised just for them by those same all encompassing and controlling local Haploids — didn't (on pain of death for the slightest of blasphemy) allow them to. Apparently, the attitude was since Jeshua hadn't himself felt it overly necessary to invent something to these effects then nobody else must bother either. On the other hand the program forced onto those men of the spot (those A-rabs) was at a place in space/time where likely they were not very willing or wanting to quickly let go of valuable information, anyway. The valuable information reference here was the mathematical use for creating beautiful and long-lasting architecture here on earth as well as being able to discern the star and planet movements in the heavens along with the magical composites to achieve metallurgical savvy that had also been passed down to them from the ancients like Hephaestus. But the Haploids were not so big in other areas of consolation and they disallowed these A-rabs to take other advantages that would have continued to propel them into the modern world alongside (if not ahead of) the Europaeans in the end. It was a cruel trick, and one that the Haploids are well known for. But it also shows the littleness that humans can stoop to. Shame on the Jeshuans of Europa, shame on their failure to become loving and compassionate beings for all things made in God's image.'

'Failure is the culprit and this reborn culprit (who we haven't come across as yet) will be Tyler, the guard outside the door (of the then be spoiled sanctum of sanctums) armed with those implements of his office the law and the lance provided by the great seal of the glorious Unified States (U S or Uncle Sham) to guard us: Instead (for its own sake of glory) and at the expense of other kingdoms and nations striving for democracy and individual freedom, it will attempt to sell us out, like the Wunschritter's Germanika.'

'But we are now getting ahead of ourselves.'

(Crusading do-gooders and the Three Stooges)

'They don't bust you that way; they work on you ways you can't fight! They put things in! They install things. They start as quick as they see you're gonna be big and go to working and installing their filthy machinery when you're little, and keep on and on and on till you're fixed.'

KEN KESEY

'So, having washed up on the northern coast of Hispana, and having traversed the Pyrenees mountain range and stomped across the Langdoc and Frankia (Francia), Dyfed finally arrived at Tournay in Flanders to discover how the House of Lucifer had fared in his absence. Remember, he had had no contact since leaving it behind since even before the reign of the Anglish king AEthelstan in old Albion. Thankfully, Dyfed found his old face-ache batman (Trachmyr) at the helm and at home and in charge of his old army that he once had timely lent to AEthelstan for the occasion of his great hurrah and triumph at the Battle of the Burh on the Wirral. Furthermore, Trachmyr had the alacrity, intelligence and presence of mind to hold onto those soldiers and bring them back to Tournay. Karatakos was also there and had taken over the disciplining of Ebreo ben Jamin the accountant and metallurgical wizard.'

'And Dyfed had just arrived home in time — it seemed — for trouble was brewing as it always was. During the last days of the Anglish West Saxen House of Cerdic (when Eadwardius the Confessor was on the throne), a certain Sweyn (also Swegen) Godwinson who due to grievous crimes committed had been exiled and (along with all his brooding sons) sought refuge and freedom outside of Albion. (Angleland) This family of felons had just arrived in Flanders at about this time. Not only was Sweyn Godwinson a contender to succeed to the throne of Angleland, he was ambitious in all ways besides. But exiled from Angleland for life meant only the life of the Confessor king of the Anglish to him — not his own life. That could be arranged so what Godwinson needed most of all now was an army to defeat either Eadwardius (Eddy the Confessor and new king) or some third party usurper (for many such creatures lurked in the shadows). Sweyn saw himself as the descendant of Sweyn Forkbeard through King Cnut (Knut) the Great that could easily place him next in line, or so he thought. He therefore looked around for a heavy cudgel or some-such fool-tool (such as an army) to make things right again. Fortunately, such things as armies lying around to be picked up at a bargain price were few and far between. That is until he happened upon Bruges, the capital of Flanders, where Sweyn Godwinson had now surfaced. Dyfed had arrived here in Bruges (prior to his intention of returning to Kent) to enter into negotiations to merge his House with that of the merchant House of Kong (Konge) controlled by the father of a player in this story named Anlaf. So it was here at this time that Dyfed came face to face with Sweyn Godwinson and Anlaf.'

'Under the circumstances he and Trachmyr cancelled their arrangements to Angleland and quickly travelled to Aachen and appealed to Emperor Henry who sometimes ruled the Second Empire from there. Fortunately Emperor Henry was home. Through his association with Childeric and Chlodovechus (Chlodio) Dyfed was able to persuade the emperor towards favouring his viewpoint on the matter and keep Sweyn from getting his hands on the House of Lucifer's army. The emperor Henry quickly intervened. He did not want trouble from any king, and that included those troublesome Anglish kings who were tactically protected by their wide and relatively deep salt water moat that didn't impede them one tiny bit to cross it in reverse and to invade Europa.'

'But Emperor Henry's favour came with a cost, although he didn't know at that time just what the cost would be. Henry took a rain check and said he would get back to Dyfed on that. Then after the emperor chastised Sweyn Godwinson, Sweyn repented and set out for Al Quds (Kadesh, also ironically known as Jebus the city of Peace). But before Sweyn could wait for the Confessor's natural (or otherwise) death, the latter died and his brother Harold stepped up to succeed Eddy the Confessor who was now the old dead king as the Anglish king before Sweyn even got wind of it. But soon after, William (also Guillaume; pronounce gee-ohm, also guy-oam) the Bastard, Duke of the province of the North men situated to the south of Flanders rushed an invasion across that moat and defeated Harold on the battlefield of the land of the south Saxen. That was in the year 1066CE or 1842, according to the calendar of the Olympiad.'

'Anyway, once Dyfed was home in the land of the Salian Franks (the Salii) he quickly settled in. With his marine enterprise in mind he kept up his contacts with old acquaintances such AEthelstan, King Henry Holy Amoran Emperor and King Karl the Magnificent now in retirement. One such gathering was at a good old knees up hootenanny shindig at Karl the Magnificent's old palace in Aachen during the holidays (holydays) over the SinterKlaas festivities that same year. Dyfed had been invited due to his successful efforts to spearhead the folksy Sinter-Klaas shtick into the burgeoning new Jeshuanism that was now being formed and fabricated by the Second Empire for its own purposes. As for himself (what with his acquisition of the House of Konge in Bruges) it was a chance to celebrate his expanding merchant and commerce branches of the House of Lucifer business plan. Of course, in respect to Sinter-Klaas Day, this festival and solstice hootenanny was a carryover from the original Saturn festival from which the Sinter-Klaas festival date originally had derived. Since the Sinter-Klaas cult and ensuing festival had caught on so well now among the hoi polloi in Europa, the acolytes (or more accurately the stakeholders) of the Church of Amor — in their attempt to capitalise on the former's huge popularity with the latter — were now re-directing the energy of that collective focus to configure Sinter-Klaas Day into an important Jeshuan holy day that would become Jeshua Adon the Nazri or Nazarean's birthday, no less. Their excuse was that Sinter-Klaas (also Santa Claus, Saint Nicholas, San Nicola, Sankt Nikolaus, Sant Nikolaz) of Demre (also, formerly Nicola of Patara (the actual and real Sinter-Klaas) had been a proponent for Jeshua Adon the Nazarean. He had been instrumental in helping to elevate the latter into the concept of an individual's Messianic true self that was one of his biggest and most important presents he dropped off of all time. At least that was how certain persons saw it. This, of course, was terribly inaccurate but was seen to help forge it into something important other than being simply a blatant identity theft of one Jeshua (the Nazri or Nazarean) the Brilliant whose philosophy Sinter-Klaas had supported.'

'This Jeshuan holy day celebration was nothing more than a blatant act to highjack the notoriety of Nicholas and pilferage all the former's good will in order to credit their own account. This of course, has become the Jeshuan cult's hallmark. Indeed, the aforementioned festival, as already mentioned, was even now being billed as Jeshua's birthday. Dyfed felt somewhat responsible for demoting Jeshua the Brilliant into Saint Nicholas. But it flourished in the end. Meanwhile, Saturn, apart from remaining a planet, and allocated to a day of the week — Saturn's day (Saturday) and also the equivalent of Saetere (Angle-Saxen equivalent of Saturn)…sabato (Jeshuan Italia's first day of the weekend or 'week's-end')…sabat (the Abramite holy day)…or Sabbath (also Abramite) — was left completely out of it now. The Jeshuans subsequently monkeyed with the Decalogue's Sabbath being appointed as the last day of week and changed it to the first day of week, the day of the sun…god's son…Sunday).'

'Saint Nicholas the Original found himself in a similar situation, and while having been pinned now onto the shirttails of the great fraud, the incomparable hoax manufactured by the Church of Amor, it really deserves more. In the end, though, the *pack,* more than any did manage to keep his identity and reputation separated and unique. And even still, to this day the *pack* fights in continuing to raise the profile of SinterKlaas (Santa Claus) in an attempt to retain that status for him that's stripped of any religious ownership such as the Church of Amor and a soda-soft drink corporate entity that don't pay out royalties or licencing fees; neither to General Account nor to the Sister and Brotherhood of the Church of Santa Claus that isn't a religion or a corporation that in turn have managed (with government help) to exempt themselves from taxes and fees.'

'So, it was to great lengths and strategies that Karl the Magnificent's descendant and successor Henry had finagled to have the hoi polloi friendly SinterKlaas re-titled the Messiah Mass. Up to this time the Church of Amor had not bothered about the birth date of their saviour god. Mostly, gods don't have birthdates, as you might have noticed. Of course, this mendacious tale of the Nazri whose birthday, according to rumour originating among his family and friends had not been shortly after the start of winter but rather on September 12th in the year 5 BCE of modern chronology (although other say that even that event was nothing more than a reoccurrence of the fame and fable of another teacher of righteousness that lived about thirteen centuries before that era).'

'It was also at this time that Henry, Emperor of the Second Empire, called in his debt to Dyfed. He wanted Dyfed to take his army to Kadesh (Al Quds also Jebus) and liberate it and the entire holy land from the grimy hands of those heathen, Saracen interloping scoundrels. Astounded at first by the request, Dyfed hesitated. But the emperor assured Dyfed that he wouldn't be alone for a crusade of tens of thousands of brave Jeshuan soldiers all clutching a get-out-of-jail-card for murder and vice and get-into-heaven-free just by participating, would be accompanying him.'

'This had all taken place not long after the North men under Williame the Bastard had successfully invaded Angleland and killed Harold who had only been a new king for a few months. Contrary to popular belief, William was a nasty sort who was un-liked and the butt of many character defining axioms and slurs. But these new lords who overran that land had new ideas as to ways of improving the old Angle and Saxen building construction method for their monumental projects, or statements of authority. These were the great un-impregnable castles and keeps and things to impress the natives that in this case were the now floundering Angle-Saxen. However, this massive 'statements' made of stone materialised into a brand new form of building blocks under the Bastard. This new building material was limestone. And it just so happened that there was a glut of limestone at Caen — a small fishing village on the coast with close access to Angleland and not too far from Bruges or even Tournay — which had and was being quarried by Anlaf's father's construction department, a wing now of the House of Lucifer. Workers from there could almost come home for lunch. So at Dyfed's behest — after he clinched the contract with William — Anlaf and his father set sail for Nova Troia one fine day to deliver the first of many barge loads to fill the contract to help provide the means for the new king and his lords fashion a new image of prestige.'

'In fact it was Anlaf who took command of seeing to the ferrying of this product; with thirty sailing barges designed to carry the stone. He also was in charge of lead hands and supervisors who managed the quarrying and Dyfed imposed on him to enforce the latter's own work oriented health and safety rules — something that had never been imposed before to help safe-guard and protect workers. Also, at about this time, or soon after, Tournay had begun to develop into a Europaean centre renowned for its exquisite tapestries and other woollen commodities, even more so than Bruges. And the House of Lucifer benefited immensely from this lucrative trade by importing wool from Albany and Angleland on the back-hauls from their limestone shipments. This now brought in silver and gold to help with the family's endeavours. Dyfed and his house were becoming rich again.'

'Back across the Helle Strait (channel) this state of affairs with trading in limestone and wool managed to quickly convert both of Dyfed's old quayside docks on the Tems into an even greater thriving and going concern than they ever had been. Now, the Hansa League Union Bank wanted to buy him and his Nova Troia Tems dockyard out, which he allowed them to do. Then Dyfed received the freedom of the City of Nova Troia shortly after. Freedom of the city in Dyfed's case meant that following an investigation as to his qualifications, he had the legal right to trade without renewing permits. He was still in AElfred's and AEthelstan's good books, it seemed. Dyfed kept his business there but sold the property, managing to negotiate the continual yet reduced use of the docks as a condition for their sale. But he was unsuccessful in moving his bank into Hansa League's lucrative spheres, although he was granted the freedom to buy more dock space if he needed it.'

'Earlier than that — and in a prelude as to what was to follow — Dyfed had been recommended for membership into the primary livery in the City of Nova Troia: This was the Worshipful Company of Mercers. In addition, he was remembered for his contribution to the city and the kingdom in general before and after the battle of Bamburh (also Brunanburh). So it wasn't a complete surprise that Dyfed had been readily sponsored by the likes of AEthelstan, AElfred and even Dunstan whose own credentials included abbot, bishop and now saint. Dyfed also reconnected with Pelagius the holy man whose inspired mores of Jeshuanism were from his own ancient roots of western philosophy. Western philosophy — notwithstanding Dyfed's differences with Pelagius' version of 'the problem of free will' — was something he had always admired and supported for it fitted in well with his own upbringing.'

'At about this time Dyfed expanded his new woollen trade from the slow, old merchant carriers into a sleek fleet of fast ships. He had also re-employed Ebreo the metallurgist again, who earlier had made himself scarce — for century or so — from Frankia and Lothar after coming under suspicion of selling knock-off Ulfberht swords to those who went a-viking. He wasn't the only metallurgist to be so accused although being the best in Europa he was a target even of lesser businesses and by the lesser astute who wanted to be rid of his competition. He was a foreigner anyway whose mother tongue was Semitic, many said, and therefore untrustworthy. Ebreo may have been a foreigner (most of us are in one fashion or another, pending where we go and when), but he wasn't a forger nor was he himself a forgery, or someone who relied solely on a velvet tongue and the gift of the gab to profit. He was certainly a magician when it came to iron-ore: He was a fabricator extraordinaire. He knew exactly how (and to what temperature) to heat the steel in order to forge the toughest steel possible. Everything was exact. He was the chemist or alchemist who (among others) forged the greatest war implement during this time. And he had come to learn of the secret ingredients and its manner of fashioning from the A-rabs of ash-Sham (Dimasqa). But anyone paying attention here will also know that Dyfed also employed Ebreo as a junior accountant disciplined by Karatakos for maintaining the books for the House of Lucifer. But fortunately Dyfed had relied on Trachmyr in this sector of his business while he was away in the new world.'

'Two other individuals now crossed his path who we have met before: Potamus Purplebal and Gizar Ankhman. Gizar was a shaman (high priest) and mesmerizer from the Land of Khem associated with the banking concern of the House of Ankhman. Apparently, he had come back to Europa from Afrika to study the protocols of Jeshuanism; although at the time nobody knew why. But in the city of Isis sprawling out on either side of the River Sen, Ankhman had been introduced rather secretly to Pepe the Hermit. Pepe the Hermit was a priest from the town called Amens, which is barely seventy Amoran miles south west of Tournay. Dyfed had never met this man who was of high status within the Church of Amor's curia and fifth column. Rather than being a man who saved souls he was an intelligence agent chosen by the now powerful Amoran curia to rabble-rouse in Northern Frankia (primarily under the control of the Dane, the Sax, the Angle and Norse men) to drum up special interest activists and militarize their volitions against the Ishlamites, those other Semites who believed in the False Prophet. These former were the tough and brutal men who had forged personal kingdoms around themselves and were on the make. The recently deceased William the Bastard's bloated body had only just been buried when Urbanite, the Vicar of Amor and head chef (chief) of the Church of Amor, wanted such men to expand Jeshuanism into the lands of the heretical Ishlamites and take back the ancient land of the Amorite Semites (that once included the Phoeniki). This acquisition would comprise an amalgamation of Canaanites including a once northern kingdom of ten tribal Amorites that were united by the common cult of Abram that had been somewhat quickly conquered by the Assyrians long ago. Numerous clans of all sorts had now absorbed this population. This modern day Jeshuan liberation of Canaan (so-called holy land) also included (at this time) a southern kingdom whose lands were called Judah. The people of Judah were also programmed into the Abramist cult that still retained some differences that distinguished them from their Amorite cousins and their relatively new Jeshuan cult, as well.'

'Along the eastern coast of the White Sea and slightly north (from where the people of Judah lived) were also the people from the sea who had arrived here almost two millennium ago and formed a federation of principalities among themselves. This republic had been called Philistria (Fill-is-tree-ah) and these peoples from the sea (possibly

Dorians from Kreta or Rhodos, and/or from Karia) who constituted this federation, were referred to as Philistines (Fill-is-teens[67]).'

'But though Pepe was a bright and intuitive man, it was the Vicar of Jeshua (also known as the supreme pontiff or Bishop of Amor) who wasn't just in charge of the operation itself but more importantly was the architect and founder of the will to crusade against his fellow man in the Levant (anciently a portion of the land of the Mar-tu, also Amorites, or Canaanites) whose god had descended from Amurru (also Aram) or Martu the shepherd, son of Anu, then subsequently to Hadad (Adad), Bel Sadé (also El Shaddai) and Ba'al then finally to Jehovah. Interestingly enough, Jehovah was the god of the Jeshuans, too, and whose son Joshua (Jeshua), like the much earlier Ba'al, was deemed the saviour of humanity. Ostensibly, the purpose of crusade then was to stem the expansion of the cult of Ishlamites founded by Mo'mad (Mohamad) the prophet, who (as far as the Jeshuans could tell) actually prophesised nothing whatsoever anyway, and opted (therefore) to reinstate the intrinsically essential rider of the clouds, the purveyor of the thunder who is the supreme storm god of storm gods who resides there upon the mount of mounts; that is either the mount of the Amorites or the mount of (A)-Moriah; (i.e. Without Moriah? whatever that means). We know where it leads, that's all. For it leads us to his pontiff, whose name (as already stated) is Urbanite. Urbanite is a title or assumed name, a positional name. Actually his real name was Giovannai Robatielle Lefbevre (Goldsmith) whose much earlier name was known to us as Judas Simon MacAbbe Junior of the MacAbbe House of Xandria whose financial arm, the Bank of MacAbbe had recently arrived from Xandria and set up shop in the city state of Venezia (Venice) upon the land of Italia. By this time the House of MacAbbe, who were referred to as Amoriot[68] Abramists, had been married into by the less successful but sly House of Medici (former pagans) also of Venezia but formerly of Hispania. Judas Simon MacAbbe Junior claimed descendancy from Og king of the Amorites, and then centuries later in time also descended from the prophet Gilead (formerly Uriah Gilead). In fact Judas Simon's first claim is thought to be a barefaced lie since neither his father nor his father's father ever made such a claim: Although his second claim may be true, Gilead, however, was himself a barefaced liar that did nothing for Judas Simon's credibility. Therefore, Giovannai Robatielle Lefbevre (aka: Judas Simon MacAbbe) was the descendant of the False Prophet. Now he was Papa, the Bishop of Amor and the Vicar of Jeshua, the so- called saviour of humanity, (although saviour from what, exactly, we don't yet know). No one's telling us, although it may be from ourselves.'

'Despite the alarm and hoop-la that rose over Ishlamite expansion the overwhelming view (coerced or not) of the public at this time (and at all times when and wherever Haploidic planning is involved) was irrelevant in determining the public interest. Urbanite's decisions here at this juncture were no exception. The Church of Amor was simply Urbanite's chosen vehicle in order for him to be able to surf high and wide over the (generally) uneducated, superstitious humans (that made up the human population the world over); those easily duped, pathetic, bleating minions of the autonomous herd. Here then was the initiation (the first major instance) of the Jeshuan Church of

---

67 The Greek name for Philistria and Philistine was Palestine (Pal-is-teen) and Palestinian (Pal-is-teen-ian) respectively. This name remains today, though sometimes mispronounced as Pal-is-tie-yn: this does not rhymn with Christine (Christeen) or gasoline (gasoleen).

68 The Amoriots are not to be confused with the Maniot folk who were Dorian and Spartan descendants from the rugged Mani peninsula of the south Pelopennes.

Amor reversing its initial theoretical precepts of saving humanity and seemingly without any conscience (whatsoever) immersed itself into the Haploidic program of enslaving those same humans instead. And enslaving the majority for the benefit of the few in the here and now was all they really believe in anyway, it seemed. Not surprisingly, protests would soon emerge, especially in Angleland, Frankia and Germanika. But we're ahead of ourselves here.'

'And in the meantime Pepe the Hermit had been instrumental in finally beating up the entire population of Europa into behaving like lunatics struck directly from the pale light of a blue moon. It was he (Pepe) who now funded directly by Gizar Ankhman through the latter's ties with the AEthling, who had successfully and single-handedly lit the fire of crusading righteous entitlement into the hearts and minds of millions of morons and fanned it into a religious firestorm which never before had been seen in these parts. It was almost a Jeshuan celebrity version of the sensational occurrence of Mo'mad the prophet and founder of the Ishmaelite movement. It's hard to read the hype around the latter but the religion fashioned him and his message into yet another psychopathic, socio-political-religious ideology spawned from the ever-illusive god of Abram. And it was at this time that Europa was most vulnerable for logic hadn't yet become a subject of fascination beyond a low percentile of the peoples here, or of the resurrection of Helleneistic philosophy (that was soon to flower into Western Philosophy) that was still a century or three away.'

'Dyfed had made it clear to the *pack* (as well as now to his friend Jack Munster to whom he was relaying this tale) that the emergence at this time of this aforementioned A-rab cult onto the world stage acted as a control method of divide and conquer that was meant to take a little shine off both the Ishlamite Mo'mads and the Jeshuans; both of whom had begun to ride high, thanks to their Amoran foundation that acted as their conduit to cultural and administrative power.'

'So, the question remains is; in respect to this Jeshuan Jihad (this self-righteous crusading fever of entitlement), that began jumping from human to human as fast as magnetic like-poles repel, why was it being fast-tracked by an A-rab himself — namely Gizar Ankhman? The answer, of course, is obvious. It's the money, stupid! This controlling element (called religion) that was invented by the Haploids was powerful in its own right, all right; but the concept of money was more powerful. And the Haploids hadn't invented that. And that was their problem, now. But they were to quickly learn to get around this by fanning the greed potential that money opened up. Although they couldn't see through the problem yet, the Haploids wanted (and began working on a manoeuvre) to eventually get rid of money, but they had no desire, nor were there any incentive to get rid of (or diminish in any way) — the Haploidic friendly vice known as greed. And the crusade (this contagious aforementioned Jeshuan Jihad) now flashed out into every Jeshuan society throughout Europa. It suddenly and quickly burgeoned them out into a fat, noisy communion of tongues that spiralled in a great tornado spewing out a crescendo of sparks and a hot gas of intolerance and affrontement that exploded eventually in the direction of Palestine (remember, pronounced Palesteen to rhyme with gasoline and Christine) and the poor, innocent and unwary folks who lived there and were minding their own business. From the point of view of the Jeshuan Jihad, even pathetic, physically challenged cripples dragged their dead legs — with an amazing elbow crawl — in the first few marches toward the so-called holy-land in their erstwhile attempt, and in their fury to liberate the kingdom of the rumoured messiah. And liberate it from whom? you may well ask: Well, the answer to that is from the evil, impure heathens, the Ishlamites, folks of the devil who had overrun it during their boisterous debut in the sixth century of the current era and new order; according to the Second Empire and their calculation of time.'

'Dyfed wasn't among the unorganised and angry mob of crusaders who rushed off bent on deliverance into Jeshuan hands of all that was holy to torment and bring about atonement for the heathens. On this first crusade many got not much further than Byzas, anyway. Instead, once they entered that great eastern Amoran Imperial city they sacked Byzas causing riot and rape among that fair city's people instead. And this was after having committed atrocities along the way against the Bulgars who were, after all, fellow Jeshuans. So it isn't surprising that this unruly, religious inspired mob quickly outlived their warm welcome from the emperor of Byzas. This man had initially invited the westerners to stop there and fly the flag of force on account of his fear of the Turks. These Turks were under the employ of the House of Seljuk and at this same time were marauding far to close to his beloved city. In fact, it had recently come under threat. But now the emperor was of the opinion that his guests couldn't vacate fast enough and leave him room to defend the city himself. All this rage and spent goodwill had taken place even before the Europaean crusade had set out to cross Anatolia with those aforementioned dangerous Turk predators at large. Alas, these Jeshuans quickly managed to provide the tough and wily Turkish Ishmaelites with the sport of target practice and the opportunity to employ the niceties of religious prejudice and slaughter. For these Turks who had already been exposed and converted over to the cult of the Ishmaelites were riding high themselves on euphoric religious intolerance, though in some ways, at this time, they were more tolerant than many. The folks under Pepe's command and direction were not closely protected with a well-trained and heavily armed militia that was needed against the Turks. The Turks, who after all had at least come trained and dressed for the occasion, generally did not die like bedraggled dogs as the western Jehuans did, and they were obviously thrilled at the opportunity to engage in safe, consensual carnage. This then was Pepe the Hermit's route. Dyfed's route, on the other hand when he came to take it, was by sea.'

'So, after another Henry, Henry king of Angleland 1068 – 1135CE and son of the bastard king William of the same kingdom, had hinted to Dyfed how a contingency of Angle Saxen and Danes — headed up by the Aethling Edgar — were to be sent by him to aid the liberation of Jebus and that he thought it would look good if Dyfed contributed a little something. Dyfed then informed Trachmyr to grab a few of their merchant ships along with a portion of his army who could be spared from their duties. Then Dyfed sent Trachmyr to ask Anlaf's father (who was currently in charge of barges and fleets of the House of Lucifer providing building material to Angleland) to select two large sailing ships with some men to man them. So, these two ships and men were to be Dyfed's show, it seemed. It was to be his somewhat light and half-hearted support effort and pause in the House of Lucifer's progressive activity for the cause. In those days, you know, you didn't have a choice when it came to abiding by decisions that the state decided upon that automatically included you. These were decisions handed down from the curia at the top of the Second Empire. For the Church of Amor administered this empire, hence its formal name, the Holy Amoran Empire. And it was, and always had been, the Vicar of Jeshua and the organization's curia who controlled this and every other trendy religious cause that emerged.'

'Would there be any tolerance for conscientious objections? Absolutely not: Objections to the Vicar of Jeshua's edicts were volitions against the Church of Amor and to buck the system would incur what?…an indictable offence, of course, punishable by having your arms and legs twisted and broken off your body while being strangled to death. Good gracious! What were you thinking? Nobody would object unless they were a fool or plain crazy. Playing the system was different mind you, and that was what Dyfed always did and did well. You had to at least pretend to play (abide by) the game while you 'played' it; but you had better be at the top of your game while you did so. Otherwise, the tantalization of extreme torture will be on you like the pox.'

'Anyway, it was on account of Anlaf's aforementioned good work and organisational skills here that his father felt confident in sending a few of the House of Lucifer's precious deep sea-going ships under his son's command to aid the Crusades. They were then to sail and row from the See-land delta, down around the coast of Hispania into the White Sea. From there Dyfed asked him to proceed east until they arrived in the vicinity of Kypress, a large island known for its copper that gave it its name. There, or somewhere thereabouts, Dyfed planned to meet up with them. So just after the following Sinter-Klaas festivities Dyfed set out from the town of Tibur in Italia where he had been commiserating with his old friend, and *pack* member, Cato. This man had subsequently bought up the villa in Tibur to use as his retreat from Alba Longa. The villa, it may be remembered, had once belonged to Emperor Hadrainus. This Purchase of Cato's was accomplished shortly after he could no longer rely on temporary digs at the Esquiline Hill hood, more formally known as the Esquiline Hill Palace Estate town-villa-residence.'

'Then catching the ferry north to Genoa where he rendezvoused with Gizar Ankhman whose fleet was anchored in Genoa's bay. Dyfed offered him money to join together in this expedition with Ankhman acting as an attaché with exceptional, if not extraordinary, privileges with which Dyfed would provide him along with a great deal of gold to help liberate the Divine Land. Ankhman, he knew, would easily see through the pretence, for the former was very wily and cunning as a fox himself. However, Dyfed knew that if Ankhman willingly supported his effort toward the Crusade, along with Anhkman's own abilities of developing trade and setting up money lending enterprises on site, partnered with him Dyfed would be in a position that would allow him to get in on the bottom floor and own the penthouse and be able to stay ahead of Ankhman while all the while the latter would be getting very rich indeed but all the while be losing the turf war of dominating the world merchant banking business. That was something Dyfed was vying for. All of this Dyfed told him in a matter of fact way without flair and exaggeration. He then suggested they could get started now and leave together in Ankhman's flagship in order to arrive early. His ships and soldiers, he told him, would follow to join them when they got closer to the Holy Land.'

'From Genoa they sailed south past Piombino to their port side and the Isle of Elba to starboard, funnelled through the Strait of Messina between Calabria and Sicilia (Si-chill-ia) and headed east sailing through the Ionian Sea. Leaving that body of water they sailed between Kythira and Kreta, going ashore and resting at Antikythira for a week. Dyfed's little fleet did not arrive. Later, at Rhodos, they stopped again, this time for almost a month: Still no sight of the merchantmen that the young Anlaf Rijk Konge was commanding. On the Island of Rhodes, while Ankhman's fleet and crew reposed at the Rhodos citadel, Dyfed chose to reside at Lindos, making his barracks near the solid and fully intact Doric temple of Athena Lindia. From there they sailed pretty much due east to the shores of ancient Lykia where they made safe harbour at a small island named Sinter-Klaas. It was a beautifully located hill of an island that lay quite close to the steeply mountainous shoreline on the southwestern coastline of Anatolia. And judging by the number of western ships floating at anchor here on the lee side of the island, they all knew that it was probably heavily fortified and armed as well. They were cheered and welcomed warmly by many Jeshuans when they arrived and they found many churches here dedicated to the Jeshuan saints. These were scattered mostly around the western tip of the isle and were very old. And there was another built on the east side of the island's summit peak that was dedicated to Sinter Klaas himself. This was reputedly the site where the saint had once been buried. The church was later dedicated to his memory. Indeed, Dyfed reminded himself that Saint Nicholas had been born at Patara. This old city was located at the mouth of the Xanthos River barely twenty-five Amoran miles southeast of here.'

'Anlaf Rijk Konge — who contributed to the tale and saga of *'In the time of Dyfed'* as part of his own memoirs *'The Daze of the Purple Haze'* that was published by Dilmun Coinminter and Apollonius Goldmin many years later — can tell you that he wasn't so sure he wanted any part of Dyfed's Crusade-and- fly-the-flag-routine to liberate Jebus. It was because of his father's pride of him and his dream of commanding a fleet of his own that brought him this far. As far as the Holy Land and AEthelstan were concerned, Dyfed knew the latter well enough to know that he could have cared less about the place never mind any of his descendant kings of the Anglish. It was all about keeping up a show for all those Karl the Magnificents of this world and their business flowing into the shires of Angleland, or for that matter, any other country. Apparently, this island kingdom (formerly of AEthelstan's but now Henry's) was not accustomed to profiting from Ishlamite business. The Island of Sinter Klaas (upon which Dyfed waited for Trachmyr and Anlaf Konge to show up with his small fleet) was very much accustomed to Mo'mad attack and bombardment. For here through the urban and market sectors there was even a stone covered main thoroughfare. This was an aboveground covered tunnel that weaved up and around the hillside. This novel contraption enabled men and women to be able to safely walk and go about their business without being seen or struck on the cheek and the eyebrow from some decapitating, death delivering blow from above as missiles rained down after being fired from ships offshore. And although the church structures per sé were placed well above ground in plain view, some of the main halls and residences were dug deep into the rock and protected and out of sight from the sea and the high cliffs above.'

'Finally, one day while sitting beside a normal man sized niche that was carved into a rock ledge at the very top of the island's summit (a tomb that Dyfed fancied may have been that of Saint Nicholas himself) he suddenly saw his ships approaching. *'Menstruating mother of messiahs, thank Apollo'*, he said to himself, even though the vernacular of the time would have properly required a hearty *by god's eyes* or *by my oath of faith* or some such pronouncement. Hooking up finally with Trachmyr, along with the boy commander Anlaf and the small battery of men afloat in his miniature war fleet comprising the two small contributions of Dyfed and Ankhman, they now set out again.

They were all afloat together and headed in the right direction even if it could not be said that they were ultimately commanded in the name of God or the Vicar of Amor or even for chief mesmerizer Pepe the Hermit who was organizing this shin-dig that was soon to be a blood-bath and a game changer when it came to Jeshuan and Mo'mad relations in the future.'

'As the fleet rounded Kypress, Dyfed's smaller fleet broke away and anchored on its eastern shore in the old harbour of Salamis. This allowed the large Genoese fleet of Ankhman's more manoeuvring room at the port of Saint Simeon. Here they planned to take on water, fresh fruit and other supplies, and sniff the air and listen for news of the whereabouts of that Jeshuan army of crusaders coming overland. But no sooner had they dropped anchor and rowed their tenders ashore when news came back to Dyfed that the ancient city of Antioch (once an outpost for the olden day Indo-Europaean speaking Mitanni, Kassite, and Hittite aristocracy, and sister city to Karkemish — both then antedated), had presently come under attack by those same crusading Jeshuan over landers as they wended their way toward Jebus. As Antioch was quite near the port of St. Simeon, the entire fleet now set out immediately from Kypress for there.'

'It should be noted, as well, that Antioch, along with the city of Xandria in the land of Khem, were the two main cities that came to become centres of wisdom because of the brilliant idea of infusing Western Philosophy with Eastern religion and the cult of Abram. Later, those deeply camouflaged individuals whose craft is secrecy and subversion further infused the Haploidic method into the western system. Quickly they took over the reins (reigns) of the burgeoning Jeshuan cult (then much later the religion of the Ishlamites) that they influenced and then enlisted certain high echelon Jeshuan priests to succumb to their will. These latter mesmerizers, who worked under their Haploid masters, had soon perverted the Nazarean's idea that was then tailor-made to program and brainwash. Thereafter, it became the main tool that helped to control the masses through a method of derision and other bullshit.'

'When Dyfed arrived at the port of St. Simon the seaboard access to Antioch, he quickly located Edgar the Aethling's fleet that was partially funded by Gizar Anhkman. When they arrived the latter were still attempting to off load at a port that was protected by the confines of the river. Some Genoese ships had already taken up anchorage there and were helping to facilitate Bohemundus the Norman prince from southern Italia who was in charge of besieging Antioch. This ancient anchorage had once been renamed Seleukia after (Seleucus) Nicator (the conqueror) and founder of the immense Seleukid Empire. As there was now little room Dyfed decided to stay clear of the port. After surveying the situation closely, he directed his fleet to hug the coast and anchor a little further up beach where a spill-way canal flowed out through the rocky hills at an ancient site called Palaeopolis (old city). Indeed, it remains so, still. So it was here Dyfed found easy access to a broad sandy beach that lay between a spillway that channelled floodwaters away from the harbour that lay to the south. This spillway helped to reduce silting along with averting dangers of flash flooding to Seleukia itself. His ships rested beside an outcropping of dark coloured jagged rock that spilled well out into the sea just to their starboard side as their bows faced west and out to sea. This spot with its rocky environs provided good protection on their north flank of his small fleet which helped to narrow their window of vulnerability should it arise.'

'The Nicator (or Seleucus I) was a fourth century BCE soldier that had once been the leading officer of Xander the Great who had died just before Dyfed's time. This seaboard city was also once the home of Dr Apollophanes a third century BCE physician to Antiochus Soter (also deceased) who was a later king of the aforementioned Hellenic Seleukid Empire: Dyfed, of course, had never known either men. They are mentioned only out of interest and for the possibility that you know something of them yourself. And regarding the spill-way that emptied out by Dyfed's ships, Titus Flavius Vespasianus Augustus had ordered his Amoran engineers (relying on Judean prisoners for its labour force) to carve and chisel out this corridor through the rocky crags thereby creating a conduit to channel the rushing flash-flood waters away from the populated area and away as well from the estuary to prevent it from silting up the harbour as already stated. And in relation to where Dyfed's ships were at anchor, the spillway emptied out directly to their port sides. This was another feature for the protection of the south side of Dyfed's fleet of two ships.'

'Once Edgar had got his men and provisions ashore and ready to march to help provide for the siege of Antioch, they gathered themselves and organised the transport of these meagre food rations and other supplies needed. Up and over the hills they then trudged into the upper valley where the city of Antioch lay. As they marched towards this ancient city the soldiers began to blow on their pipes and play other instruments. This was to alert the besieged that more besiegers were coming to complicate their lives. Then suddenly and momentarily, Dyfed harkened back to the style of B'otuk shamanism that he had been exposed to and deeply enthralled by in the new world. Without quite knowing why, Dyfed called upon a carpenter to fashion a large drum according to strict specifications and instructed soldiers to take turns beating upon it with a certain rhythm. This caused an interesting reaction among the crusading assailants that seemed to give them more energy and courage. They continued on in this way until Antioch came into view.'

(Hitch a chariot to a star)

'I will sing to the Lord…He is my God, and I will praise Him…
The Lord is a man of war;'
EXODUS 15: 1 – 2 *(SHADES OF THE VERY REVEREND JERRY FALWELL)*

'Four hundred towers were incorporated into Antioch's massive fortifications. These fortification also included Mount Silpius beneath which was huddled the city. In its fullest complexity the city was too large to successfully blockade so the soldiers camped around it's towered gates and waited for it to fall. But there were additional problems. They soon expected a relief column of three or four thousand strong Seljuks commanded by Fakhr al-Mulk Radwan to arrive. Combined with warriors inside the City of Antioch this would press the Jeshuan army to its limits. While leading Edgar's army (funded by Gizar) toward the city Dyfed's soldiers piped up and squeezed the wind from the bags attached to their recorder-type instruments with their arms as Edgar's army (that traipsed behind) pounded out the big drum beat so as to announce their arrival. These bagpipe straining sounds and drum beat piped and beat the marching army on.'

'Upon their arrival before Bridge Gate, Gizar Ankhman — who was dressed to the nine's in some self designed costume he fancied set him apart as a high commander — commiserated with one of the crusade's ad hoc field commanders in chief, a dangerous looking north-man named Bohemondus di Otranto. Bohemondus was the son of Robert the Fox of the House of Upton, a family who had conquered southern Italia and Sicilia a hundred years before and had thrown fear even into the heart of the Emperor of Byzas. These two men (father and son) could properly be counted as the Second Empire's watermark as to an appraised warrior aristocracy whose epic lives were in some way heroic even if there was generally only a personal intent involved: Either that or points for family-house-motivation-for-gain that lay behind their actions. It was that, rather than an esprit de corps for the cause and on the scale usually set aside for clan, kingdom, race, or species.'

'Anyway, Dyfed noticed immediately that Bohemondus was acutely condescending toward Gizar from the get-go, despite the haughty airs that surrounded Gizar like a strangely visible aura. When Gizar — in his own way of taking command — shouted out for Pepe the Hermit, indeed, demanded him — Bohemondus flung a ridiculing laugh into his face.'

"This, I must say,' Dyfed said to his friend Jack Galoway of Munster, 'was not on account of Gizar Ankhman's appearances which strongly reflected a man whose descent was from the land of Khem. Certainly he was a foreigner and there was something quite Ishlamite about him and his enemy-like deportment around soldiers to normally arouse their suspicions. But Bohemondus did not appear to be the type to be trifled by looks and probably not by somebody else's religion, either; but rather he'd be more concerned if Gizar was there to help or hinder Bohemundus' agenda. I realised very quickly from that point on Muns that Bohemondus was here to search out new lands for himself. It wasn't about God it was about carving out his own duchy or his own kingdom. Bohemondus, who was long on warrior fame but short on ownership of real estate, would capture his own kingdom; and what better time to do it than now? Ah, a true north-man to the core, I thought Muns, Dyfed said.'

'In fact he soon learned the aforementioned north-man had already provided troops to his nephew Tancred ordering him to attack and take Cilikia while he himself eyed Edessa. This city was an important city-state that was just east of the Euphrates River in upper Mesopotamia and was less than one hundred and fifty Amoran miles away as the crow flies. And then in addition to that, shortly afterwards he prevented Fakhr al-Mulk Radwan from being able to relieve besieged Antioch by isolating its eastern wall that prevented Radwan the reliever from entering the city. Dyfed knew then that this guy wasn't fooling around. He wasn't even here on any particularly convincing pretence, either. Obviously with taking the lead here at Antioch and claiming it for himself would suddenly put him in command of a realm of importance that could stretch from Cilikia to Edessa and from Antioch to Byzas: That last venue had already been long on his list of cities to capture. This would make him large and dangerous with a sign around his neck that read: Keep out — trespassers, forget dog (or even armies) and beware of owner. He was serious about himself and neither Gizar Ankhman nor even Pepe the Hermit were anything to him but in the way. And the sooner they were on their way to get out of his way, the better. He didn't care about their agenda. He wasn't here for that.'

'At that point Bohemondus commanded a footman to fetch and bring to him a man called the Bishop of le Puy to deal with matter of Gizar Ankhman. This man was the nuncio or apostolic legate apparent and the spiritual head of the crusade. Bohemundus hadn't even bothered to summon Pepe, as Gizar had asked but when this bishop did emerge, Dyfed suddenly had a strange physical reaction. When Bohemondus, who was conducting other business (probably allocating Edgar's troops), waved the bishop toward Gizar without even acknowledging this relatively important man, certain signals suddenly when up for Dyfed on two accounts. Firstly his disinterest and secondly that this representative of the Vicar of Jeshua and the Church of Amor who may have been seen as a simple bishop to the people around here that were manning the logistics of the Crusade, he may have even been known as a cardinal to some; but to Dyfed he was formerly Gorgeous Giorgius Gregorius Florentius that was now fully blown into the House of George Florentius Hunover Edward Sax-Goth Burgfeld (once Cardinal van Richelieu, now) Bishop du Puy instead. There was no mistaking it. Gizar, he noticed, quickly climbed down onto his knees in subservient posture as the man approached him. For Dyfed's part, as he was standing holding his wide brimmed straw hat, when suddenly he replaced it on his head so that it covered his face from this bishop's haughty gaze equally as well as from the sun. Dyfed didn't want to be recognised by him, not here, not yet for George Hunover Sax-Goth Burgfeld was the man who had a lot of secrets and knew a lot of secrets about others. Dyfed remembered that back in the fourth and fifth centuries he had been the Amoran Press pamphleteer for the Church of Amor and was a close relative of a number of church men as well as relics that were mouldering on the shelves deep in the vaults of the Vatican City at the centre of the City of Amor. And if this man wasn't a Haploid, Dyfed didn't know who was. And among his company was an infamous mascot named Athauf the Goth[69]. And Athauf (after lying low since his fifth century connivances with Galla, along with other boners and tricks he pulled for

---

69 Athauf from atta-wulf, meaning father wolf: later spelled Adolf.

self-aggrandizement as the Amoran Empire disintegrated around him) was now a regimental commander of the Knights of Germanika and was aching to bring havoc and suffering and sorrow back among sundry peoples of our planet once again. Athauf (who lived in the village of Braunau sixty Amoran miles west of the town of Linz) was now referring to himself as Athauf the Wunschritter von Braunau, the Crusading Germanik Knight of Teutonia. And along with Athauf there were two other men accompanying the House of George Florentius Hunover Edward Sax-Goth Burgfeld Bishop du Puy: The first being the former Emperor Macaronius. This former emperor had not died but with the help of Constantine III (formerly Constantine the high king in the Province of Prydain and earlier known as Bricus Maximus) he had high-tailed himself to Angleland in secret where among the shires of the Lake District he tooled himself into a wealthy lord and re-named himself Whitey H. Knight of Macaroni. Why he was with the Teutons here and not with Henry and AEthestan's Crusading contingent was anyone's guess. The second man was Publicus Servicicus Nemesis Maximus Augustus Usurperus who among many others bankrolled Ateula who called himself Arviragus, servant of Mars.'

'So there we have it then, Dyfed thought. It turned out that the crusade, that is at least the princes of Europa and their knights along with their wealth that included troops were all really just outsourced at the last minute to get the job done. Apparently, the true overseers of this campaign knew that the Church of Amor and the curia in its charge couldn't afford the initial price of securing Jebus and clearing out the city and its vicinity for Jeshuan habitation loyal to the church on their own. In other words the Church of Amor couldn't complete its contract that it had with the Haploids that were being represented here by the likes of the House of Hunover Sax-Goth Burgfeld. So outsourcing had become the only option for them, and that tactic was seemingly organised to suck in easily fooled marks and other un-expectants from Angleland and western Europa in general. But Dyfed did not include Bohemondus among the former church contractors even if he was addicted to the unique posturing inherent to Jeshuanism and its sister religions. Anyway this display was quite normal for the times. But Bohemondus was not a foolish mark that got sucked in to do the bidding of another. It was even quite likely too that this man saw the play early and took advantage of the ensuing armies to which he added his own for another and personal agenda. And as far as the outsourcing itself was concerned, Dyfed instinctively knew that it had to have been organised and accomplished by none other than the man who had now appeared and paraded in front of him conversing rapidly with Gizar. Here was the man and the genius of the Crusades; it was not Pepe and maybe not even the Vicar of Jeshua either. Dyfed was now certain that it had been the House of Hunover Sax-Goth Burgfeld who had convinced the Vicar of Jeshua to hire both Pepe the Hermit and Gizar Ankhman for logistical support services.'

'Anyway, Bohemondus, who quickly tiring of Hunover Sax-Goth Burgfeld Bishop du Puy and of Gizar Ankhman as well, shooed them both outside of his pavilion and out of his way. Meanwhile, he had found some purpose for Edgar's troops and even Dyfed's soldiers, led by Trachmyr, who now managed to become attached to Godfroi's men (through Bohemondus' help) where he knew they would at least be fed for their services. Dyfed, on the other hand, wanted to stay clear of these particular princes and their knights, especially Bohemondus Prince di Taranto, Raemon de Toulouse and Godfroi de Bouillon even while thinking they may be potentials for *pack* associates in the future. Especially he didn't want to be around George Florentius House of Sax-Goth

Burgfeld Bishop du Puy. Then Dyfed remembered that while climbing along the road to here from Seleukia by the Sea, he had passed the monastery of St. Simeon. This place, though sparse and naked, was more congenial and much to Dyfed's liking. Better there, he thought, than to be camped with a bunch of farting gruff and uncultured soldiers. This latter was Trachmyr's environment, so he allowed his batman to abandon his duties as his servant and batman to participate instead on the siege front leading men who knew him. For in some sense once a soldier always a soldier. Although his duties would likely be more administrative, it filled his soldiery urge, at least temporarily, and was more to his liking. Also, under the circumstances, it saved him face and embarrassment in the eyes of the many soldiers who he knew would judge him according. Also he was Dyfed's eyes and ears as to what and how events would unfold while allowing the latter to maintain a lower profile. And as the monks at St. Simeon's were never more than happy to wait on Dyfed hand and foot and provide him service and compatible company, he made no pretence of hesitation in accepting their invitation to join them.'

'The chief executive monk at St. Simeon's who was nothing like a high priest or a bishop or anything else like that, could clearly see that Dyfed's interests weren't with the siege along with its blood and guts of so-called manly deeds. This chief executive monk was named Simeon. Maybe it was he after whom the monastery was named, he never said. Apparently it wasn't important to him although he spoke of Jeshua the Nazarean as a friend and never referred to him as a god or messiah. Furthermore, he told Dyfed about other friends of his; men like St. Luke the Evangelist who had been born here in the City of Antioch and donated his land to the Jeshuan cause. This property swept down from the eastern slopes that overlooked the eastern loop of the Orontes River that formed the island that was old Antioch. This property included part of the flatland at the foot of these hills. It had been there — on this his donated property — that the existing church of St. Peter had been constructed, he told Dyfed. There were other notable persons as well whose life stories have been kept alive by the copious notes that Dyfed always maintained. Men like Pious Peter and the Jeshuan bounty hunter and fugitive recovery agent Saul, citizen of Amor. Saul (commonly known as Saul of Tarsus) changed his identity to Paul the Apostle after having an epiphany while undergoing an anxiety attack that temporarily blinded him. Dyfed said that he believe he may have suffered from cerebral epilepsy. During one attack he became regretful of his gifted ability of exacting cruelty upon others; then upon recovering he immediately converted to the Jeshuan cult. You have to hand it to him for, upon recovering one's normality, most people would not have honoured their earlier intent. Paul then quickly chucked his role as Jeshuan persecutor and became a Jeshuan fanatic, a born again Jeshuan fundamentalist of his time and an agitator who disrupted and threatened the system by preaching that Jeshua was the messiah. This shows just how weak the system really was and maybe still is. Although obviously misdirected and ill, Paul may not be comparable to Raimon de Toulouse, Godfroi de Bouillon, or even Pepe the Hermit and certainly not Hunover Sax-Goth Burgfeld in their over emphasised enthusiasm towards Jehsua the messiah. The Apostle Paul was clearly not well and as stated earlier, subject to cerebral epileptic attacks, also donated land to the church prior to it coming into the clutches of Amor. And his peculiar personality as a radical is obvious from his earlier convictions, convictions that fuelled his drive behind a successful career of hatred and persecution towards others who bore him no harm. So, these three men, St. Luke the Evangelist, Pious Peter and the Apostle

Paul, all who had once lived here in Antioch at one time or another and had quickly assumed sainthood in their later years, had been friends of Simeon, Dyfed's new friend. Aside from commonalities between Simeon and himself, Dyfed thought that the monks shared certain interests with him and they henceforth applied a similar level of application for debate on knowledgeable subjects in which to entertain themselves. After all there is nothing like a new and fresh player's mind and tongue injected into an old circle of conversation to liven things up a bit. They didn't always agree. He noted at this point that the Jeshuan cult's organised factors, especially within the jurisdiction of the Church of Amor, though not evident in this monastery, were very, very powerful by this time and were a law unto themselves: Furthermore, they were becoming quick to utilise the power of immediate execution without public trial.'

'Anyway, back at Antioch and adjacent to the gate of St. Paul, just where the mountains spill onto the valley, that vicious Northman Bohemondus di Otranto had set up headquarters and positioned his army. The largest armed force present was under Raemon de Toulouse, one of Bohemundus' second in command. He was camped to the west of Bohemundus by the Gate of the Dog while Godfroi de Bouillon positioned his army opposite the Gate of the Duke. This left the Gate of St. George, the Gate of the Bridge and that vicinity of the road leading to the seaports of St. Simeon and Seleukia by the Sea to be guarded by Bohemundus. For it connected his siege operations with the Genoese fleet, Edgar the Aethling's fleet and Dyfed's two ships combined with Gizar Ankhman's contribution. This access between the sea and the city of Antioch led to the Jeshuan monastery where Dyfed had now retired to and settled in. The monks, much to the latter's comfort, didn't seem the slightest bothered by any of it. Apparently, even the Turks had left them alone. So consequently they were bothered only by the death and misery that would always be present in man's struggles with each other and they prayed that humans would soon come to their senses. Their thoughts, concerns, and consideration for others, coupled with their wish for the mental act of men to wake up out of their ego encumbering slumber and work together rather than to be at odds with one another, was mighty close to Dyfed's own concept of God's so called love, or the will of the uncreated Being that works in wondrous ways. Apparently, Dyfed had found soul mates in a rather unsuspecting location working under (what was for him, anyway) a misunderstood heading. Ah, life in all its wonders.'

"I can tell you that provisions ran out early during that winter, and by spring our troops were diseased from under nutrition and dying of starvation,' Dyfed told John of Muster. 'Upon invitation, a thankful Trachmyr joined me at St. Simeon's for SinkerKlaas celebrations. And although there was little to eat we were treated by the happy monks to a fine performance of chants and singing accompanied by wonderful performance of musical instruments: Indeed, they were the St. Simeon's philharmonic orchestra at our service. At this time no relief column had succeeded and there had been no success at entering the city, either.'

'It was early June and right after a clandestine night attack by Bohemundus on the Tower of Two Sisters, accompanied by heavy bribes and treachery on both sides, that the western Europaeans (mostly referred to as Frankens) happened to enter the city victoriously. Then, on Dyfed's first visit into the citadel, and with the approach of another relief army coming to Antioch's defence, he watched from the top of Mount Silpius to where he had hiked early one morning and from where he could just make out the distant sound of 'Deus vult', the crusader battle cry, and through the smoke of many grass fires he saw the Jeshuan army rout and destroy the incoming Turks. In the meantime, Trachmyr and Dyfed's soldiers had — by Dyfed's persistent request — assumed the responsibility instead of securing the safety of the crusader ships and their anchorages back at the port of St. Simeon and that of Seleukia by the Sea. In addition, Dyfed's men provided a safe transport of whatever provisions were available on the coast into the captured city. Bohemondus and Godfroi, it seemed, had learned well from Tacitus, however, credit went neither to Tacitus, Godfroi, or Bohemondus. It went to the opportune discovery of a lance tip by Pepe the Hermit that was found, he said, in the chapel of St. Peter. This was the earlier mentioned cave like structure carved into the side of a cliff that overlooked the inner, lower city. This object was then forcibly promulgated by both the latter and especially by the Bishop du Puy (George Hunover Edward Saxgoth-Burgfeld) to have been the very lance tip that had been thrust into the side of Jeshua Adon the messiah while upon the cross to die for the sins of the hoi polloi. Dyfed saw it briefly and assumed that the startling presence of freshly dried blood still on its tip must be from either a Turk, a Jeshuan soldier, or maybe a horse; for there was nary a deer, lamb or bovine beast carcass in miles for anyone to shake a stick at never mind to stick anything into, that was for sure.'

(Armed Jeshuans set out to strike the peaceful city of Jebus with the side of their sword)

'And David and all Israel went to Jerusalem, which is Jebus, where the Jebusites were, the inhabitants of the land. But the inhabitants of Jebus said to David, 'you shall not come in here!' Nevertheless, David took the stronghold of Zion.'

1 CHRONICLES *11: 4*

'In the beginning of the new-year, according to the Jeshuan calendar anyway, they set out for Jebus (the city of Peace) from where Adoni Melchizedek once ruled. Dyfed never knew him, either. I mention him only out of interest. Gizar, who was beginning to be shown some reluctant respect from Godfroi, sided with Bohemondus' decision to remain behind and rule Antioch while the remainder stormed Jebus. I told you so. No surprise for anyone there, nor the information that Baldwin (somebody's cousin or nephew) had used treachery and the kindness and hospitality of the king of Edessa to overtake the city and kill the king's son and heir while letting the broken old man live on in misery. Now with Bohemondus distracted with the potential of an eastern principality of his own, with its capital centred at the much important Antioch, and Edessa (controlled by Baldwin) positioned as a valuable tool of defence, Godfroi assumed the role of senior field commander in charge of the combined armies' big push on Jebus. The happy and friendly monks came out to wave goodbye and then returned to their own lives that pivoted around the monastery. There they continued designing and planning for ways and means for human beings to be able to get on together that they wrote down, and filed away in their library under 'required reading. As for Dyfed's army, he was hoping to disengage it from Godfroi's clutches and turn around and sail home. That was not to happen.'

'The depleted armies now turned for Jebus. Many marched south into a blowing khamsin along the coast. Others went by ship meeting at Joippa. At Joppa the angry conjoined armies turned inland to Ram-le and Lydda. It was from those two villages that they began the ascent to Jebus. The vanguard troops of this crusading army then arrived before the gates of Jebus at the start of the fourth Rosh Chodesh of the old calendar, or the sixth month of the Jeshuan year. Decimated by starvation and still barely recovering from Antioch and their march to Jebus, they then set to and struck that city's encircling walls with the edge of their sword with a mighty whack. Meanwhile, the technical support along with many of the armies' top logicians, engineers and propagandists sailed south with the fleet. Dyfed and his regrouped army followed suit.'

'Godfroi had received news that the governor of Jebus had made full preparation for defending the city. Apparently, this man had appealed to Abd-khulid, the head sultan in the land of Khem for relief. Accordingly, the sultan of the City of Mars the Vanquisher, or Victorious as it's known in the A-rab tongue (where it is called Cairo), had dispatched an army to march to the defence of Jebus and a navy to sail to Joppa to provide the battalions with support. Since the schedule of the advancing hostiles was unknown to the Frankens, Giorgio san Giorgio di Lucca, one of the prefects who became attached to Gizar's show, volunteered his regiment to remain behind in Lydda to keep watch and guard the crusading army's rear. This was to remain in place until all the troops of the armies were made ready before the walls of the City of Jebus and all had been secured and prepared for siege battle. At that point Dyfed was given charge over the anchorage. Not all of his men were needed to attend to this duty, and as he had also accepted the position of artillery logistics support, he and some of his men quickly pushed on to the city following the first and second wave. His immediate purpose once he was settled at the siege site was to organise siege equipment construction. They had learned such arts from their stint with AEthelstan. But Dyfed refused to be drawn into the fighting at this time. They would assist with the logistics of the assault but were meant to withdraw immediately the moment the city was taken and return to the ships on the seaboard. There, they would continue in providing rear guard duties and maintain security for seaboard property, ships, anchorages, as well as provide logistical sea to shore support. As Dyfed's manservant Trachmyr remained by his side. And the two of them remained at large and apart from the community of besiegers in general.'

'This was because Dyfed's dietary habits were a far cry from those chefs who toiled solely over the culinary needs of armies. Brute strength was needed for what soldiers do and battles were fought on stomachs. Army chefs filled a hole behind each trooper's bellybutton, and nothing more. As for Trachmyr, he was well versed in all Dyfed's habits and provided him the simple yet specific food he ate. There was to be no greasy, unwashed human hair in his scrambled-egg breakfast sandwich, nor was he attracted to such things that other hungry men appeared to be oblivious to. Anyway, the regular army officer was lucky to get breakfast. There was little to eat, on the whole, but with gold that Dyfed's flag ship carried he was able to employ a baker to provide them with many loaves of daily bread baked fluffy and puffy just as he wanted it and not flat and hard. Also he employed a small contingent of local men who roamed the countryside for domesticated poultry, eggs to keep the larder stocked, as well as any game they could scare up. Dyfed could only imagine how the besiegers were scouring the vicinity of Jebus devouring everything in sight.'

'By the first quarter of the month the crusading armies had begun their siege of Jebus; so with no enemy in sight along the coast, Dyfed left the anchorage with Trachmyr in charge and rushed to join his men quartered at Samuel's Mosque, a temple on Montjoie. However, despite the rumour, and despite the appearance of the fierce crusaders before the walls of Jebus, this situation had not visited confusion and defeat upon the city's occupants as hoped, at least not at this point, and the city was still secure. In fact, long before he had drawn close, Dyfed heard the armies. But when he arrived he found a great deal of confusion in the camp of the besieging crusaders rather than a situation of normality with the due process on track. The wells around about had been poisoned prior to the arrival of our vanguard contingent, anyway, and although other watering holes were being dug, the camp was continually short of water. The situation was further complicated by an inordinate hot summer. Also the construction of mangonels and siege towers had been forced to a halt due to lack of timber and other materials. Again, prior to their arrival, most of the trees around the city had been cut down and those that had remained had been immediately harvested and milled by the crusader's tradesmen to be formed into heavy timbers; but their numbers were insufficient to finish the task. Due to the stalling of the main objective, some knights began to ride off in frustration to conquer undefended villages or carve out a fiefdom consisting of goats and sheep.'

'Amidst this turmoil the Raemon, Compt de Toulous and Godfroi were struggling to keep control of the Frankens, Germaniks, Edgar's Anglelanders and some Italians that were all living side by side in a hodge podge mixture around the city. All the while they were trying desperately (at the same time) to proceed with their plans to capture Jebus. Under the circumstances, and not wanting to spend the rest of his life here, Dyfed now pitched in and actively assisted the three princes in any way he could. He was immediately attached to the pavilion housing logistics.'

'One day Dyfed saw a man wearing his armorial insignia (that of the House of Lucifer that consisted of a gold pentangle on a red background) ride up to their pavilion and swiftly dismount. Horsemeat was at a premium and that was why there were few of them still on the hoof, so the rider never tethered the animal but held tight to its reins. It was easy to see that he was on a mission of urgency and was undecided as to which pavilion to report to. Dyfed beckoned to him. The man was a member of his lookout guard. Once he recognized Dyfed he explained that he brought word that friendly ships had just arrived at Joppa on the coast and needed directions and assistance. Once notified, Dyfed's envoy, along with Godfroi and a host of his knights, then journeyed down to Joppa to welcome another Anglelander regiment accompanied by a Norwegian contingent and two other fleets, one was Pisian and the other Venetian.'

'One morning, as Dyfed sat at his desk in the shade of the colourful pavilion that was set amid the confusion of incoming camel trains and the bustle of attendants who were reporting to him in rapid rotation, a group of Angleland west country men came riding toward him. As one of them dismounted Dyfed recognized him to be a man named Gwayne. Gwayne extended his arms from his sides and held his palms upward as though indicating the material poverty about. 'God's blood,' he said and spat out some dust onto the ground. Dyfed noticed that his manner was easy though calculated that reflected confidence. They exchanged greetings and as Dyfed looked into his intelligent face he saw a marked subtlety within the expression of his large hazel eyes. As the armorial insignia that he and his fellow men bore was unusual (a skull above two crossed thigh bones ermine [black] on a field argent), Dyfed enquired after it. The man told him that it was the escutcheon of an Anglelander named Deric, also referred to as 'the Deuce'. This man, he said, originated in the city of Brycgstow (the place of the bridge). Gwayne went on to tell Dyfed that Deric the deuce was a son of the proprietor of the up and coming House of Theudor (Tudor). This house originated in Penmynydd on Mona Major, the Isle of the Druids and the patriarch was an adopted son and part of the fifteen tribes of Gwyneth. The man added that the son's escutcheon of the skull and bones was different from his father's as the son was considered a wild and dangerous renegade and had once been cast out and ostracized by his father from his house. The escutcheon of the House of Tudor, he volunteered, was a chevron argent on a field gules.

'Presumably, then the father's name was Deric as well,' said Dyfed.

'The man told him Dyfed that his adopted clansmen called the father in question Theuder or Tudor, but that he called himself Sideric Theodoric or just Theoderic.

Apparently, the father and son had come together in this venture, he told Dyfed, and had raised an army of their own from western Angleland that comprised of men under two different heraldic arms; the prominent one being that of Theoderic (Tudor) and the lesser his son's, the skull and bones. Gwayne said that he and the other officers with him were making contact and seeking directions. Meanwhile, listening with one ear, Anlaf of Flanders and Dyfed's trusted employee was writing furiously to record the lists of materials that his attendants were reporting to him in rapid fire into the other ear. As Anlaf was writing with both hands, he suddenly put the pens down and looked up at Gwayne. He too instantly recognized the man who once had been a friend and customer of his father's house. Gwayne had bought limestone for his master who apparently had made a fortune with this commodity.'

'Dyfed immediately furthered his enquiries and came together with his old acquaintance Theoderic (once called the great) and his son. And bye the bye Dyfed learned that Deric the Deuce was the only son of Theoderic who had a different mother from his siblings. His mother, unlike the others wasn't Audofleda (the sister of Chlodio) but a local woman from Gwyneth. Her name, he told Dyfed, was Ceredwyn. And he had a half brother as well who was a poet, he told him. His name was Talsin Davie.'

(Destruction and Eviction from the City of Oblation)

> *'Furthermore, we declare, we proclaim, we define that it is absolutely necessary for salvation that every human creature be subject to the Roman Pontiff.'*
> **THE BULL:** *UNAM SANCTAM (1302 CE)*

"Let me refresh you, my dear chap,' Dyfed said to Muns as they returned again the following day to the Yeoman's Arms. 'This venture we were on was to be the liberation of the Holy City from the heretical, Ishlamite heathen, as everyone in Europa was told they must be called. Soon, the word heathen was seen to be injected into everything bad, evil, nasty and questionable. The little boys who neglected their Sunday school tasks were potentially heathens if they didn't watch their P's and Q's. Furthermore, the people of the west were informed that they had to have a name for that peculiar heathen cult because that peculiar cult had a name for them: That name was infidel. Whether any of this information was true or not is not really known or important other than it was the word game and that always led to deceit and mistrust. It is quite unlikely that the Ishlamites (who had been coerced and herded into this adopted cult during the great expansion of the Ishlamites of the seventh and eighth centuries) got together and came up with a name for the westerners any more than the westerners got together and came up with a name for them. Certainly, no one remembers it happening. Probably it was a contrived program by the Haploidic leadership who were at the same time conjuring forth Zeus,' Dyfed said to Jack of Munster.'

'Anyway, both these label-names of heathen and infidel having been introduced to them as part of their programming, it is possible that the followers on either side would have been encouraged to utilize and apply them. The crux of the situation is the question that needs to be seriously asked in order to get a true answer that will be like a light that is shone into a dark cave. And if the flash of light from the torch that's shone into that dark cave happens to illuminates anything resembling the current status quo, we can immediately identify the works of Zeus who, truthfully, is neither a friend or a believer of either, but rather a dangerous pawn of the foe who works to destroy humanity. After all, how different is the Mahdi from the Messiah? It is relatively clear that only nonsense points to any judgement in order to support one side over the other. All of which must alert us to the prospect that in their dark cave under the rock, the sponsors of Zeus must be manufacturing many compartments of hoaxes, lies and false soothsayers to pitch against each other that will bring total slavery and misery to the hoi polloi in the end if it is not stopped at once.'

'The fall of Jebus that Dyfed had come all that way to witness and record, was brutal. Godfroi de Bouillon and Robert duc de Normandie wheeled their towers up to the north wall while Raemon Compte de Toulouse was still struggling with his approach ramp from Mount Moriah. These then were the two main approaches to breach the walls of Jebus while other points were being battered and rammed by the rock hurling battery of the Crusade's 5th artillery regiment under Theoderic (Sederic) and Deric the Deuce. In addition to this were the digging and burrowing of sappers that Whitey H. Knight employed with the help of Athaulf (usually pronounced Adaulf) and his handful of Germaniks. Many of the children who accompanied the crusaders were employed in this last enterprise, for their small forms could more easily fit and crawl through the tunnels beneath the walls and into cavities within the stone abutments to place the wood that fuelled the foundation destroying fires. This was the method they employed here.'

'The aforementioned Adaulf was not the only Teutonic commander employed in this crusade. There was two other effective regiments were being commanded by Hermann von Salsa. One of these regiments was in charge of the Hungarian hand-gunners. Later, Salsa (aided by an Irish Kelt military batman named Nial O'Crockodile) returned to the port city of Acre where he actually founded the official Knights of Teuton. Interestingly enough, Salsa rejected Adaulf' von Braunau's employ and enthusiasm for assisting him in this endeavour.'

'In numerous other places around the besieged city attempts were made to scale the walls with ladders and ropes, but Godfroi's and Raemon's massive dual attack did the most to divide the city's defence. By the following mid day Godfroi and Robert had already caused a crisis along the north wall, but the defence held. The fighting continued into the night again and the entire operation was lit by the glow of burning pitch and sulphur that clung to the wooden towers in the Saracen's attempt to burn them away from the walls. Raemon de Toulouse's tower, although it had been alight with flames from the day before, wasn't attached to the wall until after midnight of that second night. Dyfed had stayed well back. Even then from his many positions (for he rapidly moved about from one camp to the other with strategic orders in hand) there arose from the city an enormous din and the earth about shook as each bombardment from the rock hurling machines struck the city's fortifications. With the clash of battle, the roar of a multitude of warriors in everyone's ears, the shaking of the earth beneath their own feet and the impact of missiles against the city's walls, Dyfed began to feel quite anxious for those people barricaded within who he imagined were huddled together in comforting groups. And now winds — blowing off from deserts far to the south — began to howl and vortex around and above the city due to the raging conflagration of flames. An eerie glow appeared above the city that night from the roaring turbulence of the many fires from which sparks of wrath showered forth into the glowing darkness. From time to time missiles of sparks and great pieces of flame broke from the towers and tumbled earthward towards the men of the Crusade and its host of bystanders.'

'Within this protracted maelstrom there were men, women and children of the Abramistic and Ishlamite cult faiths. These folks had no initial quarrel with others and were known to respect all the encouragements and laws of all the prophets and insulted and generally acted shamefully towards none. They were abiding by and living under a code fit to serve humanity. That (in their mind) also served God. Dyfed also noted that the magistrates among the inhabitants of Jebus, for reasons concerning their own security, had earlier expelled the local Jeshuans from the city and forced marched them beyond the Jordan River prior to the crusader's arrival. So, even these folks, it seemed, had being subjected to the effects of this militancy. Yet, in this act the very heathens the

Jeshuans were bent on expunging had protected those Jeshuans' fellow believers. Under these conditions Dyfed had ventured to provide a recommendation to the council who he then intentionally sought out. When that opportunity to speak came, he suggested that once the city had been taken, the Jeshuan armies ought to show consideration and succour to the non-combatants within. The princes of the crusade, on the other hand, were appalled that he had thought they would conduct themselves otherwise and quickly dismissed him.'

'That night, however, Dyfed and his co-ordinate Gizar Ankhman (that gracile man from the Land of Khem) looked upon the conflagration that raged before them in utter dismay. Dyfed suddenly felt a foreboding that some ignoble and senseless destruction was emerging as an organized entity. It was also a destruction comprised of gigantic proportions. Dyfed was unable to read his companion's thoughts as he stood like stone staring out at the destruction and breathing in the filth. Trachmyr who he had summoned and had arrived a few days before to return to his duties as batman was obviously distressed as well. Even during the darkest days when Amor was employed in the total ruination of the enemy were the acts of pure evil seldom as overwhelming as this, he had thought.'

'As Aurora of the horizon, luminous and radiating chased the long dark shadows westward and the Divine Land tilted east towards the sun, Dyfed noticed with a perplexity of emotion that apart from Raemon's tower — that during the night had come to be joined to the wall — very little other progress had been made. Many knights and soldiers from both sides lay dead and burning on the ground, the smell of their roasting flesh permeating the warm morning breezes that continued to stir up clouds of dust. With the coming of the morning light of the third day of battle, Dyfed could see the ascending clouds of billowing smoke that he assumed would be visible from very far off, perhaps even by that army sent by the sultan of the City of Xanderia on the Nile River to aid in Jebus' relief. In the dawn light he could make out the escutcheons and armorial standards of individual warriors and was able to see the Frankens frantically fighting to get off the covered tower and onto the wall. At one point he saw a young naval officer identified as Derik the Deuce. This bold man soldiered forward on an extended wooden beam and slew two Saracens before wisely retreating into the cover of the tower again. From time to time, by concentrated observation, Dyfed discerned others — which he could identify — boldly fighting for a bridgehead high upon the ramparts of the city. Then, making his way toward Mt. Zion Dyfed was able to observe the knights and footmen from the Lanquedoc and from Provence fighting for supremacy upon those battlements there. Below the partially burning towers the remainder of the troops waited their turn to ascend. They called out encouragements, passed up replacement swords, shields, and water, as well as being busy filling in as artillerymen. Raemon and Godfroi, who stopped only to shout out orders of rotation to their troops, fought on tirelessly and seldom retreated to the ground for rest and refreshments.'

'A few hours after sunrise, Raemon de Toulouse climbed down from the tower and summoned Dyfed. In turn Dyfed informed Godfroi, Robert de Normandie and Robert of Flanders that Raemon wished a council of war. These men then met to assess their position. Everywhere you looked valuable and preciously constructed siege machinery was on fire; a thousand Jeshuan soldiers alone lay dead and morale was beginning to plummet. But as Godfroi pointed out, although the Saracens defence was still holding, the witchcraft that they were employing in order to cast spells on the siege weapons and artillery ranks had been, he thought, rather unsuccessful. As the others readily agreed, they decided to continue the siege. For the time being the deciding factor in such events was no longer on their side as it was thought that relief armies for the Saracens may arrive at any moment. Robert of Flanders then suggested that when the wind was right the hay and cotton bales could be hung against the battlements and lit in order to drive the defenders back away from the wall with even more heat and smoke. Smoke and mirrors got them nowhere but this would allow the crusaders time, he thought, to drop the bridge and cross over to the wall. There was an added possibility that the entire tower may catch fire as well causing havoc with the attacker's entire operation. After this had been discussed at length Raemon said that despite Dyfed's timely reports of what was taking place along the north wall they would benefit by a better method of coordination. It was then suggested by Raemon that Dyfed take to the Mount of Olives with a signalman where he could better evaluate each tower's degree of success in breaching the fortification and be able, from there, to signal one or the other in applying supporting pressure at the appropriate time. Each siege tower was then assigned an identity letter to expedite this method. Robert of Flanders questioned Dyfed's qualifications for such a co-ordination citing the needs for proper assessment abilities in military affairs, but Godfroi, Raemon and Robert duc de Normandie quickly overruled him and Dyfed was dispatched to the location for reconnaissance.'

'From Dyfed's new vantage point he could now observe the city itself around Mount Moriah, the original site of King Arauna's altar to Tammuz where Solarman's Temple — which was actually and originally dedicated to Saturn — was located. And he could easily see the two congested knots of soldiers converging on the battlements at the two extremities of the city. Suddenly he felt the wind change course and quickly signalled Godfroi de Bouillon who had returned to the tower and who could clearly be seen now commanding the troops of the two armies. Dyfed then saw the flaming arrows stick into the bales followed by a smudge of smoke that seemed to drift listlessly about in the air that was no longer funnelling upward. The bales were soaked in oil and wax that tended to allow them to burn longer yet more violently and caused them as well to give off a black plume. Then the wind picked up again, and whooshing past in the opportune direction, flames and black smoke curled all of a sudden over the battlements driving the defenders back. Immediately Dyfed signalled to Godfroi, although he had suspected that the latter had accurately assessed the situation on his own. Dyfed then signalled Raemon de Toulouse on the other side of the city. This last act he conducted not a moment to soon for immediately afterwards this part of the city was blotted out with smoke and he could no longer see Raemon's tower. But he could easily see the hide covered drawbridge from the tower against the north wall drop and the armies of Godfroi de Bouillon and Robert, duc de Normandie make ready to surge forward. He even clearly heard their accompanying battle cry as they pored across the covered drawbridge and finally into the city.'

'An hour or so later Dyfed witnessed first-hand the awful carnage. Some knights did succumb to base or devilish instincts, but mostly it was the mercenary rabble that went berserk and bathed themselves in blood as well as disgusting and shameful acts. A grey haired berserker upon breaking into a school murdered all the children, it was said. Upon emerging shortly after into the light of day the man was summoned by a kindly and unsuspecting priest who politely asked the madman to lend a hand in assisting a frightened young woman and her child. Suddenly, to the horror of the priest, the afflicted madman whose inner voice had been pulled apart between conscience and programmed duty, thrust the bloody knife (which he had still been holding in his bloody hand) into his own neck and immediately died with a deep slashing cut to his own throat. At one point, as Trachmyr and Dyfed slowly penetrated the city behind the fighting, Dyfed quietly climbed the steps to an upper room so as to be able to look out across the front line of fighting. As he silently entered the top room he recoiled. There, a well armed Saracen soldier and what appeared to be an elderly couple lay on the carpet, their bodies opened at the throat and gushing blood. In front of them with his back turn partially towards Dyfed was a Franken soldier who Dyfed first mistook to be urinating on the floor. Then he noticed that he had become aroused with having slaughtered these people, or maybe just by viewing them, and was relieving himself in self-carnal abuse. Others were not so squeamish in regards to physical contact and often raped before or after murdering. A priest from Provence, who had entered the city with the Provencal army through the city gates that were now flung open, was discovered committing unspeakable abominations and was placed under guard. However, before the day was out he managed to throw himself off the wall to his death, possibly with some assistance.'

'In the afternoon it was learned that Raemon de Toulouse having beaten back the defenders, had clamoured into Jebus and had entered the fray from the opposite side of the city. The Saracens now pinched between the two factions were ostensibly doomed. The governor shut himself (along with some of his elite troops) in the Tower of David and eventually sought to negotiate terms of surrender with Raemon. Fighting continued throughout that day and into the next night. Tancred's knights pillaged the treasures of holy places while others massacred mindlessly. Godfroi slaughtered the defenceless governor and his imprisoned men who were under Raemon's protection before ordering that the high temple (where the remaining Abramists had gathered) was to be burned to the ground. This having been done, Godfroi thereby later claimed to have rid the city of its messiah/saviour accomplice-killers all with a single torch. It was a gruesome sight and terrifyingly awful to behold. The screams of the burning people were louder than the roar of the flames and louder even than the pounding and battering on the inside of the temple doors as the doomed people vented their fear and pleaded for mercy and deliverance from the burning pyre. Frantic cries to let their innocent children live were heard right to the awful end. Later (as Dyfed helplessly watched) the structure collapsed and raised a cloud of ash over the human destruction.'

'The soldiers, unlike the knights, had no access to rich treasures that abounded in holy places, so in their belief that the Saracens swallowed their wealth these soldiers slashed open the dead and spilled their innards upon the streets of Jebus in hopes of finding material reward in the way of gold and precious gems among the guts. Consequently men roamed the blood and guts slippery streets bloodied to the elbows from grovelling in gore. The accompanying families of the crusaders were, at this time, still outside the city and momentarily forgotten. Perhaps this was fortunate for it would not have done for wives, never mind young children, to see what vile and vulgar beasts their loved one really had become with a pull of a Haploidic lever back in Frankia, although in some cases, its quite certain that a number of these more tender ones had already guessed the truth. Just before midnight of the third night the crusaders at last made their way to the Temple of the Holy Sepulchre where knights and soldiers stood side by side to celebrate mass together. Here, before the glittering candles, the priests and congregation gave thanks to almighty god and most especially his sacrificial son Jeshua Adon for delivering unto them the Holy Sepulchre and the dome of the rock. They gave thanks also in allowing them to assist god-almighty in expelling from this holy city the primitivus ex superstitio of Ishlamitism and of the antiquated prototype of Jeshuanism, the strict Abramists' Abramism.'

(The Skull and the Cross Gnomes)

*'Then the king stood by a pillar and made a covenant
before the lord, to follow the lord and keep his commandments
and his testimonies and his statutes, with all his heart and
all his soul, to perform the words of this covenant …'*

2 KINGS 23:3

'Upon Dyfed's return from the so-called divine land, he was finally able to take up the helm of his business again in earnest and turn his full attention to remodelling it since his ad hoc improvising during that destructive era of the Great Heathen and Unwashed Horde. Now, after the distraction of the crusade, Dyfed could concentrate with help from his new (almost) family. This was Theoderic and Dyfed's own biological son's step brother, the piratical adventurer Deric the Deuce. He gathered many of these men from those who he had rubbed shoulders with during the Crusade but on second thought did not include Bohemondus. The old side and only allegiance that man employed, he thought, was his own. Using a template taken from the *pack's* own stamp and profile, Dyfed immediately envisioned and conjured up a newly formed Brotherhood of Noble Elites he called the Cross of the Gnomes. Their motto was *En to Pan* (All in One).'

'At this juncture Dyfed (who had suddenly found it lucrative to continue lending the establishment a hand via his expertize and entrepreneurship, namely through his armoured banking consolidation), decided to expand its abilities now to a new level. Now he was able to take charge of a king's chest of gold, say in Nova Troia, Isis, or Amor on one day of the week and provide the king's chamberlain or a wealthy merchant or his representative with a receipt in the form of a promissory note that was valueless to bandits, or anyone else. But that promissory note could be redeemed at some far-flung flyblown destination in the far corner on the other ends of the earth months later — or the next day if communications could be greatly enhanced. Never mind the golden calf, Dyfed knew he had a fiery lion by the tail with this enterprise. Presto! Now he would be able to safely provide credit to customers no matter where in the world they may be so long as he had a branch of the Union Bank of Commonwealth there. Dyfed's representatives in any of his banks were easily able to verify the authenticity of the promissory note and immediately remit funds in lieu and restore flushness thereof to the holder with this idea he had now formulated. Of course, as always there would be a modest, non-refundable charge for services rendered. He wasn't forcing anyone to use his banking facilities but he built it and they came.'

'This method of banking that he innovated soon proved to be safe and secure for all parties. The rich paid well to safeguard and move their money. Of course the House of Lucifer and its bank didn't have to move any gold and silver, they simply needed each banking house branch to have sufficiently large reserves of gold and silver on hand, as well as the branches grand leger for all promissory note cheques written anywhere by the bank. Every branch had the same leger copy that was continually being adjusted with new numbers for receipts for gold received by the bank and other duplicate numbered receipts being crossed off after being cashed. This was the Grand Leger. Of course a depositor could withdraw gold from the same bank with his promissory note or any other of Dyfed's banks anywhere. Derik the Deuce came in handy here for transporting gold and silver by sea to Dyfed's sundry banks and with soldiers of Dyfed's army guarding the over land caravans routes that were replenishing his bank branches inland and far from the sea. Of course customers brought gold to the bank to be deposited and that gold didn't have to go anywhere until he or another customer cashed his promissory note. But branches needed to be sure that they wouldn't run out. In Dyfed's case a run on his bank could mean a large value amount deposited in in the City of Venice and wanting to be withdrawn in the City of Lisboa. And if that branch normally deals in nickel and dime transfers and then suddenly be required to pay out a ton of gold that wasn't available, then he failed his customers. So actual gold and silver along with the very important up to date Grand Legers was on the move all over the commercial world and transported by Dyfed's fleet of Aura Maré (III to XX) floating safe-deposit boxes. They sailed here and there and every which way and were guarded by a skull and cross bones flagged fleet of war ships that was under the command of Deric the Deuce. Since the latter (now a fellow knight of the newly formed *Brotherhood of Skull and Cross Gnomes* and a registered affiliate of the *pack*) had been pirating from the Meghreb, West Afrika and along the coasts of Hispania and Gaul for the last few decades, Dyfed's partnership with him was lucrative. Even a 'gold-bank' fleet of a few ships could safely shuttle bullion either high-graded from pirating an Hispanic 'gold-ship', or being transferred legally anywhere he needed, whether around the high and dangerous seas to destinations hither and yon. But only when accompanied by a escort of one or two warships under the command of Deric the Deuce.'

'This is exactly what the newly formed Hansa League was looking into doing and Dyfed was vying for an associate membership there, at the very least. Often, now, the naval division of the House of Lucifer's Union Bank of Commonwealth would high-grade the commercial laneways of the seas under Deric the Deuce while moving gold bullion around, or waiting just off-shore and keeping a bank deposit afloat for extra security, their pirates (I mean sea captains) saw to it that any unprotected vessel heavily laden with booty that passed them by were quickly lightened of their load and liberated. This was mostly for those other ships own protection as well as for sensible safety-at-sea practices. Sometimes the House of Lucifer's bullion ships encountered dangerous loaded pirate ships from Afrika and in time from the Carib Sea and even Peru. To confuse them, instead of a flag of the House of Lucifer (that was the same as his emblazoned Crusade emblem of insignia) Dyfed's captains would quickly hoist a black skull and cross bones on a field white which was the Deuce's ensign. Soon the Deuce hit on flying the House of Lucifer flag high above his low riding designed ships that (as cargoes went) were as poor as a church mouse. Then, when they attracted foreign ships manned by swarthy pirates bent on moving in for a heist and a kill, the Deuce would swiftly out manoeuvre the mark and bring their light boats alongside their would be attackers who could neither out manoeuvre or outrun them. Now the Deuce would swing out the cannons, and the young and adventurous crews — cutlasses drawn now, daggers tightly clenched between their teeth — just waiting for the command licked their lips at the prospect of booty along with newly acquired vessels. Then with curdling screams, over the side they went to either gain possession of another ship to act as a saddlebag for their own booty, or lighten the booty that their attackers were carrying before scuttling it.'

"With the state in which the world's sea-lanes, by-ways, the valley ways and its mountain passes were in these days, even the heavily armed servants of kings and emperors could get mugged and beaten and the wealth they carried being seen to quickly disappear and vanish into thin air, Dyfed said. Especially if their servants were not as loyal as they sometimes made themselves out to be. And this poured wealth into our coffers, Muns; the better to help the poor hoi polloi and raise their standards and their expectations of what they deserve in this life on earth: equal opportunity in all things to broaden one's existence and equality before a codex of governing law. Beyond that, Muns, there is no such thing as even two humans anywhere who are equal with one another. We are all equally uniquely un-equal.'

'Also there was royal support, of course, due to the Jeshuan cult's richest henchmen not wanting to look like chumps in the face of the hoi polloi. Men such as Holy Amoran Emperor Karl the Great (retr'd), or Famous Flavius Claude Martel now Bishop of the city of Isis on the river Sen, and the ever present House of Hunover Saxe-Goth Burgfeld and George who was currently the Duke of Frankia and potentate of Burgundy West while one of his brothers or cousins, a certain Maurice van Richelieu was the acting archbishop of Aquitaine. There were other men involved who were lesser known to the hoi polloi such as Pollox Scipio, Asinius Scopalius and the former Angle-Sax king Octha (the future William Warehouser), Constantino Asinine, Lev Trotsky, Boris Karensky and last (but far from least) Charles (Carlos) Ferdinand Alfonse Metterholzenstaufenschwig. These men were all as eager as ever to hire the House of Lucifer's pirate fleets for their own ends. Even Cornelius-Felix was beginning to salivate over Dyfed's methods of gain. Trotsky and Karensky (by the way) were both later founding members of the United Industrial Workers of the World Union. So it was in Dyfed's interest to discourage them from promoting their own sea-wolf packs and use his instead. The Deuce helped Dyfed in this by pirating and sinking every vessel that was capable of being assailed with the help of the *pack* itself while being supported and advised by the likes of Count Agenbite of Inwit, Paredros of Phigalia, and Ebreo ben Jamin, who now called himself Thamus.'

'Under Hyperborean Masters of the Little Known Universe such as Dr Pel, Dr Gismo, Dr Torsionfield, Manandan and Prince Penrhyn (from Dyfed's youth) and Morgant and a host of adepts like Karatakos and Theoderic, the brotherhood of the third dimensional hoi polloi under the direction of the *pack* were now just beginning to cut the mustard and amass an incredible wealth to help wield the power they needed here in this dimension to secure their goals of destroying the Haploids and to set their less aware and less educated hoi polloi brothers and sisters free: Never mind to create a tranquil world-wide holiday resort here in this third dimension for everybody.'

'Dyfed relayed to John of Munster how when returning from the Philistine Crusade he had bumped into Ebreo in the shadow of the Pyrenees at Beziers. An up and coming Cathar stronghold, it was at Beziers just before the aforesaid Albigensian Crusade that Dyfed had learned that Ebreo had shirked and then resigned from his duties as an employee at the House of Lucifer to concentrate instead upon his two century old business of manufacturing Ulfberht designed swords to both ranks of soldiers; these were folks who were supporters of the Church of Amor's encroachment of Philistine and those who defended themselves from the Crusading Jeshuans. However, this piece of trivia in itself may have soured Ebreo's relationship with the peace loving and buggering Bognil Cathars under whose protection Ebreo (as a wandering tinker) he had sought.

Just as Dyfed had arrived there Ebreo was returning north to seek protection and re-appointment to his position of chief metallurgist in the House of Lucifer. Ebreo was a flawed character and not an easy one to read, Dyfed told him.'

'These aforementioned Cathars were a Jeshuan orientated quasi-mystical bunch who didn't appear to go out of their way to denigrate the religion of others but did not seek to become affiliated with (or believe in) the dominating Church of Amor's version of Jeshuanism, either. For that sole reason the Pontiff and Vicar of Jeshua Adon, Pope Innocent (sic), who in addition to pouring out hatred towards any who didn't bow to him (such as the Ishlamic folks of Hispania who he crusaded against, as well as the so-called Holy Land and the eventual sack of Byzas of the Fourth Crusade), he now ordered up the Albigensian Crusade against the Cathars. In this endeavour he and his submissive allies led by the Franken kings Philip and Clovis VIII who marched on these Cathars as to war with the cross of Jeshua going on before. In no time they had hunted these Albigensian (Cathar) folks down and were slaughtering them in huge numbers in their attempt to exterminate these modest reformers who hurt no one and always believed in seeking the truth in all matters and who championed education for children. It is interesting to note, too, that the massacre at Beziers that kicked off the crusade killed all twenty thousand plus souls of that city in about one day: This included women and children and even a few unlucky Church of Amor priests. The entire crusade and the ensuing holocaust lasted twenty years where somewhere between half a million to a million Cathars were exterminated: This at a time when the population of Europa was only seventy million compared to four hundred million when another holocaust occurred seven hundred years later. It is a vast and non-relative number. Relatively speaking the number is large even when compared to the unconscionable death toll of all the crusades put together. In ratio to later wars, such the Great World War, its silhouette still skyrockets to heights beyond horrendous and hideous. According to Innocent, the Vicar of Jeshua, the pontiff of Amor, this was his god's plan for the Cathars.'

(The Yeoman of the Guard Pub, Cambridge)

'Grieve not for those who live, grieve not for those who die, for life and death shall pass away.'
LORD KRISHNA

"So, there you have it Muns. At about the current time-line in our story, the Hansa or Hanseatic League (which had begun shaping up over the last half a millennium) was now reaching maturity. Yet just now, as it has just shifted into top gear and become a commercial force, Karl the Magnificent's (the establishment's name for him, not the author's) progeny have felt it necessary to quash and squash any such successful enterprise like the Hansa commerce. This was because they couldn't control the Distributionism for Profit themselves which that they meant specifically to personally profit thereby and from which to prosper exponentially more than its other participants. So certain power elites had seen to it that it was hog-tied and gagged to the point of causing it to wither. It was then put out to pasture along with its founding idea.'

'Dyfed suspected (with good reason) that for centuries this Magus, the so-called Karl the Great, was fast and furiously being mentored by certain elements among the Haploidic power elites. And Dyfed was certain that George Hunover Edward Saxe-Goth Burgfeld (the once named Georgius Gregorius Florentius, Bishop of Tours and later Cardinal van Richelieu, Bishop du Puy and later still commonly known as Giorgi Posh) was among them. He also thought that Karl the Great was probably the House of Saxe-Goth Burgfeld highest client candidate. Meanwhile, Dyfed knew that old Clovis was still in touch with his faculties despite evidence earlier on that he wouldn't be in touch for long. This man had an exceedingly sly and devious nature about him that was useful for covert machinations that were badly needed now. Dyfed had come to realize that if one came to a conclusion about the man, it was usually going to be wrong. Dyfed expected big things from Clovis (Louis). One of them being that he would rival Giorgi Posh as well as Charles (Carlos) Ferdinand Alfonse Metterholzenstaufenschwig the King of Hispania who had been preceded by Felipe the Hispanian king whose demise had freed up the seas of the world for the Virgin Queen of Angleland to flex the muscles of the male members she entertained, like Draker and Cecil and the Earls of Oxford and Essex. What he didn't know was that Giorgi Posh who served as the Hansa base in Nova Troia had hoodwinked a pivotal merchant at his Steelyard named Dickie Claude de Giese. The former had gone out of his way and borrowed heavily to secure the denarii he in turn loaned to de Giese. Giorgi Posh had managed to hit up Charles Ferdinand Alfonse Metterholzenstaufenschwig who provided him a shit-load of Hispanian Real, his very own gold coin of the realm that happened to be the international currency of it's time. Anyway, in consequence (and the upshot thereof) de Giese had become heavily indebted to George Hunover Edward Saxe-Goth Burgfeld. The climate, you see, had suddenly taken a turn for the worse again and that brought back into vogue the décor of white and frozen among the bucolic and the natural. This was later to be called the Little Ice Age. Meanwhile the fortunes Dyfed had massed had no viable conduit in place in order for him to disseminate this fortune into the hands of the needy people at least so they could make the most of their lives. It was just not working.'

'As he commiserated with John Galway of Munster at the Yeoman of the Guard Pub in Cambridge, Dyfed's thoughts had turned to the development of Merika from the Hispania Main north and up along the eastern coastal strip of the North Merikan continent. Already — over there — vast plantations, sundry agricultural sectors and new industry were underway where personal ownership (employing thousands of workers who could toil for the personal wealth of a single man) abounded. And apart from the thousands upon thousands of slaves brought in from Africa these folks were amassing fortunes. Indeed, progress was now afoot to organize and safeguard the rights and possessions of each enterprising individual. This was good and Cato had given a hand to see this through although it was still in its infant stage. Unfortunately, these possessions also included the thousands of slaves. This was not good for these slave men and women who had no freedom or equal opportunities were not provided for like other humans, namely their masters. So, it just so happened that Dyfed, who was visiting the university cities of Angleland in an effort to decimate much of his fortune through education for the masses, was now presently in the process of planning his return to Merika. He was already quite advanced with an early development of his escape plan from abject failure that had come over him in respect to his endeavours to sustain the integrity of the *pack* and further their mission In other words, this was something in which he now believed he had failed miserably.'

'Also he had growing concerns over vast Europaean bank loans that were making inroads over controlling the new world's industry and infrastructure and this was because it inevitably involved the same old names of the rich and exquisite houses of George Hunover Edward Saxe-Goth Burgfeld, Carlos Ferdinand Alfonse Metterholzenstaufenschwig (a descendant of the House of Constantine), Hipparchia Philostropodousalouspolousadous (a Canaanite Cypriot and brother of Potamus Purplebal) and Dickie Claude de Giese (of the House of Giese formerly the House of Lorraine). Furthermore, these lesser banking industrialists than himself were beginning to introduce loans to the colonists over there in Merika and were even setting up permanent business fronts in the new cities such as Cartagena (founded by Pedro de Heredia, conquistador and pirate), Bosstown (founded by Puritanical colonists from Angle-land) and the fast and vastly growing city of Megatropolis (whose port was first visited by Norse/Danes out a-Viking and Bask fishermen, then permanently recorded by the Italian Giovanni da Verrazzano, explorer). And this use of private banks — controlled by folks like the House of Saxe-Goth Burgfeld, Hipparchia Philostropodousalouspolousadous (and her brother Potamus Purplebal), Conrad Bell (Compte de Mirabelle), the House of Mettweholzenstaufenschwig, Mr Guy Julio (Magister Gaius Julius –the Jerk), Arthur Brittain (Lucius Artorius Bricus Demetia) Madam de Domrémy, and Augustus Reno III (formerly Publicus Servicicus Nemesis Maximus Augustus Usurperus XVI) — was a fast adopting trend in the use of private banks in general whose ownership wasn't fully disclosed or known. That, Dyfed then decided, would become his desk; it would become his field of operation once he got settled in. But he would need the likes of Draker and Cecil and the Earls of Oxford and Essex and Count Agenbite of Inwit, all of them among the Brotherhood of the *En to Pan* who received ever-loving support from the *pack*. He then set aside millions of Real to fund them so they could but=y up more plantations and the odd piece of mechanized industry wherever it might be found. But the more he thought of it now, the more he was concerned over the sheer volume of that responsibility and weight that it would eventually bear down upon him. He would need more help, obviously: But first things first.'

"Muns,' he said 'I have at long last located Ceredwyn. After Talsin Davie found me I knew where she and Sederic (later known as Theuder or Tudor) were located but it was not my place to make myself known to her then. Now she is recently widowed. She lives in Bristol. I am going to her and asking for her hand in marriage and we will then leave for the continent of Merika.'

"Do you know where you will go in Merika?' Muns asked: 'North or south Merika?'

"North,' said Dyfed.

"Perhaps Boss Town?'

"No. Due to reverse historic memory that was visited once on me, I know we will abide and inhabit the far western coast of North Merika. Those of us who have had access to the secrets of Whithall and the Virgin Queen's activities now know that one of Deric the Deuce's great pirates, Draker or Drago (also Dragon), during his sojourn as the first Europaean sea captain ever to return after circumnavigating the world, visited the largest island on the western coast of all the Merikas. This lies hard against the western Peaceful Ocean at approximately fifty degrees latitude north; that is North Merika. The longitude, unfortunately, is still undetermined. I will soon correct that,' he told John Galoway of Munster.'

'He then noticed that John of Munster was staring at him oddly.'

"In respect to my new life I'm going to make for myself in the new world.' Dyfed then told Muns that he was still ahead of himself, for at that point he hadn't even had the chance to become properly acquainted with Ceredwyn yet. He only had Talsin Davie's thoughts on how she still felt about him.'

'He then referred to Zuan Chabotto[70] the Italian under contract with Henry VII of Angleland, who became the first Europaean explorer during the age of discovery to step foot on the continent of Merika. Dyfed's own visit (along with those of the Norse) had occurred before that age, along with the Vascones (Basques) who had fished these waters for who knows how many decades prior to the age of discovery.

---

70 Also Giovanni Caboto (known too as John Cabot) was of a Venetian family born at Gaeta near Montagna Spaccata in the kingdom of Napoli. He explored for King Henry VII of Angleland and sailed out of Bristol making a few excursions to the new found land of Merika. In 1497 CE he first stepped foot onto Merikan soil somewhere between the 54th and 44th latitude currently now the provinces of Newfoundland and Nova Scotia of the Northern Dominion. It is fairly certain he visited Cape Breton Island. During the Age of Discovery Cristoforo Colombo didn't step foot onto the Merikan continent until 1502. Previously he visited only the islands of Lesser and Greater Antilles and had likely sighted South Merika from Trinidad.

(Prima donna)

> 'She stood to see the far-off world of cities and governments and the active scope of man...where secrets were made known and desires fulfilled. She faced outwards to where men moved dominant and creative, having turned their back on the pulsing heat of creation....'
>
> **D.H. LAWRENCE** (THE RAINBOW)

'Ceredwyn sat quietly in a pensive mood in the morning light of her boudoir. She listened to the rhythmic sound of the waves crashing onto the beach. This intrusive cadence, however, did not disrupt or intrude upon her reflections but acted more as preceptor that governed the metrics of her thoughts. Although her two sons were now long grown and worldly the woman's face was still soft and pretty and age had only added lure and sensual suggestibility to her lithe and medium form. Her hair that cascaded in large rusty ringlets upon her shoulders and tumbled down her back had lost little of it's lustre and responded with a youthful buoyancy as she pulled a brush and combed through it's massive body. As she combed and brushed she remembered her two boys as they once were compared to what they had become. Her recollections brought a gentle smile to her eyes. As she sat preening herself at her morning commode the woman began to hum an old tune that accompanied a ballad that the young shaman Dyfed had once sung. Promptly she caught herself fondly recalling the memories of that beautiful and exceptional young man who was the father of her eldest son, Talsin Davie. Those care free days seemed to be of another age the woman thought and she warmed at the memory of falling in love with that mysterious shaman and bard that had mysteriously showed up at her father's cenedl. He was heaven sent just for her, she had thought at the time, and now it seemed that that youthful dream might come true all these years later, after all. What a marvel life is with its twists and turns. Back in the day, she recalled, despite Dyfed's tender age with that peculiar air of mystique and foreign origin that he had that was decidedly not neither Keltic nor Amoran, he had come to be well placed: First at the court of Kunobelin the king of Llogia and Dux of Albion in the city of Nova Troia. This was during the early part of the Amoran occupation that lasted for half a millennium. Later she had caught snippets of information about him being in Amor itself, surrounded by a succession of emperors and their dangerous imperial henchmen and powerful bankers, along with its obligatory intrigue. Then much later right here in Albion in the kingdom of Mersha Dyfed suddenly materialized again at Hoffa's court. Dyfed, accompanied by an alert and sophisticated man named Cato, came up to Mersha from the kingdom of Kent as moneylenders in competition to Bertha who was spreading Jeshuanism along with capitalism throughout AEthelberht's growing empire. Cadwallopir, a man Ceredwyn called uncle was her sponsor and custodian. But by then she was married to Sideric with a second family. Centuries later, during the fall of the Amoran empire, Ceredwyn later discovered Sideric's paths had crossed those of Dyfed's.'

'But things had taken a turn for the worst back in the day, just about the time she found herself pregnant with Dyfed's child but unmarried to him, or anybody else, for that matter. And that was the point. And it was also at the point where her life changed. As she recalled, her father Owen MacShee still hadn't come to trust the young shaman-bard further than he could spit. Certainly she had been thankful that King Ryan, who she had initially been betrothed to (after her father refused her Dyfed), had had second thoughts and rejected her. But it hadn't relieved the real situation: Essentially the situation in which women like her — women with a certain passion for life, with its ensuing high spirit and devil may care attitude — can sometimes find themselves in when arriving upon that dividing line between careless adolescence and responsible maturity and motherhood: As if (in her case) strife over local leadership, impending large scale war and general kingdom-wide uncertainty that was also at hand were not enough. Ceredwyn's own hands were somewhat tied as well, and she was forced by the situation and by her father's gentle yet iron firm insistence to abandon her hopes and dreams and be shipped off to the kingdom of Demetia in order to marry another before it was too late.'

'However, upon arriving at that distant kingdom she discovered that the man to whom she had been betrothed had perished the day before her arrival due to circumstances and complications involving an over consumption of alcohol during a pre-celebration with friends of his impending vow exchange and marriage to her. This took place in a time long before the world caught fire from the heavens, from which ensued a great plague followed by extreme famine and cold. More than half the Cornovii, Dematae, and Deceangli people there, in that land, perished because of it, she remembered. Her father's own cenedl was decimated.'

'Her arrival at Aberteifi (the village to which she had come to be wed) had taken place just when the men of Amor were grabbing turf hand-over-fist throughout Albion and bringing the Kelts to heel in their own land. Later, she and her infant Talsin Davie along her father all narrowly escaped been slaughtered by Amoran troops who came to her father's cenedl. (Dyfed, if you remember, had been in Nova Troia when Marg had informed him of these circumstances) But at the moment to complicate her prospects for any fast and easy acceptance by the villagers of Aberteifi upon her arrival there as an already widowed bride to be, was her present and very obvious condition. For the good, teary-eyed folks of Aberteifi waiting to greet her — with handkerchiefs at the ready — had initially been anticipating something of an imminent entry (in all due respect to her) not an imminent issue. So, Talsin Davie's obvious presence within her and the child's further sudden arrival into the world — quite illegitimate and fatherless — only moments after she herself had arrived there, must have taken them all by surprise. Ceredwyn now smiled at the memory. Immediately after his birth, she now recalled, and before many thought she was fit to travel she had quickly bundled him up and accompanied her father back to his cenedl in Gwyneth. It was there that she had remained until Talsin Davie had grown and was old enough to pursue and attend to his own studies and embark upon his life. This took place first at Fort Victrix that was fondly referred to as Deva (our city), and then later at Viroconium Cornoviorum (of the Cornovii administrative civitate). Neither Powys nor Mersha, of course, were yet in existence at that time. But that was all a long time ago, now, she mused. Since then Amor had been sacked, the Amorans had long left Albion, and the few that did remain were now absorbed into the folken (folks). Not only that but a destruction of fire had then come upon the world from the sky followed by plagues and the empire of Amor (as all knew it) had faded then disappeared; albeit, emerging anew as a volatile and tribal mosaic alongside Jeshuan influences coming not only from within and from the Emerald Isle, but also from the continent and the land of the Franken. But it lacked the same power and centralised control that Amor had over the population in general, at least for the time being. That was to change with the great king AEthelstan (whose contributions capped the endeavours of forerunner kings such as AEthelfrith and AElfred) by seemingly joining opposing forces. How truly reticent are the affairs of men (what with their caveats and compromises), oh, how joyous it is how god works in wondrous ways! Anyway, the few Amorans that had remained behind tended to concentrate mainly in the middle of what was once ancient Llogia, then the general district and quasi kingdom of the Elfed.'

'After Talsin Davie was grown she journeyed north to the city of Legion in the hopes of somehow picking up Dyfed's cold trail and finding what had become of her first love. Unlike before she had quickly grown fond of the town this time, mostly on account of its memories of times past when she was a maiden, childless and in love. But also because of its old Amoran quaintness whose sector of foreign residents had long since either integrated into the people or disappeared completely. She was also befriended by Queen Carmanda who recalled meeting her at Marg's coronation years before at its strictly invitation-only midday dinner and after celebration party. Ceredwyn distinctly recalled the coronation noon luncheon but her father had prohibited her attendance to the party that was later. The queen seemed to warm towards her this time, she had thought at one point. Perhaps (she wondered later) if it wasn't because Carmen, as most called her, had taken pity on her out of the 'poor woman syndrome' because of her own fondness (and lust) for Dyfed. Ceredwyn was certain that the queen had never forgotten about Dyfed during these past many centuries. Of course (she was quickly informed) that the news was not good and the queen, apparently, couldn't tolerate even a moment's delay in announcing to Ceredwyn that Dyfed was last heard of in the Eternal City of Amor… bunked down, according to completely reliable sources, with her own step-niece Queen Marg. She told this to the still pretty Ceredwyn with a great deal of relish. "If you can just imagine! Yes siree-bub! Marg, that very same little bitch that threw the kingdom and the queen-ship of the Carvetii right back into my face just any old time when it suited her to do so,' she had said.'

'Apparently, she had spat out these words with considerable distaste and a gust of bad breath through even (but yellowing and mossy) teeth. And after all that trouble and expense that Carmen had gone to in throwing a large coronation for her! Although Ceredwyn could now smile at the memory, it irritated her to recall Carmen's lack of discretion. She never came to know that Carmen had done her the greatest of favours by talking Ryan out of marrying her, though.'

'Then, suddenly and without warning — as was always the case in these first few centuries of semi stabilization after the cataclysm — control of much of northern Albion, including Rheged where Ceredwyn and Carmanda were living at that time, fell under one of these Angle new comers. These Goths like creatures had arrived shortly after the time of great darkness and chill to the world from across the Hel. After having primarily gained a foothold in the east fens around the Wash, they had proceeded north in a succession of skirmishes and major battles by ships and by land along the coast where they carved out a territory north of the Umber River. The king that was now particularly victorious in encroaching on the ancient lands of the Kelts in this region was an Angle of great importance. His name was King AEthelfrith. Then one day in the city of Legion while she was visiting Queen Carmanda for their daily news, gossip and reports of the Angle advances, the latter had had a visitor call suddenly without notice. He appeared at first, Ceredwyn thought, to be a Goth noble of some kind or another himself. His name was Sideric. He had not appeared to be an Angle, though, possibly a Saxe the likes of whom were primarily to the south, although they were all much alike, she thought. He was tall and bearded and although his hair was blondish his general complexion was not the peculiar white as many of the Angles were. Indeed, the man later told her that he was recently from the central region of Llogia, but previously had come from Gleven where he had been in the employ of King Cadwallopir. And it was here in this central region that the kingdom once called Llogia was fast disintegrating. But ultimately the new immerging kingdom of Mersha and Carmen's visitor were to bring a welcome change to Ceredwyn's life, even more than she ever dreamed.'

'AEthelfrith, this aforementioned dangerous warrior king, already ruled much of the old Brigantes territory along the eastern shore from his base on the north east coast. This was his premier burgh or fort at the town of Bebba that he had renamed after his wife. But he was constantly making inroads even further west as well as to the north where he battled the remnants of the Wotadin. (The Wotadin it might be remembered were the quiet and elusive early iron age people that Dyfed had vaguely encountered while travelling south from Legion centuries ago)'

'AEthelfrith eventually penetrated to the southwest attacking Powys and defeating King Selyf at Fort Victrix now called Deva-Burgh. Indeed, Aethelfrith's kingdom of Bernic — which was the Anglian name for this kingdom — was actually called Brynaich by the Wotadin and by all the westerners of a like tongue (such as Ceredwyn herself and Carmen the queen). Brynaich was also their word for the Brigantes in their own Brythonic language. AEthelfrith, in effect, had usurped the Brigantes kingdom and had made it into an Angle one. Ceredwyn distinctly remembered that this aforementioned attractive man named Sideric was of Gothic ancestry whose reason to be was as a mercenary angling for a fortune through various espionage theatres. But she recalled that nobody within Carmen's circle was too certain just where his allegiance lay other than in the payments of gold that he received after providing accurate and valuable information for local concerns. Carmen had once told her that Sideric had arrived with letters of invitation signed by both Cadwallopir, king of Gwyneth and Vortimer who was the replacement king of Powys that had been reluctantly brought back (earlier he had been impeached due to his inappropriate decisions and lack of professionalism toward leading his people). But aside from these two, apparently, Sideric was also on some kind of amiable terms with AEthelfrith. He was a striking looking man, they both agreed, with his blue eyes that were darker than the Angles', with a hard body and quick and winning smile. In many ways Ceredwyn remembered thinking he looked a lot like the Amoran cavalry officers of old who she had once learned to despise but now had no need. Indeed, he looked gorgeous, what with his bright cloak over his body armour, his shining helmet, gladius and short spear. Of course, Queen Carmen had her eye on this man's gladius, too, but as soon as she saw he favoured Ceredwyn over her, the former turned quickly from friend to bitch and she was banned (accompanied by insults) from Carmen's shabby palace. It was the end for Carmen in any case. For with her status of queen lately having been generally ignored it had now vanished completely and she soon dissolved into the general great unwashed where she belonged and where she became just another bitter peasant in the new order of things. Ceredwyn now congratulated herself that she, on the other hand, had not followed suit. She had become Sideric's lover, instead, and then after the death of Autofleda she became his wife. Of course, she did not know then that Sideric was the alias of the great Theoderic, emperor of the Western Amoran Empire.'

'As she preened and combed, Ceredwyn reminisced to herself of her husband's last notable achievement following the successful invasion by that north man Guillium the Champion. Sideric's role had been to create a diversion to the civil turmoil. That piece of diversion trickery had been unique and had been accomplished for the sake of saving lives not destroying them. Unfortunately, external powers greater than his eventually took charge of the enterprise that left an indelible impression on all those who witnessed and took part in the episode. Sideric had organized a contingent of fighting men from the leaders of the different factions of society and had departed for the Divine Land in order, ostensibly, to assist in the liberation of Jebus. This simply had been a ruse to channel emotions there instead of here. With men and a ship of his own his eldest son Deric the Deuce accompanied Sideric in this venture. She was glad of this for often like many fathers and their sons the two of them had not exactly been seeing eye to eye of recent years. This brought them together, she thought.'

'After he returned to what was now called Angleland her husband plied the sea-lanes as a privateer like his son Deric the Deuce. Both had returned home as rich as King Midas with a fleet of handsome vessels and a private army of employees that enabled Deric the Deuce to begin building what became a major sea-merchant line operating somewhat in an un-orthodox manner. This line of work was essentially in trafficking in any commodity that could be bought anywhere at a good price and sold for a better one somewhere else. His specialty, however, was in pirating for profit at the expense of foreign sovereignties and giving a cut, usually about ten per cent to the crown in order to allow him to stay in business. It was a sort of tax or business permit, you might say. These sleek merchantmen with their tough and savvy crews shipped out of the Bristol Channel seaport to destinations all over the world, and often their routes were in conjunction with those arranged by Marco Zeno, Sideric's friend and a member of the Brotherhood of the *En to Pan*. She had never known that they had been hired by the House of Lucifer to transport gold and silver collateral for Dyfed's banks. Sideric then built a beautiful home on the banks of the river Avon in the heart of the city not far from the corn exchange which was set up to accommodate he and his son's flourishing enterprise and the multiple businesses that that were born from it. But she, on the other hand, having resided in the rural areas of Mersha and in Gwyneth before that had not favoured their new stately home in that Avonian city. So Sideric had acquired an estate along the north Exmoor coast for her summer use. It was here with it's rugged coast and it's woolly heaths that she had come to live following his death, for this estate was now virtually her sole possession. Her stepson Deric the Deuce showed her kind consideration and even called her mother. His fortunes were now on the wax. Anyway, aside from their main town house that she also retained, the rugged Exmoor coast estate alone had been bequeathed to her while Sedric's shipping empire and its fortunes had gone to Deric the Deuce.'

'Ceredwyn's life had not been overly easy despite her husband's wealth. But this in itself was not out of the ordinary for as was the case with most women their lives seemed never unencumbered from the wills of men folk in general and their routines seldom varied. Poorer women, she reflected, had much more variety but at what a price! Although she hadn't been aware until she had come to know Dyfed again later in life, but such treatment towards women was part of the establishment's protocol to dehumanise them by insuring that they were subservient to their master, their husband. This was what religion also taught and unlike Theoderic her husband she was a strict follower of the Jeshuan religion according to the Keltic monk Pelagius. And just as they were subservient to the worldly master in the secular sense so they were also subservient — right alongside their husbands — to that other worldly master, the ultimate master, the messiah program: the planned scheme, the system that was contrarily named as humanity's advancement by the love of Jeshua. This, then, was and remained the grand con, the great trick in helping the greedy power elites of the world established order in beating out the human spirit once and for all in its attempt to reduce all of humanity (if possible) into a mumbling, fearful and final submission. It was something, incidentally, that kings and even queens had attempted to do but had never been fully successful in setting a continent wide precedent. For in the end it wasn't the brutish wife beaters or the pitiful man that inappropriately forced unwanted sex on a woman that was the problem beyond a mild extent, it was the established order that moulded the psyche with a subtle and subliminal program that brought about the condition to begin with. So her life ticked away, not abused so much as not used –– at least in the later years with Sideric –– with little variation though equally without challenge enough to cause a ripple of concern. Seldom that is, until Sideric who, caught in a trap after being commissioned by the last King Henry to pirate un-named Europaean interests, was plummeted from two sides by so-called friendly sovereign navy war vessels in an effort to silence him forever and thereby allow other privateers easy access to powerful interests before his own.'

'Others, too, were greedy for plunder, it seemed. It didn't come out either that Sideric Tudor's own vessel that was lighter than the blown off course returning Hispanic plunder tankers (and a day ahead) happened to be the only vessel targeted that day. Nor did the leaked story of the day reveal that Tudor was leading home a fishing fleet full of salted cod from the plentiful shores of the new found land on the far side of the Atlas Sea and was not bringing back stolen gold from Hispania's King Philip's Peru in Merika. Rather, the criers said that he had drowned one stormy night in a mishap that drove his flagship upon the rocks off the Isle of Lundy. In any case, there followed a foreboding attack upon his empire from all sides that included the regular men of the establishment such as de Giese and especially a man who she only knew as Giorgi Posh. This man, thanks to Giorgi Posh had already defeated the House of Tudor's royal branch with the death of Dickie Tudor the III, also a descendant of Theoderic via his bastard line.'

(Ceredwyn the even more beautiful)

'Clouded judgement obscures the light of truth'
PARASOLO

'The early morning sun began shining into the room where (Ceredwyn) still sat brushing her hair, with her green eyes dazzling in it's light. They resembled the sparkling aquamarine sheen that lay upon the Exmouth channel in the distance. With adept movements of the comb and brush she pulled up her beautiful locks and holding them by colourful hair combs she tucked her rusty red mane under a laced coif and fidgeted about.'

'She was preparing herself more fastidiously that day, for Dyfed would be arriving by coach from his journey from Cambridge. She was nervous with anticipation as well as wanting to look her best. It was funny, she thought, he wasn't just a distant memory, for over the years their son Talsin Davie had brought her various manuscripts which featured his father's works, or comments and criticism of his works by others. This contributed somewhat to a picture she had of him which was more current than images from the past. Of course there must be other factual aspects of his life, she thought, that were not in print for he was not the kind of man to have the intention of promoting himself via an autobiography although he must have winced at the cheap prejudices and other judgemental slants and even (supposed) attitudes that were published about him that were false and definitely not him at all. Although the picture that the world had of him was pseudo scholastic in nature it was fraught with an opinionated venomosity typical of frightened little people who can't muster the strength to live without the comfort of their chewable teddy bear or their establishment/religious/cultural security blanket. Truly, his work was an idealistic aestheticism that was not generally accessed by the scholastic formulae generally at hand, or easily explained or dismissed by the usual highfalutin and pompous rhetoric that was often delivered against it with the usual condescending platitudes that passed for intelligent argument. This did not contribute to an accurate picture of the man she had once madly loved and believed him to still be. Rather, these tirades against him simply embellished a popular slant, as was the case with most composite portraits of people. Once again, truth or accuracy was not served. She did not know, of course, to what extent his appearance may have changed or how the ravages of time had affected his bearing that had once been so noble and distinguished. And it was on this subject now that her thoughts extensively turned and dwelled. It is an undisputed fact that many couples get married for the wrong reason. There will be the woman that envisions for herself some sort of future with the man in question that is unrealistic or vainly distorted: A future that will never be, a dream that cannot be fulfilled to the result of great unhappiness to both parties. And there is also the man who in placing the object of his love high upon a pedestal will be let down tremendously when his wife emerges as a human being or when his objectives change with the first of life's different stages. These selfish motives that play a large part in bringing couples together are only a glimpse at a category of general undoing of relationships that is massive in it's extent. By far the most common motive, selfishness and even greed are the marriage institution's greatest enemy, and are the antithesis of life's natural condition of love. But due no doubt to their maturity, Ceredwyn and Dyfed seem to be coming together for the sake of sharing a single dream.'

'On the ides of June and shortly after they had become reacquainted, he and Ceredwyn — two children of the forest; he a true noble prince and she a noble hoi polloi — stood alone in this temple before the high priest Aran Danmath from Powys and his acolyte Izebel (who substituting as a witness as well stood two paces behind the couple) and were married. (W)odin was present, too, of course, and Dyfed also insisted that Herecura and Nehalennia accompany Ceredwyn. This was, of course, the only form of union to which Dyfed was in agreement, and then it was all just done in symbolic nostalgia, so to speak: It was just the two of us just like all of our lovemaking ever was, she remembered later.'

'That dream which the two middle-aged lovers shared encompassed many things, but chief among them were each individual's convictions in regards to self-(hence mutual)-enlightenment and the enhancement of consciousness. His commitment was to protect her from all things; danger, anxiety, strife while hers was to see that peace and harmony was maintained within their home sphere to the best of her ability. And the prime cause within the dual form of Ceredwyn and him was their extraordinary love for each other that had long ago sloughed it's confines of puppy love and now drank, instead, from the deep source which underlay the primordial emotions of humankind. But although Ceredwyn was smitten again, his emotions towards Ceredwyn were presently ambiguous, although not indifferent by any means. He loved her as she loved him. Emotion here was firmly under the control of re-call. His attraction toward her was necessitated, one might say even regulated, and continued by bonds from the past, from a time when he was still young and impressionable and she a lithe, green-eyed beauty.'

'Besides their common desire to start afresh in the new found land, both Ceredwyn and Dyfed were inquisitive after the nature of humanity's common psyche as well as it's origin and destination and each recognized the importance of strengthening the over all karma, as Dyfed called it. True enough; with the steady inflation of population that was evident here as elsewhere, there were many newly acquired, primitive superstitions upon the heaths and around the hearths of the new civilized Angleland. These contributed to this desired state's overall condition of transgression. But Ceredwyn felt (indeed knew) that this was not her's or Dyfed's problem alone. Neither was she certain that their destiny lay in educating the population of the newfound world. After all, hadn't the immigrating Europaeans ignored the resource and wealth of native spiritualism never mind their economically sustained harmony? She knew this same indigenous animism had fascinated Dyfed since the time when he had first stumbled on it. And it had simply enraptured her when to wile away the hours of their voyage across the Atlas Sea he had described it to her with his usual exuberance. Spiritualism or animism, as it is properly known, was exclusive (at this time) only to so-called primitive peoples. So called civilized folks distained it for its primitivism. After all, they had science now. Anyway, Dyfed had long noted that they had a primitive superstition all of their own in the god of Abram. This concept of animism, although evolved and complex to the Europaean mind, lacked the multiple caused effects with which the sophisticated creeds consisted and by extension was allowed to the people in the ordinary, accepted and established superstitious beliefs. Therefore, the former had a closer proximity to its common source or archetype where an obvious effect, such as the primitive superstition, say, of Jeshuanism, was desperately lacking. This was the creative and exceptional condition for which all true adepts like Dyfed or outstanding members of the Brother and Sisterhood who resided in sophisticated societies, sought. For time had shown those who have eyes to see that in the process of dispensing with the simple while not having cognizance or consciousness to control the complex, such innovations, digged down a wall. This, the adepts knew would result in tragedy at the first stage and consequently (if the predicament was not corrected) total catastrophe for the ensuing stages. "We will come to that, in time.' For the situation will ultimately lead to objective failure and plummet the entity into a common (collective) depression; an unconditional depression that is even more dangerous to the stability of humanity and one which would effect people living in Europa as well as the new world. Indeed, it's effects, eventually, would be common to all.'

'Such was the condition at large when the two Anglelanders disembarked from the ocean going vessel and stepped onto the solid ground of the island in the new-found-land. During the last hours of their sea journey, while Dyfed peered anxiously westward from the ship's prow, Ceredwyn had contemplated what her bride groom had related to her about the trials of his life and her heart had gone out to him upon hearing of his illness that followed his internment in Amor that occurred after the Crusades. Perhaps it was possible, she had thought, that the depression that had previously enveloped him was nothing more than an anxiety attack brought on by an increase of consciousness at his arrival to the hallowed place of the present? Having left instinct (in the traditional sense) behind, consciousness had perhaps come to be on par with instinct in a total context. And in accessing the very edge of consciousness where he reached the static frontier of nothingness, instinct involuntarily welled up from his archaic depths again in defence. Ceredwyn was certain of it. For once Dyfed had found himself outside historical context he had momentarily doubted the performance of consciousness compared to that which instinct had always provided him. It would have been this very instinct which caused him to panic and retreat into confusion. My word, but who could blame him? she thought. He had every reason to fall back into fear and doubt; who wouldn't have? After all, he who heals must have been wounded and he who is life must have gone through death. However, conditions were different now for upon reaching his pinnacle, his equilibrium has had time to stabilize, she reflected confidently. The structure of his borrowed Sephiroth, to use Dyfed's own words, had become a viable and progressive form of the Ayn-soph, the one cosmic energy. In the enlightened and hallowed present (that differs subtly from the omnipresent) realities and historical effects were little more than hypothetical events. They exist, but only with a marginal affect on those who master this condition. However, historical events were less hypothetical to her and in her case depression was certainly a potential, but as is the instance of the nearly blind she (the partially enlightened) followed Dyfed's lead with the greatest of trust.'

'Ceredwyn was quite struck by Dyfed's reaction upon their arrival in the newfound land. She saw quickly that he was hurt by the manner in which his fellow countrymen (and Europaeans in general) were treating these aboriginals of whom he was apparently very fond. For he had already relayed the adventure to her of his first voyage and sojourn here in the new world over half a millennium ago. But as is customary with bullies and other shallow folk of this ilk who unable to perceive the depth of others or feel empathy towards them and not being capable of comprehending that any other members of their species (outside of themselves) have a sense of place, a code of values or a continuity with life, instead they seem bent on impinging their mores, tenets and their banal perceptiveness on those who they always regard as inferior. These newcomers quickly ridiculed the perceptions of the aboriginals who saw spiritual energy in rivers, trees and mountainous spines, and they condemned the visions of the new world people as either worthless or evil manifestations. One can understand their anxious concern only when one considers the depth of the Europaean's own deficiency of opinion in these matters and their embarrassing humility at being aesthetically dysphonetic. These are the great killjoys whose god is made entirely in their own image but is definitely not within and in any sense part of their true self. It is they who upon encountering that which is perceived to be alien are startled by a familiar emotion that it displays. And then upon recognizing a resemblance of the thing to themselves, they attempt to destroy it out of fear that it might expose that which in their superficiality they want hidden, most especially from themselves. But in attempting to destroy the childlike essence that is common to all humans they destroy instead the essence of their very being. It hurt her too to see these once noble people being actively segregated from a reality that was once second nature to them and to see their G'itchy Manitou banished as though, at best, it were only some pedestrian, semi divine pantheonic wonder. And if Dyfed was correct in his assertion that all deities are projections of psychological powers that are inside us, she mused that the common garden variety of Europaean psyche was certainly no match to these indigenous peoples in truly important matters regarding spirituality.'

'Ceredwyn and Dyfed had no sooner made landfall than he purchased a small vessel in order to search out his old B'otuk friend, Weithidic. They sailed northwest along a rugged coast, and on the third morning recognition flooded upon her husband and he excitedly pointed out to her the ramshackle mamatek of Jellyfish Bay. It was curious, he told her, for it remained much the same as he remembered although over grown now with the aged face of dereliction. Happily, he pointed out to her the quay where the Aura Maré II had once been moored and observed some B'otuks approaching. But upon closer observation Ceredwyn perceived that there was an air of listlessness about the gathering people. A tall man named Stone Deer met them at the quay and she noticed that despite Dyfed's exuberance at their reunion the B'otuk was insular in his response and there was something of a hurt look about his bearing. He appeared much like the other natives she had seen so far although his manner was less spontaneous or careless, and more orderly. She thought him very sad, as well. Dyfed told her that this man had been his first friend in the land of Abundant Codfish. It was he, he said to her, who brought me here to Jellyfish Bay to meet and confer with Weithidic the chief B'otuk. Dyfed quickly turned back toward the tall B'otuk with what she thought was an apprehensive look in his silver eyes. He spoke slowly and evenly while asking if Weithidic was well and also Telquaejit. Once again she noticed that a painful look crept back into the other man's eyes and she sensed a sudden wariness envelope her husband as his gaze shifted over Stone Deer's shoulder and took in the dishevelment of the others who had silently and watchfully gathered close by.'

"Weithidic's spirit is gone from this place,' Stone Deer told him, 'and now wanders restlessly and sad among the void. Your people took him away to the land of the Shonacks, a place that they call Cape Bretoni where they abused and tortured that gentle man by insulting our beliefs and imprisoning his spirit in a cage.' Stone Deer told Dyfed that the B'otuk people cannot be imprisoned, just as an eagle cannot dive beneath the surface of the ocean and fashion his nest there for their young. 'So, instead he died,' Stone Deer said. 'And your brothers had not even the courtesy to bring him home so that his soul could rest in peace. The sad eyes of the red man contemplated the silver-eyed white man for a moment. 'And as for Telquaejit, he said, looking down and away from Dyfed, she too is dead: Dead from a feverous pox that your brothers brought us. It was a silent and invisible tomahawk that attacked us unawares and murdered us in our sleep. No B'otuk would have stooped so low as to use such a vile and dishonourable weapon nor would even the Shonacks (reprobates that they are) have so thoroughly debased themselves in this manner. It is only the white brothers who are known to have no pride or conscience that enables them to conduct themselves in such an utterly disgraceful and ignoble manner.'

'Suddenly, the tall, noble looking B'otuk began to cry. He stood perfectly still with his arms hanging down alongside his still graceful body while the tears streamed down his cheeks. 'And they have not left off at that,' he continued, speaking through his sobs. 'They butcher our children and rape our women. Usually, the same men who do not regard them to be good enough even to stand in their presence during the light of day did the be-spoiling and rape of our girls at night. And yet it is we, they claim, who remain nothing more than crude savages who are of no use to either earthly or holy majesties.' At that point, Ceredwyn noted with a rush of emotion herself that Dyfed too began to cry, and as he stepped forward then and wrapped his arms around Stone Deer in an act of endearing condolence, Ceredwyn fought back tears and felt a strange constriction growing in her thickening throat. In the literal sense she had not understood what had passed between the two men for she knew not one word of the language in which they conversed, but in the sensorial sense she had been effected accordingly.'

'A few days after their arrival at Jellyfish Bay a young man whom Stone Deer had secretly summoned walked cautiously into the mamatek. He was a very tall and graceful young man, lithe and composed of shapely sinew as opposed to bulky muscles. He was exceedingly light skinned with strangely coloured eyes resembling the shimmering green sea in a certain light. His hair was jet black and he silently entered the longhouse that had a large kingfisher motif painted upon it. Ceredwyn knew that Dyfed had felt the man's presence immediately upon his entrance to the longhouse even though his back was to the door, for at that moment she saw him scrutinize Stone Deer's eyes. On her part she looked pleasingly at the young B'otuk who had just arrived and listened with growing amusement to Dyfed's explanation of this rather gorgeous man's presence. It turned out that he was Dyfed's own son from his union with Telquaejit and that he too had once had a wife and infant son but they had been rounded up like cattle by the other white men and were now dead. Walks on Cloud (as the man was called, due to his preference for the high mountainous terrain, far from the reach of the white brothers) now found himself in the position of being in some way emotionally attached to one of the very people who of all of man's brothers he despised the most. It is to his astute sense of virtue and his sound judgement that upon being re united with Dyfed (a father he had never actually known) he managed to quickly overcome any apprehension in this regard in the flick of an eye.'

'As is often the case in matters of love, a progeny of the loved one who is unrelated and formerly unknown to the other will quickly assume an enhanced personification to the latter and be favoured and even desired by them. Such was the case with Ceredwyn. She looked upon Walks on Cloud approvingly noticing that when this man was introduced to Dyfed by Stone Deer the former studied Dyfed intently with what she recognized as an air of respect and maybe even wonder. Dyfed then explained to her and his son that Stone Deer's wish had been for them to leave the land of Abundant Codfish and sail west up a vast river and into the watery womb of the yet undiscovered northern dominion of the new world. But Dyfed had set his sights even further a field, and wanting to distant his loved ones from the influence of the Europaeans who had congested along the Atlas seaboard, he planned to cross the continent altogether in order to discover the shores of a western ocean about which Weithidic had once told him and one in which Dyfed had been led to by the wizardry of Master Mencius from the land of Ch'in, many years before.'

(The Sovereignty that is Walks on Cloud)

"Mad dogs and Englishmen go out in the midday sun;'
NOEL COWARD

'By noon the mellow chill of early autumn was still vanishing before the warm morning sun as Ceredwyn, Dyfed, and Walks on Cloud set off from the land of Abundant Codfish. They sailed due west hugging the shore to their starboard and living off capelins, a smelt like fish, that they caught in nets. Fresh water was always on hand for in an abundance of rivers, creeks, and waterfalls, rainwater and snow melt cascaded from the land all around into the great river mouth. In a fortnight, with a warm brisk wind in their sails, the trio spotted land on both the north and south horizons for the first time since entering the river system and a few days later passed 'where river narrows'. Here they encountered the Algonkin people in great numbers whose fast canoes darted out from the north shore to greet them and warn them against continuing south into the land of the Ir'quia.'

'Although autumn was now well under way the climate was still exceedingly warm and a rich smell of forest and land blew upon the gentle winds out onto the river. This condition continued, and when some days later they smelled smoke upon an evening breeze it signalled their arrival at a well-fortified Ir'quian village called Hochelaga. The trio remained at Hochelaga a few weeks and found that the people of the Ir'quia displayed a friendly disposition towards them. During this time the harvesting of the cultivated fields that surrounded the village was enthusiastically taken up. The vegetarian staple here was a large grain plant called maize supplemented with turnips, potatoes, gourds, and cucumbers. Fish, of course, were plentiful as were fresh game, such as elk and deer that teemed in the forest all around. When the time came for them to continue up stream, Dyfed and Walks on Cloud bartered with the Ir'quia for a provision of cultivated produce and smoked fish while Ceredwyn, whose nature had endeared her to the women folk of the village, purchased material for apparel. This consisted of many different animal hides that were tanned and dyed as well as an array of woven substances that were rolled up in bolts. Game was sighted daily as they continued south up river, so there was no need to over burden themselves and their small craft with fresh meat. Finally they entered a vast and beautiful lake system and the south shore disappeared below the horizon once again. The leaves were beginning to change now and Ceredwyn and Dyfed marvelled as the forest along the north shore as it turned into striking licks of yellow, orange and red flame. With the savoury aroma that accompanied the Earth's blanket, autumn smoke was emitted forth from it's foliage that mingled and drifted lazily off shore over the stilled waters.'

'They reached the Ir'quian meeting place that was situated on the western shore of the beautiful lake, and here the air remained chilled throughout the entire day and before long the forests began to be filled up with snow. Dyfed and Walks on Cloud removed the vessel's mast and hauled the craft well up onto the shore. By the time of the winter solstice the lake was frozen solid and an extreme cold had settled upon them. A season later and as the days had lengthened sufficiently and the sun now set further to the north, the snow-white ice began to crack beneath its cover. It was then that Dyfed fashioned some wide snow boards onto the hull of their boat, and hiring a dozen Hurons to pull her along, they travelled north west through rolling forest lands until they came to an inland fresh water sea. The three waited here alone for a few weeks for the ice to give way to rolling swells again and then they sailed west, keeping close to the right hand shore. After a few weeks they came to a channel of water composed of many islands. The air was warm now, and the forests were leafy green again. Upon departing this narrow waterway, the trio entered onto another vast and superior inland fresh water sea that extended out towards the west. This time they kept close to the southern shore sailing west. Some local people they met on a point of land that jutted out in a northern direction into the lake advised them not to continue back along the coast but sail northwest across the water instead. And there, these people told them, just beyond a large offshore island they will find a shore where they can access a river and lake system to take them west. Arriving there other folks native to this land exchanged a large canoe for their sea boat. From there, Dyfed, Ceredwyn and Walks on Cloud followed this watery system through a series of smaller lakes into a country of rocky terrain and a forest comprised mainly of pine trees. Here, late in the autumn, they camped by the western shore of another big lake for the second winter. From there they set out again in the early Spring and after soon abandoning their canoe they began trudging onto a great plain that unfolded endlessly before them. Two more summers separated by another bitter winter would ensue before the landscape would alter to any noticeable degree.'

'Crossing this vast plain left an indelible mark upon Ceredwyn as well as on Walks on Cloud. The people here were nomads who lived in tepees made from hides of antelope and bison. These were game they followed from place to place throughout the seasons that was their life's blood, all the while carrying and pulling their possessions along with them as they went. For the purpose of utility the horse and the wheel were unknown to these people although Ceredwyn discovered that there was a creature of similar nature in the plains people's mythology and the wheel was not only evident in their pictographs and motifs, but was their most dominant symbol. But what really fascinated all three of these west-seeking travellers was that great beast the bison. This was an important animal for the tribal myth and the survival for these folks. It was a huge stocky animal with an enormous woolly mane and a set of symmetrically shaped crescent horns that they apparently inherited from Taurus. Bison travelled in herds consisting of a hundred thousand or more animals and when they were on the gallop the whole stepped prairie shook for miles around as these animals kicked up a cloud of dust that would spread in a column of dust storm that spread right across the wide sky and darken the sun. Soon a little coyote pup that was spied hanging around their camp one night became attached to this small party of three after Dyfed fed it. Thereafter, its presence among them provided much amusement to the local peoples. Dyfed named him Frederick. They continued west and late that following October they camped by a small lake set in a forest of willow, balsam and pine that covered a group of hills all surrounded by the bald prairie. Then as the following vernal equinox approached and just as they were getting ready to pull up stakes, Ceredwyn took sick. She had a ferocious fever and Dyfed was concerned for her while Walks on Cloud was driven to distraction with fear. By this time he had grown very fond of his stepmother, as she had of him, but he was convinced now that she would die.'

'Walks on Cloud was immensely impressed by Dyfed, but in addition to regarding him as a powerful man he viewed his father with having exemplar shamanic qualities as well. To Walks on Cloud, however, Dyfed was much more than a medicine man; he was more like a sorcerer. Early, the summer before when they had been lolling alongside the muddy banks of a racing river in preparation for the crossing, a large black fly had alighted on Dyfed shoulder. Much to Walks on Cloud's astonishment and amusement, Dyfed began to converse with the insect which remained on his shoulder not only during the river crossing but also for the rest of the day until sun down. Dyfed's explanation of the event was even more astonishing to Walks on Cloud who listened while his father told him that a plague or peste of an unusual nature was at hand and that befriending the small flying creature (which had been sent to sound out the two legged species) contributed to distancing and confusing the unknown spirit of affliction. So Walks on Cloud wondered then why his father wasn't implementing Ceredwyn's recuperation in the manner in which he had expertise? Could it be that his father had noticed the lust, just as he himself had often seen it creep into Ceredwyn eyes when she looked at him? Certainly it was the property of a sorcerer to discern the invisible thoughts within a man's mind so it was likely that Dyfed had read her thoughts as well. Walks on Cloud grounded his teeth and winced at the thought that his father was privy to his own private fantasies involving Ceredwyn even though possibly not reciprocated and certainly not realized. But what wise and knowledgeable lord would cut off his own nose to spite his face and hold these natural instincts against the offending party for evermore? Indeed, a more beautiful woman with such startling green eyes and radiant red hair Walks on Cloud had not seen among any of the other women folk of the race of the white brothers before, nor was there a more agreeable and splendid specimen to be found among the human species anywhere. It was an undeniable truth that he, Walks on Cloud, was infatuated with his stepmother.'

'When Ceredwyn continued to remain ill, Dyfed asked Walks on Cloud to fetch a medicine man from a tribe of plains people who they knew were camped nearby. By this time the sun was at the equinox and when its blazing white reflection off the snow blinded the people who followed the bison. He explained to his son the reason why it was necessary for him to have the assistance of a local shaman. The B'otuk understood well enough that an unknown spirit had inflicted his stepmother and that the antidote must somehow penetrate her unconscious. Ordinarily the duty to extract the offending spirit in this manner lay in the proficiency of a shaman whose responsibility was also to evaluate the effects of his medicine that then takes place by manifesting in the patient's conscious state. Only here can it be effectively interpreted, corrected, and extracted. Walks on Cloud, however, thought his father proficient enough alone in this field. Dyfed, however, demonstrated to Walks on Cloud that the normal state that the people of the new world enjoyed deviated from that of the white brothers where the reverse was apparent. In the latter's instance the process of influence was activated from the conscious whereupon its effects were realized in the unconscious where they remained hidden. Being in that state, problems of mispronunciations on his part or off balanced manifestations on hers could exist undetected and in turn cause adverse effects in the conscious state that now would quadruple in complexity and would be harder to analyse, understand and correct. What astounded Walks on Cloud was the fact that the Europaeans' present materialization and manifestation as human entities were different than from those of his own people. That possibility had not occurred to him. Dyfed explained that he thought it advantageous for Ceredwyn's recuperation to have an indigenous shaman present who could contribute to her accessing the local spirit of harmony, for this was something she knew very little about and he may not be able to help her. The situation would be different if Ceredwyn was back in Angleland, he told him, but being here and in the presence of the new world spirit it was necessary that the proper entrance to this entity be accessed. Of course, some of Ceredwyn (as with all Europaeans) was already receptive to this foreign entity because their unconscious state had evolved, or inappropriately progressed, towards the present condition from an earlier one that was similar to that of the people of the new world. Therefore the comprehensions and doctrines of this gallant lady are equally valid from the point of view of the universal grand mother spirit to which all local father spirits are subordinate.'

"So for us travellers from foreign lands to turn our backs on the Mother Spirit and provider of this world in which today we find ourselves, could reverse Ceredwyn's attributes as well as that of our own and induce a negative response, perhaps for all time,' said Dyfed. 'And the Father Spirit would be helpless to intervene. Since I can only glimpse the local spirit through its obvious expressions, such as the bison, the coyote, and the prairie flower, I am not familiar enough with it to be able to be a deciding influence. So I need the assistance of a true son of the plains. So, Walks on Cloud, my son,' Dyfed said lovingly, 'sally forth out onto the prairie and find me a shaman to come and make ceremony for Ceredwyn's sake.'

(Born in a Tepee at the Foot of a Rainbow)

'The two impostors, triumph and disaster…'
A. TENNYSON

'The earth breaths and fat winds swoop, rushing like wide turbulent rivers they buffeted the balsam with its driven snow and flattened the long yellow grass against a skiff of melting white laying over the warming prairie soil. Nearby a forest of bison backed into the blustery current, their woolly manes blown forward through their horns while the din of their lowing and the smell of the herd was being torn from them and scattered away across the prairie. Down wind, a crescent of tepees crouched close to the earth and Walks on Cloud could hear their hide covers fluttering in the wind that beat a hard rhythm tattoo against the support poles. Before the tepees a thick volcano of yellow sparks spew forth in a twisting column of flurry from a wide communal fire where the stern looking shaman named Born in a Tepee at the Foot of a Rainbow was busy occupying his function by making ceremony for capturing bison spirits.'

'For the occasion this shaman has donned a horned woolly head of a bison whose upper jaw protruded out beyond his forehead and the horns curled up from his ears. Part of the skull bone was bare and shone white in the light of the fire while the wool draped around it in a dark mass of ringlets. It was a mask like none other Walks on Cloud had ever seem. On this evening, the leathery skin of Born in a Tepee at the Foot of a Rainbow's face and hands were dyed white and there were striking lines marked upon them. But as usual he was dressed in his habitual coat of coyote colours. Then suddenly he heard the dogs bark and saw Walks on Cloud approach the circle from the darkened prairie; he then anxiously shook his ceremonial stick. For a moment he holds the magic wand steady in a perpendicular position before him. All eyes turn toward the pale skinned B'otuk as he willingly steps into the circle light of the fire and under the influence of the shaman's magic.'

'Through the altered and strange world of her fever Ceredwyn saw Walks on Cloud lie down on the hard snowy ground and roll around. After this he turned into a white bison with red spots on his rump and, then jumping up he galloped away to join the huge herd that was grazing nearby. She then saw a nation of people who continually migrate from the southeast towards the northwest and back again. These people follow the bison whose ancient tracks lead them to skirt the contours of the great mountain range spirit that like the white headed eagle rises high into the sky stretching his wings across the breadth of the continent. But if the bison did not prosper the people dwindled. It seemed to her that a continent wide scourge had been inflicted upon them of late and the ranks of the warriors and the hunters had been dangerously reduced. This caused further hardships to their dependants.'

'Among these people one man stood out. Ceredwyn heard his name called out by the four great winds. They are the east winds, that bring the *red* dust and where the sun is born; the north winds that is home to the *white* blizzard and where the tepee door always faces the south; the west winds of past and future that is clutched by the *black* claw or foot of the white headed eagle that brings new weather in; and the south winds who are the custodians of the pot of *yellow* metal which contains the colours of the rainbow. His name she instinctively knew was Born in a Tepee at the Foot of a Rainbow and his youth had now passed through him and was only a memory. His leathery skin was tanned by long exposure to the wind and the sun although today it was dyed white. On his part Born in a Tepee at the Foot of a Rainbow was aware of the presence of three foreign travellers who have ventured out onto his home on the Great Plains even though he saw only one. Two of these travellers appear to him to be of the race of the white brothers while he sees the other one is red. He thinks he knows the older man, so he chooses the younger one to be the acting participant in the covenant that he is preparing to re enact. This covenant has been bestowed to all the plains people by the blessing of the Mother Spirit (who was not really a spirit at all but a material density caused by the love of the Father Spirit) and takes place every season between his tribe and the life giving herd of bison with the help of the Father Spirit that is their will. The Father Spirit, of course, is that which resides in Born in a Tepee at the Foot of a Rainbow and is his talent. As well, the same spirit embodies the tribe's proficient hunters. But the Father Spirit has fallen ill in recent times and no one knows why.'

'In the dawn of the following morning, after Born in a Tepee at the Foot of a Rainbow carefully unwraps his special pointing stick from an antelope hide, a handful of hunters creep through the darkness toward the bison herd leaving their footprints in the melting snow. Even though the animals are almost motionless at this time of the day, Born in a Tepee at the Foot of a Rainbow is concerned that the tribe's hunters are too few in number to be successful in killing sufficient bison to meet the needs of his people. That this worries him even after his meticulous preparations in evoking his people's covenant with the herd by making special ceremony is indicative of the danger he perceives in the Father Spirit's illness. Although his concern for the well being of the Father Spirit is justified, he needn't be as anxious about the continuation of the covenant. For as the hunters strategically place themselves for maximum effect in the impending stampede, a white bison with red spots on his rump takes charge of a dozen cows and a half dozen young bulls and is seen by the hunters sitting on the prairie guarding them like a sentinel.'

'Suddenly the herd is spooked as a few of the animals off to one side become aware of the hunters' presence. At this, the white bull that is sitting guarding his charge stands up. As some of the other animals begin to bolt it throws the remaining herd into a panic that begins first by running conversely to each other in great circular wheels like whirlwinds before coming together with purpose in a single direction. It is in these few moments of confusion that the white bull bison misleads his charge and wheels himself and his thundering followers close to a copse of aspens and makes them accessible to the main group of hunters who are hidden there.'

'To experience this event is exhilarating, even to Born in a Tepee at the Foot of a Rainbow who in his many years of life has witnessed the hunt countless times. For these beasts are enormous and cause the ground beneath their hooves to shake while their passing-by sounds like rolling thunder. On this morning, the driven snow on the hard ground has turned to mud from the pounding of hundreds of thousands of bison hooves and as the muck flies up and out in all directions a quagmire is left in the wake of the herd whose bellies are all caked and dripping with liquid earth. Even the sense of smell is acutely employed by the hunt spirit which infuses it into perception; for it is of the freshly churned earth mixed with the potent scent of the herd whose fear and panic can influence even the seasoned hunter. Fear and smell, two totally different spheres of senses are nevertheless interchangeably connected and thereby related.'

'Of a dozen animals destined to lie dead on the plain in the wake of the stampede, the white bull falls first as an arrow pierces its left side and penetrates his heart. This honour is his alone and a melding of spirits suddenly takes place as his front legs buckle under him and he pitches forward in a spray of snow and mud as he skidded his under jaw along the fresh snow and finally came to a halt in a great upright heap. It is dangerous work for the hunters as well for they must get relatively close to the moving herd in order for their arrows to be effective and are therefore exposed to the danger of being inadvertently struck by these beasts. This activity has caused the death of many a hunter. When it is finished, and the land is quiet again, Born in a Tepee at the Foot of a Rainbow quickly re wraps his ceremonial pointing stick in the tanned antelope hide while the hunters rest and give thanks to the G'itchy Manitou and Its mysterious process of transmutation between bison and men.'

'Ceredwyn sees all of this and hears them exclaim and pass the word around even though their Siouan group linguistics is normally unknown to her. She becomes worried over Walks on Cloud and searches the blackness to the west for his presence has faded in that direction. But then suddenly he appears out of the light of the morning star in the east and walks up from the prairie into their camp by the little lake among the hills. Accompanying Walks on Cloud is the shaman Born in a Tepee at the Foot of a Rainbow. Dyfed sits quietly waiting for them while Ceredwyn watches and listens.'

'Born in a Tepee at the Foot of a Rainbow is anxious to meet his white brother who Walks on Cloud talks about at length. His red brother has told him that the white brother is his father and although he is himself a great medicine man he is soliciting Born in a Tepee at the Foot of a Rainbow's help to frighten away an evil spirit that has inflicted the white sister who is travelling with them. Here Ceredwyn pays close attention. In payment for this service Walks on Cloud tells the shaman that Dyfed will advise him on an urgent matter that involves a disruption of the mysterious forces that is effecting the Father Spirit resulting in the decimation of his people. The shaman had been reluctant at first to leave his camp and the impending feast of bison flesh that would be accompanied by much merry making, but the white brother's peculiar promise of payment was of too great an importance for him to overlook. Ceredwyn noted that the two men approaching were being accompanied by a boy; the shaman's young acolyte whose duty is to carry and guard the fire.'

'Born in a Tepee at the Foot of a Rainbow is fascinated upon meeting Dyfed who (in the interval of a few solar wheels since he and Ceredwyn left Angleland) has grown a long beard and long hair from his head folding on his shoulders. Born in a Tepee at the Foot of a Rainbow decided to give his white brother a human name; he settled on – Bearded White Skinned Man Who is Two Haircuts Behind. The meeting, however, quickly dispelled his previous notion of a physical familiarity with the white travelling brother. He then told Dyfed that on the side of his mother he is of the Blackenedfeet confederacy and a cousin to the Dakotas and a member of the Algonkin nation. But through his father's blood he counts all the Dené among his relations. He then demanded to hear

Dyfed's advise on spiritual matters before applying his medicine to cure the fiery haired white sister.'

'Ceredwyn is unsure whether she herself is relating the story through Dyfed or is listening to Dyfed tell what she already knows through a mysterious cognition. In any case from her peculiar vantage point she is able to corroborate his story that the Father Spirit has been affected due to his being sick with fear. This fear originated out of its perceiving of a great war that is pending in the mysterious shadowy world of the other side. Dyfed tells Born in a Tepee at the Foot of a Rainbow that two vastly different Father Spirits will be colliding together causing great confusion in both this and the other shadowy world. These spirits however are avatar or incarnate spirits. He cautions the shaman by telling him that unlike the spirit of the plains people, the other infused spirit is of this world and that its continuance is borne by the white brother. That is the white brother in general, he added, for not all white brothers are of the same mind. His advise to Born in a Tepee at the Foot of a Rainbow was to immediately begin teaching the youngsters of his people as though they were all destined to become medicine men or leaders; for in that way important knowledge will be instilled in them for future generations. There was a great danger, however, that their Father Spirit would suffer resounding defeat at the hands of the other and that the nature of the people of the plains, along with their cousins who were spread across the continent, would become extinct forever. The incarnate Father Spirit of the white brother, Dyfed said, has been altered by the white brothers' psyche and has become hard and made of iron and does not know of the soft ways of the other world.'

"Although it is not what I normally do,' Dyfed said, 'but here for you I will now predict that the concept of a messiah or saviour whose purpose is to deliver you as well as your nations into salvation will strike the fancy of many of your people and that will soon become all the rage as your Mother and Father Spirit fade. Don't let this happen, and to prevent this just don't be deluded or misinformed in the process,' Dyfed advised. 'For this new religion's important message and purpose will not be revealed to you by its priests because they don't appear to understand what it really is; and more telling they don't seem to even know where to look for it. But I will tell you this, Born in a Tepee at the Foot of a Rainbow, that perhaps similar to your own religion this new message that is proposed, and which the priests will fail to state out of their own ignorance, is that the Saviour is the true self and not something separate and apart from oneself. The Saviour is your connection with the Father Spirit and therefore its message is not about the universal trappings but rather it is about the specific particular: Its about you the individual and nothing more, because there is nothing more important to our Father Spirit (God) than you. Please try and remember that.'

'Born in a Tepee at the Foot of a Rainbow was grateful to Dyfed for his interpretation and he quickly, and successfully made ceremony and worked his medicine for Ceredwyn's recovery. Surprisingly she came back to being her old-self overnight, although she remained weak for some time due to her long lack of exercise. When the moon was in her first quarter prior to the month when the bison and all that live upon mother earth get fat, the Blackenedfeet arranged their provisions in order to be equipped to migrate to a spot many days to the south east to attend a great council among their people. At this same time, Dyfed, Ceredwyn and Walks on Cloud were making preparations to continue their journey west, for by then Ceredwyn had regained her strength. Shortly before their departure took place Born in a Tepee at the Foot of a

Rainbow stopped by Dyfed's camp to say goodbye. Walks on Cloud had just come up from bathing in the little lake and the shaman was taken back to see that the red man was really quite white. That reminded him of something, and he then told the two men that the grand father of the plains people, a man known as One who Passed Out from the Spirit of the Great Whirlwind to Survive the Bite of a Snake and Can Make the Sky Smile, was similarly imbued and that he, too, had customarily dyed himself red.'

"Survived a bite from a snake,' Dyfed repeated. 'Could this be the legendary B'otuk himself?' he asked.

'Born in a Tepee at the Foot of a Rainbow confirmed this. Apparently B'otuk (also One who Passed Out from the Spirit of the Great Whirlwind to Survive the Bite of a Snake and Can Make the Sky Smile) had a vision caused by the snake's poison which led him to believe that the sparsity of a nomadic life, and one that helped put its full trust in the rigors of elements both seen and unseen would deliver the practitioner to eternal salvation in harmony with the G'itchy Manitou. The shaman told Dyfed that this great and ancient man had influenced all the plains people and had been their religious and spiritual leader. Even the Dené, meaning the people (or specifically 'us'), had called them selves after the name of his god, he told Dyfed. Apparently, in failing health and being very long of tooth, he had slipped unnoticed from camp one night and had purposely curled up and fallen asleep at the foot of a bison jump. In the early hours of the following morning when the young men of his tribe separated a great number of bison from the herd and drove them over the cliff as planned, One who Passed Out from the Spirit of the Great Whirlwind to Survive the Bite of a Snake and Can Make the Sky Smile became One Who was Crushed to Death Under the Weight of Four and Twenty Bison. Everyone was very upset over the incident, but Born in a Tepee at the Foot of a Rainbow had talked the tribe out of their sorrow by suggesting that the occurrence was meant to be. After all, had it not been the man's wish that his blood be mixed with the animals who were of chief importance for the survival of his followers? Born in a Tepee at the Foot of a Rainbow had then been appointed as the tribe's chief medicine man.'

'Then looking upon Walks on Cloud's white skin as he rose to say goodbye, the shaman added:

"So it was you Walks on Cloud who embodied the white bison two moons ago. Perhaps you are the spirit of one who passed out from the spirit of the great whirlwind to survive the bite of a snake and can make the sky smile. It is you the one who was crushed to death under the weight of four and twenty bison. Well, we got only a total of one dozen bison on our last hunt although we needed two dozen. However, somehow that dozen did manage to see us through to the spring. For that we have you to thank, Walks on Cloud. You are the white sitting bull and you are now our brother. Therefore, I and the power invested in me by the brothers of our tribe, extend to you the invitation to join us and place your tepee in the spot once occupied by of our chief who died during the second moon after the last equinox.' It was to be, for Walks on Cloud (or the Quietly Sitting Bull, as he became fondly known) then reluctantly left the two people whom he now loved more than any other on Earth and remained with the plains people for some time. Among his last thoughts at this time, as he faced his father and stepmother, was that these turn of events were perhaps a blessing in disguise.'

"Catch us up in a few years, eh! Walks on Cloud,' said Dyfed. 'We'll see you soon on the coast. Don't forget. We will be looking out for you.'

(...West meets east and tall ships...)

> *The essence of the Industrial Revolution was the substitution of competition for medieval regulations which previously controlled the production and distribution of wealth.'*
>
> **ARNOLD TOYNBEE**

'One warm day in early August, a half-century or so after the rebuilding of their homestead that followed in due course after the burning down of their first one by Hispanic sailors, other tall ships appeared. Later still, another one sailed into the large inlet that opened up on their homestead waterfront. Without any warning, as he and Ceredwyn sat relaxing in the garden outside their home, Dyfed suddenly saw a jib and forecastle soar silently into view from behind the bluff, and then as it shot swiftly into full sight the billowing sails and the tall masts cut a sharp contrast against the blue haze of the coastal mountains behind it to the north. Dyfed jumped to his feet, and just as the vessel dropped anchor and swung around on the tide he noticed that the ship flew the red cross of St. George on a field argent and below it was a banner that displayed a gold field with a red lion pursuant mounted atop the insignia of the skull and the bones.'

'It was 1850 CE. Dyfed sighed, for just as the Europaean world of will and intention was filtering slowly now into this untouched frontier here a hundred and fifty years after he and Ceredwyn had first made their home alongside Xats'alanexw and Flying Sturgeon, the noble Brotherhood had come to these parts from afar at last. Here they were to make their presence felt, and perhaps be in a position to help inaugurate a social environment that would facilitate its development and progress without suppressing the natural balance that the world of mysterious design provided. This would be in addition to the social progress that the Prydainish Empire that now ruled the waves of the world from its centre in Angleland had brought forward and whose essence had augmented the pursuit of a social nobility of the current era's world-encroaching cultural stance within this the nineteenth century. This was without any doubt (by anyone anywhere in the world) the century of Rule Prytainia.'

'At once Dyfed recognized the old man sitting high in the stern of the launch as it made for the lagoon that lay alongside their homestead. It was Marco Zeno. He was very dark and his skin was quite distinct against his short, snow-white hair. Dyfed noticed, too, that his old friend had aged very little since Malta.'

"So you now seek safety under the banner of the Deuce,' Dyfed said as the former stepped shore.'

"There is grand reward today for flying the colours of Angleland either in claimed or unclaimed waters,' answered Zeno as he carefully considered Dyfed. 'But in the *don* invested trade lanes over the last few centuries of the south Atlas sea, the Hispanic Main and the waters of the Peaceful Ocean on the western coast of the Merikas off Peru, the word lucrative comes to mind as being the name of the game. And I fly whatever colours necessary to facilitate my profession and my opportunity.'

"To plunder, you mean,' said Dyfed to the old pirate.'

'Marco Zeno was a Venetian sailing captain who had shuttled soldiers from Italia to *outrmere* during the Crusades. That is where the two men met. Later Zeno worked in compliment with Deric the Deuce while sporadically under the partial protection of the Royal House of Tudor. It was said that between the two of them (and the pirate Draker who had the House of Tudor's Virgin Queen's undying love and protection) the Hispanic sea lanes King Philip used to shunt bullion from Peru in Merika all the way to Hispania had been laid waste and most of the gold shipments had suddenly been rerouted to Angleland and Elizebeth the Virgin. But there had been a time when the Virgin Queen disallowed (on the pain of death) any piracy or piratical acts against Philip's ships out of fear for the might of that king's empire that was the greatest of the grandees and host with the most within all the world. And it was one that could deal out the most devastating repercussions to a competitor at a moments notice, if need be. This was why she had sent Draker and his fleet in secrecy, not through the Hispanic Main by Cartagena, but around through the South Ocean and the tip of South Merika and up the west coast of that continent to spy on Philip's goings on there.'

'That wretched little man Draker (with all the will and temperament of a pit bull terrier crossed with a wolverine, complicated with the dominating and domineering characteristics of short-man syndrome married to a visions of grandeur complex) wrecked havoc on Philip's ships no matter where he found them, whether that be off Peru in Merika or at anchor in the harbour of Cadiz. And this was much to the chagrin of the Virgin Queen and was why she had tried to keep Draker's topographical and geological exploration (sprinkled with espionage) on a very tight leach and clouded by obscurity and secrecy.'

'However, after about a year (back in the day), Philip soon began receiving disturbing news. His well oiled and tightly controlled security conscious Merikan infrastructure that funnelled wealth back to Hispania year in and year out to help run and maintain the wealthiest and most powerful empire the western world had seen since Amor, was currently being trashed and harried by a certain Captain Draker[71]. The Hispanic king then soon began to make plans to amass together his enormous fleet and attack Angleland and Elizebeth their virgin queen, who he had once hoped to marry and whose sister it was to whom he had even once been betrothed. Unfortunately for Philip his plans for invasion developed slowly and by the time the Armada set out in the year 1588 CE to sack Angleland Draker (who had returned home from Merika decade earlier) easily managed to confound Philip's fleet captains and drove them into the wind and onto the rocks off Armorica (Britanny) before they could pick up Philip's armies who were waiting there to be transported to the coast of Kent for battle. The remainder of the fleet in their attempt to escape Draker's wrath fled north through the Hel Strait and over the top of the Isles of Prydain where some were beached upon the Emerld Isle. After that, Hispania (as we had all known it) and King Philip were toast.'

'After Draker's return from Merika that earned him the reputation of being the very first European sea captain to navigate the world[72] certain Dutch cartographers were able to easily pry some idea out of Draker about those land formations he had come

---

71   Draker: Known as Drake and Dragon to the folks of Hispania who in 1578 was the first commander to navigate his own fleet clean around the world.

72   The Portuguese explorer Fernao de Magalhaes (Ferdinand Magellan) did not himself circumnavigate the world. Only one of his ships, a carrack named Nao Victoria, did that. Magellan was killed in the Philippines before he could return to Hispania.

across. And then once the latitude and longitudes that Draker had recorded were finally corrected from their secret increment of adjustment (a method or coded tool used to maintain Elizabeth's cloak of obscurity over Draker's actual positions) these cartographers began to roughly fill in the blank white sections on the global maps. This was about two hundred and twenty years before Captain George van Couver and (shortly after him) Marco Zeno were able to find the passage on the inside of Couver Island and the waters (later known as Burrard Inlet) with the bustling Xats'alanexw's village alongside of which lay Dyfed and Ceredwyn's flourishing homestead and their anchorage in particular. And this was also located near to the mouth of the big river the locals called Sto:lo. This was about ten years after a certain Xander MacKenzie who, with his business partners that were investigating virgin lands needed for Angleland's fur trade business, became the first explorer to cross the northern Merikan continent north of Mexico.'

'But it was Captain van Couver who quickly got busy drawing some demarcation lines in the sand (and the water) to support his and Captain Cook's earlier 1778 CE's expedition here that solidly attained the ownership rights (sic) for Merika's north-western coast and to affix it forever to Angleland's Empire. And the Empire's right of might also gave Captain van Couver the right to put the run on currently marauding *dons* that were nosing and milling around by order of the now broken and denarii[73] strapped King Philip of Hispania. This king's authority, however, was still being corroborated by the powerful *caballero* Duke Francisco Gomez and helped along by the Houses of Fugga (also Fugge) and Medici. Aside from providing a mortgage for the Hispanic throne these bankers were purveyors for the exploring Visigothic Hispanic purse-snatchers and shop-lifters — the likes of Don Juan Perez and Estevan Martinez who, apparently, had followed Captain José Sebastian Ortega Fernandez and his flag ship *Buenos Noticias* here all the while looking for more morning-after left-overs. Captain van Couver's mission was to banish them altogether from doing anything here other than business with (and in favour of) the Angleland's Empire, in addition to harrying and confounding the expanding breakaway colony from Angleland now emerging in the middle of North Merika as a contentious entity that called themselves the Unified States.'

'Although Angleland was a sea and a continent away, the ramping up and powerful Anglelander navy was soon going to be somewhere and anywhere Johnny on the spot and on hand to bring swift retaliation and expungement to aggressors and grease balls everywhere. And this would include all of Angleland's large northern portion of North Merika called the Northern Dominion.'

'As Dyfed considered what Zeno had said about opportunity, he was reminded that few men had sailed under as many ensigns as this man (that included a long stint under the starched skull and bones he was now sailing under today). When Dyfed introduced him to Ceredwyn, the Italian (who was also part Arab) bowed low in the eastern Ak Sea culture fashion remarking (as he did so) on her beauty. He then told them the news. This was about the changing conditions in Europa.'

'Emperor Leone of the Frankens[74], apparently, had been on the move to obtain ownership of Europa's general account but had recently been stymied instead by the Angleland army under the command of General Field Marshall Wellingtown. Leone

---

73   The silver denarii of Amor had now been supplanted by the silver Real de Ocho (the dollar) and later the gold Doubloon (two gold escudos) that equalled 32 reales which when divided by four equalled a quarter dollar (two bits) or one eighth (or piece of eight) of a gold Doubloon.

74   Emperor Leone of the Frankens had been born on the Isle of Corsica and was of Maniot descendance.

had then been banished from Europa for life and imprisoned on a far-flung rock in the middle of an ocean that was being used as an Anglelander naval refuelling station. This victory was what kind of put the cherry on top of the Angleland Imperial multi-tiered cake. There was no stopping the newly appointed royal usurper Giorgi Posh after that, he told them. No sir! And then there was Minister Pitt who was doing everything in his extraordinary capacity for managing raw, undisciplined political power in order to rein (reign) in the notorious king/queen-maker, that same aforementioned Giorgi Posh Hunover Saxe-Goth Burgfeld and the overlord of the House of Hunover's new royal stand-in; a certain Queen Boodikka Saxe-Goth Burgfeld who was known somewhat fondly as Vikki.'

'As well as all that, Zeno said, Montesquieu and Arouet were waging wars with ferocious strokes of their pens. The new age of reason had spawned a legion of ideologies and social movements in view of replacing the old notions and while monarchs toppled naive optimism was frantically rushing in to fill the void. But these all paled when compared to the empire that the Anglelander had recently conceived, Zeno told him. This empire, of course, was due mainly to Angleland's huge advances in agriculture, medicine and a uniqueness in their industrial technology that burgeoned every little thing Anglish which allowed the latter then to set up their shop on the world's high street and not only to sell it to every nation on earth but tailor-supply and deliver it all to anywhere in the world as well; and for an astrologically proportioned profit. Advanced, individual free will and intelligence, accompanied by freedom of thought and freedom of choices that provided innovation and invention, along with an astonishing naval might that was being caused and effected by the aforementioned was then the foundational cherry directly below the Leone's vanquishing cherry all of which sat atop the multi-tiered imperial cake.'

'The Deutschritters, too, were making grand strides in the land of the Ostrogoth around Hallstatt, Zeno told Dyfed. One of these was Baron Adaulf von Braunau who had adopted the name Wunschritter (Wonderfulknight). He has had irons in the fire since the Crusades, Zeno told him, and was envisioning the resurgence of a new empire for Germanika some day. He had been much taken aback, apparently, when Angleland jumped the queue and moved quickly ahead of every other highly developed nation in the world through another of their local island inventions, *capitalized wealth*.'

'Zeno then reminded his old acquaintance how Athaulf (Adaulf, also Adolf) the Ostrogoth was at Acre and Kadesh (Jebus) during the Crusades masquerading as a Tutonic knight. But it had once looked as if Leone would be the one to stymie the Wunschritter and his front man Baron Bismark Hesse von Flot-Straupple in their endeavours. Of course, this was not to be. Meanwhile Queen Vikki, that scion of George Edward Saxe-Goth Burgfeld's House of Hunover, remained secure on the ancient Angleland throne. Giorgi Posh (as George was now better known) managed this after recently relocating their family fortress headquarters from their power position centred in the lands of the Frankens and the Germanikan Goths and relocated it to Windsor castle just outside Nova Troia. He would now strive to inaugurate a plan of isolation from the quagmire that Europa was formulating for itself. But with Pitt at the helm of her government this wasn't going to be easy for Giorgi Posh to pull it off just like that. Not with Pitt at the helm of government it wouldn't be. However with its second most valuable tool now at hand (namely Angleland's navy) all looked well for Posh for Pitt couldn't, wouldn't, shouldn't curtail the Anglish navy: So This was Vikki's day, and shades of the Virgin Queen.'

'Ceredwyn then piped up and asked the incomparable Zeno of news of her stepson Deric the Deuce. Zeno's eyes widened at this coincidence of affairs. He stated that it was on account of the new look that the navy had taken on that Deric the Deuce had reformed his operations, somewhat. They were all now semi-conjoined as opposed to partitioned as they once were. But with Leone out of the way that wasn't necessarily a favourable condition for stopping the Wunschritter; rather it encouraged him. However (he told her), Deric the Deuce had run afoul of the powerful Duke of Cromwell whose own enterprises had been affected by her stepson's successes. Somehow, they had resolved their conflict with Deric the Deuce's acceptance to help rid the high seas of all renegade (both visi and ostro-gothic profiteers) who were antagonistic to Angleland and refused to pay income tax to the crown on their profits from their shoplifting. Might is right but not necessarily correct! He told her that 'the Deuce' was as mighty and renowned a pirate as ever who was still given licence to harrow the greasy foreign merchantmen of all nations who were not paying concession to the House of Hunover. But unknown to Giorgi Posh and his queen (Vikki) he still extended that licencing to those special interests of the Brotherhood and never fully declared an income that matched reality. No, The Deuce was high grading, he was skimming the House of Hunover, that's for sure, Zeno told them.'

'The following spring, when Zeno's own cartographers had finished their surveys and Dyfed had recommended that a lucrative fur trade was in the offing with the coastal people, Zeno waved good-bye and promised to return with more trading vessels, newly engineered mining equipment for Dyfed and special all-purpose personnel to assist. In the meantime, Dyfed would clear a yard close by and provide facilities for a factor that would come out from Angleland with the new vessels. In the meantime, in addition to the volumes of written material that Zeno left for their disposal, he and Ceredwyn would catch up on the mind of Europa's new order denoted from the pen of Burke, Schopenhauer and even Emperor Leone of the Franken, that little Duke of Corse who was of Hellenic ethnic descendant.'

(Oh Merika, Merika)

> *"...banking institutions are more dangerous to our liberties than standing armies..."*
> **THOMAS JEFFERSON**

Never mind what other people say, Merika (actually 'the Merikas') is named after the Mandaean name for the evening western star and after the mystical land that lay beneath it. North Merika alone is comprised of exactly ten states. Some are independent while others are colonially ruled. South Merika with its twelve states is similarly divided. None of these states or nations are actually named Merika: all of them ARE Merika.'

After the territorial Oregon Treaty between the lands ruled over by the Angleland Empire and the usurped territory of the breakaway commonwealth (sic) that's registered in the lists as the Unified States of Merika and existed generally south of the forty-ninth and forty-fifth parallel, the dominate Merikan Fur Trading Co. of Angleland called the Heavens to Betsy Trading Company (HBTC), along with its administrating chief factor and support staff, left the Columbia River district where they had been operating. They then relocated roughly three hundred Amoran miles north to where they set up another administrative centre on the longed planned for colony of New Albion on Couver Island.[75] Zeno's arrival and the dropping of his anchor off Dyfed and Ceredwyn's waterfront had taken place about forty or so years before this. But it was here on the southern tip of the big island that the Crown of Angleland gave permission for the fur trading company to build another fort called Fort Victory or Victoria that was named after Queen Boodikka's (phonetic Gaelic for Victory or Victoria) namesake. This new queen by the same name went by Victoria; hence Vikki or Fort Vikki. This fort was situated close the tribal fort which Dyfed and Ceredwyn had visited when they watched the Visigoth captain José Sebastian Ortega Fernandez leave by sailing out through the Strait of Juan de Fuca into the Peaceful Ocean for Mexico.

Fort Vikki was situated upon the place called Camosun that was a sacred land dedicated to a spiritual sentinel they believed watched over the of the Salish Songhee people. In the bigger picture Fort Vikki and the island colony of New Albion was located at a spot just south of the forty-ninth parallel on the western coast of Merika's northern continent and it overlooked the Strait of Juan de Fuca that (according to the tides) flows water back and forth between the Salish Sea and the Peaceful Ocean. It is also proximate and opposite to the area where the River Sto:lo pours into the Salish Sea which is shielded from the open waters of the Peaceful Ocean by the aforementioned Big Island colony of New Albion.

Across the Strait over on the eastern shore of the Salish Sea lies the mainland with the settlement of Couver City. The administrative centre for the mainland Anglelander colony called New Caledonia (that was separate from the big Couver Island colony of New Albion) was located on the banks of the Sto:lo River on the Qayqayt people's land

---

75 This had initially been invisioned by Captain Draker back in 1577 or 1578 when he sailed around this island and sniffed it out.

where Flying Sturgeon lived. It was called Nova Westminster. This ideal location was at a fork in the Sto:lo River whose secondary stream arched to the north on its passage to the coastal waters. As well, this township possessed greater defences than elsewhere and easier river communication along with port facilities that ran from there down the river's mainstream course to the sheltered harbour at Stevens Town. But by our current time, however, the colonial administrative centre had relocated into the fast growing Couver City. This administrative centre on the mainland and Couver City both came about after the construction of Fort Vikki (also called Fort Vacuna[76]). After having arrived on the west coast of Merika Dyfed and Ceredwyn had remained put until the beginning of the nineteenth century CE and about the time Zeno first arrived. The colonies on the far side of the continent along the eastern seaboard south of the Bay of Towering Tides had by this time amalgamated into a Commonwealth mentality which Dyfed thought was good but was belied by this burgeoning colony's actions that became exclusive rather than inclusive. Though it is true they were very welcoming, exclusive and isolationist was a methodology they practised for two and a half centuries. Relatively early on a gentle and tame revolution eventually ensued in this Merikan commonwealth against Angleland who (on the verge of empire) was already up to their elbows in imperialism, especially on the North Merikan continent.

After the revolution[77] the local power elite exponentially expanded their influence, hence their power over others. This was aided and abetted by king-maker types and bankers (who poured in from Angleland and northern Europa, including Frisia, the Nederlands and the principalities of Germanika): Men like the aforementioned George Hunover Edward Saxe-Goth Burgfeld's House of Hunover, the House of Redshield (out of the city of Frankfort) and the House of Fugge from the city of Ulm. Dyfed, on this occasion, had missed the boat despite promptings from the likes of the Earl of Oxford, Walt Ralay and Mr Kit Marlowe.

Now called the Unified States, this former colony/commonwealth (and its citizens) began to push west and look south towards Mexico and new lands to shoplift and hard working people to liberate and exploit. Already on the west coast south from Dyfed a burgeoning civilization of plantations had now grown in the land of lotus called Caulifornicate Land. Until recently this had been a Visigothian colony controlled by Hispanic crown representatives in Mexico. Cauliflower Land was a happy and sunny place manned by suffering and miserable prisoners and outcasts that included foreigners and local indigenous peoples bound in manual slavery together. These slaves were human machines who considered themselves a likened to cauliflower vegetables row upon row who and when they weren't busy fornicating to amplify and expand their mechanical advantage for the bottom line and to increase the masters' quotas, they were busy hoeing those row upon rows themselves. But now-a-days it was being over run by Unified States citizenry and being liberated by their governing factor in New Angleland far away on the east coast of this Merikan continent who playing the word game to the

76 Vacuna (considered a Sabine goddess of victory) may have originally been either Euboean Greek or Etruscan.

77 It wasn't a revolution in the true definition, but just a change of guard. The poignant contention was that taxes were being shipped to the House of Hunover in Angleland rather than them contributing to the infrastructure at home here in some of the Angleland dominated colonies in the Merikas where the actual taxpayers resided. This did not include any territory north of the St. Lawrence River for that real estate (probably because of their smaller population) still stupidly remained loyal taxpayers to the crown.

tee conjured up high falutin' word names for their responding actions to the turmoil by that begs definition: Words such as liberty, free, emancipate, deliverance, acquit and foot-loose as in unchained! So, that is how Caulifornicate Land became Caulifornicatia. Meanwhile, stagecoach criss-crossed the territories from New Angleland to there just as tall ships set sail across the Atlas Sea in grand style that ferried passengers back and forth, to and fro, between Europa and Merika. From Merika ships departed and arrived from the territory of New Foundland, Mount Royal (Montreal) in the St. Lawrence River that were located in the titled lands of the Northern Dominion. And from to the Land of Uncle Sham (Unified States or US) it was the cities of Boss Town and Megatropolis.

Now, like their southern cousins, the implanted newcomers of the Northern Dominion were also pushing west, and rumours abounded of iron roads and great movements of people. It was true, for more than any other time since the great migrations of humanity in prehistory, Europaeans were funnelling into the new world and there was a constant stream of ships criss-crossing the Atlas Sea like bobbing little, puffy ducklings all in a row, or multiple rows, in this case. And barring flight from flood, famine and plague, peste and contagion (common calamities in Europa), the movement of millions was on a faster scale than the world had ever before seen which caused huge change in the new world. This change brought destruction to the earth people, especially in the Unified States where they were either forced into submission and uprooted entirely from their culture and concentrated en mass into camps or coerced into extinction. The latter was implemented by government approval and design and realized by expunging from the land, through the process of extermination, the great herds of bison that traditionally fed and clothed the earth people. Dyfed, who had helped finance canneries, fishing fleets off the west coast and logging shows, now handed over his operations to Walks on Cloud who had joined them quite some time before. And up to now Dyfed had practised responsible culling by taking trees down in an extremely selective manner that was guided by a program that was not only fashioned after Dyfed's integrity and responsibility to nurture mother Earth, but was also the mind-set of the local indigenous peoples who having made the local environment their home for many generations (many thousands of years, it turns out) had constantly nurtured the land always refraining from greed and abuse. It was their culture and religion, too. Dyfed and Ceredwyn felt an affinity with these vastly different Earth people in a way that they did not feel with others who appeared to be their own kind.

By this time, Couver's City and the inlet's once beautiful south shore was totally denuded of trees due to careless operations of the new developers that had moved in from Europa and even Caulifornicatia (also Caulifornika). As well, the giant forest that lay south of his home had been chopped into and so deeply scarred that the wild life had now all but disappeared. Also the hundreds of saw mills that were now operating up and down the coast were shearing the land bare and leaving ugly, clear-cut slopes while the concentrated fishing harvests were having an alarming affect on the salmon runs. Now, with every sprinkle of rain the earth flowed off those lands in muddy streams and avalanches of over-burden into the creeks and rivers and inlets. And this all poured into the sea in waves of mud that choked the fish and caused the spirit of the land to cry out. All the while, others were crying out to come to the Lord! Soon, Jeshuan churches were sprouting up on street corners everywhere and the criers and hawkers of religion were netting their catch just like the fishermen out on the choppy waters in the straits that lay off Fort Vikki and Couver City.

The coastal people of the earth stood gaping and speechless with dismay at the disrespect and chaos that the white man wrought and Dyfed noticed that they developed a disparaging attitude about themselves, as well. Now they often cast uneasy glances at the new world that had emerged around them. Dyfed asked Quail Feather, one of Flying Sturgeon's sons, about the change of mood among his people. The man answered him by saying that as the duty and task of his people was always to act as guardians and custodians over the material world that provided for them, it was now felt that they, the People of the Earth, had failed both the Father Spirit world and the Mother Material world and that the imminent death of the spirit of the land would set the precedence for their own demise.

"The white brother has failed miserably,' he told Dyfed, 'to uphold that very obligation that has been ingrained in the sons and daughters of the Earth. Like the young wife whose husband has fallen into the arms of another, the earth spirit's heart is broken. She peers at us now, incredulously, and seemingly in the throes of death she cannot understand why we have forsaken her. The truth is, however, that Mother Earth has time on her side. The real question is just how merciful will she be towards us in the end? As for us, we cannot console her and neither can we rise above the shame and the sense of worthlessness that has over come us. And it is the white brothers with the magic of machines in whom others have now placed their trust who have done this and brought this upon us, Lionman. And it is they who must now bear that responsibility,' he said.

Dyfed knew then, that he had failed these people too, yet he alone was not responsible for their state of affairs. True, in no way had he been an active participant who helped affect their predicament and cause them to be the object of derision. However, he felt shame for his white brothers and shame for the earth people too for he had always had close affinity with their concepts and faith in the tenets of their convictions. But a question nagged him in the back of his mind. Was the emerging, dominant civilization that was too quick to correct perceived transgressions of others, and who unabashedly dictated its creeds and expectations to lesser entities, capable of assuming a responsibility of this order? Was it even prepared to do so? No, Quail Feature, he thought; we have failed you and ourselves.

One day, while supervising his crew that were working in his commercial yard adjacent to his home on the inlet, two officious mannered men came and told Dyfed that they were representatives of the governing factor of the Northern Dominion and that all Sa'lish people were to be removed and registered.

"Removed to where?' asked Dyfed.

The older man of the two answered that the indigenous people were to be moved onto their own land. Dyfed replied that this was their land, although in the true sense nobody owned the land not now and not ever. The land owned us, and that they who treat the land with the utmost respect were the most desirable lodgers. However, in respect to removing the Sa'lish, as most of his workers were indigenous this meant that his business would be affected if they were forced to leave and live elsewhere. The younger man, a lawyer, spoke up and told Dyfed that it was against the law to hire the Sa'lish without special permit and that these permits weren't made available until the individuals under consideration for employment were properly registered and living on their own land which had been reserved for them.

"Anyway,' he said, 'these people will not have to work anymore for the government is going to look after them.'

"The government! What kind of government?' demanded Dyfed, of the two men. 'Since when does the government have the right to make arbitrary decisions that requires the citizen's money to be used in order to implement and uphold, never mind the right to affect the prosperity of private individual enterprise that is currently being conducted in accordance to natural and far greater law? Where is this government that is supposed to be upholding the laws of the land and prohibiting the destruction of the natural kingdom? Are these current and abortive attempts at equality and the liberation of rationality the most progressive policies that the governing factor of the age of reason can produce? And having assumed that responsibility of authority, does it now attempt to imprison the guardians of this land who for so long preserved it for us? And preserved it for what, I ask? So it can feed the superfluities of a single age before perishing forever with no further thought or concern?'

"Now listen here, Mr Lucy,' replied the older man, glancing down at the property registration that he had pulled out of his satchel. 'I sympathize with your concern, but that is the law. I did not make the law, sir, and our policy is only in enforcing it. We're not even responsible in making you aware of that or any law. However, it is your own duty, as well as obligation, to know the law and that ignorance of it does not excuse you from it.'

Dyfed was livid. Although the older man had not recognized him, Dyfed now remembered having briefly met this recent immigrant a long time ago on the quay at the port of the City of Legion. As an employee of Prince Gwyn the man had been a petty functionary and a ready servant, even then. He had strutted about with an air of importance as he took charge of the prince's property in transport at his arrival of the outpost of Legion. It occurred to Dyfed that despite change, how little the nature of such men varied. Was it simply a matter of character flaw, he wondered, that was engrained in the blueprint of their psyche, and were such pathetic creatures salvageable if fished from the mire of will and intention in which they were so totally immersed? It occurred to him, as well, that despite the age of reason, examples of such flaws of character and narrow mind-sets were not in recession, but were becoming more plentiful and profuse.

"Over there is a real governing factor,' said Dyfed, pointing to the mountainous white giant that rose into the southern sky. 'She has governed the lives of men hereabouts for ages without discrimination or even conceit. There is another,' he said pointing to the sun. 'The tides, the winds and the fluctuations of nature, whose authority far exceeds those administrators of reason, have been governing factors for all men since the beginning of time. Yet they have not seen fit to impose or implement constrictions that have reached such heights of banal incongruity as your agencies of directorship and purveyors of regulation have. Menstruating mother of Jeshua!' he exclaimed loudly. 'It seems to me that so far these paragons haven't managed to dish up anything more than a dog's breakfast.'

The two men stared at Dyfed a moment in stony silence.

"Never in my life have I heard such vulgar blasphemy against our Lord,' said the older man.

"Just hold off there a moment,' said the other, shaking a finger in Dyfed's direction. 'I'm an attorney, and a legal representative of..."

"I don't give a fig who you are,' interrupted Dyfed. 'You're trespassing, both of you. Now get the devil off my legally registered land and don't come back here ever again without a warrant signed by a legal and sane magistrate, if you can find one!'

"We won't have to come back, Mr Lucy,' replied the lawyer, 'as long as you comply with the law.'

"If you think that I'm intimidated by you gentlemen, or by the authority invested in you, congratulations; you've reached your peak of puerility and incomprehension,' said Dyfed. 'And let me also add,' he said with a thoughtful movement of his eyes. 'There are those who need no bond of chartered law to remind them of a greater duty, or for that matter of any hollow magnate to keep them just. For although it is easier to be a criminal and fare well from crimes and claim honour among thieves, sound societies are built by those who prefer to fare not as such and remain honourable to oneself. Furthermore, I'm not convinced in the slightest that the policy that your masters' promote is right or correct. I'm not convinced that I should take any consolation in knowing that they, evidently, are convinced that they are right. Quite the contrary, I'm disturbed by the prevalence of such opinions.'

"This is politics, Mr Lucy,' replied the older man, 'be careful you do not become all awash in its wake."

Dyfed's silver eyes coldly regarded the man.

"Frankly, I'm not interested in what you have to say. I've more important things to consider so please don't compound my task and just push off. However, those are words well spoken,' he said with a heavy dollop of sarcasm. 'Even that great Athenian philosopher of long ago held the opinion that wise men should stay clear of politics." With that Dyfed turned and walked briskly towards his house.

After they had gone, Dyfed spoke with Flying Sturgeon. It seemed that neither he nor his sons were aware that they were to be moved and they received the news with dejection. Flying Sturgeon then made a statement that all the Sa'lish present agreed with. With apologies to Dyfed he said that he did not understand the white man at all. He felt that they lacked something essential; some component or another was missing inside them and they were mostly freaks of nature. And as all spiritual entities had counterparts in the material world, Flying Sturgeon thought that their short comings were reflected in their anemic and sallow complexions and the sight of their thin lips and their impatient expressions worried him.

(Fire breathing dragons of the land and sea)

'If the individual has the right to govern him/herself, all external government is tyranny.'

BENJAMIN T. TUCKER

Dyfed began to make preparations to begin a venture in mineral exploration in the north. Sailing out of the inlet upon a following sea under a billowing cloud of black smoke belching from a coal fuelled boiler fire box, the steamer (with a crew of Sa'lish aboard) slipped through the narrow passages that lay between the big island and the mainland. A few days later they were steaming along towards the rugged coast east of Haida Gwaii. They skirted the coastal waters of the Tsimshian people and then entered another maze of channels and inlets that brought them to the mouth of a river that flowed out from the land of the Tahltan. The river was quite deep, so with the advantage of steam power and not having to rely on wind, they managed to easily penetrate a vast and beautiful country.

At first the sight of the vessel that breathed fire frightened the people that crowded the riverbank, but this fear was quelled when they saw aboard their Sa'lish cousins with big broad grins across their smooth brown faces. Dyfed soon began employing his unusual method of discovering rich ore bodies. He did this by carefully observing where the patterns of the brightly lit magnetism (northern lights) in the northern sky flared and fluctuated excitedly just above the earth the most. Beneath this activity this difficult procedure soon alerted him to deposits of iron ore. This unique and still unknown methodology was aided by the fact that Dyfed's prospecting was further into the northern latitude where the magnetic activity in the atmosphere was considerably stronger. This was consistent with a magnetic law that he had discovered during his recent circuit visit of Angleland and Europaean universities. At his old stomping grounds of St. John's College in Cambridge he had learned that attractive or repulsive forces between magnetic poles vary inversely as the square of the distance between the poles. He also utilized the normal method of finding ore bodies by enquiring from the locals after the existence of unusual outcroppings, or a showing of colour along the mountain slopes. He also kept an eye out for precious stones or metals that became evident by them being adorned upon the dress of the locals and their bodies. By employing these methods he made a number of important discoveries.

Dyfed enjoyed his time in the land of simple harmony and its human expression that were her people. He found the work challenging for it involved engineering skills that he had not employed since his marble quarrying days in Tuscani after the crusades and it allowed him time to immerse himself in the culture of these people before Europaism made its presence felt to an even greater extent. That would eventually change the locals and their customs forever. This event was to happen soon enough with the advent of black robed missionaries who established their first mission at a trading outpost near Riverside.

    Dyfed had made some interesting discoveries in the northlands but the work was laborious and slow. What he needed was modern drilling equipment, and if it wasn't yet designed then he would have to go ahead and design his own. Manufacturing the machinery was another matter, but as luck would have it an exposition, a movable event recently popular among the progressive cities among the world's nations, was going to be held in the city of Chic-a-go-go. This burgeoning city was relatively new and had a port on the Great Lakes. These Great Lakes fresh water system that eventual drained into the Altas Sea via (pronounced vy-ah, not vee-ah) was just off centre from being smack-dab in the middle of the eastern portion of the North Merikan continent. About a thousand Amoran miles due east of there was Putz-burg, the current the hard rock mining capital of the Unified States. The theme for this world exposition was to be strictly industrial, and thereby mirror the region's main activity. So, he and Ceredwyn set out toward the east to re cross the continent but his time by train pulled by steam locomotion.

(Vikki and the Houses of Hunover and Lucifer)

> *'I an compelled to fear that science will be used to promote the power of dominate groups rather than to make men happy.'*
> **BERTRAND RUSSELL**

Ceredwyn and Dyfed pulled out of Couver City's new train station and rolled east on the easy and slight upgrade along the Sto:lo river. They retraced almost in reverse this elongated vast and fertile valley delta that the two of them had followed to the Peaceful Ocean many years before. Now their gazes searched the landscape from their seats in the moving and swaying carriage car. From the mountainous north ridge that was steep, rocky and heavily treed, to the dark, flat alluvial land that sped away toward the south whose bordering hills in the distance were misty, their eyes scanned it all in. Below them the steel wheels scraped and jolted along the steel rails and this racket made a clickety-clack, clickety-clack sound that was punctuated every so often with the screeching sound of rubbing steel on steel as it braked or turned into a bend. Suddenly Dyfed had a vision. Once he returned to their new home, he told himself out loud so Ceredwyn would hear too, he would purchase huge tracts of this prime and fertile land and develop it into an agriculture and dairy produce holding. He would pay for it through the success of his northern mining ventures.

As they gazed out through the large light and shadow reflecting window pains of the carriage they saw the southern hills away off in the distance rising and dominating the horizon while the lofty mountain giant that once in a smoking rage threw molten rock and fire out at them (now calmed) greeted them once again. Amazingly, it was still covered in sparkling white snow though the weather was stifling hot on this month of June. For the first day there were few unscheduled stops and Ceredwyn found herself deep in thought as she gazed out at the still landscape where tiny rustling little things scurried around and where she glimpsed up close the dirty faced children who stared up at her from the occasional road crossings and pathways that wound through the tall grass growing alongside the tracks or from station platforms that rushed past as their express train they were on ploughed quickly toward the coastal mountains trailing a black plume of coal smoke that faded out into grey as it rushed passed back into the distance. Walks on Cloud would be looking after the house in Couver City while they were away, she reminded herself. And he and Quail Feather would be overseeing the building of the new ore barges for Dyfed's mineral ore transport company. Tom-Tom the Song-he medicine man would be managing Thetis, their beautiful summer home they had just recently built. It was located six Amoran miles west from Fort Vikki now a small bustling city currently called Victory on Couver Island and only about six Amoran miles from the charming fresh water lake nettled among the woodsy and rocky terrain that was close to where she and Dyfed had first camped. This quiet and peaceful location was only a mile from the spot that she and Dyfed used to tie up ashore and camp by when they were younger and more adventurous. Comforted by all this organization, Ceredwyn was happy. Apart from the iron-ore barges project she had done most of the organizing house attendance herself. Her husband was of a different nature she knew by now. With him it was more on a wing and a prayer attitude.

Once they had crossed the line and entered the nation of the Unified States their first destination would be Chic-a-go-go to attend the world exhibition; then on to Putz-burg where Dyfed would quickly locate a company that manufactured mining equipment; that's if the exhibition at Chic-a-go-go failed to turn up an adequate prospect or lead. However, on the chance that any designs did not meet with his specifications Dyfed had with him some designs of his own, as well as a letter of credit number from the City of Magatropolis' brand new branch of his Union of Commonwealth Banking Company International with an endorsement from his Nova Troia branch for good measure. If that failed, he also had funds available at the Capital Incorporated Assets Business Banking Company that had recently been purchased on his behalf by his enterprising accountant Ebreo ben Jamin in Nova Troai (or wherever he was; Dyfed wasn't sure anymore). What he did know was that at the moment a lot of his dangerously over-extended enterprises were fully drained of blood and buried under the black earth and that the rest went to bills payable. After all, this department still relied on the department of bills receivable to function properly, just like any other.

But Dyfed's current financial state of being (he sadly acknowledged to himself at this moment) was a far cry from the more desirable situation. That would be where the bills payable department was reduced to a skeleton crew, mostly part-time women who were mothers with children in school who were left bouncing around the bills payable office walls doing their nails and gossiping while their regular hours office companions were usually out to lunch: Meanwhile, over at the bills receivable department (and its overflowing annex crammed full of permanent employees) all the office doors leading to busy business rooms were permanently plastered with "Now Still Hiring" signs on each of the doors. Yup! Old Davie didn't bother his head about that since his loan department was up to its neck in searching to secure large lend outs to giant companies who were contributing in one way or another to fuel and energize the expanding industrial age. That was all he needed, borrowers and that was the easy part so long as you had the license from any nation's governing factor to print money, or at least to have the capability of demanding that dollars be printed. Dyfed knew that here in the Unified States, despite Jefferson (a colleague of his relocated friend Muns), the citizens of the Unified States supported private banking. So far only the Bank of the Unified States itself that was controlled by the people's governing factor were beyond reach of the public other than for those funds to be used specifically for the public good. At this time, he like most other enterprises, were seeking contracts to put equipment and men (that were idly standing around) to work. This was something else he would be casting around for at the exposition in Chic-a-go-go as well as in Putz-burg; for those fail-safe companies were always looking for loans to help power the new world. Then as soon as business had been taken care of they planned to travel by horse-drawn coach from Putz-burg down to Worshingtown on the Potomac River where their son Talsin Davie would meet them. Later, they would head northeast by train, first through Builtmore and then to the City of Brotherly-love and then on to Megatropolis. Then finally they would travel to Newport in the Commonwealth of New Rhodes where they hoped to connect up with Dyfed's old friend, John of Munster. Word was, he was running for governor of the commonwealth there. After he had moved from Angleland to Boss Town he then moved to Mary's Land, another commonwealth that had been founded by a charter given to an old cohort of Muns himself, a certain Baron Calvert of Builtmore. This man had once received a title of the place that was John of Munster's old stomping grounds back on the Emerald Isle. But Dyfed knew that Muns' homestead was adjacent to his salvage business on Rhode Island. The problem here was, Dyfed didn't have Muns' new address.

And since we're mentioning Rhode Island, as it turned out, Giorgi Posh, when he visited and looked over the lucrative diamond mines of the Anglelander Cecil Rhodes that were located in a South African territorial state now being named after Rhodes himself, suggested that Rhodes –– the richest man in the Angleland Empire as well as all of Europa and maybe the richest man in all the world at that time –– have his name of Rhodes also attached somehow to the nation of the Unified States. For the House of Hunover thought this attachment of Rhodes name with the US may behove Rhodes himself (if not the Unified States people) to lend a hand to alter the US government, US industrialists and the US military complex's intention toward their divine vision of manifest destiny and to go it alone when it came to conquering the world. A foolish notion at best, it was a case of divide and conquer from the Asiatic viewpoint who were all for promoting this US grown myth and drawing the US toward an attitude of false confidence and into a final and ultimate conflict for determining world order maybe within even a century. But manifest destiny was a strategy and viewpoint that the new, cheeky and still puerile Unified States believed they could accomplish on their own: it was a brash and careless attitude that showed they were full of themselves. And so with the band playing the Star Spangled Spaniard and old Glory flapping like the lips of an auctioneer, Uncle Sham (all full of piss and vinegar and newly decked out in its new striped blue, white and red duds) burgeoned forth in rank and file to beat that band was now solidly immersed in its own home grown myth of being infallible. This became its first most notable mistake. Anyway, the House of Hunover and their agents, folks like Shaw, Balfour, Stead, Curtis, Defoe and Lord Redshield attempted to bring Chatham House (controlled by the House of Hunover) and the US Foreign Relations Council together with the Institute of Pacific Relations to try getting them to work together. And in this way Rhodes' influence may somehow be able to increase the US's susceptibility to reform and join hands with the Angleland Empire where together, along with the rest of the Angleland Commonwealth that included the Northern Dominion, rule the world for hundreds of more years to come, if not a thousand. This was for the US's own good and ours, too. After all, the Land of Oz in the South Sea of the Beautiful Ocean, along with Inja and large tracts of Afrika were all pulling together and becoming part of Angleland's Empire and doing their bit. Only Uncle Sham stood apart fixated by some puerile notion that it was unique and needed nobody's help. Truth is, had they joined, maybe then together we could have tamed and subdued not only the Asiatic but also the lion of the House of Hunover and progressed from there in a more stable and fair society worldwide. Although that wasn't exactly true, but never mind, that wasn't to be! So, Hunover and the Imperial hawks' slogan of 'get on board Uncle Sham before it's too late for all of us' failed to attract. Meanwhile the Land of Ch'in and the Land of Rus were impatiently waiting and watching from the shadows, that is something we can count on.

Dyfed and Ceredwyn's train was beyond the coastal valley now and climbing high into the mountains. Up front the train's engine belched black smoke with the occasional spursh of steam from the side of the engine. Round and round it wound slowly climbing the steep grade through the dark tunnels and the cool atmosphere of the high mountainous terrain. Then on the next morning as the train rattled out through the eastern foothills of this jagged Cordilleran Mountain Range, the spine of Merika, they experienced elation and a buoyancy of spirit as they descended onto the great open plains beyond. But it was soon quelled when they passed through the bison migratory routes and saw the mountains of bones that all but remained of those noble beasts. They glanced out at the tacky towns hastily built in the bottom of coulees and along the muddy shores of brownish slow moving rivers. The towns they saw from their moving window, or from the platforms of different stations, were small and closely clustered proximate to the train station itself that was across the street from the Mercantile Dispensary and the town bank, kitty-corners to the churches Episcopalian and Presbyterian with the Pentecostal congregation meeting just up the street. As for the original Abramists and the Ishlamites, although officially welcome in the non-existent true democracy here they weren't. The bigger centres were similarly contrived with the addition of two or more banks, a barrister at law, a doctor and a dentist office and the obligatory cult centres such as the Church of Amor and the All Saints Protest Church. As already stated, they were usually the only selections. Some official buildings containing the municipal, provincial, county, state authority, with its titled lands registry and the local constabulary or sheriff and accompanying jail were ornate and had become the centre of town.

Everything was all laid out along the usual unpaved 'Front' or 'Main' street whose remaining shops were mostly mercantile enterprises. These bigger town's main streets that Ceredwyn and Dyfed explored together (during the hour or two stop-over in order to change crews, take on mail and condiments, and for the steam engine to take on boiler water) were usually wide with groups of horses tied to hitching posts that ran up and down the side of the streets where casually dressed men with dusty high boots would tip their tall wide-brimmed western felt hats to Ceredwyn and say howdy, Ma'am, and howdy pard'ner, to Dyfed. Unlike in Europa where its phase of impracticality that sported trendy styled felt (fur) hats displaying every shape and shade of ridiculousness, like the tunic of the previous generation with its thirty or so buttons running up the front requiring almost a campaign to put on or remove, the western felt hat was not quite so frivolous and top heavy but just tall an wide-brimmed enough to shield the wearer from rain and too much sun.

On this journey of theirs it was necessary to not only change trains but to change direction and take alternate steel rails that were beginning to criss-cross the country and the continent. This caused considerable delay, so it was already July when they pulled out of Chic-a-go-go on a muggy evening in a cloud of steam bound for Putz-burgh. Dyfed smacked his hand against the window of their train carriage to kill a fly whose buzzing in the lazy, hot environment was sending both of them to sleep in their seats. They had just been reminiscing aloud on their visit to the city that was disappearing behind them as they ground and jerked on the rails that was taking them through Chic-a-go-go's dilapidated outskirts. And as they commented on the world exposition Dyfed sought to disperse from his mind the trivialities and sensationalized hype that were common fare here in the Unified States and the Land of Uncle Sham.

They had neglected to book ahead (they grimaced in recollection) for their Chic-a-go-go stay, for -- through mostly a lack of necessity -- this had not yet become a custom here yet. However, that was an oversight, for due to the exposition and the lateness of their hour of arrival they found that there were no vacancies in the nicer hotels of that city. Instead they had had to take accommodations at the 'Drunken Drayman'. This hotel was a square red brick building already tarnishing from the exposure to soot and sulphur and other effluents that belched from the forest of tall brick chimneys that were all around them and poked up from the roofs of homes, businesses and factories and wherever else that contributed to the life blood of the city. Fortunately here in the Unified States money could buy anything so Dyfed had got them into a first class hotel the following day. They laughed, perishing the thought of a future repeat of the drunks who kept that hotel afloat, even if under a less than even keel. Ceredwyn laughed even harder at the memory of her husband joining them in the saloon and keeping them entertained.

At the Chic-a-go-go exposition Dyfed got his first glimpse of new age technology, and among the multitude of rotund, cigar chomping businessmen and their frivolously gilded ladies and eager gaudily dressed hawkers, he even bumped into a few old acquaintances. Jacob Fugge, though the two had never met, stood out among the others in his expensive, immaculately tailored garments. This man peered at Dyfed with sharp blue eyes under tufts of white eyebrows. After Dyfed dropped some impressive names, Fugge pieced together a story about a half-baked white man living on the far side of the Merikas a couple hundred years ago who to an imperial agent and chartered sea captain of the most powerful kingdom in Europa at the time, airily defied an important and valued client king of his: This was a certain Philip, king of Hispania, and this man in front of him was the Dyfed Lucifer. He then recalled that the House of Lucifer had broken trail when it came to world banking and how Dyfed Lucifer conjoined the concept of the banker and the pirate. Many a banker has laughed together behind closed doors over that, he recalled, and then repeated it aloud to Dyfed. The two of them bonded some and they took to touring the exposition together, often stopping at refreshment stands to quaff back libations. Both men stayed clear of a bitter tasting substance that the local inhabitants called corn whiskey. And while Ceredwyn filled her days with touring the local hospitals and orphanages with various women's groups and Jeshuan temple guilds, Dyfed and Mr J. Fugge visited the booths and viewed the exhibits of companies from all over Europa and from Angleland and the Empire to South Merika and even from Inja in Asia. But Uncle Sham tried to out do them all and in many ways did just that. And because the Land of Ch'in had recently been disciplined for being naughty and disruptive to Angleland profits, the representatives of the Angleland Empire that controlled them at the time had prohibited them from exporting any gizmos for exhibiting, other than gizmos from Angleland being manufactured in Ch'in that they had then placed in the Angleland exhibit hall. These were mostly to do with white jade sculpturing equipment and certain inventions involving harvesting. The Land of Ch'in, no matter that its backwardness was historic (so it was said), and the land there still had the world's most luscious and non-deplete able glacial silt soil that could grow anything (so it was said).

Fugge, whose presence of mind had ascended alongside the sophistication of modern Europa, displayed composure, expectancy, even imperturbability in face of the wonders that they looked on. But on the other hand Dyfed, Ceredwyn now learned as her husband told her, he had been intrigued at the sleek and way more durable railway locomotives, the steam powered lathes and gigantic reciprocating pumps that could drain huge tanks in minutes now being manufactured in the Unified States. All sorts of things he saw there at the fair that were the state of the art technology in its advanced form. And its prototypes, those same that had been available the previous twenty-five years were now incomparable, even unrecognizable in comparison. And he was absolutely amazed at the moving pictures that he saw and plans for a moving picture camera, along with the sweet sounds of popular orchestras that emitted magically from small revolving cylinders. It had already been an eye-opener to see that in the expensive hotels where they stayed, each were lighted by electricity and the city of Chic-a-go-go itself was flooded in electric light at night as well as during the day. The generation of electric power also fascinated Dyfed as he easily grasped its secrets that apparently were pure magic to most.

Sitting with Fugge at lunch later that day Dyfed recalled that way back in the seventh century CE when he was fashioning a commercial/financial industry in Albion, legal brokers in the City of Amor sold off his properties in Tuscani, Latium (Lazio) and Campania (a name which derived from Campania Felix or Fertile (lucky) Countryside), and all the funds had been confiscated by a man named Giorgio san Giorgio. Dyfed's silver eyes carefully regarded the old banker who had recently shaved off his beard and had applied an unbecoming bluish tincture to his white hair. Dyfed knew that Giorgio san Giorgio was a former employee of his and had approached Fugge at that time in order to arrange to finance the purchasing of it. But when Fugge conducted the inventory in person to assess the risk he had discovered that they all had incredible merit and potential. So, leaving Giorgio san Giorgio out of the picture altogether, he commissioned a young Franken engineer to conduct a study in view of developing the properties further.

"Yes," Dyfed had answered when the conversation between he and Fugge had touched on religious interpretations seeming in confliction with science. "The Church of Amor fleeced me clean of valuable property assets I once owned in Italia back in the seventh century, the thieving sons of bitches that they are! They picked my brains and they stole my inventions and even stooped to steal from a safe deposit box a fondly remembered keepsake and family heirloom. It was a priceless amethyst ring I would pay dearly to have returned," he said to Fugge, tapping his partially filled glass of alcohol in reference to the aforementioned amethyst.[78]

Then, in anticipation to what Fugge was about to say to him, he added:

"Buying another one isn't an option here for amethyst rings of that sort are in great shortage and new ones are no longer being cut and set anywhere or at any day as they once were when I was given mine. Mine, you see, was crafted before the beginning of the present age," he had told Fugge, wondering if the man secretly had his ring. No, he reasoned, the church wouldn't have sold it. It was probably on the finger of the Vicar of Jeshua in Amor at this very moment.

"The quartz ring consisted of three silver pyramids, two upper and one beneath where two axis lines formed a 'X' that comprised the two sides of the bottom pyramid and the V shaped inner sides of the two top pyramids, intersected across the centre of the X by a parallel line that formed the bottom lines of the upper pyramids all encompassed

---

78   The amethyst is considered to be a talisman against drunkenness for the wearer thereof.

within a silver circumscribed circle. It was a lined image, not blocked or filled in. The heavy lines were composed of quicksilver that was somehow magically fashioned within the quartz itself that in sunlight dazzled all that beheld it,' he told Fugge. Dyfed knew that the banker wasn't here as a spectator to gawk at machinery making, although new inventions and new and improved applications to meet demand were always welcomed gates that led to new capital. No, Fugge was here to sell the opportunity to anyone to help them realize their goal, their dream, and to be able to secure wealth by accessing his — Fugge's by soliciting his unique lending abilities. In other words, different from Dyfed who lent his fortune to others that found themselves without capital or without a portfolio of investments and needed his support. But he didn't hawk it like Fugge. Then telling Fugge about designs of his own for mining equipment and for engines needed to be designed for heavy work, Fugge told him he knew of such a man who most likely be able to help. But Dyfed hesitated and in the end he kept his invention ideas to himself. At this moment Dyfed found himself in the situation of being on either side of the table at the same time. He had a hundred million dollars in gold bullion but he needed an extra infusion of outside capital as well and a willing conduit of others who could chew that capital all up and absorb it to realize their intentional dream from which Dyfed in turn would receive dividends. That would help Dyfed to become solvent again. Solvent in these times by his terms meant a few trillion dollars. He knew that the *pack* were skint, too, and the Brotherhood was back on their heels at this moment; and like Zeno, who in addition to his fulltime career of high grading and piratical skimming and high-end shop-lifting from the treasuries of sundry nations, they all needed and were all keeping their eyes peeled looking for a part-time second job as well.

    Fugge told him that he was encouraged by the establishment of the Unified States to exploit. He said that the situation had been arranged for this reason and for this opportunity by those in the know. After all, he had been a charter member among the cadre of business folks in Europa. He said that he and his friend Lord Redshield had actively brought about this monetary advancement through debt arrangement. It was a well-laid plan that Dyfed had long attributed to George Hunover Edward Saxe-Goth Burgfeld and his House of Hunover as its undisputed founder. Fugge said that the general sentiment among the boys was that the situation all round was just swell!

    Once in Worshingtown he and Ceredwyn hooked up with old comrades and *pack* members. Dyfed intended too to clinch on enlisting John of Munster into the Brotherhood. If he was successful and Muns was successful in his political endeavour at the commonwealth level, he may be persuaded to run for the highest office in the land and one day become the president of the Unified States. The House of Hunover's secret aim for this office was to eventually have authority, not only over the commonwealths and sovereign states within the Union of the Unified States, but over all of the Angleland Empire and its international Commonwealth as well, with conditions, of course. This wasn't necessarily a bad idea. That Muns the Good would become the president in time didn't however forfeit any of the lingering cancerous malignance that was to eat into the fabric of social order here in this country whose original premise had been to live free and be clear of debt and subjugation and not return it back into the old order where the authority of the likes of the House of Hunover held sway over the magistrates and their courts and all the kings soldiers and all the kings men, including the Nightwatchmen and the Turnkeys under his dominion. And then there was Cecil Rhodes. Even when the land is rich, chains can be in abundance, but when liberty is more desirable than death, power doesn't help the power elite in a land populated by folks who believed freedom meant freedom from debt and where folks didn't have to conform to age old racial and prejudice restrictions. Surely these people here won't be fooled.

Meanwhile, he made a note for Ceredwyn to remind him to look into and initiate the invention of an infernal combustion engine that's both compression and spark ignition run on fuel oil and petroleum that can workout harder than O' Billio without conking out, even a high altitudes.

(The harpy and the hooker)

'The stupid are cocksure while the intelligent are full of doubt.'
BERTRAND RUSSELL

Much to Ceredwyn's surprise, when she and Dyfed stepped off the river yacht that had brought them from Cumberland to Warshingtown they were not only greeted by their son Talsin Davie but by her other son as well. This was Deric the Deuce son of Theoderic. Another man she remembered was on hand as well. That was Marco Zeno. Zeno had formed a coven of the Brotherhood (a modern version) in Warshingtown that had influenced the formation and coming together of the thirteen states to become unified under a common desire and code of life. It was this concept and design and the nobleness of it all that had influenced the notion of the constitution of the Unified States, although the Northern Dominion, along with other western social democratic leaning states followed suit similarly. Anyway, apparently having been informed that she and her husband were en route, Marco had decided to call a special meeting of the Coven of the Brotherhood to commemorate Dyfed's first official visit to this special and unique Capitol here in the Merikas. After all, Dyfed was the founder of the original Brotherhood, and the Unified States was literally the first nation born from its vague values and born also of its motto: 'en to pan'.

The couple received a happy welcome at the Warshingtown coven and Ceredwyn noted that Dyfed was pleased to see some old familiar faces among the local membership and its handful of visiting guests. Among the guests was Sallustius Culles (also formerly known as Bade), who having changed his name to Blair Black in the sixteenth century now was calling himself Blair Green. Dyfed introduced him to Ceredwyn as a friend from long ago in land of Brutus. Initially like many others that were present from abroad, he had journeyed here to the Unified States in Merika[79] to attend the ceremony of the raising of the Obelisk that was to be held the following week. It was a ceremony to which they too were invited.

Being on the roster of guest speakers during the meeting of the coven in Warshingtown, she and Dyfed were being called on to deliver erudition of their choice. Dyfed began by outlining the history of the Ancient Order of the Brotherhood and Sisterhood from its inception in the Divine Land and followed its progress to Europa and then to the Merikas and its prominent role in the founding of the Unified States and its promotion of The Universal Way. When he paused to gave up the floor to his wife she then spoke at length about her work as a care giver among the dispossessed on the west coast and noted that the donations from the Brotherhood were most valuable in facilitating the building of hospitals and providing the means to extend comfort and hope to unfortunates who ranged in ages from infancy to the extreme elderly. She also noted that the population along the Atlas Seaboard was in excess, and that although in Couver

---

[79] The tendancy was to refer to the countries within North Merika as simply Merika, while the South Merikan countries retained their polar preffix. Together, the continental Merikas consist of 22 sovereign countries, none of them are (were) named Merika.

City and along the northwest coast where the Europaean and indigenous populations still managed to merge with nature, that condition was becoming increasingly rare in the eastern portion of the Unified States in particular. She also pointed out that there were few visible signs of peoples from the Six Nations and the earth culture there in the industrialized east that had now little influence over the future of the land or had any clout whatsoever. Why was this she asked? Could this be taken as an indication and a warning of what would emerge upon continent wide Merika as the new age developed? Could the continent of Merika be doomed in a couple of centuries? People seemed out of sync with nature here, she ventured to say, and were preoccupied with themselves and their own species. Other species that shared the planet, on the other hand, and their predicaments that were primarily caused by the inconsideration of the new man, went unnoticed. Breeding grounds that were important to other branches of life were being ruthlessly obliterated and subsequently so were many species themselves. New age man seemed ignorant of the creation around him, she said, and then she launched into her knowledge of the panacea of medicinal cures which were harboured in common plants and weeds that she had learned to identify from being taught by the so called primitive, indigenous peoples.

For many solar cycles, Ceredwyn had been documenting the earth people's vast knowledge of plants, and she told the listening congregation that this cognizance bore a relationship with the Earth People's mythology that her husband Dyfed had been diligent in recording. She also told them that hereditary memory, a function that through a life long practice her husband was able to access, bore a close resemblance to the so called fantasies of these Earth People that were related (in turn) not only to the plant life but all creation of life around them. This she thought was a remarkable discovery, and she told them so. Dyfed, who had been sitting quietly observing the membership, noticed at this point that although certain members remained acutely tentative, most of them had become distracted. They were unable to comprehend where Ceredwyn was leading them; which he knew was namely to the very building blocks of matter and life itself. It had been his intention, when it came his turn to summarize, to discuss hereditary memory and its relationship to these building blocks for he believed that this function is accessible, not just to him, but to everyone and every life form. This was to lead to his closing topic; common and timeless communication, where these building blocks that Ceredwyn had discovered along with the music of the spheres and the ancient, barely remembered and non-comprehending Cabala, are united as one. This last item was a universal form of communication used by the ancient masters that Dyfed had accessed first through Manandan and now still used by the Masters of the *pack*. But due to the distracted mood that was present, when it was his turn to speak he briefly discussed the Brotherhood's motto of *'en to pan'* and its password of 'Selah', remarking only that these concepts and physical sounds (familiar to all members of the Ancient Order of Brothers and Sisters) were an intricate form of common communication between all life forms and that those who had ears to hear, hear and take note.

A few days afterwards most of the Warshingtown Brotherhood and their families including Talsin Davie gathered again for the raising of the Obelisk. The Obelisk was a monument that had been erected in the early days of the present age by a Mizr sovereign who claimed to be descended from Thoth. It had been Zeno who had been commissioned and entrusted to transport the monument from the Temple of Amen in that ancient land of Khem all the way to Merika across the Atlas Sea to be reinstated perpendicular and appear spiritually pensive here in the Unified States Capitol. The longer shadows of late fall were rapidly approaching as they, along with thousands of onlookers who were held further back, gathered for the ceremony that day in the central down town section of the city. Among the spectators was Gizar Ankhman who lost among the morass of the huge crowd remained undetected, his dark eyes carefully watching as Dyfed was called upon to deliver a prayer.

"Ladies and gentlemen,' Dyfed said. 'Please bow your heads in recognition to the god whose image and likeness each of us worship in different forms.'

'Invisible Creator Spirit and Universal Benefactor and the unity of Spirit and Matter: We thank you for your favour and furtherance, we ask that you continue to sustain us with your substance without which all life visible and invisible would perish. In addition, let the Being that is the creator of us all, direct its attention towards this, his servant nation, and give it sustenance so that it may live and thrive. Amen.'

"Amen, and so mote it be,' resounded the spectators in chorus. It was a fitting chorus.

Later, there was a banquet at the Warshingtown coven hall for members of the Brotherhood and Sisterhood and Dyfed and a visiting sister from the land of the Franken with whom he had once been briefly acquainted got into a discussion about metrology as they sat at their meal. The Franken scientist, whose name was Madam de Domrémy, was explaining to the brothers and sisters the mechanics recently used for measuring the diameter and circumference of the earth for the purpose of creating a new and more scientific unit of measurement and one that was superior over the old Amoran one and hence the Angleland measurement as well. Once the distances were correctly determined, she said, this became the key to setting this unit of measurement because the length of an earth segment was then divisible by ten with a manageable proportion being taken as the common unit itself.

"We have been endeavouring to lay out lineal measurement that is applicable to universal and unswerving delineation,' said Madam de Domrémy. 'The present Amoran mile,' she said, 'which has been made divisible into feet and inches is ambiguous and frankly, unrelated. So we have decided on the *meter* as the unit of measurement worthy of the new world age.'

Suddenly Dyfed interjected: "Your endeavour, therefore, is a make work project that true to its nature and purpose could have easily remained under considerable study for another generation or two or even twenty and could have provided employment for many more years yet to come. However, the task of actually discerning the necessary unit you claim to seek is really very simple and easily implemented, madam. And your statement in respect to the mile being ambiguous is completely and utterly untrue.'

"Easy? Untrue?' laughed the other, as she delicately wiped a white serviette around her mouth with a flutter of her delicate fingers that looked like red tipped white spider legs wiggling at the end of her hand.

"Let Dyfed Lucifer speak,' said Zeno, who was picking away at some hors-d'oeuvres as a few of the Frankish lady's very refined and politically correct cohorts began to protest Dyfed's assertiveness. It wasn't that Dyfed disagreed as to the length of the new unit itself, Ceredwyn knew, but rather to the unnecessary labour involved in discerning its value. He had discussed it with her many times since articles related to this science had began appearing in journals the world over.

"The mile is sacred,' she heard her husband reply, 'that is, this measurement has harmony with the earth and is a unit of ancient discernment based like the acre on four times *pi* times the diameter of the earth. The Hyperboreans worked out this type of science long ago long before the present age began. If you endeavour to change the unit, such as the mile or the foot and its subdivision the inch and so forth, you must remain within the parameters of that which is sacred and alter the unit only by specific ratios: This is known to all intelligent people, Madam de Domrémy. The ratio which you claim to have spent so much time and effort devising can be easily determined in a moment by the application of *phi*, the square root of five, plus one, divided by two. Its ratio is one, to one point six one and has been long known to be a universal law and a governing factor that is evident throughout creation from the origin of the human physical plan to the shape and formation of giant galaxies out on the fringy edge of the universe. Were you not at our lecture, Madam de Domrémy when I said: hearken, for those who have ears to hear? In any case, as the measurement of your new unit will be inverse to the old one, that is, one point six one, to one, then your unit, the thousand meter or *kilo meter* will be the shorter of the two, or point six one of one Amoran mile in length. This measurement, if divided by one thousand, will create the exact same measured length of the *meter* that your Francian scientists have somehow stumbled on by accident. So by utilizing this ratio against the mile you retain its sacred measurement by invoking the universal law of *phi*. But in this way I was able to discover the metric scale within a few seconds of time rather than the fifty or so solar cycles it took your group to do it in. See how simple it is? Furthermore, as the relationship between the metric system of distance and that of the mile does in fact correspond to *phi*, then we know two thing: That your laborious work sheets are at least correct, congratulations, and that the mile is not unrelated and certainly not ambiguous. So, it would seem to me, Madam de Domrémy,' Dyfed summed up, 'that you are high on instructive opinion and low on comprehension in this matter. In any case, scientists like yourself who have a curiosity of distance and time will find that the red light waves that the newly discovered krypton gas gives off will have a greater constant than other methods for measuring and thereby be more exact. For instance, we can derive lengths from fundamental physical constants. In this way we can even determine lengths at the atomic level, madam. And that is just a stop gap for the moment.' Dyfed uttered that last information involuntarily and was not sure from whence it came. This was typical, he thought, of the pattern by which hereditary memory often worked.

"You can entertain us but you can't lead us astray, Monsieur Lucifer. Pray, continue,' said the lioness from Pau in the ancient land of Aquitaine.

"Well,' replied Dyfed, 'I would point out that the information I have given you in respect to metrology happens to come from an individual who in the land of my birth was called Llanfihangel. He is also known as Michael, Abram, Hermes and Thoth; and he is the messenger. Khufu, the great pyramid alongside the river Nile was built on his instruction and his name and character have a numerical value as well. He also is made in the image of god (sic: aren't we all?) and is a jealous imitator as well. Any man would do well to aspire to his nature to which he (that is you and I) are subject in any case.'

"We know of your unorthodox views on clerical matters, Monsieur Lucifer,' the lady said, 'for it is stated somewhere in your collected works that the temple of Amor profiteered on false promulgations, and that it intentionally obscured the Holy Spirit and the true message that was sent to us from God the Creator. Also, you claim that the Church of Amor fabricated its authority as spokesman for the almighty! Indeed, its authoritarianism, so you said, perverted the rhythm and denounced the real identity of creation as well as the true sciences that brought about enlightenment.' Ceredwyn shifted her large green eyes from Madam de Domrémy towards her husband.

"Quite so,' she heard her husband reply, 'however they were said in your words, not mine.'

Then for some strange reason she seemed to notice that the greyish curls of hair that were hidden among his once fully golden hair matched the silver that gleamed from his smiling eyes.

"It was upon these cautions of yours,' continued Madam de Domremy, 'and other admissions about the demerits of the Amoran temple that prompted the establishment to excommunicate you twice, first in the seventh century and again in absentia in the tenth or eleventh century in order to preserve the spiritual well being of others who could possibly become unduly subjected to your unholy influence. Your publications, of course,' she said, accompanying it by a little laugh, 'are almost all banned and prohibited reading now by those who wish to enter the kingdom of heaven. And in the past, like a rag-a-muffin wandering willy- nilly you have been forced to seek shelter in the homes of various people who have kindly provided you with succour. And I least of all, perhaps have been among them, if you recall?' As she said this, Madam de Domremy (whose eyes wandered all over and around Dyfed) fondly remembered the time when this tall and handsome foreign felon had come and resided with her at Pamplona in Navarre. It had been there to her he had come when he sought to flee Europa and return to the land of Angleland after escaping from prison in Amor just prior to being convicted of offenses against Ecclesiastics.

"So, then let me quickly recite an unpublished piece of work which is not banned,' Dyfed offered. 'For I will make it up as I go along.' He paused, then said:

> 'An ape in purple, I see;
> there, astride a grinning donk–ey.
> A gold poitrel 'round his neck does shine,
> he watches, as Folly with her gang of nine
> by the elbow, take the aged gods out to the pit;
> the lands of plump, sleek, and glossy, they must acquit.
> But I, Daffodil, dressed as Momus, my identity so far eschew,
> dropped a golden coin at the foot of Pan, and boldly called the tune.'

Zeno and a number of others loudly applauded Dyfed's poem.

"I say,' responded the old captain, looking around him for support. He had thought that Madam de Domremy's exchange with Dyfed had betrayed her as either a harpy or a hooker. It wasn't a complimentary comparison or a fair one. 'Lucifer has a shine about him still: What? he said, still looking around for plaudit. 'This has been such a wonderful affair, has it not brethren, seeing many long absent Brothers and Sisters? Gad Azeus! What's happened to those circulating drink trays, anyway?'

They moved on from there to the City of Megatropolis. Although Dyfed was anxious to find John Munster, Ceredwyn had become attracted to the suffragette cause here, so they stayed on awhile longer. It hadn't taken much to twist Dyfed's arm for the two had become quite accustomed at the close of a full day to visiting the symphony or the cabaret each evening after taking nourishment at some of this city's most renowned social dining rooms where they were served meals prepared by the world's greatest chefs. Anyway, regarding the suffragette movement, this clique of outspoken women (with whom Ceredwyn had become associated) favoured their right to work, to receive a higher education and equal wages, as well as the right to vote no matter what race or creed it was that defined the woman in question. These women took to smoking cigars in public and wearing baggy pants that Dyfed told her reminded him of those that the mountain men in Macedonia and Albania wore. During one public episode when they had gathered in the park to take turns speaking out in support of their cause before a large gathering, Dyfed hired a photographer to take a group photo of them and record the event. In time she and her husband came to finance many of this group's ventures.

Then in November, with kisses and tears, as well as presents for their grandchildren in Angleland and a letter that Dyfed wished to be delivered to a certain Mr Michael Faraway of Nova Troika, they bid their sons good buy as the two younger men boarded a large coal fired steam vessel owned and operated by Derik the Deuce and departed Metropolis for Merseyside. Knowing his father had been involved all those years ago in and around the Wirral peninsula, Tulsan Davie noted that the Deuce's shipyards were close to the site where the Angles and the Sax-fallen had triumphed in battle and AEthelstan had changed the course Prytain and of the history of Angleland. The following day Ceredwyn and Dyfed departed for Rhodes in search of Muns.

Just as their modified chariot of horse and buggy climbed to the top of a slight ridge the name *Muns' Salvage* on a large brightly painted sign immediately caught Dyfed's eye. Salvageable junk presumably, but junk just the same was strewn around here in a big fenced yard. The junkyard was comprised of old parts of machinery mostly; they were pieces of windmills, winches, carriage chassis, wheels, pumps, and even a steam powered tug boat with her guts spilling out from one side. Old rusty boilers were stacked off to one side of the yard and large wooden spools containing cable and wire were parked everywhere along with crates of greased chain. Dyfed stopped the carriage. Across the road from the yard was an elaborate gate with a long avenue running up to a three-story white home in the distance surrounded by shady trees during the summer months. Today was a leafless November day. Dyfed turned in here and started up the drive. As they rode up they passed a black gardener dressed in a heavy long coat. He stood holding a rake alongside a pile of burning leaves that emitted a bluish, white smoke that blew across the driveway and mixed with the mid November air. The gardener nodded politely as they passed.

(Mun's Salvage: the Garden of the Fourth Path)

"Believe nothing unless it conforms with your own reasoning."
BUDDHA

"No, mistah Loocifer', said the lady who opened the door of the white three story home, 'Mistah John he not he'ah now. He and Miss Nina, dey boof done gone up to Boss Town fo' da wintah. We doan see dem no mo; least wise til nix summah. Nix summah dey be he'ah –– dat's fo' sho.'

She was a plump, dark skinned woman with round white eyes and an open and pleasant face. A colourful kerchief tied up her black crinkly hair off to one side of her head and when she smiled her big happy-face smile an even row of pearly white teeth shone in her pink mouth.

"B'ah,' she said as she waved them down the drive as Dyfed and Ceredwyn set out again to look for overnight lodgings before setting out for Boss Town the next morning. 'Ya'll come beck an' visit us a'gin…real soon nah…ya'all he'ah!'

But they had not got as far as the end of the drive when another carriage turned in and barred their way. In an impromptu action, Muns had returned to New Port unannounced to confer with his campaign advisors when Ken Tuckey, an associate of the same Jacob Fugge who Dyfed had met briefly in Putz-burg, had inadvertently informed him of Dyfed and Ceredwyn's whereabouts. So hearing that Dyfed was headed for New Port, Muns hurried alone to their summer home in hopes of connecting up with his old friends.

The two men had much to discuss and the following day they left for Boss Town where the two men retreated to the Munster's Cape Cod weekend country house while Ceredwyn and Nina at least made the appearance of putting up with one another with visitations to the homes of local high society, namely those who curried favour with others of wealth and importance such as the Munsters. The business at hand, Dyfed quickly discovered after the initial catching up of personal gossip and the reconnoitring of times gone by, was the presidential election in which Muns had just recently backed a popular candidate. As far as to when he would declare his candidacy, well…"that would be some time yet,' he said. "But it would come in time.'

It soon came to dominate the men's conversation. Dyfed told the presidential prospect of his intention to open up the great fresh water lakes above Chic-a-go-go even more than they currently were as a means to conduct trade deep in the heart of the Merikan continent that would give him the jump on commerce entering via the seaboard whether he got control of right-a-ways for railroads or not. Muns was delighted to hear that Dyfed was interested in investing a donation of a great sum to his presidential cause when it got up and running, and agreed to support Dyfed's aforementioned venture in any manner he could, but mostly by providing permits for preferences in general. He then told Dyfed that he along with a closed circle of political ideologists and entrepreneurs were writing a profile for national policy that he hoped to introduce once he was in possession of the presidential seal. Dyfed further stated that it was likely that the House of Lucifer would field supporters behind every candidate that ran for president, anyway, including him. This would go a long way in gaining an impression of neutrality. Muns then suggested that Dyfed could be appointed to his personal advisory staff, if he was elected. But Dyfed felt it better not to associate with any ring or ideological group. He promised Muns that he would be up front with everything so as to always keep him in the know.

"And as far as being your advisor, or at least your interpreter of all things regarding adversity,' said Dyfed, 'Count me in. And when you've got things organized in Warshingtown give me an idea of the cost of admission to this closed, yet growing circle of protagonists. Bye the way, you should know if you don't already, I am a charter member of the Ancient Order of the Brotherhood and Sisterhood and a member in good standing now of the Warshingtown Coven who have more than most left their stamp upon the pedestal of the great presidential seal that you seek. I dare say, Muns, that the likes of Marco Zeno as well as Blair Black, I mean Green, who you remember from the old days as Bade, are probably part of that circle of protagonists of yours. And if they are not, I can provide introductions for you.'

But Dyfed was worried about his friend now he had had a chance to evaluate him. Was it bitterness at the less than desirable manifestation that humanity and its western religion had accomplished in structuring western society that was affecting Muns? Dyfed wondered. Yes, that was it; he was disappointed in the greed of humanity and the grasping for power that was expedient in feeding that greed. His Jeshuanism was of the ancient variety and tinged strongly with not so much the Church of Amor but the teachings of Pelagius and even Cuthbert. So, at some more recent time he then had set for himself a course to consolidate his influence among the electorate so as to be given the opportunity to be put into the position to positively influence due process of the affairs of state in order to fashion a better society, a better civilization and ultimately a better world. But Dyfed wondered if this was realistic? Would it work and was Muns actually in the real world? He was strong willed, remembered Dyfed, so a greater knight or soldier of the people could scarcely be found and he was clever and his business Munsalvage had undoubtedly made him rich that could not but help either. But Dyfed now regarded his old friend with sympathy as he prepared to leave.

"But all that you contemplate with the challenges you foresee ahead does not prove that the destructive principle of the world is god,' said Dyfed devilishly. He had not meant to antagonize his friend. He found irony in his stance and pleasure in his position of opinion. 'After all,' he concluded with a Cheshire grin of the cat that ate the mouse, 'there is no god, only the ever permeating, omnipotent, and omnipresent self, the creator being from whose Omni awareness we each derive our sense of presence, indeed, any sense at all that we pick up on our preceptor receivers; for we derive nothing outside of it. Our egos on the other hand, those are superfluous in a sense yet can sometimes act to elevate us to observe, if not partaking or participating, and are simply conflation effects of the unseen portion of the third dimension that makes up about 99.99 per cent of potential phenomenon. That is easily discerned from our vantage point within the fifth dimension. And don't start again with me, Muns. I'm not interested in that born again Jeshuan punch you once so soberly served up. Add something stronger, tie on a contention with a mixed spirit or two and you might have something to be mulled over.'

Suddenly Ceredwyn entered the library and manoeuvred around to announce her and Dyfed's good-byes: and how they all must do this again, at their place –– soon.

(Wu Wei Ch'an)

> *"Wisdom is knowing when you can't be wise."*
> **PAUL ENGLE**

It wasn't until the following spring that the big steam locomotive successfully negotiated the sharp switchbacks along the mountainous western decline and brought Ceredwyn and Dyfed safely back to salt-chuck at tide-side along the coast at Couver City.

The following spring Dyfed's drilling equipment he had ordered from a company in Putz-burg arrived by ship that pulled in alongside his new docks on the north side of the inlet across from Couver City Besides this sophisticated apparatus he now also had a number of new ore and lumber barges and his steam driven paddle wheeler he used for river and sheltered inlet work had two new sisters. Both of them tunnel hulled vessels with underwater propellers powered by steam. In addition Dyfed had commissioned two larger iron hulled freighters to be built in the dockyards in the City of Vacuna (Victoria in Latin was the usual pronunciation) that he named *Ceredwyn* and *Vacuna*. But the two freighters now lay idle in his Couver City dry dock as he had intentionally (upon taking ownership) removed and re-sold their boilers and steam operated equipment in lieu of another power system he had in mind. These new contraptions were oil powered internal combustion compression engines that would soon run the huge generators he was presently designing in conjunction with the Michael Faraway Company of Nova Troia and GE (the Generic Edison Company) that was financially backed by Chesterton H. Morgan and Peter van Deroot who in turn, Dyfed knew, were backed by Potamus Purplebal, Khinglia Ephthalites and the long time industrialist named Julian Agrippa (now calling himself Brian Julianus).

These new-fashioned generators would deliver electrical power to better provide towards the ships' thrust systems than thermal or indirect mechanical power. These generators Dyfed had in mind would power up the ships' entire grid, that is all of the vessels' multiple auxiliaries such as its lighting, power for every manner of pump and winch and provide for an elaborate evaporation system for refrigerating that would be independent of block ice or cold water heat exchangers, similar to cooling radiators that were now being used for motor-chariots. These latter contraptions were quickly becoming all the rage due to their low price caused by mass production. But that was not the case with the sturdy compression engines. They were not being massed produced yet and were hugely expensive. They were mostly unknown as yet and that was why the Vacuna Dockyard Company had gone ahead and installed steam boilers that powered turbines that in turn produced electricity. Dyfed's new system, if he ever actually received his order as designed, would be a compression engine — electric system. But for the moment it was still a waiting game and in the interim he and Walks on Cloud were gearing up in readiness for a big change in the business of mining and forestry.

As he stood with his son one day waiting for some equipment to be unloaded, Dyfed found himself watching a large company of coolies disembarking from an adjacent steamer. Coolies were men of the yellow race who hailed from the land of Ch'in on the far side of the Peaceful Ocean. They were being brought here to Couver City now to work on the railroads that were being pushed through to the interior to facilitate competitive and often foreign owned mining and logging endeavours. These coolies, who were brisk, solitary go-getters when focussing on exerting themselves in this human trade, also provided cheap labour for menial work in mines and canneries. But inevitably they were shamefully exploited.

Dyfed particularly noted a dapperly dressed Ch'in-eese man that supervised the offloading of these coolies and in whose charge these migrants would remain. Although his profile was not prominent, this dapper little man did not walk with the sloppy slipper shuffle like other members of his race. He was also somewhat well known in Couver City where he had become very wealthy due to having a shrewd mind for business. His name was Wu Wei Ch'an who Dyfed had first been introduced to by Sun Tan. Dyfed knew that this man had recently funded the building of a sumptuous and expensively contrived temple whose nature was in accordance to the philosophical faith of the men of Ch'in. The building of it had seemingly been illegal at the time but ultimately it was build and had opened its doors to customers of their persuasion of religious ideology, anyway. It seemed too that he was both a slave master and an admired celebrity to his brothers and sisters of the yellow race.

Recently, at a meeting of the chamber of commerce, Dyfed had chided Wu Wei Ch'an for his trade and exploitation of humans in an endeavour to become rich. The small, alert man contemplated Dyfed without expression for a moment or two, then as he pulled at the long tuft of whiskers that hung in a clump from his chin, his face crinkled up into a broad smile. The little man from Ch'in, who was always dressed in smart Europaean styles combined with a curious round, flat topped black silk cap beneath which his pigtail fell half way down his back like a twist of greying black rope, had been somewhat taken aback by Dyfed's remark for never before had he considered that the white devil race could be aesthetic in any way and sensitive to the feelings of others; especially others of a different race. Experience in this land had taught him that so far, but he knew enough of Dyfed so as not to think the man was coveting his investments and vying for a takeover. Having himself been thoroughly schooled in aesthetic thought, however, he quickly saw the wisdom in Dyfed's concern to labour for the dignity and welfare of all men, and the two men eventually became close confidents and understanding friends. Over the next cycles in the wheels of time, Dyfed's business prospered alongside that of Wu Wei Ch'an who often supplied Dyfed with reliable specialized labour for the latter's mining camps in the interior. Mostly, they filled the positions within the camp's kitchens and laundry facilities, but also as providers of medicine as well as other needs whose practitioners among them were highly skilled in the knowledge of the body. On his part, Dyfed compensated these yellow employees with equitable wages, thereby gaining their respect.

One time on his return to Couver City from establishing new mining ventures in the north, Dyfed found his dock-side and its adjoining warehouses along the harbour on the inlet shore in front of their old homestead had been laid waste to ashes and Ceredwyn fit to be tied as she stood on what remained of their company dock anxiously wringing her hands. The fire marshal strongly suggested to Dyfed that the cause of the destruction was the savage Sa'lish who he continued to employ and who often camped on the grounds around his business. Dyfed said nothing but had no difficulty remembering that despite the many solar wheels that the local people had occupied the land around his home, it had been the so-called civilized *dons* from the Iberian Peninsula who on their brief stop over had purposely torched his dwelling, not the savage Sa'lish. So he and Ceredwyn set about again to rebuild, and the Sa'lish came out to help and so did Ch'an and other men from the land of Ch'in. Ceredwyn organized the women from her church parish that included many of the Sa'lish and also women from the land of Ch'in who didn't go to Ch'an temple, but there were some that did. The wily little man from the land of Ch'in didn't actually work himself but he did provide Dyfed with paid free labour from his work force and furnished them with steaming bowls of strangely spiced food for every day that they worked. One day as Dyfed broke off for lunch after a hard exerting morning of toil, he regarded Ch'an through a blurred vision caused by the sweat that dripped off his forehead and down through his eyebrows. He then noticed that the impeccably dressed Mr Ch'an was regarding him with amusement.

"Mos' honorable frien' and wor'ry opponent to those mos' gif'ed in art of combat and business,' Mr Ch'an said in his clipped manner of speech as his mouth chewed over words that seemed too fat to get out from around his tongue. 'I humbly enquire why mos' supreme boss man wif status mos' noble 'mong men, labour like peasant?'

Wiping the sweat off his brow with his forearm Dyfed answered.

"My dear Ch'an. To be wealthy and even powerful but to have no common purpose among the folds of the earth in keeping with those other souls, who inhabit its domain alongside you, is to be nothing. Many a powerfully rich man has built a grand house without laying a single hand of his own to help complete its form. In such a case it cannot be said that this man truly owns that which he believes to be his, nor even of those items that he believes are inherently his. Gold is for payment, not for purchase. The fruits of the field that is not harvested even in part by the labour of he who would have others regard him lord of the land is surely even less then the loathsome aphid who has no such pretensions and whose blight is most unwelcome. Ownership, Ch'an, comes from dispossession not from possession. Surely you must know this from the actions if not the words of the twenty-eighth patriarch,[80] who was something of a St Anthony[81] of the land of Ch'in, was he not? The Sa'lish will tell you the same, although the customs that these gentle people have fashioned for an age have now been averted and condemned by my own ignorant brethren among the white race. I cannot call my home, my business or anything I wish to covet to be mine, unless, besides being the captain at the helm as I steer the craft through the rip tides and dangerous shoals of phenomenon. It is I who must sound the depths as well as pull at the oar or strain my back by the furnace heat as I shovel in the coal to keep up a head of steam. And all the while I must be conscious of the souls who are in my charge and whose safety and wellbeing are in my hands and upon whose hands I must rely as they, too, rely on me. Only under these conditions and by no other can one understand ownership, my friend.'

After this, when the smaller inlet harbour had been rebuilt and Ceredwyn's roses were blooming in profusion among the holly hocks and morning glory, Mr Ch'an would often come to visit Dyfed at home and the two would walk in the garden. Mr Ch'an, dressed as always in his peculiar cap and baggy dark Europaean type clothes, his hands clasped tightly behind his back just beneath his braided rope of hair and hurrying in a shuffling manner with his short steps to keep abreast with the taller man, solicited

---

80   Bodhidarma
81   The Franciscan friar Santo Antonio de Lisboa.

Dyfed's opinions on many matters while he himself talked about Sen Dow which he referred to as Ch'an, and other enlightened ways of the east. These, he noted, were topics which Dyfed readily absorbed and grasped with ease.

"There is a change coming to the world,' Dyfed said to Mr Ch'an one warm summer morning as they sat in the garden together and breathed in the thick floral scent. 'The Wunschritter von Braunau is bringing Europa, and possibly the world, to the brink of war.'

"He velly evil man,' responded Mr Ch'an, 'in his greed for power he 'rrl-usts to haf' all the world kow tow at his feet. And to those ends he is insincere towards ah'ders, inconsiderate of doze ah'ders, and intolerant of all ah'ders, even while he forces 'dem so 'dat 'dey muss kneel to him and tongue his hole.'

Dyfed laughed at the expression and commented that Mr Ch'an was an observant fellow, indeed, for he had hit the nail on the head in regards to the Deutschritter von Wunsche, as he used to be called. He then added that it was a terrible waste of man's labour as well as material to have the resources of the world spent selfishly and carelessly on shallow egos.

"But let us not forget that it is us who are to blame, not him, for we are the ones who have made him of this world and about what the world is,' said Dyfed whimsically. 'In the end it will be seen that we have made ourselves subjected to him.

"It is the Supreme will,' said Mr Ch'an…

"Which is chosen (as always) by the people,' interrupted Dyfed. 'That undulating horde of sleepwalkers; the case of the blind leading the blind and the prisoners incarcerated for life who promise miracles outside the bars, locks and chains of the prison walls. Soon they will be coming for our materials, for our labour forces and our children, and then for our expertise, believing that we are as ignorant and foolish as they. So if in face of such aggression, and if young men the world over pluck forth the courage to issue the universally recognized middle finger salute, accompanied by a resounding chorus of *menstruating mother, you may take a flying leap*, and in solidarity then did not respond to the cry of war, would not that be an interesting situation if it were to arise, Wu Wei? Ah,' said Dyfed in a kind and funning and mimicking jest, 'the powah of mighty dollah, eh, mistah Wu Wei,'.

"Ah'so,' replied Mr Ch'an seriously. 'You mos' explessly mean almighty lending pow'ah of dollah, mis'ah Dyfed.' The blue summer sky that shone above these lands glinted off the shiny surfaces of Mr Ch'an's eyes. Compounded by the thick lens in his round, tortoise framed glasses, they were just barely visible now through the narrow and guarded slits that arrested many a would-be intruder, and could easily hold the world at bay if need be.

"We mus' be weddy and plepared, ol' flien',' said Mr Ch'an. 'I sclatch yur' back; and yoo sclatch mine. Wat say, eh?' Mr Ch'an then laughed and the two men gazed respectfully at each other. They were two men who now each held the other in high esteem.

(Pierce the Ram and...Presto!)

"No person of mortal birth is worthy to go into the house you have seen: that place is kept for the saints, where sun and moon will not rule, nor the day, but they will stand there always in the eternal realm with the holy angels."
YESHUA (JESUS) THE NAZAREAN (SPEAKING TO JUDAS: FROM THE NAG HAMMADI SCRIPTURE: 45, 14 – 24)

It was now shortly before the planned stock market crash and the setting for the opening of the second act of the world at war with itself, as if the world's nemesis was some kind of exterior alien in the physical sense rather than hordes of generations of misguided alter-egos long subjected to effects chosen at far away passed moments in space/time which the subjects have no chance now in rectifying and correcting and are seemingly equally unable to be born anew from within themselves and leave their fake realities behind. With armies of men who couldn't find their way back to the green fields of home because they lay rotting in the earthly mucky mess of petroleum, puke and the piss of battle, the Wunschritter's debut was about to open. Dyfed was suddenly summoned by the Masters among the *pack* to attend the fifth dimension for preparatory talks. These talks were being referred to as the fifth dimensional democratic resolve, or the 5-DDR. This was to be Dyfed first sojourn to that place. He would need a lot of help to get there.

In the end these talks were to become extent. They were also forced to be outside of his preferred environment, the third dimension. All of this he knew would take a toll on him. While playing the Radetsky March in solo on his viola one day, Dyfed paced slowly around his front office in disturbed anticipation of what the future held. He remained deep in thought for days because his concern was over the impending events that he knew were about to change the world forever. After his attack of heightened concern had subsided a little, and in an effort to indulge in happy thoughts to curtail his emotions, he thought about the great Southern Plateau of the Beautiful Northern Land of the Great UConn River Basin. For it was here, he knew, that valuable mineral deposits that humanity needed in order to advance their status among the living creatures of the universe lay. He wanted to get at them now or as early as possible to facilitate that level of advancement which would (as usual) be advantaged by visiting Masters and regular members of the *pack* long before the hoi polloi were anywhere near to gaining competence to do so on their own. So, he made plans to immediately return to renew his prospecting there when a certain Mr Grey, a Master and member the *pack* who was unknown to Dyfed, came for him. Irritatingly, the Fifth Dimensional Democratic Resolve now got in the way of his third density plans that had been under way.

Dyfed was the first to admit that as a shaman he was frustrated and confused at his loss of perfection in the art of transcendence. Indeed, he had no perfection whatsoever when it came to this skill; and that just wouldn't do. What he seemed to excel in here was incompetence. Long ago Manandan had insisted that as a true Master one must master the transition between here and there. But Dyfed had not mastered it and it had become a reoccurring discomfort gnawing away at his conscious every time he thought about it. Kunobelin had offered his assistance, too, but in the end he hadn't lingered long enough to help. On top of that, on the one occasion he had transcended with Kunobelin's help and it had been a disaster. Violet and Manandan, who were so looking forward to having an audience with him in the normal fifth dimensional way had to suspend the conditional phenomenon at large and send him back in great concern for his tranquillity and equilibrium. His performance as a shaman continued to be as shoddy as those mesmerisers; the priests of pretend whose display of hocus-pocus, like the latter day Druids whose unintelligible rote was nothing more than a posture without real meaning. He had disguised his performances before Owen and Ceredwyn in Gwyneth with nothing more than his drunkenness, relying solely on his musical abilities and their ignorance. But that was unacceptable now. It wouldn't cut the mustard. And he could not get to the meeting with the elders without the gift of transcendence, though in extenuating circumstances he could employ help. And that was exactly what had to happen here. But it could be very dangerous for him all the same.

A furious vibration now began to resonate Dyfed's space/time. At first his consciousness was unaware of it then suddenly upon perceiving it, it swiftly developed into a consciousness of its own which seemed to have undergone an enormous pressure drop and was expanding furiously. Indeed, the properties involving this expansion were exponential and inversely proportional compared to the tiny speck of tertiary-mover awareness that was his normal third dimensional self, a quasi self of varying alter-egos when taken in relation to the universal sense of being whose constancy remained at large but not immediately detectable. This physical world around him was momentary. There was, it seemed to him, a gentle wind that he'd seen pass through the tops of the western red cedar trees causing them to sway. The night skies were black and bejewelled with stars and the air was warm. Dyfed had a sense that a vibration had caused the wind along with the light and the material phenomenon of materialized matter in general. Then the sky was no longer above but straight down below and the trees were vibrating from their foliage to their roots in tune with the strange resonance that resembled (or even became) the notion of the dance of dervishes clad in their green cloaks of the haji. Vibration wasn't just the essence of movement that then became sound. Vibration was the essence of everything. Dyfed became aware of it as light and then sound matter.

Then an all-dimensional encompassing energy blossomed like a primeval birth, the alpha-omega and cause and effect. Tiny little grains of life unseen by the sharpest eye magnified billions of times spiralled from seeming oblivion into being. Dyfed's body seemed to reshape as he became aware of the separate existence of each tiny spiralling bio-plasma. He became aware then that his being was separate from his material shape whose fabric had somehow coalesced from the tiny spiralling bio-plasma into a coarser substance that was not at all times integral to his self. However, its material being was integral only under certain tones and was conditional according to stages and levels of those tones of vibration as defined by the universal law of life. Additionally, there was some overpowering essence, some omnipotent omniscience that defined everything specifically, such as space/time. It was this essence that had full command over his ship of finite life in an infinite abyss but could and wanted to delegate this desire.

He knew somehow that it was significant that this ship of his was founded on vibration that was its registered name. Now in relation to the ship of finite life called vibration, this infinite abyss was not really outside and around the ship. Nor was it beyond extent for it was not even included in what extent represents, for it has no meaning here where extent can only mean life; it was not included in general nothingness either — which begs for some thingness — as negative is to positive. For it is the sea of nonexistence of which we speak, and even in speaking it or thinking it we have let slip the understanding of it within the current moveable moment that's separated from the eternal moment. Indeed, we cannot now or at any time in any form or level understand it for it doesn't exist beyond that moment but instead has set the course where the die is cast. And as the commander of the ship of finite life, this was intrinsic to Dyfed's core being. He also now knew that he was something of a true being and hereby finally cognizant of his fully contained core self. He was the being of vibration. Nothing about the vibration was beyond his self, and yet, he realized with astonishment, there was nothing beyond the ship of life, nothing beyond vibration, only void, the void of non space — the abyss. Here was his true self at last.

Even the word beyond, he realised, was misleading for there is no beyond here.

He didn't wonder, either, if vibration (the ship of finite life) was the essence of all humanoids — he didn't wonder if he himself was part and parcel of the essence of all humanoids — because he knew for certain that it was so; he knew for certain that vibration and everything vibrating was the essence of all life. That is to say, the essence of everything in which finite is defined not as with end, or even limited, but rather as contained or existing. One is unable to say in this sense that non-existing exists or doesn't. Dyfed's psyche, his thoughts and their source, his essence, his self's self, all were vibration. He knew that for sure, now. Vibration he now also knew was not separated from anything, nor could it be. All life was vibration and everything which life can perceive is vibration. To belabour the point: Outside of this vibration there was nothing.

Yet, still he was capable of separate vibration as we all are but only according to the universal law of life, the only living law — beyond just and necessary — outside of which no other law needs be.

No longer weaving in and out between the conscious and subconscious of one's normal condition of animation, Dyfed's survey engines that were fuelled by forces intrinsic to unseen torsion waves within his mind's eye (representing his self) appeared to be shining a timeless laser thought through countless memory captions that were attached to the all-encompassing vibration. Not understanding his sudden and seeming ability to categorise and compartmentalise vast groupings of past formulated phenomena, he did manage to recall, of course, Manandan's prediction that in time he would have immediate access to data absorbed and correctly learned that was a form of pre-programming which, in time, would come to his aid. His universal being, his true self was centred somewhere which — after an infinitesimal passage through the spiral of the Golden Mean — Dyfed concluded that it was centred in the great learning institution of St. John's he had once attended in Anglia at Cambridge a long time ago, at least that was his impression.

The ensuing captions grouped phenomena (that were being reeled in) in a fantastic way that consisted of a debate of some kind in which he was engaged and that involved an uncertain number of individuals in a large building or ill-defined hall or large classroom. It appeared at least at first that the debaters occupied a grand position in the centre of this enormous hall, gathered (or floating, perhaps) around a large table that could seat at least fifty or more. There was something else. Spectators maybe (or assistants) were also present and they ringed this central group and communication continually passed back and forth to and from this outer ring almost as much as the main points were emphasized between those sitting around the inner ring of tabled debaters. But as the discussion, the arguments and counterpoints ensued, they appeared to break up from their central location and were flung apart as though reacting from an encompassing plasmid gravity force within the rotational field that — failing (in this) due to the tabled debater beings' emotional positions within/without the gravity force and the rotational field — pushed them out and away only to become attracted together according to each of their emotional properties. This condition caused them to end up in separate particles or small groups clustered together in likeness or compatibility that were really expressions of their collective emotions, or character vibrations. They formed and spread like fractals. Dyfed wasn't sure of the identities of those present in his little group that happened to be squashed up and crammed tightly together in a cramped position in a cluttered corner of the otherwise elegant space. Apparently, they were commiserating in a carpet discussion. Back at the central location, somewhere outside of them now, there emitted a curious light similar to a sun beam filtering through a tall window perhaps that filled with tiny dust particles was moving in slowly spiralling curves of phi. Phi was alive for the sake of vibration, for this was its characteristic. This was also the code of its psyche.

    Suddenly an un-expectant memory caption unfolded in Dyfed's psyche that suddenly displayed these same specks twisting and gyrating in great agitation around a shining glass bowl of water that sat on a table next to the windowsill. But as Dyfed's revisited phenomenon unfolded some more the elegance of the grand space and that of their individual stature quickly diminished into an uneasy fuzzy darkness on the edge of consciousness where they now all desperately clung. Cheek to jowl their mouths twisted in agony over confusing thoughts that were hard to gather, never-mind express. They seemed crunched up together, not spaced out, thereby not allowing the body's aura to breath separately but remain in communion with all the samples contained in vibration around it. At one point it seemed they had grown infinitesimally small that gave them a kind of independent reflection and Dyfed recollected crawling through a hollow yellow grass-like straw that turned out to be an amebae. They travelled this way leaving the pond behind and sought the deep darker waters of the colder lake below. Dyfed and the others of his group sought greater influences for individual expression that these new waters would provide, only to emerge in an electrified state in a sharply dendritic outline. Vibration, triumphing in its most eclectic form, cracked and zapped inside the eternal hum of its colossal extent. Again the green-cloaked dervishes whirled and twirled and the earth and the heavens turned over.

    Dyfed's memory caption-card did not fully record why they were there or who all were there, apart from himself and a few other fellows attending that college of long ago. One of those fellows in their little group, Quasi Gizmo, was scrunched up next to Professor Torsionfield who he had first both met in that submarine contraption beneath the Adriatic Sea years ago and then later at college. Professor Torsionfield flitted back and forth between all the groups, connecting their energy. Dyfed also now recalled the assistants of the outer ring that supported their local particle and suddenly he felt the presence of Manandan, Lord Huge, Morgant and even King Karatakos who somehow seemed out of place because he wasn't a fellow here among the others. Certainly he managed to recall that their little group particle exhausted mental emotions in words that were not quite adequate. They lumbered under ideas whose thoughts were incomplete and when you added something to one idea it lost another part somewhere else. They also sketched out in monosyllables rough outlines and sepia-type concepts of advanced thoughts that became either run-on or completely incomplete.

He suddenly realised with a stark reality that he hadn't made much headway and was seemingly daydreaming and wasting his time entertaining superfluous superfluities. Quasi Gizmo, on the other hand, was an accomplished multi-faceted scientist and innovator in his field of expertise. Their paths crossed often, Dyfed was thinking as he was briefly brought back to some resemblance of reality. Quasi Gizmo he reflected was without a doubt one of the world's most ingenious of scientists and had his ego — that was not strong, indeed, lacking (of all things) — wanted himself to be better known he could have been one of the world's most famous and respected scientists of all time. He easily mingled with the likes of Pri Karar Sri, John Kempster, Michael F. Faraway, and Nikki Telstar, all of who were among the leading scientists of Dyfed's era. In truth there were many more fabulous minds at large than those just mentioned, but unless there were practical reasons of the moment to bring them forward into the mind's eye they were better left where they were. Alongside these men there were many women among the former group, as well, but fewer than should be due to the civilization's prejudges. Scientists that must be placed squarely under the heading of pseudo scientists, charlatans, impostors and bull shit artists that were as thick as thieves in the third dimension were conspicuous by their absence here. These pseudo scientists average intelligence and awareness (which is intelligence) and average abilities was in cognizance and deducting. At least that was what Quasi Gizmo had said many times, and kept on saying.

Dyfed sensed that he awoke once from a deep sleep but quickly drifted off again into a shallow and troubled insubstantiality that was surrounded by more strangely distorted memories. The weird and curious vibration he had been aware of before had stopped. He heard voices differently now and realized that he had forgotten what he had easily recalled only moments before, though some para-thoughts inside him absolutely refused to define moments. He was startled to realize then that this was because there was nothing to remember. He felt that time and memory was an impediment, a suggestion really, even an involuntary condition that had been smuggled in on the sly, a programmed after-market that was being applied without authority (or was it a slight of hand?). Memory, it seemed, had become fixed more through suggestion (followed via coercion rather then by general acceptance) than was necessary. He wondered at the novel trickery of it all and he was amazed with what clarity he was presently able to see a new that was now fully available to his consciousness. This consciousness, however, seemed much sharper than normal or at least compared to his normal state within the third density wherein he struggled. But struggle through existence though he did on the average day like all people was now tremendously more endowed in cognitive powers than the average, or even the above average. In short, he soared. Although it must be said he didn't look down through prejudicial and hateful eyes upon humanity as though they were lice crawling upon a thing the way the haploids did. In fact his purpose of being there in the third dimension was in some way to help these hapless creatures to profit. Now as he expanded and shook free of temporary constraints for the space/time being he knew he wasn't succeeding, and he knew that much without being told.

King Karatakos climbed up from the bright yellow and deep gold couch and walking over to the large beautiful and decoratively adorned sideboard buffet, poured himself a glass of whisky.

"Sure, I'll have one,' said Morgant without moving. 'Make it a double, will you!'

"Yeah, me too,' said Dyfed slowly and vaguely. He was now suddenly becoming very conscious of himself upon hearing his own voice: Becoming acutely conscious of the absence of his physical self in a strange way while his mental self remained almost universally still. And inside that stillness he became quite conscious of his self's self. He had been standing staring into space literally as his gaze moved from a horizon hued like an early autumn afternoon. Then his gaze retreated across an expanse high over a beautifully treed city full of birds and banners fluttering amid warm air that was moving fair weather clouds about in the sky. Then looking back through large floor to ceiling windows into an enormous and extraordinarily well-appointed drawing room he saw King Karatakos standing beside a sideboard. He had already recognized Morgant's and Karatakos' voices which he had responded to before his vision had fully contracted that then plunged his head into a spin as he struggled with bringing himself back to an equilibrium similar to the one he knew in the third dimension. But the involuntary reflex failed as a higher awareness corrected the fault and he catapulted in the opposite direction.

"Well, well, well. Welcome, Dyfed,' said Morgant, as though he had a stutter. 'You've made it here at last. There is a soft cushioned divan directly behind you, my man, lay back and rest awhile.'

Similarly Karatakos contributed his greetings adding that Dyfed's discomfiture and confusion will pass momentarily. Dyfed was lying back comfortably now gathering his thoughts while there was some more chitchat between the other two men. All of a sudden Dyfed's dizziness abruptly dissipated.

"Hello,' said Morgant straining forward from his seated position and looking directly into Dyfed's eyes.

"How's it going, over there? queried Karatakos with his back still turned.

"He's here,' responded Morgant. 'Now Dyfed,' he said, 'the phenomenon here is all contrived. Know that.'

"Wow,' said Karatakos.

"Wow,' said Dyfed more to himself then anyone else. He sat a few more moments before uncoiling from his position on a very lavish blue and silver striped divan. He rested his soft tan leather clad feet momentarily on the dark polished hardwood floor and pushing up with his knuckles he slowly stood up to a tall standing position. 'I'll get your drink and bring it over for you. Don't get up,' he said to Morgant who as yet had made no effort to get up to retrieve it. As he said that Dyfed moved forward and made a motion with his index finger from a slightly outstretched arm toward Morgant. It was a gesture of greeting while moving away shiftily from the old sage towards King Karatakos. As Karatakos was pouring the alcohol from a sparkling crystal decanter into three large cut crystal glasses, he and Morgant had continued their quiet easy conversation. Dyfed, who was still just listening to the two other men's back and forth banter mentally adjusted himself to this place as he padded across a huge exceedingly elegant Persian carpet in his soft shoes toward the wide expanse of floor to ceiling windows where Karatakos was pouring and through which he had been staring out at the world beyond. This view through glass dominated one entire enormous wall that looked out from Karatakos' palace in a southwesterly direction onto the gigantic expanse of the city below.

The room they were in was also proportionally huge with exceedingly high ceilings hung with at least thirty or more immense and brilliantly lit chandeliers despite the sun's rays streaming through the high wall of glass at a sharp angle that indicated an hour or so shortly after midday. The ceiling was beamed in heavy dark wood that contrasted sharply with the flat white plaster that covered the walls and ceiling. Those walls were additionally decorated with the most beautiful and amazing artwork that would be recognizable to almost any middling connoisseur. Behind them, away from the windowed exterior wall, was a great dining hall with an enormous horseshoe shaped table of heavy light coloured wood that was able to seat upwards of sixty people at any one time. High above the table was an opaque glass dome set with coloured glass and prisms around the base whose diameter was the length of at least six tall men head to toe. The table was in the centre of the room and at that point two very wide corridors ran at right angles in either direction through large arched entrances. On the far side of the table, well beyond where the missing segment of the horseshoe provided room for waiters to enter the inner area and serve the seated (or access a smaller centre table that was normally reserved for desserts), lay a dance floor with more couches lining the two walls on either side while at the back of the room and away in the distance was an orchestra section.

The over all plane of the floor had (in Dyfed's mind) the impression of slanting gently down toward the windows, though it was not perceivably tilted to one's balance nor in actuality did it slant in any way. And through those windows one was able (from an enormous height) to gaze a great distance over a canopy of leafy tree tops interspaced here and there by a gothic spire or a charming palace set amidst trim green lawns all neatly cut out of the garden forest that extended as far as the eye could see. Interlaced between the occasional tiled rooftops, the glistening silver-like slate on high that composed the tips of spires decorating palaces, and there was even a gigantic crystal roof over a giant modern hippodrome in the distance. It was all neatly arranged and uncluttered and clearly laid out. Beyond and half way into the distance meandered the River Tems, its water moving slowly to the rhythm of its spirit and as it twisted and rolled it emitted flashes of silver and yellow through the gentle tan and light blue of its shimmering surface.

"I can see your palace from here Morgant,' said Karatakos, with a little laugh. He turned and glanced at Dyfed who was approaching him. Dyfed walked slowly toward one end of the long elaborately panelled buffet where he picked up the two glasses of scotch whisky that Karatakos had poured and glided back across the silk Persian carpet — handing Morgant his glass as he passed — and ignoring the divan then chose to sit down on an ornate early period Franken chair that was slightly closer to the two other men's couches. As he placed his full glass on a charming polished walnut and wicker table stand, Karatakos spoke.

"You know, Dyfed. Since your palace doesn't get any use. You should rent it out. This was followed by a burst of laughter. 'You are simply never here and we miss your company, don't we Morgant old man!'

"That's for sure,' Morgant answered. 'Everything just runs tickity-boo when you're not here. It could bore the antlers off a stage, right Karatakos? Actually, Karatakos and I have been thinking about renting your palace out to tourists!' The two other men both burst out laughing uncontrollably again. Dyfed, on the other hand felt as though he were suddenly becoming overwhelmed by a powerful hallucinogen. He smiled at the joke but did not succeed in laughing. He spoke slowly.

"If you want to see more of me you know where I am! Drop on by why don't'cha? Whether I'm in the dominion of comatose,' Dyfed stammered, winking at King Karatakos as he said that, 'or whether I'm here in the garden at the end of the fourth path, wherever the hell that is,' he said in a bewildered manner while looking around him and holding up his drink close to his chin. 'Where the devil am I, anyway? And oh yeah: You wanted to see me? Well here I am. So, what's up?'

"Nova Troia is where you are,' answered King Karatakos, 'but in its fifth dimension state of mind, to be precise.'

"Hmm,' responded Dyfed. I'd prefer my own home on the west coast of Merika,' he said.

"Ah, yes, your ideal realty. Or is it your idea of reality; somewhere out there on the fringe of the Dominion of Comatose — region…what was it? Oh yes, Merika.'

"What the hell's wrong with that?' asked Dyfed.

"You are an absolute marvel,' said Karatakos speaking through tears of laughter, 'you know that Dyfed. You really are. Danger-man! That's what we'll call you from now on. That's who you are. How do you relax anyway?' Karatakos asked Dyfed as he turned his head toward Morgant and asked him: 'Talking about the coast in the third dimension, how is your renovation coming on your palace in Massilia (Marseille)?'

"Beautifully, answered Morgant before Dyfed had figured out what was going on around him. High-end renters couldn't have better paid for the improvements so far. I visit when I can but the air is not so clean and clear there now as it used to be. The view of the White Sea is still enchanting and apart from the late summer when cooler breezes blow down from mount Meru, that season is very warm. In the fifth dimension we've now changed the port there. In the fifth dimension it looks like it did two thousand solar cycles ago when it was a commercial port for Amor. That reminds me,' Morgant stated, 'I like what you've done with Boodikka Central Station here in Nova Troia.'

"What was that?' inquired Dyfed, looking up from a deep thought.

"Bodikka Station?' Karatakos answered.

"You wouldn't have noticed when you arrived here,' said Morgant to Dyfed. 'You didn't come here by train. It doesn't run here anymore anyway.' Both Karatakos and Morgant started laughing again at the remark.

"Oh yes! I did notice, come to think of it,' Dyfed fibbed. 'But why would you do anything to it, why even keep it, he asked sarcastically, 'its just window dressing. And yes, I remember seeing it. Presumably with your wizardry I imagined it as it looked in the late nineteenth century. But at least its not falling down anymore.'

"Yes Dyfed you are right; so why do anything? Your attributes and your powers of awareness will grow and then you won't need to do anything. Probably (at least at this stage) what you see outside those windows differs immensely as to what we see. And I don't necessarily see what Morgant sees.' He laughed. Then he added: 'Soon you won't want to leave us. You will want to stay here. But yes, you are right. We seem to want to harken back to a gentler time, a more beautiful time in some ways. So we recreate and refurbish old grand styles of the third dimension into a quasi, individual function ability of the fifth density for ourselves. I mean,' Karatakos said, 'look around you. Look at this palace of mine in which you are enveloped now. So yes, it is a façade but it's an honest façade that harbours no secrets, that's all. To be modern, it now seems, is to be utility. Being modern is more about function ability than living and letting your imagination expand. There are great exceptions and great imaginations in the third density. You know them and know of them. But they are few and far in between, always have been. Modern folks who embrace the modern trend have little to no imagination within their being. In fact even their functionality is fake and plastic and is generally used only to fleece others and wouldn't exist at all if it didn't provide some exceptional personal gain for some incorporated oligarch or other.'

"Whoa, whoa! Just a moment on that,' said Morgant. 'If these people hadn't been so weak and pathetic but stood up for their own true self and not allowed themselves to be bullied into submission, things may have turned out differently. And that is hardly our fault. All right, perhaps we could have played a few things straight from our hand and slightly better.'

"Are you referring to our judicial laxity regarding the third density's stringent reaction toward culpability?' said Dyfed. Culpability is not and has never been properly defined or even understood by the hoi polloi.'

It was obvious to the two other men that Dyfed was growing stronger and thinking more clearly by the moment.

"Or somebody's laxity,' said Dyfed. 'The devil only knows that the three of us certainly tried to persuade the hoi polloi to go easy on the executions and life imprisonments. What was Thrax doing all this time?'

"Careful you don't bandy dangerous accusations around carelessly, Dyfed,' said Morgant.

"Well, you know what I mean,' replied Dyfed. Thrax has…'

"Thrax has his way of doing things, it that what you were going to say?' Morgant butted in. 'Yes, you are right, but look here! It wasn't just false justice followed by executions and life imprisonments, it was the entire corruption of the justice system where if you were rich as a lord, or whatever, or even a powerful member of the religious or political bureaucracy in general, you could buy your way out from under almost any charges brought against you. Most of the time they could buy away the accusations before the charges materialized or were known to the public at large. It was a hell of a deal. Amor did the same thing for its power elite back in its day. But that didn't mean that great and powerful men didn't fall victim, either. And, again, there were certain persons of note, lords and ladies and the like, around the kyzar, the czar or grand Pooh-Bah who were immune to any atrocity. Then their sons or their fathers were executed the next moment for someone has to pay. Round up the usual expendables, Mr Nightwatchman, and then flog them and strangle them just for good measure and practice. And it was around this maelstrom of anonymity for misdeeds done that swirled to the detriment of the folks at large that caused the break down of justice. And this was so whether or not matters were taken up before that aforementioned Pooh-Bah or some ad hoc assembly in the legislative kremlin of justice. The dice were loaded and the game was rigged. We tried. They just wouldn't listen!'

"It wasn't just the corrupt departments that made up the system in the Dominions of Comatose,' said Karatakos. Dyfed was bemused by the fact that King Karatakos had way more to say here on such matters than he had ever witnessed before. 'It isn't just the establishment that was and continues to be to blamed. It is also the responsibility of the masses to do due diligence in bringing empires to heel and under control.'

"And just how on earth is that supposed to happen when acolytes of empire brainwash the masses and fill their heads full of rubbish so they can't even reason properly,' asked Dyfed. 'How can they when the high priests conjure a separate and apart deity then fabricate a completely self imagined idea into a culture around it that the masses are forced to revere. But to spoof, ridicule or deny the established culture becomes an act of high treason punishable by strangulation moments before being drawn and quartered then hung lifeless to drip-dry from the walls of that same royal citadel/fortress (kremlin) of justice, how else are the masses to defend themselves?' asked Dyfed. I find it strange that when grown men who otherwise appear intelligent talk and question and even lecture others about what can be expected in the afterlife (not only their own but of others as well) if they continue on such and such path they've chosen. Nobody seems to suspect insanity is at work here, either. Nobody is subscribing lithium or psychotropic injections to help keep the deranged and paranoid patients who are imagining themselves dead and facing an ordeal on their journey to either heaven or hell (or some space/time unknown and undefined) on the rails with their wheels on. Here the treatment is wrongly thought to be capable of revealing a type of common sense reality that is however not common and in a condition when reality itself is an unknown. That means it's definitely composed of hypothetical structures: all of which cannot be regarded as being real. I can understand a man or woman questioning where their own path will lead them in this life, but not the afterlife. Postulating on one's probable situation in the afterlife in this our world of disassociation, apparently, isn't a symptom of insanity after all: But of course it is. It's certainly not the avenue and attitude to promotion in any kind of aspect of sanity. Anyway, there is only one avenue or path and that is one's own. Other's paths than one's own are irrelevant to all and one and can't really exist in another's reality, anyway. The truth is that as individuals on this side of the afterlife we are all probably on the same path though none of us are equal to any other, and that the path we are on is the only thing common to each of us and is the only thing relevant to us as individuals, full stop. So, we need a different strategy, a new strategy to forge ahead instead of a primitive superstitious one based on fantasy and fairy-tail type myth. Nothing is going to change in the world unless the overriding culture (that is meant to inspire and influence and appears to be innate to the order of the establishment at all times) changes drastically. Stupidity is the act of applying the exact same method over and over in the disassociated belief that somehow the result will differ. What I'm trying to say is that the establishment essentially is not changing. Time after time it remains the same. There lies the problem.'

"Ah, Dyfed, through delegation we've summoned you to relegate you to the position of Chief of Public Safety of the third dimension, not chief philosopher I'm afraid. But… here comes Lord Manandan. He is here, beside you now.'

Dyfed turned and immediately Manandan was suddenly beside him. They then embraced warmly and Lord Manandan was smiling broadly. He grasped Dyfed's hand then turning to one side the two collapsed onto the blue and silver divan that Dyfed had been reclining upon earlier. There the mature student and his old teacher basked in common memory. As space/time here is so different it could be said they talked, laughed and brought images of themselves before the present for an eternity less a moment or two. Then the discussion returned to the former one again, the matter of what was the matter with the lives of the hoi polloi.

"So, why not focus on the deity they (as we) know first-hand? To do this one must truly know one's self. We know this. Why not pierce the ram for the squalid race on their behalf, so to speak, and conjure up as best we can the perception that each can have of their own true selves behind the mask they've donned and become? This is the only deity they can know and the only one relevant to them that even matters. And of course this is the god of the all-pervading cosmic spirit (as we can only know it to be) within ourselves,' said Manandan. 'It will also help the hoi polloi to shed the mask that is not their own self.' He unclasped his hand from Dyfed's and moved his arm through latter's arm and clasped Dyfed's hand again. Now entwined Manandan was overjoyed at this long awaited reunion.

"And that was just the direction where I was headed,' said Dyfed eager to show the others his worth.

"But we've gone through all this before,' said Lord Huge who appeared now just as suddenly as Manandan had.

"I've heard about Dyfed's Sinter Klaas or Santa Claus,' said Manandan. 'I liked that, and how in their own way the hoi polloi need to identify with this beautiful fabricated concept of the giver to, and the lover of others. This, as we know, is the essence common to all hoi polloi: An essence that is now largely ignored and overlooked other than by certain pious ones and intuitive folks who love others and have compassion and empathy for their fellow hoi polloi. In other words, folks of charity.'

"Thank you Master,' Dyfed answered, 'but Nicklaus of Demre, formerly of Patara…'

"Enough,' snapped Lord Huge in a roughshod interruption. 'We know who he was as a third dimensionalist. You should be more interested in the spiritual personification that he underwent (at least in your mind, which was your idea) and the personification to which he was attracted. And it seems likely that by this very same attraction to it, it too was immediately attracted to him. And any hoi polloi can adopt agility of this quality that needs only a will of fifty per cent for it to flourish. But they need that will from the fountainhead of life to do so. So tell us, Dyfed, about Santa Claus. You conjured it up for Karl Magus so well, I thought. Do it for us. But just how is this going to change the hoi polloi's so-called debt to the Haploids, as you put it? How can we lessen the influence of the Haploids over the hoi polloi? I think this is the question you continually ask? And then we will have our convocation and later still explain the duties of the Chief of Public Safety to you and take any questions you may have at that time, despite the fact that time is irrelevant here.'

(Santa Claus)

"I have something more to do than feel."
CHARLES LAMB

It had all began of course, Dyfed stated, when he had had the responsibility of having to read everything Giorgius Florentius wrote down. After all, he couldn't accurately comment or understand the foibles common to the hoi polloi unless he knew exactly how they thought and why they thought it. And under the circumstances, and what he knew about them already, he wasn't sure he was ever going to be able to do that. But understanding what they thought was partially narrowed down to investigating what the people were being told by the chief warrior king Chlodio (at the time) along with that of his high priests all on loan from the Church of Amor. This greatly cut down Dyfed's work. There really were only a few manifestos of originality that tried to accurately explain the great lie. And the bulk of that propaganda generally followed one or two themes as put forward by talented men who embraced both the lie and the Church of Amor as the latter embraced them in return. Giorgius Gregorius Florentius was one of these men. Another was a shady character said to be descended from the House of Mistletoe who Dyfed employed from time to time. His name was Count Agenbite of Inwit and Dyfed noted he could rely on him to work (even prefer to work) during religious holidays, though Dyfed respected all men and women's religion and the established Establishment holy days and its hours of work rules thereof. It had certainly been dangerous not to acknowledge the social/religious precepts of Jeshuanism both in Europa and the Newfoundland of Merika (indeed, of all the Merikas) over the last few centuries on the pain of horrible anguish and sometimes death of one's entire family: And we all know what happened to the Cathars ten centuries ago when they bucked (some say debunked) the Church of Amor's official story-myth Idea concept that had been passed into indisputable universal truth by one or other of the Pontiff's sanctum bulls -- they were slaughtered on the beaches, the fields and in the streets, and when they were captured alive they had their hands and their feet cut off after which they were disembowelled and strangled before being hung from their fortresses and defence walls for the ravens and turkey vultures to peck them clean to pieces. And then there was the Ishlamites. But there wasn't really any more or any less propaganda there than in and among the Jeshuans, either, but at least the Ishlamists still had their translation of Homer intact. That was due to their reverence to all knowledge and it behoved them to retain Homer's work that had been devoured across Hellenic Central Asia back in the day. The Europaeans had all lost their translations not long after the fall of Amor. But to their discredit the common folks within both the Jeshuan and the Ishlamite religions were compelled to interpret signs and rumours exactly as they were told to by priests, mullahs and other mesmerizers and then to react accordingly. Here religion was a default appliance: If in doubt they should never think for themselves or believe that they could reason through the problem. Put your mind away from it as best you can during the moments of doubt; then immediately seek a priest and let him investigate and explain it to you all over once again, as before. This, after all, was the job of the priests as it was the duty of the parishioner to accept what they were being told. So, it was quite simple really. Dyfed didn't have to try and pry out the thoughts of a thousand or even a hundred common people polled around the old crumbling empire in order to conduct an accurate account of the beliefs and the temperament within the micro-organism of this new empire-aspiring state of authority that was supplanting paganism. The close approximation of the Jeshuan religion, with its hard and very fast ideals, opinions and accordant rules having been securely attached to this new establishment's power factor and elite, made it possible for Dyfed to easily fast-track his access to it by perusing and reflecting on those prolific Jeshuans of letters, such as Giorgius Florentius (Giorgi Posh) and Count Agenbite of Inwit of the House of Mistletoe, never mind the Church of Amor's and its specific precepts.

There it was, all in the propaganda handouts and required reading. Required reading that is, but only if you were an aspiring intellectual as almost everybody was and still is. That was why Giorgius wrote in the vulgar Amoran language at the time so everybody no matter how ignorant or stupid they really were could read the good news to deliver anyone and their loved ones into salvation. Never had anything like it been seen before and hardly anything has changed since. Certainly commercialism has taken a leaf out of their book, and politics too. And if there were any successful jaded and cynical writers at the time who had managed to put forward a negative spin on the encroaching and fast spreading lie(s) during its telling, our hero Dyfed was never able to pin point them. Only one man did stand out, he told them, and his spin was very positive.

For he discovered during his analysis of the mountain of propaganda which the Church of Amor pumped out (through the hard work of faithful monks and intellectualized bishops like Giorgius Florentius) that he often came face to face with many a so-called saint who he genuinely admired and praised but none so much as Nikolaos of Demre (Myra).

And all of this brought the saints from the breakaway group (that cult of Jeshua Adon, the new Abramists) into view and into perspective once and for all. But that perspective at that time was somewhat in another reflection that cast a different light from another angle. Most of these saints were trumpeted up naysayers of the old pagan unity and nothing more. Sainthood was their reward for towing the line. Others, Dyfed thought, were a breath of fresh air despite their attachment and similarity to the primitive superstition cult of the storm god Bel Shadai (Sadé), Ba'al or Jehovah. Though never having been introduced personally, at the time Morgant and Cato had provided him with reams of data on this man Nikolaus that was born in the port city of Patara located in Anatolia in the ancient land of Lykia. Dyfed remembered that he and Marg had made a brief stopover at Patara just before Effes and the Oracle of Klaros on their journey home from Xanderia. Patara was a Hellas port situated almost directly across the shallow bay from the famous and ancient city of Arnna (also Arinna now called Xanthos) of ancient Lykia. Xanthos is located where the river from Tlos flowed into the aforementioned bay. These two cities were on the White Sea coast just before the coast of Anatolia curved up from the White Sea and merged into the Aegean.

Nikolaus was a descendant and son of Hellas and had entered the Jeshuan priesthood early where he ministered to the poor, the lonely and the convicted all his life while even being persecuted (as an added cross to bear) by an *Augustus* despot. Sainthood had come posthumously and quite recently to Bishop Nikolaus.

Dyfed's interest in Saint Nikolaus led to some interesting comparisons that even the elders smiled upon from on high. Dyfed hit on the idea that this saintly man who was part and parcel of the regular folks who make up the greater element of humanity and who are not part of the Haploid psychopathic one per cent, was a legitimate symbol for whatever engine of creation one may want to look upon and praise. The black-headed people of ancient Khem often used the sun as that symbol in order to worship something tangible within the universe that they could grasp. These ancients, like the ancient Aryans of Asia before them, didn't pray to and worship the sun or planets per sé although through the Hyperborean penetration of the past they acknowledged another sun god called Saturn that they suggested once sustained the earth. Only the moderns consider doing stupid things like actually personifying planets and suns. The sun or a planet was a symbol only. And they were not alone in doing so. The Hellas, for instance revered Helios (the sun) as a god but for the sake of it being the original benefactor. This took place all over the world in ancient times. Sometimes they took the precise constellation of stars in the heavens that marked the present era such as Pisces that had a symbol or sign that they made do for this concept; and be it Taurus or Capricorn et al, each one had its own shelf in the sky. For this reason the fishes, the bull and the goat representations respectively rule not only three of the twelve segments all told of the great year, with each segment enduring for over two thousand solar cycles or years, but during each solar year itself the sun also transits each sign during a portion of that year for a duration of four weeks. This sign, therefore, rules these weeks and they are the signs under which every human is born.

It was interesting to Dyfed that Capricorn, which is one of four cardinal or hinge signs and is represented by Pan the goat, is also an earth sign that is ruled by the planet Saturn and corresponds to the festival of Saturnalia. This in many ways was the foundation for SinterKlaas. In fact (so Dyfed later discovered) Sinter Klaus was once even depicted riding a goat. Later it was a sleigh pulled by reindeer.

The sun or a planet of our system was very commonly used as symbols Dyfed knew because a long time ago the world was dominated by such a spectacle. As just mentioned, this star or sun that was once present in our sky was much different from the hot burning star that dominates our heavens today and brings us day from the dark of night. The old god (for that is what the star represents to intelligent life) was a cooler, somewhat dimmer, reddish disc that saturated the world in a green light and remained unmovable and fixed directly overhead in the north celestial pole. This was long before the time of the Hyperboreans who through magical means assembled this ancient history into the presence of their psyche. This was why the ancients always faced the north when they communicated or attempted to communicate with their creator of presence and awareness in order to give plaudit and show thankfulness. That was how the Hyperboreans did it, too, and many a pseudo high priest cult has since copied that in the ages since. But this was something he needn't advise his companions about. Mostly they had advised him.

Saint Nikolaus, who was everybody's friend and was a patron to a long list of careers and occupations (soon to be accompanied as a patron to many countries as well) with its folklore already in place, was foremost a patron to all children for which he was especially equipped. I mean –– step up to the plate any and all of you myriad of ogres and discredit that if you are insane enough to dare. And as all normal societies treasure their children, feast days that had come down from the pagan days and were now being adopted by the Jeshuans and refashioned always tipped their nature and their purpose of being in a special way toward the children no matter what language they spoke or even what religion they preached. Sinter Klaas, in person, had once bourn gifts to bring relief and joy so now in spirit form he would forever bear gifts, Dyfed had thought. He would bear gifts to children as in his symbolized form he bears life to all humanity and every living thing just as he always has done and always will. This so long as humanity and living things exist, otherwise, it won't matter. It's a Zen thing: It's also a quantum thing whatever that means: Transmissions must be received in order to actually exist in totality. A circuit open is not a circuit. But even a short circuit is still a circuit.

Anyway, Saint Nikolaus represents the giver of life in the star or sun form that hung low close to the earth long ago and dominated the north pole. And this is now where Sinter Klaas is believed to live. He dwells at the north pole dominated under the sign of the great bear as every little boy and girl knows, and from whence he comes once each and every year on SinterKlaas Day (which continues to fall within that most sacred of seasons) to smile and bring cheer to all people — little children and their proud parents and grandparents all. Happy children bring happiness to all warm-hearted, loving, empathetic and considerate folks. And this special day of Santa Klaus' (SinterKlaus) is celebrated quite close to and just prior to the winter solstice. Fortunately the Amoran festival of Saturnalia (that occurred during pagan times at the same time of year) lent itself to promote and propagate the celebration of Saint Nikolaus Day. Although pagan festivals were still being purged by those keeners in cowls who came down from the Church of Amor by various Jeshuanism schools of monks, they often turned a blind eye to some well worn customs while censoring and remodelling the rest of the festival that they thought was offensive to their fantasies. Even the northern god Wodan (Odin) to these northerners — Goths among them and Kelts too — lent elements to Saint Nikolaus (in his spirit form) and in this simple guise SinterKlaas easily became (with Dyfed and friend's promotional work) a universal love to happily embrace all of that which was available to all: For he is the celebration of humanity for humanity's sake. SinterKlaas tells us that humanity is the great celebration of the universe, for there can be no greater cause for humanity to celebrate than to celebrate humanity itself. SinterKlaas is not a religious messiah, he is much more than that, he is a human messiah for he represents us, our hopes and fears and our very existence itself. Santa Klaus is charity, the greatest of calling. But especially he represents charity within our humanity.

The Apostolic church vehemently disagrees with such a notion while often pretending to agree. This is, of course, because of strong public opinion that they fear. Strong public opinion is now, and always will be (in a free-willed, independent human oriented democratic social environment), the king of opinion, not an unconstitutional and undemocratic authoritarian religious cult. Cults don't cut public opinion well. Dyfed worked hard at this and in time came to admire and promote a second effigy alongside SinterKlaus (that of a similar iconize superman[82] that protected humanities' security the way SinterKlaas protects our passion for love). Anyway, with volunteers to spread the word he had managed to make more popular the celebration of Saint Nikolaus. Then, and only then, and with help and perseverance an actual celebration and festival day for Sinter-Klaas became possible. And he saw to it that this holy day of joy was placed back

---

82 Fictionalized by Jerry Seigel and Joe Shuster, *Superman* has appeared in comic books and the *'funnies'* section of syndicated newspapers the world over. Like Santa, no tension has ensued nor have any wars been triggered and fought over the cult of *Superman*.

where it belonged. They all agreed that this was the case. And the beauty of it all was that it was no threat to the narrow-minded established and holy government that emanated from the headquarters of the Vicar of Jeshua and the church of Amor. And as the cult of Jeshuanism gained even greater strength so did the acceptance of Santa Klaus Day. Indeed, if only half-heartedly at first, the Jeshuans soon embraced this special paraclete that Sinter Klaus represented by actually canonizing him. *'God works in mysterious ways'* is an old Jeshuan adage.

(Papa Papanasi and the paparazzi)

'There is nothing proper about what you are doing,
soldier, but do try to kill me properly'.
CICERO

"The hoi polloi, including the haploids, now finally (as you know) have a grasp not only about electrics but are now on the verge of graduating into full-blown electronics,' interjected Dyfed, solemnly, 'even if I don't. And there is a growing competency in other fields, as well. They have a rudimentary knowledge of the phenomena in which they find themselves and many even now have a partially relative definition of phenomena.'

"So, if Dyfed is correct,' said Lord Huge, 'about that and my own observations tells me that he is, and if Santa Claus has failed the hoi polloi miserably, then how's about we introduce Papa Papanasi syndrome here, into the mix, for help?

"The concept,' said Morgant, remembering his attempt to thwart Virus by incarcerating that demon within the earth somewhere in the Ethiopian highlands where it was just now beginning to leach into the Nile River and bring a succession of scourges upon the world over the next century, 'might be extremely advantageous. 'It may be that the lower echelon needs to get over the last hurdle and out from under a manifestation that only has power over them so long as the former appreciate that reality under the latter's terms. But if what I believe Lord Huge to mean by the Papa Papanashi syndrome, I heartily disagree. It is too extreme and permission to use the olden day nuclear-tipped bronze lance, or an equivalent weapon of mass destruction, would not be forth coming; though I believe that Thrax would be a strong proponent for such a deployment.'

"Furthermore, time now may be of essence, I would say,' replied Manandan, 'in more ways than one. Has not our river to the third generation…the third dimension…been one whose hallmark is of opening up? Has not each invention we've provided them led to another; have they not led to the hoi polloi's greater understanding of the universe around them? Of course it has. That is why, today, they have certain powers of perception and conceive of the phenomena of electric and mathematical physics et al as Dyfed has stated. Indeed, Lord Huge is the expert here in this field. But the use of god's oldenday lance is beyond the pale here and Thrax won't have anything to do with it. This is because the third dimension folks are well along themselves to discovering nuclear fission despite our attempts to confound them, and even if the event was secreted say somewhere in the Andes Mountains, word would get out anyway and the timing of all this is just too risky.'

"Absolutely their perception has increased,' replied Lord Huge, 'and Morgant, you used the valuable word appreciate, just now. Suppose that the Haploids, for instance, who are no further technologically advanced than the hoi polloi, that in itself is part and parcel of the cause of much of the hoi polloi's inability to shake the aforementioned Haploids off to minimize their suffering. So, suppose the Haploids take the bait of a newly devised technology of mechanized transmigration or deliverance from here into the fifth dimension where they long to be cocooned. They couldn't fully grasp it but since they are used to regular advancement over the centuries they may actually appreciate that something like that is possible now, just as the hoi polloi would. And considering the prospects of war, over population, pollution, etcetera, they may be keen to explore it.'

"But since its not technologically possible, to what advantage would this be? Said Morgant. 'To what end, I ask?'

"And let me remind you,' piped up Dyfed. 'We don't have a pollution problem in the third dimension: We have a population problem only, or soon will have; mark my words.' But as soon as he said that he bit his tongue.

"Just now you were remembering your commission to exile Virus,' said Lord huge. 'You failed, Morgant. As it happens we know that Virus is returning from isolation after a more than two millennium absence. Maybe that is enough to frighten them and want to flee the third density forever.'

"But to what advantage I ask again,' asked Morgant, 'for this task of transcending the undeveloped into this density and vibration normally cannot be done, as you know!'

"I too once failed,' said Lord Huge. 'I failed Manandan by not properly securing one of our outpost resorts on the Isle of Peace with a screen of obscurity from the prying eyes of the third dimension back when Dyvy here was born. I wish now to make amends for the sake of the hoi polloi. So, if we trick the Haploids with a ruse into thinking we can transmigrate them in mass from there to here so they can languish for an eternity in everlasting life in the fifth dimension, we have an opportunity instead to exterminate them on mass. That's to what end.'

"Whoa! and holy shit…!' came the general response from the other three men to that bombshell. It was like a black lead cloud hovering over some kill-joy, happiness-B-gone ogre which Lord Huge suddenly came to represent: it was a not so happy birthday party for a jubilant and expectant child where that same ogre had bothered to plaster the happy venue with palls of black cloth and float black balloons along the walls and ceiling just to add a touch of something far away from a child's birthday gaiety.

"Do you know what you're saying? asked Manandan.

"You can build it but they won't come,' said Morgant, thoughtfully. 'As for the Haploids, the world's situation today is not nearly dangerous enough,' he added tongue in cheek. He implied otherwise by this facial affectation though his statement was probably true, Dyfed thought. Quite soon after, Morgant's facetious sentiment came to be more than evident to others than the scientific society; even among the governments of advanced nations who claimed that the world's environment was balanced and remained healthy for human habitation: It was stay the course and full speed ahead.

"However,' replied Lord Huge, 'if they were to be convinced that comet Wormwood was discovered to be on the return, and even now on its last leg as it dived deep into our solar system yet still just out of sight, and knowing the carnage that happened on Earth due its close proximity last time this comet brushed past us on its big sling around the sun before being flung back out into space….' Lord Huge discontinued here for a pregnant pause and to contemplate a projected anticipatory thought.

'Aside from the business at hand before our convocation,' he continued, 'we now need to put this on the agenda under new business. 'So, as Chief of Public Safety, in order to further that goal, Dyvy can order up the camera toting, story telling paparazzi so as to get the word out while pretending it's a secret and that only a select few of the third dimensional region folks will have the once in a life-time opportunity to be air-lifted to a venue far away from their urban world. And there (in a secure out of the way place where) with the wave of the magic wand of technology (in this case fakery) in their general direction they will be led to believe (falsely) that they will be transmigrated out from the third density into the fifth –– presto! Ultimately, this ruse will aid and abet the hoi polloi by causing millions of Haploid flesh to disappear into vapour and out of the hoi polloi's and our hair and into extinction — Haploids every one. Good riddance, I say. And with Dr Quasi Gizmo and Professor Tortionfield's help to set the stage complete with a fake wizard in charge –– we can do this.'

'So, having said that I then propose to later nominate the one and only, that two fisting Papa Papanashi to (without delay) take up the challenge he has so often claimed was his mission and to lead his people to *saecula saeculorum*.[83] The trick being (I suppose) that we'll have to get this entire matter accomplished during the short time he'll be sober.

"So, what the devil is this? Is it an effort to make Pangaea great again? asked Dyfed sarcastically. 'And who the hell is Papa Papanashi, anyway?'

"Why, its you Dyvy, it's what you're called by us, at least by me. It is you who seek the just desserts; it's you who put the icing and the sparkle on the finished product. So I intend to nominate you Dyfed Lucifer to play the role of Two Fisting Papa Papanashi,' said Lord Huge who smiling amid an ugly visage looked around the gigantic room at the others. He then laughed a dirty laugh.

At first Dyfed did not see the necessity to broach the storehouses of Lord Huge's mind (along with those of the others) to gain access to the files therein. He was new here. But now he contemplated the image of Lord Huge. Essentially this thing was nondescript. He was, after all just a projection vibe within the vibration as a whole. But his head was ugly. It was shaped in profile as a pentagram. The line for the back of his head was straight up and down. From the top of this line (that comprised the back of his head) a second line shot off and sloped gently upward to his forehead while from the bottom of that back of head line (that was the nap of his neck) another line sloped downward at the same but opposite angle as the upper line which ended at his chin. From these two points (the forehead and the chin) his face was fashioned by two other lines that formed a triangular shape that peaked at his nose. His mouth was an ugly gash that cut the lower line of his face and in the fore-portion of the upper triangle of his head his eyes were terrible to behold. Now that he saw more plainly, it was with caution more than for reasons of courtesy that Dyfed ventured forth slowly. After a time he spoke.

"Give your head a shake, Huge' he said incredulously. 'They do called me Dyfed Nimble Wit, ya' know. What do they call you, anyway? Dull of Wit. I'll tell you right now that very few dull-of-wits are either brave enough or have reason to approach me without fear. Anyway, Solon said to Croesus (back in the day, if you recall) 'count no man happy until he be dead'. I'm beginning to see his point.'

"Thrax or Huge will not have the last word regarding this,' whispered Manandan into Dyfed's ear-hole. 'But don't get your hopes up. Oh, and by the way, if you think Lord Huge is terrifying, wait 'till you meet Thrax. He's an abomination.'

"Don't ever question to whom I extend my allegiance to the cause,' continued Dyfed with some unexpected anger, as he stared back at Lord Huge. 'But the hoi polloi do need to overcome the Haploids. This is their path to gain transmigration. Extermination isn't even the last chose for any living creature. For the definitional sum of Living Creatures is

---

83 'Unto the ages of ages'.

the Gitchy-manatoo, the Universality, Parazoa, the Great Spirit and the living God, the Absolute and the Unity. I don't see any of that in your vision and plan.'

"And how do the gods line up for you Dyvy?' Huge asked.

"Be careful, Huge,' Manandan suddenly blurted out emphatically, having just found his voice again which was shaking, but still calm. He seemed to have had to build up momentum before extrapolating. 'Dyfed, Prince of the Grove, son of Queen Violet-Eye, descendant of Lord Shirkuh the high priest-king and overlord of our race, is — least of all — my pupil, but my scholar and head of the House of Lucifer. And he was one of the best I ever had, so, I thank you not to take that tone with him for you may do so at your own peril. We need, in any case, to be concordant here. We need each of us on side and we need to set an example for approximately the half a million kshatriyas (warriors) who like Dyfed exercise almost all of their existence in the third density to fight the good fight in the manner in which they do so to the best of their ability.'

"Menstruating mother,' exclaimed Dyfed. 'Unholy anointed messiahs and prophets: Half a million? That's it; there's only half a million of us? And how many Haploids are there, not counting their hoi polloi converts, sycophants and ass-kissers.

"So, in answer to your question of how many Haploids there are,' replied Manandan, 'Thrax says more like fifty million. Apparently, there is a controversy over which percentage of the population is in fact suffering from the condition of psychopathic haploid.'

"And why am I not surprised at that,' stated Dyfed. This situation we have put ourselves in and why we are here now is the same conundrum that arises with religious thoughts and practices. But before we proceed on that subject I'll tell you this. What I've learned so far in my life in the third dimension is that I don't know if anything we do outside of the plan that's underway, and what we call phenomenon, makes any difference to it. I question how in your mind the gods stack up against phenomenon? That is my question to you,' he asked. We have the eternal ethereal spirit and the ephemeral material phenomenon and we are kind of the conjunction of its unity. I mean there's even a question as to whether or not the eternal Spirit would exist without the temporal Material and visa versa; however as I see it more simply, Lord Krishna is the ever-present Universal symbol and Lord Buddha is a symbol of the Media of unity that is the conjunction within the flux through and by which humans must navigate. As for Jeshua Adon, I see this as being the Particular that stands for the potential for each and every human. All three of these lords of the phenomenon are current and eternal axioms within the phenomenon. The Ishlamite Prophet is one more step closer to historical man and womankind and therefore is in a different sphere than the other three who are, or could have been both symbolic and material men. No so with the Prophet who already manifested individually and as such is the only historical entity here among them. Buddhahood doesn't claim to be an incarnation of the Spirit, yet it is the Spirit overcoming Material and material overcoming the spirit in a relative sense, which, if willed, every human can duplicate. This is why Buddha is the symbol of unity within the flux of phenomenon and whether he was historical or not is irrelevant. Lord Krishna assumes the symbol of universal unity and Jeshua of particular unity. Jeshua is whose potential we are, and is equally current and eternal. The Prophet is a particulate of our species and a particular individual with accompanying potential and can therefore remains a single historic entity of potentiality only; he is one who is successfully or unsuccessfully influenced by Krishna and Buddhahood and is or is not successfully on the path of Jeshua Adon. So what is around us is the noise of phenomenon within which there is silence. What we need to do individually is to never to expect influence or succour from outside it, and accept every situation within phenomenon and never retreat from it while skilfully using the thing to identify ourselves and achieve an awakened state of mind.' Having said that Dyfed remained silent for some time.

(Barbarism and the Human Erase)

My strength is that I cast my own die from an empiric lot legislated by an attitude toward veracity, and not moulded by some or other memorandum of the establishment.'

PARASOLO

Dyfed had never met Thrax face to face and he was quite taken by his strange manner. Manandan had introduced him, as was right, and warned Dyfed beforehand of what he called his 'old world conduct'. Thrax, the sacker of cities, the sacker of countries and even of civilizations had a glowering demeanour about him that would be more apparent and possibly many times more intimidating in the third dimension. In the sketchy present environment, however, it (he) was almost a sullen composure. His dark eyes were hawkish but not sharp and rapacious but rather dull which made him appear to be withdrawn inside himself, suffering perhaps from a stupor or trance. His whole body undulated slowly and almost unperceivably by expanding and contracting. He was present but he wasn't present, it seemed. From that protected spot he allowed an invisible appendage of his spark of spirit to emerge and be exposed outside his body and for it to uncoil and project out of his being like a tentacle or proboscis that felt all around him, minutely surveying and summing up the people that occupied his space. In response to some or another flattering comment that Manandan made in respect to Dyfed in order to draw that ancient warrior's attention to our hero, Thrax would only respond by allowing some visual reconnaissance to go on: His dull eyes barely sweeping over the former that seemed to sink down even deeper into himself when suddenly something akin to a psyche sneeze had occurred. Then Thrax's body moved, ever so little but incredibly swiftly and a sound came out of his mouth like a short gulp or laugh and a humorous demeanour of enhanced incredulity with caricature proportions immediately overcame him. This was followed by a good-natured expression that was obviously a brilliant mask.

"I have been watching you, Dyvy,' said Thrax. 'You remind me of your mother with your father's temperament.'

Dyfed responded by pretending to smile. He didn't like Thrax already. What else could he do, he thought. He decided to let Thrax lead this dance, at least until he caught on to the steps.

The giddiness that Dyfed had experienced had not abated over the space he shared with Thrax. If anything, it had increased, but he thought that might have had something to do with the latter's presence. Although he had automatically taken stock of the man's entity in the physical form, his psyche was well hidden under the vibration that composed his reptilian-like exterior. The companions of the *pack* now had assembled into a casual repose in the informal luncheon area and affected the imitation of nourishing their bodies and the sating of appetite in a strange and erstwhile ritual. Having moved from the lounge into the breakfast den each of the companions was seated comfortably in chairs, divans and couches of their choice with a low table of easy access before them.

They were seated fairly close together facing the wall of windows that looked out over the land interspersed with remnants (both new and old) of the ancient city that lay before them. For his seating arrangements Dyfed chose a replicated sleek and elegant Bauhaus production Brno chair. Thrax, who was somewhat beside Dyfed, appeared in the likeness of the space/time of his heyday in the third dimension and might just as well have been seated on a toadstool, for all Dyfed knew. It was difficult to assess his height and weight, as those elements were relative and not applicable here. His woolly hair was light brown beneath a headdress that resembled one that Dyfed had once seen on a stature that depicted Ares. It was open faced and crested with a griffin, and though it had side head protectors that dropped below his ears it did not appear heavy or cumbersome as its third dimensional counterpart would have been. It appeared more as a holograph that lightly surrounded his head. His body was covered in what appeared to be a heavy cloak or tunic beneath which wide trouser legs stuck out the bottom and he wore high soft leather boots. Thrax ate heartily at his intended meal that was set before him by a parade of beautiful young women and men that were mostly fair of complexion and golden haired that were dressed in light almost transparent shifts of brilliant colours. But Thrax's penetrability being otherwise too low for Dyfed to properly perceive him was unable to perceive Thrax in any meaningful way. He wasn't even sure whether the young serving staff amused him or whether they even penetrated his mental domain. Of course, this was still a confusing phenomenon for Dyfed, too. On his own part, however, Dyfed was able to choose at will from a full performing orchestra that conjured forth and played the most beautiful classical music from a recent era of the previous century: his choice. In addition, he cast the room full of the heavenly scent of hyacinth but otherwise the atmosphere was clear like mountain air and expedient to body temperature no matter how many clothes you had piled on you or not. Then, upon Dyfed's sudden recollection of a younger, dishevelled and shabbily dressed King Karatakos, Dyfed's private orchestra began to strike up a different air and belted out George Frideric Handel's Suite #5 in E major.

Dyfed had already noted that King Karatakos was well dressed and wore a simple shiny gold crown that was presently resting on the couch beside him while he sat at table. Dyfed laughed out loud, smiled and called out to those all around him and raised his glass. They, too, talked back jovially and laughed often while seemingly to consume more food and drink that normally one could have thought possible. What ambience it was that existed and surrounded each man separately, Dyfed could not tell, even with men like Manandan or Karatakos who he knew much better than the other two. In the latter's case Dyfed had shared the third dimension with him for the duration of almost two thousand solar cycles. As for the delectable edibles that Dyfed feasted on they must have astonished Thrax who spent way more time swallowing a tasty assortment of viands washed down with a variety of wines and even a Madeira than he did coughing up words. In short, Thrax ate like a starving trooper with a hollow leg and seemed to consume a sea of frothy red wine besides. Dyfed's giddiness, as stated already, had not abated and may have become enhanced not only by Thrax's presence but also by the unfamiliar vibrations of light that defined each and every individual gathered here. The result left him feeling slightly nauseous that was more of a disquieting nervousness. Dyfed ate little, opting to suck on a creamy blackberry milkshake through a wide straw and gobble down a plate of gently frittered potato fries sprinkled lightly with fermented white wine and fine milled salt that he dipped in a spicy tomato sauce. He ate this with his fingers. After awhile the remainder seemed to come to some unspoken agreement of fulfilment, then a signal was given that the congenial spectacle of sharing bread (a nostrum really) could cease and the charade all came to a close. They tipped up the glasses, dabbed the sides of their mouths with shiny white serviettes and wiped their fingers with warm wet towels that the servers brought them as they silently whisked the tables' remnants away.

As the orchestra continued to strike up beautiful and familiar airs for Dyfed in what is best described as a private performance, he spent a great deal more time talking to Manandan while they indulged strangely in the eating ritual. After that, Dyfed — who appeared to eat less than anyone else — stopped and moved to a couch where he continued to debate and reminisce with Morgant and Karatakos. Manandan occasionally joined in.

"King Karatakos!' Dyfed called out, his voice easily audible to himself above the strains of music and eager chatter all around; whereby, Karatakos — whose own head was filled with the devil only knows what immediately and hastily reach for and donned his crown again placing it on his head in a slightly tilted position that gave the impression that he couldn't be available for any discussion unless he was thus adorned.

"Yaas…brother Dyfed! What say you?' Karatakos answered, his response was then followed by a maniacal laugh. Morgant joined in with some reaction of geniality. Manandan continued to connect to him through a measured response, generally a slight laugh or — as he too had now moved and was still close at hand to Dyfed — a gentle touch to the latter's arm. But Thrax remained mute and stone-like and distant, his unreadable eyes continually shifting back and forth as he carefully watched Dyfed and Karatakos. After some time of sitting in silence, Thrax spoke.

"You three men, Morgant, because you are senior, Karatakos and Dyfed, you have a great deal on your shoulders, now. It isn't the same there as it was when Manandan, Lord Huge and I were in the thick of it. Much has changed and you were discussing just that (earlier on while I was approaching) as well as what is to be done. I know. You have good ideas and you know the lie of the land better now than we do. But do not be fooled by your ideals and do not be taken-in in any way by the enemy who lies in wait. I know of where brother Lord Huge's thoughts lie. 'Direct defiance', he would say, and I agree heartily. Consider this. We in all probability may need to annihilate the human race in the third dimension that can't transcend. Or better still let them be annihilated along with the psychopathic Haploids. Please!' he held up his hand. 'Hear me out. All of you will need to leave there completely in time, anyway. It may be that you may never be able to return to that place. I say, 'in time', that time's growing shorter and shorter. Things may change drastically in the third dimensional time that's just around the corner and you will all withdraw sooner than later. There may be some third dimensional humans there who you can help step up and realistically face the challenge and who may be able to enter into this our fifth dimension on their own or with help and eventually be come stable. But remember, it may be a favour that they will not thank you for in the end. The transition is difficult as it is and if you are not ready it is hell and there is no future to be found, anyway, not for them, not under those conditions.'

"Is that a pun?' questioned Dyfed remembering the men were laughing over it before. 'Is there a future here for us where time does not exist?'

"I know you Dyfed son of Queen Violet-Eye,' said Thrax surprisingly harshly.

"Oh!' said Morgant and Karatakos in unison, followed by a tail of almost childish laughter. Thrax waited until they had settled down, then with his eyebrows set glowering heavily over his eyelids he continued:

"Listen to me, all of you. I am a warrior. Dyfed you are a Sudra, an artisan, you have said so yourself. You claim to be a chronicler but what have you really chronicled? Nothing worth reading! And for the record, the record you have compiled will in the end be for nothing. This civilization you concern yourselves with will disappear from memory. I am Thrax, a priest-king, a sorcerer, a shaman and a warrior first and foremost but do I appear in history in the third dimension where you dwell? No. My name only remains as a place, a district and no longer even a kingdom. Oh yes, there was some grammarian named Thrax and another who was a barbarian emperor. Both adopted my name but I am hardly flattered. Not by those two imbeciles.'

"They were hardly imbeciles,' said Dyfed, knowing full well that he wasn't expected to speak, 'at least imbeciles relative to their dimension. And what is this, anyway? Is this about you? Or is it about the billions of people that the great Thrax wants to annihilate because he doesn't understand his own relativeness to them nor is there any one among them who can remember who he was?' A stunned and awkward silence followed.

"Fine,' said Thrax,' apparently unperturbed by the response, 'but all the same unless mister magician here,' he jabbed a finger in Dyfed's direction, 'can pull a hare out of a hat on queue you may all do well to remember my words. Otherwise we shall lose the future of the third dimension that is vitally important for a dimension such as ours here. A dimension like the third that has greater simplicity is a valuable asset to us. It is our heritage, too. It is our sister dimension. Surely I don't have to remind you of that. We have other options; yes we do. We can and will get by without it though if we have to, but that would be a shame.'

"So, how do you propose to conduct this mass extermination?' Dyfed asked him. Thrax looked carefully at Dyfed through strange, impenetrable eyes.

"I'm not sure I'll have to do anything,' replied Thrax. 'The cycle of destruction that goes around comes around. We (that is) you of the third density are now immanently facing an event. This event is now coming upon you so quickly that many of earth's mammal world of the larger brain will not graduate. Time is of the essence, and that is why the extermination of one of the hoi polloi's chief problems could become useful for them.'

"The idea you have seems somehow contrary to what we are trying to accomplish here,' said Dyfed. Is it the seemingly tenuous, at least from our position back in the third density, spiritual eternal probability in its eternal dance of unity what the ephemeral (temporal) material third density universe is trying with which to get a toehold grip? Or what? Remember our teachings, Thrax', Dyfed said. 'Without one there isn't the other. It's the deserted unheard forest where the falling trees make no noise; it's the deserted unheard island where the rolling breakers produce no thundering sound as they crash onto the sandy beaches and rocky shores. We make this happen, not some separate and apart god. So if there isn't any real friction that might take place within the eternal and spiritual ethereal, what then is the nature of out elementary discernment of what emanates from the aforementioned and is perceived here in the realm of the ephemeral and material tangible? It can only be that we are unity itself, we are that which interfaces with the Alfa and the Omega and by simply utilizing the fourth dimension of time we create by witnessing the phenomenon with our spiritual and material presence, both the beginning and the ending of the Universe at the same time. It is the temporal dimension along with the fourth density of time that obscures our eternity from us. No killing is necessary or acceptable at any time. It isn't the answer. It will never be the answer. Giving life is the answer; giving life and in sustaining that life in a joyous and happy environment, that's the answer.'

"Then by your own words, Dyfed,' answered Thrax, 'if anyone created the need for anything then it is written and so smote it be.'

"That is not quite what I said,' Dyfed replied. God is love and life and the incarnate action to bring this about. Where and when is it then that the singularity of God exists in your universe of staged cause and effects, Thrax? Where is god in your creative action to decide the fate of anything? Certainly it's not here, for that initial deployment, for that particular action, God is spent within the eternal moment in which it occurs. After all, the material phenomenon is a product of the reality that is imagined specifically by someone or something in all of its dimensions yet in itself this reality cannot be explained realistically unless imagination is energy that creates matter. Furthermore,' continued Dyfed, 'the material universe, it would appear, is subject to the gods of entropy wherein its form changes in one way or another throughout space/time for each and every aspect of material matter and all of its affects. Is entropy a temporal product of imagination, too? So if your energy is comparable to the divine unfolding of the eternal moment, is all then well? What about if we ask if it contradicts nature? Can it contradict nature? The answers to that then will have to be that we can't contradict anything. So it would seem that an incarnation prepared to suffer an effect upon the unfolding phenomenon is on thin ice, or should I say that the incarnation itself becomes an entirely disconnected universe within itself and at that very moment its ego-will becomes demised, and so will everything else which that entity stands for. And in being inversely proportional, being outside the eternal then its demise by definition must be an eternal demise. To decide and intend to take action to quell the phenomenon in any way will not be productive within the eternal moment of any individual, I say.'

None spoke for some time after Dyfed finished. Then Thrax looked up and spoke.

"Ah, yes,' said Thrax. 'But let us return for a moment to the reoccurring age of catastrophic returns. I know that some say it is not yet due, but I say that it is not far off. And there maybe setbacks leading up to the reoccurring age of catastrophe that will leave the hoi polloi unprepared when it is suddenly upon you.'

"What setbacks?' asked Dyfed.

"The fire of the gods,' replied Thrax.

"That would be nuclear fission not naphtha,' said Dyfed. 'And what is the reoccurring age of catastrophe?'

"That is just as bad,' answered Morgant, pleased to lend assistance. 'As the solar system moves through the galaxy the planets of our solar system periodically pass through fields of powerful electromotive force that connects the universe together. Our latter day contemporaries among the hoi polloi call these powerfully charged ions that span the universe after Citizen Birkeland who was a contemporary to Quasi Gizmo. What a genius he was for a hoi polloi. These fields contain matter or debris that play havoc with the safety of a life-developing planet such as ours. When this debris moves into our path and falls onto our speedway course it can appear as an asteroid or whatever name you want to give that debris that rain down or hurtle toward us like radioactive celestial hail. Except that this hail of meteors and comets and asteroids and bolides can range in size from being too small to survive the friction burn in our atmosphere to something the size of the moon. They are solid dense rocks composed of combined minerals that can destroy the habitation of the earth in blink of an eye even if hit only by just one of these incoming missiles. It can only take one, never mind multiple hits over a short space/time by smaller missiles streaking along at extraordinary speeds that upon impact can cause massive nuclear explosions and bring about violent, catastrophic upheavals and geologically tagged calamities. The result, if the world as be know it is left kind of intact, a sudden climate change will ensue that quickly leads to famine and aggression that ends in chaos and social destruction that has an immediate negative impact on even the most advanced civilizations. Even near passes of these celestial passer-bys from within and without our solar system could cause reduction in atmosphere and or the loss of water to the planet that could be snatched away both by gravity and forces of acceleration, as well as by the electrical magnetic field of a large celestial body with the ensuing catastrophic results of celestial reciprocity, enhanced by terrifying electrical exchanges.'

"Close encounters,' continued Thrax, 'will definitely and most certainly bring devastating storms and climate changes as well as other earth changes. These exchanges, complete with shunting of electrical charges caused by differentials between planetary bodies would certainly stun and could even kill all life on earth, as I've already said. When it happens the world will be altered not just perceivably but enormously. It will certainly bring about extinctions of one sort or another.'

"So, where was I?' said Lord Huge. 'Oh yes. The sky gods who it was incorrectly said clutched the olden day nuclear-tipped copper lance and flew around the sky raining down terror at will (more destructive even than naphtha, or any garden variety nuclear fission). They also consulted the olden day tablets of destiny that long ago were lent out and were never returned. Currently the overdue fee from the olden day library could feed the world for a century. Your job Dyvy is to announce to the world that you live in that the discovery of those olden day tablets of destiny has led the Masters to determine the return of the comet Wormwood. And technological access to the hereditary memory bank has informed the Masters of the olden day copper lance technology and tablets of destiny wisdom as to certain ingenious methods to induce transmigration from the finite world of the third density into the heaven of the fifth dimension. The tin gods that came from the sky weren't just funning their ancestors, either, or putting them on. They weren't even just taking the mickey, so to speak. Oh, no. They were down right lying through their teeth in order to control them by keeping them in debt by paying for the right to exist in the face of god and by keeping them in an ignorant and comatose state. Now we can help all you poor stupid bastards, you must tell them, and with a brilliant slight of hand we can get you past the Pearly Gates before you're missed back home: Some of them will go for it, more will follow. But its first come first served, tell 'em. We've only got the capacity for the first twenty-five million front-runners. The rest will die because you're too late or too poor. So, come on down (probably up) an' git yer ticket to heaven here, asshole! Family discounts are available with offered cash, gold, silver, diamonds, investments and waterfront properties, along with banks, ski hills and amusement parks, all are good collateral. Hurry on up now and buy your tickets before its too late. You don't have to tell 'em now that we're shootin' for expunging fifty million Haploids if we can.'

"So as a segue, this leads me to the Book of Perverts among the Books of Lists and Proverbs,' continued Thrax, 'which is not on record in the third density in the original format as it was laid out in the olden tablets of destiny. And it clearly states the following. I can repeat it by rote. Thus says the lord god: Because the children of Zeus dealt vengefully with a spiteful heart to destroy because of the old hatred, therefore, thus says the lord god: I will stretch out mine hand against the children of Zeus and I will cut off my covenant with them and destroy the remnant of the citadel of Zeus. I will execute great vengeance on them with furious rebukes and they shall know I am lord when I lay my vengeance upon them.'

"And what does this have to do with Gumcwy? Dyfed asked Manandan.

"Gumcwy?' Thrax responded excitedly upon hearing Dyfed pronounce her name. 'Gumcwy (Gum kwee),' he said, 'is the Getae name for Kubaba or Cybele who was an old consort of an ancestor of yours, Dyfed. Kubaba was the patron of Carchem during Lord Shirkuh time. So there you have it, gentlemen. You have very little time so you need to be diligent.

And so it went, Thrax and Lord Huge seized the day and a rotten stinking day it turned out to be, according to Dyfed. All in all, this episode resulted in his appointment to the *pack's* Third Dimensional position of General Secretary Select of the Committee for Public Safety. He did not understand why it should be him or why the position existed at all. As for the problem with Dyfed's transcending in order to access the venue for been versed with advice, thankfully, that was finished. He had learned that through meditation and a strange type of sleep that wasn't sleep that he could transcend at will, almost anyway. But the getting to this state on this first time event, and the trick of remaining on some kind of equilibrium while here, was only child's play compared to the affects of his immanent first return to the fifth dimension.

(Shades of a full moon and a skin-full)

> '*Those that make peaceful revolution impossible*
> *will make violent revolution inevitable.*'
> **JOHN FITZGERALD KENNEDY**

A telephone rang somewhere outside the room he was sitting in. The evening sun streamed in the two large windows that also let in a tiny percentage of the noise from the street below. As the telephone continued to ring, Dyfed sat quietly gazing out through the two windows over the trees of Hyde-Jekyll Park. Below, the grass was worn and chewed up, garbage had been dumped under bushes and beside and around the bases of trees which covered their roots with strewn rubbish: mostly metal, scrapes of wood and cardboard, broken glass and fence wire, some of which had been strewn around by scavengers. Leaves lay on the ground un-raked, flower beds were left to grow over with weeds while their old un-kept plants, all stringy and strong, had all gone to seed well before their time. The park seemed a virtual darkening jungle to Dyfed as he stared out through the two windows and through the gathering pre-gloaming that was being dampened down with a sprinkle of rain as the telephone, somewhere behind him — outside his room and down the hallway — continued to ring. He heard a muffled voice shortly after the last ring as he lay back in his sofa chair drowsily collecting his thoughts. Suddenly there was a muffled thumping on his door that led into the hallway from another room. Dyfed did not get up to answer the door but upon seeing a gardener working alone in the un-kept park across the road, he remained seated while watching him at labour. Fascinated by this man's courage against futility, Dyfed inwardly applauded and cheered him on as he sat sipping tea from a large cup. The muffled pounding at his door finally stopped and sitting in the silence of the room he heard soft ghostly footsteps fade away down the hallway from outside his door while he continued to sit and watch the gardener working in the light rain. Dyfed reached over and turned on a radio that was on the desk beside him. Immediately the room filled with beautifully recorded musical chords from Albinoni's Adagio that also seemed to add encouragement to the lonely garden attendant labouring in the rain against an opposing magnitude of which Dyfed was quite sure the gardener wasn't aware. As the man who was dressed in a long dark coat raked and bent down forward to pick objects up which he flung with a gloved hand onto a pile nearby, he worked only in one small area of the vast park nestled in the centre of this large city. From where he sat, Dyfed couldn't see clearly beyond where the man in the long coat worked, but it was possible, he supposed, that there was a tiny cleared swathe which the garden attendant had been labouring at — for only the devil would know how long — while he slowly worked his way forward inch by inch through the mountain of filth that lay scattered before him.

Dyfed noticed that the room had darkened some and shortly after that the park began to darken then fade altogether and the attendant suddenly left, carrying his rake and spade. The rain had stopped and as he looked down a nearby descending street between the buildings that lined either side, he glimpsed some silver light low down in the sky through the leafy tree branches that guarded both sides of the street. When Beethoven's Moonlight Sonata, that was presently being broadcasted, ended, Dyfed in an almost trance-like state heard the soft words the speaker was emitting into his room along with millions of other rooms in the city. Suddenly, the voice changed and it was a sharp, hollow kind of guttural sound. Dyfed stirred and sat up. He looked at his watch and noticed that it was shortly after eight o'clock before realising that it was the Wunschritter's voice he was listening to that was coming to him over the news broadcast. Dyfed suddenly felt very hungry for apart from copious pots of tea he hadn't digested anything in ages. Then he suddenly remembered that his last meal had only been an inadequate hand full of fried potatoes washed down with a milkshake. He did not turn on a light in the room but leaving the radio on he quietly left the apartment wearing only a light suede dinner jacket over an expensively embroidered short sleeved, burgundy shirt with dark coloured loose silk trousers. These were topped off with a brown Amoran fedora. He quickly made his way to the street without anybody in the neighbouring suites hearing him leave. The evening was warm and because of the recent rain Dyfed could smell the pleasant aroma of the park more sharply. No unpleasant odour was detectable from across the street but as Dyfed walked along towards the nearest underground train station, he abhorred the smells around him. It made no difference, either, when he crossed the road and followed the iron spiked fencing that separated the pavement from the overgrown park. For odours emitted out from the road's asphalt and poured forth from the motorized vehicles that whisked by as well as from the literal herds of people hacking and coughing in his direction, the stinky, sweaty beasts that crowded around him on the pavement which immediately slowed his progress as if he was walking through a corral full of pissing and swishing tailed bovine. It got worse, he noted, as he descended the stairs and escalators deep into the world under the city. Here, in addition to the pungent odour of thousands of beastly humans pressing in all around him, their arm pits and orifices reeking as well as chemicals such as ethyl benzene, snippets of methane, air bourn mercury, hexane, dimethyl sulphide, ethylene-glycol-monobutyl-ether, trimethylbenzenenes, polychlorinated biphenyls, dioxin, hydrogen sulphide, methylbenzenes and pure benzene, not to mention all the polycyclic-aromatic hydro-carbons in general, were all assailing him. These dangerous toxins were all being air bourn on warm blasts of wind created from fast moving trains in tunnels as they entered and exited the multi-levelled station platforms deep beneath the streets. Once he was stuffed and squashed into one of the underground train carriages like raisins pressed and squeezed into a jar, the environment became even worse. Without losing and being denied any of the life threatening toxins that floated around above ground, he was now further subjected to bad breaths, bad body odour, bad perfumes used yet failing to cover up both of the former, tobacco smoke — and related toxic chemicals — stale alcohol, floating skin cells from dandruff and psoriasis afflictions, phlegm, a host of viruses, all now at much closer range than before, as well, as air bourn germs along with germ microbes of faeces, urine, blood, mucus all swirling around and being breathed in and out from the soupy sludge of slimy DNA that all humans live in: That thickening marsh of putrid pus that inescapably extended from below the sea bottom up to the very tip-top of the stratosphere above.

With the fiat currency of the third dimension's emerging new world order's signatories and affiliates, the replication of a pound of sterling silver, or gold, or for that matter bronze or plug nickel was lighter in your trouser pants all rolled into a paper wad and tucked neatly away into your left testicle front pocket. If you have any testicles, that is. Of course, it had been ages since men carried around a leather satchel or money pouch, anyway, and those who did used to also carry an arsenal of weaponry to keep highwaymen and other robbers and thieves at bay, including all the king's men. Laws banning armaments were quietly passed long ago and heavily enforced when it became obvious to the crown (the establishment) along with their important executive arm of the second fiddle — those trumped up elected representatives, the wined and dined by the agents of the crown or the crown's bankers, the power elite and their opulent brothers — that they would be hard pressed to control society at large with bright, skilled and well trained men at arms at large, all of who were not the establishment's muscle, but foot loose and fancy-free-entrepreneurs who were on their own side and saw others, like the competition, including the king — especially it they were combatant — as being on the wrong side. The proverbial IOU note, bill, certificate of 'I promise to pay the bearer upon demand the value deemed herein…' was much more convenient to carry around than a bag of heavy silver or gold, and much more convenient, at least to somebody other than oneself — such as the local banker whose vault contained the gold of those very same people — particularly if it's been loaned out to others with interest. Maybe your banked money being loaned out to you with interest! But it also continued to prop up the lie that if you received the payment of such and such (now represented by that bank note) after a hard day's work, then you were fairly compensated thereof. Nothing could be further from the truth, of course. It might be one thing to be compensated with meals, roof over one's head and some money to jingle in your little pocket when you are with friends especially during times of inflation, but the worth of the labourer is always going to be misrepresented if the crown and its agents, the bankers, fix both wages and prices. Even gold prices get fixed, Dyfed reminisced, but now it's all turned around the other way. It is the bankers and cartel chiefs who are in charge and their agents are the kings, or governments of the people. This was a nasty state of affairs and one, Dyfed was very much aware, that the world of the third dimension was fast plummeting into. Indeed, it was already here. Gold or printed certificates, supposedly representing gold — if there was anyone who wanted to accept them — or money in general, was hardly of any consequence personally to Dyfed for he had access to vast sums at little notice. Dyfed's dinner, eaten that evening in the dining room of one of the city's finest hotels, cost him what a labourer's day's pay would have been in exchange of hard work preformed. In addition to the roast beef and pudding, followed by a delectable Rum-BaBa dessert pudding, he had had a few mugs of whisky at the bar before and after the meal that was all paid for with the IOU type fiat currency, the funny money, the papered over coin of the realm which was currently being called the Crown-lolly, sometimes referred to simply as the Trinket. After he paid the bill Dyfed then strolled out of the hotel's lobby with the notion of amusement on his mind.

Dyfed's body seemed to be burning up the atmosphere around him though his vibration level had begun to decrease now. This condition, of course, was the latent force of which he was ridding himself after his ordeal of descending to the third dimension from the fifth. Descending being relatively speaking, of course. All those who undergo the changes necessary to shift from one dimension to another experience this. Normally travellers are kept secluded and quiet afterwards, even, in some cases, treated like patients and are subject to strict protocols of conduct for a spell. After all, when one's physical self essentially dematerialises into the mother's womb of creation then is later re-established, the vibration levels needed to undertake such as journey are almost unfathomable! It was amazing, he thought, that the mind took it all in stride. Dyfed was not necessarily the exception; he was simply the unruly non-conforming self-asserter. Such over cautious behaviour as having to need to formally 'settle in' after the journey struck him as being silly, too pampering, too artificial. The human body was part of the universe and as such it had developed alongside the changes of cause and effect. Lightning, earthquakes, typhoons, cyclones, aurora borealis, even sunlight was subject, part and parcel, to the plasma of the cosmos that fitted tightly around every living thing — indeed, it was what made it a living thing in the first place — none of which needed pampering. They were all a state of agitation in itself in one level of vibration or another, and Dyfed was no different, he told himself. Dyfed hailed a cab and in a very loud voice gave the cabby an address. It was in a posh area of the city that the cabby delivered Dyfed where upon arriving he walked into a lobby in the middle of a large, brownstone faced building that encompassed the entire block. On his left, as he entered, was some kind of professional business that was closed for the day and in front of him across the black and white chequered tiled lobby floor there was an ornate lift. To his right was a florist shop that was open.

"Good evening, effendi,' said Dyfed, walking into the heavily scented shop. 'I'm looking for Doris.'

"She's not here,' said the other man with a Middle Eastern accent.

"Is she visiting Puck, in Myra?' Dyfed said. Without answering, the other man walked behind a counter among the hanging plants and flower arrangements and opening a drawer he handed Dyfed a card-key. Dyfed took the key and walking to the lift pushed the calling button. Somewhere within the shaft behind the doors, sounds of mechanisms coming to life were suddenly taken up and overheard by Dyfed. Shortly, the doors opened and Dyfed (after sliding open the self collapsing inner iron grid gate that enclosed the lift platform) stepped into the lift and inserted the special key he was given into a keyed slot above the six push buttons for the building's floor levels. He slid the inner cage door closed while the outer doors then closed noisily on their own; then the lift plummeted downwards. Dyfed watched as the basement light blinked on then off and the elevator car continued to drop another floor that was not marked on the registry board. Stepping through the doors Dyfed entered another lobby that was clean and decorated with potted plants that was directly two floors beneath the main lobby above. A man was seated there next to a shrub reading, but when the doors opened he jumped up to greet Dyfed, though the two were unknown to each other. Dyfed nodded to him, handed him the key, and quickly turned to the right and passing through an archway descended some wide shallow stepped spiral stairs that were covered in a sumptuous oriental carpet runner. Emerging into a fabulously decorated, high ceiling smoking room, Dyfed uncharacteristically called out to the first person he recognized. The greeting was further uncharacteristic of him in that it was loud. The stately room that had a tasteful musical trio emitting pleasantries from a staged niche was a form of men's club that happened to be full of patron members that evening. Along one shorter wall was a bar with stools in front while tables, comfortable chairs and couches and even divans were spread around the large room. Some men sat alone but mostly a few sat together smoking opium or hashish from ornate hookahs that were swiftly delivered to the seated customer by a clean and neatly dressed attendant.

"Dyfed,' said the companion he had just hailed in wide eyed wonder as the former sat down opposite to him on his own colourful and wide divan. 'Where the devil have you been? I haven't seen you in ages.' Having just sat down Dyfed looked up and over at the man sharply and replied.

"You couldn't even guess.'

"Try me,' the other retorted.

"Oh, I don't know,' Dyfed stated in a matter of fact way. 'Heading up a committee for public safety of the world, and getting ready for the rain of splattered blood from both the eunuchs severed testicles and the bulls severed throat during the sacrifice for renewal; that aged regeneration ritual of a new world order, I suppose. Will that do?'

The other man contemplated that remark momentarily with a confused expression on his face. "You are looking devilishly well, old chum,' the man then said. 'Very well, indeed, I would say and… I detect certain energy of some kind coming off you this evening that is strange and even mysterious, old boy. Could it be something to do with bulls blood or just the blood from the nut-less eunuchs; adolescent eunuchs I'm assuming?'

"Calm down, it's just latent energy,' Dyfed said smiling at his companion.

"What! Say, where the devil is that wog serving us?'

"Don't call him that,' Dyfed snapped,' anyway, here he is now. Nice looking young man, at that. Who knows, you have probably had your eye on him all evening and now wish to play the macho master for my sake! How can you be like that?' Dyfed said finishing off.

Dyfed's acquaintance suddenly went quiet. "Good evening, effendi,' said the young, nice looking attendant as he came up to them.

"Good evening to you, sir,' said Dyfed smiling politely at the man. 'Hashish, please,' he said as the attendant placed a hookah in front of Dyfed. 'You mustn't call these fellows derogative names like that,' said Dyfed after the attendant had left them.

"My humble apologies, Dyfed,' the other responded. 'How uncouth of me. Oh, it's the company I keep here, you know,' said the other man, seemingly now quite distressed and who was wildly waving his arm in their general direction with grief pouring out of his soul. 'They all call the boys wogs. I just come here for a jolly good get together, that's all.'

"Oh yeah? Really! Well it's nasty,' replied Dyfed, 'and unfair. They are nice young gentlemen who work for wages and have no money whatsoever compared to anyone of the patrons here, including the bartenders.'

With his body still burning the air around him, Dyfed ignited the attached lighter and held its flame to the bowl of the hookah. His inhale from the hookah was cool and moist on Dyfed throat from the chilled ice water in the pipe's heat exchange chamber. Some other acquaintances joined them from time to time with there never being more than five sitting around the small round table. Every few minutes Dyfed ordered whisky and cool beer which were placed on the table by his elbow.

After smoking a few grams of hashish, followed by a single pearl of opium, and forty or so doubles of scotch whisky (washed down with a pail of beer) Dyfed truly felt that he had gently re-emerged…alighted softly, you might say…on his return to the third density.

And the night was still young, at that! And even after a few more visits to some rather disreputable establishments among the amusement area of the west end of the city, nothing could have persuaded Dyfed that he was wrong in that notion. Later still, he wended his way toward the less better heeled environs of the city that was only a few streets away, feeling that he had got a little closer to knowing himself in conjunction with his subject, the people and their collective and current psyche as it hummed out; and that he was abreast of the myriad of vibrations that accompanied each and every moment of creation.

The doors of the last little pub that he had wandered into were open due to the late summer heat. It was now quite late but still short of midnight, the hour when the city would suddenly die down and go to sleep. Nova Troia was unlike big cities such as Megatropolis back in North Merika, and even some others like Humbug in Europa that partied all night long. Perhaps he should head there, he fleetingly thought: But there was work yet to be done here, he reminded himself. Loud music of some kind, music that was not particularly harmonious was blaring from somewhere into his ears that caused him difficulty in hearing others speak but did not seem to hamper their ability to hear him or each other. He shouted at the server in a very loud voice to bring more libations; some for over here and some over there for those folks, too. Hurry up now, we are parched and on death's doorstep from thirst. How can you be so slow, is it the heat? When the whisky and beer came Dyfed consumed four to one while gregariously chatting away then leaving each table or bar top host at least a free drink or two. Then he would move to another table that he had ordered for and whose drinks were just arriving. He chatted and chattered endlessly, amusing most. This lasted for another forty quick drinks, and when one youngish, large, wide and closely cropped haired working man tried to pay for a round he had ordered, Dyfed good-naturedly resisted the man's advances to do so and picking him up with one hand around his throat with his thumb knuckle and fore knuckle under the man's chin and the fingers of the other hand grasping the man's trousers at the crotch, he carried then tossed him out through the open doors into the night and onto the wet pavement outside with a bouncing thud. Dyfed followed the man out, laughing good-naturedly to the stunned expressions of the pedestrians who were mostly dressed in dark suits and carrying umbrellas as they passed by, not to mention the patrons — one or two who may have been drunk — inside the pub.

"Ah, it's starting to rain again, I see. Come on now, you'll catch your death of cold out here,' he said as he effortlessly picked the man up again and, tucking him under one arm, marched back into the pub like he was carrying a bulky rolled up mattress under his arm instead of a human.

"Here, you!' called another large man from behind the bar as Dyfed set the dazed but unhurt man back into his chair to the incredibility of the man's drinking mates. 'We don't want no trouble 'ere. Be on your way, now. Quick, hop to it or I'll call the coppers down an' they'll deal wit-chu.' A very attractive young woman who had been watching the tall middle aged man with the silver eyes with growing interest suddenly set down her lime cordial and rushing forward took Dyfed by the arm and quickly whispered, "take me out of here, quickly. Please, you can do anything you want with me. But I need your help. Take me away from here, now,' she pleaded quietly. Of course Dyfed was unable to hear anything she said, and a moment later she then began pulling at him when he didn't immediately respond due to a confrontation brewing with a table of men close by for whom he had just bought drinks. On Dyfed's part, though, it was all nothing but so much good-natured fun.

"Get your hands off that woman. And quit throwin' people about. Who the 'ell do you think you are?' One of the men from the table jumped up and just as the persistent woman distracted Dyfed, the man slugged Dyfed in the face. That did it. Dyfed gently, but firmly, removed the woman's hand from his other wrist and with a sudden backhand caught the assailant in the midst of following through with another punch that was heading towards Dyfed's face. The assailant's second punch ultimately didn't happen, or at least connect. The sudden and sickening crack to the latter's head when the top knuckles of Dyfed's closed right fist made contact with the man's right temple was only matched by the even more sickening crack his head made as the knock, which brought the man off his feet sideways and caused him to do a rotational plummet, drove his head into the slightly rounded corner of the heavy hard wood counter of the bar. The long bar shuddered and the odd empty glass that was resting on it rattled, the others splashed over. Concentric ripples occurred in the liquid under the foam of the pints that still had beer in them. The weak and loose body of the would-be assailant tumbled in a floppy manner without further glamour to the floor and remained absolutely still. As dark blood began draining out of the man's ear hole onto the tiled floor, the pub went completely quiet and the noise in Dyfed's ears stopped abruptly. Only the sounds of the street reluctantly pushed in through the opened doors; the talking and the footsteps of the people on the wet pavement outside (now thinning out a little as the evening wore on) and the swish of the chariot tires on the road and the swooshing of traffic as they quickly rolled this way and that over the wet asphalt as the different sounds of their engines (and occasionally their horns) and the brakes of the larger vehicles that laboured to bring the heavy weight above them to a standstill, was the plasma that sifted and swelled into every vacant crevice of the audio world. Dyfed stopped everything to listen. Outside the city began roaring down while here in the pub (momentarily anyway) total silence was already taking its place.

"Well, I'm heartily sorry for that man's callus stupidity,' retorted Dyfed, breaking the silence. 'May it serve others as a lesson that we all are responsible in the end for our actions whether thought out or not.' The large bartender bent the top part of his heavy body over the corner of the bar and gazed down at the man on the floor for a moment. Still in the bent-over position he then raised only his head and with a quizzical expression on his wide face, looked up at Dyfed. He saw the well dressed and obviously well to do man that despite his enormous consumption of alcohol in a short period of time yet he did not appear to be drunk at all. His voice was not thick, his words were not slurred and his eyes were clear. 'His eyes were clear and silver,' he knew he would be telling the coppers when they arrived, and arrive they would:

"He was a tall powerful man, constable.' Oh yes, indeed. Never seen anything like it. Just up and bang! Just like that. Threw that big chap effortlessly right out the door, just a few moments before, as if it weren't nobody's business. Then carted him in again like he was retrieving a little dog under his arm. 'I tell you. We were all just having a jolly old get together around a pint or two and suddenly he wandered in and caused un'oly havoc.'

"He's dead, I would say,' remarked Dyfed, screwing up his face in a comically affected but in a strained sort of way that was in response to the bartender's questioning gaze. 'Good-evening, now.' said Dyfed. He smiled faintly as tipped his hat, then quickly disappeared into the wet summer night.

(The Northern Dominion and its land of the great Ukon basin river)

"There is no joy but calm.'
ALFRED LORD TENNYSON

All of the hoop-la and its after affects that had taken a toll on Dyfed were evident when he resurfaced in Manna-hata in the city of Megatropolis with the grandfather of all hangovers. He was here to complete his business at the Jewel Banking House, the *pack's* current makeshift banking firm in Megatropolis while Dyfed's own urban office of the House of Lucifer was being constructed in downtown Manna-hata. Then, having found the hair of the dog that bit, right after that Dyfed had immediately returned to the west coast to take charge of impending damage to his own empire.

So, with further development and production stalled, Dyfed took himself off to that beautiful aforementioned northern land of the great Ukon River basin that lay north of the sixtieth parallel. Here he intended to first place a claim and then build a mining site over a rich deposit. But first he would build himself a large cabin-like abode in which he and Ceredwyn could take shelter from the impending social woes and chaos. Along with Clarence Wolf, a prospecting buddy he had met up with here earlier who had helped orient him to northern ways (along with a couple of native trappers), he laboured through the hot summer days that first year under the midnight sun searching for the ideal location. It needed to be either by a lake or a river so he could barge in building materials and supplies to keep going. Also, lakes and rivers made good thoroughfare lanes for barges and ideal airstrips for float planes between late June to early November when floats could then be changed out for skis for ice landings between the January to May air travel. For expedience he wanted to locate his private abode somewhere within a short flight or a days' travel by water in either direction to his iron ore deposits and mining facilities.

The most valuable of all the mineral deposits which Dyfed sought after were here among the Plateaus in these northlands around the Ukon River Basin, with some further afield such as in the Ukon's northern mountains. This land was rich in iron ore minerals that contained gold, silver, copper, lead, magnetite, and zinc and other earth metals as well, such as Thorium. Thorium undergoes alpha decay with a half-life of over fourteen billion years. There was Uranium, too, which has a natural occurring fissile isotope and had a half-life of about four and a half millions years. With the highest atomic weight among the primordially occurring elements, next to Plutonium, Uranium's density is seventy per cent higher than lead but it is not as dense as Tungsten, another element in abundance in Dyfed's box of mineral collections.

Unlike other prospectors Dyfed hadn't just stumbled upon his discoveries. As stated earlier he had located these deposits by observing how the Aurora Borealis repeatedly and consistently manifested over and around the white frozen tracts of mountainous land of certain areas. Specifically he sought out its display that took the frigid winter's blackish night sky Aurora Borealis to be attracted and to conflate toward high-density iron ore like magnetite. There was a subtle magnetic interaction between where the heavy minerals in the earth lay and the outward electrical disturbances wandered. What the Earth bound minerals did was to cause a disturbance-reaction in the electromagnetic field in the atmosphere up in the sky. The sparkling jewels in the Kelvin frozen firmament girded these magnificent electrical displays and he had learned to interpret the language that existed between the blood of the earth and the goddess' menstrual blood of the dawn. The trick had been to correctly understand the activity of the earth's electromagnetic field: these were the Earth's great magnetic shield which could be easily seen from the ground dancing like huge folding curtains that hung shimmering in the atmosphere. Of course they were caused by ions coming into contact with the earth's magnetic field and were also slightly affected by their attraction to those magnetic properties of the minerals within the Earth. It was a matter of learning their language. So, in this way, Dyfed had discovered the secret of locating the riches of the Earth. All he had to do was just sit silently under the black canopy of the winter sky that sparkled with a billion of diamond flashing stars in minus 50 degree Celsius (60 below zero Fahrenheit) air sipping good quality grain alcohol to keep warm. It wasn't for everybody, he noted, but it was Nirvana on Earth for him.

Anyway, in this way he had remained there in the north for the duration of eight seasons and had taken full advantage of the long daylight during the hot summer days to complete the necessary development in readiness for the production stage of these his newly acquired properties. He had also delighted in flying from site to site in his single engine aircraft equipped with floats (pontoons) that allowed him to land and take off from the plateaus' multitude of lakes and rivers. His pilot, apparently, was just as crazy as Dyfed when it came to having fun.

Then in mid June and starting into the third year he sent for Ceredwyn to join him from Couver City. They loved their home here and while Ceredwyn explored the fauna and flora that first summer, Dyfed and Clarence fashioned a barge and had a few boats built. There, among its ice-cold water they worked and played enjoying the rough and rustic work-a-relaxed-day type of life. Sometimes they sat through those days surrounded by cold water in little boats (dragging a net containing bottled beverages to keep them cold) under the northern blue summer sky and its burning sun with a retrieved, chilled beer in one hand and a fishing rod in the other. Other days Dyfed explored the environs, collected local flora with Ceredwyn or poured over the strategies and tactics he intended to employ to further his and the *pack's* enterprising interests. Although from here in the far north the tentacles connecting him to his companies elsewhere in the world were long, they were also not altogether unwieldy. Dyfed spent the summer months with drillers compiling drill samples then with geologists and mining engineers and finally with a number of rich deposits showing, they began to push roads in to these locations and then build small settlements around them to house miners and staff to keep the machinery operation, metallurgists and assayers along with cooks, carpenters and all sorts, including a doctor and nurse housed and as comfortable as possible. Dyfed, while he was in the territory, could commute from their cabin back and forth during summer and winter, if need be.

Besides his two friends, Clarence and the pilot who had facilities (if needed) at Dyfed and Ceredwyn's home, two other local men — Elijah Julius Caesar and Charlie

Johnny Charlie (accompanied by their families) — were their only relative neighbours (and occasional visitors) who lived some distance away. They were trappers and their trap lines abutted the beautiful emerald lake that Dyfed and Ceredwyn's cabin overlooked. Charlie's nephew, a shaman or medicine man (as he was generally referred to) named Johnston Robertson Jules, regularly passed through this neck of the woods once or twice a year staying for a day or two to administer his magic and maintain his status among his people that were spread out across this land. Little Jimmy, another local, expedited for any white man who could pay in coin. Dyfed approached this man who (along with their mutual friend Clarence Wolf) agreed to take on courier duties on Dyfed's behalf for an agreed price. This enterprise also attracted other locals of the To'shoni and the Quan'lin people.

A number of seasons came then passed by and then came again. Then one day, when under a stark light blue sky, the warm lengthening days saw the snow melt first from the south side of the valley slopes. Little Jimmy had just arrived again, and having broken through the heavily snowed-in pass bringing him his correspondence that had accumulated over the last winter, marked the end of that winter's isolation. After a few weeks turnaround that allowed preparation on Dyfed's part — the man who was of the wolf clan with his crow woman in tow as usual — headed back with Dyfed's return correspondence that had likewise accumulated. Within the context of the system, the world outside was just the same here where only the toughest of most powerful would survive. But how vastly different was the phenomenon at large.

Dyfed knew that worldwide chaos (beyond the mere financial woes of the people of the world) could provide those perimeters that were ideal for revolution, control and dominance, in that order. Dyfed also knew that real chaos allowed huge amounts of wealth to change hands rather quickly and usually invisibly. Reading through the sack of letters and journals of what had been happening in the world on the outside since he had been here in the north-western territory of the Northern Dominion, Dyfed was able to read between the lines and just as he had anticipated, the powers that be had now set the stage for their big move. But it was apparent to Dyfed, having historical cognizance of world financial development, that every bit of it had all been planned from the initial breakdown of investment right down to the chosen one who the opulent power elite (OPE) had invested in to pull off their greatest financial coup of all time to date. To his surprise Dyfed learned that the few individuals who the established OPE had chosen from somewhere back stage during the present intermission had been that old, many times spent, dirty old coin –– the Wunschritter. But it wasn't just the money, stupid: it was also an ideological inversion that was meant to entwine its tentacles all around the globe and strangle it into submission. The Haploids were on their game. So not only would an extreme power elite (the intrepid OPE) be the supreme governing factor that owned everything through a forced proxy, but define (and be in) total charge of the entire human race in the foreseeable future: And that was about all.

The question that remained for Dyfed was this: Was the world ready to change so drastically? It wasn't just the matter of the black entwining tentacles threatening to strangle freedom, faith and free will, it was the absurdity of its duplicity: That is — aside from the black squid — it was also its duplicate (the white squid with its white tentacles) also attempting to entwine the globe with humanity being caught off guard and the latter being entangled up in between both the others. The *pack* had anticipated this move long before but were powerless to move against it until it was implemented. The third dimensional society had not responded adequately either because the embedded OPE's fifth columnist elites had become too influential to be able to properly organise against them. And there were two schools of thought among the *pack* regarding the appropriate response, just as there were two ideological schools playing out the deadly game of total destruction. One school of thought, he reminisced, had been to try and take advantage of the situation itself with the might of any financial power that was left over and do battle. Or, to try and sabotage the whole works so that the entire system would collapse and in crashing down would burn to death taking the OPE with it. In this last scenario the impetus was for the *pack* and their package in general, to be on the ready and running the moment they landed on their feet; if in fact they did land on their feet. But in the event that a favourable situation would ensue, then there were opportunities to be had. The latter was a huge gamble that in the worst-case scenario would leave the world without either an ideological or financial engine or rudder. But would the outcome be what the Masters and the *pack* were vying for? That is, the renewed advancement of the First Advanced and Golden Era of Western Civilization falling in line directly behind the Ancient Hyperborean Civilization? Or was it to be the Third Haploidic Empire? In other words that meant more of the same: debt, despair, and slavery of the hoi polloi which would now be managed by two and a half centuries of hoi polloi advanced technology. This would ensure absolutely no wiggle room for ninety-nine per cent of the world's population who would be utterly enslaved as never before.

The frozen blanket upon the earth's north began to warm slowly that year before rapidly evaporating across open spaces of land leaving hard surfaced, bluish crusts of snow patches in the low dips that were sheltered from the burning sun's rays that rose higher and higher in the sky each day. Then in a most welcomed way the warmth penetrated the dry, high altitude air. Now Dyfed and Ceredwyn made ready and at long last set out from their not so little home nestled upon that great wind swept plateau. They travelled by dog sled across the quickly rotting ice that was receding back from the lake's bare, dark rocky shore (that attracted the heat from the sun that softened the ice first along its edges) and mushed through the fast melting snow along riverbanks. Time was of the essence now before the lakes and rivers became too dangerous with their rotting ice to travel across. As for Ceredwyn and Dyfed, the journey through the wilderness alone with the aroma of newly budding willows was going to conclude way too quickly for their liking. Like the spiritual nomads they were, both inhaled the atmosphere that gently massaged and stroked their inner psyche like an on-hands healer. They camped in the subdued light at the end of each long day under a whitish spring sky. Before them a softening, frozen light-greyish lake which caught the strengthening rays from Bel Disc the Relentless — Helios Apollo — as that phenomenal god glided slowly along the edge of the northern horizon late into the sky-light evening. Around about and next to the paleness of the flat lakes, the land's profile lay stark and bluey brown and the backdrop to the semi-solid and freezing lake was well defined as it jutted out in jagged angles into the solid and fading bland of the paling sky like a Lawren Harris oil on canvas. But here the silence and starkness was dynamic, not static; and Aurora who at this season closely guarded the horizon and would ever so slightly tip the world to one side and half fiery Helios would burst its full disc light forth again, first in red flashes then yellow spearheads and finally with streaming white shards.

Soon they had wound their way back to Galloping Whitehorse Rapids City that was near the headwaters of the mighty Ukon River and the staging ground for the recent stampede gold rush situated in the Ukon Territory Klondike of the Northern Dominion. From here, south via twisty narrow gauge rail track, the trail led to the dock nestled next to a little Alaskan village. This town was populated by rowdy Unified Statesians who easily took to liquor to help imagine their dreams. This village lay on a narrow strip of Alaskan coastal land down off from the Northern Dominion's Ukon territorial's broad southern plateau. Here was the northern terminal to which Dyfed's newly constructed tanker vessels plying the waters between here and Couver City could tie up.

(Divers arts: smoke, and mirrors on the Cutting Edge of Disaster)

"Who can refute a sneer?'
WILLIAM PALEY

Dyfed's spacious front office had a high ceiling and although it was exquisitely appointed it was sparing and simple. Comfortable and expensive furniture were poised around an enormous desk that stood almost completely uncluttered and had not so much as a pen stand or piece of paper on it, while beautifully adorned free standing lamps were strategically placed to provide un-shadowed spheres of light. The only item on the desk that day was an opened case with a beautifully polished viola resting inside. Often, when deep in though, Dyfed would wander back out here from his back (inner) office and with an absent mind pick up the instrument and play while he mulled over a problem.

On the interior walls of this front office were an array of tapestries from the lands of Italia, Arabia, and Ch'in. There were photographs and paintings, too, tastefully arranged while the northern exterior wall that lay behind the desk consisted of a panel of floor to ceiling windows that appeared as columns through which the inlet and the mountains to the north were visible. The main attraction in the room, however, was on the eastern wall at the far end of the room that faced you as you entered. It was a large painting, a masterpiece that commanded the centre of attention and focus. It hung there alone. It was called the Nascita di Venere. There was another such painting identical to it and similarly titled that also existed in the world. This latter rendition was on display in a museum far away in the land of Italia in the city of Florentia. But that one was not the original masterpiece, however, as was commonly believed, for the original in Dyfed's home — though commissioned by another — had been owned by him (paid by cash payment) for over four and a half centuries. Presumably, the artist, Sandro Botticelli, had had to work overtime to re-complete it again almost back on time so as to satisfy its powerful original commissioner, the Medici family. Though he hadn't commissioned the work, Dyfed had purchased it through the force of damaging information he had about Botticelli and the Medici. Adjacent to that particular object d' art and placed between two Arabian tapestries on the interior wall that was directly opposite the desk and the windowed exterior wall, was a large arched doorway that led into the aforementioned back room. This back office was his utility or workroom whose windows and balcony looked out to the south southwest from their homestead. It was a much larger room than the front office. This workshop had three interior walls that were covered with floor to ceiling book shelving and the occasional floor to ceiling break between the shelves for family portraits and other grand photographs of family gatherings taken at and around their summer Couver Island home. These were alongside framed maps of different regions of the world and even an early medieval suit of armour which Dyfed himself had once worn in the sixteenth century CE. And standing on the floor well out from one corner was a pedestal that was adorned with a beautiful bust of his mother Violet-Eye.

During the so-called Renaissance of Europa Dyed had commissioned this work to be sculptured by the great artist Donaletto who had once visited Perusia[84] in Umbria where Dyfed lived at the time. Dyfed had provided the artist with an exquisitely accurate image of that woman he had drawn on Arabian paper by his own fine and talented hand. That same template, too, expensively framed and mounted, was also displayed close-by.

Aside from intricate blankets made by the co-Salish native tribes around the Salish Sea, throughout this workroom were many object d'art. Large baskets woven by local women were tastefully placed here and there. Each one was either stuffed with blankets or bristling with rolled up charts, blueprints, tentative designs of prototypes of various complex mechanisms, geological and mineral surveys and the like. These baskets sat beside ancient amphorae cluttered beneath long tables that were laden down with miniature mechanical prototypes, and more books and manuscripts and a large cleared area cluttered with pens and ink and other condiments for sketching designing and writing manuscripts. A few tapestries were hung and a very fine one was spread on the back of the room's only couch. Mechanical drawings were framed and placed on either side of the only exterior door that led out of the room onto a spacious covered balcony three floors above the ground. Also, in this room there was also another enormous desk that faced south out through another column of windows like those in the front office toward the bay with the burgeoning city growing up all around. From his vantage point Dyfed could see the far shoreline. This shore now known as Xats'alanexw was home to the Swxwu7mesh. Now it was being reduced to a residential sprawl reaching out from the old centre of Couver City.

This urban blight was now spreading outward at an alarming rate towards a point of land sticking out into the sea that was usually obscured in grey fog during the winter months. But sometime before any of this had bubbled up and extending its grasping claws to gobble up the land of the Sto:lo River delta, Dyfed clearly saw the lie of the political and economical landscape from the start and from the time he had his vision from the carriage of their train as they headed east for the great Exhibition, he had begun to cast around in search of a large tracks of land to purchase.

They loved their old homestead but Dyfed was now keen to establish a safe house for himself and Ceredwyn. Now they planned to relocate. But it wasn't to be some rent-a-hide safe-house with dirty pulled across curtains and a twenty-four hour lookout posted in an upper floor gable window placed somewhere in a squalid neighbourhood invested with prostitutes, drug addicts and drunks. Instead it was the land about fifty Amoran miles inland from his Couver City homestead that Dyfed had been slowly buying up over the years that had handy canals accessible by the river Sto:lo that had access to and from his shipyard too and were set back away from roads and out of sight of the general population.

It consisted of a number of farms that included some of the most beautiful agricultural land around. The current problem was the farms weren't all available immediately to purchase. That they weren't all for sale wasn't a bad thing, though, for it allowed him to approach the farm owners individually at different times and offer them a lucrative price which he hoped they wouldn't turn down. He didn't approach them himself. The *pack* helped out here, too, and with more than one individual proposing as a land

---

84   Located in Umbria, Perusia was an Etruscan city between 500-300 BCE. Perusia was also influenced by the Sabines.

purchaser, this managed to defuse any suspicion of a mass take-over of land by some behemoth, greedy, bad-nasty with deep pockets or even an international conglomerate on the enterprising make. Indeed, it cemented the impression (not only by word of mouth among the outlying farmers that stretched out down the flat sprawling valley to the west, but also along the corridors of the lands title office and sundry insurance companies) that all was quite normal here. Normal in the sense that a positive step toward production for self-sufficiency and well being (financial and otherwise) for the local economy for the local community as a whole, was being assured, which of course it was. This conglomerated land estate of his backed up into a hilly and heavily forested area of the easterly section of the Bountiful Valley that extended west from here along the river delta for miles and miles to the coast through which the Sto:lo River flowed on its journey to the sea. But through this estate's purchase procedure (for all intent and purpose) it actually consisted of thirteen separate land holdings totalling seventy-two sections. This was considerable, for this made up a whopping forty-six thousand and eighty acres, eighteen thousand, seven hundred and twenty hectares, or seventy-two square miles of beautiful, arable land in all. And all of it registered under the Northern Dominion Land Survey (NDLS). He even set up apparent leasing tenants for different properties so as to thoroughly stump and confound any bureaucratic compilation of its true structure and ownership. This was to be the Empire Estate of the House of Lucifer, complete with warehouses, factories, foundries, kilns, stills, surrounded by its vast forty-six thousand plus acres of rich farmland.

Dyfed's plan was that once he had secured the entire area he would let it sit. War was coming, anyway. Wasn't it always? Already it was ramping up to part two of the Great World War. He also made sure that any sections of his newly acquired land that was normally productive — whether for crops of vegetables and for grain, or for fruit and vine and lastly for dairy farming — continued without any change while he devised his overall plan. Very slowly he tore down what was not needed or was below his standard. There were a number of buildings (barns of one kind or another mostly) that relevant to this new country was considered quite old. They were big and faded and often just open now to the starlings and other wildlife. These hollowly vacant, large and broad and vertical placed flat-board sided barns not only gouged out chunks of the blue sky but also the green swathes of surrounding corn fields and the thick, dark brown loam of the earth. This was so from almost any standpoint from which one might take it in, whether one was passing by in a motor chariot by road or from a barge on any of the narrow canals that adjoined the river Sto:lo. And in the evening these giant structures jutted up and out into pale, fading skies that made one — while standing in its shadow — feel excited with intrigue and playfulness within that one moment of life. In one way or another these heavily built barns with their stone foundations that lifted and rested them high and dry from the ever-present hollows such as the well worn tractor tracks or the hoof-marked, watery mud ponds, while others shored up the banks of an irrigation canal skirted with tall grass that crept slowly in straight lines across the flat valley and finished off as a pastoral scene that's often seen most cleverly transposed to canvass with swathes of smooth bright coloured paint.

From inside the lonely interior of these darkly hollow, awkwardly tall and angular gigantic barns, Dyfed strongly re-enforced and reconditioned the structure of these old barns and shop-buildings of jilted architecture so as not to alter their character and stance one iota. As such, now they seem from the exterior to have been left just as they were, acting as quiet standoffish sentinels.

Later, after the Great World War's second episode had finally come to a close, known only to Dyfed and the few close members of the *pack*, these buildings' roofs were eventually outfitted with camouflaged solar panels (not as yet invented by public industry) and placed in strategic positions among the buildings' sturdy one square foot timber beams (that spanned great distances and heights) were surveillance cameras and other high tech censors which with High Definition live feeds provided counter alternatives to unwanted trespassing and electronic snoops. They even interacted negatively to confound satellite originated electronic surveillance sweeps. These tilted, sun-bleached old structures, vacant and placed in assorted angles and positions throughout and around his entire vast estate were sentinels that acted as guardsmen like none other. Many of the outbuildings were well within public sight but not easily accessed by any easements adjoining the main right of way that the provincial government controlled for highway use. Access into Dyfed's estate was complicated as well by canals with (soon to be) electronically controlled drawbridges.

This was all put together slowly with a master plan design in mind. But with its painstaking detail of position and function and function ability, it took many years before the intricate mosaic became complete. And since money was never an issue with Dyfed, there were never any taxes owing or permits missing on this estate of many titles, either. Trachmyr (who now over here and acting as chamberlain in his capacity as Dyfed's chief assistant) saw to that. Trachmyr and Anlaf also made a career in collecting establishment lawyers onto their staff, none of whom had ever met or heard the name of Dyfed Lucifer.

Fortunately, Dyfed and the rest of *the pack*, or field force as they were called, knew beforehand what was to come. That was way easier, he had thought, than learning to read the multi dialects of the language of electromagnetic forces. A great world financial depression followed on the heels of this crash starting the very same day. This caused huge, worldwide unemployment and no bankroll whatsoever for investments that had all evaporated and were wiped out. It was subsequently accompanied by drought and pestilence, to boot; this complicated the lives of the workingman and woman in the street of the world 'as all get out', and also to no end. Meanwhile, the establishment's new man, the Wunschritter — the newly chosen one who in making up for lost time — had begun running around lighting fires all over Europa in preparation for his tenure as general in chief of the already stated act two of the Great World War. And with commerce all but shut down and hordes having become unemployed, his pitch to the revolting hordes, formerly the King's, Czar's, Kaiser's, and Caesar's complacent, had been to amalgamate the two dominate political philosophies of the age, the Ky-czar's nationalism and the socialism of the working dispossessed. It was an attempt to bamboozle and hoodwink both sides of the utopian argument. This then was his handle, another big lie. Unfortunately not enough shouted out, 'get a haircut and get a job', and way to many folks took his lie to heart.

(Homilies under the Sun & under the spell of Theoretical Assumptions)

'Opinions cannot survive if one has no chance to fight for them.'
THOMAS MANN

Awkwardly, and semi reclined, Dyfed sprawled upon and over spilled the chair in front of his big desk. His office rooms were mostly cleaned out now as he and Ceredwyn had relocated into their newly built palace tucked away in the Bountiful Valley that was fed by the waters of the Sto:lo River. At this moment he was silently reminiscing about having earlier been summoned to the fifth dimension convocation that had been held in King Kunobelin's beautiful palace. He whipped off his glasses with one hand and rubbed his eyes anxiously with the forefinger and thumb of his other before replacing his glasses again. Ever since the advent of the *pack's* Workers and Labour Division had had a hand in aiding and abetting humanity's technology — and in advancing the hoi polloi's method of making a living by improving working and product standards and by further safeguarding the integrity of apprenticeships, along with installing safety procedures, adequate pay for labour provided — resentment by the nobility (namely those who mistakenly took themselves to be noble) had quickly ensued. After all, these policies of raising the bar for the labourer, and for the consumer (too) cut deeply (too deeply for some, not deep enough for others) into the noble's and other power elitists' profits. All of this had been on the open agenda of the 3DDR held at King Kunobelin's palace in never-never land, as Dyfed sometimes termed it.

Wage increases, shorter working hours, workers' indemnity — such as paid-for company health and dental packages, paid insurance plans and widows' and orphans' compensation — along with paid holidays that guild and unionised work forces pressed for, was therefore seen by those power elite here in the third dimensional space/time as ungodly. And it was at the Twentieth Turn of the Century Nation's Summit Convocation that had been held that year in the City of Broekzele[85] where those *for* modernization towards a certain idea, and those *agin* — met head on.

"It's simply not cricket,' Lord Bastard of Stan Bastard Oil was heard to say to Giorgi Posh at that Twentieth Turn of the Century convention. 'It's not the way we play it.'

"It is an unadulterated defiance against god, and subsequently a denial of the nobility's authority,' replied the latter whose full name (if you recall) was George Hunover Edward Sax-Goth Burgfeld. 'That's what was really being challenged here.' And all things wise and wonderful — it would appear — along with all the king's horses and all the king's men who were saying that from the point of view of the establishment...that ever at hand, world-wide order — that this dastardly attitude was an act of treason: And that this state of affairs was undermining the wellbeing of the kingdom...all kingdoms and even the profits of the republics. What vile evil had been set in motion here? A motion

---

85 Broekzele (home among the marshlands) is an old Flemish town, today called Brosella (Bruxelles) that has now sprawled out over the flood lands of the river Zenne.

whereby a demand had risen in favour of the labour force (if you can just imagine it) to actually share in the profits that were being squeezed out…ripped away from…and sponged up from the earth's bounty by those chosen ones who — rightfully aided by Aristocles — had been legally decreed by god himself to have domination over the Earth and all its natural resources and creatures great and small! This was precisely what those people were saying.

'No, no, and unequivocally, categorically, indubitably and irrefutably no' Giorgi Posh had stated. 'The male god-fearing dominant men and women of the established order of the world empire have always been united,' he reiterated, almost screaming. 'We cannot…we will not…abide by such current atrocities…those extreme and dangerous trends which are now all the rage in the western world. So! We will make war. That is what we do…and that is what we do best. We make war. It is we who make war. Look to history, I say. And we don't have to look very far to see the man that can help us out there.'

Dyfed had been in attendance during Giorgi's speech. He had attained observer capacity status and had slipped in while attending another conference that was being put on by the *pack* in Broekzele at the same time. The latter's initial purpose was to open up an opportunity for the Masters to spy on the Haploidic Organization of the Unified Nations and assess some of their more undeclared motivations. To do this the former adopted the guise of an international organization itself, one to assist the wealthy to amortize debt. They called it the International Amnesty for the Wealthy. Giorgi Posh, Dyfed observed, was standing at the podium like some inanimate creation by Rodin.

'And then those jumped up, timorous little turds of Tinsel-Town will be up Shit-Creek without a fucking paddle –– just where they belong,' he shouted. 'So there! Let the Jaurés gauntlet, along with those of a host of other bloody social do-gooders, be seen now to be thrown down and chucked to the wolves. Since their mandates for the true equality of men (along with meaningful liberalism) is a threat to us, a threat to the Empire, a threat to the Establishment, and we must answer it as only we know how. Let the Establishment now utter our battle cry. Let us shout out our beloved version of Beauseant once again from the rooftops of our banks and from those of our grandest monuments that house our institutions of justice and religion: War, war, war.'

"War…war…resume the war,' the members of the elite cried out as they shot to their feet, pounding the air with their fists. And so did the cry go out. From the cosy safety of their established ideal reality and the numbers of like-minded present, the ivy-league speaking mandarins candidly solicited and influenced their minions to take up the sermon and deliver it out to all parishes and provinces for dominant alpha males and their consorts to rally 'round and put their heads together in order to seek a solution to re-rig and re-boot the system once again.

Never had there been more need and urgency in an attempt to shrug off the hood of slavery and slough the ball and chain of debt, than now, the *pack* thought. It was time to thwart the few attempting to bring low so many of the revolting masses of hoi polloi rabble and their deplorable state.

The nobility and their circle jerks of aristocrats needed mountains of money more than ever, now. That IS their sole Idea: Wealth. And in this world of theirs — and those who share this the established Idea — wealth is power that was always built on the backs of others. How else are you going to grasp power and hold on to it, they had always asked in astonishment to those un ceremonial idiots who were vulgar and common and out of the loop. So, in the past and in a fever, world industry and manufacturing had begun to be churned out faster and faster with fewer and fewer breaks or the time to smell the roses.

Soon, the industrialised world of the Empire (that segment which continued to dominate and pervert Western Civilization) that stretched from east to west and north to south was humming twenty-four/seven. After this, the quality of the environmental status in cities like Couver City and all over the world, they resumed its slide into the abyss. But it was agreed at that meeting of the Twentieth Turn of the Century Nation's Summit Convocation of the Organization of the Unified Nations that more wealth yet was needed if the hoi polloi were not to get the upper hand. In turn that concept was disputed at the secret meeting of the *pack*, the so-called International Amnesty for the Wealthy that was actually for the well being of the poor and indebted.

Anyway, at this juncture the nobility, the aristocrats and the unconscionably greedy, were more than successful, thanks to Cornelius-Felix who was in attendance here. His Idea was quite well known and Giorgius Florentius (Giorgi Posh) and his Telemachus were his strongest advocates in the Second Empire. And what with the ranks of the nobility, the aristocrats and their bureaucracy that stretched from the pulpit to parliament certainly appeared to have so far always won the day. These men who versed in the religion of the empire, complimented by sundry religious prophets such as the like of Johann Calvino whose influence served to act as a booster to their already heavily entrenched Idea's version of the phenomena around them (which included their domination over all the Earth), was propelling them to even greater heights of insanity. It was meant to cover them in glory, which is wealth and power. And so began the slide and decline of world economy into what is now called part one of the Great World War, the war to end all wars: with the convening of part two now imminent and looming equally most ugly. And in this the nobility were quite successful; they even managed to rid themselves of old wooden hangers-on and bad blood that had continued to languish among the higher echelon of the Haploid class.

As far as the on-going war was concerned, it was still intermission, but those awake and alert enough to identify the smell of the roasting coffee beans were now anticipating some small movement at the corner hem of the curtain on the world stage with some anticipation. Dyfed expected the proverbial curtain to be raised at any time now. This was because just like the posy of tulips ponzi scheme of 1608CE (when the market collapsed because prices had been pushed to an exorbitantly high level which were riding on IOU's, and not gold or bank promissory notes thereof) the market of today was way over extended. Newly posh folks who were rich in steamship companies, railways, manufacturing and industries shares, whether they lived in Isis, Nova Troia, Megatropolis or Stockholm were living lavishly on speculated credit. But this was speculated credit that certain other folks — folks who Dyfed happened to know — were about to pull the carpet out from underneath them, and millions of others with all their trillions of denarii (dollars) worth invested about to turn into mud, then smoke. That was sure to raise the curtain. And the Wunschritter was itching for it while the likes of Fugge et al salivated. And whatever else…whatever bags of tricks and cats that Fugge, Purplebal, Theo the Thug, Florentius (the incomparable Giorgi Posh) and Cornelius-Felix were going to allow the Wunschritter to let out; it was assured that once unleashed it would attack the world at large worse than any deadly virus. So, however it was all meant to transpire and transcend the societies of men into their Haploidic and Frankenstein future of a right winged conservative National Communalist dream/nightmare which the impending Act II of the Great World War would promote, it might just bring all their dreams and all they worked for crashing down. And not just the veneer of Germanika or Europa would be effected here, but eventually (and quite soon) all of Western Civilization could quickly become atrophied and wither on the vine. After all, wasn't the Great World War really anything more than a full spectrum Haploid takeover bid? Could this be the time? Dyfed wondered. It could be…it will be, but for whom; them or us? That's what they asked themselves. This had unsettled the Masters of the *pack* that were assembled there at Brosella, and it threw a pall over their normally spirited gatherings.

Meanwhile, for that past decade, Dyfed had set to and successfully — and to the best of his ability — put his house in order. This included his structure of financing which wasn't so much a problem of attainment, as he financed himself anyway, but rather to hide his tracks and remain an anonymous owner as well as donor. Dyfed provided billions of dollars into coffers to help the slaves of the Third Dimension as his mandate dictated, as did many other top dogs of the *pack*. Meanwhile, from his two private offices he handled all the transfers and conveyances of every kind. Earlier, in the midst of the still on-going worldwide marketing frenzy — when the international markets had expanded almost on air, or even the rumour of air being present; when kingdom and republic state spending and individual personal wealth had become contingent on paper investments, promises and a wing and a prayer, along with very little else — the world market was caused to crash. It was ugly and not executed very expertly, overall. But it didn't catch Dyfed off guard. This later led the *pack* to believe that such a ploy as this was still in experimental stages. So, if the aforementioned backers of the Wunschritter (for example) were successful — something that would soon become obvious — then this form of financial legerdemain would only improve. So, there wasn't an option here; they were now all thinking. The Wunschritter and company would HAVE to be defeated: And they could only be defeated by those who were the stalwart backers for the ultimate success of Western Civilization in general, and its religious backbone of Western Philosophy in particular. This credence and conviction was written in diamond, titanium and wurtzite boron nitride. It didn't isolate Confucius or Buddha, exactly, nor even to a lesser degree certain notions of Jeshuaism and Ishlamitism. But, it was obvious now that this couldn't include any of Monotheism's myriad of myths and lies about god and redemption as laid out in the Books of Lists et al. The believers in these lies had long been in open revolt against Western Civilization without realizing it; indeed, the revolt began from the inception of these very lies. And that condition had caused the latter, along with the gentle folks of the world, untold grief, suffering and misery. Fundamentalism of any kind, especially among the monotheist variety, on the other hand, was not only entirely unacceptable to Western Philosophy, by and large it was downright anathema smothered in apostasy to boot! Certainly, among the *pack* — at least at the executive level — it was unanimous believed that fundamentalism of any and all variety must be thoroughly expunged from the world, along with the memory thereof if humanity was to succeed.

(Ordering: Jeshua and a Side of Knights)

'Thus mathematics may be defined as the subject in which we never know what we are talking about, nor whether what we are saying is true.'

BERTRAND RUSSELL

Dyfed was alone in his large offices performing the Radetsky March in solo on his viola when the telephone rang in his back office. Pulling his viola away from his ear he stopped playing, set his instrument down he walked back into the other room to answer. It was Ceredwyn announcing that her youngest son Deric the Deuce had suddenly and unexpectedly arrived.

Being surprised by his presence in person (somehow and suddenly) harboured urgency, Dyfed thought. That old pirate's arrival into his office was in classic form as Dyfed strolled back into the outer office to receive him. Dyfed was standing in front of his desk as Deric the Deuce strode into his immaculate outer room. Behind Dyfed was Botticelli's the masterpiece that framed Dyfed's upper silhouette. He watched the Deuce enter and he greeted him. The Deuce was still a lithe and muscular man and almost as tall as Dyfed and the eyes in his face were blue and quick while his skin showed years of exposure to sun and sea wind. He wore loose fitting dark trousers, a roomy white shirt partially open at the neck with a scarf-like broad tie holding his collar somewhat together covered with a long, navy blue blazer opened to show his belt.

Deric the Deuce wasn't alone, and that too wasn't a complete surprise to Dyfed. Of the two men accompanied the Deuce, Trachmyr was one of them. However, the sight of Ebreo who was accompanying them was a surprise. Moreover, the condition that Ebreo was in surprised him even more for he was somewhat propped up by Deric and Trackmyr's strong arms. In fact just seeing Ebreo ben Jamin suddenly being here in his house was a kind of disjointed relevance, an un-calming deja vu more than anything. Ebreo was visibly unwell and confused, the latter condition being responsible due to his un-wellness; Dyfed guessed, maybe sea or airsickness. The Deuce and Dyfed clasped hands amiably and Dyfed led them back his into the organised clutter that was his workroom. With Ebreo's arms crooked over the other two's shoulders, together his old batman and the Deuce half carried Ebreo into the back office where they plunked him down into the closest comfortable couch. Behind them was Ceredwyn's smiling a most happy face. To this poor aging woman, as she surveyed the scene of Dyfed, her son Deric, along with her husband's batman, and this demented stranger called Ebreo who she had never seen before, appeared to her — as they huddled together in Dyfed's large study — like a scene from a painting by Caravaggio.

Over the course of a few hours (comfortably seated in deep cushioned chesterfield armchairs with a bottle of scotch and a pitcher of soda water on the less cluttered ornate cherry wood table, they now sat in a relaxed state. Mother, son and Dyfed chatted at length until Ceredwyn left the men to talk over business while she attended to the supervising of the home and in preparation for the evening meal. Ebreo had remained quiet the whole time, an unusual characteristic with him, and seemed to be seeing the two men for the first time as he slowly and without attention surveyed his truly unfamiliar surroundings.

Although Dyfed and the Deuce were not particularly close despite their connection through Ceredwyn, they were a lot alike in some ways. Both men were tough, opinionated, and unswerving in their dedication to their integrity — their first and most important responsibility — yet they were each altruistic in an idealistic way as well. Both men were also connected with the Brotherhood and Sisterhood that had been founded immediately after the terrible destruction of Kadesh (al Quds, also Jerusalem). Dyfed was a chartered member of this society, one of the few hoi polloi associations that was recognised by the *pack*. As for the old pirate, he had stowed away a lifetime of swashbuckling adventures and experience himself, all from a career on the high seas which, aside from his father Deric (Theoderic the Great had passed away) was second to none. And he had been in the employ of queens and kings and other powerful women and men who aside from kingdoms ruled powerful associations and companies. In this way Deric the Deuce was quite close to the great game in a different way than from which Dyfed was. Also, both men were fabulously wealthy from their own labours in a relative way and were in no way strangers to the affairs of men as acted out upon the world stage. But most importantly, Deric the Deuce was an initiate who had been brought on board by Morgant Carreg who, as his master, taught him the ways of sorcery as Manandan had done for Dyfed. But the Deuce had no connection to the fifth dimension.

So now, it seemed, they had been brought together as part of the big plan immerging out of the recent fifth dimensional convocation. According to the Deuce, his instructions had been to contact the newly appointed secretary select of the Committee for Public Safety of Victims of the Third Dimensional World Order. Morgant, as it now happened, had located Ebreo on orders by Thrax. Apparently, the latter was intent on doing a number on him. As the Deuce told the story, Morgant had done something to Ebreo's mind. Now with the use of certain spoken code words (of which Morgant made him aware) he or anybody else could to speak to Ebreo that was directly connected to pertinent information. But this resulted in the latter having no obvious will or volition of his own and caused him to remain in something of a stupor. Earlier, Morgant had summoned the Deuce to the Nova Metropolis that had recently been reorganized along with the boroughs and counties all around into a Megatropolis and renamed as such. There he had handed Ebreo over to the Deuce along with a small, boxed gift to be given to the secretary select of the committee that he, Deric the Deuce, had been assigned to. His instructions were to report to his mother, of all things. Apparently, at that point Morgant had drugged Ebreo sufficiently to get him from Megatropolis to here.

"What were your orders?' Dyfed asked.

"Only that in reporting to you now would give us a rushed opportunity to be able to put our heads together in order to make some sense of just what in the world was happening on the big scene and how we were going to respond. Many of those players who are now strutting forward onto the stage are well known to both you and I. After all, Dyfed, you have been tucked away out here in the western wilds for some time. I, on the other hand, while though still in the thick of it, have never really been party first hand to the financial intrigues of the social elite, at least not in the way in which you have. I'm just a pirate.

'And there was one other thing,' he said. 'Morgant was puzzled over why this former employee of yours here kept uttering the names Atta-Wulf, Ab Ram Nananda and Eonnurzazagesibababal. Also, he kept saying the name Johann Calvin, over and over.'

Dyfed was pensive.

"These are folks known to me,' he said finally in answer to the Deuce and Trachmyr's expectant silence. 'Dan Velchanos who is also known as boy Zeus controls those four aforementioned,' he said. I wonder what that means in the context in which the world finds itself today?' Dyfed thought to himself. Much to his surprise the Deuce told him that that Ebreo had been discovered to be a mole siphoning out information as to how the *pack* functions inside that is being used to confound their good works?

"That old Hun Khinglia Ephthalites may have some answers about that,' Dyfed finally said. 'Get back to Morgant. Ask him to locate Khinglia Ephthalites for me and question him in respect to the envelovment and the goings on of Ab Ram Nananda with the current status quo at large. I'm not sure I believe this.'

(...Away we go...cheerio...
wave good-bye...)

'The nature of our mind is...to superimpose sets of images; to eliminate as many of them as possible is an effort which only necessity or some yearning can make a success. Attention is less a gift than a habit, and the knowledge of this ought to encourage those who wish to live inside their own soul.'

ERNEST DIMNET

Wispy swirls of cigar smoke drifted away from the men across the warm room toward one of the large open windows. It drifted out into a sultry early summer evening where faded sepia printed angles and shapes beneath a streaky yellow horizon and a fat cobalt-blue sky was confined within the window-frame. This fixed, yet strangely dimensional object itself seemed like a transcending holograph which at the moment had become an angular noise-box that emitted hallucinated babble, grunt and bang by letting in the sounds of some strange conglomerated phenomena outside, an urbane citified world that too was another dimension in itself.

They had just been listening to the Wunschritter's hollow voice that had shrieked at them across the radio airwaves from Kolonia (western Germanika) accusing the sagging and post Empire and her sundry allies in waiting, especially US (Unified States or Uncle Sham) of unbridled aggression and self-seeking Capitalistic compliance, while warning them of swift retaliation. It was a change of heart, the two men noted, for during the interim of peace the local investments including the world labour force which the Wunschritter claimed to now represent, had initially applauded the old Angleland model and had even tried to mimic its poise and demeanour which the Wunschritter had adapted now for the purpose of his own. 'We are the Third Amoran Empire (the successor to the second or Holy Empire which itself had emerged from the great Amoran Empire), and it is we who are the world's most versatile culture of economy in this era of depression,' the Wunschritter screeched across the world to listeners. He had never been tired of saying this or of dishing out hollow promises that he stated would better mankind. They were not unlike the propaganda of Kruz Terrainsky and Vladmir Hubitchercawkoff and other pinko commie cronies of the inglorious revolution of the Rus.

"He's in possession of knowledge that we clearly don't have,' said the Deuce to Dyfed. Vibrations across the wireless from the NDBC's NorthEastWestSouth (NEWS) had just ended abruptly; then the radio began to blare out big band music. Dyfed leaned over and turned the volume down low. 'But what is it?' he asked. 'Is it part of the grand ruse, the big lie? Surely the Wunschritter is in the employ of the OPE. How else can it be? Who else would be financing him? Who else *could* finance him? You see this is why I must go to him.

"My understanding, just now,' the Deuce said after a moments reflection, 'is that you are going to the mountainous land of the Berbers with Ebreo first to seal his fate in an unmarked grave.' Here the Deuce paused. 'But to go to Barlein and the Wunschritter, this is madness. However, it is an extraordinary set of circumstances that we have all found ourselves in.'

"Actually, it is Gottengen that I will go to, not Barlein. And as far as the Berber mountains go, I am burying nobody at the moment. I told you already. I need to check this out thoroughly before I let anything happen to Ebreo. Full stop on that. Anyway, punitive action is not even my job, but it maybe yours Deric. However, I have doubts of Ebreo's guilt of those charges of treason toward the House of Lucifer.' Dyfed was referring to the command from higher up that earlier the secret Morgant code had caused Ebreo to give up. The befuddled Ebreo had himself uttered Morgant's own words to 'dispose of Ebreo on the African continent' via the code which Dyfed knew the *pack* often used.

The African continent, apparently, had long been a dumping ground for evils of every stripe. Dyfed recalled Morgant's story about Virus Ebola having been similarly sealed in Ethiopia by him in order to safe-guard humanity. It might not be working out, however, for a myriad of viruses and sexually transmitted diseases had flowed out from there to contaminate Europa over the last thousands of years and was now increasing exponentially. Virus apparently had been buried by Morgant too near the River Nile on that occasion and was leaching into it and then flowing back out into the Western Civilization. Sealing off that continent from the rest of the world had been an idea (unacceptable as it was to sound minded empathetic people) by sever and uncaring Haploids of late. Plunder Africa of its wealth, its diamonds and its rich iron ore so to improve our lot, was something Mr Rhodes had declared. But apparently he had not meant to improve the lot of Africa's people in the bargain. Or perhaps he had. Certainly then there were those who most quickly managed to stymie and stifle that idea.

In any case Dyfed was going to keep Ebreo ben Jamin here in Couver City until he could fully grasp what events had really taken place and who had been involved.

"Well, I say, said Dyfed. 'Ebreo. You are looking a little more aware now, I see. We seem to have lost you there for a while. Feeling better now, are we? You were looking peeked.'

"Where the fuck am I?' said Ebreo, uncharacteristically gruffly.

"Whoa! Easy there old boy; you had a bad turn but you are back with us now.' Dyfed pushed himself off the sofa chair while he swept up the decanter of scotch from the small table beside him. Then making a slight detour to snatch a cut crystal glass from the sideboard, he poured out a healthy slug of the rich, amber liquor while he walked over and set the glass on a small table beside the couch Ebreo was resting on.

'Drink this, old friend. Here you go. Straight up, it will make you feel better.'

Ebreo eyed Dyfed cautiously, glancing once or twice in the Deuce's direction, as well.

"Of course it will make me feel better, you two morons, so would knowing just how I got here. Where am I, anyway? I'm repeating myself, now.'

"You are in my home, Ebreo,' said Dyfed, extending his arms out to full length on either side of him. He smiled down at Ebreo ben Jamin. "Welcome to my home, at last, Ebreo,' he said.

"Thank you, Dyfed Lucifer,' Ebreo replied with emphases. He then reached for his glass of scotch and downed it in one fell swoop. He smiled back at Dyfed and held out his large glass for more.

"When I said straight up,' said Dyfed, 'I meant, it is straight, it is neat, no soda water.' Dyfed half filled the waiting glass up again.

"Thank you, Dyfed Lucifer, for your hospitality. So now, I'm at your home, in the Northern Dominion, yes?' He downed the glass once again.

"Yes,' answered Dyfed.

"So, just how the fuck did I get here, then?'

"Steady on,' replied the Deuce. 'You came with me, don't you remember? I brought you here on orders.'

"No, I don't remember, you asshole. What I do remember is being in Europa, yesterday, I think. It does seem longer somehow,' he said resignedly, brushing his right palm in front of his eyes. Dyfed filled up Ebreo's glass again that the latter had placed back on the table beside the couch.

At that moment Dyfed heard Ceredwyn come into the outer office and walk determinedly toward where they were still drinking. Derik the Deuce immediately jumped up and gave his mother another long, long hug. Releasing him she then eyed Ebreo suspiciously upon seeing that he was more alert and present. She didn't like the looks of him and gave Dyfed a certain look to convey her opinion. She had never met Ebreo before but it was not customary for people in Dyfed's outside life to visit, or for that matter be invited to their home. Nor did she believe it was customary for her son to accompany or be accompanied by others outside of his immediate sphere, especially to a safe and secure terminal, a private haven that was what their homes were. The Deuce, as he was known, had been his father's apprentice, after all. He knew business and work were separate from family life.

"Ceredwyn,' Dyfed said, 'this is Ebreo ben Jamin. He is an old, old friend from back in the days when we were young.'

Ebreo, with a resigned expression on his face, manoeuvred himself off the couch and onto his feet. He bowed quickly and curtly to Ceredwyn. Ceredwyn managed to smile somewhat at Ebreo and welcomed him and Dyfed handed her a drink he had just poured. She declined the offer.

"Don't worry,' Dyfed said. Ebreo, here, will drink it. Hurry, drink up, Ebreo. Sit down now and drink up,' he said pointing with his hand which held the other glass towards the small side table.

"What are you discussing in my house?' Ceredwyn asked looking back and forth between Dyfed and her son.

"World government,' answered her son.

"And about leaving, shortly, very shortly, maybe tonight — tomorrow night at the latest — for a brief visit to Nova Troia.'

"And then Barlein,' Ebreo added, to Dyfed's astoundment.

"What!' Ceredwyn almost shouted the exclamation.

"Yes, my dear,' exclaimed Ebreo looking directly at Dyfed before the latter could answer his own wife. Dyfed didn't like that and glared at Ebreo who was just then, sitting back down into the couch and reaching for his glass with a strange smile. This smile that appeared to have spread across his face at the first whiff of unsettlement and angst that appeared in the air. That was something that Dyfed hadn't remembered about him. 'You see,' continued Ebreo, 'I have to be… am supposed to now be in Barlein. War is starting up again. In fact I was… just now, or yesterday, or it must have been a week yesterday, I dunno…in Barlein and managed, somehow, to get momentarily side-tracked.' Ebreo briefly shot a glance at Deric the Deuce. 'Dyfed, here, so kindly invited me to drop by for a glass of scotch, since I was somehow here. I thought I would make it worth my while and have a few, but, time is ticking by,' Ebreo replaced his glass back onto the table and pulled out a pocket watch which he consulted for a moment. 'Yes, it is time I got back. Tonight would be ideal, don't you think?' He then stood up as if all set to go.

"Yes, Ebreo,' said Dyfed patiently. 'When I leave, and then come back, maybe then you can return to Europa, maybe even Barlein, if it's liveable. Don't you worry about that! Meantime, you will stay here in this country.'

"Have you forgotten something?' said Ceredwyn. She looked as if she didn't want to discuss the matter in front of Ebreo who she didn't know.

"You mean my indictment? Those papers I received by courier? The indictment begins…ah, when is that court appearance, next month? Well, that will all just have to wait now that the outbreak of war is imminent. Or better still, let them start and conduct the trial without us. After all, I'm sure they have already come up with a verdict, despite what our attorney says and despite his diligence and legerdemain.

As it happened, Dyfed's grandson Sundog was under indictment. He was Walks on Clouds' eldest son. Dyfed now made a snap decision to allow Sundog to enrol in the army of the Northern Dominion. Earlier he had been exempt. So he too would travel to Nova Troia with Trachmyr and him where he would enlist and be deployed in the war effort in a manner that Trachmyr had in mind and could arrange. It was to be light duty, though, as the young man was slight and sensitive, although otherwise tough and strong as steel. But there was a hitch, you see. Sundog had been estranged from his wife and young family due to domestic dispute and perhaps marital problems. His wife had left with their small children and having moved into an apartment had taken up with another man. Sundog, who, though concerned and wanting to act responsibly regarding the well being of his children, was less concerned about his wife having taken up with someone else (letting him off the hook, somewhat) rather than wanting to know who that someone was. His children were young and his wife (he had discovered) had poor judgement in the folks with whom she kept company without his influence. He had wanted to meet this new beau of hers, but she had denied that one existed. Sundog told her he knew about him and didn't mind but had the right to give the guy a quick look over to satisfy him that he wasn't some pervert, a child molester, for example. But she still denied Sundog access to her apartment and even denied and lied by saying she didn't have a beau on hand.

Sundog contacted the local constabulary but they had said it was a domestic dispute and at this time they could, and would, not intervene. He could file an official complaint, they had told him, and maybe after that something could be achieved, but that would take weeks if not months. So, one fine evening, shortly thereafter, Sundog rang her doorbell and said he only wanted to speak with her lover as a concerned father. She proceeded to lie and deny everything so he split the door open as he entered her domain. Now, viewing the third wheel in this arrangement as a coward who should have had every good reason to comprehend another man's concern for his children (under the circumstances), Sundog's intent was to press fear into this interloper's heart and put the run on him for his children's sake. For now he began to think that the man might be a molester, after all. It was a shame, to be sure, for whoever he was he was at least taking the heat off him. However, now the mystery man must go.

The result was a swiftly executed 'break and enter' charge that was laid against him by the local constabulary (the same men he had confided to earlier), along with an assault charge. Although Sundog's estranged wife didn't even have time to select an attorney for herself, the prosecuting attorney, aided and abetted by the police officers involved, painted her, and her children, ('never mind her innocent boyfriend,' they said) as victims who themselves were in danger of further attack and abuse from a very dangerous and jealous ne'er-do-well who was a loner, a drifter and an alcoholic.

Of course Sundog was none of these. He wasn't a wimp, either. Not like his estranged father in law, the father of his estranged wife, who cowered before his own wife's onslaught — Sundog's mother in law. This woman (as Walks on Clouds tried to warn his son beforehand) apparently wore the cock and balls in that family, even if they were fake.

Sundog was employed, not surprisingly, by the House of Lucifer, he wasn't a drifter, he wasn't a loner, and he threw up when he drank even just a little. He was an artist and was employed in advertising and also in locating impressive local art works for Dyfed to buy up. One that he found was an oil painting titled *Old and New Forest*. Of course, at first Dyfed was able to take care of this nasty business against his grandson, and after throwing a lot of money around was able to get the prosecuting attorney thrown out — along with his gibberish — for uttering statements of defamation in court as well as for certain pronouncements he made before the court which as to their validity or not, he could not have known for sure at the time of his uttering them. This was anathema to real justice. He was eventually disbarred. More importantly, Dyfed sustained a divorce for Sundog, and contrary to the narrow minded and conservatively volitional mind-set of the day, managed to get Sundog full custody of his children. But this was after the fact. At the time Sundog was ordered to face further charges stemming from his brother-in-law's murder. That man was most likely murdered by either the police themselves or by a friend of the establishment and Sundog was simply a scapegoat. So, it also meant that the lad couldn't legally accompany Dyfed overseas. But Dyfed was planning to fly to Europa in a manner independent of any carrier.

Shortly after this the Deuce received orders to take his fleet (when it arrived on the west coasts of the Northern Dominion via the Panama canal) across the Peaceful Ocean from here to Vacuna Island (Hong Kong) and to lay in wait there for events to take place. That, and to keep an eye out as to what actions all the less than friendly among the axis powers would do to complicate world trade, never mind of also confounding the *pack's* concept for advancing Western philosophy, Dyfed reminded the Deuce, along with it ideals for world democracy and equitable culture.

"And I don't think I need to caution you about being enterprising in pirating the shipping lanes and putting the pressure on the Axis powers,' Dyfed told him. 'Keep in touch with Morgant. As far as Athaulf (Adolf) von Braunau the Winschritter is concerned, I know about Atta-Wulf. As it happens, I've just had a communiqué from him.'

Then slowly he reached over and picked up a letter that lay on the little table next to the scotch decanter. The letter had arrived by yesterday morning's post. It was by registered mail and was post marked Nova Troia with no return address, but upon opening it Dyfed had been greatly surprised. It was written in the Wunschritter's own hand in the language of the northern Franken and it invited Dyfed to a secret meeting to be held at the University of Gottingen in the heartland of the Frankens in the middle of the coming month. It was already late month now.

"This is the communication I just received,' said Dyfed. He handed the letter to the Deuce.

> Das Reichstag von Barlein
> Kolonia
> May 24
>
> My dear Herr Lucifer.
>
> I hope this letter finds you well and free of virus and financial ruin.
>
> You were and remain a very able man and certain friends that we have in common tell me that this condition has in no way diminished, though you chose to live in the western wilds and have become something of a rustic recluse. I envy you, and one-day hope to visit you there and we can wander in the wilderness together if, of course, you will have me.
>
> Dyfed, you have no idea what change has come to the corridors of global powers that I, and others of the old guard, now walk. Nations have leaders who invade and ally with each other but it is nothing more than a charade. A powerful secret enclave is now at this moment storming the gates to control a world government and yours truly has become something more than just a bit player in this whole affair.
>
> I'm challenging the new order and it is I who is the master of charades. All you see on the newsreels and read in the tabloids and journals of the world is not really the true story about what is actually taking place. In fact it is just beyond the reach of comprehension by the masses on the whole. This is all propaganda for the stupid and gullible, the weak of character, and is a lullaby for the torpid and unaware. Such souls that have already succumbed and been reticently oriented, are now well beyond resuscitation, in any case. But all of this, my dear old acquaintance, I hardly need tell you. But I tell you this; that these apparitions must not be overlooked, they must be removed, cleared out of the way, culled in the name of god and the spirit of his human form and the slate to be made clean so we may clearly define friend from foe. Those not with us must be against us. My enemy's enemy must be my friend. I hardly need tell you that the ancients claimed that everything they achieved came from their gods. What claim, pray tell, can modern man possibly make other than for his own invulnerability and superiority? The claim made by the social elite is that the Will to Power is godliness itself and that likeminded souls must rise up and overthrow his suppressors and rule the world on their own terms. But the majority of those in the world are simply followers, cannon fodder, who shore up the numbers wielded by us, the socialist leaders of nations. And masses, when placed under diligent care such as ours, can be manipulated psychologically and after brutal training, they can be pressed into an array of services designed towards securing those ends that are most favourable to the soldiers of the renewed old school.
>
> This war, which I will win, must win, (for all of our sake) is a charade as well, my dear friend, and I make quite a production of it while I pretend to play the game. But listen to me and believe me when I tell you with all sincerity that I have double-crossed them all. Yes, double-crossed them, I say! The fools are greedy and want so much to believe that I have thrown my lot in with them. Alas, they are grievously

deceived, perhaps even to my own detriment. But that doesn't matter, now, for I am married to my nation and the Third Empire that is now dawning as I am married to the cause of Nation Communalism. That story, however, is too long and complex to outline here on this page, although I suspect that you have more than an inkling of what I say here.

I need your help. The great movement to avert the despicable tide and stay the course and put a stop to all those filth that are dirtying the world's gene pool of pure mankind needs your help.

To these ends we are convening a secret convocation at the palatial guesthouse at the University of Gottingen on June 13th, to be followed by a summary convocation on November 1; aptly it's the beginning of the Day of the Dead. Please come and meet old friends. All expense will be reimbursed by the great NSCP (National Socialist Communalist Party). Please contact Herr von Goethe at 11 Asmodeas Street, Nova Troia Angleland, for details.

Your old comrade in arms

Wunschritter Adolphus von Braunau

PS: Hopefully this letter will arrive in good time for you to make the necessary arrangements. For security reasons a courier will deliver this letter from my hand to Nova Troia for posting. This is in order to dispel any suspicion when it arrives in your country.

A.v.B.

Dyfed recited the letter out aloud by memory as the Deuce carefully read along.
"So what is it the Wunschritter has and what does he want of me?' he said. 'I suppose I'll have to go and find out for myself. What a lucky chance this is. Oh, Ceredwyn will hate me, of course, but she will hate the Wunschritter more.'

Dyfed had had another surprise the day following the Deuce and Ebreo's sudden arrival. And it too had been without warning. Some time earlier he had commissioned a versatile two engine aircraft for his private use between Couver City and the Beautiful Northern Land of the Great River where he would then rely on smaller float and ski planes. He had chosen the Douglas Aircraft Corporation of Caulifornicatia over de Havilland in Angleland. On the same day that Dyfed began to make his preparations for leaving for Europa, the aircraft suddenly arrived for his inspection and approval from its all Merikan, Unified Statesian manufacturer. It had been flown in from Santa Monica to Seagull City Warshingtown State a few miles south of Couver City. From there it flew to Sea Island just south and outside of Couver City where it awaited his inspection. The aircraft, one of only a hundred and ninety-eight built, was a fourteen-seat Douglas Commercial dash 2. Recently, as already mentioned, Dyfed had found a pilot he liked and trusted, a young man who had cut his teeth flying by the seat of his pants into remote areas of the north during extreme weather conditions as well as good to deliver supplies to camps in and around on the plateaus and valleys of the Beautiful Northern Land of the Great River. Dyfed had put this pilot on his payroll and kept him busy doing what the man preferred doing most of all, flying. This pilot, Hector Mayo by name, was a Unified Statesian and a friend of John of Munster by dint of fact that the former's father owned the neighbouring land to Muns Salvage. Now, Dyfed changed his plans and made immediate preparations to fly to Nova Troia on his new DC – 2 aircraft. This was as soon as it would take Hector Mayo to get to urban Couver City's airport on Sea Island from cleared field beneath the northern skies. Time was no longer on Dyfed's side, either. Upon receiving Dyfed's suggestion that he wanted him to fly his new DC – 2 aircraft across the Northern Dominion and across the Atlas Sea to Nova Troia, Captain Hector 'Heck' Mayo's metallic sounding telephone voice on the other hand had just hesitated momentarily with a pause before replying, 'yes sir'!

Meanwhile, Deric the Deuce was planning to reside with his mother in Couver City until his fleet caught up with him there. As the Deuce had been officially employed earlier by the War Commission for top-secret duties in the Far East, his being here on the western shores of Merika made him, in a sense, an undercover agent commanding a fleet capable of pirating axis powers in and around the Sea of Jay-pan and the South Ch'in Sea. In this way he could easily kill two birds with one stone if he had to. Some repair and refurbishing work would be needed on his fleet and that would be undertaken at the dockyard in Vacuna (Victoria). Then after that it was back to sea for him, for the war was on and being the captain of an armed merchant fleet, he and his ships were sorely needed off the east coast of Asia.

Dyfed and the Deuce had been listening that evening to the NDBC's news hour. It appeared that the gullible crust of society (which having gone back to the theatre) were already ordering beverages and thronging back to their ring side seats for the greatest most foolish blunder, the most devastating error they could possibly entertain in their entire lives that put each and everyone of us in abject danger and jeopardy. But they (the fools) were ignorant of all of that, for with beverage in hand they took up arms and threw themselves into a war of battles for which there was no defensive armour. Meanwhile, others were also returning to their plush boxes that inhabited the top two rows of the gallery and were set well back from the thronging masses and the turbulence that stretched out before them. Though ignorantly somewhat unsafe, here they would wait, for no one was asking anything of them. They waited the outcome, their fate, and not always too patiently, either. It was apparent now that the curtain was about to rise and war was about to resume again:

'Away we go — cheerio — wave good-bye,' sang the soldiers, their wives and the children. They were the words of the popular song of the day.

(Nicht nacht paddy-wack)

"I am homesick after mine own kind. Oh I know that there are folk about me, friendly faces. But I am homesick after mine own kind.'

EZRA LOOMIS POUND *(PERSONAE:IN DURANCE)*

This new twin-engine aircraft they were flying over the shoulder of the world to Nova Troia was a shiny silver and tan fixed wing job with extended fuel tanks. But since it wasn't meant for commercial use its interior had been designed to accommodate five or six comfortably, along with a mini lounge, kitchen and sleeping quarters for four only. The remaining space was for cargo. Dyfed named the airship the Silver-tipped Hawk. There were only the four of them, Dyfed, Trachmyr, Sundog and Heck the pilot. And there was to be only a few stops until they set down in Nova Troia. Their journey (naturally) would take them over northern Dominion land, southern Greenacres-land, then Pictland before gradually losing altitude again and landing just outside of the refurbished and expanded ancient city of Nova Troia.

Having crossed the continent in a day and a half, flying east against the time, the aircraft droned loudly as they aircraft left the west coast of the Northern Dominion heavy with fuel. Leaving Codfish Bay and nosing their way across the Atlas Sea was quite an adventure for Dyfed, though his pilot took it in stride. Ebreo, of course, had remained behind in Couver City for now under sedation and Trachmyr was to accompany him only as far as Nova Troia. The latter was also going to help Sundog enlist. Due to fuel constraints on this trip the aircraft was totally empty of anything not necessary for the flight. There were no proper beds for he and Trachmyr to rest on and Ceredwyn had packed bags of ham and egg sandwiches for them. As they flew over the ocean Dyfed gazed down from on high through the mists of clouds at its silver rippled surface glinted in the morning sunlight. He recalled the time long ago when he crossed these waters in his little ship the, Aura Maré. He faced a mutiny on that journey, and he remembered the hauling of Hakon's ashes. He laughed out loud but it was not meant to be at the expense of the poor old stupid mutineer Hakon. Once in Nova Troia Dyfed saw Trachmyr and Sundog off from Paddington station for Cardiff while he then quickly made his way to 11 Asmodeas St. to hook up with his contact, Herr Goethe (pronounced Gurt-ah). Heck Mayo preferred to remain at the airfield by the Silver-tipped Hawk and tinker and discover and keep a shine up on her.

Herr Goethe stiffened upright in Teutonic fashion as Dyfed entered the man's library just a step behind the former's batman, Karl-Heinz Heinrich, who was in the process of announcing him. Herr Goethe was a striking looking man with an old and well healed deep scar that ran from his high left temple diagonally down across his face, through his left eye — which had been replaced with a glass one — sliced the lobe of his left nostril and split his upper lip where it stopped. The right side of his face, Dyfed noticed, was smooth and cleanly shaven with a gold-wire rimmed monocle thrust in under his right eyebrow that rested on a fold in his upper cheek. After quickly contemplating Dyfed, the man relaxed the muscle in his cheek and the monocle, attached by a slender gold chain, dropped to his waistcoat. At that moment his arm automatically shot out in a horizontal salute reminiscent of ancient Amor. Dyfed ducked slightly to one side with a natural reflex as Herr Goethe's arm was flung out.

"Heil Wunschritter,' the man stammered out. Then looking more closely at Dyfed he said. 'Herr Lucifer, you don't remember me but I remember you well. You organized our ranks at the gates of Jebus, those many solar cycles ago. You were a young man, somewhat younger than I, yet the generals consulted with you, and the rumour was that you didn't billet in the camp with fellow besiegers but resided at night in one of Jebus' palaces. Of course it was just a silly rumour. But I fought hard, Herr Lucifer, I obeyed orders and helped carry the day.' The man drew out the words 'haaaard' and 'oordeeers' with a slightly guttural and throaty sound.

"A good knight — then,' stated Dyfed politely, though not sarcastically, as he offered his hand in greeting while attentively surveilling this alert and carefully presented man.

"Why — yes of course,' said Herr Goethe, seemingly a little flustered. 'I'm sorry,' he said apologetically and then suddenly appearing exasperated. 'You must be tired after all… oh, what a flight you've had…across the Atlas Sea…I say…mein gott in himmel!' He said the last four words excitedly with a glint in his one eye and a theatrically intoned quiver in his voice. 'Goodnight, Herr Lucifer,' he said. Goodnight! Now! Karl-Heinz… Heel! Now show Herr Lucifer to his quarters at vonce…'

"No! Nicht nacht (not night),' explained Dyfed. 'Ritter (knight),' he replied without showing a trace of amusement at the man's haughty and elite demeanour despite the strange magnification of his somewhat trivial misunderstanding. 'You, Herr Goethe,' Dyfed said pointing his finger at Herr Goethe, 'I said, 'you were obedient…you were subservient and faithful: a good knight. Now, do you have any brandy?'

"Aaah! Of course, mein herr,' replied the man without embarrassment. And as his face resumed its natural seriousness from its former mask-like posture of begging pardon and apology, his back straightened and he drew himself up to presumably even greater imagined magnificence while pressing his heels together with a sharp click. "Karl-Heinz…Heel! Now bring us some brandy for Herr Lucifer.'

Dyfed could easily picture the good knight Goethe…beet red from the sun, his tunic soiled, his body sweating profusely and stinking, his face eager, innocent, and ready, though decorated perhaps with a recently received ruby red welt, bulbous, ugly and jagged, tearing his face in half which he wore like a badge of honour as he stood or likely knelt, standing by and waiting patiently for his next orders. He would have been unbothered, of course, by the noise, violence and death that rose in a big filthy stink all around him. Yes sir by George! Dyfed thought. He was the ideal soldier machine. What need for psychologically designed automatons of today when you have the likes of Herr Goethe?

"Vee haff der Schnapps or brandy, Herr Lucifer?' the other now stated politely in a way of offering up a choice of poisons. This brought Dyfed quickly back. His demeanour, despite the unfortunate disfiguring injury, was not unpleasant; indeed, there was something about the man, Dyfed thought. And for the next day and a half the two men engaged themselves in the business at hand. He was the Wunschritter's listening post here in Albion, so Dyfed had been told by those in the know, but thinking back he felt that the man represented much more than that. On the second day, and with utmost care in order to remain unobserved, Dyfed made his way to a previously arranged rendezvous with an unknown man who delivered him to a man named Germanos, an old soldier and the leader now of the New Progressive Party that ruled the parliament of Angleland now referred to as the UK (also UKA (Unified Kingdom of Albion). There was a quick debriefing for Dyfed at Germanos' underground headquarters inside the city. Here he was given some pertinent advice that had come through from a multitude of fifth columns working behind enemy lines. It would not be thought odd that Dyfed might confer with the first minister, for he and Germanos were old acquaintants having corresponded openly for centuries. Dyfed had even brought up his name with Herr Goethe who had also remembered Germanos from the days in the Divine Land. Arrangements had also been made for Dyfed to hook up with Anaf Ivarsson Konge, the man who had captained Dyfed small fleet to the crusades and the son of the Northman whose merchant business at Bruges Dyfed had bought up back in tenth century. They were to meet later that same day. Anlaf had been attending to Dyfed's interests here at his Steelyards by the Tems River.

Anlaf, who was the chief executive officer for Dyfed's International Enterprise Company (IEC), a commercial-trading branch that functioned under his Commonwealth Union Banking Company (owned by a registered international company called Arcas but was in fact the property of, and solely controlled by, the House of Lucifer), was going to be accompanying him to Gottingen. Dyfed's purpose for this meeting was to brief Anlaf about his new plans, for it had only just come to pass that the latter was to accompany him to Gottingen and he needed preparation. This was all toward an effort to complete a most useful and fact-finding convocation, not necessarily accompanied by commiseration, with the Wunschritter there. Dyfed advised Anlaf that he would depart alone and first, and he Dyfed would follow later. They would be companions, Dyfed said, perhaps for a week or two. Then they would return together on the Silver-tipped Hawk, which Dyfed was using as transportation.

(What's in a name)

'The period of the Great Depression had been an inauspicious time for institutions of democracy generally. It was often democracy, not capitalism, which was seen as the root of the economic catastrophe: the people were too ignorant to elect good governments, and democracy was too inefficient to guarantee the smooth running of industry. Many in the financial and political elites of Europe and America wanted a strongman, a dictator who would guarantee a cheap supply of resources and labour.'

GREG MALONE

Anlaf walked through the marktplatz toward the hotel and found a seat near a fountain in the City of Gottingen. Here he sat to watch the comings and goings and take in the faces of the people of this unfamiliar city while waiting for Dyfed to return from his afternoon meeting. He had been given the name of the Premier Hotel in which to stay by Dyfed and the room appointed to him just happened to be adjoined with another. The folks around him didn't look sad, he thought, despite their circumstances, but they didn't look evil, either. Like elsewhere, in the world these were complicated faces on the whole, some more readable than others. Some had that unstrained matter of fact expressions upon them but others just had that raw and brutish look of stupidity about them. Behind the faces, at least of the former, he could detect minds that were churning out thoughts that he couldn't read nor cared to. And when he caught an interesting expression here or there, who knew — he thought to himself — what up-welling of emotions...what rush of subconscious or even of that unmoving, constant, inaudible tone of the unconscious (like some boisterous crowd of one handed clappers) was it that unequivocally manoeuvred these folks behind the faces forward and into one or other state of determination and perception?

Every so often, walking rigidly upright with hands behind their back, Anlaf often saw two black uniformed men together who were decorated with the identity insignia of the Protective Squad or Schutzstaffel, as they say in their language. Suddenly a small cavalcade of motor chariots (three black limousines) came screeching to a halt in front of the Hotel Premier not far away from the bench that he occupied. Doors opened and slammed and two well-dressed men in civilian suits accompanied by four or five black uniformed men piled out of the mechanised chariots. Quickly, a senior ranking black uniformed officer accompanied by the two men in civvies dashed through the entrance of the hotel and disappeared. The remaining officers remained outside by the limousines and began smoking. A short distance away, two other Protective Squad officers on foot who had walked past Anlaf only a moment or so before had halted their rounds and were standing now, hands still behind their backs. From a position across the street from the hotel Anlaf watched the two Protective Security Squad officers on foot proceeded to watch the commotion across the platz with distracted interest. These latter two were chatting in a friendly manner with each other and looked on now in mild interest at the raid which, apparently, was outside of their sphere of participation. One of the men removed his tall black cap as he spoke to the other and quickly polished the shiny silver skull badge on the front of his cap with the sleeve of his coat then wiped his brow with the sleeve as well before replacing his cap. Then they laughed at something and after a few moments they turned and sauntered on. Anlaf wasn't as concerned for the wellbeing of Dyfed or himself as might be expected under the circumstances. After all, he suspected that at that very moment Dyfed was convening with none other than the Imperial dictator of this demonstrative, radical conservative national socialist-communalist experiment that was taking place in this dangerously new and re-emerged Germanika. And this dictator had been the one who had invited Dyfed to Gottingen for an unprecedented and undetermined pow-wow. Anlaf had simply been asked by his employer and old friend to tag along. As such, his presence had also received the stamp of an official visit, so Dyfed had informed him.

The whole thing though was a strange experience, at least for Anlaf who wasn't used to being catered by top government officials as Dyfed who was much more accustomed to that. The flight over in itself was unique in that in order to pull this visit off safely it entailed that both the Royal Albion Air Force (RAAF) and the Wunschritter's Third Empire's military Loft-kafuffle needed to meet in the skies over Nova Troia together and then with each country's air force flying alongside the Silver-tipped Hawk (one air force on one side, the other air force on the opposite) to accompany the flight to Gottingen. This was for reasons of safety and security and was necessary due to the two countries being at war with one another. The Loft-kafuffle had already visited the skies over Nova Troia for the explicit purpose of dropping bombs on the civilian below in that and other Angleland cities. Not only that but the physical war with its fighting and death was taking place on land on and under the seas with battle ships and submarines. Their two armies were being employed amid rhetoric, resistance fighting and spy versus spy. So Dyfed's flight had to be neutralised by the highest authority of the warring factions involved in view of their protection and for their safe arrival. Happily, both sides of the fray desired their safe transport. Of course, by this time it wasn't just two governments and their armies that were at war. It included allies on each side, as well. In fact by this time a number of countries all over the world that had joined up to support one side or the other. It was as if civilization had divided into two camps and was facing off. There was no one theatre of war either as it had spread all over the world. But the crux of the fighting and the theatre that would determine the final outcome of hostilities was (as always) north-western Europa. Indeed, Anlaf's old hometown of Bruges, along with the first location for Dyfed's House of Lucifer at Tournay (both in Flanders) were in the thick of it. Sealand (Zeeland) along with the Rine (Rene) River valley whose name means re-birth, whose fellow companion is the River Skeid (Schelde pronounced Skeld) whose name essentially means death all empty here into the Sea of Hell that is watched over by the Keltic goddess Nehalennia. It's a bloody swathe of Europa that although not vast, encompassed the homes of many millions of folks.

In Gottingen Dyfed and Anlaf were soon settled into their sumptuous adjoining rooms at the Hotel Premier. Outside of command, Dyfed and Anlaf's presence here as aliens from a hostile nation were thoroughly unknown. Even the hotel staff thought they were Anglanders working for the Third Reich (empire).

Anlaf and the Wunschritter's parallel history went back a long way. It had been over nine hundred years since those two had first met during the scandalous First Crusade; not that the following later crusades were less scandalous, by any means. They weren't; in fact, maybe they were more scandalous. In any case it was then and there, just outside the walls of Jebus, that the Wunschritter and Anlaf –– sweating in the suffocating heat and grime that summed up the place then much like it still does today –– toiled at liberating that miserable city from the infidels for the saviour Jeshua. To those ends the crusaders toiled on behalf and at the beck and call of the Church of Amor.

Back then, of course, the Wunschritter never got even close to being invited into Dyfed's company. Anlaf was there because as stated before, earlier his father had been invited to invest into Dyfed's house. This personal enterprising tenure of Dyfed's — the House of Lucifer — was by the time of the First crusade a thriving mercantile empire that was centred in both the cities of Tourney and Nova Troia.

Tourney (the first location of the House of Lucifer) wasn't far from Bruges where Anlaf's family lived when he was born. It was here that Ivars Herakles Kongelig's (Anlaf's father) amalgamated business was centred. Anlaf's father, as already stated, had once been a Goth pirate ravaging the coasts there and around about during the time of Kysar Julius when the latter first invaded Gaul. The experience of pirating had paid Anlaf's father in dividends and by this juncture he too had been thriving for some time in shipping merchandise along the coasts from Alborg in the land of the Danes to Bruges, part of the land of the Salian Frankens. No doubt his father was honoured to have such an illustrious and prominent man such as Dyfed approach him for such a merger. Years later Dyfed approached Ivars Herakles Kongelig to help deploy a House of Lucifer fleet to at least pretend to support the mayhem and murder needed to liberate the so-called holy lands. It was here that Dyfed (with Ivars recommendation) had entrusted Anlaf to take responsibility for the fleet and the men that Ivars provided Dyfed as sailors and soldiers. Of course, once in Jebus Dyfed's attention was usually focussed on the big picture at hand. So he was virtually unaware of any puffed up minor viziers or ordinance officers such as the Wunschritter. The latter, on the other hand, was more than just a little aware of Dyfed's presence and the position that he held within the hierarchy of the Crusade at this time. But he was vastly distant and subordinate to Dyfed. Anlaf, on the other hand, because of his duties, had closer dealings with the Wunschritter while answering to Dyfed — his de facto employer — at all times. The Wunschritter (that wasn't his name then) and Anlaf were not close in any other respect. In fact Anlaf had recently told Dyfed recently he hadn't liked him at all, just that he simply passed orders down to him in order for the latter's regiment to give assistance when needed. And that's the extent as to how they had known each other. Now, almost fourteen degrees in time later, or about another thousand Earth years, this jumped up tin-pot dictator was actually daring to call his somewhat provincial, political movement cult an actual New Order with imperial overtures; in fact he was calling it The Third Empire. 'Huey, pork slap and bull-chutney,' Dyfed said upon hearing that act two of the Great War was being hailed as the rising of the Third Empire. His comment on that subject stuck, and in later days he referred to the succession of empires as the three stooges of slapstick. 'The Wunschritter doesn't get to make decisions like that,' he flatly told anyone who would listen. 'Don't worry,' he added, 'the Second Empire isn't over and is far from being finished yet, anyway. Nor will it be over either until the fat lady sings or at least until Cornelius-Felix and Giorgi Posh tells us she's done singing. And that ain't happened yet.'

Anlaf continued to while away his time on his bench by the marktplatz, speculating about the goings on at their hotel across the street. Mechanical chariots — still idling by the curb — and uniformed men continued to mill around the hotel entrance. And as he watched and waited, the city moved otherwise undisturbed around him. Nearby, once again, the two black uniformed Protective Squad officers with the silver skulls on their tall caps, the same ones that he had seen strolling passed earlier, had returned again. They had advanced now as far as the peripheral of senior authority (with its expectant commotion permeated with fear) and they were now standing motionless again. Then they each lit up a cigarette and puffed out a bellow of smoke. Apparently, they were bent on watching their fellow protective squad officers who also had silver skulls atop their tall caps, mill and smoke as they too waited. There they were, all waiting for some senior, skull-badge capped, black uniformed and stern faced protective squad officer (assisted by four plain clothed special protective squad officers carrying nine millimetre Lugar pistols in their pockets) to complete their bully type domination and terrorisation of some selected individual and quickly isolated the victim before bringing him or her outside the hotel for a quick show of domination and force only to whisk them away in the motor chariot cavalcade and into oblivion.

Since idle waiting in anticipation wasn't Anlaf's strongest point, his thoughts easily turned casually to the reminiscent discussion Dyfed and he had had on just the previous afternoon. It was shortly after they had returned to their adjoined hotel rooms, both having had a short but amiable meeting and light tea with the Wunschritter. Apart from the Crusades (and Anlaf being in the employ of the House of Lucifer for most of his life), Dyfed and Anlaf hardly knew each other. This had now become a time to rectify that.

"My first memory of you, Kongelig,' Anlaf now recalled Dyfed telling him the day before, 'was in Bruges. That beautiful house of your father's facing the Dijver canal near the Marktplaz. It was a fine home, and one fit for an old pirate king like your father, lord Ivars Herakles Kongelig: Indeed, by then he was the epitome of a merchant… home from the market, and a pirate out a Viking now come home from the seas. That was your father, all right. And like you, he was loyal to me through and through.' Dyfed could be so gentle and complimenting at times, Anlaf thought. Dyfed, he recalled, had given a non-condescending happy little laugh and pulled his glasses off. Then, with one hand lightly gripping one arm of his glasses and his alert eyes darting around him, Anlaf remembered how he twirled them around like a whirl-i-jig for a moment before putting them back on. 'Loyal,' Anlaf recalled him saying, 'that is, by hard and lean times in the early years as well as the easy and fat ones since: A time when he no longer had a need to apply himself to stay afloat. What was his background, anyway?' Dyfed had asked Anlaf.

Anlaf had assumed Dyfed had long known the answer to that question but was asking simply for the retelling and the easy conversation to while the time until supper was called. Although Anlaf knew that Dyfed regarded him as a trusted friend, he had also learned long ago that Dyfed wasn't a man to ask any man he didn't trust a question to which he didn't already know the answer. That didn't apply to him, of course, but habits die-hard.

"Father was a northern Goth as we called them then,' Anlaf answered. 'His second cousin many times removed was Sigtrig Ivarsson, the marauder of the northern seas, king of Jorvik in ancient Albion as well as Dublin and the Emerald Isle. He told Dyfed again (for who knows how many times) that his father was also related to Emma, sister of Northman Duke Richard. After the demise of her first husband AEthelred, Emma had become the wife of Knut, son of Sweyn Forkbeard who was the last great leader of the Daane people to go a viking and pocket countries as if he were shoplifting; even countries like Angleland back in the day.

"But you know all of that,' he had told him. 'Father also claimed to have had Dorian blood, too, you know. Indeed, he was a prince of the blood, which is why Herakles appears in his name. Once, long, long ago — so I've been told — these Dorians had been northerners and part of the Daane people. And this is what father told me. They were northerners in the wake of some great Earthly power shift or disappearance of civilization, possibly the Earthly desolation and devolution of the Hyperborean civilization that you, Dyfed, have referred to on occasion. It seems there was some kind of pole shift that swung it a whopping forty degrees from the north-western sector of the great Superior Lake in the eastern half of Merika to where it is today in the mid Arctic Ocean above Greenacres-land. Very quickly the entire area along the coastal regions that circumference the Arctic Ocean grew cold. It was especially noticeable in the sector from Iceland east and west as far as the Bering Strait. This coast was once much warmer than today and was once warmer than even the north coast of Merika opposite it. The climate from Iceland to the Bering was much like the White Sea is today, he told me, and it was rumoured that the Hyperboreans had pleasure resorts throughout the area. Then during the commotion that followed, thousands of Earth years ago, these Doric folk moseyed on south from our northern lands where they entered ancient history of the new age as sea going folks, occupying many of the White Seas' islands, most notably the Pelops and the southern island of Kreta. Among them was a famous man named King Albris, I was told.'

"Doctor Albaris, actually,' Dyfed interrupted to correct him. 'Yes, I know about that,' he said. 'He was a Master and the teacher of Aesculapius (also Asclepius). It may be, however, the two never met and that the latter got his hands on the formers' papers. And the name Kongelig means...what? in your language, kingly?' Dyfed stated rather than asked.

"Dad was a king, alright, and in his own right, too,' Anlaf answered. 'But I am simply a Count, and jolly glad for it. Fewer responsibilities.'

"You're the Count of Victory,' Dyfed answered, 'but privately I shall call you Parasolo. You are greater than one unaccompanied, you are an amalgamation, a combination of virtues and you have achieved the things that you have because you took responsibilities under my command, much to my satisfaction and pride. I am the chronicler that you will chronicle, Anlaf, Dyfed said. One day you will write my story.'

At that point of their conversation a knock had come to Anlaf's door, for it had been in his parlour where the two of them had been sitting. A waiter who looked Latino, possibly Catalanian, addressed him.

"Ah, Herr...I-vars-son, yes?'

"Yes,' Anlaf answered.

"Ah, zis ees evening menu, plise,' he said haltingly, pronouncing the words more or less approximately to the Anglish tongue's equivalency. He held out a tray with a large two or three page hotel menu on it.

"I'll have a spaghetti Carbonara with a Chianti,' Anlaf said without thinking or bothering to reach out for the menu.

"'They don't do a spaghetti Carbonara here,' he heard Dyfed say behind him and out of sight of the waiter. 'They do sausages, sauerkraut with beer,' Suddenly the waiter had taken on a humorous animated look. He stood stark still, his expressively animated eyes shining in his half turned head with a slight smile on his rather full lips.

"Ah,' he exclaimed, 'Herr Dyfed Lucifer ees visiting you, no? Please…'ees menu,' he said holding extending out the tray again.

"No need,' Anlaf had only just managed to say when Dyfed's voice rang out flatly from behind.

"I'll have a wiener schnitzel and sour-kraut sandwich with a couple of litres of beer. Never mind any hors d'oeuvres,' he added, 'they're already in my martini. Maybe we need to order some more kalamata olives, though, and more vodka, if this damn war will allow it, of course. Oh, and tell him to hold all strains of um-pah-pah and accordion music that seem always to be wafting up from below: That, and any other oxymoron that might come from anywhere within earshot of me and my sandwich. Thank you.'

The waiter, whose facial expression suddenly changed into a ludicrous mask of hilarity, seemed to be confused. He hesitated before saying quite carefully…"one spaghetti Carbonara with Chianti, one Wiener schnitzel and sour-kraut sandwich (he made a strange face here and slowed down his words while he verbally and mentally constructed this part) weez…ahem…wis many beers, and another bottle of fine vodka.' He quickly wrote something down and slowly backed up out from the door, bowing and scraping a couple of times as he went. He wasn't snivelling but decidedly fawning — as was the custom of waiters at this time. Anlaf then tightly closed the door.

"You were saying?' Dyfed said as Anlaf returned.

"Yes, it was a Europaean tour for one of Isabelle's and my anniversaries just before the war. Do you remember? Anyway, my highlight, I have to admit — which was my ulterior motive for vacationing— was before returning to work in Nova Troia we went to the Isle of Mona to take in the motorcycle races. Have you ever been there?' he asked Dyfed.

It was then that Dyfed told Anlaf that he had been born there. Then while Anlaf listened he told him the story of his early life over dinner. Later, Dyfed talked to Anlaf nonstop about Ebreo, as well. Apparently, so Dyfed told him, Ebreo's name had popped up the most while the *pack* had been investigating what became known as the blindsided affair. This was the sudden advance of Communalism that had damaged the *pack's* progress to bring valued succour to the hoi polloi in the new and rich industrial age. Ebreo had been fingered as the rat by investigators among the Masters in the fifth dimension who, apparently, were unknown to Dyfed. As always, this condition pivoted around a universal law dictating the 'when' and the 'if' of the need to know. But Dyfed doubted that general consensus, for he said that he couldn't make the connection between them or realise Ebreo's motive. Nor was he cognizant of any reward the man might have received, even a non-material reward that wasn't in the Haploid's vocabulary anyway. And Ebreo wasn't an idealist; rather he was pragmatic and logical. He was a skilled forger and metallurgist besides and as such he was a decided asset to, and decidedly on the side of Western Civilization. He was not our enemy. This, Dyfed told Anlaf, was what he believed. National Communalism, Dyfed had already known, would not be such an asset. The communalist part of the equation, like the three already established religions of monotheism, was in essence (Dyfed noted) the antithesis of Western Philosophy though it advertised itself as a companion to it. But it wasn't. Furthermore, the Wunscheritter's National Socialistic Communalism was merely an extension of this religion, no matter how misguided it was. And modern notions of fascist idealism or extreme Capitalism weren't assets or proponents for Western Philosophy in any way. Although rife with pseudo Western Philosophy, it actually hindered the Western Civilization due to its eroding values. And in the end it had certainly stalled the true and long awaited Golden Dawn of an advanced Western Civilization from materializing a lot more than it had helped it. Fascism and Capitalism that worked hand in hand during the Amoran Empire was only marginally different than today, Dyfed had said. Where Amor had no middle class and plunder kept the economy rolling, modern Capitalism invented the debt system (in camera) as a crutch to do much the same. In fact money, or actually money debt, was the new Capitalist slavery. With the advent of Jeshuanism and its absorption into Abramism, modern Western Philosophy and its Civilization certainly had profited by the logistics of necessities, as well as the math and the engineering needed to fabricate the great monuments which the Church of Amor (for an example) demanded in order to show off their power and the tool with which to impress the rabbling and babbling masses.

The same attributes to enhance Western Civilization took place in a similar manner during the First Empire, too. But during the time directly after the First Empire's disintegration, Europaean cities had become squalid and miserly. They were pig stys where, if the architecture around them was much higher than their heads, citizens were in constant danger of them collapsing and falling on those very heads. Since the hey-day of Amor, nothing like the Pantheon (designed and built a thousand years before) had even an outside chance of being successfully constructed. It was not until the renewal of enlightenment that buildings were once again safe to pedestrians on the street. In order to accomplish that ingenuity again, and ensure pedestrians freedom from fear of being buried under avalanches of falling destruction caused by a total failure of engineering, Western Civilization was forced to go back to the basics, to the drawing board, to redesign and improve. New infrastructure was needed, as new constructive distractions and baubles were being sought after and applauded. And a new kind of person was needed. They were folks whose decorum and morality were not to be undermined by any misunderstanding of what the *pack* called newly adopted individual rights which they were currently and furiously trying to push through and get picked up by western civilization's society with minimal ill effects. In addition, thought, the people's needs and aspirations must not become reliant on the expectations and ideals which those posh, demanding noble Haploids had. Instead they needed to embrace those of Socratic-type philosophers of early civilization and later with Kierkegaard, Nietzsche, and to a lesser degree, Sartre. As well, diversely imaginative thinkers, artists, poets and musicians, engineers, mathematicians, writers, scientific truth seekers, dreamers, and sundry teachers juxtaposed thereof desperately needed to be embraced and believed. These would not necessarily include the full works of folks like Dostoyevsky or even Lawrence but probably should include Shaw, Hume, Schweitzer, Dimnet, Ieseley, Kaufmann, among others. These, the *pack* and their company knew were the true friends of Western Civilization. These were the acolytes and the high priests of Western Philosophy: Not those tardy, trendy idealists seeking programs of religion and politics and social adjustments anymore that new-age zoot-suiting bongo-beats which their henchmen continuingly forced on the folks of the world, much –– we might add –– to the latter's distinctive disadvantage.

Other advances in matters of finance proliferated at this time, too, with debit and credit through loans and investment that had already been implemented and put into use by astute Venetian clerics in Italia, now becoming advanced even more. Known as transfer banking, by the time the successful program of the Will to Crusade and the cry to reclaim the holy land from the Saracen heretics took hold and was heard across the land, banking and redeeming credit in order to avoid the danger of robbery had become all the rage. Even Dyfed's newly up and running again Commonwealth Union Bank had been employing this service to customers, back in the day. All of this, apparently, had been some of the well-discussed topics during Dyfed's attendance at the summit meetings among the Masters recently in the fifth dimension. And yet Dyfed could still not see any association between the enemies of Western Civilization or its philosophy and Ebreo. But he trusted Cato and Morgant, and implored them to make no mistakes in the matter. But it seemed (so Dyfed was told at that time) that the accusations were coming from upon high. It was even rumoured that Thrax was behind it.

Anlaf was suddenly brought back from his daydreaming and smack dab into the middle of the marketplaz at this point of time just as a black uniformed man who was dressed in tall cap decorated with a silver skull came dashing back out of the hotel amid a lot of unnecessary noise. Anlaf noticed that two of the four emerging plain clothed officers were roughly escorting a handcuffed man out into the open. They held him tightly, showing him around briefly to the gawkers and passer-bys as if to say –– 'look here, this is the power we have over all of you.'

Anlaf quickly stood up onto the bench in order to get a better view of it over the heads of the passing pedestrians and police who surrounded the man. Suddenly, he caught a glimpse of the pale Latino waiter who had politely served he and Dyfed their last evening's supper. Just then, the clock towers that were scattered around the city all began to strike. What a false, or at least unnatural, moment in space/time it seemed to be, he thought. How humanly sterile and forced these bells sounded, not in themselves, but at this time and moment. It was the moment itself that seemed false. How overtly technical and how thoroughly unnecessary, even tragic, that moment now seemed. And it was the bells that triggered the thought and exposed it to Anlaf's inner consciousness. However, under the circumstances it provided a pleasant enough street ambiance which, for Anlaf's exterior, seemed to be its only merit.

(Bogey and Mephistopheles)

'The difference between Communism and the Hitler faith is very slight.'
PAUL JOSEPH GOEBBELS

Dyfed returned from the meeting with the Wunschritter about mid afternoon. There was fear and loathing in the air they breathed that was all over the continent now as third empire controlled media reports were all talking about an impending invasion of occupied Europa by Allied forces from the UKA. No more mention in the media of the failed blitz over the skies of Nova Troia some years back that had been in an effort by the Third Empire to bomb Angleland into submission. Neither that nor the more recently postponed, then finally cancelled sea invasion of Angleland by the pale eyed soldier machines of the self proclaimed Third Empire came to fruition. Of course, that plan could never be reinstalled now that the big mistake was in the bag. The bait had been Rus, and the Wunschritter never hesitated in his duty. Of course it was suicidal, but none of his generals or political advisers could tell him differently. The die was cast. Certain people of uncertain allegiance, somewhere, were rubbing their hands in anticipation.

Shortly after his return from his first meeting with the Wunschritter, Dyfed drank a glass of water and Anlaf ate a light snack in the hotel's Ristorante a la Mode. Immediately after leaving the hotel they crossed the street in the direction of the marktplatz and took possession of a bench on the divide between the platz and a treed park that lined the road directly opposite the hotel. In fact, it was the same bench that Anlaf had commandeered earlier when he witnessed their frail and bewildered waiter being arrested by a bevy of beefy security police. Thinking of it now, he told Dyfed what he had seen and how the hotel management had pronounced total ignorance of any such incident and denied that there had been any arrest. Only after Anlaf's insisting that he had witnessed it from across the road and how he felt concern for the unlucky man's wellbeing, had he then been told not to concern himself over it. It had been for their own safety, he had been told. Apparently, the slightly built, polite and well-mannered waiter had been a dangerous assassin. As Anlaf hadn't heard of an assassin who wasn't dangerous, his trust in the official report (it was decided then that Anlaf must be detained and informed about the report in length) was reversely proportional to the trouble they went to in order to convince him. The management explained to Anlaf that this Communalist (and former Capitalist) who was not part of the Aryan race had secured the job there at the Premier Hotel only shortly before he and Dyfed's arrival. Apparently, it was a well-organised attempt to kill them both in their sleep. Oh yes, there were witnesses. He had an accomplice, too, Anlaf was told. The police security probably already had the accomplice in custody. Anlaf told Dyfed that it was his long lingering glance at the concierge; his hesitancy to speak (though obviously having something on his mind to say) that was followed by his unconvincing statement that spooked them in the end. Anlaf said that speaking in a hoarse whisper to the concierge, he attempted to convey to the latter that he'd be sure to let Dyfed his companion know. He told Dyfed that he thought that he been very convincing in his insincerity and of his inexcitability.

Dyfed and Anlaf chatted about how Germanika had undergone immense change. It had transformed from an open and cultured nation-state into an abysmal oligarchy that was failing its folks and failing its leadership role in the world alongside other Western Civilization nation-states. Let's face it, we were all struggling with inconsistencies of democracy and coming to grips with that which gripped us all by the short and curlies, namely the great mystery of divine authority and its very human henchmen. This authority didn't put the food on the table but it did put a pecker on the post, as they say. A pecker with a long beak that attempted to peck us all into parcels of categories behind some drawn but unseen line in the sand. Somehow, this line, this divine line, with the help of agents of law and order (which was fast crumbling into order and justice — which was not the same thing) demarcated each of those categories' shifting perimeters of acceptability. And it did it in just about every theatre found in life from fun to functionality. Anyway, as for Germanika, their backsliding had not all happened since the Great War, but only in act two and the rise of the Wunschritter.

Dyfed explained how impressed the Wunschritter is about the hold which the Church of Amor has had over the masses and how they go about mesmerising them. He told Anlaf that in his initial onslaught today he had tried to put the seed in his head about questioning the wisdom of the crusades and how it was no different today. After all, it is apparent that these excursions to liberate the so called holy-land were the most memorable and glorious phase of his entire life, until now, that is. In fact a friend told me about a very prominently displayed swastika on a bridge wall that is joined to the great cathedral complex near where the Wunschritter used to live after he returned to Germanika from the land of the Philistines. I have every reason to believe that is where the Third Empire symbol originated, in his mind. I don't think he has a true concept of what it stands for other than in his mind it is an ancient Aryan symbol and one that is currently misused as much as the word Aryan is. The crusades were brutal. I don't think he ever reflected on that fact for an instant. I'm not convinced that he is a psychopath as Morgant and Karatakos are. I'll speak plainly to you Anlaf, he said.

"The Wunschritter himself is not a major player among the circle of the coven of Zeus in this theatre, but he is a pivotal one. Indeed, he may only be a patsy, a voluntary — or possibly involuntary — dupe who having been well programmed by his underlying culture in general has become easily influenced, flattered and conned. He then rose somehow to become a convenient necessity on behalf of the Haploids who are (and remain) his mentors and financiers. All the other achievements are his. From the start the secret power elite aren't going to back a loser. This doesn't excuse him of anything, of course. Ultimately he is weak and pathetic. He is the product of his mind, his fantasies. But we all have weaknesses, don't we Kongelig? I've wasted my time coming here. I'm not going to get anywhere with him, he is too far gone, I'm afraid.'

"I think he is an evil man,' Anlaf said. 'He has not only caused the death of millions with his empire building through war, he has also set out to cull and exterminate humans indiscriminately who do not follow his Idea, his faith. Other legitimate folks die in order to make room for his vision.'

"Don't be foolish,' snapped Dyfed in retort to his remark. 'That is your monotheist culture program talking: Your Jeshua the Nazarean would have never said such a thing, or thought him evil, I'm certain of that. Neither would have Sanct Niklaus (Santa Claus) or any of the great cynics and stoics that came before; all of them students of the non-monotheist, western philosophy religion. The monotheist part was obviously a temporary bridge only that was simply to provide perspective. But now the river is swollen beyond it old banks and has flooded the plains. Think about what you just said. What makes you think that the grand scheme is his vision? I'm not convinced. We are back to lesson one in reason and logical thinking all over again, dear friend. Evil is total absence of non-evil. Evil is the thorough corruption of consummate perfection that can only be considered within a universal view. Evil actually has no form and does not exist other than in a negative form. It is the absence of total perfection. Existence in the eternal moment is an unqualified Perfection, which means that life and consciousness forming cause and effect is universal but not necessary perfection. So presently for us there is only life-conscious defined by phenomenon. Nothing else exists. So what we think is real is actually relative. Bad has no form, it is just the absence of good, like moonlit darkness is the absence of full sunlight so bad and darkness don't exist. But we can create them, we can conjure up our idea of what might be and give it a genius. So our perception creates them. But whereas total absence of light is total darkness (which has no other definable form), so life-evil is the total absence of life-perfection that means too that it doesn't exist. Therefore, no human being can possibly be evil because we do exist (apparently) as such, and all because of the genius of life. No matter how weak and bad we become we still have life that defines us, and non-life has no further definition. Only in death can the physical presence be said to be evil. The Wunschritter is no different. He may be in pursuit of evil, he may be influenced by evil but he cannot be evil per sé; nobody can. They are just weak and pathetic human beings, that's all. As far as the latter is concerned, this speaks to your statement that legitimate folks die in order to make room for his vision. In this you would be correct in stating how disgusting and evil his volition is.'

'And I now know, however, that he is not the supreme architect of his rise to power. He was promoted. Yes, impressionable folks promoted him but also, and most importantly, he was promoted by powerful entities that didn't need him in order to promote humanity in general, but rather they needed him to destroy humanity. These can only be the Haploids. And as Haploids in today's vast world of two billion folks and counting, they need someone to act as their representative within the hierarchy of humanity that is strewn among the jump hoops and red tape of the modern world in order to destroy the fragile world of the third dimension. It is not as simple as it once was, say like during the Amoran Empire. Although, this hoop jumping complication is of their doing, too. However, the destruction of the order of the government of Frankia in the eighteenth century CE, no matter how poor and impinging on the hoi polloi that former government had been, it shows to what extent these Haploids could still wield power. At that time they managed to promote a committee that brought slaughter and mayhem to poor folks' lives while eliminating the pseudo contenders to what is considered by the Haploids to be their throne. You don't mess with these guys. The hoi polloi fought back, though, and Leone the Pseudo Emperor managed to get a brief foothold: But that, too, all came too naught in the end. I visited Leone on Elba and he insured me that it was only a temporary set back. I don't blame Wellington, he told me, adding that he was only doing his establishment implemented duty. And there's the bugbear. They are truly un-human devils and demons that pray upon humanity, as you know, though very few of our species comprehend this. Third dimensional species know very little, other than what cultural religion teaches and that is mostly false as the Haploids control the leading religions. I finally understood that when I came to understand the commonality that has been maintained in the messages of the ancient prophets. Jeshua the Nazarean being virtually one of the more memorable whose original script was to abolish religion and promote the word and the truth. To fulfil (in this sense) is to correct and make right.[86] And this came from sources which had not been vetted by such entities as the curia special executive of the Church of Amor, for example, and others.'

'Unfortunately, through their brilliant fabrication, we have now lost the syllabus of the word and the truth behind what earlier prophets actually said about our phenomena.'

"Ah, Dyfed,' Anlaf said. 'You forget that a long time ago my family converted from the reverence of Thor and Odin to Jeshuanism. My father didn't have your aplomb nor your sense of philosophy and background in education, nor your theosophical tendencies, either.'

"Really,' Dyfed answered. 'I don't have anything against you, my friend. Not you or any other Jeshuan, nor any Abramis or Ishlamite either, for that matter. No matter what denomination or sect of the cult-lore that folks cling to, we are all victims, after all. And I love you all for you are all my people. Its the god which your folks prop up, this tin god is what I despise and for the lie that it is,' said Dyfed. 'At least the Ishlamites got it partly right. What was it; something that the prophet said? "If you wish to further god's greatness and celebrate his (its) magnificent magnanimity, if you truly wish to serve god in this way, serve humanity! The genius of God didn't say anything further here; just serve humanity. Mo'mad the Prophet did get it right, so did Jeshua before him and so did Pythagoras, Aristippus, Socrates, Bodhidharma, Laozi (also Lao Tzu) and Zhuangzi (also Zhuang Zhou). These all symbolized the symbolic dragon which is the symbol of the highest spiritual essence that embodies wisdom, strength and the divine power of transformation; it is the square root of the substance water itself. There is only one god on the horizon, and that god is the essence of life, such as our selves. There is no life without It. Therefore nothing actually exists outside It (God's work), also known as Krishna. The mind is the only conduit to It from outside the eternal moment. When it comes to It the organized religions of the people have got it all wrong. And before I forget, I did question the Wunschritter on who his promoters and financiers were and how was it that the war started like a sports event. That didn't seem to embarrass him, either.'

"I remember,' Dyfed said, 'back when I was first thinking as to how I would respond to the Wunschritter's invitation for me to visit him in war torn Europa, I began by summoning up the description of my world. I began by prioritising my aspirations and expectations, along with planning how I intended to go forward under the circumstances. At that time I had just returned to Couver City from the north and my home away from home in the northern wilds,' he continued, 'I had half expected to have received some kind of communication by mail from you, who I had immediately written to, and from another close friend of mine, Theoderic Theoderikson, or Derik the Deuce as he was commonly known, back in the day. You may not remember him but you have certainly heard of his father, Theoderic the Great, Emperor of the Western Amoran Empire who

---

86 'Do not think I have come to abolish the Law or the Prophets; I have come…to fulfil them.' (Matthew 5:17)

was another acquaintance of mine as well. Theoderic Theoderikson is my stepson; more about him later. But instead I was suddenly surprised by his presence in person when one afternoon that old pirate's arrived in Couver City. The other occurrence, of course, had been the sudden ramping up in the direction of Scene One, Part Two of the Great World War along with a world wide outbreak of Virus that had left anything from fifty to one hundred million dead even before the fighting renewed. It became a toss up as to which calamity was the more fearful and devastating, either the war or the virus. In the end the consensus was that it was an even draw.'

"Deric the Deuce strode into my large, outer reception room. He was still a lithe and muscular man though not as tall as me and his face was leathery and weather beaten from years of exposure to sea and sun. We clasped hands amiably and I lead him back into my large, cluttered workroom. I motioned him towards two comfortable, cushioned armchairs made by Chesterfield where we made ourselves comfortable with a couple of bottles of Scotch each within easy reach. Although we hardly knew each other despite our connection through Ceredwyn, and briefly during the crusades, many said that he and I were a lot alike in some ways. We are both tough, opinionated, and unswerving in our dedication to integrity, yet we were each altruistic in an idealistic way as well. By this time in my life I have a great deal of experience, a lot more than the Deuce, but that old pirate had stowed away a lifetime of swashbuckling adventures from a career on the high seas that was second to none, never mind what he had learned from his father, Theoderic the Great. It was Deric the Deuce who alerted me of the beautiful northwestern coast of Merika. You see, he had accompanied the famed and incomparable privateer Frank Drager on his circumnavigation of the world in 1577/8 CE and had come across this paradise. The voyage had been sponsored and promoted by the old Virgin Queen herself. Anyway, all during his life Deric the Deuce had been in association with powerful men who ruled powerful companies and mercantile empires as I had done, but was close to the great game in a way that was somewhat different from me. Also, he and I were both relatively wealthy from our own labours and were in no way strangers to the affairs of men as acted out by individuals upon the world stage. So we took this time to put our heads together in order to make some sense of just what was happening on the big scene — where many of those same players were well known to us — and how it would play out. These were players such as Wunschritter, who was first up to come to mind. So, with me having being tucked out of the way over there in the western wilds for some time, Deric the Deuce had a more updated version of the Europaean program to work with than I did. But he had never been party to the elite society of world finance in quite the same way that I had despite the fact that he controlled one of the largest trading companies in the world.'

'I remember,' said Dyfed, 'I watched the wispy swirls of cigar smoke drift away from us across the warm room toward one of the large open windows that opened out into a sultry August evening. The Deuce and I had been listening to the evening news on NDBC, the national broadcasting station over there. It was apparent to us that the war would commence again soon and start off with an invasion of some kind. As we listened to the voice of the Wunschritter that shrieked at us across the radio airwaves from Barlein ... I'm sure it was all due to the poor quality of the transmission.... we heard him accuse the allies of unbridled aggression while warning us of swift retaliation. Indeed, I remember him asking specifically what should be done about these mad Anglemen who were running around Europa starting fires when typically that was what he were doing, not the Anglelander. Talk about a projection! Anyway, it was a change of heart on his part for during the previous century he had (in his own way) applauded the Angleland Empire, and had even tried to mimic its poise and demeanour. Indeed, he even adapted many of its so-called attributes for the purpose of his own. So, who changed his mind on this? I pointedly asked him this afternoon when the Wunschritter and I were face to face. But he waffled and began to strike out. 'Whoa, whoa! Hold on there Wunschritter, I said. Don't start shrieking at me over this, I've had an ear full already. Certainly, you are on record of criticising the Empire's imperial exploitation, as I have done, and many Angleman has done before you. But now you tell me just now that you intend to employ the same capitalistic tactics in your dream empire fuelled by slave labour. So, what's up with that? And the Angleland Empire isn't of the same mould as the First Empire and only casual in respect the Second Empire, the Holy Amoran Empire of which the Angleland Empire is only an extension, nothing more. The fact is this, Wunschritter; I said. The Angleland Empire is the crowning achievement of not so much ancient Albion itself — although it was to Albion that it fell to, not Germanika, neither the Lowlands nor the Highlands or even to Frankia, certainly another contender — but rather it represents the crowning achievement of specifically the Amoran Empire combined with the global Second Holy Amoran Empire.'

'So, Anlaf, I left the concept of the Third Amoran Empire hanging. When it does come it will not only be the successor to the second or Holy Empire, the heir to the First Empire, but also to the fruits of western philosophy more or less as we know it today. Otherwise there will be no Third Empire, only some form of revolution and enormous conflict and a reverting back to another First Empire or the Dark Age if not an earlier epoch. One shudders to think, Anlaf. And as the great Amoran Empire that had been ruled by the Caesars Augustus of old, and the present Holy Amoran Empire ruled first by kings and emperors, then by Vicars of Jeshua from Amor whose satellite kingdoms are is still ruled by constitutional monarchy or by constitutional republics, both governed by and large by democratic influences. Both these empires have occurred during our lives, I told the Wunschritter.'

"There is precious little difference between the first and the second empires of which we are speaking about here,' I continued to tell him this morning,' Dyfed told Anlaf. 'Precious little difference, I tell you. And that includes the current sovereign king, the son of Queen Victory and brother (some say half brother) of Giorgi Posh. Oh yes, the organized Jeshuan religion has been paramount in piloting the disaster of the Second Empire through the centuries, unlike that of the First Empire. But some good has come out of it. The Amoran Empire, however, managed only on greed. But it spawned the program of the Church of Amor and the present empire which also thrives on greed in all of its attributes as well, plus the Church of Amor's new and improved and rearranged Jeshuan cult insert that hasn't faired much better than the pagan cults.'

"But as I watched the Deuce's cigar smoke curl up toward the open window that day as we sipped out scotch whisky, and a word not having passed between us for some time as we each contemplated the future, I was suddenly brought back to Earth.

"He wants to control the world," I had heard the Deuce say to me just as I had decided to get up and turn on the high overhead electric ceiling fan. A commercial jingle was coming over the radio... 'Peoples' credit jewellers, peoples' credit jewellers," went the catchy jingle of the radio sing-song commercial.

"Why, absolutely, I answered him as I flicked off the radio and the hindrance of the silly little jingle. He actually thinks that he can control the world. Menstruating Mother of God, it's even worse than we though, by Jove.

"Surely he hasn't a chance,' the Deuce then asked me. So I told him that unless the Wunschritter knows something we don't; that is he knows somebody we don't know he knows, then he has no chance at all. And my guess is that's why he thinks I'm here now. But what the Deuce and I kept wondering that day was what was pushing him on? What glimmer of hope did he have to confidently raise the stakes at this time and to bet it all?

"Is the Wunschritter a madman?' Anlaf asked Dyfed.

That was something a lot of folks wanted to know and, again, partly it was why Dyfed was here today. However, he told Anlaf that he didn't think that he was insane, exactly, for apparently a psychiatrist, a certain Dr Ziggy Fraud had had an opportunity to examine him a few years back at the end of Act One of the world conflict when the Wunschritter was hospitalized. He has suffered during the conflict and at the end of the war had been gassed. He recovered nicely but was unable at first during the intermission to stand on his own two feet and go about his business as other soldiers had. His superiors thought he had psychological problems. After all, some said, he fancied himself as an artist but unfortunately he was a rather poor artist (and you know how artists deal with criticism and rejection). He had visions of grandeur and was angry that nobody recognized him for what he really was -- a brilliant mind gifted in originality. He thought himself a creative genius. Dr Fraud, on the other hand, did not diagnose the Wunschritter with disassociation or paranoia or any other description that more correctly painted him as a pathetic little loser who was being consumed by hatred. But here Dyfed told Anlaf that one Santa Claus day (back in the fifteenth century CE) while escaping from Italia and agents of the Curia, that he had been passing through the Arlberg when (while in a funk and total despair) he had broken his leg in a slippery fall of some distance down a rocky slope. Fortunately a man passing by towing an evergreen tree discovered him shortly before he had succumbed to hypothermia. He bundled him up and loaded him in his sleigh then took him home where he reset the broken bone and administered to his psychological well being, for, Dyfed at this point told Anlaf, at that point in his life he was in quite a state. This benefactor's name is Dr Jung who asides from medicine became a doctor of the mind. This involved and combined both biological and spiritual science. Dr Fraud and Jung kept in touch after Dyfed spent the seasonal holydays with Dr Jung and saw the local ritual of the Santa Klaus tree with presents for children hanging under it and on it for the very first time in his life. Dyfed was responsible for helping to bring that custom out of the Tyrol and introducing it to the rest of the western world. Anyway, according to this Dr Jung who having diagnosed the Wunschritter from afar with other pertinent information he had, his diagnose was that the Wunschritter was a person suffering with disassociation but stopped short of pronouncing him as an unconscionable psychopath. That's the real reason I'm here,' said Dyfed to Anlaf. 'What I need to know was who were his friends? At least people who thought he was their friend or even thought he was under their control. I felt I knew the answer to that, though. Dan Velchanos who is also known as boy Zeus came to mind first, and after him was Giorgi Posh, head of the House of Hunover that had been transplanted from Germanika to Angleland.'

"Look what the Wunschritter has done with his branch of the great socialist movement that somehow emerged with a different character from the brainchild of Charles Munze,' said Anlaf. 'We thought Terrainsky was stronger and first out of the gate near the end of Act One of the war. But now the tables are turned.'

"I told the Deuce that day that I believed the Wunschritter will invade Mother Rus a fellow non-democratic socialist regime, but for the life of me I didn't know why he would chance it, especially since they had a pact in place. And as of now he has done so. And to aggravate the Unifed Kingdom and the Unified Sates as well, by railing against them a great deal and in highly denigrating terms as to their ethnic transfusion, then he isn't mad in the sense of insane, he is simply beyond common reality in a bad and dangerous way. It isn't the first time we have seen strange, unexplainable actions taken by intelligent generals and upstart leaders. Leone di Buonaparte was an exception and a brilliant and progressive exception in many ways, too, like Tamir the Lame. But what can I say, heh? Athaulf von Braunau the Winschritter is clearly not another Leone. Yet he is in possession of certain knowledge that we clearly aren't. And that is precisely what I said to him at our meeting today. The question for me since you've invited me here, Herr Wunschritter,' I said to him, 'is will you tell me what it is that I don't know? Will you include me into your tight little circle of need-to-knows and divulge those secrets and the plans which you have in order bring your vision to fruition that will spark a new beginning and bring forth a Golden Dawn –– a new age of world order? It is you who have invited me here today; it is you who talks of a Third Amoran Empire, so now you must trust me. And you must trust me to speak the truth about this matter of what chance you have of raising an empire. But I can only do that once I have discovered those volitions of yours that is behind it. Also, who is backing you in all this? I mean the real hard-core backers. Is it Dan Velchanos, Giorgi Posh and the House of Hunover perhaps; combined maybe with other heavy weight oligarchs at large?'

(The Wunschritter)

'The belief that one person's maltreatment is isolated from the rest of us, is essential to the maintenance of state power.'
BUTLER SHAFFER

When it comes to political and sociological culture, dispassion is the path I would have recommended for you, Wunschritter, although apparently it is too late now. You should have sought me out sooner. It is to the achievement of perfection of the true self that this must also be the same path trodden by the volitions within the pretend self – the untrue self – which is at the beck and call of the ever-vacillating mind. And in this, dispassion must be the only choice. And as far as redemption goes, that comes from within oneself and manifests through actions taken only by that self. There are no third parties here. No third parties like gods or saviours and patron saints of this and that — no matter what your religion is. So, wake up Wunschritter, why don'ch-ah. The phenomenon at large is all about you, just as it is with everybody else. This is your show, and only yours, just as it's only my show, like everybody else's show. And, apparently, each show somehow impinges on the others, those two or so billions of us here in the third dimension. This is caused (I have it on good authority) by the disintegration of the universal order — entropy. Are you pickin' up what I'm putin' down here, Adaulph? Time is of the essence here and its runnin' out fast, you dig.

But the Wunschritter was having none of it. He stared unblinking at Dyfed with his hollow bright blue scaled-up lizard eyes that complimented the hollow sound of his strenuous voice. It was this voice (whose vibrations shrieked through his space/time and out over the whole world via wireless technology) that amid its post space/time moment of the actual delivery itself out from the Wunschritter's own mouth (when after having been suspended in precise and exact replication and boxed away) could be pulled down off the shelf (shelves) and by way of strangely criss-crossing space/times it could be re-transmitted again and again and again as if duplicating a moment of the Wunschritter's (and others sharing the same moment in space/time) past. It was this technology which helped get his propaganda out to greater masses than any politician before him; and what with the aircraft now in general use, he could take Haploid propaganda providing actual time voice into the actual audio/visual sphere of the moment not only to multiple locations but also utilize multiple space/times, whereby each speech could then transmitted throughout the world facilitated by multi space/time post deliveries. The Wunschritter was ahead of his time because of Master enhanced technology pirated and misused by the Haploids. But there will be consequences: and this isn't of the Wunschritter's doing either.

Dyfed explained this very phenomenon to the Wunschritter during their last ordeal. Von Braunau stated with a childish glee that he was an angel of the God of Chaos. This statement of his, of course, was rubbish; it was all hooey, pork-slap and bull-chutney and showed just how ignorant this little man really was.

(Chaos)

'Some very simple rules or equations with nothing random in them, that is, completely determined, can have outcomes that are entirely unpredictable.'

PROFESSER LORD ROBERT MAY

"Chaos,' Dyfed said to Athaulf (Adolf) von Braunau, 'was (in a sense) alien to the Newtonian mechanical universal system. Chaos isn't something introduced that would eventually be found to be caused by calculable error. The phenomenon of chaos equalled a system that is said to be completely described by mathematical equations yet is more capable of being unpredictable without any outside interference. This was because unpredictability was hardwired into every aspect of our universal phenomenon. This happens along the lines of patterns of information that are innate within nature to be able to self-organize in many unpredictable ways. It's been found to be based on simple mathematical rules that have a unique property of coupling commonly called feedback. Consequently, multiple copies create a loop through space/time that is a form of this aforementioned feedback that loops through duration. From this, certain strange things will begin to happen. The once predictable unfolding of space/time (the venue) of humanity's history (the event) will stop bearing any resemblance to what (by analytical calculation) is meant to be taking place here. Humans won't ultimately be confused by this aberration (any more than they already are) of the situation because it is actually their individual phenomenon and they aren't separate and apart from it. Phenomenon (in a sense) exists because of them and their witnessing of it.'

At this point the Wunschritter began fumbling around in his briefcase (he had noisily flopped it onto the table) for something he was pretending to search for.

"What it is unpredictable causation and effect on steroids,' continued Dyfed. 'And here and now the events in the third dimension perception become rapidly amplified. This, unfortunately, is what we must all now look forward to. It's always been this way, of course. Now we know it through a more poignant perception. Humans will in turn mysteriously also become amplified which not so subtley will drastically change the parameters of our venues and events. And even though historically we can mathematically describe each step leading us through this process, we will have no way of knowing or predicting how the changes of both venue and event will finally end up. This then, Adolf, is the Butterfly Effect in action. From our perspective, then, applying just a small, undetected tweak in the natural fabric of our phenomenon, new patterns of events will unfold. Now the system which is (mathematically exactly the same as before) based on simple rules with feedback, will (continue) to produce both chaos and order.'

"And where will that leave you?' Athaulf von Braunau the Wunschritter asked, looking up with a startled and surprised face.

"The real question is where will it leave you and millions of others who are incompetent in transcendence. You see, Adolf, this is where the true Self comes into its own and into play: for it is up to each one of us to adjust our perception accordingly within each venue and event so as to always be on the edge of transcending. This is in case our ever-present alert signal warns us that danger looms here in this resort of rest and recreation in the third dimension. At least that is how the Masters here in the third dimension work it. As for me, I'm all right Jack, I mean Adolf. You see, Adolf, transcendental action can only be activated under certain vibrations. That is to say, during certain events whose relationship with the venue is the phi equation of the genius of self pervading reason, and this was what Hermes brought to earth under the darkness of the night of Galahad[87].'

---

[87] Galahad was the grandson of the Fisher King, the perfected man, the so-called Christ (though not necessarily the acclaimed teacher of righteousness).

(The Secret of the False Empire and the Coming of the Golden Dawn)

'Is it real? Or is it some grand illusion being perpetrated by an unseen hypothesis?

RENÉ DESCARTES

"The Golden Dawn, of course, is the New World Order in the making; it is the coming, it's the re-installation of Zeus,' said the Wunschritter. 'It has now begun and it will become the Third Empire that will now unfold. And unlike the previous two empires, our fatherland's Third Empire will be a worldwide event encompassing the modern world. It will be an era, and epoch, and a worldwide new order. Accompanying the empire will be our own elite Praetorian Guards, an Aryan Regiment who (unlike the former during the First Empire who were made of flesh) ours are made of steel. Our Elite's god (state's god) will be a steely, modern, new and improved amalgamation of Thor and Zeus that follows the ideology of choice which will conform to the Third Empire's Elite's religious/political culture's ideology. This elite will be known as The Aryan Elders of Harmony. And it is from these same ancestors that we have emblazoned the sign of the swastika upon our Empire. Our codex of law (and its attached strict punitive suffix) will be the model to which every legally acknowledged nation on earth will conform. There will be no exceptions. Our official name will be the Empire of the World Union of National Socialism (WUNS) guided by the Elders of Harmony's Germanic Workers Party leadership. And they will remain at its head for a thousand years to come. Our capital will be a glorious re-built Barlein. As for the old world order whose capital's heart is located in Jebus (the City of Oblation), all the elders there and the representatives throughout the world will be finally expunged along with their ideals of Abram in favour of our new reborn Thor/Zeus. The transient folks who now horde that place, along with our own great Aryan cities of the Western Culture, will be expunged wherever they may be, as will all others who refuse to conform.'

"So you see, Dyfed Lucifer,' the Wunschritter said, 'the expiration and expunction of the old cults and their controlling clique will soon make room for the installation of the New Cult of the Golden Dawn operated and controlled by the Germanik Empire of the World Union of National Socialism under the guidance of the Elders of Harmony. As for Jebus we will turn that old order city into a toxic volcano and drive all of its inhabitants into their graves there so they may be dispersed forever, never to return. For there will be nothing to return to. And this is partly why we need you,' he blandly stated.

Dyfed didn't smile as he took up the conversation amid its foul and repulsive stink that began to suck the air from the room and choke him. He turned his head and took a deep, deep breath.

"But the re-installation of Zeus will not bring in a New World Order, Adolf,' Dyfed stated as a matter of fact. It will be a new world of disorder. Only Azeus can install order now,' he told the Wunschritter. 'Azeus is the saviour of the self. It is the curbing of the vacillations of the mind. No empire can survive for long without it. As for the Cult of the Golden Dawn,' here Dyfed paused and stifled an incredulous and de-meaning laugh. 'It's just another useless idolatry of ideology that's caused by the commonality of the ignorance of humanity. That in turn has been caused by the vacillations of the restless undisciplined mind. It is all a lie and will only bring more pain and suffering to the hoi polloi, just like all the other cults and new-fangled ideologies and religions have, including all of the organized, orthodox monotheistic cults. And as for harmony and those leaders of the Golden Dawn known as The Elders of Harmony, that wasn't going to ever happen. Give your head a shake,' he told the Wunschritter. Lose the meanderings of your mind and you will see more clearly,' he told the Wunschritter.

"Now, you talk of Aryans. Aryan simply means *civilized folks* or *noble person* in the ancient languages, primarily among the ancient Persians and also used during the Vedic period[88] in Inja. Also, the emblazoned swastika is not yours to use. And since you had no permission from the leaders of Jainism and Hinduism (among others) to borrow it and misuse it, you stole it without their permission. Now you and the Elders of Harmony, and a regime where love is conspicuous by its absence, wish to sully and tarnish this symbol that (in a sense) represents the Love of God.'

'Also,' Dyfed continued, 'under this program of Zeus and the Golden Dawn farce, money lender, money changer, money broker, and money maker will be melded into one that controls all aspects of human growth and activity, I'm sure. Phooey! Certain corporations will probably control (provide, will be their word for it) world food, world water, world energy, world technology and world media, while others will control all its transportation, all that which is available to it, its use and distribution and will also provide or withhold according to its own wishes and according to market up and down swings. Correct me won't you when I misstate. Qualified people will be needed to help run the machine with huge well-established foreign branches of authorised banks located throughout all the continents. Each branch would answer to the head office in either Barlein or Bruxelles. How am I doing so far?'

To humour Dyfed the Wunschritter suggested to him that maybe a branch will spring up in Couver City in the Northern Dominion. With turned down edges of his mouth Dyfed said he doubted that very much: That despite the Northern Dominion being rich in minerals and a land which had renewable resources galore, and apart from it being one of the most awesomely beautiful locations of anywhere in the world, it was a back eddy of world affairs with no Nightwatchmen to speak of in sight that were worth a good goddamn and the ownership of its wealth was already being quickly escorted out the door. It was being syphoned off by the proto-types of the folks of the Golden Dawn, he told Adolf the Wunschritter. And it was being done in the guise of investment corporations controlled by Unified Statesians and other foreign nationals abroad and sundry aliens who were constantly being caught with their hands in the candy-box, the cashiers' till and the ore concentrate sump-pumps all over the land; all high grading to beat the band. But none of them are yours, Wunschritter, Dyfed said.

The Wunschritter said he hoped that the Third Empire would put a lid on the Unified States in short order and said the Elders of Harmony had already had some of that country's finances consolidated. Oh yes, Dyfed understood a wink is as good as a nod which the Wunschritter had been providing for him over the course of their dialogue, but it was for nothing now since he realized that Adolf von Braunau was certifiably mad. This brought him back to the question that had been niggling him for quite some time: Who was in charge here, anyway? Who was running the show and its handpicked curia at the inner corridor of the soon to be World Central Control in the as yet not renamed City of Oblation of Barlein?

Dyfed's dull face suddenly lit up as the Wunschritter rose from his comfy chair and (now screeching and shrieking at nobody in particular) started to pull down the sumptuous and elaborate drapes that hung before the grand window case from an exceedingly high ceiling. Dyfed watched while the Wunschritter then bowed his head slightly and flashed a haunted, megalomaniacal look over one of his hunched shoulders in his direction.

And so they of the Second Empire have got themselves into a situation, it would seem, and those still engrossed in this tale can only wonder at the outcome. But all that paled to the situation that the Wunschriiter and the good and decent country folk under his charge were descending into.

So now Dyfed could see that world affairs were moving on to an even further escalation of misery. It was now the Wunschritter's own version of misery and how the Third Empire was to pan out and be implemented. Dyfed learned that in respect to this replacement authority, the dictator had ordered its design to be capable of interfacing exactly with that of the former and the Elders of Harmony were to be installed in lieu of the Golden Dawn. Dyfed now realized that this was the clique of the Haploids. Act two of the great World war was a coup and nothing more.

The Wunschritter wanted Dyfed's help and support to implement it, of course. This was why he had been invited.

The kernel of the Third Empire as the Wunschritter envisioned it was to be the ideology of the Nationalist Socialist Communalist Party itself, as opposed to just being the Golden Dawn's tool to vanquish the old world. The dictator's ego had meant to promote his alter order within the Golden Dawn itself in order to eventually emulate it and ride upon this stallion into world-wide power rather than the former one. His secret and twisted notions of empire will be the true new order that will emerge to wield the Third Empire, he told Dyfed now. Indeed, it would pounce from behind, silently in the night: It will be led by those Staffenshultz who will ruthlessly fleece and destroy these robber barons of old and raiders of the pure race such as the likes of the party membership — soon to be the extent of the world's only legal citizenship. These and any valid candidates, he told Dyfed, were descended either from Zeus and Thor. Now Dyfed knew this to be a crock of ka-ka through and through, and probably the dictator's vision was the result of huge doses of methamphetamine complicated with a host hereditary psychosis.

Apparently, once he was on top of his game, the Wunschritter was about to force the elite Elders of Harmony to first succumb through some form of ruse or change of terms, and finally (along with the will to power and the might of his racial puritans while holding the world within his iron grip) he would extirpate the most powerful of those power elite, along with endless queues of the useless eaters for all time, and without thought or compassion.

Dyfed glanced at his wristwatch. He knew he was done here so he stood up, walked around a bit then reclined in a relaxed position into a tasteful Bretz and focussed once more on the body language before him. It was obvious to Dyfed that the Wunschritter, like himself, was disappointed so far in their failed commiseration. Now he didn't think that the dictator would even bother to try and bring him around, so he quickly did a mental review of what had taken place, the results thereof and how he needed to get Anlaf and himself out of here — fast.

First, what Dyfed had gleaned from that conversations was that the Haploids planned to completely control the machinations of the Third Empire that was designed in keeping with their establishment's vision of order and their superior place in that order. Second, that they had employed the Wunschritter as their point man to head up a new cutting of the elm in order to cause sufficient chaos as a viable smokescreen: and in this way the Wunschritter's armoured order was to assist and help the Elders of Harmony (the Haploids) to process this goal and erect their new infrastructure so as to allow the latter to reign supreme over all other establishments of the third dimension worldwide.

That latter point revealed the other glaring reality. That this was the true purpose in the established elite for promoting the Wunschritter and the war effort in the first place. The sudden rise of a dominant new state, never mind an empire, under the cover of the smoke and confusion of war certainly leaves some questions, one would think. After all, to destroy through total war…that is to destroy not only lives but the real estate of brick and mortar that make up the cities of the Western civilized world, to render unto destruction its architectural beauties and mementos; its bridges, its Duomos and a host of other historic, mile post buildings, to destroy its infrastructures, to rewrite and alter its laws, to tamper with other systems and adjust attitudes, makes sense for only two reasons. It makes sense if the intention here is one; for the Haploids to wrestle to the ground full control of the world, and secondly; to position themselves for extending huge credit for unheard of sums with non-negotiable interest rates to puppet governments who will need to borrow trillions, if not zillions of gold denarii (dollars) from their bank, the single and only authorized moneylending station in the captured world, in order for nations to rebuild themselves again: therefore, to profit and otherwise immensely benefit in every and any way possible, especially from lending international mortgages.

Many of these nation states that would be targeted were already client borrowers for their war effort against the Wunschritter. Intent was written all over these transactions. Forget Euler's formula and the number e whose value of 2.71828…which when correctly used…is mathematically able to calculate and describe exponential growth, compounding interest and the cumulative effects of inflation that can be accrued for the benefit of the knowledgeable and the alert. Who needs it when you've got the deal of the millennium? Who needs it when you have traitors, arch-traitors, snakes and ladders in the grass, and conspirators within a governing organization elected by chumps who keep them there.

Dyfed knew now that this was the secret master plan. And he also knew that the Wunschritter would not best the Haploids in any case, no matter what. And the world population, currently at somewhere between two to two and a half billion would be drastically culled and pared back. Apparently the flotsam left over from the wear and tear of the war would not be wanted even as slaves, for by then the empire would have a new crop of healthy young folks, just the right age and easily programmed to work with –– lots to choose from.

But Dyfed didn't have to try and list them off. He needed to get their already well-known names to the Masters, pronto. In the meantime he needed to extract himself and Anlaf from the situation at hand.

Incredible as it was, Dyfed had followed all of what the dictator had told him, at least right up to the unmentioned terms for financing the dictator's political backing. Herr

Wunschritter told Dyfed that the hidden leaders of this world' scourge had extended him a line of credit which empowered him to unleash wanton destruction upon the societies of flesh and blood and to cull the future generations back to a manageable number. But the game changer was the dictator's double cross. That he had tricked the world's most cunning who are mid stream of an elaborate conspiracy. That was what he was telling Dyfed now. That he had tricked anybody other than the unsuspecting and vulnerable majority was assured, Dyfed thought. The rest was bullshit. For what it appeared to entail was: The white knight rides out of the castle of the Third Empire to bring his justice to the countryside of the world around. Was that it? Oh, quite so then: Jolly good and all that. Menstruating Mother of God, he'd never heard such bullshit! Dyfed thought.

'So, Wunschritter, you and your National Socialist Communalist Worker's Party of the World have set out now to dupe the Haploid power elite,' Dyfed said. 'How's that going for you? They don't know who you are!' Dyfed added sarcastically with his voice rising at the end of the sentence. He grinned.

At that point Dyfed set to with a slow, singular and hollow clapping which reverberated across the table to a most irritated Herr Wunschritter who was scowling now and grinding his teeth.

He was a false prophet, this Wunschritter, and Dyfed knew that despite some truths which this dictator Adaulf von Braunau stated, especially the evils of Capitalism and Communalism that was the plank in his own eye, along with evils he embraced in Nationalism, and those errors he saw inherent in progressive conservative liberalism and a raft of other accommodating life-buoys he was to liberate, that this civilization he envisioned had already plummeted into total insanity. And that's because most of the people were also insane and salivated after the absurd.

A century or so ago Dyfed had noticed that in Europaean society a pervading social neurosis had been evident similar to the type of widespread neurosis at the end of the First Empire. It was not just the result of not having a replacement civilization ready to step up and turn the wheels. Back then in 600CE its only saving grace had been the young, idealistic, and fresh view of humanity provided by the Jeshuan cult (that is before it was taken over by old established protocols and agendas which set it back on the old path to destruction). The present society and current situation — this suicide of Europa — was its wages. It had caused the pervading neurosis. The neurosis itself was due to the artificial strata among the hoi polloi of the Western civilised world along with its greed, its debt and suffering for millions that was in lock-step synchronization with the fruits of humanity religious cults and resultant ideologies which bore no resemblance to the reality that the hoi polloi were witnessing around them, at least not on Earth. If anything, western culture today now only alienated humanity. This same pervading condition to mismanage society and further corrupted by capitalist controlled industrialization complicated by the cause/effect of the Wunschritter's end game suddenly revealed for full display the Butterfly Effect in progress. Humanity had reason to think that just as before, exceedingly bright stars would appear and cast out a special light to show the way, put the wheels back on, and drive away on the bus. But unfortunately, as Dyfed now knew, the Butterfly Effect was all about unpredictability? It was where one could do the exact same thing with the exact same materials in the exact same way expecting a different outcome that wasn't the definition of stupidity, after all. It was the definition of the reality at hand — chaos.

PREFIX TO THE THE THIRD EMPIRE

(Johnny Rocco)

'…you're younger than that now.
DOUGLAS HORACE HOCKLEY

Harvey's face was tanned and crinkly. He was younger than the *wayfarer* but looked older, the latter thought. On the patio in front of his house Harvey reached out and the two shook hands. A warm wind blew across the land.

The prairie here, though at a higher elevation than to the east, was folding up into a rolling kind of foothills. Despite the early June heat (by this time the rodeo had been finished almost a week and a half before), the *pilgrim* had had to endure a cool ride through a national park of crammed up, high sloping mountains with snow and cold winds to get to Harvey's in Flathead from The Unified States of Merika's access portal at the border between their two countries. And as well, to get there without incident the *hombre* generally would have avoided the official designated overnight camps sites that bristled with 'no campfires allowed' signs (and the like) that was always chagrin to any real camper at heart. But that first evening as he set out for Flathead he found himself riding through a beautiful wilderness that ran along the top ridge of some mountains in the middle of nowhere with no one about. Here, it just so happened was a designated campground on the edge of a mountain high up overlooking the valley below. He even noticed that the monitor cameras common to these sites were smashed. He was completely alone. So, he chose to ride off the road apace to a rocky sparsely treed bench or ledge that was beautifully situated. No traffic had passed him nor had he seen another two or even four-wheeled chariot since the road had entered the park.

Then from the top zipped pocket of his black leather jacket he pulled out a Cuban cigar that his son-in-law had given him that morning. The *companero* however hadn't smoked it after lunch on the outskirts of Cowton but had stowed the cigar away for such an occasion as this. He then pulled out his flask and after a quick sip of whisky set the flask down, leaning it on a mossy outcropping of granite. He slowly rolled the cigar between his thumb and forefinger before clenching it between his teeth and lips. His eyes were lit from some inner thought as he gazed absentmindedly into the distant future. He then came back into himself and set the flame from his Zippo lighter onto the tip of his cigar. Then pulling with his breath he got it burning evenly. The man's mind drifted again. He thought of Aristoteles, Wittgenstein and Nietzsche. Then he pulled his mind back under control. He didn't want to go there just then. Instead he watched giant birds soar in the glint of the early evening light, knowing full well that they were only figments of the imagination of his mind in the clouds.

Later, he left his half smoked cigar and walked back to the road and battered and shook a few of the lacquered, sawed off medium sized logs which the Park's Department crew had planted upright into the ground which they used to number each campsite. To register correctly without incident at a State campsite, you needed to record the number of the campsite you occupied along with your vehicular chariot permit number and registration number on the park's registration form enclosed with your payment.

Similarly, besides the numbering of campsites, these upright logs (that extended the length of a man's arm above the ground) were also used for the demarcation between pedestrian and vehicular areas. Here they were used to cordon off and guard against mechanized traffic from the footpaths and areas once designated strictly for pedestrians, as well as beside pullovers by garbage bins and latrine sites. It should be noted here that the removal of a few of these posts wasn't done in the spirit of vandalism but rather as an expedience towards body warmth and comfort. Now that fires were prohibited at all times while camping, even the wooden woodpile shelters had been removed along with all their cut wood.

Our two wheeled, inline motor-cycle chariot riding *wayfaring pilgrim companero* and *comrade of life* saw how the white lacquer painted campsite numbers that were carved into the slanted cut at the top of the log sharply contrasted with the brown wood of the logs as he shook and pulled at them. Once these logs were loose from his shaking, he then pulled three or four of them out. These he carried back and set against a miniature rocky cave area that was sheltered beneath some low branches of conifers near to where he planned to rest for the night.

Shortly after midnight it turned quite cloudy followed by a cool rain shower that, he thought, might interfere with any forest surveillance system along with the enthusiasm of the Smoky the Bear clan Rangers who would be on the lookout for any fire and smoke in the forest park during the hot season. Contravening park regulations was (as with almost everything else) an indictable offence. But here and out there, apparently, there was no one about. So, now he put his lighter flame to some sappy, scratch-crinkly dried fuel he had scraped from the bark or rhytidome of some trees and relit his cigar at the same time. Soon he had built a bon-fire in front of the sheltered little cave on his ledge with the intention of keeping warm but mostly just to gaze into and with which to amuse himself. Then in the early morning just as the birds awoke, the grey and folding corrugated clouds were ponderous and low and reminded him of a Lawren Harris oil painting he used to have of northern Ontario in the land of the Northern Dominion.

The next morning as he rode out of the park and headed for Harvey's Montana home, he saw more mountains to the west. It was hot again here and the semi-prairie or steppe terrain undulated and rolled around as if in the middle of an ocean that was comprised of mountainous waves of earth.

He thought it pleasant here. Harvey's (aka Johnny Rocco's) beautiful palatial abode that looked as though it had been designed by Frank Lloyd Wright framed his tanned and crinkly face topped with a shock of white hair. This was further set apart by his bright Day-Glo Hawaiian shirt. The house was super modern looking and practical, but was well over a century old, now. The two men walked in the shade around his large mansion to the side patio where they sat outside in the warm shade under latticework covered in roses. Very quickly he conducted his business with Harvey. It had to do with some innovating energy producing inventions with fusion that Harvey had invested in a long time ago. This was when it remained fiction and Dyfed Lucifer had helped turn it into a fortune for him years later. It was odd that Harvey seemed confused or had forgotten all about it, the *pilgrim*, thought. Nevertheless, a prime and important duty is the duty to do the right thing here, he thought.

Then they were served lunch by a servant who (when he asked) told him she was from the Baja (bah hah, like boo hoo). Afterwards they both drank lemonade. The house was surrounded and seemed enveloped by the natural undulating land that was dry as a popcorn fart and as yeller as cornholers (on or off the cob) on Thursdays.

"How's the weather where you live, over all?' Harvey asked. 'Couver City, you say. That's on the coast, isn't it? If its anything like here,' he added, without giving any time for the *pilgrim*, to respond, 'it's at a point where we don't know where to turn anymore. The summer storms here are getting so bad now,' he said, 'the farmers find it's a waste of time to plant a crop, already. And the wild fires, holy shit, or should I say tornados. The inferno, we call it. I'm telling you, these horrific storms will be upon us any week now. And its only June! And yur on a motor cycle (pronounced sickle). You need to get a move on.'

The *wayfarer* told him that on the coast of the Peaceful Ocean, rising water was an issue along with terrific storms that blew seawater into the cities and onto the arable land that lay around.

"This land,' he said, 'was once productive agricultural land. But since its been inundated by seawater, it has soured and this fertile soil is now poisoned and made barren. Most of those vicious storms blow off the ragged sea,' he told him, 'and come in with the deluge of rain that falls continuously from the sky onto the mountains where snow once fell. The problem is,' he says, 'that the increase of rain has gorged and swollen the rivers to a point where they're washing acres upon cubic acre of valuable land out to sea each every hour and taking houses, roads and even farms with it. In fact, a large portion of the lower Sto:lo River basin and delta has disappeared altogether, along with a portion of Couver City's southern suburbia. And Dyfed H. Lucifer's old dockyard along the river has long since been washed out to sea. Then there are the forest fires,' he said. 'But due to the great current that drives the Peaceful Ocean in circular motions over more than half the surface of the earth, the winters remain mild. Apparently, that engine is still in place for the time being, anyway. But still, climate change has all but shut down trans-ocean shipping,' he says. 'And what with air travel being decimated…' his voice trailed. He saw that Johnny Rocco was staring wide eyed at him and he had a confused look on his face. Now the *hombre* felt vulnerable and insecure, somehow and wondered if there was going to suddenly be another shift. They are coming on faster now, he thought. They were increasing.

'Anyway,' he continued, 'there's that all year 'round stink to contend with as well. But soon that will end.'

Harvey's expected quizzical expression prompted him to explain.

"It's caused by millions upon millions of mammals whose home is the sea. These are, or rather were, seals, sea lions, porpoises, dolphins and Orcas and Blue whales, Fin, Minke, Right, Humpback and Sperm whales; Hubbs Beaked and Baird's Beaked whales, along with otters and the list goes on. And then there are fish of every shape and form: These are all washing up on shore where they rot in great numbers on the beaches. We're mammals, too,' the *pilgrim* said. 'And, apparently, we're next. We'll lie rotting on the lay-out of the languished and wasted land.'

With a very concerned look and manner about him Harvey then told him he had seen documentaries about such things. As Harvey spoke he leaned forward with one elbow on his knee, adding in his distinct staccato sounding voice that, "you can't always believe what they show you on televised programs anymore, you know. For it seemed,' he added, 'that everybody these days had an agenda.'

But the *comrade of life* reassured Harvey that the sea had now turned so acidic that she couldn't sustain mammals like whales, porpoises, and seals anymore and that they were struggling, panicking, and choking, and dying in droves. Even the fish, the last of Neptune's (Poseidon) food trucks from the sea are breaking down and not arriving to feed humanity.

"You know, the sword fish have become as extinct as the sailfish. Even the crustaceans such as crab, lobster and shrimp were few and far between now. Only crayfish, (crawdaddys or mudbugs) were available in markets and way over priced. Nope! No more worthwhile excursions of fishing and jolly good fun out from sunny Habana, anymore like the old days, eh Harvey? he said. 'With a boat full of rum and coke, that is the Coca-Cola company soft drink,' he added, laughing. 'And the sea bass, too, were gone. Not just in the Peaceful Ocean where sea scientists were still holding out some hope despite levels of high radiation as well. It was happening in all the oceans all over the world. They were in the same soup, or the swamped boat: Whatever you prefer. And now the advanced ocean-to-land fish were toppling off their perch; no pun intended. These are ocean-to-land fish I'm talking about here. They are not of the genus Perca of the family Percidae that like the crayfish have still survived. No, no. The Salmon were once like unto the gods, and their place within phenomenon is very reminiscent of the journey of the human species itself', he added. 'The first people here revered the Salmon. And the peoples of the Salmon have been holding a vigil ever since they noted their marked and sudden decrease among the rivers. Salmon,' he added, 'had a close association with the indigenous Salish folks who consider them to be a brother species. For they are spawned and hatched among shallow inland streambeds in the interior where the Salish live. These are the Salish folks who respect the earth and the sea just as the salmon fish once respected the sea and the earth. Not that it did them much good in the end, did it? But it wasn't their fault, was it? And so now we're next. The last of the fish to go must mean that they will still outlive humans who are destined to follow other mammals.'

"We're already next, already' Harvey suddenly said in way of it being a question, though that didn't make any sense and he knew it. It didn't even make sense with the removal of the second already, a word which Harvey had a propensity for using, especially adding it to the end of sentences. But the *pilgrim* appreciated how he said it, anyway. They then both marvelled how the world population had dropped from nine billion humans (or was it eleven?) to two and a half billion — and dropping, fast — all in just a few years. They finished their drinks and Harvey poured fresh ones.

'And by the way, who the hell is Dyfed"

The traveller looked away. He couldn't remember if Dyfed had even been around when Harvey was there. Anyway, they would talk more in the morning about that.

"And just how close are you here to the world-wide game changing caldera of Yellerstone's super-volcano?' the *pilgrim* asked Harvey.

Harvey stared at him a moment.

"Weeell,' he said, drawing out the word and ignoring the question — 'talkin' about fishin', hows about you and me pullin' in some Macs tomorrow morning. What ch'ya say? You'll stay the night now.'

Harvey was referring to the large Mackinaw trout for which Flathead Lake is renowned.

'Later my daughter and grandchildren — don't worry, they're not little children any more,' he quickly added, 'will be by. 'They're not even children at all and don't have jammy hands and fingers and won't get under foot. They will meet us at the lake before lunchtime for a barbeque in the picnic area. Its all been arranged. You'll stay over night,' he said again. 'That's all right. I'm afraid I can't accommodate you any more than that as we are driving to Cauliphornicatia the following day. I just hope that moron son-in-law of mine remembered to acquire his permits. I already reminded him twice, already. He gets mad when I do that. I have a fishin' and pal permit, so yur ok too.'

Then later, after a red sun had set, they sat inside a comfortable air-conditioned room replete with the soft ambiance of classical music and were being submerged within an even softer tone of light whose pervading vibration was interrupting yet unperceivable.

'Tell me more about Dyfed,' Harvey asked. Tell me about what happened to him?'

"Can't,' the *man* told him. 'Can't tell you something I don't know. Nobody does. His wife Ceredwyn disappeared a few years before, too. I'm the executor of the will. Everything was to stay in limbo for ten years.'

Once again Harvey looked long and hard at his visitor. It was if he couldn't quite see him. He had concern on his face, too. 'You all right?' he asked softly. When his companion didn't answer he smiled sympathetically and reaching out put his large but soft pillowed hand on the *pilgrim's* shoulder.

'I know, I know,' he said. 'It's a tough old life, ain't it?'

The *traveller* remained quiet for a moment, thinking. He didn't tell Harvey that he got money deposited into an account every month that came from a trust that Dyfed had set up for him. In addition to this pension he was also to receive the official House of Lucifer's North Merikan home in the Bountiful Valley near the Sto:lo River, along with about fifty remaining acres of land that was to be retained as part of it. Most of the huge, conglomerate farm business Dyfed had once owned was to be sold off. Previously, before the latter's disappearance, he had left the *pilgrim* strict instructions. Any money (presumably it would be in the hundreds of millions) earned from the sale was to be deposited by him into Dyfed's estate accounts receivable and then he was to place that money into a certain account at the People's Commonwealth Bank. That's all he knew. Well — not all I knew, but the man didn't breathe a word of that or mention anything of Dyfed's business arrangements whatsoever. He mentioned only that the ten years were now up and after leaving Flathead he was riding back home through the mountains, obviously. He said that on this excursion he was killing two birds with one stone, for on the way home from here he would stop in at Dyfed's home in the Bountiful Valley where lawyers and real estate brokers were soon to converge. He told Harvey that he had summoned them a few months earlier to meet with him there at the end of June. In truth, he wasn't looking forward to finishing up, but he said nothing of this, either.

Very early the following morning he and Harvey headed downhill to the lake in the latter's shiny red four wheeled recreation electric chariot that resembled a jeep. It made no noise as it purred along. Attached behind was a trailer supporting his sixteen-foot aluminium boat. This rigging under the weight of the boat was the only source of jangling noise that this chariot and its train made. The lakeshore wasn't far and as they left the house he got a glimpse of the large lake from a different angle than that which he had seen while riding in the day before on his motorcycle. Harvey backed into the water at a ramp near a playground with a beautiful camping area littered with 'no over-nite camping', 'no over-nite parking', 'no camp-fires,' and 'its against the law not to register in full (name, address, and postal code and phone number) for every person when visiting any government park no matter the duration of time spent' 'violators will be prosecuted,' signs. Standing at the water's edge he held onto a rope attached to the bow of the boat as Harvey backed the jeep in. As he backed up down the ramp, pushing the trailer deeper into the lake, the boat began to float. He then managed easily to pull it away from the trailer to one side and bring it onto the beach. As he did this, and at his command, Harvey sped silently — but for the clanging of the bouncing trailer — forward out of the water and up the ramp. As the much-lightened attached contraption accessed the driveway that connected the ramp to the designated parkade for vehicles and parked trailers, the moving trailer dripped water that poured profusely out from its hollow aluminium frame.

Other signs around indicated that it was against government park regulations (and therefore against the federal law) to off-road drive in this area. No wood burning fires were approved at any time (visitors were told) and consumption of alcohol was prohibited. There was to be no pumping of water from the lake for private use, either. A water station (actually it was nothing more than a glorified hose-bib with a card locked access valve) was available where the old woodshed (no longer in use) used to be. A credit card or bank card would activate and open the valve from which only one gallon of fresh, unpolluted potable water at a time was accessed through the tap: price (a notice said) was subject to change and would show up on consumers' card bill the following month. Another notice informed day campers and picnickers that they must remove their garbage, without exception. For that reason, no trash barrels were provided. Most of these policy statements were enhanced and qualified by acts, bylaws, and so forth, with numbers and letters (such as A-410.01, for example) attached to them in brackets. Furthermore (so the prospective reader of signs was informed), heavy fines would be levied for any and all infractions, and that the entire area, including the gazebos, the sandy beach, the sand-box areas, the swings and even the bank of restrooms and their toilets were all under constant, electronic ground to satellite surveillance.

He caught three nice sized Macs by nine o'clock compared to Harvey's five. For the remainder of the next hour they cruised around the shoreline horsing around and exploring. It was hot and calm. In fact, he noticed, it was unnaturally still as if something was brewing in the gigantic volume of atmosphere around the lake area. The air was hard here, and hot. It was electrified. He had a camera but seemed to recall that Harvey told him not to chance taking photos just yet.

"It draws attention,' Harvey was saying, and...' his voice trailed off and something shifted.

Apparently, just recently, the man thought — though Harvey hadn't actually said so — a man was taking photos of his young family who were playing together in the nude at the sand box. The exposed private parts (despite them being pre-puberty) that turned up in the surveillance reel in the same frame as their photographer dad who was filming them, signalled alarm bells built into the system. The man was tracked down by the number on his annual park access and fishing license card and was arrested along with his wife. Both were charged with taking indecent photos and movies of children and for being responsible for causing pornography to be displayed on federal televised communications; and for knowingly being in possession of child pornographic stills and motion-photos; of four accounts contributing to the corruption of youth (one charge per child); and of crossing two state borders (for the once happy vacationing family were not locals but lived in Spokane, Warshingtown State — two borders away from Flathead in Montana) while in possession of pornography as well (and while) being accompanied by under aged children; and charged (also) for corrupting youth. In addition, their children were removed from their guardianship and taken into custody from where they were placed in a state run home for protection from their parents even though the charges against the mother were later…

"You got a telephoto lens on that thing, already,' Harvey said. 'Maybe wait till we get out away from shore a bit and you can turn on the panorama mode and zoom in while we photograph ourselves holding up our catch. Hell, we gotta drink beer some time soon, anyway,' he said, gunning the engine as he swung the bow around. It glided swiftly through the water trailing a foaming white arc as Harvey headed the boat out toward the open lake. The all-watching eyes of the covert cameras weren't infallible, nothing was.

"Its only nine thirty,' the *pilgrim* told Harvey, glancing at his watch. He was funning him, obviously. Harvey was relatively quite conservative, so to rashly become a consumer of alcohol in public without the smoke and mirrors of cloak and dagger tactics was definitely not his norm. In fact he remembered the last time Harvey had exposed himself to rash and unorthodox bohemianism that had (in fact) included smoke, mirrors and a health dose of high-tech exuberated sci-fi. That had been back in the day in Denver City. And he had lived to regret it. He now reminded Harvey about that.

"Well, its twelve o'clock somewhere,' Harvey assured him as he glanced at his wrist watch without comment on events in Denver city that the *traveller* had just relayed.

"Never mind twelve,' the *companero* answered. 'The sun's over the yard arm at eleven, and since (because oppressive laws are posted) we don't have an arm or a leg to stand on, only fish; so we needn't worry about rules anymore.'

'Huh?' said Harvey.

Then as Harvey was grinning back at him, all of a sudden the *wayfarer* saw a jagged and hairy streak of living golden molten electrical convection which, having gone to the further trouble of silver plating itself, darted and did a nifty gyration of rotating cycles between a dark, slow moving and folding cloud of highly charged water molecules that underlined (and underpinned) the bright blue sky which then discharged suddenly without warning like a short circuit from the upper atmosphere to the earth. The lightning was still far off and the sound of its thunder was slower than molasses in January in closing the distance from there to the mens' ears over here. But it tumbled and rumbled when it finally came. The sound, it seemed to them, was bedraggled and drenching, yet rainless. Apart from that it was still quiet, calm and hot, but all that was about to change. They each had drunk about two beer (using an s here after the word beer is optional) which they kept encased in Styrofoam hand coolers that advertised Pepsi while they counted each vertically illuminated mega-volt jolt of negative charged induced energy formulating an electromotive force that was now encapsulated amidst a silent (cameralike) flash-pop whose properties, though not usefully labelled as ac/dc, could nevertheless define the streaking phenomena at large as it moved swiftly past them and over and across the land. They had just returned the boat onto the trailer when the wind came up.

His family, who had only arrived on the scene a quarter of an hour earlier were setting up a propane Coleman stove and their forearms were squirming like pink worms as they rummaged around a couple of boxes of lunch makings and other munchies over in the nearby picnic area. Followed around by King Bagrat, the family's Jack Russell, Harvey's son-in-law was moseying over to inspect the catch of the day. A whirly wind devil suddenly caught him unaware and blew his sun hat off which, much to the amusement of King Bagrat, swirled around in an abrupt updraft and flew high into the air. Lunch wasn't yet sorted out, let alone prepared, and already they were battling the wind.

The gusts and whirlwinds came and went. The disturbances were gentle at first with a few miniature dirt-devils rising out of nowhere and pulling at the loose sandy particles on the ground's surface and dumping it on plates of potato salad, peeled boiled eggs and into boiling pots of water for wieners or tea and coffee the moment the lids were lifted off or blown away. These whirl winds kept King Bagrat amused who thinking they were tall dirt coloured buffoons dancing around for his amusement, chased these whirly-twirlies all around the picnic grounds. Six of them finally settled beneath one of the gazebos and ate hotdogs with pollen seasoned mustard and relish, potato salad and boiled eggs a la grit, along with apple pie a la mode with a pinch of pollen and a hint of debris that stuck mainly to the a la mode portion. The family drank fruit juice and soft drinks through slurp spouts from covered containers. He and Harvey drank his son-in-laws' canned ice-cold beer straight from his cooler which they stuffed into their hand-held Pepsi 'keep cold' containers.

Despite the windy gusts that came and went, the sun and the breezy air over and around the lake were very hot and the family were set on swimming. He and Harvey watched from the gazebo then moved over to a patted down, yellow grassy area where, between brisk gales and swirling wind, they took their chances in chucking a Frisbee back and forth. The Jack Russell tore up the carpet (sort of speak) of patted down grass as he gave chase to the missile-cruising hard plastic disk. He did this much like he had done with the darkish coloured bogey men of the windy dust-devils variety. At one point the hot wind ratcheted up a few notches and ripped at the green deciduous trees, blowing up dust and snatching the Frisbee from out of the air and winging it in circles amid swirling leaves up into one of the shady trees. Being furiously attacked by the wind, the tree was violently shaking and rustling and its shorn-off leaves were swirling about the tree like a swarm of green insects or rapidly rotating leaf planets. Seeing this, King Bagrat the Jack Russell barked himself hoarse there beneath the tree expecting the men to do something about it. They opened a couple of more beers instead and wandering away they sat on the grass to watch the man's family splashing in the water.

Harvey Fulcher Brown had been (and maybe still was) a brilliant technician in the motion picture business. And he had filled that position since way back when, before sound even came to those pictures. He had worked closely with all of the great movie directors. He was a motion picture innovator and his life itself was a filmography.

"Remember back when we did that *colour red* gig thing in Colorado,' said the *traveller*, wrinkling his brow as he thought back to another segment of his life which he thought mingled with Harvey's.

"Tell me about it,' said Harvey.

What did he remember about it, the *companero* wondered.

"Who could forget it?' he answered. 'The two of us were both all wrapped up in that Colorado riddle.'

"What was that all about, anyway?' Harvey asked. 'I've never seen or known anything like it before or since, what with all those people, those technicians.' He seemed incredulous as he watched his guest.

"Scientists,' said the *traveller*, not technicians.'

"Yeah,' replied Harvey tentatively. He glanced at the man again. 'They worked for you? Is that right? Just who the fuck were those guys, anyhow, already? They scared the shit right outta me, I gotta tell ya,' he said. Then he laughed and looked up and over at his grandchildren in the water.

"They didn't work for me. They worked with the *pack*, a regiment I was just assigned to who were taking order from the scientists. Nobody, leastwise me, was happy about it. It brought out the worst in most of them.'

"And just what the hell was that project all about anyway? It was some kind of sci-fi or something. I never did know. And what came of it?"

"As far as that project went I can't tell you that much. I recall the equipment,' replied the *pilgrim*. It was the kind of equipment that you call the working tools of your trade. You were the man. But what was it? I dunno. I agree, something was amiss.' The man now wrinkled his brow under heavy concentration.

"Ah…I wasn't to touch anything unless under strict supervision,' said Harvey. 'And I even needed help turning the equipment on — and off. And when it came to sets and enhancing the illusion of set merging and converging the mixture with actors, along with overall designs — in essence, my life's work — it wasn't me who was in charge. I was nothing more than a fuckin' grip. I mean, what the fuck, already! Oh yeah. You bet'cha. There was something there that didn't meet the eye, let me tell ya.'

"I was almost scared,' the *pilgrim* answered. 'I remember that the chief technician (who everyone called the Master) telling us at length that the strange animated reality sci-fi or whatever you want to call it, was in the can and all wrapped up. That's where I thought it would end. Maybe the term should have been all washed up? I remember thinking that I had never seen such a state of trepidation and funk come over my close adjutant and close associate any time before, except for one Halloween in Megatropolis with a hurricane coming in with a heavy right hook. And it wasn't the wind that was frightening the shit out of him, either, I can tell ya. Nor was it the fate of our airship that we were trying to launch from its roof top launch pad from our skyscraper's roof all at the time. Oh yeah! A whole lot of other airships and their trappings were already wrapped around tall buildings and the stature of Liberty.'

"The advertising short film, if you want to call it that,' the pilgrim continued, 'which we did down there in Colorado was something about a comet that was dangerously approaching earth, and how scientists were going to trick the space/time and dodge the catastrophe, you remember that?'

Watching the *pilgrim* closely Harvey hesitantly concurred, saying only that he remembered it had been a propaganda campaign about a comet, all right.

"I think they lost their shirt in that strange movie venture,' Harvey said laughing a little.

The other didn't answer, but as Harvey suddenly stood up and began to hum a tune and stroll away lackadaisically toward the beach where his family were still splashing in the water, the travelling *hombre* revisited that peculiar event with some trepidation himself, even though it was only a memory to him now.

The scientists who were running the show were probably to blame for any and every screwy, cocked-up cluster-fuck-up that occurred there at that time, he mused. These were not the men who were referred to as the Masters. But they had probably taken their lead from them, he now mused, all the while he was shaking his head in the manner of incredulousness. And some of the science attributed to a certain Dr Torsionfield had indeed been employed in this unique technology that was being aired and directed toward a specific audience. He remembered, too, that he had had run-ins with some of Dr Torsionfield's inventions before. One was his first of a kind submarine, for one. Anyway, these latter day saints of science were to have been the pioneers of strange transportation and this particular endeavour, he remembered, took the cake even though he knew (in a strange way) that it was't real. But then again maybe they weren't either. But he was just vaguely aware of the implication at the time. As for himself, he thought maybe he was now coming to his senses.

Only now after reviewing his own written work during his idle hours at his daughter and son-in-law's cabin in the coulee did he become more aware that transmigration from the living body to beyond that, and then back, had been successful eons ago, even over great distances of time, whatever distances of time is. Some had even suggested that Jeshua Adon was one such transporter. Dyfed didn't believe that, of course. It was all an intuitive thing, according to Lao Tzu and others. And how different the Idea became to those so-called latter day Saints of Science. And even now, due to the imitative he had been associated with, he thought, a certain cadre of scientific masters were on the brink of discovery where once upon a time (sic) people had prostrated themselves down before some craven image of god or spiritual Idea or suggestion, or what have you. Olden day rituals …those crackling fat thighs of the burning heifer or oxen offered up to Zeus or the flayed and burnt black sheep offered up as sacrifice to the Mighty Hades, Hermes the Giant-killer god of the golden wand or the Dread Persephone… which had long been pushed to the back of the cupboard hopefully were long-john-gone just like their contemporaries, the pterodactyls, the great auk and the passenger pigeon. Today, even the ritual to some mendicant fakir or guru's ego, and the breadcrumb wafer offered up to Adon was backsliding, he believed. These superstitions were now being substituted by humanoid replicates, the grey men in grey suits with their grey eyes flashing who somehow magically descended to Earth on the wing and a prayer of a UFO crossing distances of hundreds of millions of light years in minutes. People didn't have much to sacrifice and pray for any more. Not now. For these folks *knew* that aliens had contacted their government and that medicine and the procedure for Aunty Agatha's terminal cancer had a cure that would soon be forth-coming and that soon even income and other nasty convoluted taxes would be abolished forever. Ha! Fiddlesticks, it was all pork slap and bull chutney.

Anyway, what did he know? Well, for one thing he knew that during that last space/time which he and his associate (or was it the envy of his alter-ego?) shared together in a common proximity which he couldn't explain, the latter told him in an inner voice that there were certain things that would transpire during the following decade. He was now in a position to be aware that what had been said to him had been unequivocally borne out by the passage of that strange stuff, space/time, during the last three thousand, six hundred and fifty three days (at its maximum). That alone, it seemed to him, propped up that whole fantasy with a modicum of logic: Now, in spite of it all, he laughed to himself.

And it all had something to do with a city of fantasy located as a movie set in the faraway Atacama Desert, he recalled. But it may have been the mountain of Meru, as far as he knew. In any case he and his associated alter ego were miraculously transported there to that far off place in their own space/time that was being engineered by Dr Torsionfield.

Its complicated, so bear with me, he was used to saying. He and his alter ego were to meet up again, that is, arrive or converge together (hopefully, for there were some opposing positions taken by other Masters of science on this) in the midst of this fantasy emporium of a city in the same space/time. And he was on the last lap of that road now. Here was the catch, for that didn't happen quite on the level, exactly. In fact, because it was the last time (in a common reality state of phenomenon) that he was ever conjoined with this alter-ego ever again, he was acutely aware that they were altered somehow in each others' presence. He now thought that whatever was supposed to have taken place, sort of happened and did take place (maybe not quite as it was supposed to) although he'll never really know if it did or not. After all, what is it that reality is again? What he did know, however, was that it wasn't due to any mistake or lack of expertize on the part of the great Harvey Fulcher Brown, aka Johnny H. Rocco.

Then Harvey, his family and Flathead all swirled into oblivion as a sudden fever overtook the Pilgrim.

PART 3

MORTGAGING THE BANK TO FLOAT THE TIRD EMPIRE

(Their trade is treachery with an aftermath of a view of the moon)

'It is to be believed because it is absurd.'
QUINTUS SEPTIMIUS TERTULLIANUS

Indeed, collective karma (also called the Butterfly Effect) had brought (not unexpectedly) un-calculable changes to the modern world. During the war's end and after his meetings with Athaulf von Braunau (the Wunschritter) Dyfed and Anlaf had returned safely to Nova Troia and hooked up again with Trachmyr again. Dyfed of course had to be debriefed by the allied war commission, though he had very little to say. Indeed, as for the commission's part they hardly seemed to understand the trouble Dyfed had gone to and the danger he put both himself and his employee Anlaf in by doing so. And then they added insult to potential injury and told him to go back to Merika where he belonged…

"Isn't that where you now live, old chap? What! Let's see…was it New Angleland… Boss-town or Megatropolis? By Jove…let's see…that's right, it was Cauliofornicatia.'

Dyfed blurted out that as educated folks he was utterly shocked, even astounded at just how ignorant folks of their assumed esteem as high achievers that once led the world into regression actually were about the Merikas. After all there were only just two continents of the Merikas, no more than that, to get confused over and have to cope with.

"Yes,' he said, 'I am a Merikan all right, I am now anyway…but not a Unified Statesian living in Cauliofornicatia…but rather I'm a citizen of the Northern Dominion. That's further north of the Columbo River on the west coast of North Merika. Not South Merika…Do not confuse those two, either…for that would make me either a Colombian, an Ecuadorian, a Peruvian or a Chilean Merikan: Shame on you. Shame on your misunderstanding of how the continents of the Merikas are spread across our world.'

Then with Heck back in the pilot's seat of the Silver Hawk again, now the four of them, he, Trachmyr and Sundog set out for the Isle of Peace that was set amid the Emerald Sea. As Anlaf's sphere of business was Europa, his offices were in Nova Troia and Flanders. Now he resumed his position at the head of Dyfed's House of Lucifer and its Europaean portion of his empire. Anlaf returned to Bruxelles once the clean up from the war was underway, even if it wasn't won, exactly. The only win is to win over war and minimize it, if not banish it forever. Dyfed happened to have just returned home when the great (actually disastrous and pathetic) conflagration of the olden day copper and bronze lance of the gods pierced the calm and rent the bits and pieces of material reality asunder. And that destroyed thousands of innocent lives on the islands of Honshu and Kyushu of Jay-pan for the sake of reining in a few military psychopaths and their disgusting, miserably out-of-touch-with-humanity reigning emperor. The power of the Fire of the Gods was now in the hands of the Haploids. Alas, it seemed all was lost.

There must never be another world war, for the Haploids (the fake humans) have nothing to lose and the real human Homo sapiens (reasoning folks) do. Anyway, that's how it seemed to Dyfed. Meanwhile, Dyfed's aim was then to relocate from the city into the Sto:lo's Beautiful Valley and take up his vast land-holdings and hunker down while making his assets more than just profitable. He also had to decide on Ebreo. He would let him go wherever he desired to go or stay, he decided.

With the war ended by the populated city of Hiroshima being struck down and the fallout from the mushroom cloud settled (one of two nuclear strikes against humanity in the 20th century) and of those homes all over the world except the Merikas that actually still had roofs that were now being repaired well into the night under the moon, Dyfed returned with Ceredwyn to Trapline. This home of his in the north provided him the escape he now needed to take into his own world by living in the bush, fishing the big choppy lake under the even bigger sky during the summer months and calling in bull moose during the autumn hunt. But is was there that the after-effects took hold and he was consumed with an inordinate burden of guilt for those failed responsibilities during this war operation on the far sides of both the Peaceful Ocean to the west and the Atlas Sea to the east that was destroying him. It was bad enough that the hate and violence from men who were unable to control themselves and their emotions could turn the machine of war against civilians and exterminate people they didn't want cluttering up the place which, further to the millions they burned and the mass graves outside of rural towns of eastern Europa that heaved up the crust of the earth afterwards with a great flatulence and stink, was that through an industrial process they turned a portion of the dead bodies into household and industrial soap.

    Of the dwindling few hours of daylight during that winter when tiny rice sized grains of snow continuously fell silently all around upon the white landscape like a haze, and when through the night he shivered and shuddered before the hot cabin fire contained in a raised, heavy gauged steel drum, the greatest and most foreboding gloom that cast its pall lurked no further than in his head. Then early in the spring he suffered from cabin-fever or shack-wacky, complicated with the fear of life and its imagination and what it can do and where it can lead. In time, with the constant increase of light duration throughout the northern hemisphere whose tilt toward the blessed Star began to work as a psychological salve and calmed his jittery disposition, and when the green and pink curtains of the aurora borealis' gyrating folds whose finale brought down the final curtain at winter season's end, Dyfed and Ceredwyn returned south. Taking the new dusty highway that weaved in and out from the sparse and stunted forests they drove down to the tangles of forest wood that, thick with a healthy growth of pine, fir, cedar and fern, grew like fungus on the rind of the salt-chuck itself. Here now were the vistas like *wood interior*, *red cedar* and *vanquished* that Emily Carr had once turned into stark canvases of paint. Accompanied in this fashion they drove all the way to their estate near the Sto:lo River that runs thru the Beautiful Valley just inland from Couver City in their big and plush motor-chariot.

    A few years after the Great World War, Dyfed's old acquaintance John Galoway of Munster (Muns) from Legion and latterly of Muns' Salvage, Massachusetts had being elected officially as the thirty-fifth (some say he was really the thirty-third) President and valet of Uncle Sham of the Unified States of the Merikas. First he became a representative in the House of Representatives for the state that was controlled by the city of Boss-Town. The House of Representatives is the lower house of the Unified States Congress. After a successful tenure there he rose to the upper house of the Congress to become a senator. The country was at its height at that time. Then one Fall day while beginning his upcoming campaign in the country's south west for the next election, he was brutally gunned down as he was being driven by cavalcade through a plaza past (ironically) the city's Police Headquarters and its city jail facility. It was a turkey shoot and although the Unified States House Select Committee on Assassinations agreed with the inquiring commission that concluded that a single gunman fired three shots, it also stated however that there was a high probability that two gunmen were involved. Witnesses, on the other hand, claimed that there were at least four but maybe even five or six shots with at least three fuzzy silhouettes that may have been the assassins who were at work here. The Committee was not able to identify who they may have been but did state that the investigation was seriously flawed. The US Justice Dept. on the other hand concluded (and stated) that there was no evidence to support the theory of a conspiracy to shoot the President John of Munster. There were scraps of film but up until the actual assassination itself, the most prominent broadcast taking place had been done by the city police that consisted of the city's Police Chief's announcement of the President's location as he travelled through the city.

From this point onward (though it wasn't immediately apparent) the country of the Unified States began to change radically and drastically. And although there were bastions of benevolence throughout the country whose voices rang out as did their actions, officialdom itself took a dive into oligarchical and totalitarian mannerisms such as false propaganda, concealment and other police state strategies which saw justice displaced for revenge (pending on the wealth of the accused, of course) or the necessity of the power of the state to be seen, along with a continuation of racism and loss of freedom of individual rights.

In a sense, this centralizing of control through the formation of governments was a product of the age of reason -- go figure! Anyway, it made it easier for the Haploids to penetrate and influence the population that was under the power elite's control and subsequent influence. It had obviously been a long-term strategy and was probably formulated by the educated hoi polloi minions who had been programmed by the Haploids. Dyfed, of course, had been insisting all along that religious culture was the natural spawning grounds and the medium for weakening the spirit of humanity in order to make the humanoid's will susceptible to balderdash, lies and more lies. This was not a natural condition, either, for it always needed suggestion as its cause. In a society that was properly adjusted any freakish concept or suggestion would be immediately tweaked by other well-adjusted humans who would not be sucked into a psychopath's vortex and influenced unduly. This is what Dyfed told anybody who would listen. Also at that time there was the Milgram experiment that set out to determine the likelihood and percentile for blind obedience as a common response to the commands originating from authority (and authoritive) figures. According to the experiment report, humans were a miserable failure (now in this era) when it came to individualism and in having empathy for others.

So, the *pack's* old plan to correctly and easily influence and elevate the general populace at large into an ultra consciousness fashioned for their own good that had previously seemed a certainty — a slam dunk (as they say) — was in very hot water and its head wasn't coming up for air anymore. It seemed that the Achilles' heel to that plan was the disruptive Abramist concept of god and its subsequent religious orders that (spinning out of control with unpredictability and the Butterfly Effects) were quickly being spread to the far corners of the earth, versus studious realists whose domain was for thirsting after serpent-evil knowledge (according to the monotheists) and whose faith was in the logic of calculation, investigation and observation followed by a re-enforced continued observation and re-assessment with what we know *fo'- sho' syndrome*. The rejection of the ancient concept of the practice of without expectation, without judgments and without opinions and where projecting a self vision of the future with a loose cannon will-to-power from an initial misunderstood concept of the self that formulates a false self consisting of an ego-I that doesn't actually exist and ultimately leads the dreamer astray to naught; this appears to be the innate cause of the demise of the last two empires, Dyfed thought.

It became a tug of war between those who closed their eyes and their ears and their minds and grasped at anything that elevated their common fears, and those that in abject wonderment observed everything they could with their meagre senses so to get a sense of just what the phenomenon really was about. Ironically, the latter was in the camp of the ancient Hindus and their investigation of Maya, the material cause of the world. Anyway, it turns out that in the end everything was (and remains still) in reference to how the mind perceives the reality of the phenomenon itself.

As soon as Dyfed had identified this recognizable metaphysical thread between the present and the past, he felt more secure but was not sure why. He himself had taken solace in the eastern science when it came to the touchy topic of reality and god: for here he looked to the Upanishads, the most ancient of all the sacred written scriptures on earth: More ancient even among the unwritten, so far as he knew. The Upanishads as well as the Dhamapada, the last scion of the most ancient work of craft (the Sramana of movement) is where Dyfed's portal to understanding the natural state of being, began. Interestingly enough, among the books that Zeno had left him Dyfed found a treatise from the civilization of the Indus valley that he kept in his Manna-hata apartments. He fondly remembered one of the apologues that as a youngster he was encouraged to recite. Written in Shamskar, it was called 'the Sitting at the Feet of the Master' and in one of the chapters titled 'Brihad-aranyaka' Dyfed discovered a canto that he thought complimented this very apologue. Once he had found it he wasted no time in translating it out loud to himself. It was about who dwells within the seed:

> 'He who dwells in the seed,
> And within the seed, whom the seed does not know,
> Whose body the seed is, who pulls the seed within,
> He is the self, the puller within,
> The immortal;
> Unseen, but seeing;
> Unheard, but hearing;
> Unperceived, but perceiving;
> Unknown, but knowing.
> There is no other seer but he,
> There is no other hearer but he,
> There is no other perceiver but he,
> There is no other knower but he.
> This is thy self, the ruler within,

> The immortal.
> Everything else is of evil.
> Other worlds there are,
> Joyless, enveloped in darkness.
> To these worlds, after death,
> Go those who are unwise,
> Who know not the self.
> But when the self fancies that he is a god,
> That is his highest world.
> This indeed is his true form, free from desires, free from evil,
> free from fear.'[89]

And it was in this vane — and from his nose (that for a century or more) having been in the books written by the philosophers from Europe that Dyfed set about to write another chapter into his Opus Magus. He called the chapter *Roman à clef*.[90] This chapter was to be something of a glance back into Dyfed's past, something autobiographic that (as a forward looking man) Dyfed seldom ever did. It was meant as a polemic that brushed on the differences between the life of men known as sages who in regulating their desires and other distractions so as to grasp the sense of the eternal being inside them that was the true meaning behind sentient being, and those other men and women who prolonged their misery in grasping after the eternal illusion substituted by any one of the lower material densities which they each conjured up according to the universal laws of material manifestation. John Galway of Muster was one of those men who had their feet in both camps (not unlike the majority of folks), Dyfed realized at this point. But he would write well of him, no matter what.

---

89 Wisdom and insight propounded by the Upanishads

90 The term 'à clef' is French and means a novel 'with a key' which in turn means a novel about real life, overlaid with a façade of fiction. The fictitious names in the novel represent real people, and the "key" is the relationship between the nonfiction and the fiction. This "key" may be produced separately by the author, or implied through the use of epigraphs or other literary techniques.

(Deric the Deuce and his young Pirates)

'Liberty is a beloved discipline.'
GEORGE CASPAR HOMANS

Shocked by the Muns' assassination, he and Ceredwyn hurried to Warshingtown to be by his widow's side during the funeral and internment. They returned a day later to John of Munster's home at Muns'- Salvage where they found all of the family's help wringing their hands and sobbing into kerchiefs as they were lined up to receive the widow home from the funeral. Dyfed immediately invited the widow to his and Ceredwyn's summer home close to Vacuna on the big island for a week that summer. It was a year in which Ceredwyn and Dyfed had never seen so many visitors. Even Talsin Davie arrived that year from Kent. He became a close companion for Dyfed that summer and during the little time they managed to devote to their work, his son was there working eagerly beside him. Also Derik the Deuce and his progenies of wild youths had turned up on the west coast of the Northern Dominion. They too had made the long journey over from Bristol to visit. It could be said that the latter mentioned progenies took the area by storm. Walks on clouds, Dyfed's other son, and his wife, along with a surviving son and his family and a daughter and her husband and their son, Dyfed's first great grandson, had also joined them from Couver City. That little tyke, a precocious infant named Shirkah had the large silver eyes of his great grandfather and the smoky skin of his grandparents. He proved to be a going concern and (although still a toddler) was a worthy rival to his step grandnephews, once or twice removed, or whatever! His mother called him Wolf Spirit for the night before he was born she dreamt that a she-wolf came to see her in her sleep. This youngster attracted everyone's attention.

Meanwhile, Deric the Deuce's brood immediately began to attract the attention of all their age group from the growing population of the entire district around the city of Vacuna and seemed bent on declaring war on the local establishment besides. Though neither violence against others nor theft were involved, twice Dyfed had to see that the two eldest boys, Thornborough and Pyrros, were bailed out of a Vacuna jail and even once had to make arrangements to have a lot of money paid to agents of the federal government representing the Ministry of Naval Affairs after the young pirates had commandeered (*liberated*, the boys had called it) a visiting US Marines naval Patrol Torpedo boat one night that was over here from Tacoma and tied up to a dock inside Naden, the secured property of the Northern Dominion's National Defence. It had taken naval personnel and agents of both the national and the district governments of both countries, including uniformed police, that whole evening and almost the whole the following night to almost spot them. With flags flying and horns blaring, after cordoning them off with a dangerous and heavily armed naval flotilla including two frigates and some other patrol boats in the early light of the next morning, they managed to cordon them in along a patch of sandy spit that was only a mile or so as the crow flies from Dyfed and Ceredwyn's home and less than that from where they had started out at Naden and to where, apparently, they were returning.

The spit was about two hundred or so feet across and almost twenty feet above the high tide and ran parallel to the shore in front of lawned mansion owned by Dyfed's old nemesis Baron Sir Robin Dungmute the coal baron who had always refused to show compassion towards the miners and their families who toiled to make him rich. In addition to that, Dyfed had had to shoo off one of Baron Dungmute's plain looking granddaughters who had been amorously pursuing Ceredwyn and latterly some of their female domestic help around their home. Between the spit, and the baron's shorefront was a broad tidal lagoon frequented by cranes and geese. Undeterred by the navel manoeuvre, and with the spit stretched out off their port side, the young privateers turned the vessel toward shore, revved up the engines into high speed and charged the spit. They ran their borrowed US Marines' naval Patrol Torpedo boat ashore and right up onto the sandy beach. Taking stock of their situation they found that they were fairly visible in the early morning light. So, with helicopters loudly chopping the air in circles above them in the dim light, and since they and their grounded vessel were exposed to any number of military harassments from the sea and the surrounding armada, and helicopter gunboats from the air above, they quickly scrambled over to the placid lagoon side of the spit for cover. From there they proceeded to make their getaway on foot toward a newly built bridge that spanned the natural spill way through which the lagoon tidal levels poured back and forth to and from the sea twice a day.

There in a hatch 'n tan type campsite they stumbled upon an artist woman living in a caravan parked under a large tree on the ledge overlooking a shale and shell strewn beach shore that girded the swiftly moving waters that were squeezed together there between the end of the spit and the shore. It was here that they hid out momentarily until the immediate coast was clear. The tall, manly and large boned, broad faced occidental woman (whose eyes were widely spaced apart and wore a black, traditional looking Ch'in type circular, brimless hat on her head and who went about her daily errand and business with her pet monkey on her back) quickly persuaded persistent and nosey agents (and other searchers) that she was working alone and wanted to keep it that way.

She had known that this gang of restless young men were related to Dyfed and Ceredwyn, patrons who generously purchased her paintings and whose company she enjoyed. As stated already this was very near the aforementioned wealthy coal baron's palace-mansion. Currently an annex had been built on the property and turned into a military academy and now some of the cadets had been pressed into service to help capture these dangerous criminals: Criminals who, it was later said in the local papers, were disparaging and derisive of government authority, who defied responsible behaviour without remorse and were living it up and joy riding on U.S. government property embarrassingly stolen right out from beneath the Northern Dominion's National Defence security eyes, all at the tax payer's expense of both countries which was surely (in the end) to cause some embitterment between those two countries and hamper their relationship down the road. At least, Dyfed thought, Ceredwyn's two brigand grandsons had the presence of mind to ditch the craft close to where they had shop-lifted it and then hide out in the shelter of an artist, and one of the most unconventional and socially compromising woman around.

Some of those cadets attending the academy who had been pressed into service to catch the young pirates had come to know the boys during their rest and recreation time and had often been seen around Dyfed and Ceredwyn's homestead that wasn't too far away, either. Instead of helping to track the young pirates down and blowing the whistle to summon the authorities, these boys had actively worked to help them remain at large instead, although their attempts ultimately failed. Dyfed, upon being alerted to the situation, quickly sought out those cadets and his step grandson's other friends and cautioned them to lay low and not let on to anyone that they associated or even knew the boys, never mind trying to help them. Deny association, he advised, or culpability will follow. For actions like these there are always consequences.

Before finding the boys (with a handful of local, pretty young doxies and a very large bar bill) passed out in an expensive room on the fourth floor of that grand old dame of hotels (the Empress of the Pacific) that over-looked the City of Vacuna's harbour and the buildings of parliament that (two days later at the time of their evening arrest was all lit up with their lights reflecting off the surface of the harbour), something like six hundred man hours had been utilized to expedite their capture with an expenditure of over fifty thousand dollars valued in the era of the 1950's CE. At the time this sum could buy two or three brand new beautiful and propertied homes close to the city. At least that was the dollar figure of expenditure that the treasury branch of the Department of National Defence released on behalf of the Royal Northern Dominion Navy. The City of Victory (Vacuna) and the Empress of the Pacific hotel (including its bar staff accountant) had yet to declare their full costs.

(Totalitarian Capitalism & the National Security State)

'This is the day the Lord has made: we will rejoice and be glad in it.'
PSALM 118:24

Unlike the majority of folks at this time Dyfed expertly controlled his own vibration and the aura around him, or at least almost so, or so he thought, anyway. Life of recent had become more complicated not only with the times at hand but also with age — his growing age included. A remark was no longer just a remark, it seemed, and even causal society often took on the politics and posturing of the war room or recent trendy customs and posturing. Of late he had found himself fondly watching children at play and wondered why human adults at large, who obviously envied the children's energy and ease of companionship, didn't emulate those youngsters' distain for put-ons and pretentiousness and all going it alone in a veritable free for all. More and more Dyfed shunned the excitement of unfamiliarity and more and more surrounded himself instead with those whom he loved and new well. He was also fearful that this tranquillity would soon be disrupted by renewed world hostilities that would necessarily, under the circumstances, throw him back into the tremor of its turmoil.

Already, Dyfed had detected agents of the government milling around and asking questions. He envisioned that the exclamation 'just imagine!' was being trumped in social discussions that echoed around the board rooms and drawing rooms and helped to lace the conversations of chit chat by a certain class of people of the city of Vacuna. Often this exclamation was spoken by any number of those uninvited arrivals, those very attendees whose lack of invitation, however, never deterred them from showing up and imbibing themselves at Dyfed and Ceredwyn's home of hospitality, in any case. And those same gossiping gatecrashers now let it be known that they had made plans to stay away from the Lucifer house, altogether, from then on.

"If that is what it takes,' Dyfed was heard to remark, laughing, upon hearing the gossip, 'roll on Blackbeard and the Captain Doubloon Ducats of Seville, and bring it on.'

It was early fall, by this time, and nearing the end of their extended summer season when Dyfed encouraged Derik the Deuce to begin saying his goodbyes and take his two young pirates — the two chips off the old block — back to Dunmonii. There, it seemed, 'the Deuce's' own fleet of tankers and sundry merchant ships, along with a few converted U-boats were coming more and more under the surveillance of the Unified Kingdom's national government agents. Meanwhile, Dyfed and Ceredwyn's privacy was thankfully still far from the strain and strife that cornered the world's attention at this time. Those in the know talked about how the war had been about the loss of life and miss-expenditure of funds extracted by the system as taxes from the hard working populace and the infrastructure they had built. But it was mostly all talk. It was true though that the people's earned treasure was extracted out of the infrastructure that served them by the system that they thought worked on their behalf. They forgot to remind themselves that this had always been so. True: they wanted change. But ultimately these talks concurred that this system of the established order was implemented not by the governing factor or even a king or queen but by the Haploids. And this was in order to conduct a mutually agreed financial war of personal gain, the great qualifier and saddler of debts; all of which, it seemed, was lost on all but a few. That was hardly a slur on the populace's attitude toward king and country: Quite the contrary. That the honest and hard working patrons of the establishment supported and cheered on their leaders who channelled them through the amazing corridors of the established maze system, showed an undeterred loyalty without question. A loyalty undeserving of the kings, queens, and those other leaders; those whose duty it was to guard the gate but sadly were merely yes men instead who paid lip service to the Haploid psychopaths for whom the likes of the Wunschritter were a welcome distraction, usually induced and choreographed to the tee, almost. Hurrah, for the people! Hurrah for the soldiers who hoisting the flag of their forefathers, and like all stalwart men from Aeneas to Aesenhower whose regiments donned the coat of arms of their regent. But also hurrah for all those who were cheated, lied to, bullied, and exploited no matter on whose side of the fence they fell. And fall they did, and like at no other war in history. Hurrah for the fooled who were never the foolish. The problem was the bird-blind, that labyrinth and maze of corridors within the system: That bastion of the Establishment that was conjured thence through programming and duplicity by the Haploid themselves. Dyfed's associates thought that this was the theatre of war that was being purposely ignored, and at the hoi polloi's peril. And these same disenfranchised from the Land of the Pure (as they saw it, anyway) had been mildly amused at Dyfed and Ceredwyn's grand children's antics of piracy. So now they drank heartily and drained their glasses in salute to the good fight to come that was to be led by the likes of those young pirates who showed good spirit and immunity from homogenized conditioning. This attitude inveigled by the *pack* and its associates therefore was the anecdote necessary for the established psyche surgery (brainwashing was another good word which came to mind) for a pre-approved and carefully designed generation which was planned to pilot the Haploid's new generation after the war who would bid for ultimate sovereignty as the Haploid control moved into the final stage of their coup. And these *type one* folks well out numbered the cadre of *type two* pirates (the wolves of land and sea) and it didn't look as though anybody could do anything about it. The cross hairs for the Haploids future goal were set on the paradigm where no disobedience could be tolerated. It had its trial mock-up first with the Moloch that finally found its feet of disruption first in Arabia and the Sudan under the Ishlamite Mahdi that culminated in the current era with the Haploid intellectuals and oligarchs of the Land of Rus and the Land of Ch'in. It seemed, too, that the latter were willing to politely ignore and work around each other in the silent, cold wars of intrigue and the final onslaught aggression against the west. Meanwhile, in the west it was 'tennis, anyone?' and where the social activities were forever heading out to fish on the summer oily sea or hike into Thetis's main lake to fly fish or stomp around to numerous other lakes in the area, have a drink or two and play some cards, a game of badminton…bring your swim suit and debate Wittgenstein and Descartes! One or two even fell in love.

But now the summer was finished and although the weather was generally still sunny and warm, now well behind in his work Dyfed moved in behind his desk for there was much to catch up on.

(The gadgets of Quasi Gismo)

'I am only a public entertainer who has understood his time.'
PABLO PICASSO

After being announced without warning and then ushered quickly into the library by Trachmyr, Dyfed looked up from his work and eagerly regarded King Karatakos' beaming face. Fondly gazing at the later it suddenly occurred to Dyfed just how much the former resembled a painting that was a cross between a Durer and a Van Dongen; both having been hastily left unfinished on the same canvas by their respective artist's with their paintbrushes cast aside un-cleaned. Another, a companion of the pack who Dyfed had never met before, accompanied Karatakos, on this occasion. The other man, identified as Ivan Skavinsky Skavar (who once having been a general of the XX Amoran Legion who worked alongside Trachmyr during the sixth and seventh centuries in Francia, whose large body must have been wrapped in about eight yards of a tartan kilt and topped by a waistcoat type black jacket. They both took a seat in Dyfed's library. And even still, the large, aforementioned kilt-wearing giant hadn't removed from his head the brown fedora with a tall plummy looking feather sticking up out of the hatband that had been stuck on his head at an angle. He was a strange looking man and Dyfed wasn't sure whether he'd be more comfortable exchanging his colourful kilt for a brown lederhosen or his mountain-climbing high alp type fedora for a wide be-feathered tam. The big boned and now wide girthed Skavinsky Skavar set a smallish package that he had been carrying onto Dyfed's desktop. Both men's glassy and gleaming wide eyes kept darting back and forth between it and Dyfed.

"I take it from your furtive — we've-got-a-secret-look — that you're displaying, Karatakos, that there is something important about this little gift you have brought me,' he said, not once having yet focussed his eyes on the package itself. So he absorbed the shape and size of the wrapped object as best he could through his peripheral vision as he concentrated on the faces of the two men.

"It is an electronic device,' said the old former king of Albion in a harsh tone that had more than just a hint of conspiratorial affectation in its harsh whisper.

"An electronic device!' repeated Dyfed with no pronunciation accent at the end of 'device' to indicate he wasn't asking a question but merely repeating what Karatakos had said. It was a repetitive statement than one of wonder and anticipation.

"Yaas,' answered the king more loudly now in his casual and lazy voice. 'We've recently developed it,' he said.

"You have just recently developed an electronic device?' responded Dyfed matter-of-factly. There was still no accent at the end of that word. 'Hardly, old man,' Dyfed added, whose glance shot directly into Karatakos' eyes and swept quickly passed the other man's astonished gaze as well. He had still not looked directly at the package and that, he noticed, seemed to have let them both down a bit. 'You seem to forget, Karatakos, that I once attended St. John's college.

"Yaas,' replied Karatakos again in his usual drawl. 'It was the class of sixteenth century, wasn't it, along with Bacon and Donne.' He was looking frustrated. 'Sure, on occasion you did hang around those Cambridge boys; that is when you weren't cavorting and drinking with your old pals Jonson and Ralay.'

"Yeah,' answered Dyfed, 'and don't forget Marlowe and Henry Sidney, son-in-law of that arch villain John Dudley the duke of North Umbria. It was I, unfortunately, and I don't thank you for helping me recall, who failed to get my hands first on the damning evidence against them that the agents of the crown used to have them convicted and eventually be-headed for high treason. Remember Karatakos, work and play are all part of the day…at least in our game, that is. You taught me that.' The latter's face suddenly crinkled up like a giant, wizened old prune, then just as suddenly relaxed again. 'Anyway,' Dyfed continued, 'I have returned to Cambridge since then, quite recently even, to obtain my up to date degree in physics at that my old Alma Mater. But let me say this. A device made of semi conducting material, or crystalline solids, used for the control and amplification of an electron current has been known about for some time by many of us here in the third dimension. Thanks again to a member of the *pack*. What you have apparently done — with fifth dimension logistic know-how — is you've managed to build an instrument that can utilize the physics of electronics for superconducting, and for superconducting on a specific band wave for a specific purpose. That much I will assume, although I suspect that the first of those very devices which you have here are beginning to fall off the end of the establishment's many secretly funded think-tank initiated assembly lines as we speak: or about to. You and I know that even Lord Huge understood this technology. The purpose of this thing is what then, exactly?'

For the first time he looked at the package that he now quickly picked up and unwrapped even as Karatakos' companion was reaching for it. Once the wrappings were off he beheld a device about the size of a large book, less in size than the intricately bound volumes of the old family books of sacred law that were still treasured keepsakes. With unconcealed surprise Dyfed opened it up in half just as he would a book. There was a shiny black screen on one side and a layout facsimile of a typewriter whose surface, however, was smooth, on the other side. For a moment Dyfed was somewhat puzzled.

"When it is plugged into any electric circuit such as here in your home,' he said as he bent down and plugged it in, 'and turned on like this, this screen over here, as you see, lights up. It is here where information accessed through these icons here, or where words will appear as you write them on the type board.'

"How novel,' Dyfed replied, keenly, giving them both a nod. 'This is from one of our own laboratories, then. It is much more advanced than anything I've heard about.'

"That isn't all,' said Karatakos' companion. 'Because you can plug this little device we have here into the tablet.' With that he pulled something out of his pocket twice the size of his thumb and plugged it in to the main tablet component. 'When the screen is activated, it will tell you what to do. Follow the instructions using the keyboard. Then, all written documents that are shown here on this book sized device can be electronically transferred to this little secondary device which you can then put in your pocket or keep it in a safe place, or mail/courier it out.' You can also send me your written data via a send mechanism. There aren't many selections as to where it is sent. We anticipate that soon it will not be safe to send anything electronically, hence the small portable device that can contain an encyclopaedia.'

"My word,' said Dyfed. 'Wow, that is novel, a marvel.' The other two men were now smiling broadly again.

"Once its on this tiny portable device, then all you need to do is delete the document that remains on the book sized computing tablet machine knowing that it remains safe in the little device here, and without anybody but us being able to access it.'

"Holy shit, really?' said Dyfed, now very impressed.

"What was that you said? Holy shit, what does that mean? asked King Karatakos making a nasty face.' "You need to get out more these days into the third dimension and start playing around with the word game,' replied Dyfed. 'It's an expression, an exclamation, actually, that is fashionable here in these parts, these days.'

"Ha, ha,' laughed the king. 'I like that. Holy shit!'

There was a flurry of never ending activity now that communications were increasing in quantity and quality: And the speed of communication was the big thing. Even the speed by which humanity paced itself to the frantic world that was growing around them continued to increase, but ultimately technology outpaced humanity to an exponential degree. Dyfed had been right with his first assessment of the new gadget that King Karatakos and his companion had brought to him. He had said it wasn't far from being massed produced; and that it was a skip and a jump from soon falling off the assembly line in a projectile form. It needed to, of course, to accommodate a fast approaching five billion people on earth that would soon increase to six and then seven billion in no time, and then finally mount to eight billion with virtually no science, technology, algorithm or electronic app to support the consequences. Consequences quickly came in the form of the pollution taxes levied on absolutely everything consumer able. The real problem wasn't pollution it was population under the circumstances where individualism and the will to power dominated a divided society and where balanced independence within a likeminded society was made anathema, shunned and outlawed; all to the peril of humanity. For those who remember the first pages of introduction of this tale, conditional truths were hidden from the people, as was the truth about their true genius as sentient beings. But aside from population mismanagement, even the food distribution crisis due to failing and falling water supply and water-table levels (now emerging worldwide) was ignored. It wasn't, Dyfed knew, that they couldn't do the math or figure out the logistics; it was that the power elite just couldn't be bothered because they didn't care about others enough and that they were still profiting themselves was all that mattered. It was fine when they needed brains and muscle to put the science backed infrastructures into place, but now what? And Dyfed, of course, had now become acutely aware of a 'think tank' commission on population control, accenting Haploids foremost, called 'Cloud Nine City.

(NARRATORS' PRIVILEGE)

The Butterfly Effect had brought vast change to the world since the closing days of the Great (sic) World War. This war, of course, was not great at all but was really sickening and psychotic. During this era and time/frame an Angleman scientist named Turing astonishingly discovered a pattern formation that grew out of the basic elements and atomic/molecular structures that combined to produce every kind of living mammal such as humans. Later, it was re-discovered to pervade the universe in a sense, and its innateness to all was such that it was dubbed the fingerprint of god. How, for example did molecular matter decide on its own to grow into an eyelash or an internal organ or blood or bone marrow or the retina of an eye? From this observation Turing developed mathematical biology and even went on to formalize the concept of the algorithm[91] to solve highly problematic scientific computations. But even if to the brainiest of folks this understanding of pattern formation made some kind of biological sense as to why the canine is a canine, and why leopards have certain markings that differ from tigers or hyenas and why we are what we are, an unpredictability of biological engineering was rampant nevertheless. And this was throughout nature and its environment; therefore a logical biological cause and effect regarding intrinsic areas of development for living creatures was beyond a certainty for any reliable discernity. Turning was the father of artificial intelligence (AI), and like nuclear energy (the fire of the gods and the olden day glorious copper and bronze lance) AI was an extremely dangerous tool if the operator's mind wasn't big enough for it to be out on its own, which is often the case with the hoi polloi.

But it got worse. Even if an operator was on top of it that didn't mean that the rest of humanity would be as well. Logically (with this machine now at large), they would then be under it instead. They would be subjected to a huge disadvantage throughout their entire life-long existence with this Artificial Intelligence now coming of age. In the grand scheme of things the nature of the thing itself defied the rule of safety regulation and made any kind of responsible monitoring not just impossible, but rather (the chance of it being safe) an idea cloaked in imbecility. The gay blade bloke Turing had had permission, of course, to re-invent and produce this AI tool but the Masters miscalculated the ingenuity (and the integrity) of the common hoi polloi who now at large and milling around in huge numbers were far more educated and advanced per capita than before. It had been the same with the introducing to the fire of the gods that not coincidentally occurred at the same time. And this latter re-invention wiped out two major, highly populated cities in Jay-pan during experimentation tests while the nuclear weapon itself was still under study and advanced construction. But despite what advantages Turing's work produced for his own country while at war against the Wunschritter and for a broader and brighter scientific future ahead, his own countrymen persecuted and viciously demeaned the man himself for his life style and sexual preference immediately after his brainy computerizations helped the Allies win over confrontation and aggression (that the war brought against them) by an extraordinarily abominable adversary. Turing, now isolated and shunned, soon committed suicide. Dyfed didn't think this was at all fair or

---

91 A set of instructions typically to solve problems or perform computations.

even decent. It too was abominable, he thought. And in a most egregious way it turned the countrymen of Anglelanders into an abominable adversary, not just against one of their own but also against all what Western Philosophy was about. It was crazy insane; but it was nothing more than the Butterfly Effect in action outside of nature's biological sphere. The Butterfly Effect itself has a much older name. Thousands of solar cycles ago when the great thinkers of their age, the Masters, were on a tear (pronounced tare), their noble language was Sanskrit. And the Sanskrit word equivalent to the Butterfly Effect was karma. It's not exactly a Zen thing, but if you don't look directly at your current understanding of what karma means to you, you may glimpse its reality and then understand the comparison. The Butterfly Effect pervades the universe and not just through its material reality, either. This is why is has been called the fingerprint of god. (**Parasolo)**

(The Hysterics of the Haploids)

"Carp Diem' (Pluck the day)
QUINTAS HORATIUS FLACUS

But all was not all okay-dokay or calm around the globe; not with karma (the Butterfly Effect) being what is was and which humans had been responsible for and had helped cause it to be at large more than it ever had been. But on the one-dimensional face of it, the illusion somehow seemed more than wonderful. Jobs were everywhere and accumulation and possession were fast becoming the era's flavour of greed a la mode, or was it a la carte. This Haploid environment of debt was now a faster and even less stable world- encompassing-human-activated vibration that now set the cycle creed of work, earn, buy and spend to validate one's loyalty to god, high priest and country. Now that the ethic of work, earn, buy and spend was underway, the ultimate result was — imprisonment within a de-attached attachment cocoon of frivolous trivialness. It easily managed to destroy every practitioner's soul if they weren't wise and (to a lesser degree) careful. And this vacillating mess of contagion, fuelled by the greed of corporate industry, now ramped up to beat the band so that it soon became obvious to those with clear heads who had eyes to see and ears to hear that the human aspect within their culture (no matter where in the world they were) was far from being okay-dokay. The Haploids were now back in the seat driving the bus and they now had atomic weaponry and artificial intelligence in their tool box and there was virtually nothing left to stop the sons of bitches from their ability to totally destroy the human race barring — say — a vast extinction event that would probably kill off most of the mammals and reduce the real human beings back to population numbers synonymous to pre five or ten thousand BCE. Amortized out that would probably leave only a handful of Haploids alive, with any luck. 'If we weren't careful, we will be on the extinction list ourselves soon,' was what some bright young scientist once whispered under her breath. But everybody on the streets and in the universities laughed out loud. However, in this case he who laughs first is often bound not to be around so as to laugh last. And so it was.

When the fear of the atomic warheads managed to wrestle war back to border skirmishes reminiscent of hundreds of years before with an additional help of artificial intelligence, and when the semi calm of a few generations allowed the Haploids to rein in a vast crop of university graduates, AI then became a valuable conduit to channel both knowledge and wealth right to where the Haploids wanted it; pulling along a few of the alpha male and female hoi polloi ass-lickers who thought they were entitled and more deserving to land a good deal after their long yes-man service history. It was their morning group mantra of 'yes sir, no sir three bags full sir'. In the end most of them would soon be dumped and finally expunged anyway. They were no more to the Haploids than fertilizer to help make things the Haploids wanted to take root and grow; so in the end they deserved to be tilled into the soil anyway. And seemingly, that was god's plan for them.

(The big wide vibe)

'...a world full of rucksack wandering Dharma Bums refusing to subscribe to the general demand that they consume production and therefore have to work for the privilege of consuming all that crap they didn't really want anyway...'

JACK KEROUAC

A sudden vibration of high and low pitched squeals and pings, and low base sounding static and twisting distorted musical sounds bleeped out across the land of men. Nobody, Dyfed noticed, took any notice. Nobody was aware of it. They didn't hear. They wouldn't listen. Dyfed heard the call. It was the ultimate call of distress...the ultimate SOS: Save Our Souls, it said. Hey morons, over here. Save our souls,' it said.

Dyfed knew then that it was the whales calling. All of them, or at least all that remained and who had now gathered close to the shore and were calling out for help in the hopes that the homos (homo sapiens) — fellow travellers in this life of the three dimensional phenomena, would hear them at last and act accordingly. Of course, they didn't listen and it didn't happen. Few paid any notice to Hobson's choice. Next were the seals and the porpoises and so on. But the careless and unkind man-kind went on as before — 'its business as usual' — one of the Unified Statesian presidents was said to have announced at his inauguration at the start of his tenure as the air and the oceans and the rivers and the land began to choke on and vomit toxic waste fumes.

"We are dying now." Then a little later the whales called again. 'Help us — oh arrogant man. It is you who has custodianship over all the creatures of the Earth that have now brought us to the point of extinction. So, belly up to the bar; shit or get off the pot and help us...help us...help us — you assholes,' they squealed out in their sonar sound. But no one of legal consequence was listening. Everything today was about legalities. The Haploid influenced lawyers saw to that. And none of them ever noticed that all the little song birdies were now gone. Why would they? Fake humans never listened to the sweet sound of the morning birds, anyway. And cities, in the end, made real humans into fake humans eventually, and to their detriment. In fact, cities were now being devised in such a way (and in record breaking times) to turn and make real humans into fake plastic folks.

Meanwhile the greedy narrow minded non-conservation minded politically conservative industrialist assholes, their bankers and their political yes-men up there on parliament hill, who decorated the narrow-minded corridors of fake power pretending to represent the people, along with the share-holders and their henchmen of hawkers and button-holing, corn-holing sodomizing lobbyists leaning on lean and hungry political mesmerizers with no values talking through their hat whose dwarfism handicapped their mentality as well against the greater good of the needy more hungry people while never second guessing that their dwarf-like short arms would *nevah-evah* reach the bottom of their department's deep pockets payable: and all because the buck always stopped there.

(Immaculate Ejaculation and Other Fairy Tales)

'A theory which is not refutable by any conceivable event is non-scientific'
KARL POPPER

One of the bugbears of history is the human temporary culture that is used to form and fashion our societies. And it would be bad enough if the culture of choice was uniform within a worldwide phenomenon, but it isn't. There are multiples of cultures that make up the worldwide phenomenon at large at the same time. None of them seem to see eye to eye and have hostile prejudices against those whose mandates and mission statements differ from their own. And all of them are cheesy, full of themselves and ultimately (in the face of raw phenomenon) are irrelevant in general for the well being of humankind. The ideological choice for Europa and the Merikas has been Western Philosophy with a dollop of the Cult Jeshuanism, an additive religious flavour that's stirred in. Some nations are more prone towards religion than others. Because of the Butterfly Effect within the physics of sociology, it is difficult to say who is better off. It's the old axiom: if you eat ice-cream it tastes like ice-cream. If you eat shit it tastes like shit. If you eat ice-cream mixed with a little dollop of shit, it still tastes like shit!

Certain intellectuals have said that this additive cult has had a tranquilizer-type effect upon the western world while counterpart left leaning ideologists have stated it is more like an opiate. Poets claim it's a depressant like alcohol while right wing extremities say its effect is like a constant dose of lithium. Soothsayers, on the other hand, say it's a combination of all of the above and Western Philosophy would be better off without it; especially as it is an accompaniment whose symmetry towards enhancement and compliance is obtuse and which generally acts like a rotating companion satellite whose tendency, an inertial intensity called centrifugal force, is to pull away from the centre and break down the symmetry.

Dyfed and the *pack* had long thought that religion (any religion) was highly dangerous for the well being of any society who weren't light-years ahead of the average current hoi polloi in general knowledge, logical reasoning along with those who weren't totally full of love, compassion and empathy for their fellow humans (as well as a myriad of other creatures). So in the way of this conviction, combined with both the natural world of efficacy (also causality or cause and effect) along with the unpredictability permutation and the Butterfly Effect thrown into the historic phenomenon, and what with all this right on the heels of world conflict, atomic bombs and a mass expunging of millions of lives before their time, Dyfed's life began at this point to take on newly distorted dimensions. And though it wasn't initially the result of a huge increase of worldwide population that was producing a boon of imaginative ideological and philosophical concepts along with some progressive innovations (often heavily laced with pseudo science), this contributed to it. The latter had also begun to be used as experiments on society so Dyfed now lent increasingly more and more time to sound its depths and ponder its thoughts in order to fully appreciate these occurrences. These he passed upward to Morgant, Dr Torsionfield and Quasi Gyzmo, among many other white coated wizards, some of whom Dyfed had no idea even existed, but who relied on the likes of Dyfed and the *pack*.

The present phase of the era was not easy to fully come to grips with, despite (or perhaps on account) of the curious oxy-moron it developed earlier on as its name: *the age of reason*. When gripped within a linear concept of history, Dyfed and his associates knew that reason was relative, like reality. A dangerous situation under the circumstances at any time: It was (however) innate to most states but is an especially deceptive pit-fall in the third dimension. This was hardly the first embarrassing Europaean blunder for reason and logic. Many could still remember how escalated the Moors were in knowledge of the phenomenon compared to the surrounding pedantry of Europa's Jeshuandom. But despite their advanced proficiency the Moors' god ultimately handed them the short end of the stick. Subsequently, they over-looked god's faux pas in the matter, probably because they were too far gone behind the eight ball to reset their religious culture into a medium of non-ambitendency. Further to that they then quickly developed a deep-seated fear and hatred for the *Jeshuans* and the *Ebreo* (peoples who were the original *Abramists*). This was an indication that they were as racist as the *Jeshuans* of the time, at that time. Hatred, fear and racism are not the result of advanced reasoning. So it would seem that the *Ishlamites* who were rather advanced in the natural sciences but were not so well endowed in sociology that one would think should be one of humankind's priority and most important field of study. After all, what were the tenets of Lao Tzu's *Tao* (*the way*) or *dao* and *wu wei*; or Confucius' *Hundred Schools of Thought*; and Buddha's *dharma*, the *Four Noble Truths* and the *Noble Eightfold Path* if not an advanced sociology mixed with the natural sciences? So, on the Europaean field where western philosophy was supposed to triumph, belittlement and extermination ensued because their mission statements differed. And from this same fear and loathing back a thousand year ago, there arose the words eventually translated as *'down with the infidels'* which digressed and ballooned out to *'up and at 'em brothers and make jihad* or *holy war'*, *'rise up and strike down the enemies of Allah'* and finally, *'death to Merika:* And why not? The Jeshuanist hadn't treated them any better or given their brother *Ishlamites* any kind of an out to save face. The onus should have been on integrity. Integrity was something that required truth and honour before all. Dyfed's own integrity which he demanded of the hoi polloi as well was to have the will to correct, improve, and elevate all beings locked in this phenomenal dimension into that state of consciousness which induces a specific clarity in order to be able to distinguish the true self from the ego in order to gain freedom from the claustrophobia of this phenomena and to escape from, and to exorcise and to rid oneself of one's kunderbuffer, as one enlightened philosopher of the day called it. And anyway, who knows what that really means!

Meanwhile, the Haploids were being busy promoting educated hoi polloi who were programmed and under their control to apply their talents at different times as heads of sundry departmental desks, various categories of field operations and fifth columns that had become active in new opportunities that opened up during the early days of the atomic age of reason. This new crop of humanoids now successfully stymied and confounded reason by legalized, constitutionalized nonsense that abounded. They also penetrated the hierarchy within the armed forces and other agencies, especially the departments of justice and education of the courts throughout the governments of the world when possible but concentrating on the cultural/legal infrastructure of Sino (the Land of Ch'in), Indo-Iranian-Arabian and Greater Belarus (including the Land of Rus) and its satellites, against the freedom of Western Philosophy of Europa and the Merikas that was (and remains) focussed in part on North Merika's partitioned democracy. Here the Haploid even managed to penetrate the concept of elected constitutional governments of republics and monarchies. The Unified States, that had succeeded the Angleland mini empire of ninety-nine years, had just swung into full stride in its elevated status as the world power elite when a well-planned and deliberate catastrophe struck.

But unfortunately this was all part and parcel of the kind of failures that arise, even within Western Philosophy's idealism that hadn't yet graduated from individualism and rights to independence and responsibilities.

(Homo Sapien Masters)

'Research shows that the foundations of moral functioning form early in life, and depend on the affective quality of family and community support.'

PROFESSOR DARCIA NARVAEZ

In very ancient times there was a Hyperborean civilization in northwestern Europe that remained somewhat isolated from the remainder of humans on Earth. This civilization advanced brilliantly. Long before the end of the last iceage this civilization had advanced technology that allowed them to access many fields of science. One of the more important sciences besides natural science and advanced physics was psychology. Induction into this science eventually allowed them to comprehend the full spectrum of the psyche of their genus (Homo) that was well beyond the current average level of the species (Sapiens).

The Sapiens, remember, were once relatively new inductees to treading the light fandangle of worldwide dominance. They were not the first to emerge and foraged outward from the valley of the motherland[92] to populate the planet, they were just one of a number of genus Homo types throughout the inhabited world at the time. All of them were striving to amount to something and leave their mark. The names they go by today are all modern application type names and therefore un-necessary to name here. The species that out shown the other species in the end, however, were Sapiens[93] of this Homo genus. It should be said, however, that at one point during their advancement they were neither the most intelligent nor the most proficient at expedient husbandry: And that speciality was closely related (as always) to survival. They were, however, the most adaptable. And it was this path of adaptability that set them apart. Certainly, a part of their adaptability was to learn from other species and by adopting their methods (or their tools and ideas) in order to perform better under different circumstances. This set them apart. Successful individuals of other species sought and managed to merge with the genes of the Sapiens. This did not muddy the Sapiens' gene pool in the least (in the big picture anyway). Rather it helped diversify it. Sapiens still have remnants of other species in them. Apparently adaptability is a dominant gene that's subject to variances. But it also needs a certain attitude involving self-awareness that is caused by other complexities. In any case, over many thousands of years, approximately one per cent of earth's predominately Homo sapiens population became ninety per cent more advanced than the remaining ninety-nine per cent of all Homo sapiens who dominated the Good Mother Earth. These were the Hyperboreans. It became customary to refer to them collectively as Masters. And although this was generally racial in effect, ethnicity wasn't an intrinsic component nor was it the cause, whatsoever. The component was environment. The climatic, social and cultural environment was the cause.

---

92 The lands in and around the African Greater Rift Valley area.

93 The word sapien derives from the same root as sofia (Gk) and sapienta (Latin) that means wisdom. Homo sapiens means hominoid of wisdom (sic).

Anyway, after a thousand years of labour intensive inquiries, the info that was uncovered helped them to develop an accurate data based methodology. More especially, it exposed the species' psychological past and how it merged into that of the behaviourally modern human of today. These Hyperborean magicians (scientists) were then able to identify, probe, and understand the natures of incredibly powerful archetypical images that have been busy occurring throughout the Homo genus' psychological tree of evolution. Remember, the psychological evolution of every human will parallel that of their physical evolution, which is further subject to environment that certainly includes certain biological historistics. In addition, it was found that under certain conditions infective archetypical images could be artfully injected into the human psyche and if nurtured in extraordinary ways could be artificially formed into a programmable entity that become innate in the psychological structure of susceptible Homo sapiens. It was called social engineering. There was an element of danger in this for all the Homo sapiens: But not all the creatures of this genus and species were susceptible, however. Furthermore, it was not necessarily dangerous for all the folks who were susceptible to its mutations, therefore great strides were made. Needless to say, this opened the door to understanding peculiarities about man's perceptions that influences how he thinks and what he thinks about. That exposed a range of anomalies that the unaware Homo supposedly believes to be logical conclusions of rational thinking. Rationality — the Hyperborean scientists quickly learned — was a double bladed sword with one edge being a clever illusion. For many advanced Hyperboreans who looked inward, this data allowed them to analyse their perceptions along with the resulting effects of their Ideas.

Lesser minds than the Mastermind generally mistakenly used this same process to miss-identify the phenomenon without that's within the general context and environment of our psyche. Used correctly the Master's methodology allowed the more aware to correct useless and unfocussed thought patterns or channels that have been influenced by ancient and deep-seated notions. In this way they managed to void certain inappropriate and harmful effects that were being caused by these shadowy, frightening subconscious archetypes. One example was the correction of debilitating personality due to the discovery of personal meaninglessness. Another was the rampant hatred and fear of anything outside of one's normal comfort zone within the phenomenon. Both of these appear to be indigenous to the species. In fact, it may be indigenous, but it is correctable, so it has been discovered. It is called the Kundabuffer Syndrome Correction: More recently, this idea was reintroduced by a Fakir and promising Master named Gurdjieff, but unfortunately it proceeded haphazardly as incorrect applications were taken up.

One such programmed unnatural archetype that had been introduced was the concept that each human was a lonely, isolated creature whose only salvation was in a mysterious father-figure god, the progenitor of all things that remained naturally separate and apart from humanity: And even then not everybody bought into that. The Hyperborean scientists found no sound reason for accepting this hypotenuse. Corrective explanation gravitated away from a separate and apart reasoning. In effect, the intention here was to inflict a revised condition into the species reasoning that was to help accelerate the revised influence upon the species and reverse the tendencies for it to naturally become subdued through evolution.

Anyway, the Master's system was meant to bring all citizens of the so-called Hyperborean civilization, as well as everybody else, up to speed in order to eventually advance into the ability of interpreting and transcending perceived dimensions of the phenomenon at large. Unfortunately not all individuals succeeded, or wished to succeed in this. This took place at or about the time after the geological upheavals that followed the great melt of the last glacier period. Hominid's first transcendence (or was it the first?) occurred at the start of the interglacial period of the present and fifth Ice Age (the Quaternary Ice Age) that is the era in which this story is set. This too, some say, is the fifth and last age of the hominids. What is not yet determined is whether or not the completion of the fifth Ice Age will begin a new epoch where the hominid will have joined other species in their extinction.

This condition of wanting to remain a base and beastly animal that fears insignificance of self (the non self) appears to be the quintessential human default. But (as we now know) it is relatively a newly programmed arrangement in the design system. This was the case of neither wanting full self-awareness nor of comprehending the Idea of taking control over the true self in assuming the proper level of awareness/reality that leads one to master their destiny. This was something the Master Mind called piercing the Ram, and it was mandatory in order to evolve as a species. Without this, a human being is a vacated vessel, an empty cast, and is a form of android that emotionally is being controlled remotely: or, in other words, something else that is living the human's life. And that 'something' (as we already know) is not immortal; it is death itself. And this obstinate insistence of retaining an un-relative persona and not delving into one's true potential but content to live in the foggy world of flesh and pitiful temptations is — specifically — an effect caused by certain influencing and dangerous archetypes. And this state, which was visited and remains among the folks in the third dimension, suddenly increased after the transcending of the Masters. It is obviously designed as such.

This begs the question as to what or who caused Homo sapiens' greater awareness function sphere to shrink exponentially from its projected growth potential, for the why now seems to be self-explanatory. However, the why remained unknown until our hero, Dyfed, made the discovery. Like Siddhartha, Dyfed was appalled at the state of the hoi polloi that was (and remains) in vast contrast to those advanced Hyperborean Masters who attained the knowledge of the non-return which leads eventually to the Eternal: And this is done by transcending from the third dimensional density into the fifth density where the expansion is exponential. This cannot be done where self isn't in control of volition.

Why, and by what rules or laws do Homo sapiens believe that they should outlive man's (humanity's) time-share on Earth? Is humanity something more special than that of any other life form that Mother Nature has nurtured? If (for any number of reasons) the answer to that last question is deemed to be yes, perhaps it's because of inherent human misperception and wonky ideas due to ancient archetypes that adversely affect humanity's understanding of reality as a whole? Who among us really believes that humanity's currently psyche of self-presence has a true awareness of our reality and a factual concept of our place within the full dimensions of reality?

However, that having all been said, certain folks among the Hyperboreans that transcended dimensional space/time a long time ago, were really freaks of nature. And although the latter mentioned freaks (Haploids) successfully managed to separate somewhat from the third dimension and accompany the Masters a smidgen of the way forward, they were not properly qualified to do so. This was because they hadn't sufficiently attained those special levels of proficiency (called piercing the Ram) that was necessary for a successful transcendence. Transcendence, of course, means having an advanced state of awareness that breaks down the barriers of false perceptions within phenomenon. Piercing the Ram included letting go and distancing oneself from former utterly false perceptions of self and accompanying persona, along with an unconditional love of all life force, and the conscious embodiment of relative emotions such as empathy, tenderness, charity, devotion, and compassion for everything that existed within that life force. It also means letting go of the social engineering whose indoctrination every third dimensional human has been exposed to. Again, frivolous and dangerous archetypes come to mind that have been intelligently grafted onto naturally involved host archetypes that are also worth disposing of. This was no easy accomplishment, for even though their civilization lasted for three thousand years it was only in the last remaining decades that this feat was actually accomplished by the Hyperboreans. Once this occurred, the Masters were more than able to return to the third dimension at will as well as explore their expanded sense of presence in the fifth dimension. The freaks of nature, however (as we know), were neither capable of expanding anywhere, and when (or if) they returned to the third density (which was the only thing they were able to do, and the only other direction they could go), their sense of presence and awareness were jammed and they became immoveable. These third dimensional immoveable types, these freaks of nature, are referred to here as Haploids.

As such they quickly lost many of their former human traits, especially that of empathy for fellow humans, they became fully self-centred and had no care for others and only for their own well-being. This incurable disease is known as psychopathy. With its début (and right from its first appearance) it quickly affected other humans (the hoi polloi) as well. But these aforementioned Haploids had a marked advantage over the hoi polloi hominids that were the residue of the Hyperborean citizenry. As already stated, the latter had been unable to transcend with their fellow citizenry. The marked advantage which the Haploids had here was that despite been jammed, they were now acutely aware of certain inhibitions and of the forceful nature of the human psyche over volitions that the hoi polloi were not. And today the latter are still mostly ignorant of it. This allowed the former to lay traps that easily vanquished the hoi polloi's natural veracity and godliness.

So, ever since the time of the ancients, the Haploids controlled the goings on of the world of men here in the third dimension. They had, individually and in small groupings, sought out kingdoms and formed dynasties of their own. Here they wielded wicked power where they displayed no consideration for the non-Haploids. Haploids also fought each other and allied with one another for advantages. They did this by utilizing the hoi polloi who were mangled to destruction in these skirmishes. The Earth was the Haploid's oyster and they set-to to gobble it all up for they had absolutely no future to plan for nor to economize over, for outside of this tainted and permanently jammed sphere of perception there was — at least for them — only a void. At first, the psyche of the non-advanced indigenous hominids, the homo-sapiens, quickly perceived strange and fierce gods at play here who they feared first and then later ventured to idolize. This was conveniently mixed with celestial and earthly cataclysms that visited the world of men and soon the frightened people were creating strange visions wound about with mythical legends. The Haploids took advantage of the hoi polloi's earlier programming by using their limited, but still useful, knowledge of the human psyche that the Masters gained and of which the hoi polloi were ignorant.

So, when the Masters re-visited the third dimensional Earth, usually for rest and recreation in order to enjoy the earthy, rugged elements of which this density consists, they initially steered clear of the other third dimensional folks with whom they shared this dimension. But in time these afflicted societies that were run by the Haploids began to impinge on the visiting revellers who objected to the impositions which these afflicted societies imposed. As true Masters of the Little Known Universe that they were they were dismayed and even incensed that humanoids could be so selfish, murderous, and greedy. They (and Dyfed was only just one such person) set out to find the reason for this and eventually discovered that the problem was essentially the nature of the Haploids who they quickly realized were Hyperborean freaks or failed Masters. As far as the hoi polloi were concerned, they were all subjected to the natural and shadowy archetypes of their psyche, as all hominids are before their final stage of advancement, if in fact they ever achieve that. So far — and thousands of years later — they certainly hadn't succeeded. But that opportunity was now being further confounded by the Haploid interference and hold over them. The whole of Good Mother Earth was now immersed in a violent strain of contention, a primitive behaviour even to anatomically and behaviourally modern Homo sapiens. Yet this condition didn't have to be.

Eventually, as we know, the Masters organized a fifth column against the tyranny of the present condition of Earth's human societies. This column is referred to as the *pack*. Dyfed Lucifer, the hero of this story, was destined to be indoctrinated into the *pack's* secrets due to the fact that although he was born in the third dimension, his mother and guardians were Masters who had been living in a third density 'resort' on an island called the Isle of Peace. Pushed out of the nest as the Haploidic world advances, members of the *pack* at large had been notified as to Dyfed's presence among them and of his general whereabouts. He is given independence of action so as to allow him to be able to find his own mode and way of operating, as well as for the Masters to secretly observe him and gauge the proficiency of his abilities. They were also to aid him if in dire trouble but let him take the lead otherwise for the time being. The time would soon come when he would be approached to be officially incorporated into the *pack*: That, as we know, had already happened.

As the Amoran Empire is now engaged and in full force, Dyfed gravitated from an outlander province called Albion to Amor, the so-called City of Love that is the centre of the empire that essentially controls the known western world. Those who control the Empire, for the most part, are the aforementioned Haploids who are a distinct minority, though much more numerous than the *pack*. But the Haploid influence has permeated the general masses at large, too. Once again, these are the aforementioned hoi polloi, but are called 'the rabble' by the Haploids themselves. There is also a special class or special rabble — a certain elevated hoi polloi — who have been seduced into the Haploidic mysteries and who have been employed to do the Haploidic bidding. Only select individuals of the hoi polloi are promoted into this cadre — generally the ones who have been successfully programmed, for a starter. The remainder hoi polloi (the rabble) on the other hand, are to be shamelessly exploited by the former. They are to be forced into servitude and debt and then into slavery in an endless cycle that brings misery. This must be emphasized. Also both the hoi polloi and the Haploids stink and have base needs and practices compared to the Masters. In total, the Haploids consist of almost all the greedy power elite that exists on Earth. This is the cadre that the *pack* seeks to destroy in order to bring sanity and non-violence to the people of the Earth. Only then can the hoi polloi be expected to address their predicament and turn their light around and shoot for full realization within eternity. During this entire story the Haploids have remained in charge and the *pack's* work does not go well.

(The one hundred thousand year old modern man)

'God is Dead?'
FRIEDRICH NIETZSCHE

In the modern human psyche, the religion that we as individuals embrace is akin to something like the way we adorn ourselves. It is how we clothe our body or with what we don ourselves with such as jewellery. Adorning our psychic make-up with religion (actually our psyche make up adorning us with religion) is a lot like choosing our hats and our jewellery. It satisfies both our individuality as well as our sense of belonging. This probably provided a commonality within our long ago clan or cultural grouping much as it does today along with it advertising who we are in a more individual sense. And this idea is still enhanced by cultural designers such as shamans and high priests of yesterday whose duty is to enforce and encourage the acceptance of this or that cultural program by the moral majority. In this way the status quo remains stable, for instability is the enemy of any organised clan, tribe, or civilization.

This is all well and good if the status quo is benevolent. Religion remains present within our psyche due to ancient archetypes. But in the modern human of the last hundred thousand years or so its association to us is relative to our subconscious, and our conscious lives has altered somewhat and our psyche has taken on a more personal quality. This, it would seem, coincides with the new branch of religion that has developed a personal god. This development being relatively new is understandingly causing some contradiction and confusion deep within humanity's psyche. Remember, along with physical evolution there is evolution of the psyche as well: there has to be. Imagine then the consequences in the future (if we're not fully prepared) when the personal god morphs into you, the actual person — which if the human time-share hasn't lapsed in the interim, will take place. Therefore, it is thus that in the last hundred thousand years each individual man (hu***man***-kind) has come to identify with god, even becoming godlike, something that would have been unheard of and un-thought of in the ancient past of pre one hundred thousand years ago.

The ancient Indo-Europaean culture that once extended in a swathe from central Asia to the Helle Sea in Europa's north west, with its gods like Zeus (Odin/Woden), Thor (Ares) Athena, Persephone (Herecura/Nehalennia), Hera, and so forth, show them to be *creatures* who have already taken on anthropomorphic properties. In other words, these fairy fantasies are actually real. Now don't volunteer any 'holy shit or no shit' expletive here on my account. Bearing in mind that a well-founded notion, which is probably an unequivocal fact, is that gods or god (from the human perspective) are inexpiably linked to the stars and/or one specific star: Here Saturn comes quickly to mind. Of course, Saturn, whose earlier name was Cronos, isn't a star you will say, it is a planet. But to the ancients, Saturn was a constant light in the night sky like any other star that we now know emits twice the amount of radiation than it absorbs from the brilliance of the sun's radiance. It is a gas giant that consist primarily of fluids above their critical points where distinct gas and liquid phases do not exist (the principal components are hydrogen and helium, along with methane). Gas giants are a class just beneath that of the brown-dwarf. According to the science of contemporary physics and astronomy, brown dwarfs are sub stellar objects too low in mass to sustain hydrogen −1 fusion reaction, such as our sun Radiance does. Radiance is designated as a yellow dwarf, not a brown one. Our earth may give off traces of radiation, too, but most of the radiation emitted from here is reflected radiation in the form of light coming from Radiance our sun. Radiation is the process by which electromagnet waves travel through space (which is actually not a vacuum). Light being the electromagnetic radiation waves which are visible. Radiation emitted from Radiance is a mixture of electromagnetic waves ranging from infrared (IR) to ultraviolet rays (UV). In the electromagnetic spectrum visible light is in between IR and UV. The jury, bye the way, is still out about the A to Z of stars, and their physics may still be rewritten again based (once more) on some other facts not known as yet, or not pieced together and grasped at this time. Possibly something like *'electricity for dummies'*, the handyman's bible, might be of some help for tomorrow's scientists and for those vastly confused science industry buffs of today who are gobbling up made-up fallacy theorems from those pseudo scientists who are practicing what they preach and publish in glossy science magazines for the gullible.

But for the moment, anyway, we are going forward with the help of the Hyperborean masters of the Little Known Universe (let's not forget that fact). And another thing, Saturn's holy day of the week is Saturday and is, therefore, without any doubt the origin of the god of Abram, along with a host of other gods whose catalogue is too lengthy to list here and whose holy days, starting on Friday, make up the long weekend. To sum up, in the time in which this narrative takes place, the concept of religion is essentially similar to that of the purpose of wearing bling. And the history of religion (once again, remember is a vector) is much like our science trends that we discard as we actually do learn more about the phenomenon that is our reality. Traditionally, neither one (science or religion) has helped us to grapple with that thing we refer to as god or Creator Being, if such a thing actually exists, which is doubtful: but its all in the wording — complicated by the psyche evolution of our mental concepts and constructs. Therefore, let's call god the pervading wave of the creative life of the little known universe seen by those of us who observe just that very same phenomenon at large.

But what has this got to do with god? Nothing, of course, for we make up our own god which is a Segway back to just where god (or the gods) really are, and that is inside us where they belong. And we get to make up just who and what they are and the list has long been posted or billboards everywhere, and that list is very long. We get to make the call. But then we have to live with it. Therein lies the problem.

It remains that our responsibility in the end is to insure that whatever god becomes us (one or the other) in a fit of fancy which we might want to put on and take off as we do designer glasses or necklaces from Piaget, Tiffany's, or Graff, that they do not insult or suppress those same expressional characteristics of other peoples': For this would be (and has been in the past) paramount in denying them an expression of reality that has the effect of abbreviating and curtailing the prospects of reality for the universe: And this despite the fact that all prospects of the universe have already been realized in the eternal moment. How fallacious is that? But also how different is that from the attitude of the Abramists and the ark of the lord their god who set out in holy wars (or jihad) in the lands by the great sea toward the going down of the sun in their conquest of all the kings of the Kaananite speaking Phoaneki and the Hittites, and the kings of the Amorites, and the Jebusites after having given a true token, notwithstanding the ritual of Gibeath Haaraloth (Gilgal) and the sounding of the ram's horn (trumpets), according to Joshua the pamphleteer? Or of that which is the nature of the Abramists' mind during their Jeshuan crusade begun in the eleventh century against the Ishlamites so as to liberate the holy land, followed by the entitled and obstinate nature of the caliphate mentality of the Ishlamites themselves against the world at large during the last millennium?

From the prospect of this modern man and his/her social culture in this narrative, what all this aught to have led up to was simply a recognition that religion with its god archetype is just that: Its archetypical. Its an Idea influenced by past and present conditions of these human's somewhat three-legged, long-distance race riot dimension. And in the reality that the humanoids have designed for themselves over the last hundred thousand years or so (irrespective of Aristocles [Plato] and Aristotle), god and religion has more or less settled into becoming adorning bling, but may also be somebody else's hocus-pocus — mumbo-jumbo: Hence, the slogan/axiom of ultra modern man — 'God is Dead'. No shit? Then so are you.

So, that crazy fool and certified madman Friedrich Nietzsche (of this novel), rather unsuspectingly, had it right all along, you see. Either that or something got lost in his translation, which is more likely. This is where we need to be respectful. This is where omnipotent, universal, religious, imperial, federal, or provincial Laws and Intentions that have to do with controlling and (by extension) in limiting or defining god, religion, culture, morals, preferences and visions, hopes, desires, attitudes and even philosophy (or anything, really) — so long as they don't interfere with anyone else in any way even by ostracising or in depriving anyone of liberty and livelihood — must be universally expunged. That's it. Get rid of the collective separate from humanity's notion of god and hopefully their definition of religion will follow. If not, than the human race is probably doomed for extinction. Certainly humanity won't advance forward any further than it already has. And it would appear that these hoi polloi have been stagnated in this rut now since they became behaviourally modern.

This didn't mean that in their past (or their present) that any existing culture or civil state of being didn't or couldn't accept the truth or the un-truth about any one religion, philosophy or attitude along with whatever god that was placed at its head: It simply means that it appears to have failed to protect the rights of all. Although this is not for a lack of trying on the part of either the existing sophists or the social liberals of yesterday and today — enlightened folks of the *pack* and their idealists, along with well informed and influenced hoi polloi. Now, generally speaking, though, (in the Haploidic governed world they are living in today), in the big picture they can even be seen to reverse the direction of humanising their environment. Furthermore, they refuse to seek assimilation with the rhythm of the phenomena of the universe. That is, apart from a few pockets of responsible folks here and there which is not nearly good enough. And here that mad aforementioned fiend of fame, the morose, moustachioed Nietzsche the nihilist was somewhat right once again. Folks who take the path of least resistance and adopt conformity with god and nationalism or whatever fuzzy warm comforting thing which is in vogue (placed and kept there by the greedy, conservative Haploidic power elite) simply because its easier or safer with less mess or fuss, are weak-minded slaves who favour virtues that suit their weaknesses and deprecate the virtues of the powerful individual with ethics that derive from natural Will and Ideal. The latter, whose who in the face of a controversy, select the path of their heart whose ethics and ideals draws them toward another more narrow and unsure path which offers the challenge of human advancement on a universal level toward wisdom and happiness while cognizant to and actively promoting the sum of humanity's total well-being follow The Way. This is short for the way of the Masters, those progenitors who within the era of modern behaviour paved the way. Unfortunately, there has been much waylaying, such as with those accredited fake magicians, the Druids, to name one. And even there, certain modern folks of this narrative who obviously suffer from monumental stupidity have even reverted back to the primitive superstition of the latter, a sure sign that acute atrophy-ism is currently underway among many moderns. 'It is the former, the follower of The Way,' said the potentially mind-malfunctioning Nietzsche, 'who are the strong and the masterful.' It is ironic that one of the truest of axioms about the actual status of a generalised *a priori* (god) resulting from dark archetypes electrifying the wild imagination of mankind that's come to us from a fellow modern man was uttered by a madman. It is also quite likely that he never really understood the brilliant ideal that he created.

Certainly the Wunschritter (who was at the farthest end from Nietzsche) never understood his madness. Nor in any way does Nietzsche's master thesis concept comply with the modern sense of applying eugenics to create a master race along with ideas of cleaning up the dirty gene pool: Absolutely not. The latter was terrorism encapsulated in a politician program. It became an agenda for certain special interest groups, including Totalitarianism, the federation for world domination and universal slavery and debt. A *pack* -funded organization called TERROR (The Eugenic Revolt Resisting Organised Regression) has continued to fight the good fight to squash Totalitarianism, although it has apparently been unsuccessful and so far misunderstood.

But as far as god is concerned, that archetypical thing is just a shadowy illusion of the hoi polloi struggling to make sense of their awareness: Its akin to going shopping for bling and a new hat, pending on the behavioural bent which these moderns adopt from time to time. Beware of this, all you folks who might identify with our poor hoi polloi. For at this time in the narrative the latter are now so stretched to the point where Totalitarianism strives to issue one their collar and their hat that is identical to everyone else's within their appointed, divisively purposed categories of slave ranks. One such rank may be labelled the Eagle category, another the Mouse or the Possum, while still another the Chipmunk. These designations were heralded early, usually when they first started school. The Rat always remained in charge, like the teacher or some other relative higher entity. The Rat was the one that wore the giant mask of the syndicated and trademarked Smile Face. If not given to put a smile on everyone's face it was certainly guaranteed to entice the skunk to put a smell on a non-conformist's attitude (and not a pleasant one at that). For the folks in our narrative this designation happens to signify just whose clan with whom one is now being forced to be associated. And as with everything else, past dues are owed, as always.

(Knives and axes and their hind hooves as clubs wielded by their long, strong limbs)

'The two impostors, triumph and disaster...'
A. TENNYSON

The sky from the cockpit, on that particular day, was exceedingly bright as were the white clouds below. It was almost noon according to the sun and his watch. Dyfed, flying solo, quickly descended, piercing a thin layer of crystallized moisture and then after securing his plane, he drove from his hanger to make it home in time for dinner. There, he knew, Walks on clouds and his granddaughter would be waiting for him. Down here under the clouds the day was thickly clouded over so no direct sunrays or shadows survived this far down beneath them. Only rain came through and soaked the waiting landscape. Now, with dinner finished and having moved into his working library, he sat at his desk before the machine with which he churned out his words. His son, Walks on Clouds, Walks on Clouds' daughter, his granddaughter were studiously bent over at a nearby table proof reading Dyfed's work. When he worked he summoned thoughts so fast that there were errors in the category of lacunas galore and aberrations of the type typical of disjointed thought processes that glared out on the typed out working page. These mistakes distracted from letting the readers' thoughts flow properly, and because they confused the reader in that way they needed to be caught and corrected. Dyfed was constantly reviewing his work and filling in the gaps. He knew he didn't have much time, either, and he was away behind on his report. Couriers from the fifth dimension were due to arrive at any time and did not like to arrive in vain or be kept waiting. Nor did he like to provide a report that was incomplete or essentially uninformative. Of course the rating of the latter two deficiencies were in the eye of the beholder, and with the bigger and more articulated picture before them the executive committee overseeing the squalor of the third density's sorry state of affairs was apt to marginalize anything Dyfed contributed unless it kept pace with the remainder of their reports filed and in keeping with the character of their inventory in general. That, of course — thought Dyfed — may constitute a weakness. However, as the secretary select of the Committee for Public Safety, he had a duty to record and assess in order that overall picture will be as accurate as possible. He knew that despite the impeccable character of each and every individual in the pack, that didn't mean necessarily that there weren't fallibilities within any of his or her powers of observance or deduction. Dyfed's observation and evaluation had always benefited from having been at close quarters to the characters involved and the events under scrutiny. When he reported anything he thought might be pertinent about the Wunschritter, for an example, the executive committee got the full goods. Nobody else that he knew of could have provided such as minute observation into that man's character and actions. Still, what came of it? It still wasn't clear to him how the Wunschritter could have thought that the people of the world, the average 'work-five-days-a-week' man on the street, (no matter from what nation state he originated) would come to see the true picture of the world his way. And, furthermore, in an electrified reversal of direction, be expected to abandon the Haploids, besmirch the hollow lies of the OPE and follow the glorious Wunschritter to worldwide victory under the musical strains of 'we will rise and triumph over all'. No, as far as Dyfed was concerned the Wunschritter didn't convey the confidence that somehow he had check mated the most powerful people on earth, the most secretive, the most anonymous, and in some unexplained way got the drop on them at their own game, so to speak. And on top of that, at the time now had them cornered? No, he thought. Dyfed always had thought the Wunschritter was a bit of a dupe, a pawn, actually, one who was easily flattered. In fact, Dyfed thought, the Wunschritter had sunk as low as the Haploids and their psychopathic henchmen. Talk about giving new wealth redistribution measures a black eye: Especially with an eye to the plight of the outcasts. Sure the Wunschritter redistributed wealth, but he did it in the same old-fashioned way. He slammed them up against the wall and robbed them: It's just as simple as that. Even the OPE showed a little more finesse, sometimes: Just a little, mind you. What good did his accurate reporting do then? Were mistakes made in the fifth density? Were the priest-kings, the Hyperboreans of old, that legion of sorcerers, magicians and druids, were they not infallible, after all? Despite their high standard bar that each man and woman's performance was dedicated to when it came to truth and integrity, could they turn out to be a jerry: A nincompoop? After all, Dyfed reflected with a guilty spasm, It took him forever to be adept at the transference into the fifth dimension, a personal regret or embarrassment that he didn't advertise, to be sure, once he found out how easy it was. He didn't like the effects, the hangover. If he could live with that he could deliver the communiqués himself, he thought. But the antics around his return caused Manandan to let it be known that he was going to be strictly supervised in the future when it came to transference. As Dyfed stood up Moochie the poochie, his little puppy wandered over and began playing by biting the bottoms of his trousers as Frederick, his older dog looked on with momentary mild interest before he laid his head back down on the floor under the desk with a thump. Dyfed stroked his beard as he gave himself up to creative thought around the situation at hand while he watched the rain falling from a fuzzy, bright grey, ragged sky.

Walks on Clouds suddenly looked at his watch, got up and walked to the edge of a crammed bookcase along the wall facing the desk and turned on a large box of television technology. Slowly, noises emerged with a electric-metallic resonance about them. Shortly after, a picture appeared in shades of different grey on an oval shaped glass tube that had been mottled green before being connected to power, or turned on, as they say. The picture of a man's head and torso, hued in light grey, darkened some and then strange bands of lines appeared across the picture as Walks on Clouds moved some antennae that was rigged up above the box and was draped, hanging from the bookcase. The lines went wavy and moved to the up and down position over top of the picture before Walks on Clouds thumped on the top of the box with his fist making them disappear. At that moment the fuzzy-as-the-clouds-like picture would have been described as coming over clear as a bell if it hadn't been for a glare hitting the picture tube glass. Walks on Clouds pulled a heavy window drape partially closed. The clear as a bell didn't last, apart form a fuzzy-as-the-clouds-like picture didn't last, so some more rigmarole with a knob on the side of the box and with the antennae was needed.

"Dad,' said Walks on Clouds, 'it's the news.' Dyfed was amused at this contraption, having heard about its technology in the making at the time of the world war. He was amused, mostly; because it was in his house and that he actually expended energy watching, or trying to watch it. It was frustrating, though. They are going to have to do better than this, he thought. There certainly were some advantages, though, to having this machine ply the plasma of physical creation around us as we both, and all of us, moved through the spheres of its torsion field, named after Dr Torsionfield, of course: That and the air frequency waves. Plasma made it all happen. Ether, was the ancients' name for it, Dyfed recalled, then began a long informative discourse to his son and granddaughter about it and the rudimentary principles, as he knew them to be. He explained how a man sitting at a desk a long way away could have his corresponding image and voice tele-ported to probably a few hundred or so families just in this city alone who were wealthy enough to afford such an item in their home. It was obvious that neither his son nor granddaughter were listening, or interested. He believed that, when he wasn't around, they would turn the gadget on, adjust the knobs and antennae, and sit down together and watch the wavy lines move across the motionless station signal; and all for nothing else better to do entertainment-wise! If anything, though, the television (when the signal came through loud and clear) brought the affairs of humanity, misrepresented and all, into full focus. That is if you had an eye to see it, and the brains to keep another eye out for any malignant, surreptitious agenda that may be attached. The talking head that beamed into your house wasn't something to be taken lightly or unquestioningly.

It became apparent to Dyfed, through reports, the media, especially the *cine-pathetic world newsreel* and the daily papers — and now the televised box — that the fight to control people's minds that was being thrashed out just beneath the surface of the mundane induced, distracted and artificially enhanced reality, was entering its final stages. He didn't need any head's up from anyone to see that. The fight was an unfair one, at that, for the party that was favoured to lose had been sucker punched after being hoodwinked and lied to. Worst of all, the losing side hadn't even realised yet that it was even in a fight, at all. Whoa, thought Dyfed! Those are some odds, but the winning side was still nervous and pulling out all the punches, unceasingly. Dyfed pondered awhile on this thought as he twirled his pencil over his fingers of one hand. He thought, as he gazed out into the rainy space before him, that the fight, the strategy, if you will, all hinged around the old axiom of divide and conquer. If blacks and whites, reds and yellows, heterosexual and homosexual, urban and rural, rich and poor, educated and uneducated, engaged and disengaged men and women, learn to identify their separateness from one another within a nation state or collectively within nation states, the elite will have established its power base over them. That is why agents of the state, he mused, often encourage the proliferation of divided political parties and religious entities and favour strong identification tags for minority groups based on virtually anything tangible such as skin colour, sex, sexual orientation, marital status, ethnic background, education level categories, and even profession and trade-career divisions which are then stereotyped and played up which subsequently become targets for the judgementally inclined among all of the above. This is what had been the on-going problem which had afforded an in depth discussion Dyfed had had recently had with Thrax, Manandan, Morgan, and King Karatakos, through the courier service, of course. Dyfed's position was that from that point on, within any of the above mentioned class sections or domains, those very perceived — yet essentially unrealistic and un-important — differences are exploited by the power elite as if the differences actually have some meaning, yet remain a psychological line of defence for them at the same time. When many people see a defenceless man (pick a colour, a presumed level of education and career) being savagely beaten, or being subjected to unwarranted abuse, by a sadistic psychopath in an establishment uniform of one kind or another, unless they personally know the defenceless man they will only be shocked and psychologically affected, later, in the aftermath which adds to the angst and division between people. This sometimes remains the case even if the assailant is wearing your uniform, but not always. If the assailant is wearing your uniform you pretty much know that the guy on the receiving end deserves what he's getting. In almost all instances it will be seen that this savagely beaten man, or targeted individual in some other way or another, who automatically as a stranger, will be outside your, and almost everybody else's, personal circle of influence and interest division. In addition, as well as being sharply divided from all of us who are white (or pick the same previous colour) in the sense that they are unfamiliar to us and are an unknown quality, they may well be further divided from us in an array of other ways — such as being a different colour altogether, or being heterosexual/homosexual, rural/urban, rich/poor, educated/uneducated, engaged/disengaged, or simply because they are wearing the uniform of a tinker, tailor, soldier sailor, beggar-man, thief, doctor, lawyer, or Indian chief. As such, they will be viewed by the onlookers as essentially alien. This is the ideal situation for the psychopathic haploids who Dyfed knew were fast becoming the chief executive officers that constituted the power elite. These onlookers, by the way, can have, what the power base seeking elites consider desired emotions of disassociation and insularity maximised by the advent of tele-vision, a technology just developed that can tele-vise an event, somewhere, anywhere, and broadcast that event somewhere else, anywhere else, (including the fall out, the aftermath, or repercussions of that event) knowing full well that almost everybody of millions, or even hundreds of millions of viewers could not possibly identify with the target in anything other than a superficial manner. (Superficial manner in this case is meant to be the feeling of empathy, the basic emotion that a real, non haploid, non psychopathic human being has for another, especially if they are witnessing others being marginalised or brutally beaten whether it's being televised or not) Is it right to say that this poor, beleaguered and marginalized man beaten by the hand which is infinitely more powerful then he, or even more powerful than his entire family and friends combined, is — when under duress — instantly marginalized by his fellow humans within the population because he is not our grandfather, our father or our son? Apparently, yes! The establishment zeroes in on an individual, separates him or her from the pack, so to speak, cuts them from the herd in order to mete out a beating, a beating which is televised and published widely (while pretending to hush it up or deny it, for which they rely on state funded broadcasting) for the obvious benefit to all in order to provide fear. Nothing, they believe, will come of public protest however vigorous it may appear at first. Also, because the target is conditioned, or dumbed down by carefully cultured prefabricated psychological implants of prejudges cleverly calculated to take advantage of human weaknesses and nature, his fellow humans also follow suit and marginalize him and let the beast take their sacrificial lamb. Most people seldom think who will be next. It might be their son, their daughter, or their mother. Of course, they — these new victims — will be treated by the population at large in exactly the same way as it did the other who came before. Nothing is going to change because it is your loved one. Is it possible, just maybe, that the man in the first example also had a family/friend circle? Was he someone's dad or brother, do you think? Who knows! Who cares? Apparently he wasn't his fellow's humans-at-large friend or brother. That's for sure! He wasn't their concern. The poor, crying human calling out for help from his fellow species, pleading with his assailant (who is only masquerading as a human, after all; he is not a human he is a psychopath or psychopathically induced) for mercy, only to be ignored and abandoned by most. Dyfed often wondered when seeing creatures' social interaction in the wild, or more recently in documentaries on film of beasts such as hyenas who when entering a herd of some kind or another and seeking out and dragging down an injured or vulnerable little creature, why the masses of others around it, at least the larger among them, could not easily group and counter-attack with their hooves, both front and back. The former used as knives and axes and their hind hooves as clubs wielded by their long, strong rear limbs, never mind their flesh ripping teeth or horns, on some occasions, all of which they are quite capable of doing, in order to bring relief and rescue to the assailed among their rank and file, their own kind. These intellectually challenged animals would have to learn to maximize their goals and minimize their setbacks so as not to kick the shit and bite the hell out of each other thereby allowing the assailant the freedom of continuing 'at the kill'. But that art and intuition would come in time and animals like the ibex and antelope, even the little deer, Dyfed thought, certainly have some potential there. But, of course, they don't really for they are too stupid, too dumb, too frightened of the consequences of their own skin. But if the ibex, deer, or antelope were able to think about it for a moment, if they were to get over their needless fear and did fight back together, it would be because they identified with the assailed. Because they identified with one another of their own kind (an important first factor) even if the victim did have different shaped spots on its fur. It would be because a stupid, dumb animal suddenly decided to include all of his species within a collective psyche because it was able to see the others as themselves and how each of them would hope to be defended, in return, by the others beating off the assailant if they became the next victim. Who knows, Dyfed mused, with the ibex or the antelope it might come to pass, in time. He wasn't so sure anymore about the humans, though. In fact the humans seemed hell bound for constantly creating and drawing up new and improved mutually exclusive categories in order to define endless imagined enemies, which is kind of the definition of those who are not like you in some slight or inconsequential way. In addition, that is, to those who really are your enemies and want you constantly in debt, struggling, working for and toward the infrastructure which they lay claim to and when you can work and provide and contribute no longer, then they want you dead, right there and then. Yet, if you don't or won't die willingly, well then it will become necessary to kill you, one way or another. Certainly, we know, there won't be any interference from onlookers. Those are the people I'm talking about, Dyfed wrote.

Those enemies! The human race or species had become, at least among themselves, a gigantic spread of creatures each within their own category or subspecies. But to the power elite — the powerful and intelligent beings who came down here from the fifth dimension a long, long time ago, who came down with the condition, those very same who are referred to by the pack as the Haploids, the psychopaths, Zeus worshippers, the anti-pack, the anti-humans, and the proponents of anti-life — they discern no difference whatsoever between any of the humans, not any two of them, not one iota: To them they are all everywhere at the same time, the same. This is, and continues to be, the case no matter what human-friendly yet destructive program had been downloaded into their national or cultural psyche, or individual personality, and no matter if they are black, white, yellow or red, whether they were heterosexual or homosexual, urban or rural, rich or poor, educated or uneducated and engaged or disengaged. None of these conditions matter or ever have mattered. Not to the enemies of humanity they haven't, not to *hostis humani generis* does it matter. It matters, apparently, only to the humans, and they ignore it at their own peril.

(Hazmat on the Edge of Town)

> 'A country whose population has been trained to
> accept the government's word and to shun those who question it,
> is a country without liberty in its future. In America today, and
> increasingly throughout the Western world…Only people who
> believe lies are socially approved and accepted as patriotic citizens.'
>
> **PAUL CRAIG ROBERTS**

Dyfed had been working at his writing desk for a number of weeks and the memory of Muns had incited a notion to return to Boss-town and check up on his widow and see that she was faring reasonably well under the circumstances. She wouldn't need money, he knew that much. Then one morning as he set aside his writing and prepared to make himself a poutine sandwich, the doorbell rang and he tended to that instead. When he opened the door without checking his security monitor Dyfed found two policemen standing on his doorstep staring strangely at him.

"Good morning sir,' the one on the right said as Dyfed quickly glanced casually at his wrist watch. The other, a younger policeman on the left began to step forward as to make an attempt to enter Dyfed's home. Dyfed put up is hand.

"Whoa,' he said. 'Good morning fellas, what can I do for you?' The policeman he had blocked from pushing his way in began to stare at him very hard now. The other policeman on the right then said…

"We got a call…'

"A complaint, actually,' butted in the other man still staring very confrontationally at Dyfed.

"A complaint about what, exactly?' asked Dyfed.

The policeman on the right who had started off the conversation glanced momentarily at the other and stammered:

"Well, um, actually they heard some kind of commotion.'

Dyfed who was standing in the middle of his door staring back at them kept silent. Suddenly he voluntarily convulsed as he affected three or four sneezes in succession.

"Excuse me, I'm bothered by the acridness of the air here. It is even more pronounced when the temperature rises, have you noticed that? They heard a commotion?'

Both police officers stared at him without answering. Then one of them said:

"They were concerned for you, I think… we think, I mean. They said there was a commotion.'

"Could I have been sneezing?' Dyfed asked, beginning to make it up as he went along. Despite his calm manner he was very concerned that two policemen were at his door, number one; and number two that the door was open to them. That was even more worrying. This was not good news today.

"You were sneezing loudly, a lot?' asked the policeman on the right, effecting a somewhat incredible expression on his mask which he wore.

"Can we please come in, sir,' the hard looking younger policeman on the left said, his eyes still riveted to Dyfed's face. Dyfed turned and looked directly at the man.

"You have bothered to come to my home, on a hot day, just as I am about to sit down for my lunch because they…that is what you said, wasn't it, somebody…they… complained that I was sneezing loudly, a lot?'

The two policemen stood their ground and fell silent though they continued to watch him closely. After a long gaze at the man on the left Dyfed shifted his eyes back to the other one on the right. After a moment that policeman said,

"Your neighbours, that is; that's who they are. We thought that they were concerned for you, that's all.'

"Yes, you said that already.'

Dyfed glanced around the urban street that his front door faced out on to. Normally quiet, at the moment it had suddenly come to life, as he had never seen it before. A large, dark electrically powered van with a huge white and red logo on it was just drawing up to the gates of one of two the houses directly across the street from him, just opposite of where the police car was parked in front of Dyfed's current residence, which was a safe house he was using. At this point Dyfed wasn't sure which house was to be the object of the driver of the van's attention. The van's sliding doors were open as it slowly and noiselessly drove up and stopped, and the uniformed man (who also wore a cap) began rummaging about its interior in an obvious effort to locate something he was bringing to one of the opposite houses. But that wasn't all. A thin, old lady a few doors down from him on the same side of the street, whose old and unused mail and paper box said Mortimer on it, attempted to rush by in her hobbling manner. She was heavily dressed in long dark clothes and wearing an old fashioned, green, brimless hat despite the heat of the day. She walked with a cane. Normally gregarious and nosey and wanting to engage anyone at any time in a banal conversation which never had a point nor arrived at a conclusion — her furtive eyes seeking out the little crevasses in the folds of whatever phenomena she apparently saw before her, man or beast, animate or inanimate — yet on this late morning she looked neither right nor left. But with the determination of a trooper, she wilfully forged ahead, past Dyfed's gate with not even so much as a glance in his direction, if you please, her wispy body slightly twisted in an odd way as she shuffled past.

At that moment Billy Hill (a middle aged neighbour from across the street) and his girlfriend, Patsy Putz (was what the neighbours called her, though Dyfed wasn't exactly certain it was her real name), were strolling arm in arm headed for the dark, navy blue van from which noises could now be heard as the delivery man in his uniform and cap was still rummaging around looking for whatever it was that he needed to deliver. Apparently, he was out of breath as well, for Dyfed could hear his laboured breathing.

"Thank you,' said Dyfed, pointedly lifting his left arm up in front of their faces as he pretended to be gazing at his wrist watch again. 'I must have neglected to put on the air conditioning that helps filter the indoor atmosphere, that's all. Talk about having an allergic reaction.' Dyfed made the kind of move that once again pretended he was finished with the conversation and in a hurry to get back to his lunch when without really moving at all he suddenly, and finally, pretended to have a thought.

'Say — are you here, then, about the break in?'

"A break in, sir?' said the policeman on the right.

"Yes. Somebody was in my home, you said. Didn't you? A neighbour wasn't it? Yes, apparently it was a neighbour who was in my bedroom when I had that sneezing fit in the bathroom? No. There must have been more than one. Neighbours, plural, surely! That is what you said. There were neighbours, prowlers in my bedroom or maybe just sneaking around the walls outside my home listening under my windows and waiting for their opportunity. Prowling and peeping, these, surely, are still indictable offences, never mind my stolen…' Dyfed tapered off as the younger officer on the left changed his mask to one of conciliation. Then butting in he said:

"Yes, these are serious matters. Let us come inside sir, now.'

"Oh,' replied Dyfed to the invitation to prolong this intrusion of information gathering, or whatever it was, 'I was just ascertaining as to why you were here, that's all.'

"So, sir,' said the policeman on the right, 'you have reason to believe that somebody or some persons, plural, you said, may have been in your home or prowling about listening under your windows at night? What makes you think that, sir?' The two policemen exchanged a peculiar glance as if they were talking, not to Dyfed, but to an unintelligible drunk, say, or a dazed stray known to have escaped from the home of the bewildered, or even a blithering idiot.

"Let us come in, sir,' said the policeman on the left more forcefully this time, 'for we will need more information on this.'

"You have given me reason, officers,' said Dyfed ignoring once again the insistence to enter his house, 'by saying that some neighbours that were trespassing under my window sills or from inside my house have broken in and were listening to me sneezing a lot and very loudly. So, was it a burglary? Have you recovered items that you have identified as being mine? Have you arrested these criminals in whose possession they were? Are these night prowlers my neighbours? Lets see…yes, last night I had a fit of sneezing, at least, as I said earlier, until I had remembered to switch on the air conditioning, again. My wife must have turned it off without thinking. She doesn't think, you know. She is very normal that way and terribly kind to me. You haven't said that you have arrested these prowlers, these neighbours of mine. Have you, by any chance?' Dyfed pretended to look toward one side of his house and then the other. The two policemen stared at Dyfed.

"What do you mean?' said the policeman on the right a little acidly as he quickly glanced at his watch.

"You have somewhere else you need to be, officer?' said Dyded. Then not getting an answer from the policeman he said. "What I mean is, you said the prowlers or the burglars heard or witnessed me sneezing at lot very loudly. Who are they? You have not identified which neighbours were the intruders or witnessed the intrusion upon my privacy. Frankly, officers, I don't understand exactly why you are here. I'm a little confused. Now, my neighbours don't give a damn about me, and they never complain anyway. Complaining draws attention. You people of all people must realize that! Do you have the right address, here? This is forty-five thirty-five Viewmont Street. Across the street is forty-five thirty-four. That is where Billy Hill lives. Maybe it's he you want? Look, there he is now with Patsy Putz; and the deliveryman looks as if he may be going there, too. There definitely is something going on over there. Something smells fishy, doesn't it? Doesn't seem right to me.'

Across the street the deliveryman in his uniform and cap was unloading some upholstered chairs onto the sidewalk beside a toilet that he had already unloaded. Billy and Patsy had stopped and were gawking at the commotion that was taking place on the sidewalk in front of Billy's house. She continued to have her left arm in his and both of them were talking rapidly in an eastern Europaean language to one another while gesturing with each of their other arms that they waved wildly in the direction of the uniformed delivery man and the obstacles with which he was cluttering up the sideway and walkway to the house. Dyfed feigned sudden annoyance at the protrusion upon his lunch despite actually completely hiding any real emotion and genuine concern of the presence at his door of these police soldiers who, employed at the tax payers' expense, were spread throughout the land to worry and harry and pry, or stick their noses in people's business from time to time no matter if any thing is going on or not around the targeted household. It was common, indeed, for them to arrive at an address on one or another pretence in order to snoop and assess. This was done for any number of reasons; none (or at the very least few) were genuine. Mostly it was just routine surveillance to compile data they could use later on for an array of different reasons that may not be connected to the person or persons living at that address at all, but which might very well effect them negatively for the rest of their lives if the notations collected there by the police soldiers were ever necessarily brought into use to fill a gap against some other, unconnected culprit.

"I'll be right there, dear,' Dyfed shouted over his shoulder and back into the house. 'It's just our friends, the police.'

"Let us in sir,' said the policeman on the left for the third or fourth time. This time his voice was strained and he made a move in order to better place himself in preparation for a charge at Dyfed.

"Is you wife with you now, sir?' enquired the policeman on the right, quickly pulling out a small electronic pad and consulting it. The second policeman's eyes were still riveted to Dyfed, though Dyfed could see by the expression in them that the mills of his mind were working as he thought over his plan to rush him and quickly force his way in up over the thresh-hold and into the house.

Dyfed had made a very slight and unperceived movement when he adjusted his body language a few moments before and had rested his right arm on the door jam with his index finger positioned over a button beside the door trim on the interior wall.

"My wife? Yes officer, she is here, laying out my lunch just as you called, but she wouldn't complain to you about my sneezing which in fact I don't even remember doing. No. I didn't sneeze loudly, a lot, or at all, not yesterday, anyway. Just now I did, that's all. There seems to be something in the air, some chemical or unburned molecule.' Dyfed wiggled his nostrils a bit for emphasis.

" You know,' Dyfed screwed up his face in a comical wince as though confused by something, 'I didn't even realize that sneezing was against the law if heard by burglars and snoopers, so I'm glad you officers dropped by to tell me. Oh golly! Lookie what's going on there now.'

Giving a lightening quick glance across the street at the deliveryman where Dyfed's eyes were being focussed, and seeing that the policemen were distracted momentarily, Dyfed pushed the button and an iron grill shot from his left across the door gap and clicked into the receiving mechanism with a discernable lock-mode finality. It startled both policemen but the younger one reacted first and in anger. He quickly reached out with one hand although trying to use both, but as he had just pulled out an electronic pad, like the other officer, he fumbled a bit with a left arm and a right elbow pushed forward instead. It wouldn't have done him any good, anyway. The security grill was unstoppable by human hand, arm, foot or leg unless a beam placed at Dyfed's head level was broken at which point it stopped.

"I command you to open this now,' said the officer on the left, who at the same time quickly unsnapped the securing strap of his service sidearm.

"Please, sir,' said the policeman on the right, obviously of higher intellect, as he tried to gain control of the situation. 'We are here to help. Talk to us a moment,' though his statement belied the look of hatred coupled with alarm on the other policeman's face. 'It says here that your wife is deceased, sir. It's ok that she continues to live on in your mind the way she does. We understand.'

"We are also here to assist you in getting your 'refid',' said the policeman on the left, obviously shifting to a conciliatory plan B, as he too consulted his pad, which he had inadvertently dropped as soon as the grill had shut in his face.

Refid stood for r.f.i.d, or radio frequency identification that came in the form of a micro chip (so called) that almost all humans now had implanted into their bodies according to the law. It didn't matter what country you lived in either, although some countries were stricter than others. Not strict so much in enforcing the world law — which was the United Allied States of the World's (UASW) law — which all nations enforced, but in the aspect of applying the technology in an expedient manner, everywhere. Many of the poorer states were sloppy and, therefore, infested with felons from every part of the world. All the more advanced nations, like United Kingdom of Albion (UKA), the United States (US), the Northern Dominion (ND), Greater United Europa (GUE), or the Consolidated Republics of the East (CRE) — a more loosely held together coalition of nations including Inja and Ch'in and all of the their subsidiaries, expedited the constant monitoring of all persons. These were not specific persons, of course, unless in fact a specific person was being focussed on. A specific person was a class A.

Apparently there were about two hundred and fifty thousand specific persons (class A) being closely sought or focussed on at any given moment in time and approximately four or four and a half billion lass B people being monitored around the clock under normal conditions. This was virtually the entire world's population, now down to almost half from what it was only a decade and a half before. This surveillance and monitoring of the denizens was for their own protection, of course.

Almost all people, other than the powerful elite, were B class monitors, as they called them, and every purchase they made, along with every form of credit had to be conducted through their account by law. And every communication or user charge they incurred or any transaction used to availed themselves, their exact financial status and records along with sundry records of any and all kinds, and even their exact geographically positioned whereabouts was being tracked. In essence it was being carried around individually by them always and available to the world electronic brain and eye (WEBE). This is why it was so difficult fan existence for class A persons who were being specifically sought or hunted to remain uncaught.

Normally, these people could be identified and located quickly by machines orbiting the Earth that could be engaged at once and when down loaded with the location data of an individual, a deadly beam could be shot down thereby killing the dangerous felon in question and, hence, bringing more safety to the law abiding Class B registries. All personal identification numbers were registered. Without one, one didn't exist.

Of course, some people — especially the ones who had some reason or another to fear the power elite and their machines — contracted aversion tactics and either dodged the refid implants altogether or, at some cost, had fake data entered. Dyfed, of course, was one of these people. High quality knock offs, like the one Dyfed wore (and could discard, as it was not implanted) were even able to rearrange the wearer's geographic location as well. This state of affairs, of course, allowed every manager and their underlings of each and every account of the World Bank and every single registered agency subservient to the UASW (the United Allied States of the World was one of the fronts for the global power elite whose store front is the World Bank), to be able to access the whereabouts of almost every registered person practically anywhere in the world. Dyfed, of course, was not one of these.

But those who it did impact could even have their movements traced over long spans of time due to data memory cards (DMC) often with some help from composite face similarity (CFS) kits that could be used alongside the DMCs that can 'rough in' and reduce scanning potentials as well as save time and work. Again, a huge volume of worldwide data — the comings and goings of billions — can be down loaded and run through any one of these apparatus with the result (and very quickly at that) that the culprit will often immerge into sight. His position will immerge first on the search engine then an applicable camera lens on the multitude of satellites that scour the surface of the Earth will be trained onto that exact location and then, presto!

Subsidiary cameras were part of the local scan networking that line the streets and ceilings of government and public buildings and places and are also used to hone in. Then, alongside the felon's file photo (all persons who are being hunted — for any reason — are considered felons) there will appear the current image of that same individual in situation, so long as they are within camera range. If in fact they are travelling in a vehicle such as public transit, or high volume long distant vehicles such as rapid trains, air travel and even ferries, the local scan network (LSN) that monitors the vehicle or shopping plaza in question can be spliced in to the main WEBE and the dangerous person that's jeopardizing public safety will come up on the video screen doing whatever they are doing at that very instant. And, of course, from then on all their actions can be watched closely. Washrooms are favourite locations. They can be watched while they are picking their nose, watched while being captured by the police unit that is involved who in turn are in radio contact with those monitoring him or her in live, same time-frame activities. Or, they may be watched as they are zapped and shredded by the deadly beam from one of many death machines that are floating around all over the place high above them, as well.

The target needs to be outside, of course, at least in most cases. But even on one's own vehicle laws require there to be a built in monitor that is pursuant to manufacturer standards that automatically emits a constant signal identifying the licensed owner that can be retrieved anytime (if needed) by satellite. Disabling any form of surveillance equipment anywhere without license is an indictable offence and contrary to terms of ownership and usage. Sometimes what is known as collateral damage, the establishment's terminology for the killing of innocent bystanders, occurs. But the establishment (a bureau), although it doesn't really care or feel remorse for any action, tries to avoid the fallout of aggravation such as needless demonstration or anger against the state that can result in repudiating a felony charge: This, despite the fact that any demonstration or protest activity is illegal and strictly forbidden.

Generally, however, they like to isolate the target from other people around the target either on the street, road, garden or park. In any case, the relatively quick and easy manner of locating an identifiable individual is generally due to the fact that even if the exact position is not known, certainly the general location of the felon is usually knowable, and can be broken down from there.

"My refid is in good working order and I don't need it repaired or replaced,' countered Dyfed through the grill that now separated them, speaking directly, again, to the policeman on the left. 'And as far as my mental health and my deceased wife who is actually not deceased, all is in good order there, too. Furthermore, I'm not accustomed to sneezing, normally, neither is my wife, as neither of us have allergies common to the younger generation. This affliction today has come about from modern childhood diets of highly fertilized foodstuffs where the chemicals used were controversial and or untried or just plain known to be dangerous. Never mind the CAFOs (Confined Animal Feeding Operations) and its inherent problems. No, it wasn't there in our day, my wife and I, that is. You obviously have the wrong address, you certainly have the wrong man, or… lets put it this way: The man you are looking for, well, he doesn't live here any more! So beat it!'

Dyfed couldn't believe that the establishment had found him, but they certainly had blundered into him while exercising their duty to search and watch, listen and pry here and over there and ask questions of one house about the activities of another house. He didn't waste much time thinking of these things, though, for there was only one real important matter on his mind now. He knew he didn't have much time to gather up what he needed to keep from them and get out. As he thought, he heard shots and their impact on the steel door. There was no easy way in, Dyfed knew that. Safe houses had been built to withstand a siege to some degree but it was better to get out fast. Police were using aerial vehicles capable of stationary flight that were used to launch missiles into homes. But normally in these circumstances they would take some precautions and evacuate the neighbourhood. In this case Dyfed had no worries.

But in respect to the former normal situation, that could (under different circumstance) pose a bit of a problem for an escapee, Dyfed's initial escape route was through a mad tunnel that led to another safe house — in Dyfed's case, safe house D — that lay diagonally across the main road and whose entrance faced another street running at right angles to the main road this house was on. Safe house D was another neighbour who was probably watching this scenario unfold at this very moment. He may not be out of the woods just yet, he thought as he hurriedly threw some personal items along with his computer into a large trunk with rollers. The rules were simple enough in respect to the work he did. There was no electronic communication at such times between members of *the pack* unless they used computer equipment or its download file issued to *the pack* by its trusted leaders. The problem now was they weren't as secure as they had been just a few solar cycles ago. Code words such as selah and en to pan were no longer used, indeed, they were mostly forgotten.

Outside of the download file, nothing was stored electronically. Everything was written by hand and ancient languages were preferred. No full manuscript was written in the same language. A script had been developed for these purposes (Dyfed had participated in that) that was made of symbols that didn't match or resemble any other kind of writing. There were other tricks to keep information from prying minds. *The pack* also had an extremely sophisticated key that was devised from the use of prime numbers. This method, however, was used for important flash messages to be distributed quickly worldwide between themselves or from their organizers alerting them to something important. It being public enough showed the establishment that enemy intelligence was at work but it remained totally unintelligible to all but the initiated few.

The key for this communication worked on the crypto method where two prime numbers were used as the basis. These prime numbers were then multiplied together that achieved a non prime number. That non prime number was passed around and could be made public, even published by the local media; it wouldn't matter. Dyfed often got it via the postal delivery service or from the personals on the televised rolling advertisements. In this way only the knowledge of that non prime number was needed to scramble messages which could then be printed publicly or even read over the radio, whereas, to unscramble it the two prime factors needed to be known. The two prime factor numbers used would traditionally contain approximately eighty digits each that would produce a non-prime product of over a hundred digits. It was very complicated to tackle but very simple to operate.

The pack and friends of *the pack* used this but still did not normally communicate electronically by any means as their leaders frowned upon even unintelligent communications as they could still indicate potential strengths as well as the quantities of adversity at large. The goal was to be as silent as possible before the increasingly sophisticated listening apparatus at large and remain silently as they listen to the folks of the third dimension.

Dyfed now activated his evacuee alert alarm.

(Doris and the big mosey on to Megatropolis and Manna hata)

'It is better to die on your feet than live on your knees.'
EMILIANO ZAPATA (ATTRIBUTED)

When Dyfed resurfaced from his underground conduit at his destination across the street into the fourth of a network of safe houses that had been established in this neighbourhood, some very concern faces greeted him. There had been a compromise, an imperilment, and a very dangerous one at that, it was agreed, and they were presently awaiting orders or advice of what to do next, they told him. The counsel came quickly; very quickly under the circumstances, arriving just as the homes on either side, across the street, and directly behind Dyfed's vacated safe house were been evacuated. The messenger had quickly slipped in to safe house D by taking advantage of the confusion of the melee which was just then taking place outside as people were being shuffled off to a nearby park by police. At the same time the state controlled news agencies (three, all told) arrived and not without some confusion, began to move in closer to the condoned off area in order to film the event. All of this took place in thirty minutes. This televised coverage for prime time noon hour news that was coming up in a matter of minutes necessitated the hustle and bustle that was now taking place outside. People everywhere were shouting out orders. It was even possible, thought some, that some of those who were shouting out orders were just passing by and had no authority over anyone in sight. It was part of the encouraged mind-set but it often had decidedly rude awakening consequences. This wasn't such an uncommon a situation as you might think. Each independently operated government owned and assisted news outlet jostled and jockeyed for position to best capture for their television viewers the destruction of the dangerous person or persons along with their nest, their warren, their cell. The media used all three of these descriptive nouns. In this case the house targeted for obliteration and that took place after only a few phoney attempts to mediate and flush out its human contents with gas. It almost appeared that the television crew, never mind their supervisors who were barking out commands, were more influential than the soldiery in attendance who stood around holding their automatic weapons in a vertical position, as opposed to being slung casually under their arm. The elderly messenger who arrived had no sooner let herself in through the locked door and stepped into the front hall of safe house D, and into a hushed silence, when a third air ship — its rotors heavily beating the warm humid autumn air — was heard approaching.

"There are listening vehicles swarming all over,' said the new arrival in a commanding sort of voice. She was an elderly woman who was dressed typically enough in an old fashioned manner wearing a cream coloured dress with colourful patterns covering it under a burgundy wool cardigan with matching hat and purse. She also used a cane, though she appeared sprite enough, her hosts thought. 'They comprise of different coloured vans with commercial insignia on them, as well as small, private looking electric vehicles milling around the perimeter of the action.'

"All our electronic devices are shut off," said one of the women inhabiting D house. 'We've been quiet since it was noticed that our subject had visitors at his door. And obviously we don't broadcast or receive any communications from this address in any form or another at any time, other than the programmed simulated normal traffic ruse to deflect any curiosity about our silence. We are a back-up house, here, and support group mainly,' she added, speaking directly to the elderly woman.

"I know," the other answered, 'and what program are you using to produce simulated normal traffic?'

"We recently changed to a new program,' the other answered. 'It utilizes a rotation of a hundred and twenty locations with traffic data that is the usual credit card updates and conversations pertinent to arranging for new or expanded credit or financial management. That and real live pizza deliveries.'

"Good, and in respect to the current emergency, how are the other houses doing?'

"There are only two others, B and C, and B has now been evacuated and C is sitting tight, for now. At least they — actually it is a woman and her daughter — haven't arrived here, in any case.'

"It's chaos out there right now,' said the elderly lady, 'and the uniformed police are easily equalled in force by soldiers and plain clothes experts.' The noise overhead became quite loud now that the gun ship hovered almost directly overhead.

"The other two air ships are maintaining surveillance,' said the new arrival again in a slight louder voice. 'They are positioned in stationary posts, I noted, which are advantageous to view all the comings and goings.' Just as she finished speaking there was a horrendous noise as safe house A, which Dyfed had been inhabiting, was struck by an air to surface missile fired from the recently arrived gunship that was hovering almost directly over the street in front of the targeted home. Safe house D, which had not received the anticipated order to evacuate — an opportune moment for Dyfed to get clear of the area — being relatively close to safe house A, shook violently from the ensuing explosion.

"They didn't waste much time in background checks or negotiations on that one,' said Dyfed, light heartedly and with a whimsical smile.

"No need,' said the elderly new arrival turning her attention to Dyfed. 'They realised too late that they had screwed up, and anyway, they will announce shortly, tomorrow maybe, that they recovered the burned remnants of the body of so and so. It won't be your name, that much we can be thankful for, as well as your timely escape, no matter what or whomever else they determine was inside at the time of the strike. They may find it expedient to inform the public that they extinguished three, five, or twenty-five dangerous dissidents burning with zealousness, who knows? Whatever; they already had their final report completed long before the gunship arrived, I'm sure of that.' "They won't find anybody or anything,' replied Dyfed.

"That won't change their final report, though.'

"What do you mean screwed up?' asked Dyfed.

"They were caught off guard, weren't they? They didn't know who actually inhabited that place. Not knowing means they screwed up.'

"Maybe that was why they were making enquiries; trying to find out who resided there,' responded Dyfed.

"Yes, I agree. So they screwed up twice, then, before and after,' was her response.

There was all kinds of shouting going back and forth and sirens wailing outside safe house D, now, and a few of the occupants were surreptitiously peeking out at it all through the various means they had at hand. The elderly lady motioned with her eyebrows and with a slight jerk of her head to Dyfed that implied that he step away from the others and speak with her quietly, alone.

"I know who you are,' she said flatly, when they had moved toward the arched entrance way to an empty sitting room. She spoke the common Angle language of Albion without any accent, apart from the slight local inflection indigenous to the area hereabouts. Dyfed contemplated her large, brown, attentive eyes beholding him boldly. 'I've known about you for a long, long time,' she said. My name is Doris,' she continued, 'Doris ben Jamin.'

"Really,' answered Dyfed. 'I knew a man by that name once. Haven't seen him in a long time, though.'

"You knew a man named Doris?' she asked, looking him up and down with amusement written across her face. Tell me about it.

"No, silly,' he answered, 'I knew a man by the name ben Jamin.'

"Yes, of course you do, Esau ben Jamin, my brother.'

"What? Esau? I've always called him Ebreo — he is your brother? I didn't even know he had a sister.'

"Why would you? Why would you really know anything about Esau? Why would he tell you anything about himself? That's not like him to talk about himself like that.'

"Well,' Dyfed ventured, thinking that he may be entering new terrain after all, 'I know that Esau was born in Ash Sham in southern Aram and that your mother was a princess and a Sidonite and your father an Edomite from the land of Esau, but your paternal grandfather had been a Hittite from the Taurus mountains north of Antioch.' Ebreo, Dyfed now recalled, had told him all that upon their first meeting back in the sixth century of the new era; that was fourteen centuries ago! Now, as he searched for reaction in Doris' face, he wondered for the first time if there had been any truth to that story. Doris suddenly smiled pleasantly as she looked upon Dyfed.

"My little brother held my hand as we came into the land of Canaan, we were both quite young,' she recounted, her expressive eyes showing Dyfed that she was visualizing the event of long ago. 'But he was wrong about Antioch, for Granddad came from the land around the city of Urha now known as Urfa. He was Habiru, a nomadic tribe, but was referred to as Ibrim, or Ebreo, as you say, for he was of the faith of Abram.'

"So are the followers of Jeshua Adon, of the faith of Abram, and the Ishmaelites, too,' said Dyfed.

"Yes,' she said almost hesitantly, looking up at him bashfully through her eye lashes. A strange posture, thought Dyfed, for an elderly woman though not unattractive. He thought she may have been quite a beauty, long ago, and it occurred to him at that point that she might now resemble a larger version of her pre-pubescence self. 'But the Ibrim culture conflated about the time of the Mitanni empire,' she added, 'and that was a long time before Jeshua Adon,' she added.

"I would concur that an important aspect of the Habiru culture conflated then,' replied Dyfed, 'maybe even earlier yet, however, it is unlikely that Abram's contribution was part of any of that, at least until a thousand solar cycles later when it might have begun to resemble the orthodox culture of today, although probably not.'

"I will not argue about that for I don't know, she answered, but I do know that very early on our tribe settled the affairs of its state of being. Among those affairs was a tenet regarding debt owed which was to be forgiven, that is, the debtor was to be released from his debt after seven years. Another was concerned with the protocols of justice, and the examination of an accused and evidence of the appellant, as well.'

"Yes,' replied Dyfed again. 'It was a wonderful advancement that your people undoubtedly conflated together with all the other highest of standards back as far, perhaps as Akkad, who knows! But today that influence has waned, as well as the monotheist religions in general and the Haploids have taken a leaf out of the book of the grandson of Sargon who, claiming divinity for himself, changed his name to Naram Sin, the moon god. Now we have the Naram Sin personality types.'

"Now I see you have a passion for the subject,' interjected Doris, 'but I have a responsibility to get you to safety so we must now prepare to retreat from this place.'

With Bobby Hebb's hit song 'Sunny' oozing out into the motor chariot's interior, Doris and Dyfed drove north with the Hackensack River somewhere off to the west and the plume of black smoke that was the remains of his local secure-domicile rising in the rear mirror which now disappeared from sight. Dyfed was at the wheel of the vehicle while Doris gave him directions and talked frequently, sometimes prying Dyfed about his affairs with her brother, while at other times chatting amiably about the autumn sky and the turning leaves. High powered, unmarked police vehicles, manned by heavily armed men and women, moved about constantly on the urban streets. There was nothing unusual about that, however.

"So, if you live in Megatropolis city how is it you got to where I was so soon?' Dyfed asked. 'It has to be half an hour away unless you are frozen in traffic.'

"I was already there,' she answered.

"You were?'

"Yes,' she said. 'I was coming to see you.'

"Why?'

"I was instructed to, that's why.'

They had just finished driving through a heavily secured and fenced off stretch of road that cut through a vast city (actually part of the suburb of Megatropolis) of tent and other makeshift dwellings. Then after glancing at his watch Dyfed slowly pulled into a tidy little roadhouse and parked in a lot along the pub's west wall. Armed security officers peered in at them as they passed through the gate into the compound and continued to scrutinize them while they remained in sight. However, two respectable looking people driving a late model vehicle were not the security police's normal focus.

"Since agents supposedly acting on the behalf of the government and the people of the Unified States have in every likelihood just liquidated my entire scotch, gin and vodka collection, along with some other collectables, I feel like having a macaroni and cheese sandwich washed down with a martini, how about you? Maybe a second martini for the road, what do you say? It's almost one o'clock, anyway; I'm buying.'

"Now,' –– Dyfed asked as soon as two gin martini biancos with kalamata olives were set in front of them, and after insuring that another round was on its way — 'what do you mean you were coming to see me? Who sent you?'

Doris smiled a foxy little smile and said, "Dyfed Lucifer! Why, the executive sent me, of course.'

"Who in particular?'

"Who in particular, well lets see, what's his name — ah…how about Morgant Cerrag who was accompanied at the time by Giorgi Posh.' She giggled, then after resuming her pixie smile that she kept handy she turned and looked to her left. In doing so she showed him her right profile that he noted was different from her left that he had been familiarizing himself with the past twenty minutes while driving. She had taken off her hat when they had begun to drive and her light brown hair, obviously dyed, was still fairly thick and bunched around in a youngish (mutton dressed up as lamb) style. Not that there was anything wrong about mutton being dressed up as lamb or anything like that. Girls have to work with what they've got.

"So what does he, I mean they, want?' he asked.

"Giorgi Posh wants you to go to Nova Troia,' she said bluntly. 'And Mr Cerrag agreed.'

Dyfed finished his drink then delectably and slowly ate the olive. Dyfed's opinion of Doris was that she was about as subtle as Mr Luther's ninety-five arguments against the Church of Amor, he decided.

"There is this convention of sorts and they want you there,' she answered.

"Where, at his sumptuous suite high above the city?'

"I have the address at my apartment,' she said.

Dyfed did not respond. Then the second round of martinis came.

'What are you doing in this neck of the woods, by the way?' asked Doris. 'I understand that you live, or spend most of you time somewhere out on the west coast.'

"Hmm…maybe. I wouldn't mind. I gotta get back out there one day,' he said lazily.

"So, what are you doing here, then?'

Dyfed looked over at her and held her eyes.

"So, what's it to you? What do you want to know for?' he asked matter of factly as he turned away from her and called out. 'Hey –– waiter,' he said, as the white jacketed man began to move away from their table. 'Remember, another round here before too long.'

"I saved your life,' she said affecting astonishment at his presumed ungratefulness.

"No you didn't. According to you what you did was you brought me a message from Giorgi Posh and Morgant Cerrag, that's all; and a ride back to the city. Maybe you're a spy and I've decided I've got to report you for asking questions that have nothing to do with you. Anyway, where's your cane?' She laughed heartily and so did Dyfed.

"You were lucky, today,' she said with some heart-felt emotion.

Dyfed had been thinking that to himself all the way on the drive here. He'd got out just on the skin of his teeth. As for Doris she remained quiet on the other side of the white-clothed table and watching him she waited for him to respond.

"I've been working here at different jobs, though mostly at Columbo University.'

"Ah, you are teaching?'

"No. I am a professor, but I'm not doing that. I'm combing through the physics curriculum. There are some anomalies that we've identified, anomalies in what is being taught which differs from what we know to be the truth and will play havoc with the hoi polloi's curriculum for advancement. The problem is not that the professors are not up to speed but rather that the truth, or correctness of approach and evaluation, are being intentionally sidestepped and eager young minds are being misled about knowledgeable facts which we have already attained, and have attained for some time. Although the problem is much more acute now, we think it must have been going on for a while, at least since the Great War. And it is not just Columbo, either. Other universities show a similar pattern of error. Even societies and the aero-space agencies appear tainted.'

"But why?'

"Well, if you accept the first fact then the answer is obvious. It is a matter of dumbing down the experts that will slowly sift important knowledge out of the heads and hands of the masses and leave it in the hands of the chosen few. Apparently they are the few who are descended from his lordship, Naram Sin.'

"Who?' she asked, jerking her head around.

"Yes? he answered' He looked at her looking at him, and then looked away.

'Now that so many minds have produced a plethora of knowledge,' he continued, 'which in itself has become a innovating miracle just like the discovery of bronze or the discovery of iron alloy; the invention of massing huge amounts of knowledge is power, just like those old inventions and miracles were. Greedy people gravitate and keep secretive those innovations that elevate them above the common man and woman. This is not new. You remember the fever and that all-out-scrimmage around the technology of discovering and producing iron and keeping it away from everyone else, don't you?'

Doris feigned a kick at Dyfed's shin.

"What kind of a remark is that to make to a lady?' she asked. 'It is typically banal and certainly nothing that I would come up with. Of course,' she paused a moment, 'I don't have a penis like you and your other Doris friend have to divert blood away from my brain.' She smiled at him in a facetiously tender manner then put her hand in front of her mouth as she burst out laughing. 'And who the hell is this Naram Sin, again?' she asked.

"Oh, just another believer in divine rule who decided to make himself one with the dogs — I mean gods. He was formerly a king and a general who made himself into the moon dog god!'

"Or doggone moon goddess, y' mean,' she said.

Dyfed shrugged.

'I see,' she exclaimed demonstratively. 'Just another one of your cross dresser friends from back in the day?' she dryly responded.

Dyfed marvelled that Doris did not actually look all that old at all, now. At least not nearly as old as she appeared when he first saw her. Sure, the cane and the elderly act was something of a necessary prop under the circumstances, but even so. He checked his drink. It was empty.

"Lets go,' she said. 'I'll pay. I think it is safer to use a cash card rather than debit from my account, under the circumstances.'

Since the value of fiat currency had become a hoax, cash cards had been all the rage recently. They were good so long as you spent them within a week or two before the value of the currency changed. That change was usually due to artificial alterations that were happening down at the big bank. You could purchase cash cards almost anywhere in five different denominations that would allow you to shop, rent, or procure smallish type items such as lunch or dinners for two or three people, transportation fare or a few articles of cheap clothing and the like. The value of the largest denomination, or 'heaviest' card, was equal to little more than tradesman's daily wage. Each time you used them the price was deducted from the card until you had insufficient funds left to buy anything at all; and that was just a low number on the left of the decimal. Remaining unused funds were not transferable so the card purchaser generally always lost a tiny portion each time unless they calculated their purchasing down to the last dollar. Such cards were slowly drained of credit to the advantage of the card company that was a branch of the People's World Bank. Since there was no cash or coin anymore, nobody could give or receive cold cash change from any market counter exchange.

"Why don't we have an early supper,' he said. 'I know a nice place by the river before we cross over into the city.'

Later, having dined and even danced alone at the Edge-Water Deck, as it was called, they watched the lights come on all over the city across the river and watched the ferries and little boats brighten, too, as they plied the choppy and darkening waters of the river. The restaurant was quiet and private, not too big, and Dyfed and Doris settled down and explored each other's thoughts. She was fun to be with, he thought, much different than Ceredwyn, though she was fun, too, but in a different way. A jazz band continued to play soft melodic tunes to a sparse house as though it was a command performance. Probably something they are used to in these financial harder times, he thought. His mind wandered in a relaxed way, which told him he felt secure despite the fright he had had earlier on that day. At one point Doris took his hand into hers and moved her bum over to sit beside and much closer, into him. They continued to watch the city brighten as the sky darkened and they noted the great helium zeppelins, dozens and dozens of them, that were stationed motionless high over the city with their inflated envelopes and displayed logos catching the last rays of the sun. They watched as they twisted and turned like great sea going sailing ships of old at anchor. They lay in the strata of air turbulence caused by the hot effluence funnelled skyward by tall, slim flue stacks and chimney ventilators. The skyline, in addition to the huge buildings reaching upward, was almost like a return to the old days, Dyfed thought, although the effluence was colourless rather than black smoke. Along with the billowing clouds of black smoke, the airports, which this great city had once supported, were basically no more, either. With the exception of only one of these, the central airport that was only partly in use, all the others had been dismantled. Most aircraft with gas turbines of one sort or another were vertical take-off and there was no longer the huge air traffic in and out of the city to all parts of the world as there had once been. The large billowing dirigibles that were now in prominent use fared better economically in the air at rest than on a necessary and fenced in (and guarded) ground depot whose land was at a premium, anyway. Not only that but the air above Megatropolis tended to be warmer than over the waters and land around it and this caused up currents of inflated molecules to assist in the manoeuvring of the gigantic, floating air ships in positive ways. Frequently, as he and Doris watched, one or two of these airships at a time would start their propellers (although unseen and unheard at this distance) and as their rudders controlled the ships' lateral movements, Dyfed and Doris watched as they silently rose and turned in order to glide like a silver lined cloud across the river high over head toward the Jersey air field to pick up human cargo or container shipments destined for somewhere across the continent or to the other side of the world. Other dirigibles, often in spread out groups of three or four, were constantly and silently gliding either toward the hub of the great city from one direction or another while some others were gliding away. Still the central hub of Megatropolis appeared like a birthday cake with a large shiny and brightly lit up cluster of different shaped balloons hovering well above her tallest skyscrapers as other dirigibles all brightly lit up circled around its perimeter like some kind of brightly lit-up merry-go-round in the sky. Doris kissed Dyfed gently yet passionately in the gloaming of the lounge which acted as their initiative to make the move to their final destination across the river and home.

Doris gave directions to her apartment as they turned off the turnpike onto the heavily guarded bridge and headed southeast into an inferno of activity. Here, the turnpike sailed like a thin rail high in the sky; below shimmering waters caught by moving lights chipped the surface of the wide river like some florescent, golden day-glow seafoam spreading silently over black sand. The Gold Mine, the Big and Ample Apple stood jarringly dead ahead. In the near distance -- beneath those floating giant airships -- square and vertical columns of light rose up into the now darkened sky. These structures contained the households and the commercial offices of the populace while dubbing as air docks with their ferry sized roof cleats, electrical plug-ins and hydro connections to the sky-side. Aside from this as the two of them skimmed along in her electric powered chariot traversing over Megatropolis' topside, they were serenaded by sweet sounds from musical instruments. These brilliant drops of music that sprinkled over them from the music band of the chariot's FM wireless radio, burst (or was squeezed) or simply painstakingly extracted in broad vibrating bands with an immaculate finesse from an assortment of musical instruments that pouting with a cute talk-back rhythm and chirp such as the ultra sax that mingled with fine tinkling chips of silver dollar piano chords, along with boozy bass cellos. These twisting fire brand-type chords -- if not a Tommasini keyboard composition exactly -- were certainly similar to the likes of Carlos Santana's guitar that pinched and squeezed amid the dying embers of a hot-tamales' summer salsa afternoon. That, or the rolling thunder sound of the Pink Floyd (not Dylan) complete with the beating down of cool, hard sparks of rain that tends to meld into a jolly inverted deja vu perched upon a mauve coloured valley in the hobbit distance crowned by the crimson queen. But surely it is gay and joyous as all get-out, for after all, had not the chariot's two occupants at this time (in their induced state of being) embarked on a journey of tunnel vision to spider-spooky grating guarding the wrought-iron crypt at the House of Capulet's family tomb?

Actually, on their short drive from the Hackensack to the Hud river, which only a few solar cycles ago would have taken only a few minutes, they had encountered nothing less than a dozen major security check points each manned by homeland security agents and backed up by a dozen or so soldiers. Today it had taken almost three hours, and that was why Dyfed had insisted on the pub stop for a break of normality. Now, as they entered the downtown section of Megatropolis' central hub, police and soldiers were everywhere. Often these particular government agents were employed in the detaining of younger men often just out with their girl, but the checkpoints under the authority of homeland security increased as well, and general surveillance, both from heat imaging cameras and combat clad soldiers constantly peering into vehicles, was intense. It was like entering a gigantic machine, a human machine and its roar of life around them was almost deafening. People of all looks and sizes were thronging everywhere so that Dyfed, who had not been driving very fast at any time, had to slow up even more.

"I'll need to access credit through my bank,' said Dyfed glancing at his watch and feeling weary. 'Tomorrow will do, I guess.'

The glaring lights of the city that earlier had enhanced the fading twilight that scurried quickly to the west back across the river had grown murky dark as Doris guided him to her building where she told him her apartment also looked west over the river toward the sunset. Above, and all around them, the lights from the tall buildings that shot up to the sky caught the under bellies of the flotilla of zeppelins that clustered overhead like a school of jellyfish floating near the cloud/sea surface. From this angle, however, they now appeared more spaced apart. It was also possible to see that the air ships were tiered at different heights, each layer a safe distance from those below and above. The street was also very busy and at first Dyfed was unable to park her car because of men and women sitting on the curb that was her designated spot. Some of the people were eating, others carrying on as though they were at a meeting of some kind, along with other goings on that being watched by visible and invisible agents. The latter, Dyfed knew, would appear as the quintessence of public society in general; they were the ones in smelly, unwashed clothes, eating a hotdog on the run and shouting out some or another greeting, prearrangement or defiance to superfluous buffoons or fellow agents at large.

'Don't you have secure parking?' Dyfed enquired as he craned his head and looked up at the building they had come to.

"Of course, but this is a company car and sometimes the congestion is so intense I am not able to get my vehicle out into the street in an emergency call.' Dyfed didn't say anything for a moment.

"I have an account with the Jewel Banking House at number one Fence street,' he said. I should try and get there the first thing in the morning and speak with whomever, as well as send for my pilot and my plane. I'll get in touch with Mr Morgant Cerrag tomorrow, first thing,' he said. 'Then I'll get the bank to arrange my licence that will be necessary to have him bring my jet here to Megatropolis Central. Everything I do is under corporate business, anyway, that way I don't…'

"You will come up?' she asked, interrupting him. Dyfed hesitated.

"Yes,' she added, 'I know you have an account with the bank. I'm one of its directors. I'll drive you in nice an early myself, if you want. In fact, she hesitated a moment, 'I'd do anything for a hunk of handsome man like you.'

Doris was a friend indeed when in need, it would appear. But he didn't need her now or at any other time, he reminded himself. But he also kept his cards close to his chest when he was away from hearth and home and out and about in the world. For a long time Dyfed had taken to wearing lenses that he attached right onto the cornea of the eye. This allowed him to be able to have numerous retina configurations whose colours could be blue, hazel, brown or even green in an attempt to help him remain somewhat visibly allusive. He had such lenses in all of his abodes.

"You know,' he said at last, batting large brown eyes at Doris, 'I only live just around the corner from here. Well, a few blocks, actually, not much further. You say are a director at the Jewel Banking House?' he asked suddenly, fawning incredulity.

"You live here?' she responded with an equal amount of surprise, without answering him.

"Yes,' he said, I own a building just south of here, its just west of Morningside Park and just south of Columbo University from where I look out over the Huds River. Have done for ages,' he said. 'Fortunately I purchased the property and had the high-rise structure built about a quarter century after the war long before it became mandatory by law to take out a minimum fifteen year mortgage with any and every property purchase whether you needed to or not. It was called the patriotic contribution to home finances law, remember? A useful tax to the establishment, I suppose. Yes, I have a large penthouse suite overlooking the river and the sunset. I can even see the large centrally located park behind us here, via the east west running street. It's handy to the university, too. I've never had a vehicle in this city.' Dyfed looked around and back toward the park just as Doris caught his eye. He hadn't answered her question, he knew. 'If you ever get a hankering,' he said, 'to move into new digs, I might — with the right amount of circumspect involved — be able to arrange a marvellously good price for a beautiful suite, as well.'

(Manna-hata)

*'An event has happened, upon which it is difficult to speak,
and impossible to be silent.'*

EDMUND BURKE

After arriving at Doris' apartment building Dyfed did not drive into the underground parking area as she bid him do but disembarked from behind the wheel of her chariot at the sidewalk at once. He then thanked Doris for her trouble of rescuing him and told her he would be in touch after he contacted his people. He then hailed a cab that drove him to the home he and the *pack* had here in Manna-hata.

Not an overly large building it comprised a half city block and was raised to two heights. Half of the building rose an extra hundred feet above the other and was called the Tower. It had rooftop facility, complete with gardens and pool that was also a single berth air harbour for his fleet of zeppelins that stopped here in their global circuit. The four upper most floors of the taller half was the space for the *pact's* personal abode. This was the top of the Tower and was virtually hermetically sealed off from the rest of the building that was all commercial space. The penthouse consisted of the top two floors, each of which had twelve-foot ceilings. A third of this space was opened up to one level that provided a large hall and social area with beautiful hanging chandeliers glistening above the ornate and elaborately clad furniture, rich silk Persian (four-hundred knots per square inch) carpets and ancient and delicately designed urns that sat silent and perfectly still and sprouted out voluptuous bouquets of bright, sweet smelling flowering plants. The rest of those top two levels provided kitchen facilities that one might expect in a trendy Manna-hata restaurant, as well as a library, exercise rooms and a number of well appointed bedrooms fitted out with couches, tables and saunas. Beneath this penthouse apartments were two other floors that were used as workshops, laboratories of every kind and storage facilities. Everything below that was rental. Not all of it was in use, though fake companies appeared on the books and bills receivable for rental leasing were credited rent, though this rent was being paid secretly by the Tower's bills payable department who was the landlord, though that was never entered into the books as such.

There were essentially two entrances into the *pack's* general accommodations. One was accessed from a narrower side street and was positioned between a florist shop and high-end art store that appeared customer less and always to be closed for the day. This swank high-end shop with its tidy and neat store-front display that wrapped around the north-west corner of the building towards its front entrance contained extraordinarily large subtly lit Inuit soapstone carvings alongside the rounded and shapely monstrosities of Henry Moore and Jacob Epstein and even the likes of Alexander Archipenko, Hans Bellmer and Constantin Brancusi which quietly stood in endless display behind it's large clear motionless windows. No body could access the *pack's* quarters via the front main entrance to the stately building. As already stated this was done only by two entrance-ways. One was the aforementioned simple and discreet side entrance that opened into a tidy well-appointed, extremely high ceilinged semi-circular lobby with an oval window high above the entrance. Members of the pack could only do access into the building through this door. Visitors without a *pack* escort would have to be admitted. From this foyer an elevator ran only to the top and dumped out it occupants into the sumptuous, twenty-four foot ceilinged social hall that was furnished like a palace. But the normal and usual route into the *pack's* apartment was through the street-level parkade at the back of the building. But there were two separate entrances to two separate parkades here. The corner parkade entrance under the Tower nearest the side of the building (with the classically beautifully entrance to the foyer) was the landlord entrance and nobody but the *pack* had access to enter. A slight ramp up and into the parkade led to parking arrangements that could accommodate large transport trucking chariots and such vehicles. From here there was access to two elevators. On elevator was for commercial use. It was a large, twelve by nine feet in area and ten feet high lift that could accommodate almost any large and heavy structure that needed to be placed on the top four floors. This elevator could access the rooftop so machinery brought by dirigible to the roof could be lowered to the basement. The other elevator had the normal capacity for ten people and also stopped on each of the top four floors. But this parkade had another level. To access this level a track spiralled back around and dove down beneath the first one. From here Dyfed's chariot parking area was separate and apart. Adjacent to it was another ten-person elevator that accessed the personal rooms of his apartment. But this level of the parkade was huge. It not only contained the entire area under the Tower section, it was extended also to comprise the lion's share of the entire building's footprint where mechanical and electrical maintenance shops were located, all of it invisible to the street and the user tenants. As such, this accommodated space was located under the second parkade consigned to the rental units. They were sealed to remain apart and the other parkades' entrance was on the far side of the building opposite the side with the little-used street level entrance to the Tower.

When the cab dropped Dyfed off at the main entrance at the front of the building whose lower floors flashed out bright lights onto the street, he walked around the corner glancing at the subtly lit stone carved monuments endlessly sitting in silence under their twenty-four hour evening display-case lights. He then turned and entering the private side entrance took the lift up to the grand hall. There he found Trachmyr. He had just arrived from his home near Dyfed's in the Bountiful Valley alongside the Sto:lo River. Dyfed hadn't needed to tell him about how the safe house had been demolished into a stinking, smoky ruin that was probably blighting the small community back in Jersey, for all of that had been planned. At a nearby airport to the row of the Jersey safe houses, the *pack* had an aircrew stationed as they did everywhere. And if any of the inhabited houses became compromised, before escaping to the next nearest one, an alarm was sent by the evacuee that alerted the aircrew who then immediately attended the location of the compromised house and carefully (so no bystanders were injured) demolished the house with rocketed explosions before retreating into some distant camouflage. Dyfed told him about he and Doris' drive from there into the city. As far as any bad news was concerned it was Trachmyr's duty to off-load that onto Dyfed. He told Dyfed that the expected start of Operation Cloud Nine City was on track and Dyfed and Anlaf, under code colour red, were to mosey by vehicles of conveyance along separate paths up to Denver high in the mountains in the central part of the state of Colorado (Colour-Red, in the language of the folks from Hispania). It was bad news for Dyfed because

Trachmyr knew how much Dyfed dreaded this upcoming operational event that was all about liquidating fifty million Haploids. And as far as operations of this kind went, it was the most ambitious and most costly ever.

(The — 'say ten thousand hail Marys' — device)

'The writers against religion, whilst they oppose every system, are wisely careful never to set up any of their own.'
EDMUND BURKE

As to the venue itself, Dyfed soon learned that it was a remote location on the western slopes of the Andes Mountains called the Atacama Desert. There, in a remote spot upon a remote plateau in the already remotest and driest region on Earth and placed in a gigantic five hundred foot (150 metres) deep sub-level excavated site twenty-five miles across was where the city dubbed Cloud Nine was now being hastily built. Fortunately, the geologists had found an aquifer under the desert over which they could build the city without having to install a thousand mile (sixteen hundred kilometres) water pipeline from Monte Pissis.

Although initially it was to be a one-off wham bam no-thank you man affair, it was now realized that to accommodate the prescribed number of people the event needed to be extended over a succession of ten turn-overs. That meant the city needed to have a capacity of about five million souls, or pieces of the great soul of the unbroken universe (pending how you look at it) at a time, ten times over. None of these goings-on (by the way) appealed to Dyfed. He shuddered at the very thought of it all and it made him sick to his retching stomach accompanied by a dull but highly vibrating pain to his heart. Furthermore, the initial mass electrocution originally planned was down the tubes and out the window. Now, since the mass expunging of the Haploids had to take place instead over a sequence of events the method of extermination needed to be changed. It was all to be accomplished instead by a successions of mass murders and the method now was to use relatively small enhanced radiation weapons, commonly called neutron bombs that were designed to maximize lethal radiation in the immediate vicinity of the blast while minimizing the physical power at the same time. Therefore, the city had to be assembled accordingly and with maximum strength. And as these fission-fusion-fission Neutron bombs (as they were called) would be deployed directly over the excavated Cloud Nine City itself, it was being build of reinforced concrete and steel and was designed to withstand the precise nuclear detonations that were needed to get the job done. Also the extreme arid air of this desert location complimented the destructive forces of the thermonuclear device to kill humans whose body content was ninety-eight per cent water.

Just as urgently, too, was the know-how that had been needed to judiciously search around and select chief technicians needed to assemble this mechanical transmutation from life to instant death device. An associate member of the *pack* who Dyfed had once loaned to congressman John Galway of Munster at the time to assist with the Unified States' nuclear program (something Dyfed thought would be beneficial at the time of Ivy Mike) came forward. This specialist scientist named Dr Greenworthy who had off and on been under contract by the *pack* was needed to be able to get the trigger and multiply main electrical bus devices assembled under strict directions from Master scientist Dr Torsionfield. Greenworthy, was accompanied by another electrical engineer named Dr Frankenstool. On top of that, to transport the millions of people here from all over the world would be no small feat either, even it they had a few continuous months to get the dastardly deed done. And that timeframe accounted for virtually no down time due to mishaps and engineering problems, never mind other unscheduled delays that were sure to happen. Furthermore, there wasn't a lot of time room for the entire project itself to come together from start to finish, not if they were to be ready in a timely manner to clear away Haploids. The good thing was that the Masters could manufacture scheduled delays of the comet that was bringing death to the world of men and was the bait to get the Haploids stool moving. And the excuse for schedule variations, vis a vis the fake transcendental mechanical transmutation hoax machine transporter being used for catapulting Haploids into the fifth dimension in time to escape Wormwood comet, was easily explained. It was due to 'astronomical traffic jams' and other unforeseen slow-downs that affected the comet's arrival here from space. But the message was still being hammered home like the electronic muezzin call to prayer from on high as in the A-rab state of Saud, or via the fascist and totalitarian mega-speakers of Rus and in the Land of Ch'in's methods that were constantly blaring out propaganda to the citizens on the sidewalks of their cities: the medium being the message here was…"Beware, citizens, for the comet Wormwood cometh soon to breathe its fiery breath upon the Earth and burn it asunder. Money, lots and lots of it can help you here; step up and buy our special, newly improved survival bonds now."

This death city — whose purpose by definition was anathema to what a human city actually stood for no matter where or on what continent it was located on Earth, nor by whom it was inhabited — was a facility designed for repeat user accommodation under the circumstances, as already explained. It was not to be a one off or a one shot deal. However, after the first blast, any personnel that were needed to return for the mandatory site refurbishing detail duty before the next wave of hopeful bunny-holers (as they were being called) arrived would be under duress even though the radiation decay for these low yield thermonuclear weapons was relatively rapid. However, the last blast (with all friendly personnel fully evacuated), in an effort to close the site permanently forever and bury its remnants for all time, was to be a megaton thermonuclear (fusion) weapon. This was the so-called H-bomb. This monstrous weapon of mass destruction was initially envisioned and assembled under the supervision of the theoretical physicist Edward Teller. The Hydrogen bomb was meant to do the clean-up trick here, though Dyfed was perplexed as he knew no such trick of residue able of being swept under the carpet existed in any definition of space/time; that elusive yet ever-present fourth dimension whose existence defined and encapsulated the third density — that current anchor port for all human-kind, both sane and insane.

So, the upgrade and change of strategy from mass extermination at the electric stadium holding five million cheering spectators bum-warming five million crispy-wired seats, to just the little old Neutron bomb instead, managed to function in taking the wind right out of electrical engineer Dr Frankenstool's ego trip. That softened up the good doctor of electricity's member a tad: Forthwith! This estranged doctor — who with a flare for the dramatic who had so badly wanted to be the masked executioner to close the switch on the main panel bus with more than just a flick of his wrist but with a full body press to thrust the lever up with all his strength, accompanied by a gesture of gusto (caught on film, no less), that thereby set in motion such a voracious electrical explosion to beat the band that it was able to cause the electrocution of the whole damn city of five million folks all in one fell swoop. But after being told about the new arrangements he just up and quit. Just like that! He gathered up his toys and flew home to Waco Texas. What he didn't know was that there are some jobs you just can't get fired from nor can you ever pull the plug and quit, either already.

As stated, forty-nine million Haploids, it was hoped, were seemingly preparing to be unknowingly expunged. For practical reasons and for maintaining any likelihood of a probability that spelled out a successful conclusion to this endeavour, it was always known that something more than horseshoes and the luck of the Irish were needed here. So in the likelihood that at some point when it may come to pass that the gig was up, when the penny had dropped and the charade was now being seen plainly for what it was — namely a death camp waiting silently like a Venus fly trap for its victims to alight — a contingent plan B was needed so that before the ugly truth could spread that Cloud Nine City was a hoax, certain measures then needed could be successfully taken. For it was known that once the Haploidic victims had been enclosed within a barbed-wire fenced-off bunker-like ghetto beneath the Atacama Desert, any uncontrollable, abject revolt among them would place the staff in immediate danger.

"And that, Trachmyr, is what you are in charge of, I hear: Mr pre-emptive security."

Trachmyr smiled without answering. Instead he asked…"So Doris is hooked and on board?'

"I have no idea,' Dyfed replied. 'She's interested in me and also in exposing me to the authorities,' he said. 'It appears, though, that she wasn't prepared to expose me just yet, at least perhaps until she had sounded the depths of those rumours about how to take the detour through the bunny hole and then by avoiding gravity be able to at least enter onto the frontier of some outer dimension. She knows through her own contacts that something is up. She may or may not associate me with it but we're just hoping she does. My job, according to Morgant, is to organized and perform a demonstration for her and her only, if that is the case. This is in regards to the mechanical transmutation hoax machine supposedly used to transcend and take the long detour to the land of beyond dimensions. It's easier if it's just her and not fifty sophisticated Haploids. She'll relay what she saw, you can bet on it. Now what about this Denver thing? Apparently members of the *pack* there have now built a contraption, a fake proto-type for deception and I'm supposed to turn up there soon. And then with the help of a film crew that will be on site, and will document its manufacture, along with a demonstration that I'll be given it will either lure Doris there to get a glimpse, somehow, or they'll dismantle the thing and ship it to our underground shop here to be reconstructed. I've heard it's been crassly dubbed *the ten thousand hail Marys*.'

"Just to update you, Dyfed, apparently you and I are to fly out for Denver for instructions,' Trachmyr said, 'and then you're off to the Atacama Desert next month for a tour. Morgant told me I would also accompany you there again for the opening night of the grand opening and photo Op the first big '*send off to hell*' pre-party. Presumably, you and I will be leaving just before that happens. And he suggested that you may want to put

Anlaf in charge of running your empire from your home at the Bountiful Valley control centre while you're gone?'

"For your information I prefer to remain at home in the Bountiful Valley. I don't want to go because I'm frightened,' Dyfed told Trachmyr.

"I've also been told that there was a change of plan with the show and tell of the magnificent fake transcendental mechanical transmutation hoax machine transporter,' said Trachmyr. 'There would be ten thrusts of the old copper and brass lance of the fire of the gods over the next twelve or eighteen months. So, what does that mean?' Trachmyr asked.

"It means ten thermonuclear thrusts to rent the shit out of the fabric of living matter,' Dyfed replied, visibly shaken, 'and that Wormwood has momentarily been snagged on a sky hook of some sort somewhere around the dimpled and beaming face of Jove.'

Dyfed then told Trachmyr that Morgant and Karatakos were each heading up separate committees. They were all a flurry in consolidating their plenipotentiary authority over the Haploids in respect to every aspect of the game plan. All of this was tricky business, for all Haploids — like their programmed slaves — considered themselves to be entitled and beyond the authority of others. Karatakos' responsibility was in getting certain sectors of the Haploids lined up and ready in advance of their departure but not too much in advance. Sitting around, poking around, and thinking around was dangerous too. There was danger in familiarity and close scrutiny. It meant that they needed to minimize the individual Haploids' milling around and wait to die time. Therefore, a huge orchestration was needed for so many millions of people to file, fly and fry, or in this case, to zap and pow with a heavy and deadly dose of radiation. Keeping them there in this remote part of the world in an unsuspecting and pacified state for too long was too dangerous. Logistics aside, this in itself was always going to be a compromised feat and very difficult to achieve. None of this was to be easy. Remember, many of these individuals had highly advanced special-forces type navies and armies that included squadrons of air force armed with weapons of mass destruction at their own disposal, Dyfed said. They controlled almost all the satellites and star-war-security shit, he told Trachmyr. Some had state of the art contraptions of their own which were more than beyond just high tech, and they used devices that were even unknown to the hoi polloi masses at large, though they lived side by side in the modern world. The Haploids had secret weapons and often lived in opulent mansions in the great metropolises of the world with the obligatory summer cottage or cabin at the lake carved out deep inside some remote mountain range or spread out on deserted savannahs. They were stunningly powerful people who owned and controlled ninety-nine per cent of the earth's wealth through First World finance, industry and commerce. And these in turn dominated and manipulated the hoi polloi's Third World finance, industry, and commerce. When it came to that buzz phrase, the Finance Industry (FI) and the Commerce Monopoly (CM), they *WERE* the FIC monopoly; along with the CCE, the BSOCG, the WCC, the ACS, the WJHR and the CMS, just to name a few we've already covered before.

You don't just buy these guys plane tickets or order them aboard flight 007 to nowheres-ville.

But despite their wealth and entitled status, they were ignorant of the phenomenon around them. And that was to our advantage, now. Also, now they had made this phenomenon almost unbearable for the rest of the folks who shared this state with them.

So, what to do? Well, it was a matter for a final separation. And that hinged on them all (as many as possible, anyway) convening in and around the secret venue at the same time within a short and narrow window or things would begin to fall apart fast. There couldn't be any time for reflective thought or observational intuitiveness, that's for sure: That is, if any of the expected guests even had those qualities and attributes. But they certainly were wily and often had a sixth sense about their own health and security while caring little than less about the fatal decisions they made against the well being of others and their lives with which they shared this phenomena. So, wishful thinking and other hedonistic desires had to be the name of the game here and the rule of the day. Also, large quantities of lithium were already being rounded up and readied for shipping to the Andes as an additive to the city's domestic water along with other powerful distractions. The lithium-laced water was going to be a normal procedure but after the second day the entrant's dosages would begin to be jacked sky high. Also, a short delay in the interim between the old and the incoming arrivals would allow the radiation to decay sufficiently in the city and for the staff in radiation protection gear to return to their clean up duties and get the place ready for the next wave of escapees.

Karatakos, Dyfed told Trachmyr, had already begun forming a highly skilled team of distraction innovators. This team needed to come up with a kind of dancehall, lounge, whorehouse, mega bar and grill complete with five (preferably ten) star luxurious and classy hotel accommodations to please all. The *'main venue foyer'* had to be fifty times bigger than the largest sports centres in the world plus the Dallas Fort Worth and Peking airports all joined together. Top architects like Frank Lloyd Wright the Third and his son the Fourth and Christopher Wren the XXII had been employed as well as a hundred thousand tradeswo/men, cooks and maintenance folks brought in from Ilo and Arica, Per. They also came in from the Antofagasta region of Chile. Hundreds of million tons of concrete had been shipped into the coastal city of Iquique where it had been off-loaded and muled in from there by vertical airships up into the mountains along with millions of tons of steel and glass and marble and appliances, asphalt, roofing, localized (but not outside) communication equipment, hospital facilities, hockey sticks, hot-tubs, one-armed bandits, goal posts and tennis balls; tinkers, tailors, doctors, lawyers and Indian chiefs abounded. Trillions of synapse/neuron exchanges through the neuron doctrine were evoked in order to get the place together and up and running with an energy centre to take the heat and then the chill of the highest desert on Earth off the old shack to beat the band and put the ball and chain on all the Jack Frost and Frosty the Snowman evaporation system chillers as well as domestic hot water and heating system devices they could get their sticky little hands on –– to boot. A community shuttle had been completed first and used to transport builders and workmen, along with materials around a building site more than twice the size of downtown Dusseldorf and bustling Brisbane combined. For the opening gig there was to be a virtual central park in the middle of the city. It was virtually enclosed in a bubble that rose high over the Atacama Desert that harboured Sequoia, Douglas firs, magnolias, palm trees and Japanese red dragons and a host of other flora. It would be full of butterflies fluttering full in the air here like a decretive Christmas shake-and-snow ornament, while a murder of crows would flutter back and forth zig-zag-like under a blue sky in straight lines and sharp angle corners before alighting softly on the high branches of the tall fir trees where in a barrage of shrieks they would start up a conference to loudly air their opinions and protests. Meanwhile, turkey vultures would soar high above in wide circles overhead.

As for the virtual park it was just a brief stand-in for a photo Op. and the first come first served got the benefit of it. After the first blast it wouldn't exist again.

But please, readers: The chief of promotions and director of motion picture dramas and advertisements, a certain Mr Harvey Fulcher Brown, wishes to assure all that unlike similar films showing tortured animals such large winged birds afire and aflutter as they fall in flames from palm trees proximate to the Bikini Atoll, or crushed calves and broken horse legs at round-up time, be assured that no fauna or flora were damaged or injured in any way with this slight-of-hand stint of movie-making and showmanship.

Of course, in addition to the above, the system infrastructure would have to cater to all and every whim of the self-centred and entitled sect of greedy, possessed fat-cats who were insanely detracted from the unity of the unbroken universe who the Masters were expecting to receive, comfort and bed-down while seeing to it that the whims of these Haploids were pandered to. But that they had better not pout and better not cry if they wanted the Sages of the Unknown Universe to reward them with stockings full of chance to access the bunny hole chuck and jive thing that was coming to town before Wormwood showed up. This was a daunting task but necessary for the ultimate success of the event.

Otherwise the controllers might have a Haploid revolt on their hands. And that just wouldn't do. Morgant left the responsibility for selecting the chosen ones to the Haploid executive central committee themselves, but retained the job of surreptitiously contacting those persons who fancied themselves as being entitled to VIP treatment. Their names and addresses were forwarded to him and he took charge of organising and arranging transportation to the venue for them when the time came. Any loose talk about what they were up to with other folks, and they were then struck off the list. It was expressly impressed upon the Haploid elite that in the end the greater the secrecy the greater likelihood of over-all success. This erroneous tip — the *pack* discovered — went a long way. Condition number one: no self motivated transportation. Condition two: bring only the clothes you are wearing, all will be provided. Condition three: all other private and corporate property of the candidate is to be transferred to Jewel Banking House before being accepted by the Cloud Nine City host executives. It was not only going to be forty-nine million people, but they would be coming from all over the globe. Great imagination was put in charge of third dimensional logistics just to get this show on the road. This inevitably, involved the dispersion of non-virtual honey to dress up the considerably virtual and ultimately dull bunny-hole…that dimensional gateway… that port of entry and exit to death, dressed up as eternity. Remember, the fascination around the ability to cheat death and live cannot be exaggerated. Then add to that the added fascination of time shifting and you have your hook. But the hook needed to splash out a bit but it mustn't be available to any serious scrutiny either. So that was where Dr Torsionfield, Dr Tesla and Dr Greenback came in. Even Dr Frankenstein, once thought to be in his dotage, was consulted from time to time on this matter. Their somewhat complicated job was to figure out the mechanism of use that essentially was to rig up a brilliant variety of smoke and mirrors, complete with impressive holographs of celestial outer space and even Ice Age earth. These would be splashed across neo-Pathy News Update smart screens that would be prominent fixtures everywhere within the city. Some of this had already been worked out and gotten underway even before the

Antarctic hoax-preparation-workshop sessions that passed the budget. The icing for this Andean project would be a magnetic field bubble that when placed over and around the city would virtually paralyse the inhabitants and fix them permanently to the spot until their exposure to sudden, intensively high radiation that would finish them off. Obviously, the promotional advertising and preview shorts were everything.

When the time came and they finally all started to arrived one by one it wasn't going to be Vegas; it was even more brighter than that with fatter pomp and ceremony, with noisier clubs and curb-side jingo-jango fandangos, jumpier bands shells, fantastic music halls and darkened lizard-haven jazz-jive lounges combined with a more connected hub-bub of variety adult entertainment distractions than Moe Green, Bugsy Siegel or even little ol' Wayne Newton (all in a row) could ever raise compared to Marilyn Monroe's skirt above her hips while charmed by Charles Laughton and Frank Sinatra and the rat pack: This was Cloud Nine City, Bub!...right here in the Atacama Desert... Andes Mountains...Chile...South Merika...You betcha!...and don't you forget it!

(Papa Papanasi and the paparazzi)

'The end had come, but it was not yet in sight.'
JOHN KENNETH GALBRAITH

Other Masters of the Little Known Universe scientists were employed in contributing to the situation at hand, too. They worked behind the scenes. Often their job was the dissimulation needed to counteract pertinent and persistent questioning in regards to the *pack's* claim to be capable of assisting the Haploids in this endeavour in the first place. Cross culture soldiers had been routinely trounced by the Haploid's upper hand for centuries, everyone knew. And when it came to keeping their secrets, the *pack* — along with their handlers (the Masters) — knew what they were doing. Even the hapless Haploids knew when and how to keep a secret in order to keep the public soothed and ignorant. They had written the book on it. So the duty of everyone in the know was to provide wide spread disinformation about perceived proceedings and rumours thereof. And the Haploids were to have as little self-determination and control over this entire aspect as possible. This was of crucial importance. The advice was to make it known that during the intended time, the candidate was simply going to be away somewhere on holiday. 'That golf game…when?…sorry Mr Greenworm, business calls me away for a few weeks, I'll take a rain check'. The trick was to make it happen as instantaneously as possible…to get as many of the Haploid kingpins together in the newly constructed Cloud Nine City as they could… then, get them pacified and chilled out as much as a Haploid could ever be chilled out…then…hit the switch. Pow…Zap…Kapute.

It should be pointed out at this time that tens of thousands of other scientists worldwide who were controlled by the Haploid systemised establishment (and had been so for many, many years) were about as useless as tits on old Taurus when it came to being able to help out in any way in this regard. They weren't wanted anyway. This was because their science had been all about snow jobs and whitewash for curriculum income and misappropriation and syphon-offs of massive tax-denarii/dollars rather than real science expenditure conducted for the understanding of the truth of the real and virtual phenomenon that's around us. A slow and very subtle transformation was the hallmark of the Haploid's new world order that consisted of the establishment's corridors of authority. Such a corridor, and one of the first to be reshaped and redirected, was the World department of Justice and Human Rights. World Justice and Human Rights had long become the Haploid's Supreme Court and the supreme authority to which every Attorney General's office and every related agency in the world was subordinate. Even county, provincial, sovereign state and dominion law enforcement agencies — often erroneously referred to as Peace Enforcement Officers, who are public sector — along with the aforementioned departments of justice and sundry welfare, and human development ministries, were now easily trumped by the agency for Capital Crimes Ulterior-eNforcemenT [or *CCUNT* for short]. This was a World Government agency which now analysed and controlled all financial transactions which took place anywhere in the world. Transactions outside of their cognizance, or unsanctioned by

CCUNT, were deemed unlawful and considered to be felonies. Even numbered and licenced transactions from the past could be retroactively deemed illegal and felonious. That status would depend on any status change among the participants themselves. Someone — say — who may have spoken up and brought critical attention directed towards some wrong-doing by a merited individual of the establishment, especially if that merited individual was a Haploid, could (and in fact would) suffer an immediate status shift to that of non-gratis and by definition become an instant felon themselves. All transactions by that felon — forward and backward — would then be deemed illegal. Anyway, those magistrates (like the aforementioned pseudo scientists) now acted as a glut that bogged down justice and civil liberties just as it bogged down real science. This had had a devastating effect on the world economy (if you could call it that any more) that played havoc with development of industry and commerce at the hoi polloi level. The Haploid game was a much higher league, as earlier discussed. However, the world situation did enable the Haploid's ability to tweak the hoi polloi's game as often as needed. In either case, this — in turn — produced huge unrest and worldwide insurgencies that — if not fully confounding the Haploid's new world order, had caught them off guard. It also stumped those folks adrift over at Iron Mountain who had earlier entered the great game on their own terms quite unprepared. It was, however, a game that — to their peril — was well above their league. Their providence of authority was called Iron Mountain because as typical theists and believers in the cult of the god of Abram their authority was perceived to resonate within the mind-set of the age of iron. They were the Unified States' proponents to Morning Prayer. These were the typical re-scripture-scribed devotees of halleluiah; praise the lord, hurrah for god, rah, rah, fucking rah! The Iron Mountain insurgency now even included members of all three components of Abramism — Jeshuans, Abramis, and Ishlamites, all Jeshua freaks each and every one. The *pack* sympathized with their hapless condition but considered them status non-gratis due to their extremely successful indoctrination by the Haploid induced religion/culture monopoly. Happily, along with Father Papanasi and sundry paparazzi, all of this acted to help the *pact's* attempts to dissimulate, escape, and evade direct Haploidic action of scrutiny and vengeance in the day to day combat on civvy street that battled on in the jungle of life while the *pack* weaved their tangled web of deception in, around and about the distant Cloud Nine City.

(The charge of the chimichanga)

> *"In silence man can most readily preserve his integrity.'*
> **MEISTER ECKHART**

The next morning Dyfed was up as usual well before the crack of dawn. Unlike others his age who rose out of bed and medicated, he slowly and deliberately exercised then meditated in Zazen. Then as his mind was still empty he let his breath breathe and define him in this moment by breathing through him. Then once again he was empty and ready to be filled with the goings on of the day. But the filling up wasn't going to be forced on him or dumped into him in any haphazard way. He would be standing on guard and controlling the senses he perceived and imagined.

The after a breakfast of a spring-roll and fries sandwich he sat quietly alone in the darkness of his apartment looking out into the early morning's pale light. Despite it being late October the mean temperature of the outside air was quite warm.

Soon Megatropolis had fully awakened and was on the move so Dyfed now began to prepare for his day. As one of the hubs of this world, Megatropolis was the great celebration of the Haploidian culture. Therefore it was here where a victory of any kind for Dyfed (and the *pack*) was badly needed. Even if Lower Lothar was the Haploids' head office, Megatropolis was their great wielding crutch, or more likely the rocket booster of the Haploid's world system. Where else on earth did a city hum along at full speed twenty-four seven? Where else in the world was there such a collection of the arts in all of it expressions that represented and miss-represented all ethnic cultures of the world in such an important way all at the same time: With the exception of music that was thus far insurmountable (yet, though unable to be distorted it managed to be socially-degradable). Where else in the world, exactly, was this to be found?

Megatropolis, the venue of the world's greatest night shows bar none, and all night bars show and tell: it was the establishment's great machine which churned out its virtual culture yet was reliant at the same time on the hoi polloi, as with everything else. Like a castaway from humanity's norm, here Captain Cult — all flashily gilded out — managed to ferret out an abnormal existence like a Morning gecko upon a volcanic island located far out to sea, or a fox feeding on fat six year old rabbits galore.

Megatropolis the glittering; Megatropolis the golden plated idol — it seemed to exist only to entice one and all into the Haploidic matrix. Megatropolis the designer distraction — the box-office hit to the Haploid's greatest movie script ever told.

Come one, come all…pick a role now. Then face your partner…everybody ready? Yessiree bub…and away we go with an allemande left and an allemande right…now take your partner and…dos a dos!

(Cuvée cognac for two)

'The wind cried: Hey, Joe, where are you going with that gun.'
JIMMY HENDRIX

As the noise of the awakening city grew a little louder, Dyfed was good to go. His plans having now been made, his stretch exercises to get the blood moving, followed by a quick bath that was followed by a quicker shower was all done. He now stood dressed in slim, dark loosely fitting silk trousers dusted lightly with tiny grains of silver thread that was complimented with a somewhat scruffy dark hoodie and cap. With his satchel slung over his shoulders and resting on his lower back, Dyfed set out on foot first for number one Fence Street, the address of the Jewel Banking House. The latter was a subsidiary of Dyfed's Commonwealth Union Banking House.

The moment he stepped away from the building he noticed that a wind had picked up. It gusted up and down through the narrow channels of the streets which with imagination could resemble an urban version of a Poussin in the wilds of Frankia, or van Gogh's waves of an incoming tide as it throws white capped rollers up and down a chilly beach blowing the sun-brellas over and lifting the sides of sandy towels that rolled over and over and away like discarded clothes across the sand. He walked slowly, limping slightly, with gnarled walking stick in hand as he breathed in the newly exchanged and relatively clean, early morning autumn air. Lately, Dyfed noticed that as his age increased the injury he had sustained over eight centuries earlier in the Tyrol caused a marked debilitation a his stride though it did not effect his still tall and erect stature.

Only a decade before the storefronts around him here had still been open to quick take-away breakfast and such food such as pizzas by the slice, toasted bagels with cheese or slaw and hamburgers with poutine or vinegar sprinkled fries. A passer-by would have been greeted by music and loud diners with full, sit-down breakfasts and early lunch patrons spilling out onto the sidewalks with full bellies, wiping their mouths with the backs of their hands or their sleeves. Food trucks adorned sections of the sidewalks. Mostly, though, commercial businesses thrived hereabouts like rising bread with fresh produce grocery filler sandwiched between them or a newsstand and a fruit vendor's wares that impeded pedestrians' passage on the sidewalks both here and across the street. Here, too, had once been expensive shops jammed with fine merchant wares from Inja, Land of Ch'in, Frankia and Sweden. But now — here and there — there were gaping and gutted-out shops at street level (some burned and smelling of tar or fuel) which like sturdy hunchbacks now propped up weighty overburdens of dilapidated hulks that resembled derelict high rises succumbing to demolition. Above, either abandoned, broken down or its operators on strike for higher wages, derricks and cranes towered tall into the sky exposing a profile of dangerous and forebodingly fragility. This in itself was sufficient enough to jar Dyfed into a reality that he was struggling to fight off. As he made for the subway transit station, all around him the streets and sidewalks were being cleared of glass and litter by brightly dressed minimum wage earners whose jobs each morning never varied. Monotonously they brushed debris from the thoroughfares and shovelled it into large, smelly, shrill-noise emitting trucks whose diesel engines never shut off. And in concert with thousands of other vehicles, the refuge was collectively disposed at a giant refuge burn facility annexed to a power generating plant downtown and not dumped as it used to be at any number of expanding refuge and rubbish sites out somewhere beyond the suburbs. Recycle, though promoted by the people for a generation before being adopted by the governing factors here and across the Western world, was rampant, and not just by the homeless.

Dyfed noticed that above the streets and the heads of workers, bystanders and other folks that were just hurrying past on their way to work, were a myriad of small, noiseless drones, watching, recording, compiling, and endlessly active. Some of these drones, however, were commercial. They were delivering boxed-up mail such as pharmaceuticals, toasters, toys and new or repaired clothing. There were industrial products, private correspondences, pizzas, birthday-cakes and sundry other items all flying through the air attached to little drones which themselves needed to respond to instructions and obey traffic rules and not hinder or cause accidents all the while being closely monitored by the State Security drones that incessantly watched on, unblinkingly.

Beneath ground, and after many stops and starts and with a great mixing and stirring of multitudes of folks being forced along passage-ways, escalators and into subway trains that whisked them hither and yon to somewhere approximate to their desired location, suddenly the public address system — speaking in a smooth, slow feminine voice — announced Dyfed's stop as it zipped into his station. He disembarked from the transit train beneath the city and as he climbed a motionless escalator to the street he noticed it had a section removed and two intelligent looking workmen dressed in dark jumpsuits and caps were poking around inside. Presumably they were preparing for some operative function in the near future. At this juncture he was at his destination. But not wanting to be followed from their high-rise to here, and believing that a disguise was in his favour, he couldn't immediately try to enter the bank looking common and scruffy. Once at the street level he glanced at its huge glassy entrance artfully placed between its half-engaged Doric facsimile-type columns that fronted both of the exposed sides of the lower five floors. Above these rose a glistening high-rise office tower whose top floors — having just caught the sun — shone out like a beacon over Manna-hata. It was all such a long way away and a long time ago from back in the day, he then thought, when he casually walked or charioted to work from either his Palatine palace or their Esquiline compound and apartments down to the forum in Amor where his first bank was located.

As Dyfed marched along he remained alert to any specific human agents or tails that he may have attracted and picked up who might be observing and detailing him while he was on the move. These dangerous folks were the real business end and they were the extension of the mechanical drones hovering and milling about above. However (he had found), they were not necessarily authorized to second-guess a decision already made nor were they the ones upon whose virtual desk the buck stopped, either: They could stop a armed and dangerous perpetrator, they could stop a bull, hell they could probably even stop a tank! But they couldn't stop that little wee buck when it came down to it. Their duty was to do what they were told and to pass it on. They were security-type special force bureaucrats in limbo. This meant they were probably a more unpredictable force of non-habit working in what is normally a highly predictable environment of employment for most of its top-heavy staff. They were the boots on the ground, a glorified one step up from the common *go-to* Nightwatchmen for the office shut-ins of the higher level (and more intelligent) staff that monitored everything the machines of surveillance transmitted back.

On this morning the uniformed security who at present were successfully keeping loud and strangely affected humans who routinely performed and acted out in plain public view upon the congested streets the most bizarre acts and insane motions, seemingly without rhyme nor reason, pretty much under control. Dyfed sensed a carnival-type atmosphere in the air on this fine top of the morning: And this, too, gave up no suspicious gestures of untoward, at least in his immediate direction. Now, since the prince of the grove and of the forest who could merge and camouflage among the files and pigeon-holes of men here just as easily as he could among the forests and mountains, he now set-to to do his thing, his slight of hand, his legerdemain.

Dyfed quickly unslung his ruck-sack/satchel from his back as he jousted rigorously among the enormous presence of uniformed officers and plain-clothed agents at large that milled here and there and every which way betwixed in their uneasy, thin blue-lined postured presence among the milieu in an effort to divide the less-fortunate from the genuinely purposeful pedestrians. Now, from out of his rucksack shaped satchel (that could just as easily be converted back from his satchel into a ruck-sack again by turning it inside out and by the manner in which he carried or wore it) Dyfed pulled out a finely tailored silk suit jacket and a fedora. With these he quickly replaced his dark hoodie and mariner's cap. Now, newly attired in an expensive suit carrying an expensive looking business satchel, he moved back, breaking through the sloppy cordon of blue ribbon in the direction of his bank. Passing a swanky and popular evening restaurant for the well heeled called *Typhoid Mary's* he emerged now exhibiting frustration and infuriation, a measured posturing intent topped with a hint of self-importance that mainly emulated the intent of others, specifically about who they thought they were and where they thought they were going. He dodged back and forth in between legions of street maintenance workers dressed in their assigned bright yellow jackets that were pulled over their shabby worn out personal duds.

At the corner of Fence Street, where his bank was located directly behind the subway station entrance from which he had surfaced minutes earlier, he stopped. He had returned appropriately dressed but was now kitty-corner to it. He looked over at it and at the classical styled building next to it. This was the home branch of the Centre for Cultural Decontamination, while immediately across the street from his bank, and just off to his right, was the head office for the Association for Progressive Initiatives. All around him men and women were idly standing around mostly busy consulting and talking to their tele-pads. Few folks talked to each other on the street. Indeed, the streets of this vast and bustling city seemed to lack the sound of human voices compared to the past. Only electronic voices were most evident. They were predominating wherever humans walked or waited nowadays, so that Dyfed's journey on foot through the streets was like some endless, virtual electronic circus passing by his ears. Most evident, however, was the monotone human voice being constantly and monotonously broadcasted as pedestrians went about their business. It was a barrage of propaganda consisting of subliminal hints and explanations of courtesy and political/cultural procedure whose thyme (if there was one) was no more apparent than card suits in a shuffled deck faced down. Only the ever-present electronic video recording monitors were silent as, in addition to the drones, they continually scanned the coming and going of every moving thing along every stretch of street and sidewalk, every doorway entrances, subway platforms and the interiors of every transit vehicle throughout the city.

The street was packed with people and even the security police lining the streets couldn't keep the pickpockets and panhandlers at bay. Across the street in front of the street level subway entrance and his bank behind that, two large official looking vans had pulled up and stopped illegally along the *no-parking he*re curb. A man from the front van wearing a dark uniform and matching cap that looked like a captain's cap or that of a high-end chauffeur's walked back and approached the rear van. At this point Dyfed stepped out to cross the street and walk toward the subway entrance that was in front of the bank's revolving main glass and brass doors. But he didn't get that far. As Dyfed skirted behind the rear van, and as his forward left foot stepped onto the curb only ten feet from the subway's entrance and its security guards, the uniformed and capped chauffeur (he had first seen) grabbed him forcefully. Then suddenly the van's rear doors were violently flung open and another man jumped out. After thrusting a needle into Dyfed's neck, and being assisted by the chauffeur, he and the chauffeur lifted Dyfed horizontal and manhandled him into the rear van.

Something spongy was then quickly placed over his nose and mouth. He went loose and his synapse pulsations weren't function right. His body seemed enclosed in cotton batten and his vision became fuzzy and it appeared he was gazing through a culvert with a cloud of fog rushing at him. Then he felt bodies closing in on him. After that he was unaware of anything further until after an undisclosed space of time when he opened his eyes and found himself in a bare room with the ceiling light on and his wrists and ankles shackled to the frame of a raised and narrow bed. It's a hospital, he quickly hoped. He could only hope, as his eyes searched out for hospital accoutrements, like friendly nurses. But he could only see the metal collapsible sides of the bed he was in that were both pulled up like a baby's crib.

Much later he saw a male nurse in dark glasses approach. Seeing he was awake the man turned and quickly walked away. A few moments later somebody in green loose fitting overalls poked his nose into Dyfed's vision. He was wearing a green cap and green protective mask over his mouth. Moment later he was accompanied by another nurse similarly attired. Each stared at him from opposite sides of his crib. The man on the right spoke to Dyfed.

"Hello, sir,' he said pleasantly, 'how are you feeling now? What's your name and do you know what day it is?' He picked up Dyfed's hand and held it gently before feeling his pulse. 'Hmm?' he said, as he reached up and gently pulled the skin away slightly from the bottom of one of Dyfed's eyes.

"Can you focus on us ok?' said lefty from the other side of the crib. 'Can you hear us alright, sir?'

Dyfed's eyes opened wider and keeping his head on the pillow he jerked his head slightly to indicate the affirmative. Two other men were then summoned who were orderlies but Dyfed noticed they had names pinned onto their uniforms while the first two did not. Still strapped to the bed they wheeled him down a hall and into another room that was more of a clinical office. Those two orderlies then quickly exited the room. He then heard somebody breathing and then from somewhere a man in a white coat appeared above and to the right of him. Without a word he raised the bed so Dyfed's torso was half way between lying down as he had been and sitting upright. When that was done he left the room and Dyfed could hear him conduct a short discussion with two other men in the hallway outside the door who Dyfed assumed were the two men in the flimsy loose fitting green jumpsuits.

"Mr Newhouse H. Easystreet, is it?' the Doctor asked. His eyebrows arched when he asked the question. Apparently, he was reading from an electronic file that was attached to the bed.

A sort of grimace appeared on Dyfed's face as though he was thinking hard, but he did not reply. 'Well, we are here to help you, whoever you are. Can you hear me alright?' He stood up and pulled a small light out of his breast pocket that he shone into each of Dyfed's eyes. As he wandered back, presumably to his station or his desk, he began to speak.

"They picked you up on the street. Apparently, you had collapsed and we thought it might have been a drug overdose. It doesn't seem to have been, though. How has your health been, Mr Easystreet, eh? Any problems of late — you can think of,' he asked. Then when Dyfed didn't answer he added: 'You know we can provide the best treatment for alcoholism or delusion right out of our clinic here in Megatropolis. You had been drinking we know that although the blood/alcohol content in your body was not high. What affiliations do you have, now, if any, Mr Easystreet? Hmm.?' The doctor in the white coat had come back to the bedside and was looking down at the electronic file, again. 'We couldn't help notice that your body is covered with some very exquisite tattoos. Were you in the armed forces? Were you in the navy or do you belong to some undisclosed secret cult, Mr Easystreet? Of course I know they are illegal, but I am a doctor of medicine, Mr Easystreet. You can, and will, tell me everything because it's all confidential.'

At that point he summoned the two men in the green loose fitting overalls without nametags on their uniforms to enter the room.

"So, we can put him on a program,' said the doctor to lefty and righty who were just visible now to Dyfed at the end of his bed, 'and keep him medicated for a few weeks. That's what I'm recommending.'

"We don't think that will be acceptable,' said one of the light and loose green uniformed men. 'He has some pretty serious charges pending and he is considered dangerous. Very dangerous.'

"We'll take some more blood tests,' continued the doctor. 'He needs to dry out and be put on a proper diet before we fish around in his mind. We'll get the body functioning in a more congenial fashion first then I can work on his mind later and see what's what. I won't start that examination, though, not until he is feeling a bit more chipper, shall we say. And all that has to be done before he is released into your care, Sergeant Greengrape.'

"It doesn't look like there's anything wrong with him,' one of the green men said. He acted pretty chipper when he came to, and his physique, despite him being a relatively old man, is remarkably preserved and strong.'

"You're a physician now?' the doctor snapped back at one of the green men.

"There is nothing wrong with my mind nor my body. What kind of a doctor are you, anyway?' said Dyfed in a slightly sounding irritated manner. 'Furthermore, I wasn't passed out in the street, either. Some thugs jumped me and drugged me. You did the tests, so you said. You tell me; what was it they put in me? Oh, and bye the way, I'd like to make a call so I need my torc and my hands free. And how long exactly have I been in here in this state, anyway?'

"You had been drinking,' repeated the doctor in a definitive manner, 'and then you were rushed here in an intoxicated state this morning by street medics which, fortunately for you, is a service our establishment still provides some of us, at least.'

"The devil I was,' replied Dyfed. 'I was jumped and drugged from a needle stuck into my neck and bundled into one of two black vans that were waiting for me on Fence Street downtown in front of the People's Union and Commonwealth Bank. That I can recall well, but I remember nothing after that.'

The doctor showed no expression although it was obvious he was not taken with Dyfed's statement.

"I think I understand your predicament, sir,' the doctor said. 'After all you are hardly the only poor devil out there struggling, are you?'

"What do you mean, poor devil,' said Dyfed. What poor devil do you know wears a suit jacket and pants the likes of what I was wearing? What down on his luck, fleeced to the bone, marginalized wino eats a caviar and rose jelly sandwich washed down with a bottle of Cuvée cognac for breakfast this morning, might I ask? Say, what did you say you were? A doctor? What kind of doctor are you? A doctor of particle physics, doctor of chemistry, of music, a spin-doctor or witch doctor? I'm a doctor too. So what does that mean. And if you could discern alcohol about my presence, Herr doctor, why couldn't you recognize the smell of a splash of cognac worth two and a half thousand dollars a bottle? Hmm? For a doctor you aren't very observant, are you! Obviously, you aren't a doctor of cognac, anyway. So, what kind of doctor did you not say you were? Huh! My dollar says you're a psychiatrist or a psychopath?'

"Hmm, maybe! Either that or I can't afford to drink Cuvée cognac at two and a half thousand dollars a bottle and wouldn't recognize it if I was swimming in it,' snapped the doctor in response. 'Furthermore, I know nothing of an expensive suit. My understanding, since you were already in hospital clothes when I looked in on you, was that you were dressed by any one of the big box stores around the city just like those other middle class folks who can still afford store-bought clothes from K-Mart.' His eyebrows shot up again and his face slackened into that assuming look that people often outwardly and purposely posture: It was his doctor face, Dyfed came to realize.

"Ah,' replied the latter in quick response. 'We, that is you and I, are both victims then it would seem. You're pathetic and paltry palette is keeping you away from decent cognac by dint of its price: Poor, poor doctor skint. Either that or your pockets are too deep for your little short arms that don't allow your hands to reach anywhere near the bottom of your pocket where the money is. And I'm drugged and robbed of my untidy brightly-coloured threads bought in a clothing-for-convenience store like Discount Warehouse that I wouldn't dare shop in, never mind even wearing in my private dreams.'

The doctor then began to furiously write something down by tap tap tapping on the keys of his small electronic file.

"I see,' he interrupted. 'What kind of employment did you have when you worked? That is, the kind of job you did during the majority of your life; your career, shall we say?'

" You know,' responded Dyfed, 'that a social system which is oriented toward victimizing individuals — such as what we appear to have here — requires a certain amount of co-operation from the individual victim themself to either let become, or let continue this practise into general acceptance. Since I do not wish to see this condition continue I will not contribute to the situation. So, of course I will not co-operate with your line of questioning or commit to participate other than to aid my advantage in order to clearly establish that your utterances are composed of pure, syllogistic fallacy. But I will provide the essentials so we can speed up my release process. I need to have the office of my attorney at law notified of my situation immediately. The contact information to accomplish this is with my personals of which I have been divested. First, at this time it is not my intention, nor do I feel compelled by any compunction, to divulge that which has, or will, be asked of me until such time that I have found by due trial, strict examination or sure information that you or any other questioner is worthy of that confidence, which at this time I do not. Therefore, as such, I will not comply with your questioning until my attorney is present. Until then, I will conform to her advice and instructions of silence to which she has informed me to commit. Now, as my attorney is on a tour of relaxation and recreation somewhere in and around La Paz in Bolivia enjoying extreme camping, mountaineering and rock-climbing and won't be back to North Merika for another four or five weeks, my bank will be able to immediately provide bail for my release from custody no matter at what amount it will be set for.'

"Oh really? said the doctor without any emotion. 'How is your relationship with other people? Are you married? Do you live in a cordial arrangement of any kind? Hmm?'

"And how would my lawyer respond to that, do you think?' said Dyfed. 'Where's my privilege before the law?' Beyond that, and since the doctor didn't question him further, Dyfed did not answer any more questions.

'No, I didn't think so, Mister whoever you really are. Mr Easystreet! — Really? I didn't think you had anybody close to you. Lookit! I'm not saying I don't believe you,' the doctor continued while tapping at his pad board, 'and that you are a liar, not at all. I do believe you. At least I believe that you think that you do own expensive clothes and consume expensive cognac for breakfast with your — what was it — financial adviser? Oh yes, bank manager, with whom you were brokering an earth shattering deal, I suppose. It is even possible that you were well educated, but who you really think you are?' Here he let his voice trail off before saying: 'What was the first statement you said to me, do you remember Mr Easystreet? You said there is nothing wrong with my mind. That is what you said. Don't deny it. It is on record,' he said after clearing his throat. 'You told me that there was nothing wrong with your mind. That alerts me to the probable fact that you are pretty cocksure of yourself, Mr Easystreet. What is it that someone once said about the trouble of the world being that the stupid are cocksure and the intelligent full of doubt? You see in my profession the cocksure types are radical, foolish and/ or insane. And even then some of them are highly intelligent and rich enough to swill cognac for breakfast. Gee whiz, Mr Easystreet, I don't think that you differ much from my last mental patient, or the one before that, even. Alas! They are — one and all — the victims of society to which you allude, or so you might think. Perhaps, to some degree that is so. But really, let's be honest Mr Easystreet, we are the architects of our own failing in the end. You have given in, thrown care to the wind, tossed in the towel. You've lost your ideals, lost your pride and sense of purpose and have created yourself into something you want to be but aren't! You have lost your true identity, Mr Easystreet, for that is precisely what insanity is. But take heart; there are many degrees of insanity and you appear to be still on a fairly even keel. We have drugs for medication and medication for procedures that you need to follow so you can erase your delusional world and shake out the bugs, so to speak. We can re-fashion you anew. Now, how does that sound to you?'

"Hey, that sounds just swell, but it still sounds like I need to speak to my attorney at law,' replied Dyfed, 'As I've said, if you won't release me, if you won't tell me why you're holding me that's more credible than your fabricated story about finding me prone and dying in the gutter from overdosing on phyntnol (fentanyl) laced heroin along with a binge of excessive sauce-lapping of libations of the highly proofed spirit persuasion that causes these delusions of fantastic fantasia to which you elude, then I hereby now demand you summon my council through some arrangement this moment with the office of my personal attorney and direct her or him to visit me ASAP?'

At a point during their brief conversation Dyfed realised that the doctor had just learned that his patient was to be arraigned. Dyfed had never been sure just what route his enemies would take if they ever got him fully in their sights and then came at him. But he had no doubt that it would likely be a direct route to annihilation. At this point he wasn't quite sure in whose hands he was, either. But the Haploids wouldn't employ unprofessional people, or agencies that did. Professional operators like the Haploids themselves would narrow the window for mistake and carelessness by either properly securing him down or take the shortcut and kill him quickly. So what's the arraignment all about? he wondered. The people he knew wouldn't waste time sending him into a clinic, either, and they wouldn't waste time in trying to drain his brain in a psyche ward, that's for sure. His mind turned in this direction because he knew he was in some kind of ward run by a doctor of psychiatry who was either toying with him in a belief which was either pure, beyond-reasoning superstition, or simply worthy of any broken down run of the mill sick moron who actually believed that a Rorschach ink blot test could help any run of the mill shrink figure out what made him tick. So, could it possibly be that unprofessional people of an unknown origin were involved instead? That may be, he concluded, but the heavies could still weigh in soon enough. He wondered about Doris again. Was his abduction related to her in any way? It seemed likely that it was but maybe not in the uncomplicated way he would have expected the Haploids to operate. Who then had hired her for the bump? he wondered. Maybe she was contracting or running her own show. Was he going to be sold off? Perhaps Doris was negotiating his price. He knew that his men would be coming sooner than eventually; there was no doubt about that. And he could take his choice when it came to summoning back into his memory some of those hired psychopaths who had strutted their stuff across the world stage on numerous occasions that the *pack* had often been forced to use, even if it just took them out of the game for the Haploid's to utilize. These agents would probably be under the strict direction of Morgant and Deric the Deuce with Trachmyr acting as the accompanying agent who operated and controlled them in the field.

Oh where oh where were those dangerous agents of the *pack*, when you needed them? All would be lost if somebody among them didn't show up soon. He was putting on a good face, he was holding up, but how long could it last? he wondered. In the end he might have to rely once again specifically on the good Count Agenbite of Inwit, though up until now Dyfed was only experienced in holding him at bay.

(Their trade is treachery)

'Spare all I have, and take my life.'
GEORGE FARQUHAR

"I have been asked by people who are concerned for your health,' the doctor began later that day, 'to ask you a few questions that will indicate to me your state of mind. Presumably, your answers will allow me to determine if in fact you can stand trial.' He smiled elfishly at Dyfed while one of the orderlies coughed loudly. But Dyfed, whose head and torso was so tightly bound to a wheel chair that he could only look straight a head, saw only the good doctor in his vision. He was also aware that a third man had joined this friendly little group therapy session they were now having. Dyfed had not heard the man enter the room but had only become aware of him by hearing an extra set of breathing. Wondering just who the person was, suddenly Mr anonymous began to speak. Dyfed then knew instantly who he was.

"So, I have a list here of questions,' said the voice who was speaking a little absent-mindedly as if he was mentally scanning the items on it. This told Dyfed that it wasn't his list or there wasn't a list at all. But it was the good doctor who read the questions out aloud.

"Do you recognise the authority of the government of the Unified States over you as an individual?'

"The question is relative even if you were to define authority and define the parameters of this term government,' said Dyfed.

The doctor, who was in Dyfed's plain view, looked thoughtfully at him for a moment or two.

"Do you recognise the fact that a military agency or a court of this nation has an unquestionable authority to hold you and deny and prevent you any freedom of movement? Do you recognise the fact that both of them have the authority to judge you in what the latter call a people's court of law and punish you if necessary with proper peer representation and an appeal process, all terms of which are defined by the establishment itself? Do you recognize that the court can legally confiscate and appropriate everything you own, including your DNA, and profit thereby at your expense at once, if found guilty by our courts?'

"All relative to an independent individual like me, perhaps even to an individualist, I dunno?'

"Do you deny that you are a felon who has been charged with molestation and of having illicit sexual intercourse with a young child in a room at the Hotel Strait Menai a few years back?'

"A few years back, you say?' He snorted a little laugh. 'I deny ever having such an encounter. And again, acting as my own substitute attorney, I hereby advise myself to not answer anything further until my really inventive and skilled attorney has had an opportunity to remind me once again in person of her advise of not saying anything unless she or a colleague is present. I undertake this measure as I know anything I say will be used against me, will likely be misconstrued with a biased miss-interpretation, supported by false witnesses for the state to embellish and fabricate upon later. I therefore refuse to say anything for fear of incriminating myself. Unless, the speaker has come to act…'

Dyfed quickly started to jerk and bounce the whole stump of his bounded and shackled body around in order to catch the eyes of the now not so mysterious visitor with the voice. It didn't appear to the doctor that he was able to move fast enough before the orderlies that were also sitting behind him on each side even more quickly responded by smothering Dyfed with their arms and torsos as the man with the elderly voice jumped up as fast as he could and beat a hastily exit out of the examining room.

'Menstruating mother of Adon, exclaimed Dyfed in surprise.' The doctor also jumped up at this point and attempted to be seen to put an immediate end to the questioning.

Shortly after, the two orderlies with the nametags were summoned who then wheeled Dyfed into a small brightly lit, pale green room. When the door closed Dyfed noted that it was very, very quiet and now it was only his own breathing that he could hear. Well, well, he mused. So far there has been clumsy, clumsier, and clumsiest. I might have an outside chance yet, he thought to himself.

Once alone, the doctor reviewed his notes then left the examination room and strolled down the hall back to the main office he was temporarily using. For a long hour or two he sat pondering the last events of the day. Something was troubling him. It was much later than usual, therefore, when he decided to take his thoughts home. Once there, with his wife doting over her clever and successful husband, he could nurse them along with a scotch on his sealed air-conditioned deck overlooking his private lawn in the suburb of Kings. As he left he paused at the employees entrance to the admitting office. Walking into the files room on an impulse he was, for some reason, startled to see the receptionist working quietly alone. He began to ask her poignant questions about the patient Mr Easystreet. He asked her questions he hadn't asked earlier as he tried to draw as much knowledge from her observation of Dyfed's arrival as possible. Leaning over to a desk computer he asked her to electronically transfer the man's full admitting file over so he could look it over some more for it seemed, he told her, that the patient had arrived by a local precinct ambulance of the City of Megatropolis on a Medic on Wheels initiative. The accompanying medics, the good doctor knew, would have signed the form alongside their identification numbers that had been download electronically from the official identification tags they wore that was part of their uniform. Even the caption of the man and woman team caught on camera as they typed in their report in that very office was attached. Everything seemed in order and he saw that the man's clothes were listed as one very expensive silvery silk suit, dark silk expensive shirt, and a cravat-like tie that was purchased, like the rest of his garments, from a high end retailer who hired the finest garment makers and tailors in the world. Along with these there were some items o identification: Specifically this was a Unified States Freedom to Purchase citizen's card, a motorised vehicle operator's licence and two bankcards. Even the make and size of his shoes were recorded here, as well. There was also a photo of the patient. He appeared asleep or dead. The doctor quickly looked and found the clinic attorney's signature on that page which was strictly to help verify the data and identification for the admitting patient.

"I need this patient to be properly photographed while awake,' he said to the receptionist as he clicked on the close function of the file and headed for the door. 'And finger printed, first thing in the morning after he has awakened,' he added. 'Contact one of our units right now on the double and make the appointment. Don't wait until tomorrow to phone over, this is a priority. Do you understand? Also, I want to speak to the medics that brought the patient in. Oh, and send his updated file to me as soon as it is completed. I'll need it by nine o'clock tomorrow morning. Good night,' he said. 'Oh, and just one other thing: Here is a phone number.' He reached into his pocket and handed her a page ripped from his notebook. 'Please call it, and keep calling if you don't get an answer. It may be his attorney, although I doubt it. Try it and find out more about him if you can.'

(Disassociation by Paranoid-type Schizophrenia)

"The three greatest dolts in the world:
Jesus Christ, Don Quixote and me.'
SIMON BOLIVAR (ATTRIBUTED)

"How the devil are we going to pull this off?' said a new associate attached to the *pack*. His name was Rhodrie MacGwryon and he had once fought alongside those who rode with Bricus at the gallop under the former's screaming wolf and boar windsock banner that was his family insignia. This was the same Bricus who had prematurely declared himself king of ancient Prydain known as Constantine. Rhodrie had seen action in the sixth, seventh and eighth centuries to either slaughtering or putting the run on any Druids who took up practice in those lands that now stretched from Gwyneth to Nova Troia while helping to forge a new kingdom under AEthelstan. Later while soldiering at the Battle of Catal against Atala with Trachmyr, he had become known as General Germanos.

General Germanos (retired) spoke directly to Morgant and King Karatakos. Sucking on a huge cigar Rhodrie Germanos was now twisting it from one side of his mouth to the other as he sat on a plush Chesterfield chair in Dyfed's apartment high-rise in Manna-hata. He then began looking for somewhere to knock off a growing ash. The three had arrived together and had immediately gained secret access to Dyfed's building and keyed their way up the private elevator to the top floors. Although they took nothing for granted, they knew they were safe here due to the diligent work of the local team who were part of the *pack*. It was true that some adverse agents who were never properly identified had already earlier concentrated their attention on the building. Presumably this was after Doris had been debriefed and Dyfed nabbed, but nothing came of it. Everything had looked in order, even to these motivated glorified Night watchmen who were incorporated by Corporate World and their Haploid masters that were highly suspicious, ultra security conscious folks who took themselves very seriously indeed. Serious, dark suited men with serious dark glasses who carried serious automatic weapons as easily as though they were umbrellas or brief cases. But as for the intent here, even those who didn't have a limited imagination wouldn't have uncovered anything, not even so much as a hot computer or a fingerprint, never mind a DNA swab that could match a sample that a lab technician of the establishment could come up with. They never so much as got a foot in the door never mind expediting a search warrant of the premise. Even a thorough examination of registered names on permits, bills, lease documents at City Hall and records from The Megatropolis Energy Corp. as well as data gathered elsewhere. None of it had turned up anything other than a fat resounding zilch. The skeleton crew (which was the hallmark of the *pack*) were extremely helpful to all and any in the former's inquiries that never took place face to face. But even that defence for the cause all paled compared to the observation intelligence and personal security the local *pack* provided for the executive members of this division who had just arrived, along with Trachmyr and his field lieutenant, General Rhodrie Germanos. The field unit was meant to be led by Deric the Deuce, but everybody thought it was doubtful that he and his men would actually show up, which (however) they did. The information that Morgant and Karatakos had received was that the Deuce and his field crew were living just off shore near the bottom of the sea in a submarine from where they were able to slip back and forth from there into local waters around Megatropolis at ease and unseen: And staying put kept them unseen.

"We will probably end up using the National Defence Appropriations Act, amendment #10-04 for sure, at some point,' said Germanos as he flipped through some old laminated, card type electrical schematics and scrolled down through an electronic file on his computer at the same time. 'It is a powerful piece of legislature and will be useful in cutting into the flank of their onslaught to appropriate this building, which in all likelihood will be almost iron clad.'

"We don't know what the Deuce and his crew will turn up yet, either,' said King Karatakos.

"I'm very concerned at this point for Dyfed,' said Morgant, 'but I'm also afraid that once we've got him free we still have no way to get him out and away. And let's face it, we aren't going to be able to employ the olden day shifting dimension machine, either, that fake transcendental mechanical transmutation hoax machine transporter as promised. Its arrival has already been delayed. Now its not supposed to arrive from Denver until the day after tomorrow, and we need to rescue Dyfed and get him clear of this place and into somewhere else fast — and long before then.'

The crew around him suddenly burst out laughing. This seemed to take the edge off their long, ascending row to hoe in order to free Dyfed from some unknown agent of the Haploid establishment.

"Oh, and be ready to keep your ears open. When the olden day machine I mentioned will be delivered, it will be come in three parts dangling from three Sokorskis that will arrive in relays above the roof launch pad. We will have to weigh anchor, too, and move the airship Samsara across the river to our Jersey compound for now. And I'm not certain the olde transcending machine is even fake-functional any more,' he said with resignation and concern. 'Dr Torsionfield had it assembled many solar cycles ago for a private summer-school college camp think-tank he was once intent on setting up. We'll have a lot of work ahead of us to make it appear impressive.'

"Sure it will be impressively fake-functional,' said Germanos who having accessed pertinent data from a secret vault was busy familiarizing himself with the mechanical and electrical schematics. 'If it worked as a prototype mock-up once, we can get it to work again. I suspect it will need reprogramming, or at least re-tuning, that's all. But that is definitely do-able. I'll probably end up using probabilistic adduces on top of extended super-positioning if I'm going to pretend to get it off the third dimension. Of course, but I have the perfect quantum program here in my computer for that. Where are we setting this old machine up, anyway?' he asked.

"Down in the basement's basement,' said Morgant. 'The mechanical service elevator is large enough to take it down piecemeal in three parts as delivered.'

"Good,' said Germanos. 'All we need to do is get Dyfed out of whatever hot water he is sitting in, clear the aisle of those no-good-get-in-the-way-circle-jerks and head back up here and after giving this woman Doris a tour, ship Dyfed out. Is that the plan, then?'

"Well, kind of,' responded Trachmyr, with King Karatakos standing by and looking amused.

"Good,' said Germanos, 'the Deuce is on it now, too, so there shouldn't be a problem. Does anyone see a problem?' Germanos had cast aside his computer onto a couch, and letting some of the paper schematics fall onto an ornate little table he was working over. He stood up and stretched, then after picking up his cigar he walked over to the huge picture window that Dyfed had been gazing out of three days earlier. He then stuck his cigar back in between his teeth again as he listened to Morgant run through a program that they had been working on to secure Dyfed's freedom. Morgant was holding a tele-pad in his hand and was also in touch with Deric the Deuce as he spoke. As Germanos listened he watched some serious faced, dark suited and dark glasses clad men climb in and out of large, specially manufactured internal combustion driven motor chariots that were parked a long way down below on the sidewalks around another commercial-tenement building that was across the street and which rose into the air beside Dyfed's building. Armed men guarded the vehicles, and as the others filed up and down among its floors, some had computers at the ready that they plugged in here and there while others had automatic rifles also at the ready with handguns strapped to their leg calves and hips. They appeared to be rifling through computer files, and frightened office workers were being shoed away from their desks while angry managers were punching their tele-pads to summon corporate higher ups in order to protest or demand of them new directions in dealing with the onslaught of this army; this division of an aggressive Department of Public Safety, of dark suit and shades that labelled this special variety of Nightwatchmen. This particular division, also funded by lucrative tax credit cash transfers wielded by Corporate World, was an elite unit that was hand picked from its own agency for central intelligence. None of this of course was anything unusual in the day-to-day activity in any city of the world. Germanos put the binoculars down and relit his cigar.

Dyfed was lying motionless on his side when he heard the door open. Although the footsteps were quiet he could tell that there were a few people just outside his room.

"He has been subdued for over twelve-four hours, now,' said a young female as she closed the security ward door between his little alcove and the main ward.

From then on, Dyfed knew, they would be observing him through the one-way windows that looked into his alcove but prevented him from looking out.

"I noticed his I.V. bag emptied out late last night and I asked nurse Jackson to remove his apparatus at that time.'

"Good, thank you doctor Morscher,' said the good doctor. 'He won't need any more.' Then turning toward two well dressed men, the doctor continued. 'He was photographed again earlier and went back to sleep. He will be coming around and ready shortly, gentle-men and then you can have him. Give him an hour and then we can freshen him up. I'll need to look over your release and transfer permits so lets go back to the office. Dr Morscher, inform the secretary now that I'll need the attorney present.'

"He doesn't get to have an attorney present, at least not here and not now,' said the younger of the two men once they were outside the ward room number 101B and walking down the hall in the direction they had come.

"Oh, it's not for him,' replied the doctor. 'It's our attorney, actually,' he said laughing a little, 'the clinic's attorney. She will be the adviser on any legal matters such as admissions, transfers, terminations, and the like. She will also witness all signatures. That is our policy, gentlemen.'

"I'm sorry, doctor, but we are not authorized to sign anything. Indeed, we are specifically instructed not to sign anything. That is our policy.'

"Whose policy is that,' asked Dr Morscher. 'I'll need administrative approval for this release. You know that, surely?' she said. 'You do have that in writing, don't you?' she asked. Specifically, I'll need a Megatropolis District Attorney's office application for release, too. I understand from what you have said that Mr Easystreet is to be arraigned in a court of law, so I will also need that jurisdiction's application and permit for release that is signed by a judge along with an accompanying specific reason for release that is sealed and dated. You know how things work. The indictment registration number should do, but our attorney will be able to advise you on that.'

"I'm...sorry, doctor,' said the other man who had been doing all the speaking. 'You, that is, we are continually referring to a Mr Easystreet. Well, actually that isn't his real name. That is it isn't the name that actually appears on the official paperwork. It is his paperwork, be sure of that, doctor. That is, it is Mr Easystreet's paperwork. The two names we will be dealing with here actually refer to one and the same man. We could get it changed, but that would only take time, court time, for we would not be able to reveal any other name for the time being other than Easystreet and without an affidavit as such. Now, his photo identification will be useful, thank you doctor for upgrading it, but what I'm getting at is that all of this might pose a problem at this end. You may need to take our word at face value over it. What I'm trying to say, doctor, is this: We might find a corroborating photo with Mr Easystreet's real name attached which would then match the photo of your patient which would verify to you — that is you and the clinic's attorney — that we are in fact dealing with one and the same man. Of course, his real name at this time will be redacted, you understand. You and the attorney would need to be sworn to secrecy in any case. But again, that may take time and this pseudonym of his, or code name — as we refer to it as — works to our advantage in keeping his identity under wraps, at least for now. Also, the time delay in any format does not work for us. He's our man all right. I viewed him myself, as you know.' The man quickly darted a look at his companion.

"What do you mean a code name?' asked the doctor.

"It's our policy,' the man replied, 'to keep a low profile on this. We don't wish any untoward embarrassment to the family if it should go public, at least at this time, prior to any convictions. You see?'

"Not really,' answered the doctor, looking a little disconcerted as his gaze moved back and forth between the man who had just spoken and the mysterious older man, a Mr Purplebal. 'You see,' continued the good doctor, 'because Mr Easystreet was the photo, fingerprint, and retina secure identification match that the patient was carrying when he arrived. At least that was the case with his motorised vehicle operator's licence, his bankcards, and his Unified Statesian Freedom to Purchase citizen's card. So, what are you saying? You had them planted on him before he arrived here a few days ago, and for what reason, again?'

"Listen here, doctor. I've tried to explain it as succinctly as I can. Ah, — is doctor Soros back yet, bye the way?'

"No,' replied the doctor.

"You don't want to involve yourself too deeply in this, believe me, doctor.'

"Believe you? Why?'

"Look-it! You are out of you depth here. Do you follow?'

The doctor turned and led them on again toward the secure main door with its card swipe that led out of the ward.

"You can explain your position and your policies yourself to our attorney. I cannot release anyone until she has signed the release first. But she won't sign it until she knows that I am favourable to releasing him. It's a medical thing, you understand. Whatever she is going to require is what you will have to deal with first. Ah. There she is now,' he said.

"Good morning Madam attorney,' the doctor said, as the two male guests and himself exited through the secure main door. She was just coming from the next office and turning, he motioned for her to enter a very large office first, while the two guests followed her and he walked in last. There he introduced the attorney to the two men. The pretty attorney smiled and shook hands with the other men as the introductions were made. The office was littered with packing boxes and some of them the doctor moved with his foot, sliding them over in order to make room for people's feet. They then shuffled around a small conference table that easily managed the four of them.

"These men are here about securing the release of Mr Easystreet,' he said, throwing a glance at the two other men. 'He is a patient here whose file I've already sent to you this morning. It would appear that there may be two identities and I am recommending now that you look into that first. Please keep me informed. I'm afraid, gentlemen,' the doctor now glanced over at the two men briefly, 'from what I've picked up from our short talk it would appear that this release is going to be a little more complicated than either of us thought.' The two other men carefully eyed the attractive attorney who was pulling things out of her over-the-shoulder case as the younger man who normally did the talking suddenly spoke.

"How many doctors are there on staff here, doctor?' he asked.

"Four… ah, pardon me, three,' the doctor answered, volunteering no more information.

"Isn't that a lot, really?' the other man countered. The doctor, who was checking his calls on his tele-pad while their attorney was getting ready, looked up at the man.

"Not really,' he replied.

"Oh, really?' the man said. 'Who is Mr Easystreet's doctor, doctor?'

"I am,' the doctor replied, not looking at the man. 'At least I'm the doctor responsible for him. Why do you ask?'

"But there was another doctor, just now, who accompanied us to the patient's room.

"Yes,' replied the doctor, 'how observant of you.'

"So who is she?'

"She is a doctor; Dr Uschi Morscher. I have already introduced you to her, just earlier.' He glanced over at the man's quiet companion who was watching them both with those emotionless eyes, and then he looked over at Madam attorney who sat adjacent to the latter man. It was a strange contrast between the two, the doctor thought. She, young, pretty and milky pink with her clear blue eyes and brown wavy hair, he old and craggy with frighteningly strange eyes and dark, stiffly hardened skin contrasting with his shock of short white hair that seemed to stand up in an old fashioned brush-cut fashion.

The other man, the talkative one — Madam attorney had already decided — had those hard, cold eyes of a falsely smiling Jeshuan evangelical fundamentalist salesman canvassing for his political life. She was also aware that he was extremely uncomfortable about the other man's presence, as was the doctor. She did not know why that should be the case for either man.

"Do we have a collective and accurate report of the patient, considering the varied input? the man asked.

"I don't understand,' replied the doctor. 'Input is a combination of test results, many of which were done at either one or two of the labs we use that are across town, as well as observations recorded during the time that Mr Easystreet has been closely monitored here. And the input also includes other physical data that either accompanied him in here or by verbal statements; things he has stated during his stay here that have all been recorded.' The visiting man looked down at the table top directly in front of him.

"In order to release Mr Easystreet,' said the attorney, taking advantage of the momentary lull, 'as you know we will need a signed application for release from the district attorney's office. It says here,' she was indicating her computer screen with a slight jerk of her head, 'that Mr Easystreet is to be arraigned, so I'll need a copy of the arraignment order with a Department of Justice seal on it, too.'

"Is all this really necessary?' the younger man asked seeming exasperated. He emitted a little incredulous type laugh as he leaned back in his chair.

"It's the law,' she replied. 'Why don't you know that? It is also our policy to conform to the law. And as this man's medical well being takes precedence, in our opinion, over any other matters we would not release him in any case under any circumstance until we, that is, the doctor,' she motioned toward the good doctor, 'felt it was safe to do so. That also includes the police, accompanied by a judge's writ, from any court of law in the city, but not outside it. Otherwise, we would not be prepared to release him.'

"You don't know who you are dealing with here,' the man suddenly said nastily. 'And anyway, what you just stated probably wouldn't happen, not in our world it wouldn't.' The young attorney, the doctor noted, was obviously quite taken aback by the man's rude manner.

"Who are we dealing with then?' asked the doctor. 'Who in fact are you, exactly?' The doctor looked up and right into the older man's dead eyes.

"It's not who we are,' the younger man started to explain, 'I'm a deputized officer of state security, as you well know, doctor. I am on loan from the military. Mr Purplebal here,' he said, indicating the older man, 'is an extremely important man, an adviser to our government, no less and a personal friend of the president and the CEO of Monsignor the SaintlyÔ, one of the most influential corporations in the world who helps fund the World Food bank account. Something very much in need right now, wouldn't you say? He is also the director head of the Chasen Whorbegger Bank, as well as a major stockholder in Schiffly, Shiny & Shack. Right there you have two of this country's largest banks, as you no doubt know. Mr Purplebal's presence should be an indication of the seriousness in which the state views this felon and wants him brought before justice, immediately.' He paused a moment for effect. 'Oh no, it's not who we are, doctor, it is who Mr Easystreet is.

"Well, then, let's start there, shall we! Who, then, is my patient? And let's start with his real name.'

"I'm afraid,' said the other man, 'that the information we have on him is classified, doctor. But he is a very dangerous man who is wanted by the guardians of our country as well as others.'

"Who are these guardians and why does our country want him, exactly?'

"I'm sorry, doctor, 'that information is also classified.'

"Why is it classified?'

"Because it is a matter involving national security, that's why.'

"I see. How convenient for you.'

"You will find that that is the way it will always be when you deal with us,' the man said.

"But you were here the other evening when I began interviewing Mr Easystreet. If you remember,' continued the good doctor, 'he told us that thugs had attacked him downtown and they had stuck a needle into his neck. Do you remember?' The doctor looked pointedly at Mr Purplebal.

"Of course he is going to say that,' answered the other man. 'Remember doctor, as we have told you, he is intelligent, dangerous and insane. We have information that he suffers from psychopathy.'

"Yes, as you have said. And a loner, a drifter, and an alcoholic as well, I believe. However,' continued the good doctor, 'this is the part where it is very convenient for him, and not you.'

"What are you talking about?' asked the man.

"I'm talking about the needle wound in his neck,' responded the doctor.

"Of course he faked it,' interjected the man.

"I'm talking about the scopolamine that came out of that needle. I'm talking about chloroform that was found in abundance in his system along with the traces of that scopolamine he had been injected with. That's what I'm talking about. Furthermore, in respect to his identity, I am even more confused. Madam attorney, please pay attention to this as I have tasked you with shining a light on this conundrum. You told me, sir,' the doctor met the eyes of the younger man, 'when you contacted me the day before yesterday, that you wanted to view a Mr Easystreet who had been admitted here earlier that day. Do you remember?'

"Yes, yes, of course I remember. What has this got…'

"You arrived that evening,' continued the doctor after interrupting the other man. Then turning to look at the older Mr Purplebal, he said: 'And although paying close attention to his photo identification which I showed you, you listened to him while I did an unimportant spot interview with him yet you neither spoke to him nor did you ask me any questions about him. Isn't that right? You also asked to view him a moment or two behind a one-way mirror after he returned to his room and before he was mildly medicated again. In addition Mr Purplebal also viewed Mr Easystreet surreptitiously while keeping his identity from the patient, as well.'

"I have no idea where you are going with this,' the younger man replied.

"Then let me tell you by asking you this. How did you know that Mr Easystreet was here in the first place? Who told you?'

The other man looked vaguely bewildered for a moment and then glancing over at his quiet companion said; "I think I got a call from someone at this office. You have got to realise doctor, I'm a busy man and furthermore, this file was handed to me. I wasn't even the first on it. Maybe someone within our office told me or sent me a memo. Who knows? What does it matter, doctor?'

"Our record shows, sir, that no one contacted your department. Nor at any time was Mr Easystreet's name given out to anybody. We did contact missing persons and asked them to send over a list to us, but we gave out no name. Also, Mr Easystreet's description didn't match some eleven hundred odd people reported missing that day in the general area. Nobody but nobody should have known he was here other than the medics and they have stated earlier today that they did not inform you or anybody else. They also said they collected him after receiving a call which specifically gave his whereabouts which was close to here, not downtown. That's in their admission record. The question remains, how did you come to know that Mr Easystreet was here?'

"Ok. Listen, doctor,' the man said, adjusting himself in his chair and looking slightly angry and uncomfortable. 'We want to speak to Dr Soros. Why isn't he here, incidentally? We understand that he is running this place, not you.'

"Dr Soros. Yes you asked me about him the other evening, as well as a few minutes ago. I told you then that he wasn't here. What has Dr Soros got to do with you or the patient? Did he contact you about our patient?' the doctor cautiously inquired. As he did so he shot a quick look at the silent, older man, but was unable to read him. The talkative man seemed uncharacteristically tongue tied for a few seconds and even managed a raised eye browed glance at his companion. The doctor waited patiently, looking away from the man and at the young attorney instead.

"Yes, it must have been Dr Soros who contacted our office.' the other man responded. 'Yes, that's right I'm sure it was now. He didn't contact me in person, you understand. That I know. You see, he would have been worried about a man like Mr Easystreet.'

"I see,' said the doctor, whimsically.

There was a quick rap at the door and it opened and the receptionist poked her nose through the partly opened door.

"Good gracious! Madam receptionist. Can't you see I'm in an important meeting?' said the good doctor.

"I'm terribly sorry, sir, but there is a gentleman here to see you and I thought it was important enough to interrupt, under the circumstances.' The two men had their backs to the door and couldn't see the receptionist quickly rolling her eyes as she spoke the last three words.

"Alright, tell 'em I'll be there in a few minutes.' The tall silent man suddenly stood up and tried to put on a congenial air. His eyes, however, didn't change.

"I beg your pardon, doctor, for coming unprepared. We will have to get a court order allowing for the patient in question to be released into the hands of agents of our national security. That is clear to me now. Doctor, do not think for one minute that we will return empty handed. And we will return shortly and we will relieve you of your patient. Please do not be foolish enough to think to stop us.'

The doctor was dumbfounded for he hadn't realised that all this time this quite, unspeaking man's mouth had been so full of words and had so much to let out and say. "How is that, then?' he answered.

"Well, one reason,' the man named Purplebal continued, 'is on account of this man's dangerous nature. You see, you just aren't capable or well equipped enough for me to be comfortable about him being left here unguarded the way he is. I'm concerned for the safety of you and your staff, to be truthful. And for that same reason I'm anxious to get him secured.'

"I'll need a deposition from a federal court, in that case, not just any court, since it is a matter of national defence,' said the pretty Madam attorney, smiling gently with her chin resting lightly on her entwined fingers that were propped up by her bared elbows. 'But the name — Mr Easystreet — must appear on it just the same as it does on our documents. Either that or you must procure an official change of name document.' The elderly man started to move quickly toward the door with his companion beginning to stumble to his feet. The doctor, still not moving from his chair, held up a hand.

"Whoa, just a moment fellas. Look-it; I know you aren't going to like this but I have to tell you anyway. The way I see it right now is that our patient won't be going anywhere soon, not with you or anyone else. Don't waste your time running around getting any paperwork done if you got something better to do. Ok? You will need to inform your chief officer to contact me ASAP, though. There is one other thing, you see. Dr Soros didn't call anybody about the patient. That much I know for certain. Dr Soros never knew, saw or heard of Mr Easystreet: So you see, he couldn't have. This is because Dr Soros was dead before Mr Easystreet crossed our threshold the other morning. Unless, of course, somehow he knew he was going to be coming! But how could that be?' He looked sharply at the elderly Mr Purplebal. 'As for me, well, the patient crossed the threshold and came in here even before I did. You see Dr Soros died three nights ago and about eight or nine hours before our patient in question arrived here. This was Dr Soros' office and as you can see his stuff is being packed up and made ready to be moved out. As far as my involvement is concerned, I was brought over here from my clinic to help out. I also manage another clinic, you see! Although maybe Dr Uschi Morscher should have succeeded to chief in this clinic, it was I who the state health board chose instead. Just what the real reason was for channelling Mr Easystreet through here… well, I don't know and unfortunately Dr Soros didn't even have the opportunity to lie to me about it, had he wanted to.'

The doctor then stared at the two men who glared back at him.

"We will be back soon enough and you will accept what documents we present,' the talkative man said. 'I'll be leaving some guards that I will post outside. Be very careful doctor. Goodbye to you.'

(The Trial and escape of the Free Radical)

'It's dangerous to be right in matters where established men are wrong.'
VOLTAIRE

Only after the doctor had watched the men leave and saw that soldier type security troops had been placed in front of the clinic did he look around for the visitor that the receptionist had announced. In the reception room there was a tall, strong young man with a winning smile who still standing since his entry here. The young man told the receptionist that his name was Thornborough Derikson, and in a world — never mind a city — where people went around wearing almost anything most of the time (Kimonos over jeans and jump suits under raincoats along with sneakers, always sneakers), Thornborough Derikson was well and exquisitely dressed. The doctor noted that in addition to expensive well made black boots that could be seen riding high under his trouser legs, he also wore a navy blue sea cap with no insignia on it and a partly opened tan coloured raincoat even though it was broiling hot out.

"What can I do for you Mr Derikson?' the doctor asked.

"I'm looking for a man who has gone missing and we received a call that this clinic had recently been searching for the proper identification of an inmate. The message we received was that this patient has asked for an attorney and would someone please respond immediately. Unfortunately we were out of town for a day or two, that is why the delay. Sorry,' Thornborough Derikson said.

The doctor thought for a moment. How strange, he concluded, thinking to himself.

"What is this man's name? he then asked.

"He is a big man,' Mr Derikson continued, 'that is, he is tall and he has silver eyes. He goes by...'

"Well, well, well! You are here for Mr Easystreet, then. I thought as much,' replied the good doctor.

"Ah, — yes, that would be him,' the younger man answered, smiling broadly. He noticed that the doctor was eyeing him closely.

"Yes,' said the doctor, 'he was checked in fairly early in the morning a couple of days ago by some medics, I'm afraid.'

"So, how is he doing, now?' the young man nonchalantly inquired.

"Not bad,' the doctor said, slowly. The conversation was conducted in a searching manner by both sides and this was apparent to both the men.

"What did you say your relationship with him was?' asked the doctor.

"I'm not his attorney,' said Mr Derikson. Actually I'm a step-grandson, you could say. My grandmother is his wife, or became his wife after my biological grandfather was killed.'

"You don't say!' said the doctor. Sorry to hear that. So, what line of work was your step-grandfather in?' the doctor asked. The young man noticed that the doctor was slightly distracted: He was checking his tele-pad for incoming messages, once again.

"He's a merchant banker,' the young man answered. 'But we are wasting time. He can come with me now. If he's unable to walk, we have facilities parked just outside. I can pay all cost now with card or cash, if you wish.

"That wouldn't be a good idea, you see, for those security men who are also outside who you passed on your way in would nab him as quick as a wink of an eye. Yes, faster than you could say Jack Robinson. Would you happen to know why that is, by any chance? Would you know the reason for all this controversy which is surrounding your step-grandfather?'

"No...I...don't...ah...not...off-hand,' said Mr Derikson slowly and hesitantly, all the while well imagining just how fast a couple of the boys from the *pack* could dispatch that professional troop of special agents outside.

"Did you know that your family member is being arraigned?' asked the doctor.

"Heavens, no. What on Earth for?' Thornborough replied, laughing slightly.

"I don't know and your family member and I aren't on close terms, yet. The security officers, though, are reciting the national security excuse for not telling us, I know that much.'

Thornborough Derikson, the son of Deric the Deuce, thought about that for a moment and concluded that everything wasn't as bad as they thought it might be.

"No,' he said, after a moment, 'I wasn't completely truthful with you, I'm afraid, doctor. You see my grandfather's real name is Dyfed Lucifer, not Mr Easystreet. I do know that powerful and dangerous people are framing him and that you don't want to get involved with this, doctor, believe me. Uncle Dyfed, as I call him, is a friend of the good people of the Unified Sates, you can be sure of that. He was also a friend of President John Munster. They were friends practically back to childhood, at least for almost two thousand years until the time of the latter's assassination during the Great Uncle Sham Coup, back in '63. They were still friends then. So,' Thornborough said, quickly changing the subject, 'can you get someone, a nurse maybe, to bring him out so I can see him now?'

"Please, Mr Derikson. Come into my office and have a seat for a few minutes. There are some things we need to talk about and we may need to do it quickly.'

"Yes, you are right, we need to do this very quickly. I'm not so sure we have enough time even to talk,' Derikson said, suddenly looking slightly agitated.

"But there are some big problems,' the doctor countered. 'Have you forgotten that I said he is to be arraigned?'

"True, said the younger man, 'but have you been served with the proper papers, or do you just have it on somebody else's say so?'

The doctor thought about that for a moment then said,

"So, this is what I'm prepared to do.' The doctor then immediately buzzed nurse Jackson to ask her to bring the patient into the visiting room, immediately. 'We will get a few things straightened out right now then you will need to get your attorney here, ASAP. I may not be able to hold on to him much longer, I'm afraid.'

The patient visiting room was adjacent to the reception area and was cordoned off from the entrance and reception area with large panes of one-way glass looking out and a normal glass door with Venetian blinds running down the length. As they turned towards this door the doctor asked Thornborough Derikson to spell Dyfed's last name.

"Lucifer,' he repeated, 'spelled, el, ewe, cee, aye eff, ee, arr.

"Oh," said the doctor, as if he had suddenly remembered something. 'Why is he using an alias and has gone to the trouble of illegally procuring an alternative set of identification if he has nothing to hide?'

"Ah, that is a little more complicated," replied Thornborough Derikson, 'but not unusual for Grandpa. After all, you see the circumstances he is in, yourself. With my presence here, I'm quite sure he will now explain it all to you, himself. Please hurry him up.'

"So, I will let you see him for a few moments," said the doctor, 'but he isn't going anywhere. In fact, I'm frightened by the situation he is in. And, frankly, I don't know where or who to turn to. These people are military of some kind, you know. Can you contact his lawyer now?'

"No worries, doctor. We're here, now. Let me see Dyfed and let's take it from there."

A moment later a door opened and Thornborough saw Dyfed being wheeled into the room. Upon seeing his surrogate grandson a big smile came over Dyfed's face. It was what the doctor would have ordered and just what he was looking for, too. The nurse wheeled him up to the two men and left. Thornborough scrutinized Dyfed carefully for a moment, looking at the former's large boned frame that was collapsed carelessly yet comfortably for a body too big for the chair.

"What are YOU doing here?" said Dyfed, casually.

"Good morning Mr Lucifer," said the doctor. 'You can identify this man, I assume?' He was smiling and feeling a little more confident now.

"Of course," replied Dyfed, 'he is my wife's grandson, Thornborough.'

"Good," replied the doctor. 'Now we are getting somewhere.'

Suddenly, while still regarding his older kin with a smile, Thornborough pulled out his tele-pad and punching in some keys soon began to speak.

"So, he is here," they all heard Thornborough say. 'What? No, he is right beside me. But we have to hurry. Where are you? Ok, so you are pretty much in place, then? Ok. How many?' 'Ok. What? Where? Ok. How many? So, there's a tall old guy and a younger one? Ok. Give me a couple of seconds.' He then turned to Dyfed and said: 'Say, old man. Can you get up out of that thing and walk at all?'

Still slumped awkwardly and spilling out of the wheel chair, Dyfed didn't move a muscle other than the smile on his face.

"Now listen to me, Mr Derikson," the doctor cut in, 'we have discussed this. I know what you are thinking but Mr Lucifer must stay right…'

"I'm sorry, doctor," interrupted Thornborough Derikson. 'And I…that is, we want to thank you for your concern for my grandpa, believe me. We all want to thank you. And I'm sure Dyfed will make a huge donation to your clinic to compensate for any expenses incurred. If this is you clinic he will donate an enormous amount of money to you in way of his thanks. Believe me. It could have gone a lot worse, that's for sure. So, here's the thing. I can do anything you want. Fire a couple of shots in the ceiling, whatever it takes to let you off the hook. You and your staff won't be harmed by me, I can say that much. I can't speak for the others who are on their way in here right now though, but chances are more than good that I'll get the drop on them as easy peasy as pie and see that you're all right.'

"What do you mean?" said the doctor now fully in alarm. 'What do you mean on their way here now?'

"I'm about to vacate the premises and grandpa here is coming with me,' said Thornborough. 'That's it: That's all. There is no negotiation, no ifs, no ands and no buts. This is how I work. This is no reflection on you, by the way, or your integrity or your honesty, doctor. The men that left your office less than half an hour ago will be back with even more re-enforcements then are already waiting outside. I can make a show of it so it appears that you fought to keep Dyfed here, but please take caution, I'm dealing with dangerous men here.

"Including the old codger,' said Dyfed all of a sudden, 'who is the deadliest of all.'

"What old codger?' asked Thornborough. He turned toward the outer set of glass sliding doors and saw an elderly man with cold eyes who he saw leaving the doctors' office shortly after he himself had arrived here. 'You mean you know that elderly man who is just now stepping through the outer door?' He turned and looked back again at the intruding man.

"You bet I do,' said Dyfed. 'I've known him for at least seventeen or eighteen hundred years, anyway. I'll introduce you to Potamus Purplebal the moment he steps in here,' said Dyfed who still had not moved.

The doctor's head snapped around taking in first the sight of the senior man coming through the outer doors who had been negotiating to relieve the clinic of the erstwhile Mr Easystreet, then returning his eyes that suddenly riveted on Dyfed.

"And you had better listen to my young step-grandson, doctor,' Dyfed added. 'Don't judge him by his looks and manners. He's a pirate, a real honest to dog-gone son-of-a-bitchin' pirate just like his dad, who steals oil tankers and other gargantuan container carrying vessels. He's even been known to steal military aircraft carriers and submarines. Watch out for him!' The doctor stood absolutely still now and stared at both of them in amazement and disbelief. His wife, he thought for just a split second, won't believe him tonight when he gets home and tells her about his day. And he had had some really crazy ones in his time, too!

"Here they come,' said Dyfed, interrupting the doctor's thoughts. Through the one way glass Dyfed watched two men in suits coming through the doors into the reception room accompanied by three uniformed officers whose insignia he couldn't make out.

"Ok, they're in,' Thornborough said into his tele-pad. 'Let's rock and roll.' Thornborough cautioned the doctor by extending his arm a little and holding his hand so the fingers were pointing down and then gently waved them away from his body, motioning the doctor back. The doctor quickly stepped back with a look of fear and confusion on his face just as Dyfed sprung up out of the wheelchair. Thornborough then opened his rain coat and for the first time Dyfed saw the short barrelled, pump action twelve gauge shotgun slung from his neck which he quickly freed. Then gripping it in his left hand Thornborough thrust it in front of him. Holding the weapon perpendicular by the handgrip with barrel pointing up. Then he jerked his arm with a quick up and down motion and the sliding grip moved up and down as the heavy action part of the gun remain stationary. The shotgun was now cocked and ready for action. Derikson then lowered the barrel from the perpendicular to the horizontal. The men were now all inside the reception room and Dyfed strode quickly toward the field of the door's auto-motion controller and it jerked open.

"Well, well; lookie here,' he said pleasantly. 'It's the old codger Potamus Purplebal himself. Not even taking proper precaution, either,' he added, as all five of the other men appeared startled as they began to swing around to face the voice. Thornborough walked through the door first with a smile on his face, keeping his eyes on the three officers. The youngest and fattest officer who had a head and neck like an inverted elephant's foot nervously began to swing his automatic rifle around.

"Don't do that,' Thornborough shouted. The man's arm did not stop and the blast from the Derikson's shotgun must have broken the staff's eardrums as it tore off a large piece of the man's neck including the top of his spine. The remnants were instantly sprayed across the short space behind the remains of the man still standing and were partly imbedded into the wall behind him that was across some of the glass of the outer doors. The man's head, that momentarily remained partially attached to the body by some skin from the man's throat, finally pulled loose and thumped as it hit the floor and rolled slightly. A spit second later Thornborough had already positioned another shell into the breach from the magazine by quickly pulling down and pushing up with his fist. This motion ejected the spent shell while with an upward thrust and the definite sound of a shell being slammed back into the chamber readied the shotgun to be fired again. This was all done only by the use of Thornborough's right arm. He had repeated this noisy forward and back reload motion before the rest of the plummeting officer's body had hit the wall and then flopped to a heavy landing thud at foot level where it never voluntarily moved again. All the while black coloured blood was being pumped out of his neck. Meanwhile, Dyfed had rushed forward with lightening action and had torn the briefcase that Purplebal was carrying out of his hand.

The other man in the suit, the talkative one, never so much as uttered a single word though Dyfed had the impression that he was frantically trying to say something. He also recognised him as the man he took to be a military senior official who had been climbing out of the limousine van that had been parked outside the Jewel Banking House the other day. No mistake about that, he thought. Meanwhile, gunshots galore began to wring out all over the place outside. Thornborough motioned with his head and Dyfed moved back.

"Over here by the wall, Potamus,' Dyfed said, 'where I can see you better.' Yet he never took his eyes off the other officers. 'That's fine right there. I can see you.'

"Do you want to keep him, Grandpa Dyfed?' he said.

Dyfed looked across at Purplebal. He looked into those eyes of his where he saw no emotion whatsoever.

"It's been a long journey, eh, Potamus?' he said very nicely and calmly. 'Do you ever have regrets over your unconscionable behaviour towards the human race? Has your beastly and unconscionable behaviour towards other people who trusted you and over whom you had polipotential authority and power managed to humble you any?' Dyfed glanced at the Thornborough. 'We could try him, I suppose, but I'd sooner have him tell me from his own mouth the identity of the chief Haploid,' he answered.

"He'll never do that, Grandpa Dyfed,' he said. 'And we're fast running out of time here. Is he guilty of something bad?' Thornborough asked again.

"Oh yes, Thorborough, he is,' replied Dyfed, 'he's guilty all right.'

"I mean really guilty of something bad?

"Yes, he is guilty of horrendous crimes. He's guilty of destroying the dreams of others less advantaged than himself and interfering with them. Always interfering. He is guilty of finding new ways to program innocent people, of brainwashing children and destroying their individual independence and their pure thought process and imagination. He is guilty, too, of incurring incalculable debt upon the backs of the poor masses that had no means to climb out from under it. And all for his own clan's benefit to remain wealthy and powerful.'

"So,' said the young man who was facing Purplebal, 'guilty as charged, then.' Thornborough now fired a second shot and caught Potamus Purplebal in the heart that blew it right out his back and splattered blood, tissue and ribcage bone all over the same wall. The heart, still partially attached to him with arteries, thumped twice as it hit first the wall then the floor behind Purplebal's slumped back before his body, now thrown backwards, fell to the floor. The body lay next to the torso of the uniformed security agent whose separated head was now crooked under Purplebal's armpit. Purplebal's neck — that was broken with the fall — was twisted at an awkward angle that left his head propped up against the base of the bloodied wall.

"Drop your weapons, you two, or die,' Thornborough said calmly to the two other uniformed men. 'It doesn't matter to me, though. Make your move, but do it now — right now — for time is up.' Their weapons clattered to the ground immediately and Dyfed bent down and grabbed the automatic rifles from the floor and clutched them under his arm in which he also held the Purplebal's briefcase. He then kicked the handguns out through the sliding doors that were just opening. Suddenly, aptly dodging the small side arms that were skating across the pavement under his feet, Derik the Deuce himself came rushing in sweating a little and out of breath.

"Dyfed,' said the Deuce, 'you're looking good! And how about you son, you making out okay?' he said to Thornbourgh.

"Okay d-okay,' was the latter's simple four syllable replied. That said it all, as far as the Deuce was concerned.

"Good,' the former said. 'Looks like you cleaned up here. My word! Isn't that Purplebal way down there on the floor?' he asked, leaning over and looking down at the thin elderly man in a black suit that lay among a growing blotch of dark red gore. 'Geewillikers! He's not looking so good, though. What happened to him, anyway? Did he put up a fight, fellas?' He asked this question as he looked around at both Dyfed and his son. Dyfed shrugged as though he were completely mystified as to how it all came about.

"No, not really,' Dyfed then decided to say. 'His heart wasn't in it, that's all. He had his day, he had his trial and then he was found guilty and that's about it.'

"C'mon, then,' said the Deuce, 'let's get the hell out of here while the going is good.'

"Hey Doc,' Dyfed called over his shoulder as they quickly left the clinic and headed toward the street to their waiting vehicles, 'thanks for everything, eh. I'll send you a promissory note. Will a million dollars do it?'

Once outside, as the three of them fled from the clinic and into the street, Dyfed noticed a voracious wind was now air blasting the City of Megatropolis. Banners were being torn from their lanyards and along with garbage and peoples' personal affects even the metal dispensing machines, carousels and advertisements were doing loop-de-loops in the air and catching on fences and wires and bouncing off the streets like a snow blizzard of Frisbees. About ten men, their clothes furiously fluttering and flapping in the wind, were converging together beside three high powered vehicles whose large, illegal, eight litre, petroleum gas fuelled internal combustion engines were idling away… waiting. The wind mixed a stunning turmoil of sounds and flung them around like when an eggbeater swirls the ingredients of a Cheese-Bix soufflé. Suddenly, this orchestrated cacophony brought to Dyfed's ears snatches of a squad of wailing sirens in the distance. And even in the short time it took to dash from the clinic's office doors across the street against the wind to the waiting motorised chariots, it was apparent that the sirens were quickly growing louder and would be upon them momentarily.

'I'll accompany Dyfed back to his place,' said the Deuce, shouting loudly to make himself heard by all the men, 'the rest of you know what to do. Follow Thornborough, he's in charge now. Afterwards,' he said in a softer voice as he addressed his son. 'The *pack is throwin*' a Halloween release from mental psychiatric clinic party for Dyfed back at his place, so I'll be stayin' here in Megatropolis for a bit. See you later, though. You sure you'll be okay without me? Just make sure you get back safe, son,' he said.

'I'll be fine, Dad. It's all worked out, anyway,' the younger man replied. 'The moment we get the signal we'll be on it. I'll get control of the atomic sub that's presently submerged in the Hudson River. Then we will get it back to our enclave at Madeira as fast as we can.'

"Okay, Thorny," he said. 'Stay safe.'

"Don't worry, Dad. So long as we can keep reprogramming the anti-tracking system they have on board, we'll stay safe. See you at home in a few weeks and hey, have a good time at the Halloween party. Oh…hey,' Thornborough had turned around to face the formidable Deric the Deuce as he continued to slowly stride backwards toward the motorised chariot that were waiting for him. 'At this dress-up Halloween party for Dyfed …you're doing the Batman routine again?' he called out. It was as if a second or spontaneous thought had necessitated this parting gesture and The Deuce quickly nodded as to say; so, what's up?

"So who,' said Thornborough in jest through a Cheshire cat-like grin, 'will be accompanying you as the sodomite Robin?'

"Get out of here,' the Deuce playfully snarled at his son. Nobody else on earth but he would have dared toy with the deuce like that, the latter thought, smiling to himself. 'Don't you worry, dear,' he replied teasingly to Thornborough. 'If I wanted a cute young man that looks good in earrings and lipstick I'd be taking you.'

"Yeah…yeah. Wish I could come and see that,' Thornborough flung back over his shoulder to his dad as he turned and collapsed into the driver's seat behind six hundred and fifty cubic inches of ignited gasified petroleum that powered this motorized chariot. The Deuce then quickly climbed into another and sat beside Dyfed.

"Home, Jeeves,' the latter said to the outwardly casual but heavily armed driver, 'and don't spare the horses.'

Then in great haste they began to head for Dyfed's Manna-hata skyscraper as Thornborough pulled a wide and screeching turn in the street in front of the clinic and sped off in another direction. The third car, a decoy, waited until the police were on top of them before speeding off in another all the while blazing away with automatic weapons that shot out the tires of their pursuers.

Morgant Cerrag answered a signal coming from his torc.

"So what's happening out there? he said urgently as he held it up to the side of his head and listened.

"You've GOT Dyfed…and you're on your way back here now? Just like that, huh,' he added. What…all right…when? Good, see you soon then,' he said. 'They'll be here anytime now,' said Morgant turning to Trachmyr as he shoved his tele-pad back into his pocket.

Although excessively windy, it was a beautiful autumn day and they were enjoying the sunshine on the roof gardens of Dyfed's mini skyscraper while they waited anxiously for news of the operation. Before turning to the rooftop elevator, Morgant glanced up at the huge zeppelins that were jostling violently in the sky overhead like fluttering banners on tall poles in the wind.

"We got our delivery and the Samsara airship back and anchored overhead just in time.

"What a damnable time for a hurricane to blow in he said. If only it could have been delayed somewhere else for a day or two. It seems hurricanes are hurtling in any old time of the year now. Hurricane season is all seasons.'

"Yeah,' said Trachmyr with a grin, 'they've even got a hotel chain named after them now.'

"Don't be an idiot,' snapped Morgant who was holding a shivering little dog named Many Bones under his arm. He knew Many Bones would be making a beeline for Dyfed the moment he heard his master's voice. 'Its nothing to laugh about,' said Morgant.

"Whose an idiot?' asked one of the House of Lucifer's trusty security men who was standing by the elevator as Morgant and Trachmyr stepped out into the guest living room. 'What's happening out there, anyway?'

"It's the Hurricane All Seasons,' answered Trachmyr, winking at the security officer, 'and the airships are beginning to drag anchor. It's going to get dirty and dangerous soon. Oh…and the boss is arriving at any moment.'

"What?' the words were like an electric jolt that simultaneously zapped the house crew out of their sluggish demure. 'Far out, man!' A cry of exuberance went up among the small house crew of special agents that Dyfed kept here. 'Now,' continued the chatty agent acting as elevator sentinel, 'if we could — nonchalantly like — say tonight float up and out of sight in the airship under the cover of darkness and storm, what with the coming hurricane and the distraction of a chaotic melee of airships tugged loose from their moorings, we could quickly spirit Mr Lucifer away without detection.'

Morgant turned abruptly and flung a disapproving look in the direction of the agent. It had *watch your place* written all over it. Seeing the look, the agent reigned himself in.

"That's a hell of an idea,' said Trachmyr. 'I like it. We can get him out tonight. General Rhodri Germanos, that old Amoran centurion, can entertain Doris and do the show-and-tell and tow her around after dinner.'

"Just saying, sir,' the *pack* security guard added again. 'Excuuuse me'.

"She won't come if Dyfed's not here,' said Morgant.

"Don't tell her until she's here,' suggested Trachmyr. He glanced over at Morgant who at that moment was looking more like a full life-sized garden gnome than he had ever done.

(Agitated Trolls that were mutant monsters at best)

'Old dragons live in mounds guarding buried treasure.'
OLD ENGLISH PROVERB

Dyfed was having a naked brunch when they came…a caravan of them arrived…a cavalcade of mutant monsters descending upon his estate early one morning as he watched from above in his sanctuary nestled in the Bountiful Valley by the Sto:lo River. They came in a caravan of four black chariots and one by one they pulled up behind each other at the gate, one behind the other. When they were all stopped, only then did two individuals (one being a woman) get out of the first chariot and in presenting their credentials confront the gatekeeper. Dyfed saw them there in the distance.

There would be no repeat here of that safe-house business in Jersey, he knew that much. Dyfed was relatively safe where he was and he had means of escape if and when push came to shove. And unless combat troops (backed by highly advanced technology such as high decibel subduing machines, and air-cover complete with heavy artillery all controlled by advanced artificial intelligence) were waiting in the wings to be called in to assist, and where under such conditions a clean escape would become more difficult to retain, Dyfed's Western Right of Free Movement was assured, for now.

Although entropy and the cause and effect syndrome of reality which is illusion provided a lead up to the big reversal for the hoi polloi of being able to manage and maintain some vestiges of their natural right to privacy (during all this time over the ages) had changed noticeably in modern man during the start of the 20th century, at least according to Dyfed Lucifer and what he wrote in his Magnum opus: Again, this was due to one of the chief Haploids in the third dimension, Giorgi Posh and his worldwide interests.

Major impingements and infringements to the hoi polloi's privacy and to his natural right as a human being began in earnest at this time that was accompanied also by an exponential dis-integration of their free will. To use a Vespasansius phrase it was the quintessential Publicus Servicicus Nemesis Maximus Augustus Usurperus chief of chiefs that brought sacred life to the depths of becoming a new-reality prisoner within its own natural environment. This in obstinate rebellion directed against the God chosen by all who love all life and are outside (and inside) who have no part in hate and cause and effect. But the victims (it must be said) chose to abide and follow this direction willingly, even if done ignorantly. In other words, it's the individual's own fault for believing in the illusions of their delusions. And who was this (or these) PSNMAUs and the chief of chiefs of illusions? That was still the sixty-four trillion dollar question. And what, then, is the illusion?

Mind-bogglingly, Giorgi Posh and Secular ideology wasn't just to blame. A new and improved mythos/religious concept that reared it ugly and frightening head also appeared at this time around the 20th century. Its worldwide beck and call catchphrase was Hallelujah praise the lord, hurrah for God, rah rah rah! This phrase wasn't actually related to Shalom Aleichem or As-salam alaykum in any way whatsoever, either. It was a connived and fake Idea only. God had nothing to do with it. It was the individual's dis-illusional form of god: It was a homemade mock up, and nothing more. Dyfed recognized it at its conception as Zeus and had long demurred the concept. As for the concept of Ba'al and the Messiah Saviour, they were a particulate; and particularly of oneself and oneself only who by their symbolic presence could enjoy everlasting life by the grace of Azeus. But not by having being embedded in a one time event such as yesterday or on some day two or four thousand years ago. The true paraclete or avatar of demi-god(s) representing God Azeus that the misguided monotheist religions exhorted (but got it wrong) wasn't an event. Rather than be represented by "event' paracletes, the coming of 'the Lord' IS (not was) something like the rays of the sun. A ray from the sun a minute ago is meaningless: Now, is all that's important. The sunray of the current now is all that ever matters. God's love of life and the world that every living creature bathes in is happening now and is all that matters. The god and its representations are in truth not a yesterday's or even a tomorrow's event, but something that is constantly and continuously impinging and bombarding every single living creature of Earth and the Universe every single nano-second. This is the It, because we can't use the word reality because it is an illusion. The new religions don't teach this truth any longer, and the effect from that is the nature of entropy. Now the cry and call to god was more than like heil Wunscheritter or Hail Krauz Terrainski, the new Communalist totalitarian leader of Rus, or even pseudo political correctness! For delusion means one is unenlightened and has no real awareness nor true realization or understanding of their fundamental self. Realization and understanding of self and of the mind and objects around them means that false conceptions are pushed away. No longer deluded, beginninglessness of all things becomes accepted and one will need nothing more, not even an opinion: And one won't need somebody else's opinion, either. That's detachment for you.

Advancement in world technology, although a boon to the organizations enforcing the Haploid's program have continued gaining greater and greater authority over all people in general, at this time, who have survived. It has surely most assuredly brought about huge limitations for the *pack*. Hundreds if not thousands of *pack* members had been killed worldwide in conflict now or murdered by Haploidic agents of terror in the past few decades, alone.

But these mutant monsters Dyfed was observing now wandering aimlessly around his estate were only marginally dangerous compared to the psychopathic, mutant monster Trolls of the Modern Nightwatchmen of the militant clone persuasion who imbued special services and counter-terrorist organizations. Interestingly enough, the Establishment of the West, who following the examples of nationalized unites such as those of the Land of Ch'in's Establishment, as well as those of Rus and Araby in the east, those definitions of terror, terrorist and terrorism have been kept buoyant and were allowed to float. Giorgi Posh, who was allied to the former and who now heavily controlled the west, had seen to this. This allowed for an industry of cherry-picking by the likes of Ministries and Departments within government. In the Unified States, for example, the Department of Apple-Pie and Home Land Security regularly had to provide special forces of counter-terrorism to rigorously cherry-pick now that all un-entitled aliens, such as free and foot-loose travelling folk, unskilled immigrants and the odd snow-bird vacationers from the Northern Dominion, the Unified Kingdom,

Francia, Germanika and Mexico; some of whom were employed cherry-picking in Cauliphornicatia and elsewhere that had all now been banned and squeezed out of the country and thereby were unavailable for general farm work. This too was a boon to the government there, for now not only could they define terrorism to justify their own agenda (the word game again) but they could define cherry-picking as well. So now, no such cherry-picking will take place again. So, there! Billie boy, Billie boy, you can forget about that young thing with a dimple in her chin that cannot leave her mother, charming Billie. For cherry-picking has now been made into a bad thing and an indictable offence according to how authority defines it for you. And for that (at least in the 'States') you have no one else other than Uncle Sham to thank for it, or its namesake asleep at the wheel. Good-bye to cherry pickers, Billie boy.

But anyway, what Dyfed had here on his doorstep, were simple Northern Dominion bureaucratic petty ordnance enforcing monsters of the domestic office variety which Dyfed could clearly see (with the aid of his security monitors) were comprised of a relatively small, unarmed troop of pencil pushers and key plodders led by a smallish woman who assumed the position of commander-in-chief.

"I'm in charge here,' gushed Alice the attendant-in-chief at Dyfed's gate, upon being rebuffed.

"But we have orders and warrants along with letters of special privileges from the local government giving us permission to enter and evaluate,' responded the bureaucratic petty ordnance commander-in-chief in response. 'So, I need to speak with a Mr Greengarden,' she said quickly casting her eyes down at her hand-held electronic torc she used as a memo file.

Dyfed's recent re-distribution of identity had aimed at providing him a different name for each of his locations where he had any registered ownership. In the Megatropolis area his permits and deeds were under the name Easystreet, here it was Greengarden and over on Couver Island it was Greenstreet.

"We're sorry,' said Alice pleasantly with a fake smile, 'but Mr Greengarden — the master of the residence and owner of this estate and its businesses — is too busy today to disagree with you on whatever recently adjusted by-laws, regulations or professional advice you have about running and minding his business, that, of course, is his own. I now have your contact information, here. Please go away and wait for his call. Thank you and you have yourself a nice day, eh. Too-d-loo!'

This was her standard rehearsed answer that she had needed to learn and was required to state for any enquiries after Dyfed. Generally it stumped and confounded soliciting and bothersome salesmen and the like at the door. This had all come about years before when a religious proselyting biker who, not getting any answer at the door bell, left his message on the door answering machine, instead. Later, when accessing the recording Dyfed heard the unmistakable rumple of a Harley whose engine was doing the... *potato...potato* serenade as it rested lazily on its kick-stand close-by on the driveway near the message machine speaker while all the while a gravelly old voice crackled into his ear hole and told him to fuck right off! So, when some unwanted solicitor knocks on your door and tells you to fuck off, that's when the gate goes up and when it actually went up at Dyfed's House of Lucifer's estate. But unfortunately it didn't cut it with this cavalcade of deluded and watered-down mutant monsters and their pretty in pink commander-in-chief on this day.

"But you simply don't understand,' said the well dressed officious woman, 'and you have no authority here. We have permits giving us permission for entry.' She then shielded her eyes with her hand and cast her gaze upward. A feint sound of approaching helicopters was evident in the morning bird-song air.

Dyfed and his staff heard it too.

This woman was accompanied by fifteen men, four people in each dark chariot, but only her and the three others she rode with that led the cavalcade had any governmental authority. The others were scientists, mostly agricultural earth scientists, chemists and two biologists. Of the lead chariot and the group of four, including the commander-in-chief, one of the other men of authority was tall and thin while the other two were fat and medium sized. One was the financial adviser from the Provincial Department of Finance who was an economist. The other two were an ecologist and an attorney. The woman was tallish and attractive wearing militaristic outdoor clothing with a pink scarf tied around her neck to help her appear feminine. Her three companions were her advisors who also consulted with the other twelve persons. The four elites were impeccably dressed in large, tall yellow gumboots. Though the others were merely a host of aids for the former, they were a knot of very commanding looking gloved men dressed in khaki shorts from which their muscular legs pillaring down into sturdy hiking boots. Essentially, these twelve were field officers and two of them pulled along something like a golf-cart, each loaded with instruments. The remaining ten aids had degrees in ecology and such and were basically impact assessors. In addition to these sixteen officials, there was also an assessment for expedience analysis contingent that just then had arrived in two helicopters that Dyfed had heard coming from a distance. This air-borne group, led by a chief over-all analyst (of who knows what), along with his staff whose purpose was unknown to Dyfed, lurked a little behind of the main body of first arrivers where they pretended to be sorting themselves out in an effort to remain technically dis-attached to the other officials. This was done possibly to appear more professional than they expected the others to look and act. Both were responding to political motivation by being here, Dyfed reasoned, but the choppered-in crew (who were decidedly more militaristic in appearance) were more likely to lean heavily in favour of political enthusiasm than any economical or ecological equivalent.

No, these folks this morning, Dyfed thought, were just glorified petty ordnance enforcers, at best. These particular mutant monsters were the normally devolved replicas of the mother monster itself that acted as an advanced defence line. In fact, all these mutant monsters were just trolls. For the monster is within, and trolls were the natural host to entertain them and give them succour. The real Nightwatchmen (he remembered those of the Pretorian Guard of Amor), on the other hand, were actually highly agitated Trolls in the physical bodied sense that were psychopathic mutant monsters at best and virtual demons of anti-life at worst. These paled only to the Haploids themselves, those high priests of the Idea of the Trend and the program of cult Mythos, and sometimes to a lesser extent, their lackeys, the emperor kings with their Turn-keys, magistrates and such — all a dime-a-dozen serving the Haploidic power elite.

It was already nine o'clock in the morning and beginning to get hot. Dyfed, who had just returned from his long late morning walk and pensive hour realized that these unwanted guests must have been well prepared and had left Couver City early for the drive up the Sto:lo River to his Bountiful Valley estate. They were, of course, just the tip of the iceberg; he knew that. There was little doubt in Dyfed's mind that this activity that employed thousands and thousands of bureaucrats back in the big smoke whose job seldom took them any further than their desk, their computer and relevant offices in their building (seldom to other buildings) that almost looked exactly alike, had probably begun months before, if not years ago where scads of probers had been probably weeks into their plan of today's pounce. Now, in the final stage of their endeavour to pry into his affairs of estate, their campaign's semi-final phase of discovery and confrontation had opened this fine June morning. And to *these people*, as far as they were concerned, everybody and everything was their business, and their duty was to place it all under a powerful magnifying lens and painfully (if at all possible) dissect and expose every little move of the lowliest pawn of every active House, ma and pa business operation and ad hoc pocket-money economics of any given individual, if necessary. In this environment even inactive Houses and Houses that had become defunct or their owners deceased were still considered fair game to be put under scrutiny, spied on and (in an effort to place an estate into debt). On a few instances they even charged a defunct estate post humorously. Apparently the attorneys working for the Department of Finance Recovery in this western sector of the Northern Dominion had easily convinced the politicians of its expedient strategy since in the defunct case-file they didn't expect the defence to put up much of a defence case — or for that matter, even to show up for court.

Dyfed ate two meals a day — always had done, probably always will — especially during the warm summers months: an early breakfast around five-thirty or six in the morning followed by a nine o'clock brunch and a late light supper just before the gloaming set in. And aside from his exercise, everything from a pleasant walk and stretch to a gentle form of callisthenics complicated with kundalini; this was his only association with routine. Outside of that there was nothing predictable or routine about Dyfed. And outside his palace on this bright morning that shone through the large windows of his luxuriously home, the bright azure sky — propped up along the entire horizon by a blinding yellowish glaze growing out of the dark earth, shored up here and there by a henge of mountain ramparts (one of which lay just to the south had recently begun, once again, to puff out Vulcan's white vapours) — engulfed Radiance that blazed down from above: Then suddenly nothing became routine. Around this terrain of tidy tackiness was an assortment of red, silver, and chunks of black…buildings of different sorts, an airdrome, silos among green laurel hedges and tall, shimmering poplars…shining out like strange holographic pieces of picture-puzzle on a giant slanted card table, now traipsed upon by the citified gang of bureaucrats. Along with a vista chuck full of fields of produce dancing to the horizons in summer bloom, made these bureaucrats hoof it around and build up a sweat all the while surrounded by sections for dairy cows to pasture in, and not shackled in a tight stall and connected to a machine the way many of the far distant neighbouring farmers housed — out of sight — their bovine residents. The warm fragrant air heaved and hummed and throughout the vast tract of Dyfed's estate, set here upon the Bountiful Valley, were the constant movement of tractors and trucks and a hundred farm employees on sight consisting of pickers and post-holers, veterinarians and modern nine to five vassals all currently on day-shift, hustling and bustling, all of who stumbled over, veered off track so not to run-over or back over sundry bureaucrats crawling around under-foot and getting in the way.

Mack Greenacres was in charge of both incoming and outgoing tractor-trailers that came and left the estate. The transport company under contract was part of Dyfed's conglomerate run by another employee, Sidney Greengrass. This rolling stock were huge wagons, pulled by motorized chariots that could transport a hundred livestock or tons and tons of corn, wheat and fruit to a market-board terminal railhead. These steel rails then helped to guide the product/produce across the land in even more gigantic machines. These vehicular machines, which were way beyond the chariot class, and could pull millions of tons of goods stored in rolling-stock-type gigantic steel wagons hitched together to form a mile long train, shot natural and cultivated resources like grain, fish, livestock, refrigerated meat, processed foodstuffs, fruits, vegetables as well as steel, lumber, processed wood, oil, coal and newly fabricated mechanized equipment all wrapped up, from city to city all over the continents of the Merikas and to their refiners, distributors, and ultimately to consumers. This Daedalusian artifice of steel was the labyrinth and left over vestiges of Capitalist expedience extraordinaire, like the great floating steel sea vessels all of which the House of Lucifer accessed and renamed Enterprise expedience extraordinaire.

Meanwhile, Albert Greenthumb was responsible for all employee time schedules and hours worked. Mack and Albert were only two among thirty employees in mid management level dealing with production. This included waste material for removal and redistribution but did not include the veterinarians, biologists, chemists, and a host of others that contributed to production. Then there was the development division. Obviously, it goes without saying, that the House of Lucifer was a twenty-four hour operation, and this was just the tip of his iceberg.

The House of Lucifer's personal residence where Dyfed resided was situated on a slight hillock ringed by a forest of thickly girthed cottonwoods. This property was set away somewhat from the goings on of industry at hand, though it looked down upon them. By the time Dyfed had arrived in the main office foyer via an underground escalator, his two front men, Anlaf Konge and Trachmyr, were busy organising the fiasco into a controllable event and were baring the brunt of the official, unannounced and ready made government bureaucracy's complimentary, illogical and contradictory pronouncements.

"From now on it will have to be the government's own policies that entertain vast change and get into line with the real world,' said Anlaf acting Virtual Chief Executive Officer. 'This is the world that Harvey Heavy was already working with. We can no longer sustain the constant policy reversals and government increase of costs that are growing exponentially a few times a year,' Anlaf abruptly told these measly mutant monsters. 'It won't be Harvey Heavy, the prize and jewel of Bountiful Valley, that is the main consortium contributing to the feeding of the Northern Dominion's western provinces that takes it up the ass, anymore,' said Anlaf in a matter of fact way. No sir! Our annual budget is bigger than the entire pay and pension and provincial income-tax division of our entire province. You bureaucrats need to wake up because if we don't exist, you don't eat, the provincial government won't receive a third of their taxes, plus recriminations thereof that may affect another third dealing with personal income taxes. Oh yes, and along with millions of others you people won't have a job and like your children, you won't have a future beyond tomorrow afternoon, or the day after. So, wake up! Harvey Heavy grosses billions and is by far the province's largest licence purchaser and employer next to the Government of (and for) Bureaucracy. The chairman's committee of the board has informed you that we won't be doing provincial petty ordinance dances of *do si do and swing your partner* anymore. 'No sir!' said Anlaf managing to feign a incredulous laugh as he spoke to respond to the bureaucrat's commander-in-chief rebuttal and final demand to speak with Mr Harvey Heavy since Mr Greengarden isn't available, then. 'You can't speak with a Mr Harvey Heavy. It's a brand name, a corporate name, you cute and pretty in pink moron,' he stated.

Strangely, the gestating hands and arms, the queerly glazed luminous and staring eyes and the twisting of their ugly mouths that accompanied the talking heads of these mutant monsters, were all done in orchestrated sync. They took turns, they banded together, babbling — first these few then another few. They didn't laugh. They couldn't. They didn't know how. They postured, constantly. Their mouths pulled back exposing gleaming, white pearly teeth paid for by the government employee plan: And for what? But this gesture wasn't a response to any volition of merriment or humour. All of this façade was accompanied with their needling reactions and their exposition of official grandeur and by their by-the-book account and the mandatory word game-speak that was now accompanying almost every conversation all over the world among the hoi polloi, even at home with discussion among family and friends. The phenomenon was now quite absurd. These absurdities included preposterously ponderous proclivities complicated with bumptious presumptions which the new modern wo/man was now using to justify his pseudo political correctness with which 99% of the world's population now occupied 99% of their social life conversation by doing just that. None of it was able to obscure the general lack of these people to function in the world of competing disorder capable of organizing anything responsibly or to responsibly manage in order to operate such an elaborate and on-going concern such as a multifaceted business and firm that Harvey Heavy was, not to mention what Dyfed easily held together within the workings of the House of Lucifer all told — on a daily basis — for the past fifteen hundred years without causing any of the well known dysfunctions the latter bureaucrats were famous for. These blunders were oil spills and other escaped toxins, lay-offs, under budgeting, abuse of employees, lack of leadership, lack of foresight, unsafe work practices, unfair work practices, union bashing, and financial scandals and general mismanagement of almost everything from natural resources to human resources. This also included pilfering employees' pension funds. Dyfed was capable of flying way above the heights of all these pretenders without even thinking about it. So, forget about it! Anlaf laughed out loud. He then suddenly saw Dyfed mingling with the monsters that were spread out in a large semi-circle facing Anlaf and Trachmyr who had now been joined by the chief office manager, Albert Greenacre.

When Dyfed arrived on the scene — without so much as a hint of being in a rush to find out what was going on, looking distracted and un-interested in the goings-on and the on-going hub-bub at hand — old Trachmyr had been explaining to Anlaf that they should probably get the staff lawyer here.

"They will become suspicious if we don't summon a lawyer,' he said under his breath. Anlaf then handed the wheel to Trachmyr. Trachmyr began then to field out some questions for which he was hungrily eager to sensibly block out any reasonable questions and answers and for any systematic righteousness for which all respectable mutant monsters were programmed to extoll, verbally and in an assumed posturing of body language. Then surrounded by one of the estate's lawyers, and an accountant who quickly joined him, Trachmyr, this lanky, scarred-faced old reprobate who looked more like a war-lord bandit biker on steroids and apple-jack, or even a shotgun riding, whisky sucking, drug smuggling trucker renegade from hell (at least one might think judging from the looks on his audience's stupid, unlived, bureaucratic faces that were full of pure incredulousness mixed with anxiety and confusion and maybe a hint of fear — there is always the fear with *these people*). Trachmyr began to speak the straightforward language of an Amoran general and legion commander. His nerves, on the other hand, were like steel and rightly so. Aside from his batman duties to Dyfed that was no small task in itself, Trachmyr now mostly dealt in fake certificates of deposit that amounted into the hundreds of millions of dollars. This was on the side (a hobby), you might say. The money wasn't for him. He didn't need any money. It was his little bit to help the big cause. Dyfed (ostensive a zillionaire), who was presently (although unintentionally disguised) dressed as a casually dressed farm labourer's shop steward would be (has been) would look like — albeit an old and retired one at that — who, apparently took to hanging around his old security blanket job like a bad smell with nothing else to do but see that the shop conducted itself according to Hoyle, and had nowhere else to go anyway. He removed his wide brimmed straw fedora-shaped hat once or twice and wiped his forehead with a handkerchief while he listened, always setting his hat back on his head at a slight angle.

Meanwhile, back in an office on a high floor of a tall building in Cover City, Johnny Rocco (no relation to any other known Rocco) was scrutinizing a file on Dyfed Lucifer. Originally from the Unified States, of course (there's no Roccos in the Northern Dominion), he was a thin medium sized man with slicked back shortish brown hair who wore strangely coloured but well tailored suits. He was a plant sent from Warshingtown and he worked for what in the Northern Dominion would be called the Ministry of Interior.

"Poor mixing skills with his peers and general age group,' the official read aloud, looking over at the monitor screen. 'An early and disappointing tendency to ignore advice from his elders, whether or not they were of a lower or higher class or whether or not they were very much less educated or more educated. He displays a disappointing tendency to withdraw from participation with almost all of the establishment's programs. Nothing here about any activity one would expect from a wellborn youth. There is, on the other hand, a mention about two possible felonies concerning paedophilia and pederasty. The first felony concerned a young child. It wasn't recent, it seems. According to the file this deep-seated sexual perversion, however, has never being addressed through mandatory programs at any time. So, the psychiatrists that have signed off on this indicate that today this disgusting perversion remains active within this patient who is even more at risk re-offending than ever. Later, we see that during the First Empire, that he was non compliant towards accepting the religion of Amor. Furthermore, in fact, he has shown no interest in any religion whatsoever. He is obviously a shallow human being. He has no love in his life. He is a sick sex pervert, greedy to fulfil a want of lust and desire. He also has a poor showing with other hallmarks of the Establishment's order; and even a notation here of an un-resolved accusation of interfering with other youngsters. Apparently, he and some emperor named Gaius Kyser Augustus Germanicus, I've never heard of him, committed some very offensive crimes for which Dyfed Lucifer was apparently indicted. But since there is no record of that conviction, it is thought that the emperor, his bumboy, must have either got him off, or more likely got the record destroyed. Emperors could do those kinds of things back then, you know. These people don't live in the real world. Neither does Dyfed H. Lucifer which all sums up to make him a very dangerous criminal who is highly likely to re-offend without remorse: They're not from Merika…I mean North Merika. As for people like him, we just caint trust 'em.'

The person to whom Johnny Rocco was relaying Dyfed's bogus file to was someone who in turn was acknowledging the conversation in monosyllables. Uh-huh, uh-huh, she kept saying until she soon developed a sudden lack of poignant interest in the conversation. The file showed that later in life, the official continued to state, that Dyfed held some junior position within the First Empire, he continued. But as he never achieved Amoran status this never went anywhere. That he has consistently showed poor judgement in friendships and allegiances was quite clear, it stated, and he was even a cohort of some kind with the great purveyor of misery, the failed and destitute retch, the chief representative of anti-Establishment itself, the Wunschritter von Brauneau. Why Mr Lucifer was never taken into custody immediately after the war and charged with crimes of association with mayhem and for war baiting, we'll never know. 'Strangely, it is not recorded here. I wonder why?' Rocco now said out loud to himself. 'Somehow, he managed to dodge being tried at Nuremburg, during that great embrace and display of justice for these crimes committed. But it is quite possible — and more than likely — that a bribe was involved for it is known that he is and always has been extravagantly rich.'

At that moment his own secretary walked into his office with an electric disc. Rocco immediately struck up the conversation with her at the same time shooing (at least in his eyes) the dull pandering in-house obsequious sycophant out the door. 'Which brings us to another thing,' he now said; 'how did Mr Lucifer actually amass such a fortune? I ask you! Do you know anybody with trillions and trillions of dollars at their disposal: A neighbour or a friend maybe? Of course not! Nobody does. How could you? How could they? You…they…are good slaves providing for the Establishment, you slave to make it work for the benefit of all, especially the hard working chiefs at the very top. And all this while, all your hard working life you have been in debt, poor things. Just like me. No. Mr Lucifer, it seems, is a full-fledged crook, a briber, a corrupter of children and an embezzler who misappropriates the most enormous of sums on a continual basis. He steals from your pocket just as he steals from mine. He is an all round felon. There is no doubt — your honour, your worship and your most gracious henchman of the Establishment; there is no doubt in my mind at all about that. And look at this. Here it is signed — auditor in chief, third quarter, second millennium, for Chief justice Mr Doomsday and associates. P.S. Please forward current correspondence receipt (form attached) and payment to World Bank, Western Division, Denver City. Ok, Sugar Tits,' he said to a tall sepia stamped blond dressed in pale yellow, 'here it is. We got 'em. It's not just us who are suspicious. The time zone centre of the continent is suspicious, too. Now, pay attention to what the attached letter says. See, here. So, the correspondence must be clearly marked — Couver City branch. It says here, that their records show that somebody's, probably his, records may be in arrears as to previous requested correspondence. Please contact the registry, it says, of the In Arrears Division, of the Accounts section of the World Bank, immediately.'

"Quick, Sugar Tits, saddle up and dial me the number for federal Emergency. Somebody's gotta take action on this. We can't have a guy like this roamin' around unsupervised. What the devil!' he leaned back and lit a cigar.

The secretary who didn't like her boss and worked hard at not reprimanding him regarding his inappropriate and disgusting manner towards her, obediently dialled on her torc. Her lips hadn't moved in all this time. Then she made a face and put the speakerphone on and held the tork out close to Mr Johnny Rocco's ear hole. 'All our agents at the Federal Emergency Help & Life-Line are currently busy: Please hold. Your call is important to us: Someone will be with you shortly. Thank you for waiting: Your call will be monitored once answered by the next available agent. We're sorry, your call cannot be completed as dialled: Please hang up and try again, later.'

"What the fuck! Johnny Rocco screamed, tearing the lopsidedly lit cigar from his wide ugly mouth and throwing it at the computer screen that glanced off it and knocked over a deck picture frame. 'What other displays of trickery born of brain children of the wizards of miscommunication and the likes of the House of Lucifer were to be most evident here in the long run?' he asked himself out loud. Clearly he was a raving lunatic. His secretary bent down and picked up the knocked off eight by eleven framed photo that had been sitting on the side of her boss's desk. As well as noticing the price sticker was still on the lower right corner of the frame which threw immediate suspicion onto the actual relevance here of the supposed family of his in the photo; she then noticed that the smiling and happy looking family was generic and part of the wrapped advertisement. Most purchasers of photo frames (if not every single one except Johnny Rocco) tore that glossy photo out to put in one of their own loved ones. He hadn't bothered. She didn't bother to pick up the cigar that landed in a rather obsolete wastepaper basket.

Suddenly, the secretary in the yellow dress spoke. Her voice was clear and because of the words that she chose, consequently it was obvious that the thoughts and the person behind those words were intelligent and concise and possibly a lot more alert than her boss had ever realized.

"Mr Rocco,' she said in a very pleasant sounding voice, not looking at her nails or taking gum out of her mouth before she spoke. She made direct eye contact with Johnny Rocco whose own restless eyes darted back and forth avoiding (at all costs) her beautiful dark eyes that were burrowing into him. 'Mr Rocco, there is still nothing in any of this that points a finger, or in any way states, or proves, that the subject here, a Mr Dyfed Lucifer is in any way part of — a board of director of — or a beneficiary of — never mind controlling officer of — Harvey Heavy, ah… general enterprise consortium whose head office is here in Couver City.

Rocco, who was tirelessly twisting something that looked like it may have been an envelope, suddenly shifted his blurry and bulging eyes in his secretary's direction. It didn't look to her, though, as though Rocco was even seeing her. She wondered if this bitter little man who it seemed may be suffering from cerebral epilepsy was in fact having an epileptic seizure. And then she wondered if she should summon advice or help. She wasn't a cold-hearted vixen, quite the contrary. She had love in her heart, and pity, too, for him; and she was compassionate about the ills and suffering of other people as well. That was why the people who promoted her put her there. That was why she was in Rocco's office as his assistant. But Rocco was a selfish pig. He was in the right business, she thought. She noticed now that the cigar that had landed in the wastepaper basket alongside of Rocco's large desk was smouldering. The secretary turned and left the office.

(Absurdly incarnate)

'I don't like people who are indifferent to the truth.'
BORIS PASTERNAK

Dyfed lifted off from his private heli-pad and headed straight for his head office in downtown Couver City where he landed on the roof. The floor below was his office and when he arrived Rose was there to greet him. She was a beautiful woman, dark eyes and hair but fair skin covering a sleek body. She was exquisitely dressed in a beautiful yellow dress that set off her natural colour. She wore a string of large, shiny jade stones around her neck that complimented everything about her. He was there because he needed more re-assurance that this thing that happened this morning wasn't going to blow up and out of control. She was there because he had summoned her. He had suggested that she make an excuse that she was ill. He needed to see her immediately because she had told him that she had put her hands on some confidential information about him, including that of his local business, Harvey Heavy. She then began to disclose what her immediate office manager had unearthed. Dyfed was surprised they didn't have more.

From Dyfed's sound proofed office the silent motions of this large west-coast city that was spread out all around beneath them ticked on like an old grandfather clock.

"Say, what's that commotion that's going on over there all about?' Dyfed said, pointing.

Smoke was billowing from the top third of a towering structure while a hodgepodge of fire engines and conspicuous looking black vans surrounded it.

"Oh that. That's the Howe-Ashcroft building,' answered Rose. 'It's on fire, I'd say.'

"Yaas,' drawled Dyfed, 'so would I. Isn't that where one of those dreadful security agencies that the Establishment conceals and supports with public taxes is housed is located?'

"Why, that's correct,' replied Rose. 'Golly!

"And isn't that where you work?' he added.

"You know, I should be getting back there,' she answered. They'll miss me...they might think that I've been burned alive with my boss.'

"You need to stay right where you are and not go back there ever again,' said Dyfed. 'Phone around and chat a little; that will alert folks you're alive and well and getting on with business. Now, how's my grandson, Shirkah?' asked Dyfed, changing the subject. Then reverting back again to the earlier subject he said: 'With the highly dangerous cancer causing fire retardants they use in buildings nowadays from carpet clue to ceiling sealant, nobody coming out of that building under these conditions are going to be dead,' he said; 'at least not right away and not yet, and not from the fire either. Death will take a few years and maybe a few more fires for the toxins to accumulate in one's body. You're lucky you're here and not breathing in those dangerous chemicals over there, though. But you had better get start circulating a little. Don't stay anywhere too long and don't go back there. Say, why not get pregnant and give me a great granddaughter as pretty as you? Better still: why not just tell your employer over there that you've got a change in plans to increase your family. Then air kiss them and their job goodbye because your grandfather-in-law is going to flip you and your son a golden goose.' Dyfed laughed at himself. 'Heh. How would you two like to take over the running of Harvey Heavy's?'

(Heidi — Heidi — Heidi — ho)

'Nice work if you can get it.'
GEORGE AND IRA GERSHWIN (ATTRIBUTED)

Dyfed looked up from the dwellings of his mind and peered outside. Slowly he got up and pushed aside the heavy sliding glass door out onto the outside patio. Standing there in the warm early evening…the serene sky above with verdant fields below which struck out into the distance beyond…it was with some difficulty he managed to open a portal within him which allowed him access to an internal susceptibility that passes all self understanding. This state of being is beyond understanding for most humans within the phenomena of the third dimension: But not for Dyfed. This ability enabled him to communicate with Earth eternal in some common yet uniquely personal way beyond the Eternal Return. Spring, having bloomed in the hedges while summer began to sew a sprinkling of budding green among the conifers, was finished. Dyfed's idea of summer now charged the warm evening air. Surrounded by the quiet of his vast estate at the head of the Sto:lo River basin and the Bountiful Valley, his mind flashed unimpeded while he searched high and low through the shifting fields, the crops or generations upon which the ghosts of history flitted, pausing for him to contemplate, then to fast forward or reverse (as necessary) as he mentally searched for the pertinent reel/space/time he sought after among the jagged journey, that haunted corridor of tears where only the initiated could find alcoves of peace and solitude. He then heard the heavy solid work that was being churned out by a long, slow freight train that was snaking the distant edge of his property-estate. Once again he suddenly remembered his pet dogs, Many Bones and Sweet Lorraine that he had let out hours before. Often now in old age mode Many Bones suffered from a succession of senior moments and he was worried that she had got herself lost again. As for Sweet Lorraine, she was just a puppy and wouldn't leave poor old lost Many Bones' side. He was lonely enough with the absence of Ceredwyn so he didn't want to be here completely alone. Trachmyr, his old batman was here, of course, and looking after him. Though on that account Dyfed wasn't sure who was looking after whom. Anlaf had just left for Couver City. He wouldn't be back until just before he and Trachmyr had to leave for Cloud-Nine City to face the horror that was planned to occur there. It would be something, he thought, which would surely cloud every sweet day that unfolded thereafter for the remainder of his life. But he was chief security of public safety. He shivered despite the thick warmth that pressed in on him. And the recent memory of dodging capture by the skin of his teeth in Megatropolis had left his shaken, he admitted to himself. "I'm getting to old for this,' he said. 'Here little Miss Sweet Lorraine,' Dyfed called. 'Many Bones, where are you?'

Surely, Dyfed had been thinking, the Haploids were on their last legs before their fall and hopefully potential extinction. But what did it really matter anymore. Nobody cared, did they? He didn't think so. They didn't seem to. But he did once. What had happened? Everything else was going to hell in a hand basket. Although extinctions are a regular occurrence here on earth and always have been, the rate had now jumped immensely and the cycle had shrunk exponentially. Mammals, the top factors of the food chain on earth, were now dying like flies that in fact were not themselves dying but so far their larvae was increasing.

This was worrisome, indeed. The mammals were going the way of the frogs, Pterodactyls, the Great auks and the passenger pigeons, it seemed. Dyfed had always thought that when whales, porpoises, and dolphins started down this slippery slope and dead-end track, humans wouldn't be far behind. Virtually every living mammal on Earth was edging up to the starting line for the race to extinction. Birds, too, the remnants who had endured since the age of dinosaurs had now become depleted in astounding numbers. Gone were the hummingbird, the robin and all the little songbirds, the swan, the hawk, the eagle and the heron. Only the turkey remained now, usually basted and stuffed, and even then many of those were just a turkey flavoured chemical added to tofu. And why was this? Mostly it was to do with biochemical corporations who displayed no conscience when it came to their products that were exterminating forever these vulnerable and unsuspecting creatures of earth in order to line their pockets and make flush the lives of a few company directors and their investors for perhaps a handful of years at most. Elephants, rhinoceroses and the great apes had now virtually all gone from outside of captivity. Once again the rape and depletion of resources and forests along with grasslands and natural wetlands were nothing compared to the firestorms that came with the intensity once associated with hurricanes. Since the vast forests of the world were now gone there was no propagation ability for them to come back, either. The wilds of planet earth were denuded and quiet for the first time in a way that they had never been during the entire history of humankind right from the dawn of time. The natural world was depleted and fading while the humans — who once had domination over all could hardly claim to rule supreme over anything, less even of themselves — now lived in cities that had morphed into a complex of hutches or cells reminiscent to the honey comb where bees (now quickly becoming extinct) once lived. And here they were required to stay and could travel only with special permits which were only available to a very few who in thinking themselves more important than others who managed to fool and convince others of just that. Extinction this time around was due to an irresponsible attitude, not a comet or bolide striking the Earth. It was the worldwide use of insecticides that man couldn't be bothered to make friendly so that the bees and other insects that the great Absolute Creator Being provided by design to pollinate and provide foodstuffs for man's initial survival could retain their survival. Nope, the chief executive officers in charge of everything couldn't manage that, either. We were all doomed. Soon the earth in the third dimension wouldn't be worth saving, never mind living in, though it may even be too late for the flourishing again of humanity. Of course, it all depended on what papers you read and what televised media you tuned into. It also depended on the potential of the knowledgeable and hence civilized world's doctrine. If countries of the commonwealth and their western ideology could survive, if they could shrug off the un-charitable nature of their Idea and those nightmares of their singularly little, imaginatively cramped, egotistical leaders, then the illusion of the phenomenon might be disenfranchised enough for the hoi polloi to re-begin their climb again.

Dyfed's silver eyes, glittered midst his bronze old face wrinkled and lined as he now finished explaining to Anlaf all that was needed of him towards his duties to keep the farm from being sold while he was away at Cloud Nine City in the Anacana desert. He then looked up from the dwellings of his mind where space/time past was being eclipsed by the uncomfortable present and peered outside into the late afternoon.

He saw the suns reflected light, which at that particular moment in the gloaming after sunset he thought was peculiar of all things magical. Dyfed looked around as though he was seeing the world for the first time. The immediate absence of Many Bones and Sweet Lorraine, his faithful canine companions, suddenly came to mind again within him outside of its time frame. This, in addition to the pain of the absence of his long companion, Ceredwyn, had left him sad, but not fearful in the twilight hours of his life. Slowly he got up and, pushing aside the heavy sliding glass door, stepped back out onto the outside patio. He breathed in the warm, early evening air. For a second he saw in the darkening sky those whitecaps like tiny beacons of light that lit up the dark sea as they once did just for him. Swiftly he manoeuvred to his natural space/time where he was surrounded by verdant fields that struck out into the distance beyond in the quickly fading light and glanced at the serene, supernatural sky dancing above. It was with some difficulty that Dyfed managed to open a portal within him that allowed him access to an internal susceptibility that passes all self-understanding. For this state of being is beyond understanding for most mortal humans within the phenomena of the third dimension: But generally this was not the case with Dyfed. His ability as an experienced homognostic with not a completely unimpeded access to the homo-spiritus world enabled him to communicate with earth incarnate and eternal in some common yet uniquely personal way beyond the Eternal Return.

Spring bloomed once, long, long ago, and it was decided then and there that it should be repeated for the duration of his life. Quite recently, in fact, spring had once been in the hedges around the gardens — there in the appropriate space/time — while an eternity of summer beginnings had sewn a sprinkling of budding green among the conifers. On this evening they were long gone and finished. Now, within Dyfed's Idea, the last glimmers of the late summer sun that had once pierced the air of a warm evening had slide away. This contributed a distinct and agitated charge to Dyfed Lucifer's separate and stand-alone psyche as it probed the density around him.

Surrounded by the quiet of his once vast estate at the head of the Sto:lo River basin amid the Bountiful Valley, the old gentleman's mind flashed unimpeded…searching high and low through the shifting fields, the crops, the generations upon which the ghosts of history flitted…pausing for him to contemplate…then to fast forward (or reverse as necessary) as he mentally searched for the pertinent real (reel)/space/time he sought after there among the waves upon waves of jagged journeys which haunted the corridor of tears. Here, hysterical laughter once cried out to him in despair. This is where only the wise and experienced could find alcoves of peace and solitude. Others, less fortunate and fast-forwarding to a returning death, froze in fear, their souls shivering to pieces amid the temperature less hollow of the abstract and silvery moonlight.

Dyfed turned slightly as he heard that faint but distinct and solid sound of heavy work being caused just as Trachmyr came out and handed him a gin and tonic with a wedge of lime in one hand and handed him the half full decanter with the other before turning and heading back inside again. The solid noise came at first from afar. It was work being undertaken…and accomplished…somewhere distant, but its effect was also close at hand at the same time. He felt its vibration. It was the kind of sound that's only given off in this manner here, in the third density. He recognised it, he felt it…he moved passed it...then came back to it. He analysed its phenomena. He sensed the noise and felt the energy generated that was being pressed upon him...at him. From its space/time the aforementioned expending work's prevailing influence impinged closely upon matter in the third dimension in such as way that affected the atmosphere around him even here, far away from the source. This work was being churned and grated out — accompanied by clap and clashes and blinding squeals of grinding steel — by some long, slow unseen train hauling freight through the murky shade of the evening's sun-loss. He knew this work was providing motion for that giant machine which snaked along the distant northern edge of his once vast estate. Despite the fact that the grit of work was being accomplished somewhere out beyond his immediate space, Dyfed could smell it. It was somewhere out there. Though out of sight, he imagined it crawling like a thin river of mercury toward the mountains, that great spine of the continent that the folks of this world called Merika.

He then knew the world around him again, momentarily, when suddenly the memory of Cloud-Nine City, his only regret at this juncture of his long life, punctured his memory as a future potential which he hated, once more; and then it thrust itself directly at the heart of his Idea, but not at his heart of hearts, the lotus of his heart. That remained untouched and unaffected. Damn that Thrax! he suddenly thought.

Although a tried and approved method, the conduct of the osmosis he physically struggled with in order to apply and manage the diocotron instability affecting the plasma of any given phenomena (the precise method by which the adepts controlled personal entropy), he still wasn't exactly certain of what ultimate truth he had discerned about Cloud-Nine City. It was a troubling and worrying episode, he thought. A trouble that would surely cloud every sweet moment that unfolded before him now for the next few remaining days; precious remaining days they were, and which were all that was left of his long life here in this world that was coming quickly to its end. For Dyfed, Cloud Nine City was the Idea akin to the Great Flood, and like at the end of that world, it was a dangerous notion to entertain. For Dyfed knew that ideas and wishes actually do materialize in this world.

He had not long returned from Denver City where he commiserated with a Mr Greenhorn from Denver who real name was Harvey F. Brown who was later known as Johnny Rocco as almost all red blooded Unified Statians liked to be called. Once he was there Dyfed and the aforementioned underwent individual training to perform what was billed as a section shoot for a supposedly up-coming block-buster of a motion picture starring another Johnny Rocco the movie star opposite Veronica Pond. These two actors had just rocketed to Follywood fame and stardom in typical Cauliofornicatia style following their debut there on account of the film Bogey, Betsie and Bacall that was about two other real long ago Follywood stars and their common alter ego Betsie. Both were now long dead but the alter ego was rumoured to be still alive, somewhere. The scene that cinematographer Johnny Rocco of Denver (not any of the multitude of actors, or anybody else of the same name) was to supposed to supervise from scratch and get the thing done and into the can on space/time and on budget, was the dramatic ending of the movie and the final shoot. It entailed the devastation destruction of a city with an H-bomb, supposedly on another planet whose alien inhabitants were planning to invade Earth. And although Dyfed wasn't going to be present during the actual final shoot, but because he was in charge of health and safety on the set for all the personnel during the first episode, to be relieved by Trachmyr for the remaining episodes, his instructions too would be part of the undressed rehearsal. And as the rehearsal would remain undressed until the actual shoot got under way, and because there would only be a one shot chance at the final explosion, a lot of work was needed to be accomplished in Denver. At one point Dyfed had confided in Mr Johnny Rocco (the chief cinematographer) and told him he would put aside valuable shares in a company he controlled just for him if he would only tweak the cinematography as Dyfed asked, and not as the script called for. Then back home again in the Bountiful Valley Dyfed toiled at bringing Anlaf up to speed about his empire-of-the-farm while keeping a low profile and under the radar himself. Then he began planning to leave for Cloud Nine City where, it seemed, he'd meet up with a few old acquaintances and where Trachmyr would be joining him later.

(Divers arts: smoke, and mirrors on the Cutting Edge of Disaster)

"To be not as eloquent would be more eloquent.'
CHRISTOPHER WEILAND

Dyfed's mind wandered again. With a sudden jolt he recalled the journey's start. Much to his chagrin, fear, and loathing, never mind lollygagging and procrastinating and generally side-stepping the umph to push off, had meant that he was finally sharply ordered then quickly dispatched to Cloud Nine City by Morgant: that much was clear. Then he had the recollection of walking alone high in some mountainous area that he presumed to be the Andes. He had no idea where the city he was searching for was. Menstruating Mother! Why wasn't he just flown there like everyone else? What the fig? At that moment it appeared to him that he was walking on the top of the world where in the distance, and in the direction he was moving, the shape of the horizon hinted that the path would plunge down into a very deep ravine or shelf-like lands below.

He imagined a desolate dry desert there and beyond that was an ocean. The sky was almost azure in colour despite it being a clear sunny day. This condition of sky was due, he thought, to the altitude. In the early years of the last century he and some of the tougher members of G — Squadron had masterminded an ascent of a string of the highest mountains in the world which were in Asia. It had been glorious fun and despite Dyfed's advancing age, he had performed admirably. There he had learned about dark skies even on bright days like here today, and a little thing about oxygen depletion which can bring on edema (both pulmonary and cerebral) that will cause death if not rectified by decreasing one's altitude without too much delay. This appeared to be the exact same conditions of those suffering from cerebral epilepsy. These latter folks, though, only fancied that they are at a great altitude above others and at a place where they took advantage of the opportunity to discuss human matters with god: these were the unenviable afflicted hen-pecked hermits, philosophers without borders and vision, high priests of primitive superstition, soothsayers long out of vogue who had lost their insight, fake and false prophets and others whose suffering was further complicated by messianic envy. It didn't seem to be the case here. Rather, it was much more gentle than the aforementioned, and he wasn't entirely sure if he was actually in third dimensional reality, either.

But the place he was in, along with its atmosphere, was very pleasant. It had a dream-like character about it. It was just on the edge of night now as he continued to walk toward the world's western abyss. Here the sky was tinged with orange and mottled brown.

He quickly tried to give up thinking about anything. He thought it better that way. Nevertheless, the place and its atmosphere where he happened to be were very pleasant and congenial: it had a dream-like character about it. So as he walked the thought of Mr Greenhorn suddenly came to Dyfed's mind. The man from Denver was (at the fake supposed time of Wormwood's approach to destroy Earth) to be brought by members of the *pack* to this Haploidic stage portal send off to oblivion in order to shoot the event for posterity; or as Mr Greehorn was led to believe, for the grand finale of a Paradoxical new motion picture. Dyfed didn't marvel over the fact that pulling the wool over Mr Greenhorn's eyes seemed to be a piece of cake because he was quite used to these things. But Mr Greenhorn and his personal crew of dudes and dandies, Doreens and dollies were more than just popcorn and Pepsi pushers. Even the Coca-Cola Company of Merika wasn't in their league when it came to sensationalism and putting on the spin. And for good reason, for the movie business wasn't just habit forming, it was an addiction. And that addiction could be just about anything a man or woman wanted: an alternative to reality being one of its major headings. Under this pretence an array of subjects could list well on into the night: cartoons, drama, porn, soap, more porn, more soap, girl meets boy, boy meets boy, detective, search for adventure, sports, police squad and its twin — law enforcement, law and order (another fantasy), travel, culinary, talk show and host, gamers-win a million, pseudo science and fantasy in a thousand other different flavours and as long as sponsors were available — children's education. In many folks minds this might not hand-jive with encroachments on advanced quantum sciences that propel people into other dimensions reachable from their present state. But positively insane looking people who just because they have no reality grip on how others who they work for who are negatively insane, put up with them anyway so long as it's an alternative to reality as we the public know it.

Dyfed had come to be vaguely aware that at this point in space/time that the subject matter might be Mr Greenhorn's technology but it was his (Dyfed's) movie. And Mr Greenhorn, just like all the hundreds of thousands of people he had personally encountered throughout his life, were all in his movie, memories and all. That makes me a surviving victim of life, he thought. So, that means I'm not a recovering victim of the established order, after all. And although Mr Greenhorn didn't know it, Dyfed had once known of him from afar and had personally recommended him for the job. Dyfed had known him once as Edom or Jerry Shusterman who had been Ebreo's assistant during his Wulfberht manufacturing escapade days.

As he mulled these things over in his mind's eye Dyfed continued to follow the smooth, patted down path that wended somewhere at high altitude among the mountains.

At this point Dyfed felt relaxed as he joined the past with the present again. The first purpose he had for himself was to reconnoitre and be safe. He walked on still in anticipation of approaching the edge of the world to peer out from a great height over at a distant and motion-frozen sea. But the anticipation of certain emotional expectations plays tricks and like climbing to the last rise, scrambling up the final hump, you eventually gain its height only to see yet another hill up ahead. As stated, it was now at the edge of night, here, and Dyfed was roaming in the gloaming, or as certain writers might insist — creeping into the crepuscular. Then — all of a sudden — he saw a shallow dished hollow. It was padded with lichen and mosses and was partially surrounded by scrubby little bushes which one finds at higher altitudes where ferocious winds can sculpture the hardy, rough flora into bent and twisted shapes. Dyfed stepped off the pathway and settled down into it. Here he cast his eyes about and softly felt the ground. As a prince of the grove and the forest and in nature in general, Dyfed knew that animals have a sense of mother Earth that have become atrophied in modern humans who have artificially endeavoured to separate themselves from the natural environment. The Earth is a molten droplet, now chilled and crusted on the outside some. This planet floats in a more-or-less fixed position within the environment of the solar system. This granulated molten glob is held in any one place not just by gravitation, as the hoi polloi believe (an almost four hundred year old theorem of theirs) but by the plasmid atmosphere of the solar system itself which is electrified and full of electromagnetic forces. In, on and around the Earth itself, Field Aligned Currents (FAC's) were in play here connecting the Earth's magnetosphere to the high latitude ionosphere. Currents in the Earth's magnetosphere are driven by the interplanetary magnetic field along with plasma streaming out from the sun. The solar system is wired with magnetism, the sun being its pile which is a very important factor and feature of the Apollo the Sun. But its strength and source of its strength is not so easy to explain. Ancient folks who lived closer to nature knew about the lines of force that gird the Earth. In the Land of Ch'in, even until recently, wizards knew of these power corridors which girded the planet like a grid, although the adopted intricacies that were dispensed later by rout were heavily flawed and not fully understood by the so-called experts. Still, these opinionated experts sought to advise the rulers of the land as to where and how to build, where not to construct roads, dams or excavate mines and quarries (like Dyfed's quarry at Carrara in Italia) so as not to challenge these force lines and evoke bad karma and unlucky Joss. Lao Tzu and Confucius were both aware of these features (at work here). Animals, too, were fully aware of them and used them for natural migration orientation, energy and strength gathering, along with wellness centres and ideal spots to calve or to relieve disquiet and even die. Caribou, bison, wolves and foxes all knew about this attribution that Mother Earth shared with them. Dyfed also knew, just like the Masters who taught him did. Quickly he realized that this slightly hollowed enclave he had discovered was such a station. It was a lair which animals hereabouts frequented in order to sustain energy or clear their primitive minds. Dyfed knew instinctively that such a natural charging Earth station would bode well for him, too. Feeling around he managed to find the position that received the most powerful energy just as animals had done before him. He curled up and made himself warm as he looked out toward the orange and mottled brown haze in the direction his intuition told him an ancient ocean lapped against the continent far, far below. Soon he fell fast asleep.

Dyfed awakened early before Aurora's light and set out again along the pathway. Then, when he crested a rocky rigid hillock — suddenly far in the distance before him — was the brilliant light of Cloud Nine City set in what looked like a gigantic silver coloured dish. And that dish was recessed into the desert floor with its shiny rim that circumscribed the city's perimeter set flush with the plateau's surface above which no buildings or towers protruded. From where Dyfed got his first glimpse it could have dubbed for the capital of planet Krypton, if not Tinsel-Town itself for its light energy glinted in a livid bluish frosty glow that shone upward like a vast search light.

After walking for some time Dyfed surveyed the scene before him. It was no longer still dark and now a bright and sunny day shone down from behind him on the city and the desert all around. He could now see that the city was further away than he had first thought and what he couldn't see before, even with the sun above, that a rapid river flowed between himself and his destination. An hour or two of rough hiking passed before the sound of its rushing rapids was heard clearly and he could now feel the cool air that the flowed downstream with the river. Suddenly, a hermit darted out from behind a rocky crag. The hermit was wearing a Phrygian cap of revolution red and appeared beside him again like magic and pointing toward the river he led the way toward it. At the river's edge was a wooden dock that ran a short space along the riverbank. A cry went up and looking upstream, Dyfed saw a wide raft-like riverboat being jostled by the rapids with their curly-waves caused by the currents rushing over boulders strewn over the uneven riverbed beneath. As the riverboat approached, Dyfed noticed that it was filled with folks wearing strange masks that watched eerily out over the low sides of the vessel with stark, unfaltering stares as they approached. Only the helmsman, the river ferryman, was unmasked and he shouted out orders to certain designated crewmembers (also masked) that frantically paddled the white-water river ferry towards the riverbank's dock. Then with a splash and the banging of wooden timbers and the squeak of planks, the ferry arrived with a sudden cease of violent motion. And as the helmsman held the ferry steady with a long pole-oar, the boat crowd disembarked onto the dock in a rough and ready manner of pushing and shoving. The commotion was overwhelming and then suddenly Dyfed was alone at the ferry dock. Even the hermit had disappeared.

Dyfed then noticed the ferryman's eyes were transfixed on him. This caused a strange affect like a tingling up and down his spine, for the wide-brimmed hatted ferryman somehow (he didn't know why) looked familiar somehow.

"Ahoy, ferryman,' said Dyfed. 'I am in need of your services.'

"Can't help you cross until I have almost a full boat,' the man answered in a gravelly voice. 'The current is too swift and the rapids too dangerous without the weight of a ferry full of passengers.'

Beside the dock was a tall, sturdy post. Attached to the top of the post was a cable that stretched across to the far side of the river to a similar post there. Hanging down at each end on the cable were large pulleys with ropes.

"I mean only to cross to the other side,' said Dyfed to the strange ferryman, 'not to travel up or down stream.'

"Is it your time? Is it time enough?' were the ferryman's only words as he beckoned Dyfed aboard. He then smiled to himself.

Soon the helmsman was busy effortlessly ferrying him slowly to the other side. At first he didn't speak. But when Dyfed asked him again if they had once met, he answered that they had.

"You don't remember me,' he said, 'for it was a time long before now and the situation we are in. But I remember us.'

"My master was Manandan,' Dyfed told him, surprised at the defence mechanism he had summoned.

"I am well aware of that,' the man replied. 'Have you done well by him?

This question puzzled Dyfed at first then began to worry him after a moment of reflection. There was something very familiar about this man that Dyfed couldn't put his finger on.

"When did we know each other? Dyfed asked.

"That is not important today,' he answered. 'I dare say,' he continued, that you recall the middle of the Iron Age with the rise of Amoran Empire. But can you recall the end of the Bronze Age? Can you remember when the spirit of men became bitter and sharp and unrelenting with the advent of iron? Of course, it's much the same today, isn't it?

Now it's called economizing and progress, as it was way back when, too; back in the days of King Shamaniser Assyr, cousin to Nebuchadnezzar, latterly the fast food giant mogul. What has changed? Time is denarii and the responsible buck stops here. Soon, they all had a social/religious culture to match that was further fashioned by Amor, remember? And before Amor and before Assyr…the dark age of marauding sea-folks that changed the age from bronze to iron: And before the age of bronze… and before the age of silver was the Golden Age. What, if anything do you remember of them? Nothing? Wake up Dyfed H. Lucifer. Don't you remember the essence function of the twelfth century Chinul where Nirvana is the sublime essence that is present in all beings? And what of the Indus civilization, what of the transcendence and the sense of effacement from effacement itself? Long ago at the celestial fair we opted for a thrill seeker ride on the olden day celestial Ferris wheel together. We knew there was an allotted time before the thrill ended. But we could pay our fare and we could be gripped into the reoccurrence of figurative phenomena to our heart's content, some enjoying, others screaming, one fool fantasying himself a king, another fooled into the fantasy of wealth. We took it upon ourselves, after all, if you recall. We revelled in the idea of momentarily and utter ignorance of all else, an ignorance by which we once said we could not be fooled. Remember the words of our friend the mystic and saint, Kabir':

'Oh Friend, hope for knowledge of God the Absolute while you live, know while you live, understand while you live: for in life deliverance abides. If your bonds be not broken while you live, what hope of deliverance in death? It is but an empty dream that the soul shall have union with God because it has passed from the body. If God is found now, God is found then: If not, we do but go to dwell in the City of Death.'

"Who are you?' asked Dyfed again.

"We have now crossed over,' said the ferryman. 'Your final journey begins here and now your metanoia is about to happen. As for my name, it is Yagnavalkya. I am also referred to as Purusha and sometimes Akshara. We will meet again soon. Good-bye,' he said silently to Dyfed's back as the latter clambered ashore.

After an hour or so, with the sun dipping below the horizon, Dyfed suddenly saw the sparkling brightness of a white spot shining up out of the desert. As for those lavish urban frills it processed, it had been wrought by a no-expense-spared expenditure taken to outfit C9C that bathed it in a glorious electrical halo. Darkness, once again, approached though he was still quite some way off. He got himself under the superstructure of an arching monorail. This lit-up viaduct on high struck an eerie contrast between it and the dark sky behind. He got beneath it and followed it to the brim of the giant excavation dug into the desert into which this bright humming city nestled. This led him to the city's pedestrian disembark station and its bank of vernaculars down which all guests descended into this city of the valley (or pit) of death.

(Clad in Wedding Garments, Zeus's Chosen Comes Forth by Day)

'Then I saw an angel standing in the sun; and he cried with a loud voice, saying to all the birds that fly in the midst of heaven, "Come and gather together for the supper of the great God, that you may eat the flesh of kings, the flesh of captains, the flesh of the mighty men...and the flesh of all people..." '...and fire came down from God out of heaven and devoured them.'

JOHN *(ANON)*

Though bright, the city was quiet and seductive. Dyfed felt he was completely enclosed by it even while his spirit raged to soar quickly away and to escape it. The anchor that confounded his will in the pursuit for immediate escape wasn't so much his word that he'd given to Morgant and others that they could count on him being here, but rather it was about his duty here. Dyfed was chief occupational health and safety officer for the entire first operation and it behoved (pronounced bee-hooved) him to honour himself by plying his responsibility, obviously if not to the Haploid guests, then at least to the personnel who were keeping the show running and gliding smoothly without a hitch as evenly as possible along the tracks.

In a way that was a paradox, this strange and frightening place that had been dug into the rocky desert plateau was nonetheless a bright shining beacon of intense light. There was nothing in C9C that for Dyfed would be relatively coherent in respect to what it actual represented, either then or for the remainder of his stint and tenure there. For it to become relative, that would be either too demeaning or too horrifying and probably both. And it wasn't a matter that its targeted victims were the very monsters who were the cause of most of the suffering and sorrow in the big, wide world throughout history, either. His going concern was the effect it was to have on him and the others by just being here to facilitate this monstrosity of their own doing. What goes around comes around, as the saying goes. You see, this was because there had been none of the normal preparation and desensitising period to lead him up to this monstrous event compared to what was generally happening to the hoi polloi by that handy slight of hand which the Haploids had managed to master so well. This desensitizing of violence against fellow and loving human beings was part of their core programming and was promoted by political and cultural ideology and disseminated by audio and televised waves that permeated not only the workplace, the public space and the privacy of the home, but even impinged on the peace of the individual private/personal space at rest and at play. Along with raucous vibrations that substituted for music, those multiple flavours of medication ranging from lithium (that was stockpiled here for other uses as well) to dangerous psychotropic drugs and the titanic increase of formats, formulas, unnatural expectations and beyond reasonable responsibilities and technical information overloads, all of which doesn't even scratch the surface here of that disillusioned prison of acceptance and belonging that was necessary (not) for young men and young women's well-being in their lives that lay stretched out and lonely before them and how inescapable it all was, it was no wonder the normal universal human psych had recently collapsed suddenly that left the new generation of establishment to resemble trolls and medicated schizophrenic psychopaths running amok and all the futile while they were also trying to dodge monstrous archetypical constructs created in moments passed that had become neigh impossible to revisit and correct without free will that was now lost to them in the fog of unknowing that lay between their physiological intelligence and its inferential knowledge that belongs to humanity, that the true (but now more than any time hidden) self or non self, and god.

Although Morgant had brought Dyfed and Trachmyr to this despicable and detestable spot here in the desert only nine months before the present, it seemed that he'd been gone so long now that he didn't recognise the place. And it didn't recognize him. Security was tight. The fact is he hadn't wanted to remember. And under the circumstances there was nothing relative about Cloud Nine City to recognize anyway with or without which to feel comfortable. On that previous advent which happened shortly after their escape from the *pack's* Manna-hata penthouse suites, they had done a quick site visit to take a gander as to how the city's construction was unfolding and to orient themselves for their future duties here. It was his responsibility, Dyfed told himself, to at least protect the staff. Massive amounts of construction material had been on hand then that was waiting to be summoned and placed alongside another brick in the wall as relative to their purpose. All this material was stacked neatly in a filing system proximate to their destined location all of which occupied over five thousand hectares of flat, excavated land beneath the desert on this high plateau where Cloud Nine City had been quickly on the rise then. A monorail from the airship terminal that ran to and fro the city terminal had been completed to help to shuttle manpower and more contained material like pharmaceuticals, alcohol, recreational drugs and items considered necessary condiments, into the centre's hub storerooms and warehouses.

Aside from that, at that time there had been heavy equipment everywhere moving and shifting chunky pieces of the plateau and granulated piles of blasted rock in enormous wheeled buggies. Other gigantic trucks were delivering wet-porridge-like concrete to be poured into forms that smelled of fresh pine and fir that were filled with bundles of steel and iron re-bar that stuck up into the air or formed a massive grid of steel netting that ran for miles and miles and miles in every direction. For twenty miles by twenty miles the industrial noise of manufacturing and building was constant twenty-four seven. There were rows and rows of fantastical cranes standing like huge iron mechano soldiers. These were for lifting unheard of loads from the subterranean floor up and up toward the excavated crater's rim or materials from the rim down to its floor, as the metropolis took shape. Ten road ramps (that were actually switch-backs) creeping down its sidewalls from the top brim substituted for the thorough-fare needed to facilitate the bumper to bumper traffic jam descending gradually down from the desert plateau into the giant excavation to deliver its cargo on one side while another line of bumper to bumper traffic-jam of ten other road-ramps were ascending with the rattle that reminded Dyfed of a train of empty box-cars. These were ascending on the other side of the man-made crater almost twenty miles across the way and with hardly any more speed than the former. And take shape it had done but in an uncharacteristic way, he noted. On that day he had stood looking down at the partially constructed foundations that was spreading out in a giant shiny grid like an industrial metallic creeping moss covering the depressed footprint foundation of the city that then began to grow upward like some kind of expanding crystallization reaching for the lip of the huge man-made depression. From their vantage point he and Trachmyr were able to watch the big earthmovers crawl back and forth beneath them and hear them clear their deep gravely throats and see the corresponding spurts of blue effluents which discharged from their massive compression engines through an exhaust stack that towered over the cab. This happened as each machine encountered reaction that — upon engagement — affected their output. From their position upon the rim they watched as heavy gas and diesel internal combustion engines growled and coughed, choked and sputtered, as they gouged and glided, cutting and smoothening the earth and shifting conical piles of heavy material. While over yonder, small electric engines bussed workers around from site to site in multi seated chariots decked out with bobbing and side to side shaking sun-shade carousels with colourful fringes on top, while still smaller machines were busy at work in the gloved hands of men, cutting, grinding, drilling and pounding. The hauling chariots were of varying sizes, from small run-abouts to large earthmovers, the latter were the ones equipped with big diesel engines. All around the invisible smell from their exhaust reached Dyfed's nostrils, as did the smell of freshly excavated earth and the odour of cordite from the explosives that detonated all around as they blasted the rigid and immovable bones of the Earth into a whitish rock powder.

All of these smells hung in the rare Andean air. Then all of a sudden, memory from another time flooded into him and filled up his multi-dimensional nostalgia vessels. He was able to differentiate between the differences in the visible and invisible vapours that spewed forth from the oily machines. This was because of his alertness and unique cognizance. It enabled him to discern which engines were four cycle or two cycles, and which were diesel compression engines and petroleum gas ignition engines. But with the disappearance years ago of those big compression engines that consumed raw fossil fuel at the rate of one imperial gallon (4.5 litres) every six minutes, the presence on that day of these unique machines and the environment they caused of sound and smell, along with all he and Trachmyr associated with that, was a poignant reminder of happier days and these flash-moments from the past were strangely cherished by the two onlookers. It was like a museum of nostalgia for both Dyfed and Trachmyr who were sensitive to this emotion that rippled through this phenomena of theirs and spread out before them. Was it a fitting finalé or not? they wondered, for nostalgia like this to be found here in this strange and creepy city. The irony in this was not lost on them.

As stated, all of these aforementioned mechanical inventions that ran on oil had long since disappeared from normal use in the world outside. They had run their course in polluting the atmosphere and were rumoured by the more ignorant to be the single main cause of why the mean temperature of the Earth had risen monumentally in the last hundred years. Also, as the Earth's magnetic field had been drastically reduced along with an oxygen depletion, and what with dangerous solar winds penetrating deeper and deeper into the atmosphere from the power of the sun, rising temperatures that brought ferocious storms that scoured across sea and land and caused the black funnelled tornadoes and the super scary fire tornadoes raging over hundreds of millions of hectares dotted with farms and cities all over the continents of the Earth including the mighty

Amazon, that one-stop shop panacea for every illness known to man. As well as being the lungs of the world the Amazon and a number of other of Earth's natural barometric safety valves meant to guard our atmosphere (and everything under it) were all in tatters now. However, that, along with chain extinctions that had become rampant, weren't all because of the iron machines. But it had been this generation of iron and steel machines along with their (and the civilization's) ferocity for fossil fuel consumption that had truly helped make those key Haploids (who benefited from this Earth-ravishing technology) rich beyond imagination. But on the other hand raging fires could add fresh new nutrients into the Amazonian earth and now maybe having once leaned heavily on our newly acquired knowledge and its technology we may have now learned that in our haste to consume and experiment we run the risk of presumption that will expose our towering ignorance, not only about our global life-raft in space but even about ourselves, and maybe then we need to exhaust not our resources but our powers of observation towards what effects our enthusiastic intentions and volitions might have and their repercussions and consequences down the road.

In addition to internal combustion and compression engines the two men had noticed that the inexhaustible electric power generated by the earth that could be practically and safely converted into a gigantic conductor (as Tesla had demonstrated in vain) were now in common use everywhere including here. But here the built-in meters whose purpose was to summon up monthly sums of debit to the receiver were not installed, as they were everywhere else in the world. That was the corporate-capitalist way, along with its slogan, 'pay as you go', which was also their password to prosperity. That wasn't needed here. The password to human prosperity here was to complete this project on time and flick the on switch so that Cloud Nine City can ramp up and begin exterminating the Haploids on schedule.

And as for power, there would be no concern here of being under powered, that's for sure. Available electrical energy was never going to be a problem here. Isolating it and keeping safe zones would be. Twenty-five hundred mega watts was power enough to run a million homes outside that on average housed five people back home. And yet here at C9C its capacity would be capable of providing service with a supply equalling tera and peta coulombs per sec. The whole city would be capable of glowing in a dazzle of light brighter than even Vegas used to be back in its heyday before it dimmed. And once everything was connected and jacked up, the dynamo and supporting apparatus could turn the entire city into an extremely hot and brilliant flashbulb. The network was further webbed with super step-up transformers designed by particle physicist Quantum Gizmo III, Quasi Gizmo's nephew.

By the time of that earlier visit, Dr Tesla and Dr Torsionfield along with their battery of scientists had already completed the installation that would provide the magnetic field that would help generate the cycles of vibration to maintain the constant electrical energy needed here and to stabilize the situation for the lifestyle to which the Haploids had long been accustomed. In addition, due to the team's innovative insulating methods, the city itself and the single connecting monorail system that allowed a commuter train to operate between the airport and the city's main terminal were all run on electricity. Once the commuters were on the floor of C9C another lower transit system was able to deliver them to all the different sections of the city. This lower transit system use was intended to be for guests and for any of the temporary inhabitants as well; but the

Haploid guests were not to be permitted to return to crater's rim or return to the airport for any reason. For this return passage to the airport required a ticket with a special password. It was used much like an elevator key-lock that was capable of accessing specially protected floors of a building, say, or in this case the escape hatch airport. You had to have the key code and only special staff would be armed with that.

Back nine months earlier as Dyfed had watched, he saw the team was finishing off what looked to be insulating platforms for the mono-rail as well as the pivotal, high energy connections from the magnifying step-up transmitters. Each of these transmitters was atop a gigantic concrete and steel support structure that looked like (and each one was equal in size to) the Eifel Tower. And they almost stuck out above the mean level of the desert floor. Even from that distance, Dyfed remembered he had seen huge black bottles with tiny little ant-sized workers moving around dressed in bright yellow bio-suits. He presumed that these might be the lithium containers used for drugging the inhabitants. They were that and more. Aside from large quantities of lithium to mix with the Haploid's domestic drinking water to help keep them passive and calm, heavy hydrogen isotopes such as lithium deuteride was being stored here as well. The latter is the primary fusion fuel in thermonuclear devices, namely the hydrogen bomb that is colloquially called the H-bomb.[94]

From where he stood Dyfed hadn't been able to properly see what was being housed in these and other similar silos throughout the foundations of the city. Nor could he see what the workmen were doing, but the electronic torc-like tablet he's been given contained all the as-built prints and the over-all plans of the entire project, as well as updated information as to the progress of each work site. From it he had learned that the black bottles (that were within sight prior to becoming enclosed in a warehouse) contained methyl iodide. They were being kept in black bottles to inhibit degradation that occurs from any light source. Over top of the bottle's exterior workers were constructing shiny silver reflective jackets before they were to be enclosed in a windowless building that was to be constructed around them. Dyfed knew that this product was stabilised by silver wire. He explained to Trachmyr that when this product is water doped and used with a ramped up irradiation process it creates a Coulomb explosion. Ionised by a lazar field, it is used, he told him, as a method for coupling electronic excitation energy from intense electromagnetic fields into atomic motion. This procedure can break the bonds that hold solids together. For this operation, he had said that they would have to greatly ramp up and magnify the methyl iodide, coulomb explosion process. This lazar procedure of being able to break the bonds of solids was an ideal method of attacking and stripping the heavy metal insulation coating on key leg foundation rods on which the city rested. This was to be used in conjunction with the final H-bomb in order to eradicate and erase any remnants and evidence of the city after its final use. As the last of the unsuspecting Haploid victims went about their day (possibly night) in the last day in the life of C9C, this open-switch death-trap collective domicile would be all ready and set to go SNAP! CRACKLE! and POP! Directly after the preamble of that jingle is the main event; that is the heat of the H-bomb. Since these high efficient devices produce plasma temperatures at over 500 million degrees kelvin (K), the overall temperature of

---

94 A modern fusion devices used for weapons consist of 2 main components: a nuclear fission primary stage fuelled by uranium-235 or plutonium-239, along with a separate second stage nuclear fusion containing the thermonuclear fuel. This fuel is the heavy hydrogen isotopes lithium deuteride.

the city upon the moment of crisis would become exceedingly high. Zapped with those kinds of temperatures any given handy mercury thermometer gauge on the wall somewhere in any one of Cloud Nine City's many air-conditioned spas, lizard lounges or a bedroom en-suite could be exposed to temperatures of over 85000 times hotter than the surface of the sun.[95] So, there you have it. Once the switch was flipped, and the nuclear devise illuminated into a candlepower with radiation greater than the sun, the circuit would be closed on this puppy. Then all there would be left to say was…Adios Haploid motherfuckers, he thought. But somehow that wasn't uplifting enough.

"No shit?' Trachmyr had responded with a jerk of his head to Dyfed's tablet consultant data. And are they trying to hide it and their dirty little secret about it from god… and on that tablet? Isn't reality part of god anyway, oh *captain*?'

"And am I comfortable with this?' Dyfed had challenged his companion back, without giving Trachmyr an answer. 'Absolutely not! I'm nowhere near comfortable. But Thrax, that old Marsian red warrior himself, he is the one in charge here. I mean, really. Anyway, this is his show, not ours.'

"Just who the fuck then is this Thrax asshole, anyway? asked Trachmyr. 'I don't like him already. And the fact that I can do that without having met him even once means something's wrong here. Oh Dyfed my pilgrim, is it me or him?'

"The last thing you want, or need, is to meet Thrax,' replied Dyfed. 'He's a scary legend.

"He's a legend?' enquired Trachmyr.

"Yuh,' replied Dyfed, 'just like all those old legendary ones, men like Atreus and Polypheides king of Sicyon to whom Agamemnon and Menelaus were sent after the murder of their father Atreas king of Mycenae. And then there is the legendary Perseus (the half brother of the aforementioned Herakles' as well as being his great-grandfather. Perseus murdered Medusa with a beheading which in turn caused the justified death of Polydectes who had earlier raped Perseus' mother, Danae. And then last but not least there was Alkaios (also Alkeides) son of Zeus who was given the name Herakles (glory or pride of Hera[96]) And who do you think was more legendary than MacAchilles or MacAlcides (aka Alkeidesson)? Just kidding,' he volunteered with a laugh.

"Is this actually a laughing matter, after all?' queried Trachmyr.

"No more than the Marquise de Sade's slave, Sir Belvedere, was the laughing stock of that *pulchra femina* of the river Sen, that is to say, gay old Isis, by Jove!'

'But what we have here,' responded Trachmyr, 'is that we come from afar across a world full of natural commotion to the centre of a cluster fuck of organized evil commotion by human machination.'

Dyfed, the once and future Paisley of Tulip, the captain of pilgrims, paused characteristically before replying here to his companion's statement.

"Even when the day comes, Trachmyr, I say to you…if Thrax sacrifices two dozen sheep, eight white-whiskered boars and two shambling and shaggy buffalos which are flayed after their fatty thighs are burned in sacrifice, and then when all is made ready for our ceremony table to deprive life even to the Haploids' reality (which has never been mine, nor do I wish to invite it into my life)…it's a mission I'm not willing to except, it's one I'm most willing to postpone and one whose agenda (in the end) I do not expect

---

95   The sun's surface is just over five thousand seven hundred degrees Kelvin.
96   Though she was the wife and consort of Zeus, Hera was not Alkeides' mother, after all.

to win. As you say, Trachmyr; reality is god, or the window of cognizance thereof, and this — what we have here in the quietude among natural disturbances of the Atacama Desert — is a cluster fuck of organized evil commotion: I couldn't have said it better myself, oh companion mine! Haploid profit before safety and greed before empathy is in poor form, but the idea of the unsuspecting invited and visiting guests (even if they aren't the stranger in the midst, exactly) who into the temenos of evil they steppeth and strayeth whereupon they're deemed unwelcome, ineligible to remain, their visa expired and their exit blocked, is of even worse form. And in itself this has all the hallmarks of Haploidism written all over it,' said Dyfed. 'If it's a thing whose original use has become redundant but instead is now utilized as a trend and its realization is subject to and accomplished by rote, then a rose by a different name is the name of the game. The question remains; what then is the reality of the Masters of the Unkown Unbroken Universe, if indeed it actually is unbroken to them or is this too just another rote and a lie?'

Dyfed remembered nothing after that. Trachmyr informed him later that he had passed out and Morgant had been summoned. Then becoming fearful for whatever the reason that wasn't made known to Trachmyr, Morgant quickly evacuated Dyfed out of C9C and shuffled the two of them off to Buffalo.

(NARRATOR'S PRIVILEGE)

What would anybody think after reading or hearing about something like this? It's all right to speculate, I guess. There's no test afterwards. Nor will there be any consequence that's likely to travel down the pike or start coming through the rye. Nobody's going to start or stop a bullet because of it, not on anyone's account. That's an expectation and an order, no exception. Indeed, just touching on it lightly, just running the tips of your mind's fingers across its tapestry ever so softly can be the answer to the confusion it raises. There is no need here to boldly postulate or procrastinate or tear it open. Here we can resist metonymy and banish metaphor from any state of endemicity. We can also discard any mellifluousness or the need to entertain any superfluous posture. Nor can there be any closure here through investigation, by debate or by analysing it for the purpose of providing some kind of pass or fail against the lists of literature: that, or any other fake, trumped-up drivel to help make some idiot somewhere into some pseudo, lame-brain intellectual. I'm even a prime subject, of course. Its potential to remain a festering or bleeding wound to those who contemplate it is too real. But in no way is it a lame duck. Its composition is that of the dark and murky mire that encases those least settled, generally fraught with angst and anger, the land of the lost and undisciplined, the weakest of the weaklings and those who are most unhappy. Any-who!! How is it always that some asshole from an obscure shit hole in the ground overshadowed by a forgotten back eddy on the far side of the Earth gets to be a silver screen motion-picture celebrity writer/poet to claim their fifteen minutes or fifteen years of ill gained fame over here where we are, anyway? Surely, there must be about two hundred million or more folks around these parts…folks who've been lining up at the doors to this event for years who were front-centre and ahead of Mr Nobody over there who should have had first dibs, for goodness sake. There's no justice in this world. If you set your mind to something the first thing you will learn is that life's not fair, either for you or because of you. The second lesson is that you're a loser. So, this is not about Joyce, Picasso, Beckett, Euripedes or even Cambell or Jung. There isn't supposed to be any intellectualism here in this part. This is an intellectual free zone, please. Enjoy its degeneracy or clean up the reception. That's up to you. It's all about the reader, who can make with it whatever they choose, and whether he/she is intelligent or not is irrelevant. No permission has been given for this tale to either sore or shine, crash and burn on the analogy of the metaphoric circuit…'that's *foe show!*' as they say in the trade. I forbid it.

So, was it true then? Is it that the Earth and all in it are profane just as certain priests of Jeshua had proclaimed? And the heavens; were they sacred? The irony was that in a sense any bogus or real incoming dark comet — wormwood, or by any other name — the so-called witch on a furry tailed broomstick or the dragon guarding the mound that was a speck of dust in a vast void, it was all taken as a harbinger of a god sent to mete out justice and revenge, at last. Never mind rape and pillage and set the thatch on fire. Clearly, it was thought to mean to be a divine volition to force a clean sweep of those key backsliders and torturers of a debilitated humanity who were not driving the bus. **Parasolo.**

(Mack the Knife)

'Where have all the young men gone? Long time passing...Where have all the young men gone? Long time ago...Where have all the young men gone? Gone for soldiers everyone...When will they ever learn? When will they ever learn?'

PETE SEEGER

Across the blue and frosty looking fake cobblestone street that lay before him was a vast brightly lit venue called 'The Club Palace'. It glared out giant, brightly coloured lights that spelled out its name for the benefit of all. Just then, Dyfed was remembering a gigantic limousine had silently pulled up between him and the Palace. This quickly converted the image of the limousine into something that resembled a burning building or carriage where only the supporting timbers showed through against the fierce and blinding blaze behind it. Besides being huge the limousine was also an ostentatious looking motor chariot with high rear fins and red-dwarf like lights glowing like burning embers aft. Two heavily faded beams of yellow, conical pyramids were projected through the absence of evening darkness invisibly forward unseen onto the road in front. They had started from smallish points at the shiny chrome ringed headlight domes and expanded invisibly out. Automatically Dyfed captured the image of these funnel shaped beams of energy that widened in ratio to their projected distance. Painted robin's egg blue, the motor chariot was clad with a decorative icing resembling chrome Christmas tree trim, chrome bulbous bumpers at each end, with a brilliant pink canvas ragtop and an aerial on the front passenger fender with a yellow and navy-blue teddy bear mounted from it like a banner. Finally, it had wide, pink tire walls that were further set off by the remaining visible crust of the tires' black, shiny new rubber. Peering into the limo's burning and spacious interior, Dyfed had thought he had recognised the shape of the darkly glowing silhouette there, which despite its wavy mirage appearances he assumed must resemble the man actually sitting alone in the back seat eating what looked like an ice-cream cone. But because his silhouette suddenly altered as the occupant turned his head the other way just then to look out toward the light that shone out from the Club Palace's façade and streamed through the limousine, suddenly Dyfed had been unsure of himself for a change. For he discerned a glowing, fibrous doorman that looked like a twisting microbe being magnified on a burning petri dish as he quickly rushed forward and curving his arm in a demonstrative manner, indicated to the unseen driver of the vast motor chariot to push on and turn down the lane to his left. The whole, brilliant but grainy picture before Dyfed was like something out of the movie Lawrence of Arabia @ the Imax, with a light exposure increase somewhere around ten to the power of five magnification. Interestingly, even though all the folks close to the venue shimmered and danced like cinders they appeared to absorb nary a joule of heat. Right over there, the doorman had pointed without saying the words. Right there his finger said it all without any lips moving. Presumably, Dyfed remembered thinking at the time, the lane must lead to the performers' entrance at the side. The limousine slowly and silently moved ahead again. As he had watched, the gaiety of bright light from the Club Palace had moved through the moving limousine like a spreading fire storm and the motor chariot's sharp, high rear fins cut a jagged angle in the beckoning door of the night/day club's white swimming brilliance beyond. As it cleared the Club Palace's entrance, Dyfed had been certain that he had been right about the man in the back seat. Yes it was. It WAS Mack the Knife.

In his mind, Dyfed recalled quickly crossing the blue, frosty looking street. He laughed to himself over the sensation of feeling like some animated-come-to-life Dick Tracy as he moved across the crimson road. He had flicked his wrist and looked at his Dick Tracy watch. He wasn't wearing a watch. At that moment he had suddenly realised that he was in bare feet and wearing shorts and an open, loosely fitting short sleeve, dark shirt which had some sparkling silver threads sewn every which way into it. These were the only things hanging in the room closet of the hotel that Morgant had him checked into shortly after he had arrived. The front desk had at his request sent his travelling clothes out to be laundered. Not to worry, the evening (or was it morning) under Cloud Nine City's environmental and insolating bubble was an ideal temperature for such attire. But at that moment he saw a man wearing a huge, knee length fur coat and fur hat with quilted seal skin leggings tucked into high laced caribou moccasins and heavy moose hide gloves hanging from his arm sleeves. Quickly the north man was absorbed in the blazing quicksilver-like pool of the Palace's entrance lights where he dissolved like egg white into a massive sunny-side up on a hot skittle. This north man was accompanied by a shapely young woman, a blond, who — from Dyfed's disadvantaged position — may not have had anything on, he wasn't quite sure. Hesitating a moment while he pondered that thought (the expression that a moment in time is relative, is quite relative here, if not fitting), he began to walk in the direction following the limousine. He stopped at the alley corner. Straining his vision he looked over the heads of some freaks that were crouching in the shadows and were probably high on crystal meth or shooting up some other popular and trendy phenomenon boosting substance called *the crack of dawn*. He watched as another doorman rushed forward. The glittery dressed doorman opened the rear door to allow Mack the Knife to step gingerly from the limousine onto the curb. Dyfed saw him fling the ice-cream cone in a sharp curve onto the curb and enter the Club Palace where he disappeared out of sight. Perpendicular to the wall above that side door he saw a small, lit sign that read: Club Palace. Back in front, a firestorm of flashing multi-coloured lights that took a whole block to spell out *Club Palace* mesmerized patrons inside the club and out like a country preacher or some other salesman hawking for the chance of his next meal. This must be called the Palace Club, Dyfed thought. Whew! Why! Look, he said to himself. Aren't those two men over there that are entering the club none other than Julius the Jerk and Flav the Finger? Imagine, he thought, Mack the Knife and those two all in one night's caste.

Besides the light which Neon and Incandescent caused to shine out, the light shining in from the cosmos was much blurred and greatly diminished. And that cosmic light had a bluish hue about it. Of course, as we now know, like the constant rain of short wave radiant energy — energy that we absorb to our detriment throughout our lives — it was that blue vibration from the cosmos beyond which aside from keeping us stressed out and awake right to the end of our days was at least capable of attributing to our collective discernment of the cosmos itself. Anyway, whatever it was it was a mega version of the ultimate attention grabber and Dyfed knew it was a condition that could be filtered out even if violet blue was his favourite colour.

"So,' he spoke now seemingly to another persona of himself in his own defence, 'I'm not a recovering victim of the established order here, you know. Far from it: I'm a self-made survivor who remains fully intact, so there! As you should know, Parasolus, in a sense, the establishment has all the tools to get something right but they almost always get it wrong. Indeed, we have reports from the establishment that individuals in society can be violent under stressful situations: Situations and conditions that we have today, for instance. Yet, for well over 2000 years the establishment has proved that collectively, it — itself — is always violent under these same stressful situations and that generally we, the hoi polloi or whomever, are powerless in the face of it. This is why the long planned for mental state of imprisonment forced onto humanity via culture and financial necessity — which was eventually and successfully implemented some years back — that has finally and certifiably been complicated now with the new situational state of open-air physical imprisonment as well and why the inevitable psyche crash came to pass. And the lock down of society right across the board and its borders then ensued without a ripple or a hitch. All with the help and design, I might add, of The World's Department of Public Safety and their illustrious and fearless underwriters, The World Limited Liability Company (LLC). Of course their liability is limited; it is directly funded by taxpayers' dollars straight from the World Treasury. Where else?' he added, grinning outwardly.

Staring up and around Dyfed saw the big wide brim above that lined the deep excavated depression in which this city (this man-cave of total distraction with a myriad of material amusements of every flavour for every mind set and every form of pleasure) sprawled and huddled. Dyfed thought that the unlucky Haploids were denied at least one pleasure; those rambunctious rummage sales with ladies in rubber boots or sneakers, all emotionally highly charged and fleshing out pressure building queues of folks all in a row. Then he saw them. Just past the Club Palace he caught sight of a queue that lined up down the street and around the squarest of blocks. Apparently, they were waiting for the doors to open on some gigantic seventh day of the week blow-out-shopping-day count down into the first day of next week. It was a…help get us into the Black Sabbath/Sunday weekend shop-fest. Lighting the candles at sundown to start Shabbat, or Sunday-go-to-meeting clothes of snazzy blazer over grey…had been put on hold, here and everywhere. The slogan had long been…shop till you drop, my fine consumer fiends. No work tomorrow or today your love has gone away to stay, so spend, spend and spend your money away. Only the Ishlamite culture lagged about a thousand years behind this frenzy. But they too were being fast-forward into the present day. God help them. No word yet on the complimentary and highly anticipated reward of a thousand and one blowjobs from a thousand and one virgins as you pass through the Pearly Gates after shedding blood for Allah. Shake your head Jihad Habib! I mean, really…virgins giving blowjobs? How good could that be and even god wouldn't bestow his daughters to some wing nut without a job or a place of respect among the community around the masjid who doesn't have a pulse. Being dead from the third dimension and expecting third dimensional delights elsewhere beyond here in the hereafter is just plain stupid. Hello?

(Blond up and Red down with a Pink Martini strutting the Drag-strip of Pop Culture)

> 'All I have I would have given gladly not to be standing here today.'
> **LYNDON BAINES JOHNSON**

"Hey, baby. You my baby?' the voice said. She was a blond up and a red head down kind of girl. Since that doesn't sound right, it occurred to Dyfed later that it might have been the other way around. There's no telling sometimes what you think you see. She had a pink martini in one hand that was for sure. It matched her tight crotch-less shorts that matched the ragtop and tire walls on Mack the Knife's otherwise robin's egg blue motor chariot. Was there a connection, he wondered, fleetingly. And getting back to Hey baby You My Baby; in her other hand she had a tall milkshake glass of something that looked like a chemistry lab experiment that was in the process of reacting and vomiting sparkling white fog from the rim like a volcano.

"Yummy, huh?' Dyfed remarked rather blandly as he tried to push by her. He was looking for Trachmyr. This, he thought, might be a place he would visit for their last night in town. Thinking about that for a moment he then wondered where the time had gone, as if time was capable of just up and going somewhere without people noticing. Was that even possible? Retroactively yes, I guess. Since he crossed the river on the ferry and had arrived following the monorail to the brimming outskirts of Cloud Nine City, what had he actually accomplished in the interim? That was the question, but it was fleeting and shortly he had brushed (if not pushed) past the crotch less pantied no bra babe, this time blond down and red up, and moved on, scraping the partial exposed portion of his bare chest against her rough nipples as he went by.

"Hey baby. You my baby?' she said again like a windup doll, her eyes fixed and unblinking and incredibly sharp and lucid that were sparkling like the drink in her left hand. He was certain that she saw him but not that she remembered him. He knew she sensed him being there, even from the moment he stepped from the sidewalk across the road. Dyfed thought she was pretending to be a cyborg (cybernetic organism), but he knew exactly who she was — it was Eleanor, once the queen consort of Francia and Albion who was a duchess in her own right. Cyborgs he thought were all the rage now for those poor, pathetic and lonely men and women and were an upgrade from the Barbie-doll blow up for those who wanted something more like the real thing without brains and back-talk and no ability to have personal or affectionate contact or anything dangerous as that. But that was no Eleanor, no sir; he knew that much.

The area Dyfed was in was virtually an unbroken bar that circled around a huge open centre as large a rodeo arena ring that looked down into a vast subterranean space below. Gambling was available to patrons here, as well. But Dyfed had long ago learned to gamble on the big things in life from the heart, not among the soul-destroying squalor of mere greed and distraction, a commodity that was kind of like peripheral vision filler to his imagination. Bar tables hosting couples of different kinds were placed beside the glass guard rim enclosing the pit hole. Here folks sought an optimum view of the performance stage and activity beyond and beneath. A large multi-coloured sun disc dominated the apex above. It was obviously not supported by anything and because of the reverse season of the southern hemisphere it was decorated with a white Santa beard and eyebrows and topped with a red toque whose pointy end was fastened with a flashing snowball that rested beside and separate from the sun's disc. From here it loomed, hanging down from a realistic sky. It shone very brightly in sequins of silver and gold. Their were food vendors of different culinary tastes interspersed in neat segments that were sandwiched between the peripherally placed liquor bars that were next to a beer bar to its left and a wine bar to its right: And so forth. This sequence, along with slot machine and keno TVs kept replicating in a three sixty-degree circle around him, apart from the front lobby. There was a similar bar, food vending and gambling facilities arrangement down underneath in the main music and dancing arena, too: As above, so below. As it was directly under the upper lounge and what with the brightly shining disc, he couldn't make out much below other than the central positioned performance stage. One would have to have the advantage of being comfortably placed inside the central glowing sun to get a good perspective of seeing the full layout.

The central sun became a cartouche above Dick Tracy's slicked back haired head somewhere in his mind. Then another cartouche: This is where the probing security circuit cameras were probably positioned, he thought. The thunderous chatter all around was thick but not ear splittingly loud, nor was the live music from below that was piped up from the musicians performing there. This quickly brought him back. How could he drift so easily, he wondered sleepily. How easily I digress, he thought. Dyfed knew always to be careful about what he thought as he realized that there was no need for security cameras here. Really, Dyfed knew that there was only just him and his tangled web he'd woven over a lifetime of thoughts. Where the hell is Trachmyr, anyway?

Choosing the closest corridor of wide up and down escalators, he embarked on a steep descent into the central pit and punctured the vast arena. About half way down what had before been the comfortable strains of audible music was suddenly pushed up a ton of decibels. It was as if an invisible sound padded door has been un-expectantly jerked open. He waited for someone to close it. It didn't happen. It only got louder as he descended. The light down here was different, too, he thought, almost like moonlight and immediately he saw the 'hey baby, you my baby' woman again — who must have followed him, unless it was a clone. He noted that her tight hot pink crotch-less shorts were day-glow and tattoos that he hadn't noticed she had when he first saw her topside, but now shone out from her naked skin in vibrant colours of the rainbow. She had obviously downed the pink martini or spilled it, for she had two others instead. Each one vomited a different colour fog: One red and the other blue. Anyway, it now appeared that she held one in each hand high up over the height of her shoulders as she gyrated obscenely.

Just like above, after a space for promenade and strut your stuff exhibiting walkway for show-offs that wound around inside the inner rim of bar stools that were two or three thick and lined the belly-up-to bar casual stance area, individual bar tables were spread out in the direction towards the central stage. The lounge area was bigger down here than above. There was still a huge dance area beyond the last of the tables all of which circled the raised stage. The dance floor was more like a curved football field cut lengthwise and joined together at both ends with the plug in the hole of the donut centre performing stage that belted forth mega decibels. This circular football field was also open to the artificial sky. From the dance floor — as one did the chimi…chimi…changa…shake, or the chuck and jive — one could look up high above and see little dots of folk's heads around a glass rim looking down. But as for the dance floor, he could see that these extreme vibrations so agitated the dancers (some being couples, others, singles and groupies) that they shook and rattled like popcorn on a hot popping plate. He watched disinterested.

The next time he saw the crotch-less hot pants woman — it the same woman Surely, no Eleanor — she was sitting on a bar stool that was set back a little from the bar. He had wandered into the Solar Wind Hotel section of this plaza that provided many bars and substance abuse nooks. This one was named The Comet Debris Bar and was next to the Wormwood Game Changer. He saw that the lady who had caught his interest was now having to lean forward towards the bar top in order to set down an exhausted Volcano which the bartender was replacing with another. As Dyfed brushed by on his way to order a Free Dram (scotch whisky), her head swivelled and her dead eyes reached out and said: "Hey baby, you my baby? Then added, relax; take a load off, mister. Say, do you wanna push in my stool?' Suddenly, shrill peals of flat shrieking single layered laughter tore away from her blood red rouged-up lipsticked upper most lips. True, both upper and lower lips were, after all, glossy red but for the moment only the upper lips were talking. Dyfed knocked back his whisky and was just about to race up the nearest escalator for the safety of somewhere else and open a new dream chapter in his search for Trachmyr when the music, or whatever, suddenly ended and the reverberations and vibrations quietened down. He couldn't hear any more laughter coming from crotch-less hot pants, either, and he didn't dare look over. The band quickly sank into the stage via a mechanical up and down lift and a deep voice from somewhere, being transmitted through an electronic conduit, said:

> "We have a really big show for you folks here today, tomorrow and everyday of your life after that. And now, heeeeere's — Mack the Knife.

Meanwhile, ignoring Hotpants as best he could, Dyfed scrutinized the drink list. At a glance he noticed he had come to a place with a healthy choice of beverages, even if every one of them was likely detrimental to his health, aside from their names. Looking at the menu and he saw the Impact martini, the Radioactive Isotope (locally brewed beer), the Cosmic Radiation, the ^{14}C (radio carbon cocktail), the ^{10}Be (beryllium-10) aperitif, the ^{36}Cl, the ^{26}Al, the Gamma Ray (liqueur), and the Enriched Plutonium and the Volcano, both shooters. Furious finger and fast food was available here, too. The bar drink list informed one and all that it came fresh from the adjoining Gamma Ray Restaurant that also provided full cost meals twenty-four seven. Dyfed's choice became a toss-up between a Supernova (hamburger) with poutine or the popular Extinction (16 oz. tenderloin anyway you want it) with fries. He chose the former and was about to bite in when…

"Sir,' he heard a voice say behind him. Turning he now saw the same bartender dressed in a neat short white jacket was talking to a man beside him as he indicated a fog spewing milkshake glass on the bar. This drink was apparently for the man whose back was to him. But that broad back was unmistakably Trachmyr's back. Dyfed had found him at last.

'The lady here ordered you a Chemistry Lab Experiment Gone Wrong. It's not on that old drink menu list, yet,' he added. He inched the foaming and throthing fountain of uncertainty towards the edge of the bar closer to Trachmyr with a crooked finger that protruded from a soft lilywhite hand. Trachmyr seemed to be staring at the steamy broiling day-glo white vaporizing tall drink for some time before he reacted. With no satisfying or intelligent conclusion as to what was going through Trachmyr mind, Dyfed was about to call out to him but quickly changed his mind and looked on instead. Then in a single involuntary motion Trachmyr snatched up the drink. Dyfed then saw the eyes of Crotch-less Hot Pants unblinkingly probing Trachmyr's total entirety. Then quickly he tipped the tall foaming milkshake sized glass to his lips and pulled a Dyfed Lucifer. This was something Trachmyr called what he had seen Dyfed do so many times in years gone by. It was almost the same technique that's used to shotgun a can of beer: That is, he would gorge the entire drink in one humongous inhaling draught, but then — instead of crunching the collapsible can against lips and teeth like a biker or a Cauliafornicatian surfer beach bum — he slammed the damn empty thing back onto the bar and wiped his mouth with a long fell swoop of his right arm from elbow to hand.

Suddenly with a mechanical motion, Trachmyr spun around to face the stage and get his swaying body stance under control and was just on time to catch sight of Mack the Knife rise up from somewhere down below in the bowels of Abandon all Hope. The thought that he'd finally come to the Comet Debris Bar entertainment stage at the far edge of his reality, must have scrambled illicitly through his befuddled mind at the same time. Without moving a muscle other than his eyes, Trachmyr glanced to his left to look at (maybe in gesture of polite acknowledgement) the dead eyed Hey Baby Are You My Baby in the tight hot pink crotch-less pants when the concoction he'd just sucked back hit bottom. He had told Dyfed later that the same second a signal from his stomach that it had arrived was sent to his brain that in shock failed to adequately take over. The slight delay here must have been caused by the beverage's negative density, or something!

"Holy shit,' Trachmyr involuntarily shouted out. The words left his mouth and instantly expanded both in physical sight and sound like some dark creature, maybe a gigantic black heron or pterodactyl that had come from within him and out through his parted lips. Then having immediately flown up into the void it was as instantly absorbed (possibly joined in union…indelibly mixing) with the local phenomenon at large. Unknowingly Trachmyr had just made an involuntary contribution to an unidentified version of the unknown universe. Instinctively knowing that that wasn't good, he continued to err. In a flash the woman with the tight, day glow, hot pink, crotch-less pantyshorts was on her feet holding both of Trachmyr's hands in hers and gyrating her hips while rubbing her rough nipples against his exposed skin.

Holy shit, thought Dyfed.

"Yummy, huh? she said, mimicking Dyfed's words to her earlier. Now cowboy lets you and me boogie. With that she dragged Trachmyr swiftly to a spot well beyond the tables and directly in front of Mack the Knife who was just beginning his performance of — what else but — Mack the Knife, as only he, Mack the Knife, can.

The two of them boogie-woogied and gyrated along with the best of them, and the best of them was Hey Baby Are You My Baby in the hot pink crotch-less panty shorts. Mack the Knife quickly swung into his hottie routine, laying it on thick and heavy that was what everyone wanted. He strutted and flirted with his groin out in the direction of the audience, he traipsed back and forth along the stage and minced this way and that and prowled the other. As he flung out his bump and grind he even lit a cigarette, stuffing it into a long black and pearl holder and holding it between a sparkling be-ringed forefinger and thumb like some coifed and perfumed Madam Pontchartrain clapped-out old has-been would do. It was then, as he held the cigarette holder up to his mouth, that Dyfed saw the pale, flat horse-like face of the real Mack the Knife. It wasn't a horse face it was a donkey face, the face of a mule, a burro, he finally decided.

"Hee haw, hee haw, was all Dyfed could only hear now in a rhythmic, jazzy beat. And as he glanced up, he beheld Mack the Knife as an apparition with his long white donkey face and the slow motion, hop-step gyrating loins of a Mick Jagger all rolled into one and doing the shimmy shimmy shake with a rattle and rock and roll like Jigs with a bowl of bubble and squeak (squeek). Where the hell did those names come from, anyway? he suddenly wondered. Speaking of that, anyway, it didn't stop Trachmyr and his new fun found gal, the volcano drinking chick in the tight hot pink, crotch-less panty shorts and no top rough nipples from dancing up a storm like two dust devils in heat, accompanied by flashes of jagged lightning.

Oh my god and menstruating mother, to boot, thought Dyfed. Here we go.

Later, Dyfed had followed them back up in the upper lounge area that seemed almost quiet in comparison. Here he paused momentarily to decide whether to rescue or not to rescue, after all, Trachmyr needed to unwind too. They weren't able to see him for Genghis Khan, who was cooing sweet nothings to a giant green gecko whose knee he was sitting on, shielded him. Close by he then caught sight of Sweyn Forkbeard the berserker Dane king doing the Rumba with a transvestite Shirley Temple and her anima, Dorothy from Kansas. Or was it Alice in Wonderland? No, wait a minute, Dyfed thought, that's my anima. He had decided that on the spot. Also, there was some pious old Oriental Zen monk close by with shaved scalp wearing a lion's mane wig playing backgammon over a small short table by himself and drinking shooters along with a fierce looking man from the land of Ch'in with a knot of pig tail growing out of the back of his otherwise bald head that hung down to his tail bone who was telling him what and where to move. There was a pirate sitting on a cushy stool swilling rum from a giant pitcher with a chick on his knee who on and off was playfully sticking her soft beak into his ear. I mean, a chick, a giant, yellow chick (as in daughter of a mother red hen) also wearing tight hot pink, crotch-less shorts (it was all the Elton John rage here at that time). And through a hole under her beak this thing was occasionally sucking on a vodka and grape Popsicle that the old pirate was holding up for her from his lap. He had a sticker on his poke-a-dot head bandana that read, 'Hi, I'm Blue Beard'. The corporate-type looking sticker had the skull and cross-bones logo on it that seemed to indicate that he was part of the Buccaneer party. Funny, Dyfed thought, he hadn't seen their bus outside. Seemingly unperturbed that he was being blown here in fake virtual reality instead of somewhere far, far out on the ocean blue where he obviously belonged, Dyfed leaned over and whispered into his ear: "Har, Billie, have you ever been blown off shore?'

"You finally took off your mask,' Dyfed heard Trachmyr say to her. Then as they slinked from the bar over and sank back into a deep waiting couch, he watched them entwined together like Python and a deer in shock and wondered at that moment if Trachmyr was conscious that he was the wide-eyed deer startled by the bright lights.

"No,' she answered, insipidly. It was you who took your mask off, silly. I didn't alter an itzi bitzi teeny-weeny thing,' she added.

I'm otta here, Dyfed thought in exasperation as he up and left. Meanwhile, downstairs the Follywood the Somebodys were belting out the original rendition of the old quasi country tune Alley Oop.

(Eonnurzazagesibababal)

'I would far rather be ignorant than knowledgeable of evil.'
AESCHYLUS

"Holy shit. Wasn't it a party?' Trachmyr said out loud to himself and to no one in particular the moment he felt himself awake. He then struggled through a series of fluctuant movements. 'Where am I anyway?' he said as he raised himself against an unknown weight. It was the red up blond down (or whatever) sans her crotch-less hot pink dayglow panty shorts, now in all her glory and dressed up in her birthday suit. She had been lying across his chest but now she rolled down off him with a thud.

"How would I know,' he suddenly heard Dyfed say as the latter walked into his vision just then. 'You wandered,' said Dyfed. I told you not to wander the last night of all nights. I told you to stay close. Where did you go? Anyway, I know where you went and why are you sleeping with Mack the Knife's wife?'

"Holy shit,' Trachmyr said. Then hey, baby, you my baby's head popped up.

"Can I tell you something?' said Dyfed.

"Don't pretend that I have a choice,' Trachmyr answered, groggily. And whatever it is my answer to that is, I know, an Occam's razor, as always. Don't go on with me, I'm hung-over.'

"It isn't the morning of the big day,' said Dyfed. 'It's this evening of the big day and you and I and others have got a venue we need to be at soon. You need to get dressed and you can't bring what's her name with you, either dressed or undressed.'

"Her name is Doreen,' slurred Trachmyr.

"No its not,' said Dyfed, 'but anyway, Doreen, you have to go home. You too need to get ready. You can't be here in this city after another six hours from now. Do you hear me? The last train leaves here at midnight, be on it. Here's your hot pink split shorts. You don't seem to have brought anything else with you,' he said as he chucked them in her direction and they landed flung over one of her shoulders. 'Now get out. And you Trachmyr,' Dyfed said when they were finally alone, 'I will need assistance in getting a kingpin Haploid masquerading as a Master into # 6 powerhouse trailer immediately after our private and secret wind-up party. That will be around 18 hundred hours. He will need to be handcuffed and then locked in the trailer. We also need to grab his VIP pass from him, too, so he will be blocked and can't make it to back through the escape route to the airfield on time and leave C9C. That's just in case he is able somehow, presumably with help, to escape from the trailer. In this we leave no stone unturned. This guy has to die.'

"You want an elite with a VIP pass to fry with the Haploids?' said Trachmyr. 'Why?'

"Listen, Trachmyr,' said Dyfed. This VIP is actually Eonnurzazagesibababal, chief of staff and numero uno Haploid. He's living on the edge, here. It's the first time in seven thousand years, I think, since he's been in this dimension and thinks he can leave here and go back, so he can come back again after that as many times as he wants, or at least his alter ego Thrax can. But he's not going to leave. He's going to fry, here, later sometime tomorrow night. Is that clear?

"Yessir,' replied Trachmyr.

"Are you ready for this, my old companion? Dyfed asked Trachmyr later. The two of them had left their apartments and were alone in a large motor chariot. He looked at Trachmyr with concern and then leaned forward and said softly to the uniformed driver that was seated up front.

"What is this chariot?' he asked. 'A Chevy one fifty, I believe. Am I right?'

"Yes, sir,' answered the driver who was one of thousands of personnel that Dyfed was responsible for. 'Its a virtual one fifty, four door station wagon,' the driver answered. It was much bigger than Dyfed remembered them being. Then he asked Trachmyr if he remembered back in the day when they had had a fleet of these.

"Hell of a good engine. It was powered by a three eighty three cubic inch super Turbo-Fire V-eight with overhead valves and a Rochester Ram-Jet fuel injection system rated at two hundred and eighty-three horsepower (211kW), if I remember right,' Trachmyr said, glancing away from Dyfed and out the side window. 'They were a big improvement on the '55 and the '56, I'll tell you,' he followed up saying, as he turned back toward Dyfed. The driver flashed a glimpse at him from his mirror.

"Do you remember the '58 Chevy Delray models? Dyfed asked Trachmyr. Then I ordered a '59 Impala sport coupe, my choice for a much subdued and low profile chauffeur-type chariot,' he said to the driver again as he leaned forward. This was after I had long retired my old electric chariots that I had designed and built myself. Of course I never gave up my other fleet of personal toys: my model 11 Rolls Silver Ghost, for example; my model 13 golden Minerva tourer with its back, triple bucket seating arrangement; my '32 Ford Deus phaeton, my '40 Deluxe station wagon woody, I had a fleet of then once, incidentally, they replaced an older fleet of '15 Ford Model T depot hacks that I had, d' ya' remember Trachmyr?,' he said turning to him. 'Oh and my 1910 Velie Racytype Roadster powered by a four cylinder, four hundred cubic inch John Deere engine with a three speed Brown & Lippe selective transmission to a Timken rear end; and finally my '04 Waverly Electric that I always thought was an unscrupulously bold manufacturing infringement of my first un-horsed chariot that I designed, the Electra Chariot.'

"You didn't register any patents on it you told me,' Trachmyr said to him.

"Then there was my Bugatti two door sports saloon,' Dyfed continued without answering, 'and that '24 Itala 61 coupe de ville by Garavini that I don't have any more. But I still have my '09 Model 5D V-Twin Harley Davidson and my '50 Indian Chief Blackhawk motorcycle; my Ducati…oh, no I smashed that up when I skinned my elbow right through my heavy leather jacket to the bone, remember? But I still have my Indian 842, the '63 Corvette Grand Sport 001, my '94 Lamborghini Diablo VT, a Maserati Grancorsa and finally a '65 Chevelle SS396 two door hardtop… ah, what the hell. Whether I have them or not it's all gone now. So, here we are. And we've arrived safe and sound here in a Chevy one-fifty instead.

They had arrived at the venue which had been dubbed as the wind up party of season # one, complete with a sumptuous nosh-up of left overs and whatever liquor remained in the city. Leaving only what was necessary, mostly freezable and storable goods along with other reusable condiments. The rest of the usables had been silently and surreptitiously removed from the city over the last few weeks to a user friendly cache about two hundred Amoran miles across the desert from C9C. The time had come. The place to which Dyfed and Trachmyr had arrived was in another otherworldly environment it seemed to Trachmyr. Once Dyfed was ushered in, Karatakos and Morgant quickly greeted him. These two people with whom he had associated for many years were standing waiting for him to arrive. But Trachmyr's eyes popped out when I saw Doreen, the last person he expected to see here at this high-end gathering. As soon as Morgant had finished speaking something of importance to Dyfed in a language Trachmyr didn't understand, Dyfed leaned over closely to Trachmyr and said,

"We arrived before I had finished our little chat. I see your girlfriend is here, by the way. I wasn't expecting her to be here but I wasn't not expecting her, either.' Before Trachmyr could protest at Dyfed's inference that Doreen was his girlfriend, he continued. 'Now, she maybe here simply because she heard me remind you of our engagement: If that's the case she would have known the 'what and the where' without being told. I was intending to enlighten you as to her real name, which is not Doreen. She tells everybody who doesn't know her that she is Doreen. I've known her a long, long time. I can handle her and you can't either. Under the circumstances she is poison to you, though she might relent, there's no telling. But you must know this. Faye is a very dangerous woman, who goes by other names, too, such as Aenor or Alienor and even Eleanor all of which are derived from the Amoran language. She has been the wife of a king of Albion and a king of Francia. Two of her sons were also kings of Albion and her other numerous children were movers and shakers often with the appellations of Duke and Duchess before their names. Of course she looks elegant, and — incidentally — she speaks many languages elegantly as well. Do not try to make anything of her for you already underestimate her cunning and shrewdness. She was one of the establishment's greatest spies that ever was, probably the greatest, who knows? Unknown to the Haploids she has been playing them along for a couple of thousand years anyway. Fortunately, she is on *our* side, but to her the word *our* suddenly becomes blurred when it refers to someone like you. Although you are an adjutant and friend of mine, to her all you are is just a hoi polloi. Do you follow? Are you pickin' up here what I'm layin' down here, Trachmyr?' Dyfed smiled at this turn of phrase. 'Even double and triple agent spooks like Sid Really, Maclean Maclean and Mo Berg pale compared to her; the old stand-by and my favourite…Bond: The name's Bond…James Bond!

All of these are just so many crude and sloppy copies compared to her. Alienor would eat the likes of those aforementioned as fast as a spider rushing to the kill can suck the juicy, goo-ey, god-awful goodness out of a fly. All that would be left of you would be a shrivelled dried up carcass. She has slept with more than half of Europa's established hierarchy; both men and women, both our side and the Haploid side. And besides being responsible for many deaths she was the creator and patron of the young Jeanne, the martyr of Leon. This was one of her greatest coups. Our woman Alienor studied under her mother-in-law, Matilda, mother of the incomparable King Henry II of Albion and wife of Godfroi XII of Frankia. Matilda was one of the sharpest, rough and tough skinned and haughty dames that ever walked. She taught Alienor (Eleanor) how to wield power among already very powerful folks, so hey babe are you my babe learned from the best while creating people in her own image, women like Helen Gone, for instance; a shrewd bitch, that one. You're no match for Alienor no matter what name she goes by or how she spells it, friend,' Dyfed said. What happened between you earlier was her doing. The result being, that she now has a window into your soul; that is to say, your programmed psyche, since souls are a third dimensional invention. Guard that breech, Mr Trachmyr, and guard it well is my advice to you. We all resent such things even when those close to us achieve only minimum access.'

"What kind of a place is this that you have you brought me to? Trachmyr said quite loudly. He had been diligently employed but his errands and responsibilities were a little less demanding in dealing with the general management and the movers and shakers in attendance here.

"Stay close. You see that old warrior up there? He pointed to a man who seemed like some kind of specimen from the ancient past contained in an open door cage contraption. He appeared immobile and unperceivable as a human touchstone for any recognizable emotion and whose projection was one where he appeared suspended, floating in mid air like it came out of some kind of museum curio where it had once been contained in formaldehyde within a giant jar. Strangely, only his eyes of glowing red coals moved while the remainder of his giant, squat body was like a flat dead rat or beetle. Yet somehow, though he spoke to no one, he managed to impel or inject an extremely perceivable presence, albeit somewhat a harsh and very sharp one, into the entire huge room. Everybody, even the dead beats among this high stratus of Haploids, the rich and powerful drunks and the stoners all intensely felt his presence and feared him.

"Is that the son of Mars?' asked Trachmyr. Is that Thrax?

Turning again to look more closely at him Dyfed was suddenly taken over by feeling of fear that stuck pins and needles into his armpits. Then a wave of some unknown emotion rippled through him.

'That's not Thrax,' he said, as he seemed to shudder. Dyfed's eyes now shot directly into Morgant's eyes.

"The Master called Thrax wouldn't come to something like this, exactly,' said Morgant, addressing Trachmyr. This is his troll Eonnurzazagesibababal that lingers here in the third density. Then seeing Dyfed's sudden reaction of dysfunction, Morgant added for Dyfed's benefit, 'do either of you remember anything about Eonnurzazagesibababal? he asked.

"Eonnurzazagesibababal? Yes,' answered Dyfed, 'and I remember Cornelius-Felix enquiring whether I knew a certain Eonnurzazagesibababal, too. That was nineteen or so centuries ago in Tibur. He is the arch enemy, the supreme fiend.'

"Exactly,' stated Morgant. And here he is, fooled like the best of them have been, including Augustus Cornelius-Felix, Giorgy Posh, Jihad Habib, Dan Velchanos (also known as boy Zeus)...oh my goodness, so many of the king-pins are on this round robin's roster who have contrived to enslave and destroy and terrorize humanity...all here, today: None of them late for their own funeral. And there's more to come next time. Another five million, and another ten times over,' said Morgant.

"So, Thrax is the villain of villains yet we didn't get him here? 'stated Trachmyr.

"No,' said Dyfed, 'he did not come here to Cloud Nine City. According to Morgant he sent his troll here to watch on and participate instead.' The three of them glanced up to the cage hanging from the high ceiling to look upon Eonnurzazagesibababal who was watching them. 'You see,' continued Dyfed, 'Thrax too fears death, even though he dwells in the fifth dimension. But he couldn't leave it, you see, even while he craved the elements and wants to brush with a reality so far fetched from the fifth dimension. He wants more than to actually rape and murder and drink the blood of his victims, along with other bodily fluids. He wants to sup to the extent of gorging his body with the tastiest of cuisines and sip the finest of wines and whiskeys unto utter inebriation and then to ride his charge of pride and swagger and the chariot of enviable luxury and power at full gallop and feel the wind in his face. Apparently, he believed that if his troll came here to the third dimension C9C and transmuted from here into the fifth dimensional space/time reel accompanied by everlasting life, it would be a win win and then he personally for the first time in forever could traverse back and forth between the fifth and third dimensions like a true Master. But he knew he had to do it now or forever hold his peace and remain imprisoned. And as billions face certain death, he believes that if his troll is trans-mutated by our machine, then he too, by association, will ride on into nirvana. If his troll doesn't make it, and even Thrax may suspect a hoax here, still, he believes that he will remain as he is now, albeit, perhaps without a troll, his only companion by his side. But unknowingly, by doing that, instead the troll has come to follow Captains Crash and Crunch,' Dyfed told Trachmyr.

"We couldn't expunge him in the fifth dimension, you see, but we could here,' said Morgant. 'Thrax once informed me that he was the architect of Zeus and wanted to look onto his works again here from the perspective of the third density just one more time. He was the quintessential Haploid, but we couldn't get at Thrax/Eonnurzazagesibababal where he was. So you see, we lured his troll here in a hoax as big as anything we've ever wrought. We will restrain Eonnurzazagesibababal this evening. I know Dyfed has discussed this with you. Our belief and our hope is that when Thrax's troll is expunged, Thrax, without the ego and support of his troll will shrivel and die even though he remains in the fifth density. But if Thrax manages to survive Eonnurzazagesibababal's expiration, we have lost nothing and he has lost everything he has in the way of companionship. But it is more likely that once he has lost Eonnurzazagesibababal, then he will shrivel and die.'

"Hurrah for our side,' Dyfed said, his silver eyes glistening. 'And herein he will sustain more than just road rash on his chin and, theoretically speaking, it will be his own pain he feels and this own blood he smells and tastes for once. Oh bliss!'

"This strange and mysterious Eonnurzazagesibababal,' continued Morgant, 'was also known for most of the last thirty-five hundred years as Eurynomius (Yuri) Moloch, and he was apparently either a close companion of, or related to, Ares somehow. And for certain Potamus Purplebal and a host of others are avatars or clones of some kind to this forbearing Eonnurzazagesibababal.'

"Perish the thought that that thing ever wants to speak with me again,' said Dyfed.

"He confounded my attempt to successfully lay away Virus forever by forcefully recommending the site I picked to entomb that menacing and dastardly scourge upon humanity,' said Morgant. 'My valiant attempt failed for Virus seeped back into the River Ab (Nile) via one of that river's upper tributaries coming from the mountainous terrain of Ethiopia from where it spread influenza (under a thousand different names) throughout the world even in our modern time. I know now that he knew it would. Don't worry,' he showed some teeth as he grinned. Then slowly shaking his head he looked into those silver eyes of Dyfed's that shone beneath his shaggy head of silver hair flecked with gold glistening under the bright incandescent light. 'He doesn't want to talk to you,' said Morgant, 'and he's not personnel. And he's not going anywhere, either, except straight from here to what men call a fiery storm filled personalized hell called oblivion.'

"Manandan taught me, Morgant,' said Dyfed, 'not to say anything about somebody if you couldn't say something good about them.'

"There's nothing good about him,' Morgant retorted.

"Well,' replied Dyfed, 'he at least kept our world population in check, something the moderns have been unable to do. And look at the result.'

"Yeah!' replied Morgant, 'along with the brutality of war, suffering, misery and suicide, and somewhat at my expense.'

"Just sayin',' said Dyfed.

(Eviction from the City of Anti-Oblation called Entropy C9C)

> *'What is hell? Hell is oneself.'*
> T.S. ELLIOT

Morgant had called a series of impromptu and last minute staff meetings throughout the city that was to take place during this wind up party. The venue where the meetings were to be held was in an annex attached to the venue where the gala was being held on this the eve of space/time zero and the first destructive shock and awe meant to eradicate the first round of hosting and toasting and roasting the Haploid elite into oblivion. All of the executive staff was needed to be debriefed here and the high number meant a revolving meeting.

"Now listen,' said Morgant, when they were all together in their meeting room. Dr Torsionfield and Quasi Gismo were in attendance alongside Karatakos and a host of others that included Dyfed and Trachmyr. 'We are going to get out now: Get out as planned and while the going is good. Under the distraction of this gala all two hundred and fifty of us here need to push off as fast as we can as soon as we are finished here with this debrief.'

Dyfed then stated that as the *Pack* Initiative Logistics Group Responsible for Information & Maintenance (PILGRIM) captain, his responsibility was for all C9C staff safety: And that now this current and first round in a series of ten rounds was coming to a close, his job was finished. But his authority and responsibility (the two are inseparable) extended fully to the time of evacuation from the Atacama Desert itself. To do this, and to minimize any glitches, they would all meet up together forty miles away across the desert at C9C's only securely guarded air portal.

"I will depart from this meeting here momentarily,' Dyfed said, and as captain of this unit I will make my own way alone. I've just got some last minute business to attend to first, a few loose ends to tie up and that's it. The rest of you will follow your orders as group leaders. And as group leaders you will safely deliver your crews to the terminal as originally planned if you follow all of your instructions. It's all arranged. Once the first five thousand of all seventy thousand of us staff have safely arrived, the relay flights to Ikiki on the Peaceful Ocean coast will begin. This will take about twenty-four hours before we will finish transporting all seventy thousand of us by midnight tomorrow. This completion of our staff evacuation is roughly about six hours prior to countdown zero and the moment of detonation of the first of a total of nine small precision thermonuclear devices that come later in successions over the next eighteen months to eradicate any human life that's left in this city each time. That's to be followed finally by an H-bomb. This event was to hide our tracks from history, as we all know. Once we arrive at the terminal, preparation to board the waiting cavalcade (that should be copter-cade, there's no horses involved here) that will consist of a fleet of Mil Mi 26 helicopter aircrafts will then begin. Accompanying us on each relay will be dozens of

CH-53K Sikorsky King Stallion helicopter flying gunboats on escort duty. We will begin final flight departure at twenty-three hundred hours, just about four hours from now. It will take just over an hour and a half for all of us to be airborne and clear of the air field in order to make room for the cross-shift replacement aircrafts coming in to land. The next five thousand personnel will follow within an hour or two. We've made allowances for unscheduled delays. Guard and use your photo pass, it gives you full clearance. Take orders or directions from nobody of than Trachmyr or Karatatos. You have their contact number, so keep them posted. If a problem arises and you run into a glitch, immediately contact Trachmyr or Karatakos on your neo-astrolabe (palm held android).'

'I don't get to make any calls other than those affecting your safety,' he said out loud to the group. 'Some of you will be back and forth for a while over the next year and a half. I won't be, so I want to thank you again for your dedication. It's a downright dirty job, but some capable bodies have to see that its done right. For those of you who are coming back to raise C9C from the ashes like a Phoenix, our hopes and prayers and condolences go out to you. That's it, that's all, good bye.'

Shortly after he and Trachmyr had completed their restraining of Thrax's troll Eonnurzazagesibababal, Dyfed, the harried looking unit captain suddenly looked very glum and Trachmyr who knew him better than anyone else knew that he was thinking of Ceredwyn and his family. Not because he wasn't expecting to survive and never see them again, but because he was expecting to see them all too soon and was afraid of facing them and embarrassed and ashamed of his part he played here. He couldn't save the city — Trachmyr knew he was thinking — or the people in it, even if he tried — because they were all thinking that. Anyway, this isn't Murtlewood, Follywood or even Wormwood television. This was the real MacCoy that was centre and front and in the present. Apparently, it had come to this.

The exhaustion that the aged captain of the Staff Health and Safety division underwent during the last weeks and months at Cloud Nine City was so extent that he collapsed in the monorail carriage enroute to the departure terminal. Trachmyr remembered he had done the same thing a year ago when they were here before on reconnaissance. Dyfed was never to recall travelling to Ikiki where he was transferred by ambulance to a hospital for the night. This bustling seaport city of Ikiki was about four hundred lineal miles as the crow flies from the thermonuclear blast that was to be detonated on the following dawn. Ikiki was also about fifteen thousand feet (five thousand metres) below the detonation site of C9C. Therefore, as Ikiki was in the clear and the event itself at C9C was deemed completely safe, everything was a go. But of course that status per sé had been in place long before the first excavator chipped away up at the Atacama Desert.

Some of the recovery personnel who would be returning would wait out the radiation decay delay sequence in Ikiki before returning to C9C for its refurbishing brush and tidy-up in preparation for the next turn-around cycle of five million more Haploids that would continue until all fifty million had been processed. But never mind the safe distance that the City of Ikiki was from C9C, the remainder (that included Dyfed delivered again by ambulance from the hospital to the air terminal) climbed or were carried aboard a chain of Boeing 737s that ferried them from Ikiki to Boise Idaho in the Unified States from where they could make their connection for flights to anywhere whether it was Francia, the Unified Kingdom, Inja, or to the Land of Ch'in via change-overs at two other Merikan cities, Couver City and Megatropolis.

He spent almost a week in hospital in Boise. Dyfed had brought along from home The Oresteia that he was rereading for the um-teenth time. It was a work of four plays by Aeschylus and his copy was the only copied edition that included the fourth play, Proteus. And inserted into that book at the beginning of Proteus was a note from Trachmyr that wished him well and stated he needed to return to Megatropolis immediately but said that he'd be in touch with him soon. Morgant, too, stopped in about a week later when he flew up from Ikiki having settled arrangements there for the return staff with that city's Welfare and Public Works departments. And now he had to pay the horrendous hospital bill issued to this beleaguered travelling pilgrim from South Merika before this old friend could be discharged without the *pilgrim* being charged and then him having to defend himself in court.

As soon as Morgant had bailed him out, the *traveller* was now on his own and somewhat lost in thought, yet he was cognizant of the fact that he had some pressing business to conduct under his new identification that had come about due to the Megatropolis fiasco. He needed to get in touch with a certain Harvey Fulcher Brown (aka Johnny Rocco whose alias was Mr Greenhorn) who resided at Flathead Lake. There, he needed to get an urgent business transaction completed. Furthermore, he needed to return home immediately afterwards to the Bountiful Valley to secure his property that had been the centre of his empire. But problems in this had arisen under the guise of new titles due to his new identity.

That night he took a room in the finest hotel that the City of Boise had available. Then after a quick egg foo young sandwich washed down by a bottle of Peroni beer in the hotel's insipid and antiseptically atmosphere-tinged lounge, he left there to carouse around the other bars for a while. Spiralling quickly out of control and into a greater depression that was paralleled by a decreasing decorum with each new pub, bar, beer parlour he entered, and where the over all condition were shades of Nova Troia on his return from the big 5D back in the day, he found himself finally at the carpeted-in-filth Rock Bottom Booze and Babes Bar, Boise's notorious most-down-and-out scuzz pit. Here, full of vomiting drunks, heroin, phentanyl and Borax injecting addicts along with the brain damaged, the lurking psychopaths and the insane, he felt quite at home as was his ability to neatly fit right in anywhere. Now weakened, distracted and desperately seeking solace from a sterile pain that tore is heart and his brain apart, the *pilgrim's* dream started to fall apart, not at the seams but from the inside out. Succumbing to primitive, basic and natural or even bestial urges he gave a young home-bar-stool girl with super starched and ironed fake blond hair above dead eyes, dressed only in a skimpy, light fabric and light coloured loose pinafore dress the nod and out they went into the night. Around the corner they went where she quickly pointed out a more than convenient flophouse type hotel called Johnny On the Spot just at hand that for a room and a bed they charged by the half hour, even for a quarter of an hour, but it advertised that half an hour was a better deal. She immediately asked him for one hundred dollars. Since he was undressing and didn't answer she poked at him in a zombie mechanical motion and again in a zombie mechanical type of speech demanded fifty dollars from him. Since he still didn't answer she said, "Ok, asshole, I'll suck your cock for twenty-five dollars and you'd bedder give it to me right now, or else,' she said to him, slurring as she spoke.

The *traveller* pulled out more than three thousand loose dollars in fifties and hundred dollar bills in cash from his pocket and shoved it all the way down the front of the drowsy, victimized girl's pinafore and told her to fuck off. What took place in his mind after that was bizarre, even from the standards concerning a tale where the john who as an instigator, and one of the designers of situation where a city of five million unsuspecting people who by design were destroyed in seconds by a weapon of mass destruction that was now preparing for another (the second of ten such events in total), it was more than insane.

In the battered *pilgrim's* mind she was like stiff plastic, cold yet giving without being not-withholding. She yielded with him without complying. At no time did he make love to her: he fucked her only, that was all he did, in his mind. He fucked her only to experience the sweet emission of his semen and nothing more. Creative and imaginative volitions exploded in his head as the greatest of all illusions — that pinnacle of sensation and sexual release — mounted. In for a penny, in for a pound: his lust soared beyond his control and extended even beyond the physical. The three thousand dollars he laid out for this was meaningless and non-negotiable with his conscience while being incompatible with his self-esteem. He became almost insane and to ensure that the pinnacle of mental sexual feeling would be reached he would have stopped at nothing: not just by ravishing her or physically debasing her as he was already doing, but more. He would kill her if need be. In his mind's eye he conjured up forms of ugly images, he not only nipped and bit but like a wolf at the kill he lunged and lunched and gobbled her up. He found himself biting and tearing and ripping her open. He then began to devour her from the bottom up and up, further and further into her warm bloodied body. At that point sweet emission erupted.

But this wasn't sweet at all. It was cruel, it was wicked and it was debasing for both of them. This was the game to which only the most extremely pathetic humans succumb, he knew. Yet aside from gungy brothels you can find them in palaces, mansions and the courts and at the head of every high official level of government and in every priesthood of every religion. So, here he was at last, no better than any of them. Yes, he now recalled, frantic and frightened by his post climax thoughts that rushed in: he had seen ferocious carnivores bring down deer, antelope and moose and eat them from their anal cavity up and into their warm insides. This was the preferred edible of choice and only the dominant animals managed to get the opportunity to indulge. Even the northern indigenous peoples when hunting for their survival — once the hunted beast was down and the prayers of the family of hunters had been given up in praise of the beast — the skilled hunter would open and gut the animal then go first for the main intestine which was immediately incised, pulled out from the animal, sliced and thoroughly washed by responsible children who at this point delivered handfuls of it to the women who wrapped it around peeled sticks to roast over the hot fires or to fry the pieces of gut in sizzling pans. This was all accompanied by song and family chatter and as the men skinned off the hide and cut up the quarters of the feast beast they consumed the main intestine gut as they worked and listened to the old story tellers while others consuming fermented blackberry juice sang with merriment in their hearts and in their voices. This scenario was a happy family occasion, his — conducted in such a way that it was — was not, it was pathetic and lonely.

Then suddenly the *travelling pilgrim* remembered how the crusading soldiers acted when they were over come with bloodlust and carnal madness after the defeat of Jebus (Kadesh) almost eleven hundred years ago. He then remembered his uncontained disgust at such deplorable actions. Had he become them?

(The road to Hellen Gone)

'For the first time the old man's mouth was full of words.'
THOMAS EDWARD LAWRENCE (SEVEN PILLARS OF WISDOM)

The *pilgrim's* awareness of the outside came slowly to the surface.
"Your back among the living again,' said a face he was trying to remember the name of. 'I'm Harvey; at least that's what you kept calling me. 'You've been with a high fever for just over a day and have been chattering nonsense the whole time,' he said. 'Maybe a touch of heat or sunstroke caused it. It was hot out there on the lake, and you didn't have a hat. I'm sorry,' he added, I feel responsible.'
After he left Flathead the *pilgrim* headed northwest back into Idaho as he headed toward the Kootenay. This place was back across the line in the Northern Dominion. But before he got there and close to the line in northern Idaho he was pulled over by two police/security-come-axillary Nightwatchmen that caught him up by helicopter from the sky. This particular sky patrol, he reasoned, were part of the 24/7 piloted choppers in the-vicinity-air-security-surveillance of the Columbia pipeline that also was correlated with military special forces boots-on-the-ground. This corridor consisted of sixteen giant culverts bundled together that carried billions of metric tons of fresh water run-offs from North Merika's spine mountainous valleys across the line in the Northern Dominion down to southern Cauliphornicatia about twelve hundred Amoran miles away as the crow flies. These guys now noisily glided over him and set their machine down on the undulating road pavement in front of him where the watery asphalt spread out like shining liquid in the heat. There was no traffic. There was nobody but him on the road nor were there any farms or anyone else in sight. Other than the necessary licenses, the permits, and copies of inspection under the authority of motor-vehicle safety documents (and such) these Nightwatchmen paid scant attention to anything else around them; such as the warm morning wind bringing relief to the already stifling air that wafted around them and stirred the glint of the sun that glanced off the land shaped by the wide yellow rough that bordered the twisted and flashing ribbon of highway. The ascending sky chariot machine loomed like hallucination in the foreground with its two propeller blades drooping in the warmth of the sun. These horizontal propellers were shaped like giant Shasta daisy petals that faded into a dull mat steel grey yet they still seemed to shine like mirrors in the morning light. This, not to mention his beautifully leather scented shiny black riding gear that contrasting with the *pilgrim's* silver eyes and his fading hair flecked now with wisdom grey and moving in the wind. And (of course) there was the even more beautiful two wheeled, shiny-black and chrome gear-oil scented machine that was his chariot of choice, powered by its side-valve engine. Leaning casually and quietly still on its side-kick prop, this perky looking gadget that intermittently emitted tiny, sharp pinging sounds as this sparkling mechanical contraption sat separate and strangely alone, cooling in the hot sun from where it emitted the subtle scent of gear oil and of burnt petroleum and engine oil whose musty combination could threaten to

bring on a sneeze. And this, aside from the prairie land under the hot burning sun, was what the three men standing around it inhaled and exhaled through their lungs.

Meanwhile, what was concurrently taking place now was the rustling and clashing and the matching and mating of torcs as they electronically passed back and forth permits and other identification appliances. As this took place the *traveller* surveyed and scrutinized the two members of the sky police patrol. In contrast to himself who now quite re-environed after his short sickness and finding himself free at last from his bed ridden stint and was back at large in the outdoors again to pursue once more his passion of riding through the warm wind of summer, these two unsmiling Nightwatchmen stood in the middle of the hot road and in his way and neither acknowledged him personally or any other thing that was not part of their job. Nor did a jot of friendly emotion pass through their eyes or pass over their lips in his direction in any way and they showed no inquisitiveness whatsoever about anything other then establishment's documents and protocols and everything else of no importance. It was as though he and they were two different species indifferently confronting each other for the very first time; it was like a moment of contact, so to speak, except it wasn't. But for the two officers of the Nightwatchman brigade it would not be a memory, it would be a notation, a procedure (actually) of muster-census and due process. It was quite like a numeration exercise. Yet the wily and unorthodox *pilgrim* knew that if physical impact were to quickly follow this encounter, it would not be he who would come a cropper and undergo agitation and anxiety on account of it. There was going to be no leg irons for him for he was prepared as always.

Prior to them landing on the road and pulling him over, they had caught sight of him riding dippity dive over the hot undulating land beneath them like some fantasized quixotic horseman. He was the fly and they were the Frog of the Long Tongue. Even now, as he and the machine were fixed before their eyes, inquisitiveness was an emotion they apparently lacked. As for them, one would think, the spectacle that the rider and machine caused to ripple through the phenomenon — initially as well as presently — would have been utterly unique in itself. In truth the phenomenon that was before them was something from out of the past that was operating in the present, something that to many who are awake is always intriguing, he thought. But these bureaucrats from the sky police division of the Nightwatchman patrol showed no curiosity in something which they couldn't understand, anyway; and that something was the joy in taking individual pleasure in just being. Their sole and only interest wasn't in blending with the out of the ordinary that they by chance happened upon. On their part there was no individual intrigue that needed celebrating or even enhancing apart from the seriousness of their duty. What interested them was something that needed to be investigated immediately on account of protocol. It was in order for them to apprise as to whether or not regularities, statues and permissions and so forth were (or were not) being dangerously challenged here. And this led to whether or not (that in some possible way) legalities (somehow) were being squashed asunder which were quickly to lead to misconduct. Therefore, it could be concluded, mischief was afoot and needed an immediate intromit for contrary persuasion, accompanied by the strong arm of the law to intervene and rein the prospective culprit into abeyance. It's the old adage; we don't know yet what crime has been committed here, but the culprit does; we need to find out by looking closer and by getting it out of him, one way or the other.

But above all, the incident of the happened-upon-phenomena-at-large needed categorizing. For them, he supposed, there was a lot not to understand about riding a motorcycle. He was certain these men wouldn't have wanted to ride a horse (either) unless it was a group outing, probably with their friends (other members of the force and their families, that is) at some popular and well advertised hobby farm. These would probably be their only opportunities for horse riding under supervision, but only after half an hour instruction. Of course, these came with the obligatory photo opportunities and kumbaya bon-fire for the evening's finalé. These men, he thought — who living in not even a parallel universe to him, or so it seemed — were very much unlike him in every way possible, anyway. Who were they? What had they to do with anything about him? It wasn't so much as where the boundaries of authority were but rather what were the boundaries of authority? For him it was all about aesthetics and being in the moment even as he applied all the nuances of natural law and its expectation of decency and non-entitlement over the privacy and personal sovereignty of others. Could they have understood that for him it was about the connection to Mother Earth while having the agility of a deer and the speed of a mountain lion that made him ride? The first hurdle that arose by chance for these psychologically truncated automated Nightwatchmen would be the first of many. He was sure that their puzzlement was more likely to be, why here, why so alone, and why bother? Didn't this loner loser have a job or a retirement cubicle to go to like normal people? Even Aristotle refrained from describing normal; after all, unlike these men, he was no fool.

That this particular lonely little party standing around out there on the prairie did the ritualistic security Nightwatchmen-like dance, and that it was recorded and filed in the repository of the eternal registrar of lists before the antagonists reluctantly released the *pilgrim* again under his own re-cognizance (as they put it, somewhat incorrectly), is assured. He knew they had been summoned by other white collar Nightwatchmen taking orders and authority from Turn-keys that were tracking him via unmanned spy-cams and armed drones in the sky which they controlled from great distances away.

Again, finally away and motoring on his own with still no evidence of any population — no friendly and willing community or confrontational and un-willing congregation — in sight for a new world order government to rule or restrict in any way, and certainly still no signs of traffic on a road that appeared to be laying down under a farmer's fallow as it bent and meandered into the evening, the *pilgrim's* concern was now elsewhere. This 'elsewhere' was his fuel tank, or at least the amount of smelly liquid stuff remaining in it to keep making his engine run. And that led to his problem. It was the shortage of what they used to call gas stations that had the *pilgrim* worried about. He knew that once he crossed the line again just south of Kootenay Lake he would be subjected to the guards of the Northern Dominion to a similar degree he was here. But he knew the lie of the land better there, and accessing benzene or petroleum gasoline (gas-o-leen, not gas-o-lyne) was imperative if he was to stay on schedule. Fortunately, he knew that stashes had been set up and set aside years ago on the north side of the line. He knew of none south of the line. His concern generally was about the petroleum liquid's shelf life before its natural chemical deterioration caused a failure for a continuous and clean combustion to power his machine. He had set out carrying five imperial gallons (approximately twenty-two and a half litres, or roughly eight and a half Unified States standard gallons) of benzene gas (liquid petroleum) in a jerry can in addition to the full capacity of the machine's gas tank. But at the present moment his jerry can was dust-dry empty and his tank was plummeting quickly to the same level.

Though the engine machine was an early design, because the two-wheeled chariot it powered up was smaller and lighter than later models of similar chariots, it was more fuel-efficient. Furthermore, the tinker that had refurbished and improved the automotive parts and its over all performance was a highly trained Master. For this two-wheeled chariot (the companero recalled now) had once been owned by Dyfed who had given it to him for a Halloween present, a festive and feasting day the *pack* always tried to celebrate together. In turn, he treasured it and aside from its hidden enhanced electrics, he always applied a chemical additive enhancer to the petroleum that gave him more miles to the imperial gallon. He had filled up last from a stash Harvey had offered him in order to make Kootenay. But he would need more to get him from Kootenay Lake to the Bountiful Valley. Without gas, a motorcycle (like any contraption that needs to consume energy) would stop functioning and assume the stance of down time. And that would leave him on foot. And that was dangerous when he considered his precarious position here. May the old adage of *chrome will get you home*, hold up, he thought. It could become his mantra today for in reality his chariot was a chromed beast clad in slapped over glossy black.

As he rode (with mountains, tall forests, rough road surfaces and sky clouds starting to whirl and twirl around him), he mulled over something Harvey told him. He then cast his mind into this swirling state for the sake of taking his mind off such pressing concerns about having to abandon his motorcycle somewhere in the middle of nowhere and having to shank's mare it to the Bountiful Valley through a virtual wilderness unknown to him and made dangerous with snipers in helicopters or unmanned drones overhead. He was already a stranger in an alien land denuded of compassionate and of happy folks who would not be available to lend one a hand and willing to dish out a bite to eat and a bed in which to rest the night like Harvey had done. He didn't want to be the one on foot. The most he could do if the need arose would be to summon help through his torc. And even if his torc's positioning apparatus was switched on to stealth mode it would be dangerous to break from the black: don't ever break from the black was good advise which Dyfed had told him he had learned back during his early finance marketing days.

Anyway, he had to mull something over to take his mind off his fast dwindling fuel. Then he remembered one of the things Harvey told him. It was that when the white Caucasians arrived here just over two hundred years ago, they claimed they found that some indigenous peoples were accustomed to practicing the peculiarity (or barbarity) known as artificial cranial deformation. Flattening the top front of the head back in a sloping fashion was decorative and thought to be either attractive, or possibly intimidating. This occurred world wide, of course. The word Salish meant 'the people' in the language of those of this area. Their nation extended from the big island (later known as Couver Island) on the northwest coast of the Peaceful Ocean (and not to be confused with the big smoke later called Couver City on the mainland), and continued all the way inland to Kootenay territory and to Flathead territory now south of the line. Harvey told him archaeologists delving into the Salish culture assert that it is a civilization. In fact their civilization was the oldest of all and had existed for thirteen or fourteen thousand years to this point. Furthermore, it was the most advanced culture throughout the entirety of the two continents of the Merikas. Anyway, the name Flathead became an unfair slur for the Salish people in general but odder still since the people of the Flathead region did not actually practice cranial deformation at all, although some on the coast did.

As mentioned, with the population contracting, once the initial violence and chaos in the urban areas subsided, folks flocked to the now shrunken urban centres in an effort to survive. Most folks could not manage to make their life happen without enormous support and props. Among the people who had no difficulty with this and still remained at great distances from urban centres and maintained an unbroken way of life unlike the others, were the Salish folks. They were not hungry while others were starving to death, and they seemed partially oblivious to the sudden and huge life change which shit-happening brought about. In fact, they seemed to thrive. These were people who Dyfed (known once as prince of the grove) had befriended long, long ago and who loved him. An easily believed rumour had it that some of the younger chiefs were directly descended from Dyfed himself. Dyfed was sometimes referred to as a tinker for his people; the Hyperborean masters (so it was rumoured) tinkered with the fabric of reality and the universe at large. It was said that these local descendants of his went straight from tinker to chief, avoiding tailor, soldier, sailor, begger man, thief (also known as lawyer, if you prefer).

So, in the end it was to be these folks who would be providing him with petrol once he had crossed the line and hopefully coasted into their village on gas fumes which (as he calculated it) would be just by the skin of his teeth. Then when this happened, and he finally did pull up before Beaver Joes and the large dirty white building across the road with wide open bay doors and a gas pump out front, he saw the familiar figure he had seen a few times before when he took the time to visit here. At that moment three workmen, two of whom were welding and a third who was wrenching and tinkering, stopped what they were doing and looked up at him in surprise. He hardly noticed them because his eyes were on a fourth enormous form that stood watching him in baggy dungarees. This was a large and heavy woman wearing a red and black plaid logger's shirt with either a white Smith-built or Stetson hat perched on her head while her black straight hair streamed down out from under it in every direction. This large fat woman was standing in front of a gigantic shell of a building and through the open doors the *traveller* could see past her to where his vision fell on enormous olden day cargo carrying chariots and trailing wagons that were undergoing both mechanical and body work as sparks and rainbow colours showered and flew about in a gaseous and bluish atmospheric haze punctured only by sharp hammer blows that were only slightly deadened by a nearby whining generator. A cool smell of water coming off the lake nearby acted as a welcomed filter that dampened the village air here which smelled of diesel exhaust and forest fir. However, most disconcertingly, there was the constant, terrific noise of that powerful generator that assaulted his ears in a cacophony of surround-sound. This machine, of course, not only kept the lights on in the village but also powered the sawmill and ran tools for all sorts of repair service. This included automotive repair, sheet metal working and the like.

The three workmen watched the *pilgrim* pull up and stall. They dropped their tools and congregated around the big woman and the *pilgrim* could see their rapid moving lips working a quick conversation about him. These were *injuns*, as the Salish were often called. This term was better than savages that they were also once often referred to. They were neither. For injuns were inhabitants of Inja, an ancient land in Asia washed by the river Indus, and secondly it took a long time for the white man to realize that those very same Homo Sapiens which the Europaeans called savages on this continent weren't. It was quite the contrary, for more often than not it was the new arrivals themselves who exhorted and demonstratively displayed savagery. In fact, it was now known that the indigenous people of the Merikas were uniquely Merikan, unlike any other Homo sapiens walking around anywhere on Good Mother Earth. Although Aristotle had not sufficiently defined law and justice, he hadn't defined savages, either; not at all. In fact he might have defined savages as those separated from any human that was noble in purpose or honourable of character towards their fellow living species, or all and any species whoever they were. They would be folks for which primary and fundamental natural law would be an intrinsic ingredient for any meaningful, long lasting civilization, such as were the Salish people themselves. But the so-called civilizers of this continent failed to understand what living piety truly meant. And the reason for this ignorant disconnect? Their false mythos is more than partially to blame. Of course, the self-destruction of their civilization proved it.

 The *Pilgrim* shouted out a password that Dyfed had provided him years earlier in the direction of the enormous woman blocking his way. Its affect was immediate. The large western-hatted Salish woman beamed a big smile showing very white false teeth and ambled stiltingly forward while the others suddenly dropped their affected demeanour of concern and possible confrontation. Then managing an incredulous shrug and a shaking of their heads returned to their work in an unassuming manner. This mobilization was accompanied, however, by a glance or two over their shoulder towards the motorcyclist, just in case.

 Aside from gasoline and diesel fuel, these inland Salish people had many mechanical parts on hand that were of no more use to modern folks anymore or to themselves: Which was why almost everything they had was for sale. And these old abandoned warehouses took the shape of caves and culverts beneath ground that were spread out all over hell's half acre in overgrown underbrush or in refuge dumps and quarries — come parts department stores — where they were stock-piled and stashed far away and out of sight of agents of the modern world to steal or tax. Meanwhile, as a small horde of native entrepreneurs encircled him like turkey vultures trying to sell him make-believe enabled torcs that had been cleaned up and dusted off (basically useless) along with other hardware artefacts he (or anybody else) didn't need or want, he filled up his tank and jerry can. 'I'm not a tourist,' he shouted out at them as the big chief who wore the big Smith-built hat grinned with amusement. Big Hat, whose real name was Hellen Gone, then pointed to a small neon sign that flashed on and off and read 'Big Beaver Joe's — *open*' in pink coloured cursive written lettering that was sandwiched in between the pulled curtains and the steamed up window glass of a low, tar-papered roofed wood-framed building. Over a quick cup of black coffee and the house specialty, deep-fried elk and moose bum-gut and fries all smothered in tomato ketchup or gravy, Big Hat pointed out to him a number of new back trails on a map she kept in her wide pocket and had unfolded onto the red and white chequered plastic table cloth. She told the *pilgrim* in her deep manly voice that the trails were kept relatively clean of brush for the next forty miles or so as they wound through the bush. Cleanliness of assortment of yard gatherables may not have been a natural Salish trait, but cleanliness of the trails here in this instance allowed their horse drawn wagons and winter dog sleds (sleights) access through the bush.

At one point an old injun who the *travelling companero* recognized and who had never before spoken to him when they met, immediately came over to their table and opened his mouth. Whereupon, words began to endlessly spill out. The *traveller* couldn't understand his language, but that made no difference, the man kept on talking anyway. It didn't make any difference to Hellen Gone, either. She too kept on into her discussion with her white friend over changes he'll encounter on his route.

So, it was in this manner that the *traveller* had in no time moved slowly in a westerly direction just north of the border on his motorized in lined two wheeled chariot. And it was these same Salish folks who had later (in the Skagit area) directed him to the old paved and broken down road on which he was currently travelling and where long ago our tall tale began.

(The old House of Lucifer)

'My strength is gone. Bold and weak am I'
JOSEPH HAYDN

The pilgrim gazed into the distance from his lookout on this old back road he'd been creeping along ever so slowly since yesterday. He even thought he could see Dyfed's farms now as he looked out across the flat and lush Bountiful Valley cut by irrigation channels with water still spilling through them. These were being fed by the Sto:lo River. It had once been a great salmon river, but no more. But many dairy and vegetable farms were still active here for although the area's local population had declined from about three million, Couver City was still half a million living people who needed a viable agricultural industry in place. He walked over to the side of the road to answer the call of nature. That twigged his memory, so afterwards he returned to his motorcycle and pulled a can of beer out of one of the pockets of his jacket. Earlier, he had purchased a can of beer for each of his two outside pockets from the Skagit people for a low on fuel Ronson lighter he'd been carting around for years. He'd wrapped the cans in wet handkerchiefs which had hoped would help keep their coolness from attracting his body heat as well as from the warm outside air. Then before he sat down in the shade to sip beer he pulled a dog-eared pocket book from the same black leather jacket. The novel entitled Under the Volcano was by Malcolm Lowry. Once again, half slumbering, the man's sleepy eyes flitted over the prose in an attempt to grip and experience the unctuousness of Lowry's epic account of a single day in the life that was (and remains) his four hundred-page masterpiece:

> "...a loudspeaker mounted on a van blaring the Washington Post March...there was a savage scribble of lightening...M. Laruelle...stood, out of breath...into a graveyard darkness, stabbed by flashes of torchlight...The van with the loudspeaker slithered away into the rain and thunder... the sound echoed away like coal sliding down a chute...Las Manos de Orlac said a poster: 6 y 8:30. Las Manos de Orlac, con Peter Lorre..."

It had been perhaps the sixth time during the past two weeks that he'd pulled out this novel and started to read. Yet after re-reading the last few pages he still couldn't get past page thirty-three. He was confused. He seemed to recognize the characters and the events but the characters were wrongly melded somehow with events misappropriated in a twisted time frame. It was much like his life, now. They weren't supposed to meld, he thought: The event(s) were separate and apart from each other as well as juxtipositined from segments within the lives of the characters and were reminiscent like an echo, they were reflective. Fascinating, he thought, and then following earlier procedures (while thus engaged) he began to dose and drift off.

The lawyers and real estate agents wouldn't be swarming onto Dyfed's place until tomorrow. So his arrival the day before was good. This, the man thought, would gave him time for the opportunity to touch old memories without the interference of others. Those others would cramp the flexibility of his imagination and he already felt a sense of hostility toward them. He knew that somebody had been hired unseen to take over caretaking the place, but the *pilgrim* didn't know whom that was. He had already decided to introduce himself as Dyfed Lucifer; after all, his old boss had suggested that. The *travelling companero's* job had been to see to it that the books for overseeing the estate were properly kept. In a sense, it was no longer the House of Lucifer but Dyfed Lucifer's house. The former was all about business; the latter was simply a roof overhead. So, under the heat of the June sun, with his gloves tucked into his jacket pockets, his jacket off and lying across his upper thighs and the chariot's fuel sloshing around the bottom of an almost an empty gas tank again, he slowly wound his way through the thick hot air stuffed with the smell of fertilizers and dairy stock along the old road toward Dyfed's central abode tucked in among his farms. Equally poignant to his senses were the sounds of insects buzzing furiously in the atmosphere and the long drawn-out audio-ordeal of miles of sprinklers that automatically sprayed columns of water onto the rich and darkened soil accompanied by a strangely metallic staccato sound much likened to *wapp…wapp…trigga trigga…chink chink*. What he didn't hear were birdsongs. There were none. Even the meadowlark was gone from here now. But the smell of the cottonwoods, the ones that hadn't yet burned, lay thick in the air.

The *companion of the road* introduced himself as Dyfed Lucifer when the elderly caretaker came to the door. He had half expected it to be Anlaf, for some reason, but couldn't remember why. The strange caretaker was a pleasant sort of chap, though, middling in age and could have passed for a store clerk. People, it seemed, got old faster today. When he asked him if Anlaf was home the man just shrugged and smiled at him. He noticed that there were still House of Lucifer security personnel present (both physically on site as well as actively providing surveillance electronically from afar via satellite as well, if needs be). This was necessary if one meant to keep the bad-nasties of the establishment and other unfriendly and uncompromising individuals away and at bay. And because preventative maintenance of the premise needed to be kept up there were kitchen staff available at all times, too. But the mansion site was off limits to the farming personnel, the agriculturists, the mechanics and so forth. He fished out a ham sandwich lunch from an inside pocket of his jacket and drank ice tea as this strangely animated old caretaker kept him company and forever closely watched him. Later they played backgammon in the library and the superintendent (as he now jovially called himself) told him that he had never heard the name Dyfed Lucifer before or Anlaf. The caretaker asked him too many questions, he thought.

Later, after supper and proffering subtle hints about resting and being meditative, the *pilgrim* finally found himself alone again. He noticed that the liquor decanters were half full, much the way they had been the last time he was here, he suddenly remembered. That was just before he and Trachmyr had left for Colorado to meet up with Harvey Fulcher Brown known as Mr Greenhorn who went by Johnny Rocco. Then he hoped that his wife Wanda would come home soon, wherever she was. Wait a minute: she must be back on Couver Island. Yes, he remembered. He then thought of phoning her and leaving a message but picked up a liquor decanter instead and lit his last Cuban cigar before sliding open the patio door. For some reason he expected a cold gust of air to blow in from outside, but it was warm. For the first time (in a long while, it seemed) he thought of Many Bones and Sweet Lorraine. And where the hell is Anlaf, anyway?

Pulling aside the sliding glass patio door he stepped out onto the patio and into the evening light. It was quiet, too quiet, yet he was unable to discern a modicum of traffic flow from the direction of the highway or the unforgettable sound, that low, highly charged hum of a railway engine as it slaved away through the grade, pulling its mile and a half long burden behind through the warm evening air with that accompanying rattle and squeaking noises peculiar to the boxcar wheel set assemblies. Here, on this night, all was quiet.

Then suddenly he thought he heard the unmistakable sound of Sweet Lorraine barking nearby.

"Here little Miss Sweet Lorraine," he called out. He thought of pinching himself to see if he was dreaming. Suddenly, he felt his mind move quite unimpeded and flashing like an old camera flash bulb beside him just somewhere beyond his peripheral limit. To contemplate it more closely he turned slightly that caused what he wanted to look at to move out of range. What he felt was an invisible light that was undetected here in the third dimension as it searched high and low through the crops or generations upon which the ghosts of history flitted...pausing to contemplate, fast forwarding or reversing as necessary...as he (apparently) was mentally searching for the pertinent reel/space/time he sought after that lay somewhere among the jagged shards of his journey...that strangely haunted corridor of tears where only the initiated could find alcoves of peace and solitude.

It was then that he heard the heavy, solid work that was being churned out by a long, slow freight train that was snaking the distant edge of the estate somewhere in the darkness. And in a flashback he then remembered that he was expecting his faithful old batman (willing servant) Trachmyr to call him soon.

Suddenly he felt a dizzy spell rush into his head. He fancied himself leaning back against a wall of rock to steady his vertigo. His feet gripped a narrow ledge that sloped away towards a bottomless precipice. And around him rock began to break off and plummeted into space. He dropped his glass of gin but somehow managed to hold onto the decanter that he now placed on the concrete patio. He was already on his hands and knees but could feel something buffeting and jarring him. He quickly noted there was no pain in his head. The patio furniture, though, which had obviously been set out for his stay rattled and shook and he could hear a horrendous noise which came from the direction of the mountains beyond the flat farming land that lay round about. And that awful noise which he heard even drowned (drou-nd not dround-ed) out the heavy, high pressure sound of enormous energy being consumed and expired by actively materializing the work of pulling that very long train that was out there somewhere across the land, passing by fences, tall grass and scooting quickly over canals.

Again, there was a dizzy shock that convinced him not to try and get to his feet as he had just been doing. What the devil! he thought. He could still hear that horrific rumbling noise and supposed then that he hadn't been wrong in any imaginings, just momentarily mistaken. It was just the train after all. Of course it is, for he had heard it a minute ago...a minute ago when he was waiting for a call. He suddenly became aware that he had lost track of time and had, for a moment or two, forgotten about something that he now no longer felt. He then heard a loud flapping and banging sound. It came from afar, possibly down by the farm buildings. He recalled that a supervisor of some kind had come to the house while the property chief caretaker and he were playing backgammon earlier on. He was expecting Anlaf, he remembered. It was something about all the cattle, the man had said. There was something wrong. They were all acting strangely, he said. 'And we're talking of thousands of head of dairy cows here which have to be milked,' he had added. Maybe the banging is connected to that, he thought. Something has happened down there and they're on it, fixing whatever it is.

But that didn't account for his dizziness and why he was crouched down on his hands and knees with the overturned patio furniture, along with the rattling of the house and the shaking and trembling of the large cottonwood trees that circled all around the house. Then he saw a huge spiky bolt of lightning off to his right, and though the weather had warranted it, there was no pending rain and no wind. And it was spiky lightning, he recalled, not scribbly or sketchy. But now he heard voices shouting out. Some came from afar and others were somewhere in the house where alarms were going off. Oh dear! He thought. Then he distinctly heard someone calling his name. He then called out Sun Tan's name. Then he realized it was the chief caretaker. What the devil does he want, anyway, he wondered.

Then it struck him. What he was reeling under…what was causing his dizziness and his inability to stand, were shock waves from an enormous earthquake, one that was over due, according to some scientists. And they were still rippling through the earth; on and on and on they went. Oh dear! he thought again. Why it might even set off the big mountain just over there, he thought, and cause it to erupt. That's why the cattle are unsettled.

"Mr Lucifer? Hello! Are you here? Are you all right?'

It was definitely the strange caretaker. He was aware as well of searchlights that were obviously moving around in the darkening evening. The noise was still deafening so he did not answer. After quite some time the noises and rumblings stopped. He still heard voices in the house. It sounded to him as though some folks were looking for someone. What the hell were they doing? Who the devil were they looking for, anyway? Who were these folks that were responsible for breaking the peace of this normally quite house, aside from that devastating sudden natural disaster, just now: It was an event, surely, outside of human control…this act of god to render insurance policies null and void across the entire epi-centre to its furthest periphery. Then he thought that perhaps there had been a rupture — somewhere in the plumbing — and water (or worse yet, sewer sludge) that may be coursing out over the Persian silk carpets, spraying onto rich tapestries and splashing onto priceless masterpieces which hung on the walls of his beautiful home. Masterpieces and other objects d'art that were consigned to him to insure and secure until they could be sold to the highest bidders, some of whom would be here tomorrow, he now remembered.

Panic struck him suddenly and hard in the stage-fright zone and he felt he had to pee uncontrollably. He was, after all, a recovering earthquake victim and all that which entailed. A moment later he calmed down. After all, it was he who had to take charge here for there was no one else qualified to delegate the way he was entitled to do so. He'll have to get the farm hands in here and on it, he thought. They will know what to do. Farm boys and girls make the best of everything; whether as soldiers or generals or politicians to world leaders, inventors, scientists, artisans, tinkers and poets, farms boys and girls are almost always the top qualifiers. If only we had more farm boys and girls. City slickers are no good: Useless, in fact that brings out the worst in themselves and in everybody else, too. But the silly and trendy city slickers aren't here yet. They will be arriving tomorrow, he remind himself again as he took charge of forming a plan. Get up off the patio and get moving, he told himself.

At the patio door with the forgotten decanter still hanging loosely from one hand, he encountered the chief property manager. He noticed, too, that the interior lights had come back on. He couldn't hear the emergency generator running, so apparently they still had power. Then probably having checked the breaker switch, the caretaker had come back looking for him.

"Are you all right, sir?" the man said.

Ignoring the question the *pilgrim* asked, "Is everything holding together ok?" He did this (he was quite sure) with dire concern written across his face. He noticed, however, that the elderly caretaker looked very alarmed but seemed to have put on a brave face possibly on his account.

'How are the carpets and wall hangings?' he asked this aged superintending custodian that stood before him with genuine concern. 'Is there any water damage?' The caretaker now stared at him hesitatingly. Then suddenly something of a good-humouring condescension crept over his startled face.

"There are some men here to see you,' he said.

"What, all ready. Nobody was supposed to arrive until tomorrow,' he said. Then remembering his memory time-lapse, he asked. 'What time is it? Or should I say, what day is it?' He laughed self-consciously and remembered he still needed to urinate.

At that moment a tall, youngish man poked his nose and mouth around the door jam from across the room. Maybe the farm boys have been summoned already the man thought when he saw him.

"Hello. Is everything all right, Mr Woodruff?' the mouth said to the caretaker. The entire man himself then stepped into the room followed by another man. Both men were dressed in the accustomed uniform of the Royal Northern Dominion Nightwatchman. Each man was armed with sidearm and steel handcuffs that dangled by their side. One of the wireless communicating devices fastened on to the belts of each of the uniformed police appeared suddenly to have a cold: without warning it proceeded in an irritatingly manner to blow its nose. The uniformed man quickly quieted his radio down by fiddling the thing with his fingers. These men reeked of officiality but they were holding their official caps casually in hand by their right knees which gave them a softer, more gentile profile, he thought. That didn't fool him, though, he reflected. They looked relaxed and were even smiling like they were just regular, not particularly bright, not too much education or imagination type cops, he noticed. That didn't fool him either. What he had here, without a doubt, were uniformed guards — security police by the looks of them. Suddenly he began to tremble.

"Sir,' said the first officer looking directly at him. 'I'm Sergeant Henky of the Northern Dominion Police. We will need you to finish up here and come along with us right away, sir. If you wouldn't mind.' He smiled at him pleasantly in a business-like manner. But the pilgrim could see that there was no nonsense about him whatsoever. He was a trim and tough looking man who wore his uniform with pride and with taste.

Menstruating mother of god, he thought, as he involuntarily began to urinate in his trousers. What went wrong here? I'm fucked!' he said aloud. He prepared to be trundled out in irons and paddy-wagoned to some drab, naked cell washed in a dirty coat of pale (reduced-for-paint-sale) green where without a doubt he'd be water boarded by two sweating thugs, one (in every likelihood) would be a certain Captain Kowalski, while he had little doubt that the other would be called Corporal Rudichuk. And both of these doses of human scopolamine would be stripped down to their white, sleeveless wife-beater undershirts that they wore tucked carelessly into their belted trousers while they alternatingly choked and drowned him half to death one moment while the next moment played a no trump dummy hand of Russian roulette with the six inch barrel of a Ruger Blackhawk revolver that they would suddenly brandish. This semi-automatic had a full cylinder of live, .44 Magnum ammo that would be alternatingly shoved either half way down his throat between his clenched teeth to make him talk or else up his ass to make him shit bricks.

Oh dear, he thought. Suddenly he felt very exposed and weak and frightened. He thought of his worrying wife. Yeah, she would come back and be there when he needed her. He then remembered his memoirs that were lying around in a not very secure drawer of his desk in their Quw'utsun River home on Couver Island where she would be. Memoirs that figured and fingered individuals and named names of people who had manipulated the history of the world; dangerous felons all who had contributed to the cause of the world's greatest wars and were responsible for the suffering and the misery of quite a few hundred million people or more over two thousand years, were among them. And there wasn't any prospect of the established authorities (who Sergeant Henky of the Northern Dominion Police answered to) doing anything about it other than deep six all the evidence and seeing that they never surface again or see the light of day for historians or investigators alike. Perhaps at that very moment, back there in his neck of the woods, those Nightwatchmen were swarming over his personals, pushing his wife away from protecting the privacy of his home and his office desk and ordering her to sit down and shut up! They might already even have his memoirs in hand by now.

Suddenly, after having already urinated down the left leg of his trousers, he began to throw up on the expensive, silvery Persian silk carpet under foot. At this juncture he was fit to be tied as only moments before he had been expecting to be. As his toughness failed him he was no longer manning up or mustering together and getting down to it as the going got tougher. He was trembling noticeably, feeling that he had already been pricked over by these greasy bastards. Almost gone was his resolve; gone was all that steely, ramrod stiff stuff he once thought he had. Now he was reduced to no more than a wanked willie that more or less left him wet below the crotch. Nevertheless, he had what it took to fling out one last and final remark to proffer some meagre trace of resolve and fling it into the face of the enemy of Nightwatchmen, those soldiers of the established order, for his own sake. It was done as a last ditch effort if only to delay the ultimate for a moment.

"You'll have a current and signed warrant on you to search the premise, I presume,' the *pilgrim* said shakily, and with a little intended despondence so as to proffer false bravado before Sergeant Henky's eyes. 'Make sure you get the boys and the girls in from forensics, eh! You hear? I don't want anything broken or misplaced as they rifle through my shit.'

(Homilies under the Sun & under the spell of Theoretical Assumptions)

'The conscious mind allows itself to be trained like a parrot, but the unconscious mind does not:'

CARL JUNG

The *wayfaring pilgrim* went with Sergeant Henky of the Royal Northern Dominion Police. Outside it was dark now but the walkway and roadway lamps were burning. Upon reflection he mentally corrected his vernacular of the idea of burning into how the lamps were actually shining out radiated energy at sixty hertz a second. There was no smoke and nothing was smouldering or on fire. It was like a miracle. The fire and smoke thing was back in the old days, when he was young, he recalled then. But it was years ago now since he had gotten used to miracles. And although the present situation provided adequate illumination for comfortable seeing where one was walking, he made note anyway of the sepia subdued hash-tag, mish- mash of night shadows being cast all about in every direction in varying shades of darkish grey.

Suddenly he remembered the animals; especially the cattle that he had been told were acting peculiarly on this evening. He was worried about them. And then he noticed his motorcycle that was parked in the drive where he had left it. He looked at it longingly. Familiarity was his association to it, it was his and he knew every inch of it. Now, what with the rude interjection of some foreign presence and authority, we (this familiar thing and himself) seemed apart, separated by a different state of being. But it remained familiar so he was anxious to re-pair the two states back into one by manipulating the former state to become dominate over the latter one.

The officer accompanying Sergeant Henky saw the *pilgrim* glancing whimsically toward his two wheeled chariot and stated in a friendly voice that he would make arrangements with the property owner to have the motorcycle stored here until the *wayfarer* had made arrangement with a friend to see that its picked up and shipped home. Then he was helped into a police helicopter that quickly rose into the night air and the *pilgrim* was whisked away. Once he was airborne he looked to see if sparks of lava and other pyro tectonics were happening out of the big White Mountain just across the line as its god was throwing a tantrum. All was quiet on that front, he thought. A policeman then offered him headphones to dampen the noise of the engine directly over his head. The *pilgrim* had not spoken a word of plaudit as yet, and wisely chose to continue not to do so.

Once their pilot had achieved the posted altitude for their flight they sped west following the Bountiful Valley. He could see the lights of individual chariots crawling along the Trans Dominion highway. The Sto:lo River was a ribbon of darkness that snaked across the land below and was bisected by the occasional illuminated bridge. It was most probable, he thought, that as they approached the infrastructure of Couver City, it would be a scene of frightening carnage plagued by disruptions and delay that spread across the land below. Geological disruptions like volcanoes and earthquakes always brought immediate disorganization to our society, he knew. He had seen this before. He also saw groupings of wide spread light below as they quickly flew over towns and industry. Less than an hour later the vast lit up expanse of Cover City became visible. Apart from some banter between the chopper pilot and helicopter dispatch — at first upon departure and again approaching arrival — no conversation took place during this trip.

Earthquake caused fires so the *wayfarer* kept an eye out for them especially as he almost flew directly over the harboured bitumen fuel terminal at tide-side where oil was pumped aboard waiting tankers destined for foreign lands. Quakes also cause gas circulating within the infrastructure of big cities to explode, but he couldn't see any traces of that from his seat in the chopper in the sky. It was possible, too that the city could have by now been struck by a tsunami, devastating much of the lower lying areas of the city. This would have caused wide spread flooding which would have doused out any fires along with possibly dousing out thousands of innocent people's lives into an inky pool of darkness, the *pilgrim* reasoned. Because it was dark, despite (never mind not withstanding) the glowing lights of the city, the *companero* was unable to discern any extended damage to highways or buildings from the air whatsoever. He had no doubt, however, that some devastation would later be evident and probably quite extent.

Since he had felt the quake hit he had been worried about his wife Wanda and her well being in general. Now that he was closer to home that worrying took on a dimension of over-powering imminence. The man feared that she might not be all right, that maybe their home had collapsed in the shake or caught fire and she was trapped. What would he do without her? he asked himself. And then there was the extended family to deal with. He'll have to get it to them straight right off the bat…no, they're not going to look after me, he thought. Stay where you are. I'll look after myself. Don't you worry; I'll be all right.

From the heli-pad area atop a tall building's large roof, *the man* was whisked down an elevator from which he stepped out into a large, very busy, well-lit room full of commotion. Under these circumstances he had expected as much, though he expected to see more uniforms. This would be the kind of hubbub in any emergency response centre such as the headquarters for the Nightwatchmen (the equivalent of a guard's command centre) that was also especially used for interrogation, usually run by the military. He wasn't sure which one it was at that moment. He wasn't worried. He would figure it out in a moment. Nor was he under any illusion that it wouldn't be to a highly proficient sovereign security detention centre run by special branch officers of the governing factor of the authority under the Northern Dominion's charter of governance. This would be the compartment at the end of the long hall to which he would be ultimately brought. After all, what was the definition of a uniformed guard of the established order if not to protect the tools of control, the rights, rules and possessions of the governing factor? And those who embody those positions were necessary to help maintain that control. This was yet another throwback to a thousand years ago and a glaring example of worldwide sociological failure. What the *pilgrim* had been pleasantly surprised about (and it hadn't been the politeness of the two arresting officers, who actually didn't officially arrested him) was that he hadn't been given a mild injection of some kind to take the fight out of him, nor was he shackled in hand and leg irons; at least not yet. Let them try — for they would soon find out that that wouldn't be as easy as they thought. It would become a struggle followed by mountains of dreaded paperwork. That was one thing that was not on their side, the aftermath of a mountain of bureaucratic paperwork. Even Lev Davidovich Bronstein threw up regularly due to its effects, never mind Joe Citizen with short hair with no imagination (or curiosity) and in uniform. Anyway, as for the politeness of professional Nightwatchmen and policing officers, along with the administrators of their protective agencies in general, the real professionals who are astute are always polite, hadn't anyone noticed? the *pilgrim* asked himself. And (as a rule of thumb) if during an arrest it happens that the restraining officers are not professional, then one — especially a smart and agile felon that one might be — may even have an outside chance of making good a quick escape leaving them looking like chumps that they are. In the *traveller's* mind, there were far too many arresting and restraining officers of the law that were not professionals; at least not any more they weren't. Not like back in the day, anyway.

Historically, however, it has been shown that in most arrest cases when unprofessional officers of the law are involved, one had a greater chance of being beaten, shot or tasered to death by the said officers. And this, after it had been determined that the would be felon or perpetrator was unarmed or at least not dangerously disposed and probably clasped and restrained in hand and leg irons. In other words, not dangerously disposed according to the standards of trained, competent, professionals that nowadays many of the day and Nightwatchmen were decidedly not. To those modern ranks of the untrained, incompetent and unprofessional policemen, along with other members of the department of Justice, dangerously disposed is now meant to be a suspect of any kind; it didn't matter whether the perp was at large or secured fast in iron fetters or even fast asleep.

(Is Paradise Lost?)

'But now the time has come and we must go hence: I to die, and you to live. Whether life or death is better is known to god, and to god alone.'
SOCRATES (ATTRIBUTED)[97]

At about this point the *pilgrim* was taken by the kindly polite officers of the law to a desk clerk who summoned a male orderly who took the man to an even more brightly lit room (if that was possible) down a short hallway.

Here it comes, the *man* thought. I'm now going to be beaten, interrogated or debriefed, as they say. Apparently going black hadn't done the *man* much good, after all, in the end. At that moment he was quite sure that he would be plied with some form of barbiturates that fall under the "truth serum" category complimented with electric probes to his testicles. He automatically suspected scopolamine or sodium pentothal to start off the party. He looked over at his accompanying orderly and saw the glaring cruel and contemptuous eyes of the eminent psychopathic beast that lurked inside this interrogator as he averted his eyes away from him while (undoubtedly) he was salivating over the imminent torture to which he the *prisoner* was about to be subjected. And that was whether or not if the serums produced the effects that they wanted.

The tall, silent orderly waited with the *prisoner* until a woman who was either a doctor of psychiatry or a psychologist had arrived. Seeing her make her swift entrance and immediately seat herself without a word, the *imprisoned traveller* thought for sure she was going to order that he (the *prisoner*) be girdled up in a suit of geriatric diapers covered over with a snazzy and bright coloured restraint jacket decked out with a radio frequency device for good measure. But instead the doctor was quite pleasant and, after she dismissed the orderly, instead she spent a few moments reading something off on a small computer screen. Much to the *prisoner's* utter surprise the strict by-the-book orderly touched the prisoner gently and respectfully and said 'good luck, sir,' as he took his leave of them, glancing politely at both of them. The crisp looking young woman doctor then turned slightly to address him. The *prisoner* thought that when she turned her head he would then see that the woman would appear much differently; she would be beastly and devilishly, manly. These harsh-like people always appeared in some form like that. These people!

But this did not take place for she pleasantly (with a matching pleasant face — to boot) then asked some very simple and uncompromising questions in a pleasant voice. The first question was his name. He hesitated and she gave him the institutionally renowned raised-eyebrow-look. Since he thought that there would be no harm in giving her his name, he told her. Quickly she nodded and seemed satisfied.

"I don't know why,' she said smiling, 'but somehow, due to my earlier quick debrief I expected you to be somebody somewhat different. Either that,' she said with laughing eyes and a wide smile, 'or someone dressed up in a giant, Halloween gorilla costume and

---

[97] Sentenced to either retract his life's teachings or die, by order of the magistrates of Athena who accused him of atheism, Socrates chose to preserve his legacy and died willingly.

itching to hang from a tall building to look for your lost beauty and the love/lust of your life.' She laughed unabashedly and the *man* was suddenly reassured of something but couldn't quite remember what. But he quickly told her that he didn't equate gorillas with Halloween and although he hadn't read the book he had once seen the movie.

She then asked him if he knew what day of the week it was, and if he remember where he had been for the last five days, and what was the name of his wife? She then asked him who Dyfed Lucifer was, and Anlaf? She also was recording everything he said. She had told him that she would be doing that at the beginning of their little chat. The questions she asked him were so matter of fact; the *prisoner/patient* didn't feel it was necessary to avoid them. In respect to who Dyfed Lucifer was, however, he hesitated and did not answer. As she was still otherwise engaged with some memo or instruction that he couldn't see but was on the monitor from which she was reading, it was a moment or two before she looked up at him inquisitively.

"Perhaps,' she said after a moments pause, 'the officer had written it incorrectly, or perhaps Mister...' she glanced down at the screen again...'ah, Mr Woodruff had misunderstood what you said. I have his statement here, you see,' she said without showing him.

"I have no idea what you are talking about,' the *man* responded, having decided to be a little more careful and coy about his answers in the future.

"Ah...the man you gave info to?' she suggested, speaking slowly while looking directly into his eyes,. 'He was the man who owned the home you inappropriately accommodated earlier today. Mr Woodruff...who is not pressing charges against you, nor are the police, sir...but you apparently gave him a scare when you entered uninvited to his home,' she stated plainly to him. She then gave the fixed address of the property that she read off the computer screen. 'And this Dyfed Lucifer?' she continued, 'according to this report was a name you kept on repeating,' she said. She then looked at the *man* again expectantly.

"Ah, that's ah, doctor...,' the *man* began to stutter before he halted again and set about to collect his thoughts as to how he would address this question.

"Ah, I see...right?' she suddenly stated. And seeing that he didn't look perplexed she continued.

'Dyfed Lucifer is your doctor.'

"Absolutely,' the man answered in a heartbeat, smiling broadly. I might add that Dr Lucifer was a graduate of St. John's college, Cambridge, you know,' but he didn't volunteer that his doctorate wasn't medicine.

"Do you still feel ill now? she asked.

"Ill? No,' he said. 'Heavens to Betsy! No I don't feel ill at all.'

"Do you feel frightened?'

"Frightened?' He thought about that for a moment. It's not good to show your hand in these things. 'No,' he said, finally. 'At least no more than anyone else does, under the circumstances.'

She hesitated. "Do you want to go home, or to a hospital?'

"A hospital? Good gracious — no,' he told her. 'Why would I want to go to a hospital?' I want to go home, he thought. Then I want to collect my motorcycle. What on earth is going on here?

"Well that's good, then sir,' she said. 'Your wife is here now to pick you up, I understand.'

"My wife? Here?'

The doctor got up and went to another door in the room and opened it. After a moment Wanda walked in. She looked worried, he thought.

"Oh for heaven's sake dear,' she said, tears immediately welling up into her eyes. "I've...I mean...we've been so worried about you.' She then turned angry for a moment. 'You and your antics and sudden absence has been most distressing. Really! We didn't know what had happened to you. I mean...I was meant to fly to Cowton on tonight's flight to be with out daughter Ophelia,' she said glancing at the pretty doctor, 'from where a two province-wide search was to begin looking for you.' She glared again at him. 'Mac flew out here this afternoon to accompany me there,' she added. 'He's here now. Then we got the call from a nice policeman. He told me you were found confused, somewhat, and had happened onto...or actually ventured uninvited into the living room of a private estate over in the Bountiful Valley. What on earth, dear? You were wandering around in someone else's home until a Sgt Henky got the wind of your location there and rescued you and brought you back here to me by chopper...I mean helicopter, not your motorcycle. I was confused about that at first. I think the policeman thought that it was funny...but I have no idea why. He then quickly changed the subject and asked if in fact you actually owned a motorbike. I assured him you did. I thanked him and he put me in touch with the kindly Mr Woodruff, such a nice decent man. He owns the estate you were trespassing on, dear. I spoke with him shortly after you and the policeman had left his home just after supper tonight. He was very understanding. He said it was probably nothing for me to worry about.' She glanced over at the doctor who was watching them both.

Shortly after this he and Wanda headed for the car where Mac was waiting. The *traveller*, home from his journeys, noted with amusement that there were no traces of fire and flood permeating the mild summer evening air but there was a student demonstration taking place close by.

"The premier is flying in tonight and these young people are concerned about our economy and climate change,' said Wanda.

"They're being disruptive,' said Mac.

"No. They're concerned for their future,' said the *pilgrim*.

Mac said nothing but insisted on taking the wheel and Wanda climbed into the back seat behind Mac so she could see her husband more clearly.

"Mr Woodruff said that your motorcycle will be safe and sound in his garage,' she said leaning back when they were on their way. 'But he asked me if I could arrange for someone to pick it up? There was no immediate rush. What on earth? Dear. Did you run out of gas again? Its no good you riding that old contraption...nobody rides them anymore; do they Mac? At least not men your age — do they Mac? They are way too dangerous and they are always running out of gas — aren't they Mac? Oh, and your friends from that metaphysical society you belong to,' she said to him as they motored south away from the airport toward the ferry terminal, 'ah.... what's their name again?'

"The Unbroken Unity of the Universe group, you mean? he answered slowly.

"Yeah, that's right dear,' she said. 'You've got a meeting tomorrow night. Had you forgotten? You were to deliver a speech at your symposium about the categories of how and why humans unconsciously create their own reality during their day-to-day life. Something about a word game, too, I believe. Did you forget? Are you prepared for that? She threw a concerned glance at him as he sat all hunched against the side of the passenger door up front.

'Oh, and you had a phone call. Someone named — David, I think he said it was. He was probably from your group. He said you'd know what it was about. Do you, dear?'

Now it was Mac's turn to throw an expectant glance over at him.

The *traveller* laughed silently to himself and quickly turning his head looked out the side window at the passing lights in the distance. Slowly he turned back to look forward through the windshield. He then lifted his hand and rubbed under his nose with the topside of his crooked index finger.

"Not really,' he said. 'It's a hard enough job knowing exactly who it is I am and what I'm really about, what with all the kerfuffle and hubbub and distractions. I've discovered that opinions, whether they are either mine or somebody else's, aren't important to me anymore. So I'm going to quit the boring Unbroken Unity group and stop writing my weekly letters to the editor, too. And on those rare happen-stances when I get a true glimpse of myself, let me tell you just so you know: It's a frightening exposé of what you are outside the mindness of your true Self where the ego-self makes a whole lot of *to-do* about nothing, for nothing. If you were to say to me that it appears that a single thought of the undisciplined ego mind encompasses the direct route to all fear, suffering and delusion, I'd say to you; tell me about it! Today I feel as if I've just woken up from an ineradicable dream, an illusion.'

"I see,' said Wanda. 'So, welcome back into the real world of the living, then.'

"Is that where I am?' he answered.

End

Deryck Douglas Hockley: poet, engineer, part-time humourist and amateur ontological philosopher, is a transcending world-travelling adventurer whose only concern for himself and other humans is in the present moment as he seeks the ruins and echos of our history via a myriad of twisty rural byways and urban highways. Hockley believes humanity's semi-permanent predicament of world social instability caused by ignorance, fear, hatred and insufferable debt is the effect from long exposure to bogus mythical, religious and historical fabrications and personal deceptive illusions that are either individually created both mistakenly and intentionally, or absorbed unnaturally. His mission for this *protest novel* edition is "to enact subterfuge that can perhaps help people ignore the path of least resistance in this world and enable them instead to shun senseless wealth and egotistical ceremony," and to help individuals flex their right to express (and have accepted) their personal expressions of nonconformity and uphold their private independence within the context of common normality and its accepted decency.

In addition to pursuits of the mind, Deryck Hockley is a husband and a father who enjoys and prefers the wilderness and the outdoors in general to urban settings. A former mountaineer and once an avid rock-climber, now motorcycling, yachting, classical music, writing and oil painting remain his passions today; especially he is a friend of dogs and other gentle animals.

Deryck lives with his wife on Pender Island, British Columbia. *The Gods of Entropy* is his second book. (Circa: 2020)

CPSIA information can be obtained
at www.ICGtesting.com
Printed in the USA
BVHW041153040121
596016BV00010B/2